RAYMOND CHANDLER

# RAYMOND CHANDLER

## LATER NOVELS AND OTHER WRITINGS

*The Lady in the Lake*
*The Little Sister*
*The Long Goodbye*
*Playback*
*Double Indemnity*
*Selected Essays and Letters*

THE LIBRARY OF AMERICA

First Printing
The Library of America — 80

Manufactured in the United States of America

FRANK MACSHANE
WROTE THE NOTES FOR THIS VOLUME

# Contents

# THE LADY IN THE LAKE

# I

THE TRELOAR BUILDING was, and is, on Olive Street, near Sixth, on the west side. The sidewalk in front of it had been built of black and white rubber blocks. They were taking them up now to give to the government, and a hatless pale man with a face like a building superintendent was watching the work and looking as if it was breaking his heart.

I went past him through an arcade of specialty shops into a vast black and gold lobby. The Gillerlain Company was on the seventh floor, in front, behind swinging double plate glass doors bound in platinum. Their reception room had Chinese rugs, dull silver walls, angular but elaborate furniture, sharp shiny bits of abstract sculpture on pedestals and a tall display in a triangular showcase in the corner. On tiers and steps and islands and promontories of shining mirror-glass it seemed to contain every fancy bottle and box that had ever been designed. There were creams and powders and soaps and toilet waters for every season and every occasion. There were perfumes in tall thin bottles that looked as if a breath would blow them over and perfumes in little pastel phials tied with ducky satin bows, like little girls at a dancing class. The cream of the crop seemed to be something very small and simple in a squat amber bottle. It was in the middle at eye height, had a lot of space to itself, and was labelled *Gillerlain Regal, The Champagne of Perfumes.* It was definitely the stuff to get. One drop of that in the hollow of your throat and the matched pink pearls started falling on you like summer rain.

A neat little blonde sat off in a far corner at a small PBX, behind a railing and well out of harm's way. At a flat desk in line with the doors was a tall, lean, dark-haired lovely whose name, according to the tilted embossed plaque on her desk, was Miss Adrienne Fromsett.

She wore a steel gray business suit and under the jacket a dark blue shirt and a man's tie of lighter shade. The edges of the folded handkerchief in the breast pocket looked sharp enough to slice bread. She wore a linked bracelet and no other jewelry. Her dark hair was parted and fell in loose but

3

not unstudied waves. She had a smooth ivory skin and rather severe eyebrows and large dark eyes that looked as if they might warm up at the right time and in the right place.

I put my plain card, the one without the tommy gun in the corner, on her desk and asked to see Mr. Derace Kingsley.

She looked at the card and said: "Have you an appointment?"

"No appointment."

"It is very difficult to see Mr. Kingsley without an appointment."

That wasn't anything I could argue about.

"What is the nature of your business, Mr. Marlowe?"

"Personal."

"I see. Does Mr. Kingsley know you, Mr. Marlowe?"

"I don't think so. He may have heard my name. You might say I'm from Lieutenant M'Gee."

"And does Mr. Kingsley know Lieutenant M'Gee?"

She put my card beside a pile of freshly typed letterheads. She leaned back and put one arm on the desk and tapped lightly with a small gold pencil.

I grinned at her. The little blonde at the PBX cocked a shell-like ear and smiled a small fluffy smile. She looked playful and eager, but not quite sure of herself, like a new kitten in a house where they don't care much about kittens.

"I'm hoping he does," I said. "But maybe the best way to find out is to ask him."

She initialed three letters rapidly, to keep from throwing her pen set at me. She spoke again without looking up.

"Mr. Kingsley is in conference. I'll send your card in when I have an opportunity."

I thanked her and went and sat in a chromium and leather chair that was a lot more comfortable than it looked. Time passed and silence descended on the scene. Nobody came in or went out. Miss Fromsett's elegant hand moved over her papers and the muted peep of the kitten at the PBX was audible at moments, and the little click of the plugs going in and out.

I lit a cigarette and dragged a smoking stand beside the chair. The minutes went by on tiptoe, with their fingers to their lips. I looked the place over. You can't tell anything about an outfit like that. They might be making millions, and they might have the sheriff in the back room, with his chair tilted against the safe.

Half an hour and three or four cigarettes later a door opened behind Miss Fromsett's desk and two men came out backwards laughing. A third man held the door for them and helped them laugh. They all shook hands heartily and the two men went across the office and out. The third man dropped the grin off his face and looked as if he had never grinned in his life. He was a tall bird in a gray suit and he didn't want any nonsense.

"Any calls?" he asked in a sharp bossy voice.

Miss Fromsett said softly: "A Mr. Marlowe to see you. From Lieutenant M'Gee. His business is personal."

"Never heard of him," the tall man barked. He took my card, didn't even glance at me, and went back into his office. His door closed on the pneumatic closer and made a sound like 'phooey.' Miss Fromsett gave me a sweet sad smile and I gave it back to her in the form of an obscene leer. I ate another cigarette and more time staggered by. I was getting to be very fond of The Gillerlain Company.

Ten minutes later the same door opened again and the big shot came out with his hat on and sneered that he was going to get a hair-cut. He started off across the Chinese rug in a swinging athletic stride, made about half the distance to the door and then did a sharp cutback and came over to where I was sitting.

"You want to see me?" he barked.

He was about six feet two and not much of it soft. His eyes were stone gray with flecks of cold light in them. He filled a large size in smooth gray flannel with a narrow chalk stripe, and filled it elegantly. His manner said he was very tough to get along with.

I stood up. "If you're Mr. Derace Kingsley."

"Who the hell did you think I was?"

I let him have that trick and gave him my other card, the one with the business on it. He clamped it in his paw and scowled down at it.

"Who's M'Gee?" he snapped.

"He's just a fellow I know."

"I'm fascinated," he said, glancing back at Miss Fromsett. She liked it. She liked it very much. "Anything else you would care to let drop about him?"

"Well, they call him Violets M'Gee," I said. "On account of he chews little throat pastilles that smell of violets. He's a big man with soft silvery hair and a cute little mouth made to kiss babies with. When last seen he was wearing a neat blue suit, wide-toed brown shoes, gray homburg hat, and he was smoking opium in a short briar pipe."

"I don't like your manner," Kingsley said in a voice you could have cracked a Brazil nut on.

"That's all right," I said. "I'm not selling it."

He reared back as if I had hung a week-old mackerel under his nose. After a moment he turned his back on me and said over his shoulder:

"I'll give you exactly three minutes. God knows why."

He burned the carpet back past Miss Fromsett's desk to his door, yanked it open and let it swing to in my face. Miss Fromsett liked that too, but I thought there was a little sly laughter behind her eyes now.

## 2

The private office was everything a private office should be. It was long and dim and quiet and air-conditioned and its windows were shut and its gray venetian blinds half-closed to keep out the July glare. Gray drapes matched the gray carpeting. There was a large black and silver safe in the corner and a low row of low filing cases that exactly matched it. On the wall there was a huge tinted photograph of an elderly party with a chiselled beak and whiskers and a wing collar. The Adam's apple that edged through his wing collar looked harder than most people's chins. The plate underneath the photograph read: *Mr. Matthew Gillerlain 1860 –1934.*

Derace Kingsley marched briskly behind about eight hundred dollars' worth of executive desk and planted his backside in a tall leather chair. He reached himself a panatela out of a copper and mahogany box and trimmed it and lit it with a fat copper desk lighter. He took his time about it. It didn't matter about my time. When he had finished this, he leaned back and blew a little smoke and said:

"I'm a business man. I don't fool around. You're a licensed detective your card says. Show me something to prove it."

I got my wallet out and handed him things to prove it. He looked at them and threw them back across the desk. The celluloid holder with the photostat of my license in it fell to the floor. He didn't bother to apologize.

"I don't know M'Gee," he said. "I know Sheriff Petersen. I asked for the name of a reliable man to do a job. I suppose you are the man."

"M'Gee is in the Hollywood sub-station of the sheriff's office," I said. "You can check on that."

"Not necessary. I guess you might do, but don't get flip with me. And remember when I hire a man he's my man. He does exactly what I tell him and he keeps his mouth shut. Or he goes out fast. Is that clear? I hope I'm not too tough for you."

"Why not leave that an open question?" I said.

He frowned. He said sharply: "What do you charge?"

"Twenty-five a day and expenses. Eight cents a mile for my car."

"Absurd," he said. "Far too much. Fifteen a day flat. That's plenty. I'll pay the mileage, within reason, the way things are now. But no joyriding."

I blew a little gray cloud of cigarette smoke and fanned it with my hand. I said nothing. He seemed a little surprised that I said nothing.

He leaned over the desk and pointed with his cigar. "I haven't hired you yet," he said, "but if I do, the job is absolutely confidential. No talking it over with your cop friends. Is that understood?"

"Just what do you want done, Mr. Kingsley?"

"What do you care? You do all kinds of detective work, don't you?"

"Not all kinds. Only the fairly honest kinds."

He stared at me level-eyed, his jaw tight. His gray eyes had an opaque look.

"For one thing I don't do divorce business," I said. "And I get a hundred down as a retainer—from strangers."

"Well, well," he said, in a voice suddenly soft. "Well, well."

"And as for your being too tough for me," I said, "most of the clients start out either by weeping down my shirt or bawling me out to show who's boss. But usually they end up very reasonable—if they're still alive."

"Well, well," he said again, in the same soft voice, and went on staring at me. "Do you lose very many of them?" he asked.

"Not if they treat me right," I said.

"Have a cigar," he said.

I took a cigar and put it in my pocket.

"I want you to find my wife," he said. "She's been missing for a month."

"Okay," I said. "I'll find your wife."

He patted his desk with both hands. He stared at me solidly. "I think you will at that," he said. Then he grinned. "I haven't been called down like that in four years," he said.

I didn't say anything.

"Damn it all," he said, "I liked it. I liked it fine." He ran a hand through his thick dark hair. "She's been gone a whole month," he said. "From a cabin we have in the mountains. Near Puma Point. Do you know Puma Point?"

I said I knew Puma Point.

"Our place is three miles from the village," he said, "partly over a private road. It's on a private lake. Little Fawn Lake. There's a dam three of us put up to improve the property. I own the tract with two other men. It's quite large, but undeveloped and won't be developed now for some time, of course. My friends have cabins, I have a cabin and a man named Bill Chess lives with his wife in another cabin rent free and looks after the place. He's a disabled veteran with a pension. That's all there is up there. My wife went up the middle of May, came down twice for weekends, was due down the 12th of June for a party and never showed up. I haven't seen her since."

"What have you done about it?" I asked.

"Nothing. Not a thing. I haven't even been up there." He waited, wanting me to ask why.

I said: "Why?"

He pushed his chair back to get a locked drawer open. He took out a folded paper and passed it over. I unfolded it and saw it was a Postal Telegraph form. The wire had been filed at El Paso on June 14th. at 9.19 A.M. It was addressed to Derace Kingsley, 965 Carson Drive, Beverly Hills, and read:

"AM CROSSING TO GET MEXICAN DIVORCE STOP WILL MARRY CHRIS STOP GOOD LUCK AND GOODBY CRYSTAL."

I put this down on my side of the desk and he was handing me a large and very clear snapshot on glazed paper which showed a man and a woman sitting on the sand under a beach umbrella. The man wore trunks and the woman what looked like a very daring white sharkskin bathing suit. She was a slim blonde, young and shapely and smiling. The man was a hefty dark handsome lad with fine shoulders and legs, sleek dark hair and white teeth. Six feet of a standard type of home-wrecker. Arms to hold you close and all his brains in his face. He was holding a pair of dark glasses in his hand and smiling at the camera with a practised and easy smile.

"That's Crystal," Kingsley said, "and that's Chris Lavery. She can have him and he can have her and to hell with them both."

I put the photo down on the telegram. "All right, what's the catch?" I asked him.

"There's no telephone up there," he said, "and there was nothing important about the affair she was coming down for. So I got the wire before I gave much thought to it. The wire surprised me only mildly. Crystal and I have been washed up for years. She lives her life and I live mine. She has her own money and plenty of it. About twenty thousand a year from a family holding corporation that owns valuable oil leases in Texas. She plays around and I knew Lavery was one of her playmates. I might have been a little surprised that she would actually marry him, because the man is noth-ing but a professional chaser. But the picture looked all right so far, you understand?"

"And then?"

"Nothing for two weeks. Then the Prescott Hotel in San Bernardino got in touch with me and said a Packard Clipper registered to Crystal Grace Kingsley at my address was unclaimed in their garage and what about it. I told them to keep it and I sent them a check. There was nothing much in that either. I figured she was still out of the state and that if they had gone in a car at all, they had gone in Lavery's car. The day before yesterday, however, I met Lavery in front of the Athletic Club down on the corner here. He said he didn't know where Crystal was."

Kingsley gave me a quick look and reached a bottle and two tinted glasses up on the desk. He poured a couple of drinks and pushed one over. He held his against the light and said slowly:

"Lavery said he hadn't gone away with her, hadn't seen her in two months, hadn't had any communication with her of any kind."

I said, "You believed him?"

He nodded, frowning, and drank his drink and pushed the glass to one side. I tasted mine. It was Scotch. Not very good Scotch.

"If I believed him," Kingsley said, " — and I was probably wrong to do it — it wasn't because he's a fellow you have to believe. Far from it. It's because he's a no good son of a bitch who thinks it is smart to lay his friends' wives and brag about it. I feel he would have been tickled pink to stick it into me and break it off that he had got my wife to run away with him and leave me flat. I know these tomcats and I know this one too well. He rode a route for us for a while and he was in trouble all the time. He couldn't keep his hands off the office help. And apart from all that there was this wire from El Paso and I told him about it and why would he think it worth while to lie about it?"

"She might have tossed him out on his can," I said. "That would have hurt him in his deep place — his Casanova complex."

Kingsley brightened up a little, but not very much. He shook his head. "I still more than half way believe him," he said. "You'll have to prove me wrong. That's part of why I wanted you. But there's another and very worrying angle. I have a good job here, but a job is all it is. I can't stand scandal. I'd be out of here in a hurry if my wife got mixed up with the police."

"Police?"

"Among her other activities," Kingsley said grimly, "my wife occasionally finds time to lift things in department stores. I think it's just a sort of delusion of grandeur she gets when she has been hitting the bottle too hard, but it happens, and we have had some pretty nasty scenes in managers' offices. So far I've been able to keep them from filing charges, but if something like that happened in a strange city where nobody knew her——" He lifted his hands and let them fall with a smack on the desk——"well, it might be a prison matter, mightn't it?"

"Has she ever been fingerprinted?"

"She has never been arrested," he said.

"That's not what I mean. Sometimes in large department stores they make it a condition of dropping shoplifting charges that you give them your prints. It scares the amateurs and builds up a file of kleptomaniacs in their protective association. When the prints come in a certain number of times they call time on you."

"Nothing like that has happened to my knowledge," he said.

"Well, I think we might almost throw the shoplifting angle out of this for the time being," I said. "If she got arrested, she would get searched. Even if the cops let her use a Jane Doe name on the police blotter, they would be likely to get in touch with you. Also she would start yelling for help when she found herself in a jam." I tapped the blue and white telegraph form. "And this is a month old. If what you are thinking about happened around that time, the case would have been settled by now. If it was a first offense, she would get off with a scolding and a suspended sentence."

He poured himself another drink to help him with his worrying. "You're making me feel better," he said.

"There are too many other things that could have happened," I said. "That she did go away with Lavery and they split up. That she went away with some other man and the wire is a gag. That she went away alone or with a woman. That she drank herself over the edge and is holed up in some private sanatorium taking a cure. That she got into some jam we have no idea of. That she met with foul play."

"Good God, don't say that," Kingsley exclaimed.

"Why not? You've got to consider it. I get a very vague idea of Mrs. Kingsley—that she is young, pretty, reckless, and wild. That she drinks and does dangerous things when she drinks. That she is a sucker for the men and might take up with a stranger who might turn out to be a crook. Does that fit?"

He nodded. "Every word of it."

"How much money would she have with her?"

"She liked to carry enough. She has her own bank and her own bank account. She could have any amount of money."

"Any children?"

"No children."

"Do you have the management of her affairs?"

He shook his head. "She hasn't any—excepting depositing checks and drawing out money and spending it. She never invests a nickel. And her money certainly never does me any good, if that's what you are thinking." He paused and then said: "Don't think I haven't tried. I'm human and it's not fun to watch twenty thousand a year go down the drain and nothing to show for it but hangovers and boy friends of the class of Chris Lavery."

"How are you with her bank? Could you get a detail of the checks she has drawn for the past couple of months?"

"They wouldn't tell me. I tried to get some information of the sort once, when I had an idea she was being blackmailed. All I got was ice."

"We can get it," I said, "and we may have to. It will mean going to the Missing Persons Bureau. You wouldn't like that?"

"If I had liked that, I wouldn't have called you," he said.

I nodded, gathered my exhibits together and put them away in my pockets. "There are more angles to this than I can even see now," I said, "but I'll start by talking to Lavery and then taking a run up to Little Fawn Lake and asking questions there. I'll need Lavery's address and a note to your man in charge at the mountain place."

He got a letterhead out of his desk and wrote and passed it over. I read: "Dear Bill: This will introduce Mr. Philip

Marlowe who wishes to look over the property. Please show him my cabin and assist him in every way. Yrs. Derace Kingsley."

I folded this up and put it in the envelope he had addressed while I was reading it. "How about the other cabins up there?" I asked.

"Nobody up this year so far. One man's in government service in Washington and the other is at Fort Leavenworth. Their wives are with them."

"Now Lavery's address," I said.

He looked at a point well above the top of my head. "In Bay City. I could find the house but I forget the address. Miss Fromsett can give it to you, I think. She needn't know why you want it. She probably will. And you want a hundred dollars, you said."

"That's all right," I said. "That's just something I said when you were tramping on me."

He grinned. I stood up and hesitated by the desk looking at him. After a moment I said: "You're not holding anything back, are you—anything important?"

He looked at his thumb. "No. I'm not holding anything back. I'm worried and I want to know where she is. I'm damn worried. If you get anything at all, call me any time, day or night."

I said I would do that, and we shook hands and I went back down the long cool office and out to where Miss Fromsett sat elegantly at her desk.

"Mr. Kingsley thinks you can give me Chris Lavery's address," I told her and watched her face.

She reached very slowly for a brown leather address book and turned the leaves. Her voice was tight and cold when she spoke.

"The address we have is 623 Altair Street, in Bay City. Telephone Bay City 12523. Mr. Lavery has not been with us for more than a year. He may have moved."

I thanked her and went on to the door. From there I glanced back at her. She was sitting very still, with her hands clasped on her desk, staring into space. A couple of red spots burned in her cheeks. Her eyes were remote and bitter.

I got the impression that Mr. Chris Lavery was not a pleasant thought to her.

# 3

Altair Street lay on the edge of the V forming the inner end of a deep canyon. To the north was the cool blue sweep of the bay out to the point above Malibu. To the south the beach town of Bay City was spread out on a bluff above the coast highway.

It was a short street, not more than three or four blocks, and ended in a tall iron fence enclosing a large estate. Beyond the gilded spikes of the fence I could see trees and shrubs and a glimpse of lawn and part of a curving driveway, but the house was out of sight. On the inland side of Altair Street the houses were well kept and fairly large, but the few scattered bungalows on the edge of the canyon were nothing much. In the short half block ended by the iron fence were only two houses, on opposite sides of the street and almost directly across from each other. The smaller was number 623.

I drove past it, turned the car in the paved half circle at the end of the street and came back to park in front of the lot next to Lavery's place. His house was built downwards, one of those clinging vine effects, with the front door a little below street level, the patio on the roof, the bedrooms in the basement, and a garage like the corner pocket on a pool table. A crimson bougainvillea was rustling against the front wall and the flat stones of the front walk were edged with Korean moss. The door was narrow, grilled and topped by a lancet arch. Below the grill there was an iron knocker. I hammered on it.

Nothing happened. I pushed the bell at the side of the door and heard it ring inside not very far off and waited and nothing happened. I worked on the knocker again. Still nothing. I went back up the walk and along to the garage and lifted the door far enough to see that a car with white side-walled tires was inside. I went back to the front door.

A neat black Cadillac coupe came out of the garage across

the way, backed, turned and came along past Lavery's house, slowed, and a thin man in dark glasses looked at me sharply, as if I hadn't any business to be there. I gave him my steely glare and he went on his way.

I went down Lavery's walk again and did some more hammering on his knocker. This time I got results. The Judas window opened and I was looking at a handsome bright-eyed number through the bars of the grill.

"You make a hell of a lot of noise," a voice said.

"Mr. Lavery?"

He said he was Mr. Lavery and what about it. I poked a card through the grill. A large brown hand took the card. The bright brown eyes came back and the voice said: "So sorry. Not needing any detectives today please."

"I'm working for Derace Kingsley."

"The hell with both of you," he said, and banged the Judas window.

I leaned on the bell beside the door and got a cigarette out with my free hand and had just struck the match on the woodwork beside the door when it was yanked open and a big guy in bathing trunks, beach sandals, and a white terrycloth bathrobe started to come out at me.

I took my thumb off the bell and grinned at him. "What's the matter?" I asked him. "Scared?"

"Ring that bell again," he said, "and I'll throw you clear across the street."

"Don't be childish," I told him. "You know perfectly well I'm going to talk to you and you're going to talk to me."

I got the blue and white telegram out of my pocket and held it in front of his bright brown eyes. He read it morosely, chewed his lip and growled:

"Oh for Chrissake, come on in then."

He held the door wide and I went in past him, into a dim pleasant room with an apricot Chinese rug that looked expensive, deepsided chairs, a number of white drum lamps, a big Capehart in the corner, a long and very wide davenport in pale tan mohair shot with dark brown, and a fireplace with a copper screen and an overmantel in white wood. A fire was laid behind the screen and partly masked by a large spray of manzanita bloom. The bloom was turning yellow in places, but was still pretty. There was a bottle of Vat 69 and glasses on a tray and a copper icebucket on a low round burl walnut table with a glass top. The room went clear to the back of the house and ended in a flat arch through which showed three narrow windows and the top few feet of the white iron railing of the staircase going down.

Lavery swung the door shut and sat on the davenport. He grabbed a cigarette out of a hammered silver box and lit it and looked at me irritably. I sat down opposite him and looked him over. He had everything in the way of good looks the snapshot had indicated. He had a terrific torso and magnificent thighs. His eyes were chestnut brown and the whites of them slightly gray-white. His hair was rather long and curled a little over his temples. His brown skin showed no signs of dissipation. He was a nice piece of beef, but to me that was all he was. I could understand that women would think he was something to yell for.

"Why not tell us where she is?" I said. "We'll find out eventually anyway and if you tell us now, we won't be bothering you."

"It would take more than a private dick to bother me," he said.

"No, it wouldn't. A private dick can bother anybody. He's persistent and used to snubs. He's paid for his time and he would just as soon use it to bother you as any other way."

"Look," he said, leaning forward and pointing his cigarette at me. "I know what that wire says, but it's the bunk. I didn't go to El Paso with Crystal Kingsley. I haven't seen her in a long time—long before the date of that wire. I haven't had any contact with her. I told Kingsley that."

"He didn't have to believe you."

"Why would I lie to him?" He looked surprised.

"Why wouldn't you?"

"Look," he said earnestly, "it might seem so to you, but you don't know her. Kingsley has no strings on her. If he doesn't like the way she behaves he has a remedy. These proprietary husbands make me sick."

"If you didn't go to El Paso with her," I said, "why did she send this telegram?"

"I haven't the faintest idea."

"You can do better than that," I said. I pointed to the spray of manzanita in the fireplace. "You pick that up at Little Fawn Lake?"

"The hills around here are full of manzanita," he said contemptuously.

"It doesn't bloom like that down here."

He laughed. "I was up there the third week in May. If you have to know. I suppose you can find out. That's the last time I saw her."

"You didn't have any idea of marrying her?"

He blew smoke and said through it: "I've thought of it, yes. She has money. Money is always useful. But it would be too tough a way to make it."

I nodded, but didn't say anything. He looked at the manzanita spray in the fireplace and leaned back to blow smoke in the air and show me the strong brown line of his throat. After a moment, when I still didn't say anything, he began to get restless. He glanced down at the card I had given him and said:

"So you hire yourself out to dig up dirt? Doing well at it?"

"Nothing to brag about. A dollar here, a dollar there."

"And all of them pretty slimy," he said.

"Look, Mr. Lavery, we don't have to get into a fight. Kingsley thinks you know where his wife is, but won't tell him. Either out of meanness or motives of delicacy."

"Which way would he like it?" the handsome brown-faced man sneered.

"He doesn't care, as long as he gets the information. He doesn't care a great deal what you and she do together or where you go or whether she divorces him or not. He just wants to feel sure that everything is all right and that she isn't in trouble of any kind."

Lavery looked interested. "Trouble? What kind of trouble?" He licked the word around on his brown lips, tasting it.

"Maybe you won't know the kind of trouble he is thinking of."

"Tell me," he pleaded sarcastically. "I'd just love to hear about some kind of trouble I didn't know about."

"You're doing fine," I told him. "No time to talk business, but always time for a wisecrack. If you think we might try to get a hook into you because you crossed a state line with her, forget it."

"Go climb up your thumb, wise guy. You'd have to prove I paid the freight, or it wouldn't mean anything."

"This wire has to mean something," I said stubbornly. It seemed to me that I had said it before, several times.

"It's probably just a gag. She's full of little tricks like that. All of them silly, and some of them vicious."

"I don't see any point in this one."

He flicked cigarette ash carelessly at the glass top table. He gave me a quick up from under look and immediately looked away.

"I stood her up," he said slowly. "It might be her idea of a way to get back at me. I was supposed to run up there one week-end. I didn't go. I was—sick of her."

I said: "Uh-huh," and gave him a long steady stare. "I don't like that so well. I'd like it better if you did go to El Paso with her and had a fight and split up. Could you tell it that way?"

He flashed solidly behind the sunburn.

"God damn it," he said, "I told you I didn't go anywhere with her. Not anywhere. Can't you remember that?"

"I'll remember it when I believe it."

He leaned over to snub out his cigarette. He stood up with an easy movement, not hurried at all, pulled the belt of his robe tight, and moved out to the end of the davenport.

"All right," he said in a clear tight voice. "Out you go. Take the air. I've had enough of your third-degree tripe. You're wasting my time and your own—if it's worth anything."

I stood up and grinned at him. "Not a lot, but for what it's worth I'm being paid for it. It couldn't be, for instance, that you ran into a little unpleasantness in some department store—say at the stocking or jewelry counter."

He looked at me very carefully, drawing his eyebrows down at the corners and making his mouth small.

"I don't get it," he said, but there was thought behind his voice.

"That's all I wanted to know," I said. "And thanks for listening. By the way, what line of business are you in—since you left Kingsley?"

"What the hell business is it of yours?"

"None. But of course I can always find out," I said, and moved a little way towards the door, not very far.

"At the moment I'm not doing anything," he said coldly. "I expect a commission in the navy almost any day."

"You ought to do well at that," I said.

"Yeah. So long, snooper. And don't bother to come back. I won't be at home."

I went over to the door and pulled it open. It stuck on the lower sill, from the beach moisture. When I had it open, I looked back at him. He was standing there narrow-eyed, full of muted thunder.

"I may have to come back," I said. "But it won't be just to swop gags. It will be because I find something out that needs talking over."

"So you still think I'm lying," he said savagely.

"I think you have something on your mind. I've looked at too many faces not to know. It may not be any of my business. If it is, you're likely to have to throw me out again."

"A pleasure," he said. "And next time bring somebody to drive you home. In case you land on your fanny and knock your brains out."

Then without any rhyme or reason that I could see, he spat on the rug in front of his feet.

It jarred me. It was like watching the veneer peel off and leave a tough kid in an alley. Or like hearing an apparently refined woman start expressing herself in four-letter words.

"So long, beautiful hunk," I said, and left him standing there. I closed the door, had to jerk it to get it shut, and went up the path to the street. I stood on the sidewalk looking at the house across the way.

# 4

It was a wide shallow house with rose stucco walls faded out to a pleasant pastel shade and trimmed with dull green at the window frames. The roof was of green tiles, round rough ones. There was a deeply inset front door framed in a mosaic of multi-colored pieces of tiling and a small flower garden in front, behind a low stucco wall topped by an iron railing which the beach moisture had begun to corrode. Outside the wall to the left was the three-car garage, with a door opening inside the yard and a concrete path going from there to a side door of the house.

Set into the gate post was a bronze tablet which read: "Albert S. Almore, M.D."

While I was standing there staring across the street, the black Cadillac I had already seen came purring around the corner and then down the block. It slowed and started to sweep outwards to get turning space to go into the garage, decided my car was in the way of that, and went on to the end of the road and turned in the widened-out space in front of the ornamental iron railing. It came back slowly and went into the empty third of the garage across the way.

The thin man in sun glasses went along the sidewalk to the house, carrying a double-handled doctor's bag. Halfway along he slowed down to stare across at me. I went along towards my car. At the house he used a key and as he opened the door he looked across at me again.

I got into the Chrysler and sat there smoking and trying to make up my mind whether it was worth while hiring somebody to pull a tail on Lavery. I decided it wasn't, not the way things looked so far.

Curtains moved at a lower window close to the side door Dr. Almore had gone in at. A thin hand held them aside and I caught the glint of light on glasses. They were held aside for quite some time, before they fell together again.

I looked along the street at Lavery's house. From this angle I could see that his service porch gave on a flight of painted wooden steps to a sloping concrete walk and a flight of concrete steps ending in the paved alley below.

I looked across at Dr. Almore's house again, wondering idly if he knew Lavery and how well. He probably knew him, since theirs were the only two houses in the block. But being a doctor, he wouldn't tell me anything about him. As I looked, the curtains which had been lifted apart were now completely drawn aside.

The middle segment of the triple window they had masked had no screen. Behind it, Dr. Almore stood staring across my way, with a sharp frown on his thin face. I shook cigarette ash out of the window and he turned abruptly and sat down at a desk. His double-handled bag was on the desk in front of him. He sat rigidly, drumming on the desk beside the bag. His hand reached for the telephone, touched it and came away again. He lit a cigarette and shook the match violently, then strode to the window and stared out at me some more.

This was interesting, if at all, only because he was a doctor. Doctors, as a rule, are the least curious of men. While they are still internes they hear enough secrets to last them a lifetime. Dr. Almore seemed interested in me. More than interested, bothered.

I reached down to turn the ignition key, then Lavery's front door opened and I took my hand away and leaned back again. Lavery came briskly up the walk of his house, shot a glance down the street and turned to go into his garage. He was dressed as I had seen him. He had a rough towel and a steamer rug over his arm. I heard the garage door lift up, then the car door open and shut, then the grind and cough of the starting car. It backed up the steep incline to the street, white steamy exhaust pouring from its rear end. It was a cute little blue convertible, with the top folded down and Lavery's sleek dark head just rising above it. He was now wearing a natty pair of sun-goggles with very wide white sidebows. The convertible swooped off down the block and danced around the corner.

There was nothing in that for me. Mr. Christopher Lavery was bound for the edge of the broad Pacific, to lie in the sun and let the girls see what they didn't necessarily have to go on missing.

I gave my attention back to Dr. Almore. He was on the telephone now, not talking, holding it to his ear, smoking and waiting. Then he leaned forward as you do when the voice comes back, listened, hung up and wrote something on a pad in front of him. Then a heavy book with yellow sides appeared on his desk and he opened it just about in the middle. While he was doing this he gave one quick look out of the window, straight at the Chrysler.

He found his place in the book, leaned down over it and quick puffs of smoke appeared in the air over the pages. He wrote something else, put the book away, and grabbed for the telephone again. He dialed, waited, began to speak quickly, pushing his head down and making gestures in the air with his cigarette.

He finished his call and hung up. He leaned back and sat there brooding, staring down at his desk, but not forgetting to look out of the window every half minute. He was waiting, and I waited with him, for no reason at all. Doctors make many phone calls, talk to many people. Doctors look out of their front windows, doctors frown, doctors show nervousness, doctors have things on their mind and show the strain. Doctors are just people, born to sorrow, fighting the long grim fight like the rest of us.

But there was something about the way this one behaved that intrigued me. I looked at my watch, decided it was time to get something to eat, lit another cigarette and didn't move.

It took about five minutes. Then a green sedan whisked around the corner and bore down the block. It coasted to a stop in front of Dr. Almore's house and its tall buggywhip aerial quivered. A big man with dusty blond hair got out and went up to Dr. Almore's front door. He rang the bell and leaned down to strike a match on the step. His head came around and he stared across the street exactly at where I was sitting.

The door opened and he went into the house. An invisible hand gathered the curtains at Dr. Almore's study window and blanked the room. I sat there and stared at the sun-darkened lining of the curtains. More time trickled by.

The front door opened again and the big man loafed casually down the steps and through the gate. He snapped his cigarette end off into the distance and rumpled his hair. He shrugged once, pinched the end of his chin, and walked diagonally across the street. His steps in the quiet were leisurely and distinct. Dr. Almore's curtains moved apart again behind him. Dr. Almore stood in his window and watched.

A large freckled hand appeared on the sill of the car door at my elbow. A large face, deeply-lined hung above it. The man had eyes of metallic blue. He looked at me solidly and spoke in a deep harsh voice.

"Waiting for somebody?" he asked.

"I don't know," I said. "Am I?"

"I'll ask the questions."

"Well, I'll be damned," I said. "So that's the answer to the pantomime."

"What pantomime?" He gave me a hard level unfriendly stare from his very blue eyes.

I pointed across the street with my cigarette. "Nervous Nellie and the telephone. Calling the cops, after first getting my name from the Auto Club, probably, then looking it up in the city directory. What goes on?"

"Let me see your driver's license."

I gave him back his stare. "You fellows ever flash a buzzer—or is acting tough all the identification you need?"

"If I have to get tough, fellow, you'll know it."

I leaned down and turned my ignition key and pressed the starter. The motor caught and idled down.

"Cut that motor," he said savagely, and put his foot on the running-board.

I cut the motor again and leaned back and looked at him.

"God damn it," he said, "do you want me to drag you out of there and bounce you on the pavement?"

I got my wallet out and handed it to him. He drew the celluloid pocket out and looked at my driver's license, then turned the pocket over and looked at the photostat of my other license on the back. He rammed it contemptuously back into the wallet and handed me the wallet. I put it away. His hand dipped and came up with a blue and gold police badge.

"Degarmo, detective-lieutenant," he said in his heavy brutal voice.

"Pleased to meet you, lieutenant."

"Skip it. Now tell why you're down here casing Almore's place."

"I'm not casing Almore's place, as you put it, lieutenant. I never heard of Dr. Almore and I don't know of any reason why I should want to case his house."

He turned his head to spit. I was meeting the spitting boys today.

"What's your grift then? We don't like peepers down here. We don't have one in town."

"Is that so?"

"Yeah, that's so. So come on, talk it up. Unless you want to ride down to the clubhouse and sweat it out under the bright lights."

I didn't answer him.

"Her folks hire you?" he asked suddenly.

I shook my head.

"The last boy that tried it ended up on the road gang, sweetheart."

"I bet it's good," I said, "if only I could guess. Tried what?"

"Tried to put the bite on him," he said thinly.

"Too bad I don't know how," I said. "He looks like an easy man to bite."

"That line of talk don't buy you anything," he said.

"All right," I said. "Let's put it this way. I don't know Dr. Almore, never heard of him, and I'm not interested in him. I'm down here visiting a friend and looking at the view. If I'm doing anything else, it doesn't happen to be any of your business. If you don't like that, the best thing to do is to take it down to headquarters and see the day captain."

He moved a foot heavily on the running-board and looked doubtful. "Straight goods?" he asked slowly.

"Straight goods."

"Aw hell, the guy's screwy," he said suddenly and looked back over his shoulder at the house. "He ought to see a doctor." He laughed, without any amusement in the laugh. He took his foot off my runningboard and rumpled his wiry hair.

"Go on—beat it," he said. "Stay off our reservation, and you won't make any enemies."

I pressed the starter again. When the motor was idling gently I said: "How's Al Norgaard these days?"

He stared at me. "You knew Al?"

"Yeah. He and I worked on a case down here a couple of years ago—when Wax was chief of police."

"Al's in the military police. Wish I was," he said bitterly. He started to walk away and then swung sharply on his heel. "Go on, beat it before I change my mind," he snapped.

He walked heavily across the street and through Dr. Almore's front gate again.

I let the clutch in and drove away. On the way back to the city, I listened to my thoughts. They moved fitfully in and out, like Dr. Almore's thin nervous hands pulling at the edges of his curtains.

Back in Los Angeles I ate lunch and went up to my office in the Cahuenga Building to see what mail there was. I called Kingsley from there.

"I saw Lavery," I told him. "He told me just enough dirt to sound frank. I tried to needle him a little, but nothing came of it. I still like the idea that they quarreled and split up and that he hopes to fix it up with her yet."

"Then he must know where she is," Kingsley said.

"He might, but it doesn't follow. By the way a rather curious thing happened to me on Lavery's street. There are only two houses. The other belongs to a Dr. Almore." I told him briefly about the rather curious thing.

He was silent for a moment at the end and then he said: "Is this Dr. Albert Almore?"

"Yes?"

"He was Crystal's doctor for a time. He came to the house several times when she was—well, when she had been over-drinking. I thought him a little too quick with a hypodermic needle. His wife—let me see, there was something about his wife. Oh yes, she committed suicide."

I said, "When?"

"I don't remember. Quite a long time ago. I never knew them socially. What are you going to do now?"

I told him I was going up to Puma Lake, although it was a little late in the day to start.

He said I would have plenty of time and that they had an hour more of daylight in the mountains.

I said that was fine and we hung up.

# 5

San Bernardino baked and shimmered in the afternoon heat. The air was hot enough to blister my tongue. I drove through it gasping, stopped long enough to buy a pint of liquor in case I fainted before I got to the mountains, and started up the long grade to Crestline. In fifteen miles the road climbed five thousand feet, but even then it was far from cool. Thirty miles of mountain driving brought me to the tall pines and a place called Bubbling Springs. It had a clapboard store and a gas pump, but it felt like paradise. From there on it was cool all the way.

The Puma Lake dam had an armed sentry at each end and one in the middle. The first one I came to had me close all the windows of the car before crossing over the dam. About a hundred yards from the dam a rope with cork floats barred the pleasure boats from coming any closer. Beyond these details the war did not seem to have done anything much to Puma Lake.

Canoes paddled about on the blue water and rowboats with outboard motors put-putted and speed boats showing off like fresh kids made wide swathes of foam and turned on a dime and girls in them shrieked and dragged their hands in the water. Jounced around in the wake of the speedboats people who had paid two dollars for a fishing license were trying to get a dime of it back in tired-tasting fish.

The road skimmed along a high granite outcrop and dropped to meadows of coarse grass in which grew what was left of the wild irises and white and purple lupine and bugle flowers and columbine and penny-royal and desert paint brush. Tall yellow pines probed at the clear blue sky. The road dropped again to lake level and the landscape began to be full of girls in gaudy slacks and snoods and peasant handkerchiefs and rat rolls and fatsoled sandals and fat white thighs. People on bicycles wobbled cautiously over the highway and now and then an anxious-looking bird thumped past on a power-scooter.

A mile from the village the highway was joined by another lesser road which curved back into the mountains. A rough wooden sign under the highway sign said: *Little Fawn Lake 1¾ miles*. I took it. Scattered cabins were perched along the slopes for the first mile and then nothing. Presently another very narrow road debouched from this one and another rough wood sign said: *Little Fawn Lake. Private Road. No Trespassing*.

I turned the Chrysler into this and crawled carefully around huge bare granite rocks and past a little waterfall and through a maze of black oak trees and ironwood and manzanita and silence. A bluejay squawked on a branch and a squirrel scolded at me and beat one paw angrily on the pine cone it was holding. A scarlet-topped woodpecker stopped probing in the bark long enough to look at me with one beady eye and then dodge behind the tree trunk to look at me with the other one. I came to a five-barred gate and another sign.

Beyond the gate the road wound for a couple of hundred yards through trees and then suddenly below me was a small oval lake deep in trees and rocks and wild grass, like a drop of dew caught in a curled leaf. At the near end of it was a rough concrete dam with a rope hand-rail across the top and an old millwheel at the side. Near that stood a small cabin of native pine with the bark on it.

Across the lake the long way by the road and the short way by the top of the dam a large redwood cabin overhung the water and farther along, each well separated from the others, were two other cabins. All three were shut up and quiet, with drawn curtains. The big one had orange-yellow venetian blinds and a twelve-paned window facing on the lake.

At the far end of the lake from the dam was what looked like a small pier and band pavilion. A warped wooden sign on it was painted in large white letters: *Camp Kilkare*. I couldn't see any sense in that in these surroundings, so I got out of the car and started down towards the nearest cabin. Somewhere behind it an axe thudded.

I pounded on the cabin door. The axe stopped. A man's voice yelled from somewhere. I sat down on a rock and lit a cigarette. Steps came around the corner of the cabin, uneven steps. A man with a harsh face and a swarthy skin came into view carrying a double-bitted axe.

He was heavily-built and not very tall and he limped as he

walked, giving his right leg a little kick out with each step and swinging the foot in a shallow arc. He had a dark unshaven chin and steady blue eyes and grizzled hair that curled over his ears and needed cutting badly. He wore blue denim pants and a blue shirt open on a brown muscular neck. A cigarette hung from the corner of his mouth. He spoke in a tight tough city voice.

"Yeah?"

"Mr. Bill Chess?"

"That's me."

I stood up and got Kingsley's note of introduction out of my pocket and handed it to him. He squinted at the note, then clumped into the cabin and came back with glasses perched on his nose. He read the note carefully and then again. He put it in his shirt pocket, buttoned the flap of the pocket, and put his hand out.

"Pleased to meet you, Mr. Marlowe."

We shook hands. He had a hand like a wood rasp.

"You want to see Kingsley's cabin, huh? Glad to show you. He ain't selling for Chrissake?" He eyed me steadily and jerked a thumb across the lake.

"He might," I said. "Everything's for sale in California."

"Ain't that the truth? That's his—the redwood job. Lined with knotty pine, composition roof, stone foundations and porches, full bath and shower, venetian blinds all around, big fireplace, oil stove in the big bedroom—and brother, you need it in the spring and fall—Pilgrim combination gas and wood range, everything first class. Cost about eight thousand and that's money for a mountain cabin. And private reservoir in the hills for water."

"How about electric light and telephone?" I asked, just to be friendly.

"Electric light, sure. No phone. You couldn't get one now. If you could, it would cost plenty to string the lines out here."

He looked at me with steady blue eyes and I looked at him. In spite of his weathered appearance he looked like a drinker. He had the thickened and glossy skin, the too noticeable veins, the bright glitter in the eyes.

I said: "Anybody living there now?"

"Nope. Mrs. Kingsley was here a few weeks back. She went down the hill. Back any day, I guess. Didn't he say?"

I looked surprised. "Why? Does she go with the cabin?"

He scowled and then put his head back and burst out laughing. The roar of his laughter was like a tractor backfiring. It blasted the woodland silence to shreds.

"Jesus, if that ain't a kick in the pants!" he gasped. "Does she go with the—" He put out another bellow and then his mouth shut tight as a trap.

"Yeah, it's a swell cabin," he said, eyeing me carefully.

"The beds comfortable?" I asked.

He leaned forward and smiled. "Maybe you'd like a face full of knuckles," he said.

I stared at him with my mouth open. "That one went by me too fast," I said, "I never laid an eye on it."

"How would I know if the beds are comfortable?" he snarled, bending down a little so that he could reach me with a hard right, if it worked out that way.

"I don't know why you wouldn't know," I said. "I won't press the point. I can find out for myself."

"Yah," he said bitterly, "think I can't smell a dick when I meet one? I played hit and run with them in every state in the Union. Nuts to you, pal. And nuts to Kingsley. So he hires himself a dick to come up here and see am I wearing his pajamas, huh? Listen, Jack, I might have a stiff leg and all, but the women I could get—"

I put a hand out, hoping he wouldn't pull it off and throw it in the lake.

"You're slipping your clutch," I told him. "I didn't come up here to enquire into your love life. I never saw Mrs. Kingsley. I never saw Mr. Kingsley until this morning. What the hell's the matter with you?"

He dropped his eyes and rubbed the back of his hand viciously across his mouth, as if he wanted to hurt himself. Then he held the hand in front of his eyes and squeezed it into a hard fist and opened it again and stared at the fingers. They were shaking a little.

"Sorry, Mr. Marlowe," he said slowly. "I was out on the

roof last night and I've got a hangover like seven Swedes. I've been up here alone for a month and it's got me talking to myself. A thing happened to me."

"Anything a drink would help?"

His eyes focussed sharply on me and glinted. "You got one?"

I pulled the pint of rye out of my pocket and held it so that he could see the green label over the cap.

"I don't deserve it," he said. "God damn it, I don't. Wait till I get a couple of glasses or would you come into the cabin?"

"I like it out here. I'm enjoying the view."

He swung his stiff leg and went into his cabin and came back carrying a couple of small cheese glasses. He sat down on the rock beside me smelling of dried perspiration.

I tore the metal cap off the bottle and poured him a stiff drink and a light one for myself. We touched glasses and drank. He rolled the liquor on his tongue and a bleak smile put a little sunshine into his face.

"Man that's from the right bottle," he said. "I wonder what made me sound off like that. I guess a guy gets the blues up here all alone. No company, no real friends, no wife." He paused and added with a sidewise look. "Especially no wife."

I kept my eyes on the blue water of the tiny lake. Under an overhanging rock a fish surfaced in a lance of light and a circle of widening ripples. A light breeze moved the tops of the pines with a noise like a gentle surf.

"She left me," he said slowly. "She left me a month ago. Friday the 12th of June. A day I'll remember."

I stiffened, but not too much to pour more whiskey into his empty glass. Friday the 12th of June was the day Mrs. Crystal Kingsley was supposed to have come into town for a party.

"But you don't want to hear about that," he said. And in his faded blue eyes was the deep yearning to talk about it, as plain as anything could possibly be.

"It's none of my business," I said. "But if it would make you feel any better —"

He nodded sharply. "Two guys will meet on a park bench," he said, "and start talking about God. Did you ever notice that? Guys that wouldn't talk about God to their best friend."

"I know that," I said.

He drank and looked across the lake. "She was one swell kid," he said softly. "A little sharp in the tongue sometimes, but one swell kid. It was love at first sight with me and Muriel. I met her in a joint in Riverside, a year and three months ago. Not the kind of joint where a guy would expect to meet a girl like Muriel, but that's how it happened. We got married. I loved her. I knew I was well off. And I was too much of a skunk to play ball with her."

I moved a little to show him I was still there, but I didn't say anything for fear of breaking the spell. I sat with my drink untouched in my hand. I like to drink, but not when people are using me for a diary.

He went on sadly: "But you know how it is with marriage—any marriage. After a while a guy like me, a common no good guy like me, he wants to feel a leg. Some other leg. Maybe it's lousy, but that's the way it is."

He looked at me and I said I had heard the idea expressed.

He tossed his second drink off. I passed him the bottle. A blue jay went up a pine tree hopping from branch to branch without moving his wings or even pausing to balance.

"Yeah," Bill Chess said. "All these hillbillies are half crazy and I'm getting that way too. Here I am sitting pretty, no rent to pay, a good pension check every month, half my bonus money in war bonds, I'm married to as neat a little blonde as ever you clapped an eye on and all the time I'm nuts and I don't know it. I go for *that*." He pointed hard at the redwood cabin across the lake. It was turning the color of oxblood in the late afternoon light. "Right in the front yard," he said, "right under the windows, and a showy little tart that means no more to me than a blade of grass. Jesus, what a sap a guy can be."

He drank his third drink and steadied the bottle on a rock. He fished a cigarette out of his shirt, fired a match on his thumbnail and puffed rapidly. I breathed with my mouth open, as silent as a burglar behind a curtain.

"Hell," he said at last, "you'd think if I had to jump off the dock, I'd go a little ways from home and pick me a change in types at least. But little roundheels over there ain't even that. She's a blonde like Muriel, same size and weight, same type, almost the same color eyes. But, brother, how different from then on in. Pretty, sure, but no prettier to anybody and not half so pretty to me. Well, I'm over there burning trash that morning and minding my own business, as much as I ever mind it. And she comes to the back door of the cabin in peekaboo pajamas so thin you can see the pink of her nipples against the cloth. And she says in her lazy, no-good voice: 'Have a drink, Bill. Don't work so hard on such a beautiful morning.' And me, I like a drink too well and I go to the kitchen door and take it. And then I take another and then I take another and then I'm in the house. And the closer I get to her the more bedroom her eyes are."

He paused and swept me with a hard level look.

"You asked me if the beds over there were comfortable and I got sore. You didn't mean a thing. I was just too full of remembering. Yeah—the bed I was in was comfortable."

He stopped talking and I let his words hang in the air. They fell slowly and after them was silence. He leaned to pick the bottle off the rock and stare at it. He seemed to fight with it in his mind. The whiskey won the fight, as it always does. He took a long savage drink out of the bottle and then screwed the cap on tightly, as if that meant something. He picked up a stone and flicked it into the water.

"I came back across the dam," he said slowly, in a voice already thick with alcohol. "I'm as smooth as a new piston head. I'm getting away with something. Us boys can be so wrong about those little things, can't we? I'm not getting away with anything at all. Not anything at all. I listen to Muriel telling me and she don't even raise her voice. But she tells me things about myself I didn't even imagine. Oh yeah, I'm getting away with it lovely."

"So she left you," I said, when he fell silent.

"That night. I wasn't even here. I felt too mean to stay even half sober. I hopped into my Ford and went over to the north side of the lake and holed up with a couple of no-goods like myself and got good and stinking. Not that it did me any good. Along about 4 a.m. I got back home and Muriel is gone, packed up and gone, nothing left but a note on the bureau and some cold cream on the pillow."

He pulled a dog-eared piece of paper out of a shabby old

wallet and passed it over. It was written in pencil on blue-lined paper from a note book. It read:

"I'm sorry, Bill, but I'd rather be dead than live with you any longer. Muriel."

I handed it back. "What about over there?" I asked, pointing across the lake with a glance.

Bill Chess picked up a flat stone and tried to skip it across the water, but it refused to skip.

"Nothing over there," he said. "She packed up and went down the same night. I didn't see her again. I don't want to see her again. I haven't heard a word from Muriel in the whole month, not a single word. I don't have any idea at all where she's at. With some other guy, maybe. I hope he treats her better than I did."

He stood up and took keys out of his pocket and shook them. "So if you want to go across and look at Kingsley's cabin, there isn't a thing to stop you. And thanks for listening to the soap opera. And thanks for the liquor. Here." He picked the bottle up and handed me what was left of the pint.

# 6

We went down the slope to the bank of the lake and the narrow top of the dam. Bill Chess swung his stiff leg in front of me, holding on to the rope handrail set in iron stanchions. At one point water washed over the concrete in a lazy swirl.

"I'll let some out through the wheel in the morning," he said over his shoulder. "That's all the darn thing is good for. Some movie outfit put it up three years ago. They made a picture up here. That little pier down at the other end is some more of their work. Most of what they built is torn down and hauled away, but Kingsley had them leave the pier and the millwheel. Kind of gives the place a touch of color."

I followed him up a flight of heavy wooden steps to the porch of the Kingsley cabin. He unlocked the door and we went into hushed warmth. The closed up room was almost hot. The light filtering through the slatted blinds made narrow bars across the floor. The living room was long and cheerful and had Indian rugs, padded mountain furniture with metal-strapped joints, chintz curtains, a plain hardwood floor, plenty of lamps and a little built-in bar with round stools in one corner. The room was neat and clean and had no look of having been left at short notice.

We went into the bedrooms. Two of them had twin beds and one a large double bed with a cream-colored spread having a design in plum-colored wool stitched over it. This was the master bed room, Bill Chess said. On a dresser of varnished wood there were toilet articles and accessories in jade green enamel and stainless steel, and an assortment of cosmetic oddments. A couple of cold cream jars had the wavy gold brand of the Gillerlain Company on them. One whole side of the room consisted of closets with sliding doors. I slid one open and peeked inside. It seemed to be full of women's clothes of the sort they wear at resorts. Bill Chess watched me sourly while I pawed them over. I slid the door shut and pulled open a deep shoe drawer underneath. It contained at least half a dozen pairs of new-looking shoes. I heaved the drawer shut and straightened up.

Bill Chess was planted squarely in front of me, with his chin pushed out and his hard hands in knots on his hips.

"So what did you want to look at the lady's clothes for?" he asked in an angry voice.

"Reasons," I said. "For instance Mrs. Kingsley didn't go home when she left here. Her husband hasn't seen her since. He doesn't know where she is."

He dropped his fists and twisted them slowly at his sides. "Dick it is," he snarled. "The first guess is always right. I had myself about talked out of it. Boy, did I open up to you. Nellie with her hair in her lap. Boy, am I a smart little egg!"

"I can respect a confidence as well as the next fellow," I said, and walked around him into the kitchen.

There was a big green and white combination range, a sink of lacquered yellow pine, an automatic water heater in the service porch, and opening off the other side of the kitchen a cheerful breakfast room with many windows and an expansive plastic breakfast set. The shelves were gay with colored dishes and glasses and a set of pewter serving dishes.

Everything was in apple-pie order. There were no dirty cups or plates on the drain board, no smeared glasses or empty liquor bottles hanging around. There were no ants and no flies. Whatever loose living Mrs. Derace Kingsley indulged in she managed without leaving the usual Greenwich Village slop behind her.

I went back to the living room and out on the front porch again and waited for Bill Chess to lock up. When he had done that and turned to me with his scowl well in place I said:

"I didn't ask you to take your heart out and squeeze it for me, but I didn't try to stop you either. Kingsley doesn't have to know his wife made a pass at you, unless there's a lot more behind all this than I can see now."

"The hell with you," he said, and the scowl stayed right where it was.

"All right, the hell with me. Would there be any chance your wife and Kingsley's wife went away together?"

"I don't get it," he said.

"After you went to drown your troubles they could have had a fight and made up and cried down each other's necks. Then Mrs. Kingsley might have taken your wife down the hill. She had to have something to ride in, didn't she?"

It sounded silly, but he took it seriously enough.

"Nope. Muriel didn't cry down anybody's neck. They left the weeps out of Muriel. And if she did want to cry on a shoulder, she wouldn't have picked little roundheels. And as for transportation she has a Ford of her own. She couldn't drive mine easily on account of the way the controls are switched over for my stiff leg."

"It was just a passing thought," I said.

"If any more like it pass you, let them go right on," he said.

"For a guy that takes his long wavy hair down in front of complete strangers, you're pretty damn touchy," I said.

He took a step towards me. "Want to make something of it?"

"Look, pal," I said, "I'm working hard to think you are a fundamentally good egg. Help me out a little, can't you?"

He breathed hard for a moment and then dropped his hands and spread them helplessly.

"Boy, can I brighten up anybody's afternoon," he sighed. "Want to walk back around the lake?"

"Sure, if your leg will stand it."

"Stood it plenty of times before."

We started off side by side, as friendly as puppies again. It would probably last all of fifty yards. The roadway, barely wide enough to pass a car, hung above the level of the lake and dodged between high rocks. About half way to the far end another smaller cabin was built on a rock foundation. The third was well beyond the end of the lake, on a patch of almost level ground. Both were closed up and had that long-empty look.

Bill Chess said after a minute or two: "That straight goods little roundheels lammed off?"

"So it seems."

"You a real dick or just a shamus?"

"Just a shamus."

"She go with some guy?"

"I should think it likely."

"Sure she did. It's a cinch. Kingsley ought to be able to guess that. She had plenty of friends."

"Up here?"

He didn't answer me.

"Was one of them named Lavery?"

"I wouldn't know," he said.

"There's no secret about this one," I said. "She sent a wire from El Paso saying she and Lavery were going to Mexico." I dug the wire out of my pocket and held it out. He fumbled his glasses loose from his shirt and stopped to read it. He handed the paper back and put his glasses away again and stared out over the blue water.

"That's a little confidence for you to hold against some of what you gave me," I said.

"Lavery was up here once," he said slowly.

"He admits he saw her a couple of months ago, probably up here. He claims he hasn't seen her since. We don't know whether to believe him. There's no reason why we should and no reason why we shouldn't."

"She isn't with him now, then?"

"He says not."

"I wouldn't think she would fuss with little details like getting married," he said soberly. "A Florida honeymoon would be more in her line."

"But you can't give me any positive information? You didn't see her go or hear anything that sounded authentic?"

"Nope," he said. "And if I did, I doubt if I would tell. I'm dirty, but not that kind of dirty."

"Well, thanks for trying," I said.

"I don't owe you any favors," he said. "The hell with you and every other God damn snooper."

"Here we go again," I said.

We had come to the end of the lake now. I left him standing there and walked out on the little pier. I leaned on the wooden railing at the end of it and saw that what had looked like a band pavilion was nothing but two pieces of propped up wall meeting at a flat angle towards the dam. About two feet deep of overhanging roof was stuck on the wall, like a coping. Bill Chess came up behind me and leaned on the railing at my side.

"Not that I don't thank you for the liquor," he said.

"Yeah. Any fish in the lake?"

"Some smart old bastards of trout. No fresh stock. I don't go for fish much myself. I don't bother with them. Sorry I got tough again."

I grinned and leaned on the railing and stared down into the deep still water. It was green when you looked down into it. There was a swirl of movement down there and a swift greenish form moved in the water.

"There's Granpa," Bill Chess said. "Look at the size of that old bastard. He ought to be ashamed of himself getting so fat."

Down below the water there was what looked like an underwater flooring. I couldn't see the sense of that. I asked him.

"Used to be a boat landing before the dam was raised. That lifted the water level so far the old landing was six feet under."

A flat-bottomed boat dangled on a frayed rope tied to a post of the pier. It lay in the water almost without motion, but not quite. The air was peaceful and calm and sunny and held a quiet you don't get in cities. I could have stayed there for hours doing nothing but forgetting all about Derace Kingsley and his wife and her boy friends.

There was a hard movement at my side and Bill Chess said, "Look there!" in a voice that growled like mountain thunder.

His hard fingers dug into the flesh of my arm until I started to get mad. He was bending far out over the railing, staring down like a loon, his face as white as the weather tan would let it get. I looked down with him into the water at the edge of the submerged staging.

Languidly at the edge of this green and sunken shelf of wood something waved out from the darkness, hesitated, waved back again out of sight under the flooring.

The something had looked far too much like a human arm.

Bill Chess straightened his body rigidly. He turned without a sound and clumped back along the pier. He bent to a loose pile of stones and heaved. His panting breath reached me. He got a big one free and lifted it breast high and started back out on the pier with it. It must have weighed a hundred pounds. His neck muscles stood out like ropes under canvas under his taut brown skin. His teeth were clamped tight and his breath hissed between them.

He reached the end of the pier and steadied himself and lifted the rock high. He held it a moment poised, his eyes staring down now, measuring. His mouth made a vague distressful sound and his body lurched forward hard against the quivering rail and the heavy stone smashed down into the water.

The splash it made went over both of us. The rock fell straight and true and struck on the edge of the submerged planking, almost exactly where we had seen the thing wave in and out.

For a moment the water was a confused boiling, then the ripples widened off into the distance, coming smaller and smaller with a trace of froth at the middle, and there was a dim sound as of wood breaking under water, a sound that seemed to come to us a long time after it should have been audible. An ancient rotted plank popped suddenly through the surface, stuck out a full foot of its jagged end, and fell back with a flat slap and floated off.

The depths cleared again. Something moved in them that

was not a board. It rose slowly, with an infinitely careless languor, a long dark twisted something that rolled lazily in the water as it rose. It broke surface casually, lightly, without haste. I saw wool, sodden and black, a leather jerkin blacker than ink, a pair of slacks. I saw shoes and something that bulged nastily between the shoes and the cuffs of the slacks. I saw a wave of dark blond hair straighten out in the water and hold still for a brief instant as if with a calculated effect, and then swirl into a tangle again.

The thing rolled over once more and an arm flapped up barely above the skin of the water and the arm ended in a bloated hand that was the hand of a freak. Then the face came. A swollen pulpy gray white mass without features, without eyes, without mouth. A blotch of gray dough, a nightmare with human hair on it.

A heavy necklace of green stones showed on what had been a neck, half imbedded, large rough green stones with something that glittered joining them together.

Bill Chess held the handrail and his knuckles were polished bones.

"Muriel!" his voice said croakingly. "Sweet Christ, it's Muriel!"

His voice seemed to come to me from a long way off, over a hill, through a thick silent growth of trees.

# 7

Behind the window of the board shack one end of a counter was piled with dusty folders. The glass upper half of the door was lettered in flaked black paint. *Chief of Police. Fire Chief. Town Constable. Chamber of Commerce.* In the lower corners a USO card and a Red Cross emblem were fastened to the glass.

I went in. There was a pot-bellied stove in the corner and a rolltop desk in the other corner behind the counter. There was a large blue print map of the district on the wall and beside that a board with four hooks on it, one of which supported a frayed and much mended mackinaw. On the counter beside the dusty folders lay the usual sprung pen, exhausted blotter and smeared bottle of gummy ink. The end wall beside the desk was covered with telephone numbers written in hard-bitten figures that would last as long as the wood and looked as if they had been written by a child.

A man sat at the desk in a wooden armchair whose legs were anchored to flat boards, fore and aft, like skis. A spittoon big enough to coil a hose in was leaning against the man's right leg. He had a sweat-stained Stetson on the back of his head and his large hairless hands were clasped comfortably over his stomach, above the waistband of a pair of khaki pants that had been scrubbed thin years ago. His shirt matched the pants except that it was even more faded. It was buttoned tight to the man's thick neck and undecorated by a tie. His hair was mousy brown except at the temples, where it was the color of old snow. He sat more on his left hip than his right, because there was a hip holster down inside his right hip pocket, and a half foot of forty-five gun reared up and bored into his solid back. The star on his left breast had a bent point.

He had large ears and friendly eyes and his jaws munched slowly and he looked as dangerous as a squirrel and much less nervous. I liked everything about him. I leaned on the counter and looked at him and he looked at me and nodded and loosed half a pint of tobacco juice down his right leg into the spittoon. It made a nasty sound of something falling into water.

I lit a cigarette and looked around for an ash tray.

"Try the floor, son," the large friendly man said.

"Are you Sheriff Patton?"

"Constable and deputy sheriff. What law we got to have around here I'm it. Come election anyways. There's a couple of good boys running against me this time and I might get whupped. Job pays eighty a month, cabin, firewood and electricity. That ain't hay in these little old mountains."

"Nobody's going to whip you," I said. "You're going to get a lot of publicity."

"That so?" he asked indifferently and ruined the spittoon again.

"That is, if your jurisdiction extends over to Little Fawn Lake."

"Kingsley's place. Sure. Something bothering over there, son?"

"There's a dead woman in the lake."

That shook him to the core. He unclasped his hands and scratched one ear. He got to his feet by grasping the arms of his chair and deftly kicking it back from under him. Standing up he was a big man and hard. The fat was just cheerfulness.

"Anybody I know?" he enquired uneasily.

"Muriel Chess. I guess you know her. Bill Chess's wife."

"Yep, I know Bill Chess." His voice hardened a little.

"Looks like suicide. She left a note which sounded as if she was just going away. But it could be a suicide note just as well. She's not nice to look at. Been in the water a long time, about a month, judging by the circumstances."

He scratched his other ear. "What circumstances would that be?" His eyes were searching my face now, slowly and calmly, but searching. He didn't seem in any hurry to blow his whistle.

"They had a fight a month ago. Bill went over to the north shore of the lake and was gone some hours. When he got home she was gone. He never saw her again."

"I see. Who are you, son?"

"My name is Marlowe. I'm up from L.A. to look at the property. I had a note from Kingsley to Bill Chess. He took me around the lake and we went out on that little pier the movie people built. We were leaning on the rail and looking down into the water and something that looked like an arm waved out under the submerged flooring, the old boat landing. Bill dropped a heavy rock in and the body popped up."

Patton looked at me without moving a muscle.

"Look, sheriff, hadn't we better run over there? The man's half crazy with shock and he's there all alone."

"How much liquor has he got?"

"Very little when I left. I had a pint but we drank most of it talking."

He moved over to the rolltop desk and unlocked a drawer. He brought up three or four bottles and held them against the light.

"This baby's near full," he said, patting one of them. "Mount Vernon. That ought to hold him. County don't allow me no money for emergency liquor, so I just have to seize a little here and there. Don't use it myself. Never could understand folks letting theirselves get gummed up with it."

He put the bottle on his left hip and locked the desk up and lifted the flap in the counter. He fixed a card against the inside of the glass door panel. I looked at the card as we went out. It read: *Back in Twenty Minutes—Maybe.*

"I'll run down and get Doc Hollis," he said. "Be right back and pick you up. That your car?"

"Yes."

"You can follow along then, as I come back by."

He got into a car which had a siren on it, two red spotlights, two foglights, a red and white fire plate, a new air raid horn on top, three axes, two heavy coils of rope and a fire extinguisher in the back seat, extra gas and oil and water cans in a frame on the running board, an extra spare tire roped to the one on the rack, the stuffing coming out of the upholstery in dingy wads, and half an inch of dust over what was left of the paint.

Behind the right hand lower corner of the windshield there was a white card printed in block capitals. It read:

"VOTERS, ATTENTION! KEEP JIM PATTON CONSTABLE. HE IS TOO OLD TO GO TO WORK."

He turned the car and went off down the street in a swirl of white dust.

# 8

He stopped in front of a white frame building across the road from the stage depot. He went into the white building and presently came out with a man who got into the back seat with the axes and the rope. The official car came back up the street and I fell in behind it. We sifted along the main stem through the slacks and shorts and French sailor jerseys and

knotted bandannas and knobby knees and scarlet lips. Beyond
the village we went up a dusty hill and stopped at a cabin.
Patton touched the siren gently and a man in faded blue
overalls opened the cabin door.

"Get in, Andy. Business."

The man in blue overalls nodded morosely and ducked
back into the cabin. He came back out wearing an oyster-gray
lion hunter's hat and got in under the wheel of Patton's car
while Patton slid over. He was about thirty, dark, lithe, and
had the slightly dirty and slightly underfed look of the native.

We drove out to Little Fawn Lake with me eating enough
dust to make a batch of mud pies. At the five-barred gate
Patton got out and let us through and we went on down to
the lake. Patton got out again and went to the edge of the
water and looked along towards the little pier. Bill Chess was
sitting naked on the floor of the pier, with his head in his
hands. There was something stretched out on the wet planks
beside him.

"We can ride a ways more," Patton said.

The two cars went on to the end of the lake and all four of
us trouped down to the pier from behind Bill Chess's back.
The doctor stopped to cough rackingly into a handkerchief
and then look thoughtfully at the handkerchief. He was an
angular bug-eyed man with a sad sick face.

The thing that had been a woman lay face down on the
boards with a rope under the arms. Bill Chess's clothes lay to
one side. His stiff leg, flat and scarred at the knee, was
stretched out in front of him, the other leg bent up and his
forehead resting against it. He didn't move or look up as we
came down behind him.

Patton took the pint bottle of Mount Vernon off his hip
and unscrewed the top and handed it.

"Drink hearty, Bill."

There was a horrible, sickening smell in the air. Bill Chess
didn't seem to notice it, nor Patton nor the doctor. The man
called Andy got a dusty brown blanket out of the car and
threw it over the body. Then without a word he went and
vomited under a pine tree.

Bill Chess drank a long drink and sat holding the bottle
against his bare bent knee. He began to talk in a stiff wooden

voice, not looking at anybody, not talking to anybody in particular. He told about the quarrel and what happened after it, but not why it had happened. He didn't mention Mrs. Kingsley even in the most casual way. He said that after I left him he had got a rope and stripped and gone down into the water and got the thing out. He had dragged it ashore and then got it up on his back and carried it out on the pier. He didn't know why. He had gone back into the water again then. He didn't have to tell us why.

Patton put a cut of tobacco into his mouth and chewed on it silently, his calm eyes full of nothing. Then he shut his teeth tight and leaned down to pull the blanket off the body. He turned the body over carefully, as if it might come to pieces. The late afternoon sun winked on the necklace of large green stones that were partly imbedded in the swollen neck. They were roughly carved and lustreless, like soapstone or false jade. A gilt chain with an eagle clasp set with small brilliants joined the ends. Patton straightened his broad back and blew his nose on a tan handkerchief.

"What you say, Doc?"

"About what?" the bug-eyed man snarled.

"Cause and time of death."

"Don't be a damn fool, Jim Patton."

"Can't tell nothing, huh?"

"By looking at that? Good God!"

Patton sighed. "Looks drowned all right," he admitted. "But you can't always tell. There's been cases where a victim would be knifed or poisoned or something, and they would soak him in the water to make things look different."

"You get many like that up here?" the doctor enquired nastily.

"Only honest to God murder I ever had up here," Patton said, watching Bill Chess out of the corner of his eye, "was old Dad Meacham over on the north shore. He had a shack in Sheedy Canyon, did a little panning in summer on an old placer claim he had back in the valley near Belltop. Folks didn't see him around for a while in late fall, then come a heavy snow and his roof caved in to one side. So we was over there trying to prop her up a bit, figuring Dad had gone down the hill for the winter without telling anybody, the way them old prospectors do things. Well by gum, old Dad never went down the hill at all. There he was in bed with most of a kindling axe in the back of his head. We never did find out who done it. Somebody figured he had a little bag of gold hid away from the summer's panning."

He looked thoughtfully at Andy. The man in the lion hunter's hat was feeling a tooth in his mouth. He said:

"'Course we know who done it. Guy Pope done it. Only Guy was dead nine days of pneumonia before we found Dad Meacham."

"Eleven days," Patton said.

"Nine," the man in the lion hunter's hat said.

"Was all of six years ago, Andy. Have it your own way, son. How you figure Guy Pope done it?"

"We found about three ounces of small nuggets in Guy's cabin along with some dust. Never was anything bigger'n sand on Guy's claim. Dad had nuggets all of a pennyweight, plenty of times."

"Well, that's the way it goes," Patton said, and smiled at me in a vague manner. "Fellow always forgets something, don't he? No matter how careful he is."

"Cop stuff," Bill Chess said disgustedly and put his pants on and sat down again to put on his shoes and shirt. When he had them on he stood up and reached down for the bottle and took a good drink and laid the bottle carefully on the planks. He thrust his hairy wrists out towards Patton.

"That's the way you guys feel about it, put the cuffs on and get it over," he said in a savage voice.

Patton ignored him and went over to the railing and looked down. "Funny place for a body to be," he said. "No current here to mention, but what there is would be towards the dam."

Bill Chess lowered his wrists and said quietly: "She did it herself, you darn fool. Muriel was a fine swimmer. She dived down in and swum under the boards there and just breathed water in. Had to. No other way."

"I wouldn't quite say that, Bill," Patton answered him mildly. His eyes were as blank as new plates.

Andy shook his head. Patton looked at him with a sly grin. "Crabbin' again, Andy?"

"Was nine days, I tell you. I just counted back," the man in the lion hunter's hat said morosely.

The doctor threw his arms up and walked away, with one hand to his head. He coughed into his handkerchief again and again looked into the handkerchief with passionate attention.

Patton winked at me and spat over the railing. "Let's get on to this one, Andy."

"You ever try to drag a body six feet under water?"

"Nope, can't say I ever did, Andy. Any reason it couldn't be done with a rope?"

Andy shrugged. "If a rope was used, it will show on the corpse. If you got to give yourself away like that, why bother to cover up at all?"

"Question of time," Patton said. "Fellow has his arrangements to make."

Bill Chess snarled at them and reached down for the whiskey. Looking at their solemn mountain faces I couldn't tell what they were really thinking.

Patton said absently: "Something was said about a note."

Bill Chess rummaged in his wallet and drew the folded piece of ruled paper loose. Patton took it and read it slowly.

"Don't seem to have any date," he observed.

Bill Chess shook his head sombrely. "No. She left a month ago. June 12th."

"Left you once before, didn't she?"

"Yeah." Bill Chess stared at him fixedly. "I got drunk and stayed with a chippy. Just before the first snow last December. She was gone a week and came back all prettied up. Said she just had to get away for a while and had been staying with a girl she used to work with in L.A."

"What was the name of this party?" Patton asked.

"Never told me and I never asked her. What Muriel did was all silk with me."

"Sure. Note left that time, Bill?" Patton asked smoothly.

"No."

"This note here looks middling old," Patton said, holding it up.

"I carried it a month," Bill Chess growled. "Who told you she left me before?"

"I forget," Patton said. "You know how it is in a place like this. Not much folks don't notice. Except maybe in summer time where there's a lot of strangers about."

Nobody said anything for a while and then Patton said absently: "June 12th you say she left? Or you thought she left? Did you say the folks across the lake were up here then?"

Bill Chess looked at me and his face darkened again. "Ask this snoopy guy—if he didn't already spill his guts to you."

Patton didn't look at me at all. He looked at the line of mountains far beyond the lake. He said gently: "Mr. Marlowe here didn't tell me anything at all, Bill, except how the body come up out of the water and who it was. And that Muriel went away, as you thought, and left a note you showed him. I don't guess there's anything wrong in that, is there?"

There was another silence and Bill Chess stared down at the blanket-covered corpse a few feet away from him. He clenched his hands and a thick tear ran down his cheek.

"Mrs. Kingsley was here," he said. "She went down the hill that same day. Nobody was in the other cabins. Perrys and Farquars ain't been up at all this year."

Patton nodded and was silent. A kind of charged emptiness hung in the air, as if something that had not been said was plain to all of them and didn't need saying.

Then Bill Chess said wildly: "Take me in, you sons of bitches! Sure I did it! I drowned her. She was my girl and I loved her. I'm a heel, always was a heel, always will be a heel, but just the same I loved her. Maybe you guys wouldn't understand that. Just don't bother to try. Take me in, damn you!"

Nobody said anything at all.

Bill Chess looked down at his hard brown fist. He swung it up viciously and hit himself in the face with all his strength.

"You rotten son of a bitch," he breathed in a harsh whisper.

His nose began to bleed slowly. He stood and the blood ran down his lip, down the side of his mouth, to the point of his chin. A drop fell sluggishly to his shirt.

Patton said quietly: "Got to take you down the hill for questioning, Bill. You know that. We ain't accusing you of anything, but the folks down there have got to talk to you."

Bill Chess said heavily: "Can I change my clothes?"

"Sure. You go with him, Andy. And see what you can find to kind of wrap up what he got here."

They went off along the path at the edge of the lake. The doctor cleared his throat and looked out over the water and sighed.

"You'll want to send the corpse down in my ambulance, Jim, won't you?"

Patton shook his head. "Nope. This is a poor county, Doc. I figure the lady can ride cheaper than what you get for that ambulance."

The doctor walked away from him angrily, saying over his shoulder: "Let me know if you want me to pay for the funeral."

"That ain't no way to talk," Patton sighed.

# 9

The Indian Head Hotel was a brown building on a corner across from the new dance hall. I parked in front of it and used its rest room to wash my face and hands and comb the pine needles out of my hair, before I went into the dining-drinking parlor that adjoined the lobby. The whole place was full to overflowing with males in leisure jackets and liquor breaths and females in highpitched laughs, oxblood fingernails and dirty knuckles. The manager of the joint, a low budget tough guy in shirt sleeves and a mangled cigar, was prowling the room with watchful eyes. At the cash desk a pale-haired man was fighting to get the war news on a small radio that was as full of static as the mashed potatoes were full of water. In the deep back corner of the room, a hillbilly orchestra of five pieces, dressed in ill-fitting white jackets and purple shirts, was trying to make itself heard above the brawl at the bar and smiling glassily into the fog of cigarette smoke and the blur of alcoholic voices. At Puma Point summer, that lovely season, was in full swing.

I gobbled what they called the regular dinner, drank a

brandy to sit on its chest and hold it down, and went out on to the main street. It was still broad daylight but some of the neon signs had been turned on, and the evening reeled with the cheerful din of auto horns, children screaming, bowls rattling, skeeballs clunking, .22's snapping merrily in shooting galleries, juke boxes playing like crazy, and behind all this out on the lake the hard barking roar of the speedboats going nowhere at all and acting as though they were racing with death.

In my Chrysler a thin, serious-looking, brown-haired girl in dark slacks was sitting smoking a cigarette and talking to a dude ranch cowboy who sat on my running board. I walked around the car and got into it. The cowboy strolled away hitching his jeans up. The girl didn't move.

"I'm Birdie Keppel," she said cheerfully, "I'm the beautician here daytimes and evenings I work on the Puma Point Banner. Excuse me sitting in your car."

"That's all right," I said. "You want to just sit or you want me to drive you somewhere?"

"You can drive down the road a piece where it's quieter, Mr. Marlowe. If you're obliging enough to talk to me."

"Pretty good grapevine you've got up here," I said and started the car.

I drove down past the post office to a corner where a blue and white arrow marked *Telephone* pointed down a narrow road towards the lake. I turned down that, drove down past the telephone office, which was a log cabin with a tiny railed lawn in front of it, passed another small cabin and pulled up in front of a huge oak tree that flung its branches all the way across the road and a good fifty feet beyond it.

"This do, Miss Keppel?"

"Mrs. But just call me Birdie. Everybody does. This is fine. Pleased to meet you, Mr. Marlowe. I see you come from Hollywood, that sinful city."

She put a firm brown hand out and I shook it. Clamping bobbie pins into fat blondes had given her a grip like a pair of iceman's tongs.

"I was talking to Doc Hollis," she said, "about poor Muriel Chess. I thought you could give me some details. I understand you found the body."

"Bill Chess found it really. I was just with him. You talk to Jim Patton?"

"Not yet. He went down the hill. Anyway I don't think Jim would tell me much."

"He's up for re-election," I said. "And you're a newspaper woman."

"Jim's no politician, Mr. Marlowe, and I could hardly call myself a newspaper woman. This little paper we get out up here is a pretty amateurish proposition."

"Well, what do you want to know?" I offered her a cigarette and lit it for her.

"You might just tell me the story."

"I came up here with a letter from Derace Kingsley to look at his property. Bill Chess showed me around, got talking to me, told me his wife had moved out on him and showed me the note she left. I had a bottle along and he punished it. He was feeling pretty blue. The liquor loosened him up, but he was lonely and aching to talk anyway. That's how it happened. I didn't know him. Coming back around the end of the lake we went out on the pier and Bill spotted an arm waving out from under the planking down in the water. It turned out to belong to what was left of Muriel Chess. I guess that's all."

"I understand from Doc Hollis she had been in the water a long time. Pretty badly decomposed and all that."

"Yes. Probably the whole month he thought she had been gone. There's no reason to think otherwise. The note's a suicide note."

"Any doubt about that, Mr. Marlowe?"

I looked at her sideways. Thoughtful dark eyes looked out at me under fluffed out brown hair. The dusk had begun to fall now, very slowly. It was no more than a slight change in the quality of the light.

"I guess the police always have doubts in these cases," I said.

"How about you?"

"My opinion doesn't go for anything."

"But for what it's worth?"

"I only met Bill Chess this afternoon," I said. "He struck me as a quick-tempered lad and from his own account he's no saint. But he seems to have been in love with his wife. And I can't see him hanging around there for a month knowing she was rotting down in the water under that pier. Coming out of his cabin in the sunlight and looking along that soft blue water and seeing in his mind what was under it and what was happening to it. And knowing he put it there."

"No more can I," Birdie Keppel said softly. "No more could anybody. And yet we know in our minds that such things have happened and will happen again. Are you in the real estate business, Mr. Marlowe?"

"No."

"What line of business are you in, if I may ask?"

"I'd rather not say."

"That's almost as good as saying," she said. "Besides Doc Hollis heard you tell Jim Patton your full name. And we have an L.A. city directory in our office. I haven't mentioned it to anyone."

"That's nice of you," I said.

"And what's more, I won't," she said. "If you don't want me to."

"What does it cost me?"

"Nothing," she said. "Nothing at all. I don't claim to be a very good newspaper man. And we wouldn't print anything that would embarrass Jim Patton. Jim's the salt of the earth. But it does open up, doesn't it?"

"Don't draw any wrong conclusions," I said. "I had no interest in Bill Chess whatever."

"No interest in Muriel Chess?"

"Why would I have any interest in Muriel Chess?"

She snuffed her cigarette out carefully into the ash tray under the dashboard. "Have it your own way," she said. "But here's a little item you might like to think about, if you don't know it already. There was a Los Angeles copper named De Soto up here about six weeks back, a big roughneck with damn poor manners. We didn't like him and we didn't open up to him much. I mean the three of us in the Banner office didn't. He had a photograph with him and he was looking for a woman called Mildred Haviland, he said. On police business. It was an ordinary photograph, an enlarged snapshot, not a police photo. He said he had information the woman was staying up here. The photo looked a good deal like Muriel Chess. The hair seemed to be reddish and in a very different style than she has worn it here, and the eyebrows were all plucked to narrow arches, and that changes a woman a good deal. But it did look a good deal like Bill Chess's wife."

I drummed on the door of the car and after a moment I said, "What did you tell him?"

"We didn't tell him anything. First off, we couldn't be sure. Second, we didn't like his manner. Third, even if we had been sure and had liked his manner, we likely would not have sicked him on to her. Why would we? Everybody's done something to be sorry for. Take me. I was married once—to a professor of classical languages at Redlands University." She laughed lightly.

"You might have got yourself a story," I said.

"Sure. But up here we're just people."

"Did this man De Soto see Jim Patton?"

"Sure, he must have. Jim didn't mention it."

"Did he show you his badge?"

She thought and then shook her head. "I don't recall that he did. We just took him for granted, from what he said. He certainly acted like a tough city cop."

"To me that's a little against his being one. Did anybody tell Muriel about this guy?"

She hesitated, looking quietly out through the windshield for a long moment before she turned her head and nodded.

"I did. Wasn't any of my damn business, was it?"

"What did she say?"

"She didn't say anything. She gave a funny little embarrassed laugh, as if I had been making a bad joke. Then she walked away. But I did get the impression that there was a queer look in her eyes, just for an instant. You still not interested in Muriel Chess, Mr. Marlowe?"

"Why should I be? I never heard of her until I came up here this afternoon. Honest. And I never heard of anybody named Mildred Haviland either. Drive you back to town?"

"Oh no, thanks. I'll walk. It's only a few steps. Much obliged to you. I kind of hope Bill doesn't get into a jam. Especially a nasty jam like this."

She got out of the car and hung on one foot, then tossed her head and laughed. "They say I'm a pretty good beauty operator," she said. "I hope I am. As an interviewer I'm terrible. Goodnight."

I said goodnight and she walked off into the evening. I sat there watching her until she reached the main street and turned out of sight. Then I got out of the Chrysler and went over towards the telephone company's little rustic building.

## 10

A tame doe deer with a leather dog collar on wandered across the road in front of me. I patted her rough hairy neck and went into the telephone office. A small girl in slacks sat at a small desk working on the books. She got me the rate to Beverly Hills and the change for the coin box. The booth was outside, against the front wall of the building.

"I hope you like it up here," she said. "It's very quiet, very restful."

I shut myself into the booth. For ninety cents I could talk to Derace Kingsley for five minutes. He was at home and the call came through quickly but the connection was full of mountain static.

"Find anything up there?" he asked me in a three highball voice. He sounded tough and confident again.

"I've found too much," I said. "And not at all what we want. Are you alone?"

"What does that matter?"

"It doesn't matter to me. But I know what I'm going to say. You don't."

"Well, get on with it, whatever it is," he said.

"I had a long talk with Bill Chess. He was lonely. His wife had left him—a month ago. They had a fight and he went out and got drunk and when he came back she was gone. She left a note saying she would rather be dead than live with him any more."

"I guess Bill drinks too much," Kingsley's voice said from very far off.

"When he got back, both the women had gone. He has no idea where Mrs. Kingsley went. Lavery was up here in May, but not since. Lavery admitted that much himself. Lavery could, of course, have come up again while Bill was out getting drunk, but there wouldn't be a lot of point to that and there would be two cars to drive down the hill. And I thought that possibly Mrs. K. and Muriel Chess might have gone away together, only Muriel also had a car of her own. But that idea, little as it was worth, has been thrown out by another development. Muriel Chess didn't go away at all. She went down into your little private lake. She came back up today. I was there."

"Good God!" Kingsley sounded properly horrified. "You mean she drowned herself?"

"Perhaps. The note she left could be a suicide note. It would read as well that way as the other. The body was stuck down under that old submerged landing below the pier. Bill was the one who spotted an arm moving down there while we were standing on the pier looking down into the water. He got her out. They've arrested him. The poor guy's pretty badly broken up."

"Good God!" Kingsley said again. "I should think he would be. Does it look as if he—" He paused as the operator came in on the line and demanded another forty-five cents. I put in two quarters and the line cleared.

"Look as if he what?"

Suddenly very clear, Kingsley's voice said: "Look as if he murdered her?"

I said: "Very much. Jim Patton, the constable up here, doesn't like the note not being dated. It seems she left him once before over some woman. Patton sort of suspects Bill might have saved up an old note. Anyhow they've taken Bill down to San Bernardino for questioning and they've taken the body down to be post-mortemed."

"And what do you think?" he asked slowly.

"Well, Bill found the body himself. He didn't have to take me around by that pier. She might have stayed down in the water very much longer, or forever. The note could be old because Bill had carried it in his wallet and handled it from time to time, brooding over it. It could just as easily be undated this time as another time. I'd say notes like that are undated more often than not. The people who write them are apt to be in a hurry and not concerned with dates."

"The body must be pretty far gone. What can they find out now?"

"I don't know how well equipped they are. They can find out if she died by drowning, I guess. And whether there are any marks of violence that wouldn't be erased by water and decomposition. They could tell if she had been shot or stabbed. If the hyoid bone in the throat was broken, they could assume she was throttled. The main thing for us is that I'll have to tell why I came up here. I'll have to testify at an inquest."

"That's bad," Kingsley growled. "Very bad. What do you plan to do now?"

"On my way home I'll stop at the Prescott Hotel and see if I can pick up anything there. Were your wife and Muriel Chess friendly?"

"I guess so. Crystal's easy enough to get along with most of the time. I hardly knew Muriel Chess."

"Did you ever know anybody named Mildred Haviland?"

"What?"

I repeated the name.

"No," he said. "Is there any reason why I should?"

"Every question I ask you ask another right back," I said. "No, there isn't any reason why you should know Mildred Haviland. Especially if you hardly knew Muriel Chess. I'll call you in the morning."

"Do that," he said, and hesitated. "I'm sorry you had to walk into such a mess," he added, and then hesitated again and said goodnight and hung up.

The bell rang again immediately and the long distance operator told me sharply I had put in five cents too much money. I said the sort of thing I would be likely to put into an opening like that. She didn't like it.

I stepped out of the booth and gathered some air into my lungs. The tame doe with the leather collar was standing in the gap in the fence at the end of the walk. I tried to push her out of the way, but she just leaned against me and wouldn't push. So I stepped over the fence and went back to the Chrysler and drove back to the village.

There was a hanging light in Patton's headquarters but the shack was empty and his "Back in Twenty Minutes" sign was still against the inside of the glass part of the door. I kept on going down to the boat landing and beyond to the edge of a deserted swimming beach. A few put-puts and speedboats were still fooling around on the silky water. Across the lake tiny yellow lights began to show in toy cabins perched on miniature slopes. A single bright star glowed low in the north east above the ridge of the mountains. A robin sat on the spike top of a hundred foot pine and waited for it to be dark enough for him to sing his goodnight song.

In a little while it was dark enough and he sang and went away into the invisible depths of sky. I snapped my cigarette into the motionless water a few feet away and climbed back into the car and started back in the direction of Little Fawn Lake.

## II

The gate across the private road was padlocked. I put the Chrysler between two pine trees and climbed the gate and pussy-footed along the side of the road until the glimmer of the little lake bloomed suddenly at my feet. Bill Chess's cabin was dark. The three cabins on the other side were abrupt shadows against the pale granite outcrop. Water gleamed white where it trickled across the top of the dam, and fell almost soundlessly along the sloping outer face to the brook below. I listened, and heard no other sound at all.

The front door of the Chess cabin was locked. I padded along to the back and found a brute of a padlock hanging at that. I went along the walls feeling window screens. They were all fastened. One window higher up was screenless, a small double cottage window half way down the north wall.

This was locked too. I stood still and did some more listening. There was no breeze and the trees were as quiet as their shadows.

I tried a knife blade between the two halves of the small window. No soap. The catch refused to budge. I leaned against the wall and thought and then suddenly I picked up a large stone and smacked it against the place where the two frames met in the middle. The catch pulled out of dry wood with a tearing noise. The window swung back into darkness. I heaved up on the sill and wangled a cramped leg over and edged through the opening. I rolled and let myself down into the room. I turned, grunting a little from the exertion at that altitude, and listened again.

A blazing flash beam hit me square in the eyes.

A very calm voice said: "I'd rest right there, son. You must be all tuckered out."

The flash pinned me against the wall like a squashed fly. Then a light switch clicked and a table lamp glowed. The flash went out. Jim Patton was sitting in an old brown Morris chair beside the table. A fringed brown scarf hung over the end of the table and touched his thick knee. He wore the same clothes he had worn that afternoon, with the addition of a leather jerkin which must have been new once, say about the time of Grover Cleveland's first term. His hands were empty except for the flash. His eyes were empty. His jaws moved in gentle rhythm.

"What's on your mind, son—besides breaking and entering?"

I poked a chair out and straddled it and leaned my arms on the back and looked around the cabin.

"I had an idea," I said. "It looked pretty good for a while, but I guess I can learn to forget it."

The cabin was larger than it had seemed from outside. The part I was in was the living room. It contained a few articles of modest furniture, a rag rug on the pineboard floor, a round table against the end wall and two chairs set against it. Through an open door the corner of a big black cookstove showed.

Patton nodded and his eyes studied me without rancor. "I

heard a car coming," he said. "I knew it had to be coming here. You walk right nice though. I didn't hear you walk worth a darn. I've been a mite curious about you, son."

I said nothing.

"I hope you don't mind me callin' you 'son,'" he said. "I hadn't ought to be so familiar, but I got myself into the habit and I can't seem to shake it. Anybody that don't have a long white beard and arthritis is 'son' to me."

I said he could call me anything that came to mind. I wasn't sensitive.

He grinned. "There's a mess of detectives in the L.A. phone book," he said. "But only one of them is called Marlowe."

"What made you look?"

"I guess you might call it lowdown curiosity. Added to which Bill Chess told me you was some sort of dick. You didn't bother to tell me yourself."

"I'd have got around to it," I said. "I'm sorry it bothered you."

"It didn't bother me none. I don't bother at all easy. You got any identification with you?"

I got my wallet out and showed him this and that.

"Well, you got a good build on you for the work," he said satisfied. "And your face don't tell a lot of stories. I guess you was aiming to search the cabin."

"Yeah."

"I already pawed around considerable myself. Just got back and come straight here. That is, I stopped by my shack a minute and then come. I don't figure I could let you search the place, though." He scratched his ear. "That is, dum if I know whether I could or not. You telling who hired you?"

"Derace Kingsley. To trace his wife. She skipped out on him a month ago. She started from here. So I started from here. She's supposed to have gone away with a man. The man denies it. I thought maybe something up here might give me a lead."

"And did anything?"

"No. She's traced pretty definitely as far as San Bernardino and then El Paso. There the trail ends. But I've only just started."

Patton stood up and unlocked the cabin door. The spicy smell of the pines surged in. He spat outdoors and sat down again and rumpled the mousy brown hair under his Stetson. His head with the hat off had the indecent look of heads that are seldom without hats.

"You didn't have no interest in Bill Chess at all?"

"None whatever."

"I guess you fellows do a lot of divorce business," he said. "Kind of smelly work, to my notion."

I let that ride.

"Kingsley wouldn't have asked help from the police to find his wife, would he?"

"Hardly," I said. "He knows her too well."

"None of what you've been saying don't hardly explain your wanting to search Bill's cabin," he said judiciously.

"I'm just a great guy to poke around."

"Hell," he said, "you can do better than that."

"Say I am interested in Bill Chess then. But only because he's in trouble and rather a pathetic case—in spite of being a good deal of a heel. If he murdered his wife, there's something here to point that way. If he didn't, there's something to point that way too."

He held his head sideways, like a watchful bird. "As for instance what kind of thing?"

"Clothes, personal jewelry, toilet articles, whatever a woman takes with her when she goes away, not intending to come back."

He leaned back slowly. "But she didn't go away, son."

"Then the stuff should be still here. But if it was still here, Bill would have noticed she hadn't taken it. He would know she hadn't gone away."

"By gum, I don't like it either way," he said.

"But if he murdered her," I said, "then he would have to get rid of the things she ought to have taken with her, if she had gone away."

"And how do you figure he would do that, son?" The yellow lamplight made bronze of one side of his face.

"I understand she had a Ford car of her own. Except for that I'd expect him to burn what he could burn and bury what he could not burn out in the woods. Sinking it in the lake might be dangerous. But he couldn't burn or bury her car. Could he drive it?"

Patton looked surprised. "Sure. He can't bend his right leg at the knee, so he couldn't use the footbrake very handy. But he could get by with the handbrake. All that's different on Bill's own Ford is the brake pedal is set over on the left side of the post, close to the clutch, so he can shove them both down with one foot."

I shook ash from my cigarette into a small blue jar that had once contained a pound of orange honey, according to the small gilt label on it.

"Getting rid of the car would be his big problem," I said. "Wherever he took it he would have to get back, and he would rather not be seen coming back. And if he simply abandoned it on a street, say, down in San Bernardino, it would be found and identified very quickly. He wouldn't want that either. The best stunt would be to unload it on a hot car dealer, but he probably doesn't know one. So the chances are he hid it in the woods within walking distance of here. And walking distance for him would not be very far."

"For a fellow that claims not to be interested, you're doing some pretty close figuring on all this," Patton said dryly. "So now you've got the car hid out in the woods. What then?"

"He has to consider the possibility of its being found. The woods are lonely, but rangers and woodcutters get around in them from time to time. If the car is found, it would be better for Muriel's stuff to be found in it. That would give him a couple of outs—neither one very brilliant but both at least possible. One, that she was murdered by some unknown party who fixed things to implicate Bill when and if the murder was discovered. Two, that Muriel did actually commit suicide, but fixed things so that he would be blamed. A revenge suicide."

Patton thought all this over with calm and care. He went to the door to unload again. He sat down and rumpled his hair again. He looked at me with solid scepticism.

"The first one's possible like you say," he admitted. "But only just, and I don't have anybody in mind for the job. There's that little matter of the note to be got over."

I shook my head. "Say Bill already had the note from

another time. Say she went away, as he thought, without leaving a note. After a month had gone by without any word from her he might be just worried and uncertain enough to show the note, feeling it might be some protection to him in case anything had happened to her. He didn't say any of this, but he could have had it in his mind."

Patton shook his head. He didn't like it. Neither did I. He said slowly: "As to your other notion, it's just plain crazy. Killing yourself and fixing things so as somebody else would get accused of murdering you don't fit in with my simple ideas of human nature at all."

"Then your ideas of human nature are too simple," I said. "Because it has been done, and when it has been done, it has nearly always been done by a woman."

"Nope," he said, "I'm a man fifty-seven years old and I've seen a lot of crazy people, but I don't go for that worth a peanut shell. What I like is that she did plan to go away and did write the note, but he caught her before she got clear and saw red and finished her off. Then he would have to do all them things we been talking about."

"I never met her," I said. "So I wouldn't have any idea what she would be likely to do. Bill said he met her in a place in Riverside something over a year ago. She may have had a long and complicated history before that. What kind of girl was she?"

"A mighty cute little blonde when she fixed herself up. She kind of let herself go with Bill. A quiet girl, with a face that kept its secrets. Bill says she had a temper, but I never seen any of it. I seen plenty of nasty temper in him."

"And did you think she looked like the photo of somebody called Mildred Haviland?"

His jaws stopped munching and his mouth became almost primly tight. Very slowly he started chewing again.

"By gum," he said, "I'll be might careful to look under the bed before I crawl in tonight. To make sure you ain't there. Where did you get that information?"

"A nice little girl called Birdie Keppel told me. She was interviewing me in the course of her spare time newspaper job. She happened to mention that an L.A. cop named De Soto was showing the photo around."

Patton smacked his thick knee and hunched his shoulders forward.

"I done wrong there," he said soberly, "I made one of my mistakes. This big bruiser showed his picture to darn near everybody in town before he showed it to me. That made me kind of sore. It looked some like Muriel, but not enough to be sure by any manner of means. I asked him what she was wanted for. He said it was police business. I said I was in that way of business myself, in an ignorant countrified kind of way. He said his instructions were to locate the lady and that was all he knew. Maybe he did wrong to take me up short like that. So I guess I done wrong to tell him I didn't know anybody that looked like his little picture."

The big calm man smiled vaguely at the corner of the ceiling, then brought his eyes down and looked at me steadily.

"I'll thank you to respect this confidence, Mr. Marlowe. You done right nicely in your figuring too. You ever happen to go over to Coon Lake?"

"Never heard of it."

"Back about a mile," he said, pointing over his shoulder with a thumb, "there's a little narrow wood road turns over west. You can just drive it and miss the trees. It climbs about five hundred feet in another mile and comes out by Coon Lake. Pretty little place. Folks go up there to picnic once in a while, but not often. It's hard on tires. There's two three small shallow lakes full of reeds. There's snow up there even now in the shady places. There's a bunch of old handhewn log cabins that's been falling down ever since I recall, and there's a big broken down frame building that Montclair University used to use for a summer camp maybe ten years back. They ain't used it in a very long time. This building sits back from the lakes in heavy timber. Round at the back of it there's a wash house with an old rusty boiler and along of that there's a big woodshed with a sliding door hung on rollers. It was built for a garage but they kept their wood in it and they locked it up out of season. Wood's one of the few things people will steal up here, but folks who might steal it off a pile wouldn't break a lock to get it. I guess you know what I found in that woodshed."

"I thought you went down to San Bernardino."

"Changed my mind. Didn't seem right to let Bill ride down there with his wife's body in the back of the car. So I sent it down in Doc's ambulance and I sent Andy down with Bill. I figured I kind of ought to look around a little more before I put things up to the sheriff and the coroner."

"Muriel's car was in the woodshed?"

"Yep. And two unlocked suitcases in the car. Packed with clothes and packed kind of hasty, I thought. Women's clothes. The point is, son, no stranger would have known about that place."

I agreed with him. He put his hand into the slanting side pocket of his jerkin and brought out a small twist of tissue paper. He opened it up on his palm and held the hand out flat.

"Take a look at this."

I went over and looked. What lay on the tissue was a thin gold chain with a tiny lock hardly larger than a link of the chain. The gold had been snipped through, leaving the lock intact. The chain seemed to be about seven inches long. There was white powder sticking to both chain and paper.

"Where would you guess I found that?" Patton asked.

I picked the chain up and tried to fit the cut ends together. They didn't fit. I made no comment on that, but moistened a finger and touched the powder and tasted it.

"In a can or box of confectioner's sugar," I said. "The chain is an anklet. Some women never take them off, like wedding rings. Whoever took this one off didn't have the key."

"What do you make of it?"

"Nothing much," I said. "There wouldn't be any point in Bill cutting it off Muriel's ankle and leaving that green necklace on her neck. There wouldn't be any point in Muriel cutting it off herself—assuming she had lost the key—and hiding it to be found. A search thorough enough to find it wouldn't be made unless her body was found first. If Bill cut it off, he would have thrown it into the lake. But if Muriel wanted to keep it and yet hide it from Bill, there's some sense in the place where it was hidden."

Patton looked puzzled this time. "Why is that?"

"Because it's a woman's hiding place. Confectioner's sugar

is used to make cake icing. A man would never look there. Pretty clever of you to find it, sheriff."

He grinned a little sheepishly. "Hell, I knocked the box over and some of the sugar spilled," he said. "Without that I don't guess I ever would have found it." He rolled the paper up again and slipped it back into his pocket. He stood up with an air of finality.

"You staying up here or going back to town, Mr. Marlowe?"

"Back to town. Until you want me for the inquest. I suppose you will."

"That's up to the coroner, of course. If you'll kind of shut that window you bust in, I'll put this lamp out and lock up."

I did what he said and he snapped his flash on and put out the lamp. We went out and he felt the cabin door to make sure the lock had caught. He closed the screen softly and stood looking across the moonlit lake.

"I don't figure Bill meant to kill her," he said sadly. "He could choke a girl to death without meaning to at all. He has mighty strong hands. Once done he has to use what brains God gave him to cover up what he done. I feel real bad about it, but that don't alter the facts and the probabilities. It's simple and natural and the simple and natural things usually turn out to be right."

I said: "I should think he would have run away. I don't see how he could stand it to stay here."

Patton spat into the black velvet shadow of a manzanita bush. He said slowly: "He had a government pension and he would have to run away from that too. And most men can stand what they've got to stand, when it steps up and looks them straight in the eye. Like they're doing all over the world right now. Well, goodnight to you. I'm going to walk down to that little pier again and stand there awhile in the moonlight and feel bad. A night like this, and we got to think about murders."

He moved quietly off into the shadows and became one of them himself. I stood there until he was out of sight and then went back to the locked gate and climbed over it. I got into the car and drove back down the road looking for a place to hide.

## 12

Three hundred yards from the gate a narrow track, sifted over with brown oak leaves from last fall, curved around a granite boulder and disappeared. I followed it around and bumped along the stones of the outcrop for fifty or sixty feet, then swung the car around a tree and set it pointing back the way it had come. I cut the lights and switched off the motor and sat there waiting.

Half an hour passed. Without tobacco it seemed a long time. Then far off I heard a car motor start up and grow louder and the white beam of headlights passed below me on the road. The sound faded into the distance and a faint dry tang of dust hung in the air for a while after it was gone.

I got out of my car and walked back to the gate and to the Chess cabin. A hard push opened the sprung window this time. I climbed in again and let myself down to the floor and poked the flash I had brought across the room to the table lamp. I switched the lamp on and listened a moment, heard nothing, and went out to the kitchen. I switched on a hanging bulb over the sink.

The woodbox beside the stove was neatly piled with split wood. There were no dirty dishes in the sink, no foul-smelling pots on the stove. Bill Chess, lonely or not, kept his house in good order. A door opened from the kitchen into the bedroom, and from that a very narrow door led into a tiny bathroom which had evidently been built on to the cabin fairly recently. The clean celotex lining showed that. The bathroom told me nothing.

The bedroom contained a double bed, a pinewood dresser with a round mirror on the wall above it, a bureau, two straight chairs, and a tin waste basket. There were two oval rag rugs on the floor, one on each side of the bed. On the walls Bill Chess had tacked up a set of war maps from the National Geographic. There was a silly-looking red and white flounce on the dressing table.

I poked around in the drawers. An imitation leather trinket box with an assortment of gaudy costume jewelry had not been taken away. There was the usual stuff women use on their faces and fingernails and eyebrows, and it seemed to me that there was too much of it. But that was just guessing. The bureau contained both man's and woman's clothes, not a great deal of either. Bill Chess had a very noisy check shirt with starched matching collar, among other things. Underneath a sheet of blue tissue paper in one corner I found something I didn't like. A seemingly brand new peach-colored silk slip trimmed with lace. Silk slips were not being left behind that year, not by any woman in her senses.

This looked bad for Bill Chess. I wondered what Patton had thought of it.

I went back to the kitchen and prowled the open shelves above and beside the sink. They were thick with cans and jars of household staples. The confectioner's sugar was in a square brown box with a torn corner. Patton had made an attempt to clean up what was spilled. Near the sugar were salt, borax, baking soda, cornstarch, brown sugar and so on. Something might be hidden in any of them.

Something that had been clipped from a chain anklet whose cut ends did not fit together.

I shut my eyes and poked a finger out at random and it came to rest on the baking soda. I got a newspaper from the back of the woodbox and spread it out and dumped the soda out of the box. I stirred it around with a spoon. There seemed to be an indecent lot of baking soda, but that was all there was. I funnelled it back into the box and tried the borax. Nothing but borax. Third time lucky. I tried the cornstarch. It made too much fine dust, and there was nothing but cornstarch.

The sound of distant steps froze me to the ankles. I reached up and yanked the light out and dodged back into the living room and reached for the lamp switch. Much too late to be of any use, of course. The steps sounded again, soft and cautious. The hackles rose on my neck.

I waited in the dark, with the flash in my left hand. A deadly long two minutes crept by. I spent some of the time breathing, but not all.

It wouldn't be Patton. He would walk up to the door and

open it and tell me off. The careful quiet steps seemed to move this way and that, a movement, a long pause, another movement, another long pause. I sneaked across to the door and twisted the knob silently. I yanked the door wide and stabbed out with the flash.

It made golden lamps of a pair of eyes. There was a leaping movement and a quick thudding of hoofs back among the trees. It was only an inquisitive deer.

I closed the door again and followed my flashlight beam back into the kitchen. The small round glow rested squarely on the box of confectioner's sugar.

I put the light on again, lifted the box down and emptied it on the newspaper.

Patton hadn't gone deep enough. Having found one thing by accident he had assumed that was all there was. He hadn't seemed to notice that there ought to be something else.

Another twist of white tissue showed in the fine white powdered sugar. I shook it clean and unwound it. It contained a tiny gold heart, no larger than a woman's little fingernail.

I spooned the sugar back into the box and put the box back on the shelf and crumpled the piece of newspaper into the stove. I went back to the living room and turned the table lamp on. Under that brighter light the tiny engraving on the back of the little gold heart could just be read without a magnifying glass.

It was in script. It read: "Al to Mildred. June 28th 1938. With all my love."

Al to Mildred. Al somebody to Mildred Haviland. Mildred Haviland was Muriel Chess. Muriel Chess was dead—two weeks after a cop named De Soto had been looking for her.

I stood there, holding it, wondering what it had to do with me. Wondering, and not having the faintest glimmer of an idea.

I wrapped it up again and left the cabin and drove back to the village.

Patton was in his office telephoning when I got around there. The door was locked. I had to wait while he talked. After a while he hung up and came to unlock the door.

I walked in past him and put the twist of tissue paper on his counter and opened it up.

"You didn't go deep enough into the powdered sugar," I said.

He looked at the little gold heart, looked at me, went around behind the counter and got a cheap magnifying glass off his desk. He studied the back of the heart. He put the glass down and frowned at me.

"Might have known if you wanted to search that cabin, you was going to do it," he said gruffly. "I ain't going to have trouble with you, am I, son?"

"You ought to have noticed that the cut ends of the chain didn't fit," I told him.

He looked at me sadly. "Son, I don't have your eyes." He pushed the little heart around with his square blunt finger. He stared at me and said nothing.

I said: "If you were thinking that anklet meant something Bill could have been jealous about, so was I—provided he ever saw it. But strictly on the cuff I'm willing to bet he never did see it and that he never heard of Mildred Haviland."

Patton said slowly: "Looks like maybe I owe this De Soto party an apology, don't it?"

"If you ever see him," I said.

He gave me another long empty stare and I gave it right back to him. "Don't tell me, son," he said. "Let me guess all for myself that you got a brand new idea about it."

"Yeah. Bill didn't murder his wife."

"No?"

"No. She was murdered by somebody out of her past. Somebody who had lost track of her and then found it again and found her married to another man and didn't like it. Somebody who knew the country up here—as hundreds of people do who don't live here—and knew a good place to hide the car and the clothes. Somebody who hated and could dissimulate. Who persuaded her to go away with him and when everything was ready and the note was written, took her around the throat and gave her what he thought was coming to her and put her in the lake and went his way. Like it?"

"Well," he said judiciously, "it does make things kind of

complicated, don't you think? But there ain't anything impossible about it. Not one bit impossible."

"When you get tired of it, let me know. I'll have something else," I said.

"I'll just be doggone sure you will," he said, and for the first time since I had met him he laughed.

I said goodnight again and went out, leaving him there moving his mind around with the ponderous energy of a homesteader digging up a stump.

## 13

At somewhere around eleven I got down to the bottom of the grade and parked in one of the diagonal slots at the side of the Prescott Hotel in San Bernardino. I pulled an overnight bag out of the boot and had taken three steps with it when a bellhop in braided pants and a white shirt and black bow tie yanked it out of my hand.

The clerk on duty was an eggheaded man with no interest in me or in anything else. He wore parts of a white linen suit and he yawned as he handed me the desk pen and looked off into the distance as if remembering his childhood.

The hop and I rode a four by four elevator to the second floor and walked a couple of blocks around corners. As we walked it got hotter and hotter. The hop unlocked a door into a boy's size room with one window on an air shaft. The air-conditioner inlet up in the corner of the ceiling was about the size of a woman's handkerchief. The bit of ribbon tied to it fluttered weakly, just to show that something was moving.

The hop was tall and thin and yellow and not young and as cool as a slice of chicken in aspic. He moved his gum around in his face, put my bag on a chair, looked up at the grating and then stood looking at me. He had eyes the color of a drink of water.

"Maybe I ought to have asked for one of the dollar rooms," I said. "This one seems a mite close-fitting."

"I reckon you're lucky to get one at all. This town's fair bulgin' at the seams."

"Bring us up some ginger ale and glasses and ice," I said.

"Us?"

"That is, if you happen to be a drinking man."

"I reckon I might take a chance this late."

He went out. I took off my coat, tie, shirt and undershirt and walked around in the warm draft from the open door. The draft smelled of hot iron. I went into the bathroom sideways—it was that kind of bathroom—and doused myself with tepid cold water. I was breathing a little more freely when the tall languid hop returned with a tray. He shut the door and I brought out a bottle of rye. He mixed a couple of drinks and we made the usual insincere smiles over them and drank. The perspiration started from the back of my neck down my spine and was halfway to my socks before I put the glass down. But I felt better all the same. I sat on the bed and looked at the hop.

"How long can you stay?"

"Doin' what?"

"Remembering."

"I ain't a damn bit of use at it," he said.

"I have money to spend," I said, "in my own peculiar way." I got my wallet unstuck from the lower part of my back and spread tired-looking dollar bills along the bed.

"I beg yore pardon," the hop said. "I reckon you might be a dick."

"Don't be silly," I said. "You never saw a dick playing solitaire with his own money. You might call me an investigator."

"I'm interested," he said. "The likker makes my mind work."

I gave him a dollar bill. "Try that on your mind. And can I call you Big Tex from Houston?"

"Amarillo," he said. "Not that it matters. And how do you like my Texas drawl? It makes me sick, but I find people go for it."

"Stay with it," I said. "It never lost anybody a dollar yet."

He grinned and tucked the folded dollar neatly into the watch pocket of his pants.

"What were you doing on Friday, June 12th?" I asked him. "Late afternoon or evening. It was a Friday."

He sipped his drink and thought, shaking the ice around gently and drinking past his gum. "I was right here, six to twelve shift," he said.

"A woman, slim, pretty blonde, checked in here and stayed until time for the night train to El Paso. I think she must have taken that because she was in El Paso Sunday morning. She came here driving a Packard Clipper registered to Crystal Grace Kingsley, 965 Carson Drive, Beverly Hills. She may have registered as that, or under some other name, and she may not have registered at all. Her car is still in the hotel garage. I'd like to talk to the boys that checked her in and out. That wins another dollar—just thinking about it."

I separated another dollar from my exhibit and it went into his pocket with a sound like caterpillars fighting.

"Can do," he said calmly.

He put his glass down and left the room, closing the door. I finished my drink and made another. I went into the bathroom and used some more warm water on my torso. While I was doing this the telephone on the wall tinkled and I wedged myself into the minute space between the bathroom door and the bed to answer it.

The Texas voice said: "That was Sonny. He was inducted last week. Another boy we call Les checked her out. He's here."

"Okay. Shoot him up, will you?"

I was playing with my second drink and thinking about the third when a knock came and I opened the door to a small, green-eyed rat with a tight, girlish mouth.

He came in almost dancing and stood looking at me with a faint sneer.

"Drink?"

"Sure," he said coldly. He poured himself a large one and added a whisper of ginger ale, put the mixture down in one long swallow, tucked a cigarette between his smooth little lips and snapped a match alight while it was coming up from his pocket. He blew smoke and went on staring at me. The corner of his eye caught the money on the bed, without looking directly at it. Over the pocket of his shirt, instead of a number, the word *Captain* was stitched.

"You Les?" I asked him.

"No." He paused. "We don't like dicks here," he added. "We don't have one of our own and we don't care to bother with dicks that are working for other people."

"Thanks," I said. "That will be all."

"Huh?" The small mouth twisted unpleasantly.

"Beat it," I said.

"I thought you wanted to see me," he sneered.

"You're the bell captain?"

"Check."

"I wanted to buy you a drink. I wanted to give you a buck. Here." I held it out to him. "Thanks for coming up."

He took the dollar and pocketed it, without a word of thanks. He hung there, smoke trailing from his nose, his eyes tight and mean.

"What I say here goes," he said.

"It goes as far as you can push it," I said. "And that couldn't be very far. You had your drink and you had your graft. Now you can scram out."

He turned with a swift tight shrug and slipped out of the room noiselessly.

Four minutes passed, then another knock, very light. The tall boy came in grinning. I walked away from him and sat on the bed again.

"You didn't take to Les, I reckon?"

"Not a great deal. Is he satisfied?"

"I reckon so. You know what captains are. They have to have their cut. Maybe you better call me Les, Mr. Marlowe."

"So you checked her out."

"No, that was all a stall. She never checked in at the desk. But I remember the Packard. She gave me a dollar to put it away for her and to look after her stuff until train time. She ate dinner here. A dollar gets you remembered in this town. And there's been talk about the car bein' left so long."

"What was she like to look at?"

"She wore a black and white outfit, mostly white, and a panama hat with a black and white band. She was a neat blonde lady like you said. Later on she took a hack to the station. I put her bags into it for her. They had initials on them but I'm sorry I can't remember the initials."

"I'm glad you can't," I said. "It would be too good. Have a drink. How old would she be?"

He rinsed the other glass and mixed a civilized drink for himself.

"It's mighty hard to tell a woman's age these days," he said. "I reckon she was about thirty, or a little more or a little less."

I dug in my coat for the snapshot of Crystal and Lavery on the beach and handed it to him.

He looked at it steadily and held it away from his eyes, then close.

"You won't have to swear to it in court," I said.

He nodded. "I wouldn't want to. These small blondes are so much of a pattern that a change of clothes or light or makeup makes them all alike or all different." He hesitated, staring at the snapshot.

"What's worrying you?" I asked.

"I'm thinking about the gent in this snap. He enter into it at all?"

"Go on with that," I said.

"I think this fellow spoke to her in the lobby, and had dinner with her. A tall good-lookin' jasper, built like a fast light-heavy. He went in the hack with her too."

"Quite sure about that?"

He looked at the money on the bed.

"Okay, how much does it cost?" I asked wearily.

He stiffened, laid the snapshot down and drew the two folded bills from his pocket and tossed them on the bed.

"I thank you for the drink," he said, "and to hell with you." He started for the door.

"Oh sit down and don't be so touchy," I growled.

He sat down and looked at me stiff-eyed.

"And don't be so damn southern," I said. "I've been knee deep in hotel hops for a lot of years. If I've met one who wouldn't pull a gag, that's fine. But you can't expect me to expect to meet one that wouldn't pull a gag."

He grinned slowly and nodded quickly. He picked the snapshot up again and looked at me over it.

"This gent takes a solid photo," he said. "Much more so than the lady. But there was another little item that made me remember him. I got the impression the lady didn't quite like him walking up to her so openly in the lobby."

I thought that over and decided it didn't mean anything much. He might have been late or have missed some earlier appointment. I said:

"There's a reason for that. Did you notice what jewelry the lady was wearing? Rings, ear-pendants, anything that looked conspicuous or valuable?"

He hadn't noticed, he said.

"Was her hair long or short, straight or waved or curly, natural blonde or bleached?"

He laughed. "Hell, you can't tell that last point, Mr. Marlowe. Even when it's natural they want it lighter. As to the rest, my recollection is it was rather long, like they're wearing it now and turned in a little at the bottom and rather straight. But I could be wrong." He looked at the snapshot again. "She has it bound back here. You can't tell a thing."

"That's right," I said. "And the only reason I asked you was to make sure you didn't over-observe. The guy that sees too much detail is just as unreliable a witness as the guy that doesn't see any. He's nearly always making half of it up. You check just about right, considering the circumstances. Thanks very much."

I gave him back his two dollars and a five to keep them company. He thanked me, finished his drink and left softly. I finished mine and washed off again and decided I would rather drive home than sleep in that hole. I put my shirt and coat on again and went downstairs with my bag.

The redheaded rat of a captain was the only hop in the lobby. I carried my bag over to the desk and he didn't move to take it off my hands. The eggheaded clerk separated me from two dollars without even looking at me.

"Two bucks to spend the night in this manhole," I said, "when for free I could have a nice airy ashcan."

The clerk yawned, got a delayed reaction, and said brightly: "It gets quite cool here about three in the morning. From then on until eight, or even nine, it's quite pleasant."

I wiped the back of my neck and staggered out to the car. Even the seat of the car was hot, at midnight.

I got home about two-forty-five and Hollywood was an icebox. Even Pasadena had felt cool.

# 14

I dreamed I was far down in the depths of icy green water with a corpse under my arm. The corpse had long blond hair that kept floating around in front of my face. An enormous fish with bulging eyes and a bloated body and scales shining with putrescence swam around leering like an elderly roué. Just as I was about to burst from the lack of air, the corpse came alive under my arm and got away from me and then I was fighting with the fish and the corpse was rolling over and over in the water, spinning its long hair.

I woke up with a mouth full of sheet and both hands hooked on the head-frame of the bed and pulling hard. The muscles ached when I let go and lowered them. I got up and walked the room and lit a cigarette, feeling the carpet with bare toes. When I had finished the cigarette, I went back to bed.

It was nine o'clock when I woke up again. The sun was on my face. The room was hot. I showered and shaved and partly dressed and made the morning toast and eggs and coffee in the dinette. While I was finishing up there was a knock at the apartment door.

I went to open it with my mouth full of toast. It was a lean, serious-looking man in a severe gray suit.

"Floyd Greer, lieutenant, Central Detective Bureau," he said and walked into the room.

He put out a dry hand and I shook it. He sat down on the edge of a chair, the way they do, and turned his hat in his hands and looked at me with the quiet stare they have.

"We got a call from San Bernardino about that business up at Puma Lake. Drowned woman. Seems you were on hand when the body was discovered."

I nodded and said, "Have some coffee?"

"No thanks. I had breakfast two hours ago."

I got my coffee and sat down across the room from him.

"They asked us to look you up," he said. "Give them a line on you."

"Sure."

"So we did that. Seems like you have a clean bill of health so far as we are concerned. Kind of coincidence a man in your line would be around when the body was found."

"I'm like that," I said. "Lucky."

"So I just thought I'd drop around and say howdy."

"That's fine. Glad to know you, lieutenant."

"Kind of a coincidence," he said again, nodding. "You up there on business, so to speak?"

"If I was," I said, "my business had nothing to do with the girl who was drowned, so far as I know."

"But you couldn't be sure?"

"Until you've finished with a case, you can't ever be quite sure what its ramifications are, can you?"

"That's right." He circled his hat brim through his fingers again, like a bashful cowboy. There was nothing bashful about his eyes. "I'd like to feel sure that if these ramifications you speak of happened to take in this drowned woman's affairs, you would put us wise."

"I hope you can rely on that," I said.

He bulged his lower lip with his tongue. "We'd like a little more than a hope. At the present time you don't care to say?"

"At the present time I don't know anything that Patton doesn't know."

"Who's he?"

"The constable up at Puma Point."

The lean serious man smiled tolerantly. He cracked a knuckle and after a pause said: "The San Berdoo D.A. will likely want to talk to you—before the inquest. But that won't be very soon. Right now they're trying to get a set of prints. We lent them a technical man."

"That will be tough. The body's pretty far gone."

"It's done all the time," he said. "They worked out the system back in New York where they're all the time pulling in floaters. They cut patches of skin off the fingers and harden them in a tanning solution and make stamps. It works well enough as a rule."

"You think this woman had a record of some kind?"

"Why, we always take prints of a corpse," he said. "You ought to know that."

I said: "I didn't know the lady. If you thought I did and that was why I was up there, there's nothing in it."

"But you wouldn't care to say just why you *were* up there," he persisted.

"So you think I'm lying to you," I said.

He spun his hat on a bony forefinger. "You got me wrong, Mr. Marlowe. We don't think anything at all. What we do is investigate and find out. This stuff is just routine. You ought to know that. You been around long enough." He stood up and put his hat on. "You might let me know if you have to leave town. I'd be obliged."

I said I would and went to the door with him. He went out with a duck of his head and a sad half-smile. I watched him drift languidly down the hall and punch the elevator button.

I went back out to the dinette to see if there was any more coffee. There was about two-thirds of a cup. I added cream and sugar and carried my cup over to the telephone. I dialed Police Headquarters downtown and asked for the Detective Bureau and then for Lieutenant Floyd Greer.

The voice said: "Lieutenant Greer is not in the office. Anybody else do?"

"De Soto in?"

"Who?"

I repeated the name.

"What's his rank and department?"

"Plain clothes something or other."

"Hold the line."

I waited. The burring male voice came back after a while and said: "What's the gag? We don't have a De Soto on the roster. Who's this talking?"

I hung up, finished my coffee and dialed the number of Derace Kingsley's office. The smooth and cool Miss Fromsett

said he had just come in and put me through without a
murmur.

"Well," he said, loud and forceful at the beginning of a
fresh day, "what did you find out at the hotel?"

"She was there all right. And Lavery met her there. The
hop who gave me the dope brought Lavery into it himself,
without any prompting from me. He had dinner with her and
went with her in a cab to the railroad station."

"Well, I ought to have known he was lying," Kingsley said
slowly. "I got the impression he was surprised when I told
him about the telegram from El Paso. I was just letting my
impressions get too sharp. Anything else?"

"Not there. I had a cop calling on me this morning, giving
me the usual looking over and warning not to leave town
without letting him know. Trying to find out why I went to
Puma Point. I didn't tell him and as he wasn't even aware of
Jim Patton's existence, it's evident that Patton didn't tell
anybody."

"Jim would do his best to be decent about it," Kingsley
said. "Why were you asking me last night about some
name—Mildred something or other?"

I told him, making it brief. I told him about Muriel Chess's
car and clothes being found and where.

"That looks bad for Bill," he said. "I know Coon Lake
myself, but it would never have occurred to me to use that
old woodshed—or even that there was an old woodshed. It
not only looks bad, it looks premeditated."

"I disagree with that. Assuming he knew the country well
enough it wouldn't take him any time to search his mind for a
likely hiding place. He was very restricted as to distance."

"Maybe. What do you plan to do now?" he asked.

"Go up against Lavery again, of course."

He agreed that that was the thing to do. He added: "This
other, tragic as it is, is really no business of ours, is it?"

"Not unless your wife knew something about it."

His voice sounded sharply, saying: "Look here, Marlowe, I
think I can understand your detective instinct to tie everything that happens into one compact knot, but don't let it
run away with you. Life isn't like that at all—not life as I have
known it. Better leave the affairs of the Chess family to

the police and keep your brains working on the Kingsley family."

"Okay," I said.

"I don't mean to be domineering," he said.

I laughed heartily, said goodby, and hung up. I finished dressing and went down to the basement for the Chrysler. I started for Bay City again.

## 15

I drove past the intersection of Altair Street to where the cross street continued to the edge of the canyon and ended in a semi-circular parking place with a sidewalk and a white wooden guard fence around it. I sat there in the car a little while, thinking, looking out to sea and admiring the blue gray fall of the foothills towards the ocean. I was trying to make up my mind whether to try handling Lavery with a feather or go on using the back of my hand and the edge of my tongue. I decided I could lose nothing by the soft approach. If that didn't produce for me—and I didn't think it would—nature could take its course and we could bust up the furniture.

The paved alley that ran along halfway down the hill below the houses on the outer edge was empty. Below that, on the next hillside street, a couple of kids were throwing a boomerang up the slope and chasing it with the usual amount of elbowing and mutual insult. Farther down still a house was enclosed in trees and a red brick wall. There was a glimpse of washing on the line in the backyard and two pigeons strutted along the slope of the roof bobbing their heads. A blue and tan bus trundled along the street in front of the brick house and stopped and a very old man got off with slow care and settled himself firmly on the ground and tapped with a heavy cane before he started to crawl back up the slope.

The air was clearer than yesterday. The morning was full of peace. I left the car where it was and walked along Altair Street to No. 623.

The venetian blinds were down across the front windows and the place had a sleepy look. I stepped down over the Korean moss and punched the bell and saw that the door was not quite shut. It had dropped in its frame, as most of our doors do, and the spring bolt hung a little on the lower edge of the lock plate. I remembered that it had wanted to stick the day before, when I was leaving.

I gave the door a little push and it moved inward with a light click. The room beyond was dim, but there was some light from west windows. Nobody answered my ring. I didn't ring again. I pushed the door a little wider and stepped inside.

The room had a hushed warm smell, the smell of late morning in a house not yet opened up. The bottle of Vat 69 on the round table by the davenport was almost empty and another full bottle waited beside it. The copper ice bucket had a little water in the bottom. Two glasses had been used, and half a siphon of carbonated water.

I fixed the door about as I had found it and stood there and listened. If Lavery was away I thought I would take a chance and frisk the joint. I didn't have anything much on him, but it was probably enough to keep him from calling the cops.

In the silence time passed. It passed in the dry whirr of the electric clock on the mantel, in the far-off toot of an auto horn on Aster Drive, in the hornet drone of a plane over the foothills across the canyon, in the sudden lurch and growl of the electric refrigerator in the kitchen.

I went farther into the room and stood peering around and listening and hearing nothing except those fixed sounds belonging to the house and having nothing to do with the humans in it. I started along the rug towards the archway at the back.

A hand in a glove appeared on the slope of the white metal railing, at the edge of the archway, where the stairs went down. It appeared and stopped.

It moved and a woman's hat showed, then her head. The woman came quietly up the stairs. She came all the way up, turned through the arch and still didn't seem to see me. She was a slender woman of uncertain age, with untidy brown hair, a scarlet mess of a mouth, too much rouge on her cheekbones, shadowed eyes. She wore a blue tweed suit that looked like the dickens with the purple hat that was doing its best to hang on to the side of her head.

She saw me and didn't stop or change expression in the slightest degree. She came slowly on into the room, holding her right hand away from her body. Her left hand wore the brown glove I had seen on the railing. The right hand glove that matched it was wrapped around the butt of a small automatic.

She stopped then and her body arched back and a quick distressful sound came out of her mouth. Then she giggled, a high nervous giggle. She pointed the gun at me, and came steadily on.

I kept on looking at the gun and not screaming.

The woman came close. When she was close enough to be confidential she pointed the gun at my stomach and said:

"All I wanted was my rent. The place seems well taken care of. Nothing broken. He has always been a good tidy careful tenant. I just didn't want him to get too far behind in the rent."

A fellow with a kind of strained and unhappy voice said politely: "How far behind is he?"

"Three months," she said. "Two hundred and forty dollars. Eighty dollars is very reasonable for a place as well furnished as this. I've had a little trouble collecting before, but it always came out very well. He promised me a check this morning. Over the telephone. I mean he promised to give it to me this morning."

"Over the telephone," I said. "This morning."

I shuffled around a bit in an inconspicuous sort of way. The idea was to get close enough to make a side swipe at the gun, knock it outwards, and then jump in fast before she could bring it back in line. I've never had a lot of luck with the technique, but you have to try it once in a while. This looked like the time to try it.

I made about six inches, but not nearly enough for a first down. I said: "And you're the owner?" I didn't look at the gun directly. I had a faint, a very faint hope that she didn't know she was pointing it at me.

"Why, certainly. I'm Mrs. Fallbrook. Who did you think I was?"

"Well, I thought you might be the owner," I said. "You talking about the rent and all. But I didn't know your name." Another eight inches. Nice smooth work. It would be a shame to have it wasted.

"And who are you, if I may enquire?"

"I just came about the car payment," I said. "The door was open just a teensy weensy bit and I kind of shoved in. I don't know why."

I made a face like a man from the finance company coming about the car payment. Kind of tough, but ready to break into a sunny smile.

"You mean Mr. Lavery is behind in his car payments?" she asked, looking worried.

"A little. Not a great deal," I said soothingly.

I was all set now. I had the reach and I ought to have the speed. All it needed was a clean sharp sweep inside the gun and outward. I started to take my left foot out of the rug.

"You know," she said, "it's funny about this gun. I found it on the stairs. Nasty oily things, aren't they? And the stair carpet is a very nice gray chenille. Quite expensive."

And she handed me the gun.

My hand went out for it, as stiff as an eggshell, almost as brittle. I took the gun. She sniffed with distaste at the glove which had been wrapped around the butt. She went on talking in exactly the same tone of cockeyed reasonableness. My knees cracked, relaxing.

"Well of course it's much easier for you," she said. "About the car, I mean. You can just take it away, if you have to. But taking a house with nice furniture in it isn't so easy. It takes time and money to evict a tenant. There is apt to be bitterness and things get damaged, sometimes on purpose. The rug on this floor cost over two hundred dollars, secondhand. It's only a jute rug, but it has a lovely coloring, don't you think? You'd never know it was only jute, secondhand. But that's silly too because they're always secondhand after you've used them. And I walked over here too, to save my tires for the government. I could have taken a bus part way, but the darn things never come along except going in the wrong direction."

I hardly heard what she said. It was like surf breaking beyond a point, out of sight. The gun had my interest.

I broke the magazine out. It was empty. I turned the gun and looked into the breech. That was empty too. I sniffed the muzzle. It reeked.

I dropped the gun into my pocket. A six-shot .25 caliber automatic. Emptied out. Shot empty, and not too long ago. But not in the last half hour either.

"Has it been fired?" Mrs. Fallbrook enquired pleasantly. "I certainly hope not."

"Any reason why it should have been fired?" I asked her. The voice was steady, but the brain was still bouncing.

"Well, it was lying on the stairs," she said. "After all, people do fire them."

"How true that is," I said. "But Mr. Lavery probably had a hole in his pocket. He isn't home, is he?"

"Oh no." She shook her head and looked disappointed. "And I don't think it's very nice of him. He promised me the check and I walked over — "

"When was it you phoned him?" I asked.

"Why, yesterday evening." She frowned, not liking so many questions.

"He must have been called away," I said.

She stared at a spot between my big brown eyes.

"Look, Mrs. Fallbrook," I said. "Let's not kid around any more, Mrs. Fallbrook. Not that I don't love it. And not that I like to say this. But you didn't shoot him, did you — on account of he owed you three months' rent?"

She sat down very slowly on the edge of a chair and worked the tip of her tongue along the scarlet slash of her mouth.

"Why, what a perfectly horrid suggestion," she said angrily. "I don't think you are nice at all. Didn't you say the gun had not been fired?"

"All guns have been fired sometime. All guns have been loaded sometime. This one is not loaded now."

"Well, then — " she made an impatient gesture and sniffed at her oily glove.

"Okay, my idea was wrong. Just a gag anyway. Mr. Lavery was out and you went through the house. Being the owner, you have a key. Is that correct?"

"I didn't mean to be interfering," she said, biting a finger.

"Perhaps I ought not to have done it. But I have a right to see how things are kept."

"Well, you looked. And you're sure he's not here?"

"I didn't look under the beds or in the icebox," she said coldly. "I called out from the top of the stairs when he didn't answer my ring. Then I went down to the lower hall and called out again. I even peeped into the bedroom." She lowered her eyes as if bashfully and twisted a hand on her knee.

"Well, that's that," I said.

She nodded brightly. "Yes, that's that. And what did you say your name was?"

"Vance," I said. "Philo Vance."

"And what company are you employed with, Mr. Vance?"

"I'm out of work right now," I said. "Until the police commissioner gets in a jam again."

She looked startled. "But you said you came about a car payment."

"That's just part-time work," I said. "A fill-in job."

She rose to her feet and looked at me steadily. Her voice was cold saying: "Then in that case I think you had better leave now."

I said: "I thought I might take a look around first, if you don't mind. There might be something you missed."

"I don't think that is necessary," she said. "This is my house. I'll thank you to leave now, Mr. Vance."

I said: "And if I don't leave, you'll get somebody who will. Take a chair again, Mrs. Fallbrook. I'll just glance through. This gun, you know, is kind of queer."

"But I told you I found it lying on the stairs," she said angrily. "I don't know anything else about it. I don't know anything about guns at all. I—I never shot one in my life." She opened a large blue bag and pulled a handkerchief out of it and sniffled.

"That's your story," I said. "I don't have to get stuck with it."

She put her left hand out to me with a pathetic gesture, like the erring wife in East Lynne.

"Oh, I shouldn't have come in!" she cried. "It was horrid of me. I know it was. Mr. Lavery will be furious."

"What you shouldn't have done," I said, "was let me find out the gun was empty. Up to then you were holding everything in the deck."

She stamped her foot. That was all the scene lacked. That made it perfect.

"Why, you perfectly loathsome man," she squawked. "Don't you dare touch me! Don't you take a single step towards me! I won't stay in this house another minute with you. How *dare* you be so insulting—"

She caught her voice and snapped it in mid-air like a rubber band. Then she put her head down, purple hat and all, and ran for the door. As she passed me she put a hand out as if to stiff arm me, but she wasn't near enough and I didn't move. She jerked the door wide and charged out through it and up the walk to the street. The door came slowly shut and I heard her rapid steps above the sound of its closing.

I ran a fingernail along my teeth and punched the point of my jaw with a knuckle, listening. I didn't hear anything anywhere to listen to. A six-shot automatic, fired empty.

"Something," I said out loud, "is all wrong with this scene."

The house seemed now to be abnormally still. I went along the apricot rug and through the archway to the head of the stairs. I stood there for another moment and listened again.

I shrugged and went quietly down the stairs.

# 16

The lower hall had a door at each end and two in the middle side by side. One of these was a linen closet and the other was locked. I went along to the end and looked in at a spare bedroom with drawn blinds and no sign of being used. I went back to the other end of the hall and stepped into a second bedroom with a wide bed, a cafe-au-lait rug, angular furniture in light wood, a box mirror over the dressing table and a long fluorescent lamp over the mirror. In the corner a crystal greyhound stood on a mirror-top table and beside him a crystal box with cigarettes in it.

Face powder was spilled around on the dressing table. There was a smear of dark lipstick on a towel hanging over the waste basket. On the bed were pillows side by side, with depressions in them that could have been made by heads. A woman's handkerchief peeped from under one pillow. A pair of sheer black pajamas lay across the foot of the bed. A rather too emphatic trace of chypre hung in the air.

I wondered what Mrs. Fallbrook had thought of all this.

I turned around and looked at myself in the long mirror of a closet door. The door was painted white and had a crystal knob. I turned the knob in my handkerchief and looked inside. The cedar-lined closet was fairly full of man's clothes. There was a nice friendly smell of tweed. The closet was not entirely full of man's clothes.

There was also a woman's black and white tailored suit, mostly white, black and white shoes under it, a panama with a black and white rolled band on a shelf above it. There were other woman's clothes, but I didn't examine them.

I shut the closet door and went out of the bedroom, holding my handkerchief ready for more doorknobs.

The door next the linen closet, the locked door, had to be the bathroom. I shook it, but it went on being locked. I bent down and saw there was a short, slit-shaped opening in the middle of the knob. I knew then that the door was fastened by pushing a button in the middle of the knob inside, and that the slit-like opening was for a metal key without wards that would spring the lock open in case somebody fainted in the bathroom, or the kids locked themselves in and got sassy.

The key for this ought to be kept on the top shelf of the linen closet, but it wasn't. I tried my knife blade, but that was too thin. I went back to the bedroom and got a flat nail file off the dresser. That worked. I opened the bathroom door.

A man's sand-colored pajamas were tossed over a painted hamper. A pair of heelless green slippers lay on the floor. There was a safety razor on the edge of the washbowl and a tube of cream with the cap off. The bathroom window was shut, and there was a pungent smell in the air that was not quite like any other smell.

Three empty shells lay bright and coppery on the nile green tiles of the bathroom floor, and there was a nice clean hole in the frosted pane of the window. To the left and a little above the window were two scarred places in the plaster where the white showed behind the paint and where something, such as a bullet, had gone in.

The shower curtain was green and white oiled silk and it hung on shiny chromium rings and it was drawn across the shower opening. I slid it aside, the rings making a thin scraping noise, which for some reason sounded indecently loud.

I felt my neck creak a little as I bent down. He was there all right—there wasn't anywhere else for him to be. He was huddled in the corner under the two shining faucets, and water dripped slowly on his chest, from the chromium shower-head.

His knees were drawn up but slack. The two holes in his naked chest were dark blue and both of them were close enough to his heart to have killed him. The blood seemed to have been washed away.

His eyes had a curiously bright and expectant look, as if he smelled the morning coffee and would be coming right out.

Nice efficient work. You have just finished shaving and stripped for the shower and you are leaning in against the shower curtain and adjusting the temperature of the water. The door opens behind you and somebody comes in. The somebody appears to have been a woman. She has a gun. You look at the gun and she shoots it.

She misses with three shots. It seems impossible, at such short range, but there it is. Maybe it happens all the time. I've been around so little.

You haven't anywhere to go. You could lunge at her and take a chance, if you were that kind of fellow, and if you were braced for it. But leaning in over the shower faucets, holding the curtains closed, you are off balance. Also you are apt to be somewhat petrified with panic, if you are at all like other people. So there isn't anywhere to go, except into the shower.

That is where you go. You go into it as far as you can, but a shower stall is a small place and the tiled wall stops you. You are backed up against the last wall there is now. You are all out of space, and you are all out of living. And then there are two more shots, possibly three, and you slide down the wall, and your eyes are not even frightened any more now. They are just the empty eyes of the dead.

She reaches in and turns the shower off. She sets the lock of the bathroom door. On her way out of the house she throws the empty gun on the stair carpet. She should worry. It is probably your gun.

Is that right? It had better be right.

I bent and pulled at his arm. Ice couldn't have been any colder or any stiffer. I went out of the bathroom, leaving it unlocked. No need to lock it now. It only makes work for the cops.

I went into the bedroom and pulled the handkerchief out from under the pillow. It was a minute piece of linen rag with a scalloped edge embroidered in red. Two small initials were stitched in the corner, in red. *A.F.*

"Adrienne Fromsett," I said. I laughed. It was a rather ghoulish laugh.

I shook the handkerchief to get some of the chypre out of it and folded it up in a tissue and put it in a pocket. I went back upstairs to the living room and poked around in the desk against the wall. The desk contained no interesting letters, phone numbers or provocative match folders. Or if it did, I didn't find them.

I looked at the phone. It was on a small table against the wall beside the fireplace. It had a long cord so that Mr. Lavery could be lying on his back on the davenport, a cigarette between his smooth brown lips, a tall cool one at the table at his side, and plenty of time for a nice long cosy conversation with a lady friend. An easy, languid, flirtatious, kidding, not too subtle and not too blunt conversation, of the sort he would be apt to enjoy.

All that wasted too. I went away from the telephone to the door and set the lock so I could come in again and shut the door tight, pulling it hard over the sill until the lock clicked. I went up the walk and stood in the sunlight looking across the street at Dr. Almore's house.

Nobody yelled or ran out of the door. Nobody blew a police whistle. Everything was quiet and sunny and calm. No cause for excitement whatever. It's only Marlowe, finding another body. He does it rather well by now. Murder-a-day Marlowe, they call him. They have the meat wagon following him around to follow up on the business he finds.

A nice enough fellow, in an ingenuous sort of way.

I walked back to the intersection and got into my car and started it and backed it and drove away from there.

## 17

The bellhop at the Athletic Club was back in three minutes with a nod for me to come with him. We rode up to the fourth floor and went around a corner and he showed me a half open door.

"Around to the left, sir. As quietly as you can. A few of the members are sleeping."

I went into the club library. It contained books behind glass doors and magazines on a long central table and a lighted portrait of the club's founder. But its real business seemed to be sleeping. Outward-jutting bookcases cut the room into a number of small alcoves and in the alcoves were high backed leather chairs of an incredible size and softness. In a number of the chairs old boys were snoozing peacefully, their faces violet with high blood pressure, thin racking snores coming out of their pinched noses.

I climbed over a few feet and stole around to the left. Derace Kingsley was in the very last alcove in the far end of the room. He had two chairs arranged side by side, facing into the corner. His big dark head just showed over the top of one of them. I slipped into the empty one and gave him a quick nod.

"Keep your voice down," he said. "This room is for after-luncheon naps. Now what is it? When I employed you it was to save me trouble, not to add trouble to what I already had. You made me break an important engagement."

"I know," I said, and put my face close to his. He smelled of highballs, in a nice way. "She shot him."

His eyebrows jumped and his face got that stony look. His teeth clamped tight. He breathed softly and twisted a large hand on his kneecap.

"Go on," he said, in a voice the size of a marble.

I looked back over the top of my chair. The nearest old geezer was sound asleep and blowing the dusty fuzz in his nostrils back and forth as he breathed.

"No answer at Lavery's place," I said. "Door slightly open. But I noticed yesterday it sticks on the sill. Pushed it open. Room dark, two glasses with drinks having been in them. House very still. In a moment a slim dark woman calling herself Mrs. Fallbrook, landlady, came up the stairs with her glove wrapped around a gun. Said she had found it on the stairs. Said she came to collect her three months' back rent. Used her key to get in. Inference is she took the chance to snoop around and look the house over. Took the gun from her and found it had been fired recently, but didn't tell her so. She said Lavery was not home. Got rid of her by making her mad and she departed in high dudgeon. She may call the police, but it's much more likely she will just go out and hunt butterflies and forget the whole thing—except the rent."

I paused. Kingsley's head was turned towards me and his jaw muscles bulged with the way his teeth were clamped. His eyes looked sick.

"I went downstairs. Signs of a woman having spent the night. Pajamas, face powder, perfume, and so on. Bathroom locked, but got it open. Three empty shells on the floor, two shots in the wall, one in the window. Lavery in the shower stall, naked and dead."

"My God!" Kingsley whispered. "Do you mean to say he had a woman with him last night and she shot him this morning in the bathroom?"

"Just what did you think I was trying to say?" I asked.

"Keep your voice down," he groaned. "It's a shock, naturally. Why in the bathroom?"

"Keep your own voice down," I said. "Why not in the bathroom? Could you think of a place where a man would be more completely off guard?"

He said: "You don't know that a woman shot him. I mean, you're not sure, are you?"

"No," I said. "That's true. It might have been somebody who used a small gun and emptied it carelessly to look like a woman's work. The bathroom is downhill, facing outwards on space and I don't think shots down there would be easily heard by anyone not in the house. The woman who spent the night might have left—or there need not have been any woman at all. The appearances could have been faked. *You* might have shot him."

"What would I want to shoot him for?" he almost bleated, squeezing both kneecaps hard. "I'm a civilized man."

That didn't seem to be worth an argument either. I said: "Does your wife own a gun?"

He turned a drawn miserable face to me and said hollowly: "Good God, man, you can't really think that!"

"Well does she?"

He got the words out in small gritty pieces. "Yes—she does. A small automatic."

"You buy it locally?"

"I—I didn't buy it at all. I took it away from a drunk at a party in San Francisco a couple of years ago. He was waving it around, with an idea that that was very funny. I never gave it back to him." He pinched his jaw hard until his knuckles whitened. "He probably doesn't even remember how or when he lost it. He was that kind of a drunk."

"This is working out almost too neatly," I said. "Could you recognize this gun?"

He thought hard, pushing his jaw out and half closing his eyes. I looked back over the chairs again. One of the elderly snoozers had waked himself up with a snort that almost blew him out of his chair. He coughed, scratched his nose with a thin dried-up hand, and fumbled a gold watch out of his vest. He peered at it bleakly, put it away, and went to sleep again.

I reached in my pocket and put the gun on Kingsley's hand. He stared down at it miserably.

"I don't know," he said slowly. "It's like it, but I can't tell."

"There's a serial number on the side," I said.

"Nobody remembers the serial numbers of guns."

"I was hoping you wouldn't," I said. "It would have worried me very much."

His hand closed around the gun and he put it down beside him in the chair.

"The dirty rat," he said softly. "I suppose he ditched her."

"I don't get it," I said. "The motive was inadequate for you, on account of you're a civilized man. But it was adequate for her."

"It's not the same motive," he snapped. "And women are more impetuous than men."

"Like cats are more impetuous than dogs."

"How?"

"Some women are more impetuous than some men. That's all that means. We'll have to have a better motive, if you want your wife to have done it."

He turned his head enough to give me a level stare in which there was no amusement. White crescents were bitten into the corners of his mouth.

"This doesn't seem to me a very good spot for the light touch," he said. "We can't let the police have this gun. Crystal had a permit and the gun was registered. So they will know the number, even if I don't. We can't let them have it."

"But Mrs. Fallbrook knows I had the gun."

He shook his head stubbornly. "We'll have to chance that. Yes, I know you're taking a risk. I intend to make it worth your while. If the set-up were possible for suicide, I'd say put the gun back. But the way you tell it, it isn't."

"No. He'd have to have missed himself with the first three shots. But I can't cover up a murder, even for a ten-dollar bonus. The gun will have to go back."

"I was thinking of more money than that," he said quietly. "I was thinking of five hundred dollars."

"Just what did you expect to buy with it?"

He leaned close to me. His eyes were serious and bleak, but not hard. "Is there anything in Lavery's place, apart from the gun, that might indicate Crystal has been there lately?"

"A black and white dress and a hat like the bellhop in Bernardino described on her. There may be a dozen things I don't know about. There almost certainly will be fingerprints. You say she was never printed, but that doesn't mean they won't get her prints to check. Her bedroom at home will be full of them. So will the cabin at Little Fawn Lake. And her car."

"We ought to get the car—" he started to say. I stopped him.

"No use. Too many other places. What kind of perfume does she use?"

He looked blank for an instant. "Oh—Gillerlain Regal, the Champagne of Perfumes," he said woodenly. "A Chanel number once in a while."

"What's this stuff of yours like?"

"A kind of chypre. Sandalwood chypre."

"The bedroom reeks with it," I said. "It smelled like cheap stuff to me. But I'm no judge."

"Cheap?" he said, stung to the quick. "My God, cheap? We get thirty dollars an ounce for it."

"Well, this stuff smelled more like three dollars a gallon."

He put his hands down hard on his knees and shook his head. "I'm talking about money," he said. "Five hundred dollars. A check for it right now."

I let the remark fall to the ground, eddying like a soiled feather. One of the old boys behind us stumbled to his feet and groped his way wearily out of the room.

Kingsley said gravely: "I hired you to protect me from scandal, and of course to protect my wife, if she needed it. Through no fault of yours the chance to avoid scandal is pretty well shot. It's a question of my wife's neck now. I don't believe she shot Lavery. I have no reason for that belief. None at all. I just feel the conviction. She may even have been there last night, this gun may even be her gun. It doesn't prove she killed him. She would be as careless with the gun as with anything else. Anybody could have got hold of it."

"The cops down there won't work very hard to believe that," I said. "If the one I met is a fair specimen, they'll just pick the first head they see and start swinging with their blackjacks. And hers will certainly be the first head they see when they look the situation over."

He ground the heels of his hands together. His misery had a theatrical flavor, as real misery so often has.

"I'll go along with you up to a point," I said. "The set-up

down there is almost too good, at first sight. She leaves clothes there she has been seen wearing and which can probably be traced. She leaves the gun on the stairs. It's hard to think she would be as dumb as that."

"You give me a little heart," Kingsley said wearily.

"But none of that means anything," I said. "Because we are looking at it from the angle of calculation, and people who commit crimes of passion or hatred, just commit them and walk out. Everything I have heard indicates that she is a reckless foolish woman. There's no sign of planning in any of the scene down there. There's every sign of a complete lack of planning. But even if there wasn't a thing down there to point to your wife, the cops would tie her up to Lavery. They will investigate his background, his friends, his women. Her name is bound to crop up somewhere along the line, and when it does, the fact that she has been out of sight for a month will make them sit up and rub their horny palms with glee. And of course they'll trace the gun, and if it's her gun—"

His hand dived for the gun in the chair beside him.

"Nope," I said. "They'll have to have the gun. Marlowe may be a very smart guy and very fond of you personally, but he can't risk the suppression of such vital evidence as the gun that killed a man. Whatever I do has to be on the basis that your wife is an obvious suspect, but that the obviousness can be wrong."

He groaned and put his big hand out with the gun on it. I took it and put it away. Then I took it out again and said: "Lend me your handkerchief. I don't want to use mine. I might be searched."

He handed me a stiff white handkerchief and I wiped the gun off carefully all over and dropped it into my pocket. I handed him back the handkerchief.

"My prints are all right," I said. "But I don't want yours on it. Here's the only thing I can do. Go back down there and replace the gun and call the law. Ride it out with them and let the chips fall where they have to. The story will have to come out. What I was doing down there and why. At the worst they'll find her and prove she killed him. At the best they'll find her a lot quicker than I can and let me use my energies proving that she didn't kill him, which means, in effect, proving that somebody else did. Are you game for that?"

He nodded slowly. He said: "Yes—and the five hundred stands. For showing Crystal didn't kill him."

"I don't expect to earn it," I said. "You may as well understand that now. How well did Miss Fromsett know Lavery? Out of office hours?"

His face tightened up like a charleyhorse. His fists went into hard lumps on his thighs. He said nothing.

"She looked kind of queer when I asked her for his address yesterday morning," I said.

He let a breath out slowly.

"Like a bad taste in the mouth," I said. "Like a romance that fouled out. Am I too blunt?"

His nostrils quivered a little and his breath made noise in them for a moment. Then he relaxed and said quietly:

"She—she knew him rather well—at one time. She's a girl who would do about what she pleased in that way. Lavery was, I guess, a fascinating bird—to women."

"I'll have to talk to her," I said.

"Why?" he asked shortly. Red patches showed in his cheeks.

"Never mind why. It's my business to ask all sorts of questions of all sorts of people."

"Talk to her then," he said tightly. "As a matter of fact she knew the Almores. She knew Almore's wife, the one who killed herself. Lavery knew her too. Could that have any possible connection with this business?"

"I don't know. You're in love with her, aren't you?"

"I'd marry her tomorrow, if I could," he said stiffly.

I nodded and stood up. I looked back along the room. It was almost empty now. At the far end a couple of elderly relics were still blowing bubbles. The rest of the soft chair boys had staggered back to whatever it was they did when they were conscious.

"There's just one thing," I said, looking down at Kingsley. "Cops get very hostile when there is a delay in calling them after a murder. There's been delay this time and there will be more. I'd like to go down there as if it was the first visit today. I think I can make it that way, if I leave the Fallbrook woman out."

"Fallbrook?" He hardly knew what I was talking about. "Who the hell—oh yes, I remember."

"Well, don't remember. I'm almost certain they'll never hear a peep from her. She's not the kind to have anything to do with the police of her own free will."

"I understand," he said.

"Be sure you handle it right then. Questions will be asked you *before* you are told Lavery is dead, before I'm allowed to get in touch with you—so far as they know. Don't fall into any traps. If you do, I won't be able to find anything out. I'll be in the clink."

"You could call me from the house down there—before you call the police," he said reasonably.

"I know. But the fact that I don't will be in my favor. And they'll check the phone calls one of the first things they do. And if I call you from anywhere else, I might just as well admit that I came up here to see you."

"I understand," he said again. "You can trust me to handle it."

We shook hands and I left him standing there.

# 18

The Athletic Club was on a corner across the street and half a block down from the Treloar Building. I crossed and walked north to the entrance. They had finished laying rose-colored concrete where the rubber sidewalk had been. It was fenced around, leaving a narrow gangway in and out of the building. The space was clotted with office help going in from lunch.

The Gillerlain Company's reception room looked even emptier than the day before. The same fluffy little blonde was tucked in behind the PBX in the corner. She gave me a quick smile and I gave her the gunman's salute, a stiff forefinger pointing at her, the three lower fingers tucked back under it, and the thumb wiggling up and down like a western gunfighter fanning his hammer. She laughed heartily, without making a sound. This was more fun than she had had in a week.

I pointed to Miss Fromsett's empty desk and the little blonde nodded and pushed a plug in and spoke. A door opened and Miss Fromsett swayed elegantly out to her desk and sat down and gave me her cool expectant eyes.

"Yes, Mr. Marlowe? Mr. Kingsley is not in, I'm afraid."

"I just came from him. Where do we talk?"

"Talk?"

"I have something to show you."

"Oh, yes?" She looked me over thoughtfully. A lot of guys had probably tried to show her things, including etchings. At another time I wouldn't have been above taking a flutter at it myself.

"Business," I said. "Mr. Kingsley's business."

She stood up and opened the gate in the railing. "We may as well go into his office then."

We went in. She held the door for me. As I passed her I sniffed. Sandalwood. I said:

"Gillerlain Regal, the Champagne of Perfumes?"

She smiled faintly, holding the door. "On my salary?"

"I didn't say anything about your salary. You don't look like a girl who has to buy her own perfume."

"Yes, that's what it is," she said. "And if you want to know, I detest wearing perfume in the office. He makes me."

We went down the long dim office and she took a chair at the end of the desk. I sat where I had sat the day before. We looked at each other. She was wearing tan today, with a ruffled jabot at her throat. She looked a little warmer, but still no prairie fire.

I offered her one of Kingsley's cigarettes. She took it, took a light from his lighter, and leaned back.

"We needn't waste time being cagey," I said. "You know by now who I am and what I am doing. If you didn't know yesterday morning, it's only because he loves to play big shot."

She looked down at the hand that lay on her knee, then lifted her eyes and smiled almost shyly.

"He's a great guy," she said. "In spite of the heavy executive act he likes to put on. He's the only guy that gets fooled by it after all. And if you only knew what he has stood from that little tramp—" She waved her cigarette—"well, perhaps I'd better leave that out. What was it you wanted to see me about?"

"Kingsley said you knew the Almores."

"I knew Mrs. Almore. That is, I met her a couple of times."

"Where?"

"At a friend's house. Why?"

"At Lavery's house?"

"You're not going to be insolent, are you, Mr. Marlowe?"

"I don't know what your definition of that would be. I'm going to talk business as if it was business, not international diplomacy."

"Very well." She nodded slightly. "At Chris Lavery's house, yes. I used to go there—once in a while. He had cocktail parties."

"Then Lavery knew the Almores—or Mrs. Almore."

She flushed very slightly. "Yes. Quite well."

"And a lot of other women—quite well, too. I don't doubt that. Did Mrs. Kingsley know her too?"

"Yes, better than I did. They called each other by their first names. Mrs. Almore is dead, you know. She committed suicide, about a year and a half ago."

"Any doubt about that?"

She raised her eyebrows, but the expression looked artificial to me, as if it just went with the question I asked, as a matter of form.

She said: "Have you any particular reason for asking that question in that particular way? I mean, has it anything to do with—with what you are doing?"

"I didn't think so. I still don't know that it has. But yesterday Dr. Almore called a cop just because I looked at his house. After he had found out from my car license who I was. The cop got pretty tough with me, just for being there. He didn't know what I was doing and I didn't tell him I had been calling on Lavery. But Dr. Almore must have known that. He had seen me in front of Lavery's house. Now why would he think it necessary to call a cop? And why would the cop think it smart to say that the last fellow who tried to put the bite on Almore ended up on the road gang? And why would the cop ask me if her folks—meaning Mrs. Almore's folks, I suppose—had hired me? If you can answer any of those questions, I might know whether it's any of my business."

She thought about it for a moment, giving me one quick glance while she was thinking, and then looking away again.

"I only met Mrs. Almore twice," she said slowly. "But I think I can answer your questions—all of them. The last time I met her was at Lavery's place, as I said, and there were quite a lot of people there. There was a lot of drinking and loud talk. The women were not with their husbands and the men were not with their wives, if any. There was a man there named Brownwell who was very tight. He's in the navy now, I heard. He was ribbing Mrs. Almore about her husband's practice. The idea seemed to be that he was one of those doctors who run around all night with a case of loaded hypo-dermic needles, keeping the local fast set from having pink elephants for breakfast. Florence Almore said she didn't care how her husband got his money as long as he got plenty of it and she had the spending of it. She was tight too and not a very nice person sober, I should imagine. One of these slinky glittering females who laugh too much and sprawl all over their chairs, showing a great deal of leg. A very light blonde with a high color and indecently large baby-blue eyes. Well, Brownwell told her not to worry, it would always be a good racket. In and out of the patient's house in fifteen minutes and anywhere from ten to fifty bucks a trip. But one thing bothered him, he said, how ever a doctor could get hold of so much dope without underworld contacts. He asked Mrs. Almore if they had many nice gangsters to dinner at their house. She threw a glass of liquor in his face."

I grinned, but Miss Fromsett didn't. She crushed her cigarette out in Kingsley's big copper and glass tray and looked at me soberly.

"Fair enough," I said. "Who wouldn't, unless he had a large hard fist to throw?"

"Yes. A few weeks later Florence Almore was found dead in the garage late at night. The door of the garage was shut and the car motor was running." She stopped and moistened her lips slightly. "It was Chris Lavery who found her. Coming home at God knows what o'clock in the morning. She was lying on the concrete floor in pajamas, with her head under a blanket which was also over the exhaust pipe of the car. Dr. Almore was out. There was nothing about the affair in the papers, except that she had died suddenly. It was well hushed up."

She lifted her clasped hands a little and then let them fall slowly into her lap again. I said:

"Was something wrong with it, then?"

"People thought so, but they always do. Some time later I heard what purported to be the lowdown. I meet this man Brownwell on Vine Street and he asked me to have a drink with him. I didn't like him, but I had half an hour to kill. We sat at the back of Levy's bar and he asked me if I remembered the babe who threw the drink in his face. I said I did. The conversation then went something very like this. I remember it very well.

"Brownwell said: 'Our pal Chris Lavery is sitting pretty, if he ever runs out of girl friends he can touch for dough.'

"I said: 'I don't think I understand.'

"He said: 'Hell, maybe you don't want to. The night the Almore woman died she was over at Lou Condy's place losing her shirt at roulette. She got into a tantrum and said the wheels were crooked and made a scene. Condy practically had to drag her into his office. He got hold of Dr. Almore through the Physicians' Exchange and after a while the doc came over. He shot her with one of his busy little needles. Then he went away, leaving Condy to get her home. It seems he had a very urgent case. So Condy took her home and the doc's office nurse showed up, having been called by the doc, and Condy carried her upstairs and the nurse put her to bed. Condy went back to his chips. So she had to be carried to bed and yet the same night she got up and walked down to the family garage and finished herself off with monoxide. What do you think of that?' Brownwell was asking me.

"I said: 'I don't know anything about it. How do you?'

"He said: 'I know a reporter on the rag they call a newspaper down there. There was no inquest and no autopsy. If any tests were made, nothing was told about them. They don't have a regular coroner down there. The undertakers take turns at being acting coroner, a week at a time. They're pretty well subservient to the political gang naturally. It's easy to fix a thing like that in a small town, if anybody with any pull wants it fixed. And Condy had plenty at that time. He didn't want the publicity of an investigation and neither did the doctor.'"

Miss Fromsett stopped talking and waited for me to say something. When I didn't, she went on: "I suppose you know what all this meant to Brownwell."

"Sure. Almore finished her off and then he and Condy between them bought a fix. It has been done in cleaner little cities than Bay City ever tried to be. But that isn't all the story, is it?"

"No. It seems Mrs. Almore's parents hired a private detective. He was a man who ran a night watchman service down there and he was actually the second man on the scene that night, after Chris. Brownwell said he must have had something in the way of information but he never got a chance to use it. They arrested him for drunk driving and he got a jail sentence."

I said: "Is that all?"

She nodded. "And if you think I remember it too well, it's part of my job to remember conversations."

"What I was thinking was that it doesn't have to add up to very much. I don't see where it has to touch Lavery, even if he was the one who found her. Your gossipy friend Brownwell seems to think what happened gave somebody a chance to blackmail the doctor. But there would have to be some evidence, especially when you're trying to put the bite on a man who has already cleared himself with the law."

Miss Fromsett said: "I think so too. And I'd like to think blackmail was one of the nasty little tricks Chris Lavery didn't quite run to. I think that's all I can tell you, Mr. Marlowe. And I ought to be outside."

She started to get up. I said: "It's not quite all. I have something to show you."

I got the little perfumed rag that had been under Lavery's pillow out of my pocket and leaned over to drop it on the desk in front of her.

# 19

She looked at the handkerchief, looked at me, picked up a pencil and pushed the little piece of linen around with the eraser end.

"What's on it?" she asked. "Flyspray?"

"Some kind of sandalwood, I thought."

"A cheap synthetic. Repulsive is a mild word for it. And why did you want me to look at this handkerchief, Mr. Marlowe?" She leaned back again and stared at me with level cool eyes.

"I found it in Chris Lavery's house, under the pillow on his bed. It has initials on it."

She unfolded the handkerchief without touching it by using the rubber tip of the pencil. Her face got a little grim and taut.

"It has two letters embroidered on it," she said in a cold angry voice. "They happen to be the same letters as my initials. Is that what you mean?"

"Right," I said. "He probably knows half a dozen women with the same initials."

"So you're going to be nasty after all," she said quietly.

"Is it your handkerchief—or isn't it?"

She hesitated. She reached out to the desk and very quietly got herself another cigarette and lit it with a match. She shook the match slowly, watching the small flame creep along the wood.

"Yes, it's mine," she said, "I must have dropped it there. It's a long time ago. And I assure you I didn't put it under a pillow on his bed. Is that what you wanted to know?"

I didn't say anything, and she added: "He must have lent it to some woman who—who would like this kind of perfume."

"I get a mental picture of the woman," I said. "And she doesn't quite go with Lavery."

Her upper lip curled a little. It was a long upper lip. I like long upper lips.

"I think," she said, "you ought to do a little more work on your mental picture of Chris Lavery. Any touch of refinement you may have noticed is purely coincidental."

"That's not a nice thing to say about a dead man," I said.

For a moment she just sat there and looked at me as if I hadn't said anything and she was waiting for me to say something. Then a slow shudder started at her throat and passed over her whole body. Her hands clenched and the cigarette bent into a crook. She looked down at it and threw it into the ashtray with a quick jerk of her arm.

"He was shot in his shower," I said. "And it looks as if it was done by some woman who spent the night there. He had just been shaving. The woman left a gun on the stairs and this handkerchief on the bed."

She moved very slightly in her chair. Her eyes were perfectly empty now. Her face was as cold as a carving.

"And did you expect me to be able to give you information about that?" she asked me bitterly.

"Look, Miss Fromsett, I'd like to be smooth and distant and subtle about all this too. I'd like to play this sort of game just once the way somebody like you would like it to be played. But nobody will let me—not the clients, nor the cops, nor the people I play against. However hard I try to be nice I always end up with my nose in the dirt and my thumb feeling for somebody's eye."

She nodded as if she had only just barely heard me. "When was he shot?" she asked, and then shuddered slightly again.

"This morning, I suppose. Not long after he got up. I said he had just shaved and was going to take a shower."

"That," she said, "would probably have been quite late. I've been here since eight-thirty."

"I didn't think you shot him."

"Awfully kind of you," she said. "But it is my handkerchief, isn't it? Although not my perfume. But I don't suppose policemen are very sensitive to quality in perfume—or in anything else."

"No—and that goes for private detectives too," I said. "Are you enjoying this a lot?"

"God," she said, and put the back of her hand hard against her mouth.

"He was shot at five or six times," I said. "And missed all but twice. He was cornered in the shower stall. It was a pretty grim scene, I should think. There was a lot of hate on one side of it. Or a pretty cold-blooded mind."

"He was quite easy to hate," she said emptily. "And poisonously easy to love. Women—even decent women—make such ghastly mistakes about men."

"All you're telling me is that you once thought you loved him, but not any more, and that you didn't shoot him."

"Yes?" Her voice was light and dry now, like the perfume she didn't like to wear at the office. "I'm sure you'll respect the confidence." She laughed shortly and bitterly. "Dead," she said. "The poor, egotistical, cheap, nasty, handsome, treacherous guy. Dead and cold and done with. No, Mr. Marlowe, I didn't shoot him."

I waited, letting her work it out of her. After a moment she said quietly: "Does Mr. Kingsley know?"

I nodded.

"And the police, of course."

"Not yet. At least not from me. I found him. The house door wasn't quite shut. I went in. I found him."

She picked the pencil up and poked at the handkerchief again. "Does Mr. Kingsley know about this scented rag?"

"Nobody knows about that, except you and I, and whoever put it there."

"Nice of you," she said dryly. "And nice of you to think what you thought."

"You have a certain quality of aloofness and dignity that I like," I said. "But don't run it into the ground. What would you expect me to think? Do I pull the hankie out from under the pillow and sniff it and hold it out and say, 'Well, well, Miss Adrienne Fromsett's initials and all. Miss Fromsett must have known Lavery, perhaps very intimately. Let's say, just for the book, as intimately as my nasty little mind can conceive. And that would be pretty damn intimately. But this is cheap synthetic sandalwood and Miss Fromsett wouldn't use cheap scent. And this was under Lavery's pillow and Miss Fromsett just never keeps her hankies under a man's pillow. Therefore this has absolutely nothing to do with Miss Fromsett. It's just an optical delusion.'"

"Oh shut up," she said.

I grinned.

"What kind of girl do you think I am?" she snapped.

"I came in too late to tell you."

She flushed, but delicately and all over her face this time. Then, "Have you any idea who did it?"

"Ideas, but that's all they are. I'm afraid the police are going to find it simple. Some of Mrs. Kingsley's clothes are hanging in Lavery's closet. And when they know the whole story—including what happened at Little Fawn Lake yesterday—I'm afraid they'll just reach for the handcuffs. They have to find her first. But that won't be so hard for them."

"Crystal Kingsley," she said emptily. "So he couldn't be spared even that."

I said: "It doesn't have to be. It could be an entirely different motivation, something we know nothing about. It could have been somebody like Dr. Almore."

She looked up quickly, then shook her head. "It could be," I insisted. "We don't know anything against it. He was pretty nervous yesterday, for a man who has nothing to be afraid of. But, of course, it isn't only the guilty who are afraid."

I stood up and tapped on the edge of the desk looking down at her. She had a lovely neck. She pointed to the handkerchief.

"What about that?" she asked dully.

"If it was mine, I'd wash that cheap scent out of it."

"It has to mean something, doesn't it? It might mean a lot."

I laughed. "I don't think it means anything at all. Women are always leaving their handkerchiefs around. A fellow like Lavery would collect them and keep them in a drawer with a sandalwood sachet. Somebody would find the stock and take one out to use. Or he would lend them, enjoying the reactions to the other girls' initials. I'd say he was that kind of a heel. Goodby, Miss Fromsett, and thanks for talking to me."

I started to go, then I stopped and asked her: "Did you hear the name of the reporter down there who gave Brownwell all his information?"

She shook her head.

"Or the name of Mrs. Almore's parents?"

"Not that either. But I could probably find that out for you. I'd be glad to try."

"How?"

"Those things are usually printed in death notices, aren't they? There is pretty sure to have been a death notice in the Los Angeles papers."

"That would be very nice of you," I said. I ran a finger along the edge of the desk and looked at her sideways. Pale ivory skin, dark and lovely eyes, hair as light as hair can be and as dark as night can be.

I walked back down the room and out. The little blonde at the PBX looked at me expectantly, her small red lips parted, waiting for more fun.

I didn't have any more. I went on out.

## 20

No police cars stood in front of Lavery's house, nobody hung around on the sidewalk and when I pushed the front door open there was no smell of cigar or cigarette smoke inside. The sun had gone away from the windows and a fly buzzed softly over one of the liquor glasses. I went down to the end and hung over the railing that led downstairs. Nothing moved in Mr. Lavery's house. Nothing made sound except very faintly down below in the bathroom the quiet trickle of water dripping on a dead man's shoulder.

I went to the telephone and looked up the number of the police department in the directory. I dialed and while I was waiting for an answer, I took the little automatic out of my pocket and laid it on the table beside the telephone.

When the male voice said: "Bay City police—Smoot talking," I said: "There's been a shooting at 623 Altair Street. Man named Lavery lives there. He's dead."

"Six-two-three Altair. Who are you?"

"The name is Marlowe."

"You there in the house?"

"Right."

"Don't touch anything at all."

I hung up, sat down on the davenport and waited.

Not very long. A siren whined far off, growing louder with great surges of sound. Tires screamed at a corner, and the siren wail died to a metallic growl, then to silence, and the tires screamed again in front of the house. The Bay City police conserving rubber. Steps hit the sidewalk and I went over to the front door and opened it.

Two uniformed cops barged into the room. They were the usual large size and they had the usual weathered faces and suspicious eyes. One of them had a carnation tucked under his cap, behind his right ear. The other one was older, a little gray and grim. They stood and looked at me warily, then the older one said briefly:

"All right, where is it?"

"Downstairs in the bathroom, behind the shower curtain."

"You stay here with him, Eddie."

He went rapidly along the room and disappeared. The other one looked at me steadily and said out of the corner of his mouth:

"Don't make any false moves, buddy."

I sat down on the davenport again. The cop ranged the room with his eyes. There were sounds below stairs, feet walking. The cop with me suddenly spotted the gun lying on the telephone table. He charged at it violently, like a downfield blocker.

"This the death gun?" he almost shouted.

"I should imagine so. It's been fired."

"Ha!" He leaned over the gun, baring his teeth at me, and put his hand to his holster. His finger tickled the flap off the stud and he grasped the butt of the black revolver.

"You should what?" he barked.

"I should imagine so."

"That's very good," he sneered. "That's very good indeed."

"It's not that good," I said.

He reeled back a little. His eyes were being careful of me. "What you shoot him for?" he growled.

"I've wondered and wondered."

"Oh, a wisenheimer."

"Let's just sit down and wait for the homicide boys," I said. "I'm reserving my defense."

"Don't give me none of that," he said.

"I'm not giving you any of anything. If I had shot him, I wouldn't be here. I wouldn't have called up. You wouldn't have found the gun. Don't work so hard on the case. You won't be on it more than ten minutes."

His eyes looked hurt. He took his cap off and the carnation dropped to the floor. He bent and picked it up and twirled it between his fingers, then dropped it behind the fire screen.

"Better not do that," I told him. "They might think it's a clue and waste a lot of time on it."

"Aw hell." He bent over the screen and retrieved the carnation and put it in his pocket. "You know all the answers, don't you, buddy?"

The other cop came back up the stairs, looking grave. He stood in the middle of the floor and looked at his wrist watch and made a note in a notebook and then looked out of the front windows, holding the venetian blinds to one side to do it.

The one who had stayed with me said: "Can I look now?"

"Let it lie, Eddie. Nothing in it for us. You call the coroner?"

"I thought homicide would do that."

"Yeah, that's right. Captain Webber will be on it and he likes to do everything himself." He looked at me and said: "You're a man named Marlowe?"

I said I was a man named Marlowe.

"He's a wise guy, knows all the answers," Eddie said.

The older one looked at me absently, looked at Eddie absently, spotted the gun lying on the telephone table and looked at that not at all absently.

"Yeah, that's the death gun," Eddie said. "I ain't touched it."

The other nodded. "The boys are not so fast today. What's your line, mister? Friend of his?" He made a thumb towards the floor.

"Saw him yesterday for the first time. I'm a private operative from L.A."

"Oh." He looked at me very sharply. The other cop looked at me with deep suspicion.

"Cripes, that means everything will be all balled up," he said.

That was the first sensible remark he had made. I grinned at him affectionately.

The older cop looked out of the front window again. "That's the Almore place across the street, Eddie," he said.

Eddie went and looked with him. "Sure is," he said. "You can read the plate. Say, this guy downstairs might be the guy—"

"Shut up," the other one said and dropped the venetian blind. They both turned around and stared at me woodenly.

A car came down the block and stopped and a door slammed and more steps came down the walk. The older of the prowl car boys opened the door to two men in plain clothes, one of whom I already knew.

## 21

The one who came first was a small man for a cop, middle-aged, thin-faced, with a permanently tired expression. His nose was sharp and bent a little to one side, as if somebody had given it the elbow one time when it was into something. His blue pork pie hat was set very square on his head and chalk-white hair showed under it. He wore a dull brown suit and his hands were in the side pockets of the jacket, with the thumbs outside the seam.

The man behind him was Degarmo, the big cop with the dusty blond hair and the metallic blue eyes and the savage, lined face who had not liked my being in front of Dr. Almore's house.

The two uniformed men looked at the small man and touched their caps.

"The body's in the basement, Captain Webber. Been shot twice after a couple of misses, looks like. Dead quite some time. This party's name is Marlowe. He's a private eye from Los Angeles. I didn't question him beyond that."

"Quite right," Webber said sharply. He had a suspicious voice. He passed a suspicious eye over my face and nodded briefly. "I'm Captain Webber," he said. "This is Lieutenant Degarmo. We'll look at the body first."

He went along the room. Degarmo looked at me as if he had never seen me before and followed him. They went downstairs, the older of the two prowl car men with them. The cop called Eddie and I stared each other down for a while.

I said: "This is right across the street from Dr. Almore's place, isn't it?"

All the expression went out of his face. There hadn't been much to go. "Yeah. So what?"

"So nothing," I said.

He was silent. The voices came up from below, blurred and indistinct. The cop cocked his ear and said in a more friendly tone: "You remember that one?"

"A little."

He laughed. "They killed that one pretty," he said. "They wrapped it up and hid it in back of the shelf. The top shelf in the bathroom closet. The one you can't reach without standing on a chair."

"So they did," I said. "I wonder why."

The cop looked at me sternly. "There was good reasons, pal. Don't think there wasn't. You know this Lavery well?"

"Not well."

"On to him for something?"

"Working on him a little," I said. "You knew him?"

The cop called Eddie shook his head. "Nope. I just remembered it was a guy from this house found Almore's wife in the garage that night."

"Lavery may not have been here then," I said.

"How long's he been here?"

"I don't know," I said.

"Would be about a year and a half," the cop said, musingly. "The L.A. papers give it any play?"

"Paragraph on the Home Counties page," I said, just to be moving my mouth.

He scratched his ear and listened. Steps were coming back up the stairs. The cop's face went blank and he moved away from me and straightened up.

Captain Webber hurried over to the telephone and dialed

the number and spoke, then held the phone away from his ear and looked back over his shoulder.

"Who's deputy coroner this week, Al?"

"Ed Garland," the big lieutenant said woodenly.

"Call Ed Garland," Webber said into the phone. "Have him come over right away. And tell the flash squad to step on it."

He put the phone down and barked sharply: "Who handled this gun?"

I said: "I did."

He came over and teetered on his heels in front of me and pushed his small sharp chin up at me. He held the gun delicately on a handkerchief in his hand.

"Don't you know enough not to handle a weapon found at the scene of a crime?"

"Certainly," I said. "But when I handled it I didn't know there had been a crime. I didn't know the gun had been fired. It was lying on the stairs and I thought it had been dropped."

"A likely story," Webber said bitterly. "You get a lot of that sort of thing in your business?"

"A lot of what sort of thing?"

He kept his hard stare on me and didn't answer.

I said: "How would it be for me to tell you my story as it happened?"

He bridled at me like a cockerel. "Suppose you answer my questions exactly as I choose to put them."

I didn't say anything to that. Webber swivelled sharply and said to the two uniformed men: "You boys can get back to your car and check in with the despatcher."

They saluted and went out, closing the door softly until it stuck, then getting as mad at it as anybody else. Webber listened until their car went away. Then he put the bleak and callous eye on me once more.

"Let me see your identification."

I handed him my wallet and he rooted in it. Degarmo sat in a chair and crossed his legs and stared up blankly at the ceiling. He got a match out of his pocket and chewed the end of it. Webber gave me back my wallet. I put it away.

"People in your line make a lot of trouble," he said.

"Not necessarily," I said.

He raised his voice. It had been sharp enough before. "I said they made a lot of trouble, and a lot of trouble is what I meant. But get this straight. You're not going to make any in Bay City."

I didn't answer him. He jabbed a forefinger at me.

"You're from the big town," he said. "You think you're tough and you think you're wise. Don't worry. We can handle you. We're a small place, but we're very compact. We don't have any political tug-of-war down here. We work on the straight line and we work fast. Don't worry about us, mister."

"I'm not worrying," I said. "I don't have anything to worry about. I'm just trying to make a nice clean dollar."

"And don't give me any of the flip talk," Webber said. "I don't like it."

Degarmo brought his eyes down from the ceiling and curled a forefinger to stare at the nail. He spoke in a heavy bored voice.

"Look, chief, the fellow downstairs is called Lavery. He's dead. I knew him a little. He was a chaser."

"What of it?" Webber snapped, not looking away from me.

"The whole set-up indicates a dame," Degarmo said. "You know what these private eyes work at. Divorce stuff. Suppose we'd let him tie into it, instead of just trying to scare him dumb."

"If I'm scaring him," Webber said, "I'd like to know it. I don't see any signs of it."

He walked over to the front window and yanked the venetian blind up. Light poured into the room almost dazzlingly, after the long dimness. He came back bouncing on his heels and poked a thin hard finger at me and said:

"Talk."

I said, "I'm working for a Los Angeles business man who can't take a lot of loud publicity. That's why he hired me. A month ago his wife ran off and later a telegram came which indicated she had gone with Lavery. But my client met Lavery in town a couple of days ago and he denied it. The client believed him enough to get worried. It seems the lady is pretty reckless. She might have taken up with some bad company and got into a jam. I came down to see Lavery and he denied to me that he had gone with her. I half believed him but later I got reasonable proof that he had been with her in a San Bernardino hotel the night she was believed to have left the mountain cabin where she had been staying. With that in my pocket I came down to tackle Lavery again. No answer to the bell, the door was slightly open. I came inside, looked around, found the gun and searched the house. I found him. Just the way he is now."

"You had no right to search the house," Webber said coldly.

"Of course not," I agreed. "But I wouldn't be likely to pass up the chance either."

"The name of this man you're working for?"

"Kingsley." I gave him the Beverly Hills address. "He manages a cosmetic company in the Treloar Building on Olive. The Gillerlain Company."

Webber looked at Degarmo. Degarmo wrote lazily on an envelope. Webber looked back at me and said: "What else?"

"I went up to this mountain cabin where the lady had been staying. It's at a place called Little Fawn Lake, near Puma Point, forty-six miles into the mountains from San Bernardino."

I looked at Degarmo. He was writing slowly. His hand stopped a moment and seemed to hang in the air stiffly, then it dropped to the envelope and wrote again. I went on:

"About a month ago the wife of the caretaker at Kingsley's place up there had a fight with him and left, as everybody thought. Yesterday she was found drowned in the lake."

Webber almost closed his eyes and rocked on his heels. Almost softly he asked: "Why are you telling me this? Are you implying a connection?"

"There's a connection in time. Lavery had been up there. I don't know of any other connection, but I thought I'd better mention it."

Degarmo was sitting very still, looking at the floor in front of him. His face was tight and he looked even more savage than usual. Webber said:

"This woman that was drowned? Suicide?"

"Suicide or murder. She left a goodby note. But her husband has been arrested on suspicion. The name is Chess. Bill and Muriel Chess, his wife."

"I don't want any part of that," Webber said sharply. "Let's confine ourselves to what went on here."

"Nothing went on here," I said, looking at Degarmo. "I've been down here twice. The first time I talked to Lavery and didn't get anywhere. The second time I didn't talk to him and didn't get anywhere."

Webber said slowly: "I'm going to ask you a question and I want an honest answer. You won't want to give it, but now will be as good a time as later. You know I'll get it eventually. The question is this. You have looked through the house and I imagine pretty thoroughly. Have you seen anything that suggests to you that this Kingsley woman has been here?"

"That's not a fair question," I said. "It calls for a conclusion of the witness."

"I want an answer to it," he said grimly. "This isn't a court of law."

"The answer is yes," I said. "There are women's clothes hanging in a closet downstairs that have been described to me as being worn by Mrs. Kingsley at San Bernardino the night she met Lavery there. The description was not exact though. A black and white suit, mostly white, and a panama hat with a rolled black and white band."

Degarmo snapped a finger against the envelope he was holding. "You must be a great guy for a client to have working for him," he said. "That puts the woman right in this house where a murder has been committed and she is the woman he's supposed to have gone away with. I don't think we'll have to look far for the killer, chief."

Webber was staring at me fixedly, with little or no expression on his face but a kind of tight watchfulness. He nodded absently to what Degarmo had said.

I said: "I'm assuming you fellows are not a pack of damn fools. The clothes are tailored and easy to trace. I've saved you an hour by telling you, perhaps even no more than a phone call."

"Anything else?" Webber asked quietly.

Before I could answer, a car stopped outside the house, and then another. Webber skipped over to open the door. Three men came in, a short, curly-haired man and a large ox-like man, both carrying heavy black leather cases. Behind them a tall thin man in a dark gray suit and black tie. He had very bright eyes and a poker face.

Webber pointed a finger at the curly-haired man and said: "Downstairs in the bathroom, Busoni. I want a lot of prints from all over the house, particularly any that seem to be made by a woman. It will be a long job."

"I do all the work," Busoni grunted. He and the ox-like man went along the room and down the stairs.

"We have a corpse for you, Garland," Webber said to the third man. "Let's go down and look at him. You've ordered the wagon?"

The bright-eyed man nodded briefly and he and Webber went downstairs after the other two.

Degarmo put the envelope and pencil away. He stared at me woodenly.

I said: "Am I supposed to talk about our conversation yesterday—or is that a private transaction?"

"Talk about it all you like," he said. "It's our job to protect the citizen."

"You talk about it," I said. "I'd like to know more about the Almore case."

He flushed slowly and his eyes got mean. "You said you didn't know Almore."

"I didn't yesterday, or know anything about him. Since then I've learned that Lavery knew Mrs. Almore, that she committed suicide, that Lavery found her dead, and that Lavery has at least been suspected of blackmailing him—or of being in a position to blackmail him. Also both your prowl-car boys seemed interested in the fact that Almore's house was across the street from here. And one of them remarked that the case had been killed pretty, or words to that effect."

Degarmo said in a slow deadly tone: "I'll have the badge off the son of a bitch. All they do is flap their mouths. God damn empty-headed bastards."

"Then there's nothing in it," I said.

He looked at his cigarette. "Nothing in what?"

"Nothing in the idea that Almore murdered his wife, and had enough pull to get it fixed."

Degarmo came to his feet and walked over to lean down at me. "Say that again," he said softly.

I said it again.

He hit me across the face with his open hand. It jerked my head around hard. My face felt hot and large.

"Say it again," he said softly.

I said it again. His hand swept and knocked my head to one side again.

"Say it again."

"Nope. Third time lucky. You might miss." I put a hand up and rubbed my cheek.

He stood leaning down, his lips drawn back over his teeth, a hard animal glare in his very blue eyes.

"Any time you talk like that to a cop," he said, "you know what you got coming. Try it on again and it won't be the flat of a hand I'll use on you."

I bit hard on my lips and rubbed my cheek.

"Poke your big nose into our business and you'll wake up in an alley with the cats looking at you," he said.

I didn't say anything. He went and sat down again, breathing hard. I stopped rubbing my face and held my hand out and worked the fingers slowly, to get the hard clench out of them.

"I'll remember that," I said. "Both ways."

## 22

It was early evening when I got back to Hollywood and up to the office. The building had emptied out and the corridors were silent. Doors were open and the cleaning women were inside with their vacuum cleaners and their dry mops and dusters.

I unlocked the door to mine and picked up an envelope that lay in front of the mail slot and dropped it on the desk without looking at it. I ran the windows up and leaned out, looking at the early neon lights glowing, smelling the warm, foody air that drifted up from the alley ventilator of the coffee shop next door.

I peeled off my coat and tie and sat down at the desk and got the office bottle out of the deep drawer and bought myself a drink. It didn't do any good. I had another, with the same result.

By now Webber would have seen Kingsley. There would be a general alarm out for his wife, already, or very soon. The thing looked cut and dried to them. A nasty affair between two rather nasty people, too much loving, too much drinking, too much proximity ending in a savage hatred and a murderous impulse and death.

I thought this was all a little too simple.

I reached for the envelope and tore it open. It had no stamp. It read: "Mr. Marlowe: Florence Almore's parents are a Mr. and Mrs. Eustace Grayson, presently residing at the Rossmore Arms, 640 South Oxford Avenue. I checked this by calling the listed phone number. Yrs. Adrienne Fromsett."

An elegant handwriting, like the elegant hand that wrote it. I pushed it to one side and had another drink. I began to feel a little less savage. I pushed things around on the desk. My hands felt thick and hot and awkward. I ran a finger across the corner of the desk and looked at the streak made by the wiping off of the dust. I looked at the dust on my finger and wiped that off. I looked at my watch. I looked at the wall. I looked at nothing.

I put the liquor bottle away and went over to the washbowl to rinse the glass out. When I had done that I washed my hands and bathed my face in cold water and looked at it. The flush was gone from the left cheek, but it looked a little swollen. Not very much, but enough to make me tighten up again. I brushed my hair and looked at the gray in it. There was getting to be plenty of gray in it. The face under the hair had a sick look. I didn't like the face at all.

I went back to the desk and read Miss Fromsett's note again. I smoothed it out on the glass and sniffed it and smoothed it out some more and folded it and put it in my coat pocket.

I sat very still and listened to the evening grow quiet outside the open windows. And very slowly I grew quiet with it.

## 23

The Rossmore Arms was a gloomy pile of dark red brick built around a huge forecourt. It had a plush-lined lobby containing silence, tubbed plants, a bored canary in a cage as big as a dog-house, a smell of old carpet dust and the cloying fragrance of gardenias long ago.

The Graysons were on the fifth floor in front, in the north wing. They were sitting together in a room which seemed to be deliberately twenty years out of date. It had fat overstuffed furniture and brass doorknobs, shaped like eggs, a huge wall mirror in a gilt frame, a marble-topped table in the window and dark red plush side drapes by the windows. It smelled of tobacco smoke and behind that the air was telling me they had had lamb chops and broccoli for dinner.

Grayson's wife was a plump woman who might once have had big baby-blue eyes. They were faded out now and dimmed by glasses and slightly protuberant. She had kinky white hair. She sat darning socks with her thick ankles crossed, her feet just reaching the floor, and a big wicker sewing basket in her lap.

Grayson was a long stooped yellow-faced man with high shoulders, bristly eyebrows and almost no chin. The upper part of his face meant business. The lower part was just saying goodby. He wore bifocals and he had been gnawing fretfully at the evening paper. I had looked him up in the city directory. He was a C.P.A. and looked it every inch. He even had ink on his fingers and there were four pencils in the pocket of his open vest.

He read my card carefully for the seventh time and looked me up and down and said slowly:

"What is it you want to see us about, Mr. Marlowe?"

"I'm interested in a man named Lavery. He lives across the street from Dr. Almore. Your daughter was the wife of Dr. Almore. Lavery is the man who found your daughter the night she—died."

They both pointed like bird dogs when I deliberately hesitated on the last word. Grayson looked at his wife and she shook her head.

"We don't care to talk about that," Grayson said promptly. "It is much too painful to us."

I waited a moment and looked gloomy with them. Then I said: "I don't blame you. I don't want to make you. I'd like to get in touch with the man you hired to look into it, though."

They looked at each other again. Mrs. Grayson didn't shake her head this time.

Grayson asked: "Why?"

"I'd better tell you a little of my story." I told them what I had been hired to do, not mentioning Kingsley by name. I told them the incident with Degarmo outside Almore's house the day before. They pointed again on that.

Grayson said sharply: "Am I to understand that you were unknown to Dr. Almore, had not approached him in any way, and that he nevertheless called a police officer because you were outside his house?"

I said: "That's right. Had been outside for at least an hour though. That is, my car had."

"That's very queer," Grayson said.

"I'd say that was one very nervous man," I said. "And Degarmo asked me if her folks—meaning your daughter's folks—had hired me. Looks as if he didn't feel safe yet, wouldn't you say?"

"Safe about what?" He didn't look at me saying this. He re-lit his pipe, slowly, then tamped the tobacco down with the end of a big metal pencil and lit it again.

I shrugged and didn't answer. He looked at me quickly and looked away. Mrs. Grayson didn't look at me, but her nostrils quivered.

"How did he know who you were?" Grayson asked suddenly.

"Made a note of the car license, called the Auto Club, looked up the name in the directory. At least that's what I'd have done and I saw him through his window making some of the motions."

"So he has the police working for him," Grayson said.

"Not necessarily. If they made a mistake that time, they wouldn't want it found out now."

"Mistake!" He laughed almost shrilly.

"Okay," I said. "The subject is painful but a little fresh air won't hurt it. You've always thought he murdered her, haven't you? That's why you hired this dick—detective."

Mrs. Grayson looked up with quick eyes and ducked her head down and rolled up another pair of mended socks.

Grayson said nothing.

I said: "Was there any evidence, or was it just that you didn't like him?"

"There was evidence," Grayson said bitterly, and with a sudden clearness of voice, as if he had decided to talk about it after all. "There must have been. We were told there was. But we never got it. The police took care of that."

"I heard they had this fellow arrested and sent up for drunk driving."

"You heard right."

"But he never told you what he had to go on?"

"No."

"I don't like that," I said. "That sounds a little as if this fellow hadn't made up his mind whether to use his information for your benefit or keep it and put a squeeze on the doctor."

Grayson looked at his wife again. She said quietly: "Mr. Talley didn't impress me that way. He was a quiet unassuming little man. But you can't always judge, I know."

I said: "So Talley was his name. That was one of the things I hoped you would tell me."

"And what were the others?" Grayson asked.

"How can I find Talley—and what it was that laid the groundwork of suspicion in your minds. It must have been there, or you wouldn't have hired Talley without a better showing from him that *he* had grounds."

Grayson smiled very thinly and primly. He reached for his little chin and rubbed it with one long yellow finger.

Mrs. Grayson said: "Dope."

"She means that literally," Grayson said at once, as if the single word had been a green light. "Almore was, and no doubt is, a dope doctor. Our daughter made that clear to us. In his hearing too. He didn't like it."

"Just what do you mean by a dope doctor, Mr. Grayson?"

"I mean a doctor whose practice is largely with people who are living on the raw edge of nervous collapse, from drink and dissipation. People who have to be given sedatives and narcotics all the time. The stage comes when an ethical physician refuses to treat them any more, outside a sanatorium. But not the Dr. Almores. *They* will keep on as long as the money comes in, as long as the patient remains alive and reasonably sane, even if he or she becomes a hopeless addict in the process. A lucrative practice," he said primly, "and I imagine a dangerous one to the doctor."

"No doubt of that," I said. "But there's a lot of money in it. Did you know a man named Condy?"

"No. We know who he was. Florence suspected he was a source of Almore's narcotic supply."

I said: "Could be. He probably wouldn't want to write himself too many prescriptions. Did you know Lavery?"

"We never saw him. We knew who he was."

"Ever occur to you that Lavery might have been blackmailing Almore?"

It was a new idea to him. He ran his hand over the top of his head and brought it down over his face and dropped it to his bony knee. He shook his head.

"No. Why should it?"

"He was first to the body," I said. "Whatever looked wrong to Talley must have been equally visible to Lavery."

"Is Lavery that kind of man?"

"I don't know. He has no visible means of support, no job. He gets around a lot, especially with women."

"It's an idea," Grayson said. "And those things can be handled very discreetly." He smiled wryly. "I have come across traces of them in my work. Unsecured loans, long outstanding. Investments on the face of them worthless made by men who would not be likely to make worthless investments. Bad debts that should obviously be charged off and have not been, for fear of inviting scrutiny from the income tax people. Oh yes, those things can easily be arranged."

I looked at Mrs. Grayson. Her hands had never stopped working. She had a dozen pairs of darned socks finished. Grayson's long bony feet would be hard on socks.

"What's happened to Talley? Was he framed?"

"I don't think there's any doubt about it. His wife was very bitter. She said he had been given a doped drink in a bar and he had been drinking with a policeman. She said a police car was waiting across the street for him to start driving and that he was picked up at once. Also that he was given only the most perfunctory examination at the jail."

"That doesn't mean too much. That's what he told her after he was arrested. He'd tell her something like that automatically."

"Well, I hate to think the police are not honest," Grayson said. "But these things are done, and everybody knows it."

I said: "If they made an honest mistake about your daughter's death, they would hate to have Talley show them up. It might mean several lost jobs. If they thought what he was really after was blackmail, they wouldn't be too fussy about how they took care of him. Where is Talley now? What it all boils down to is that if there was any solid clue, he either had it or was on the track of it and knew what he was looking for."

Grayson said: "We don't know where he is. He got six months, but that expired long ago."

"How about his wife?"

He looked at his own wife. She said briefly: "1618½ Westmore Street, Bay City. Eustace and I sent her a little money. She was left bad off."

I made a note of the address and leaned back in my chair and said:

"Somebody shot Lavery this morning in his bathroom."

Mrs. Grayson's pudgy hands became still on the edges of the basket. Grayson sat with his mouth open, holding his pipe in front of it. He made a noise of clearing his throat softly, as if in the presence of the dead. Nothing ever moved slower than his old black pipe going back between his teeth.

"Of course it would be too much to expect," he said and let it hang in the air and blew a little pale smoke at it, and then added, "that Dr. Almore had any connection with that."

"I'd like to think he had," I said. "He certainly lives at a handy distance. The police think my client's wife shot him. They have a good case too, when they find her. But if Almore had anything to do with it, it must surely arise out of your daughter's death. That's why I'm trying to find out something about that."

Grayson said: "A man who has done one murder wouldn't have more than twenty-five per cent of the hesitation in doing another." He spoke as if he had given the matter considerable study.

I said: "Yeah, maybe. What was supposed to be the motive for the first one?"

"Florence was wild," he said sadly. "A wild and difficult girl. She was wasteful and extravagant, always picking up new and rather doubtful friends, talking too much and too loudly, and generally acting the fool. A wife like that can be very dangerous to a man like Albert S. Almore. But I don't believe that was the prime motive, was it, Lettie?"

He looked at his wife, but she didn't look at him. She jabbed a darning needle into a round ball of wool and said nothing.

Grayson sighed and went on: "We had reason to believe he was carrying on with his office nurse and that Florence had threatened him with a public scandal. He couldn't have anything like that, could he? One kind of scandal might too easily lead to another."

I said: "How did he do the murder?"

"With morphine, of course. He always had it, he always used it. He was an expert in the use of it. Then when she was in a deep coma he would have placed her in the garage and started the car motor. There was no autopsy, you know. But if there had been, it was known that she had been given a hypodermic injection that night."

I nodded and he leaned back satisfied and ran his hand over his head and down his face and let it fall slowly to his bony knee. He seemed to have given a lot of study to this angle too.

I looked at them. A couple of elderly people sitting there quietly, poisoning their minds with hate, a year and a half after it had happened. They would like it if Almore had shot Lavery. They would love it. It would warm them clear down to their ankles.

After a pause I said: "You're believing a lot of this because you want to. It's always possible that she committed suicide, and that the cover-up was partly to protect Condy's gambling club and partly to prevent Almore having to be questioned at a public hearing."

"Rubbish," Grayson said sharply. "He murdered her all right. She was in bed, asleep."

"You don't know that. She might have been taking dope herself. She might have established a tolerance for it. The effect wouldn't last long in that case. She might have got up in the middle of the night and looked at herself in the glass and seen devils pointing at her. These things happen."

"I think you have taken up enough of our time," Grayson said.

I stood up. I thanked them both and made a yard towards the door and said: "You didn't do anything more about it after Talley was arrested?"

"Saw an assistant district attorney named Leach," Grayson grunted. "Got exactly nowhere. He saw nothing to justify his office in interfering. Wasn't even interested in the narcotic angle. But Condy's place was closed up about a month later. That might have come out of it somehow."

"That was probably the Bay City cops throwing a little smoke. You'd find Condy somewhere else, if you knew where to look. With all his original equipment intact."

I started for the door again and Grayson hoisted himself out of his chair and dragged across the room after me. There was a flush on his yellow face.

"I didn't mean to be rude," he said. "I guess Lettie and I oughtn't to brood about this business the way we do."

"I think you've both been very patient," I said. "Was there anybody else involved in all this that we haven't mentioned by name?"

He shook his head, then looked back at his wife. Her hands were motionless holding the current sock on the darning egg. Her head was tilted a little to one side. Her attitude was of listening, but not to us.

I said: "The way I got the story, Dr. Almore's office nurse put Mrs. Almore to bed that night. Would that be the one he was supposed to be playing around with?"

Mrs. Grayson said sharply: "Wait a minute. We never saw the girl. But she had a pretty name. Just give me a minute."

We gave her a minute. "Mildred something," she said, and snapped her teeth.

I took a deep breath. "Would it be Mildred Haviland, Mrs. Grayson?"

She smiled brightly and nodded. "Of course, Mildred Haviland. Don't you remember, Eustace?"

He didn't remember. He looked at us like a horse that has got into the wrong stable. He opened the door and said: "What does it matter?"

"And you said Talley was a small man," I bored on. "He wouldn't for instance be a big loud bruiser with an overbearing manner?"

"Oh no," Mrs. Grayson said. "Mr. Talley is a man of not more than medium height, middle-aged, with brownish hair and a very quiet voice. He had a sort of worried expression. I mean, he looked as if he always had it."

"Looks as if he needed it," I said.

Grayson put his bony hand out and I shook it. It felt like shaking hands with a towel rack.

"If you get him," he said and clamped his mouth hard on his pipe stem, "call back with a bill. If you get Almore, I mean, of course."

I said I knew he meant Almore, but that there wouldn't be any bill.

I went back along the silent hallway. The self-operating elevator was carpeted in red plush. It had an elderly perfume in it, like three widows drinking tea.

## 24

The house on Westmore Street was a small frame bungalow behind a larger house. There was no number visible on the smaller house, but the one in front showed a stencilled *1618* beside the door, with a dim light behind the stencil. A narrow concrete path led along under windows to the house at the back. It had a tiny porch with a single chair on it. I stepped up on the porch and rang the bell.

It buzzed not very far off. The front door was open behind the screen but there was no light. From the darkness a querulous voice said:

"What is it?"

I spoke into the darkness. "Mr. Talley in?"

The voice became flat and without tone. "Who wants him?"

"A friend."

The woman sitting inside in the darkness made a vague sound in her throat which might have been amusement. Or she might just have been clearing her throat.

"All right," she said. "How much is this one?"

"It's not a bill, Mrs. Talley. I suppose you are Mrs. Talley?"

"Oh, go away and let me alone," the voice said. "Mr. Talley isn't here. He hasn't been here. He won't be here."

I put my nose against the screen and tried to peer into the room. I could see the vague outlines of its furniture. From where the voice came from also showed the shape of a couch. A woman was lying on it. She seemed to be lying on her back and looking up at the ceiling. She was quite motionless.

"I'm sick," the voice said. "I've had enough trouble. Go away and leave me be."

I said: "I've just come from talking to the Graysons."

There was a little silence, but no movement, then a sigh. "I never heard of them."

I leaned against the frame of the screen door and looked back along the narrow walk to the street. There was a car across the way with parking lights burning. There were other cars along the block.

I said: "Yes, you have, Mrs. Talley. I'm working for them. They're still in there pitching. How about you? Don't you want something back?"

The voice said: "I want to be let alone."

"I want information," I said. "I'm going to get it. Quietly if I can. Loud, if it can't be quiet."

The voice said: "Another copper, eh?"

"You know I'm not a copper, Mrs. Talley. The Graysons wouldn't talk to a copper. Call them up and ask them."

"I never heard of them," the voice said. "I don't have a

phone, if I knew them. Go away, copper. I'm sick. I've been sick for a month."

"My name is Marlowe," I said. "Philip Marlowe. I'm a private eye in Los Angeles, I've been talking to the Graysons. I've got something, but I want to talk to your husband."

The woman on the couch let out a dim laugh which barely reached across the room. "You've got something," she said. "That sounds familiar. My God it does! You've got something. George Talley had something too—once."

"He can have it again," I said, "if he plays his cards right."

"If that's what it takes," she said, "you can scratch him off right now."

I leaned against the doorframe and scratched my chin instead. Somebody back on the street had clicked a flashlight on. I didn't know why. It went off again. It seemed to be near my car.

The pale blur of face on the couch moved and disappeared. Hair took its place. The woman had turned her face to the wall.

"I'm tired," she said, her voice now muffled by talking at the wall. "I'm so damn tired. Beat it, mister. Be nice and go away."

"Would a little money help any?"

"Can't you smell the cigar smoke?"

I sniffed. I didn't smell any cigar smoke. I said "No."

"They've been here. They were here two hours. God, I'm tired of it all. Go away."

"Look, Mrs. Talley—"

She rolled on the couch and the blur of her face showed again. I could almost see her eyes, not quite.

"Look yourself," she said. "I don't know you. I don't want to know you. I have nothing to tell you. I wouldn't tell it, if I had. I live here, mister, if you call it living. Anyway it's the nearest I can get to living. I want a little peace and quiet. Now you get out and leave me alone."

"Let me in the house," I said. "We can talk this over. I think I can show you—"

She rolled suddenly on the couch again and feet struck the floor. A tight anger came into her voice.

"If you don't get out," she said. "I'm going to start yelling my head off. Right now. Now!"

"Okay," I said quickly. "I'll stick my card in the door. So you won't forget my name. You might change your mind."

I got the card out and wedged it into the crack of the screen door. I said: "Well goodnight, Mrs. Talley."

No answer. Her eyes were looking across the room at me, faintly luminous in the dark. I went down off the porch and back along the narrow walk to the street.

Across the way a motor purled gently in the car with the parking lights on it. Motors purl gently in thousands of cars on thousands of streets, everywhere.

I got into the Chrysler and started it up.

## 25

Westmore was a north and south street on the wrong side of town. I drove north. At the next corner I bumped over disused interurban tracks and on into a block of junk yards. Behind wooden fences the decomposing carcases of old automobiles lay in grotesque designs, like a modern battlefield. Piles of rusted parts looked lumpy under the moon. Roof high piles, with alleys between them.

Headlights glowed in my rear view mirror. They got larger. I stepped on the gas and reached keys out of my pocket and unlocked the glove compartment. I took a .38 out and laid it on the car seat close to my leg.

Beyond the junk yards there was a brick field. The tall chimney of the kiln was smokeless, far off over waste land. Piles of dark bricks, a low wooden building with a sign on it, emptiness, no one moving, no light.

The car behind me gained. The low whine of a lightly touched siren growled through the night. The sound loafed over the fringes of a neglected golf course to the east, across the brick yard to the west. I speeded up a bit more, but it wasn't any use. The car behind me came up fast and a huge red spotlight suddenly glared all over the road.

The car came up level and started to cut in. I stood the Chrysler on its nose, swung out behind the police car, and made a U turn with half an inch to spare. I gunned the motor the other way. Behind me sounded the rough clashing of gears, the howl of an infuriated motor, and the red spotlight swept for what seemed miles over the brickyard.

It wasn't any use. They were behind me and coming fast again. I didn't have any idea of getting away. I wanted to get back where there were houses and people to come out and watch and perhaps to remember.

I didn't make it. The police car heaved up alongside again and a hard voice yelled:

"Pull over, or we'll blast a hole in you!"

I pulled over to the curb and set the brake. I put the gun back in the glove compartment and snapped it shut. The police car jumped on its springs just in front of my left front fender. A fat man slammed out of it roaring.

"Don't you know a police siren when you hear one? Get out of that car!"

I got out of the car and stood beside it in the moonlight. The fat man had a gun in his hand.

"Gimme your license!" he barked in a voice as hard as the blade of a shovel.

I took it out and held it out. The other cop in the car slid out from under the wheel and came around beside me and took what I was holding out. He put a flash on it and read.

"Name of Marlowe," he said. "Hell, the guy's a shamus. Just think of that, Cooney."

Cooney said: "Is that all? Guess I won't need this." He tucked the gun back in his holster and buttoned the leather flap down over it. "Guess I can handle this with my little flippers," he said. "Guess I can at that."

The other one said: "Doing fifty-five. Been drinking, I wouldn't wonder."

"Smell the bastard's breath," Cooney said.

The other one leaned forward with a polite leer. "Could I smell the breath, shamus?"

I let him smell the breath.

"Well," he said judiciously, "he ain't staggering. I got to admit that."

"'S a cold night for summer. Buy the boy a drink, Officer Dobbs."

"Now that's a sweet idea," Dobbs said. He went to the car and got a half pint bottle out of it. He held it up. It was a third full. "No really solid drinking here," he said. He held the bottle out. "With our compliments, pal."

"Suppose I don't want a drink," I said.

"Don't say that," Cooney whined. "We might get the idea you wanted feetprints on your stomach."

I took the bottle and unscrewed the cap and sniffed. The liquor in the bottle smelled like whiskey. Just whiskey.

"You can't work the same gag all the time," I said.

Cooney said: "Time is eight twenty-seven. Write it down, Officer Dobbs."

Dobbs went to the car and leaned in to make a note on his report. I held the bottle up and said to Cooney: "You insist that I drink this?"

"Naw. You could have me jump on your belly instead."

I tilted the bottle, locked my throat, and filled my mouth with whiskey. Cooney lunged forward and sank a fist in my stomach. I sprayed the whiskey and bent over choking. I dropped the bottle.

I bent to get it and saw Cooney's fat knee rising at my face. I stepped to one side and straightened and slammed him on the nose with everything I had. His left hand went to his face and his voice howled and his right hand jumped to his gun holster. Dobbs ran at me from the side and his arm swung low. The blackjack hit me behind the left knee, the leg went dead and I sat down hard on the ground, gritting my teeth and spitting whiskey.

Cooney took his hand away from his face full of blood.

"Jesus," he cracked in a thick horrible voice. "This is blood. My blood." He let out a wild roar and swung his foot at my face.

I rolled far enough to catch it on my shoulder. It was bad enough taking it there.

Dobbs pushed between us and said: "We got enough, Charlie. Better not get it all gummed up."

Cooney stepped backwards three shuffling steps and sat down on the running board of the police car and held his face. He groped for a handkerchief and used it gently on his nose.

"Just gimme a minute," he said through the handkerchief. "Just a minute, pal. Just one little minute."

Dobbs said, "Pipe down. We got enough. That's the way it's going to be." He swung the blackjack slowly beside his leg. Cooney got up off the running board and staggered forward. Dobbs put a hand against his chest and pushed him gently. Cooney tried to knock the hand out of his way.

"I gotta see blood," he croaked. "I gotta see more blood."

Dobbs said sharply, "Nothing doing. Pipe down. We got all we wanted."

Cooney turned and moved heavily away to the other side of the police car. He leaned against it muttering through his handkerchief. Dobbs said to me:

"Up on the feet, boy friend."

I got up and rubbed behind my knee. The nerve of the leg was jumping like an angry monkey.

"Get in the car," Dobbs said. "Our car."

I went over and climbed into the police car.

Dobbs said: "You drive the other heap, Charlie."

"I'll tear every god damn fender off'n it," Cooney roared.

Dobbs picked the whiskey bottle off the ground, threw it over the fence, and slid into the car beside me. He pressed the starter.

"This is going to cost you," he said. "You hadn't ought to have socked him."

I said: "Just why not?"

"He's a good guy," Dobbs said. "A little loud."

"But not funny," I said. "Not at all funny."

"Don't tell him," Dobbs said. The police car began to move. "You'd hurt his feelings."

Cooney slammed into the Chrysler and started it and clashed the gears as if he was trying to strip them. Dobbs tooled the police car smoothly around and started north again along the brickyard.

"You'll like our new jail," he said.

"What will the charge be?"

He thought a moment, guiding the car with a gentle hand

and watching in the mirror to see that Cooney followed along behind.

"Speeding," he said. "Resisting arrest. H.B.D." H.B.D. is police slang for "had been drinking."

"How about being slammed in the belly, kicked in the shoulder, forced to drink liquor under threat of bodily harm, threatened with a gun and struck with a blackjack while unarmed? Couldn't you make a little something more out of that?"

"Aw forget it," he said wearily. "You think this sort of thing is my idea of a good time?"

"I thought they cleaned this town up," I said. "I thought they had it so that a decent man could walk the streets at night without wearing a bullet proof vest."

"They cleaned it up some," he said. "They wouldn't want it too clean. They might scare away a dirty dollar."

"Better not talk like that," I said. "You'll lose your union card."

He laughed. "The hell with them," he said. "I'll be in the army in two weeks."

The incident was over for him. It meant nothing. He took it as a matter of course. He wasn't even bitter about it.

# 26

The cell block was almost brand new. The battleship gray paint on the steel walls and door still had the fresh gloss of newness disfigured in two or three places by squirted tobacco juice. The overhead light was sunk in the ceiling behind a heavy frosted panel. There were two bunks on one side of the cell and a man snored in the top bunk, with a dark gray blanket wrapped around him. Since he was asleep that early and didn't smell of whiskey or gin and had chosen the top berth where he would be out of the way, I judged he was an old lodger.

I sat on the lower bunk. They had tapped me for a gun but they hadn't stripped my pockets. I got out a cigarette and rubbed the hot swelling behind my knee. The pain radiated all the way to the ankle. The whiskey I had coughed on my coat front had a rank smell. I held the cloth up and breathed smoke into it. The smoke floated up around the flat square of lighted glass in the ceiling. The jail seemed very quiet. A woman was making a shrill racket somewhere very far off, in another part of the jail. My part was as peaceful as a church.

The woman was screaming, wherever she was. The screaming had a thin sharp unreal sound, something like the screaming of coyotes in the moonlight, but it didn't have the rising keening note of the coyote. After a while the sound stopped.

I smoked two cigarettes through and dropped the butts into the small toilet in the corner. The man in the upper berth still snored. All I could see of him was damp greasy hair sticking out over the edge of the blanket. He slept on his stomach. He slept well. He was one of the best.

I sat down on the bunk again. It was made of flat steel slats with a thin hard mattress over them. Two dark gray blankets were folded on it quite neatly. It was a very nice jail. It was on the twelfth floor of the new city hall. It was a very nice city hall. Bay City was a very nice place. People lived there and thought so. If I lived there, I would probably think so. I would see the nice blue bay and the cliffs and the yacht harbor and the quiet streets of houses, old houses brooding under old trees and new houses with sharp green lawns and wire fences and staked saplings set into the parkway in front of them. I knew a girl who lived on Twenty-fifth Street. It was a nice street. She was a nice girl. She liked Bay City.

She wouldn't think about the Mexican and Negro slums stretched out on the dismal flats south of the old interurban tracks. Nor of the waterfront dives along the flat shore south of the cliffs, the sweaty little dance halls on the pike, the marihuana joints, the narrow fox faces watching over the tops of newspapers in far too quiet hotel lobbies, nor the pickpockets and grifters and con men and drunk rollers and pimps and queens on the board walk.

I went over to stand by the door. There was nobody

stirring across the way. The lights in the cell block were bleak and silent. Business in the jail was rotten.

I looked at my watch. Nine fifty-four. Time to go home and get your slippers on and play over a game of chess. Time for a tall cool drink and a long quiet pipe. Time to sit with your feet up and think of nothing. Time to start yawning over your magazine. Time to be a human being, a householder, a man with nothing to do but rest and suck in the night air and rebuild the brain for tomorrow.

A man in the blue-gray jail uniform came along between the cells reading numbers. He stopped in front of mine and unlocked the door and gave me the hard stare they think they have to wear on their pans forever and forever and forever. I'm a cop, brother, I'm tough, watch your step, brother, or we'll fix you up so you'll crawl on your hands and knees, brother, snap out of it, brother, let's get a load of the truth, brother, let's go, and let's not forget we're tough guys, we're cops, and we do what we like with punks like you.

"Out," he said.

I stepped out of the cell and he relocked the door and jerked his thumb and we went along to a wide steel gate and he unlocked that and we went through and he relocked it and the keys tinkled pleasantly on the big steel ring and after a while we went through a steel door that was painted like wood on the outside and battleship gray on the inside.

Degarmo was standing there by the counter talking to the desk sergeant.

He turned his metallic blue eyes on me and said: "How you doing?"

"Fine."

"Like our jail?"

"I like your jail fine."

"Captain Webber wants to talk to you."

"That's fine," I said.

"Don't you know any words but fine?"

"Not right now," I said. "Not in here."

"You're limping a little," he said. "You trip over something?"

"Yeah," I said. "I tripped over a blackjack. It jumped up and bit me behind the left knee."

"That's too bad," Degarmo said, blank-eyed. "Get your stuff from the property clerk."

"I've got it," I said. "It wasn't taken away from me."

"Well, that's fine," he said.

"It sure is," I said. "It's fine."

The desk sergeant lifted his shaggy head and gave us both a long stare. "You ought to see Cooney's little Irish nose," he said. "If you want to see something fine. It's spread over his face like syrup on a waffle."

Degarmo said absently: "What's the matter? He get in a fight?"

"I wouldn't know," the desk sergeant said. "Maybe it was the same blackjack that jumped up and bit him."

"For a desk sergeant you talk too damn much," Degarmo said.

"A desk sergeant always talks too God damn much," the desk sergeant said. "Maybe that's why he isn't a lieutenant on homicide."

"You see how we are here," Degarmo said. "Just one great big happy family."

"With beaming smiles on our faces," the desk sergeant said, "and our arms spread wide in welcome, and a rock in each hand."

Degarmo jerked his head at me and we went out.

## 27

Captain Webber pushed his sharp bent nose across the desk at me and said: "Sit down."

I sat down in a round-backed wooden armchair and eased my left leg away from the sharp edge of the seat. It was a large neat corner office. Degarmo sat at the end of the desk and crossed his legs and rubbed his ankle thoughtfully, looked out of a window.

Webber went on: "You asked for trouble, and you got it. You were doing fifty-five miles an hour in a residential zone and you attempted to get away from a police car that signaled you to stop with its siren and red spotlight. You were abusive when stopped and you struck an officer in the face."

I said nothing. Webber picked a match off his desk and broke it in half and threw the pieces over his shoulder.

"Or are they lying—as usual?" he asked.

"I didn't see their report," I said. "I was probably doing fifty-five in a residential district, or anyhow within city limits. The police car was parked outside a house I visited. It followed me when I drove away and I didn't at that time know it was a police car. It had no good reason to follow me and I didn't like the look of it. I went a little fast, but all I was trying to do was get to a better lighted part of town."

Degarmo moved his eyes to give me a bleak meaningless stare. Webber snapped his teeth impatiently.

He said: "After you knew it was a police car you made a half turn in the middle of the block and still tried to get away. Is that right?"

I said: "Yes. It's going to take a little frank talk to explain that."

"I'm not afraid of a little frank talk," Webber said. "I tend to kind of specialize in frank talk."

I said: "These cops that picked me up were parked in front of the house where George Talley's wife lives. They were there before I got there. George Talley is the man who used to be a private detective down here. I wanted to see him. Degarmo knows why I wanted to see him."

Degarmo picked a match out of his pocket and chewed on the soft end of it quietly. He nodded, without expression. Webber didn't look at him.

I said: "You are a stupid man, Degarmo. Everything you do is stupid, and done in a stupid way. When you went up against me yesterday in front of Almore's house you had to get tough when there was nothing to get tough about. You had to make me curious when I had nothing to be curious about. You even had to drop hints which showed me how I could satisfy that curiosity, if it became important. All you had to do to protect your friends was keep your mouth shut until I made a move. I never would have made one, and you would have saved all this."

Webber said: "What the devil has all this got to do with

your being arrested in the twelve hundred block on Westmore Street?"

"It has to do with the Almore case," I said. "George Talley worked on the Almore case—until he was pinched for drunk driving."

"Well, I never worked on the Almore case," Webber snapped. "I don't know who stuck the first knife into Julius Caesar either. Stick to the point, can't you?"

"I am sticking to the point. Degarmo knows about the Almore case and he doesn't like it talked about. Even your prowl car boys know about it. Cooney and Dobbs had no reason to follow me unless it was because I visited the wife of a man who had worked on the Almore case. I wasn't doing fifty-five miles an hour when they started to follow me. I tried to get away from them because I had a good idea I might get beaten up for going there. Degarmo had given me that idea."

Webber looked quickly at Degarmo. Degarmo's hard blue eyes looked across the room at the wall in front of him.

I said: "And I didn't bust Cooney in the nose until after he had forced me to drink whiskey and then hit me in the stomach when I drank it, so that I would spill it down my coat front and smell of it. This can't be the first time you have heard of that trick, captain."

Webber broke another match. He leaned back and looked at his small tight knuckles. He looked again at Degarmo and said: "If you got made chief of police today, you might let me in on it."

Degarmo said: "Hell, the shamus just got a couple of playful taps. Kind of kidding. If a guy can't take a joke—"

Webber said: "You put Cooney and Dobbs over there?"

"Well—yes, I did," Degarmo said. "I don't see where we have to put up with these snoopers coming into our town and stirring up a lot of dead leaves just to promote themselves a job and work a couple of old suckers for a big fee. Guys like that need a good sharp lesson."

"Is that how it looks to you?" Webber asked.

"That's exactly how it looks to me," Degarmo said.

"I wonder what fellows like you need," Webber said. "Right now I think you need a little air. Would you please take it, lieutenant?"

Degarmo opened his mouth slowly. "You mean you want me to breeze on out?"

Webber leaned forward suddenly and his sharp little chin seemed to cut the air like the forefoot of a cruiser. "Would you be so kind?"

Degarmo stood up slowly, a dark flush staining his cheekbones. He leaned a hard hand flat on the desk and looked at Webber. There was a little charged silence. He said:

"Okay, captain. But you're playing this wrong."

Webber didn't answer him. Degarmo walked to the door and out. Webber waited for the door to close before he spoke.

"Is it your line that you can tie this Almore business a year and a half ago to the shooting in Lavery's place today? Or is it just a smoke screen you're laying down because you know damn well Kingsley's wife shot Lavery?"

I said: "It was tied to Lavery before he was shot. In a rough sort of way, perhaps only with a granny knot. But enough to make a man think."

"I've been into this matter a little more thoroughly than you might think," Webber said coldly. "Although I never had anything personally to do with the death of Almore's wife and I wasn't chief of detectives at that time. If you didn't even know Almore yesterday morning, you must have heard a lot about him since."

I told him exactly what I had heard, both from Miss Fromsett and from the Graysons.

"Then it's your theory that Lavery may have blackmailed Dr. Almore?" he asked at the end. "And that that may have something to do with the murder?"

"It's not a theory. It's no more than a possibility. I wouldn't be doing a job if I ignored it. The relations, if any, between Lavery and Almore might have been deep and dangerous or just the merest acquaintance, or not even that. For all I positively know they may never even have spoken to each other. But if there was nothing funny about the Almore case, why get so tough with anybody who shows an interest in it? It could be coincidence that George Talley was hooked for drunk driving just when he was working on it. It could be coincidence that Almore called a cop because I stared at his house, and that Lavery was shot before I could talk to him a second time. But it's no coincidence that two of your men were watching Talley's home tonight, ready, willing and able to make trouble for me, if I went there."

"I grant you that," Webber said. "And I'm not done with that incident. Do you want to file charges?"

"Life's too short for me to be filing charges of assault against police officers," I said.

He winced a little. "Then we'll wash all that out and charge it to experience," he said. "And as I understand you were not even booked, you're free to go home any time you want to. And if I were you, I'd leave Captain Webber to deal with the Lavery case and with any remote connection it might turn out to have with the Almore case."

I said: "And with any remote connection it might have with a woman named Muriel Chess being found drowned in a mountain lake near Puma Point yesterday?"

He raised his little eyebrows. "You think that?"

"Only you might not know her as Muriel Chess. Supposing that you knew her at all you might have known her as Mildred Haviland, who used to be Dr. Almore's office nurse. Who put Mrs. Almore to bed the night she was found dead in the garage, and who, if there was any hanky-panky about that, might know who it was, and be bribed or scared into leaving town shortly thereafter."

Webber picked up two matches and broke them. His small bleak eyes were fixed on my face. He said nothing.

"And at that point," I said, "you run into a real basic coincidence, the only one I'm willing to admit in the whole picture. For this Mildred Haviland met a man named Bill Chess in a Riverside beer parlor and for reasons of her own married him and went to live with him at Little Fawn Lake. And Little Fawn Lake was the property of a man whose wife was intimate with Lavery, who had found Mrs. Almore's body. That's what I call a real coincidence. It can't be anything else, but it's basic, fundamental. Everything else flows from it."

Webber got up from his desk and went over to the water cooler and drank two paper cups of water. He crushed the cups slowly in his hand and twisted them into a ball and dropped the ball into a brown metal basket under the cooler.

He walked to the windows and stood looking out over the bay. This was before the dim-out went into effect, and there were many lights in the yacht harbor.

He came slowly back to the desk and sat down. He reached up and pinched his nose. He was making up his mind about something.

He said slowly: "I can't see what the hell sense there is in trying to mix that up with something that happened a year and a half later."

"Okay," I said, "and thanks for giving me so much of your time." I got up to go.

"Your leg feel pretty bad?" he asked, as I leaned down to rub it.

"Bad enough, but it's getting better."

"Police business," he said almost gently, "is a hell of a problem. It's a good deal like politics. It asks for the highest type of men, and there's nothing in it to attract the highest type of men. So we have to work with what we get—and we get things like this."

"I know," I said. "I've always known that. I'm not bitter about it. Goodnight, Captain Webber."

"Wait a minute," he said. "Sit down a minute. If we've got to have the Almore case in this, let's drag it out into the open and look at it."

"It's about time somebody did that," I said. I sat down again.

# 28

Webber said quietly: "I suppose some people think we're just a bunch of crooks down here. I suppose they think a fellow kills his wife and then calls me up on the phone and says: 'Hi, Cap, I got a little murder down here cluttering up the front room. And I've got five hundred iron men that are not working.' And then I say: 'Fine. Hold everything and I'll be right down with a blanket.'"

"Not quite that bad," I said.

"What did you want to see Talley about when you went to his house tonight?"

"He had some line on Florence Almore's death. Her parents hired him to follow it up, but he never told them what it was."

"And you thought he would tell you?" Webber asked sarcastically.

"All I could do was try."

"Or was it just that Degarmo getting tough with you made you feel like getting tough right back at him?"

"There might be a little of that in it too," I said.

"Talley was a petty blackmailer," Webber said contemptuously. "On more than one occasion. Any way to get rid of him was good enough. So I'll tell you what it was he had. He had a slipper he had stolen from Florence Almore's foot."

"A slipper?"

He smiled faintly. "Just a slipper. It was later found hidden in his house. It was a green velvet dancing pump with some little stones set into the heel. It was custom made, by a man in Hollywood who makes theatrical footwear and such. Now ask me what was important about this slipper?"

"What was important about it, captain?"

"She had two pair of them, exactly alike, made on the same order. It seems that is not unusual. In case one of them gets scuffed or some drunken ox tries to walk up a lady's leg." He paused and smiled thinly. "It seems that one pair had never been worn."

"I think I'm beginning to get it," I said.

He leaned back and tapped the arms of his chair. He waited.

"The walk from the side door of the house to the garage is rough concrete," I said. "Fairly rough. Suppose she didn't walk it, but was carried. And suppose whoever carried her put her slippers on—and got one that had not been worn."

"Yes?"

"And suppose Talley noticed this while Lavery was telephoning to the doctor, who was out on his rounds. So he took the unworn slipper, regarding it as evidence that Florence Almore had been murdered."

Webber nodded his head. "It was evidence if he left it

where it was, for the police to find it. After he took it, it was just evidence that he was a rat."

"Was a monoxide test made of her blood?"

He put his hands flat on his desk and looked down at them. "Yes," he said. "And there was monoxide all right. Also the investigating officers were satisfied with appearances. There was no sign of violence. They were satisfied that Dr. Almore had not murdered his wife. Perhaps they were wrong. I think the investigation was a little superficial."

"And who was in charge of it?" I asked.

"I think you know the answer to that."

"When the police came, didn't they notice that a slipper was missing?"

"When the police came there was no slipper missing. You must remember that Dr. Almore was back at his home, in response to Lavery's call, before the police were called. All we know about the missing shoe is from Talley himself. He might have taken the unworn shoe from the house. The side door was unlocked. The maids were asleep. The objection to that is that he wouldn't have been likely to know there was an unworn slipper to take. I wouldn't put it past him to think of it. He's a sharp sneaky little devil. But I can't fix the necessary knowledge on him."

We sat there and looked at each other, thinking about it.

"Unless," Webber said slowly, "we can suppose that this nurse of Almore's was involved with Talley in a scheme to put the bite on Almore. It's possible. There are things in favor of it. There are more things against it. What reason have you for claiming that the girl drowned up in the mountains was this nurse?"

"Two reasons, neither one conclusive separately, but pretty powerful taken together. A tough guy who looked and acted like Degarmo was up there a few weeks ago showing a photograph of Mildred Haviland that looked something like Muriel Chess. Different hair and eyebrows and so on, but a fair resemblance. Nobody helped him much. He called himself De Soto and said he was a Los Angeles cop. There isn't any Los Angeles cop named De Soto. When Muriel Chess heard about it, she looked scared. If it was Degarmo, that's easily established. The other reason is that a golden anklet with a heart on it was hidden in a box of powdered sugar in the Chess cabin. It was found after her death, after her husband had been arrested. On the back of the heart was engraved: *"Al to Mildred. June 28th. 1938. With all my love."*

"It could have been some other Al and some other Mildred," Webber said.

"You don't really believe that, captain."

He leaned forward and made a hole in the air with his forefinger. "What do you want to make of all this exactly?"

"I want to make it that Kingsley's wife didn't shoot Lavery. That his death had something to do with the Almore business. And with Mildred Haviland. And possibly with Dr. Almore. I want to make it that Kingsley's wife disappeared because something happened that gave her a bad fright, that she may or may not have guilty knowledge, but that she hasn't murdered anybody. There's five hundred dollars in it for me, if I can determine that. It's legitimate to try."

He nodded. "Certainly it is. And I'm the man that would help you, if I could see any grounds for it. We haven't found the woman, but the time has been very short. But I can't help you put something on one of my boys."

I said: "I heard you call Degarmo Al. But I was thinking of Almore. His name's Albert."

Webber looked at his thumb. "But he was never married to the girl," he said quietly. "Degarmo was. I can tell you she led him a pretty dance. A lot of what seems bad in him is the result of it."

I sat very still. After a moment I said: "I'm beginning to see things I didn't know existed. What kind of a girl was she?"

"Smart, smooth and no good. She had a way with men. She could make them crawl over her shoes. The big boob would tear your head off right now, if you said anything against her. She divorced him, but that didn't end it for him."

"Does he know she is dead?"

Webber sat quiet for a long moment before he said: "Not from anything he has said. But how could he help it, if it's the same girl?"

"He never found her in the mountains — so far as we know."

I stood up and leaned down on the desk. "Look, captain, you're not kidding me, are you?"

"No. Not one damn bit. Some men are like that and some women can make them like it. If you think Degarmo went up there looking for her because he wanted to hurt her, you're as wet as a bar towel."

"I never quite thought that," I said. "It would be possible, provided Degarmo knew the country up there pretty well. Whoever murdered the girl did."

"This is all between us," he said. "I'd like you to keep it that way."

I nodded, but I didn't promise him. I said goodnight again and left. He looked after me as I went down the room. He looked hurt and sad.

The Chrysler was in the police lot at the side of the building with the keys in the ignition and none of the fenders smashed. Cooney hadn't made good on his threat. I drove back to Hollywood and went up to my apartment in the Bristol. It was late, almost midnight.

The green and ivory hallway was empty of all sound except that a telephone bell was ringing in one of the apartments. It rang insistently and got louder as I came near to my door. I unlocked the door. It was my telephone.

I walked across the room in darkness to where the phone stood on the ledge of an oak desk against the side wall. It must have rung at least ten times before I got to it.

I lifted it out of the cradle and answered, and it was Derace Kingsley on the line.

His voice sounded tight and brittle and strained. "Good Lord, where in hell have you been?" he snapped. "I've been trying to reach you for hours."

"All right. I'm here now," I said. "What is it?"

"I've heard from her."

I held the telephone very tight and drew my breath in slowly and let it out slowly. "Go ahead," I said.

"I'm not far away. I'll be over there in five or six minutes. Be prepared to move."

He hung up.

I stood there holding the telephone halfway between my

ear and the cradle. Then I put it down very slowly and looked at the hand that had held it. It was half open and clenched stiff, as if it was still holding the instrument.

## 29

The discreet midnight tapping sounded on the door and I went over and opened it. Kingsley looked as big as a horse in a creamy shetland sports coat with a green and yellow scarf around the neck inside the loosely turned up collar. A dark reddish brown snapbrim hat was pulled low on his forehead and under its brim, his eyes looked like the eyes of a sick animal.

Miss Fromsett was with him. She was wearing slacks and sandals and a dark green coat and no hat and her hair had a wicked lustre. In her ears hung ear drops made of a pair of tiny artificial gardenia blooms, hanging one above the other, two on each ear. Gillerlain Regal, the Champagne of Perfumes, came in at the door with her.

I shut the door and indicated the furniture and said: "A drink will probably help."

Miss Fromsett sat in an armchair and crossed her legs and looked around for cigarettes. She found one and lit it with a long casual flourish and smiled bleakly at a corner of the ceiling.

Kingsley stood in the middle of the floor trying to bite his chin. I went out to the dinette and mixed three drinks and brought them in and handed them. I went over to the chair by the chess table with mine.

Kingsley said: "What have you been doing and what's the matter with the leg?"

I said: "A cop kicked me. A present from the Bay City police department. It's a regular service they give down there. As to where I've been—in jail for drunk driving. And from the expression on your face, I think I may be right back there soon."

"I don't know what you're talking about," he said

shortly. "I haven't the foggiest idea. This is no time to kid around."

"All right, don't," I said. "What did you hear and where is she?"

He sat down with his drink and flexed the fingers of his right hand and put it inside his coat. It came out with an envelope, a long one.

"You have to take this to her," he said. "Five hundred dollars. She wanted more, but this is all I could raise. I cashed a check at a night club. It wasn't easy. She has to get out of town."

I said: "Out of what town?"

"Bay City somewhere. I don't know where. She'll meet you at a place called the Peacock Lounge, on Arguello Boulevard, at Eighth Street, or near it."

I looked at Miss Fromsett. She was still looking at the corner of the ceiling as if she had just come along for the ride.

Kingsley tossed the envelope across and it fell on the chess table. I looked inside it. It was money all right. That much of his story made sense. I let it lie on the small polished table with its inlaid squares of brown and pale gold.

I said: "What's the matter with her drawing her own money? Any hotel would clear a check for her. Most of them would cash one. Has her bank account got lockjaw or something?"

"That's no way to talk," Kingsley said heavily. "She's in trouble. I don't know how she knows she's in trouble. Unless a pick-up order has been broadcast. Has it?"

I said I didn't know. I hadn't had much time to listen to police calls. I had been too busy listening to live policemen.

Kingsley said: "Well, she won't risk cashing a check now. It was all right before. But not now." He lifted his eyes slowly and gave me one of the emptiest stares I had ever seen.

"All right, we can't make sense where there isn't any," I said. "So she's in Bay City. Did you talk to her?"

"No. Miss Fromsett talked to her. She called the office. It was just after hours but that cop from the beach, Captain Webber, was with me. Miss Fromsett naturally didn't want her to talk at all then. She told her to call back. She wouldn't give any number we could call."

I looked at Miss Fromsett. She brought her glance down from the ceiling and pointed it at the top of my head. There was nothing in her eyes at all. They were like drawn curtains.

Kingsley went on: "I didn't want to talk to her. She didn't want to talk to me. I don't want to see her. I guess there's no doubt she shot Lavery. Webber seemed quite sure of it."

"That doesn't mean anything," I said. "What he says and what he thinks don't even have to be on the same map. I don't like her knowing the cops were after her. It's a long time since anybody listened to the police short wave for amusement. So she called back later. And then?"

"It was almost half-past six," Kingsley said. "We had to sit there in the office and wait for her to call. You tell him." He turned his head to the girl.

Miss Fromsett said: "I took the call in Mr. Kingsley's office. He was sitting right beside me, but he didn't speak. She said to send the money down to the Peacock place and asked who would bring it."

"Did she sound scared?"

"Not in the least. Completely calm. I might say, icily calm. She had it all worked out. She realized somebody would have to bring the money she might not know. She seemed to know Derry—Mr. Kingsley wouldn't bring it."

"Call him Derry," I said. "I'll be able to guess who you mean."

She smiled faintly. "She will go into this Peacock Lounge every hour about fifteen minutes past the hour. I—I guess I assumed you would be the one to go. I described you to her. And you're to wear Derry's scarf. I described that. He keeps some clothes at the office and this was among them. It's distinctive enough."

It was all of that. It was an affair of fat green kidneys laid down on an egg yolk background. It would be almost as distinctive as if I went in there wheeling a red, white and blue wheelbarrow.

"For a blimp brain she's doing all right," I said.

"This is no time to fool around," Kingsley put in sharply.

"You said that before," I told him. "You've got a hell of a crust assuming I'll go down there and take a getaway stake to somebody I know the police are looking for."

He twisted a hand on his knee and his face twisted into a crooked grin.

"I admit it's a bit thick," he said. "Well, how about it?"

"It makes accessories after the fact out of all three of us. That might not be too tough for her husband and his confidential secretary to talk out of, but what they would do to me would be nobody's dream of a vacation."

"I'm going to make it worth your while," he said. "And we wouldn't be accessories, if she hasn't done anything."

"I'm willing to suppose it," I said. "Otherwise I wouldn't be talking to you. And in addition to that, if I decide she did do any murder, I'm going to turn her over to the police."

"She won't talk to you," he said.

I reached for the envelope and put it in my pocket. "She will, if she wants this." I looked at my strap watch. "If I start right away, I might make the one-fifteen deadline. They must know her by heart in that bar after all these hours. That makes it nice too."

"She's dyed her hair dark brown," Miss Fromsett said. "That ought to help a little."

I said: "It doesn't help me to think she is just an innocent wayfarer." I finished my drink and stood up. Kingsley swallowed his at a gulp and stood up and got the scarf off his neck and handed it to me.

"What did you do to get the police on your neck down there?" he asked.

"I was using some information Miss Fromsett very kindly got for me. And that led to my looking for a man named Talley who worked on the Almore case. And that led to the clink. They had the house staked. Talley was the dick the Graysons hired," I added, looking at the tall dark girl. "You'll probably be able to explain to him what it's all about. It doesn't matter anyway. I haven't time to go into it now. You two want to wait here?"

Kingsley shook his head. "We'll go to my place and wait for a call from you."

Miss Fromsett stood up and yawned. "No. I'm tired, Derry. I'm going home and going to bed."

"You'll come with me," he said sharply. "You've got to keep me from going nuts."

"Where do you live, Miss Fromsett?" I asked.

"Bryson Tower on Sunset Place. Apartment 716. Why?" She gave me a speculative look.

"I might want to reach you some time."

Kingsley's face looked bleakly irritated, but his eyes still were the eyes of a sick animal. I wound his scarf around my neck and went out to the dinette to switch off the light. When I came back they were both standing by the door. Kingsley had his arm around her shoulders. She looked very tired and rather bored.

"Well, I certainly hope—" he started to say, then took a quick step and put his hand out. "You're a pretty level guy, Marlowe."

"Go on, beat it," I said. "Go away. Go far away."

He gave a queer look and they went out.

I waited until I heard the elevator come up and stop, and the doors open and close again, and the elevator start down. Then I went out myself and took the stairs down to the basement garage and got the Chrysler awake again.

## 30

The Peacock Lounge was a narrow front next to a gift shop in whose window a tray of small crystal animals shimmered in the street light. The Peacock had a glass brick front and soft light glowed out around the stained glass peacock that was set into the brick. I went in around a Chinese screen and looked along the bar and then sat at the outer edge of a small booth. The light was amber, the leather was Chinese red and the booths had polished plastic tables. In one booth four soldiers were drinking beer moodily, a little glassy in the eyes and obviously bored even with drinking beer. Across from them a party of two girls and two flashy-looking men were making the only noise in the place. I saw nobody that looked like my idea of Crystal Kingsley.

A wizened waiter with evil eyes and a face like a gnawed bone put a napkin with a printed peacock on it down on the table in front of me and gave me a bacardi cocktail. I sipped it and looked at the amber face of the bar clock. It was just past one-fifteen.

One of the men with the two girls got up suddenly and stalked along to the door and went on. The voice of the other man said:

"What did you have to insult the guy for?"

A girl's tinny voice said: "Insult him? I like that. He propositioned me."

The man's voice said complainingly: "Well, you didn't have to insult him, did you?"

One of the soldiers suddenly laughed deep in his chest and then wiped the laugh off his face with a brown hand and drank a little more beer. I rubbed the back of my knee. It was hot and swollen still but the paralyzed feeling had gone away.

A tiny, white-faced Mexican boy with enormous black eyes came in with morning papers and scuttled along the booths trying to make a few sales before the barman threw him out. I bought a paper and looked through it to see if there were any interesting murders. There were not.

I folded it and looked up as a slim, brown-haired girl in coal black slacks and a yellow shirt and a long gray coat came out of somewhere and passed the booth without looking at me. I tried to make up my mind whether her face was familiar or just such a standard type of lean, rather hard, prettiness that I must have seen it ten thousand times. She went out of the street door around the screen. Two minutes later the little Mexican boy came back in, shot a quick look at the barman, and scuttled over to stand in front of me.

"Mister," he said, his great big eyes shining with mischief. Then he made a beckoning sign and scuttled out again.

I finished my drink and went after him. The girl in the gray coat and yellow shirt and black slacks was standing in front of the gift shop, looking in at the window. Her eyes moved as I went out. I went and stood beside her.

She looked at me again. Her face was white and tired. Her hair looked darker than dark brown. She looked away and spoke to the window.

"Give me the money, please." A little mist formed on the plate glass from her breath.

I said: "I'd have to know who you are."

"You know who I am," she said softly. "How much did you bring?"

"Five hundred."

"It's not enough," she said. "Not nearly enough. Give it to me quickly. I've been waiting half of eternity for somebody to get here."

"Where can we talk?"

"We don't have to talk. Just give me the money and go the other way."

"It's not that simple. I'm doing this at quite a risk. I'm at least going to have the satisfaction of knowing what goes on and where I stand."

"Damn you," she said acidly, "why couldn't he come himself? I don't want to talk. I want to get away as soon as I can."

"You didn't want him to come himself. He understood that you didn't even want to talk to him on the phone."

"That's right," she said quickly and tossed her head.

"But you've got to talk to me," I said. "I'm not as easy as he is. Either to me or to the law. There's no way out of it. I'm a private detective and I have to have some protection too."

"Well, isn't he charming," she said. "Private detective and all." Her voice held a low sneer.

"He did the best he knew how. It wasn't easy for him to know what to do."

"What do you want to talk about?"

"You, and what you've been doing and where you've been and what you expect to do. Things like that. Little things, but important."

She breathed on the glass of the shop window and waited while the mist of her breath disappeared.

"I think it would be much better," she said in the same cool empty voice, "for you to give me the money and let me work things out for myself."

"No."

She gave me another sharp sideways glance. She shrugged the shoulders of the gray coat impatiently.

"Very well, if it has to be that way. I'm at the Granada, two blocks north on Eighth. Apartment 618. Give me ten minutes. I'd rather go in alone."

"I have a car."

"I'd rather go alone." She turned quickly and walked away.

She walked back to the corner and crossed the boulevard and disappeared along the block under a line of pepper trees. I went and sat in the Chrysler and gave her her ten minutes before I started it.

The Granada was an ugly gray building on a corner. The plate glass entrance door was level with the street. I drove around the corner and saw a milky globe with *Garage* painted on it. The entrance to the garage was down a ramp into the hard rubber-smelling silence of parked cars in rows. A lanky Negro came out of a glassed-in office and looked the Chrysler over.

"How much to leave this here a short time? I'm going upstairs."

He gave me a shady leer. "Kinda late, boss. She needs a good dustin' too. Be a dollar."

"What goes on here?"

"Be a dollar," he said woodenly.

I got out. He gave me a ticket. I gave him the dollar. Without my asking him he said the elevator was in back of the office, by the Men's Room.

I rode up to the sixth floor and looked at numbers on doors and listened to stillness and smelled beach air coming in at the ends of corridors. The place seemed decent enough. There would be a few happy ladies in any apartment house. That would explain the lanky Negro's dollar. A great judge of character, that boy.

I came to the door of Apartment 618 and stood outside it a moment and then knocked softly.

# 31

She still had the gray coat on. She stood back from the door and I went past her into a square room with twin wall beds and a minimum of uninteresting furniture. A small lamp on a

window table made a dim yellowish light. The window behind it was open.

The girl said: "Sit down and talk then."

She closed the door and went to sit in a gloomy Boston
rocker across the room. I sat down on a thick davenport. There
was a dull green curtain hanging across an open door space, at
one end of the davenport. That would lead to dressing room
and bathroom. There was a closed door at the other end. That
would be the kitchenette. That would be all there was.

The girl crossed her ankles and leaned her head back
against the chair and looked at me under long beaded lashes.
Her eyebrows were thin and arched and as brown as her hair.
It was a quiet, secret face. It didn't look like the face of a
woman who would waste a lot of motion.

"I got a rather different idea of you," I said. "From
Kingsley."

Her lips twisted a little. She said nothing.

"From Lavery too," I said. "It just goes to show that we
talk different languages to different people."

"I haven't time for this sort of talk," she said. "What is it
you have to know?"

"He hired me to find you. I've been working on it. I supposed you would know that."

"Yes. His office sweetie told me that over the phone. She
told me you would be a man named Marlowe. She told me
about the scarf."

I took the scarf off my neck and folded it up and slipped it
into a pocket. I said:

"So I know a little about your movements. Not very
much. I know you left your car at the Prescott Hotel in San
Bernardino and that you met Lavery there. I know you sent
a wire from El Paso. What did you do then?"

"All I want from you is the money he sent. I don't see that
my movements are any of your business."

"I don't have to argue about that," I said. "It's a question
of whether you want the money."

"Well, we went to El Paso," she said, in a tired voice. "I
thought of marrying him then. So I sent that wire. You saw
the wire?"

"Yes."

"Well, I changed my mind. I asked him to go home and leave me. He made a scene."

"Did he go home and leave you?"

"Yes. Why not?"

"What did you do then?"

"I went to Santa Barbara and stayed there a few days. Over a week, in fact. Then to Pasadena. Same thing. Then to Hollywood. Then I came down here. That's all."

"You were alone all this time?"

She hesitated a little and then said: "Yes."

"Not with Lavery—any part of it?"

"Not after he went home."

"What was the idea?"

"Idea of what?" Her voice was a little sharp.

"Idea of going these places and not sending any word. Didn't you know he would be very anxious?"

"Oh, you mean my husband," she said coolly. "I don't think I worried much about him. He'd think I was in Mexico, wouldn't he? As for the idea of it all—well, I just had to think things out. My life had got to be a hopeless tangle. I had to be somewhere quite alone and try to straighten myself out."

"Before that," I said, "you spent a month at Little Fawn Lake trying to straighten it out and not getting anywhere. Is that it?"

She looked down at her shoes and then up at me and nodded earnestly. The wavy brown hair surged forward along her cheeks. She put her left hand up and pushed it back and then rubbed her temple with one finger.

"I seemed to need a new place," she said. "Not necessarily an interesting place. Just a strange place. Without associations. A place where I would be very much alone. Like a hotel."

"How are you getting on with it?"

"Not very well. But I'm not going back to Derace Kingsley. Does he want me to?"

"I don't know. Why did you come down here, to the town where Lavery was?"

She bit a knuckle and looked at me over her hand.

"I wanted to see him again. He's all mixed up in my mind.

I'm not in love with him, and yet—well, I suppose in a way I am. But I don't think I want to marry him. Does that make sense?"

"That part of it makes sense. But staying away from home in a lot of crummy hotels doesn't. You've lived your own life for years, as I understand it."

"I had to be alone, to—to think things out," she said a little desperately and bit the knuckle again, hard. "Won't you please give me the money and go away?"

"Sure. Right away. But wasn't there any other reason for your going away from Little Fawn Lake just then? Anything connected with Muriel Chess, for instance?"

She looked surprised. But anyone can look surprised. "Good heavens, what would there be? That frozen-faced little drip—what is she to me?"

"I thought you might have had a fight with her—about Bill."

"Bill? Bill Chess?" She seemed even more surprised. Almost too surprised.

"Bill claims you made a pass at him."

She put her head back and let out a tinny and unreal laugh. "Good heavens, that muddy-faced boozer?" Her face sobered suddenly. "What's happened? Why all the mystery?"

"He might be a muddy-faced boozer," I said. "The police think he's a murderer too. Of his wife. She's been found drowned in the lake. After a month."

She moistened her lips and held her head on one side, staring at me fixedly. There was a quiet little silence. The damp breath of the Pacific slid into the room around us.

"I'm not too surprised," she said slowly. "So it came to that in the end. They fought terribly at times. Did you think that had something to do with my leaving?"

I nodded. "There was a chance of it."

"It didn't have anything to do with it at all," she said seriously, and shook her head back and forth. "It was just the way I told you. Nothing else."

"Muriel's dead," I said. "Drowned in the lake. You don't get much of a boot out of that, do you?"

"I hardly knew the girl," she said. "Really. She kept to herself. After all—"

"I don't suppose you knew she had once worked in Dr. Almore's office?"

She looked completely puzzled now. "I was never in Dr. Almore's office," she said slowly. "He made a few house calls a long time ago. I—what are you talking about?"

"Muriel Chess was really a girl called Mildred Haviland, who had been Dr. Almore's office nurse."

"That's a queer coincidence," she said wonderingly. "I knew Bill met her in Riverside. I didn't know how or under what circumstances or where she came from. Dr. Almore's office, eh? It doesn't have to mean anything, does it?"

I said, "No. I guess it's a genuine coincidence. They do happen. But you see why I had to talk to you. Muriel being found drowned and you having gone away and Muriel being Mildred Haviland who was connected with Dr. Almore at one time—as Lavery was also, in a different way. And of course Lavery lives across the street from Dr. Almore. Did he, Lavery, seem to know Muriel from somewhere else?"

She thought about it, biting her lower lip gently. "He saw her up there," she said finally. "He didn't act as if he had ever seen her before."

"And he would have," I said. "Being the kind of guy he was."

"I don't think Chris had anything to do with Dr. Almore," she said. "He knew Dr. Almore's wife. I don't think he knew the doctor at all. So he probably wouldn't know Dr. Almore's office nurse."

"Well, I guess there's nothing in all this to help me," I said. "But you can see why I had to talk to you. I guess I can give you the money now."

I got the envelope out and stood up to drop it on her knee. She let it lie there. I sat down again.

"You do this character very well," I said. "This confused innocence with an undertone of hardness and bitterness. People have made a bad mistake about you. They have been thinking of you as a reckless little idiot with no brains and no control. They have been very wrong."

She stared at me, lifting her eyebrows. She said nothing. Then a small smile lifted the corners of her mouth. She reached for the envelope, tapped it on her knee, and laid it aside on the table. She stared at me all the time.

"You did the Fallbrook character very well too," I said. "Looking back on it, I think it was a shade overdone. But at the time it had me going all right. That purple hat that would have been all right on blonde hair but looked like hell on straggly brown, that messed-up makeup that looked as if it had been put on in the dark by somebody with a sprained wrist, the jittery screwball manner. All very good. And when you put the gun in my hand like that—I fell like a brick."

She snickered and put her hands in the deep pockets of her coat. Her heels tapped on the floor.

"But why did you go back at all?" I asked. "Why take such a risk in broad daylight, in the middle of the morning?"

"So you think I shot Chris Lavery?" she said quietly.

"I don't think it. I know it."

"Why did I go back? Is that what you want to know?"

"I don't really care," I said.

She laughed. A sharp cold laugh. "He had all my money," she said. "He had stripped my purse. He had it all, even silver. That's why I went back. There wasn't any risk at all. I know how he lived. It was really safer to go back. To take in the milk and the newspaper for instance. People lose their heads in these situations. I don't, I didn't see why I should. It's so very much safer not to."

"I see," I said. "Then of course you shot him the night before. I ought to have thought of that, not that it matters. He had been shaving. But guys with dark beards and lady friends sometimes shave the last thing at night, don't they?"

"It has been heard of," she said almost gaily. "And just what are you going to do about it?"

"You're a cold-blooded little bitch if ever I saw one," I said. "Do about it? Turn you over to the police naturally. It will be a pleasure."

"I don't think so." She threw the words out, almost with a lilt. "You wondered why I gave you the empty gun. Why not? I had another one in my bag. Like this."

Her right hand came up from her coat pocket and she pointed it at me.

I grinned. It may not have been the heartiest grin in the world, but it was a grin.

"I've never liked this scene," I said. "Detective confronts murderer. Murderer produces gun, points same at detective. Murderer tells detective the whole sad story, with the idea of shooting him at the end of it. Thus wasting a lot of valuable time, even if in the end murderer did shoot detective. Only murderer never does. Something always happens to prevent it. The gods don't like this scene either. They always manage to spoil it."

"But this time," she said softly and got up and moved towards me softly across the carpet, "suppose we make it a little different. Suppose I don't tell you anything and nothing happens and I do shoot you?"

"I still wouldn't like the scene," I said.

"You don't seem to be afraid," she said, and slowly licked her lips coming towards me very gently without any sound of footfalls on the carpet.

"I'm not afraid," I lied. "It's too late at night, too still, and the window is open and the gun would make too much noise. It's too long a journey down to the street and you're not good with guns. You would probably miss me. You missed Lavery three times."

"Stand up," she said.

I stood up.

"I'm going to be too close to miss," she said. She pushed the gun against my chest. "Like this. I really can't miss now, can I? Now be very still. Hold your hands up by your shoulders and then don't move at all. If you move at all, the gun will go off."

I put my hands up beside my shoulders. I looked down at the gun. My tongue felt a little thick, but I could still wave it.

Her probing left hand didn't find a gun on me. It dropped and she bit her lip, staring at me. The gun bored into my chest. "You'll have to turn around now," she said, polite as a tailor at a fitting.

"There's something a little off key about everything you do," I said. "You're definitely not good with guns. You're much too close to me, and I hate to bring this up — but there's that old business of the safety catch not being off. You've overlooked that too."

So she started to do two things at once. To take a long step backwards and to feel with her thumb for the safety-catch, without taking her eyes off my face. Two very simple things, needing only a second to do. But she didn't like my telling her. She didn't like my thought riding over hers. The minute confusion of it jarred her.

She let out a small choked sound and I dropped my right hand and yanked her face hard against my chest. My left hand smashed down on her right wrist, the heel of my hand against the base of her thumb. The gun jerked out of her hand to the floor. Her face writhed against my chest and I think she was trying to scream.

Then she tried to kick me and lost what little balance she had left. Her hands came up to claw at me. I caught her wrist and began to twist it behind her back. She was very strong, but I was very much stronger. So she decided to go limp and let her whole weight sag against the hand that was holding her head. I couldn't hold her up with one hand. She started to go down and I had to bend down with her.

There were vague sounds of our scuffling on the floor by the davenport, and hard breathing, and if a floor board creaked I didn't hear it. I thought a curtain ring checked sharply on a rod. I wasn't sure and I had no time to consider the question. A figure loomed up suddenly on my left, just behind, and out of range of clear vision. I knew there was a man there and that he was a big man.

That was all I knew. The scene exploded into fire and darkness. I didn't even remember being slugged. Fire and darkness and just before the darkness a sharp flash of nausea.

## 32

I smelled of gin. Not just casually, as if I had taken four or five drinks of a winter morning to get out of bed on, but as if the Pacific Ocean was pure gin and I had nose-dived off the boat deck. The gin was in my hair and eyebrows, on my chin and under my chin. It was on my shirt. I smelled like dead toads.

My coat was off and I was lying flat on my back beside the davenport on somebody's carpet and I was looking at a framed picture. The frame was of cheap soft wood varnished and the picture showed part of an enormously high pale yellow viaduct across which a shiny black locomotive was dragging a Prussian blue train. Through one lofty arch of the viaduct a wide yellow beach showed and was dotted with sprawled bathers and striped beach umbrellas. Three girls walked close up, with paper parasols, one girl in cerise, one in pale blue, one in green. Beyond the beach a curving bay was bluer than any bay has any right to be. It was drenched with sunshine and flecked and dotted with aching white sails. Beyond the inland curve of the bay three ranges of hills rose in three precisely opposed colors, gold and terra cotta and lavender.

Across the bottom of the picture was printed in large capitals SEE THE FRENCH RIVIERA BY THE BLUE TRAIN.

It was a fine time to bring that up.

I reached up wearily and felt the back of my head. It felt pulpy. A shoot of pain from the touch went clear to the soles of my feet. I groaned, and made a grunt out of the groan, from professional pride—what was left of it. I rolled over slowly and carefully and looked at the foot of a pulled down wall bed; one twin, the other being still up in the wall. The flourish of design on the painted wood was familiar. The picture had hung over the davenport and I hadn't even looked at it.

When I rolled a square gin bottle rolled off my chest and hit the floor. It was water white, and empty. It didn't seem possible there could be so much gin in just one bottle.

I got my knees under me and stayed on all fours for a while, sniffing like a dog who can't finish his dinner, but hates to leave it. I moved my head around on my neck. It hurt. I moved it around some more and it still hurt, so I climbed up on my feet and discovered I didn't have any shoes on.

The shoes were lying against the baseboard, looking as dissipated as shoes ever looked. I put them on wearily. I was an old man now. I was going down the last long hill. I still had a tooth left though. I felt it with my tongue. It didn't seem to taste of gin.

"It will all come back to you," I said. "Some day it will all come back to you. And you won't like it."

There was the lamp on the table by the open window. There was the fat green davenport. There was the doorway with the green curtain across it. Never sit with your back to a green curtain. It always turns out badly. Something always happens. Who had I said that to? A girl with a gun. A girl with a clear empty face and dark brown hair that had been blonde.

I looked around for her. She was still there. She was lying on the pulled-down twin bed.

She was wearing a pair of tan stockings and nothing else. Her hair was tumbled. There were dark bruises on her throat. Her mouth was open and a swollen tongue filled it to over-flowing. Her eyes bulged and the whites of them were not white.

Across her naked belly four angry scratches leered crimson red against the whiteness of flesh. Deep angry scratches, gouged out by four bitter fingernails.

On the davenport there were tumbled clothes, mostly hers. My coat was there also. I disentangled it and put it on. Something crackled under my hand in the tumbled clothes. I drew out a long envelope with money still in it. I put it in my pocket. Marlowe, five hundred dollars. I hoped it was all there. There didn't seem much else to hope for.

I stepped on the balls of my feet softly, as if walking on very thin ice. I bent down to rub behind my knee and wondered which hurt most, my knee, or my head when I bent down to rub the knee.

Heavy feet came along the hallway and there was a hard mutter of voices. The feet stopped. A hard fist knocked on the door.

I stood there leering at the door, with my lips drawn back tight against my teeth. I waited for somebody to open the door and walk in. The knob was tried, but nobody walked in. The knocking began again, stopped, the voices muttered again. The steps went away. I wondered how long it would take to get the manager with a pass key. Not very long.

Not nearly long enough for Marlowe to get home from the French Riviera.

I went to the green curtain and brushed it aside and looked down a short dark hallway into a bathroom. I went in there and put the light on. Two wash rugs on the floor, a bath mat folded over the edge of the tub, a pebbled glass window at the corner of the tub. I shut the bathroom door and stood on the edge of the tub and eased the window up. This was the sixth floor. There was no screen. I put my head out and looked into darkness and a narrow glimpse of a street with trees. I looked sideways and saw that the bathroom window of the next apartment was not more than three feet away. A well-nourished mountain goat could make it without any trouble at all.

The question was whether a battered private detective could make it, and if so, what the harvest would be.

Behind me a rather remote and muffled voice seemed to be chanting the policeman's litany: "Open it up or we'll kick it in." I sneered back at the voice. They wouldn't kick it in because kicking in a door is hard on the feet. Policemen are kind to their feet. Their feet are about all they are kind to.

I grabbed a towel off the rack and pulled the two halves of the window down and eased out on the sill. I swung half of me over to the next sill, holding on to the frame of the open window. I could just reach to push the next window down, if it was unlocked. It wasn't unlocked. I got my foot over there and kicked the glass over the catch. It made a noise that ought to have been heard in Reno. I wrapped the towel around my left hand and reached in to turn the catch. Down on the street a car went by, but nobody yelled at me.

I pushed the broken window down and climbed across to the other sill. The towel fell out of my hand and fluttered down into the darkness to a strip of grass far below, between the two wings of the building.

I climbed in at the window of the other bathroom.

# 33

I climbed down into darkness and groped through darkness to a door and opened it and listened. Filtered moonlight coming through north windows showed a bedroom with twin beds, made up and empty. Not wall beds. This was a larger apartment. I moved past the beds to another door and into a living room. Both rooms were closed up and smelled musty. I felt my way to a lamp and switched it on. I ran a finger along the wood of a table edge. There was a light film of dust, such as accumulates in the cleanest room when it is left shut up.

The room contained a library dining table, an armchair radio, a book rack built like a hod, a big bookcase full of novels with their jackets still on them, a dark wood highboy with a siphon and a cut glass bottle of liquor and four striped glasses upside down on an Indian brass tray. Beside this paired photographs in a double silver frame, a youngish middle-aged man and woman, with round healthy faces and cheerful eyes. They looked out at me as if they didn't mind my being there at all.

I sniffed the liquor, which was Scotch, and used some of it. It made my head feel worse but it made the rest of me feel better. I put light on the bedroom and poked into closets. One of them had a man's clothes, tailor-made, plenty of them. The tailor's label inside a coat pocket declared the owner's name to be H. G. Talbot. I went to the bureau and poked around and found a soft blue shirt that looked a little small for me. I carried it into the bathroom and stripped mine off and washed my face and chest and wiped my hair off with a wet towel and put the blue shirt on. I used plenty of Mr. Talbot's rather insistent hair tonic on my hair and used his brush and comb to tidy it up. By that time I smelled of gin only remotely, if at all.

The top button of the shirt wouldn't meet its buttonhole so I poked into the bureau again and found a dark blue crepe tie and strung it around my neck. I got my coat back on and looked at myself in the mirror. I looked slightly too neat for that hour of the night, even for as careful a man as Mr. Talbot's clothes indicated him to be. Too neat and too sober.

I rumpled my hair a little and pulled the tie loose, and went back to the whisky decanter and did what I could about being too sober. I lit one of Mr. Talbot's cigarettes and hoped that

Mr. and Mrs. Talbot, wherever they were, were having a much better time than I was. I hoped I would live long enough to come and visit them.

I went to the living room door, the one giving on the hallway, and opened it and leaned in the opening smoking. I didn't think it was going to work. But I didn't think waiting there for them to follow my trail through the window was going to work any better.

A man coughed a little way down the hall and I poked my head out farther and he was looking at me. He came towards me briskly, a small sharp man in a neatly pressed police uniform. He had reddish hair and red-gold eyes.

I yawned and said languidly: "What goes on, officer?"

He stared at me thoughtfully. "Little trouble next door to you. Hear anything?"

"I thought I heard knocking. I just got home a little while ago."

"Little late," he said.

"That's a matter of opinion," I said. "Trouble next door, ah?"

"A dame," he said. "Know her?"

"I think I've seen her."

"Yeah," he said. "You ought to see her now . . ." He put his hands to his throat and bulged his eyes out and gurgled unpleasantly. "Like that," he said. "You didn't hear nothing, huh?"

"Nothing I noticed—except the knocking."

"Yeah. What was the name?"

"Talbot."

"Just a minute, Mr. Talbot. Wait there just a minute."

He went along the hallway and leaned into an open doorway through which light streamed out. "Oh, lieutenant," he said. "The man next door is on deck."

A tall man came out of the doorway and stood looking along the hall straight at me. A tall man with rusty hair and very blue, blue eyes. Degarmo. That made it perfect.

"Here's the guy lives next door," the small neat cop said helpfully. "His name's Talbot."

Degarmo looked straight at me, but nothing in his acid blue eyes showed that he had ever seen me before. He came quietly along the hall and put a hard hand against my chest and pushed me back into the room. When he had me half a dozen feet from the door he said over his shoulder:

"Come in here and shut the door, Shorty."

The small cop came in and shut the door.

"Quite a gag," Degarmo said lazily. "Put a gun on him, Shorty."

Shorty flicked his black belt holster open and had his .38 in his hand like a flash. He licked his lips.

"Oh boy," he said softly, whistling a little. "Oh boy. How'd you know, lieutenant?"

"Know what?" Degarmo asked, keeping his eyes fixed on mine. "What were you thinking of doing, pal—going down to get a paper—to find out if she was dead?"

"Oh boy," Shorty said. "A sex-killer. He pulled the girl's clothes off and choked her with his hands, lieutenant. How'd you know?"

Degarmo didn't answer him. He just stood there, rocking a little on his heels, his face empty and granite-hard.

"Yah, he's the killer, sure," Shorty said suddenly. "Sniff the air in here, lieutenant. The place ain't been aired out for days. And look at the dust on those bookshelves. And the clock on the mantel's stopped, lieutenant. He come in through the— lemme look a minute, can I, lieutenant?"

He ran out of the room into the bedroom. I heard him fumbling around. Degarmo stood woodenly.

Shorty came back. "Come in at the bathroom window. There's broken glass in the tub. And something stinks of gin in there something awful. You remember how that apartment smelled of gin when we went in? Here's a shirt, lieutenant. Smells like it was washed in gin."

He held the shirt up. It perfumed the air rapidly. Degarmo looked at it vaguely and then stepped forward and yanked my coat open and looked at the shirt I was wearing.

"I know what he done," Shorty said. "He stole one of the guy's shirts that lives here. You see what he done, lieutenant?"

"Yeah." Degarmo held his hand against my chest and let it fall slowly. They were talking about me as if I was a piece of wood.

"Frisk him, Shorty."

Shorty ran around me feeling here and there for a gun. "Nothing on him," he said.

"Let's get him out the back way," Degarmo said. "It's our pinch, if we make it before Webber gets here. That lug Reed couldn't find a moth in a shoe box."

"You ain't even detailed on the case," Shorty said doubtfully. "Didn't I hear you was suspended or something?"

"What can I lose?" Degarmo asked, "if I'm suspended?"

"I can lose this here uniform," Shorty said.

Degarmo looked at him wearily. The small cop blushed and his bright red-gold eyes were anxious.

"Okay, Shorty. Go and tell Reed."

The small cop licked his lip. "You say the word, lieutenant, and I'm with you. I don't have to know you got suspended."

"We'll take him down ourselves, just the two of us," Degarmo said.

"Yeah, sure."

Degarmo put his finger against my chin. "A sex killer," he said quietly. "Well, I'll be damned." He smiled at me thinly, moving only the extreme corners of his wide brutal mouth.

# 34

We went out of the apartment and along the hall the other way from Apartment 618. Light streamed from the still open door. Two men in plain clothes now stood outside it smoking cigarettes inside their cupped hands, as if a wind was blowing. There was a sound of wrangling voices from the apartment.

We went around the bend of the hall and came to the elevator. Degarmo opened the fire door beyond the elevator shaft and we went down echoing concrete steps, floor after floor. At the lobby floor Degarmo stopped and held his hand on the doorknob and listened. He looked back over his shoulder.

"You got a car?" he asked me.

"In the basement garage."

"That's an idea."

We went on down the steps and came out into the shadowy basement. The lanky Negro came out of the little office and I gave him my car check. He looked furtively at the police uniform on Shorty. He said nothing. He pointed to the Chrysler.

Degarmo climbed under the wheel of the Chrysler. I got in beside him and Shorty got into the back seat. We went up the ramp and out into the damp cool night air. A big car with twin red spotlights was charging towards us from a couple of blocks away.

Degarmo spat out of the car window and yanked the Chrysler the other way. "That will be Webber," he said. "Late for the funeral again. We sure skinned his nose on that one, Shorty."

"I don't like it too well, lieutenant. I don't, honest."

"Keep the chin up, kid. You might get back on homicide."

"I'd rather wear buttons and eat," Shorty said. The courage was oozing out of him fast.

Degarmo drove the car hard for ten blocks and then slowed a little. Shorty said uneasily:

"I guess you know what you're doing, lieutenant, but this ain't the way to the Hall."

"That's right," Degarmo said. "It never was, was it?"

He let the car slow down to a crawl and then turned into a residential street of small exact houses squatting behind small exact lawns. He braked the car gently and coasted over to the curb and stopped about the middle of the block. He threw an arm over the back of the seat and turned his head to look back at Shorty.

"You think this guy killed her, Shorty?"

"I'm listening," Shorty said in a tight voice.

"Got a flash?"

"No."

I said: "There's one in the car pocket on the left side."

Shorty fumbled around and metal clicked and the white beam of the flashlight came on. Degarmo said:

"Take a look at the back of this guy's head."

The beam moved and settled. I heard the small man's breathing behind me and felt it on my neck. Something felt for and touched the bump on my head. I grunted. The light went off and the darkness of the street rushed in again.

Shorty said: "I guess maybe he was sapped, lieutenant. I don't get it."

"So was the girl," Degarmo said. "It didn't show much but it's there. She was sapped so she could have her clothes pulled off and be clawed up before she was killed. So the scratches would bleed. Then she was throttled. And none of this made any noise. Why would it? And there's no telephone in that apartment. Who reported it, Shorty?"

"How the hell would I know? A guy called up and said a woman had been murdered in 618 Granada Apartments on Eighth. Reed was still looking for a cameraman when you come in. The desk said a guy with a thick voice, likely disguised. Didn't give any name at all."

"All right then," Degarmo said. "If you had murdered the girl, how would you get out of there?"

"I'd walk out," Shorty said. "Why not? Hey," he barked at me suddenly, "why didn't you?"

I didn't answer him. Degarmo said tonelessly: "You wouldn't climb out of a bathroom window six floors up and then bust in another bathroom window into a strange apartment where people would likely be sleeping, would you? You wouldn't pretend to be the guy that lived there and you wouldn't throw away a lot of your time by calling the police, would you? Hell, that girl could have laid there for a week. You wouldn't throw away the chance of a start like that, would you, Shorty?"

"I don't guess I would," Shorty said cautiously. "I don't guess I would call up at all. But you know these sex fiends do funny things, lieutenant. They ain't normal like us. And this guy could have had help and the other guy could have knocked him out to put him in the middle."

"Don't tell me you thought that last bit up all by yourself," Degarmo grunted. "So here we sit, and the fellow that knows all the answers is sitting here with us and not saying a word." He turned his big head and stared at me. "What were you doing there?"

"I can't remember," I said. "The crack on the head seems to have blanked me out."

"We'll help you to remember," Degarmo said. "We'll take

you up back in the hills a few miles where you can be quiet and look at the stars and remember. You'll remember all right."

Shorty said: "That ain't no way to talk, lieutenant. Why don't we just go back to the Hall and play this the way it says in the rule book?"

"To hell with the rule book," Degarmo said. "I like this guy. I want to have one long sweet talk with him. He just needs a little coaxing, Shorty. He's just bashful."

"I don't want any part of it," Shorty said.

"What you want to do, Shorty?"

"I want to go back to the Hall."

"Nobody's stopping you, kid. You want to walk?"

Shorty was silent for a moment. "That's right," he said at last, quietly. "I want to walk." He opened the car door and stepped out on to the curbing. "And I guess you know I have to report all this, lieutenant?"

"Right," Degarmo said. "Tell Webber I was asking for him. Next time he buys a hamburger, tell him to turn down an empty plate for me."

"That don't make any sense to me," the small cop said. He slammed the car door shut. Degarmo let the clutch in and gunned the motor and hit forty in the first block and a half. In the third block he hit fifty. He slowed down at the boulevard and turned east and began to cruise along at a legal speed. A few late cars drifted by both ways, but for the most part the world lay in the cold silence of early morning.

After a little while we passed the city limits and Degarmo spoke. "Let's hear you talk," he said quietly. "Maybe we can work this out."

The car topped a long rise and dipped down to where the boulevard wound through the parklike grounds of the veteran's hospital. The tall triple electroliers had halos from the beach fog that had drifted in during the night. I began to talk.

"Kingsley came over to my apartment tonight and said he had heard from his wife over the phone. She wanted some money quick. The idea was I was to take it to her and get her out of whatever trouble she was in. My idea was a little different. She was told how to identify me and I was to be at the Peacock Lounge at Eighth and Arguello at fifteen minutes past the hour. Any hour."

Degarmo said slowly: "She had to breeze and that meant she had something to breeze from, such as murder." He lifted his hands lightly and let them fall on the wheel again.

"I went down there, hours after she had called. I had been told her hair was dyed brown. She passed me going out of the bar, but I didn't know her. I had never seen her in the flesh. All I had seen was what looked like a pretty good snapshot, but could be that and still not a very good likeness. She sent a Mexican kid in to call me out. She wanted the money and no conversation. I wanted her story. Finally she saw she would have to talk a little and told me she was at the Granada. She made me wait ten minutes before I followed her over."

Degarmo said: "Time to fix up a plant."

"There was a plant all right, but I'm not sure she was in on it. She didn't want me to come up there, didn't want to talk. Yet she ought to have known I would insist on some explanation before I gave up the money, so her reluctance could have been just an act, to make me feel that I was controlling the situation. She could act all right. I found that out. Anyhow I went and we talked. Nothing she said made very much sense until we talked about Lavery getting shot. Then she made too much sense too quick. I told her I was going to turn her over to the police."

Westwood Village, dark except for one all night service station and a few distant windows in apartment houses, slid away to the north of us.

"So she pulled a gun," I said. "I think she meant to use it, but she got too close to me and I got a headlock on her. While we were wrestling around, somebody came out from behind a green curtain and slugged me. When I came out of that the murder was done."

Degarmo said slowly: "You get any kind of a look at who slugged you?"

"No. I felt or half saw he was a man and a big one. And this lying on the davenport, mixed in with clothes." I reached Kingsley's yellow and green scarf out of my pocket and draped it over his knee. "I saw Kingsley wearing this earlier this evening," I said.

Degarmo looked down at the scarf. He lifted it under the dashlight. "You wouldn't forget that too quick," he said. "It steps right up and smacks you in the eye. Kingsley, huh? Well, I'm damned. What happened then?"

"Knocking on the door. Me still woozy in the head, not too bright and a bit panicked. I had been flooded with gin and my shoes and coat stripped off and maybe I looked and smelled a little like somebody who would yank a woman's clothes off and strangle her. So I got out through the bathroom window, cleaned myself up as well as I could, and the rest you know."

Degarmo said: "Why didn't you lie dormy in the place you climbed into?"

"What was the use? I guess even a Bay City cop would have found the way I had gone in a little while. If I had any chance at all, it was to walk out before that was discovered. If nobody was there who knew me, I had a fair chance of getting out of the building."

"I don't think so," Degarmo said. "But I can see where you didn't lose much trying. What's your idea of the motivation here?"

"Why did Kingsley kill her—if he did? That's not hard. She had been cheating on him, making him a lot of trouble, endangering his job and now she had killed a man. Also, she had money and Kingsley wanted to marry another woman. He might have been afraid that with money to spend she could beat the rap and be left laughing at him. If she didn't beat the rap, and got sent up, her money would be just as thoroughly beyond his reach. He'd have to divorce her to get rid of her. There's plenty of motive for murder in all that. Also he saw a chance to make me the goat. It wouldn't stick, but it would make confusion and delay. If murderers didn't think they could get away with their murders, very few would be committed."

Degarmo said: "All the same it could be somebody else, somebody who isn't in the picture at all. Even if he went down there to see her, it could still be somebody else. Somebody else could have killed Lavery too."

"If you like it that way."

He turned his head. "I don't like it any way at all. But if I crack the case, I'll get by with a reprimand from the police board. If I don't crack it, I'll be thumbing a ride out of town. You said I was dumb. Okay, I'm dumb. Where does Kingsley live? One thing I know is how to make people talk."

"965 Carson Drive, Beverly Hills. About five blocks on you turn north to the foothills. It's on the left side, just below Sunset. I've never been there, but I know how the block numbers run."

He handed me the green and yellow scarf. "Tuck that back into your pocket until we want to spring it on him."

# 35

It was a two-storied white house with a dark roof. Bright moonlight lay against its wall like a fresh coat of paint. There were wrought iron grilles against the lower halves of the front windows. A level lawn swept up to the front door, which was set diagonally into the angle of a jutting wall. All the visible windows were dark.

Degarmo got out of the car and walked along the parkway and looked back along the drive to the garage. He moved down the driveway and the corner of the house hid him. I heard the sound of a garage door going up, then the thud as it was lowered again. He reappeared at the corner of the house, shook his head at me, and walked across the grass to the front door. He leaned his thumb on the bell and juggled a cigarette out of his pocket with one hand and put it between his lips.

He turned away from the door to light it and the flare of the match cut deep lines into his face. After a while there was light on the fan over the door. The peephole in the door swung back. I saw Degarmo holding up his shield. Slowly and as if unwillingly the door was opened. He went in.

He was gone four or five minutes. Light went on behind various windows, then off again. Then he came out of the house and while he was walking back to the car the light went off in the fan and the whole house was again as dark as we had found it.

He stood beside the car smoking and looking off down the curve of the street.

"One small car in the garage," he said. "The cook says it's hers. No sign of Kingsley. They say they haven't seen him since this morning. I looked in all the rooms. I guess they told the truth. Webber and a print man were there late this afternoon and the dusting powder is still all over the main bedroom. Webber would be getting prints to check against what we found in Lavery's house. He didn't tell me what he got. Where would he be—Kingsley?"

"Anywhere," I said. "On the road, in a hotel, in a Turkish bath getting the kinks out of his nerves. But we'll have to try his girl friend first. Her name is Fromsett and she lives at the Bryson Tower on Sunset Place. That's away downtown, near Bullock's Wilshire."

"She does what?" Degarmo asked, getting in under the wheel.

"She holds the fort in his office and holds his hand out of office hours. She's no office cutie, though. She has brains and style."

"This situation is going to use all she has," Degarmo said. He drove down to Wilshire and we turned east again.

Twenty-five minutes brought us to the Bryson Tower, a white stucco palace with fretted lanterns in the forecourt and tall date palms. The entrance was in an L, up marble steps, through a Moorish archway, and over a lobby that was too big and a carpet that was too blue. Blue Ali Baba oil jars were dotted around, big enough to keep tigers in. There was a desk and a night clerk with one of those mustaches that get stuck under your fingernail.

Degarmo lunged past the desk towards an open elevator beside which a tired old man sat on a stool waiting for a customer. The clerk snapped at Degarmo's back like a terrier.

"One moment, please. Whom did you wish to see?"

Degarmo spun on his heel and looked at me wonderingly. "Did he say 'whom'?"

"Yeah, but don't hit him," I said. "There is such a word."

Degarmo licked his lips. "I knew there was," he said. "I often wondered where they kept it. Look, buddy," he said to the clerk, "we want up to seven-sixteen. Any objection?"

"Certainly I have," the clerk said coldly. "We don't announce guests at—" he lifted his arm and turned it neatly to look at the narrow oblong watch on the inside of his wrist,—"at twenty-three minutes past four in the morning."

"That's what I thought," Degarmo said. "So I wasn't going to bother you. You get the idea?" He took his shield out of his pocket and held it so that the light glinted on the gold and the blue enamel. "I'm a police lieutenant."

The clerk shrugged. "Very well. I hope there isn't going to be any trouble. I'd better announce you then. What names?"

"Lieutenant Degarmo and Mr. Marlowe."

"Apartment 716. That will be Miss Fromsett. One moment."

He went behind a glass screen and we heard him talking on the phone after a longish pause. He came back and nodded.

"Miss Fromsett is in. She will receive you."

"That's certainly a load off my mind," Degarmo said. "And don't bother to call your house peeper and send him up to the scatter. I'm allergic to house peepers."

The clerk gave a small cold smile and we got into the elevator.

The seventh floor was cool and quiet. The corridor seemed a mile long. We came at last to a door with 716 on it in gilt numbers in a circle of gilt leaves. There was an ivory button beside the door. Degarmo pushed it and chimes rang inside the door and it was opened.

Miss Fromsett wore a quilted blue robe over her pajamas. On her feet were small tufted slippers with high heels. Her dark hair was fluffed out engagingly and the cold cream had been wiped from her face and just enough makeup applied.

We went past her into a rather narrow room with several handsome oval mirrors and gray period furniture upholstered in blue damask. It didn't look like apartment house furniture. She sat down on a slender love seat and leaned back and waited calmly for somebody to say something.

I said: "This is Lieutenant Degarmo of the Bay City police. We're looking for Kingsley. He's not at his house. We thought you might be able to give us an idea where to find him."

She spoke to me without looking at me. "Is it that urgent?"

"Yes. Something has happened."

"What has happened?"

Degarmo said bluntly: "We just want to know where Kingsley is, sister. We don't have time to build up a scene."

The girl looked at him with a complete absence of expression. She looked back at me and said:

"I think you had better tell me, Mr. Marlowe."

"I went down there with the money," I said. "I met her as arranged. I went to her apartment to talk to her. While there I was slugged by a man who was hidden behind a curtain. I didn't see the man. When I came out of it she had been murdered."

"Murdered?"

I said: "Murdered."

She closed her fine eyes and the corners of her lovely mouth drew in. Then she stood up with a quick shrug and went over to a small, marble-topped table with spindly legs. She took a cigarette out of a small embossed silver box and lit it, staring emptily down at the table. The match in her hand was waved more and more slowly until it stopped, still burning, and she dropped it into a tray. She turned and put her back to the table.

"I suppose I ought to scream or something," she said. "I don't seem to have any feeling about it at all."

Degarmo said: "We don't feel so interested in your feelings right now. What we want to know is where Kingsley is. You can tell us or not tell us. Either way you can skip the attitudes. Just make your mind up."

She said to me quietly: "The lieutenant here is a Bay City officer?"

I nodded. She turned at him slowly, with a lovely contemptuous dignity. "In that case," she said, "he has no more right in my apartment than any other loud-mouthed bum that might try to toss his weight around."

Degarmo looked at her bleakly. He grinned and walked across the room and stretched his long legs from a deep downy chair. He waved his hand at me.

"Okay, you work on her. I can get all the co-operation I need from the L.A. boys, but by the time I had things explained to them, it would be a week from next Tuesday."

I said: "Miss Fromsett, if you know where he is, or where he started to go, please tell us. You can understand that he has to be found."

She said calmly, "Why?"

Degarmo put his head back and laughed. "This babe is good," he said. "Maybe she thinks we should keep it a secret from him that his wife has been knocked off."

"She's better than you think," I told him. His face sobered and he bit his thumb. He looked her up and down insolently.

She said: "Is it just because he has to be told?"

I took the yellow and green scarf out of my pocket and shook it out loose and held it in front of her.

"This was found in the apartment where she was murdered. I think you have seen it."

She looked at the scarf and she looked at me, and in neither of the glances was there any meaning. She said: "You ask for a great deal of confidence, Mr. Marlowe. Considering that you haven't been such a very smart detective after all."

"I ask for it," I said, "and I expect to get it. And how smart I've been is something you don't really know anything about."

"This is cute," Degarmo put in. "You two make a nice team. All you need is acrobats to follow you. But right now—"

She cut through his voice as if he didn't exist. "How was she murdered?"

"She was strangled and stripped naked and scratched up."

"Derry wouldn't have done anything like that," she said quietly.

Degarmo made a noise with his lips. "Nobody ever knows what anybody else will do, sister. A cop knows that much."

She still didn't look at him. In the same level tone she asked: "Do you want to know where we went after we left your apartment and whether he brought me home—things like that?"

"Yes."

"Because if he did, he wouldn't have had time to go down to the beach and kill her? Is that it?"

I said, "That's a good part of it."

"He didn't bring me home," she said slowly. "I took a taxi on Hollywood Boulevard, not more than five minutes after we left your place. I didn't see him again. I supposed he went home."

Degarmo said: "Usually the bim tries to give her boy friend a bit more alibi than that. But it takes all kinds, don't it?"

Miss Fromsett said to me: "He wanted to bring me home, but it was a long way out of his way and we were both tired. The reason I was telling you this is because I know it doesn't matter in the least. If I thought it did, I wouldn't tell you."

"So he did have time," I said.

She shook her head. "I don't know. I don't know how much time was needed. I don't know how he could have known where to go. Not from me, not from her through me. She didn't tell me." Her dark eyes were on mine, searching, probing. "Is this the kind of confidence you ask for?"

I folded the scarf up and put it back in my pocket. "We want to know where he is now."

"I can't tell you because I have no idea." Her eyes had followed the scarf down to my pocket. They stayed there. "You say you were slugged. You mean knocked unconscious?"

"Yes. By somebody who was hidden out behind a curtain. We still fall for it. She pulled a gun on me and I was busy trying to take it away from her. There's no doubt she shot Lavery."

Degarmo stood up suddenly: "You're making yourself a nice smooth scene, fellow," he growled. "But you're not getting anywhere. Let's blow."

I said: "Wait a minute. I'm not finished. Suppose he had something on his mind, Miss Fromsett, something that was eating pretty deep into him. That was how he looked tonight. Suppose he knew more about all this than we realized—or than I realized—and knew things were coming to a head. He would want to go somewhere quietly and try to figure out what to do. Don't you think he might?"

I stopped and waited, looking sideways at Degarmo's impatience. After a moment the girl said tonelessly: "He wouldn't run away or hide, because it wasn't anything he could run away and hide from. But he might want a time to himself to think."

"In a strange place, in a hotel," I said, thinking of the story that had been told me in the Granada. "Or in a much quieter place than that."

I looked around for the telephone.

"It's in my bedroom," Miss Fromsett said, knowing at once what I was looking for.

I went down the room and through the door at the end. Degarmo was right behind me. The bedroom was ivory and ashes of roses. There was a big bed with no footboard and a pillow with the rounded hollow of a head. Toilet articles glistened on a built-in dresser with paneled mirrors on the wall above it. An open door showed mulberry bathroom tiles. The phone was on a night table by the bed.

I sat down on the edge of the bed and patted the place where Miss Fromsett's head had been and lifted the phone and dialed long distance. When the operator answered I asked for Constable Jim Patton at Puma Point, person to person, very urgent. I put the phone back in the cradle and lit a cigarette. Degarmo glowered down at me, standing with his legs apart, tough and tireless and ready to be nasty. "What now?" he grunted.

"Wait and see."

"Who's running this show?"

"You're asking me shows that. I am—unless you want the Los Angeles police to run it."

He scratched a match on his thumbnail and watched it burn and tried to blow it out with a long steady breath that just bent the flame over. He got rid of that match and put another between his teeth and chewed on it. The phone rang in a moment.

"Ready with your Puma Point call."

Patton's sleepy voice came on the line. "Yes? This is Patton at Puma Point."

"This is Marlowe in Los Angeles," I said. "Remember me?"

"Sure I remember you, son. I ain't only half awake though."

"Do me a favor," I said. "Although I don't know why you should. Go or send over to Little Fawn Lake and see if Kingsley is there. Don't let him see you. You can spot his car outside the cabin or maybe see lights. And see that he stays put. Call me back as soon as you know. I'm coming up. Can you do that?"

Patton said: "I got no reason to stop him if he wants to leave."

"I'll have a Bay City police officer with me who wants to question him about a murder. Not your murder, another one."

There was a drumming silence along the wire. Patton said: "You ain't just bein' tricky, are you, son?"

"No. Call me back at Tunbridge 2722."

"Should likely take me half an hour," he said.

I hung up. Degarmo was grinning now. "This babe flash you a signal I couldn't read?"

I stood up off the bed. "No. I'm just trying to read his mind. He's no cold killer. Whatever fire there was is all burned out of him by now. I thought he might go to the quietest and most remote place he knows—just to get a grip of himself. In a few hours he'll probably turn himself in. It would look better for you if you got to him before he did that."

"Unless he puts a slug in his head," Degarmo said coldly. "Guys like him are very apt to do that."

"You can't stop him until you find him."

"That's right."

We went back into the living room. Miss Fromsett poked her head out of her kitchenette and said she was making coffee, and did we want any. We had some coffee and sat around looking like people seeing friends off at the railroad station.

The call from Patton came through in about twenty-five minutes. There was light in the Kingsley cabin and a car was parked beside it.

# 36

We ate some breakfast at Alhambra and I had the tank filled. We drove out Highway 70 and started moving past the trucks into the rolling ranch country. I was driving. Degarmo sat moodily in the corner, his hands deep in his pockets.

I watched the fat straight rows of orange trees spin by like the spokes of a wheel. I listened to the whine of the tires on the pavement and I felt tired and stale from lack of sleep and too much emotion.

We reached the long slope south of San Dimas that goes up to a ridge and drops down into Pomona. This is the ultimate end of the fog belt, and the beginning of that semi-desert region where the sun is as light and dry as old sherry in the morning, as hot as a blast furnace at noon, and drops like an angry brick at nightfall.

Degarmo stuck a match in the corner of his mouth and said almost sneeringly:

"Webber gave me hell last night. He said he was talking to you and what about."

I said nothing. He looked at me and looked away again. He waved a hand outwards. "I wouldn't live in this damn country if they gave it to me. The air's stale before it gets up in the morning."

"We'll be coming to Ontario in a minute. We'll switch over to Foothill Boulevard and you'll see five miles of the finest grevillea trees in the world."

"I wouldn't know one from a fireplug," Degarmo said.

We came to the center of town and turned north on Euclid, along the splendid parkway. Degarmo sneered at the grevillea trees.

After a while he said: "That was my girl that drowned in the lake up there. I haven't been right in the head since I heard about it. All I can see is red. If I could get my hands on that guy Chess—"

"You made enough trouble," I said, "letting her get away with murdering Almore's wife."

I stared straight ahead through the windshield. I knew his head moved and his eyes froze on me. I didn't know what his hands were doing. I didn't know what expression was on his face. After a long time his words came. They came through tight teeth and edgeways, and they scraped a little as they came out.

"You a little crazy or something?"

"No," I said. "Neither are you. You know as well as anybody could know anything that Florence Almore didn't get up out of bed and walk down to that garage. You know she was carried. You know that was why Talley stole her slipper, the slipper that had never walked on a concrete path. You knew that Almore gave his wife a shot in the arm at Condy's place and that it was just enough and not any too much. He knew his shots in the arm the way you know how to rough up a bum that hasn't any money or any place to sleep. You know that Almore didn't murder his wife with morphine and that if he wanted to murder her, morphine would be the last thing in the world he would use. But you know that somebody else did, and that Almore carried her down to the garage and put her there—technically still alive to breathe in some monoxide, but medically just as dead as though she had stopped breathing. You know all that."

Degarmo said softly: "Brother, how did you ever manage to live so long?"

I said: "By not falling for too many gags and not getting too much afraid of professional hard guys. Only a heel would have done what Almore did, only a heel and a badly scared man who had things on his soul that wouldn't stand daylight. Technically he may even have been guilty of murder. I don't think the point has ever been settled. Certainly he would have a hell of a time proving that she was in such a deep coma that she was beyond any possibility of help. But as a practical matter of who killed her, you know the girl killed her."

Degarmo laughed. It was a grating unpleasant laugh, not only mirthless, but meaningless.

We reached Foothill Boulevard and turned east again. I thought it was still cool, but Degarmo was sweating. He couldn't take his coat off because of the gun under his arm.

I said: "The girl, Mildred Haviland, was playing house with Almore and his wife knew it. She had threatened him. I got that from her parents. The girl, Mildred Haviland, knew all about morphine and where to get all of it she needed and how much to use. She was alone in the house with Florence Almore, after she put her to bed. She was in a perfect spot to load a needle with four or five grains and shoot it into an unconscious woman through the same puncture Almore had already made. She would die, perhaps while Almore was still out of the house, and he would come home and find her dead. The problem would be his. He would have to solve it. Nobody would believe anybody else had doped his wife to death. Nobody that didn't know all the circumstances. But you knew. I'd have to think you much more of a damn fool than I think you are to believe you didn't know. You covered the girl up. You were in love with her still. You scared her out of town, out of danger, out of reach, but you covered up for her. You let the murder ride. She had you that way. Why did you go up to the mountains looking for her?"

"And how did I know where to look?" he said harshly. "It wouldn't bother you to add an explanation of that, would it?"

"Not at all," I said. "She got sick of Bill Chess and his boozing and his tempers and his down-at-heels living. But she had to have money to make a break. She thought she was safe, now that she had something on Almore that was safe to use. So she wrote him for money. He sent you up to talk to her. She didn't tell Almore what her present name was or any details or where or how she was living. A letter addressed to Mildred Haviland at Puma Point would reach her. All she had to do was ask for it. But no letter came and nobody connected her with Mildred Haviland. All you had was an old photo and your usual bad manners, and they didn't get you anywhere with those people."

Degarmo said gratingly: "Who told you she tried to get money from Almore?"

"Nobody. I had to think of something to fit what happened. If Lavery or Mrs. Kingsley had known who Muriel Chess had been, and had tipped it off, you would have known where to find her and what name she was using. You didn't know those things. Therefore the lead had to come from the only person up there who knew who she was, and that was herself. So I assume she wrote to Almore."

"Okay," he said at last. "Let's forget it. It doesn't make any difference any more now. If I'm in a jam, that's my business. I'd do it again, in the same circumstances."

"That's all right," I said. "I'm not planning to put the bite on anybody myself. Not even on you. I'm telling you this mostly so you won't try to hang any murders on Kingsley that don't belong on him. If there is one that does, let it hang."

"Is that why you're telling me?" he asked.

"Yeah."

"I thought maybe it was because you hated my guts," he said.

"I'm all done with hating you," I said. "It's all washed out of me. I hate people hard, but I don't hate them very long."

We were going through the grape country now, the open sandy grape country along the scarred flanks of the foothills. We came in a little while to San Bernardino and I kept on through it without stopping.

## 37

At Crestline, elevation 5000 feet, it had not yet started to warm up. We stopped for a beer. When we got back into the car, Degarmo took the gun from his underarm holster and looked it over. It was a .38 Smith and Wesson on a .44 frame, a wicked weapon with a kick like a .45 and a much greater effective range.

"You won't need that," I said. "He's big and strong, but he's not that kind of tough."

He put the gun back under his arm and grunted. We didn't talk any more now. We had no more to talk about. We rolled around the curves and along the sharp sheer edges walled with white guard rails and in some places with walls of field stone and heavy iron chains. We climbed through the tall oaks and on to the altitudes where the oaks are not so tall and the pines are taller and taller. We came at last to the dam at the end of Puma Lake.

I stopped the car and the sentry threw his piece across his body and stepped up to the window.

"Close all the windows of your car before proceeding across the dam, please."

I reached back to wind up the rear window on my side. Degarmo held his shield up. "Forget it, buddy. I'm a police officer," he said with his usual tact.

The sentry gave him a solid expressionless stare. "Close all windows, please," he said in the same tone he had used before.

"Nuts to you," Degarmo said. "Nuts to you, soldier boy."

"It's an order," the sentry said. His jaw muscles bulged very slightly. His dull grayish eyes stared at Degarmo. "And I didn't write the order, mister. Up with the windows."

"Suppose I told you to go jump in the lake," Degarmo sneered.

The sentry said: "I might do it. I scare easily." He patted the breech of his rifle with a leathery hand.

Degarmo turned and closed the windows on his side. We drove across the dam. There was a sentry in the middle and one at the far end. The first one must have flashed them some kind of signal. They looked at us with steady watchful eyes, without friendliness.

I drove on through the piled masses of granite and down through the meadows of coarse grass where cows grazed. The same gaudy slacks and short shorts and peasant handkerchiefs as yesterday, the same light breeze and golden sun and clear blue sky, the same smell of pine needles, the same cool softness of a mountain summer. But yesterday was a hundred years ago, something crystallized in time, like a fly in amber.

I turned off on the road to Little Fawn Lake and wound around the huge rocks and past the little gurgling waterfall. The gate into Kingsley's property was open and Patton's car was standing in the road pointing towards the lake, which was invisible from that point. There was nobody in it. The card sign on the windshield still read *"Keep Jim Patton Constable. He Is Too Old To Go To Work."*

Close to it and pointed the other way was a small battered coupe. Inside the coupe a lion hunter's hat. I stopped my car behind Patton's and locked it and got out. Andy got out of the coupe and stood staring at us woodenly.

I said: "This is Lieutenant Degarmo of the Bay City police."

Andy said: "Jim's just over the ridge. He's waiting for you. He ain't had any breakfast."

We walked up the road to the ridge as Andy got back into his coupe. Beyond it the road dropped to the tiny blue lake. Kingsley's cabin across the water seemed to be without life.

"That's the lake," I said.

Degarmo looked down at it silently. His shoulders moved in a heavy shrug. "Let's go get the bastard," was all he said.

We went on and Patton stood up from behind a rock. He was wearing the same old Stetson and khaki pants and shirt buttoned to his thick neck. The star on his left breast still had a bent point. His jaws moved slowly, munching.

"Nice to see you again," he said, not looking at me, but at Degarmo.

He put his hand out and shook Degarmo's hard paw. "Last time I seen you, lieutenant, you was wearing another name. Kind of undercover, I guess you'd call it. I guess I didn't treat you right neither. I apologize. Guess I know who that photo of yours was all the time."

Degarmo nodded and said nothing.

"Likely if I'd of been on my toes and played the game right, a lot of trouble would have been saved," Patton said. "Maybe a life would have been saved. I feel kind of bad about it, but then again I ain't a fellow that feels too bad about anything very long. Suppose we sit down here and you tell me what it is we're supposed to be doing now."

Degarmo said: "Kingsley's wife was murdered in Bay City last night. I have to talk to him about it."

"You mean you suspect him?" Patton asked.

"And how," Degarmo grunted.

Patton rubbed his neck and looked across the lake. "He ain't showed outside the cabin at all. Likely he's still asleep. Early this morning I snuck around the cabin. There was a radio goin' then and I heard sounds like a man would make playing with a bottle and a glass. I stayed away from him. Was that right?"

"We'll go over there now," Degarmo said.

"You got a gun, lieutenant?"

Degarmo patted under his left arm. Patton looked at me. I shook my head, no gun.

"Kingsley might have one too," Patton said. "I don't hanker after no fast shooting around here, lieutenant. It wouldn't do me no good to have a gunfight. We don't have that kind of community up here. You look to me like a fellow who would jack his gun out kind of fast."

"I've got plenty of swift, if that's what you mean," Degarmo said. "But I want this guy talking."

Patton looked at Degarmo, looked at me, looked back at Degarmo and spat tobacco juice in a long stream to one side.

"I ain't heard enough to even approach him," he said stubbornly.

So we sat down on the ground and told him the story. He listened silently, not blinking an eye. At the end he said to me: "You got a funny way of working for people, seems to me. Personally I think you boys are plumb misinformed. We'll go over and see. I'll go in first—in case you would know what you are talking about and Kingsley would have a gun and would be a little desperate. I got a big belly. Makes a nice target."

We stood up off the ground and started around the lake the long way. When we came to the little pier I said:

"Did they autopsy her yet, sheriff?"

Patton nodded. "She drowned all right. They say they're satisfied that's how she died. She wasn't knifed or shot or had her head cracked in or anything. There's marks on the body, but too many to mean anything. And it ain't a very nice body to work with."

Degarmo looked white and angry.

"I guess I oughtn't to have said that, lieutenant," Patton added mildly. "Kind of tough to take. Seeing you knew the lady pretty well."

Degarmo said: "Let's get it over and do what we have to do."

We went on along the shore of the lake and came to Kingsley's cabin. We went up the heavy steps. Patton went quietly across the porch to the door. He tried the screen. It was not hooked. He opened it and tried the door. That was unlocked also. He held the door shut, with the knob turned in his hand, and Degarmo took hold of the screen and pulled it wide. Patton opened the door and we walked into the room.

Derace Kingsley lay back in a deep chair by the cold fireplace with his eyes closed. There was an empty glass and an almost empty whiskey bottle on the table beside him. The room smelled of whiskey. A dish near the bottle was choked with cigarette stubs. Two crushed empty packs lay on top of the stubs.

All the windows in the room were shut. It was already close and hot in there. Kingsley was wearing a sweater and his face was flushed and heavy. He snored and his hands hung lax outside the arms of the chair, the fingertips touching the floor.

Patton moved to within a few feet of him and stood looking silently down at him for a long moment before he spoke.

"Mr. Kingsley," he said then, in a calm steady voice, "we got to talk to you a little."

# 38

Kingsley moved with a kind of jerk, and opened his eyes and moved them without moving his head. He looked at Patton, then at Degarmo, lastly at me. His eyes were heavy, but the light sharpened in them. He sat up slowly in the chair and rubbed his hands up and down the sides of his face.

"I was asleep," he said. "Fell asleep a couple of hours ago. I was as drunk as a skunk, I guess. Anyway, much drunker than I like to be." He dropped his hands and let them hang.

Patton said: "This is Lieutenant Degarmo of the Bay City police. He has to talk to you."

Kingsley looked briefly at Degarmo and his eyes came around to stare at me. His voice when he spoke again sounded sober and quiet and tired to death.

"So you let them get her?" he said.

I said: "I would have, but I didn't."

Kingsley thought about that, looking at Degarmo. Patton had left the front door open. He pulled the brown Venetian blinds up at two front windows and pulled the windows up. He sat in a chair near one of them and clasped his hands over his stomach. Degarmo stood glowering down at Kingsley.

"Your wife is dead, Kingsley," he said brutally. "If it's any news to you."

Kingsley stared at him and moistened his lips.

"Takes it easy, don't he?" Degarmo said. "Show him the scarf."

I took the green and yellow scarf out and dangled it. Degarmo jerked a thumb. "Yours?"

Kingsley nodded. He moistened his lips again.

"Careless of you to leave it behind you," Degarmo said. He was breathing a little hard. His nose was pinched and deep lines ran from his nostrils to the corners of his mouth.

Kingsley said very quietly: "Leave it behind me where?" He had barely glanced at the scarf. He hadn't looked at all at me.

"In the Granada Apartments, on Eighth Street, in Bay City. Apartment 716. Am I telling you something?"

Kingsley now very slowly lifted his eyes to meet mine. "Is that where she was?" he breathed.

I nodded. "She didn't want me to go there. I wouldn't give her the money until she talked to me. She admitted she killed Lavery. She pulled a gun and planned to give me the same treatment. Somebody came from behind the curtain and knocked me out without letting me see him. When I came to she was dead." I told him how she was dead and how she looked. I told him what I had done and what had been done to me.

He listened without moving a muscle of his face. When I had done talking he made a vague gesture towards the scarf.

"What has that got to do with it?"

"The lieutenant regards it as evidence that you were the party hidden out in the apartment."

Kingsley thought that over. He didn't seem to get the implications of it very quickly. He leaned back in the chair and rested his head against the back. "Go on," he said at length. "I suppose you know what you're talking about. I'm quite sure I don't."

Degarmo said: "All right, play dumb. See what it gets you. You could begin by accounting for your time last night after you dropped your biddy at her apartment house."

Kingsley said evenly: "If you mean Miss Fromsett, I didn't. She went home in a taxi. I was going home myself, but I didn't. I came up here instead. I thought the trip and the night air and the quiet might help me to get straightened out."

"Just think of that," Degarmo jeered. "Straightened out from what, if I might ask?"

"Straightened out from all the worry I had been having."

"Hell," Degarmo said, "a little thing like strangling your wife and clawing her belly wouldn't worry you that much, would it?"

"Son, you hadn't ought to say things like that," Patton put in from the background. "That ain't no way to talk. You ain't produced anything yet that sounds like evidence."

"No?" Degarmo swung his hard head at him. "What about this scarf, fatty? Isn't that evidence?"

"You didn't fit it in to anything—not that I heard," Patton said peacefully. "And I ain't fat either, just well covered."

Degarmo swung away from him disgustedly. He jabbed his finger at Kingsley.

"I suppose you didn't go down to Bay City at all," he said harshly.

"No. Why should I? Marlowe was taking care of that. And I don't see why you are making a point of the scarf. Marlowe was wearing it."

Degarmo stood rooted and savage. He turned very slowly and gave me his bleak angry stare.

"I don't get this," he said. "Honest, I don't. It wouldn't be that somebody is kidding me, would it? Somebody like you?"

I said: "All I told about the scarf was that it was in the apartment and that I had seen Kingsley wearing it earlier this evening. That seemed to be all you wanted. I might have added that I had later worn the scarf myself, so the girl I was to meet could identify me that much easier."

Degarmo backed away from Kingsley and leaned against the wall at the end of the fireplace. He pulled his lower lip out with thumb and forefinger of his left hand. His right hand hung lax at his side, the fingers slightly curved.

I said: "I told you all I had ever seen of Mrs. Kingsley was a snapshot. One of us had to be sure of being able to identify the other. The scarf seemed obvious enough for identification. As a matter of fact I had seen her once before, although I didn't know it when I went to meet her. But I didn't recognize her at once," I turned to Kingsley. "Mrs. Fallbrook," I said.

"I thought you said Mrs. Fallbrook was the owner of the house," he answered slowly.

"That's what she said at the time. That's what I believed at the time. Why wouldn't I?"

Degarmo made a sound in his throat. His eyes were a little crazy. I told him about Mrs. Fallbrook and her purple hat and her fluttery manner and the empty gun she had been holding and how she gave it to me.

When I stopped, he said very carefully: "I didn't hear you tell Webber any of that."

"I didn't tell him. I didn't want to admit I had already been in the house three hours before. That I had gone to talk it over with Kingsley before I reported it to the police."

"That's something we're going to love you for," Degarmo said with a cold grin. "Jesus, what a sucker I've been. How much you paying this shamus to cover up your murders for you, Kingsley?"

"His usual rates," Kingsley told him emptily. "And a five hundred dollar bonus if he can prove my wife didn't murder Lavery."

"Too bad he can't earn that," Degarmo sneered.

"Don't be silly," I said. "I've already earned it."

There was a silence in the room. One of those charged silences which seem about to split apart with a peal of thunder. It didn't. It remained, hung heavy and solid, like a wall. Kingsley moved a little in his chair, and after a long moment, he nodded his head.

"Nobody could possibly know that better than you know it, Degarmo," I said.

Patton had as much expression on his face as a chunk of wood. He watched Degarmo quietly. He didn't look at Kingsley at all. Degarmo looked at a point between my eyes, but not as if that was anything in the room with him. Rather as if he was looking at something very far away, like a mountain across a valley.

After what seemed a very long time, Degarmo said quietly: "I don't see why. I don't know anything about Kingsley's wife. To the best of my knowledge I never laid eyes on her—until last night."

He lowered his eyelids a little and watched me broodingly. He knew perfectly well what I was going to say. I said it anyway.

"And you never saw her last night. Because she had already been dead for over a month. Because she had been drowned in Little Fawn Lake. Because the woman you saw dead in the Granada Apartments was Mildred Haviland, and Mildred Haviland was Muriel Chess. And since Mrs. Kingsley was dead long before Lavery was shot, it follows that Mrs. Kingsley did not shoot him."

Kingsley clenched his fists on the arms of his chair, but he made no sound, no sound at all.

# 39

There was another heavy silence. Patton broke it by saying in his careful slow voice: "That's kind of a wild statement, ain't it? Don't you kind of think Bill Chess would know his own wife?"

I said: "After a month in the water? With his wife's clothes on her and some of his wife's trinkets? With water-soaked blonde hair like his wife's hair and almost no recognizable face? Why would he even have a doubt about it? She left a note that might be a suicide note. She was gone away. They had quarreled. Her clothes and car had gone away. During the month she was gone, he had heard nothing from her. He had no idea where she had gone. And then this corpse comes up out of the water with Muriel's clothes on it. A blonde woman about his wife's size. Of course there would be differences and if any substitution had been suspected, they would have been found and checked. But there was no reason to suspect any such thing. Crystal Kingsley was still alive. She had gone off with Lavery. She had left her car in San Bernardino. She had sent a wire to her husband from El Paso. She was all taken care of, so far as Bill Chess was concerned. He had no thoughts about her at all. She didn't enter the picture anywhere for him. Why should she?"

Patton said: "I ought to of thought of it myself. But if I had, it would be one of those ideas a fellow would throw away almost as quick as he thought of it. It would look too kind of far-fetched."

"Superficially yes," I said. "But only superficially. Suppose the body had not come up out of the lake for a year, or not at all, unless the lake was dragged for it. Muriel Chess was gone and nobody was going to spend much time looking for her. We might never have heard of her again. Mrs. Kingsley was a different proposition. She had money and connections and an anxious husband. She would be searched for, as she was, eventually. But not very soon, unless something happened to start suspicion. It might have been a matter of months before anything was found out. The lake might have been dragged, but if a search along her trail seemed to indicate that she had actually left the lake and gone down the hill, even as far as San Bernardino, and the train from there east, then the lake might never have been dragged. And even if it was and the body was found, there was rather better than an even chance that the body would not be correctly identified. Bill Chess was arrested for his wife's murder. For all I know he might even have been convicted of it, and that would have been that, as far as the body in the lake was concerned. Crystal Kingsley would still be missing, and it would be an unsolved mystery. Eventually it would be assumed that something had happened to her and that she was no longer alive. But nobody would know where or when or how it had happened. If it hadn't been for Lavery, we might not be here talking about it now. Lavery is the key to the whole thing. He was in the Prescott Hotel in San Bernardino the night Crystal Kingsley was supposed to have left here. He saw a woman there who had Crystal Kingsley's car, who was wearing Crystal Kingsley's clothes, and of course he knew who she was. But he didn't have to know there was anything wrong.

He didn't have to know they were Crystal Kingsley's clothes or that the woman had put Crystal Kingsley's car in the hotel garage. All he had to know was that he met Muriel Chess. Muriel took care of the rest."

I stopped and waited for somebody to say anything. Nobody did. Patton sat immovable in his chair, his plump, hairless hands clasped comfortably across his stomach. Kingsley leaned his head back and he had his eyes half closed and he was not moving. Degarmo leaned against the wall by the fireplace, taut and white-faced and cold, a big hard solemn man whose thoughts were deeply hidden.

I went on talking.

"If Muriel Chess impersonated Crystal Kingsley, she murdered her. That's elementary. All right, let's look at it. We know who she was and what kind of woman she was. She had already murdered before she met and married Bill Chess. She had been Dr. Almore's office nurse and his little pal and she had murdered Dr. Almore's wife in such a neat way that Almore had to cover up for her. And she had been married to a man in the Bay City police who also was sucker enough to cover up for her. She got the men that way, she could make them jump through hoops. I didn't know her long enough to see why, but her record proves it. What she was able to do with Lavery proves it. Very well, she killed people who got in her way, and Kingsley's wife got in her way too. I hadn't meant to talk about this, but it doesn't matter much now. Crystal Kingsley could make the men do a little jumping through hoops too. She made Bill Chess jump and Bill Chess's wife wasn't the girl to take that and smile. Also, she was sick to death of her life up here—she must have been—and she wanted to get away. But she needed money. She had tried to get it from Almore, and that sent Degarmo up here looking for her. That scared her a little. Degarmo is the sort of fellow you are never quite sure of. She was right not to be sure of him, wasn't she, Degarmo?"

Degarmo moved his foot on the ground. "The sands are running against you, fellow," he said grimly. "Speak your little piece while you can."

"Mildred didn't positively have to have Crystal Kingsley's

car and clothes and credentials and what not, but they helped. What money she had must have helped a great deal, and Kingsley says she liked to have a good deal of money with her. Also she must have had jewelry which could eventually be turned into money. All this made killing her a rational as well as an agreeable thing to do. That disposes of motive, and we come to means and opportunity.

"The opportunity was made to order for her. She had quarreled with Bill and he had gone off to get drunk. She knew her Bill and how drunk he could get and how long he would stay away. She needed time. Time was of the essence. She had to assume that there was time. Otherwise the whole thing flopped. She had to pack her own clothes and take them in her car to Coon Lake and hide them there, because they had to be gone. She had to walk back. She had to murder Crystal Kingsley and dress her in Muriel's clothes and get her down in the lake. All that took time. As to the murder itself, I imagine she got her drunk or knocked her on the head and drowned her in the bathtub in this cabin. That would be logic and simple too. She was a nurse, she knew how to handle things like bodies. She knew how to swim—we have it from Bill that she was a fine swimmer. And a drowned body will sink. All she had to do was guide it down into the deep water where she wanted it. There is nothing in all this beyond the powers of one woman who could swim. She did it, she dressed in Crystal Kingsley's clothes, packed what else of hers she wanted, got into Crystal Kingsley's car and departed. And at San Bernardino she ran into her first snag, Lavery.

"Lavery knew her as Muriel Chess. We have no evidence and no reason whatever to assume that he knew her as anything else. He had seen her up here and he was probably on his way up here again when he met her. She wouldn't want that. All he would find would be a locked up cabin but he might get talking to Bill and it was part of her plan that Bill should not know positively that she had ever left Little Fawn Lake. So that when, and if, the body was found, he would identify it. So she put her hooks into Lavery at once, and that wouldn't be too hard. If there is one thing we know for certain about Lavery, it is that he couldn't keep his hands off the women. The more of them, the better. He would be easy for a smart girl like Mildred Haviland. So she played him and took him away with her. She took him to El Paso and there sent a wire he knew nothing about. Finally she played him back to Bay City. She probably couldn't help that. He wanted to go home and she couldn't let him get too far from her. Because Lavery was dangerous to her. Lavery alone could destroy all the indications that Crystal Kingsley had actually left Little Fawn Lake. When the search for Crystal Kingsley eventually began, it had to come to Lavery, and at that moment Lavery's life wasn't worth a plugged nickel. His first denials might not be believed, as they were not, but when he opened up with the whole story, that would be believed, because it could be checked. So the search began and immediately Lavery was shot dead in his bathroom, the very night after I went down to talk to him. That's about all there is to it, except why she went back to the house the next morning. That's just one of those things that murderers seem to do. She said he had taken her money, but I don't believe it. I think more likely she got to thinking he had some of his own hidden away, or that she had better edit the job with a cool head and make sure it was all in order and pointing the right way; or perhaps it was just what she said, and to take in the paper and the milk. Anything is possible. She went back and I found her there and she put on an act that left me with both feet in my mouth."

Patton said: "Who killed her, son? I gather you don't like Kingsley for that little job."

I looked at Kingsley and said: "You didn't talk to her on the phone, you said. What about Miss Fromsett? Did she think she was talking to your wife?"

Kingsley shook his head. "I doubt it. It would be pretty hard to fool her that way. All she said was that she seemed very changed and subdued. I had no suspicion then. I didn't have any until I got up here. When I walked into this cabin last night, I felt there was something wrong. It was too clean and neat and orderly. Crystal didn't leave things that way. There would have been clothes all over the bedroom, cigarette stubs all over the house, bottles and glasses all over the kitchen. There would have been unwashed dishes and ants and flies. I thought Bill's wife might have cleaned up, and then I remembered that Bill's wife wouldn't have, not on that particular day. She had been too busy quarreling with Bill and being murdered, or committing suicide, whichever it was. I thought about all this in a confused sort of way, but I don't claim I actually made anything of it."

Patton got up from his chair and went out on the porch. He came back wiping his lips with his tan handkerchief. He sat down again, and eased himself over on his left hip, on account of the hip holster on the other side. He looked thoughtfully at Degarmo. Degarmo stood against the wall, hard and rigid, a stone man. His right hand still hung down at his side, with the fingers curled.

Patton said: "I still ain't heard who killed Muriel. Is that part of the show or is that something that still has to be worked out?"

I said: "Somebody who thought she needed killing, somebody who had loved her and hated her, somebody who was too much of a cop to let her get away with any more murders, but not enough of a cop to pull her in and let the whole story come out. Somebody like Degarmo."

# 40

Degarmo straightened away from the wall and smiled bleakly. His right hand made a hard clean movement and was holding a gun. He held it with a lax wrist, so that it pointed down at the floor in front of him. He spoke to me without looking at me.

"I don't think you have a gun," he said. "Patton has a gun but I don't think he can get it out fast enough to do him any good. Maybe you have a little evidence to go with that last guess. Or wouldn't that be important enough for you to bother with?"

"A little evidence," I said. "Not very much. But it will grow. Somebody stood behind that green curtain in the Granada for more than half an hour and stood as silently as only a cop on a stake-out knows how to stand. Somebody who had a blackjack. Somebody who knew I had been hit with one without looking at the back of my head. You told Shorty, remember? Somebody who knew the dead girl had been hit with one too, although it wouldn't have showed and he wouldn't have been likely at that time to have handled the body enough to find out. Somebody who stripped her and raked her body with scratches in the kind of sadistic hate a man like you might feel for a woman who had made a small private hell for him. Somebody who has blood and cuticle under his fingernails right now, plenty enough for a chemist to work on. I bet you won't let Patton look at the fingernails of your right hand, Degarmo."

Degarmo lifted the gun a little and smiled. A wide white smile.

"And just how did I know where to find her?" he asked.

"Almore saw her—coming out of, or going into Lavery's house. That's what made him so nervous, that's why he called you when he saw me hanging around. As to how exactly you trailed her to the apartment, I don't know. I don't see anything difficult about it. You could have hid out in Almore's house and followed her, or followed Lavery. All that would be routine work for a copper."

Degarmo nodded and stood silent for a moment, thinking. His face was grim, but his metallic blue eyes held a light that was almost amusement. The room was hot and heavy with a disaster that could no longer be mended. He seemed to feel it less than any of us.

"I want to get out of here," he said at last. "Not very far maybe, but no hick cop is going to put the arm on me. Any objections?"

Patton said quietly: "Can't be done, son. You know I got to take you. None of this ain't proved, but I can't just let you walk out."

"You have a nice big belly, Patton. I'm a good shot. How do you figure to take me?"

"I been trying to figure," Patton said and rumpled his hair under his pushed back hat. "I ain't got very far with it. I don't want no holes in my belly. But I can't let you make a monkey of me in my own territory either."

"Let him go," I said. "He can't get out of these mountains. That's why I brought him up here."

Patton said soberly: "Somebody might get hurt taking him. That wouldn't be right. If it's anybody, it's got to be me."

Degarmo grinned. "You're a nice boy, Patton," he said. "Look, I'll put the gun back under my arm and we'll start from scratch. I'm good enough for that too."

He tucked the gun under his arm. He stood with his arms hanging, his chin pushed forward a little, watching. Patton chewed softly, with his pale eyes on Degarmo's vivid eyes.

"I'm sitting down," he complained. "I ain't as fast as you anyways. I just don't like to look yellow." He looked at me sadly. "Why the hell did you have to bring this up here? It ain't any part of my troubles. Now look at the jam I'm in." He sounded hurt and confused and rather feeble.

Degarmo put his head back a little and laughed. While he was still laughing, his right hand jumped for his gun again.

I didn't see Patton move at all. The room throbbed with the roar of his frontier Colt.

Degarmo's arm shot straight out to one side and the heavy Smith and Wesson was torn out of his hand and thudded against the knotty pine wall behind him. He shook his numbed right hand and looked down at it with wonder in his eyes.

Patton stood up slowly. He walked slowly across the room and kicked the revolver under a chair. He looked at Degarmo sadly. Degarmo was sucking a little blood off his knuckles.

"You give me a break," Patton said sadly. "You hadn't ought ever to give a man like me a break. I been a shooter more years than you been alive, son."

Degarmo nodded to him and straightened his back and started for the door.

"Don't do that," Patton told him calmly.

Degarmo kept on going. He reached the door and pushed on the screen. He looked back at Patton and his face was very white now.

"I'm going out of here," he said. "There's only one way you can stop me. So long, fatty."

Patton didn't move a muscle.

Degarmo went out through the door. His feet made heavy sounds on the porch and then on the steps. I went to the front window and looked out. Patton still hadn't moved. Degarmo came down off the steps and started across the top of the little dam.

"He's crossing the dam," I said. "Has Andy got a gun?"

"I don't figure he'd use one if he had," Patton said calmly. "He don't know any reason why he should."

"Well, I'll be damned," I said.

Patton sighed. "He hadn't ought to have given me a break like that," he said. "Had me cold. I got to give it back to him. Kind of puny too. Won't do him a lot of good."

"He's a killer," I said.

"He ain't that kind of killer," Patton said. "You lock your car?"

I nodded. "Andy's coming down to the other end of the dam," I said. "Degarmo has stopped him. He's speaking to him."

"He'll take Andy's car maybe," Patton said sadly.

"Well, I'll be damned," I said again. I looked back at Kingsley. He had his head in his hands and he was staring at the floor. I turned back to the window. Degarmo was out of sight beyond the rise. Andy was half way across the dam, coming slowly, looking back over his shoulder now and then. The sound of a starting car came distantly. Andy looked up at the cabin, then turned back and started to run back along the dam.

The sound of the motor died away. When it was quite gone, Patton said: "Well, I guess we better go back to the office and do some telephoning."

Kingsley got up suddenly and went out to the kitchen and came back with a bottle of whiskey. He poured himself a stiff drink and drank it standing. He waved a hand at it and walked heavily out of the room. I heard bed springs creak.

Patton and I went quietly out of the cabin.

# 41

Patton had just finished putting his calls through to block the highways when a call came through from the sergeant in charge of the guard detail at Puma Lake dam. We went out and got into Patton's car and Andy drove very fast along the lake road through the village and along the lake shore back to the big dam at the end. We were waved across the dam to where the sergeant was waiting in a jeep beside the head-quarters hut.

The sergeant waved his arm and started the jeep and we followed him a couple of hundred feet along the highway to where a few soldiers stood on the edge of the canyon looking down. Several cars had stopped there and a cluster of people was grouped near the soldiers. The sergeant got out of the jeep and Patton and Andy and I climbed out of the official car and went over by the sergeant.

"Guy didn't stop for the sentry," the sergeant said, and there was bitterness in his voice. "Damn near knocked him off the road. The sentry in the middle of the bridge had to jump fast to get missed. The one at this end had enough. He called the guy to halt. Guy kept going."

The sergeant chewed his gum and looked down into the canyon.

"Orders are to shoot in a case like that," he said. "The sentry shot." He pointed down to the grooves in the shoulder at the edge of the drop. "This is where he went off."

A hundred feet down in the canyon a small coupe was smashed against the side of a huge granite boulder. It was almost upside down, leaning a little. There were three men down there. They had moved the car enough to lift something out.

Something that had been a man.

# THE LITTLE SISTER

# I

THE PEBBLED glass door panel is lettered in flaked black paint: *"Philip Marlowe . . . Investigations."* It is a reasonably shabby door at the end of a reasonably shabby corridor in the sort of building that was new about the year the all-tile bathroom became the basis of civilization. The door is locked, but next to it is another door with the same legend which is not locked. Come on in—there's nobody in here but me and a big bluebottle fly. But not if you're from Manhattan, Kansas.

It was one of those clear, bright summer mornings we get in the early spring in California before the high fog sets in. The rains are over. The hills are still green and in the valley across the Hollywood hills you can see snow on the high mountains. The fur stores are advertising their annual sales. The call houses that specialize in sixteen-year-old virgins are doing a land-office business. And in Beverly Hills the jacaranda trees are beginning to bloom.

I had been stalking the bluebottle fly for five minutes, waiting for him to sit down. He didn't want to sit down. He just wanted to do wing-overs and sing the prologue to *Pagliacci.* I had the fly swatter poised in midair and I was all set. There was a patch of bright sunlight on the corner of the desk and I knew that sooner or later that was where he was going to light. But when he did, I didn't even see him at first. The buzzing stopped and there he was. And then the phone rang.

I reached for it inch by inch with a slow and patient left hand. I lifted the phone slowly and spoke into it softly: "Hold the line a moment, please."

I laid the phone down gently on the brown blotter. He was still there, shining and blue-green and full of sin. I took a deep breath and swung. What was left of him sailed halfway across the room and dropped to the carpet. I went over and picked him up by his good wing and dropped him into the wastebasket.

"Thanks for waiting," I said into the phone.

"Is this Mr. Marlowe, the detective?" It was a small, rather hurried, little-girlish voice. I said it was Mr. Marlowe, the detective. "How much do you charge for your services, Mr. Marlowe?"

"What was it you wanted done?"

The voice sharpened a little. "I can't very well tell you that over the phone. It's—it's very confidential. Before I'd waste time coming to your office I'd have to have some idea—"

"Forty bucks a day and expenses. Unless it's the kind of job that can be done for a flat fee."

"That's far too much," the little voice said. "Why, it might cost hundreds of dollars and I only get a small salary and—"

"Where are you now?"

"Why, I'm in a drugstore. It's right next to the building where your office is."

"You could have saved a nickel. The elevator's free."

"I—I beg your pardon?"

I said it all over again. "Come on up and let's have a look at you," I added. "If you're in my kind of trouble, I can give you a pretty good idea—"

"I have to know something about you," the small voice said very firmly. "This is a very delicate matter, very personal. I couldn't talk to just anybody."

"If it's that delicate," I said, "maybe you need a lady detective."

"Goodness, I didn't know there were any." Pause. "But I don't think a lady detective would do at all. You see, Orrin was living in a very tough neighborhood, Mr. Marlowe. At least I thought it was tough. The manager of the rooming house is a most unpleasant person. He smelled of liquor. Do you drink, Mr. Marlowe?"

"Well, now that you mention it—"

"I don't think I'd care to employ a detective that uses liquor in any form. I don't even approve of tobacco."

"Would it be all right if I peeled an orange?"

I caught the sharp intake of breath at the far end of the line. "You might at least talk like a gentleman," she said.

"Better try the University Club," I told her. "I heard they had a couple left over there, but I'm not sure they'll let you handle them." I hung up.

It was a step in the right direction, but it didn't go far enough. I ought to have locked the door and hid under the desk.

## 2

Five minutes later the buzzer sounded on the outer door of the half-office I use for a reception room. I heard the door close again. Then I didn't hear anything more. The door between me and there was half open. I listened and decided somebody had just looked in at the wrong office and left without entering. Then there was a small knocking on wood. Then the kind of cough you use for the same purpose. I got my feet off the desk, stood up and looked out. There she was. She didn't have to open her mouth for me to know who she was. And nobody ever looked less like Lady Macbeth. She was a small, neat, rather prissy-looking girl with primly smooth brown hair and rimless glasses. She was wearing a brown tailor-made and from a strap over her shoulder hung one of those awkward-looking square bags that make you think of a Sister of Mercy taking first aid to the wounded. On the smooth brown hair was a hat that had been taken from its mother too young. She had no make-up, no lipstick and no jewelry. The rimless glasses gave her that librarian's look.

"That's no way to talk to people over the telephone," she said sharply. "You ought to be ashamed of yourself."

"I'm just too proud to show it," I said. "Come on in." I held the door for her. Then I held the chair for her.

She sat down on about two inches of the edge. "If I talked like that to one of Dr. Zugsmith's patients," she said, "I'd lose my position. He's most particular how I speak to the patients — even the difficult ones."

"How is the old boy? I haven't seen him since that time I fell off the garage roof."

She looked surprised and quite serious. "Why surely you can't know Dr. Zugsmith." The tip of a rather anemic tongue came out between her lips and searched furtively for nothing.

"I know a Dr. George Zugsmith," I said, "in Santa Rosa."

"Oh no. This is Dr. Alfred Zugsmith, in Manhattan. Manhattan, Kansas, you know, not Manhattan, New York."

"Must be a different Dr. Zugsmith," I said. "And your name?"

"I'm not sure I'd care to tell you."

"Just window shopping, huh?"

"I suppose you could call it that. If I have to tell my family affairs to a total stranger, I at least have the right to decide whether he's the kind of person I could trust."

"Anybody ever tell you you're a cute little trick?"

The eyes behind the rimless cheaters flashed. "I should hope not."

I reached for a pipe and started to fill it. "Hope isn't exactly the word," I said. "Get rid of that hat and get yourself a pair of those slinky glasses with colored rims. You know, the ones that are all cockeyed and oriental—"

"Dr. Zugsmith wouldn't permit anything like that," she said quickly. Then, "Do you really think so?" she asked, and blushed ever so slightly.

I put a match to the pipe and puffed smoke across the desk. She winced back.

"If you hire me," I said, "I'm the guy you hire. Me. Just as I am. If you think you're going to find any lay readers in this business, you're crazy. I hung up on you, but you came up here all the same. So you need help. What's your name and trouble?"

She just stared at me.

"Look," I said. "You come from Manhattan, Kansas. The last time I memorized the *World Almanac* that was a little town not far from Topeka. Population around twelve thousand. You work for Dr. Alfred Zugsmith and you're looking for somebody named Orrin. Manhattan is a small town. It has to be. Only half a dozen places in Kansas are anything else. I already have enough information about you to find out your whole family history."

"But why should you want to?" she asked, troubled.

"Me?" I said. "I don't want to. I'm fed up with people telling me histories. I'm just sitting here because I don't have any place to go. I don't want to work. I don't want anything."

"You talk too much."

"Yes," I said, "I talk too much. Lonely men always talk too much. Either that or they don't talk at all. Shall we get down to business? You don't look like the type that goes to see private detectives, and especially private detectives you don't know."

"I know that," she said quietly. "And Orrin would be absolutely livid. Mother would be furious too. I just picked your name out of the phone book——"

"What principle?" I asked. "And with the eyes closed or open?"

She stared at me for a moment as if I were some kind of freak. "Seven and thirteen," she said quietly.

"How?"

"Marlowe has seven letters," she said, "and Philip Marlowe has thirteen. Seven together with thirteen——"

"What's *your* name?" I almost snarled.

"Orfamay Quest." She crinkled her eyes as if she could cry. She spelled the first name out for me, all one word. "I live with my mother," she went on, her voice getting rapid now as if my time is costing her. "My father died four years ago. He was a doctor. My brother Orrin was going to be a surgeon, too, but he changed into engineering after two years of medical. Then a year ago Orrin came out to work for the Cal-Western Aircraft Company in Bay City. He didn't have to. He had a good job in Wichita. I guess he just sort of wanted to come out here to California. Most everybody does."

"*Al*most everybody," I said. "If you're going to wear those rimless glasses, you might at least try to live up to them."

She giggled and drew a line along the desk with her finger-tip, looking down. "Did you mean those slanting kind of glasses that make you look kind of oriental?"

"Uh-huh. Now about Orrin. We've got him to California, and we've got him to Bay City. What do we do with him?"

She thought a moment and frowned. Then she studied my face as if making up her mind. Then her words came with a burst: "It wasn't like Orrin not to write to us regularly. He only wrote twice to mother and three times to me in the last six months. And the last letter was several months ago. Mother and I got worried. So it was my vacation and I came

out to see him. He'd never been away from Kansas before."
She stopped. "Aren't you going to take any notes?" she
asked.

I grunted.

"I thought detectives always wrote things down in little
notebooks."

"I'll make the gags," I said. "You tell the story. You came
out on your vacation. Then what?"

"I'd written to Orrin that I was coming but I didn't get
any answer. Then I sent a wire to him from Salt Lake City but
he didn't answer that either. So all I could do was go down
where he lived. It's an awful long way. I went in a bus. It's in
Bay City. No. 449 Idaho Street."

She stopped again, then repeated the address, and I still
didn't write it down. I just sat there looking at her glasses and
her smooth brown hair and the silly little hat and the fingernails with no color and her mouth with no lipstick and the tip
of the little tongue that came and went between the pale lips.

"Maybe you don't know Bay City, Mr. Marlowe."

"Ha," I said. "All I know about Bay City is that every time
I go there I have to buy a new head. You want me to finish
your story for you?"

"Wha-a-at?" Her eyes opened so wide that the glasses made
them look like something you see in the deep-sea fish tanks.

"He's moved," I said. "And you don't know where he's
moved to. And you're afraid he's living a life of sin in a penthouse on top of the Regency Towers with something in a
long mink coat and an interesting perfume."

"Well for goodness' sakes!"

"Or am I being coarse?" I asked.

"Please, Mr. Marlowe," she said at last, "I don't think
anything of the sort about Orrin. And if Orrin heard you say
that you'd be sorry. He can be awfully mean. But I know
something has happened. It was just a cheap rooming house,
and I didn't like the manager at all. A horrid kind of man. He
said Orrin had moved away a couple of weeks before and he
didn't know where to and he didn't care, and all he wanted
was a good slug of gin. I don't know why Orrin would even
live in a place like that."

"Did you say slug of gin?" I asked.

She blushed. "That's what the manager said. I'm just telling you."

"All right," I said. "Go on."

"Well, I called the place where he worked. The Cal-Western Company, you know. And they said he'd been laid off like a lot of others and that was all they knew. So then I went to the post office and asked if Orrin had put in a change of address to anywhere. And they said they couldn't give me any information. It was against the regulations. So I told them how it was and the man said, well if I was his sister he'd go look. So he went and looked and came back and said no. Orrin hadn't put in any change of address. So then I began to get a little frightened. He might have had an accident or something."

"Did it occur to you to ask the police about that?"

"I wouldn't dare ask the police. Orrin would never forgive me. He's difficult enough at the best of times. Our family—" She hesitated and there was something behind her eyes she tried not to have there. So she went on breathlessly: "Our family's not the kind of family—"

"Look," I said wearily, "I'm not talking about the guy lifting a wallet. I'm talking about him getting knocked down by a car and losing his memory or being too badly hurt to talk."

She gave me a level look which was not too admiring. "If it was anything like that, we'd know," she said. "Everybody has things in their pockets to tell who they are."

"Sometimes all they have left is the pockets."

"Are you trying to scare me, Mr. Marlowe?"

"If I am, I'm certainly getting nowhere fast. Just what do you think might have happened?"

She put her slim forefinger to her lips and touched it very carefully with the tip of that tongue. "I guess if I knew that I wouldn't have to come and see you. How much would you charge to find him?"

I didn't answer for a long moment, then I said: "You mean alone, without telling anybody?"

"Yes. I mean alone, without telling anybody."

"Uh-huh. Well that depends. I told you what my rates were."

She clasped her hands on the edge of the desk and

squeezed them together hard. She had about the most meaningless set of gestures I had ever laid eyes on. "I thought you being a detective and all you could find him right away," she said. "I couldn't possibly afford more than twenty dollars. I've got to buy my meals here and my hotel and the train going back and you know the hotel is so terribly expensive and the food on the train—"

"Which one are you staying at?"

"I—I'd rather not tell you, if you don't mind."

"Why?"

"I'd just rather not. I'm terribly afraid of Orrin's temper. And, well I can always call you up, can't I?"

"Uh-huh. Just what is it you're scared of, besides Orrin's temper, Miss Quest?" I had let my pipe go out. I struck a match and held it to the bowl, watching her over it.

"Isn't pipe-smoking a very dirty habit?" she asked.

"Probably," I said. "But it would take more than twenty bucks to have me drop it. And don't try to side-step my questions."

"You can't talk to me like that," she flared up. "Pipe-smoking *is* a dirty habit. Mother never let father smoke in the house, even the last two years after he had his stroke. He used to sit with that empty pipe in his mouth sometimes. But she didn't like him to do that really. We owed a lot of money too and she said she couldn't afford to give him money for useless things like tobacco. The church needed it much more than he did."

"I'm beginning to get it," I said slowly. "Take a family like yours and somebody in it has to be the dark meat."

She stood up sharply and clasped the first-aid kit to her body. "I don't like you," she said. "I don't think I'm going to employ you. If you're insinuating that Orrin has done something wrong, well I can assure you that it's not Orrin who's the black sheep of our family."

I didn't move an eyelash. She swung around and marched to the door and put her hand on the knob and then she swung around again and marched back and suddenly began to cry. I reacted to that just the way a stuffed fish reacts to cut bait. She got out her little handkerchief and tickled the corners of her eyes.

"And now I suppose you'll call the p-police," she said with a catch in her voice. "And the Manhattan p-paper will hear all about it and they'll print something n-nasty about us."

"You don't suppose anything of the sort. Stop chipping at my emotions. Let's see a photo of him."

She put the handkerchief away in a hurry and dug something else out of her bag. She passed it across the desk. An envelope. Thin, but there could be a couple of snapshots in it. I didn't look inside.

"Describe him the way you see him," I said.

She concentrated. That gave her a chance to do something with her eyebrows. "He was twenty-eight years old last March. He has light brown hair, much lighter than mine, and lighter blue eyes, and he brushes his hair straight back. He's very tall, over six feet. But he only weighs about a hundred and forty pounds. He's sort of bony. He used to wear a little blond mustache but mother made him cut it off. She said—"

"Don't tell me. The minister needed it to stuff a cushion."

"You can't talk like that about my mother," she yelped, getting pale with rage.

"Oh stop being silly. There's a lot of things about you I don't know. But you can stop pretending to be an Easter lily right now. Does Orrin have any distinguishing marks on him, like moles or scars, or a tattoo of the Twenty-Third Psalm on his chest? And don't bother to blush."

"Well you don't have to yell at me. Why don't you look at the photograph?"

"He probably has his clothes on. After all, you're his sister. You ought to know."

"No he hasn't," she said tightly. "He has a little scar on his left hand where he had a wen removed."

"What about his habits? What does he do for fun—besides not smoking or drinking or going out with girls?"

"Why—how did you know that?"

"Your mother told me."

She smiled. I was beginning to wonder if she had one in her. She had very white teeth and she didn't wave her gums. That was something. "Aren't you silly," she said. "He studies a lot and he has a very expensive camera he likes to snap people with when they don't know. Sometimes it makes them mad. But Orrin says people ought to see themselves as they really are."

"Let's hope it never happens to him," I said. "What kind of camera is it?"

"One of those little cameras with a very fine lens. You can take snaps in almost any kind of light. A Leica."

I opened the envelope and took out a couple of small prints, very clear. "These weren't taken with anything like that," I said.

"Oh no. Philip took those, Philip Anderson. A boy I was going with for a while." She paused and sighed. "And I guess that's really why I came here, Mr. Marlowe. Just because your name's Philip too."

I just said: "Uh-huh," but I felt touched in some vague sort of way. "What happened to Philip Anderson?"

"But it's about Orrin—"

"I know," I interrupted. "But what happened to Philip Anderson?"

"He's still there in Manhattan." She looked away. "Mother doesn't like him very much. I guess you know how it is."

"Yes," I said, "I know how it is. You can cry if you want to. I won't hold it against you. I'm just a big soft slob myself."

I looked at the two prints. One of them was looking down and was no good to me. The other was a fairly good shot of a tall angular bird with narrow-set eyes and a thin straight mouth and a pointed chin. He had the expression I expected to see. If you forgot to wipe the mud off your shoes, he was the boy who would tell you. I laid the photos aside and looked at Orfamay Quest, trying to find something in her face even remotely like his. I couldn't. Not the slightest trace of family resemblance, which of course meant absolutely nothing. It never has.

"All right," I said. "I'll go down there and take a look. But you ought to be able to guess what's happened. He's in a strange city. He's making good money for a while. More than he's ever made in his life, perhaps. He's meeting a kind of people he never met before. And it's not the kind of town— believe me it isn't, I know Bay City—that Manhattan, Kansas, is. So he just broke training and he doesn't want his family to know about it. He'll straighten out."

She just stared at me for a moment in silence, then she shook her head. "No. Orrin's not the type to do that, Mr. Marlowe."

"Anyone is," I said. "Especially a fellow like Orrin. The small-town sanctimonious type of guy who's lived his entire life with his mother on his neck and the minister holding his hand. Out here he's lonely. He's got dough. He'd like to buy a little sweetness and light, and not the kind that comes through the east window of a church. Not that I have anything against that. I mean he already had enough of that, didn't he?"

She nodded her head silently.

"So he starts to play," I went on, "and he doesn't know how to play. That takes experience too. He's got himself all jammed up with some floozy and a bottle of hootch and what he's done looks to him as if he'd stolen the bishop's pants. After all, the guy's going on twenty-nine years old and if he wants to roll in the gutter that's his business. He'll find somebody to blame it on after a while."

"I hate to believe you, Mr. Marlowe," she said slowly. "I'd hate for mother—"

"Something was said about twenty dollars," I cut in.

She looked shocked. "Do I have to pay you now?"

"What would be the custom in Manhattan, Kansas?"

"We don't have any private detectives in Manhattan. Just the regular police. That is, I don't think we do."

She probed in the inside of her tool kit again and dragged out a red change purse and from that she took a number of bills, all neatly folded and separate. Three fives and five ones. There didn't seem to be much left. She kind of held the purse so I could see how empty it was. Then she straightened the bills out on the desk and put one on top of the other and pushed them across. Very slowly, very sadly, as if she was drowning a favorite kitten.

"I'll give you a receipt," I said.

"I don't need a receipt, Mr. Marlowe."

"I do. You won't give me your name and address, so I want something with your name on it."

"What for?"

"To show I'm representing you." I got the receipt book

out and made the receipt and held the book for her to sign the duplicate. She didn't want to. After a moment reluctantly she took the hard pencil and wrote "Orfamay Quest" in a neat secretary's writing across the face of the duplicate.

"Still no address?" I asked.

"I'd rather not."

"Call me any time then. My home number is in the phone book, too. Bristol Apartments, Apartment 428."

"I shan't be very likely to visit you," she said coldly.

"I haven't asked you yet," I said. "Call me around four if you like. I might have something. And then again I might not."

She stood up. "I hope mother won't think I've done wrong," she said, picking at her lip now with the pale fingernail. "Coming here, I mean."

"Just don't tell me any more of the things your mother won't like," I said. "Just leave that part out."

"Well really!"

"And stop saying 'well really.'"

"I think you are a very offensive person," she said.

"No, you don't. You think I'm cute. And I think you're a fascinating little liar. You don't think I'm doing this for any twenty bucks, do you?"

She gave me a level, suddenly cool stare. "Then why?" Then when I didn't answer she added, "Because spring is in the air?"

I still didn't answer. She blushed a little. Then she giggled.

I didn't have the heart to tell her I was just plain bored with doing nothing. Perhaps it *was* the spring too. And something in her eyes that was much older than Manhattan, Kansas.

"I think you're very nice — really," she said softly. Then she turned quickly and almost ran out of the office. Her steps along the corridor outside made tiny, sharp pecky sounds, kind of like mother drumming on the edge of the dinner table when father tried to promote himself a second piece of pie. And him with no money any more. No nothing. Just sitting in a rocker on the front porch back there in Manhattan, Kansas, with his empty pipe in his mouth. Rocking on the front porch, slow and easy, because when you've had a stroke you have to take it slow and easy. And wait for the next one. And the empty pipe in his mouth. No tobacco. Nothing to do but wait.

I put Orfamay Quest's twenty hard-earned dollars in an envelope and wrote her name on it and dropped it in the desk drawer. I didn't like the idea of running around loose with that much currency on me.

# 3

You could know Bay City a long time without knowing Idaho Street. And you could know a lot of Idaho Street without knowing Number 449. The block in front of it had a broken paving that had almost gone back to dirt. The warped fence of a lumberyard bordered the cracked sidewalk on the opposite side of the street. Halfway up the block the rusted rails of a spur track turned in to a pair of high, chained wooden gates that seem not to have been opened for twenty years. Little boys with chalk had been writing and drawing pictures on the gates and all along the fence.

Number 449 had a shallow, paintless front porch on which five wood and cane rockers loafed dissolutely, held together with wire and the moisture of the beach air. The green shades over the lower windows of the house were two thirds down and full of cracks. Beside the front door there was a large printed sign "No Vacancies." That had been there a long time too. It had got faded and flyspecked. The door opened on a long hall from which stairs went up a third of the way back. To the right there was a narrow shelf with a chained, indelible pencil hanging beside it. There was a push button and a yellow and black sign above which read "Manager," and was held up by three thumbtacks no two of which matched. There was a pay phone on the opposite wall.

I pushed the bell. It rang somewhere near by but nothing happened. I rang it again. The same nothing happened. I prowled along to a door with a black and white metal sign on it—"Manager." I knocked on that. Then I kicked it. Nobody seemed to mind my kicking it.

I went back out of the house and down around the side where a narrow concrete walk led to the service entrance. It looked as if it was in the right place to belong to the manager's apartment. The rest of the house would be just rooms. There was a dirty garbage pail on the small porch and a wooden box full of liquor bottles. Behind the screen the back door of the house was open. It was gloomy inside. I put my face against the screen and peered in. Through the open inner door beyond the service porch I could see a straight chair with a man's coat hanging over it and in the chair a man in shirtsleeves with his hat on. He was a small man. I couldn't see what he was doing, but he seemed to be sitting at the end of the built-in breakfast table in the breakfast nook.

I banged on the screen door. The man paid no attention. I banged again, harder. This time he tilted his chair back and showed me a small pale face with a cigarette in it. "Whatcha want?" he barked.

"Manager."

"Not in, bub."

"Who are you?"

"What's it to you?"

"I want a room."

"No vacancies, bub. Can't you read large print?"

"I happen to have different information," I said.

"Yeah?" He shook ash from his cigarette by flicking it with a nail without removing it from his small sad mouth. "Go fry your head in it."

He tilted his chair forward again and went on doing whatever it was he was doing.

I made noise getting down off the porch and none whatever coming back up on it. I felt the screen door carefully. It was hooked. With the open blade of a penknife I lifted the hook and eased it out of the eye. It made a small tinkle but louder tinkling sounds were being made beyond, in the kitchen.

I stepped into the house, crossed the service porch, went through the door into the kitchen. The little man was too busy to notice me. The kitchen had a three-burner gas stove, a few shelves of greasy dishes, a chipped icebox and the breakfast nook. The table in the breakfast nook was covered with money. Most of it was paper, but there was silver also, in all sizes up to dollars. The little man was counting and stacking it and making entries in a small book. He wetted his pencil without bothering the cigarette that lived in his face.

There must have been several hundred dollars on that table.

"Rent day?" I asked genially.

The small man turned very suddenly. For a moment he smiled and said nothing. It was the smile of a man whose mind is not smiling. He removed the stub of cigarette from his mouth, dropped it on the floor and stepped on it. He reached a fresh one out of his shirt and put it in the same hole in his face and started fumbling for a match.

"You came in nice," he said pleasantly.

Finding no match, he turned casually in his chair and reached into a pocket of his coat. Something heavy knocked against the wood of the chair. I got hold of his wrist before the heavy thing came out of the pocket. He threw his weight backwards and the pocket of the coat started to lift towards me. I yanked the chair out from under him.

He sat down hard on the floor and knocked his head against the end of the breakfast table. That didn't keep him from trying to kick me in the groin. I stepped back with his coat and took a .38 out of the pocket he had been playing with.

"Don't sit on the floor just to be chummy," I said.

He got up slowly, pretending to be groggier than he was. His hand fumbled at the back of his collar and light winked on metal as his arm swept towards me. He was a game little rooster.

I sideswiped his jaw with his own gun and he sat down on the floor again. I stepped on the hand that held the knife. His face twisted with pain but he didn't make a sound. So I kicked the knife into a corner. It was a long thin knife and it looked very sharp.

"You ought to be ashamed of yourself," I said. "Pulling guns and knives on people that are just looking for a place to live. Even for these times that's out of line."

He held his hurt hand between his knees and squeezed it and began to whistle through his teeth. The slap on the jaw didn't seem to have hurt him. "O.K.," he said, "O.K. I ain't supposed to be perfect. Take the dough and beat it. But don't ever think we won't catch up with you."

I looked at the collection of small bills and medium bills and silver on the table. "You must meet a lot of sales resistance, the weapons you carry," I told him. I walked across to the inner door and tried it. It was not locked. I turned back.

"I'll leave your gun in the mailbox," I said. "Next time ask to see the buzzer."

He was still whistling gently between his teeth and holding his hand. He gave me a narrow, thoughtful eye, then shoveled the money into a shabby briefcase and slipped its catch. He took his hat off, straightened it around, put it back jauntily on the back of his head and gave me a quiet efficient smile.

"Never mind about the heater," he said. "The town's full of old iron. But you could leave the skiv with Clausen. I've done quite a bit of work on it to get it in shape."

"And with it?" I said.

"Could be." He flicked a finger at me airily. "Maybe we meet again some day soon. When I got a friend with me."

"Tell him to wear a clean shirt," I said. "And lend you one."

"My, my," the little man said chidingly. "How tough we get how quick once we get that badge pinned on."

He went softly past me and down the wooden steps from the back porch. His footsteps tapped to the street and faded. They sounded very much like Orfamay's heels clicking along the corridor in my office building. And for some reason I had that empty feeling of having miscounted the trumps. No reason for it at all. Maybe it was the steely quality about the little man. No whimper, no bluster, just the smile, the whistling between the teeth, the light voice and the unforgetting eyes.

I went over and picked up the knife. The blade was long and round and thin, like a rattailed file that has been ground smooth. The handle and guard were lightweight plastic and seemed all one piece. I held the knife by the handle and gave it a quick flip at the table. The blade came loose and quivered in the wood.

I took a deep breath and slid the handle down over the end again and worked the blade loose from the table. A curious knife, with design and purpose in it, and neither of them agreeable.

I opened the door beyond the kitchen and went through it with the gun and knife in one hand.

It was a wall-bed living room, with the wall bed down and rumpled. There was an overstuffed chair with a hole burnt in the arm. A high oak desk with tilted doors like old-fashioned cellar doors stood against the wall by the front window. Near this there was a studio couch and on the studio couch lay a man. His feet hung over the end of the couch in knobby gray socks. His head had missed the pillow by two feet. It was nothing much to miss from the color of the slip on it. The upper part of him was contained in a colorless shirt and a threadbare gray coat-sweater. His mouth was open and his face was shining with sweat and he breathed like an old Ford with a leaky head gasket. On a table beside him was a plate full of cigarette stubs, some of which had a homemade look. On the floor a near full gin bottle and a cup that seemed to have contained coffee but not at all recently. The room was full mostly of gin and bad air, but there was also a reminiscence of marijuana smoke.

I opened a window and leaned my forehead against the screen to get a little cleaner air into my lungs and looked out into the street. Two kids were wheeling bicycles along the lumberyard fence, stopping from time to time to study the examples of restroom art on the boarding. Nothing else moved in the neighborhood. Not even a dog. Down at the corner was dust in the air as though a car had passed that way.

I went over to the desk. Inside it was the house register, so I leafed back until I came to the name "Orrin P. Quest," written in a sharp meticulous handwriting, and the number 214 added in pencil by another hand that was by no means sharp or meticulous. I followed on through to the end of the register but found no new registration for Room 214. A party named G. W. Hicks had Room 215. I shut the register in the desk and crossed to the couch. The man stopped his snoring and bubbling and threw his right arm across his body as if he thought he was making a speech. I leaned down and gripped his nose tight between my first and second fingers and stuffed a handful of his sweater into his mouth. He stopped snoring and jerked his eyes open. They were glazed and bloodshot. He struggled against my hand. When I was sure he was fully awake I let go of him, picked the bottle full of gin off the floor and poured some into a glass that lay on its side near the bottle. I showed the glass to the man.

His hand came out to it with the beautiful anxiety of a mother welcoming a lost child.

I moved it out of his reach and said: "You the manager?"

He licked his lips stickily and said: "Gr-r-r-r."

He made a grab for the glass. I put it on the table in front of him. He grasped it carefully in both hands and poured the gin into his face. Then he laughed heartily and threw the glass at me. I managed to catch it and up-end it on the table again. The man looked me over with a studied but unsuccessful attempt at sternness.

"What gives?" he croaked in an annoyed tone.

"Manager?"

He nodded and almost fell off the couch. "Must be I'm drunky," he said. "Kind of a bit of a little bit drunky."

"You're not bad," I said. "You're still breathing."

He put his feet on the ground and pushed himself upright. He cackled with sudden amusement, took three uneven steps, went down on his hands and knees and tried to bite the leg of a chair.

I pulled him up on his feet again, set him down in the overstuffed chair with the burned arm and poured him another slug of his medicine. He drank it, shuddered violently and all at once his eyes seemed to get sane and cunning. Drunks of his type have a certain balanced moment of reality. You never know when it will come or how long it will last.

"Who the hell are you?" he growled.

"I'm looking for a man named Orrin P. Quest."

"Huh?"

I said it again. He smeared his face with his hands and said tersely: "Moved away."

"Moved away when?"

He waved his hand, almost fell out of his chair and waved it again the other way to restore his balance. "Gimme a drink," he said.

I poured another slug of the gin and held it out of his reach.

"Gimme," the man said urgently. "I'm not happy."

"All I want is the present address of Orrin P. Quest."

"Just think of that," he said wittily and made a loose pass at the glass I was holding.

I put the glass down on the floor and got one of my business cards out for him. "This might help you to concentrate," I told him.

He peered at the card closely, sneered, bent it in half and bent it again. He held it on the flat of his hand, spit on it, and tossed it over his shoulder.

I handed him the glass of gin. He drank it to my health, nodded solemnly, and threw the glass over his shoulder too. It rolled along the floor and thumped the baseboard. The man stood up with surprising ease, jerked a thumb towards the ceiling, doubled the fingers of his hand under it and made a sharp noise with his tongue and teeth.

"Beat it," he said. "I got friends." He looked at the telephone on the wall and back at me with cunning. "A couple of boys to take care of you," he sneered. I said nothing. "Don't believe me, huh?" he snarled, suddenly angry. I shook my head.

He started for the telephone, clawed the receiver off the hook, and dialed the five digits of a number. I watched him. One-three-five-seven-two.

That took all he had for the time being. He let the receiver fall and bang against the wall and he sat down on the floor beside it. He put it to his ear and growled at the wall: "Lemme talk to the Doc." I listened silently. "Vince! The Doc!" he shouted angrily. He shook the receiver and threw it away from him. He put his hands down on the floor and started to crawl in a circle. When he saw me he looked surprised and annoyed. He got shakily to his feet again and held his hand out. "Gimme a drink."

I retrieved the fallen glass and milked the gin bottle into it. He accepted it with the dignity of an intoxicated dowager, drank it down with an airy flourish, walked calmly over to the couch and lay down, putting the glass under his head for a pillow. He went to sleep instantly.

I put the telephone receiver back on its hook, glanced out in the kitchen again, felt the man on the couch over and dug some keys out of his pocket. One of them was a passkey. The door to the hallway had a spring lock and I fixed it so that I could come in again and started up the stairs. I paused on the way to write "Doc—Vince, 13572" on an envelope. Maybe it was a clue.

The house was quite silent as I went on up.

# 4

The manager's much filed passkey turned the lock of Room 214 without noise. I pushed the door open. The room was not empty. A chunky, strongly built man was bending over a suitcase on the bed, with his back to the door. Shirts and socks and underwear were laid out on the bed cover, and he was packing them leisurely and carefully, whistling between his teeth in a low monotone.

He stiffened as the door hinge creaked. His hand moved fast for the pillow on the bed.

"I beg your pardon," I said. "The manager told me this room was vacant."

He was as bald as a grapefruit. He wore dark gray flannel slacks and transparent plastic suspenders over a blue shirt. His hands came up from the pillow, went to his head, and down again. He turned and he had hair.

It looked as natural as hair ever looked, smooth, brown, not parted. He glared at me from under it.

"You can always try knocking," he said.

He had a thick voice and a broad careful face that had been around.

"Why would I? If the manager said the room was empty?"

He nodded, satisfied. The glare went out of his eyes.

I came further into the room without invitation. An open

love-pulp magazine lay face down on the bed near the suitcase. A cigar smoked in a green glass ash tray. The room was
careful and orderly, and, for that house, clean.

"He must have thought you had already moved out," I
said, trying to look like a well-meaning party with some talent
for the truth.

"Have it in half an hour," the man said.

"O.K. if I look around?"

He smiled mirthlessly. "Ain't been in town long, have you?"

"Why?"

"New around here, ain't you?"

"Why?"

"Like the house and the neighborhood?"

"Not much," I said. "The room looks all right."

He grinned, showing a porcelain jacket crown that was too
white for his other teeth. "How long you been looking?"

"Just started," I said. "Why all the questions?"

"You make me laugh," the man said, not laughing. "You
don't look at rooms in this town. You grab them sight un-
seen. This burg's so jam-packed even now that I could get ten
bucks just for telling there's a vacancy here."

"That's too bad," I said. "A man named Orrin P. Quest
told me about the room. So there's one sawbuck you don't
get to spend."

"That so?" Not a flicker of an eye. Not a movement of a
muscle. I might as well have been talking to a turtle.

"Don't get tough with me," the man said. "I'm a bad man
to get tough with."

He picked his cigar out of the green glass ash tray and blew
a little smoke. Through it he gave me the cold gray eye. I got
a cigarette out and scratched my chin with it.

"What happens to people that get tough with you?" I asked
him. "You make them hold your toupee?"

"You lay off my toupee," he said savagely.

"So sorry," I said.

"There's a 'No Vacancy' sign on the house," the man said.
"So what makes you come here and find one?"

"You didn't catch the name," I said. "Orrin P. Quest." I
spelled it for him. Even that didn't make him happy. There
was a dead-air pause.

He turned abruptly and put a pile of handkerchiefs into his suitcase. I moved a little closer to him. When he turned back there was what might have been a watchful look on his face. But it had been a watchful face to start with.

"Friend of yours?" he asked casually.

"We grew up together," I said.

"Quiet sort of guy," the man said easily. "I used to pass the time of day with him. Works for Cal-Western, don't he?"

"He did," I said.

"Oh. He quit?"

"Let out."

We went on staring at each other. It didn't get either of us anywhere. We both had done too much of it in our lives to expect miracles.

The man put the cigar back in his face and sat down on the side of the bed beside the open suitcase. Glancing into it I saw the square butt of an automatic peeping out from under a pair of badly folded shorts.

"This Quest party's been out of here ten days," the man said thoughtfully. "So he still thinks the room is vacant, huh?"

"According to the register it *is* vacant," I said.

He made a contemptuous noise. "That rummy downstairs probably ain't looked at the register in a month. Say—wait a minute." His eyes sharpened and his hand wandered idly over the open suitcase and gave an idle pat to something that was close to the gun. When the hand moved away, the gun was no longer visible.

"I've been kind of dreamy all morning or I'd have wised up," he said. "You're a dick."

"All right. Say I'm a dick."

"What's the beef?"

"No beef at all. I just wondered why you had the room."

"I moved from 215 across the hall. This here is a better room. That's all. Simple. Satisfied?"

"Perfectly," I said, watching the hand that could be near the gun if it wanted to.

"What kind of dick? City? Let's see the buzzer."

I didn't say anything.

"I don't believe you got no buzzer."

"If I showed it to you, you're the type of guy would say it was counterfeit. So you're Hicks."

He looked surprised.

"George W. Hicks," I said. "It's in the register. Room 215. You just got through telling me you moved from 215." I glanced around the room. "If you had a blackboard here, I'd write it out for you."

"Strictly speaking, we don't have to get into no snarling match," he said. "Sure I'm Hicks. Pleased to meetcha. What's yours?"

He held his hand out. I shook hands with him, but not as if I had been longing for the moment to arrive.

"My name's Marlowe," I said. "Philip Marlowe."

"You know something," Hicks said politely, "you're a God-damn liar."

I laughed in his face.

"You ain't getting no place with that breezy manner, bub. What's your connection?"

I got my wallet out and handed him one of my business cards. He read it thoughtfully and tapped the edge against his porcelain crown.

"He coulda went somewhere without telling me," he mused.

"Your grammar," I said, "is almost as loose as your toupee."

"You lay off my toupee, if you know what's good for you," he shouted.

"I wasn't going to eat it," I said. "I'm not that hungry."

He took a step towards me, and dropped his right shoulder. A scowl of fury dropped his lip almost as far.

"Don't hit me. I'm insured," I told him.

"Oh hell. Just another screwball." He shrugged and put his lip back up on his face. "What's the lay?"

"I have to find this Orrin P. Quest," I said.

"Why?"

I didn't answer that.

After a moment he said: "O.K. I'm a careful guy myself. That's why I'm movin' out."

"Maybe you don't like the reefer smoke."

"That," he said emptily, "and other things. That's why Quest left. Respectable type. Like me. I think a couple of hard boys threw a scare into him."

"I see," I said. "That would be why he left no forwarding address. And why did they throw a scare into him?"

"You just mentioned reefer smoke, didn't you? Wouldn't he be the type to go to headquarters about that?"

"In Bay City?" I asked. "Why would he bother? Well, thanks a lot, Mr. Hicks. Going far?"

"Not far," he said. "No. Not very far. Just far enough."

"What's your racket?" I asked him.

"Racket?" He looked hurt.

"Sure. What do you shake them for? How do you make your dibs?"

"You got me wrong, brother. I'm a retired optometrist."

"That why you have the .45 gun in there?" I pointed to the suitcase.

"Nothing to get cute about," he said sourly. "It's been in the family for years." He looked down at the card again. "Private investigator, huh?" he said thoughtfully. "What kind of work do you do mostly?"

"Anything that's reasonably honest," I said.

He nodded. "Reasonably is a word you could stretch. So is honest."

I gave him a shady leer. "You're so right," I agreed. "Let's get together some quiet afternoon and stretch them." I reached out and slipped the card from between his fingers and dropped it into my pocket. "Thanks for the time," I said.

I went out and closed the door, then stood against it listening. I don't know what I expected to hear. Whatever it was I didn't hear it. I had a feeling he was standing exactly where I had left him and looking at the spot where I had made my exit. I made noise going along the hall and stood at the head of the stairs.

A car drove away from in front of the house. Somewhere a door closed. I went quietly back to Room 215 and used the passkey to enter. I closed and locked its door silently, and waited just inside.

# 5

Not more than two minutes passed before Mr. George W. Hicks was on his way. He came out so quietly that I wouldn't have heard him if I hadn't been listening for precisely that kind of movement. I heard the slight metallic sound of the doorknob turning. Then slow steps. Then very gently the door was closed. The steps moved off. The faint distant creak of the stairs. Then nothing. I waited for the sound of the front door. It didn't come. I opened the door of 215 and moved along the hall to the stairhead again. Below there was the careful sound of a door being tried. I looked down to see Hicks going into the manager's apartment. The door closed behind him. I waited for the sound of voices. No voices.

I shrugged and went back to 215.

The room showed signs of occupancy. There was a small radio on a night table, an unmade bed with shoes under it, and an old bathrobe hung over the cracked, pull-down green shade to keep the glare out.

I looked at all this as if it meant something, then stepped back into the hall and relocked the door. Then I made another pilgrimage into Room 214. Its door was now unlocked. I searched the room with care and patience and found nothing that connected it in any way with Orrin P. Quest. I didn't expect to. There was no reason why I should. But you always have to look.

I went downstairs, listened outside the manager's door, heard nothing, went in and crossed to put the keys on the desk. Lester B. Clausen lay on his side on the couch with his face to the wall, dead to the world. I went through the desk, found an old account book that seemed to be concerned with rent taken in and expenses paid out and nothing else. I looked at the register again. It wasn't up to date but the party on the couch seemed enough explanation for that. Orrin P. Quest had moved away. Somebody had taken over his room. Somebody else had the room registered to Hicks. The little man counting money in the kitchen went nicely with the neighborhood. The fact that he carried a gun and a knife was a social eccentricity that would cause no comment at all on Idaho Street.

I reached the small Bay City telephone book off the hook beside the desk. I didn't think it would be much of a job to sift out the party that went by the name of "Doc" or "Vince" and the phone number one-three-five-seven-two. First of all I leafed back through the register. Something which I ought to have done first. The page with Orrin Quest's registration had been torn out. A careful man, Mr. George W. Hicks. Very careful.

I closed the register, glanced over at Lester B. Clausen again, wrinkled my nose at the stale air and the sickly sweetish smell of gin and of something else, and started back to the entrance door. As I reached it, something for the first time penetrated my mind. A drunk like Clausen ought to be snoring very loudly. He ought to be snoring his head off with a nice assortment of checks and gurgles and snorts. He wasn't making any sound at all. A brown army blanket was pulled up around his shoulders and the lower part of his head. He looked very comfortable, very calm. I stood over him and looked down. Something which was not an accidental fold held the army blanket away from the back of his neck. I moved it. A square yellow wooden handle was attached to the back of Lester B. Clausen's neck. On the side of the yellow handle were printed the words "Compliments of the Crumsen Hardware Company." The position of the handle was just below the occipital bulge.

It was the handle of an ice pick. . . .

I did a nice quiet thirty-five getting away from the neighborhood. On the edge of the city, a frog's jump from the line, I shut myself in an outdoor telephone booth and called the Police Department.

"Bay City Police. Moot talking," a furry voice said.

I said: "Number 449 Idaho Street. In the apartment of the manager. His name's Clausen."

"Yeah?" the voice said. "What do we do?"

"I don't know," I said. "It's a bit of a puzzle to me. But the man's name is Lester B. Clausen. Got that?"

"What makes it important?" the furry voice said without suspicion.

"The coroner will want to know," I said, and hung up.

# 6

I drove back to Hollywood and locked myself in the office with the Bay City telephone book. It took me a quarter-hour to find out that the party who went with the telephone number one-three-five-seven-two in Bay City was a Dr. Vincent Lagardie, who called himself a neurologist, had his home and offices on Wyoming Street, which according to my map was not quite in the best residential neighborhood and not quite out of it. I locked the Bay City telephone book up in my desk and went down to the corner drugstore for a sandwich and a cup of coffee and used a pay booth to call Dr. Vincent Lagardie. A woman answered and I had some trouble getting through to Dr. Lagardie himself. When I did his voice was impatient. He was very busy, in the middle of an examination he said. I never knew a doctor who wasn't. Did he know Lester B. Clausen? He never heard of him. What was the purpose of my inquiry?

"Mr. Clausen tried to telephone you this morning," I said. "He was too drunk to talk properly."

"But I don't know Mr. Clausen," the doctor's cool voice answered. He didn't seem to be in quite such a hurry now.

"Well that's all right then," I said. "Just wanted to make sure. Somebody stuck an ice pick into the back of his neck."

There was a quiet pause. Dr. Lagardie's voice was now almost unctuously polite. "Has this been reported to the police?"

"Naturally," I said. "But it shouldn't bother you — unless of course it was your ice pick."

He passed that one up. "And who is this speaking?" he inquired suavely.

"The name is Hicks," I said. "George W. Hicks. I just moved out of there. I don't want to get mixed up with that sort of thing. I just figured when Clausen tried to call you — this was before he was dead you understand — that you might be interested."

"I'm sorry, Mr. Hicks," Dr. Lagardie's voice said, "but I don't *know* Mr. Clausen. I have never *heard* of Mr. Clausen or had any contact with him whatsoever. And I have an excellent memory for names."

"Well, that's fine," I said. "And you won't meet him now. But somebody *may* want to know why he tried to telephone you—unless I forget to pass the information along."

There was a dead pause. Dr. Lagardie said: "I can't think of any comment to make on that."

I said: "Neither can I. I may call you again. Don't get me wrong, Dr. Lagardie. This isn't any kind of a shake. I'm just a mixed-up little man who needs a friend. I kind of felt that a doctor—like a clergyman—"

"I'm at your entire disposal," Dr. Lagardie said. "Please feel free to consult me."

"Thank you, doctor," I said fervently. "Thank you very very much."

I hung up. If Dr. Vincent Lagardie was on the level, he would now telephone the Bay City Police Department and tell them the story. If he didn't telephone the police, he wasn't on the level. Which might or might not be useful to know.

# 7

The phone on my desk rang at four o'clock sharp.

"Did you find Orrin yet, Mr. Marlowe?"

"Not yet. Where are you?"

"Why I'm in the drugstore next to—"

"Come on up and stop acting like Mata Hari," I said.

"Aren't you ever polite to anybody?" she snapped.

I hung up and fed myself a slug of Old Forester to brace my nerves for the interview. As I was inhaling it I heard her steps tripping along the corridor. I moved across and opened the door.

"Come in this way and miss the crowd," I said.

She seated herself demurely and waited.

"All I could find out," I told her, "is that the dump on Idaho Street is peddling reefers. That's marijuana cigarettes."

"Why, how disgusting," she said.

"We have to take the bad with the good in this life," I said. "Orrin must have got wise and threatened to report it to the police."

"You mean," she said in her little-girl manner, "that they might hurt him for doing that?"

"Well, most likely they'd just throw a scare into him first."

"Oh, they couldn't scare Orrin, Mr. Marlowe," she said decisively. "He just gets mean when people try to run him."

"Yeah," I said. "But we're not talking about the same things. You can scare anybody—with the right technique."

She set her mouth stubbornly. "No, Mr. Marlowe. They couldn't scare Orrin."

"Okay," I said. "So they didn't scare him. Say they just cut off one of his legs and beat him over the head with it. What would he do then—write to the Better Business Bureau?"

"You're making fun of me," she said politely. Her voice was as cool as boarding-house soup. "Is that all you did all day? Just find Orrin had moved and it was a bad neighborhood? Why I found that out for myself, Mr. Marlowe. I thought you being a detective and all—" She trailed off, leaving the rest of it in the air.

"I did a little more than that," I said. "I gave the landlord a little gin and went through the register and talked to a man named Hicks. George W. Hicks. He wears a toupee. I guess maybe you didn't meet him. He has, or had, Orrin's room. So I thought maybe—" It was my turn to do a little trailing in the air.

She fixed me with her pale blue eyes enlarged by the glasses. Her mouth was small and firm and tight, her hands clasped on the desk in front of her over her large square bag, her whole body stiff and erect and formal and disapproving.

"I paid you twenty dollars, Mr. Marlowe," she said coldly. "I understood that was in payment of a day's work. It doesn't seem to me that you've done a day's work."

"No," I said. "That's true. But the day isn't over yet. And don't bother about the twenty bucks. You can have it back if you like. I didn't even bruise it."

I opened the desk drawer and got out her money. I pushed

it across the desk. She looked at it but didn't touch it. Her eyes came up slowly to meet mine.

"I didn't mean it like that. I know you're doing the best you can, Mr. Marlowe."

"With the facts I have."

"But I've told you all I know."

"I don't think so," I said.

"Well I'm sure I can't help what you think," she said tartly. "After all, if I knew what I wanted to know already, I wouldn't have come here and asked you to find it out, would I?"

"I'm not saying you know all you want to know," I answered. "The point is I don't know all I want to know in order to do a job for you. And what you tell me doesn't add up."

"What doesn't add up? I've told you the truth. I'm Orrin's sister. I guess I know what kind of person he is."

"How long did he work for Cal-Western?"

"I've told you that. He came out to California just about a year ago. He got work right away because he practically had the job before he left."

"He wrote home how often? Before he stopped writing."

"Every week. Sometimes oftener. He'd take turns writing to mother and me. Of course the letters were for both of us."

"About what?"

"You mean what did he write about?"

"What did you think I meant?"

"Well, you don't have to snap at me. He wrote about his work and the plant and the people there and sometimes about a show he'd been to. Or it was about California. He'd write about church too."

"Nothing about girls?"

"I don't think Orrin cared much for girls."

"And lived at the same address all this time?"

She nodded, looking puzzled.

"And he stopped writing how long ago?"

That took thought. She pressed her lips and pushed a fingertip around the middle of the lower one. "About three or four months," she said at last.

"What was the date of his last letter?"

"I—I'm afraid I can't tell you exactly the date. But it was like I said, three or four—"

I waved a hand at her. "Anything out of the ordinary in it? Anything unusual said or anything unusual unsaid?"

"Why no. It seemed just like all the rest."

"Don't you have any friends or relatives in this part of the country?"

She gave me a funny stare, started to say something, then shook her head sharply. "No."

"Okay. Now I'll tell you what's wrong. I'll skip over your not telling me where you're staying, because it might be just that you're afraid I'll show up with a quart of hooch under my arm and make a pass at you."

"That's not a very nice way to talk," she said.

"Nothing I say is nice. I'm not nice. By your standards nobody with less than three prayerbooks could be nice. But I *am* inquisitive. What's wrong with this picture is that you're not scared. Neither you personally nor your mother. And you ought to be scared as hell."

She clutched her bag to her bosom with tight little fingers. "You mean something has happened to him?" Her voice faded off into a sort of sad whisper, like a mortician asking for a down payment.

"I don't know that anything has. But in your position, knowing the kind of guy Orrin was, the way his letters came through and then didn't, I can't see myself waiting for my summer vacation to come around before I start asking questions. I can't see myself by-passing the police who have an organization for finding people. And going to a lone-wolf operator you never heard of, asking him to root around for you in the rubble. And I can't see your dear old mother just sitting there in Manhattan, Kansas, week after week darning the minister's winter underwear. No letter from Orrin. No news. And all she does about it is take a long breath and mend up another pair of pants."

She came to her feet with a lunge. "You're a horrid, disgusting person," she said angrily. "I think you're vile. Don't you dare say mother and I weren't worried. Just don't you dare."

I pushed the twenty dollars' worth of currency a little closer to the other side of the desk. "You were worried twenty dollars' worth, honey," I said. "But about what I wouldn't know. I guess I don't really want to know. Just put this hunk of the folding back in your saddlebag and forget you ever met me. You might want to lend it to another detective tomorrow."

She snapped her bag shut viciously on the money. "I'm not very likely to forget your rudeness," she said between her teeth. "Nobody in the world's ever talked to me the way you have."

I stood up and wandered around the end of the desk. "Don't think about it too much. You might get to like it."

I reached up and twitched her glasses off. She took half a step back, almost stumbled, and I reached an arm around her by pure instinct. Her eyes widened and she put her hands against my chest and pushed. I've been pushed harder by a kitten.

"Without the cheaters those eyes are really something," I said in an awed voice.

She relaxed and let her head go back and her lips open a little. "I suppose you do this to all the clients," she said softly. Her hands now had dropped to her sides. The bag whacked against my leg. She leaned her weight on my arm. If she wanted me to let go of her, she had her signals mixed.

"I just didn't want you to lose your balance," I said.

"I knew you were the thoughtful type." She relaxed still more. Her head went back now. Her upper lids drooped, fluttered a bit and her lips came open a little farther. On them appeared the faint provocative smile that nobody ever has to teach them. "I suppose you thought I did it on purpose," she said.

"Did what on purpose?"

"Stumbled, sort of."

"Wel-l-l-l."

She reached a quick arm around my neck and started to pull. So I kissed her. It was either that or slug her. She pushed her mouth hard at me for a long moment, then quietly and very comfortably wriggled around in my arms and nestled. She let out a long easy sigh.

"In Manhattan, Kansas, you could be arrested for this," she said.

"If there was any justice, I could be arrested just for being there," I said.

She giggled and poked the end of my nose with a fingertip. "I suppose you really prefer fast girls," she said, looking up at me sideways. "At least you won't have to wipe off any lip rouge. Maybe I'll wear some next time."

"Maybe we'd better sit down on the floor," I said. "My arm's getting tired."

She giggled again and disengaged herself gracefully. "I guess you think I've been kissed lots of times," she said.

"What girl hasn't?"

She nodded, gave me the up-from-under look that made her eyelashes cut across the iris. "Even at the church socials they play kissing games," she said.

"Or there wouldn't be any church socials," I said.

We looked at each other with no particular expression.

"Well-l-l—" she began at last. I handed her back her glasses. She put them on. She opened her bag, looked at herself in a small mirror, rooted around in her bag and came out with her hand clenched.

"I'm sorry I was mean," she said, and pushed something under the blotter of my desk. She gave me another little frail smile and marched to the door and opened it.

"I'll call you," she said intimately. And out she went, tap, tap, tap down the hall.

I went over and lifted the blotter and smoothed out the crumpled currency that lay under it. It hadn't been much of a kiss, but it looked like I had another chance at the twenty dollars.

The phone rang before I had quite started to worry about Mr. Lester B. Clausen. I reached for it absently. The voice I heard was an abrupt voice, but thick and clogged, as if it was being strained through a curtain or somebody's long white beard.

"You Marlowe?" it said.

"Speaking."

"You got a safe-deposit box, Marlowe?"

I had enough of being polite for one afternoon. "Stop asking and start telling," I said.

"I asked you a question, Marlowe."

"I didn't answer it," I said. "Like this." I reached over and pressed down the riser on the phone. Held it that way while I fumbled around for a cigarette. I knew he would call right back. They always do when they think they're tough. They haven't used their exit line. When it rang again I started right in.

"If you have a proposition, state it. And I get called 'mister' until you give me some money."

"Don't let that temper ride you so hard, friend. I'm in a jam. I need help. I need something kept in a safe place. For a few days. Not longer. And for that you make a little quick money."

"How little?" I asked. "And how quick?"

"A C note. Right here and waiting. I'm warming it for you."

"I can hear it purr," I said. "Right where and waiting?" I was listening to the voice twice, once when I heard it and once when it echoed in my mind.

"Room 332, Van Nuys Hotel. Knock two quick ones and two slow ones. Not too loud. I got to have live action. How fast can you—"

"What is it you want me to keep?"

"That'll wait till you get here. I said I was in a hurry."

"What's your name?"

"Just Room 332."

"Thanks for the time," I said. "Goodbye."

"Hey. Wait a minute, dope. It's nothing hot like you think. No ice. No emerald pendants. It just happens to be worth a lot of money to me—and nothing at all to anybody else."

"The hotel has a safe."

"Do you want to die poor, Marlowe?"

"Why not? Rockefeller did. Goodbye again."

The voice changed. The furriness went out of it. It said sharply and swiftly: "How's every little thing in Bay City?"

I didn't speak. Just waited. There was a dim chuckle over the wire. "Thought that might interest you, Marlowe. Room 332 it is. Tramp on it friend. Make speed."

The phone clicked in my ear. I hung up. For no reason a pencil rolled off the desk and broke its point on the glass doohickey under one of the desk legs. I picked it up and slowly and carefully sharpened it in the Boston sharpener screwed to the edge of the window frame, turning the pencil around to get it nice and even. I laid it down in the tray on the desk and dusted off my hands. I had all the time in the world. I looked out of the window. I didn't see anything. I didn't hear anything.

And then, for even less reason, I saw Orfamay Quest's face without the glasses, and polished and painted and with blonde hair piled up high on the forehead with a braid around the middle of it. And bedroom eyes. They all have to have bedroom eyes. I tried to imagine this face in a vast close-up being gnawed by some virile character from the wide-open spaces of Romanoff's bar.

It took me twenty-nine minutes to get to the Van Nuys Hotel.

# 8

Once, long ago, it must have had a certain elegance. But no more. The memories of old cigars clung to its lobby like the dirty gilt on its ceiling and the sagging springs of its leather lounging chairs. The marble of the desk had turned a yellowish brown with age. But the floor carpet was new and had a hard look, like the room clerk. I passed him up and strolled over to the cigar counter in the corner and put down a quarter for a package of Camels. The girl behind the counter was a straw blonde with a long neck and tired eyes. She put the cigarettes in front of me, added a packet of matches, dropped my change into a slotted box marked "The Community Chest Thanks You."

"You'd want me to do that, wouldn't you," she said, smiling patiently. "You'd want to give your change to the poor little underprivileged kids with bent legs and stuff, wouldn't you?"

"Suppose I didn't," I said.

"I dig up seven cents," the girl said, "and it would be very painful." She had a low lingering voice with a sort of moist caress in it like a damp bath towel. I put a quarter after the seven cents. She gave me her big smile then. It showed more of her tonsils.

"You're nice," she said. "I can see you're nice. A lot of fellows would have come in here and made a pass at a girl. Just think. Over seven cents. A pass."

"Who's the house peeper here now?" I asked her, without taking up the option.

"There's two of them." She did something slow and elegant to the back of her head, exhibiting what seemed like more than one handful of blood-red fingernails in the process. "Mr. Hady is on nights and Mr. Flack is on days. It's day now so it would be Mr. Flack would be on."

"Where could I find him?"

She leaned over the counter and let me smell her hair, pointing with a half-inch fingernail towards the elevator bank. "It's down along that corridor there, next to the porter's room. You can't miss the porter's room on account of it has a half-door and says PORTER on the upper part in gold letters. Only that half is folded back like, so I guess maybe you can't see it."

"I'll see it," I said. "Even if I have to get a hinge screwed to my neck. What does this Flack look like?"

"Well," she said, "he's a little squatty number, with a bit of a mustache. A sort of chunky type. Thick-set like, only not tall." Her fingers moved languidly along the counter to where I could have touched them without jumping. "He's not interesting," she said. "Why bother?"

"Business," I said, and made off before she threw a half-nelson on me.

I looked back at her from the elevators. She was staring after me with an expression she probably would have said was thoughtful.

The porter's room was halfway down the corridor to the Spring Street entrance. The door beyond it was half open. I looked around its edge, then went in and closed it behind me.

A man was sitting at a small desk which had dust on it, a very large ash tray and very little else. He was short and thick-set. He had something dark and bristly under his nose about an inch long. I sat down across from him and put a card on the desk.

He reached for the card without excitement, read it, turned it over and read the back with as much care as the front. There was nothing on the back to read. He picked half of a cigar out of his ash tray and burned his nose lighting it.

"What's the gripe?" he growled at me.

"No gripe. You Flack?"

He didn't bother to answer. He gave me a steady look which may or may not have concealed his thoughts, depending on whether he had any to conceal.

"Like to get a line on one of the customers," I said.

"What name?" Flack asked, with no enthusiasm.

"I don't know what name he's using here. He's in Room 332."

"What name was he using before he came here?" Flack asked.

"I don't know that either."

"Well, what did he look like?" Flack was suspicious now. He reread my card but it added nothing to his knowledge.

"I never saw him, so far as I know."

Flack said: "I must be overworked. I don't get it."

"I had a call from him," I said. "He wanted to see me."

"Am I stopping you?"

"Look, Flack. A man in my business makes enemies at times. You ought to know that. This party wants something done. Tells me to come on over, forgets to give his name, and hangs up. I figured I'd do a little checking before I went up there."

Flack took the cigar out of his mouth and said patiently: "I'm in terrible shape. I still don't get it. Nothing makes sense to me any more."

I leaned over the desk and spoke to him slowly and distinctly: "The whole thing could be a nice way to get me into a hotel room and knock me off and then quietly check out. You wouldn't want anything like that to happen in your hotel, would you, Flack?"

"Supposing I cared," he said, "you figure you're that important?"

"Do you smoke that piece of rope because you like it or because you think it makes you look tough?"

"For forty-five bucks a week," Flack said, "would I smoke anything better?" He eyed me steadily.

"No expense account yet," I told him. "No deal yet."

He made a sad sound and got up wearily and went out of the room. I lit one of my cigarettes and waited. He came back in a short time and dropped a registration card on the desk. *Dr. G. W. Hambleton, El Centro, California* was written on it in a firm round hand in ink. The clerk had written other things on it, including the room number and daily rate. Flack pointed a finger that needed a manicure or failing that a nailbrush.

"Came in at 2.47 P.M.," he said. "Just today, that is. Nothing on his bill. One day's rent. No phone calls. No nothing. That what you want?"

"What does he look like?" I asked.

"I didn't see him. You think I stand out there by the desk and take pictures of them while they register?"

"Thanks," I said. "Dr. G. W. Hambleton, El Centro. Much obliged." I handed him back the registration card.

"Anything I ought to know," Flack said as I went out, "don't forget where I live. That is, if you call it living."

I nodded and went out. There are days like that. Everybody you meet is a dope. You begin to look at yourself in the glass and wonder.

# 9

Room 332 was at the back of the building near the door to the fire escape. The corridor which led to it had a smell of old carpet and furniture oil and the drab anonymity of a thousand shabby lives. The sand bucket under the racked fire hose was full of cigarette and cigar stubs, an accumulation of several days. A radio pounded brassy music through an open transom. Through another transom people were laughing fit to kill themselves. Down at the end by Room 332 it was quieter.

I knocked the two longs and two shorts as instructed. Nothing happened. I felt jaded and old. I felt as if I had spent my life knocking at doors in cheap hotels that nobody bothered to open. I tried again. Then turned the knob and walked in. A key with a red fiber tab hung in the inside keyhole.

There was a short hall with a bathroom on the right. Beyond the hall the upper half of a bed was in view and a man lay on it in shirt and pants.

I said: "Dr. Hambleton?"

The man didn't answer. I went past the bathroom door towards him. A whiff of perfume reached me and I started to turn, but not quickly enough. A woman who had been in the bathroom was standing there holding a towel in front of the lower part of her face. Dark glasses showed above the towel. And then the brim of a wide-brimmed straw hat in a sort of dusty delphinium blue. Under that was fluffed-out pale blond hair. Blue earbuttons lurked somewhere back in the shadows. The sunglasses were in white frames with broad flat sidebows. Her dress matched her hat. An embroidered silk or rayon coat was open over the dress. She wore gauntleted gloves and there was an automatic in her right hand. White bone grip. Looked like a .32.

"Turn around and put your hands behind you," she said through the towel. The voice muffled by the towel meant as little to me as the dark glasses. It was not the voice which had talked to me on the telephone. I didn't move.

"Don't ever think I'm fooling," she said. "I'll give you exactly three seconds to do what I say."

"Couldn't you make it a minute? I like looking at you."

She made a threatening gesture with the little gun. "Turn around," she snapped. "But fast."

"I like the sound of your voice too."

"All right," she said, in a tight dangerous tone. "If that's the way you want it, that's the way you want it."

"Don't forget you're a lady," I said, and turned around and put my hands up to my shoulders. A gun muzzle poked into the back of my neck. Breath almost tickled my skin. The perfume was an elegant something or other, not strong, not decisive. The gun against my neck went away and a white flame burned for an instant behind my eyes. I grunted and fell forward on my hands and knees and reached back quickly. My hand touched a leg in a nylon stocking but slipped off, which seemed a pity. It felt like a nice leg. The jar of another blow on the head took the pleasure out of this and I made the hoarse sound of a man in desperate shape. I collapsed on the floor. The door opened. A key rattled. The door closed. The key turned. Silence.

I climbed up to my feet and went into the bathroom. I bathed my head with a towel from the rack soaked with cold water. It felt as if the heel of a shoe had hit me. Certainly it was not a gun butt. There was a little blood, not much. I rinsed the towel out and stood there patting the bruise and wondering why I didn't run after her screaming. But what I was doing was staring into the open medicine cabinet over the basin. The upper part of a can of talcum had been pried off the shoulder. There was talcum all over the shelf. A toothpaste tube had been cut open. Someone had been looking for something.

I went back to the little hallway and tried the room door. Locked from the outside. I bent down and looked through the keyhole. But it was an up-and-down lock, with the outer and inner keyholes on different levels. The girl in the dark glasses with the white rims didn't know much about hotels. I twisted the night latch, which opened the outside lock, opened the door, looked along the empty corridor, and closed the door again.

Then I went towards the man on the bed. He had not moved during all this time, for a somewhat obvious reason.

Beyond the little hallway the room widened towards a pair of windows through which the evening sun slanted in a shaft that reached almost across the bed and came to a stop under the neck of the man that lay there. What it stopped on was blue and white and shining and round. He lay quite comfortably half on his face with his hands down at his sides and his shoes off. The side of his face was on the pillow and he seemed relaxed. He was wearing a toupee. The last time I had talked to him his name had been George W. Hicks. Now it was Dr. G. W. Hambleton. Same initials. Not that it mattered any more. I wasn't going to be talking to him again. There was no blood. None at all, which is one of the few nice things about an expert ice-pick job.

I touched his neck. It was still warm. While I was doing it the shaft of sunlight moved away from the knob of the ice pick towards his left ear. I turned away and looked the room over. The telephone bell box had been opened and left open. The Gideon Bible was thrown in the corner. The desk had been searched. I went to a closet and looked into that. There were clothes in it and a suitcase I had seen before. I found nothing that seemed important. I picked a snap-brim hat off the floor and put it on the desk and went back to the bath-room. The point of interest now was whether the people who had ice-picked Dr. Hambleton had found what they came for. They had had very little time.

I searched the bathroom carefully. I moved the top of the toilet tank and drained it. There was nothing in it. I peered down the overflow pipe. No thread hung there with a small object at the end of it. I searched the bureau. It was empty except for an old envelope. I unhooked the window screens and felt under the sills outside. I picked the Gideon Bible off the floor and leafed through it again. I examined the backs of three pictures and studied the edge of the carpet. It was tacked close to the wall and there were little pockets of dust in the depressions made by the tacks. I got down on the floor and examined the part under the bed. Just the same. I stood on a chair, looked into the bowl of the light fixture. It con-tained dust and dead moths. I looked the bed over. It had been made up by a professional and not touched since. I felt the pillow under the dead man's head, then got the extra pillow out of the closet and examined its edges. Nothing.

Dr. Hambleton's coat hung over a chair back. I went through that, knowing it was the least likely place to find any-thing. Somebody with a knife had worked on the lining and the shoulder padding. There were matches, a couple of cigars, a pair of dark glasses, a cheap handkerchief not used, a Bay City movie theater ticket stub, a small comb, an unopened package of cigarettes. I looked at it in the light. It showed no sign of having been disturbed. I disturbed it. I tore off the cover, went through it, found nothing but cigarettes.

That left Dr. Hambleton himself. I eased him over and got into his trouser pockets. Loose change, another handkerchief, a small tube of dental floss, more matches, a bunch of keys, a folder of bus schedules. In a pigskin wallet was a book of stamps, a second comb (here was a man who really took care of his toupee), three flat packages of white powder, seven printed cards reading *Dr. G. W. Hambleton, O. D. Tustin Building, El Centro, California, Hours 9–12 and 2–4, and by Appointment. Telephone El Centro 50406.* There was no driver's license, no social-security card, no insurance cards, no real identification at all. There was $164 in currency in the wallet. I put the wallet back where I found it.

I lifted Dr. Hambleton's hat off the desk and examined the sweatband and the ribbon. The ribbon bow had been picked loose with a knife point, leaving hanging threads. There was nothing hidden inside the bow. No evidence of any previous ripping and restitching.

This was the take. If the killers knew what they were looking for, it was something that could be hidden in a book, a telephone box, a tube of toothpaste, or a hatband. I went back into the bathroom and looked at my head again. It was still oozing a tiny trickle of blood. I gave it more cold water and dried the cut with toilet paper and flushed that down the bowl. I went back and stood a moment looking down on Dr. Hambleton, wondering what his mistake had been. He had seemed a fairly wise bird. The sunlight had moved over to the far edge of the room now, off the bed and down into a sad dusty corner.

I grinned suddenly, bent over and quickly and with the grin still on my face, out of place as it was, pulled off Dr. Hambleton's toupee and turned it inside out. As simple as all that. To the lining of the toupee a piece of orange-colored paper was fastened by Scotch tape, protected by a square of cellophane. I pulled it loose, turned it over, and saw that it was a numbered claim check belonging to the Bay City Camera Shop. I put it in my wallet and put the toupee carefully back on the dead egg-bald head.

I left the room unlocked because I had no way to lock it.

Down the hall the radio still blared through the transom and the exaggerated alcoholic laughter accompanied it from across the corridor.

# IO

Over the telephone the Bay City Camera Shop man said: "Yes, Mr. Hicks. We have them for you. Six enlarged prints on glossy from your negative."

"What time do you close?" I asked.

"Oh in about five minutes. We open at nine in the morning."

"I'll pick them up in the morning. Thanks."

I hung up, reached mechanically into the slot and found somebody else's nickel. I walked over to the lunch counter and bought myself a cup of coffee with it, and sat there sipping and listening to the auto horns complaining on the street outside. It was time to go home. Whistles blew. Motors raced. Old brake linings squeaked. There was a dull steady mutter of feet on the sidewalk outside. It was just after five-thirty. I finished the coffee, stuffed a pipe, and strolled a half-block back to the Van Nuys Hotel. In the writing room I folded the orange camera-shop check into a sheet of hotel stationery and addressed an envelope to myself. I put a special-delivery stamp on it and dropped it in the mail chute by the elevator bank. Then I went along to Flack's office again.

Again I closed his door and sat down across from him. Flack didn't seem to have moved an inch. He was chewing morosely on the same cigar butt and his eyes were still full of nothing. I relit my pipe by striking a match on the side of his desk. He frowned.

"Dr. Hambleton doesn't answer his door," I said.

"Huh?" Flack looked at me vacantly.

"Party in 332. Remember? He doesn't answer his door."

"What should I do—bust my girdle?" Flack asked.

"I knocked several times," I said. "No answer. Thought he

might be taking a bath or something, although I couldn't hear anything. Went away for a while, then tried again. Same no answer again."

Flack looked at a turnip watch he got from his vest. "I'm off at seven," he said. "Jesus. A whole hour to go, and more. Boy, am I hungry."

"Working the way you do," I said, "you must be. You have to keep your strength up. Do I interest you at all in Room 332?"

"You said he wasn't in," Flack said irritably. "So what? He wasn't in."

"I didn't say he wasn't in. I said he didn't answer his door."

Flack leaned forward. Very slowly he removed the débris of the cigar from his mouth and put it in the glass tray. "Go on. Make me like it," he said, carefully.

"Maybe you'd like to run up and look," I said. "Maybe you didn't see a first-class ice-pick job lately."

Flack put his hands on the arms of his chair and squeezed the wood hard. "Aw," he said painfully, "aw." He got to his feet and opened the desk drawer. He took out a large black gun, flicked the gate open, studied the cartridges, squinted down the barrel, snapped the cylinder back into place. He unbuttoned his vest and tucked the gun down inside his waistband. In an emergency he could probably have got to it in less than a minute. He put his hat on firmly and jerked a thumb at the door.

We went up to the third floor in silence. We went down the corridor. Nothing had changed. No sound had increased or diminished. Flack hurried along to 332 and knocked from force of habit. Then tried the door. He looked back at me with a twisted mouth.

"You said the door wasn't locked," he complained.

"I didn't exactly say that. It *was* unlocked, though."

"It ain't now," Flack said, and unshipped a key on a long chain. He unlocked the door and glanced up and down the hall. He twisted the knob slowly without sound and eased the door a couple of inches. He listened. No sounds came from within. Flack stepped back, took the black gun out of his waistband. He removed the key from the door, kicked it wide open, and brought the gun up hard and straight, like the wicked foreman of the Lazy Q. "Let's go," he said out of the corner of his mouth.

Over his shoulder I could see that Dr. Hambleton lay exactly as before, but the ice-pick handle didn't show from the entrance. Flack leaned forward and edged cautiously into the room. He reached the bathroom door and put his eye to the crack, then pushed the door open until it bounced against the tub. He went in and came out, stepped down into the room, a tense and wary man who was taking no chances.

He tried the closet door, leveled his gun and jerked it wide open. No suspects in the closet.

"Look under the bed," I said.

Flack bent swiftly and looked under the bed.

"Look under the carpet," I said.

"You kidding me?" Flack asked nastily.

"I just like to watch you work."

He bent over the dead man and studied the ice pick.

"Somebody locked that door," he sneered. "Unless you're lying about its being unlocked."

I said nothing.

"Well I guess it's the cops," he said slowly. "No chance to cover up on this one."

"It's not your fault," I told him. "It happens even in good hotels."

## II

The redheaded intern filled out a DOA form and clipped his stylus to the outside pocket of his white jacket. He snapped the book shut with a faint grin on his face.

"Punctured spinal cord just below the occipital bulge, I'd say," he said carelessly. "A very vulnerable spot. If you know how to find it. And I suppose you do."

Detective Lieutenant Christy French growled. "Think it's the first time I've seen one?"

"No, I guess not," the intern said. He gave a last quick

look at the dead man, turned and walked out of the room. "I'll call the coroner," he said over his shoulder. The door closed behind him.

"What a stiff means to those birds is what a plate of warmed-up cabbage means to me," Christy French said sourly to the closed door. His partner, a cop named Fred Beifus, was down on one knee by the telephone box. He had dusted it for fingerprints and blown off the loose powder. He was looking at the smudge through a small magnifying glass. He shook his head, then picked something off the screw with which the box had been fastened shut.

"Gray cotton undertaker's gloves," he said disgustedly. "Cost about four cents a pair wholesale. Fat lot of good printing this joint. They were looking for something in the telephone box, huh?"

"Evidently something that could be there," French said. "I didn't expect prints. These ice-pick jobs are a specialty. We'll get the experts after a while. This is just a quick-over."

He was stripping the dead man's pockets and laying what had been in them out on the bed beside the quiet and already waxy corpse. Flack was sitting in a chair by the window, looking out morosely. The assistant manager had been up, said nothing with a worried expression, and gone away. I was leaning against the bathroom wall and sorting out my fingers.

Flack said suddenly: "I figure an ice-pick job's a dame's work. You can buy them anywhere. Ten cents. If you want one fast, you can slip it down inside a garter and let it hang there."

Christy French gave him a brief glance which had a kind of wonder in it. Beifus said: "What kind of dames you been running around with, honey? The way stockings cost nowadays a dame would as soon stick a saw down her sock."

"I never thought of that," Flack said.

Beifus said: "Leave us do the thinking sweetheart. It takes equipment."

"No need to get tough," Flack said.

Beifus took his hat off and bowed. "You mustn't deny us our little pleasures, Mr. Flack."

Christy French said: "Besides, a woman would keep on jabbing. She wouldn't even know how much was enough. Lots of the punks don't. Whoever did this one was a performer. He got the spinal cord the first try. And another thing—you have to have the guy quiet to do it. That means more than one guy, unless he was doped, or the killer was a friend of his."

I said: "I don't see how he could have been doped, if he's the party that called me on the phone."

French and Beifus both looked at me with the same expression of patient boredom. "If," French said, "and since you didn't know the guy—according to you—there's always the faint possibility that you wouldn't know his voice. Or am I being too subtle?"

"I don't know," I said. "I haven't read your fan mail."

French grinned.

"Don't waste it on him," Beifus told French. "Save it for when you talk to the Friday Morning Club. Some of them old ladies in the shiny-nose league go big for the nicer angles of murder."

French rolled himself a cigarette and lit it with a kitchen match he struck on the back of a chair. He sighed.

"They worked the technique out in Brooklyn," he explained. "Sunny Moe Stein's boys specialized in it, but they run it into the ground. It got so you couldn't walk across a vacant lot without finding some of their work. Then they came out here, what was left of them. I wonder why did they do that."

"Maybe we just got more vacant lots," Beifus said.

"Funny thing, though," French said, almost dreamily. "When Weepy Moyer had the chill put on Sunny Moe Stein over on Franklin Avenue last February, the killer used a gun. Moe wouldn't have liked that at all."

"I betcha that was why his face had that disappointed look, after they washed the blood off," Beifus remarked.

"Who's Weepy Moyer?" Flack asked.

"He was next to Moe in the organization," French told him. "This could easily be his work. Not that he'd have done it personal."

"Why not?" Flack asked sourly.

"Don't you guys ever read a paper? Moyer's a gentleman now. He knows the nicest people. Even has another name.

And as for the Sunny Moe Stein job, it just happened we had him in jail on a gambling rap. We didn't get anywhere. But we did make him a very sweet alibi. Anyhow he's a gentleman like I said, and gentlemen don't go around sticking ice picks into people. They hire it done."

"Did you ever have anything on Moyer?" I asked.

French looked at me sharply. "Why?"

"I just had an idea. But it's very fragile," I said.

French eyed me slowly. "Just between us girls in the powder room," he said, "we never even proved the guy we had *was* Moyer. But don't broadcast it. Nobody's supposed to know but him and his lawyer and the D.A. and the police beat and the city hall and maybe two or three hundred other people."

He slapped the dead man's empty wallet against his thigh and sat down on the bed. He leaned casually against the corpse's leg, lit a cigarette and pointed with it.

"That's enough time on the vaudeville circuit. Here's what we got, Fred. First off, the customer here was not too bright. He was going by the name of Dr. G. W. Hambleton and had the cards printed with an El Centro address and a phone number. It took just two minutes to find out there ain't any such address or any such phone number. A bright boy doesn't lay open that easy. Next, the guy is definitely not in the chips. He has fourteen smackeroos folding in here and about two bucks loose change. On his key ring he don't have any car key or any safe-deposit key or any house key. All he's got is a suitcase key and seven filed Yale master keys. Filed fairly recently at that. I figure he was planning to sneak the hotel a little. Do you think these keys would work in your dump, Flack?"

Flack went over and stared at the keys. "Two of them are the right size," he said. "I couldn't tell if they'd work by just looking. If I want a master key I have to get it from the office. All I carry is a passkey. I can only use that if the guest is out." He took a key out of his pocket, a key on a long chain, and compared it. He shook his head. "They're no good without more work," he said. "Far too much metal on them."

French flicked ash into the palm of his hand and blew it off as dust. Flack went back to his chair by the window.

"Next point," Christy French announced. "He don't have a driver's license or any identification. None of his outside clothes were bought in El Centro. He had some kind of a grift, but he don't have the looks or personality to bounce checks."

"You didn't really see him at his best," Beifus put in.

"And this hotel is the wrong dump for that anyway," French went on. "It's got a crummy reputation."

"Now wait a minute!" Flack began.

French cut him short with a gesture. "I know every hotel in the metropolitan district, Flack. It's my business to know. For fifty bucks I could organize a double-strip act with French trimmings inside of an hour in any room in this hotel. Don't kid me. You earn your living and I'll earn mine. Just don't kid me. All right. The customer had something he was afraid to keep around. That means he knew somebody was after him and getting close. So he offers Marlowe a hundred bucks to keep it for him. But he doesn't have that much money on him. So what he must have been planning on was getting Marlowe to gamble with him. It couldn't have been hot jewelry then. It had to be something semi-legitimate. That right, Marlowe?"

"You could leave out the semi," I said.

French grinned faintly. "So what he had was something that could be kept flat or rolled up—in a phone box, a hatband, a Bible, a can of talcum. We don't know whether it was found or not. But we do know there was very little time. Not much more than half an hour."

"If Dr. Hambleton did the phoning," I said. "You opened that can of beans yourself."

"It's kind of pointless any other way. The killers wouldn't be in a hurry to have him found. Why should they ask anybody to come over to his room?" He turned to Flack. "Any chance to check his visitors?"

Flack shook his head gloomily. "You don't even have to pass the desk to get to the elevators."

Beifus said: "Maybe that was one reason he came here. That, and the homey atmosphere."

"All right," French said. "Whoever knocked him off could come and go without any questions asked. All he had to know was his room number. And that's about all we know. Okay, Fred?"

Beifus nodded.

I said: "Not quite all. It's a nice toupee, but it's still a toupee."

French and Beifus both swung around quickly. French reached, carefully removed the dead man's hair, and whistled. "I wondered what that damn intern was grinning at," he said. "The bastard didn't even mention it. See what I see, Fred?"

"All I see is a guy without no hair," Beifus answered.

"Maybe you never knew him at that. Mileaway Marston. Used to be a runner for Ace Devore."

"Why sure enough," Beifus chuckled. He leaned over and patted the dead bald head gently. "How you been all this time, Mileaway? I didn't see you in so long I forgot. But you know me, pal. Once a softy always a softy."

The man on the bed looked old and hard and shrunken without his toupee. The yellow mask of death was beginning to set his face into rigid lines.

French said calmly: "Well, that takes a load off my mind. This punk ain't going to be no twenty-four-hour-a-day job. The hell with him." He replaced the toupee over one eye and stood up off the bed. "That's all for you two," he said to Flack and me.

Flack stood up.

"Thanks for the murder, honey," Beifus told him. "You get any more in your nice hotel, don't forget our service. Even when it ain't good, it's quick."

Flack went down the short hall and yanked the door open. I followed him out. On the way to the elevator we didn't speak. Nor on the way down. I walked with him along to his little office, followed him in and shut the door. He seemed surprised.

He sat down at his desk and reached for his telephone. "I got to make a report to the Assistant Manager," he said. "Something you want?"

I rolled a cigarette around on my fingers, put a match to it and blew smoke softly across the desk. "One hundred and fifty dollars," I said.

Flack's small, intent eyes became round holes in a face

washed clean of expression. "Don't get funny in the wrong place," he said.

"After those two comedians upstairs, you could hardly blame me if I did. But I'm not being funny." I beat a tattoo on the edge of the desk and waited.

Tiny beads of sweat showed on Flack's lip above his little mustache. "I got business to attend to," he said, more throatily this time. "Beat it and keep going."

"Such a tough little man," I said. "Dr. Hambleton had $164 currency in his wallet when I searched him. He promised me a hundred as retainer, remember? Now, in the same wallet, he has fourteen dollars. And I *did* leave the door of his room unlocked. And somebody else locked it. You locked it, Flack."

Flack took hold of the arms of his chair and squeezed. His voice came from the bottom of a well saying: "You can't prove a damn thing."

"Do I have to try?"

He took the gun out of his waistband and laid it on the desk in front of him. He stared down at it. It didn't have any message for him. He looked up at me again. "Fifty-fifty, huh?" he said brokenly.

There was a moment of silence between us. He got his old shabby wallet out and rooted in it. He came up with a handful of currency and spread bills out on the desk, sorted them into two piles and pushed one pile my way.

I said: "I want the whole hundred and fifty."

He hunched down in his chair and stared at a corner of the desk. After a long time, he sighed. He put the two piles together and pushed them over—to my side of the desk.

"It wasn't doing him any good," Flack said. "Take the dough and breeze. I'll remember you, buddy. All you guys make me sick to my stomach. How do I know you didn't take half a grand off him."

"I'd take it all. So would the killer. Why leave fourteen dollars?"

"So why did I leave fourteen dollars?" Flack asked, in a tired voice, making vague movements along the desk edge with his fingers. I picked up the money, counted it and threw it back at him.

"Because you're in the business and could size him up. You knew he'd at least have room rent, and a few dollars for loose change. The cops would expect the same thing. Here, I don't want the money. I want something else."

He stared at me with his mouth open.

"Put that dough out of sight," I said.

He reached for it and crammed it back in his wallet. "What something else?" His eyes were small and thoughtful. His tongue pushed out his lower lip. "It don't seem to me *you're* in a very hot trading position either."

"You could be a little wrong about that. If I have to go back up there and tell Christy French and Beifus I was up there before and searched the body, I'd get a tongue-lashing all right. But he'd understand that I haven't been holding out just to be smart. He'd know that somewhere in the background I had a client I was trying to protect. I'd get tough talk and bluster. But that's not what *you'd* get." I stopped and watched the faint glisten of moisture forming on his forehead now. He swallowed hard. His eyes were sick.

"Cut out the wise talk and lay your deal on the deck," he said. He grinned suddenly, rather wolfishly. "Got here a little late to protect her, didn't you?" The fat sneer he lived with was coming home again, but slowly, but gladly.

I killed my cigarette and got another one out and went through all the slow futile face-saving motions of lighting it, getting rid of the match, blowing smoke off to one side, inhaling deeply as though that scrubby little office was a hill-top overlooking the bouncing ocean—all the tired clichéd mannerisms of my trade.

"All right," I said. "I'll admit it was a woman. I'll admit she must have been up there while he was dead, if that makes you happy. I guess it was just shock that made her run away."

"Oh sure," Flack said nastily. The fat sneer was all the way home now. "Or maybe she hadn't ice-picked a guy in a month. Kind of lost touch."

"But why would she take his key?" I said, talking to myself. "And why leave it at the desk? Why not just walk away and leave the whole thing? What if she did think she had to lock the door? Why not drop the key in a sand jar and cover it up? Or take it away with her and lose it? Why do anything with

that key that would connect her with that room?" I brought
my eyes down and gave Flack a thick leaden stare. "Unless of
course she was seen to leave the room—with the key in her
hand—and followed out of the hotel."

"What for would anybody do that?" Flack asked.

"Because whoever saw her could have got into that room at
once. He had a passkey."

Flack's eyes flicked up at me and dropped all in one
motion.

"So he must have followed her," I said. "He must have
seen her dump the key at the desk and stroll out of the hotel
and he must have followed her a little further than that."

Flack said derisively: "What makes you so wonderful?"

I leaned down and pulled the telephone towards me. "I'd
better call Christy and get this over with," I said. "The more I
think about it the scareder I get. Maybe she did kill him.
I can't cover up for a murderer."

I took the receiver off the hook. Flack slammed his moist
paw down hard on top of my hand. The phone jumped on
the desk. "Lay off." His voice was almost a sob. "I followed
her to a car parked down the street. Got the number. Christ
sake, pal, give me some kind of a break." He was fumbling
wildly in his pockets. "Know what I make on this job? Cigarette and cigar money and hardly a dime more. Wait a minute
now. I think—" He looked down and played solitaire with
some dirty envelopes, finally selected one and tossed it over
to me. "License number," he said wearily, "and if it's any
satisfaction to you, I can't even remember what it was."

I looked down at the envelope. There was a scrawled license number on it all right. Ill-written and faint and oblique,
the way it would be written hastily on a paper held in a man's
hand on the street. 6N333. California 1947.

"Satisfied?" This was Flack's voice. Or it came out of his
mouth. I tore the number off and tossed the envelope back to
him.

"4P 327," I said, watching his eyes. Nothing flicked in
them. No trace of derision or concealment. "But how do I
know this isn't just some license number you had already?"

"You just got to take my word for it."

"Describe the car," I said.

"Caddy convertible, not new, top up. About 1942 model. Sort of dusty blue color."

"Describe the woman."

"Want a lot for your dough, don't you, peeper?"

"Dr. Hambleton's dough."

He winced. "All right. Blonde. White coat with some colored stitching on it. Wide blue straw hat. Dark glasses. Height about five two. Built like a Conover model."

"Would you know her again—without the glasses?" I asked carefully.

He pretended to think. Then shook his head, no.

"What was that license number again, Flackie?" I caught him off guard.

"Which one?" he said.

I leaned across the desk and dropped some cigarette ash on his gun. I did some more staring into his eyes. But I knew he was licked now. He seemed to know too. He reached for his gun, blew off the ash and put it back in the drawer of his desk.

"Go on. Beat it," he said between his teeth. "Tell the cops I frisked the stiff. So what? Maybe I lose a job. Maybe I get tossed in the fishbowl. So what? When I come out I'm solid. Little Flackie don't have to worry about coffee and crullers. Don't think for a minute those dark cheaters fool little Flackie. I've seen too many movies to miss that lovely puss. And if you ask me that babe'll be around for a long time. She's a comer—and who knows—" he leered at me triumphantly—"she'd need a bodyguard one of these days. A guy to have around, watch things, keep her out of jams. Somebody that knows the ropes and ain't unreasonable about dough. . . . What's the matter?"

I had put my head on one side and was leaning forward. I was listening. "I thought I heard a church bell," I said.

"There ain't any church around here," he said contemptuously. "It's that platinum brain of yours getting cracks in it."

"Just one bell," I said. "Very slow. Tolling is the word, I believe."

Flack listened with me. "I don't hear anything," he said sharply.

"Oh you wouldn't hear it," I said. "You'd be the one guy in the whole world who wouldn't hear it."

He just sat there and stared at me with his nasty little eyes half closed and his nasty little mustache shining. One of his hands twitched on the desk, an aimless movement.

I left him to his thoughts, which were probably as small, ugly and frightened as the man himself.

## 12

The apartment house was over on Doheny Drive, just down the hill from the Strip. It was really two buildings, one behind the other, loosely connected by a floored patio with a fountain, and a room built over the arch. There were mailboxes and bells in the imitation marble foyer. Three out of the sixteen had no names over them. The names that I read meant nothing to me. The job needed a little more work. I tried the front door, found it unlocked, and the job still needed more work.

Outside stood two Cadillacs, a Lincoln Continental and a Packard Clipper. Neither of the Cadillacs had the right color or license. Across the way a guy in riding breeches was sprawled with his legs over the door of a low-cut Lancia. He was smoking and looking up at the pale stars which know enough to keep their distance from Hollywood. I walked up the steep hill to the boulevard and a block east and smothered myself in an outdoor sweat-box phone booth. I dialed a man named Peoria Smith, who was so-called because he stuttered—another little mystery I hadn't had time to work out.

"Mavis Weld," I said. "Phone number. This is Marlowe."

"S-s-s-ure," he said. "M-M-Mavis Weld huh? You want h-h-her ph-ph-phone number?"

"How much?"

"Be-b-b-be ten b-b-b-bucks," he said.

"Just forget I called," I said.

"W-W-Wait a minute! I ain't supposed to give out with

them b-b-babes' phone numbers. An assistant prop man is taking a hell of a chance."

I waited and breathed back my own breath.

"The address goes with it naturally," Peoria whined, forgetting to stutter.

"Five bucks," I said. "I've got the address already. And don't haggle. If you think you're the only studio grifter in the business of selling unlisted telephone numbers—"

"Hold it," he said wearily, and went to get his little red book. A left-handed stutterer. He only stuttered when he wasn't excited. He came back and gave it to me. A Crestview number of course. If you don't have a Crestview number in Hollywood you're a bum.

I opened up the steel-and-glass cell to let in some air while I dialed again. After two rings a drawling sexy voice answered. I pulled the door shut.

"Ye-e-e-s," the voice cooed.

"Miss Weld, please."

"And who is calling Miss Weld if you please?"

"I have some stills Whitey wants me to deliver tonight."

"Whitey? And who is Whitey, amigo?"

"The head still-photographer at the studio," I said. "Don't you know that much? I'll come up if you'll tell me which apartment. I'm only a couple of blocks away."

"Miss Weld is taking a bath." She laughed. I guess it was a silvery tinkle where she was. It sounded like somebody putting away saucepans where I was. "But of course bring up the photographs. I am sure she is dying to see them. The apartment number is fourteen."

"Will you be there too?"

"But of course. But naturally. Why do you ask that?"

I hung up and staggered out into the fresh air. I went down the hill. The guy in the riding breeches was still hanging out of the Lancia but one of the Cadillacs was gone and two Buick convertibles had joined the cars in front. I pushed the bell to number fourteen, went on through the patio where scarlet Chinese honeysuckle was lit by a peanut spotlight. Another light glowed down on the big ornamental pool full of fat goldfish and silent lily pads, the lilies folded tight for the night. There were a couple of stone seats and a lawn swing. The place didn't look very expensive except that every place was expensive that year. The apartment was on the second floor, one of two doors facing across a wide landing.

The bell chimed and a tall dark girl in jodhpurs opened the door. Sexy was very faint praise for her. The jodhpurs, like her hair, were coal black. She wore a white silk shirt with a scarlet scarf loose around her throat. It was not as vivid as her mouth. She held a long brown cigarette in a pair of tiny golden tweezers. The fingers holding it were more than adequately jeweled. Her black hair was parted in the middle and a line of scalp as white as snow went over the top of her head and dropped out of sight behind. Two thick braids of her shining black hair lay one on each side of her slim brown neck. Each was tied with a small scarlet bow. But it was a long time since she was a little girl.

She looked sharply down at my empty hands. Studio stills are usually a little too big to put in your pocket.

I said: "Miss Weld please."

"You can give me the stills." The voice was cool, drawling and insolent, but the eyes were something else. She looked almost as hard to get as a haircut.

"For Miss Weld personally. Sorry."

"I told you she was taking a bath."

"I'll wait."

"Are you quite sure you have the stills, amigo?"

"As sure as I'll ever be. Why?"

"Your name?" Her voice froze on the second word, like a feather taking off in a sudden draft. Then it cooed and hovered and soared and eddied and the silent invitation of a smile picked delicately at the corners of her lips, very slowly, like a child trying to pick up a snowflake.

"Your last picture was wonderful, Miss Gonzales."

The smile flashed like lightning and changed her whole face. The body came erect and vibrant with delight. "But it was stinking," she glowed. "Positively God-damned stinking, you sweet lovely man. You know but positively God-damn well it was stinking."

"Nothing with you in it stinks for me, Miss Gonzales."

She stood away from the door and waved me in. "We will

have a drink," she said. "The God-damnest drink we will have. I adore flattery, however dishonest."

I went in. A gun in the kidney wouldn't have surprised me a bit. She stood so that I had to practically push her mammaries out of the way to get through the door. She smelled the way the Taj Mahal looks by moonlight. She closed the door and danced over to a small portable bar.

"Scotch? Or would you prefer a mixed drink? I mix a perfectly loathsome Martini," she said.

"Scotch is fine, thanks."

She made a couple of drinks in a couple of glasses you could almost have stood umbrellas in. I sat down in a chintz chair and looked around. The place was old-fashioned. It had a false fireplace with gas logs and a marble mantel, cracks in the plaster, a couple of vigorously colored daubs on the walls that looked lousy enough to have cost money, an old black chipped Steinway and for once no Spanish shawl on it. There were a lot of new-looking books in bright jackets scattered around and a double-barreled shotgun with a handsomely carved stock stood in the corner with a white satin bow tied around the barrels. Hollywood wit.

The dark lady in the jodhpurs handed me a glass and perched on the arm of my chair. "You may call me Dolores if you wish," she said, taking a hearty swig out of her own tumbler.

"Thanks."

"And what may I call you?"

I grinned.

"Of course," she said, "I am most fully aware that you are a God-damn liar and that you have no stills in your pockets. Not that I wish to inquire into your no doubt very private business."

"Yeah?" I inhaled a couple of inches of my liquor. "Just what kind of bath is Miss Weld taking? An old-fashioned soap or something with Arabian spices in it?"

She waved the remains of the brown cigarette in the small gold clasp. "Perhaps you would like to help her. The bathroom is over there—through the arch and to the right. Most probably the door is not locked."

"Not if it's that easy," I said.

"Oh," she gave me the brilliant smile again. "You like to do the difficult things in life. I must remember to be less approachable, must I not?" She removed herself elegantly from the arm of my chair and ditched her cigarette, bending over enough so that I could trace the outline of her hips.

"Don't bother, Miss Gonzales. I'm just a guy who came here on business. I don't have any idea of raping anybody."

"No?" The smile became soft, lazy and, if you can't think of a better word, provocative.

"But I'm sure as hell working up to it," I said.

"You are an amusing son-of-a-bitch," she said with a shrug and went off through the arch, carrying her half-quart of Scotch and water with her. I heard a gentle tapping on a door and her voice: "Darling, there's a man here who says he has some stills from the studio. He says. Muy simpático. Muy guapo también. Con cojones."

A voice I had heard before said sharply: "Shut up, you little bitch. I'll be out in a second."

The Gonzales came back through the archway humming. Her glass was empty. She went to the bar again. "But you are not drinking," she cried, looking at my glass.

"I ate dinner. I only have a two-quart stomach anyway. I understand a little Spanish."

She tossed her head. "You are shocked?" Her eyes rolled. Her shoulders did a fan dance.

"I'm pretty hard to shock."

"But you heard what I said? Madre de Dios. I'm so terribly sorry."

"I'll bet," I said.

She finished making herself another highball.

"Yes. I am so sorry," she sighed. "That is, I think I am. Sometimes I am not sure. Sometimes I do not give a good god-damn. It is so confusing. All my friends tell me I am far too outspoken. I do shock you, don't I?" She was on the arm of my chair again.

"No. But if I wanted to be shocked I'd know right where to come." She reached her glass behind her indolently and leaned towards me.

"But I do not live here," she said. "I live at the Chateau Bercy."

"Alone?"

She slapped me delicately across the tip of my nose. The next thing I knew I had her in my lap and she was trying to bite a piece off my tongue. "You are a very sweet son-of-a-bitch," she said. Her mouth was as hot as ever a mouth was. Her lips burned like dry ice. Her tongue was driving hard against my teeth. Her eyes looked enormous and black and the whites showed under them.

"I am so tired," she whispered into my mouth. "I am so worn, so incredibly tired."

I felt her hand in my breast pocket. I shoved her off hard, but she had my wallet. She danced away with it laughing, flicked it open and went through it with fingers that darted like little snakes.

"So glad you two got acquainted," a voice off to one side said coolly. Mavis Weld stood in the archway.

Her hair was fluffed out carelessly and she hadn't bothered with make-up. She wore a hostess gown and very little else. Her legs ended in little green and silver slippers. Her eyes were empty, her lips contemptuous. But she was the same girl all right, dark glasses on or off.

The Gonzales gave her a quick darting glance, closed my wallet and tossed it. I caught it and put it away. She strolled to a table and picked up a black bag with a long strap, hooked it over her shoulder and moved towards the door.

Mavis Weld didn't move, didn't look at her. She looked at me. But there was no emotion of any kind in her face. The Gonzales opened the door and glanced outside and almost closed it and turned.

"The name is Philip Marlowe," she said to Mavis Weld. "Nice don't you think?"

"I didn't know you bothered to ask them their names," Mavis Weld said. "You so seldom know them long enough."

"I see," the Gonzales answered gently. She turned and smiled at me faintly. "Such a charming way to call a girl a whore, don't you think?"

Mavis Weld said nothing. Her face had no expression.

"At least," the Gonzales said smoothly as she pulled the door open again, "I haven't been sleeping with any gunmen lately."

"Are you sure you can remember?" Mavis Weld asked her in exactly the same tone. "Open the door, honey. This is the day we put the garbage out."

The Gonzales looked back at her slowly, levelly, and with a knife in her eyes. Then she made a faint sound with her lips and teeth and yanked the door wide. It closed behind her with a jarring smash. The noise didn't even flicker the steady dark-blue glare in Mavis Weld's eyes.

"Now suppose you do the same—but more quietly," she said.

I got out a handkerchief and scrubbed the lipstick over my face. It looked exactly the color of blood, fresh blood. "That could happen to anybody," I said. "I wasn't petting her. She was petting me."

She marched to the door and heaved it open. "On your way, dreamboat. Make with the feet."

"I came here on business, Miss Weld."

"Yes. I can imagine. Out. I don't know you. I don't want to know you. And if I did, this wouldn't be either the day or the hour."

"Never the time and place and the loved one all together," I said.

"What's that?" She tried to throw me out with the point of her chin, but even she wasn't that good.

"Browning. The poet, not the automatic. I feel sure you'd prefer the automatic."

"Look little man, do I have to call the manager to bounce you downstairs like a basketball?"

I went over and pushed the door shut. She held on to the last moment. She didn't quite kick me, but it cost her an effort not to. I tried to ease her away from the door without appearing to. She didn't ease worth a darn. She stood her ground, one hand still reaching for the doorknob, her eyes full of dark-blue rage.

"If you're going to stand that close to me," I said, "maybe you'd better put some clothes on."

She took her hand back and swung it hard. The slap sounded like Miss Gonzales slamming the door, but it stung. And it reminded me of the sore place on the back of my head.

"Did I hurt you?" she said softly.

I nodded.

"That's fine." She hauled off and slapped me again, harder if anything. "I think you'd better kiss me," she breathed. Her eyes were clear and limpid and melting. I glanced down casually. Her right hand was balled into a very businesslike fist. It wasn't too small to work with, either.

"Believe me," I said. "There's only one reason I don't. Even if you had your little black gun with you. Or the brass knuckles you probably keep on your night table."

She smiled politely.

"I might just happen to be working for you," I said. "And I don't go whoring around after every pair of legs I see." I looked down at hers. I could see them all right and the flag that marked the goal line was no larger than it had to be. She pulled the hostess gown together and turned and walked over to the little bar shaking her head.

"I'm free, white and twenty-one," she said. "I've seen all the approaches there are. I think I have. If I can't scare you, lick you, or seduce you, what the hell can I buy you with?"

"Well—"

"Don't tell me," she interrupted sharply and turned with a glass in her hand. She drank and tossed the loose hair around and smiled a thin little smile. "Money, of course. How damned stupid of me to overlook that."

"Money would help," I said.

Her mouth twisted in wry disgust but the voice was almost affectionate. "How much money?"

"Oh a hundred bucks would do to start with."

"You're cheap. It's a cheap little bastard, isn't it? A hundred bucks it says. Is a hundred bucks money in your circle, darling?"

"Make it two hundred then. I could retire on that."

"Still cheap. Every week of course. In a nice clean envelope?"

"You could skip the envelope. I'd only get it dirty."

"And just what would I get for this money, my charming little gum-shoe? I'm quite sure of what you are, of course."

"You'd get a receipt. Who told you I was a gum-shoe?"

She stared out of her own eyes for a brief instant before the act dropped over her again. "It must have been the smell." She sipped her drink and stared at me over it with a faint smile of contempt.

"I'm beginning to think you write your own dialogue," I said. "I've been wondering just what was the matter with it."

I ducked. A few drops splattered me. The glass splintered on the wall behind me. The broken pieces fell soundlessly.

"And with that," she said, completely calm, "I believe I must have used up my entire stock of girlish charm."

I went over and picked up my hat. "I never thought *you* killed him," I said. "But it would help to have some sort of reason for not telling you were there. It's a help to have enough money for a retainer just to establish myself. And enough information to justify my accepting the retainer."

She picked a cigarette out of a box, tossed it in the air, caught it between her lips effortlessly and lit it with a match that came from nowhere.

"My goodness. Am I supposed to have killed somebody?" she asked. I was still holding the hat. It made me feel foolish. I don't know why. I put it on and started for the door.

"I trust you have carfare home," the contemptuous voice said behind me.

I didn't answer. I just kept going. When I had the door ready to open she said: "I also trust Miss Gonzales gave you her address and phone number. You should be able to get almost anything out of her—including, I am told, money."

I let go of the doorknob and went back across the room fast. She stood her ground and the smile on her lips didn't slip a millimeter.

"Look," I said. "You're going to find this hard to believe. But I came over here with the quaint idea that you might be a girl who needed some help—and would find it rather hard to get anyone you could bank on. I figured you went to that hotel room to make some kind of a pay-off. And the fact that you went by yourself and took chances on being recognized—and *were* recognized by a house dick whose standard of ethics would take about as much strain as a very tired old cobweb—all this made me think you might be in one of those Hollywood jams that really mean curtains. But you're not in any jam. You're right up front under the baby spot pulling every tired ham gesture you ever used in the most tired B-picture you ever acted in—if acting is the word—"

"Shut up," she said, between teeth so tight they grated. "Shut up, you slimy, blackmailing keyhole peeper."

"You don't need me," I said. "You don't need anybody. You're so God-damn smart you could talk your way out of a safe-deposit box. Okay. Go ahead and talk your way out. I won't stop you. Just don't make me listen to it. I'd burst out crying to think a mere slip of an innocent little girl like you should be so clever. You do things to me, honey. Just like Margaret O'Brien."

She didn't move or breathe when I reached the door, nor when I opened it. I don't know why. The stuff wasn't *that* good.

I went down the stairs and across the court and out of the front door, almost bumping into a slim dark-eyed man who was standing there lighting a cigarette.

"Excuse me," he said quietly, "I'm afraid I'm in your way."

I started to go around him, then I noticed that his lifted right hand held a key. I reached out and snapped it out of his hand for no reason at all. I looked at the number stamped on it. No. 14. Mavis Weld's apartment. I threw it off behind some bushes.

"You don't need that," I said. "The door isn't locked."

"Of course," he said. There was a peculiar smile on his face. "How stupid of me."

"Yeah," I said. "We're both stupid. Anybody's stupid that bothers with that tramp."

"I wouldn't quite say that," he answered quietly, his small sad eyes watching me without any particular expression.

"You don't have to," I said. "I just said it for you. I beg your pardon. I'll get your key." I went over behind the bushes, picked it up and handed it to him.

"Thank you very much," he said. "And by the way—" He stopped. I stopped. "I hope I don't interrupt an interesting quarrel," he said. "I should hate to do that. No?" He smiled. "Well, since Miss Weld is a friend in common, may I introduce myself. My name is Steelgrave. Haven't I seen you somewhere?"

"No you haven't seen me anywhere, Mr. Steelgrave," I said. "My name's Marlowe, Philip Marlowe. It's extremely unlikely that we've met. And strange to relate I never heard of you, Mr. Steelgrave. And I wouldn't give a damn, even if your name was Weepy Moyer." I never knew quite why I said that. There was nothing to make me say it, except that the name had been mentioned. A peculiar stillness came over his face. A peculiar fixed look in his silent black eyes. He took the cigarette out of his mouth, looked at the tip, flicked a little ash off it, although there was no ash to flick off, looking down as he said: "Weepy Moyer? Peculiar name. I don't think I ever heard that. Is he somebody I should know?"

"Not unless you're unusually fond of ice picks," I said, and left him. I went on down the steps, crossed to my car, looked back before I got in. He was standing there looking down at me, the cigarette between his lips. From that distance I couldn't see whether there was any expression on his face. He didn't move or make any kind of gesture when I looked back at him. He didn't even turn away. He just stood there. I got in and drove off.

# 13

I drove east on Sunset but I didn't go home. At La Brea I turned north and swung over to Highland, out over Cahuenga Pass and down on to Ventura Boulevard, past Studio City and Sherman Oaks and Encino. There was nothing lonely about the trip. There never is on that road. Fast boys in stripped-down Fords shot in and out of the traffic streams, missing fenders by a sixteenth of an inch, but somehow always missing them. Tired men in dusty coupés and sedans winced and tightened their grip on the wheel and ploughed on north and west towards home and dinner, an evening with the sports page, the blatting of the radio, the whining of their spoiled children and the gabble of their silly wives. I drove on past the gaudy neons and the false fronts behind them, the sleazy hamburger joints that look like palaces under the colors, the circular drive-ins as gay as circuses with the chipper hard-eyed car-hops, the brilliant counters, and the sweaty greasy kitchens that would have poisoned a toad. Great double trucks rumbled down over Sepulveda from Wilmington and San Pedro and crossed towards the Ridge Route, starting up in low-low from the traffic lights with a growl of lions in the zoo.

Behind Encino an occasional light winked from the hills through thick trees. The homes of screen stars. Screen stars, phooey. The veterans of a thousand beds. Hold it, Marlowe, you're not human tonight.

The air got cooler. The highway narrowed. The cars were so few now that the headlights hurt. The grade rose against chalk walls and at the top a breeze, unbroken from the ocean, danced casually across the night.

I ate dinner at a place near Thousand Oaks. Bad but quick. Feed 'em and throw 'em out. Lots of business. We can't bother with you sitting over your second cup of coffee, mister. You're using money space. See those people over there behind the rope? They want to eat. Anyway they think they have to. God knows why they want to eat here. They could do better home out of a can. They're just restless. Like you. They have to get the car out and go somewhere. Sucker-bait for the racketeers that have taken over the restaurants. Here we go again. You're not human tonight, Marlowe.

I paid off and stopped in a bar to drop a brandy on top of the New York cut. Why New York, I thought. It was Detroit where they made machine tools. I stepped out into the night air that nobody had yet found out how to option. But a lot of people were probably trying. They'd get around to it.

I drove on to the Oxnard cut-off and turned back along the ocean. The big eight-wheelers and sixteen-wheelers were streaming north, all hung over with orange lights. On the right the great fat solid Pacific trudging into shore like a scrubwoman going home. No moon, no fuss, hardly a sound of the surf. No smell. None of the harsh wild smell of the sea. A California ocean. California, the department-store state. The most of everything and the best of nothing. Here we go again. You're not human tonight, Marlowe.

All right. Why would I be? I'm sitting in that office, playing with a dead fly and in pops this dowdy little item from Manhattan, Kansas, and chisels me down to a shop-worn twenty to find her brother. He sounds like a creep but she wants to find him. So with this fortune clasped to my chest, I trundle down to Bay City and the routine I go through is so tired I'm half asleep on my feet. I meet nice people, with and without ice picks in their necks. I leave, and I leave myself wide-open too. Then she comes in and takes the twenty away from me and gives me a kiss and gives it back to me because I didn't do a full day's work.

So I go see Dr. Hambleton, retired (and how) optometrist from El Centro, and meet again the new style in neckwear. And I don't tell the cops. I just frisk the customer's toupee and put on an act. Why? Who am I cutting my throat for this time? A blonde with sexy eyes and too many door keys? A girl from Manhattan, Kansas? I don't know. All I know is that something isn't what it seems and the old tired but always reliable hunch tells me that if the hand is played the way it is dealt the wrong person is going to lose the pot. Is that my business? Well, what is my business? Do I know? Did I ever know? Let's not go into that. You're not human tonight, Marlowe. Maybe I never was or ever will be. Maybe I'm an ectoplasm with a private license. Maybe we all get like this in the cold half-lit world where always the wrong thing happens and never the right.

Malibu. More movie stars. More pink and blue bathtubs. More tufted beds. More Chanel No. 5. More Lincoln Continentals and Cadillacs. More wind-blown hair and sunglasses and attitudes and pseudo-refined voices and waterfront morals. Now, wait a minute. Lots of nice people work in pictures. You've got the wrong attitude, Marlowe. You're not human tonight.

I smelled Los Angeles before I got to it. It smelled stale and old like a living room that had been closed too long. But the colored lights fooled you. The lights were wonderful. There ought to be a monument to the man who invented neon lights. Fifteen stories high, solid marble. There's a boy who really made something out of nothing.

So I went to a picture show and it had to have Mavis Weld
in it. One of those glass-and-chromium deals where everybody smiled too much and talked too much and knew it. The
women were always going up a long curving staircase to
change their clothes. The men were always taking monogrammed cigarettes out of expensive cases and snapping
expensive lighters at each other. And the help was round-
shouldered from carrying trays with drinks across the terrace
to a swimming pool about the size of Lake Huron but a lot
neater.

The leading man was an amiable ham with a lot of charm,
some of it turning a little yellow at the edges. The star was a
bad-tempered brunette with contemptuous eyes and a couple
of bad close-ups that showed her pushing forty-five backwards almost hard enough to break a wrist. Mavis Weld
played second lead and she played it with wraps on. She was
good, but she could have been ten times better. But if she
had been ten times better half her scenes would have been
yanked out to protect the star. It was as neat a bit of tightrope
walking as I ever saw. Well it wouldn't be a tightrope she'd be
walking from now on. It would be a piano wire. It would
be very high. And there wouldn't be any net under it.

# 14

I had a reason for going back to the office. A special-delivery
letter with an orange claim check ought to have arrived there
by now. Most of the windows were dark in the building, but
not all. People work nights in other businesses than mine. The
elevator man said "Howdy" from the depths of his throat and
trundled me up. The corridor had lighted open doors where
the scrubwomen were still cleaning up the débris of the
wasted hours. I turned a corner past the slobbery hum of a
vacuum cleaner, let myself into my dark office and opened the
windows. I sat there at the desk doing nothing, not even
thinking. No special-delivery letter. All the noise of the building, except the vacuum cleaner, seemed to have flowed out

into the street and lost itself among the turning wheels of innumerable cars. Then somewhere along the hall outside a man started whistling "Lili Marlene" with elegance and virtuosity. I knew who that was. The night man checking office doors. I switched the desk lamp on and he passed without trying mine. His steps went away, then came back with a different sound, more of a shuffle. The buzzer sounded in the other office which was still unlocked. That would be special delivery. I went out to get it, only it wasn't.

A fat man in sky-blue pants was closing the door with that beautiful leisure only fat men ever achieve. He wasn't alone, but I looked at him first. He was a large man and wide. Not young nor handsome, but he looked durable. Above the sky-blue gabardine slacks he wore a two-tone leisure jacket which would have been revolting on a zebra. The neck of his canary-yellow shirt was open wide, which it had to be if his neck was going to get out. He was hatless and his large head was decorated with a reasonable amount of pale salmon-colored hair. His nose had been broken but well set and it hadn't been a collector's item in the first place.

The creature with him was a weedy number with red eyes and sniffles. Age about twenty, five feet nine, thin as a broom straw. His nose twitched and his mouth twitched and his hands twitched and he looked very unhappy.

The big man smiled genially. "Mr. Marlowe, no doubt?"

I said: "Who else?"

"It's a little late for a business call," the big man said and hid half the office by spreading out his hands. "I hope you don't mind. Or do you already have all the business you can handle?"

"Don't kid me. My nerves are frayed," I said. "Who's the junky?"

"Come along, Alfred," the big man said to his companion. "And stop acting girlish."

"In a pig's valise," Alfred told him.

The big man turned to me placidly. "Why do all these punks keep saying that? It isn't funny. It isn't witty. It doesn't mean anything. Quite a problem, this Alfred. I got him off the stuff, you know, temporarily at least. Say 'how do you do' to Mr. Marlowe, Alfred."

"Screw him," Alfred said.

The big man sighed. "My name's Toad," he said. "Joseph P. Toad."

I didn't say anything.

"Go ahead and laugh," the big man said. "I'm used to it. Had the name all my life." He came towards me with his hand out. I took it. The big man smiled pleasantly into my eyes. "O.K. Alfred," he said without looking back.

Alfred made what seemed to be a very slight and unimportant movement at the end of which a heavy automatic was pointing at me.

"Careful, Alfred," the big man said, holding my hand with a grip that would have bent a girder. "Not yet."

"In a pig's valise," Alfred said. The gun pointed at my chest. His finger tightened around the trigger. I watched it tighten. I knew at precisely what moment that tightening would release the hammer. It didn't seem to make any difference. This was happening somewhere else in a cheesy program picture. It wasn't happening to me.

The hammer of the automatic clicked dryly on nothing. Alfred lowered the gun with a grunt of annoyance and it disappeared whence it had come. He started to twitch again. There was nothing nervous about his movements with the gun. I wondered just what junk he was off of.

The big man let go of my hand, the genial smile still over his large healthy face.

He patted a pocket. "I got the magazine," he said. "Alfred ain't reliable lately. The little bastard might have shot you."

Alfred sat down in a chair and tilted it against the wall and breathed through his mouth.

I let my heels down on the floor again.

"I bet he scared you," Joseph P. Toad said.

I tasted salt on my tongue.

"You ain't so tough," Toad said, poking me in the stomach with a fat finger.

I stepped away from the finger and watched his eyes.

"What does it cost?" he asked almost gently.

"Let's go into my parlor," I said.

I turned my back on him and walked through the door into the other office. It was hard work but I made it. I sweat all

the way. I went around behind the desk and stood there waiting. Mr. Toad followed me in placidly. The junky came
twitching in behind him.

"You don't have a comic book around, do you?" Toad
asked. "Keeps him quiet."

"Sit down," I said. "I'll look."

He reached for the chair arms. I jerked a drawer open and
got my hand around the butt of a Luger. I brought it up
slowly, looking at Alfred. Alfred didn't even look at me. He
was studying the corner of the ceiling and trying to keep his
mouth out of his eye.

"This is as comic as I get," I said.

"You won't need that," the big man said, genially.

"That's fine," I said, like somebody else talking, far away
behind a wall. I could just barely hear the words. "But if I do,
here it is. And this one's loaded. Want me to prove it to you?"

The big man looked as near worried as he would ever look.
"I'm sorry you take it like that," he said. "I'm so used to
Alfred I hardly notice him. Maybe you're right. Maybe I
ought to do something about him."

"Yeah," I said. "Do it this afternoon before you come up
here. It's too late now."

"Now wait a minute, Mr. Marlowe." He put his hand out.
I slashed at it with the Luger. He was fast, but not fast
enough. I cut the back of his hand open with the sight on the
gun. He grabbed at it and sucked at the cut. "Hey, please!
Alfred's my nephew. My sister's kid. I kind of look after him.
He wouldn't hurt a fly, really."

"Next time you come up I'll have one for him not to hurt,"
I said.

"Now don't be like that, mister. Please don't be like that.
I've got quite a nice little proposition—"

"Shut up," I said. I sat down very slowly. My face burned. I
had difficulty speaking clearly at all. I felt a little drunk. I said,
slowly and thickly: "A friend of mine told me about a fellow
that had something like this pulled on him. He was at a desk
the way I am. He had a gun, just the way I have. There were
two men on the other side of the desk, like you and Alfred.
The man on my side began to get mad. He couldn't help
himself. He began to shake. He couldn't speak a word. He

just had this gun in his hand. So without a word he shot twice under the desk, right where your belly is."

The big man turned a sallow green color and started to get up. But he changed his mind. He got a violent-looking handkerchief out of his pocket and mopped his face. "You seen that in a picture," he said.

"That's right," I said. "But the man who made the picture told me where he got the idea. *That* wasn't in any picture." I put the Luger down on the desk in front of me and said in a more natural voice: "You've got to be careful about firearms, Mr. Toad. You never know but what it may upset a man to have an Army .45 snapped in his face—especially when he doesn't know it's not loaded. It made me kind of nervous for a minute. I haven't had a shot of morphine since lunch time."

Toad studied me carefully with narrow eyes. The junky got up and went to another chair and kicked it around and sat down and tilted his greasy head against the wall. But his nose and hands kept on twitching.

"I heard you were kind of hard-boiled," Toad said slowly, his eyes cool and watchful.

"You heard wrong. I'm a very sensitive guy. I go all to pieces over nothing."

"Yeah. I understand." He stared at me a long time without speaking. "Maybe we played this wrong. Mind if I put my hand in my pocket? I don't wear a gun."

"Go ahead," I said. "It would give me the greatest possible pleasure to see you try to pull a gun."

He frowned, then very slowly got out a flat pigskin wallet and drew out a crisp new one-hundred-dollar bill. He laid it on the edge of the glass top, drew out another just like it, then one by one three more. He laid them carefully in a row along the desk, end to end. Alfred let his chair settle to the floor and stared at the money with his mouth quivering.

"Five C's," the big man said. He folded his wallet and put it away. I watched every movement he made. "For nothing at all but keeping the nose clean. Check?"

I just looked at him.

"You ain't looking for nobody," the big man said. "You couldn't find nobody. You don't have time to work for nobody. You didn't hear a thing or see a thing. You're clean. Five C's clean. Okay?"

There was no sound in the office but Alfred's sniffling. The big man half turned his head. "Quiet Alfred. I'll give you a shot when we leave," the big man told him. "Try to act nice." He sucked again at the cut on the back of his hand.

"With you for a model that ought to be easy," I said.

"Screw you," Alfred said.

"Limited vocabulary," the big man told me. "Very limited. Get the idea, chum?" He indicated the money. I fingered the butt of the Luger. He leaned forward a little. "Relax, can't you. It's simple. This is a retainer. You don't do a thing for it. Nothing is what you do. If you keep on doing nothing for a reasonable length of time you get the same amount later on. That's simple, isn't it?"

"And who am I doing this nothing for?" I asked.

"Me. Joseph P. Toad."

"What's your racket?"

"Business representative, you might call me."

"What else could I call you? Besides what I could think up myself?"

"You could call me a guy that wants to help out a guy that don't want to make trouble for a guy."

"And what could I call that lovable character?" I asked.

Joseph P. Toad gathered the five hundred-dollar bills together, lined up the edges neatly and pushed the packet across the desk. "You can call him a guy that would rather spill money than blood," he said. "But he don't mind spilling blood if it looks like that's what he's got to do."

"How is he with an ice pick?" I asked. "I can see how lousy he is with a .45."

The big man chewed his lower lip, then pulled it out with a blunt forefinger and thumb and nibbled on the inside of it softly, like a milch cow chewing her cud. "We're not talking about ice picks," he said at length. "All we're talking about is how you might get off on the wrong foot and do yourself a lot of harm. Whereas if you don't get off on no foot at all, you're sitting pretty and money coming in."

"Who is the blonde?" I asked.

He thought about that and nodded. "Maybe you're into

this too far already," he sighed. "Maybe it's too late to do business."

After a moment he leaned forward and said gently: "Okay. I'll check back with my principal and see how far out he wants to come. Maybe we can still do business. Everything stands as it is until you hear from me. Check?"

I let him have that one. He put his hands on the desk and very slowly stood up, watching the gun I was pushing around on the blotter.

"You can keep the dough," he said. "Come on, Alfred." He turned and walked solidly out of the office.

Alfred's eyes crawled sideways watching him, then jerked to the money on the desk. The big automatic appeared with the same magic in his thin right hand. Dartingly as an eel he moved over to the desk. He kept the gun on me and reached for the money with his left hand. It disappeared into his pocket. He gave me a smooth cool empty grin, nodded and moved away, apparently not realizing for a moment that I was holding a gun too.

"Come on, Alfred," the big man called sharply from outside the door. Alfred slipped through the door and was gone.

The outer door opened and closed. Steps went along the hall. Then silence. I sat there thinking back over it, trying to make up my mind whether it was pure idiocy or just a new way to toss a scare.

Five minutes later the telephone rang.

A thick pleasant voice said: "Oh by the way, Mr. Marlowe, I guess you know Sherry Ballou, don't you?"

"Nope."

"Sheridan Ballou, Incorporated. The big agent? You ought to look him up sometime."

I held the phone silently for a moment. Then I said: "Is he her agent?"

"He might be," Joseph P. Toad said, and paused a moment. "I suppose you realize we're just a couple of bit players, Mr. Marlowe. That's all. Just a couple of bit players. Somebody wanted to find out a little something about you. It seemed the simplest way to do it. Now, I'm not so sure."

I didn't answer. He hung up. Almost at once the phone rang again.

A seductive voice said: "You do not like me so well, do you, amigo?"

"Sure I do. Just don't keep biting me."

"I am at home at the Chateau Bercy. I am lonely."

"Call an escort bureau."

"But please. That is no way to talk. This is business of a great importance."

"I bet. But not the business I'm in."

"That slut— What does she say about me?" she hissed.

"Nothing. Oh, she might have called you a Tijuana hooker in riding pants. Would you mind?"

That amused her. The silvery giggle went on for a little while. "Always the wisecrack with you. Is it not so? But you see I did not then know you were a detective. That makes a very big difference."

I could have told her how wrong she was. I just said: "Miss Gonzales, you said something about business. What kind of business, if you're not kidding me?"

"Would you like to make a great deal of money? A very great deal of money?"

"You mean without getting shot?" I asked.

Her incaught breath came over the wire. "Sí," she said thoughtfully. "There is also that to consider. But you are so brave, so big, so—"

"I'll be at my office at nine in the morning, Miss Gonzales. I'll be a lot braver then. Now if you'll excuse me—"

"You have a date? Is she beautiful? More beautiful than I am?"

"For Christ's sake," I said. "Don't you ever think of anything but one thing?"

"The hell with you, darling," she said and hung up in my face.

I turned the lights out and left. Halfway down the hall I met a man looking at numbers. He had a special delivery in his hand. So I had to go back to the office and put it in the safe. And the phone rang again while I was doing this.

I let it ring. I had had enough for one day. I just didn't care. It could have been the Queen of Sheba with her cellophane pajamas on—or off—I was too tired to bother. My brain felt like a bucket of wet sand.

It was still ringing as I reached the door. No use. I had to go back. Instinct was stronger than weariness. I lifted the receiver.

Orfamay Quest's twittery little voice said: "Oh Mr. Marlowe I've been trying to get you for just the longest time. I'm so upset. I'm—"

"In the morning," I said. "The office is closed."

"Please, Mr. Marlowe—just because I lost my temper for a moment—"

"In the morning."

"But I tell you I have to see you." The voice didn't quite rise to a yell. "It's terribly important."

"Unhuh."

She sniffled. "You—you kissed me."

"I've kissed better since," I said. To hell with her. To hell with all women.

"I've heard from Orrin," she said.

That stopped me for a moment, then I laughed. "You're a nice little liar," I said. "Goodbye."

"But really I have. He called me. On the telephone. Right here where I'm staying."

"Fine," I said. "Then you don't need a detective at all. And if you did, you've got a better one than I am right in the family. I couldn't even find out where you were staying."

There was a little pause. She still had me talking to her anyway. She'd kept me from hanging up. I had to give her that much.

"I wrote to him where I'd be staying," she said at last.

"Unhuh. Only he didn't get the letter because he had moved and he didn't leave any forwarding address. Remember? Try again some time when I'm not so tired. Goodnight, Miss Quest. And you don't have to tell me where you are staying now. I'm not working for you."

"Very well, Mr. Marlowe. I'm ready to call the police now. But I don't think you'll like it. I don't think you'll like it at all."

"Why?"

"Because there's murder in it, Mr. Marlowe, and murder is a very nasty word—don't you think?"

"Come on up," I said. "I'll wait."

I hung up. I got the bottle of Old Forester out. There was nothing slow about the way I poured myself a drink and dropped it down my throat.

## 15

She came in briskly enough this time. Her motions were small and quick and determined. There was one of those thin little, bright little smiles on her face. She put her bag down firmly, settled herself in the customer's chair and went on smiling.

"It's nice of you to wait for me," she said. "I bet you haven't had your dinner yet, either."

"Wrong," I said. "I have had my dinner. I am now drinking whiskey. You don't approve of whiskey-drinking do you?"

"I certainly do not."

"That's just dandy," I said. "I hoped you hadn't changed your mind." I put the bottle up on the desk and poured myself another slug. I drank a little of it and gave her a leer above the glass.

"If you keep on with that you won't be in any condition to listen to what I have to say," she snapped.

"About this murder," I said. "Anybody I know? I can see you're not murdered—yet."

"Please don't be unnecessarily horrid. It's not my fault. You doubted me over the telephone so I had to convince you. Orrin did call me up. But he wouldn't tell me where he was or what he was doing. I don't know why."

"He wanted you to find out for yourself," I said. "He's building your character."

"That's not funny. It's not even smart."

"But you've got to admit it's nasty," I said. "Who was murdered? Or is that a secret too?"

She fiddled a little with her bag, not enough to overcome her embarrassment, because she wasn't embarrassed. But enough to needle me into taking another drink.

"That horrid man in the rooming house was murdered. Mr.—Mr.—I forget his name."

"Let's both forget it," I said. "Let's do something together for once." I dropped the whiskey bottle into the desk drawer and stood up. "Look, Orfamay, I'm not asking you how you know all this. Or rather how Orrin knows it all. Or if he *does* know it. You've found him. That's what you wanted me to do. Or he's found you, which comes to the same thing."

"It's not the same thing," she cried. "I haven't really found him. He wouldn't tell me where he was living."

"Well if it is anything like the last place, I don't blame him."

She set her lips in a firm line of distaste. "He wouldn't tell me anything really."

"Just about murders," I said. "Trifles like that."

She laughed bubblingly. "I just said that to scare you. I don't really mean anybody was murdered, Mr. Marlowe. You sounded so cold and distant. I thought you wouldn't help me any more. And—well, I just made it up."

I took a couple of deep breaths and looked down at my hands. I straightened out the fingers slowly. Then I stood up. I didn't say anything.

"Are you mad at me?" she asked timidly, making a little circle on the desk with the point of a finger.

"I ought to slap your face off," I said. "And quit acting innocent. Or it mightn't be your face I'd slap."

Her breath caught with a jerk. "Why, how dare you!"

"You used that line," I said. "You used it too often. Shut up and get the hell out of here. Do you think I enjoy being scared to death? Oh—there's this." I yanked a drawer open, got out her twenty dollars and threw them down in front of her. "Take this money away. Endow a hospital or a research laboratory with it. It makes me nervous having it around."

Her hand reached automatically for the money. Her eyes behind the cheaters were round and wondering. "Goodness," she said, assembling her handbag with a nice dignity. "I'm sure I didn't know you scared that easy. I thought you were tough."

"That's just an act," I growled, moving around the desk. She leaned back in her chair away from me. "I'm only tough with little girls like you that don't let their fingernails grow too long. I'm all mush inside." I took hold of her arm and yanked her to her feet. Her head went back. Her lips parted. I was hell with the women that day.

"But you will find Orrin for me, won't you?" she whispered. "It was all a lie. Everything I've told you was a lie. He didn't call me up. I—I don't know anything."

"Perfume," I said sniffing. "Why, you little darling. You put perfume behind your ears—and all for me!"

She nodded her little chin half an inch. Her eyes were melting. "Take my glasses off," she whispered, "Philip. I don't mind if you take a little whiskey once in a while. Really I don't."

Our faces were about six inches apart. I was afraid to take her glasses off. I might have socked her on the nose.

"Yes," I said in a voice that sounded like Orson Welles with his mouth full of crackers. "I'll find him for you, honey, if he's still alive. And for free. Not a dime of expense involved. I only ask one thing."

"What, Philip?" she asked softly and opened her lips a little wider.

"Who was the black sheep in your family?"

She jerked away from me like a startled fawn might, if I had a startled fawn and it jerked away from me. She stared at me stony-faced.

"You said Orrin wasn't the black sheep in your family. Remember? With a very peculiar emphasis. And when you mentioned your sister Leila, you sort of passed on quickly as if the subject was distasteful."

"I—I don't remember saying anything like that," she said very slowly.

"So I was wondering," I said. "What name does your sister Leila use in pictures?"

"Pictures?" she sounded vague. "Oh you mean motion pictures? Why I never said she was in pictures. I never said anything about her like that."

I gave her my big homely lopsided grin. She suddenly flew into a rage.

"Mind your own business about my sister Leila," she spit at me. "You leave my sister Leila out of your dirty remarks."

"What dirty remarks?" I asked. "Or should I try to guess?"

"All you think about is liquor and women," she screamed.

"I hate you!" She rushed to the door and yanked it open and went out. She practically ran down the hall.

I went back around my desk and slumped into the chair. A very strange little girl. Very strange indeed. After a while the phone started ringing again, as it would. On the fourth ring I leaned my head on my hand and groped for it, fumbled it to my face.

"Utter McKinley Funeral Parlors," I said.

A female voice said: "Wha-a-t?" and went off into a shriek of laughter. That one was a riot at the police smoker in 1921. What a wit. Like a hummingbird's beak. I put the lights out and went home.

# 16

Eight-forty-five the next morning found me parked a couple of doors from the Bay City Camera Shop, breakfasted and peaceful and reading the local paper through a pair of sunglasses. I had already chewed my way through the Los Angeles paper, which contained no item about ice picks in the Van Nuys or any other hotel. Not even MYSTERIOUS DEATH IN DOWNTOWN HOTEL, with no names or weapons specified. The Bay City *News* wasn't too busy to write up a murder. They put it on the first page, right next to the price of meat.

### LOCAL MAN FOUND STABBED
### IN IDAHO STREET ROOMING HOUSE

*An anonymous telephone call late yesterday sent police speeding to an address on Idaho Street opposite the Seamans and Jansing Company's lumber yard. Entering the unlocked door of his apartment, officers found Lester B. Clausen, 45, manager of the rooming house, dead on the couch. Clausen had been stabbed in the neck with an ice pick which was still in his body. After a preliminary examination, Coroner Frank L. Crowdy announced that Clausen had been drinking heavily and may have been unconscious at the time of his death. No signs of struggle were observed by the police.*

*Detective Lieutenant Moses Maglashan immediately took charge and questioned tenants of the rooming house on their return from work, but no light has so far been thrown on the circumstances of the crime. Interviewed by this reporter, Coroner Crowdy stated that Clausen's death might have been suicide but that the position of the wound made this unlikely. Examination of the rooming-house register disclosed that a page had recently been torn out. Lieutenant Maglashan, after questioning the tenants at length, stated that a thick-set middle-aged man with brown hair and heavy features had been noticed in the hallway of the rooming house on several occasions, but that none of the tenants knew his name or occupation. After carefully checking all rooms, Maglashan further gave it as his opinion that one of the roomers had left recently and in some haste. The mutilation of the register, however, the character of the neighborhood, the lack of an accurate description of the missing man, made the job of tracing him extremely difficult.*

*"I have no idea at present why Clausen was murdered," Maglashan announced at a late hour last night. "But I have had my eye on this man for some time. Many of his associates are known to me. It's a tough case, but we'll crack it."*

It was a nice piece and only mentioned Maglashan's name twelve times in the text and twice more in picture captions. There was a photo of him on page three holding an ice pick and looking at it with profound thought wrinkling his brows. There was a photo of 449 Idaho Street which did it more than justice, and a photo of something with a sheet over it on a couch and Lieutenant Maglashan pointing at it sternly. There was also a close-up of the mayor looking as executive as hell behind his official desk and an interview with him on the subject of post-war crime. He said just what you would expect a mayor to say—a watered-down shot of J. Edgar Hoover with some extra bad grammar thrown in.

At three minutes to nine the door of the Bay City Camera Shop opened and an elderly Negro began to sweep dirt across the sidewalk into the gutter. At nine A.M. a neat-appearing young guy in glasses fixed the lock on the door and I went in there with the black-and-orange check Dr. G. W. Hambleton had pasted to the inside of his toupee.

The neat-appearing young man gave me a searching glance as I exchanged the check and some money for an envelope containing a tiny negative and half a dozen shiny prints blown up to eight times the size of the negative. He didn't say anything, but the way he looked at me gave me the impression that he remembered I was not the man who had left the negative.

I went out and sat in my car and looked over the catch. The prints showed a man and a blond girl sitting in a rounded booth in a restaurant with food in front of them. They were looking up as though their attention had suddenly been attracted and they had only just had time to react before the camera had clicked. It was clear from the lighting that no flashbulb had been used.

The girl was Mavis Weld. The man was rather small, rather dark, rather expressionless. I didn't recognize him. There was no reason why I should. The padded leather seat was covered with tiny figures of dancing couples. That made the restaurant THE DANCERS. This added to the confusion. Any amateur camera hound that tried to flash a lens in there without getting an okay from the management would have been thrown out so hard that he would have bounced all the way down to Hollywood and Vine. I figured it must have been the hidden-camera trick, the way they took Ruth Snyder in the electric chair. He would have the little camera up hanging by a strap under his coat collar, the lens just peeping out from his open jacket, and he would have rigged a bulb release that he could hold in his pocket. It wasn't too hard for me to guess who had taken the picture. Mr. Orrin P. Quest must have moved fast and smooth to get out of there with his face still in front of his head.

I put the pictures in my vest pocket and my fingers touched a crumpled piece of paper. I got it out and read: "Doctor Vincent Lagardie, 965 Wyoming Street, Bay City." That was the Vince I had talked to on the phone, the one Lester B. Clausen might have been trying to call.

An elderly flatfoot was strolling down the line of parked cars, marking tires with yellow chalk. He told me where Wyoming Street was. I drove out there. It was a cross-town street well out beyond the business district, parallel with two numbered streets. Number 965, a gray-white frame house, was on a corner. On its door a brass plate said *Vincent Lagardie, M.D., Hours 10.00 to 12.00 and 2.30 to 4.00.*

The house looked quiet and decent. A woman with an unwilling small boy was going up the steps. She read the plate, looked at a watch pinned to her lapel and chewed irresolutely on her lip. The small boy looked around carefully, then kicked her on the ankle. She winced but her voice was patient. "Now, Johnny, you mustn't do that to Aunty Fern," she said mildly.

She opened the door and dragged the little ape in with her. Diagonally across the intersection was a big white colonial mansion with a portico which was roofed and much too small for the house. Floodlight reflectors were set into the front lawn. The walk was bordered by tree roses in bloom. A large black and silver sign over the portico said: *"The Garland Home of Peace."* I wondered how Dr. Lagardie liked looking out of his front windows at a funeral parlor. Maybe it made him careful.

I turned around at the intersection and drove back to Los Angeles, and went up to the office to look at my mail and lock my catch from the Bay City Camera Shop up in the battered green safe—all but one print. I sat down at the desk and studied this through a magnifying glass. Even with that and the camera shop blow-up the detail was still clear. There was an evening paper, a *News-Chronicle*, lying on the table in front of the dark thin expressionless man who sat beside Mavis Weld. I could just read the headline. LIGHT HEAVYWEIGHT CONTENDER SUCCUMBS TO RING INJURIES. Only a noon or late sports edition would use a headline like that. I pulled the phone towards me. It rang just as I got my hand on it.

"Marlowe? This is Christy French downtown. Any ideas this morning?"

"Not if your teletype's working. I've seen a Bay City paper."

"Yeah, we got that," he said casually. "Sounds like the same guy, don't it? Same initials, same description, same method of murder, and the time element seems to check. I hope to

Christ this doesn't mean Sunny Moe Stein's mob have started in business again."

"If they have, they've changed their technique," I said. "I was reading up on it last night. The Stein mob used to jab their victims full of holes. One of them had over a hundred stab wounds in him."

"They could learn better," French said a little evasively, as if he didn't want to talk about it. "What I called you about was Flack. Seen anything of him since yesterday afternoon?"

"No."

"He skipped out. Didn't come to work. Hotel called his landlady. Packed up and left last night. Destination unknown."

"I haven't seen him or heard from him," I said.

"Didn't it strike you as kind of funny our stiff only had fourteen bucks in his kick?"

"It did a little. You answered that yourself."

"I was just talking. I don't buy that any more. Flack's either scared out or come into money. Either he saw something he didn't tell and got paid to breeze, or else he lifted the customer's case dough, leaving the fourteen bucks to make it look better."

I said: "I'll buy either one. Or both at the same time. Whoever searched that room so thoroughly wasn't looking for money."

"Why not?"

"Because when this Dr. Hambleton called me up I suggested the hotel safe to him. He wasn't interested."

"A type like that wouldn't have hired you to hold his dough anyway," French said. "He wouldn't have hired you to keep anything for him. He wanted protection or he wanted a sidekick—or maybe just a messenger."

"Sorry," I said. "He told me just what I told you."

"And seeing he was dead when you got over there," French said with a too casual drawl, "you couldn't hardly have given him one of your business cards."

I held the phone too tight and thought back rapidly over my talk with Hicks in the Idaho Street rooming house. I saw him holding my card between his fingers, looking down at it. And then I saw myself taking it out of his hand quickly, before he froze to it. I took a deep breath and let it out slowly.

"Hardly," I said. "And stop trying to scare me to death."

"He had one, chum. Folded twice across in his pants watch pocket. We missed it the first time."

"I gave Flack a card," I said, stiff-lipped.

There was silence. I could hear voices in the background and the clack of a typewriter. Finally French said dryly: "Fair enough. See you later." He hung up abruptly.

I put the phone down very slowly in its cradle and flexed my cramped fingers. I stared down at the photo lying on the desk in front of me. All it told me was that two people, one of whom I knew, were having lunch at The Dancers. The paper on the table told me the date, or would.

I dialed the *News-Chronicle* and asked for the sports section. Four minutes later I wrote on a pad: "Ritchy Belleau, popular young light heavyweight contender, died in the Sisters Hospital just before midnight February 19 as a result of ring injuries sustained the previous evening in the main event at the Hollywood Legion Stadium. The *News-Chronicle* Noon Sports Edition for February 20 carried the headlines."

I dialed the same number again and asked for Kenny Haste in the City Room. He was an ex-crime reporter I had known for years. We chatted around for a minute and then I said:

"Who covered the Sunny Moe Stein killing for you?"

"Tod Barrow. He's on the *Post-Despatch* now. Why?"

"I'd like the details, if any."

He said he would send to the morgue for the file and call me, which he did ten minutes later. "He was shot twice in the head, in his car, about two blocks from the Chateau Bercy on Franklin. Time, about 11.15 P.M."

"Date, February 20," I said, "or was it?"

"Check, it was. No witnesses, no arrests except the usual police stock company of book-handlers, out-of-work fight managers and other professional suspects. What's in it?"

"Wasn't a pal of his supposed to be in town about that time?"

"Nothing here says so. What name?"

"Weepy Moyer. A cop friend of mine said something about a Hollywood money man being held on suspicion and then released for lack of evidence."

Kenny said: "Wait a minute. Something's coming back to me — yeah. Fellow named Steelgrave, owns The Dancers, supposed to be a gambler and so on. Nice guy. I've met him. That was a bust."

"How do you mean, a bust?"

"Some smart monkey tipped the cops he was Weepy Moyer and they held him for ten days on an open charge for Cleveland. Cleveland brushed it off. That didn't have anything to do with the Stein killing. Steelgrave was under glass all that week. No connection at all. Your cop friend has been reading pulp magazines."

"They all do," I said. "That's why they talk so tough. Thanks, Kenny."

We said goodbye and hung up and I sat leaning back in my chair and looking at my photograph. After a while I took scissors and cut out the piece that contained the folded newspaper with the headline. I put the two pieces in separate envelopes and put them in my pocket with the sheet from the pad.

I dialed Miss Mavis Weld's Crestview number. A woman's voice answered after several rings. It was a remote and formal voice that I might or might not have heard before. All it said was, "Hello?"

"This is Philip Marlowe. Is Miss Weld in?"

"Miss Weld will not be in until late this evening. Do you care to leave a message?"

"Very important. Where could I reach her?"

"I'm sorry. I have no information."

"Would her agent know?"

"Possibly."

"You're quite sure *you're* not Miss Weld?"

"Miss Weld is not in." She hung up.

I sat there and listened to the voice. At first I thought yes, then I thought no. The longer I thought the less I knew. I went down to the parking lot and got my car out.

## 17

On the terrace at The Dancers a few early birds were getting ready to drink their lunch. The glass-fronted upstairs room had the awning let down in front of it. I drove on past the curve that goes down into the Strip and stopped across the street from a square building of two stories of rose-red brick with small white leaded bay windows and a Greek porch over the front door and what looked, from across the street, like an antique pewter doorknob. Over the door was a fanlight and the name Sheridan Ballou, Inc., in black wooden letters severely stylized. I locked my car and crossed to the front door. It was white and tall and wide and had a keyhole big enough for a mouse to crawl through. Inside this keyhole was the real lock. I went for the knocker, but they had thought of that too. It was all in one piece and didn't knock.

So I patted one of the slim fluted white pillars and opened the door and walked directly into the reception room which filled the entire front of the building. It was furnished in dark antique-looking furniture and many chairs and settees of quilted chintz-like material. There were lace curtains at the windows and chintz boxes around them that matched the chintz of the furniture. There was a flowered carpet and a lot of people waiting to see Mr. Sheridan Ballou.

Some of them were bright and cheerful and full of hope. Some looked as if they had been there for days. One small dark girl was sniffling into her handkerchief in the corner. Nobody paid any attention to her. I got a couple of profiles at nice angles before the company decided I wasn't buying anything and didn't work there.

A dangerous-looking redhead sat languidly at an Adam desk talking into a pure-white telephone. I went over there and she put a couple of cold blue bullets into me with her eyes and then stared at the cornice that ran around the room.

"No," she said into the phone. "No. So sorry. I'm afraid it's no use. Far, far too busy." She hung up and ticked off something on a list and gave me some more of her steely glance.

"Good morning. I'd like to see Mr. Ballou," I said. I put my plain card on her desk. She lifted it by one corner, smiled at it amusedly.

"Today?" she inquired amiably. "This week?"

"How long does it usually take?"

"It *has* taken six months," she said cheerfully. "Can't somebody else help you?"

"No."

"So sorry. Not a chance. Drop in again won't you? Somewhere about Thanksgiving." She was wearing a white wool skirt, a burgundy silk blouse and a black velvet over-jacket with short sleeves. Her hair was a hot sunset. She wore a golden topaz bracelet and topaz earrings and a topaz dinner ring in the shape of a shield. Her fingernails matched her blouse exactly. She looked as if it would take a couple of weeks to get her dressed.

"I've got to see him," I said.

She read my card again. She smiled beautifully. "Everyone has," she said. "Why—er—Mr. Marlowe. Look at all these lovely people. Every one of them has been here since the office opened two hours ago."

"This is important."

"No doubt. In what way if I may ask?"

"I want to peddle a little dirt."

She picked a cigarette out of a crystal box and lit it with a crystal lighter. "Peddle? You mean for money—in Hollywood?"

"Could be."

"What kind of dirt? Don't be afraid to shock me."

"It's a bit obscene, Miss—Miss—" I screwed my head around to read the plaque on her desk.

"Helen Grady," she said. "Well, a little well-bred obscenity never did any harm, did it?"

"I didn't say it was well-bred."

She leaned back carefully and puffed smoke in my face.

"Blackmail in short." She sighed. "Why the hell don't you lam out of here, bud? Before I throw a handful of fat coppers in your lap?"

I sat on the corner of her desk, grabbed a double handful of her cigarette smoke and blew it into her hair. She dodged angrily. "Beat it, lug," she said in a voice that could have been used for paint remover.

"Oh oh. What happened to the Bryn Mawr accent?"

Without turning her head she said sharply: "Miss Vane."

A tall slim elegant dark girl with supercilious eyebrows looked up. She had just come through an inner door camouflaged as a stained-glass window. The dark girl came over. Miss Grady handed her my card: "Spink."

Miss Vane went back through the stained-glass window with the card.

"Sit down and rest your ankles, big stuff," Miss Grady informed me. "You may be here all week."

I sat down in a chintz winged chair, the back of which came eight inches above my head. It made me feel shrunken. Miss Grady gave me her smile again, the one with the hand-honed edge, and bent to the telephone once more.

I looked around. The little girl in the corner had stopped crying and was making up her face with calm unconcern. A very tall distinguished-looking party swung up a graceful arm to stare at his elegant wrist watch and oozed gently to his feet. He set a pearl-gray homburg at a rakish angle on the side of his head, checked his yellow chamois gloves and his silver-knobbed cane, and strolled languidly over to the red-headed receptionist.

"I have been waiting two hours to see Mr. Ballou," he said icily in a rich sweet voice that had been modulated by a lot of training. "I'm not accustomed to waiting two hours to see anybody."

"So sorry, Mr. Fortescue. Mr. Ballou is just too busy for words this A.M."

"I'm sorry I cannot leave him a check," the elegant tall party remarked with a weary contempt. "Probably the only thing that would interest him. But in default of that—"

"Just a minute, kid." The redhead picked up a phone and said into it: "Yes? . . . Who says so besides Goldwyn? Can't you reach somebody that's not crazy? . . . Well try again." She slammed the telephone down. The tall party had not moved.

"In default of that," he resumed as if he had never stopped speaking, "I should like to leave a short personal message."

"Please do," Miss Grady told him. "I'll get it to him somehow."

"Tell him with my love that he is a dirty polecat."

"Make it skunk, darling," she said. "He doesn't know any English words."

"Make it skunk and double skunk," Fortescue told her. "With a slight added nuance of sulphurated hydrogen and a very cheap grade of whore-house perfume." He adjusted his hat and gave his profile the once over in a mirror. "I now bid you good morning and to hell with Sheridan Ballou, Incorporated."

The tall actor stalked out elegantly, using his cane to open the door.

"What's the matter with him?" I asked.

She looked at me pityingly. "Billy Fortescue? Nothing's the matter with him. He isn't getting any parts so he comes in every day and goes through that routine. He figures somebody might see him and like it."

I shut my mouth slowly. You can live a long time in Hollywood and never see the part they use in pictures.

Miss Vane appeared through the inner door and made a chin-jerk at me. I went in past her. "This way. Second on the right." She watched me while I went down the corridor to the second door which was open. I went in and closed the door.

A plump white-haired Jew sat at the desk smiling at me tenderly. "Greetings," he said. "I'm Moss Spink. What's on the thinker, pal? Park the body. Cigarette?" He opened a thing that looked like a trunk and presented me with a cigarette which was not more than a foot long. It was in an individual glass tube.

"No thanks," I said. "I smoke tobacco."

He sighed. "All right. Give. Let's see. Your name's Marlowe. Huh? Marlowe. Marlowe. Have I ever heard of anybody named Marlowe?"

"Probably not," I said. "I never heard of anybody named Spink. I asked to see a man named Ballou. Does that sound like Spink? I'm not looking for anybody named Spink. And just between you and me, the hell with people named Spink."

"Anti-Semitic huh?" Spink said. He waved a generous hand

on which a canary-yellow diamond looked like an amber traffic light. "Don't be like that," he said. "Sit down and dust off the brains. You don't know me. You don't want to know me. O.K. I ain't offended. In a business like this you got to have somebody around that don't get offended."

"Ballou," I said.

"Now be reasonable, pal. Sherry Ballou's a very busy guy. He works twenty hours a day and even then he's way behind schedule. Sit down and talk it out with little Spinky."

"You're what around here?" I asked him.

"I'm his protection, pal. I gotta protect him. A guy like Sherry can't see everybody. I see people for him. I'm the same as him—up to a point you understand."

"Could be I'm past the point you're up to," I said.

"Could be," Spink agreed pleasantly. He peeled a thick tape off an aluminum individual cigar container, reached the cigar out tenderly and looked it over for birthmarks. "I don't say not. Why not demonstrate a little? Then we'll know. Up to now all you're doing is throwing a line. We get so much of that in here it don't mean a thing to us."

I watched him clip and light the expensive-looking cigar. "How do I know you wouldn't double-cross him?" I asked cunningly.

Spink's small tight eyes blinked and I wasn't sure but that there were tears in them. "Me cross Sherry Ballou?" he asked brokenly in a hushed voice, like a six-hundred-dollar funeral. "Me? I'd sooner double-cross my own mother."

"That doesn't mean anything to me either," I said. "I never met your mother."

Spink laid his cigar aside in an ash tray the size of a bird bath. He waved both his arms. Sorrow was eating into him. "Oh pal. What a way to talk," he wailed. "I love Sherry Ballou like he was my own father. Better. My father—well, skip it. Come on, pal. Be human. Give with a little of the old trust and friendliness. Spill the dirt to little Spinky, huh?"

I drew an envelope from my pocket and tossed it across the desk to him. He pulled the single photograph from it and stared at it solemnly. He laid it down on the desk. He looked up at me, down at the photo, up at me. "Well," he said woodenly, in a voice suddenly empty of the old trust and friendliness he had been talking about. "What's it got that's so wonderful?"

"Do I have to tell you who the girl is?"

"Who's the guy?" Spink snapped.

I said nothing.

"I said who's the guy?" Spink almost yelled at me. "Cough up, mug. Cough up."

I still didn't say anything. Spink reached slowly for his telephone, keeping his hard bright eyes on my face.

"Go on. Call them," I said. "Call downtown and ask for Lieutenant Christy French in the homicide bureau. There's another boy that's hard to convince."

Spink took his hand off the phone. He got up slowly and went out with the photograph. I waited. Outside on Sunset Boulevard traffic went by distantly, monotonously. The minutes dropped silently down a well. The smoke of Spink's freshly lit cigar played in the air for a moment, then was sucked through the vent of the air-conditioning apparatus. I looked at the innumerable inscribed photos on the walls, all inscribed to Sherry Ballou with somebody's eternal love. I figured they were back numbers if they were in Spink's office.

# 18

After a while Spink came back and gestured to me. I followed him along the corridor through double doors into an anteroom with two secretaries. Past them towards more double doors of heavy black glass with silver peacocks etched into the panels. As we neared the doors they opened of themselves.

We went down three carpeted steps into an office that had everything in it but a swimming pool. It was two stories high, surrounded by a balcony loaded with book shelves. There was a concert grand Steinway in the corner and a lot of glass and bleached-wood furniture and a desk about the size of a badminton court and chairs and couches and tables and a man lying on one of the couches with his coat off and his shirt open over a Charvet scarf you could have found in the dark by listening to it purr. A white cloth was over his eyes and forehead and a lissome blond girl was wringing out another in a silver bowl of ice water at a table beside him.

The man was a big shapely guy with wavy dark hair and a strong brown face below the white cloth. An arm dropped to the carpet and a cigarette hung between fingers, wisping a tiny thread of smoke.

The blond girl changed the cloth deftly. The man on the couch groaned. Spink said: "This is the boy, Sherry. Name of Marlowe."

The man on the couch groaned. "What does he want?"

Spink said: "Won't spill."

The man on the couch said: "What did you bring him in for then? I'm tired."

Spink said: "Well you know how it is, Sherry. Sometimes you kind of got to."

The man on the couch said: "What did you say his beautiful name was?"

Spink turned to me. "You can tell us what you want now. And make it snappy, Marlowe."

I said nothing.

After a moment the man on the couch slowly raised the arm with the cigarette at the end of it. He got the cigarette wearily into his mouth and drew on it with the infinite languor of a decadent aristocrat moldering in a ruined château.

"I'm talking to you, pal," Spink said harshly. The blonde changed the cloth again, looking at nobody. The silence hung in the room as acrid as the smoke of the cigarette. "Come on, lug. Snap it up."

I got one of my Camels out and lit it and picked out a chair and sat down. I stretched my hand out and looked at it. The thumb twitched up and down slowly every few seconds.

Spink's voice cut into this furiously: "Sherry don't have all day, you."

"What would he do with the rest of the day?" I heard myself asking. "Sit on a white satin couch and have his toenails gilded?"

The blonde turned suddenly and stared at me. Spink's mouth fell open. He blinked. The man on the couch lifted a slow hand to the corner of the towel over his eyes. He removed enough so that one seal-brown eye looked at me. The towel fell softly back into place.

"You can't talk like that in here," Spink said in a tough voice.

I stood up. I said: "I forgot to bring my prayer book. This is the first time I knew God worked on commission."

Nobody said anything for a minute. The blonde changed the towel again.

From under it the man on the couch said calmly: "Get the Jesus out of here, darlings. All but the new chum."

Spink gave me a narrow glare of hate. The blonde left silently.

Spink said: "Why don't I just toss him out on his can?"

The tired voice under the towel said: "I've been wondering about that so long I've lost interest in the problem. Beat it."

"Okay, boss," Spink said. He withdrew reluctantly. He paused at the door, gave me one more silent snarl and disappeared.

The man on the couch listened to the door close and then said: "How much?"

"You don't want to buy anything."

He pushed the towel off his head, tossed it to one side and sat up slowly. He put his bench-made pebble-grain brogues on the carpet and passed a hand across his forehead. He looked tired but not dissipated. He fumbled another cigarette from somewhere, lit it and stared morosely through the smoke at the floor.

"Go on," he said.

"I don't know why you wasted all the build-up on me," I said. "But I credit you with enough brains to know you couldn't buy anything, and know it would stay bought."

Ballou picked up the photo that Spink had put down near him on a long low table. He reached out a languid hand. "The piece that's cut out would be the punch line, no doubt," he said.

I got the envelope out of my pocket and gave him the cut out corner, watched him fit the two pieces together.

"With a glass you can read the headline," I said.

"There's one on my desk. Please."

I went over and got the magnifying glass off his desk. "You're used to a lot of service, aren't you, Mr. Ballou?"

"I pay for it." He studied the photograph through the glass and sighed. "Seems to me I saw that fight. They ought to take more care of these boys."

"Like you do of your clients," I said.

He laid down the magnifying glass and leaned back to stare at me with cool untroubled eyes.

"That's the chap that owns The Dancers. Name's Steelgrave. The girl is a client of mine, of course." He made a vague gesture towards a chair. I sat down in it. "What were you thinking of asking, Mr. Marlowe?"

"For what?"

"All the prints and the negative. The works."

"Ten grand," I said, and watched his mouth. The mouth smiled, rather pleasantly.

"It needs a little more explanation, doesn't it? All I see is two people having lunch in a public place. Hardly disastrous to the reputation of my client. I assume that was what you had in mind."

I grinned. "You can't buy anything, Mr. Ballou. I could have had a positive made from the negative and another negative from the positive. If that snap is evidence of something, you could never know you had suppressed it."

"Not much of a sales talk for a blackmailer," he said, still smiling.

"I always wonder why people pay blackmailers. They can't buy anything. Yet they do pay them, sometimes over and over and over again. And in the end are just where they started."

"The fear of today," he said, "always overrides the fear of tomorrow. It's a basic fact of the dramatic emotions that the part is greater than the whole. If you see a glamour star on the screen in a position of great danger, you fear for her with one part of your mind, the emotional part. Notwithstanding that your reasoning mind knows that she is the star of the picture and nothing very bad is going to happen to her. If suspense and menace didn't defeat reason, there would be very little drama."

I said: "Very true, I guess," and puffed some of my Camel smoke around.

His eyes narrowed a little. "As to really being able to buy anything, if I paid you a substantial price and didn't get what I bought, I'd have you taken care of. Beaten to a pulp. And when you got out of the hospital, if you felt aggressive enough, you could try to get me arrested."

"It's happened to me," I said. "I'm a private eye. I know what you mean. Why are you talking to me?"

He laughed. He had a deep pleasant effortless laugh. "I'm an agent, sonny. I always tend to think traders have a little something in reserve. But we won't talk about any ten grand. She hasn't got it. She only makes a grand a week so far. I admit she's very close to the big money, though."

"That would stop her cold," I said, pointing to the photo. "No big money, no swimming pool with underwater lights, no platinum mink, no name in neons, no nothing. All blown away like dust."

He laughed contemptuously.

"Okay if I show this to the johns down town, then?" I said.

He stopped laughing. His eyes narrowed. Very quietly he asked:

"Why would they be interested?"

I stood up. "I don't think we're going to do any business, Mr. Ballou. And you're a busy man. I'll take myself off."

He got up off the couch and stretched, all six feet two of him. He was a very fine hunk of man. He came over and stood close to me. His seal-brown eyes had little gold flecks in them. "Let's see who you are, sonny."

He put his hand out. I dropped my open wallet into it. He read the photostat of my license, poked a few more things out of the wallet and glanced at them. He handed it back.

"What would happen, if you did show your little picture to the cops?"

"I'd first of all have to connect it up with something they're working on—something that happened in the Van Nuys Hotel yesterday afternoon. I'd connect it up through the girl—who won't talk to me—that's why I'm talking to you."

"She told me about it last night," he sighed.

"Told you how much?" I asked.

"That a private detective named Marlowe had tried to force her to hire him, on the ground that she was seen in a downtown hotel inconveniently close to where a murder was committed."

"How close?" I asked.

"She didn't say."

"Nuts she didn't."

He walked away from me to a tall cylindrical jar in the corner. From this he took one of a number of short thin malacca canes. He began to walk up and down the carpet, swinging the cane deftly past his right shoe.

I sat down again and killed my cigarette and took a deep breath. "It could only happen in Hollywood," I grunted.

He made a neat about turn and glanced at me. "I beg your pardon."

"That an apparently sane man could walk up and down inside the house with a Piccadilly stroll and a monkey stick in his hand."

He nodded. "I caught the disease from a producer at MGM. Charming fellow. Or so I've been told." He stopped and pointed the cane at me. "You amuse the hell out of me, Marlowe. Really you do. You're so transparent. You're trying to use me for a shovel to dig yourself out of a jam."

"There's some truth in that. But the jam I'm in is nothing to the jam your client would be in if I hadn't done the thing that put me in the jam."

He stood quite still for a moment. Then he threw the cane away from him and walked over to a liquor cabinet and swung the two halves of it open. He poured something into a couple of pot-bellied glasses. He carried one of them over to me. Then went back and got his own. He sat down with it on the couch.

"Armagnac," he said. "If you knew me, you'd appreciate the compliment. This stuff is pretty scarce. The Krauts cleaned most of it out. Our brass got the rest. Here's to you."

He lifted the glass, sniffed and sipped a tiny sip. I put mine down in a lump. It tasted like good French brandy.

Ballou looked shocked. "My God, you sip that stuff, you don't swallow it whole."

"I swallow it whole," I said. "Sorry. She also told you that if somebody didn't shut my mouth, she would be in a lot of trouble."

He nodded.

"Did she suggest how to go about shutting my mouth?"

"I got the impression she was in favor of doing it with some kind of heavy blunt instrument. So I tried out a mixture of threat and bribery. We have an outfit down the street that specializes in protecting picture people. Apparently they didn't scare you and the bribe wasn't big enough."

"They scared me plenty," I said. "I damn near fanned a Luger at them. That junky with the .45 puts on a terrific act. And as for the money not being big enough, it's all a question of how it's offered to me."

He sipped a little more of his Armagnac. He pointed at the photograph lying in front of him with the two pieces fitted together.

"We got to where you were taking that to the cops. What then?"

"I don't think we got that far. We got to why she took this up with you instead of with her boy friend. He arrived just as I left. He has his own key."

"Apparently she just didn't." He frowned and looked down into his Armagnac.

"I like that fine," I said. "I'd like it still better if the guy didn't have her doorkey."

He looked up rather sadly. "So would I. So would we all. But show business has always been like that—any kind of show business. If these people didn't live intense and rather disordered lives, if their emotions didn't ride them too hard—well, they wouldn't be able to catch those emotions in flight and imprint them on a few feet of celluloid or project them across the footlights."

"I'm not talking about her love life," I said. "She doesn't have to shack up with a redhot."

"There's no proof of that, Marlowe."

I pointed to the photograph. "The man that took that is missing and can't be found. He's probably dead. Two other men who lived at the same address are dead. One of them was trying to peddle those pictures just before he got dead. She went to his hotel in person to take delivery. So did whoever killed him. She didn't get delivery and neither did the killer. They didn't know where to look."

"And you did?"

"I was lucky. I'd seen him without his toupee. None of this is what I call proof, maybe. You could build an argument against it. Why bother? Two men have been killed, perhaps three. She took an awful chance. Why? She wanted that picture. Getting it was worth an awful chance. Why, again? It's just two people having lunch on a certain day. The day Moe Stein was shot to death on Franklin Avenue. The day a character named Steelgrave was in jail because the cops got a tip he was a Cleveland redhot named Weepy Moyer. That's what the record shows. But the photo says he was out of jail. And by saying that about him on that particular day it says who is he. And she knows it. And he still has her doorkey."

I paused and we eyed each other solidly for a while. I said:

"You don't really want the cops to have that picture, do you? Win, lose or draw, they'd crucify her. And when it was all over it wouldn't make a damn bit of difference whether Steelgrave was Moyer or whether Moyer killed Stein or had him killed or just happened to be out on a jail pass the day he was killed. If he got away with it, there'd always be enough people to think it was a fix. She wouldn't get away with anything. She's a gangster's girl in the public mind. And as far as your business is concerned, she's definitely and completely through."

Ballou was silent for a moment, staring at me without expression. "And where are you all this time?" he asked softly.

"That depends a good deal on you, Mr. Ballou."

"What do you really want?" His voice was thin and bitter now.

"What I wanted from her and couldn't get. Something that gives me a colorable right to act in her interests up to the point where I decided I can't go any farther."

"By suppressing evidence?" he asked tightly.

"If it *is* evidence. The cops couldn't find out without smearing Miss Weld. Maybe I can. They wouldn't be bothered to try; they don't care enough. I do."

"Why?"

"Let's say it's the way I earn my living. I might have other motives, but that one's enough."

"What's your price?"

"You sent it to me last night. I wouldn't take it then. I'll take it now. With a signed letter employing my services to investigate an attempt to blackmail one of your clients."

I got up with my empty glass and went over and put it down on the desk. As I bent down I heard a soft whirring noise. I went around behind the desk and yanked upon a drawer. A wire recorder slid out on a hinged shelf. The motor was running and the fine steel wire was moving steadily from one spool to the other. I looked across at Ballou.

"You can shut it off and take the record with you," he said. "You can't blame me for using it."

I moved the switch over to rewind and the wire reversed direction and picked up speed until the wire was winding so fast I couldn't see it. It made a sort of high keening noise, like a couple of pansies fighting for a piece of silk. The wire came loose and the machine stopped. I took the spool off and dropped it into my pocket.

"You might have another one," I said. "I'll have to chance that."

"Pretty sure of yourself, aren't you, Marlowe?"

"I only wish I was."

"Press that button on the end of the desk, will you?"

I pressed it. The black glass doors opened and a dark girl came in with a stenographer's notebook.

Without looking at her Ballou began to dictate. "Letter to Mr. Philip Marlowe, with his address. Dear Mr. Marlowe: This agency herewith employs you to investigate an attempt to blackmail one of its clients, particulars of which have been given to you verbally. Your fee is to be one hundred dollars a day with a retainer of five hundred dollars, receipt of which you acknowledge on the copy of this letter. Blah, blah, blah. That's all, Eileen. Right away please."

I gave the girl my address and she went out.

I took the wire spool out of my pocket and put it back in the drawer.

Ballou crossed his knees and danced the shiny tip of his

shoe up and down staring at it. He ran his hand through crisp dark hair.

"One of these days," he said, "I'm going to make the mistake which a man in my business dreads above all other mistakes. I'm going to find myself doing business with a man I can trust and I'm going to be just too god-damn smart to trust him. Here you'd better keep this." He held out the two pieces of the photograph.

Five minutes later I left. The glass doors opened when I was three feet from them. I went past the two secretaries and down the corridor past the open door of Spink's office. There was no sound in there, but I could smell his cigar smoke. In the reception room exactly the same people seemed to be sitting around in the chintzy chairs. Miss Helen Grady gave me her Saturday-night smile. Miss Vane beamed at me.

I had been forty minutes with the boss. That made me as gaudy as a chiropractor's chart.

# 19

The studio cop at the semicircular glassed-in desk put down his telephone and scribbled on a pad. He tore off the sheet and pushed in through the narrow slit not more than three quarters of an inch wide where the glass did not quite meet the top of his desk. His voice coming through the speaking device set into the glass panel had a metallic ring.

"Straight through to the end of the corridor," he said, "you'll find a drinking fountain in the middle of the patio. George Wilson will pick up there."

I said: "Thanks. Is this bullet-proof glass?"

"Sure. Why?"

"I just wondered," I said. "I never heard of anybody shooting his way into the picture business."

Behind me somebody snickered. I turned to look at a girl in slacks with a red carnation behind her ear. She was grinning.

"Oh brother, if a gun was all it took."

I went over to an olive-green door that didn't have any handle. It made a buzzing sound and let me push it open. Beyond was an olive-green corridor with bare walls and a door at the far end. A rat trap. If you got into that and something was wrong, they could still stop you. The far door made the same buzz and click. I wondered how the cop knew I was at it. So I looked up and found his eyes staring at me in a tilted mirror. As I touched the door the mirror went blank. They thought of everything.

Outside in the hot midday sun flowers rioted in a small patio with tiled walks and a pool in the middle and a marble seat. The drinking fountain was beside the marble seat. An elderly and beautifully dressed man was lounging on the marble seat watching three tan-colored boxers root up some tea-rose begonias. There was an expression of intense but quiet satisfaction on his face. He didn't glance at me as I came up. One of the boxers, the biggest one, came over and made a wet on the marble seat beside his pants leg. He leaned down and patted the dog's hard short-haired head.

"You Mr. Wilson?" I asked.

He looked up at me vaguely. The middle-sized boxer trotted up and sniffed and wet after the first one.

"Wilson?" He had a lazy voice with a touch of drawl to it. "Oh no. My name's not Wilson. Should it be?"

"Sorry." I went over to the drinking fountain and hit myself in the face with a stream of water. While I was wiping it off with a handkerchief the smallest boxer did his duty on the marble bench.

The man whose name was not Wilson said lovingly, "Always do it in the exact same order. Fascinates me."

"Do what?" I asked.

"Pee," he said. "Question of seniority it seems. Very orderly. First Maisie. She's the mother. Then Mac. Year older than Jock, the baby. Always the same. Even in my office."

"In your office?" I said, and nobody ever looked stupider saying anything.

He lifted his whitish eyebrows at me, took a plain brown cigar out of his mouth, bit the end off and spit it into the pool.

"That won't do the fish any good," I said.

He gave me an up-from-under look. "I raise boxers. The hell with fish."

I figured it was just Hollywood. I lit a cigarette and sat down on the bench. "In your office," I said. "Well, every day has its new idea, hasn't it."

"Up against the corner of the desk. Do it all the time. Drives my secretaries crazy. Gets into the carpet, they say. What's the matter with women nowadays? Never bothers me. Rather like it. You get fond of dogs, you even like to watch them pee."

One of the dogs heaved a full-blown begonia plant into the middle of the tiled walk at his feet. He picked it up and threw it into the pool.

"Bothers the gardeners, I suppose," he remarked as he sat down again. "Oh well, if they're not satisfied, they can always—" He stopped dead and watched a slim mail girl in yellow slacks deliberately detour in order to pass through the patio. She gave him a quick side glance and went off making music with her hips.

"You know what's the matter with this business?" he asked me.

"Nobody does," I said.

"Too much sex," he said. "All right in its proper time and place. But we get it in carload lots. Wade through it. Stand up to our necks in it. Gets to be like flypaper." He stood up. "We have too many flies too. Nice to have met you, Mister—"

"Marlowe," I said. "I'm afraid you don't know me."

"Don't know anybody," he said. "Memory's going. Meet too many people. Name's Oppenheimer."

"Jules Oppenheimer?"

He nodded. "Right. Have a cigar." He held one out to me. I showed my cigarette. He threw the cigar into the pool, then frowned. "Memory's going," he said sadly. "Wasted fifty cents. Oughtn't to do that."

"You run this studio," I said.

He nodded absently. "Ought to have saved that cigar. Save fifty cents and what have you got?"

"Fifty cents," I said, wondering what the hell he was talking about.

"Not in this business. Save fifty cents in this business and all you have is five dollars worth of bookkeeping." He paused and made a motion to the three boxers. They stopped whatever they were rooting at and watched him. "Just run the financial end," he said. "That's easy. Come on children, back to the brothel." He sighed. "Fifteen hundred theaters," he added.

I must have been wearing my stupid expression again. He waved a hand around the patio. "Fifteen hundred theaters is all you need. A damn sight easier than raising purebred boxers. The motion-picture business is the only business in the world in which you can make all the mistakes there are and still make money."

"Must be the only business in the world where you can have three dogs pee up against your office desk," I said.

"You have to have the fifteen hundred theaters."

"That makes it a little harder to get a start," I said.

He looked pleased. "Yes. That *is* the hard part." He looked across the green clipped lawn at a four-story building which made one side of the open square. "All offices over there," he said. "I never go there. Always redecorating. Makes me sick to look at the stuff some of these people put in their suites. Most expensive talent in the world. Give them anything they like, all the money they want. Why? No reason at all. Just habit. Doesn't matter a damn what they do or how they do it. Just give me fifteen hundred theaters."

"You wouldn't want to be quoted on that, Mr. Oppenheimer?"

"You a newspaper man?"

"No."

"Too bad. Just for the hell of it I'd like to see somebody try to get that simple elementary fact of life into the papers." He paused and snorted. "Nobody'd print it. Afraid to. Come on, children!"

The big one, Maisie, came over and stood beside him. The middle-sized one paused to ruin another begonia and then trotted up beside Maisie. The little one, Jock, lined up in order, then with a sudden inspiration, lifted a hind leg at the cuff of Oppenheimer's pants. Maisie blocked him off casually.

"See that?" Oppenheimer beamed. "Jock tried to get out of

turn. Maisie wouldn't stand for it." He leaned down and patted Maisie's head. She looked up at him adoringly.

"The eyes of your dog," Oppenheimer mused. "The most unforgettable thing in the world."

He strolled off down the tiled path towards the executive building, the three boxers trotting sedately beside him.

"Mr. Marlowe?"

I turned to find that a tall sandy-haired man with a nose like a straphanger's elbow had sneaked up on me.

"I'm George Wilson. Glad to know you. I see you know Mr. Oppenheimer."

"Been talking to him. He told me how to run the picture business. Seems all it takes is fifteen hundred theaters."

"I've been working here five years. I've never even spoken to him."

"You just don't get pee'd on by the right dogs."

"You could be right. Just what can I do for you, Mr. Marlowe?"

"I want to see Mavis Weld."

"She's on the set. She's in a picture that's shooting."

"Could I see her on the set for a minute?"

He looked doubtful. "What kind of pass did they give you?"

"Just a pass, I guess." I held it out to him. He looked it over.

"Ballou sent you. He's her agent. I guess we can manage. Stage 12. Want to go over there now?"

"If you have time."

"I'm the unit publicity man. That's what my time is for." We walked along the tiled path towards the corners of two buildings. A concrete roadway went between them towards the back lot and the stages.

"You in Ballou's office?" Wilson asked.

"Just came from there."

"Quite an organization, I hear. I've thought of trying that business myself. There's nothing in this but a lot of grief."

We passed a couple of uniformed cops, then turned into a narrow alley between two stages. A red wigwag was swinging in the middle of the alley, a red light was on over a door marked 12, and a bell was ringing steadily above the red light.

Wilson stopped beside the door. Another cop in a tilted-back chair nodded to him, and looked me over with that dead gray expression that grows on them like scum on a water tank.

The bell and the wigwag stopped and the red light went off. Wilson pulled a heavy door open and I went in past him. Inside was another door. Inside that what seemed after the sunlight to be pitch-darkness. Then I saw a concentration of lights in the far corner. The rest of the enormous sound stage seemed to be empty.

We went towards the lights. As we drew near the floor seemed to be covered with thick black cables. There were rows of folding chairs, a cluster of portable dressing rooms with names on the doors. We were wrong way on to the set and all I could see was the wooden backing and on either side a big screen. A couple of back-projection machines sizzled off to the side.

A voice shouted: "Roll 'em." A bell rang loudly. The two screens came alive with tossing waves. Another calmer voice said: "Watch your positions, please, we may have to end up matching this little vignette. All right, action."

Wilson stopped dead and touched my arm. The voices of the actors came out of nowhere, neither loud nor distinct, an unimportant murmur with no meaning.

One of the screens suddenly went blank. The smooth voice, without change of tone, said: "Cut."

The bell rang again and there was a general sound of movement. Wilson and I went on. He whispered in my ear: "If Ned Gammon doesn't get this take before lunch, he'll bust Torrance on the nose."

"Oh. Torrance in this?" Dick Torrance at the time was a ranking star of the second grade, a not uncommon type of Hollywood actor that nobody really wants but a lot of people in the end have to take for lack of better.

"Care to run over the scene again, Dick?" the calm voice asked, as we came around the corner of the set and saw what it was—the deck of a pleasure yacht near the stern. There were two girls and three men in the scene. One of the men was middle-aged, in sport clothes, lounging in a deck chair. One wore whites and had red hair and looked like the yacht's captain. The third was the amateur yachtsman, with the handsome cap, the blue jacket with gold buttons, the white shoes and slacks and the supercilious charm. This was Torrance. One of the girls was a dark beauty who had been younger; Susan Crawley. The other was Mavis Weld. She wore a wet white sharkskin swim suit, and had evidently just come aboard. A make-up man was spraying water on her face and arms and the edges of her blond hair.

Torrance hadn't answered. He turned suddenly and stared at the camera. "You think I don't know my lines?"

A gray-haired man in gray clothes came forward into the light from the shadowy background. He had hot black eyes, but there was no heat in his voice.

"Unless you changed them intentionally," he said, his eyes steady on Torrance.

"It's just possible that I'm not used to playing in front of a back projection screen that has a habit of running out of film only in the middle of a take."

"That's a fair complaint," Ned Gammon said. "Trouble is he only has two hundred and twelve feet of film, and that's my fault. If you could take the scene just a little faster—"

"Huh." Torrance snorted. "If *I* could take it a little faster. Perhaps Miss Weld could be prevailed upon to climb aboard this yacht in rather less time than it would take to build the damn boat."

Mavis Weld gave him a quick, contemptuous look.

"Weld's timing is just right," Gammon said. "Her performance is just right too."

Susan Crawley shrugged elegantly. "I had the impression she could speed it up a trifle, Ned. It's good, but it *could* be better."

"If it was any better, darling," Mavis Weld told her smoothly, "somebody might call it acting. You wouldn't want anything like that to happen in *your* picture, would you."

Torrance laughed. Susan Crawley turned and glared at him. "What's funny, Mister Thirteen?"

Torrance's face settled into an icy mask. "The name again?" he almost hissed.

"Good heavens, you mean you didn't know," Susan Crawley said wonderingly. "They call you Mister Thirteen because any time you play a part it means twelve other guys have turned it down."

"I see," Torrance said coolly, then burst out laughing again. He turned to Ned Gammon. "Okay, Ned. Now everybody's got the rat poison out of their system, maybe we can give it to you the way you want it."

Ned Gammon nodded. "Nothing like a little hamming to clear the air. All right here we go."

He went back beside the camera. The assistant shouted "roll 'em" and the scene went through without a hitch.

"Cut," Gammon said. "Print that one. Break for lunch everybody."

The actors came down a flight of rough wooden steps and nodded to Wilson. Mavis Weld came last, having stopped to put on a terry-cloth robe and a pair of beach sandals. She stopped dead when she saw me. Wilson stepped forward.

"Hello, George," Mavis Weld said, staring at me. "Want something from me?"

"Mr. Marlowe would like a few words with you. Okay?"

"Mr. Marlowe?"

Wilson gave me a quick sharp look. "From Ballou's office. I supposed you knew him."

"I may have seen him." She was still staring at me. "What is it?"

I didn't speak.

After a moment she said, "Thanks, George. Better come along to my dressing room, Mr. Marlowe."

She turned and walked off around the far side of the set. A green and white dressing room stood against the wall. The name on the door was Miss Weld. At the door she turned and looked around carefully. Then she fixed her lovely blue eyes on my face.

"And now, Mr. Marlowe?"

"You *do* remember me?"

"I believe so."

"Do we take up where we left off—or have a new deal with a clean deck?"

"Somebody let you in here. Who? Why? That takes explaining."

"I'm working for you. I've been paid a retainer and Ballou has the receipt."

"How very thoughtful. And suppose I don't want you to work for me? Whatever your work is."

"All right, be fancy," I said. I took the Dancers photo out of my pocket and held it out. She looked at me a long steady moment before she dropped her eyes. Then she looked at the snapshot of herself and Steelgrave in the booth. She looked at it gravely without movement. Then very slowly she reached up and touched the tendrils of damp hair at the side of her face. Ever so slightly she shivered. Her hand came out and she took the photograph. She stared at it. Her eyes came up again slowly, slowly.

"Well?" she asked.

"I have the negative and some other prints. You would have had them, if you had had more time and known where to look. Or if he had stayed alive to sell them to you."

"I'm a little chilly," she said. "And I have to eat some lunch." She held the photo out to me.

"You're a little chilly and you have to eat some lunch," I said.

I thought a pulse beat in her throat. But the light was not too good. She smiled very faintly. The bored-aristocrat touch.

"The significance of all this escapes me," she said.

"You're spending too much time on yachts. What you mean is I know you and I know Steelgrave, so what has this photo got that makes anybody give me a diamond dog collar?"

"All right," she said. "What?"

"I don't know," I said. "But if finding out is what it takes to shake you out of this duchess routine, I'll find out. And in the meantime you're still chilly and you still have to eat some lunch."

"And you've waited too long," she said quietly. "You haven't anything to sell. Except perhaps your life."

"I'd sell that cheap. For love of a pair of dark glasses and a delphinium-blue hat and a crack on the head from a high-heeled slipper."

Her mouth twitched as if she was going to laugh. But there was no laughter in her eyes.

"Not to mention three slaps in the face," she said. "Goodbye, Mr. Marlowe. You came too late. Much, much too late."

"For me—or for you?" She reached back and opened the door of the dressing room.

"I think for both of us." She went in quickly, leaving the door open.

"Come in and shut the door," her voice said from the dressing room.

I went in and shut the door. It was no fancy custom-built star's dressing room. Strictly utility only. There was a shabby couch, one easy chair, a small dressing table with mirror and two lights, a straight chair in front of it, a tray that had held coffee.

Mavis Weld reached down and plugged in a round electric heater. Then she grabbed up a towel and rubbed the damp edges of her hair. I sat down on the couch and waited.

"Give me a cigarette." She tossed the towel to one side. Her eyes came close to my face as I lit the cigarette for her. "How did you like that little scene we ad libbed on the yacht?"

"Bitchy."

"We're all bitches. Some smile more than others, that's all. Show business. There's something cheap about it. There always has been. There was a time when actors went in at the back door. Most of them still should. Great strain, great urgency, great hatred, and it comes out in nasty little scenes. They don't mean a thing."

"Cat talk," I said.

She reached up and pulled a fingertip down the side of my cheek. It burned like a hot iron. "How much money do you make, Marlowe?"

"Forty bucks a day and expenses. That's the asking price. I take twenty-five. I've taken less." I thought about Orfamay's worn twenty.

She did that with her finger again and I just didn't grab hold of her. She moved away from me and sat in the chair, drawing the robe close. The electric heater was making the little room warm.

"Twenty-five dollars a day," she said wonderingly.

"Little lonely dollars."

"Are they very lonely?"

"Lonely as lighthouses."

She crossed her legs and the pale glow of her skin in the light seemed to fill the room.

"So ask me the questions," she said, making no attempt to cover her thighs.

"Who's Steelgrave?"

"A man I've known for years. And liked. He owns things. A restaurant or two. Where he comes from—that I don't know."

"But you know him very well."

"Why don't you ask me if I sleep with him?"

"I don't ask that kind of questions."

She laughed and snapped ash from her cigarette. "Miss Gonzales would be glad to tell you."

"The hell with Miss Gonzales."

"She's dark and lovely and passionate. And very, very kind."

"And exclusive as a mailbox," I said. "The hell with her. About Steelgrave—has he ever been in trouble?"

"Who hasn't?"

"With the police."

Her eyes widened a little too innocently. Her laugh was a little too silvery. "Don't be ridiculous. The man is worth a couple of million dollars."

"How did he get it?"

"How would I know?"

"All right. You wouldn't. That cigarette's going to burn your fingers." I leaned across and took the stub out of her hand. Her hand lay open on her bare leg. I touched the palm with a fingertip. She drew away from me and tightened the hand into a fist.

"Don't do that," she said sharply.

"Why? I used to do that to girls when I was a kid."

"I know." She was breathing a little fast. "It makes me feel very young and innocent and kind of naughty. And I'm far from being young and innocent any more."

"Then you don't really know anything about Steelgrave."

"I wish you'd make up your mind whether you are giving me a third degree or making love to me."

"My mind has nothing to do with it," I said.

After a silence she said: "I really do have to eat something, Marlowe. I'm working this afternoon. You wouldn't want me to collapse on the set, would you?"

"Only stars do that." I stood up. "Okay, I'll leave. Don't forget I'm working for you. I wouldn't be if I thought you'd killed anybody. But you were there. You took a big chance. There was something you wanted very badly."

She reached the photo out from somewhere and stared at it, biting her lip. Her eyes came up without her head moving.

"It could hardly have been this."

"That was the one thing he had so well hidden that it was not found. But what good is it? You and a man called Steelgrave in a booth at The Dancers. Nothing in that."

"Nothing at all," she said.

"So it has to be something about Steelgrave—or something about the date."

Her eyes snapped down to the picture again. "There's nothing to tell the date," she said quickly. "Even if it meant something. Unless the cut-out piece—"

"Here." I gave her the cut-out piece. "But you'll need a magnifier. Show it to Steelgrave. Ask *him* if it means anything. Or ask Ballou."

I started towards the exit of the dressing room. "Don't kid yourself the date can't be fixed," I said over my shoulder. "Steelgrave won't."

"You're just building a sand castle, Marlowe."

"Really?" I looked back at her, not grinning. "You really think that? Oh no you don't. You went there. The man was murdered. You had a gun. He was a known crook. And I found something the police would love to have me hide from them. Because it must be as full of motive as the ocean is full of salt. As long as the cops don't find it I have a license. And as long as somebody else doesn't find it I don't have an ice pick in the back of my neck. Would you say I was in an overpaid profession?"

She just sat there and looked at me, one hand on her kneecap, squeezing it. The other moving restlessly, finger by finger, on the arm of the chair.

All I had to do was turn the knob and go on out. I don't know why it had to be so hard to do.

## 20

There was the usual coming and going in the corridor outside my office and when I opened the door and walked into the musty silence of the little waiting room there was the usual feeling of having been dropped down a well dried up twenty years ago to which no one would come back ever. The smell of old dust hung in the air as flat and stale as a football interview.

I opened the inner door and inside there it was the same dead air, the same dust along the veneer, the same broken promise of a life of ease. I opened the windows and turned on the radio. It came up too loud and when I had it tuned down to normal the phone sounded as if it had been ringing for some time. I took my hat off it and lifted the receiver.

It was high time I heard from her again. Her cool compact voice said: "This time I really mean it."

"Go on."

"I lied before. I'm not lying now. I really have heard from Orrin."

"Go on."

"You're not believing me. I can tell by your voice."

"You can't tell anything by my voice. I'm a detective. Heard from him how?"

"By phone from Bay City."

"Wait a minute." I put the receiver down on the stained brown blotter and lit my pipe. No hurry. Lies are always patient. I took it up again.

"We've been through that routine," I said. "You're pretty forgetful for your age. I don't think Dr. Zugsmith would like it."

"Please don't tease me. This is very serious. He got my letter. He went to the post office and asked for his mail. He knew where I'd be staying. And about when I'd be here. So he called up. He's staying with a doctor he got to know down there. Doing some kind of work for him. I told you he had two years medical."

"Doctor have a name?"

"Yes. A funny name. Dr. Vincent Lagardie."

"Just a minute. There's somebody at the door."

I laid the phone down very carefully. It might be brittle. It might be made of spun glass. I got a handkerchief out and wiped the palm of my hand, the one that had been holding it. I got up and went to the built-in wardrobe and looked at my face in the flawed mirror. It was me all right. I had a strained look. I'd been living too fast.

Dr. Vincent Lagardie, 965 Wyoming Street. Catty-corners from The Garland Home of Peace. Frame house on the corner. Quiet. Nice neighborhood. Friend of the extinct Clausen. Maybe. Not according to him. But still maybe.

I went back to the telephone and squeezed the jerks out of my voice. "How would you spell that?" I asked.

She spelled it—with ease and precision. "Nothing to do then, is there?" I said. "All jake to the angels—or whatever they say in Manhattan, Kansas."

"Stop sneering at me. Orrin's in a lot of trouble. Some—" her voice quivered a little and her breath came quickly, "some gangsters are after him."

"Don't be silly, Orfamay. They don't have gangsters in Bay City. They're all working in pictures. What's Dr. Lagardie's phone number?"

She gave it to me. It was right. I won't say the pieces were beginning to fall into place, but at least they were getting to look like parts of the same puzzle. Which is all I ever get or ask.

"Please go down there and see him and help him. He's afraid to leave the house. After all I did pay you."

"I gave it back."

"Well, I offered it to you again."

"You more or less offered me other things that are more than I'd care to take."

There was silence.

"All right," I said. "All right. If I can stay free that long. I'm in a lot of trouble myself."

"Why?"

"Telling lies and not telling the truth. It always catches up with me. I'm not as lucky as some people."

"But I'm not lying, Philip. I'm not lying. I'm frantic."

"Take a deep breath and get frantic so I can hear it."

"They might kill him," she said quietly.

"And what is Dr. Vincent Lagardie doing all this time?"

"He doesn't know, of course. Please, please go at once. I have the address here. Just a moment."

And the little bell rang, the one that rings far back at the end of the corridor, and is not loud, but you'd better hear it. No matter what other noises there are you'd better hear it.

"He'll be in the phone book," I said. "And by an odd coincidence I have a Bay City phone book. Call me around four. Or five. Better make it five."

I hung up quickly. I stood up and turned the radio off, not having heard a thing it said. I closed the windows again. I opened the drawer of my desk and took out the Luger and strapped it on. I fitted my hat on my head. On the way out I had another look at the face in the mirror.

I looked as if I had made up my mind to drive off a cliff.


## 21


They were just finishing a funeral service at The Garland Home of Peace. A big gray hearse was waiting at the side entrance. Cars were clotted along both sides of the street, three black sedans in a row at the side of Dr. Vincent Lagardie's establishment. People were coming sedately down the walk from the funeral chapel to the corner and getting into their cars. I stopped a third of a block away and waited. The cars didn't move. Then three people came out with a woman heavily veiled and all in black. They half carried her down to a big limousine. The boss mortician fluttered around making elegant little gestures and body movements as graceful as a Chopin ending. His composed gray face was long enough to wrap twice around his neck.

The amateur pallbearers carried the coffin out the side door and professionals eased the weight from them and slid it into the back of the hearse as smoothly as if it had no more weight than a pan of butter rolls. Flowers began to grow into a mound over it. The glass doors were closed and motors started all over the block.

A few moments later nothing was left but one sedan across the way and the boss mortician sniffing a tree-rose on his way back to count the take. With a beaming smile he faded into his neat colonial doorway and the world was still and empty again. The sedan that was left hadn't moved. I drove along and made a U-turn and came up behind it. The driver wore blue serge and a soft cap with a shiny peak. He was doing a crossword puzzle from the morning paper. I stuck a pair of those diaphanous mirror sunglasses on my nose and strolled past him toward Dr. Lagardie's place. He didn't look up. When I was a few yards ahead I took the glasses off and pretended to polish them on my handkerchief. I caught him in one of the mirror lenses. He still didn't look up. He was just a guy doing a crossword puzzle. I put the mirror glasses back on my nose, and went around to Dr. Lagardie's front door.

The sign over the door said: Ring and Enter. I rang, but the door wouldn't let me enter. I waited. I rang again. I waited again. There was silence inside. Then the door opened a crack very slowly, and the thin expressionless face over a white uniform looked out at me.

"I'm sorry. Doctor is not seeing any patients today." She blinked at the mirror glasses. She didn't like them. Her tongue moved restlessly inside her lips.

"I'm looking for a Mr. Quest. Orrin P. Quest."

"Who?" There was a dim reflection of shock behind her eyes.

"Quest. Q as in quintessential, U as in uninhibited, E as in Extrasensory, S as in Subliminal, T as in Toots. Put them all together and they spell Brother."

She looked at me as if I had just come up from the floor of the ocean with a drowned mermaid under my arm.

"I beg your pardon. Dr. Lagardie is not—"

She was pushed out of the way by invisible hands and a thin dark haunted man stood in the half-open doorway.

"I am Dr. Lagardie. What is it, please?"

I gave him a card. He read it. He looked at me. He had the white pinched look of a man who is waiting for a disaster to happen.

"We talked over the phone," I said. "About a man named Clausen."

"Please come in," he said quickly. "I don't remember, but come in."

I went in. The room was dark, the blinds drawn, the windows closed. It was dark, and it was cold.

The nurse backed away and sat down behind a small desk. It was an ordinary living room with light painted woodwork which had once been dark, judging by the probable age of the house. A square arch divided the living room from the dining room. There were easy chairs and a center table with magazines. It looked like what it was—the reception room of a doctor practicing in what had been a private home.

The telephone rang on the desk in front of the nurse. She started and her hand went out and then stopped. She stared at the telephone. After a while it stopped ringing.

"What was the name you mentioned?" Dr. Lagardie asked me softly.

"Orrin Quest. His sister told me he was doing some kind of work for you, Doctor. I've been looking for him for days. Last night he called her up. From here, she said."

"There is no one of that name here," Dr. Lagardie said politely. "There hasn't been."

"You don't know him at all?"

"I have never heard of him."

"I can't figure why he would say that to his sister."

The nurse dabbed at her eyes furtively. The telephone on her desk burred and made her jump again. "Don't answer it," Dr. Lagardie said without turning his head.

We waited while it rang. Everybody waits while a telephone rings. After a while it stopped.

"Why don't you go home, Miss Watson? There's nothing for you to do here."

"Thank you, Doctor." She sat without moving, looking down at the desk. She squeezed her eyes shut and blinked them open. She shook her head hopelessly.

Dr. Lagardie turned back to me. "Shall we go into my office?"

We went across through another door leading to a hallway. I walked on eggs. The atmosphere of the house was charged with foreboding. He opened a door and ushered me into what must have once been a bedroom, but nothing suggested a bedroom. It was a small compact doctor's office. An open door showed a part of an examination room. A sterilizer was working in the corner. There were a lot of needles cooking in it.

"That's a lot of needles," I said, always quick with an idea.

"Sit down, Mr. Marlowe."

He went behind the desk and sat down and picked up a long thin letter-opening knife.

He looked at me levelly from his sorrowful eyes. "No, I don't know anyone named Orrin Quest, Mr. Marlowe. I can't imagine any reason in the world why a person of that name should say he was in my house."

"Hiding out," I said.

His eyebrows went up. "From what?"

"From some guys that might want to stick an ice pick in the back of his neck. On account of he is a little too quick with his little Leica. Taking people's photographs when they want to be private. Or it could be something else, like peddling reefers and he got wise. Am I talking in riddles?"

"It was you who sent the police here," he said coldly.

I didn't say anything.

"It was you who called up and reported Clausen's death."

I said the same as before.

"It was you who called me up and asked me if I knew Clausen. I said I did not."

"But it wasn't true."

"I was under no obligation to give you information, Mr. Marlowe."

I nodded and got a cigarette out and lit it. Dr. Lagardie glanced at his watch. He turned in his chair and switched off the sterilizer. I looked at the needles. A lot of needles. Once before I had had trouble in Bay City with a guy who cooked a lot of needles.

"What makes it?" I asked him. "The yacht harbor?"

He picked up the wicked-looking paper knife with a silver handle in the shape of a nude woman. He pricked the ball of his thumb. A pearl of dark blood showed on it. He put it to his mouth and licked it. "I like the taste of blood," he said softly.

There was a distant sound as of the front door opening and closing. We both listened to it carefully. We listened to retreating steps on the front steps of the house. We listened hard.

"Miss Watson has gone home," Dr. Lagardie said. "We are all alone in the house." He mulled that over and licked his thumb again. He laid the knife down carefully on the desk blotter. "Ah, the question of the yacht harbor," he added. "The proximity of Mexico you are thinking of, no doubt. The ease with which marihuana—"

"I wasn't thinking so much of marihuana any more." I stared again at the needles. He followed my stare. He shrugged.

I said: "Why so many of them?"

"Is it any of your business?"

"Nothing's any of my business."

"But you seem to expect your questions to be answered."

"I'm just talking," I said. "Waiting for something to happen. Something's going to happen in this house. It's leering at me from corners."

Dr. Lagardie licked another pearl of blood off his thumb.

I looked hard at him. It didn't buy me a way into his soul. He was quiet, dark and shuttered and all the misery of life was in his eyes. But he was still gentle.

"Let me tell you about the needles," I said.

"By all means." He picked the long thin knife up again.

"Don't do that," I said sharply. "It gives me the creeps. Like petting snakes."

He put the knife down again gently and smiled. "We do seem to talk in circles," he suggested.

"We'll get there. About the needles. A couple of years back I had a case that brought me down here and mixed me up with a doctor named Almore. Lived over on Altair Street. He had a funny practice. Went out nights with a big case of hypodermic needles—all ready to go. Loaded with the stuff.

He had a peculiar practice. Drunks, rich junkies, of whom there are far more than people think, overstimulated people who had driven themselves beyond the possibility of relaxing. Insomniacs—all the neurotic types that can't take it cold. Have to have their little pills and little shots in the arm. Have to have help over the humps. It gets to be all humps after a while. Good business for the doctor. Almore was the doctor for them. It's all right to say it now. He died a year or so back. Of his own medicine."

"And you think I may have inherited his practice?"

"Somebody would. As long as there are the patients, there will be the doctor."

He looked even more exhausted than before. "I think you are an ass, my friend. I did not know Dr. Almore. And I do not have the sort of practice you attribute to him. As for the needles—just to get that trifle out of the way—they are in somewhat constant use in the medical profession today, often for such innocent medicaments as vitamin injections. And needles get dull. And when they are dull they are painful. Therefore in the course of the day one may use a dozen or more. Without narcotics in a single one."

He raised his head slowly and stared at me with a fixed contempt.

"I can be wrong," I said. "Smelling that reefer smoke over at Clausen's place yesterday, and having him call your number on the telephone—and call you by your first name—all this probably made me jump to wrong conclusions."

"I have dealt with addicts," he said. "What doctor has not? It is a complete waste of time."

"They get cured sometimes."

"They can be deprived of their drug. Eventually after great suffering they can do without it. That is not curing them, my friend. That is not removing the nervous or emotional flaw which made them become addicts. It is making them dull negative people who sit in the sun and twirl their thumbs and die of sheer boredom and inanition."

"That's a pretty raw theory, doctor."

"You raised the subject. I have disposed of it. I will raise another subject. You may have noticed a certain atmosphere and strain about this house. Even with those silly mirror glasses on. Which you may now remove. They don't make you look in the least like Cary Grant."

I took them off. I'd forgotten all about them.

"The police have been here, Mr. Marlowe. A certain Lieutenant Maglashan, who is investigating Clausen's death. He would be pleased to meet you. Shall I call him? I'm sure he would come back."

"Go ahead, call him," I said. "I just stopped off here on my way to commit suicide."

His hand went towards the telephone but was pulled to one side by the magnetism of the paper knife. He picked it up again. Couldn't leave it alone, it seemed.

"You could kill a man with that," I said.

"Very easily," and he smiled a little.

"An inch and a half in the back of the neck, square in the center, just under the occipital bulge."

"An ice pick would be better," he said. "Especially a short one, filed down very sharp. It would not bend. If you miss the spinal cord, you do no great damage."

"Takes a bit of medical knowledge then?" I got out a poor old package of Camels and untangled one from the cellophane.

He just kept on smiling. Very faintly, rather sadly. It was not the smile of a man in fear. "That would help," he said softly. "But any reasonably dexterous person could acquire the technique in ten minutes."

"Orrin Quest had a couple of years medical," I said.

"I told you I did not know anybody of that name."

"Yeah, I know you did. I didn't quite believe you."

He shrugged his shoulders. But his eyes as always went to the knife in the end.

"We're a couple of sweethearts," I said. "We just sit here making with the old over-the-desk dialogue. As though we hadn't a care in the world. Because both of us are going to be in the clink by nightfall."

He raised his eyebrows again. I went on:

"You, because Clausen knew you by your first name. And you may have been the last man he talked to. Me, because I've been doing all the things a P.I. never gets away with. Hiding evidence, hiding information, finding bodies and not

coming in with my hat in my hand to these lovely incorrupt-
ible Bay City cops. Oh, I'm through. Very much through. But
there's a wild perfume in the air this afternoon. I don't seem
to care. Or I'm in love. I just don't seem to care."

"You have been drinking," he said slowly.

"Only Chanel No. 5, and kisses, and the pale glow of lovely
legs, and the mocking invitation in deep blue eyes. Innocent
things like that."

He just looked sadder than ever. "Women can weaken a
man terribly, can they not?" he said.

"Clausen."

"A hopeless alcoholic. You probably know how they are.
They drink and drink and don't eat. And little by little the
vitamin deficiency brings on the symptoms of delirium. There
is only one thing to do for them." He turned and looked at
the sterilizer. "Needles, and more needles. It makes me feel
dirty. I am a graduate of the Sorbonne. But I practice among
dirty little people in a dirty little town."

"Why?"

"Because of something that happened years ago—in
another city. Don't ask me too much, Mr. Marlowe."

"He used your first name."

"It is a habit with people of a certain class. Onetime actors
especially. And onetime crooks."

"Oh," I said. "That all there is to it?"

"All."

"Then the cops coming here doesn't bother you on account of Clausen. You're just afraid of this other thing that
happened somewhere else long gone. Or it could even be
love."

"Love?" He dropped the word slowly off the end of his
tongue, tasting it to the last. A bitter little smile stayed after
the word, like powder smell in the air after a gun is fired. He
shrugged and pushed a desk cigarette box from behind a
filing tray and over to my side of the desk.

"Not love then," I said. "I'm trying to read your mind.
Here you are a guy with a Sorbonne degree and a cheap little
practice in a cheap and nasty little town. I know it well. So
what are you doing here? What are you doing with people like
Clausen? What was the rap, Doctor? Narcotics, abortions, or

were you by any chance a medic for the gang boys in some hot Eastern city?"

"As for instance?" he smiled thinly.

"As for instance Cleveland."

"A very wild suggestion, my friend." His voice was like ice now.

"Wild as all hell," I said. "But a fellow like me with very limited brains tends to try to fit the things he knows into a pattern. It's often wrong, but it's an occupational disease with me. It goes like this, if you want to listen."

"I am listening." He picked the knife up again and pricked lightly at the blotter on his desk.

"You knew Clausen. Clausen was killed very skillfully with an ice pick, killed while I was in the house, upstairs talking to a grifter named Hicks. Hicks moved out fast taking a page of the register with him, the page that had Orrin Quest's name on it. Later that afternoon Hicks was killed with an ice pick in L.A. His room had been searched. There was a woman there who had come to buy something from him. She didn't get it. I had more time to search. I did get it. Presumption A: Clausen and Hicks killed by same man, not necessarily for same reason. Hicks killed because he muscled in on another guy's racket and muscled the other guy out. Clausen killed because he was a babbling drunk and might know who would be likely to kill Hicks. Any good so far?"

"Not the slightest interest to me," Dr. Lagardie said.

"But you *are* listening. Sheer good manners, I suppose. Okay. Now what did I find? A photo of a movie queen and an ex-Cleveland gangster, maybe, now a Hollywood restaurant owner, etc., having lunch on a particular day. Day when this ex-Cleveland gangster was supposed to be in hock at the County Jail, also day when ex-Cleveland gangster's onetime sidekick was shot dead on Franklin Avenue in Los Angeles. Why was he in hock? Tip-off that he was who he was, and say what you like against the L.A. cops they do try to run back-East hot shots out of town. Who gave them the tip? The guy they pinched gave it to them himself, because his ex-partner was being troublesome and had to be rubbed out, and being in jail was a first-class alibi when it happened."

"All fantastic," Dr. Lagardie smiled wearily. "Utterly fantastic."

"Sure. It gets worse. Cops couldn't prove anything on ex-gangster. Cleveland police not interested. The L.A. cops turn him loose. But they wouldn't have turned him loose if they'd seen that photo. Photo therefore strong blackmail material, first against ex-Cleveland character, if he really is the guy; secondly against movie queen for being seen around with him in public. A good man could make a fortune out of that photo. Hicks not good enough. Paragraph. Presumption B: Orrin Quest, the boy I'm trying to find, took that photo. Taken with Contax or Leica, without flashbulb, without subjects knowing they were being photographed. Quest had a Leica and liked to do things like that. In this case of course he had a more commercial motive. Question, how did he get a chance to take photo? Answer, the movie queen was his sister. She would let him come up and speak to her. He was out of work, needed money. Likely enough she gave him some and made it a condition he stay away from her. She wants no part of her family. Is it still utterly fantastic, Doctor?"

He stared at me moodily. "I don't know," he said slowly. "It begins to have possibilities. But why are you telling this rather dangerous story to me?"

He reached a cigarette out of the box and tossed me one casually. I caught it and looked it over. Egyptian, oval and fat, a little rich for my blood. I didn't light it, just sat holding it between my fingers, watching his dark unhappy eyes. He lit his own cigarette and puffed nervously.

"I'll tie you in on it now," I said. "You knew Clausen. Professionally, you said. I showed him I was a dick. He tried at once to call you up: He was too drunk to talk to you. I caught the number and later told you he was dead. Why? If you were on the level, you would call the cops. You didn't. Why? You knew Clausen, you could have known some of his roomers. No proof either way. Paragraph. Presumption C: you knew Hicks or Orrin Quest or both. The L.A. cops couldn't or didn't establish identity of ex-Cleveland character—let's give him his new name, call him Steelgrave. But *somebody* had to be able to—if that photo was worth killing people over. Did you ever practice medicine in Cleveland, Doctor?"

"Certainly not." His voice seemed to come from far off. His eyes were remote too. His lips opened barely enough to admit his cigarette. He was very still.

I said: "They have a whole roomful of directories over at the telephone office. From all over the country. I checked you up."

"A suite in a downtown office building," I said. "And now this—an almost furtive practice in a little beach town. You'd have liked to change your name—but you couldn't and keep your license. Somebody had to mastermind this deal, Doctor. Clausen was a bum, Hicks a stupid lout, Orrin Quest a nasty-minded creep. But they could be used. You couldn't go up against Steelgrave directly. You wouldn't have stayed alive long enough to brush your teeth. You had to work through pawns—expendable pawns. Well—are we getting anywhere?"

He smiled faintly and leaned back in his chair with a sigh. "Presumption D, Mr. Marlowe," he almost whispered. "You are an unmitigated idiot."

I grinned and reached for a match to light his fat Egyptian cigarette.

"Added to all the rest," I said, "Orrin's sister calls me up and tells me he is in your house. There are a lot of weak arguments taken one at a time, I admit. But they do seem to sort of focus on you." I puffed peacefully on the cigarette.

He watched me. His face seemed to fluctuate and become vague, to move far off and come back. I felt a tightness in my chest. My mind had slowed to a turtle's gallop.

"What's going on here?" I heard myself mumble.

I put my hands on the arms of the chair and pushed myself up. "Been dumb, haven't I?" I said, with the cigarette still in my mouth and me still smoking it. Dumb was hardly the word. Have to coin a new word.

I was out of the chair and my feet were stuck in two barrels of cement. When I spoke my voice seemed to come through cottonwool.

I let go of the arms of the chair and reached for the cigarette. I missed it clean a couple of times, then got my hand

around it. It didn't feel like a cigarette. It felt like the hind leg
of an elephant. With sharp toenails. They stuck into my hand.
I shook my hand and the elephant took his leg away.

A vague but enormously tall figure swung around in front
of me and a mule kicked me in the chest. I sat down on the
floor.

"A little potassium hydrocyanide," a voice said, over the
transatlantic telephone. "Not fatal, not even dangerous.
Merely relaxing. . . ."

I started to get up off the floor. You ought to try it sometime. But have somebody nail the floor down first. This one
looped the loop. After a while it steadied a little. I settled for
an angle of forty-five degrees. I took hold of myself and
started to go somewhere. There was a thing that might have
been Napoleon's tomb on the horizon. That was a good
enough objective. I started that way. My heart beat fast and
thick and I was having trouble opening my lungs. Like after
being winded at football. You think your breath will never
come back. Never, never, never.

Then it wasn't Napoleon's tomb any more. It was a raft on
a swell. There was a man on it. I'd seen him somewhere. Nice
fellow. We'd got on fine. I started towards him and hit a wall
with my shoulder. That spun me around. I started clawing for
something to hold on to. There was nothing but the carpet.
How did I get down there? No use asking. It's a secret. Every
time you ask a question they just push the floor in your face.
Okay, I started to crawl along the carpet. I was on what formerly had been my hands and knees. No sensation proved it.
I crawled towards a dark wooden wall. Or it could have been
black marble. Napoleon's tomb again. What did I ever do to
Napoleon? What for should he keep shoving his tomb at me?

"Need a drink of water," I said.

I listened for the echo. No echo. Nobody said anything.
Maybe I didn't say it. Maybe it was just an idea I thought
better of. Potassium cyanide. That's a couple of long words to
be worrying about when you're crawling through tunnels.
Nothing fatal, he said. Okay, this is just fun. What you might
call semi-fatal. Philip Marlowe, 38, a private license operator
of shady reputation, was apprehended by police last night
while crawling through the Ballona Storm Drain with a grand

piano on his back. Questioned at the University Heights Police station Marlowe declared he was taking the piano to the Maharajah of Coot-Berar. Asked why he was wearing spurs Marlowe declared that a client's confidence was sacred. Marlowe is being held for investigation. Chief Hornside said police were not yet ready to say more. Asked if the piano was in tune Chief Hornside declared that he had played the Minute Waltz on it in thirty-five seconds and so far as he could tell there were no strings in the piano. He intimated that something else was. A complete statement to the press will be made within twelve hours, Chief Hornside said abruptly. Speculation is rife that Marlowe was attempting to dispose of a body.

A face swam towards me out of the darkness. I changed direction and started for the face. But it was too late in the afternoon. The sun was setting. It was getting dark rapidly. There was no face. There was no wall, no desk. Then there was no floor. There was nothing at all.

I wasn't even there.

## 22

A big black gorilla with a big black paw had his big black paw over my face and was trying to push it through the back of my neck. I pushed back. Taking the weak side of an argument is my specialty. Then I realized that he was trying to keep me from opening my eyes.

I decided to open my eyes just the same. Others have done it, why not me? I gathered my strength and very slowly, keeping the back straight, flexing the thighs and knees, using the arms as ropes, I lifted the enormous weight of my eyelids.

I was looking at the ceiling, lying on my back on the floor, a position in which my calling has occasionally placed me. I rolled my head. My lungs felt stiff and my mouth felt dry. The room was just Dr. Lagardie's consulting room. Same chair, same desk, same walls and window. There was a shuttered silence hanging around.

I got up on my haunches and braced myself on the floor and shook my head. It went into a flat spin. It spun down about five thousand feet and then I dragged it out and leveled off. I blinked. Same floor, same desk, same walls. But no Dr. Lagardie.

I wet my lips and made some kind of a vague noise to which nobody paid any attention. I got up on my feet. I was as dizzy as a dervish, as weak as a worn-out washer, as low as a badger's belly, as timid as a titmouse, and as unlikely to succeed as a ballet dancer with a wooden leg.

I groped my way over behind the desk and slumped into Lagardie's chair and began to paw fitfully through his equipment for a likely-looking bottle of liquid fertilizer. Nothing doing. I got up again. I was as hard to lift as a dead elephant. I staggered around looking into cabinets of shining white enamel which contained everything somebody else was in a hurry for. Finally, after what seemed like four years on the road gang, my little hand closed around six ounces of ethyl alcohol. I got the top off the bottle and sniffed. Grain alcohol. Just what the label said. All I needed now was a glass and some water. A good man ought to be able to get that far. I started through the door to the examination room. The air still had the aromatic perfume of overripe peaches. I hit both sides of the doorway going through and paused to take a fresh sighting.

At that moment I was aware that steps were coming down the hall. I leaned against the wall wearily and listened.

Slow, dragging steps, with a long pause between each. At first they seemed furtive. Then they just seemed very, very tired. An old man trying to make it to his last armchair. That made two of us. And then I thought, for no reason at all, of Orfamay's father back there on the porch in Manhattan, Kansas, moving quietly along to his rocking chair with his cold pipe in his hand, to sit down and look out over the front lawn and have himself a nice economical smoke that required no matches and no tobacco and didn't mess up the living-room carpet. I arranged his chair for him. In the shade at the end of the porch where the bougainvillaea was thick I helped him sit down. He looked up and thanked me with the good side of his face. His fingernails scratched on the arms of the chair as he leaned back.

The fingernails scratched, but it wasn't on the arm of any chair. It was a real sound. It was close by, on the outside of a closed door that led from the examination room to the hallway. A thin feeble scratch, possibly a young kitten wanting to be let in. Okay, Marlowe, you're an old animal lover. Go over and let the kitten in. I started. I made it with the help of the nice examination couch with the rings on the end and the nice clean towels. The scratching had stopped. Poor little kitten, outside and wanting in. A tear formed itself in my eye and trickled down my furrowed cheek. I let go of the examination table and made a smooth four yards to the door. The heart was bumping inside me. And the lungs still had that feeling of having been in storage for a couple of years. I took a deep breath and got hold of the doorknob and opened it. Just at the last moment it occurred to me to reach for a gun. It occurred to me but that's as far as I got. I'm a fellow that likes to take an idea over by the light and have a good look at it. I'd have had to let go of the doorknob. It seemed like too big an operation. I just twisted the knob and opened the door instead.

He was braced to the doorframe by four hooked fingers made of white wax. He had eyes an eighth of an inch deep, pale gray-blue, wide open. They looked at me but they didn't see me. Our faces were inches apart. Our breathing met in midair. Mine was quick and harsh, his was the far-off whisper which has not yet begun to rattle. Blood bubbled from his mouth and ran down his chin. Something made me look down. Blood drained slowly down the inside of his trouser leg and out on his shoe and from his shoe it flowed without haste to the floor. It was already a small pool.

I couldn't see where he had been shot. His teeth clicked and I thought he was going to speak, or try to speak. But that was the only sound from him. He had stopped breathing. His jaw fell slack. Then the rattle started. It isn't a rattle at all, of course. It isn't anything like a rattle.

Rubber heels squeaked on the linoleum between the rug and the door sill. The white fingers slid away from the door frame. The man's body started to wind up on the legs. The legs refused to hold it. They scissored. His torso turned in midair, like a swimmer in a wave, and jumped at me.

In the same moment his other arm, the one that had been out of sight, came up and over in a galvanic sweep that seemed not to have any possible living impetus behind it. It fell across my left shoulder as I reached for him. A bee stung me between the shoulder blades. Something besides the bottle of alcohol I had been holding thumped to the floor and rattled against the bottom of the wall.

I clamped my teeth hard and spread my feet and caught him under the arms. He weighed like five men. I took a step back and tried to hold him up. It was like trying to lift one end of a fallen tree. I went down with him. His head bumped the floor. I couldn't help it. There wasn't enough of me working to stop it. I straightened him out a bit and got away from him. I climbed up on my knees, and bent down and listened. The rattle stopped. There was a long silence. Then there was a muted sigh, very quiet and indolent and without urgency. Another silence. Another still slower sigh, languid and peaceful as a summer breeze drifting past the nodding roses.

Something happened to his face and behind his face, the indefinable thing that happens in that always baffling and inscrutable moment, the smoothing out, the going back over the years to the age of innocence. The face now had a vague inner amusement, an almost roguish lift at the corners of the mouth. All of which was very silly, because I knew damn well, if I ever knew anything at all, that Orrin P. Quest had not been that kind of boy.

In the distance a siren wailed. I stayed kneeling and listened. It wailed and went away. I got to my feet and went over and looked out of the side window. In front of The Garland Home of Peace another funeral was forming up. The street was thick with cars again. People walked slowly up the path past the tree roses. Very slowly, the men with their hats in their hands long before they reached the little colonial porch.

I dropped the curtain and went over and picked up the bottle of ethyl alcohol and wiped it off with my handkerchief and laid it aside. I was no longer interested in alcohol. I bent down again and the bee-sting between my shoulder blades reminded me that there was something else to pick up. A thing with a round white wooden handle that lay against the baseboard. An ice pick with a filed-down blade not more than three inches long. I held it against the light and looked at the needle-sharp tip. There might or might not have been a faint stain of my blood on it. I pulled a finger gently beside the point. No blood. The point was very sharp.

I did some more work with my handkerchief and then bent down and put the ice pick on the palm of his right hand, white and waxy against the dull nap of the carpet. It looked too arranged. I shook his arm enough to make it roll off his hand to the floor. I thought about going through his pockets, but a more ruthless hand than mine would have done that already.

In a flash of sudden panic I went through mine instead. Nothing had been taken. Even the Luger under my arm had been left. I dragged it out and sniffed at it. It had not been fired, something I should have known without looking. You don't walk around much after being shot with a Luger.

I stepped over the dark red pool in the doorway and looked along the hall. The house was still silent and waiting. The blood trail led me back and across to a room furnished like a den. There was a studio couch and a desk, some books and medical journals, an ash tray with five fat oval stubs in it. A metallic glitter near the leg of the studio couch turned out to be a used shell from an automatic — .32 caliber. I found another under the desk. I put them in my pocket.

I went back out and up the stairs. There were two bedrooms both in use, one pretty thoroughly stripped of clothes. In an ash tray more of Dr. Lagardie's oval stubs. The other room contained Orrin Quest's meager wardrobe, his spare suit and overcoat neatly hung in the closet, his shirts and socks and underwear equally neat in the drawers of a chest. Under the shirts at the back I found a Leica with an F.2 lens.

I left all these things as they were and went back downstairs into the room where the dead man lay indifferent to these trifles. I wiped off a few more doorknobs out of sheer perverseness, hesitated over the phone in the front room, and left without touching it. The fact that I was still walking around was a pretty good indication that the good Dr. Lagardie hadn't killed anybody.

People were still crawling up the walk to the oddly under-sized colonial porch of the funeral parlors across the street. An organ was moaning inside.

I went around the corner of the house and got into my car and left. I drove slowly and breathed deeply from the bottom of my lungs, but I still couldn't seem to get enough oxygen.

Bay City ends about four miles from the ocean. I stopped in front of the last drugstore. It was time for me to make one more of my anonymous phone calls. Come and pick up the body, fellows. Who am I? Just a lucky boy who keeps finding them for you. Modest too. Don't even want my name mentioned.

I looked at the drugstore and in through the plate-glass front. A girl with slanted cheaters was reading at a magazine. She looked something like Orfamay Quest. Something tightened up my throat.

I let the clutch in and drove on. She had a right to know first, law or no law. And I was far outside the law already.

# 23

I stopped at the office door with the key in my hand. Then I went noiselessly along to the other door, the one that was always unlocked, and stood there and listened. She might be in there already, waiting, with her eyes shining behind the slanted cheaters and the small moist mouth willing to be kissed. I would have to tell her a harder thing than she dreamed of, and then after a while she would go and I would never see her again.

I didn't hear anything. I went back and unlocked the other door and picked the mail up and carried it over and dumped it on the desk. Nothing in it made me feel any taller. I left it and crossed to turn the latch in the other door and after a long slow moment I opened it and looked out. Silence and emptiness. A folded piece of paper lay at my feet. It had been pushed under the door. I picked it up and unfolded it.

"Please call me at the apartment house. Most urgent. I must see you." It was signed D.

I dialed the number of the Chateau Bercy and asked for Miss Gonzales. Who was calling, please? One moment please, Mr. Marlowe. Buzz, buzz. Buzz, buzz.

" 'Allo?"

"The accent's a bit thick this afternoon."

"Ah, it is you, amigo. I waited so long in your funny little office. Can you come over here and talk to me?"

"Impossible. I'm waiting for a call."

"Well, may I come there?"

"What's it all about?"

"Nothing I could discuss on the telephone, amigo."

"Come ahead."

I sat there and waited for the telephone to ring. It didn't ring. I looked out of the window. The crowd was seething on the boulevard, the kitchen of the coffee shop next door was pouring the smell of Blue Plate Specials out of its ventilator shaft. Time passed and I sat there hunched over the desk, my chin in a hand, staring at the mustard-yellow plaster of the end wall, seeing on it the vague figure of a dying man with a short ice pick in his hand, and feeling the sting of its point between my shoulder blades. Wonderful what Hollywood will do to a nobody. It will make a radiant glamour queen out of a drab little wench who ought to be ironing a truck driver's shirts, a he-man hero with shining eyes and brilliant smile reeking of sexual charm out of some overgrown kid who was meant to go to work with a lunchbox. Out of a Texas car hop with the literacy of a character in a comic strip it will make an international courtesan, married six times to six millionaires and so blasé and decadent at the end of it that her idea of a thrill is to seduce a furniture mover in a sweaty undershirt.

And by remote control it might even take a small-town prig like Orrin Quest and make an ice-pick murderer out of him in a matter of months, elevating his simple meanness into the classic sadism of the multiple killer.

It took her a little over ten minutes to get there. I heard the door open and close and I went through to the waiting room and there she was, the All-American Gardenia. She hit me right between the eyes. Her own were deep and dark and unsmiling.

She was all in black, like the night before, but a tailor-made outfit this time, a wide black straw hat set at a rakish angle, the collar of a white silk shirt folded out over the collar of her jacket, and her throat brown and supple and her mouth as red as a new fire engine.

"I waited a long time," she said. "I have not had any lunch."

"I had mine," I said. "Cyanide. Very satisfying. I've only just stopped looking blue."

"I am not in an amusing mood this morning, amigo."

"You don't have to amuse me," I said. "I amuse myself. I do a brother act that has me rolling in the aisle. Let's go inside."

We went into my private thinking parlor and sat down.

"You always wear black?" I asked.

"But yes. It is more exciting when I take my clothes off."

"Do you have to talk like a whore?"

"You do not know much about whores, amigo. They are always most respectable. Except of course the very cheap ones."

"Yeah," I said. "Thanks for telling me. What is the urgent matter we have to talk about? Going to bed with you is not urgent. It can be done any day."

"You are in a nasty mood."

"Okay. I'm in a nasty mood."

She got one of her long brown cigarettes out of her bag and fitted it carefully into the golden tweezers. She waited for me to light it for her. I didn't so she lit it herself with a golden lighter.

She held this doohickey in a black gauntleted glove and stared at me out of depthless black eyes that had no laughter in them now.

"Would you like to go to bed with me?"

"Most anyone would. But let's leave sex out of it for now."

"I do not draw a very sharp line between business and sex," she said evenly. "And you cannot humiliate me. Sex is a net with which I catch fools. Some of these fools are useful and generous. Occasionally one is dangerous."

She paused thoughtfully.

I said: "If you're waiting for me to say something that lets on I know who a certain party is—okay, I know who he is."

"Can you prove it?"

"Probably not. The cops couldn't."

"The cops," she said contemptuously, "do not always tell all they know. They do not always prove everything they could prove. I suppose you know he was in jail for ten days last February."

"Yes."

"Did it not occur to you as strange that he did not get bail?"

"I don't know what charge they had him on. If it was as a material witness—"

"Do you not think he could get the charge changed to something bailable—if he really wanted to?"

"I haven't thought much about it," I lied. "I don't know the man."

"You have never spoken to him?" she asked idly, a little too idly.

I didn't answer.

She laughed shortly. "Last night, amigo. Outside Mavis Weld's apartment. I was sitting in a car across the street."

"I may have bumped into him accidentally. Was that the guy?"

"You do not fool me at all."

"Okay. Miss Weld was pretty rough with me. I went away sore. Then I meet this ginzo with her doorkey in his hand. I yank it out of his hand and toss it behind some bushes. Then I apologize and go get it for him. He seemed like a nice little guy too."

"Ver-ry nice," she drawled. "He was *my* boy friend also."

I grunted.

"Strange as it may seem I'm not a hell of a lot interested in your love life, Miss Gonzales. I assume it covers a wide field—all the way from Stein to Steelgrave."

"Stein?" she asked softly. "Who is Stein?"

"A Cleveland hot shot that got himself gunned in front of your apartment house last February. He had an apartment there. I thought perhaps you might have met him."

She let out a silvery little laugh. "Amigo, there are men I do not know. Even at the Chateau Bercy."

"Reports say he was gunned two blocks away," I said. "I like it better that it happened right in front. And you were looking out of the window and saw it happen. And saw the killer run away and just under a street light he turned back and the light caught his face and darned if it wasn't old man Steelgrave. You recognized him by his rubber nose and the fact that he was wearing his tall hat with the pigeons on it."

She didn't laugh.

"You like it better that way," she purred.

"We could make more money that way."

"But Steelgrave was in jail," she smiled. "And even if he was not in jail—even if, for example, I happened to be friendly with a certain Dr. Chalmers who was county jail physician at the time and he told me, in an intimate moment, that he had given Steelgrave a pass to go to the dentist—with a guard of course, but the guard was a reasonable man—on the very day Stein was shot—even if this happened to be true, would it not be a very poor way to use the information by blackmailing Steelgrave?"

"I hate to talk big," I said, "but I'm not afraid of Steelgrave—or a dozen like him in one package."

"But I am, amigo. A witness to a gang murder is not in a very safe position in this country. No, we will not blackmail Steelgrave. And we will not say anything about Mr. Stein, whom I may or may not have known. It is enough that Mavis Weld is a close friend of a known gangster and is seen in public with him."

"We'd have to prove he was a known gangster," I said.

"Can we not do that?"

"How?"

She made a disappointed mouth. "But I felt sure that was what you had been doing these last couple of days."

"Why?"

"I have private reasons."

"They mean nothing to me while you keep them private."

She got rid of the brown cigarette stub in my ash tray. I leaned over and squashed it out with the stub of a pencil. She touched my hand lightly with a gauntleted finger. Her smile was the reverse of anesthetic. She leaned back and crossed her legs. The little lights began to dance in her eyes. It was a long time between passes—for her.

"Love is such a dull word," she mused. "It amazes me that the English language so rich in the poetry of love can accept such a feeble word for it. It has no life, no resonance. It suggests to me little girls in ruffled summer dresses, with little pink smiles, and little shy voices, and probably the most unbecoming underwear."

I said nothing. With an effortless change of pace she became businesslike again.

"Mavis will get $75,000 a picture from now on, and eventually $150,000. She has started to climb and nothing will stop her. Except possibly a bad scandal."

"Then somebody ought to tell her who Steelgrave is," I said. "Why don't you? And incidentally, suppose we did have all this proof, what's Steelgrave doing all the time we're putting the bite on Weld?"

"Does he have to know? I hardly think she would tell him. In fact, I hardly think she would go on having anything to do with him. But that would not matter to us—if we had our proof. And if she knew we had it."

Her black gauntleted hand moved towards her black bag, stopped, drummed lightly on the edge of the desk, and so got back to where she could drop it in her lap. She hadn't looked at the bag. I hadn't either.

I stood up. "I might happen to be under some obligation to Miss Weld. Ever think of that?"

She just smiled.

"And if that was so," I said, "don't you think it's about time you got the hell out of my office?"

She put her hands on the arms of her chair and started to get up, still smiling. I scooped the bag before she could change direction. Her eyes filled with glare. She made a spitting sound.

I opened the bag and went through and found a white envelope that looked a little familiar. Out of it I shook the photo at The Dancers, the two pieces fitted together and pasted on another piece of paper.

I closed the bag and tossed it across to her.

She was on her feet now, her lips drawn back over her teeth. She was very silent.

"Interesting," I said and snapped a digit at the glazed surface of the print. "If it's not a fake. Is that Steelgrave?"

The silvery laugh bubbled up again. "You are a ridiculous character, amigo. You really are. I did not know they made such people any more."

"Prewar stock," I said. "We're getting scarcer every day. Where did you get this?"

"From Mavis Weld's purse in Mavis Weld's dressing room. While she was on the set."

"She know?"

"She does not know."

"I wonder where she got it."

"From you."

"Nonsense." I raised my eyebrows a few inches. "Where would *I* get it?"

She reached the gauntleted hand across the desk. Her voice was cold. "Give it back to me, please."

"I'll give it back to Mavis Weld. And I hate to tell you this, Miss Gonzales, but I'd never get anywhere as a blackmailer. I just don't have the engaging personality."

"Give it back to me!" she said sharply. "If you do not—"

She cut herself off. I waited for her to finish. A look of contempt showed on her smooth features.

"Very well," she said. "It is my mistake. I thought you were smart, I can see that you are just another dumb private eye. This shabby little office," she waved a black gloved hand at it, "and the shabby little life that goes on here—they ought to tell me what sort of idiot you are."

"They do," I said.

She turned slowly and walked to the door. I got around the desk and she let me open it for her.

She went out slowly. The way she did it hadn't been learned at business college.

She went on down the hall without looking back. She had a beautiful walk.

The door bumped against the pneumatic doorcloser and very softly clicked shut. It seemed to take a long time to do that. I stood there watching it as if I had never seen it happen before. Then I turned and started back towards my desk and the phone rang.

I picked it up and answered it. It was Christy French. "Marlowe? We'd like to see you down at headquarters."

"Right away?"

"If not sooner," he said and hung up.

I slipped the pasted-together print from under the blotter and went over to put it in the safe with the others. I put my hat on and closed the window. There was nothing to wait for. I looked at the green tip on the sweep hand of my watch. It was a long time until five o'clock. The sweep hand went around and around the dial like a door-to-door salesman. The hands stood at four-ten. You'd think she'd have called up by now. I peeled my coat off and unstrapped the shoulder harness and locked it with the Luger in the desk drawer. The cops don't like you to be wearing a gun in their territory. Even if you have the right to wear one. They like you to come in properly humble, with your hat in your hand, and your voice low and polite, and your eyes full of nothing.

I looked at the watch again. I listened. The building seemed quiet this afternoon. After a while it would be silent and then the madonna of the dark-gray mop would come shuffling along the hall, trying doorknobs.

I put my coat back on and locked the communicating door and switched off the buzzer and let myself out into the hallway. And then the phone rang. I nearly took the door off its hinges getting back to it. It was her voice all right, but it had a tone I had never heard before. A cool balanced tone, not flat or empty or dead, or even childish. Just the voice of a girl I didn't know and yet did know. What was in that voice I knew before she said more than three words.

"I called you up because you told me to," she said. "But you don't have to tell me anything. I went down there."

I was holding the phone with both hands.

"You went down there," I said. "Yes. I heard that. So?"

"I—borrowed a car," she said. "I parked across the street. There were so many cars you would never have noticed me. There's a funeral home there. I wasn't following you. I tried to go after you when you came out but I don't know the streets down there at all. I lost you. So I went back."

"What did you go back for?"

"I don't really know. I thought you looked kind of funny when you came out of the house. Or maybe I just had a feeling. He being my brother and all. So I went back and rang the bell. And nobody answered the door. I thought that was funny too. Maybe I'm psychic or something. All of a sudden I seemed to have to get into that house. And I didn't know how to do it, but I had to."

"That's happened to me," I said, and it was my voice, but somebody had been using my tongue for sandpaper.

"I called the police and told them I had heard shots," she said. "They came and one of them got into the house through a window. And then he let the other one in. And after a while they let me in. And then they wouldn't let me go. I had to tell them all about it, who he was, and that I had lied about the shots, but I was afraid something had happened to Orrin. And I had to tell them about you too."

"That's all right," I said. "I'd have told them myself as soon as I could get a chance to tell *you*."

"It's kind of awkward for you, isn't it?"

"Yes."

"Will they arrest you or something?"

"They could."

"You left him lying there on the floor. Dead. You had to, I guess."

"I had my reasons," I said. "They won't sound too good, but I had them. It made no difference to him."

"Oh you'd have your reasons all right," she said. "You're very smart. You'd always have reasons for things. Well, I guess you'll have to tell the police your reasons too."

"Not necessarily."

"Oh yes, you will," the voice said, and there was a ring of pleasure in it I couldn't account for. "You certainly will. They'll make you."

"We won't argue about that," I said. "In my business a fellow does what he can to protect a client. Sometimes he goes a little too far. That's what I did. I've put myself where they can hurt me. But not entirely for you."

"You left him lying on the floor, dead," she said. "And I

don't care what they do to you. If they put you in prison, I think I would like that. I bet you'll be awfully brave about it."

"Sure," I said. "Always a gay smile. Do you see what he had in his hand?"

"He didn't have anything in his hand."

"Well, lying near his hand."

"There wasn't anything. There wasn't anything at all. What sort of thing?"

"That's fine," I said. "I'm glad of that. Well, goodbye. I'm going down to headquarters now. They want to see me. Good luck, if I don't see you again."

"You'd better keep your good luck," she said. "You might need it. And I wouldn't want it."

"I did my best for you," I said. "Perhaps if you'd given me a little more information in the beginning—"

She hung up while I was saying it.

I put the phone down in its cradle as gently as if it was a baby. I got out a handkerchief and wiped the palms of my hands. I went over to the washbasin and washed my hands and face. I sloshed cold water on my face and dried it off hard with the towel and looked at it in the mirror.

"You drove off a cliff all right," I said to the face.

## 24

In the center of the room was a long yellow oak table. Its edges were unevenly grooved with cigarette burns. Behind it was a window with wire over the stippled glass. Also behind it with a mess of papers spread out untidily in front of him was Detective-Lieutenant Fred Beifus. At the end of the table leaning back on two legs of an armchair was a big burly man whose face had for me the vague familiarity of a face previously seen in a halftone on newsprint. He had a jaw like a park bench. He had the butt end of a carpenter's pencil between his teeth. He seemed to be awake and breathing, but apart from that he just sat.

There were two rolltop desks at the other side of the table and there was another window. One of the rolltop desks was backed to the window. A woman with orange-colored hair was typing out a report on a typewriter stand beside the desk. At the other desk, which was endways to the window, Christy French sat in a tilted-back swivel chair with his feet on the corner of the desk. He was looking out of the window, which was open and afforded a magnificent view of the police parking lot and the back of a billboard.

"Sit down there," Beifus said, pointing.

I sat down across from him in a straight oak chair without arms. It was far from new and when new had not been beautiful.

"This is Lieutenant Moses Maglashan of the Bay City police," Beifus said. "He don't like you any better than we do."

Lieutenant Moses Maglashan took the carpenter's pencil out of his mouth and looked at the teeth marks in the fat octagonal pencil butt. Then he looked at me. His eyes went over me slowly exploring me, noting me, cataloguing me. He said nothing. He put the pencil back in his mouth.

Beifus said: "Maybe I'm a queer, but for me you don't have no more sex appeal than a turtle." He half turned to the typing woman in the corner. "Millie."

She swung around from the typewriter to a shorthand notebook. "Name's Philip Marlowe," Beifus said. "With an 'e' on the end, if you're fussy. License number?"

He looked back at me. I told him. The orange queen wrote without looking up. To say she had a face that would have stopped a clock would have been to insult her. It would have stopped a runaway horse.

"Now if you're in the mood," Beifus told me, "you could start in at the beginning and give us all the stuff you left out yesterday. Don't try to sort it out. Just let it flow natural. We got enough stuff to check you as you go along."

"You want me to make a statement?"

"A very full statement," Beifus said. "Fun, huh?"

"This statement is to be voluntary and without coercion?"

"Yeah. They all are." Beifus grinned.

Maglashan looked at me steadily for a moment. The orange

queen turned back to her typing. Nothing for her yet. Thirty years of it had perfected her timing.

Maglashan took a heavy worn pigskin glove out of his pocket and put it on his right hand and flexed his fingers.

"What's that for?" Beifus asked him.

"I bite my nails times," Maglashan said. "Funny. Only bite 'em on my right hand." He raised his slow eyes to stare at me. "Some guys are more voluntary than others," he said idly. "Something to do with the kidneys, they tell me. I've known guys of the not so voluntary type that had to go to the can every fifteen minutes for weeks after they got voluntary. Couldn't seem to hold water."

"Just think of that," Beifus said wonderingly.

"Then there's the guys can't talk above a husky whisper," Maglashan went on. "Like punch-drunk fighters that have stopped too many with their necks."

Maglashan looked at me. It seemed to be my turn.

"Then there's the type that won't go to the can at all," I said. "They try too hard. Sit in a chair like this for thirty hours straight. Then they fall down and rupture a spleen or burst a bladder. They overco-operate. And after sunrise court, when the tank is empty, you find them dead in a dark corner. Maybe they ought to have seen a doctor, but you can't figure everything, can you, Lieutenant?"

"We figure pretty close down in Bay City," he said. "When we got anything to figure with."

There were hard lumps of muscle at the corners of his jaws. His eyes had a reddish glare behind them.

"I could do lovely business with you," he said staring at me. "Just lovely."

"I'm sure you could, Lieutenant. I've always had a swell time in Bay City—while I stayed conscious."

"I'd keep you conscious a long long time, baby. I'd make a point of it. I'd give it my personal attention."

Christy French turned his head slowly and yawned. "What makes you Bay City cops so tough?" he asked. "You pickle your nuts in salt water or something?"

Beifus put his tongue out so that the tip showed and ran it along his lips.

"We've always been tough," Maglashan said, not looking at

him. "We like to be tough. Jokers like this character here keep us tuned up." He turned back to me. "So you're the sweetheart that phoned in about Clausen. You're right handy with a pay phone, ain't you, sweetheart?"

I didn't say anything.

"I'm talking to you, sweetheart," Maglashan said. "I asked you a question, sweetheart. When I ask a question I get answered. Get that, sweetheart?"

"Keep on talking and you'll answer yourself," Christy French said. "And maybe you won't like the answer, and maybe you'll be so damn tough you'll have to knock yourself out with that glove. Just to prove it."

Maglashan straightened up. Red spots the size of half-dollars glowed dully on his cheeks.

"I come up here to get co-operation," he told French slowly. "The big razzoo I can get to home. From my wife. Here I don't expect the wise numbers to work out on me."

"You'll get co-operation," French said. "Just don't try to steal the picture with that nineteen-thirty dialogue." He swung his chair around and looked at me. "Let's take out a clean sheet of paper and play like we're just starting this investigation. I know all your arguments. I'm no judge of them. The point is do you want to talk or get booked as a material witness?"

"Ask the questions," I said. "If you don't like the answers, you can book me. If you book me, I get to make a phone call."

"Correct," French said, "*if* we book you. But we don't have to. We can ride the circuit with you. It might take days."

"And canned cornbeef hash to eat," Beifus put in cheerfully.

"Strictly speaking, it wouldn't be legal," French said. "But we do it all the time. Like you do a few things which you hadn't ought to do maybe. Would you say you were legal in this picture?"

"No."

Maglashan let out a deep throated, "Ha!"

I looked across at the orange queen who was back to her notebook, silent and indifferent.

"You got a client to protect," French said.

"Maybe."

"You mean you did have a client. She ratted on you."

I said nothing.

"Name's Orfamay Quest," French said, watching me.

"Ask your questions," I said.

"What happened down there on Idaho Street?"

"I went there looking for her brother. He'd moved away, she said, and she'd come out here to see him. She was worried. The manager, Clausen, was too drunk to talk sense. I looked at the register and saw another man had moved into Quest's room. I talked to this man. He told me nothing that helped."

French reached around and picked a pencil off the desk and tapped it against his teeth. "Ever see this man again?"

"Yes. I told him who I was. When I went back downstairs Clausen was dead. And somebody had torn a page out of the register. The page with Quest's name on it. I called the police."

"But you didn't stick around?"

"I had no information about Clausen's death."

"But you didn't stick around," French repeated. Maglashan made a savage noise in his throat and threw the carpenter's pencil clear across the room. I watched it bounce against the wall and floor and come to a stop.

"That's correct," I said.

"In Bay City," Maglashan said, "we could murder you for that."

"In Bay City you could murder me for wearing a blue tie," I said.

He started to get up. Beifus looked sideways at him and said: "Leave Christy handle it. There's always a second show."

"We could break you for that," French said to me without inflexion.

"Consider me broke," I said. "I never liked the business anyway."

"So you came back to your office. What then?"

"I reported to the client. Then a guy called me up and asked me over to the Van Nuys Hotel. He was the same guy I had talked to down on Idaho Street, but with a different name."

"You could have told us that, couldn't you?"

"If I had, I'd have had to tell you everything. That would have violated the conditions of my employment."

French nodded and tapped his pencil. He said slowly: "A murder wipes out agreements like that. Two murders ought to do it double. And two murders by the same method, treble. You don't look good, Marlowe. You don't look good at all."

"I don't even look good to the client," I said, "after today."

"What happened today?"

"She told me her brother had called her up from this doctor's house. Dr. Lagardie. The brother was in danger. I was to hurry on down and take care of him. I hurried on down. Dr. Lagardie and his nurse had the office closed. They acted scared. The police had been there." I looked at Maglashan.

"Another of his phone calls," Maglashan snarled.

"Not me this time," I said.

"All right. Go on," French said, after a pause.

"Lagardie denied knowing anything about Orrin Quest. He sent his nurse home. Then he slipped me a doped cigarette and I went away from there for a while. When I came to I was alone in the house. Then I wasn't. Orrin Quest, or what was left of him, was scratching at the door. He fell through it and died as I opened it. With his last ounce of strength he tried to stick me with an ice pick." I moved my shoulders. The place between them was a little stiff and sore, nothing more.

French looked hard at Maglashan. Maglashan shook his head, but French kept on looking at him. Beifus began to whistle under his breath. I couldn't make out the tune at first, and then I could. It was "Old Man Mose is Dead."

French turned his head and said slowly: "No ice pick was found by the body."

"I left it where it fell," I said.

Maglashan said: "Looks like I ought to be putting on my glove again." He stretched it between his fingers. "Somebody's a goddam liar and it ain't me."

"All right," French said. "All right. Let's not be theatrical.

Suppose the kid did have an ice pick in his hand, that doesn't prove he was born holding one."

"Filed down," I said. "Short. Three inches from the handle to the tip of the point. That's not the way they come from the hardware store."

"Why would he want to stick you?" Beifus asked with his derisive grin. "You were his pal. You were down there to keep him safe for his sister."

"I was just something between him and the light," I said. "Something that moved and could have been a man and could have been the man that hurt him. He was dying on his feet. I'd never seen him before. If he ever saw me, I didn't know it."

"It could have been a beautiful friendship," Beifus said with a sigh. "Except for the ice pick, of course."

"And the fact that he had it in his hand and tried to stick me with it could mean something."

"For instance what?"

"A man in his condition acts from instinct. He doesn't invent new techniques. He got me between the shoulder blades, a sting, the feeble last effort of a dying man. Maybe it would have been a different place and a much deeper penetration if he had had his health."

Maglashan said: "How much longer we have to barber round with this monkey? You talk to him like he was human. Leave me talk to him my way."

"The captain doesn't like it," French said casually.

"Hell with the captain."

"The captain doesn't like small-town cops saying the hell with him," French said.

Maglashan clamped his teeth tight and the line of his jaw showed white. His eyes narrowed and glistened. He took a deep breath through his nose.

"Thanks for the co-operation," he said and stood up. "I'll be on my way." He rounded the corner of the table and stopped beside me. He put his left hand out and tilted my chin up again.

"See you again, sweetheart. In *my* town."

He lashed me across the face twice with the wrist end of the glove. The buttons stung sharply. I put my hand up and rubbed my lower lip.

French said: "For Chrissake, Maglashan, sit down and let the guy speak his piece. And keep your hands off him."

Maglashan looked back at him and said: "Think you can make me?"

French just shrugged. After a moment Maglashan rubbed his big hand across his mouth and strolled back to his chair. French said:

"Let's have your ideas about all this, Marlowe."

"Among other things Clausen was probably pushing reefers," I said. "I sniffed marihuana smoke in his apartment. A tough little guy was counting money in the kitchen when I got there. He had a gun and a sharpened rat-tail file, both of which he tried to use on me. I took them away from him and he left. He would be the runner. But Clausen was liquored to a point where you wouldn't want to trust him any more. They don't go for that in the organizations. The runner thought I was a dick. Those people wouldn't want Clausen picked up. He would be too easy to milk. The minute they smelled dick around the house Clausen would be missing."

French looked at Maglashan. "That make any sense to you?"

"It could happen," Maglashan said grudgingly.

French said: "Suppose it was so, what's it got to do with this Orrin Quest?"

"Anybody can smoke reefers," I said. "If you're dull and lonely and depressed and out of a job, they might be very attractive. But when you smoke them you get warped ideas and calloused emotions. And marihuana affects different people different ways. Some it makes very tough and some it just makes never-no-mind. Suppose Quest tried to put the bite on somebody and threatened to go to the police. Quite possibly all three murders are connected with the reefer gang."

"That don't jibe with Quest having a filed-down ice pick," Beifus said.

I said: "According to the lieutenant here he didn't have one. So I must have imagined that. Anyhow, he might just have picked it up. They might be standard equipment around Dr. Lagardie's house. Get anything on him?"

He shook his head. "Not so far."

"He didn't kill me, probably he didn't kill anybody," I said. "Quest told his sister—according to her—that he was working for Dr. Lagardie, but that some gangsters were after him."

"This Lagardie," French said, prodding at his blotter with a pen point, "what do you make of him?"

"He used to practise in Cleveland. Downtown in a large way. He must have had his reasons for hiding out in Bay City."

"Cleveland, huh?" French drawled and looked at a corner of the ceiling. Beifus looked down at his papers. Maglashan said:

"Probably an abortionist. I've had my eye on him for some time."

"Which eye?" Beifus asked him mildly.

Maglashan flushed.

French said: "Probably the one he didn't have on Idaho Street."

Maglashan stood up violently. "You boys think you're so goddam smart it might interest you to know that we're just a small town police force. We got to double in brass once in a while. Just the same I like that reefer angle. It might cut down my work considerable. I'm looking into it right now."

He marched solidly to the door and left. French looked after him. Beifus did the same. When the door closed they looked at each other.

"I betcha they pull that raid again tonight," Beifus said.

French nodded.

Beifus said: "In a flat over a laundry. They'll go down on the beach and pull in three or four vagrants and stash them in the flat and then they'll line them up for the camera boys after they pull the raid."

French said: "You're talking too much, Fred."

Beifus grinned and was silent. French said to me: "If you were guessing, what would you guess they were looking for in that room at the Van Nuys?"

"A claim check for a suitcase full of weed."

"Not bad," French said. "And still guessing where would it have been?"

"I thought about that. When I talked to Hicks down at Bay City he wasn't wearing his muff. A man doesn't around the house. But he was wearing it on the bed at the Van Nuys. Maybe he didn't put it on himself."

French said: "So?"

I said: "Wouldn't be a bad place to stash a claim check."

French said: "You could pin it down with a piece of scotch tape. Quite an idea."

There was a silence. The orange queen went back to her typing. I looked at my nails. They weren't as clean as they might be. After the pause French said slowly:

"Don't think for a minute you're in the clear, Marlowe. Still guessing, how come Dr. Lagardie to mention Cleveland to you?"

"I took the trouble to look him up. A doctor can't change his name if he wants to go on practicing. The ice pick made you think of Weepy Moyer. Weepy Moyer operated in Cleveland. Sunny Moe Stein operated in Cleveland. It's true the ice-pick technique was different, but it was an ice pick. You said yourself the boys might have learned. And always with these gangs there's a doctor somewhere in the background."

"Pretty wild," French said. "Pretty loose connection."

"Would I do myself any good if I tightened it up?"

"Can you?"

"I can try."

French sighed. "The little Quest girl is okay," he said. "I talked to her mother back in Kansas. She really did come out here to look for her brother. And she really did hire you to do it. She gives you a good write-up. Up to a point. She really did suspect her brother was mixed up in something wrong. You make any money on the deal?"

"Not much," I said. "I gave her back the fee. She didn't have much."

"That way you don't have to pay income tax on it," Beifus said.

French said, "Let's break this off. The next move is up to the D.A. And if I know Endicott, it will be a week from Tuesday before he decides how to play it." He made a gesture towards the door.

I stood up. "Will it be all right if I don't leave town?" I asked.

They didn't bother to answer that one.

I just stood there and looked at them. The ice-pick wound between my shoulders had a dry sting, and the flesh around the place was stiff. The side of my face and mouth smarted where Maglashan had sideswiped me with his well-used pig-skin glove. I was in the deep water. It was dark and unclear and the taste of the salt was in my mouth.

They just sat there and looked back at me. The orange queen was clacking her typewriter. Cop talk was no more treat to her than legs to a dance director. They had the calm weathered faces of healthy men in hard condition. They had the eyes they always have, cloudy and gray like freezing water. The firm set mouth, the hard little wrinkles at the corners of the eyes, the hard hollow meaningless stare, not quite cruel and a thousand miles from kind. The dull ready-made clothes, worn without style, with a sort of contempt; the look of men who are poor and yet proud of their power, watching always for ways to make it felt, to shove it into you and twist it and grin and watch you squirm, ruthless without malice, cruel and yet not always unkind. What would you expect them to be? Civilization had no meaning for them. All they saw of it was the failures, the dirt, the dregs, the aberrations and the disgust.

"What you standing there for?" Beifus asked sharply. "You want us to give you a great big spitty kiss? No snappy come-back, huh? Too bad." His voice fell away into a dull drone. He frowned and reached a pencil off the desk. With a quick motion of his fingers he snapped it in half and held the two halves out on his palm.

"We're giving you that much break," he said thinly, the smile all gone. "Go on out and square things up. What the hell you think we're turning you loose for? Maglashan bought you a rain check. Use it."

I put my hand up and rubbed my lip. My mouth had too many teeth in it.

Beifus lowered his eyes to the table, picked up a paper and began to read it. Christy French swung around in his chair and put his feet on the desk and stared out of the open window at the parking lot. The orange queen stopped typing. The room was suddenly full of heavy silence, like a fallen cake.

I went on out, parting the silence as if I was pushing my way through water.

## 25

The office was empty again. No leggy brunettes, no little girls with slanted glasses, no neat dark men with gangster's eyes.

I sat down at the desk and watched the light fade. The going-home sounds had died away. Outside the neon signs began to glare at one another across the boulevard. There was something to be done, but I didn't know what. Whatever it was it would be useless. I tidied up my desk, listening to the scrape of a bucket on the tiling of the corridor. I put my papers away in the drawer, straightened the pen stand, got out a duster and wiped off the glass and then the telephone. It was dark and sleek in the fading light. It wouldn't ring tonight. Nobody would call me again. Not now, not this time. Perhaps not ever.

I put the duster away folded with the dust in it, leaned back and just sat, not smoking, not even thinking. I was a blank man. I had no face, no meaning, no personality, hardly a name. I didn't want to eat. I didn't even want a drink. I was the page from yesterday's calendar crumpled at the bottom of the waste basket.

So I pulled the phone towards me and dialed Mavis Weld's number. It rang and rang and rang. Nine times. That's a lot of ringing, Marlowe. I guess there's nobody home. Nobody home to you. I hung up. Who would you like to call now? You got a friend somewhere that might like to hear your voice? No. Nobody.

Let the telephone ring, please. Let there be somebody to call up and plug me into the human race again. Even a cop. Even a Maglashan. Nobody has to like me. I just want to get off this frozen star.

The telephone rang.

"Amigo," her voice said. "There is trouble. Bad trouble. She wants to see you. She likes you. She thinks you are an honest man."

"Where?" I asked. It wasn't really a question, just a sound I made. I sucked on a cold pipe and leaned my head on my hand, brooding at the telephone. It was a voice to talk to anyway.

"You will come?"

"I'd sit up with a sick parrot tonight. Where do I go?"

"I will come for you. I will be before your building in fifteen minutes. It is not easy to get where we go."

"How is it coming back," I asked, "or don't we care?"

But she had already hung up.

Down at the drugstore lunch counter I had time to inhale two cups of coffee and a melted-cheese sandwich with two slivers of ersatz bacon imbedded in it, like dead fish in the silt at the bottom of a drained pool.

I was crazy. I liked it.

## 26

It was a black Mercury convertible with a light top. The top was up. When I leaned in at the door Dolores Gonzales slid over towards me along the leather seat.

"You drive please, amigo. I do not really ever like to drive."

The light from the drugstore caught her face. She had changed her clothes again, but it was still all black, save for a flame-colored shirt. Slacks and a kind of loose coat like a man's leisure jacket.

I leaned on the door of the car. "Why didn't she call me?"

"She couldn't. She did not have the number and she had very little time."

"Why?"

"It seemed to be while someone was out of the room for just a moment."

"And where is this place she called from?"

"I do not know the name of the street. But I can find the house. That is why I come. Please get into the car and let us hurry."

"Maybe," I said. "And again maybe I am not getting into the car. Old age and arthritis have made me cautious."

"Always the wisecrack," she said. "It is a very strange man."

"Always the wisecrack where possible," I said, "and it is a

very ordinary guy with only one head—which has been rather harshly used at times. The times usually started out like this."

"Will you make love to me tonight?" she asked softly.

"That again is an open question. Probably not."

"You would not waste your time. I am not one of these synthetic blondes with a skin you could strike matches on. These ex-laundresses with large bony hands and sharp knees and unsuccessful breasts."

"Just for half an hour," I said, "let's leave the sex to one side. It's great stuff, like chocolate sundaes. But there comes a time you would rather cut your throat. I guess maybe I'd better cut mine."

I went around the car and slid under the wheel and started the motor.

"We go west," she said, "through the Beverly Hills and then farther on."

I let the clutch in and drifted around the corner to go south to Sunset. Dolores got one of her long brown cigarettes out.

"Did you bring a gun?" she asked.

"No. What would I want a gun for?" The inside of my left arm pressed against the Luger in the shoulder harness.

"It is better not perhaps." She fitted the cigarette into the little golden tweezer thing and lit it with the golden lighter. The light flaring in her face seemed to be swallowed up by her depthless black eyes.

I turned west on Sunset and swallowed myself up in three lanes of race-track drivers who were pushing their mounts hard to get nowhere and do nothing.

"What kind of trouble is Miss Weld in?"

"I do not know. She just said that it was trouble and she was much afraid and she needed you."

"You ought to be able to think up a better story than that."

She didn't answer. I stopped for a traffic signal and turned to look at her. She was crying softly in the dark.

"I would not hurt a hair of Mavis Weld's head," she said. "I do not quite expect that you would believe me."

"On the other hand," I said, "maybe the fact that you don't have a story helps."

She started to slide along the seat towards me.

"Keep to your own side of the car," I said. "I've got to drive this heap."

"You do not want my head on your shoulder?"

"Not in this traffic."

I stopped at Fairfax with the green light to let a man make a left turn. Horns blew violently behind. When I started again the car that had been right behind swung out and pulled level and a fat guy in a sweatshirt yelled:

"Aw go get yourself a hammock!"

He went on, cutting in so hard that I had to brake.

"I used to like this town," I said, just to be saying something and not to be thinking too hard. "A long time ago. There were trees along Wilshire Boulevard. Beverly Hills was a country town. Westwood was bare hills and lots offering at eleven hundred dollars and no takers. Hollywood was a bunch of frame houses on the interurban line. Los Angeles was just a big dry sunny place with ugly homes and no style, but goodhearted and peaceful. It had the climate they just yap about now. People used to sleep out on porches. Little groups who thought they were intellectual used to call it the Athens of America. It wasn't that, but it wasn't a neon-lighted slum either."

We crossed La Cienega and went into the curve of the Strip. The Dancers was a blaze of light. The terrace was packed. The parking lot was like ants on a piece of overripe fruit.

"Now we get characters like this Steelgrave owning restaurants. We get guys like that fat boy that balled me out back there. We've got the big money, the sharp shooters, the percentage workers, the fast-dollar boys, the hoodlums out of New York and Chicago and Detroit—and Cleveland. We've got the flash restaurants and night clubs they run, and the hotels and apartment houses they own, and the grifters and con men and female bandits that live in them. The luxury trades, the pansy decorators, the Lesbian dress designers, the riffraff of a big hardboiled city with no more personality than a paper cup. Out in the fancy suburbs dear old Dad is reading the sports page in front of a picture window, with his shoes off, thinking he is high class because he has a three-car garage. Mom is in front of her princess dresser trying to paint the suitcases out from under her eyes. And Junior is clamped onto the telephone calling up a succession of high school girls that talk pigeon English and carry contraceptives in their make-up kit."

"It is the same in all big cities, amigo."

"Real cities have something else, some individual bony structure under the muck. Los Angeles has Hollywood—and hates it. It ought to consider itself damn lucky. Without Hollywood it would be a mail-order city. Everything in the catalogue you could get better somewhere else."

"You are bitter tonight, amigo."

"I've got a few troubles. The only reason I'm driving this car with you beside me is that I've got so much trouble a little more will seem like icing."

"You have done something wrong?" she asked and came close to me along the seat.

"Well, just collecting a few bodies," I said. "Depends on the point of view. The cops don't like the work done by us amateurs. They have their own service."

"What will they do to you?"

"They might run me out of town and I couldn't care less. Don't push me so hard. I need this arm to shift gears with."

She pulled away in a huff. "I think you are very nasty to get along with," she said. "Turn right at the Lost Canyon Road."

After a while we passed the University. All the lights of the city were on now, a vast carpet of them stretching down the slope to the south and on into the almost infinite distance. A plane droned overhead losing altitude, its two signal lights winking on and off alternately. At Lost Canyon I swung right skirting the big gates that led into Bel-Air. The road began to twist and climb. There were too many cars; the headlights glared angrily down the twisting white concrete. A little breeze blew down over the pass. There was the odor of wild sage, the acrid tang of eucalyptus, and the quiet smell of dust. Windows glowed on the hillside. We passed a big white two storied Monterey house that must have cost $70,000 and had a cut-out illuminated sign in front: "Cairn Terriers."

"The next to the right," Dolores said.

I made the turn. The road got steeper and narrower. There were houses behind walls and masses of shrubbery but you couldn't see anything. Then we came to the fork and there was a police car with a red spotlight parked at it and across the right side of the fork two cars parked at right angles. A torch waved up and down. I slowed the car and stopped level with the police car. Two cops sat in it smoking. They didn't move.

"What goes on?"

"Amigo, I have no idea at all." Her voice had a hushed withdrawn sound. She might have been a little scared. I didn't know what of.

A tall man, the one with the torch, came around the side of the car and poked the flash at me, then lowered it.

"We're not using this road tonight," he said. "Going anywhere in particular?"

I set the brake, reached for a flash which Dolores got out of the glove compartment. I snapped the light on to the tall man. He wore expensive-looking slacks, a sport shirt with initials on the pocket and a polka-dot scarf knotted around his neck. He had horn-rimmed glasses and glossy wavy black hair. He looked as Hollywood as all hell.

I said: "Any explanation—or are you just making law?"

"The law is over there, if you want to talk to them." His voice held a tone of contempt. "We are merely private citizens. We live around here. This is a residential neighborhood. We mean to keep it that way."

A man with a sporting gun came out of the shadows and stood beside the tall man. He held the gun in the crook of his left arm, pointed muzzle down. But he didn't look as if he just had it for ballast.

"That's jake with me," I said. "I didn't have any other plans. We just want to go to a place."

"What place?" the tall man asked coolly.

I turned to Dolores. "What place?"

"It is a white house on the hill, high up," she said.

"And what did you plan to do up there?" the tall man asked.

"The man who lives there is my friend," she said tartly.

He shone the flash in her face for a moment. "You look swell," he said. "But we don't like your friend. We don't like characters that try to run gambling joints in this kind of neighborhood."

"I know nothing about a gambling joint," Dolores told him sharply.

"Neither do the cops," the tall man said. "They don't even want to find out. What's your friend's name, darling?"

"That is not of your business," Dolores spit at him.

"Go on home and knit socks, darling," the tall man said. He turned to me.

"The road's not in use tonight," he said. "Now you know why."

"Think you can make it stick?" I asked him.

"It will take more than you to change our plans. You ought to see our tax assessments. And those monkeys in the prowl car—and a lot more like them down at the City Hall—just sit on their hands when we ask for the law to be enforced."

I unlatched the car door and swung it open. He stepped back and let me get out. I walked over to the prowl car. The two cops in it were leaning back lazily. Their loudspeaker was turned low, just audibly muttering. One of them was chewing gum rhythmically.

"How's to break up this road block and let the citizens through?" I asked him.

"No orders, buddy. We're just here to keep the peace. Anybody starts anything, we finish it."

"They say there's a gambling house up the line."

"They say," the cop said.

"You don't believe them?"

"I don't even try, buddy," he said, and spat past my shoulder.

"Suppose I have urgent business up there."

He looked at me without expression and yawned.

"Thanks a lot, buddy," I said.

I went back to the Mercury, got my wallet out and handed the tall man a card. He put his flash on it, and said: "Well?"

He snapped the flash off and stood silent. His face began to take form palely in the darkness.

"I'm on business. To me it's important business. Let me through and perhaps you won't need this block tomorrow."

"You talk large, friend."

"Would I have the kind of money it takes to patronize a private gambling club?"

"*She* might," he flicked an eye at Dolores. "She might have brought you along for protection."

He turned to the shotgun man. "What do you think?"

"Chance it. Just two of them and both sober."

The tall one snapped his flash on again and made a side-sweep with it back and forth. A car motor started. One of the block cars backed around on to the shoulder. I got in and started the Mercury, went on through the gap and watched the block car in the mirror as it took up position again, then cut its high beam lights.

"Is this the only way in and out of here?"

"They think it is, amigo. There is another way, but it is a private road through an estate. We would have had to go around by the valley side."

"We nearly didn't get through," I told her. "This can't be very bad trouble anybody is in."

"I knew you would find a way, amigo."

"Something stinks," I said nastily. "And it isn't wild lilac."

"Such a suspicious man. Do you not even want to kiss me?"

"You ought to have used a little of that back at the road block. That tall guy looked lonely. You could have taken him off in the bushes."

She hit me across the mouth with the back of her hand. "You son of a bitch," she said casually. "The next driveway on the left, if you please."

We topped a rise and the road ended suddenly in a wide black circle edged with whitewashed stones. Directly ahead was a wire fence with a wide gate in it, and a sign on the gate: Private Road. No Trespassing. The gate was open and a padlock hung from one end of a loose chain on the posts. I turned the car around a white oleander bush and was in the motor yard of a long low white house with a tile roof and a four-car garage in the corner, under a walled balcony. Both the wide garage doors were closed. There was no light in the house. A high moon made a bluish radiance on the white stucco walls. Some of the lower windows were shuttered. Four packing cases full of trash stood in a row at the foot of the steps. There was a big garbage can upended and empty. There were two steel drums with papers in them.

There was no sound from the house, no sign of life. I stopped the Mercury, cut the lights and the motor, and just sat. Dolores moved in the corner. The seat seemed to be shaking. I reached across and touched her. She was shivering.

"What's the matter?"

"Get—get out, please," she said as if her teeth chattered.

"How about you?"

She opened the door on her side and jumped out. I got out my side and left the door hanging open, the keys in the lock. She came around the back of the car and as she got close to me I could almost feel her shaking before she touched me. Then she leaned up against me hard thigh to thigh and breast to breast. Her arms went around my neck.

"I am being very foolish," she said softly. "He will kill me for this—just as he killed Stein. Kiss me."

I kissed her. Her lips were hot and dry. "Is he in there?"

"Yes."

"Who else?"

"Nobody else—except Mavis. He will kill her too."

"Listen—"

"Kiss me again. I have not very long to live, amigo. When you are the finger for a man like that—you die young."

I pushed her away from me, but gently.

She stepped back and lifted her right hand quickly. There was a gun in it now.

I looked at the gun. There was a dull shine on it from the high moon. She held it level and her hand wasn't shaking now.

"What a friend I would make if I pulled this trigger," she said.

"They'd hear the shot down the road."

She shook her head. "No, there is a little hill between. I do not think they would hear, amigo."

I thought the gun would jump when she pulled the trigger. If I dropped just at the right moment—

I wasn't that good. I didn't say anything. My tongue felt large in my mouth.

She went on slowly, in a soft tired voice: "With Stein it did not matter. I would have killed him myself, gladly. That filth. To die is not much, to kill is not much. But to entice people to their deaths—" She broke off with what might have been a sob. "Amigo, I liked you for some strange reason. I should be far beyond such nonsense. Mavis took him away from me, but I did not want him to kill her. The world is full of men who have enough money."

"He seems like a nice little guy," I said, still watching the hand that held the gun. Not a quiver in it now.

She laughed contemptuously. "Of course he does. That is why he is what he is. You think you are tough, amigo. You are a very soft peach compared with Steelgrave." She lowered the gun and now it was my time to jump. I still wasn't good enough.

"He has killed a dozen men," she said. "With a smile for each one. I have known him for a long time. I knew him in Cleveland."

"With ice picks?" I asked.

"If I give you the gun, will you kill him for me?"

"Would you believe me if I promised?"

"Yes." Somewhere down the hill there was the sound of a car. But it seemed as remote as Mars, as meaningless as the chattering of monkeys in the Brazilian jungle. It had nothing to do with me.

"I'd kill him if I had to," I said licking along my lips.

I was leaning a little, knees bent, all set for a jump again.

"Good night, amigo. I wear black because I am beautiful and wicked—and lost."

She held the gun out to me. I took it. I just stood there holding it. For another silent moment neither of us moved. Then she smiled and tossed her head and jumped into the car. She started the motor and slammed the door shut. She idled the motor down and sat looking out at me. There was a smile on her face now.

"I was pretty good in there, no?" she said softly.

Then the car backed violently with a harsh tearing of the tires on the asphalt paving. The lights jumped on. The car curved away and was gone past the oleander bush. The lights turned left, into the private road. The lights drifted off among trees and the sound faded into the long-drawn whee of tree frogs. Then that stopped and for a moment there was no sound at all. And no light except the tired old moon.

I broke the magazine from the gun. It had seven shells in it. There was another in the breach. Two less than a full load. I sniffed at the muzzle. It had been fired since it was cleaned. Fired twice, perhaps.

I pushed the magazine into place again and held the gun on the flat of my hand. It had a white bone grip. .32 caliber.

Orrin Quest had been shot twice. The two exploded shells I picked up on the floor of the room were .32 caliber.

And yesterday afternoon, in Room 332 of the Hotel Van Nuys, a blonde girl with a towel in front of her face had pointed a .32-caliber automatic with a white bone grip at me.

You can get too fancy about these things. You can also not get fancy enough.

## 27

I walked on rubber heels across to the garage and tried to open one of the two wide doors. There were no handles, so it must have been operated by a switch. I played a tiny pencil flash on the frame, but no switch looked at me.

I left that and prowled over to the trash barrels. Wooden steps went up to a service entrance. I didn't think the door would be unlocked for my convenience. Under the porch was another door. This was unlocked and gave on darkness and the smell of corded eucalyptus wood. I closed the door behind me and put the little flash on again. In the corner there was another staircase, with a thing like a dumb-waiter beside it. It wasn't dumb enough to let me work it. I started up the steps.

Somewhere remotely something buzzed. I stopped. The buzzing stopped. I started again. The buzzing didn't. I went on up to a door with no knob, set flush. Another gadget.

But I found the switch to this one. It was an oblong movable plate set into the door frame. Too many dusty hands had touched it. I pressed it and the door clicked and fell back off the latch. I pushed it open, with the tenderness of a young intern delivering his first baby.

Inside was a hallway. Through shuttered windows moon-light caught the white corner of a stove and the chromed griddle on top of it. The kitchen was big enough for a danc-ing class. An open arch led to a butler's pantry tiled to the ceiling. A sink, a huge icebox set into the wall, a lot of elec-trical stuff for making drinks without trying. You pick your poison, press a button, and four days later you wake up on the rubbing table in a reconditioning parlor.

Beyond the butler's pantry a swing door. Beyond the swing door a dark dining room with an open end to a glassed-in lounge into which the moonlight poured like water through the floodgates of a dam.

A carpeted hall led off somewhere. From another flat arch a flying buttress of a staircase went up into more darkness, but shimmered as it went in what might have been glass brick and stainless steel.

At last I came to what should be the living room. It was curtained and quite dark, but it had the feel of great size. The darkness was heavy in it and my nose twitched at a lin-gering odor that said somebody had been there not too long ago. I stopped breathing and listened. Tigers could be in the darkness watching me. Or guys with large guns, standing flat-footed, breathing softly with their mouths open. Or nothing and nobody and too much imagination in the wrong place.

I edged back to the wall and felt around for a light switch. There's always a light switch. Everybody has light switches. Usually on the right side as you go in. You go into a dark room and you want light. Okay, you have a light switch in a natural place at a natural height. This room hadn't. This was a different kind of house. They had odd ways of handling doors and lights. The gadget this time might be something fancy like having to sing A above high C, or stepping on a flat button under the carpet, or maybe you just spoke and said: "Let there be light," and a mike picked it up and turned the voice vibration into a low-power electrical impulse and a transformer built that up to enough voltage to throw a silent mercury switch.

I was psychic that night. I was a fellow who wanted com-pany in a dark place and was willing to pay a high price for it.

The Luger under my arm and the .32 in my hand made me tough. Two-gun Marlowe, the kid from Cyanide Gulch.

I took the wrinkles out of my lips and said aloud:

"Hello again. Anybody here needing a detective?"

Nothing answered me, not even a stand-in for an echo. The sound of my voice fell on silence like a tired head on a swansdown pillow.

And then amber light began to grow high up behind the cornice that circumnavigated the huge room. It brightened very slowly, as if controlled by a rheostat panel in a theater. Heavy apricot-colored curtains covered the windows.

The walls were apricot too. At the far end was a bar off to one side, a little catty-corner, reaching back into the space by the butler's pantry. There was an alcove with small tables and padded seats. There were floor lamps and soft chairs and love seats and the usual paraphernalia of a living room, and there were long shrouded tables in the middle of the floor space.

The boys back at the road block had something after all. But the joint was dead. The room was empty of life. It was almost empty. Not quite empty.

A blonde in a pale cocoa fur coat stood leaning against the side of a grandfather's chair. Her hands were in the pockets of the coat. Her hair was fluffed out carelessly and her face was not chalk-white because the light was not white.

"Hello again yourself," she said in a dead voice. "I still think you came too late."

"Too late for what?"

I walked towards her, a movement which was always a pleasure. Even then, even in that too silent house.

"You're kind of cute," she said. "I didn't think you were cute. You found a way in. You—" Her voice clicked off and strangled itself in her throat.

"I need a drink," she said after a thick pause. "Or maybe I'll fall down."

"That's a lovely coat," I said. I was up to her now. I reached out and touched it. She didn't move. Her mouth moved in and out, trembling.

"Stone marten," she whispered. "Forty thousand dollars. Rented. For the picture."

"Is this part of the picture?" I gestured around the room.

"This is the picture to end all pictures—for me. I—I do need that drink. If I try to walk—" the clear voice whispered away into nothing. Her eyelids fluttered up and down.

"Go ahead and faint," I said. "I'll catch you on the first bounce."

A smile struggled to arrange her face for smiling. She pressed her lips together, fighting hard to stay on her feet.

"Why did I come too late?" I asked. "Too late for what?"

"Too late to be shot."

"Shucks, I've been looking forward to it all evening. Miss Gonzales brought me."

"I know."

I reached out and touched the fur again. Forty thousand dollars is nice to touch, even rented.

"Dolores will be disappointed as hell," she said, her mouth edged with white.

"No."

"She put you on the spot—just as she did Stein."

"She may have started out to. But she changed her mind."

She laughed. It was a silly pooped-out little laugh like a child trying to be supercilious at a playroom tea party.

"What a way you have with the girls," she whispered. "How the hell do you do it, wonderful? With doped cigarettes? It can't be your clothes or your money or your personality. You don't have any. You're not too young, nor too beautiful. You've seen your best days and—"

Her voice had been coming faster and faster, like a motor with a broken governor. At the end she was chattering. When she stopped a spent sigh drifted along the silence and she caved at the knees and fell straight forward into my arms.

If it was an act it worked perfectly. I might have had guns in all nine pockets and they would have been as much use to me as nine little pink candles on a birthday cake.

But nothing happened. No hard characters peeked at me with automatics in their hands. No Steelgrave smiled at me with the faint dry remote killer's smile. No stealthy footsteps crept up behind me.

She hung in my arms as limp as a wet tea towel and not as heavy as Orrin Quest, being less dead, but heavy enough to make the tendons in my knee joints ache. Her eyes were closed when I pushed her head away from my chest. Her breath was inaudible and she had that bluish look on the parted lips.

I got my right hand under her knees and carried her over to a gold couch and spread her out on it. I straightened up and went along to the bar. There was a telephone on the corner of it but I couldn't find the way through to the bottles. So I had to swing over the top. I got a likely-looking bottle with a blue and silver label and five stars on it. The cork had been loosened. I poured dark and pungent brandy into the wrong kind of glass and went back over the bar top, taking the bottle with me.

She was lying as I had left her, but her eyes were open.

"Can you hold a glass?"

She could, with a little help. She drank the brandy and pressed the edge of the glass hard against her lips as if she wanted to hold them still. I watched her breathe into the glass and cloud it. A slow smile formed itself on her mouth.

"It's cold tonight," she said.

She swung her legs over the edge of the couch and put her feet on the floor.

"More," she said, holding the glass out. I poured into it. "Where's yours?"

"Not drinking. My emotions are being worked on enough without that."

The second drink made her shudder. But the blue look had gone away from her mouth and her lips didn't glare like stop lights and the little etched lines at the corners of her eyes were not in relief any more.

"Who's working on your emotions?"

"Oh, a lot of women that keep throwing their arms around my neck and fainting on me and getting kissed and so forth. Quite a full couple of days for a beat-up gumshoe with no yacht."

"No yacht," she said. "I'd hate that. I was brought up rich."

"Yeah," I said. "You were born with a Cadillac in your mouth. And I could guess where."

Her eyes narrowed. "Could you?"

"Didn't think it was a very tight secret, did you?"

"I—I—" She broke off and made a helpless gesture. "I can't think of any lines tonight."

"It's the technicolor dialogue," I said. "It freezes up on you."

"Aren't we talking like a couple of nuts?"

"We could get sensible. Where's Steelgrave?"

She just looked at me. She held the empty glass out and I took it and put it somewhere or other without taking my eyes off her. Nor she hers off me. It seemed as if a long long minute went by.

"He was here," she said at last, as slowly as if she had to invent the words one at a time. "May I have a cigarette?"

"The old cigarette stall," I said. I got a couple out and put them in my mouth and lit them. I leaned across and tucked one between her ruby lips.

"Nothing's cornier than that," she said. "Except maybe butterfly kisses."

"Sex is a wonderful thing," I said. "When you don't want to answer questions."

She puffed loosely and blinked, then put her hand up to adjust the cigarette. After all these years I can never put a cigarette in a girl's mouth where she wants it.

She gave her head a toss and swung the soft loose hair around her cheeks and watched me to see how hard that hit me. All the whiteness had gone now. Her cheeks were a little flushed. But behind her eyes things watched and waited.

"You're rather nice," she said, when I didn't do anything sensational. "For the kind of guy you are."

I stood that well too.

"But I don't really know what kind of guy you are, do I?" She laughed suddenly and a tear came from nowhere and slid down her cheek. "For all I know you might be nice for any kind of guy." She snatched the cigarette loose and put her hand to her mouth and bit on it. "What's the matter with me? Am I drunk?"

"You're stalling for time," I said. "But I can't make up my mind whether it's to give someone time to get here—or to give somebody time to get far away from here. And again it could just be brandy on top of shock. You're a little girl and you want to cry into your mother's apron."

"Not my mother," she said. "I could get as far crying into a rain barrel."

"Dealt and passed. So where is Steelgrave?"

"You ought to be glad wherever he is. He had to kill you. Or thought he had."

"You wanted me here, didn't you? Were you that fond of him?"

She blew cigarette ash off the back of her hand. A flake of it went into my eye and made me blink.

"I must have been," she said, "once." She put a hand down on her knee and spread the fingers out, studying the nails. She brought her eyes up slowly without moving her head. "It seems like about a thousand years ago I met a nice quiet little guy who knew how to behave in public and didn't shoot his charm around every bistro in town. Yes, I liked him. I liked him a lot."

She put her hand up to her mouth and bit a knuckle. Then she put the same hand into the pocket of the fur coat and brought out a white-handled automatic, the brother of the one I had myself.

"And in the end I liked him with this," she said.

I went over and took it out of her hand. I sniffed the muzzle. Yes. That made two of them fired around.

"Aren't you going to wrap it up in a handkerchief, the way they do in the movies?"

I just dropped it into my other pocket, where it could pick up a few interesting crumbs of tobacco and some seeds that grow only on the southeast slope of the Beverly Hills City Hall. It might amuse a police chemist for a while.

# 28

I watched her for a minute, biting at the end of my lip. She watched me. I saw no change of expression. Then I started prowling the room with my eyes. I lifted up the dust cover on one of the long tables. Under it was a roulette layout but no wheel. Under the table was nothing.

"Try that chair with the magnolias on it," she said.

She didn't look towards it so I had to find it myself. Surprising how long it took me. It was a high-backed wing chair, covered in flowered chintz, the kind of chair that a long time ago was intended to keep the draft off while you sat crouched over a fire of cannel coal.

It was turned away from me. I went over there walking softly, in low gear. It almost faced the wall. Even at that it seemed ridiculous that I hadn't spotted him on my way back from the bar. He leaned in the corner of the chair with his head tilted back. His carnation was red and white and looked as fresh as though the flower girl had just pinned it into his lapel. His eyes were half open as such eyes usually are. They stared at a point in the corner of the ceiling. The bullet had gone through the outside pocket of his double-breasted jacket. It had been fired by someone who knew where the heart was.

I touched his cheek and it was still warm. I lifted his hand and let it fall. It was quite limp. It felt like the back of somebody's hand. I reached for the big artery in his neck. No blood moved in him and very little had stained his jacket. I wiped my hands off on my handkerchief and stood for a little longer looking down at his quiet little face. Everything I had done or not done, everything wrong and everything right— all wasted.

I went back and sat down near her and squeezed my kneecaps.

"What did you expect me to do?" she asked. "He killed my brother."

"Your brother was no angel."

"He didn't have to kill him."

"Somebody had to—and quick."

Her eyes widened suddenly.

I said: "Didn't you ever wonder why Steelgrave never went after me and why he let you go to the Van Nuys yesterday instead of going himself? Didn't you ever wonder why a fellow with his resources and experience never tried to get hold of those photographs, no matter what he had to do to get them?"

She didn't answer.

"How long have you known the photographs existed?" I asked.

"Weeks, nearly two months. I got one in the mail a couple of days after—after that time we had lunch together."

"After Stein was killed."

"Yes, of course."

"Did you think Steelgrave had killed Stein?"

"No. Why should I? Until tonight, that is."

"What happened after you got the photo?"

"My brother Orrin called me up and said he had lost his job and was broke. He wanted money. He didn't say anything about the photo. He didn't have to. There was only one time it could have been taken."

"How did he get your number?"

"Telephone? How did you?"

"Bought it."

"Well—" She made a vague movement with her hand. "Why not call the police and get it over with."

"Wait a minute. Then what? More prints of the photo?"

"One every week. I showed them to *him*." She gestured toward the chintzy chair. "He didn't like it. I didn't tell him about Orrin."

"He must have known. His kind find things out."

"I suppose so."

"But not where Orrin was hiding out," I said. "Or he wouldn't have waited this long. *When* did you tell Steelgrave?"

She looked away from me. Her fingers kneaded her arm. "Today," she said in a distant voice.

"Why today?"

Her breath caught in her throat. "Please," she said. "Don't ask me a lot of useless questions. Don't torment me. There's nothing you can do. I thought there was—when I called Dolores. There isn't now."

I said: "All right. There's something you don't seem to understand. Steelgrave knew that whoever was behind that photograph wanted money—a lot of money. He knew that sooner or later the blackmailer would have to show himself. That was what Steelgrave was waiting for. He didn't care anything about the photo itself, except for your sake."

"He certainly proved that," she said wearily.

"In his own way," I said.

Her voice came to me with glacial calm. "He killed my brother. He told me so himself. The gangster showed through then all right. Funny people you meet in Hollywood, don't you—including me."

"You were fond of him once," I said brutally.

Red spots flared on her cheeks.

"I'm not fond of anybody," she said. "I'm all through being fond of people." She glanced briefly towards the high-backed chair. "I stopped being fond of him last night. He asked me about you, who you were and so on. I told him. I told him that I would have to admit that I was at the Van Nuys Hotel when that man was lying there dead."

"You were going to tell the police that?"

"I was going to tell Julius Oppenheimer. He would know how to handle it."

"If he didn't one of his dogs would," I said.

She didn't smile. I didn't either.

"If Oppenheimer couldn't handle it, I'd be through in pictures," she added without interest. "Now I'm through everywhere else as well."

I got a cigarette out and lit it. I offered her one. She didn't want one. I wasn't in any hurry. Time seemed to have lost its grip on me. And almost everything else. I was flat out.

"You're going too fast for me," I said, after a moment. "You didn't know when you went to the Van Nuys that Steelgrave was Weepy Moyer."

"No."

"Then what did you go there for?"

"To buy back those photographs."

"That doesn't check. The photographs didn't mean anything to you then. They were just you and him having lunch."

She stared at me and winked her eyes tight, then opened them wide. "I'm not going to cry," she said. "I said I didn't *know*. But when he was in jail that time, I had to know there was something about him that he didn't care to have known. I knew he had been in some kind of racket, I guess. But not killing people."

I said: "Uh-huh." I got up and walked around the high-backed chair again. Her eyes traveled slowly to watch me. I leaned over the dead Steelgrave and felt under his arm on the left side. There was a gun there in the holster. I didn't touch it. I went back and sat down opposite her again.

"It's going to cost a lot of money to fix this," I said.

For the first time she smiled. It was a very small smile, but it was a smile. "I don't have a lot of money," she said. "So that's out."

"Oppenheimer has. You're worth millions to him by now."

"He wouldn't chance it. Too many people have their knives into the picture business these days. He'll take his loss and forget it in six months."

"You said you'd go to him."

"I said if I got into a jam and hadn't really done anything, I'd go to him. But I have done something now."

"How about Ballou? You're worth a lot to him too."

"I'm not worth a plugged nickel to anybody. Forget it, Marlowe. You mean well, but I know these people."

"That puts it up to me," I said. "That would be why you sent for me."

"Wonderful," she said. "You fix it, darling. For free." Her voice was brittle and shallow again.

I went and sat beside her on the davenport. I took hold of her arm and pulled her hand out of the fur pocket and took hold of that. It was almost ice cold, in spite of the fur.

She turned her head and looked at me squarely. She shook her head a little. "Believe me, darling, I'm not worth it—even to sleep with."

I turned the hand over and opened the fingers out. They were stiff and resisted. I opened them out one by one. I smoothed the palm of her hand.

"Tell me why you had the gun with you."

"The gun?"

"Don't take time to think. Just tell me. Did you mean to kill him?"

"Why not, darling? I thought I meant something to him. I guess I'm a little vain. He fooled me. Nobody means anything to the Steelgraves of this world. And nobody means anything to the Mavis Welds of this world any more."

She pulled away from me and smiled thinly. "I oughtn't to have given you that gun. If I killed you I might get clear yet."

I took it out and held it towards her. She took it and stood up quickly. The gun pointed at me. The small tired smile moved her lips again. Her finger was very firm on the trigger.

"Shoot high," I said. "I'm wearing my bullet-proof underwear."

She dropped the gun to her side and for a moment she just stood staring at me. Then she tossed the gun down on the davenport.

"I guess I don't like the script," she said. "I don't like the lines. It just isn't me, if you know what I mean."

She laughed and looked down at the floor. The point of her shoe moved back and forth on the carpeting. "We've had a nice chat, darling. The phone's over there at the end of the bar."

"Thanks, do you remember Dolores's number?"

"Why Dolores?"

When I didn't answer she told me. I went along the room to the corner of the bar and dialed. The same routine as before. Good evening, the Chateau Bercy, who is calling Miss Gonzales please. One moment, please, buzz, buzz, and then a sultry voice saying: "Hello?"

"This is Marlowe. Did you really mean to put me on a spot?"

I could almost hear her breath catch. Not quite. You can't really hear it over the phone. Sometimes you think you can.

"Amigo, but I am glad to hear your voice," she said. "I am so very very glad."

"Did you or didn't you?"

"I—I don't know. I am very sad to think that I might have. I like you very much."

"I'm in a little trouble here."

"Is he—" Long pause. Apartment house phone. Careful. "Is he there?"

"Well—in a way. He is and yet he isn't."

I really did hear her breath this time. A long indrawn sigh that was almost a whistle.

"Who else is there?"

"Nobody. Just me and my homework. I want to ask you

something. It is deadly important. Tell me the truth. Where did you get that thing you gave me tonight?"

"Why, from him. He gave it to me."

"When?"

"Early this evening. Why?"

"How early?"

"About six o'clock, I think."

"*Why* did he give it to you?"

"He asked me to keep it. He always carried one."

"Asked you to keep it why?"

"He did not say, amigo. He was a man that did things like that. He did not often explain himself."

"Notice anything unusual about it? About what he gave you?"

"Why—no, I did not."

"Yes, you did. You noticed that it had been fired and that it smelled of burned powder."

"But I did not—"

"Yes, you did. Just like that. You wondered about it. You didn't like to keep it. You didn't keep it. You gave it back to him. You don't like them around anyhow."

There was a long silence. She said at last, "But of course. But why did he want me to have it? I mean, if that was what happened."

"He didn't tell you why. He just tried to ditch a gun on you and you weren't having any. Remember?"

"That is something I have to tell?"

"Sí."

"Will it be safe for me to do that?"

"When did you ever try to be safe?"

She laughed softly. "Amigo, you understand me very well."

"Goodnight," I said.

"One moment, you have not told me what happened."

"I haven't even telephoned you."

I hung up and turned.

Mavis Weld was standing in the middle of the floor watching me.

"You have your car here?" I asked.

"Yes."

"Get going."

"And do what?"

"Just go home. That's all."

"You can't get away with it," she said softly.

"You're my client."

"I can't let you. I killed him. Why should you be dragged into it?"

"Don't stall. And when you leave go the back way. Not the way Dolores brought me."

She stared me straight in the eyes and repeated in a tense voice, "But I killed him."

"I can't hear a word you say."

Her teeth took hold of her lower lip and held it cruelly. She seemed hardly to breathe. She stood rigid. I went over close to her and touched her cheek with a fingertip. I pressed it hard and watched the white spot turn red.

"If you want to know my motive," I said, "it has nothing to do with you. I owe it to the johns. I haven't played clean cards in this game. They know. I know. I'm just giving them a chance to use the loud pedal."

"As if anyone ever had to give them that," she said, and turned abruptly and walked away. I watched her to the arch and waited for her to look back. She went on through without turning. After a long time I heard a whirring noise. Then the bump of something heavy—the garage door going up. A car started a long way off. It idled down and after another pause the whirring noise again.

When that stopped the motor faded off into the distance. I heard nothing now. The silence of the house hung around me in thick loose folds like that fur coat around the shoulders of Mavis Weld.

I carried the glass and bottle of brandy over to the bar and climbed over it. I rinsed the glass in a little sink and set the bottle back on the shelf. I found the trick catch this time and swung the door open at the end opposite the telephone. I went back to Steelgrave.

I took out the gun Dolores had given me and wiped it off and put his small limp hand around the butt, held it there and let go. The gun thudded to the carpet. The position looked natural. I wasn't thinking about fingerprints. He would have learned long ago not to leave them on any gun.

That left me with three guns. The weapon in his holster I took out and went and put it on the bar shelf under the counter, wrapped in a towel. The Luger I didn't touch. The other white-handled automatic was left. I tried to decide about how far away from him it had been fired. Beyond scorching distance, but probably very close beyond. I stood about three feet from him and fired two shots past him. They nicked peacefully into the wall. I dragged the chair around until it faced into the room. I laid the small automatic down on the dust cover of one of the roulette tables. I touched the big muscle in the side of his neck, usually the first to harden. I couldn't tell whether it had begun to set or not. But his skin was colder than it had been.

There was not a hell of a lot of time to play around with.

I went to the telephone and dialed the number of the Los Angeles Police Department. I asked the police operator for Christy French. A voice from homicide came on, said he had gone home and what was it. I said it was a personal call he was expecting. They gave me his phone number at home, reluctantly, not because they cared, but because they hate to give anybody anything any time.

I dialed and a woman answered and screamed his name. He sounded rested and calm.

"This is Marlowe. What were you doing?"

"Reading the funnies to my kid. He ought to be in bed. What's doing?"

"Remember over at the Van Nuys yesterday you said a man could make a friend if he got you something on Weepy Moyer?"

"Yeah."

"I need a friend."

He didn't sound very interested. "What you got on him?"

"I'm assuming it's the same guy. Steelgrave."

"Too much assuming, kid. We had him in the fishbowl because we thought the same. It didn't pan any gold."

"You got a tip. He set that tip up himself. So the night Stein was squibbed off he would be where you knew."

"You just making this up—or got evidence?" He sounded a little less relaxed.

"If a man got out of jail on a pass from the jail doctor, could you prove that?"

There was a silence. I heard a child's voice complaining and a woman's voice speaking to the child.

"It's happened," French said heavily. "I dunno. That's a tough order to fill. They'd send him under guard. Did he get to the guard?"

"That's my theory."

"Better sleep on it. Anything else?"

"I'm out at Stillwood Heights. In a big house where they were setting up for gambling and the local residents didn't like it."

"Read about it. Steelgrave there?"

"He's here. I'm here alone with him."

Another silence. The kid yelled and I thought I heard a slap. The kid yelled louder. French yelled at somebody.

"Put him on the phone," French said at last.

"You're not bright tonight, Christy. Why would I call *you?*"

"Yeah," he said. "Stupid of me. What's the address there?"

"I don't know. But it's up at the end of Tower Road in Stillwood Heights and the phone number is Halldale 9-5033. I'll be waiting for you."

He repeated the number and said slowly: "This time you wait, huh?"

"It had to come sometime."

The phone clicked and I hung up.

I went back through the house putting on lights as I found them and came out at the back door at the top of the stairs. There was a floodlight for the motor yard. I put that on. I went down the steps and walked along to the oleander bush. The private gate stood open as before. I swung it shut, hooked up the chain and clicked the padlock. I went back, walking slowly, looking up at the moon, sniffing the night air, listening to the tree frogs and the crickets. I went into the house and found the front door and put the light on over that. There was a big parking space in front and a circular lawn with roses. But you had to slide back around the house to the rear to get away.

The place was a dead end except for the driveway through the neighboring grounds. I wondered who lived there. A long way off through trees I could see the lights of a big house. Some Hollywood big shot, probably, some wizard of the slobbery kiss, and the pornographic dissolve.

I went back in and felt the gun I had just fired. It was cold enough. And Mr. Steelgrave was beginning to look as if he meant to stay dead.

No siren. But the sound of a car coming up the hill at last. I went out to meet it, me and my beautiful dream.

# 29

They came in as they should, big, tough and quiet, their eyes flickering with watchfulness and cautious with disbelief.

"Nice place," French said. "Where's the customer?"

"In there," Beifus said, without waiting for me to answer.

They went along the room without haste and stood in front of him looking down solemnly.

"Dead, wouldn't you say?" Beifus remarked, opening up the act.

French leaned down and took the gun that lay on the floor with thumb and finger on the trigger guard. His eyes flicked sideways and he jerked his chin. Beifus took the other white-handled gun by sliding a pencil into the end of the barrel.

"Fingerprints all in the right places, I hope," Beifus said. He sniffed. "Oh yeah, this baby's been working. How's yours, Christy?"

"Fired," French said. He sniffed again. "But not recently." He took a clip flash from his pocket and shone it into the barrel of the black gun. "Hours ago."

"Down at Bay City, in a house on Wyoming Street," I said.

Their heads swung around to me in unison.

"Guessing?" French asked slowly.

"Yes."

He walked over to the covered table and laid the gun down

some distance from the other. "Better tag them right away, Fred. They're twins. We'll both sign the tags."

Beifus nodded and rooted around in his pockets. He came up with a couple of tie-on tags. The things cops carry around with them.

French moved back to me. "Let's stop guessing and get to the part you know."

"A girl I know called me this evening and said a client of mine was in danger up here—from him." I pointed with my chin at the dead man in the chair. "This girl rode me up here. We passed the road block. A number of people saw us both. She left me in back of the house and went home."

"Somebody with a name?" French asked.

"Dolores Gonzales, Chateau Bercy Apartments. On Franklin. She's in pictures."

"Oh-ho," Beifus said and rolled his eyes.

"Who's your client? Same one?" French asked.

"No. This is another party altogether."

"She have a name?"

"Not yet."

They stared at me with hard bright faces. French's jaw moved almost with a jerk. Knots of muscles showed at the sides of his jaw bone.

"New rules, huh?" he said softly.

I said, "There has to be some agreement about publicity. The D.A. ought to be willing."

Beifus said, "You don't know the D.A. good, Marlowe. He eats publicity like I eat tender young garden peas."

French said, "We don't give you any undertaking whatsoever."

"She hasn't any name," I said.

"There's a dozen ways we can find out, kid," Beifus said. "Why go into this routine that makes it tough for all of us?"

"No publicity," I said, "unless charges are actually filed."

"You can't get away with it, Marlowe."

"God damn it," I said, "this man killed Orrin Quest. You take that gun downtown and check it against the bullets in Quest. Give me that much at least, before you force me into an impossible position."

"I wouldn't give you the dirty end of a burnt match," French said.

I didn't say anything. He stared at me with cold hate in his eyes. His lips moved slowly and his voice was thick saying, "You here when he got it?"

"No."

"Who was?"

"He was," I said looking across at the dead Steelgrave.

"Who else?"

"I won't lie to you," I said. "And I won't tell you anything I don't want to tell—except on the terms I stated. I don't know who was here when he got it."

"Who was here when you got here?"

I didn't answer. He turned his head slowly and said to Beifus: "Put the cuffs on him. Behind."

Beifus hesitated. Then he took a pair of steel handcuffs out of his left hip pocket and came over to me. "Put your hands behind you," he said in an uncomfortable voice.

I did. He clicked the cuffs on. French walked over slowly and stood in front of me. His eyes were half closed. The skin around them was grayish with fatigue.

"I'm going to make a little speech," he said. "You're not going to like it."

I didn't say anything.

French said: "It's like this with us, baby. We're coppers and everybody hates our guts. And as if we didn't have enough trouble, we have to have you. As if we didn't get pushed around enough by the guys in the corner offices, the City Hall gang, the day chief, the night chief, the Chamber of Commerce, His Honor the Mayor in his paneled office four times as big as the three lousy rooms the whole homicide staff has to work out of. As if we didn't have to handle one hundred and fourteen homicides last year out of three rooms that don't have enough chairs for the whole duty squad to sit down in at once. We spend our lives turning over dirty underwear and sniffing rotten teeth. We go up dark stairways to get a gun punk with a skinful of hop and sometimes we don't get all the way up, and our wives wait dinner that night and all the other nights. We don't come home any more. And nights we do come home, we come home so goddam tired we can't eat or sleep or even read the lies the papers print about us. So we lie awake in the dark in a cheap house on a cheap street and listen to the drunks down the block having fun. And just about the time we drop off the phone rings and we get up and start all over again. Nothing we do is right, not ever. Not once. If we get a confession, we beat it out of the guy, they say, and some shyster calls us Gestapo in court and sneers at us when we muddle our grammar. If we make a mistake they put us back in uniform on Skid Row and we spend the nice cool summer evenings picking drunks out of the gutter and being yelled at by whores and taking knives away from grease-balls in zoot suits. But all that ain't enough to make us entirely happy. We got to have you."

He stopped and drew in his breath. His face glistened a little as if with sweat. He leaned forward from his hips.

"We got to have you," he repeated. "We got to have sharpers with private licenses hiding information and dodging around corners and stirring up dust for us to breathe in. We got to have you suppressing evidence and framing set-ups that wouldn't fool a sick baby. You wouldn't mind me calling you a goddam cheap double-crossing keyhole peeper, would you, baby?"

"You want me to mind?" I asked him.

He straightened up. "I'd love it," he said. "In spades redoubled."

"Some of what you say is true," I said. "Not all. Any private eye wants to play ball with the police. Sometimes it's a little hard to find out who's making the rules of the ball game. Sometimes he doesn't trust the police, and with cause. Sometimes he just gets in a jam without meaning to and has to play his hand out the way it's dealt. He'd usually rather have a new deal. He'd like to keep on earning a living."

"Your license is dead," French said. "As of now. That problem won't bother you any more."

"It's dead when the commission that gave it to me says so. Not before."

Beifus said quietly, "Let's get on with it, Christy. This could wait."

"I'm getting on with it," French said. "My way. This bird hasn't cracked wise yet. I'm waiting for him to crack wise.

The bright repartee. Don't tell me you're all out of the quick stuff, Marlowe."

"Just what is it you want me to say?" I asked him.

"Guess," he said.

"You're a man eater tonight," I said. "You want to break me in half. But you want an excuse. And you want me to give it to you?"

"That might help," he said between his teeth.

"What would you have done in my place?" I asked him.

"I couldn't imagine myself getting that low."

He licked at the point of his upper lip. His right hand was hanging loose at his side. He was clenching and unclenching the fingers without knowing it.

"Take it easy, Christy," Beifus said. "Lay off."

French didn't move. Beifus came over and stepped between us. French said, "Get out of there, Fred."

"No."

French doubled his fist and slugged him hard on the point of the jaw. Beifus stumbled back and knocked me out of the way. His knees wobbled. He bent forward and coughed. He shook his head slowly in a bent-over position. After a while he straightened up with a grunt. He turned and looked at me. He grinned.

"It's a new kind of third degree," he said. "The cops beat hell out of each other and the suspect cracks up from the agony of watching."

His hand went up and felt the angle of his jaw. It already showed swelling. His mouth grinned but his eyes were still a little vague. French stood rooted and silent.

Beifus got out a pack of cigarettes and shook one loose and held the pack out to French. French looked at the cigarette, looked at Beifus.

"Seventeen years of it," he said. "Even my wife hates me."

He lifted his open hand and slapped Beifus across the cheek with it lightly. Beifus kept on grinning.

French said: "Was it you I hit, Fred?"

Beifus said: "Nobody hit me, Christy. Nobody that I can remember."

French said: "Take the cuffs off him and take him out to

the car. He's under arrest. Cuff him to the rail if you think it's necessary."

"Okay." Beifus went around behind me. The cuffs came loose. "Come along, baby," Beifus said.

I stared hard at French. He looked at me as if I was the wallpaper. His eyes didn't seem to see me at all.

I went out under the archway and out of the house.

# 30

I never knew his name, but he was rather short and thin for a cop, which was what he must have been, partly because he was there, and partly because when he leaned across the table to reach a card I could see the leather underarm holster and the butt end of a police .38.

He didn't speak much, but when he did he had a nice voice, a soft-water voice. And he had a smile that warmed the whole room.

"Wonderful casting," I said, looking at him across the cards.

We were playing double Canfield. Or he was. I was just there, watching him, watching his small and very neat and very clean hands go out across the table and touch a card and lift it delicately and put it somewhere else. When he did this he pursed his lips a little and whistled without tune, a low soft whistle, like a very young engine that is not yet sure of itself.

He smiled and put a red nine on a black ten.

"What do you do in your spare time?" I asked him.

"I play the piano a good deal," he said. "I have a seven-foot Steinway. Mozart and Bach mostly. I'm a bit old-fashioned. Most people find it dull stuff. I don't."

"Perfect casting," I said, and put a card somewhere.

"You'd be surprised how difficult some of that Mozart is," he said. "It sounds so simple when you hear it played well."

"Who can play it well?" I asked.

"Schnabel."

"Rubinstein?"

He shook his head. "Too heavy. Too emotional. Mozart is just music. No comment needed from the performer."

"I bet you get a lot of them in the confession mood," I said. "Like the job?"

He moved another card and flexed his fingers lightly. His nails were bright but short. You could see he was a man who loved to move his hands, to make little neat inconspicuous motions with them, motions without any special meaning, but smooth and flowing and light as swansdown. They gave him a feel of delicate things delicately done, but not weak. Mozart, all right. I could see that.

It was about five-thirty, and the sky behind the screened window was getting light. The rolltop desk in the corner was rolled shut. The room was the same room I had been in the afternoon before. Down at the end of the table the square carpenter's pencil was lying where somebody had picked it up and put it back after Lieutenant Maglashan of Bay City threw it against the wall. The flat desk at which Christy French had sat was littered with ash. An old cigar butt clung to the extreme edge of a glass ash tray. A moth circled around the overhead light on a drop cord that had one of those green and white glass shades they still have in country hotels.

"Tired?" he asked.

"Pooped."

"You oughtn't to get yourself involved in these elaborate messes. No point in it that I can see."

"No point in shooting a man?"

He smiled the warm smile. "You never shot anybody."

"What makes you say that?"

"Common sense—and a lot of experience sitting here with people."

"I guess you do like the job," I said.

"It's night work. Gives me the days to practice. I've had it for twelve years now. Seen a lot of funny ones come and go."

He got another ace out, just in time. We were almost blocked.

"Get many confessions?"

"I don't take confessions," he said. "I just establish a mood."

"Why give it all away?"

He leaned back and tapped lightly with the edge of a card on the edge of the table. The smile came again. "I'm not giving anything away. We got you figured long ago."

"Then what are they holding me for?"

He wouldn't answer that. He looked around at the clock on the wall. "I think we could get some food now." He got up and went to the door. He half opened it and spoke softly to someone outside. Then he came back and sat down again and looked at what we had in the way of cards.

"No use," he said. "Three more up and we're blocked. Okay with you to start over?"

"Okay with me if we never started at all. I don't play cards. Chess."

He looked up at me quickly. "Why didn't you say so? I'd rather have played chess too."

"I'd rather drink some hot black coffee as bitter as sin."

"Any minute now. But I won't promise the coffee's what you're used to."

"Hell, I eat anywhere. . . . Well, if I didn't shoot him, who did?"

"Guess that's what is annoying them."

"They ought to be glad to have him shot."

"They probably are," he said. "But they don't like the way it was done."

"Personally I thought it was as neat a job as you could find."

He looked at me in silence. He had the cards between his hands, all in a lump. He smoothed them out and flicked them over on their faces and dealt them rapidly into the two decks. The cards seemed to pour from his hands in a stream, in a blur.

"If you were that fast with a gun," I began.

The stream of cards stopped. Without apparent motion a gun took their place. He held it lightly in his right hand pointed at a distant corner of the room. It went away and the cards started flowing again.

"You're wasted in here," I said. "You ought to be in Las Vegas."

He picked up one of the packs and shuffled it slightly and quickly, cut it, and dealt me a king high flush in spades.

"I'm safer with a Steinway," he said.

The door opened and a uniformed man came in with a tray.

We ate canned cornbeef hash and drank hot but weak coffee. By that time it was full morning.

At eight-fifteen Christy French came in and stood with his hat on the back of his head and dark smudges under his eyes.

I looked from him to the little man across the table. But he wasn't there any more. The cards weren't there either. Nothing was there but a chair pushed in neatly to the table and the dishes we had eaten off gathered on a tray. For a moment I had that creepy feeling.

Then Christy French walked around the table and jerked the chair out and sat down and leaned his chin on his hand. He took his hat off and rumpled his hair. He stared at me with hard morose eyes. I was back in coptown again.

# 31

"The D.A. wants to see you at nine o'clock," he said. "After that I guess you can go on home. That is, if he doesn't hang a pinch on you. I'm sorry you had to sit up in that chair all night."

"It's all right," I said. "I needed the exercise."

"Yeah, back in the groove again," he said. He stared moodily at the dishes on the tray.

"Got Lagardie?" I asked him.

"No. He's a doctor all right, though." His eyes moved to mine. "He practiced in Cleveland."

I said: "I hate it to be that tidy."

"How do you mean?"

"Young Quest wants to put the bite on Steelgrave. So he just by pure accident runs into the one guy in Bay City that could prove who Steelgrave was. *That's* too tidy."

"Aren't you forgetting something?"

"I'm tired enough to forget my name. What?"

"Me too," French said. "*Somebody* had to tell him who

Steelgrave was. When that photo was taken Moe Stein hadn't been squibbed off. So what good was the photo unless somebody knew who Steelgrave was?"

"I guess Miss Weld knew," I said. "And Quest was her brother."

"You're not making much sense, chum." He grinned a tired grin. "Would she help her brother put the bite on her boy friend and on her too?"

"I give up. Maybe the photo was just a fluke. His other sister—my client that was—said he liked to take candid camera shots. The candider the better. If he'd lived long enough you'd have had him up for mopery."

"For murder," French said indifferently.

"Oh?"

"Maglashan found that ice pick all right. He just wouldn't give out to you."

"There'd have to be more than that."

"There is, but it's a dead issue. Clausen and Mileaway Marston both had records. The kid's dead. His family's respectable. He had an off streak in him and he got in with the wrong people. No point in smearing his family just to prove the police can solve a case."

"That's white of you. How about Steelgrave?"

"That's out of my hands." He started to get up. "When a gangster gets his how long does the investigation last?"

"Just as long as it's front-page stuff," I said. "But there's a question of identity involved here."

"No."

I stared at him. "How do you mean, no?"

"Just no. We're sure." He was on his feet now. He combed his hair with his fingers and rearranged his tie and hat. Out of the corner of his mouth he said in a low voice: "Off the record—we were always sure. We just didn't have a thing on him."

"Thanks," I said, "I'll keep it to myself. How about the guns?"

He stopped and stared down at the table. His eyes came up to mine rather slowly. "They both belonged to Steelgrave. What's more he had a permit to carry a gun. From the sheriff's office in another county. Don't ask me why. One of them—" he paused and looked up at the wall over my head—"one of them killed Quest. . . . The same gun killed Stein."

"Which one?"

He smiled faintly. "It would be hell if the ballistics man got them mixed up and we didn't know," he said.

He waited for me to say something. I didn't have anything to say. He made a gesture with his hand.

"Well, so long. Nothing personal you know, but I hope the D.A. takes your hide off—in long thin strips."

He turned and went out.

I could have done the same, but I just sat there and stared across the table at the wall, as if I had forgotten how to get up. After a while the door opened and the orange queen came in. She unlocked her rolltop desk and took her hat off of her impossible hair and hung her jacket on a bare hook in the bare wall. She opened the window near her and uncovered her typewriter and put paper in it. Then she looked across at me.

"Waiting for somebody?"

"I room here," I said. "Been here all night."

She looked at me steadily for a moment. "You were here yesterday afternoon. I remember."

She turned to her typewriter and her fingers began to fly. From the open window behind her came the growl of cars filling up the parking lot. The sky had a white glare and there was not much smog. It was going to be a hot day.

The telephone rang on the orange queen's desk. She talked into it inaudibly, and hung up. She looked across at me again.

"Mr. Endicott's in his office," she said. "Know the way?"

"I worked there once. Not for him, though. I got fired."

She looked at me with that City Hall look they have. A voice that seemed to come from anywhere but her mouth said:

"Hit him in the face with a wet glove."

I went over near her and stood looking down at the orange hair. There was plenty of gray at the roots.

"Who said that?"

"It's the wall," she said. "It talks. The voices of the dead men who have passed through on the way to hell."

I went out of the room walking softly and shut the door against the closer so that it wouldn't make any noise.

## 32

You go in through double swing doors. Inside the double doors there is a combination PBX and information desk at which sits one of those ageless women you see around municipal offices everywhere in the world. They were never young and will never be old. They have no beauty, no charm, no style. They don't have to please anybody. They are safe. They are civil without ever quite being polite and intelligent and knowledgeable without any real interest in anything. They are what human beings turn into when they trade life for existence and ambition for security.

Beyond this desk there is a row of glassed-in cubicles stretching along one side of a very long room. On the other side is the waiting room, a row of hard chairs all facing one way, towards the cubicles.

About half of the chairs were filled with people waiting and the look of long waiting on their faces and the expectation of still longer waiting to come. Most of them were shabby. One was from the jail, in denim, with a guard. A white-faced kid built like a tackle, with sick, empty eyes.

At the back of the line of cubicles a door was lettered SEWELL ENDICOTT DISTRICT ATTORNEY. I knocked and went on into a big airy corner room. A nice enough room, old-fashioned with padded black leather chairs and pictures of former D.A.'s and governors on the walls. Breeze fluttered the net curtains at four windows. A fan on a high shelf purred and swung slowly in a languid arc.

Sewell Endicott sat behind a flat dark desk and watched me come. He pointed to a chair across from him. I sat down. He was tall, thin and dark with loose black hair and long delicate fingers.

"You're Marlowe?" he said in a voice that had a touch of the soft South.

I didn't think he really needed an answer to that. I just waited.

"You're in a bad spot, Marlowe. You don't look good at all. You've been caught suppressing evidence helpful to the solution of a murder. That is obstructing justice. You could go up for it."

"Suppressing what evidence?" I asked.

He picked a photo off his desk and frowned at it. I looked across at the other two people in the room. They sat in chairs side by side. One of them was Mavis Weld. She wore the dark glasses with the wide white bows. I couldn't see her eyes, but I thought she was looking at me. She didn't smile. She sat very still.

By her side sat a man in an angelic pale-gray flannel suit with a carnation the size of a dahlia in his lapel. He was smoking a monogrammed cigarette and flicking the ashes on the floor, ignoring the smoking stand at his elbow. I knew him by pictures I had seen in the papers. Lee Farrell, one of the hottest trouble-shooting lawyers in the country. His hair was white but his eyes were bright and young. He had a deep outdoor tan. He looked as if it would cost a thousand dollars to shake hands with him.

Endicott leaned back and tapped the arm of his chair with his long fingers. He turned with polite deference to Mavis Weld.

"And how well did you know Steelgrave, Miss Weld?"

"Intimately. He was very charming in some ways. I can hardly believe—" She broke off and shrugged.

"And you are prepared to take the stand and swear as to the time and place when this photograph was taken?" He turned the photograph over and showed it to her.

Farrell said indifferently, "Just a moment. Is that the evidence Mr. Marlowe is supposed to have suppressed?"

"I ask the questions," Endicott said sharply.

Farrell smiled. "Well, in case the answer is yes, that photo isn't evidence of anything."

Endicott said softly: "Will you answer my question, Miss Weld?"

She said quietly and easily: "No, Mr. Endicott, I couldn't

swear when that picture was taken or where. I didn't know it was being taken."

"All you have to do is look at it," Endicott suggested.

"And all I know is what I get from looking at it," she told him.

I grinned. Farrell looked at me with a twinkle. Endicott caught the grin out of the corner of his eye. "Something you find amusing?" he snapped at me.

"I've been up all night. My face keeps slipping," I said.

He gave me a stern look and turned to Mavis Weld again.

"Will you amplify that, Miss Weld?"

"I've had a lot of photos taken of me, Mr. Endicott. In a lot of different places and with a lot of different people. I have had lunch and dinner at The Dancers with Mr. Steelgrave and with various other men. I don't know what you want me to say."

Farrell put in smoothly, "If I understand your point, you would like Miss Weld to be your witness to connect this photo up. In what kind of proceeding?"

"That's my business," Endicott said shortly. "Somebody shot Steelgrave to death last night. It could have been a woman. It could even have been Miss Weld. I'm sorry to say that, but it seems to be in the cards."

Mavis Weld looked down at her hands. She twisted a white glove between her fingers.

"Well, let's assume a proceeding," Farrell said. "One in which that photo is part of your evidence—if you can get it in. But you can't get it in. Miss Weld won't get it in for you. All she knows about the photo is what she sees by looking at it. What anybody can see. You'd have to connect it up with a witness who could swear as to when, how and where it was taken. Otherwise I'd object—if I happened to be on the other side. I could even introduce experts to swear the photo was faked."

"I'm sure you could," Endicott said dryly.

"The only man who could connect it up for you is the man who took it," Farrell went on without haste or heat. "I understand he's dead. I suspect that was why he was killed."

Endicott said: "This photo is clear evidence of itself that at a certain time and place Steelgrave was not in jail and therefore had no alibi for the killing of Stein."

Farrell said: "It's evidence when and if you get it introduced in evidence, Endicott. For Pete's sake, I'm not trying to tell you the law. You know it. Forget that picture. It proves nothing whatsoever. No paper would dare print it. No judge would admit it in evidence, because no competent witness can connect it up. And if that's the evidence Marlowe suppressed, then he didn't in a legal sense suppress evidence at all."

"I wasn't thinking of trying Steelgrave for murder," Endicott said dryly. "But I *am* a little interested in who killed him. The police department, fantastically enough, also has an interest in that. I hope our interest doesn't offend you."

Farrell said: "Nothing offends me. That's why I'm where I am. Are you sure Steelgrave was murdered?"

Endicott just stared at him. Farrell said easily: "I understand two guns were found, both the property of Steelgrave."

"Who told you?" Endicott asked sharply. He leaned forward frowning.

Farrell dropped his cigarette into the smoking stand and shrugged. "Hell, these things come out. One of these guns had killed Quest and also Stein. The other had killed Steelgrave. Fired at close quarters too. I admit those boys don't as a rule take that way out. But it could happen."

Endicott said gravely: "No doubt. Thanks for the suggestion. It happens to be wrong."

Farrell smiled a little and was silent. Endicott turned slowly to Mavis Weld.

"Miss Weld, this office—or the present incumbent of it at least—doesn't believe in seeking publicity at the expense of people to whom a certain kind of publicity might be fatal. It is my duty to determine whether anyone should be brought to trial for any of these murders, and to prosecute them, if the evidence warrants it. It is not my duty to ruin your career by exploiting the fact that you had the bad luck or bad judgment to be the friend of a man who, although never convicted or even indicted for any crime, was undoubtedly a member of a criminal mob at one time. I don't think you have been quite candid with me about this photograph, but I won't press the matter now. There is not much point in my asking you whether you shot Steelgrave. But I do ask you whether you have any knowledge that would point to who may have or might have killed him."

Farrell said quickly: "Knowledge, Miss Weld—not mere suspicion."

She faced Endicott squarely. "No."

He stood up and bowed. "That will be all for now then. Thanks for coming in."

Farrell and Mavis Weld stood up. I didn't move. Farrell said: "Are you calling a press conference?"

"I think I'll leave that to you, Mr. Farrell. You have always been very skillful in handling the press."

Farrell nodded and went to open the door. They went out. She didn't seem to look at me when she went out, but something touched the back of my neck lightly. Probably accidental. Her sleeve.

Endicott watched the door close. He looked across the desk at me. "Is Farrell representing you? I forgot to ask him."

"I can't afford him. So I'm vulnerable."

He smiled thinly. "I let them take all the tricks and then salve my dignity by working out on you, eh?"

"I couldn't stop you."

"You're not exactly proud of the way you have handled things, are you, Marlowe?"

"I got off on the wrong foot. After that I just had to take my lumps."

"Don't you think you owe a certain obligation to the law?"

"I would—if the law was like you."

He ran his long pale fingers through his tousled black hair.

"I could make a lot of answers to that," he said. "They'd all sound about the same. The citizen is the law. In this country we haven't got around to understanding that. We think of the law as an enemy. We're a nation of cop-haters."

"It'll take a lot to change that," I said. "On both sides."

He leaned forward and pressed a buzzer. "Yes," he said quietly. "It will. But somebody has to make a beginning. Thanks for coming in."

As I went out a secretary came in at another door with a fat file in her hand.

# 33

A shave and a second breakfast made me feel a little less like the box of shavings the cat had had kittens in. I went up to the office and unlocked the door and sniffed in the twice-breathed air and the smell of dust. I opened a window and inhaled the fry-cook smell from the coffee shop next door. I sat down at my desk and felt the grit on it with my fingertips. I filled a pipe and lit it and leaned back and looked around.

"Hello," I said.

I was just talking to the office equipment, the three green filing cases, the threadbare piece of carpet, the customer's chair across from me, and the light fixture in the ceiling with three dead moths in it that had been there for at least six months. I was talking to the pebbled glass panel and the grimy wood-work and the pen set on the desk and the tired, tired telephone. I was talking to the scales on an alligator, the name of the alligator being Marlowe, a private detective in our thriving little community. Not the brainiest guy in the world, but cheap. He started out cheap and he ended cheaper still.

I reached down and put the bottle of Old Forester up on the desk. It was about a third full. Old Forester. Now who gave you that, pal? That's green-label stuff. Out of your class entirely. Must have been a client. I had a client once.

And that got me thinking about her, and maybe I have stronger thoughts than I know. The telephone rang, and the funny little precise voice sounded just as it had the first time she called me up.

"I'm in that telephone booth," she said. "If you're alone, I'm coming up."

"Uh-huh."

"I suppose you're mad at me," she said.

"I'm not mad at anybody. Just tired."

"Oh yes you are," her tight little voice said. "But I'm coming up anyway. I don't care if you *are* mad at me."

She hung up. I took the cork out of the bottle of Old Forester and gave a sniff at it. I shuddered. That settled it. Any time I couldn't smell whiskey without shuddering I was through.

I put the bottle away and got up to unlock the communicating door. Then I heard her tripping along the hall. I'd know those tight little footsteps anywhere. I opened the door and she came up to me and looked at me shyly.

It was all gone. The slanted cheaters, and the new hair-do and the smart little hat and the perfume and the prettied-up touch. The costume jewelry, the rouge, the everything. All gone. She was right back where she started that first morning. Same brown tailor-made, same square bag, same rimless glasses, same prim little narrow-minded smile.

"It's me," she said. "I'm going home."

She followed me into my private thinking parlor and sat down primly and I sat down just any old way and stared at her.

"Back to Manhattan," I said. "I'm surprised they let you."

"I may have to come back."

"Can you afford it?"

She gave a quick little half-embarrassed laugh. "It won't cost me anything," she said. She reached up and touched the rimless glasses. "These feel all wrong now," she said. "I liked the others. But Dr. Zugsmith wouldn't like them at all." She put her bag on the desk and drew a line along the desk with her fingertip. That was just like the first time too.

"I can't remember whether I gave you back your twenty dollars or not," I said. "We kept passing it back and forth until I lost count."

"Oh, you gave it to me," she said. "Thank you."

"Sure?"

"I never make mistakes about money. Are you all right? Did they hurt you?"

"The police? No. And it was as tough a job as they ever didn't do."

She looked innocently surprised. Then her eyes glowed. "You must be awfully brave," she said.

"Just luck," I said. I picked up a pencil and felt the point. It was a good sharp point, if anybody wanted to write anything. I didn't. I reached across and slipped the pencil through the strap of her bag and pulled it towards me.

"Don't touch my bag," she said quickly and reached for it.

I grinned and drew it out of her reach. "All right. But it's such a cute little bag. It's so like you."

She leaned back. There was a vague worry behind her eyes, but she smiled. "You think I'm cute—Philip? I'm so ordinary."

"I wouldn't say so."

"You wouldn't?"

"Hell no, I think you're one of the most unusual girls I ever met." I swung the bag by its strap and set it down on the corner of the desk. Her eyes fastened on it quickly, but she licked her lip and kept on smiling at me.

"And I bet you've known an awful lot of girls," she said. "Why—" she looked down and did that with her fingertip on the desk again—"why didn't you ever get married?"

I thought of all the ways you answer that. I thought of all the women I had liked that much. No, not all. But some of them.

"I suppose I know the answer," I said. "But it would just sound corny. The ones I'd maybe like to marry—well, I haven't what they need. The others you don't have to marry. You just seduce them—if they don't beat you to it."

She flushed to the roots of her mousy hair.

"You're horrid when you talk like that."

"That goes for some of the nice ones too," I said. "Not what you said. What I said. You wouldn't have been so hard to take yourself."

"Don't talk like that, please!"

"Well, would you?"

She looked down at the desk. "I wish you'd tell me," she said slowly, "what happened to Orrin. I'm all confused."

"I told you he probably went off the rails. The first time you came in. Remember?"

She nodded slowly, still blushing.

"Abnormal sort of home life," I said. "Very inhibited sort of guy and with a very highly developed sense of his own importance. It looked at you out of the picture you gave me. I don't want to go psychological on you, but I figure he was just the type to go very completely haywire, if he went haywire at all. Then there's that awful money hunger that runs in your family—all except one."

She smiled at me now. If she thought I meant her, that was jake with me.

"There's one question I want to ask you," I said. "Was your father married before?"

She nodded, yes.

"That helps. Leila had another mother. That suits me fine. Tell me some more. After all I did a lot of work for you, for a very low fee of no dollars net."

"You got paid," she said sharply. "Well paid. By Leila. And don't expect me to call her Mavis Weld. I won't do it."

"You didn't know I was going to get paid."

"Well—" there was a long pause, during which her eyes went to her bag again—"you did get paid."

"Okay, pass that. Why wouldn't you tell me who she was?"

"I was ashamed. Mother and I were both ashamed."

"Orrin wasn't. He loved it."

"Orrin?" There was a tidy little silence while she looked at her bag again. I was beginning to get curious about that bag. "But he had been out here and I suppose he'd got used to it."

"Being in pictures isn't that bad, surely."

"It wasn't just that," she said swiftly, and her tooth came down on the outer edge of her lower lip and something flared in her eyes and very slowly died away. I just put another match to my pipe. I was too tired to show emotions, even if I felt any.

"I know. Or anyway I kind of guessed. How did Orrin find out something about Steelgrave that the cops didn't know?"

"I—I don't know," she said slowly, picking her way among her words like a cat on a fence. "Could it have been that doctor?"

"Oh sure," I said, with a big warm smile. "He and Orrin got to be friends somehow. A common interest in sharp tools maybe."

She leaned back in her chair. Her little face was thin and angular now. Her eyes had a watchful look.

"Now you're just being nasty," she said. "Every so often you have to be that way."

"Such a pity," I said. "I'd be a lovable character if I'd let myself alone. Nice bag." I reached for it and pulled it in front of me and snapped it open.

She came up out of her chair and lunged.

"You let my bag alone!"

I looked her straight in the rimless glasses. "You want to go home to Manhattan, Kansas, don't you? Today? You got your ticket and everything?"

She worked her lips and slowly sat down again.

"Okay," I said. "I'm not stopping you. I just wondered how much dough you squeezed out of the deal."

She began to cry. I opened the bag and went through it. Nothing until I came to the zipper pocket at the back. I unzipped and reached in. There was a flat packet of new bills in there. I took them out and riffled them. Ten centuries. All new. All nice. An even thousand dollars. Nice traveling money.

I leaned back and tapped the edge of the packet on my desk. She sat silent now, staring at me with wet eyes. I got a handkerchief out of her bag and tossed it across to her. She dabbed at her eyes. She watched me around the handkerchief. Once in a while she made a nice little appealing sob in her throat.

"Leila gave the money to me," she said softly.

"What size chisel did you use?"

She just opened her mouth and a tear ran down her cheek into it.

"Skip it," I said. I dropped the pack of money back into the bag, snapped the bag shut and pushed it across the desk to her. "I guess you and Orrin belong to that class of people that can convince themselves that everything they do is right. He can blackmail his sister and then when a couple of small-time crooks get wise to his racket and take it away from him, he can sneak up on them and knock them off with an ice pick in the back of the neck. Probably didn't even keep him awake that night. You can do much the same. Leila didn't give you that money. Steelgrave gave it to you. For what?"

"You're filthy," she said. "You're vile. How dare you say such things to me?"

"Who tipped off the law that Dr. Lagardie knew Clausen? Lagardie thought I did. I didn't. So you did. Why? To smoke out your brother who was not cutting you in—because right then he had lost his deck of cards and was hiding out. I'd like to see some of those letters he wrote home. I bet they're meaty. I can see him working at it, watching his sister, trying to get her lined up for his Leica, with the good Doctor Lagardie waiting quietly in the background for his share of the take. What did you hire me for?"

"I didn't know," she said evenly. She wiped her eyes again and put the handkerchief away in the bag and got herself all collected and ready to leave. "Orrin never mentioned any names. I didn't even know Orrin had lost his pictures. But I knew he had taken them and that they were very valuable. I came out to make sure."

"Sure of what?"

"That Orrin treated me right. He could be awfully mean sometimes. He might have kept all the money himself."

"Why did he call you up night before last?"

"He was scared. Dr. Lagardie wasn't pleased with him any more. He didn't have the pictures. Somebody else had them. Orrin didn't know who. But he was scared."

"I had them. I still have," I said. "They're in that safe."

She turned her head very slowly to look at the safe. She ran a fingertip questioningly along her lip. She turned back.

"I don't believe you," she said, and her eyes watched me like a cat watching a mousehole.

"How's to split that grand with me. You get the pictures."

She thought about it. "I could hardly give you all that money for something that doesn't belong to you," she said, and smiled. "Please give them to me. Please, Philip. Leila ought to have them back."

"For how much dough?"

She frowned and looked hurt.

"She's my client now," I said. "But double-crossing her wouldn't be bad business—at the right price."

"I don't believe you have them."

"Okay." I got up and went to the safe. In a moment I was back with the envelope. I poured the prints and the negative out on the desk—my side of the desk. She looked down at them and started to reach.

I picked them up and shuffled them together and held one so that she could look at it. When she reached for it I moved it back.

"But I can't see it so far away," she complained.

"It costs money to get closer."

"I never thought you were a crook," she said with dignity.

I didn't say anything. I relit my pipe.

"I could make you give them to the police," she said.

"You could try."

Suddenly she spoke rapidly. "I couldn't give you this money I have, really I couldn't. We—well mother and I owe money still on account of father and the house isn't clear and—"

"What did you sell Steelgrave for the grand?"

Her mouth fell open and she looked ugly. She closed her lips and pressed them together. It was a tight hard little face that I was looking at.

"You had one thing to sell," I said. "You knew where Orrin was. To Steelgrave that information was worth a grand. Easy. It's a question of connecting up evidence. You wouldn't understand. Steelgrave went down there and killed him. He paid you the money for the address."

"Leila told him," she said in a faraway voice.

"Leila told me she told him," I said. "If necessary Leila would tell the world she told him. Just as she would tell the world she killed Steelgrave—if that was the only way out. Leila is a sort of free-and-easy Hollywood babe that doesn't have very good morals. But when it comes to bedrock guts—she has what it takes. She's not the ice-pick type. And she's not the blood-money type."

The color flowed away from her face and left her as pale as ice. Her mouth quivered, then tightened up hard into a little knot. She pushed her chair back and leaned forward to get up.

"Blood money," I said quietly. "Your own brother. And you set him up so they could kill him. A thousand dollars blood money. I hope you'll be happy with it."

She stood away from the chair and took a couple of steps backward. Then suddenly she giggled.

"Who could prove it?" she half squealed. "Who's alive to prove it? You? Who are you? A cheap shyster, a nobody." She went off into a shrill peal of laughter. "Why even twenty dollars buys you."

I was still holding the packet of photos. I struck a match

and dropped the negative into the ash tray and watched it flare up.

She stopped dead, frozen in a kind of horror. I started to tear the pictures up into strips. I grinned at her.

"A cheap shyster," I said. "Well, what would you expect. I don't have any brothers or sisters to sell out. So I sell out my clients."

She stood rigid and glaring. I finished my tearing-up job and lit the scraps of paper in the tray.

"One thing I regret," I said. "Not seeing your meeting back in Manhattan, Kansas, with dear old Mom. Not seeing the fight over how to split that grand. I bet that would be something to watch."

I poked at the paper with a pencil to keep it burning. She came slowly, step by step, to the desk and her eyes were fixed on the little smoldering heap of torn prints.

"I could tell the police," she whispered. "I could tell them a lot of things. They'd believe me."

"I could tell them who shot Steelgrave," I said. "Because I know who didn't. They might believe *me*."

The small head jerked up. The light glinted on the glasses. There were no eyes behind them.

"Don't worry," I said. "I'm not going to. It wouldn't cost me enough. And it would cost somebody else too much."

The telephone rang and she jumped a foot. I turned and reached for it and put my face against it and said, "Hello."

"Amigo, are you all right?"

There was a sound in the background. I swung around and saw the door click shut. I was alone in the room.

"Are you all right, amigo?"

"I'm tired. I've been up all night. Apart from—"

"Has the little one called you up?"

"The little sister? She was just in here. She's on her way back to Manhattan with the swag."

"The swag?"

"The pocket money she got from Steelgrave for fingering her brother."

There was a silence, then she said gravely, "You cannot know that, amigo."

"Like I know I'm sitting leaning on this desk holding on to

this telephone. Like I know I hear your voice. And not quite so certainly, but certainly enough like I know who shot Steelgrave."

"You are somewhat foolish to say that to me, amigo. I am not above reproach. You should not trust me too much."

"I make mistakes, but this won't be one. I've burned all the photographs. I tried to sell them to Orfamay. She wouldn't bid high enough."

"Surely you are making fun, amigo."

"Am I? Who of?"

She tinkled her laugh over the wire. "Would you like to take me to lunch?"

"I might. Are you home?"

"Sí."

"I'll come over in a little while."

"But I shall be delighted."

I hung up.

The play was over. I was sitting in the empty theater. The curtain was down and projected on it dimly I could see the action. But already some of the actors were getting vague and unreal. The little sister above all. In a couple of days I would forget what she looked like. Because in a way she *was* so unreal. I thought of her tripping back to Manhattan, Kansas, and dear old Mom, with that fat little new little thousand dollars in her purse. A few people had been killed so she could get it, but I didn't think that would bother her for long. I thought of her getting down to the office in the morning—what was the man's name? Oh yes. Dr. Zugsmith—and dusting off his desk before he arrived and arranging the magazines in the waiting room. She'd have her rimless cheaters on and a plain dress and her face would be without make-up and her manners to the patients would be most correct.

"Dr. Zugsmith will see you now, Mrs. Whoosis."

She would hold the door open with a little smile and Mrs. Whoosis would go in past her and Dr. Zugsmith would be sitting behind his desk as professional as hell with a white coat on and his stethoscope hanging around his neck. A case file would be in front of him and his note pad and prescription pad would be neatly squared off. Nothing that Dr. Zugsmith didn't know. You couldn't fool him. He had it all at his fingertips. When he looked at a patient he knew the answers to all the questions he was going to ask just as a matter of form.

When he looked at his receptionist, Miss Orfamay Quest, he saw a nice quiet young lady, properly dressed for a doctor's office, no red nails, no loud make-up, nothing to offend the old-fashioned type of customer. An ideal receptionist, Miss Quest.

Dr. Zugsmith, when he thought about her at all thought of her with self-satisfaction. He had made her what she was. She was just what the doctor ordered.

Most probably he hadn't made a pass at her yet. Maybe they don't in those small towns. Ha, ha! I grew up in one.

I changed position and looked at my watch and got that bottle of Old Forester up out of the drawer after all. I sniffed it. It smelled good. I poured myself a good stiff jolt and held it up against the light.

"Well, Dr. Zugsmith," I said out loud, just as if he was sitting there on the other side of the desk with a drink in his hand, "I don't know you very well and you don't know me at all. Ordinarily I don't believe in giving advice to strangers, but I've had a short intensive course of Miss Orfamay Quest and I'm breaking my rule. If ever that little girl wants anything from you, give it to her quick. Don't stall around or gobble about your income tax and your overhead. Just wrap yourself in a smile and shell out. Don't get involved in any discussions about what belongs to who. Keep the little girl happy, that's the main thing. Good luck to you, Doctor, and don't leave any harpoons lying around the office."

I drank off half of my drink and waited for it to warm me up. When it did that I drank the rest and put the bottle away.

I knocked the cold ashes out of my pipe and refilled it from the leather humidor an admirer had given me for Christmas, the admirer by an odd coincidence having the same name as mine.

When I had the pipe filled I lit it carefully, without haste, and went on out and down the hall, as breezy as a Britisher coming in from a tiger hunt.

# 34

The Chateau Bercy was old but made over. It had the sort of lobby that asks for plush and india-rubber plants, but gets glass brick, cornice lighting, three-cornered glass tables, and a general air of having been redecorated by a parolee from a nut hatch. Its color scheme was bile green, linseed-poultice brown, sidewalk gray and monkey-bottom blue. It was as restful as a split lip.

The small desk was empty but the mirror behind it could be diaphanous, so I didn't try to sneak up the stairs. I rang a bell and a large soft man oozed out from behind a wall and smiled at me with moist soft lips and bluish-white teeth and unnaturally bright eyes.

"Miss Gonzales," I said. "Name's Marlowe. She's expecting me."

"Why, yes of course," he said, fluttering his hands. "Yes, of course. I'll telephone up at once." He had a voice that fluttered too.

He picked up the telephone and gurgled into it and put it down.

"Yes, Mr. Marlowe. Miss Gonzales says to come right up. Apartment 412." He giggled. "But I suppose you know."

"I know now," I said. "By the way were you here last February?"

"Last February? Last February? Oh yes, I was here last February." He pronounced it exactly as spelled.

"Remember the night Stein got chilled out front?"

The smile went away from the fat face in a hurry. "Are you a police officer?" His voice was now thin and reedy.

"No. But your pants are unzipped, if you care."

He looked down with horror and zipped them up with hands that almost trembled.

"Why thank you," he said. "Thank you." He leaned across the low desk. "It was not exactly out front," he said. "That is not exactly. It was almost to the next corner."

"Living here, wasn't he?"

"I'd really rather not talk about it. Really I'd rather not talk about it." He paused and ran his pinkie along his lower lip. "Why do you ask?"

"Just to keep you talking. You want to be more careful, bud. I can smell it on your breath."

The pink flowed all over him right down to his neck. "If you suggest I have been drinking—"

"Only tea," I said. "And not from a cup."

I turned away. He was silent. As I reached the elevator I looked back. He stood with his hands flat on the desk and his head strained around to watch me. Even from a distance he seemed to be trembling.

The elevator was self-service. The fourth floor was cool gray, the carpet thick. There was a small bell push beside Apartment 412. It chimed softly inside. The door was swung open instantly. The beautiful deep dark eyes looked at me and the red red mouth smiled at me. Black slacks and the flame-colored shirt, just like last night.

"Amigo," she said softly. She put her arms out. I took hold of her wrists and brought them together and made her palms touch. I played patacake with her for a moment. The expression in her eyes was languorous and fiery at the same time.

I let go of her wrists, closed the door with my elbow and slid past her. It was like the first time.

"You ought to carry insurance on those," I said touching one. It was real enough. The nipple was as hard as a ruby.

She went into her joyous laugh. I went on in and looked the place over. It was French gray and dusty blue. Not her colors, but very nice. There was a false fireplace with gas logs, and enough chairs and tables and lamps, but not too many. There was a neat little cellarette in the corner.

"You like my little apartment, amigo?"

"Don't say little apartment. That sounds like a whore too."

I didn't look at her. I didn't want to look at her. I sat down on a davenport and rubbed a hand across my forehead.

"Four hours sleep and a couple of drinks," I said. "And I'd be able to talk nonsense to you again. Right now I've barely strength to talk sense. But I've got to."

She came to sit close to me. I shook my head. "Over there. I really do have to talk sense."

She sat down opposite and looked at me with grave dark eyes. "But yes, amigo, whatever you wish. I am your girl—at least I would gladly be your girl."

"Where did you live in Cleveland?"

"In Cleveland?" Her voice was very soft, almost cooing. "Did I say I had lived in Cleveland?"

"You said you knew him there."

She thought back and then nodded. "I was married then, amigo. What is the matter?"

"You did live in Cleveland then?"

"Yes," she said softly.

"You got to know Steelgrave how?"

"It was just that in those days it was fun to know a gangster. A form of inverted snobbery, I suppose. One went to the places where they were said to go and if one was lucky, perhaps some evening—"

"You let him pick you up."

She nodded brightly. "Let us say I picked him up. He was a very nice little man. Really, he was."

"What about the husband? Your husband. Or don't you remember?"

She smiled. "The streets of the world are paved with discarded husbands," she said.

"Isn't it the truth? You find them everywhere. Even in Bay City."

That bought me nothing. She shrugged politely. "I would not doubt it."

"Might even be a graduate of the Sorbonne. Might even be mooning away in a measly small-town practice. Waiting and hoping. That's one coincidence I'd like to eat. It has a touch of poetry."

The polite smile stayed in place on her lovely face.

"We've slipped far apart," I said. "Ever so far. And we got to be pretty clubby there for a while."

I looked down at my fingers. My head ached. I wasn't even forty per cent of what I ought to be. She reached me a crystal cigarette box and I took one. She fitted one for herself into the golden tweezers. She took it from a different box.

"I'd like to try one of yours," I said.

"But Mexican tobacco is so harsh to most people."

"As long as it's tobacco," I said, watching her. I made up my mind. "No, you're right. I wouldn't like it."

"What," she asked carefully, "is the meaning of this by-play?"

"Desk clerk's a muggle-smoker."

She nodded slowly. "I have warned him," she said. "Several times."

"Amigo," I said.

"What?"

"You don't use much Spanish do you? Perhaps you don't know much Spanish. Amigo gets worn to shreds."

"We are not going to be like yesterday afternoon, I hope," she said slowly.

"We're not. The only thing Mexican about you is a few words and a careful way of talking that's supposed to give the impression of a person speaking a language they had to learn. Like saying 'do not' instead of 'don't.' That sort of thing."

She didn't answer. She puffed gently on her cigarette and smiled.

"I'm in bad trouble downtown," I went on. "Apparently Miss Weld had the good sense to tell it to her boss—Julius Oppenheimer—and he came through. Got Lee Farrell for her. I don't think they think she shot Steelgrave. But they think I know who did, and they don't love me any more."

"And do you know, amigo?"

"Told you over the phone I did."

She looked at me steadily for a longish moment. "I was there." Her voice had a dry serious sound for once.

"It was very curious, really. The little girl wanted to see the gambling house. She had never seen anything like that and there had been in the papers—"

"She was staying here—with you?"

"Not in my apartment, amigo. In a room I got for her here."

"No wonder she wouldn't tell me," I said. "But I guess you didn't have time to teach her the business."

She frowned very slightly and made a motion in the

air with the brown cigarette. I watched its smoke write something unreadable in the still air.

"Please. As I was saying she wanted to go to that house. So I called him up and he said to come along. When we got there he was drunk. I have never seen him drunk before. He laughed and put his arm around little Orfamay and told her she had earned her money well. He said he had something for her, then he took from his pocket a billfold wrapped in a cloth of some kind and gave it to her. When she unwrapped it there was a hole in the middle of it and the hole was stained with blood."

"That wasn't nice," I said. "I wouldn't even call it characteristic."

"You did not know him very well."

"True. Go on."

"Little Orfamay took the billfold and stared at it and then stared at him and her white little face was very still. Then she thanked him and opened her bag to put the billfold in it, as I thought—it was all very curious—"

"A scream," I said. "It would have had me gasping on the floor."

"—but instead she took a gun out of her bag. It was a gun he had given Mavis, I think. It was like the one—"

"I know exactly what it was like," I said. "I played with it some."

"She turned around and shot him dead with one shot. It was very dramatic."

She put the brown cigarette back in her mouth and smiled at me. A curious, rather distant smile, as if she was thinking of something far away.

"You made her confess to Mavis Weld," I said.

She nodded.

"Mavis wouldn't have believed *you*, I guess."

"I did not care to risk it."

"It wasn't you gave Orfamay the thousand bucks, was it, darling? To make her tell? She's a little girl who would go a long way for a thousand bucks."

"I do not care to answer that," she said with dignity.

"No. So last night when you rushed me out there, you already knew he was dead and there wasn't anything to be afraid of and all that act with the gun was just an act."

"I do not like to play God," she said softly. "There was a situation and I knew that somehow or other you would get Mavis out of it. There was no one else who would. Mavis was determined to take the blame."

"I better have a drink," I said. "I'm sunk."

She jumped up and went to the little cellarette. She came back with a couple of huge glasses of Scotch and water. She handed me one and watched me over her glass as I tried it out. It was wonderful. I drank some more. She sank down into her chair again, and reached for the golden tweezers.

"I chased her out," I said, finally. "Mavis, I'm talking about. She told me she had shot him. She had the gun. The twin of the one you gave me. You didn't probably notice that yours had been fired."

"I know very little about guns," she said softly.

"Sure. I counted the shells in it, and assuming it had been full to start with, two had been fired. Quest was killed with two shots from a .32 automatic. Same caliber. I picked up the empty shells in the den down there."

"Down where, amigo?"

It was beginning to grate. Too much amigo, far too much.

"Of course I couldn't know it was the same gun, but it seemed worth trying out. Only confuse things up a little anyhow, and give Mavis that much break. So I switched guns on him, and put his behind the bar. His was a black .38. More like what he would carry, if he carried one at all. Even with a checked grip you can leave prints, but with an ivory grip you're apt to leave a fair set of finger marks on the left side. Steelgrave wouldn't carry that kind of gun."

Her eyes were round and empty and puzzled. "I am afraid I am not following you too well."

"And if he killed a man he would kill him dead, and be sure of it. This guy got up and walked a bit."

A flash of something showed in her eyes and was gone.

"I'd like to say he talked a bit," I went on. "But he didn't. His lungs were full of blood. He died at my feet. Down there."

"But down where? You have not told me where it was that this—"

"Do I have to?"

She sipped from her glass. She smiled. She put the glass down. I said:

"You were present when little Orfamay told him where to go."

"Oh yes, of course." Nice recovery. Fast and clean. But her smile looked a little more tired.

"Only he didn't go," I said.

Her cigarette stopped in midair. That was all. Nothing else. It went on slowly to her lips. She puffed elegantly.

"That's what's been the matter all along," I said. "I just wouldn't buy what was staring me in the face. Steelgrave is Weepy Moyer. That's solid, isn't it?"

"Most certainly. And it can be proved."

"Steelgrave is a reformed character and doing fine. Then this Stein comes out bothering him, wanting to cut in. I'm guessing, but that's about how it would happen. Okay, Stein has to go. Steelgrave doesn't want to kill anybody—and he has never been accused of killing anybody. The Cleveland cops wouldn't come out and get him. No charges pending. No mystery—except that he had been connected with a mob in some capacity. But he has to get rid of Stein. So he gets himself pinched. And then he gets out of jail by bribing the jail doctor, and he kills Stein and goes back into jail at once. When the killing shows up whoever let him out of jail is going to run like hell and destroy any records there might be of his going out. Because the cops will come over and ask questions."

"Very naturally, amigo."

I looked her over for cracks, but there weren't any yet.

"So far so good. But we've got to give this lad credit for a few brains. Why did he let them hold him in jail for ten days? Answer One, to make himself an alibi. Answer Two, because he knew that sooner or later this question of him being Moyer was going to get aired, so why not give them the time and get it over with? That way any time a racket boy gets blown down around here they're not going to keep pulling Steelgrave in and trying to hang the rap on him."

"You like that idea, amigo?"

"Yes. Look at it this way. Why would he have lunch in a public place the very day he was out of the cooler to knock

Stein off? And if he did, why would young Quest happen around to snap that picture? Stein hadn't been killed, so the picture wasn't evidence of anything. I like people to be lucky, but that's *too* lucky. Again, even if Steelgrave didn't know his picture had been taken, he knew who Quest was. Must have. Quest had been tapping his sister for eating money since he lost his job, maybe before. Steelgrave had a key to her apartment. He must have known something about this brother of hers. Which simply adds up to the result, that *that* night of all nights Steelgrave would *not* have shot Stein—even if he had planned to."

"It is now for me to ask you who did," she said politely.

"Somebody who knew Stein and could get close to him. Somebody who already knew that photo had been taken, knew who Steelgrave was, knew that Mavis Weld was on the edge of becoming a big star, knew that her association with Steelgrave was dangerous, but would be a thousand times more dangerous if Steelgrave could be framed for the murder of Stein. Knew Quest, because he had been to Mavis Weld's apartment, and had met him there and given him the works, and he was a boy that could be knocked clean out of his mind by that sort of treatment. Knew that those bone-handled .32's were registered to Steelgrave, although he had only bought them to give to a couple of girls, and if he carried a gun himself, it would be one that was not registered and could not be traced to him. Knew—"

"Stop!" Her voice was a sharp stab of sound, but neither frightened nor even angry. "You will stop at once, please! I will not tolerate this another minute. You will now go!"

I stood up. She leaned back and a pulse beat in her throat. She was exquisite, she was dark, she was deadly. And nothing would ever touch her, not even the law.

"Why did you kill Quest?" I asked her.

She stood up and came close to me, smiling again. "For two reasons, amigo. He was more than a little crazy and in the end he would have killed me. And the other reason is that none of this—absolutely none of it—was for money. It was for love."

I started to laugh in her face. I didn't. She was dead serious. It was out of this world.

"No matter how many lovers a woman may have," she said softly, "there is always one she cannot bear to lose to another woman. Steelgrave was the one."

I just stared into her lovely dark eyes. "I believe you," I said at last.

"Kiss me, amigo."

"Good God!"

"I must have men, amigo. But the man I loved is dead. I killed him. That man I would not share."

"You waited a long time."

"I can be patient—as long as there is hope."

"Oh, nuts."

She smiled a free, beautiful and perfectly natural smile. "And you cannot do a damn thing about all this, darling, unless you destroy Mavis Weld utterly and finally."

"Last night she proved she was willing to destroy herself."

"If she was not acting." She looked at me sharply and laughed. "That hurt, did it not? You are in love with her."

I said slowly, "That would be kind of silly. I could sit in the dark with her and hold hands, but for how long? In a little while she will drift off into a haze of glamour and expensive clothes and froth and unreality and muted sex. She won't be a real person any more. Just a voice from a sound track, a face on a screen. I'd want more than that."

I moved towards the door without putting my back to her. I didn't really expect a slug. I thought she liked better having me the way I was—and not being able to do a damn thing about any of it.

I looked back as I opened the door. Slim, dark and lovely and smiling. Reeking with sex. Utterly beyond the moral laws of this or any world I could imagine.

She was one for the book all right. I went out quietly. Very softly her voice came to me as I closed the door.

"Querido—I have liked you very much. It is too bad."

I shut the door.

# 35

As the elevator opened at the lobby a man stood there waiting for it. He was tall and thin and his hat was pulled low over his eyes. It was a warm day but he wore a thin topcoat with the collar up. He kept his chin low.

"Dr. Lagardie," I said softly.

He glanced at me with no trace of recognition. He moved into the elevator. It started up.

I went across to the desk and banged the bell. The large fat soft man came out and stood with a pained smile on his loose mouth. His eyes were not quite so bright.

"Give me the phone."

He reached down and put it on the desk. I dialed Madison 7911. The voice said: "Police." This was the Emergency Board.

"Chateau Bercy Apartments, Franklin and Girard in Hollywood. A man named Dr. Vincent Lagardie wanted for questioning by homicide, Lieutenants French and Beifus, has just gone up to Apartment 412. This is Philip Marlowe, a private detective."

"Franklin and Girard. Wait there please. Are you armed?"

"Yes."

"Hold him if he tries to leave."

I hung up and wiped my mouth off. The fat softy was leaning against the counter, white around the eyes.

They came fast—but not fast enough. Perhaps I ought to have stopped him. Perhaps I had a hunch what he would do, and deliberately let him do it. Sometimes when I'm low I try to reason it out. But it gets too complicated. The whole damn case was that way. There was never a point where I could do the natural obvious thing without stopping to rack my head dizzy with figuring how it would affect somebody I owed something to.

When they cracked the door he was sitting on the couch holding her pressed against his heart. His eyes were blind and there was bloody foam on his lips. He had bitten through his tongue.

Under her left breast and tight against the flame-colored shirt lay the silver handle of a knife I had seen before. The handle was in the shape of a naked woman. The eyes of Miss Dolores Gonzales were half open and on her lips there was the dim ghost of a provocative smile.

"The Hippocrates smile," the ambulance intern said, and sighed. "On her it looks good."

He glanced across at Dr. Lagardie who saw nothing and heard nothing, if you could judge by his face.

"I guess somebody lost a dream," the intern said. He bent over and closed her eyes.

THE LONG GOODBYE

# I

THE FIRST TIME I laid eyes on Terry Lennox he was drunk in a Rolls-Royce Silver Wraith outside the terrace of The Dancers. The parking lot attendant had brought the car out and he was still holding the door open because Terry Lennox's left foot was still dangling outside, as if he had forgotten he had one. He had a young-looking face but his hair was bone white. You could tell by his eyes that he was plastered to the hairline, but otherwise he looked like any other nice young guy in a dinner jacket who had been spending too much money in a joint that exists for that purpose and for no other.

There was a girl beside him. Her hair was a lovely shade of dark red and she had a distant smile on her lips and over her shoulders she had a blue mink that almost made the Rolls-Royce look like just another automobile. It didn't quite. Nothing can.

The attendant was the usual half-tough character in a white coat with the name of the restaurant stitched across the front of it in red. He was getting fed up.

"Look, mister," he said with an edge to his voice, "would you mind a whole lot pulling your leg into the car so I can kind of shut the door? Or should I open it all the way so you can fall out?"

The girl gave him a look which ought to have stuck at least four inches out of his back. It didn't bother him enough to give him the shakes. At The Dancers they get the sort of people that disillusion you about what a lot of golfing money can do for the personality.

A low-swung foreign speedster with no top drifted into the parking lot and a man got out of it and used the dash lighter on a long cigarette. He was wearing a pullover check shirt, yellow slacks, and riding boots. He strolled off trailing clouds of incense, not even bothering to look towards the Rolls-Royce. He probably thought it was corny. At the foot of the steps up to the terrace he paused to stick a monocle in his eye.

The girl said with a nice burst of charm: "I have a wonderful idea, darling. Why don't we just take a cab to your place and get your convertible out? It's such a wonderful night for a run up the coast to Montecito. I know some people there who are throwing a dance around the pool."

The white-haired lad said politely: "Awfully sorry, but I don't have it any more. I was compelled to sell it." From his voice and articulation you wouldn't have known he had had anything stronger than orange juice to drink.

"Sold it, darling? How do you mean?" She slid away from him along the seat but her voice slid away a lot farther than that.

"I mean I had to," he said. "For eating money."

"Oh, I see." A slice of spumoni wouldn't have melted on her now.

The attendant had the white-haired boy right where he could reach him—in a low-income bracket. "Look, buster," he said, "I've got to put a car away. See you some more some other time—maybe."

He let the door swing open. The drunk promptly slid off the seat and landed on the blacktop on the seat of his pants. So I went over and dropped my nickel. I guess it's always a mistake to interfere with a drunk. Even if he knows and likes you he is always liable to haul off and poke you in the teeth. I got him under the arms and got him up on his feet.

"Thank you so very much," he said politely.

The girl slid under the wheel. "He gets so goddam English when he's loaded," she said in a stainless-steel voice. "Thanks for catching him."

"I'll get him in the back of the car," I said.

"I'm terribly sorry. I'm late for an engagement." She let the clutch in and the Rolls started to glide. "He's just a lost dog," she added with a cool smile. "Perhaps you can find a home for him. He's housebroken—more or less."

And the Rolls ticked down the entrance driveway on to Sunset Boulevard, made a right turn, and was gone. I was looking after her when the attendant came back. And I was still holding the man up and he was now sound asleep.

"Well, that's one way of doing it," I told the white coat.

"Sure," he said cynically. "Why waste it on a lush? Them curves and all."

"You know him?"

"I heard the dame call him Terry. Otherwise I don't know him from a cow's caboose. But I only been here two weeks."

"Get my car, will you?" I gave him the ticket.

By the time he brought my Olds over I felt as if I was holding up a sack of lead. The white coat helped me get him into the front seat. The customer opened an eye and thanked us and went to sleep again.

"He's the politest drunk I ever met," I said to the white coat.

"They come all sizes and shapes and all kinds of manners," he said. "And they're all bums. Looks like this one had a plastic job one time."

"Yeah." I gave him a dollar and he thanked me. He was right about the plastic job. The right side of my new friend's face was frozen and whitish and seamed with thin fine scars. The skin had a glossy look along the scars. A plastic job and a pretty drastic one.

"Whatcha aim to do with him?"

"Take him home and sober him up enough to tell me where he lives."

The white coat grinned at me. "Okay, sucker. If it was me, I'd just drop him in the gutter and keep going. Them booze hounds just make a man a lot of trouble for no fun. I got a philosophy about them things. The way the competition is nowadays a guy has to save his strength to protect hisself in the clinches."

"I can see you've made a big success out of it," I said.

He looked puzzled and then he started to get mad, but by that time I was in the car and moving.

He was partly right of course. Terry Lennox made me plenty of trouble. But after all that's my line of work.

I was living that year in a house on Yucca Avenue in the Laurel Canyon district. It was a small hillside house on a dead-end street with a long flight of redwood steps to the front door and a grove of eucalyptus trees across the way. It was furnished, and it belonged to a woman who had gone to Idaho to live with her widowed daughter for a while. The rent was low, partly because the owner wanted to be able to come back on short notice, and partly because of the steps. She was getting too old to face them every time she came home.

I got the drunk up them somehow. He was eager to help but his legs were rubber and he kept falling asleep in the middle of an apologetic sentence. I got the door unlocked and dragged him inside and spread him on the long couch, threw a rug over him and let him go back to sleep. He snored like a grampus for an hour. Then he came awake all of a sudden and wanted to go to the bathroom. When he came back he looked at me peeringly, squinting his eyes, and wanted to know where the hell he was. I told him. He said his name was Terry Lennox and that he lived in an apartment in Westwood and no one was waiting up for him. His voice was clear and unslurred.

He said he could handle a cup of black coffee. When I brought it he sipped it carefully holding the saucer close under the cup.

"How come I'm here?" he asked, looking around.

"You squiffed out at The Dancers in a Rolls. Your girl friend ditched you."

"Quite," he said. "No doubt she was entirely justified."

"You English?"

"I've lived there. I wasn't born there. If I might call a taxi, I'll take myself off."

"You've got one waiting."

He made the steps on his own going down. He didn't say much on the way to Westwood, except that it was very kind of me and he was sorry to be such a nuisance. He had probably said it so often and to so many people that it was automatic.

His apartment was small and stuffy and impersonal. He might have moved in that afternoon. On a coffee table in front of a hard green davenport there was a half empty Scotch bottle and melted ice in a bowl and three empty fizzwater bottles and two glasses and a glass ash tray loaded with stubs with and without lipstick. There wasn't a photograph or a personal article of any kind in the place. It might have been a hotel room rented for a meeting or a farewell, for a few drinks and a talk, for a roll in the hay. It didn't look like a place where anyone lived.

He offered me a drink. I said no thanks. I didn't sit down. When I left he thanked me some more, but not as if I had climbed a mountain for him, nor as if it was nothing at all. He was a little shaky and a little shy but polite as hell. He stood in the open door until the automatic elevator came up and I got into it. Whatever he didn't have he had manners.

He hadn't mentioned the girl again. Also, he hadn't mentioned that he had no job and no prospects and that almost his last dollar had gone into paying the check at The Dancers for a bit of high class fluff that couldn't stick around long enough to make sure he didn't get tossed in the sneezer by some prowl car boys, or rolled by a tough hackie and dumped out in a vacant lot.

On the way down in the elevator I had an impulse to go back up and take the Scotch bottle away from him. But it wasn't any of my business and it never does any good anyway. They always find a way to get it if they have to have it.

I drove home chewing my lip. I'm supposed to be tough but there was something about the guy that got me. I didn't know what it was unless it was the white hair and the scarred face and the clear voice and the politeness. Maybe that was enough. There was no reason why I should ever see him again. He was just a lost dog, like the girl said.

## 2

It was the week after Thanksgiving when I saw him again. The stores along Hollywood Boulevard were already beginning to fill up with overpriced Christmas junk, and the daily papers were beginning to scream about how terrible it would be if you didn't get your Christmas shopping done early. It would be terrible anyway; it always is.

It was about three blocks from my office building that I

saw a cop car double-parked and the two buttons in it staring at something over by a shop window on the sidewalk. The something was Terry Lennox—or what was left of him—and that little was not too attractive.

He was leaning against a store front. He had to lean against something. His shirt was dirty and open at the neck and partly outside his jacket and partly not. He hadn't shaved for four or five days. His nose was pinched. His skin was so pale that the long thin scars hardly showed. And his eyes were like holes poked in a snowbank. It was pretty obvious that the buttons in the prowl car were about ready to drop the hook on him, so I went over there fast and took hold of his arm.

"Straighten up and walk," I said, putting on the tough. I winked at him from the side. "Can you make it? Are you stinko?"

He looked me over vaguely and then smiled his little one-sided smile. "I have been," he breathed. "Right now I guess I'm just a little—empty."

"Okay, but make with the feet. You're halfway into the drunk tank already."

He made the effort and let me walk him through the sidewalk loafers to the edge of the curb. There was a taxi stand there and I yanked open the door.

"He goes first," the hackie said, jerking a thumb at the cab ahead. He swung his head around and saw Terry. "If at all," he added.

"This is an emergency. My friend is sick."

"Yeah," the hackie said. "He could get sick somewheres else."

"Five bucks," I said, "and let's see that beautiful smile."

"Oh well," he said, and stuck a magazine with a Martian on the cover behind his mirror. I reached in and got the door open. I got Terry Lennox in and the shadow of the prowl car blocked the far window. A gray-haired cop got out and came over. I went around the taxi and met him.

"Just a minute, Mac. What have we got here? Is the gentleman in the soiled laundry a real close friend of yours?"

"Close enough for me to know he needs a friend. He's not drunk."

"For financial reasons, no doubt," the cop said. He put his

hand out and I put my license in it. He looked at it and handed it back. "Oh-oh," he said. "A P.I. picking up a client." His voice changed and got tough. "That tells a little something about you, Mr. Marlowe. What about him?"

"His name's Terry Lennox. He works in pictures."

"That's nice." He leaned into the taxi and stared at Terry back in the corner. "I'd say he didn't work too lately. I'd say he didn't sleep indoors too lately. I'd even say he was a vag and so maybe we ought to take him in."

"Your arrest record can't be that low," I said. "Not in Hollywood."

He was still looking in at Terry. "What's your friend's name, buddy?"

"Philip Marlowe," Terry said slowly. "He lives on Yucca Avenue, Laurel Canyon."

The cop pulled his head out of the window space. He turned, and made a gesture with his hand. "You could of just told him."

"I could have, but I didn't."

He stared at me for a second or two. "I'll buy it this time," he said. "But get him off the street." He got into the police car and the police car went away.

I got into the taxi and we went the three-odd blocks to my parking lot and shifted to my car. I held out the five-spot to the hackie. He gave me a stiff look and shook his head.

"Just what's on the meter, Jack, or an even buck if you feel like it. I been down and out myself. In Frisco. Nobody picked me up in no taxi either. There's one stony-hearted town."

"San Francisco," I said mechanically.

"I call it Frisco," he said. "The hell with them minority groups. Thanks." He took the dollar and went away.

We went to a drive-in where they made hamburgers that didn't taste like something the dog wouldn't eat. I fed Terry Lennox a couple and a bottle of beer and drove him home. The steps were still tough on him but he grinned and panted and made the climb. An hour later he was shaved and bathed and he looked human again. We sat down over a couple of very mild drinks.

"Lucky you remembered my name," I said.

"I made a point of it," he said. "I looked you up too. Could I do less?"

"So why not give me a ring? I live here all the time. I have an office as well."

"Why should I bother you?"

"Looks like you had to bother somebody. Looks like you don't have many friends."

"Oh I have friends," he said, "of a sort." He turned his glass on the table top. "Asking for help doesn't come easy— especially when it's all your own fault." He looked up with a tired smile. "Maybe I can quit drinking one of these days. They all say that, don't they?"

"It takes about three years."

"Three years?" He looked shocked.

"Usually it does. It's a different world. You have to get used to a paler set of colors, a quieter lot of sounds. You have to allow for relapses. All the people you used to know well will get to be just a little strange. You won't even like most of them, and they won't like you too well."

"That wouldn't be much of a change," he said. He turned and looked at the clock. "I have a two-hundred-dollar suit-case checked at the Hollywood bus station. If I could bail it out I could buy a cheap one and pawn the one that's checked for enough to get to Vegas on the bus. I can get a job there."

I didn't say anything. I just nodded and sat there nursing my drink.

"You're thinking that idea might have come to me a little sooner," he said quietly.

"I'm thinking there's something behind all this that's none of my business. Is the job for sure or just a hope?"

"It's for sure. Fellow I knew very well in the army runs a big club there, the Terrapin Club. He's part racketeer, of course, they all are—but the other part is a nice guy."

"I can manage the bus fare and something over. But I'd just as soon it bought something that would stay bought for a while. Better talk to him on the phone."

"Thank you, but it's not necessary. Randy Starr won't let me down. He never has. And the suitcase will pawn for fifty dollars. I know from experience."

"Look," I said, "I'd put up what you need. I'm no big

soft-hearted slob. So you take what's offered and be good. I want you out of my hair because I've got a feeling about you."

"Really?" He looked down into his glass. He was only sipping the stuff. "We've only met twice and you've been more than white to me both times. What sort of feeling?"

"A feeling that next time I'll find you in worse trouble than I can get you out of. I don't know just why I have the feeling, but I have it."

He touched the right side of his face gently with two fingertips. "Maybe it's this. It does make me look a little sinister, I suppose. But it's an honorable wound—or anyhow the result of one."

"It's not that. That doesn't bother me at all. I'm a private dick. You're a problem that I don't have to solve. But the problem is there. Call it a hunch. If you want to be extra polite, call it a sense of character. Maybe that girl didn't walk out on you at The Dancers just because you were drunk. Maybe she had a feeling too."

He smiled faintly. "I was married to her once. Her name is Sylvia Lennox. I married her for her money."

I stood up scowling at him. "I'll fix you some scrambled eggs. You need food."

"Wait a minute, Marlowe. You're wondering why if I was down and out and Sylvia had plenty I couldn't ask her for a few bucks. Did you ever hear of pride?"

"You're killing me, Lennox."

"Am I? My kind of pride is different. It's the pride of a man who has nothing else. I'm sorry if I annoy you."

I went out to my kitchen and cooked up some Canadian bacon and scrambled eggs and coffee and toast. We ate in the breakfast nook. The house belonged to the period that always had one.

I said I had to go to the office and would pick up his suitcase on the way back. He gave me the check ticket. His face now had a little color and the eyes were not so far back in his head that you had to grope for them.

Before I went out I put the whiskey bottle on the table in front of the couch. "Use your pride on that," I said. "And call Vegas, if only as a favor to me."

He just smiled and shrugged his shoulders. I was still sore going down the steps. I didn't know why, any more than I knew why a man would starve and walk the streets rather than pawn his wardrobe. Whatever his rules were he played by them.

The suitcase was the damndest thing you ever saw. It was bleached pigskin and when new had been a pale cream color. The fittings were gold. It was English made and if you could buy it here at all, it would cost more like eight hundred than two.

I planked it down in front of him. I looked at the bottle on the cocktail table. He hadn't touched it. He was as sober as I was. He was smoking, but not liking that very well.

"I called Randy," he said. "He was sore because I hadn't called him before."

"It takes a stranger to help you," I said. "A present from Sylvia?" I pointed at the suitcase.

He looked out of the window. "No. That was given to me in England, long before I met her. Very long ago indeed. I'd like to leave it with you, if you could lend me an old one."

I got five double sawbucks out of my wallet and dropped them in front of him. "I don't need security."

"That wasn't the idea at all. You're no pawnbroker. I just don't want it with me in Vegas. And I don't need this much money."

"Okay. You keep the money and I'll keep the suitcase. But this house is easy to burgle."

"It wouldn't matter," he said indifferently. "It wouldn't matter at all."

He changed his clothes and we ate dinner at Musso's about five-thirty. No drinks. He caught the bus on Cahuenga and I drove home thinking about this and that. His empty suitcase was on my bed where he had unpacked it and put his stuff in a lightweight job of mine. His had a gold key which was in one of the locks. I locked the suitcase up empty and tied the key to the handle and put it on the high shelf on my clothes closet. It didn't feel quite empty, but what was in it was no business of mine.

It was a quiet night and the house seemed emptier than

usual. I set out the chessmen and played a French defense against Steinitz. He beat me in forty-four moves, but I had him sweating a couple of times.

The phone rang at nine-thirty and the voice that spoke was one I had heard before.

"Is this Mr. Philip Marlowe?"

"Yeah. I'm Marlowe."

"This is Sylvia Lennox, Mr. Marlowe. We met very briefly in front of The Dancers one night last month. I heard afterwards that you had been kind enough to see that Terry got home."

"I did that."

"I suppose you know that we are not married any more, but I've been a little worried about him. He gave up the apartment he had in Westwood and nobody seems to know where he is."

"I noticed how worried you were the night we met."

"Look, Mr. Marlowe, I've been married to the man. I'm not very sympathetic to drunks. Perhaps I was a little unfeeling and perhaps I had something rather important to do. You're a private detective and this can be put on a professional basis, if you prefer it."

"It doesn't have to be put on any basis at all, Mrs. Lennox. He's on a bus going to Las Vegas. He has a friend there who will give him a job."

She brightened up very suddenly. "Oh—to Las Vegas? How sentimental of him. That's where we were married."

"I guess he forgot," I said, "or he would have gone somewhere else."

Instead of hanging up on me she laughed. It was a cute little laugh. "Are you always as rude as this to your clients?"

"You're not a client, Mrs. Lennox."

"I might be someday. Who knows? Let's say to your lady friends, then."

"Same answer. The guy was down and out, starving, dirty, without a bean. You could have found him if it had been worth your time. He didn't want anything from you then and he probably doesn't want anything from you now."

"That," she said coolly, "is something you couldn't possibly know anything about. Good night." And she hung up.

She was dead right, of course, and I was dead wrong. But I didn't feel wrong. I just felt sore. If she had called up half an hour earlier I might have been sore enough to beat the hell out of Steinitz—except that he had been dead for fifty years and the chess game was out of a book.

# 3

Three days before Christmas I got a cashier's check on a Las Vegas bank for $100. A note written on hotel paper came with it. He thanked me, wished me a Merry Christmas and all kinds of luck and said he hoped to see me again soon. The kick was in a postscript. "Sylvia and I are starting a second honeymoon. She says please don't be sore at her for wanting to try again."

I caught the rest of it in one of those snob columns in the society section of the paper. I don't read them often, only when I run out of things to dislike.

"Your correspondent is all fluttery at the news that Terry and Sylvia Lennox have rehitched at Las Vegas, the dears. She's the younger daughter of multimillionaire Harlan Potter of San Francisco and Pebble Beach, of course. Sylvia is having Marcel and Jeanne Duhaux redecorate the entire mansion in Encino from basement to roof in the most *devastatingly* dernier cri. Curt Westerheym, Sylvia's last but one, my dears, gave her the little eighteen-room shack for a wedding present, you may remember. And whatever happened to Curt, you ask? Or do you? St. Tropez has the answer, and permanently I hear. Also a certain very, *very* blue-blooded French duchess with two perfectly adorable children. And what does Harlan Potter think of the remarriage, you may also ask? One can only guess. Mr. Potter is one person who but *never* gives an interview. How exclusive can you get, darlings?"

I threw the paper into the corner and turned on the TV set. After the society page dog vomit even the wrestlers looked good. But the facts were probably right. On the society page they better be.

I had a mental picture of the kind of eighteen-room shack that would go with a few of the Potter millions, not to mention decorations by Duhaux in the latest subphallic symbolism. But I had no mental picture at all of Terry Lennox loafing around one of the swimming pools in Bermuda shorts and phoning the butler by R/T to ice the champagne and get the grouse atoasting. There was no reason why I should have. If the guy wanted to be somebody's woolly bear, it was no skin off my teeth. I just didn't want to see him again. But I knew I would—if only on account of his goddam gold-plated pigskin suitcase.

It was five o'clock of a wet March evening when he walked into my down-at-heels brain emporium. He looked changed. Older, very sober and severe and beautifully calm. He looked like a guy who had learned to roll with a punch. He wore an oyster-white raincoat and gloves and no hat and his white hair was as smooth as a bird's breast.

"Let's go to some quiet bar and have a drink," he said, as if he had been in ten minutes before. "If you have the time, that is."

We didn't shake hands. We never did. Englishmen don't shake hands all the time like Americans and although he wasn't English he had some of the mannerisms.

I said: "Let's go by my place and pick up your fancy suitcase. It kind of worries me."

He shook his head. "It would be kind of you to keep it for me."

"Why?"

"I just feel that way. Do you mind? It's a sort of link with a time when I wasn't a no-good waster."

"Nuts to that," I said. "But it's your business."

"If it bothers you because you think it might be stolen—"

"That's your business too. Let's go get that drink."

We went to Victor's. He drove me in a rust-colored Jupiter-Jowett with a flimsy canvas rain top under which there was only just room for the two of us. It had pale leather upholstery and what looked like silver fittings. I'm not too fussy about cars, but the damn thing did make my mouth water a little. He said it would do sixty-five in second. It had a squatty little gear shift that barely came up to his knee.

"Four speeds," he said. "They haven't invented an automatic shift that will work for one of these jobs yet. You don't really need one. You can start it in third even uphill and that's as high as you can shift in traffic anyway."

"Wedding present?"

"Just a casual 'I happened to see this gadget in a window' sort of present. I'm a very pampered guy."

"Nice," I said. "If there's no price tag."

He glanced at me quickly and then put his eyes back on the wet pavement. Double wipers swished gently over the little windscreen. "Price tag? There's always a price tag, chum. You think I'm not happy maybe?"

"Sorry. I was out of line."

"I'm rich. Who the hell wants to be happy?" There was a bitterness in his voice that was new to me.

"How's your drinking?"

"Perfectly elegant, old top. For some strange reason I seem to be able to handle the stuff. But you never know, do you?"

"Perhaps you were never really a drunk."

We sat in a corner of the bar at Victor's and drank gimlets. "They don't know how to make them here," he said. "What they call a gimlet is just some lime or lemon juice and gin with a dash of sugar and bitters. A real gimlet is half gin and half Rose's Lime Juice and nothing else. It beats martinis hollow."

"I was never fussy about drinks. How did you get on with Randy Starr? Down my street he's called a tough number."

He leaned back and looked thoughtful. "I guess he is. I guess they all are. But it doesn't show on him. I could name you a couple of lads in the same racket in Hollywood that act the part. Randy doesn't bother. In Las Vegas he's a legitimate businessman. You look him up next time you're there. He'll be your pal."

"Not too likely. I don't like hoodlums."

"That's just a word, Marlowe. We have that kind of world. Two wars gave it to us and we are going to keep it. Randy and I and another fellow were in a jam once. It made a sort of bond between us."

"Then why didn't you ask him for help when you needed it?"

He drank up his drink and signaled the waiter. "Because he couldn't refuse."

The waiter brought fresh drinks and I said: "That's just talk to me. If by any chance the guy owed you something, think of *his* end. He'd like a chance to pay something back."

He shook his head slowly. "I know you're right. Of course I did ask him for a job. But I worked at it while I had it. As for asking favors or handouts, no."

"But you'll take them from a stranger."

He looked me straight in the eye. "The stranger can keep going and pretend not to hear."

We had three gimlets, not doubles, and it didn't do a thing to him. That much would just get a real souse started. So I guess maybe he was cured at that.

Then he drove me back to the office.

"We have dinner at eight-fifteen," he said. "Only millionaires can afford it. Only millionaires' servants will stand for it nowadays. Lots of lovely people coming."

From then on it got to be a sort of habit with him to drop in around five o'clock. We didn't always go to the same bar, but oftener to Victor's than anywhere else. It may have had some association for him that I didn't know about. He never drank too much, and that surprised him.

"It must be something like the tertian ague," he said. "When it hits you it's bad. When you don't have it, it's as though you never did have it."

"What I don't get is why a guy with your privileges would want to drink with a private eye."

"Are you being modest?"

"Nope. I'm just puzzled. I'm a reasonably friendly type but we don't live in the same world. I don't even know where you hang out except that it's Encino. I should guess your home life is adequate."

"I don't have any home life."

We were drinking gimlets again. The place was almost empty. There was the usual light scattering of compulsive drinkers getting tuned up at the bar on the stools, the kind that reach very slowly for the first one and watch their hands so they won't knock anything over.

"I don't get that. Am I supposed to?"

"Big production, no story, as they say around the movie lots. I guess Sylvia is happy enough, though not necessarily with me. In our circle that's not too important. There's always something to do if you don't have to work or consider the cost. It's no real fun but the rich don't know that. They never had any. They never want anything very hard except maybe somebody else's wife and that's a pretty pale desire compared with the way a plumber's wife wants new curtains for the living room."

I didn't say anything. I let him carry the ball.

"Mostly I just kill time," he said, "and it dies hard. A little tennis, a little golf, a little swimming and horseback riding, and the exquisite pleasure of watching Sylvia's friends trying to hold out to lunch time before they start killing their hangovers."

"The night you went to Vegas she said she didn't like drunks."

He grinned crookedly. I was getting so used to his scarred face that I only noticed it when some change of expression emphasized its one-sided woodenness.

"She meant drunks without money. With money they are just heavy drinkers. If they vomit in the lanai, that's for the butler to handle."

"You didn't have to have it the way it is."

He finished his drink at a gulp and stood up. "I've got to run, Marlowe. Besides I'm boring you and God knows I'm boring myself."

"You're not boring me. I'm a trained listener. Sooner or later I may figure out why you like being a kept poodle."

He touched his scars gently with a fingertip. He had a remote little smile. "You should wonder why she wants me around, not why I want to be there, waiting patiently on my satin cushion to have my head patted."

"You like satin cushions," I said, as I stood up to leave with him. "You like silk sheets and bells to ring and the butler to come with his deferential smile."

"Could be. I was raised in an orphanage in Salt Lake City."

We went out into the tired evening and he said he wanted to walk. We had come in my car, and for once I had been fast enough to grab the check. I watched him out of sight. The light from a store window caught the gleam of his white hair for a moment as he faded into the light mist.

I liked him better drunk, down and out, hungry and beaten and proud. Or did I? Maybe I just liked being top man. His reasons for things were hard to figure. In my business there's a time to ask questions and a time to let your man simmer until he boils over. Every good cop knows that. It's a good deal like chess or boxing. Some people you have to crowd and keep off balance. Some you just box and they will end up beating themselves.

He would have told me the story of his life if I had asked him. But I never even asked him how he got his face smashed. If I had and he told me, it just possibly might have saved a couple of lives. Just possibly, no more.

# 4

The last time we had a drink in a bar was in May and it was earlier than usual, just after four o'clock. He looked tired and thinner but he looked around with a slow smile of pleasure.

"I like bars just after they open for the evening. When the air inside is still cool and clean and everything is shiny and the barkeep is giving himself that last look in the mirror to see if his tie is straight and his hair is smooth. I like the neat bottles on the bar back and the lovely shining glasses and the anticipation. I like to watch the man mix the first one of the evening and put it down on a crisp mat and put the little folded napkin beside it. I like to taste it slowly. The first quiet drink of the evening in a quiet bar—that's wonderful."

I agreed with him.

"Alcohol is like love," he said. "The first kiss is magic, the second is intimate, the third is routine. After that you take the girl's clothes off."

"Is that bad?" I asked him.

"It's excitement of a high order, but it's an impure emotion—impure in the aesthetic sense. I'm not sneering at sex. It's necessary and it doesn't have to be ugly. But it always has to be managed. Making it glamorous is a billion-dollar industry and it costs every cent of it."

He looked around and yawned. "I haven't been sleeping well. It's nice in here. But after a while the lushes will fill the place up and talk loud and laugh and the goddam women will start waving their hands and screwing up their faces and tinkling their goddam bracelets and making with the packaged charm which will later on in the evening have a slight but unmistakable odor of sweat."

"Take it easy," I said. "So they're human, they sweat, they get dirty, they have to go to the bathroom. What did you expect—golden butterflies hovering in a rosy mist?"

He emptied his glass and held it upside down and watched a slow drop form on the rim and then tremble and fall.

"I'm sorry for her," he said slowly. "She's such an absolute bitch. Could be I'm fond of her too in a remote sort of way. Some day she'll need me and I'll be the only guy around not holding a chisel. Likely enough then I'll flunk out."

I just looked at him. "You do a great job of selling yourself," I said after a moment.

"Yeah, I know. I'm a weak character, without guts or ambition. I caught the brass ring and it shocked me to find out it wasn't gold. A guy like me has one big moment in his life, one perfect swing on the high trapeze. Then he spends the rest of his time trying not to fall off the sidewalk into the gutter."

"What's this in favor of?" I got out a pipe and started to fill it.

"She's scared. She's scared stiff."

"What of?"

"I don't know. We don't talk much any more. Maybe of the old man. Harlan Potter is a coldhearted son of a bitch. All Victorian dignity on the outside. Inside he's as ruthless as a Gestapo thug. Sylvia is a tramp. He knows it and he hates it and there's nothing he can do about it. But he waits and he watches and if Sylvia ever gets into a big mess of scandal he'll break her in half and bury the two halves a thousand miles apart."

"You're her husband."

He lifted the empty glass and brought it down hard on the edge of the table. It smashed with a sharp ping. The barman stared, but didn't say anything.

"Like that, chum. Like that. Oh sure, I'm her husband. That's what the record says. I'm the three white steps and the big green front door and the brass knocker you rap one long and two short and the maid lets you into the hundred-dollar whorehouse."

I stood up and dropped some money on the table. "You talk too damn much," I said, "and it's too damn much about you. See you later."

I walked out leaving him sitting there shocked and white-faced as well as I could tell by the kind of light they have in bars. He called something after me, but I kept going.

Ten minutes later I was sorry. But ten minutes later I was somewhere else. He didn't come to the office any more. Not at all, not once. I had got to him where it hurt.

I didn't see him again for a month. When I did it was five o'clock in the morning and just beginning to get light. The persistent ringing of the doorbell yanked me out of bed. I plowed down the hall and across the living room and opened up. He stood there looking as if he hadn't slept for a week. He had a light topcoat on with the collar turned up and he seemed to be shivering. A dark felt hat was pulled down over his eyes.

He had a gun in his hand.

# 5

The gun wasn't pointed at me, he was just holding it. It was a medium-caliber automatic, foreign made, certainly not a Colt or a Savage. With the white tired face and the scars and the turned-up collar and the pulled-down hat and the gun he could have stepped right out of an old-fashioned kick-em-in-the-teeth gangster movie.

"You're driving me to Tijuana to get a plane at ten-fifteen," he said. "I have a passport and visa and I'm all set except for transportation. For certain reasons I can't take a train or a bus or a plane from L.A. Would five hundred bucks be a reasonable taxi fare?"

I stood in the doorway and didn't move to let him in. "Five hundred plus the gat?" I asked.

He looked down at it rather absently. Then he dropped it into his pocket.

"It might be a protection," he said, "for you. Not for me."

"Come on in then." I stood to one side and he came in with an exhausted lunge and fell into a chair.

The living room was still dark, because of the heavy growth of shrubbery the owner had allowed to mask the windows. I put a lamp on and mooched a cigarette. I lit it. I stared down at him. I rumpled my hair which was already rumpled. I put the old tired grin on my face.

"What the hell's the matter with me sleeping such a lovely morning away? Ten-fifteen, huh? Well, there's plenty of time. Let's go out to the kitchen and I'll brew some coffee."

"I'm in a great deal of trouble, shamus." Shamus, it was the first time he had called me that. But it kind of went with his style of entry, the way he was dressed, the gun and all.

"It's going to be a peach of a day. Light breeze. You can hear those tough old eucalyptus trees across the street whispering to each other. Talking about old times in Australia when the wallabies hopped about underneath the branches and the koala bears rode piggyback on each other. Yes, I got the general idea you were in some trouble. Let's talk about it after I've had a couple of cups of coffee. I'm always a little lightheaded when I first wake up. Let us confer with Mr. Huggins and Mr. Young."

"Look, Marlowe, this is not the time—"

"Fear nothing, old boy. Mr. Huggins and Mr. Young are two of the best. They make Huggins-Young coffee. It's their life work, their pride and joy. One of these days I'm going to see that they get the recognition they deserve. So far all they're making is money. You couldn't expect that to satisfy them."

I left him with that bright chatter and went out to the kitchen at the back. I turned the hot water on and got the coffee maker down off the shelf. I wet the rod and measured the stuff into the top and by that time the water was steaming. I filled the lower half of the dingus and set it on the flame. I set the upper part on top and gave it a twist so it would bind.

By that time he had come in after me. He leaned in the doorway a moment and then edged across to the breakfast nook and slid into the seat. He was still shaking. I got a bottle of Old Grand-Dad off the shelf and poured him a shot in a big glass. I knew he would need a big glass. Even with that he had to use both hands to get it to his mouth. He swallowed, put the glass down with a thud, and hit the back of the seat with a jar.

"Almost passed out," he muttered. "Seems like I've been up for a week. Didn't sleep at all last night."

The coffee maker was almost ready to bubble. I turned the flame low and watched the water rise. It hung a little at the bottom of the glass tube. I turned the flame up just enough to get it over the hump and then turned it low again quickly. I stirred the coffee and covered it. I set my timer for three minutes. Very methodical guy, Marlowe. Nothing must interfere with his coffee technique. Not even a gun in the hand of a desperate character.

I poured him another slug. "Just sit there," I said. "Don't say a word. Just sit."

He handled the second slug with one hand. I did a fast wash-up in the bathroom and the bell of the timer went just as I got back. I cut the flame and set the coffee maker on a straw mat on the table. Why do I go into such detail? Because the charged atmosphere made every little thing stand out as a performance, a movement distinct and vastly important. It was one of those hypersensitive moments when all your automatic movements, however long established, however habitual, become separate acts of will. You are like a man learning to walk after polio. You take nothing for granted, absolutely nothing at all.

The coffee was all down and the air rushed in with its usual fuss and the coffee bubbled and then became quiet. I removed the top of the maker and set it on the drainboard in the socket of the cover.

I poured two cups and added a slug to his. "Black for you,

Terry." I added two lumps of sugar and some cream to mine. I was coming out of it by now. I wasn't conscious of how I opened the Frig and got the cream carton.

I sat down across from him. He hadn't moved. He was propped in the corner of the nook, rigid. Then without warning his head came down on the table and he was sobbing.

He didn't pay any attention when I reached across and dug the gun out of his pocket. It was a Mauser 7.65, a beauty. I sniffed it. I sprang the magazine loose. It was full. Nothing in the breach.

He lifted his head and saw the coffee and drank some slowly, not looking at me. "I didn't shoot anybody," he said.

"Well—not recently anyhow. And the gun would have had to be cleaned. I hardly think you shot anybody with this."

"I'll tell you about it," he said.

"Wait just a minute." I drank my coffee as quickly as the heat would let me. I refilled my cup. "It's like this," I said. "Be very careful what you tell me. If you really want me to ride you down to Tijuana, there are two things I must not be told. One—are you listening?"

He nodded very slightly. He was looking blank-eyed at the wall over my head. The scars were very livid this morning. His skin was almost dead white but the scars seemed to shine out of it just the same.

"One," I repeated slowly, "if you have committed a crime or anything the law calls a crime—a serious crime, I mean—I can't be told about it. Two, if you have essential knowledge that such a crime has been committed, I can't be told about that either. Not if you want me to drive you to Tijuana. That clear?"

He looked me in the eye. His eyes focused, but they were lifeless. He had the coffee inside him. He had no color, but he was steady. I poured him some more and loaded it the same way.

"I told you I was in a jam," he said.

"I heard you. I don't want to know what kind of jam. I have a living to earn, a license to protect."

"I could hold the gun on you," he said.

I grinned and pushed the gun across the table. He looked down at it but didn't touch it.

"Not to Tijuana you couldn't hold it on me, Terry. Not across the border, not up the steps into a plane. I'm a man who occasionally has business with guns. We'll forget about the gun. I'd look great telling the cops I was so scared I just had to do what you told me to. Supposing, of course, which I don't know, that there was anything to tell the cops."

"Listen," he said, "it will be noon or even later before anybody knocks at the door. The help knows better than to disturb her when she sleeps late. But by about noon her maid would knock and go in. She wouldn't be in her room."

I sipped my coffee and said nothing.

"The maid would see that her bed hadn't been slept in," he went on. "Then she would think of another place to look. There's a big guest house pretty far back from the main house. It has its own driveway and garage and so on. Sylvia spent the night there. The maid would eventually find her there."

I frowned. "I've got to be very careful what questions I ask you, Terry. Couldn't she have spent the night away from home?"

"Her clothes would be thrown all over her room. She never hangs anything up. The maid would know she had put a robe over her pajamas and gone out that way. So it would only be to the guest house."

"Not necessarily," I said.

"It would be to the guest house. Hell, do you think they don't know what goes on in the guest house? Servants always know."

"Pass it," I said.

He ran a finger down the side of his good cheek hard enough to leave a red streak. "And in the guest house," he went on slowly, "the maid would find—"

"Sylvia dead drunk, paralyzed, spifflicated, iced to the eyebrows," I said harshly.

"Oh." He thought about it. Big think. "Of course," he added, "that's how it would be. Sylvia is not a souse. When she does get over the edge it's pretty drastic."

"That's the end of the story," I said. "Or almost. Let me improvise. The last time we drank together I was a bit rough with you, walked out if you recall. You irritated the hell out of me. Thinking it over afterwards I could see that you were just trying to sneer yourself out of a feeling of disaster. You say you have a passport and a visa. It takes a little time to get a visa to Mexico. They don't let just anybody in. So you've been planning to blow for some time. I was wondering how long you would stick."

"I guess I felt some vague kind of obligation to be around, some idea she might need me for something more than a front to keep the old man from nosing around too hard. By the way, I tried to call you in the middle of the night."

"I sleep hard. I didn't hear."

"Then I went to a Turkish bath place. I stayed a couple of hours, had a steam bath, a plunge, a needle shower, a rubdown and made a couple of phone calls from there. I left the car at La Brea and Fountain. I walked from there. Nobody saw me turn into your street."

"Do these phone calls concern me?"

"One was to Harlan Potter. The old man flew down to Pasadena yesterday, some business. He hadn't been to the house. I had a lot of trouble getting him. But he finally talked to me. I told him I was sorry, but I was leaving." He was looking a little sideways when he said this, towards the window over the sink and the tecoma bush that fretted against the screen.

"How did he take it?"

"He was sorry. He wished me luck. Asked if I needed any money." Terry laughed harshly. "Money. Those are the first five letters of his alphabet. I said I had plenty. Then I called Sylvia's sister. Much the same story there. That's all."

"I want to ask this," I said. "Did you ever find her with a man in that guest house?"

He shook his head. "I never tried. It would not have been difficult. It never has been."

"Your coffee's getting cold."

"I don't want any more."

"Lots of men, huh? But you went back and married her again. I realize that she's quite a dish, but all the same—"

"I told you I was no good. Hell, why did I leave her the first time? Why after that did I get stinking every time I saw her? Why did I roll in the gutter rather than ask her for money? She's been married five times, not including me. Any one of them would go back at the crook of her finger. And not just for a million bucks."

"She's quite a dish," I said. I looked at my watch. "Just why does it have to be ten-fifteen at Tijuana?"

"There's always space on that flight. Nobody from L.A. wants to ride a DC-3 over mountains when he can take a Connie and make it in seven hours to Mexico City. And the Connies don't stop where I want to go."

I stood up and leaned against the sink. "Now let's add it up and don't interrupt me. You came to me this morning in a highly emotional condition and wanted to be driven to Tijuana to catch an early plane. You had a gun in your pocket, but I needn't have seen it. You told me you had stood things as long as you could but last night you blew up. You found your wife dead drunk and a man had been with her. You got out and went to a Turkish bath to pass the time until morning and you phoned your wife's two closest relatives and told them what you were doing. Where you went was none of my business. You had the necessary documents to enter Mexico. How you went was none of my business either. We are friends and I did what you asked me without much thought. Why wouldn't I? You're not paying me anything. You had your car but you felt too upset to drive yourself. That's your business too. You're an emotional guy and you got yourself a bad wound in the war. I think I ought to pick up your car and shove it in a garage somewhere for storage."

He reached into his clothes and pushed a leather keyholder across the table.

"How does it sound?" he asked.

"Depends who's listening. I haven't finished. You took nothing but the clothes you stood up in and some money you had from your father-in-law. You left everything she had given you including that beautiful piece of machinery you parked at La Brea and Fountain. You wanted to go away as clean as it was possible for you to go and still go. All right. I'll buy it. Now I shave and get dressed."

"Why are you doing it, Marlowe?"

"Buy yourself a drink while I shave."

I walked out and left him sitting there hunched in the corner of the nook. He still had his hat and light topcoat on. But he looked a lot more alive.

I went into the bathroom and shaved. I was back in the bedroom knotting my tie when he came and stood in the doorway. "I washed the cups just in case," he said. "But I got thinking. Maybe it would be better if you called the police."

"Call them yourself. I haven't anything to tell them."

"You want me to?"

I turned around sharply and gave him a hard stare. "God damn it!" I almost yelled at him. "Can't you for Chrissake just leave it lay?"

"I'm sorry."

"Sure you're sorry. Guys like you are always sorry, and always too late."

He turned and walked back along the hall to the living room.

I finished dressing and locked up the back part of the house. When I got to the living room he had fallen asleep in a chair, his head on one side, his face drained of color, his whole body slack with exhaustion. He looked pitiful. When I touched his shoulder he came awake slowly as if it was a long way from where he was to where I was.

When I had his attention I said, "What about a suitcase? I still got that white pigskin job on the top shelf in my closet."

"It's empty," he said without interest. "Also it's too conspicuous."

"You'd be more conspicuous without any baggage."

I walked back to the bedroom and stood up on the steps in the clothes closet and pulled the white pigskin job down off the high shelf. The square ceiling trap was right over my head, so I pushed that up and reached in as far as I could and dropped his leather keyholder behind one of the dusty tie beams or whatever they were.

I climbed down with the suitcase, dusted it off, and shoved some things into it, a pair of pajamas never worn, toothpaste, an extra toothbrush, a couple of cheap towels and washcloths, a package of cotton handkerchiefs, a fifteen-cent tube of shaving cream, and one of the razors they give away with a package of blades. Nothing used, nothing marked, nothing conspicuous, except that his own stuff would be better. I added a pint of bourbon still in its wrapping paper. I locked the suitcase and left the key in one of the locks and carried it up front. He had gone to sleep again. I opened the door without waking him and carried the suitcase down to the garage and put it in the convertible behind the front seat. I got the car out and locked the garage and went back up the steps to wake him. I finished locking up and we left.

I drove fast but not fast enough to get tagged. We hardly spoke on the way down. We didn't stop to eat either. There wasn't that much time.

The border people had nothing to say to us. Up on the windy mesa where the Tijuana Airport is I parked close to the office and just sat while Terry got his ticket. The propellers of the DC-3 were already turning over slowly, just enough to keep warm. A tall dreamboat of a pilot in a gray uniform was chatting with a group of four people. One was about six feet four and carried a gun case. There was a girl in slacks beside him, and a smallish middle-aged man and a gray-haired woman so tall that she made him look puny. Three or four obvious Mexicans were standing around as well. That seemed to be the load. The steps were at the door but nobody seemed anxious to get in. Then a Mexican flight steward came down the steps and stood waiting. There didn't seem to be any loudspeaker equipment. The Mexicans climbed into the plane but the pilot was still chatting with the Americans.

There was a big Packard parked next to me. I got out and took a gander at the license on the post. Maybe someday I'll learn to mind my own business. As I pulled my head out I saw the tall woman staring in my direction.

Then Terry came across the dusty gravel.

"I'm all set," he said. "This is where I say goodbye."

He put his hand out. I shook it. He looked pretty good now, just tired, just tired as all hell.

I lifted the pigskin suitcase out of the Olds and put it down on the gravel. He stared at it angrily.

"I told you I didn't want it," he said snappishly.

"There's a nice pint of hooch in it, Terry. Also some pajamas and stuff. And it's all anonymous. If you don't want it, check it. Or throw it away."

"I have reasons," he said stiffly.

"So have I."

He smiled suddenly. He picked up the suitcase and squeezed my arm with his free hand. "Okay, pal. You're the boss. And remember, if things get tough, you have a blank check. You don't owe me a thing. We had a few drinks together and got to be friendly and I talked too much about me. I left five C notes in your coffee can. Don't be sore at me."

"I'd rather you hadn't."

"I'll never spend half of what I have."

"Good luck, Terry."

The two Americans were going up the steps into the plane. A squatty guy with a wide dark face came out of the door of the office building and waved and pointed.

"Climb aboard," I said. "I know you didn't kill her. That's why I'm here."

He braced himself. His whole body got stiff. He turned slowly, then looked back.

"I'm sorry," he said quietly. "But you're wrong about that. I'm going to walk quite slowly to the plane. You have plenty of time to stop me."

He walked. I watched him. The guy in the doorway of the office was waiting, but not too impatient. Mexicans seldom are. He reached down and patted the pigskin suitcase and grinned at Terry. Then he stood aside and Terry went through the door. In a little while Terry came out through the door on the other side, where the customs people are when you're coming in. He walked, still slowly, across the gravel to the steps. He stopped there and looked towards me. He didn't signal or wave. Neither did I. Then he went up into the plane, and the steps were pulled back.

I got into the Olds and started it and backed and turned and moved halfway across the parking space. The tall woman and the short man were still out on the field. The woman had a handkerchief out to wave. The plane began to taxi down to the end of the field raising plenty of dust. It turned at the far end and the motors revved up in a thundering roar. It began to move forward picking up speed slowly.

The dust rose in clouds behind it. Then it was airborne. I watched it lift slowly into the gusty air and fade off into the naked blue sky to the southeast.

Then I left. Nobody at the border gate looked at me as if my face meant as much as the hands on a clock.

# 6

It's a long drag back from Tijuana and one of the dullest drives in the state. Tijuana is nothing; all they want there is the buck. The kid who sidles over to your car and looks at you with big wistful eyes and says, "One dime, please, mister," will try to sell you his sister in the next sentence. Tijuana is not Mexico. No border town is anything but a border town, just as no waterfront is anything but a waterfront. San Diego? One of the most beautiful harbors in the world and nothing in it but navy and a few fishing boats. At night it is fairyland. The swell is as gentle as an old lady singing hymns. But Marlowe has to get home and count the spoons.

The road north is as monotonous as a sailor's chantey. You go through a town, down a hill, along a stretch of beach, through a town, down a hill, along a stretch of beach.

It was two o'clock when I got back and they were waiting for me in a dark sedan with no police tags, no red light, only the double antenna, and not only police cars have those. I was halfway up the steps before they came out of it and yelled at me, the usual couple in the usual suits, with the usual stony leisure of movement, as if the world was waiting hushed and silent for them to tell it what to do.

"Your name Marlowe? We want to talk to you."

He let me see the glint of a badge. For all I caught of it he might have been Pest Control. He was gray blond and looked sticky. His partner was tall, good-looking, neat, and had a precise nastiness about him, a goon with an education. They had watching and waiting eyes, patient and careful eyes, cool disdainful eyes, cops' eyes. They get them at the passing-out parade at the police school.

"Sergeant Green, Central Homicide. This is Detective Dayton."

I went on up and unlocked the door. You don't shake hands with big city cops. That close is too close.

They sat in the living room. I opened the windows and the breeze whispered. Green did the talking.

"Man named Terry Lennox. Know him, huh?"

"We have a drink together once in a while. He lives in Encino, married money. I've never been where he lives."

"Once in a while," Green said. "How often would that be?"

"It's a vague expression. I meant it that way. It could be once a week or once in two months."

"Met his wife?"

"Once, very briefly, before they were married."

"You saw him last when and where?"

I took a pipe off the end table and filled it. Green leaned forward close to me. The tall lad sat farther back holding a ball-point poised over a red-edged pad.

"This is where I say, 'What's this all about?' and you say, 'We ask the questions.'"

"So you just answer them, huh?"

I lit the pipe. The tobacco was a little too moist. It took me some time to light it properly and three matches.

"I got time," Green said, "but I already used up a lot of it waiting around. So snap it up, mister. We know who you are. And you know we ain't here to work up an appetite."

"I was just thinking," I said. "We used to go to Victor's fairly often, and not so often to The Green Lantern and The Bull and Bear—that's the place down at the end of the Strip that tries to look like an English inn—"

"Quit stalling."

"Who's dead?" I asked.

Detective Dayton spoke up. He had a hard, mature, don't-try-to-fool-with-me voice. "Just answer the questions, Marlowe. We are conducting a routine investigation. That's all you need to know."

Maybe I was tired and irritable. Maybe I felt a little guilty. I could learn to hate this guy without even knowing him. I could just look at him across the width of a cafeteria and want to kick his teeth in.

"Shove it, Jack," I said. "Keep that guff for the juvenile bureau. It's a horse laugh even to them."

Green chuckled. Nothing changed in Dayton's face that you could put a finger on but he suddenly looked ten years older and twenty years nastier. The breath going through his nose whistled faintly.

"He passed the bar examination," Green said. "You can't fool around with Dayton."

I got up slowly and went over to the bookshelves. I took down the bound copy of the California Penal Code. I held it out to Dayton.

"Would you kindly find me the section that says I have to answer the questions?"

He was holding himself very still. He was going to slug me and we both knew it. But he was going to wait for the break. Which meant that he didn't trust Green to back him up if he got out of line.

He said: "Every citizen has to co-operate with the police. In all ways, even by physical action, and especially by answering any questions of a non-incriminating nature the police think it necessary to ask." His voice saying this was hard and bright and smooth.

"It works out that way," I said. "Mostly by a process of direct or indirect intimidation. In law no such obligation exists. Nobody has to tell the police anything, any time, anywhere."

"Aw shut up," Green said impatiently. "You're crawfishing and you know it. Sit down. Lennox's wife has been murdered. In a guest house at their place in Encino. Lennox has skipped out. Anyway he can't be found. So we're looking for a suspect in a murder case. That satisfy you?"

I threw the book in a chair and went back to the couch across the table from Green. "So why come to me?" I asked. "I've never been near the house. I told you that."

Green patted his thighs, up and down, up and down. He grinned at me quietly. Dayton was motionless in the chair. His eyes ate me.

"On account of your phone number was written on a pad in his room during the past twenty-four hours," Green said. "It's a date pad and yesterday was torn off but you could see the impression on today's page. We don't know when he called you up. We don't know where he went or why or when. But we got to ask, natch."

"Why in the guest house?" I asked, not expecting him to answer, but he did.

He blushed a little. "Seems she went there pretty often. At night. Had visitors. The help can see down through the trees where the lights show. Cars come and go, sometimes late, sometimes very late. Too much is enough, huh? Don't kid yourself. Lennox is our boy. He went down that way about one in the A.M. The butler happened to see. He come back alone, maybe twenty minutes later. After that nothing. The lights stayed on. This morning no Lennox. The butler goes down by the guest house. The dame is as naked as a mermaid on the bed and let me tell you he don't recognize her by her face. She practically ain't got one. Beat to pieces with a bronze statuette of a monkey."

"Terry Lennox wouldn't do anything like that," I said. "Sure she cheated on him. Old stuff. She always had. They'd been divorced and remarried. I don't suppose it made him happy but why should he go crazy over it now?"

"Nobody knows that answer," Green said patiently. "It happens all the time. Men and women both. A guy takes it and takes it and takes it. Then he don't. He probably don't know why himself, why at that particular instant he goes berserk. Only he does, and somebody's dead. So we got business to do. So we ask you one simple question. So quit horsing around or we take you in."

"He's not going to tell you, Sergeant," Dayton said acidly. "He read that law book. Like a lot of people that read a law book he thinks the law is in it."

"You make the notes," Green said, "and leave your brains alone. If you're real good we'll let you sing 'Mother Machree' at the police smoker."

"The hell with you, Sarge, if I may say so with proper respect for your rank."

"Let's you and him fight," I said to Green. "I'll catch him when he drops."

Dayton laid his note pad and ball-point aside very carefully. He stood up with a bright gleam in his eyes. He walked over and stood in front of me.

"On your feet, bright boy. Just because I went to college don't make me take any guff from a nit like you."

I started to get up. I was still off balance when he hit me. He hooked me with a neat left and crossed it. Bells rang, but not for dinner. I sat down hard and shook my head. Dayton was still there. He was smiling now.

"Let's try again," he said. "You weren't set that time. It wasn't really kosher."

I looked at Green. He was looking at his thumb as if studying a hangnail. I didn't move or speak, waiting for him to look up. If I stood up again, Dayton would slug me again. He might slug me again anyhow. But if I stood up and he slugged me, I would take him to pieces, because the blows proved he was strictly a boxer. He put them in the right place but it would take a lot of them to wear me down.

Green said almost absently: "Smart work, Billy boy. You gave the man exactly what he wanted. Clam juice."

Then he looked up and said mildly: "Once more, for the record, Marlowe. Last time you saw Terry Lennox, where and how and what was talked about, and where did you come from just now. Yes—or no?"

Dayton was standing loosely, nicely balanced. There was a soft sweet sheen in his eyes.

"How about the other guy?" I asked, ignoring him.

"What other guy was that?"

"In the hay, in the guest house. No clothes on. You're not saying she had to go down there to play solitaire."

"That comes later—when we get the husband."

"Fine. If it's not too much trouble when you already have a patsy."

"You don't talk, we take you in, Marlowe."

"As a material witness?"

"As a material my foot. As a suspect. Suspicion of accessory after the fact of murder. Helping a suspect escape. My guess is you took the guy somewhere. And right now a guess is all I need. The skipper is tough these days. He knows the rule book but he gets absent-minded. This could be a misery for you. One way or another we get a statement from you. The harder it is to get, the surer we are we need it."

"That's a lot of crap to him," Dayton said. "He knows the book."

"It's a lot of crap to everybody," Green said calmly. "But it still works. Come on, Marlowe. I'm blowing the whistle on you."

"Okay," I said. "Blow it. Terry Lennox was my friend. I've got a reasonable amount of sentiment invested in him. Enough not to spoil it just because a cop says come through. You've got a case against him, maybe far more than I hear from you. Motive, opportunity, and the fact that he skipped out. The motive is old stuff, long neutralized, almost part of the deal. I don't admire that kind of deal, but that's the kind of guy he is—a little weak and very gentle. The rest of it means nothing except that if he knew she was dead he knew he was a sitting duck for you. At the inquest if they have one and if they call me, I'll have to answer questions. I don't have to answer yours. I can see you're a nice guy, Green. Just as I can see your partner is just another goddam badge flasher with a power complex. If you want to get me in a real jam, let him hit me again. I'll break his goddam pencil for him."

Green stood up and looked at me sadly. Dayton hadn't moved. He was a one-shot tough guy. He had to have time out to pat his back.

"I'll use the phone," Green said. "But I know what answer I'll get. You're a sick chicken, Marlowe. A very sick chicken. Get the hell outa my way." This last to Dayton. Dayton turned and went back and picked up his pad.

Green crossed to the phone and lifted it slowly, his plain face creased with the long slow thankless grind. That's the trouble with cops. You're all set to hate their guts and then you meet one that goes human on you.

The Captain said to bring me in, and rough.

They put handcuffs on me. They didn't search the house, which seemed careless of them. Possibly they figured I would be too experienced to have anything there that could be dangerous to me. In which they were wrong. Because if they had made any kind of job of it they would have found Terry Lennox's car keys. And when the car was found, as it would be sooner or later, they would fit the keys to it and know he had been in my company.

Actually, as it turned out, that meant nothing. The car was never found by any police. It was stolen sometime in the night, driven most probably to El Paso, fitted with new keys and forged papers, and put on the market eventually in Mexico City. The procedure is routine. Mostly the money comes back in the form of heroin. Part of the good-neighbor policy, as the hoodlums see it.

## 7

The homicide skipper that year was a Captain Gregorius, a type of copper that is getting rarer but by no means extinct, the kind that solves crimes with the bright light, the soft sap, the kick to the kidneys, the knee to the groin, the fist to the solar plexus, the night stick to the base of the spine. Six months later he was indicted for perjury before a grand jury, booted without trial, and later stamped to death by a big stallion on his ranch in Wyoming.

Right now I was his raw meat. He sat behind his desk with his coat off and his sleeves rolled almost to his shoulders. He was as bald as a brick and getting heavy around the waist like all hard-muscled men in middle age. His eyes were fish gray. His big nose was a network of burst capillaries. He was drinking coffee and not quietly. His blunt strong hands had hairs thick on their backs. Grizzled tufts stuck out of his ears. He pawed something on his desk and looked at Green.

Green said: "All we got on him is he won't tell us nothing, skipper. The phone number makes us look him up. He's out riding and don't say where. He knows Lennox pretty well and don't say when he saw him last."

"Thinks he's tough," Gregorius said indifferently. "We

could change that." He said it as if he didn't care one way or another. He probably didn't. Nobody was tough to him. "Point is the D.A. smells a lot of headlines on this one. Can't blame him, seeing who the girl's old man is. I guess we better pick this fellow's nose for him."

He looked at me as if I was a cigarette stub, or an empty chair. Just something in his line of vision, without interest for him.

Dayton said respectfully: "It's pretty obvious that his whole attitude was designed to create a situation where he could refuse to talk. He quoted law at us and needled me into socking him. I was out of line there, Captain."

Gregorius eyed him bleakly. "You must needle easy if this punk can do it. Who took the cuffs off?"

Green said he did. "Put them back on," Gregorius said. "Tight. Give him something to brace him up."

Green put the cuffs back on or started to. "Behind the back," Gregorius barked. Green cuffed my hands behind my back. I was sitting in a hard chair.

"Tighter," Gregorius said. "Make them bite."

Green made them tighter. My hands started to feel numb.

Gregorius looked at me finally. "You can talk now. Make it snappy."

I didn't answer him. He leaned back and grinned. His hand went out slowly for his coffee cup and went around it. He leaned forward a little. The cup jerked but I beat it by going sideways out of the chair. I landed hard on my shoulder, rolled over and got up slowly. My hands were quite numb now. They didn't feel anything. The arms above the cuffs were beginning to ache.

Green helped me back into the chair. The wet smear of the coffee was over the back and some of the seat, but most of it was on the floor.

"He don't like coffee," Gregorius said. "He's a swifty. He moves fast. Good reflexes."

Nobody said anything. Gregorius looked me over with fish eyes.

"In here, mister, a dick license don't mean any more than a calling card. Now let's have your statement, verbal at first. We'll take it down later. Make it complete. Let's have, say, a full account of your movements since ten P.M. last night. I mean full. This office is investigating a murder and the prime suspect is missing. You connect with him. Guy catches his wife cheating and beats her head to raw flesh and bone and blood-soaked hair. Our old friend the bronze statuette. Not original but it works. You think any goddam private eye is going to quote law at me over this, mister, you got a hell of a tough time coming your way. There ain't a police force in the country could do its job with a law book. You got information and I want it. You could of said no and I could of not believed you. But you didn't even say no. You're not dummying up on me, my friend. Not six cents worth. Let's go."

"Would you take the cuffs off, Captain?" I asked. "I mean if I made a statement?"

"I might. Make it short."

"If I told you I hadn't seen Lennox within the last twenty-four hours, hadn't talked to him and had no idea where he might be—would that satisfy you, Captain?"

"It might—if I believed it."

"If I told you I had seen him and where and when, but had no idea he had murdered anyone or that any crime had been committed, and further had no idea where he might be at this moment, that wouldn't satisfy you at all, would it?"

"With more detail I might listen. Things like where, when, what he looked like, what was talked about, where he was headed. It might grow into something."

"With your treatment," I said, "it would probably grow into making me an accessory."

His jaw muscles bulged. His eyes were dirty ice. "So?"

"I don't know," I said. "I need legal advice. I'd like to co-operate. How would it be if we had somebody from the D.A.'s office here?"

He let out a short raucous laugh. It was over very soon. He got up slowly and walked around the desk. He leaned down close to me, one big hand on the wood, and smiled. Then without change of expression he hit me on the side of the neck with a fist like a piece of iron.

The blow traveled eight or ten inches, no more. It nearly took my head off. Bile seeped into my mouth. I tasted blood mixed with it. I heard nothing but a roaring in my head. He leaned over me still smiling, his left hand still on the desk. His voice seemed to come from a long way off.

"I used to be tough but I'm getting old. You take a good punch, mister, and that's all you get from me. We got boys over at the City Jail that ought to be working in the stockyards. Maybe we hadn't ought to have them because they ain't nice clean powder-puff punchers like Dayton here. They don't have four kids and a rose garden like Green. They live for different amusements. It takes all kinds and labor's scarce. You got any more funny little ideas about what you might say, if you bothered to say it?"

"Not with the cuffs on, Captain." It hurt even to say that much.

He leaned farther towards me and I smelled his sweat and the gas of corruption. Then he straightened and went back around the desk and planted his solid buttocks in his chair. He picked up a three-cornered ruler and ran his thumb along one edge as if it was a knife. He looked at Green.

"What are you waiting for, Sergeant?"

"Orders." Green ground out the word as if he hated the sound of his own voice.

"You got to be told? You're an experienced man, it says in the records. I want a detailed statement of this man's movements for the past twenty-four hours. Maybe longer, but that much at first. I want to know what he did every minute of the time. I want it signed and witnessed and checked. I want it in two hours. Then I want him back here clean, tidy, and unmarked. And one thing more, Sergeant."

He paused and gave Green a stare that would have frozen a fresh-baked potato.

"—next time I ask a suspect a few civil questions I don't want you standing there looking as if I had torn his ear off."

"Yes, sir." Green turned to me. "Let's go," he said gruffly.

Gregorius bared his teeth at me. They needed cleaning— badly. "Let's have the exit line, chum."

"Yes, sir," I said politely. "You probably didn't intend it, but you've done me a favor. With an assist from Detective Dayton. You've solved a problem for me. No man likes to betray a friend but I wouldn't betray an enemy into your hands. You're not only a gorilla, you're an incompetent. You don't know how to operate a simple investigation. I was balanced on a knife edge and you could have swung me either way. But you had to abuse me, throw coffee in my face, and use your fists on me when I was in a spot where all I could do was take it. From now on I wouldn't tell you the time by the clock on your own wall."

For some strange reason he sat there perfectly still and let me say it. Then he grinned. "You're just a little old cop-hater, friend. That's all you are, shamus, just a little old cop-hater."

"There are places where cops are not hated, Captain. But in those places you wouldn't be a cop."

He took that too. I guess he could afford it. He'd probably taken worse many times. Then the phone rang on his desk. He looked at it and gestured. Dayton stepped smartly around the desk and lifted the receiver.

"Captain Gregorius' office. Detective Dayton speaking."

He listened. A tiny frown drew his handsome eyebrows together. He said softly: "One moment, please, sir."

He held the phone out to Gregorius. "Commissioner Allbright, sir."

Gregorius scowled. "Yeah? What's that snotty bastard want?" He took the phone, held it a moment and smoothed his face out. "Gregorius, Commissioner."

He listened. "Yeah, he's here in my office, Commissioner. I been asking him a few questions. Not co-operative. Not co-operative at all . . . How's that again?" A sudden ferocious scowl twisted his face into dark knots. The blood darkened his forehead. But his voice didn't change in tone by a fraction. "If that's a direct order, it ought to come through the Chief of Detectives, Commissioner . . . Sure, I'll act on it until it's confirmed. Sure . . . Hell, no. Nobody laid a glove on him . . . Yes, sir. Right away."

He put the phone back in its cradle. I thought his hand shook a little. His eyes moved up and across my face and then to Green. "Take the cuffs off," he said tonelessly.

Green unlocked the cuffs. I rubbed my hands together, waiting for the pins and needles of circulation.

"Book him in the county jail," Gregorius said slowly. "Suspicion of murder. The D.A. has glommed the case right out of our hands. Lovely system we got around here."

Nobody moved. Green was close to me, breathing hard. Gregorius looked up at Dayton.

"Whatcha waiting for, cream puff? An ice-cream cone maybe?"

Dayton almost choked. "You didn't give me any orders, skipper."

"Say sir to me, damn you! I'm skipper to sergeants and better. Not to you, kiddo. Not to you. Out."

"Yes, sir." Dayton walked quickly to the door and went out. Gregorius heaved himself to his feet and moved to the window and stood with his back to the room.

"Come on, let's drift," Green muttered in my ear.

"Get him out of here before I kick his face in," Gregorius said to the window.

Green went to the door and opened it. I started through. Gregorius barked suddenly: "Hold it! Shut that door!"

Green shut it and leaned his back to it.

"Come here, you!" Gregorius barked at me.

I didn't move. I stood and looked at him. Green didn't move either. There was a grim pause. Then very slowly Gregorius walked across the room and stood facing me toe to toe. He put his big hard hands in his pockets. He rocked on his heels.

"Never laid a glove on him," he said under his breath, as if talking to himself. His eyes were remote and expressionless. His mouth worked convulsively.

Then he spat in my face.

He stepped back. "That will be all, thank you."

He turned and went back to the window. Green opened the door again.

I went through it reaching for my handkerchief.

# 8

Cell No. 3 in the felony tank has two bunks, Pullman style, but the tank was not very full and I had the cell to myself. In the felony tank they treat you pretty well. You get two blankets, neither dirty nor clean, and a lumpy mattress two inches thick which goes over crisscrossed metal slats. There is a flush toilet, a washbasin, paper towels and gritty gray soap. The cell block is clean and doesn't smell of disinfectant. The trusties do the work. The supply of trusties is always ample.

The jail deputies look you over and they have wise eyes. Unless you are a drunk or a psycho or act like one you get to keep your matches and cigarettes. Until preliminary you wear your own clothes. After that you wear the jail denim, no tie, no belt, no shoelaces. You sit on the bunk and wait. There is nothing else to do.

In the drunk tank it is not so good. No bunk, no chair, no blankets, no nothing. You lie on the concrete floor. You sit on the toilet and vomit in your own lap. That is the depth of misery. I've seen it.

Although it was still daylight the lights were on in the ceiling. Inside the steel door of the cell block was a basket of steel bars around the Judas window. The lights were controlled from outside the steel door. They went out at nine P.M. Nobody came through the door or said anything. You might be in the middle of a sentence in a newspaper or magazine. Without any sound of a click or any warning—darkness. And there you were until the summer dawn with nothing to do but sleep if you could, smoke if you had anything to smoke, and think if you had anything to think about that didn't make you feel worse than not thinking at all.

In jail a man has no personality. He is a minor disposal problem and a few entries on reports. Nobody cares who loves or hates him, what he looks like, what he did with his life. Nobody reacts to him unless he gives trouble. Nobody abuses him. All that is asked of him is that he go quietly to the right cell and remain quiet when he gets there. There is nothing to fight against, nothing to be mad at. The jailers are quiet men without animosity or sadism. All this stuff you read about men yelling and screaming, beating against the bars, running spoons along them, guards rushing in with clubs— all that is for the big house. A good jail is one of the quietest places in the world. You could walk through the average cell block at night and look in through the bars and see a huddle of brown blanket, or a head of hair, or a pair of eyes looking at nothing. You might hear a snore. Once in a long while you might hear a nightmare. The life in a jail is in suspension, without purpose or meaning. In another cell you might see a man who cannot sleep or even try to sleep. He is sitting on the edge of his bunk doing nothing. He looks at you or doesn't. You look at him. He says nothing and you say nothing. There is nothing to communicate.

In the corner of the cell block there may be a second steel door that leads to the show-up box. One of its walls is wire mesh painted black. On the back wall are ruled lines for height. Overhead are floodlights. You go in there in the morning as a rule, just before the night captain goes off duty. You stand against the measuring lines and the lights glare at you and there is no light behind the wire mesh. But plenty of people are out there: cops, detectives, citizens who have been robbed or assaulted or swindled or kicked out of their cars at gun point or conned out of their life savings. You don't see or hear them. You hear the voice of the night captain. You receive him loud and clear. He puts you through your paces as if you were a performing dog. He is tired and cynical and competent. He is the stage manager of a play that has had the longest run in history, but it no longer interests him.

"All right, you. Stand straight. Pull your belly in. Pull your chin in. Keep your shoulders back. Hold your head level. Look straight front. Turn left. Turn right. Face front again and hold your hands out. Palms up. Palms down. Pull your sleeves back. No visible scars. Hair dark brown, some gray. Eyes brown. Height six feet, one half inch. Weight about one ninety. Name, Philip Marlowe. Occupation private detective. Well, well, nice to see you, Marlowe. That's all. Next man."

Much obliged, Captain. Thanks for the time. You forgot to have me open my mouth. I have some nice inlays and one very high-class porcelain jacket crown. Eighty-seven dollars worth of porcelain jacket crown. You forgot to look inside my nose too, Captain. A lot of scar tissue in there for you. Septum operation and was that guy a butcher! Two hours of it in those days. I hear they do it in twenty minutes now. I got it playing football, Captain, a slight miscalculation in an attempt to block a punt. I blocked the guy's foot instead—after he kicked the ball. Fifteen yards penalty, and that's about how much stiff bloody tape they pulled out of my nose an inch at a time the day after the operation. I'm not bragging, Captain. I'm just telling you. It's the little things that count.

On the third day a deputy unlocked my cell in the middle of the morning.

"Your lawyer's here. Kill the butt—and not on the floor."

I flushed it down the toilet. He took me to the conference room. A tall pale dark-haired man was standing there looking out of the window. There was a fat brown briefcase on the table. He turned. He waited for the door to close. Then he sat down near his briefcase on the far side of a scarred oak table that came out of the Ark. Noah bought it secondhand. The lawyer opened a hammered silver cigarette case and put it in front of him and looked me over.

"Sit down, Marlowe. Care for a cigarette? My name is Endicott. Sewell Endicott. I've been instructed to represent you without cost or expense to you. I guess you'd like to get out of here, wouldn't you?"

I sat down and took one of the cigarettes. He held a lighter for me.

"Nice to see you again, Mr. Endicott. We've met before—while you were D.A."

He nodded. "I don't remember, but it's quite possible." He smiled faintly. "That position was not quite in my line. I guess I don't have enough tiger in me."

"Who sent you?"

"I'm not at liberty to say. If you accept me as your attorney, the fee will be taken care of."

"I guess that means they've got him."

He just stared at me. I puffed at the cigarette. It was one of those things with filters in them. It tasted like a high fog strained through cotton wool.

"If you mean Lennox," he said, "and of course you do, no—they haven't got him."

"Why the mystery, Mr. Endicott? About who sent you."

"My principal wishes to remain anonymous. That is the privilege of my principal. Do you accept me?"

"I don't know," I said. "If they haven't got Terry, why are they holding me? Nobody has asked me anything, nobody has been near me."

He frowned and looked down at his long white delicate fingers. "District Attorney Springer has taken personal charge of this matter. He may have been too busy to question you yet. But you are entitled to arraignment and a preliminary hearing. I can get you out on bail on a habeas corpus proceeding. You probably know what the law is."

"I'm booked on suspicion of murder."

He shrugged impatiently. "That's just a catch-all. You could have been booked in transit to Pittsburgh, or any one of a dozen charges. What they probably mean is accessory after the fact. You took Lennox somewhere, didn't you?"

I didn't answer. I dropped the tasteless cigarette on the floor and stepped on it. Endicott shrugged again and frowned.

"Assume you did then, just for the sake of argument. To make you an accessory they have to prove intent. In this case that would mean knowledge that a crime had been committed and that Lennox was a fugitive. It's bailable in any case. Of course what you really are is a material witness. But a man can't be held in prison as a material witness in this state except by court order. He's not a material witness unless a judge so declares. But the law enforcement people can always find a way to do what they want to do."

"Yeah," I said. "A detective named Dayton slugged me. A homicide captain named Gregorius threw a cup of coffee at me, hit me in the neck hard enough to bust an artery—you can see it's still swollen, and when a call from Police Commissioner Allbright kept him from turning me over to the wrecking crew, he spat in my face. You're quite right, Mr. Endicott. The law boys can always do what they want to do."

He looked at his wrist watch rather pointedly. "You want out on bail or don't you?"

"Thanks. I don't think I do. A guy out on bail is already half guilty in the public mind. If he gets off later on, he had a smart lawyer."

"That's silly," he said impatiently.

"Okay, it's silly. I'm silly. Otherwise I wouldn't be here. If you're in touch with Lennox, tell him to quit bothering about me. I'm not in here for him. I'm in here for me. No complaints. It's part of the deal. I'm in a business where people come to me with troubles. Big troubles, little troubles, but always troubles they don't want to take to the cops. How long would they come if any bruiser with a police shield could hold me upside down and drain my guts?"

"I see your point," he said slowly. "But let me correct you on one thing. I am not in touch with Lennox. I scarcely know him. I'm an officer of the court, as all lawyers are. If I knew where Lennox was, I couldn't conceal the information from the District Attorney. The most I could do would be to agree to surrender him at a specified time and place after I had had an interview with him."

"Nobody else would bother to send you here to help me."

"Are you calling me a liar?" He reached down to rub out his cigarette stub on the underside of the table.

"I seem to remember that you're a Virginian, Mr. Endicott. In this country we have a sort of historical fixation about Virginians. We think of them as the flower of southern chivalry and honor."

He smiled. "That was nicely said. I only wish it was true. But we're wasting time. If you had had a grain of sense you'd have told the police you hadn't seen Lennox for a week. It didn't have to be true. Under oath you could always have told the real story. There's no law against lying to the cops. They expect it. They feel much happier when you lie to them than when you refuse to talk to them. That's a direct challenge to their authority. What do you expect to gain by it?"

I didn't answer. I didn't really have an answer. He stood up and reached for his hat and snapped his cigarette case shut and put it in his pocket.

"You had to play the big scene," he said coldly. "Stand on your rights, talk about the law. How ingenuous can a man get, Marlowe? A man like you who is supposed to know his way around. The law isn't justice. It's a very imperfect mechanism. If you press exactly the right buttons and are also lucky, justice may show up in the answer. A mechanism is all the law was ever intended to be. I guess you're not in any mood to be helped. So I'll take myself off. You can reach me if you change your mind."

"I'll stick it out for a day or two longer. If they catch Terry they won't care how he got away. All they'll care about is the circus they can make of the trial. The murder of Mr. Harlan Potter's daughter is headline material all over the country. A crowd-pleaser like Springer could ride himself right into Attorney General on that show, and from there into the governor's chair and from there—" I stopped talking and let the rest of it float in the air.

Endicott smiled a slow derisive smile. "I don't think you know very much about Mr. Harlan Potter," he said.

"And if they don't get Lennox, they won't *want* to know how he got away, Mr. Endicott. They'll just want to forget the whole thing fast."

"Got it all figured out, haven't you, Marlowe?"

"I've had the time. All I know about Mr. Harlan Potter is that he is supposed to be worth a hundred million bucks, and that he owns nine or ten newspapers. How's the publicity going?"

"The publicity?" His voice was ice cold saying it.

"Yeah. Nobody's interviewed me from the press. I expected to make a big noise in the papers out of this. Get lots of business. Private eye goes to jail rather than split on a pal."

He walked to the door and turned with his hand on the knob. "You amuse me, Marlowe. You're childish in some ways. True, a hundred million dollars can buy a great deal of publicity. It can also, my friend, if shrewdly employed, buy a great deal of silence."

He opened the door and went out. Then a deputy came in and took me back to Cell No. 3 in the felony block.

"Guess you won't be with us long, if you've got Endicott," he said pleasantly as he locked me in. I said I hoped he was right.

# 9

The deputy on the early night shift was a big blond guy with meaty shoulders and a friendly grin. He was middle-aged and had long since outlived both pity and anger. He wanted to put in eight easy hours and he looked as if almost anything would be easy down his street. He unlocked my door.

"Company for you. Guy from the D.A.'s office. No sleep, huh?"

"It's a little early for me. What time is it?"

"Ten-fourteen." He stood in the doorway and looked over the cell. One blanket was spread on the lower bunk, one was folded for a pillow. There were a couple of used paper towels in the trash bucket and a small wad of toilet paper on the edge of the washbasin. He nodded approval. "Anything personal in here?"

"Just me."

He left the cell door open. We walked along a quiet corridor to the elevator and rode down to the booking desk. A fat man in a gray suit stood by the desk smoking a corncob. His fingernails were dirty and he smelled.

"I'm Spranklin from the D.A.'s office," he told me in a tough voice. "Mr. Grenz wants you upstairs." He reached behind his hip and came up with a pair of bracelets. "Let's try these for size."

The jail deputy and the booking clerk grinned at him with deep enjoyment. "What's the matter, Sprank? Afraid he'll mug you in the elevator?"

"I don't want no trouble," he growled. "Had a guy break from me once. They ate my ass off. Let's go, boy."

The booking clerk pushed a form at him and he signed it with a flourish. "I never take no unnecessary chances," he said. "Man never knows what he's up against in this town."

A prowl car cop brought in a drunk with a bloody ear. We went towards the elevator. "You're in trouble, boy," Spranklin told me in the elevator. "Heap bad trouble." It seemed to give him a vague satisfaction. "A guy can get hisself in a lot of trouble in this town."

The elevator man turned his head and winked at me. I grinned.

"Don't try nothing, boy," Spranklin told me severely. "I shot a man once. Tried to break. They ate my ass off."

"You get it coming and going, don't you?"

He thought it over. "Yeah," he said. "Either way they eat your ass off. It's a tough town. No respect."

We got out and went in through the double doors of the D.A.'s office. The switchboard was dead, with lines plugged in for the night. There was nobody in the waiting chairs. Lights were on in a couple of offices. Spranklin opened the door of a small lighted room which contained a desk, a filing case, a hard chair or two, and a thick-set man with a hard chin and stupid eyes. His face was red and he was just pushing something into the drawer of his desk.

"You could knock," he barked at Spranklin.

"Sorry, Mr. Grenz," Spranklin bumbled. "I was thinkin' about the prisoner."

He pushed me into the office. "Should I take the cuffs off, Mr. Grenz?"

"I don't know what the hell you put them on for," Grenz said sourly. He watched Spranklin unlock the cuffs on my wrist. He had the key on a bunch the size of a grapefruit and it troubled him to find it.

"Okay, scram," Grenz said. "Wait outside to take him back."

"I'm kind of off duty, Mr. Grenz."

"You're off duty when I say you're off duty."

Spranklin flushed and edged his fat bottom out through the door. Grenz looked after him savagely, then when the door closed he moved the same look to me. I pulled a chair over and sat down.

"I didn't tell you to sit down," Grenz barked.

I got a loose cigarette out of my pocket and stuck it in my mouth. "And I didn't say you could smoke," Grenz roared.

"I'm allowed to smoke in the cell block. Why not here?"

"Because this is my office. *I* make the rules here." A raw smell of whiskey floated across the desk.

"Take another quick one," I said. "It'll calm you down. You got kind of interrupted when we came in."

His back hit the back of the chair hard. His face went dark red. I struck a match and lit my cigarette.

After a long minute Grenz said softly, "Okay, tough boy. Quite a man, aren't you? You know something? They're all sizes and shapes when they come in here, but they all go out the same size—small. And the same shape—bent."

"What did you want to see me about, Mr. Grenz? And

don't mind me if you feel like hitting that bottle. I'm a fellow that will take a snort myself, if I'm tired and nervous and overworked."

"You don't seem much impressed by the jam you're in."

"I don't figure I'm in any jam."

"We'll see about that. Meantime I want a very full statement from you." He flicked a finger at a recording set on a stand beside his desk. "We'll take it now and have it transcribed tomorrow. If the Chief Deputy is satisfied with your statement, he may release you on your own undertaking not to leave town. Let's go." He switched on the recorder. His voice was cold, decisive, and as nasty as he knew how to make it. But his right hand kept edging towards the desk drawer. He was too young to have veins in his nose, but he had them, and the whites of his eyes were a bad color.

"I get so tired of it," I said.

"Tired of what?" he snapped.

"Hard little men in hard little offices talking hard little words that don't mean a goddam thing. I've had fifty-six hours in the felony block. Nobody pushed me around, nobody tried to prove he was tough. They didn't have to. They had it on ice for when they needed it. And why was I in there? I was booked on suspicion. What the hell kind of legal system lets a man be shoved in a felony tank because some cop didn't get an answer to some questions? What evidence did he have? A telephone number on a pad. And what was he trying to prove by locking me up? Not a damn thing except that he had the power to do it. Now you're on the same pitch—trying to make me feel what a lot of power you generate in this cigar box you call your office. You send this scared baby sitter over late at night to bring me in here. You think maybe sitting alone with my thoughts for fifty-six hours has made gruel out of my brains? You think I'm going to cry in your lap and ask you to stroke my head because I'm so awful goddam lonely in the great big jail? Come off it, Grenz. Take your drink and get human; I'm willing to assume you are just doing your job. But take the brass knuckles off before you start. If you're big enough you don't need them, and if you need them you're not big enough to push me around."

He sat there and listened and looked at me. Then he grinned sourly. "Nice speech," he said. "Now you've got the crap out of your system, let's get that statement. You want to answer specific questions or just tell it your own way?"

"I was talking to the birds," I said. "Just to hear the breeze blow. I'm not making any statement. You're a lawyer and you know I don't have to."

"That's right," he said coolly. "I know the law. I know police work. I'm offering you a chance to clear yourself. If you don't want it, that's jake with me too. I can arraign you tomorrow morning at ten A.M. and have you set for a preliminary hearing. You may get bail, although I'll fight it, but if you do, it will be stiff. It'll cost you plenty. That's one way we can do it."

He looked down at a paper on his desk, read it, and turned it face down.

"On what charge?" I asked him.

"Section thirty-two. Accessory after the fact. A felony. It rates up to a five-spot in Quentin."

"Better catch Lennox first," I said carefully. Grenz had something and I sensed it in his manner. I didn't know how much, but he had something all right.

He leaned back in his chair and picked up a pen and twirled it slowly between his palms. Then he smiled. He was enjoying himself.

"Lennox is a hard man to hide, Marlowe. With most people you need a photo and a good clear photo. Not with a guy that has scars all over one side of his face. Not to mention white hair, and not over thirty-five years old. We got four witnesses, maybe more."

"Witnesses to what?" I was tasting something bitter in my mouth, like the bile I had tasted after Captain Gregorius slugged me. That reminded me that my neck was still sore and swollen. I rubbed it gently.

"Don't be a chump, Marlowe. A San Diego superior court judge and his wife happened to be seeing their son and daughter-in-law off on that plane. All four saw Lennox and the judge's wife saw the car he came in and who came with him. You don't have a prayer."

"That's nice," I said. "How did you get to them?"

"Special bulletin on radio and TV. A full description was all it took. The judge called in."

"Sounds good," I said judicially. "But it takes a little more than that, Grenz. You have to catch him and prove he committed a murder. Then you have to prove I knew it."

He snapped a finger at the back of the telegram. "I think I will take that drink," he said. "Been working nights too much." He opened the drawer and put a bottle and a shot glass on the desk. He poured it full to the brim and knocked it back in a lump. "Better," he said. "Much better. Sorry I can't offer you one while you're in custody." He corked the bottle and pushed it away from him, but not out of reach. "Oh yeah, we got to prove something, you said. Well, it could be we already got a confession, chum. Too bad, huh?"

A small but very cold finger moved the whole length of my spine, like an icy insect crawling.

"So why do you need a statement from me?"

He grinned. "We like a tidy record. Lennox will be brought back and tried. We need everything we can get. It's not so much what we want from you as what we might be willing to let you get away with—if you co-operate."

I stared at him. He did a little paper-fiddling. He moved around in his chair, looked at his bottle, and had to use up a lot of will power not grabbing for it. "Maybe you'd like the whole libretto," he said suddenly with an off-key leer. "Well, smart guy, just to show you I'm not kidding, here it is."

I leaned across his desk and he thought I was reaching for his bottle. He grabbed it away and put it back in the drawer. I just wanted to drop a stub in his ash tray. I leaned back again and lit another pill. He spoke rapidly.

"Lennox got off the plane at Mazatlán, an airline junction point and a town of about thirty-five thousand. He disappeared for two or three hours. Then a tall man with black hair and a dark skin and what might have been a lot of knife scars booked to Torreón under the name of Silvano Rodriguez. His Spanish was good but not good enough for a man of his name. He was too tall for a Mexican with such a dark skin. The pilot turned in a report on him. The cops were too slow at Torreón. Mex cops are no balls of fire. What they do best is shoot people. By the time they got going the man had chartered a plane and gone on to a little mountain town called Otatoclán, a small time summer resort with a lake. The pilot of the charter plane had trained as a combat pilot in Texas. He spoke good English. Lennox pretended not to catch what he said."

"If it *was* Lennox," I put in.

"Wait a while, chum. It was Lennox all right. Okay, he gets off at Otatoclán and registers at the hotel there, this time as Mario de Cerva. He was wearing a gun, a Mauser 7.65, which doesn't mean too much in Mexico, of course. But the charter pilot thought the guy didn't seem kosher, so he had a word with the local law. They put Lennox under surveillance. They did some checking with Mexico City and then they moved in."

Grenz picked up a ruler and sighted along it, a meaningless gesture which kept him from looking at me.

I said, "Uh-huh. Smart boy, your charter pilot, and nice to his customers. The story stinks."

He looked up at me suddenly. "What we want," he said dryly, "is a quick trial, a plea of second degree which we will accept. There are some angles we'd rather not go into. After all, the family is pretty influential."

"Meaning Harlan Potter."

He nodded briefly. "For my money the whole idea is all wet. Springer could have a field day with it. It's got every-thing. Sex, scandal, money, beautiful unfaithful wife, wounded war hero husband—I suppose that's where he got the scars—hell, it would be front page stuff for weeks. Every rag in the country would eat it up. So we shuffle it off to a fast fade." He shrugged. "Okay, if the chief wants it that way, it's up to him. Do I get that statement?" He turned to the re-cording machine which had been humming away softly all this time, with the light showing in front.

"Turn it off," I said.

He swung around and gave me a vicious look. "You like it in jail?"

"It's not too bad. You don't meet the best people, but who the hell wants to? Be reasonable, Grenz. You're trying to make a fink out of me. Maybe I'm obstinate, or even senti-mental, but I'm practical too. Suppose you had to hire a private eye—yeah, yeah, I know how you would hate the idea—but just suppose you were where it was your only out. Would you want one that finked on his friends?"

He stared at me with hate.

"A couple more points. Doesn't it strike you that Lennox's evasion tactics were just a little too transparent? If he wanted to be caught, he didn't have to go to all that trouble. If he didn't want to be caught, he had brains enough not to disguise himself as a Mexican in Mexico."

"Meaning what?" Grenz was snarling at me now.

"Meaning you could just be filling me up with a lot of hooey you made up, that there wasn't any Rodriguez with dyed hair and there wasn't any Mario de Cerva at Otatoclán, and you don't know any more about where Lennox is than where Black Beard the Pirate buried his treasure."

He got his bottle out again. He poured himself a shot and drank it down quickly, as before. He relaxed slowly. He turned in his chair and switched off the recording machine.

"I'd like to have tried you," he said gratingly. "You're the kind of wise guy I like to work over. This rap will be hanging over you for a long long time, cutie. You'll walk with it and eat with it and sleep with it. And next time you step out of line we'll murder you with it. Right now I got to do something that turns my guts inside out."

He pawed on his desk and pulled the face-down paper to him, turned it over and signed it. You can always tell when a man is writing his own name. He has a special way of moving. Then he stood up and marched around the desk and threw the door of his shoe box open and yelled for Spranklin.

The fat man came in with his B.O. Grenz gave him the paper.

"I've just signed your release order," he said. "I'm a public servant and sometimes I have unpleasant duties. Would you care to know why I signed it?"

I stood up. "If you want to tell me."

"The Lennox case is closed, mister. There ain't any Lennox case. He wrote out a full confession this afternoon in his hotel room and shot himself. In Otatoclán, just like I said."

I stood there looking at nothing. Out of the corner of my eye I saw Grenz back away slowly as if he thought I might be going to slug him. I must have looked pretty nasty for a moment. Then he was behind his desk again and Spranklin had grabbed onto my arm.

"Come on, move," he said in a whining kind of voice. "Man likes to get to home nights once in a while."

I went out with him and closed the door. I closed it quietly as if on a room where someone had just died.

## 10

I dug out the carbon of my property slip and turned it over and receipted on the original. I put my belongings back in my pockets. There was a man draped over the end of the booking desk and as I turned away he straightened up and spoke to me. He was about six feet four inches tall and as thin as a wire.

"Need a ride home?"

In the bleak light he looked young-old, tired and cynical, but he didn't look like a grifter. "For how much?"

"For free. I'm Lonnie Morgan of the *Journal.* I'm knocking off."

"Oh, police beat," I said.

"Just this week. The City Hall is my regular beat."

We walked out of the building and found his car in the parking lot. I looked up at the sky. There were stars but there was too much glare. It was a cool pleasant night. I breathed it in. Then I got into his car and he drove away from there.

"I live way out in Laurel Canyon," I said. "Just drop me anywhere."

"They ride you in," he said, "but they don't worry how you get home. This case interests me, in a repulsive sort of way."

"It seems there isn't any case," I said. "Terry Lennox shot himself this afternoon. So they say. So they say."

"Very convenient," Lonnie Morgan said, staring ahead through the windshield. His car drifted quietly along quiet streets. "It helps them build their wall."

"What wall?"

"Somebody's building a wall around the Lennox case, Marlowe. You're smart enough to see that, aren't you? It's not getting the kind of play it rates. The D.A. left town tonight for Washington. Some kind of convention. He walked out on the sweetest hunk of publicity he's had in years. Why?"

"No use to ask me. I've been in cold storage."

"Because somebody made it worth his while, that's why. I don't mean anything crude like a wad of dough. Somebody promised him something important to him and there's only one man connected with the case in a position to do that. The girl's father."

I leaned my head back in a corner of the car. "Sounds a little unlikely," I said. "What about the press? Harlan Potter owns a few papers, but what about the competition?"

He gave me a brief amused glance and then concentrated on his driving. "Ever been a newspaperman?"

"No."

"Newspapers are owned and published by rich men. Rich men all belong to the same club. Sure, there's competition—hard tough competition for circulation, for newsbeats, for exclusive stories. Just so long as it doesn't damage the prestige and privilege and position of the owners. If it does, down comes the lid. The lid, my friend, is down on the Lennox case. The Lennox case, my friend, properly built up, could have sold a hell of a lot of papers. It has everything. The trial would have drawn feature writers from all over the country. But there ain't going to be no trial. On account of Lennox checked out before it could get moving. Like I said—very convenient—for Harlan Potter and his family."

I straightened up and gave him a hard stare.

"You calling the whole thing a fix?"

He twisted his mouth sardonically. "Could just be Lennox had some help committing suicide. Resisting arrest a little. Mexican cops have very itchy trigger fingers. If you want to lay a little bet, I'll give you nice odds that nobody gets to count the bullet holes."

"I think you're wrong," I said. "I knew Terry Lennox pretty well. He wrote himself off a long time ago. If they brought him back alive, he would have let them have it their way. He'd have copped a manslaughter plea."

Lonnie Morgan shook his head. I knew what he was going to say and he said it. "Not a chance. If he had shot her or cracked her skull, maybe yes. But there was too much brutality. Her face was beaten to a pulp. Second degree murder would be the best he could get, and even that would raise a stink."

I said: "You could be right."

He looked at me again. "You say you knew the guy. Do you go for the setup?"

"I'm tired. I'm not in a thinking mood tonight."

There was a long pause. Then Lonnie Morgan said quietly: "If I was a real bright guy instead of a hack newspaperman, I'd think maybe he didn't kill her at all."

"It's a thought."

He stuck a cigarette in his mouth and lit it by scratching a match on the dashboard. He smoked silently with a fixed frown on his thin face. We reached Laurel Canyon and I told him where to turn off the boulevard and where to turn again into my street. His car churned up the hill and stopped at the foot of my redwood steps.

I got out. "Thanks for the ride, Morgan. Care for a drink?"

"I'll take a rain check. I figure you'd rather be alone."

"I've got lots of time to be alone. Too damn much."

"You've got a friend to say goodbye to," he said. "He must have been that if you let them toss you into the can on his account."

"Who said I did that?"

He smiled faintly. "Just because I can't print it don't mean I didn't know it, chum. So long. See you around."

I shut the car door and he turned and drove off down the hill. When his tail lights vanished around the corner I climbed the steps, picked up newspapers, and let myself into the empty house. I put all the lamps on and opened all the windows. The place was stuffy.

I made some coffee and drank it and took the five C notes out of the coffee can. They were rolled tight and pushed down into the coffee at the side. I walked up and down with a cup of coffee in my hand, turned the TV on, turned it off, sat, stood, and sat again. I read through the papers that had piled up on the front steps. The Lennox case started out big, but by that morning it was a Part Two item. There was a photo of Sylvia, but none of Terry. There was a snap of me that I didn't know existed. "L.A. Private Detective Held for Questioning." There was a large photo of the Lennox home in Encino. It was pseudo English with a lot of peaked roof and it would have cost a hundred bucks to wash the windows. It stood on a knoll in a big two acres, which is a lot of real estate for the Los Angeles area. There was a photo of the guest house, which was a miniature of the main building. It was hedged in with trees. Both photos had obviously been taken from some distance off and then blown up and trimmed. There was no photo of what the papers called the "death room."

I had seen all this stuff before, in jail, but I read it and looked at it again with different eyes. It told me nothing except that a rich and beautiful girl had been murdered and the press had been pretty thoroughly excluded. So the influence had started to work very early. The crime beat boys must have gnashed their teeth and gnashed them in vain. It figured. If Terry talked to his father-in-law in Pasadena the very night she was killed, there would have been a dozen guards on the estate before the police were even notified.

But there was something that didn't figure at all—the way she had been beaten up. Nobody could sell me that Terry had done that.

I put the lamps out and sat by an open window. Outside in a bush a mockingbird ran through a few trills and admired himself before settling down for the night.

My neck itched, so I shaved and showered and went to bed and lay on my back listening, as if far off in the dark I might hear a voice, the kind of calm and patient voice that makes everything clear. I didn't hear it and I knew I wasn't going to. Nobody was going to explain the Lennox case to me. No explanation was necessary. The murderer had confessed and he was dead. There wouldn't even be an inquest.

As Lonnie Morgan of the *Journal* had remarked—very convenient. If Terry Lennox had killed his wife, that was fine. There was no need to try him and bring out all the unpleasant details. If he hadn't killed her, that was fine too. A dead man is the best fall guy in the world. He never talks back.

## II

In the morning I shaved again and dressed and drove down-town in the usual way and parked in the usual place and if the parking lot attendant happened to know that I was an important public character he did a top job in hiding it. I went upstairs and along the corridor and got keys out to unlock my door. A dark smooth-looking guy watched me.

"You Marlowe?"

"So?"

"Stick around," he said. "A guy wants to see you." He unplastered his back from the wall and strolled off languidly.

I stepped inside the office and picked up the mail. There was more of it on the desk where the night cleaning woman had put it. I slit the envelopes after I opened windows, and threw away what I didn't want, which was practically all of it. I switched on the buzzer to the other door and filled a pipe and lit it and then just sat there waiting for somebody to scream for help.

I thought about Terry Lennox in a detached sort of way. He was already receding into the distance, white hair and scarred face and weak charm and his peculiar brand of pride. I didn't judge him or analyze him, just as I had never asked him questions about how he got wounded or how he ever happened to get himself married to anyone like Sylvia. He was like somebody you meet on board ship and get to know very well and never really know at all. He was gone like the same fellow when he says goodbye at the pier and let's keep in touch, old man, and you know you won't and he won't. Likely enough you'll never even see the guy again. If you do he will be an entirely different person, just another Rotarian in a club car. How's business? Oh, not too bad. You look good. So do you. I've put on too much weight. Don't we all? Remember that trip in the *Franconia* (or whatever it was)? Oh sure, swell trip, wasn't it?

The hell it was a swell trip. You were bored stiff. You only talked to the guy because there wasn't anybody around that interested you. Maybe it was like that with Terry Lennox and me. No, not quite. I owned a piece of him. I had invested time and money in him, and three days in the icehouse, not to mention a slug on the jaw and a punch in the neck that I felt every time I swallowed. Now he was dead and I couldn't even give him back his five hundred bucks. That made me sore. It is always the little things that make you sore.

The door buzzer and the telephone rang at the same time. I answered the phone first because the buzzer meant only that somebody had walked into my pint-size waiting room.

"Is this Mr. Marlowe? Mr. Endicott is calling you. One moment please."

He came on the line. "This is Sewell Endicott," he said, as if he didn't know his goddam secretary had already fed me his name.

"Good morning, Mr. Endicott."

"Glad to hear they turned you loose. I think possibly you had the right idea not to build any resistance."

"It wasn't an idea. It was just mulishness."

"I doubt if you'll hear any more about it. But if you do and need help, let me hear from you."

"Why would I? The man is dead. They'd have a hell of a time proving he ever came near me. Then they'd have to prove I had guilty knowledge. And then they'd have to prove he had committed a crime or was a fugitive."

He cleared his throat. "Perhaps," he said carefully, "you haven't been told he left a full confession."

"I was told, Mr. Endicott. I'm talking to a lawyer. Would I be out of line in suggesting that the confession would have to be proved too, both as to genuineness and as to veracity?"

"I'm afraid I have no time for a legal discussion," he said sharply. "I'm flying to Mexico with a rather melancholy duty to perform. You can probably guess what it is?"

"Uh-huh. Depends who you're representing. You didn't tell me, remember."

"I remember very well. Well, goodbye, Marlowe. My offer of help is still good. But let me also offer you a little advice. Don't be too certain you're in the clear. You're in a pretty vulnerable business."

He hung up. I put the phone back in its cradle carefully. I sat for a moment with my hand on it, scowling. Then I wiped the scowl off my face and got up to open the communicating door into my waiting room.

A man was sitting by the window ruffling a magazine. He wore a bluish-gray suit with an almost invisible pale blue check. On his crossed feet were black moccasin-type ties, the kind with two eyelets that are almost as comfortable as strollers and don't wear your socks out every time you walk a block. His white handkerchief was folded square and the end of a pair of sunglasses showed behind it. He had thick dark wavy hair. He was tanned very dark. He looked up with bird-bright eyes and smiled under a hairline mustache. His tie was a dark maroon tied in a pointed bow over a sparkling white shirt.

He threw the magazine aside. "The crap these rags go for," he said. "I been reading a piece about Costello. Yeah, they know all about Costello. Like I know all about Helen of Troy."

"What can I do for you?"

He looked me over unhurriedly. "Tarzan on a big red scooter," he said.

"What?"

"You. Marlowe. Tarzan on a big red scooter. They rough you up much?"

"Here and there. What makes it your business?"

"After Allbright talked to Gregorius?"

"No. Not after that."

He nodded shortly. "You got a crust asking Allbright to use ammunition on that slob."

"I asked you what made it your business. Incidentally I don't know Commissioner Allbright and I didn't ask him to do anything. Why would he do anything for me?"

He stared at me morosely. He stood up slowly, graceful as a panther. He walked across the room and looked into my office. He jerked his head at me and went in. He was a guy who owned the place where he happened to be. I went in after him and shut the door. He stood by the desk looking around, amused.

"You're small time," he said. "Very small time."

I went behind my desk and waited.

"How much you make in a month, Marlowe?"

I let it ride, and lit my pipe.

"Seven-fifty would be tops," he said.

I dropped a burnt match into a tray and puffed tobacco smoke.

"You're a piker, Marlowe. You're a peanut grifter. You're so little it takes a magnifying glass to see you."

I didn't say anything at all.

"You got cheap emotions. You're cheap all over. You pal around with a guy, eat a few drinks, talk a few gags, slip him a little dough when he's strapped, and you're sold out to him. Just like some school kid that read *Frank Merriwell*. You got no guts, no brains, no connections, no savvy, so you throw out a phony attitude and expect people to cry over you. Tarzan on a big red scooter." He smiled a small weary smile. "In my book you're a nickel's worth of nothing."

He leaned across the desk and flicked me across the face backhanded, casually and contemptuously, not meaning to hurt me, and the small smile stayed on his face. Then when I didn't even move for that he sat down slowly and leaned an elbow on the desk and cupped his brown chin in his brown hand. The bird-bright eyes stared at me without anything in them but brightness.

"Know who I am, cheapie?"

"Your name's Menendez. The boys call you Mendy. You operate on the Strip."

"Yeah? How did I get so big?"

"I wouldn't know. You probably started out as a pimp in a Mexican whorehouse."

He took a gold cigarette case out of his pocket and lit a brown cigarette with a gold lighter. He blew acrid smoke and nodded. He put the gold cigarette case on the desk and caressed it with his fingertips.

"I'm a big bad man, Marlowe. I make lots of dough. I got to make lots of dough to juice the guys I got to juice in order to make lots of dough to juice the guys I got to juice. I got a place in Bel-Air that cost ninety grand and I already spent more than that to fix it up. I got a lovely platinum-blond wife and two kids in private schools back east. My wife's got a hundred and fifty grand in rocks and another seventy-five in furs and clothes. I got a butler, two maids, a

cook, a chauffeur, not counting the monkey that walks behind me. Everywhere I go I'm a darling. The best of everything, the best food, the best drinks, the best hotel suites. I
got a place in Florida and a seagoing yacht with a crew of five
men. I got a Bentley, two Cadillacs, a Chrysler station wagon,
and an MG for my boy. Couple of years my girl gets one too.
What you got?"

"Not much," I said. "This year I have a house to live in—
all to myself."

"No woman?"

"Just me. In addition to that I have what you see here and
twelve hundred dollars in the bank and a few thousand in
bonds. That answer your question?"

"What's the most you ever made on a single job?"

"Eight-fifty."

"Jesus, how cheap can a guy get?"

"Stop hamming and tell me what you want."

He killed his cigarette half smoked and immediately lit
another. He leaned back in his chair. His lip curled at me.

"We were three guys in a foxhole eating," he said. "It was
cold as hell, snow all around. We eat out of cans. Cold food.
A little shelling, more mortar fire. We are blue with the cold,
and I mean blue, Randy Starr and me and this Terry Lennox.
A mortar shell plops right in the middle of us and for some
reason it don't go off. Those jerries have a lot of tricks. They
got a twisted sense of humor. Sometimes you think it's a dud
and three seconds later it ain't a dud. Terry grabs it and he's
out of the foxhole before Randy and me can even start to get
unstuck. But I mean quick, brother. Like a good ball handler.
He throws himself face down and throws the thing away from
him and it goes off in the air. Most of it goes over his head
but a hunk gets the side of his face. Right then the krauts
mount an attack and the next thing we know we ain't there
any more."

Menendez stopped talking and gave me the bright steady
glare of his dark eyes.

"Thanks for telling me," I said.

"You take a good ribbing, Marlowe. You're okay. Randy
and me talked things over and we decided that what happened to Terry Lennox was enough to screw up any guy's

brains. For a long time we figured he was dead but he wasn't. The krauts got him. They worked him over for about a year and a half. They did a good job but they hurt him too much. It cost us money to find out, and it cost us money to find him. But we made plenty in the black market after the war. We could afford it. All Terry gets out of saving our lives is half of a new face, white hair, and a bad case of nerves. Back east he hits the bottle, gets picked up here and there, kind of goes to pieces. There's something on his mind but we never know what. The next thing we know he's married to this rich dame and riding high. He unmarries her, hits bottom again, marries her again, and she gets dead. Randy and me can't do a thing for him. He won't let us except for that short job in Vegas. And when he gets in a real jam he don't come to us, he goes to a cheapie like you, a guy that cops can push around. So then *he* gets dead, and without telling us goodbye, and without giving us a chance to pay off. I got connections in Mexico that could have buried him forever. I could have got him out of the country faster than a card sharp can stack a deck. But he goes crying to you. It makes me sore. A cheapie, a guy cops can push around."

"The cops can push anybody around. What do you want me to do about it?"

"Just lay off," Menendez said tightly.

"Lay off what?"

"Trying to make yourself dough or publicity out of the Lennox case. It's finished, wrapped up. Terry's dead and we don't want him bothered any more. The guy suffered too much."

"A hoodlum with sentiment," I said. "That slays me."

"Watch your lip, cheapie. Watch your lip. Mendy Menendez don't argue with guys. He tells them. Find yourself another way to grab a buck. Get me?"

He stood up. The interview was finished. He picked up his gloves. They were snow-white pigskin. They didn't look as if he ever had them on. A dressy type, Mr. Menendez. But very tough behind it all.

"I'm not looking for publicity," I said. "And nobody's offered me any dough. Why would they and for what?"

"Don't kid me, Marlowe. You didn't spend three days in

the freezer just because you're a sweetheart. You got paid off. I ain't saying who by but I got a notion. And the party I'm thinking about has plenty more of the stuff. The Lennox case is closed and it stays closed even if—" He stopped dead and flipped his gloves at the desk edge.

"Even if Terry didn't kill her," I said.

His surprise was as thin as the gold on a weekend wedding ring. "I'd like to go along with you on that, cheapie. But it don't make any sense. But if it did make sense—and Terry wanted it the way it is—then that's how it stays."

I didn't say anything. After a moment he grinned slowly. "Tarzan on a big red scooter," he drawled. "A tough guy. Lets me come in here and walk all over him. A guy that gets hired for nickels and dimes and gets pushed around by anybody. No dough, no family, no prospects, no nothing. See you around, cheapie."

I sat still with my jaws clamped, staring at the glitter of his gold cigarette case on the desk corner. I felt old and tired. I got up slowly and reached for the case.

"You forgot this," I said, going around the desk.

"I got half a dozen of them," he sneered.

When I was near enough to him I held it out. His hand reached for it casually. "How about half a dozen of these?" I asked him and hit him as hard as I could in the middle of his belly.

He doubled up mewling. The cigarette case fell to the floor. He backed against the wall and his hands jerked back and forth convulsively. His breath fought to get into his lungs. He was sweating. Very slowly and with an intense effort he straightened up and we were eye to eye again. I reached out and ran a finger along the bone of his jaw. He held still for it. Finally he worked a smile onto his brown face.

"I didn't think you had it in you," he said.

"Next time bring a gun—or don't call me cheapie."

"I got a guy to carry the gun."

"Bring him with you. You'll need him."

"You're a hard guy to get sore, Marlowe."

I moved the gold cigarette case to one side with my foot and bent and picked it up and handed it to him. He took it and dropped it into his pocket.

"I couldn't figure you," I said. "Why it was worth your time to come up here and ride me. Then it got monotonous. All tough guys are monotonous. Like playing cards with a deck that's all aces. You've got everything and you've got nothing. You're just sitting there looking at yourself. No wonder Terry didn't come to you for help. It would be like borrowing money from a whore."

He pressed delicately on his stomach with two fingers. "I'm sorry you said that, cheapie. You could crack wise once too often."

He walked to the door and opened it. Outside the bodyguard straightened from the opposite wall and turned. Menendez jerked his head. The bodyguard came into the office and stood there looking me over without expression.

"Take a good look at him, Chick," Menendez said. "Make sure you know him just in case. You and him might have business one of these days."

"I already saw him, Chief," the smooth dark tight-lipped guy said in the tight-lipped voice they all affect. "He wouldn't bother me none."

"Don't let him hit you in the guts," Menendez said with a sour grin. "His right hook ain't funny."

The bodyguard just sneered at me. "He wouldn't get that close."

"Well, so long, cheapie," Menendez told me and went out.

"See you around," the bodyguard told me coolly. "The name's Chick Agostino. I guess you'll know me."

"Like a dirty newspaper," I said. "Remind me not to step on your face."

His jaw muscles bulged. Then he turned suddenly and went out after his boss.

The door closed slowly on the pneumatic gadget. I listened but I didn't hear their steps going down the hall. They walked as softly as cats. Just to make sure, I opened the door again after a minute and looked out. But the hall was quite empty.

I went back to my desk and sat down and spent a little time wondering why a fairly important local racketeer like Menendez would think it worth his time to come in person to my office and warn me to keep my nose clean, just minutes after I had received a similar though differently expressed warning from Sewell Endicott.

I didn't get anywhere with that, so I thought I might as well make it a perfect score. I lifted the phone and put in a call to the Terrapin Club at Las Vegas, person to person, Philip Marlowe calling Mr. Randy Starr. No soap. Mr. Starr was out of town, and would I talk to anyone else? I would not. I didn't even want to talk to Starr very badly. It was just a passing fancy. He was too far away to hit me.

After that nothing happened for three days. Nobody slugged me or shot at me or called me up on the phone and warned me to keep my nose clean. Nobody hired me to find the wandering daughter, the erring wife, the lost pearl necklace, or the missing will. I just sat there and looked at the wall. The Lennox case died almost as suddenly as it had been born. There was a brief inquest to which I was not summoned. It was held at an odd hour, without previous announcement and without a jury. The coroner entered his own verdict, which was that the death of Sylvia Potter Westerheym di Giorgio Lennox had been caused with homicidal intent by her husband, Terence William Lennox, since deceased outside the jurisdiction of the coroner's office. Presumably a confession was read into the record. Presumably it was verified enough to satisfy the coroner.

The body was released for burial. It was flown north and buried in the family vault. The press was not invited. Nobody gave any interviews, least of all Mr. Harlan Potter, who never gave interviews. He was about as hard to see as the Dalai Lama. Guys with a hundred million dollars live a peculiar life, behind a screen of servants, bodyguards, secretaries, lawyers, and tame executives. Presumably they eat, sleep, get their hair cut, and wear clothes. But you never know for sure. Everything you read or hear about them has been processed by a public relations gang of guys who are paid big money to create and maintain a usable personality, something simple and clean and sharp, like a sterilized needle. It doesn't have to be true. It just has to be consistent with the known facts, and the known facts you could count on your fingers.

Late afternoon of the third day the telephone rang and I

was talking to a man who said his name was Howard Spencer, that he was a representative of a New York publishing house in California on a brief business trip, that he had a problem he would like to discuss with me and would I meet him in the bar of the Ritz-Beverly Hotel at eleven A.M. the next morning.

I asked him what sort of problem.

"Rather a delicate one," he said, "but entirely ethical. If we don't agree, I shall expect to pay you for your time, naturally."

"Thank you, Mr. Spencer, but that won't be necessary. Did someone I know recommend me to you?"

"Someone who knows about you—including your recent brush with the law, Mr. Marlowe. I might say that that was what interested me. My business, however, has nothing to do with that tragic affair. It's just that—well, let's discuss it over a drink, rather than over the telephone."

"You sure you want to mix it with a guy who has been in the cooler?"

He laughed. His laugh and his voice were both pleasant. He talked the way New Yorkers used to talk before they learned to talk Flatbush.

"From my point of view, Mr. Marlowe, that is a recommendation. Not, let me add, the fact that you were, as you put it, in the cooler, but the fact, shall I say, that you appear to be extremely reticent, even under pressure."

He was a guy who talked with commas, like a heavy novel. Over the phone anyway.

"Okay, Mr. Spencer, I'll be there in the morning."

He thanked me and hung up. I wondered who could have given me the plug. I thought it might be Sewell Endicott and called him to find out. But he had been out of town all week, and still was. It didn't matter much. Even in my business you occasionally get a satisfied customer. And I needed a job because I needed the money—or thought I did, until I got home that night and found the letter with a portrait of Madison in it.

## 12

The letter was in the red and white birdhouse mailbox at the foot of my steps. A woodpecker on top of the box attached to the swing arm was raised and even at that I might not have looked inside because I never got mail at the house. But the woodpecker had lost the point of his beak quite recently. The wood was fresh broken. Some smart kid shooting off his atom gun.

The letter had Correo Aéreo on it and a flock of Mexican stamps and writing that I might or might not have recognized if Mexico hadn't been on my mind pretty constantly lately. I couldn't read the postmark. It was hand-stamped and the ink pad was pretty far gone. The letter was thick. I climbed my steps and sat down in the living room to read it. The evening seemed very silent. Perhaps a letter from a dead man brings its own silence with it.

It began without date and without preamble.

I'm sitting beside a second-floor window in a room in a not too clean hotel in a town called Otatoclán, a mountain town with a lake. There's a mailbox just below the window and when the mozo comes in with some coffee I've ordered he is going to mail the letter for me and hold it up so that I can see it before he puts it in the slot. When he does that he gets a hundred-peso note, which is a hell of a lot of money for him.

Why all the finagling? There's a swarthy character with pointed shoes and a dirty shirt outside the door watching it. He's waiting for something, I don't know what, but he won't let me out. It doesn't matter too much as long as the letter gets posted. I want you to have this money because I don't need it and the local gendarmerie would swipe it for sure. It is not intended to buy anything. Call it an apology for making you so much trouble and a token of esteem for a pretty decent guy. I've done everything wrong as usual, but I still have the gun. My hunch is that you have probably made up your mind on a certain point. I might have killed her and perhaps I did, but I never could have done the other thing. That kind of brutality is not in my line. So something is very sour. But it doesn't matter, not in the least. The main thing now is to save an unnecessary and useless scandal. Her father and her sister never did me any harm. They have their lives to live and I'm up to here in disgust with mine. Sylvia didn't make a bum out of me, I was one already. I can't give you any very clear answer about why she married me. I suppose it was just a whim. At least she died young and beautiful. They say lust makes a man old, but keeps a woman young. They say a lot of nonsense. They say the rich can always protect themselves and that in their world it is always summer. I've lived with them and they are bored and lonely people.

I have written a confession. I feel a little sick and more than a little scared. You read about these situations in books, but you don't read the truth. When it happens to you, when all you have left is the gun in your pocket, when you are cornered in a dirty little hotel in a strange country, and have only one way out—believe me, pal, there is nothing elevating or dramatic about it. It is just plain nasty and sordid and gray and grim.

So forget it and me. But first drink a gimlet for me at Victor's. And the next time you make coffee, pour me a cup and put some bourbon in it and light me a cigarette and put it beside the cup. And after that forget the whole thing. Terry Lennox over and out. And so goodbye.

A knock at the door. I guess it will be the mozo with the coffee. If it isn't, there will be some shooting. I like Mexicans, as a rule, but I don't like their jails. So long.

TERRY

That was all. I refolded the letter and put it back in the envelope. It had been the mozo with the coffee all right. Otherwise I would never have had the letter. Not with a portrait of Madison in it. A portrait of Madison is a $5000 bill.

It lay in front of me green and crisp on the table top. I had never even seen one before. Lots of people who work in banks haven't either. Very likely characters like Randy Starr and Menendez wear them for folding money. If you went to a bank and asked for one, they wouldn't have it. They'd have to get it for you from the Federal Reserve. It might take several days. There are only about a thousand of them in circulation in the whole U.S.A. Mine had a nice glow around it. It created a little private sunshine all its own.

I sat there and looked at it for a long time. At last I put it away in my letter case and went out to the kitchen to make that coffee. I did what he asked me to, sentimental or not. I poured two cups and added some bourbon to his and set it down on the side of the table where he had sat the morning I

took him to the plane. I lit a cigarette for him and set it in an
ash tray beside the cup. I watched the steam rise from the
coffee and the thin thread of smoke rise from the cigarette.
Outside in the tecoma a bird was gussing around, talking to
himself in low chirps, with an occasional brief flutter of wings.

Then the coffee didn't steam any more and the cigarette
stopped smoking and was just a dead butt on the edge of an
ash tray. I dropped it into the garbage can under the sink. I
poured the coffee out and washed the cup and put it away.

That was that. It didn't seem quite enough to do for five
thousand dollars.

I went to a late movie after a while. It meant nothing. I
hardly saw what went on. It was just noise and big faces.
When I got home again I set out a very dull Ruy Lopez and
that didn't mean anything either. So I went to bed.

But not to sleep. At three A.M. I was walking the floor and
listening to Khachaturyan working in a tractor factory. He
called it a violin concerto. I called it a loose fan belt and
the hell with it.

A white night for me is as rare as a fat postman. If it hadn't
been for Mr. Howard Spencer at the Ritz-Beverly I would
have killed a bottle and knocked myself out. And the next
time I saw a polite character drunk in a Rolls-Royce Silver
Wraith, I would depart rapidly in several directions. There is
no trap so deadly as the trap you set for yourself.

# 13

At eleven o'clock I was sitting in the third booth on the right-
hand side as you go in from the dining-room annex. I had my
back against the wall and I could see anyone who came in or
went out. It was a clear morning, no smog, no high fog even,
and the sun dazzled the surface of the swimming pool which
began just outside the plate-glass wall of the bar and stretched
to the far end of the dining room. A girl in a white sharkskin
suit and a luscious figure was climbing the ladder to the high
board. I watched the band of white that showed between the

tan of her thighs and the suit. I watched it carnally. Then she was out of sight, cut off by the deep overhang of the roof. A moment later I saw her flash down in a one and a half. Spray came high enough to catch the sun and make rainbows that were almost as pretty as the girl. Then she came up the ladder and unstrapped her white helmet and shook her bleach job loose. She wobbled her bottom over to a small white table and sat down beside a lumberjack in white drill pants and dark glasses and a tan so evenly dark that he couldn't have been anything but the hired man around the pool. He reached over and patted her thigh. She opened a mouth like a firebucket and laughed. That terminated my interest in her. I couldn't hear the laugh but the hole in her face when she unzipped her teeth was all I needed.

The bar was pretty empty. Three booths down a couple of sharpies were selling each other pieces of Twentieth Century—Fox, using double-arm gestures instead of money. They had a telephone on the table between them and every two or three minutes they would play the match game to see who called Zanuck with a hot idea. They were young, dark, eager and full of vitality. They put as much muscular activity into a telephone conversation as I would put into carrying a fat man up four flights of stairs.

There was a sad fellow over on a bar stool talking to the bartender, who was polishing a glass and listening with that plastic smile people wear when they are trying not to scream. The customer was middle-aged, handsomely dressed, and drunk. He wanted to talk and he couldn't have stopped even if he hadn't really wanted to talk. He was polite and friendly and when I heard him he didn't seem to slur his words much, but you knew that he got up on the bottle and only let go of it when he fell asleep at night. He would be like that for the rest of his life and that was what his life was. You would never know how he got that way because even if he told you it would not be the truth. At the very best a distorted memory of the truth as he knew it. There is a sad man like that in every quiet bar in the world.

I looked at my watch and this high-powered publisher man was already twenty minutes late. I would wait half an hour and then I would leave. It never pays to let the customer make all the rules. If he can push you around, he will assume other people can too, and that is not what he hires you for. And right now I didn't need the work badly enough to let some fathead from back east use me for a horse-holder, some executive character in a paneled office on the eighty-fifth floor, with a row of pushbuttons and an intercom and a secretary in a Hattie Carnegie Career Girl's Special and a pair of those big beautiful promising eyes. This was the kind of operator who would tell you to be there at nine sharp and if you weren't sitting quietly with a pleased smile on your pan when he floated in two hours later on a double Gibson, he would have a paroxysm of outraged executive ability which would necessitate five weeks at Acapulco before he got back the hop on his high hard one.

The old bar waiter came drifting by and glanced softly at my weak Scotch and water. I shook my head and he bobbed his white thatch, and right then a dream walked in. It seemed to me for an instant that there was no sound in the bar, that the sharpies stopped sharping and the drunk on the stool stopped burbling away, and it was like just after the conductor taps on his music stand and raises his arms and holds them poised.

She was slim and quite tall in a white linen tailormade with a black and white polka-dotted scarf around her throat. Her hair was the pale gold of a fairy princess. There was a small hat on it into which the pale gold hair nestled like a bird in its nest. Her eyes were cornflower blue, a rare color, and the lashes were long and almost too pale. She reached the table across the way and was pulling off a white gauntleted glove and the old waiter had the table pulled out in a way no waiter ever will pull a table out for me. She sat down and slipped the gloves under the strap of her bag and thanked him with a smile so gentle, so exquisitely pure, that he was damn near paralyzed by it. She said something to him in a very low voice. He hurried away, bending forward. There was a guy who really had a mission in life.

I stared. She caught me staring. She lifted her glance half an inch and I wasn't there any more. But wherever I was I was holding my breath.

There are blondes and blondes and it is almost a joke word

nowadays. All blondes have their points, except perhaps the metallic ones who are as blond as a Zulu under the bleach and as to disposition as soft as a sidewalk. There is the small cute blonde who cheeps and twitters, and the big statuesque blonde who straight-arms you with an ice-blue glare. There is the blonde who gives you the up-from-under look and smells lovely and shimmers and hangs on your arm and is always very very tired when you take her home. She makes that help-less gesture and has that goddamned headache and you would like to slug her except that you are glad you found out about the headache before you invested too much time and money and hope in her. Because the headache will always be there, a weapon that never wears out and is as deadly as the bravo's rapier or Lucrezia's poison vial.

There is the soft and willing and alcoholic blonde who doesn't care what she wears as long as it is mink or where she goes as long as it is the Starlight Roof and there is plenty of dry champagne. There is the small perky blonde who is a little pal and wants to pay her own way and is full of sunshine and common sense and knows judo from the ground up and can toss a truck driver over her shoulder without missing more than one sentence out of the editorial in the *Saturday Review*. There is the pale, pale blonde with anemia of some non-fatal but incurable type. She is very languid and very shadowy and she speaks softly out of nowhere and you can't lay a finger on her because in the first place you don't want to and in the second place she is reading *The Waste Land* or Dante in the original, or Kafka or Kierkegaard or studying Provençal. She adores music and when the New York Philharmonic is playing Hindemith she can tell you which one of the six bass viols came in a quarter of a beat too late. I hear Toscanini can also. That makes two of them.

And lastly there is the gorgeous show piece who will outlast three kingpin racketeers and then marry a couple of million-aires at a million a head and end up with a pale rose villa at Cap Antibes, an Alfa-Romeo town car complete with pilot and co-pilot, and a stable of shopworn aristocrats, all of whom she will treat with the affectionate absent-mindedness of an elderly duke saying goodnight to his butler.

The dream across the way was none of these, not even of

that kind of world. She was unclassifiable, as remote and clear as mountain water, as elusive as its color. I was still staring when a voice close to my elbow said:

"I'm shockingly late. I apologize. You must blame it on this. My name's Howard Spencer. You're Marlowe, of course."

I turned my head and looked at him. He was middle-aged, rather plump, dressed as if he didn't give any thought to it, but well shaved and with thin hair smoothed back carefully over a head that was wide between the ears. He wore a flashy double-breasted vest, the sort of thing you hardly ever see in California except perhaps on a visiting Bostonian. His glasses were rimless and he was patting a shabby old dog of a briefcase which was evidently the "this."

"Three brand new book-length manuscripts. Fiction. It would be embarrassing to lose them before we have a chance to reject them." He made a signal to the old waiter who had just stepped back from placing a tall green something or other in front of the dream. "I have a weakness for gin and orange. A silly sort of drink really. Will you join me? Good."

I nodded and the old waiter drifted away.

Pointing to the briefcase I said: "How do you know you are going to reject them?"

"If they were any good, they wouldn't be dropped at my hotel by the writers in person. Some New York agent would have them."

"Then why take them at all?"

"Partly not to hurt feelings. Partly the thousand-to-one chance all publishers live for. But mostly you're at a cocktail party and get introduced to all sorts of people, and some of them have novels written and you are just liquored up enough to be benevolent and full of love for the human race, so you say you'd love to see the script. It is then dropped at your hotel with such sickening speed that you are forced to go through the motions of reading it. But I don't suppose you are much interested in publishers and their problems."

The waiter brought the drinks. Spencer grabbed for his and took a healthy swig. He wasn't noticing the golden girl across the way. I had all his attention. He was a good contact man.

"If it's part of the job," I said. "I can read a book once in a while."

"One of our most important authors lives around here," he said casually. "Maybe you've read his stuff. Roger Wade."

"Uh-huh."

"I see your point." He smiled sadly. "You don't care for historical romances. But they sell brutally."

"I don't have any point, Mr. Spencer. I looked at one of his books once. I thought it was tripe. Is that the wrong thing for me to say?"

He grinned. "Oh no. There are many people who agree with you. But the point is at the moment that he's an automatic best seller. And every publisher has to have a couple with the way costs are now."

I looked across at the golden girl. She had finished her limeade or whatever it was and was glancing at a microscopic wrist watch. The bar was filling up a little, but not yet noisy. The two sharpies were still waving their hands and the solo drinker on the bar stool had a couple of pals with him. I looked back at Howard Spencer.

"Something to do with your problem?" I asked him. "This fellow Wade, I mean."

He nodded. He was giving me a careful once over. "Tell me a little about yourself, Mr. Marlowe. That is, if you don't find the request objectionable."

"What sort of thing? I'm a licensed private investigator and have been for quite a while. I'm a lone wolf, unmarried, getting middle-aged, and not rich. I've been in jail more than once and I don't do divorce business. I like liquor and women and chess and a few other things. The cops don't like me too well, but I know a couple I get along with. I'm a native son, born in Santa Rosa, both parents dead, no brothers or sisters, and when I get knocked off in a dark alley sometime, if it happens, as it could to anyone in my business, and to plenty of people in any business or no business at all these days, nobody will feel that the bottom has dropped out of his or her life."

"I see," he said. "But all that doesn't exactly tell me what I want to know."

I finished the gin and orange. I didn't like it. I grinned at him. "I left out one item, Mr. Spencer. I have a portrait of Madison in my pocket."

"A portrait of Madison? I'm afraid I don't—"

"A five-thousand-dollar bill," I said. "Always carry it. My lucky piece."

"Good God," he said in a hushed voice. "Isn't that terribly dangerous?"

"Who was it said that beyond a certain point all dangers are equal?"

"I think it was Walter Bagehot. He was talking about a steeplejack." Then he grinned. "Sorry, but I *am* a publisher. You're all right, Marlowe. I'll take a chance on you. If I didn't you would tell me to go to hell. Right?"

I grinned back at him. He called the waiter and ordered another pair of drinks.

"Here it is," he said carefully. "We are in bad trouble over Roger Wade. He can't finish a book. He's losing his grip and there's something behind it. The man seems to be going to pieces. Wild fits of drinking and temper. Every once in a while he disappears for days on end. Not very long ago he threw his wife downstairs and put her in the hospital with five broken ribs. There's no trouble between them in the usual sense, none at all. The man just goes nuts when he drinks." Spencer leaned back and looked at me gloomily. "We have to have that book finished. We need it badly. To a certain extent my job depends on it. But we need more than that. We want to save a very able writer who is capable of much better things than he has ever done. Something is very wrong. This trip he won't even see me. I realize this sounds like a job for a psychiatrist. Mrs. Wade disagrees. She is convinced that he is perfectly sane but that something is worrying him to death. A blackmailer, for instance. The Wades have been married five years. Something from his past may have caught up with him. It might even be—just as a wild guess—a fatal hit-and-run accident and someone has the goods on him. We don't know what it is. We want to know. And we are willing to pay well to correct the trouble. If it turns out to be a medical matter, well—that's that. If not, there has to be an answer. And in the meantime Mrs. Wade has to be protected. He might kill her the next time. You never know."

The second round of drinks came. I left mine untouched and watched him gobble half of his in one swallow. I lit a cigarette and just stared at him.

"You don't want a detective," I said. "You want a magician. What the hell could I do? If I happened to be there at exactly the right time, and if he isn't too tough for me to handle, I might knock him out and put him to bed. But I'd have to *be* there. It's a hundred to one against. You know that."

"He's about your size," Spencer said, "but he's not in your condition. And you could be there all the time."

"Hardly. And drunks are cunning. He'd be certain to pick a time when I wasn't around to throw his wingding. I'm not in the market for a job as a male nurse."

"A male nurse wouldn't be any use. Roger Wade is not the kind of man to accept one. He is a very talented guy who has been jarred loose from his self-control. He has made too much money writing junk for halfwits. But the only salvation for a writer is to write. If there is anything good in him, it will come out."

"Okay, I'm sold on him," I said wearily. "He's terrific. Also he's damn dangerous. He has a guilty secret and he tries to drown it in alcohol. It's not my kind of problem, Mr. Spencer."

"I see." He looked at his wrist watch with a worried frown that knotted his face and made it look older and smaller. "Well, you can't blame me for trying."

He reached for his fat briefcase. I looked across at the golden girl. She was getting ready to leave. The white-haired waiter was hovering over her with the check. She gave him some money and a lovely smile and he looked as if he had shaken hands with God. She touched up her lips and put her white gauntlets on and the waiter pulled the table halfway across the room for her to stroll out.

I glanced at Spencer. He was frowning down at the empty glass on the table edge. He had the briefcase on his knees.

"Look," I said. "I'll go see the man and try to size him up, if you want me to. I'll talk to his wife. But my guess is he'll throw me out of the house."

A voice that was not Spencer's said: "No, Mr. Marlowe, I

don't think he would do that. On the contrary I think he might like you."

I looked up into the pair of violet eyes. She was standing at the end of the table. I got up and canted myself against the back of the booth in that awkward way you have to stand when you can't slide out.

"Please don't get up," she said in a voice like the stuff they use to line summer clouds with. "I know I owe you an apology, but it seemed important for me to have a chance to observe you before I introduced myself. I am Eileen Wade."

Spencer said grumpily: "He's not interested, Eileen."

She smiled gently. "I disagree."

I pulled myself together. I had been standing there off balance with my mouth open and me breathing through it like a sweet girl graduate. This was really a dish. Seen close up she was almost paralyzing.

"I didn't say I wasn't interested, Mrs. Wade. What I said or meant to say was that I didn't think I could do any good, and it might be a hell of a mistake for me to try. It might do a lot of harm."

She was very serious now. The smile had gone. "You are deciding too soon. You can't judge people by what they do. If you judge them at all, it must be by what they are."

I nodded vaguely. Because that was exactly the way I had thought about Terry Lennox. On the facts he was no bargain, except for that one brief flash of glory in the foxhole—if Menendez told the truth about that—but the facts didn't tell the whole story by any means. He had been a man it was impossible to dislike. How many do you meet in a lifetime that you can say that about?

"And you have to know them for that," she added gently. "Goodbye, Mr. Marlowe. If you should change your mind—" She opened her bag quickly and gave me a card— "and thank you for being here."

She nodded to Spencer and walked away. I watched her out of the bar, down the glassed-in annex to the dining room. She carried herself beautifully. I watched her turn under the archway that led to the lobby. I saw the last flicker of her white linen skirt as she turned the corner. Then I eased myself down into the booth and grabbed the gin and orange.

Spencer was watching me. There was something hard in his eyes.

"Nice work," I said, "but you ought to have looked at her once in a while. A dream like that doesn't sit across the room from you for twenty minutes without your even noticing."

"Stupid of me, wasn't it?" He was trying to smile, but he didn't really want to. He didn't like the way I had looked at her. "People have such queer ideas about private detectives. When you think of having one in your home—"

"Don't think of having this one in your home," I said. "Anyhow, think up another story first. You can do better than trying to make me believe anybody, drunk or sober, would throw that gorgeous downstairs and break five ribs for her."

He reddened. His hands tightened on the briefcase. "You think I'm a liar?"

"What's the difference? You've made your play. You're a little hot for the lady yourself, maybe."

He stood up suddenly. "I don't like your tone," he said. "I'm not sure I like *you*. Do me a favor and forget the whole idea. I think this ought to pay you for your time."

He threw a twenty on the table, and then added some ones for the waiter. He stood a moment staring down at me. His eyes were bright and his face was still red. "I'm married and have four children," he said abruptly.

"Congratulations."

He made a swift noise in his throat and turned and went. He went pretty fast. I watched him for a while and then I didn't. I drank the rest of my drink and got out my cigarettes and shook one loose and stuck it in my mouth and lit it. The old waiter came up and looked at the money.

"Can I get you anything else, sir?"

"Nope. The dough is all yours."

He picked it up slowly. "This is a twenty-dollar bill, sir. The gentleman made a mistake."

"He can read. The dough is all yours, I said."

"I'm sure I'm very grateful. If you are quite sure, sir—"

"Quite sure."

He bobbed his head and went away, still looking worried. The bar was filling up. A couple of streamlined demi-virgins went by caroling and waving. They knew the two hotshots in the booth farther on. The air began to be spattered with darlings and crimson fingernails.

I smoked half of my cigarette, scowling at nothing, and then got up to leave. I turned to reach back for my cigarettes and something bumped into me hard from behind. It was just what I needed. I swung around and I was looking at the profile of a broad-beamed crowd-pleaser in an overdraped Oxford flannel. He had the outstretched arm of the popular character and the two-by-six grin of the guy who never loses a sale.

I took hold of the outstretched arm and spun him around. "What's the matter, Jack? Don't they make the aisles wide enough for your personality?"

He shook his arm loose and got tough. "Don't get fancy, buster. I might loosen your jaw for you."

"Ha, ha," I said. "You might play center field for the Yankees and hit a home run with a breadstick."

He doubled a meaty fist.

"Darling, think of your manicure," I told him.

He controlled his emotions. "Nuts to you, wise guy," he sneered. "Some other time, when I have less on my mind."

"Could there be less?"

"G'wan, beat it," he snarled. "One more crack and you'll need new bridgework."

I grinned at him. "Call me up, Jack. But with better dialogue."

His expression changed. He laughed. "You in pictures, chum?"

"Only the kind they pin up in the post office."

"See you in the mug book," he said, and walked away, still grinning.

It was all very silly, but it got rid of the feeling. I went along the annex and across the lobby of the hotel to the main entrance. I paused inside to put on my sunglasses. It wasn't until I got into my car that I remembered to look at the card Eileen Wade had given me. It was an engraved card, but not a formal calling card, because it had an address and a telephone number on it. Mrs. Roger Stearns Wade, 1247 Idle Valley Road. Tel. Idle Valley 5-6324.

I knew a good deal about Idle Valley, and I knew it had

changed a great deal from the days when they had the gate-house at the entrance and the private police force, and the gambling casino on the lake, and the fifty-dollar joy girls. Quiet money had taken over the tract after the casino was closed out. Quiet money had made it a subdivider's dream. A club owned the lake and the lake frontage and if they didn't want you in the club, you didn't get to play in the water. It was exclusive in the only remaining sense of the word that doesn't mean merely expensive.

I belonged in Idle Valley like a pearl onion on a banana split.

Howard Spencer called me up late in the afternoon. He had got over his mad and wanted to say he was sorry and he hadn't handled the situation very well, and had I perhaps any second thoughts.

"I'll go see him if he asks me to. Not otherwise."

"I see. There would be a substantial bonus—"

"Look, Mr. Spencer," I said impatiently, "you can't hire destiny. If Mrs. Wade is afraid of the guy, she can move out. That's *her* problem. Nobody could protect her twenty-four hours a day from her own husband. There isn't that much protection in the world. But that's not all you want. You want to know why and how and when the guy jumped the rails, and then fix it so that he doesn't do it again—at least until he finishes that book. And that's up to him. If he wants to write the damn book bad enough, he'll lay off the hooch until he does it. You want too damn much."

"They all go together," he said. "It's all one problem. But I guess I understand. It's a little oversubtle for your kind of operation. Well, goodbye. I'm flying back to New York tonight."

"Have a smooth trip."

He thanked me and hung up. I forgot to tell him I had given his twenty to the waiter. I thought of calling back to tell him, then I thought he was miserable enough already.

I closed the office and started off in the direction of Victor's to drink a gimlet, as Terry had asked me to in his letter. I changed my mind. I wasn't feeling sentimental enough. I went to Lowry's and had a martini and some prime ribs and Yorkshire pudding instead.

When I got home I turned on the TV set and looked at the fights. They were no good, just a bunch of dancing masters who ought to have been working for Arthur Murray. All they did was jab and bob up and down and feint one another off balance. Not one of them could hit hard enough to wake his grandmother out of a light doze. The crowd was booing and the referee kept clapping his hands for action, but they went right on swaying and jittering and jabbing long lefts. I turned to another channel and looked at a crime show. The action took place in a clothes closet and the faces were tired and over familiar and not beautiful. The dialogue was stuff even Mono-gram wouldn't have used. The dick had a colored houseboy for comic relief. He didn't need it, he was plenty comical all by himself. And the commercials would have sickened a goat raised on barbed wire and broken beer bottles.

I cut it off and smoked a long cool tightly packed cigarette. It was kind to my throat. It was made of fine tobacco. I forgot to notice what brand it was. I was about ready to hit the hay when Detective-Sergeant Green of homicide called me up.

"Thought you might like to know they buried your friend Lennox a couple of days ago right in that Mexican town where he died. A lawyer representing the family went down there and attended to it. You were pretty lucky this time, Marlowe. Next time you think of helping a pal skip the country, don't."

"How many bullet holes did he have in him?"

"What's that?" he barked. Then he was silent for a space. Then he said rather too carefully: "One, I should say. It's usually enough when it blows a guy's head off. The lawyer is bringing back a set of prints and whatever was in his pockets. Anything more you'd like to know?"

"Yeah, but you can't tell me. I'd like to know who killed Lennox's wife."

"Cripes, didn't Grenz tell you he left a full confession? It was in the papers, anyway. Don't you read the papers any more?"

"Thanks for calling me, Sergeant. It was real kind of you."

"Look, Marlowe," he said raspingly. "You got any funny ideas about this case, you could buy yourself a lot of grief talking about them. The case is closed, finalized, and laid away in mothballs. Damn lucky for you it is. Accessory after the fact is good for five years in this state. And let me tell you something else. I've been a cop a long time and one thing I've learned for sure is it ain't always what you do that gets you sent up. It's what it can be made to look like when it comes in to court. Goodnight."

He hung up in my ear. I replaced the phone thinking that an honest cop with a bad conscience always acts tough. So does a dishonest cop. So does almost anyone, including me.

# 14

Next morning the bell rang as I was wiping the talcum off an earlobe. When I got to the door and opened up I looked into a pair of violet-blue eyes. She was in brown linen this time, with a pimento-colored scarf, and no earrings or hat. She looked a little pale, but not as though anyone had been throwing her downstairs. She gave me a hesitant little smile.

"I know I shouldn't have come here to bother you, Mr. Marlowe. You probably haven't even had breakfast. But I had a reluctance to go to your office and I hate telephoning about personal matters."

"Sure. Come in, Mrs. Wade. Would you go for a cup of coffee?"

She came into the living room and sat on the davenport without looking at anything. She balanced her bag on her lap and sat with her feet close together. She looked rather prim. I opened windows and pulled up venetian blinds and lifted a dirty ash tray off the cocktail table in front of her.

"Thank you. Black coffee, please. No sugar."

I went out to the kitchen and spread a paper napkin on a green metal tray. It looked as cheesy as a celluloid collar. I crumpled it up and got out one of those fringed things that come in sets with little triangular napkins. They came with the house, like most of the furniture. I set out two Desert Rose coffee cups and filled them and carried the tray in.

She sipped. "This is very nice," she said. "You make good coffee."

"Last time anyone drank coffee with me was just before I went to jail," I said. "I guess you knew I'd been in the cooler, Mrs. Wade."

She nodded. "Of course. You were suspected of having helped him escape, wasn't it?"

"They didn't say. They found my telephone number on a pad in his room. They asked me questions I didn't answer— mostly because of the way they were asked. But I don't suppose you are interested in that."

She put her cup down carefully and leaned back and smiled at me. I offered her a cigarette.

"I don't smoke, thank you. Of course I'm interested. A neighbor of ours knew the Lennoxes. He must have been insane. He doesn't sound at all like that kind of man."

I filled a bulldog pipe and lit it. "I guess so," I said. "He must have been. He was badly wounded in the war. But he's dead and it's all done with. And I don't think you came here to talk about that."

She shook her head slowly. "He was a friend of yours, Mr. Marlowe. You must have a pretty strong opinion. And I think you are a pretty determined man."

I tamped the tobacco in my pipe and lit it again. I took my time and stared at her over the pipe bowl while I was doing it.

"Look, Mrs. Wade," I said finally. "My opinion means nothing. It happens every day. The most unlikely people commit the most unlikely crimes. Nice old ladies poison whole families. Clean-cut kids commit multiple holdups and shootings. Bank managers with spotless records going back twenty years are found out to be long-term embezzlers. And successful and popular and supposedly happy novelists get drunk and put their wives in the hospital. We know damn little about what makes even our best friends tick."

I thought it would burn her up, but she didn't do much more than press her lips together and narrow her eyes.

"Howard Spencer shouldn't have told you that," she said. "It was my own fault. I didn't know enough to keep away from him. I've learned since that the one thing you can never do to a man who is drinking too much is to try to stop him. You probably know that much better than I do."

"You certainly can't stop him with words," I said. "If you're lucky, and *if* you have the strength, you can sometimes keep him from hurting himself or someone else. Even that takes luck."

She reached quietly for her coffee cup and saucer. Her hands were lovely, like the rest of her. The nails were beautifully shaped and polished and only very slightly tinted.

"Did Howard tell you he hadn't seen my husband this time?"

"Yeah."

She finished her coffee and put the cup carefully back on the tray. She fiddled with the spoon for a few seconds. Then she spoke without looking up at me.

"He didn't tell you why, because he didn't know. I am very fond of Howard but he is the managing type, wants to take charge of everything. He thinks he is very executive."

I waited, not saying anything. There was another silence. She looked at me quickly then looked away again. Very softly she said: "My husband has been missing for three days. I don't know where he is. I came here to ask you to find him and bring him home. Oh, it has happened before. One time he drove himself all the way to Portland and got sick in a hotel there and had to get a doctor to sober him up. It's a wonder how he ever got that far without getting into trouble. He hadn't eaten anything for three days. Another time he was in a Turkish bath in Long Beach, one of those Swedish places where they give high colonics. And the last time it was some sort of small private and probably not very reputable sanitarium. This was less than three weeks ago. He wouldn't tell me the name of it or where it was, just said he had been taking a cure and was all right. But he looked deadly pale and weak. I got a brief glimpse of the man who brought him home. A tall young man dressed in the sort of overelaborate cowboy outfit you would only see on the stage or in a technicolor musical film. He let Roger out in the driveway and backed out and drove away at once."

"Could have been a dude ranch," I said. "Some of these tame cowpunchers spend every dime they make on a fancy outfit like that. The women go crazy over them. That's what they're there for."

She opened her bag and took out a folded paper. "I've brought you a check for five hundred dollars, Mr. Marlowe. Will you accept it as a retainer?"

She put the folded check down on the table. I looked at it, but didn't touch it. "Why?" I asked her. "You say he has been gone three days. It takes three or four to sober a man up and get some food into him. Won't he come back the way he did before? Or does something make this time different?"

"He can't stand much more of it, Mr. Marlowe. It will kill him. The intervals are getting shorter. I'm badly worried. I'm more than worried, I'm scared. It's unnatural. We've been married for five years. Roger was always a drinker, but not a psychopathic drinker. Something is all wrong. I want him found. I didn't sleep more than an hour last night."

"Any idea *why* he drinks?"

The violet eyes were looking at me steadily. She seemed a bit fragile this morning, but certainly not helpless. She bit her lower lip and shook her head. "Unless it's me," she said at last, almost in a whisper. "Men fall out of love with their wives."

"I'm only an amateur psychologist, Mrs. Wade. A man in my racket has to be a little of that. I'd say it's more likely he has fallen out of love with the kind of stuff he writes."

"It's quite possible," she said quietly. "I imagine all writers have spells like that. It's true that he can't seem to finish a book he is working on. But it isn't as if he had to finish it for the rent money. I don't think that is quite enough reason."

"What sort of guy is he sober?"

She smiled. "Well, I'm rather prejudiced. *I* think he is a very nice guy indeed."

"And how is he drunk?"

"Horrible. Bright and hard and cruel. He thinks he is being witty when he is only being nasty."

"You left out violent."

She raised her tawny eyebrows. "Just once, Mr. Marlowe. And too much has been made of that. I'd never have told Howard Spencer. Roger told him himself."

I got up and walked around in the room. It was going to be a hot day. It already was hot. I turned the blinds on one of the windows to keep the sun out. Then I gave it to her straight.

"I looked him up in *Who's Who* yesterday afternoon. He's forty-two years old, yours is his only marriage, no children. His people are New Englanders, he went to Andover and Princeton. He has a war record and a good one. He has written twelve of these fat sex-and-swordplay historical novels and every damn one of them has been on the best-seller lists. He must have made plenty of the folding. If he had fallen out of love with his wife, he sounds like the type who would say so and get a divorce. If he was haring around with another woman, you would probably know about it, and anyway he wouldn't have to get drunk just to prove he felt bad. If you've been married five years, then he was thirty-seven when that happened. I'd say he knew most of what there is to know about women by that time. I say most, because nobody ever knows all of it."

I stopped and looked at her and she smiled at me. I wasn't hurting her feelings. I went on.

"Howard Spencer suggested—on what grounds I have no idea—that what's the matter with Roger Wade is something that happened a long time ago before you were married and that it has caught up with him now, and is hitting him harder than he can take. Spencer thought of blackmail. Would you know?"

She shook her head slowly. "If you mean would I know if Roger had been paying out a lot of money to someone—no, I wouldn't know that. I don't meddle with his bookkeeping affairs. He could give away a lot of money without my knowing it."

"Okay then. Not knowing Mr. Wade I can't have much idea how he would react to having the bite put on him. If he has a violent temper, he might break somebody's neck. If the secret, whatever it is, might damage his social or professional standing or even, to take an extreme case, made the law boys drop around, he might pay off—for a while anyhow. But none of this gets us anywhere. You want him found, you're worried, you're more than worried. So how do I go about finding him? I don't want your money, Mrs. Wade. Not now anyway."

She reached into her bag again and came up with a couple of pieces of yellow paper. They looked like second sheets, folded, and one of them looked crumpled. She smoothed them out and handed them to me.

"One I found on his desk," she said. "It was very late, or rather early in the morning. I knew he had been drinking and I knew he hadn't come upstairs. About two o'clock I went down to see if he was all right—or comparatively all right, passed out on the floor or the couch or something. He was gone. The other paper was in the wastebasket or rather caught on the edge, so that it hadn't fallen in."

I looked at the first piece, the one not crumpled. There was a short typewritten paragraph on it, no more. It read: "I do not care to be in love with myself and there is no longer anyone else for me to be in love with. Signed: Roger (F. Scott Fitzgerald) Wade. P.S. This is why I never finished *The Last Tycoon*."

"That mean anything to you, Mrs. Wade?"

"Just attitudinizing. He has always been a great admirer of Scott Fitzgerald. He says Fitzgerald is the best drunken writer since Coleridge, who took dope. Notice the typing, Mr. Marlowe. Clear, even, and no mistakes."

"I did. Most people can't even write their names properly when soused." I opened the crumpled paper. More typing, also without any errors or unevenness. This one read: "I do not like you, Dr. V. But right now you're the man for me."

She spoke while I was still looking at it. "I have no idea who Dr. V. is. We don't know any doctor with a name beginning that way. I suppose he is the one who has that place where Roger was the last time."

"When the cowpoke brought him home? Your husband didn't mention any names at all—even place names?"

She shook her head. "Nothing. I've looked in the directory. There are dozens of doctors of one sort or another whose names begin with V. Also, it may not be his surname."

"Quite likely he's not even a doctor," I said. "That brings up the question of ready cash. A legitimate man would take a check, but a quack wouldn't. It might turn into evidence. And a guy like that wouldn't be cheap. Room and board at his house would come high. Not to mention the needle."

She looked puzzled. "The needle?"

"All the shady ones use dope on their clients. Easiest way to handle them. Knock them out for ten or twelve hours and when they come out of it, they're good boys. But using narcotics without a license can get you room and board with Uncle Sam. And that comes very high indeed."

"I see. Roger probably would have several hundred dollars. He always keeps that much in his desk. I don't know why. I suppose it's just a whim. There's none there now."

"Okay," I said. "I'll try to find Dr. V. I don't know just how, but I'll do my best. Take the check with you, Mrs. Wade."

"But why? Aren't you entitled—"

"Later on, thanks. And I'd rather have it from Mr. Wade. He's not going to like what I do in any case."

"But if he's sick and helpless—"

"He could have called his own doctor or asked you to. He didn't. That means he didn't want to."

She put the check back in her bag and stood up. She looked very forlorn. "Our doctor refused to treat him," she said bitterly.

"There are hundreds of doctors, Mrs. Wade. Any one of them would handle him once. Most of them would stay with him for some time. Medicine is a pretty competitive affair nowadays."

"I see. Of course you must be right." She walked slowly to the door and I walked with her. I opened it.

"You could have called a doctor on your own. Why didn't you?"

She faced me squarely. Her eyes were bright. There might have been a hint of tears in them. A lovely dish and no mistake.

"Because I love my husband, Mr. Marlowe. I'd do anything in the world to help him. But I know what sort of man he is too. If I called a doctor every time he took too many drinks, I wouldn't have a husband very long. You can't treat a grown man like a child with a sore throat."

"You can if he's a drunk. Often you damn well have to."

She was standing close to me. I smelled her perfume. Or thought I did. It hadn't been put on with a spray gun. Perhaps it was just the summer day.

"Suppose there *is* something shameful in his past," she said, dragging the words out one by one as if each of them had a bitter taste. "Even something criminal. It would make no difference to me. But I'm not going to be the means of its being found out."

"But it's all right if Howard Spencer hires me to find out?"

She smiled very slowly. "Do you really think I expected you to give Howard any answer but the one you did—a man who went to jail rather than betray a friend?"

"Thanks for the plug, but that wasn't why I got jugged."

She nodded after a moment of silence, said goodbye, and started down the redwood steps. I watched her into her car, a slim gray Jaguar, very new looking. She drove it up to the end of the street and swung around in the turning circle there. Her glove waved at me as she went by down the hill. The little car whisked around the corner and was gone.

There was a red oleander bush against part of the front wall of the house. I heard a flutter in it and a baby mockingbird started cheeping anxiously. I spotted him hanging on to one of the top branches, flapping his wings as if he was having trouble keeping his balance. From the cypress trees at the corner of the wall there was a single harsh warning chirp. The cheeping stopped at once and the little fat bird was silent.

I went inside and shut the door and left him to his flying lesson. Birds have to learn too.

# 15

No matter how smart you think you are, you have to have a place to start from: a name, an address, a neighborhood, a background, an atmosphere, a point of reference of some sort. All I had was typing on a crumpled yellow page that said, "I do not like you, Dr. V. But right now you're the man for me." With that I could pinpoint the Pacific Ocean, spend a month wading through the lists of half a dozen county medical associations, and end up with the big round o. In our town quacks breed like guinea pigs. There are eight counties within a hundred miles of the City Hall and in every town in every single one of them there are doctors, some genuine medical men, some just mail-order mechanics with a license to cut corns or jump up and down on your spine. Of the real doctors some are prosperous and some poor, some ethical, others not sure they can afford it. A well-heeled patient with incipient D.T.'s could be money from home to plenty of old geezers who have fallen behind in the vitamin and antibiotic trade. But without a clue there was no place to start. I didn't have the clue and Eileen Wade either didn't have it or didn't know she had it. And even if I found somebody that fitted and had the right initial, he might turn out to be a myth, so far as Roger Wade was concerned. The jingle might be something that just happened to run through his head while he was getting himself stewed up. Just as the Scott Fitzgerald allusion might be merely an off-beat way of saying goodbye.

In a situation like that the small man tries to pick the big man's brains. So I called up a man I knew in The Carne Organization, a flossy agency in Beverly Hills that specialized in protection for the carriage trade—protection meaning almost anything with one foot inside the law. The man's name was George Peters and he said he could give me ten minutes if I made it fast.

They had half the second floor of one of these candy-pink four-storied buildings where the elevator doors open all by themselves with an electric eye, where the corridors are cool and quiet, and the parking lot has a name on every stall, and the druggist off the front lobby has a sprained wrist from filling bottles of sleeping pills.

The door was French gray outside with raised metal lettering, as clean and sharp as a new knife. THE CARNE ORGANIZATION, INC. GERALD C. CARNE, PRESIDENT. Below and smaller: *Entrance*. It might have been an investment trust.

Inside was a small and ugly reception room, but the ugliness was deliberate and expensive. The furniture was scarlet and dark green, the walls were a flat Brunswick green, and the pictures hung on them were framed in a green about three shades darker than that. The pictures were guys in red coats on big horses that were just crazy to jump over high fences. There were two frameless mirrors tinted a slight but disgusting shade of rose pink. The magazines on the table of polished primavera were of the latest issue and each one was enclosed in a clear plastic cover. The fellow who decorated that room was not a man to let colors scare him. He probably wore a pimento shirt, mulberry slacks, zebra shoes, and vermilion drawers with his initials on them in a nice Mandarin orange.

The whole thing was just window-dressing. The clients of The Carne Organization were charged a minimum of one hundred fish *per diem* and they expected service in their homes. They didn't go sit in no waiting rooms. Carne was an ex-colonel of military police, a big pink and white guy as hard as a board. He had offered me a job once, but I never got desperate enough to take it. There are one hundred and ninety ways of being a bastard and Carne knew all of them.

A rubbed glass partition slid open and a receptionist looked out at me. She had an iron smile and eyes that could count the money in your hip wallet.

"Good morning. May I help you?"

"George Peters, please. My name is Marlowe."

She put a green leather book on the ledge. "Is he expecting you, Mr. Marlowe? I don't see your name on the appointment list."

"It's a personal matter. I just talked to him on the phone."

"I see. How do you spell your name, Mr. Marlowe? And your first name, please?"

I told her. She wrote it down on a long narrow form, then slipped the edge under a clock punch.

"Who's that supposed to impress?" I asked her.

"We are very particular about details here," she said coldly. "Colonel Carne says you never know when the most trivial fact may turn out to be vital."

"Or the other way around," I said, but she didn't get it. When she had finished her book work she looked up and said:

"I will announce you to Mr. Peters."

I told her that made me very happy. A minute later a door in the paneling opened and Peters beckoned me into a battleship-gray corridor lined with little offices that looked like cells. His office had soundproofing on the ceiling, a gray steel desk with two matching chairs, a gray dictating machine on a gray stand, a telephone and pen set of the same color as the walls and floor. There were a couple of framed photographs on the walls, one of Carne in uniform, with his snow-drop helmet on, and one of Carne as a civilian seated behind a desk and looking inscrutable. Also framed on the wall was a small inspirational legend in steely letters on a gray background. It read:

A CARNE OPERATIVE DRESSES, SPEAKS AND BEHAVES LIKE A GENTLEMAN AT ALL TIMES AND IN ALL PLACES. THERE ARE NO EXCEPTIONS TO THIS RULE.

Peters crossed the room in two long steps and pushed one of the pictures aside. Set into the gray wall behind it was a gray microphone pickup. He pulled it out, unclipped a wire, and pushed it back in place. He moved the picture in front of it again.

"Right now I'd be out of a job," he said, "except that the son of a bitch is out fixing a drunk-driving rap for some actor. All the mike switches are in his office. He has the whole joint wired. The other morning I suggested to him that he have a microfilm camera installed with infra red light behind a di-aphanous mirror in the reception room. He didn't like the idea too well. Maybe because somebody else had it."

He sat down in one of the hard gray chairs. I stared at him. He was a gawky long-legged man with a bony face and receding hair. His skin had the worn weathered look of a man who has been out of doors a great deal, in all kinds of weather. He had deep-set eyes and an upper lip almost as long as his nose. When he grinned the bottom half of his face disappeared into two enormous ditches that ran from his nostrils to the ends of his wide mouth.

"How can you take it?" I asked him.

"Sit down, pal. Breathe quietly, keep your voice down, and remember that a Carne operative is to a cheap shamus like you what Toscanini is to an organ grinder's monkey." He paused and grinned. "I take it because I don't give a damn. It's good money and any time Carne starts acting like he thought I was doing time in that maximum-security prison he ran in England during the war, I'll pick up my check and blow. What's your trouble? I hear you had it rough a while back."

"No complaints about that. I'd like to look at your file on the barred-window boys. I know you have one. Eddie Dowst told me after he quit here."

He nodded. "Eddie was just a mite too sensitive for The Carne Organization. The file you mention is top secret. In no circumstances must any confidential information be disclosed to outsiders. I'll get it at once."

He went out and I stared at the gray wastebasket and the gray linoleum and the gray leather corners of the desk blotter. Peters came back with a gray cardboard file in his hand. He put it down and opened it.

"For Chrissake, haven't you got anything in this place that isn't gray?"

"The school colors, my lad. The spirit of the organization. Yeah, I have something that isn't gray."

He pulled a desk drawer open and took out a cigar about eight inches long.

"An Upman Thirty," he said. "Presented to me by an elderly gent from England who has been forty years in California and still says 'wireless.' Sober he is just an old swish with a good deal of superficial charm, which is all right with me, because most people don't have any, superficial or otherwise, including Carne. He has as much charm as a steel puddler's underpants. Not sober, the client has a strange habit of writing checks on banks which never heard of him. He always makes good and with my fond help he has so far stayed out of the icebox. He gave me this. Should we smoke it together, like a couple of Indian chiefs planning a massacre?"

"I can't smoke cigars."

Peters looked at the huge cigar sadly. "Same here," he said. "I thought of giving it to Carne. But it's not really a one-man cigar, even when the one man is Carne." He frowned. "You know something? I'm talking too much about Carne. I must be edgy." He dropped the cigar back in the drawer and looked at the open file. "Just what do we want from this?"

"I'm looking for a well-heeled alcoholic with expensive tastes and money to gratify them. So far he hasn't gone in for check-bouncing. I haven't heard so anyway. He has a streak of violence and his wife is worried about him. She thinks he's hid out in some sobering-up joint but she can't be sure. The only clue we have is a jingle mentioning a Dr. V. Just the initial. My man is gone three days now."

Peters stared at me thoughtfully. "That's not too long," he said. "What's to worry about?"

"If I find him first, I get paid."

He looked at me some more and shook his head. "I don't get it, but that's okay. We'll see." He began to turn the pages of the file. "It's not too easy," he said. "These people come and go. A single letter ain't much of a lead." He pulled a page out of the folder, turned some more pages, pulled another, and finally a third. "Three of them here," he said. "Dr. Amos Varley, an osteopath. Big place in Altadena. Makes or used to make night calls for fifty bucks. Two registered nurses. Was in a hassle with the State Narcotics people a couple of years back, and turned in his prescription book. This information is not really up to date."

I wrote down the name and address in Altadena.

"Then we have Dr. Lester Vukanich. Ear, Nose, and Throat, Stockwell Building, on Hollywood Boulevard. This one's a dilly. Office practice mostly, and seems to sort of specialize in chronic sinus infections. Rather a neat routine. You go in and complain of a sinus headache and he washes out your antrums for you. First of course he has to anesthetize with Novocain. But if he likes your looks it don't have to be Novocain. Catch?"

"Sure." I wrote that one down.

"This is good," Peters went on, reading some more. "Obviously his trouble would be supplies. So our Dr. Vukanich does a lot of fishing off Ensenada and flies down in his own plane."

"I wouldn't think he'd last long if he brings the dope in himself," I said.

Peters thought about that and shook his head. "I don't

think I agree. He could last forever if he's not too greedy. His only real danger is a discontented customer—pardon me, I mean patient—but he probably knows how to handle that. He's had fifteen years in the same office."

"Where the hell do you get this stuff?" I asked him.

"We're an organization, my boy. Not a lone wolf like you. Some we get from the clients themselves, some we get from the inside. Carne's not afraid to spend money. He's a good mixer when he wants to be."

"He'd love this conversation."

"Screw him. Our last offering today is a man named Verringer. The operative who filed on him is long gone. Seems a lady poet suicided at Verringer's ranch in Sepulveda Canyon one time. He runs a sort of art colony for writers and such who want seclusion and a congenial atmosphere. Rates moderate. He sounds legit. He calls himself doctor, but doesn't practice medicine. Could be a Ph.D. Frankly, I don't know why he's in here. Unless there was something about this suicide." He picked up a newspaper clipping pasted to a blank sheet. "Yeah, overdose of morphine. No suggestion Verringer knew anything about it."

"I like Verringer," I said. "I like him very much."

Peters closed the file and slapped it. "You haven't seen this," he said. He got up and left the room. When he came back I was standing up to leave. I started to thank him, but he shook it off.

"Look," he said, "there must be hundreds of places where your man could be."

I said I knew that.

"And by the way, I heard something about your friend Lennox that might interest you. One of our boys ran across a fellow in New York five or six years ago that answers the description exactly. But the guy's name was not Lennox, he says. It was Marston. Of course he could be wrong. The guy was drunk all the time, so you couldn't really be sure."

I said: "I doubt if it was the same man. Why would he change his name? He had a war record that could be checked."

"I didn't know that. Our man's in Seattle right now. You

can talk to him when he gets back, if it means anything to you. His name is Ashterfelt."

"Thanks for everything, George. It was a pretty long ten minutes."

"I might need *your* help some day."

"The Carne Organization," I said, "never needs anything from anybody."

He made a rude gesture with his thumb. I left him in his metallic gray cell and departed through the waiting room. It looked fine now. The loud colors made sense after the cell block.

# 16

Back from the highway at the bottom of Sepulveda Canyon were two square yellow gateposts. A five-barred gate hung open from one of them. Over the entrance was a sign hung on wire: PRIVATE ROAD. NO ADMITTANCE. The air was warm and quiet and full of the tomcat smell of eucalyptus trees.

I turned in and followed a graveled road around the shoulder of a hill, up a gentle slope, over a ridge and down the other side into a shallow valley. It was hot in the valley, ten or fifteen degrees hotter than on the highway. I could see now that the graveled road ended in a loop around some grass edged with stones that had been lime-washed. Off to my left there was an empty swimming pool, and nothing ever looks emptier than an empty swimming pool. Around three sides of it there was what remained of a lawn dotted with redwood lounging chairs with badly faded pads on them. The pads had been of many colors, blue, green, yellow, orange, rust red. Their edge bindings had come loose in spots, the buttons had popped, and the pads were bloated where this had happened. On the fourth side there was the high wire fence of a tennis court. The diving board over the empty pool looked knee-sprung and tired. Its matting covering hung in shreds and its metal fittings were flaked with rust.

I came to the turning loop and stopped in front of a redwood building with a shake roof and a wide front porch. The entrance had double screen doors. Large black flies dozed on the screens. Paths led off among the ever green and always dusty California oaks and among the oaks there were rustic cabins scattered loosely over the side of the hill, some almost completely hidden. Those I could see had that desolate out-of-season look. Their doors were shut, their windows were blanked by drawn curtains of monk's cloth or something on that order. You could almost feel the thick dust on their sills.

I switched off the ignition and sat there with my hands on the wheel listening. There was no sound. The place seemed to be as dead as Pharaoh, except that the doors behind the double screens were open and something moved in the dimness of the room beyond. Then I heard a light accurate whistling and a man's figure showed against the screen, pushed it open and strolled down the steps. He was something to see.

He wore a flat black gaucho hat with the woven strap under his chin. He wore a white silk shirt, spotlessly clean, open at the throat, with tight wristlets and loose puffed sleeves above. Around his neck a black fringed scarf was knotted unevenly so that one end was short and the other dropped almost to his waist. He wore a wide black sash and black pants, skin-tight at the hips, coal black, and stitched with gold thread down the side to where they were slashed and belled out loosely with gold buttons along both sides of the slash. On his feet he wore patent-leather dancing pumps.

He stopped at the foot of the steps and looked at me, still whistling. He was as lithe as a whip. He had the largest and emptiest smoke-colored eyes I had ever seen, under long silky lashes. His features were delicate and perfect without being weak. His nose was straight and almost but not quite thin, his mouth was a handsome pout, there was a dimple in his chin, and his small ears nestled gracefully against his head. His skin had that heavy pallor which the sun never touches.

He struck an attitude with his left hand on a hip and his right made a graceful curve in the air.

"Greetings," he said. "Lovely day, isn't it?"

"Pretty hot in here for me."

"I like it hot." The statement was flat and final and closed the discussion. What I liked was beneath his notice. He sat down on a step, produced a long file from somewhere, and began to file his fingernails. "You from the bank?" he asked without looking up.

"I'm looking for Dr. Verringer."

He stopped working with the file and looked off into the warm distance. "Who's he?" he asked with no possible interest.

"He owns the place. Laconic as hell, aren't you? As if you didn't know."

He went back to his file and fingernails. "You got told wrong, sweetie. The bank owns the place. They done foreclosed it or it's in escrow or something. I forget the details."

He looked up at me with the expression of a man to whom details mean nothing. I got out of the Olds and leaned against the hot door, then I moved away from that to where there was some air.

"Which bank would that be?"

"You don't know, you don't come from there. You don't come from there, you don't have any business here. Hit the trail, sweetie. Buzz off but fast."

"I have to find Dr. Verringer."

"The joint's not operating, sweetie. Like it says on the sign, this is a private road. Some gopher forgot to lock the gate."

"You the caretaker?"

"Sort of. Don't ask any more questions, sweetie. My temper's not reliable."

"What do you do when you get mad—dance a tango with a ground squirrel?"

He stood up suddenly and gracefully. He smiled a minute, an empty smile. "Looks like I got to toss you back in your little old convertible," he said.

"Later. Where would I find Dr. Verringer about now?"

He pocketed his file in his shirt and something else took its place in his right hand. A brief motion and he had a fist with shining brass knuckles on it. The skin over his cheekbones was tighter and there was a flame deep in his large smoky eyes.

He strolled towards me. I stepped back to get more room. He went on whistling but the whistle was high and shrill.

"We don't have to fight," I told him. "We don't have anything to fight about. And you might split those lovely britches."

He was as quick as a flash. He came at me with a smooth leap and his left hand snaked out very fast. I expected a jab and moved my head well enough but what he wanted was my right wrist and he got it. He had a grip too. He jerked me off balance and the hand with the brass knucks came around in a looping bolo punch. A crack on the back of the head with those and I would be a sick man. If I pulled he would catch me on the side of the face or on the upper arm below the point of the shoulder. It would have been a dead arm or a dead face, whichever it happened to be. In a spot like that there is only one thing to do.

I went with the pull. In passing I blocked his left foot from behind, grabbed his shirt and heard it tear. Something hit me on the back of the neck, but it wasn't the metal. I spun to the left and he went over sideways and landed catlike and was on his feet again before I had any kind of balance. He was grinning now. He was delighted with everything. He loved his work. He came for me fast.

A strong beefy voice yelled from somewhere: "Earl! Stop that at once! At once, do you hear me?"

The gaucho boy stopped. There was a sort of sick grin on his face. He made a quick motion and the brass knucks disappeared into the wide sash around the top of his pants.

I turned and looked at a solid chunk of man in a Hawaiian shirt hurrying towards us down one of the paths waving his arms. He came up breathing a little fast.

"Are you crazy, Earl?"

"Don't ever say that, Doc," Earl said softly. Then he smiled, turned away, and went to sit on the steps of the house. He took off the flat-crowned hat, produced a comb, and began to comb his thick dark hair with an absent expression. In a second or two he started to whistle softly.

The heavy man in the loud shirt stood and looked at me. I stood and looked at him.

"What's going on here?" he growled. "Who are you, sir?"

"Name's Marlowe. I was asking for Dr. Verringer. The lad you call Earl wanted to play games. I figure it's too hot."

"I am Dr. Verringer," he said with dignity. He turned his head. "Go in the house, Earl."

Earl stood up slowly. He gave Dr. Verringer a thoughtful studying look, his large smoky eyes blank of expression. Then he went up the steps and pulled the screen door open. A cloud of flies buzzed angrily and then settled on the screen again as the door closed.

"Marlowe?" Dr. Verringer gave me his attention again. "And what can I do for you, Mr. Marlowe?"

"Earl says you are out of business here."

"That is correct. I am just waiting for certain legal formalities before moving out. Earl and I are alone here."

"I'm disappointed," I said, looking disappointed. "I thought you had a man named Wade staying with you."

He hoisted a couple of eyebrows that would have interested a Fuller Brush man. "Wade? I might possibly know somebody of that name—it's a common enough name—but why should he be staying with me?"

"Taking the cure."

He frowned. When a guy has eyebrows like that he can really do you a frown. "I am a medical man, sir, but no longer in practice. What sort of cure did you have in mind?"

"The guy's a wino. He goes off his rocker from time to time and disappears. Sometimes he comes home under his own power, sometimes he gets brought home, and sometimes he takes a bit of finding." I got a business card out and handed it to him.

He read it with no pleasure.

"What goes with Earl?" I asked him. "He think he's Valentino or something?"

He made with the eyebrows again. They fascinated me. Parts of them curled off all by themselves as much as an inch and a half. He shrugged his meaty shoulders.

"Earl is quite harmless, Mr. Marlowe. He is—at times—a little dreamy. Lives in a play world, shall we say?"

"You say it, Doc. From where I stand he plays rough."

"Tut, tut, Mr. Marlowe. You exaggerate surely. Earl likes to dress himself up. He is childlike in that respect."

"You mean he's a nut," I said. "This place some kind of sanitarium, isn't it? Or was?"

"Certainly not. When it was in operation it was an artists' colony. I provided meals, lodging, facilities for exercise and entertainment, and above all seclusion. And for moderate fees. Artists, as you probably know, are seldom wealthy people. In the term artists I of course include writers, musicians, and so on. It was a rewarding occupation for me—while it lasted."

He looked sad when he said this. The eyebrows drooped at the outer corners to match his mouth. Give them a little more growth and they would be *in* his mouth.

"I know that," I said. "It's in the file. Also the suicide you had here a while back. A dope case, wasn't it?"

He stopped drooping and bristled. "What file?" he asked sharply.

"We've got a file on what we call the barred-window boys, Doctor. Places where you can't jump out of when the French fits take over. Small private sanitariums or what have you that treat alcoholics and dopers and mild cases of mania."

"Such places must be licensed by law," Dr. Verringer said harshly.

"Yeah. In theory anyway. Sometimes they kind of forget about that."

He drew himself up stiffly. The guy had a kind of dignity, at that. "The suggestion is insulting, Mr. Marlowe. I have no knowledge of why my name should be on any such list as you mention. I must ask you to leave."

"Let's get back to Wade. Could he be here under another name, maybe?"

"There is no one here but Earl and myself. We are quite alone. Now if you will excuse me—"

"I'd like to look around."

Sometimes you can get them mad enough to say something off key. But not Dr. Verringer. He remained dignified. His eyebrows went all the way with him. I looked towards the house. From inside there came a sound of music, dance music. And very faintly the snapping of fingers.

"I bet he's in there dancing," I said. "That's a tango. I bet you he's dancing all by himself in there. Some kid."

"Are you going to leave, Mr. Marlowe? Or shall I have to ask Earl to assist me in putting you off my property?"

"Okay, I'll leave. No hard feelings, Doctor. There were only three names beginning with V and you seemed the most promising of them. That's the only real clue we had—Dr. V. He scrawled it on a piece of paper before he left: Dr. V."

"There must be dozens," Dr. Verringer said evenly.

"Oh sure. But not dozens in our file of the barred-window boys. Thanks for the time, Doctor. Earl bothers me a little."

I turned and went over to my car and got into it. By the time I had the door shut Dr. Verringer was beside me. He leaned in with a pleasant expression.

"We need not quarrel, Mr. Marlowe. I realize that in your occupation you often have to be rather intrusive. Just what bothers you about Earl?"

"He's so obviously a phony. Where you find one thing phony you're apt to expect others. The guy's a manic-depressive, isn't he? Right now he's on the upswing."

He stared at me in silence. He looked grave and polite. "Many interesting and talented people have stayed with me, Mr. Marlowe. Not all of them were as level-headed as you may be. Talented people are often neurotic. But I have no facilities for the care of lunatics or alcoholics, even if I had the taste for that sort of work. I have no staff except Earl, and he is hardly the type to care for the sick."

"Just what would say he is the type for, Doctor? Apart from bubble-dancing and stuff?"

He leaned on the door. His voice got low and confidential. "Earl's parents were dear friends of mine, Mr. Marlowe. Someone has to look after Earl and they are no longer with us. Earl has to live a quiet life, away from the noise and temptations of the city. He is unstable but fundamentally harmless. I control him with absolute ease, as you saw."

"You've got a lot of courage," I said.

He sighed. His eyebrows waved gently, like the antennae of some suspicious insect. "It has been a sacrifice," he said. "A rather heavy one. I thought Earl could help me with my work here. He plays beautiful tennis, swims and dives like a champion, and can dance all night. Almost always he is amiability itself. But from time to time there were—incidents." He waved a broad hand as if pushing painful memories into the background. "In the end it was either give up Earl or give up my place here."

He held both hands palms up, spread them apart, turned them over and let them fall to his sides. His eyes looked moist with unshed tears.

"I sold out," he said. "This peaceful little valley will become a real estate development. There will be sidewalks and lampposts and children with scooters and blatting radios. There will even"—he heaved a forlorn sigh—"be Television." He waved his hand in a sweeping gesture. "I hope they will spare the trees," he said, "but I'm afraid they won't. Along the ridges there will be television aerials instead. But Earl and I will be far away, I trust."

"Goodbye, Doctor. My heart bleeds for you."

He put out his hand. It was moist but very firm. "I appreciate your sympathy and understanding, Mr. Marlowe. And I regret I am unable to help you in your quest for Mr. Slade."

"Wade," I said.

"Pardon me, Wade, of course. Goodbye and good luck, sir."

I started up and drove back along the graveled road by the way I had come. I felt sad, but not quite as sad as Dr. Verringer would have liked me to feel.

I came out through the gates and drove far enough around the curve of the highway to park out of sight of the entrance. I got out and walked back along the edge of the paving to where I could just see the gates from the barbed-wire boundary fence. I stood there under a eucalyptus and waited.

Five minutes or so passed. Then a car came down the private road churning gravel. It stopped out of sight from where I was. I pulled back still farther into the brush. I heard a creaking noise, then the click of a heavy catch and the rattle of a chain. The car motor revved up and the car went back up the road.

When the sound of it had died I went back to my Olds and did a U turn to face back towards town. As I drove past the entrance to Dr. Verringer's private road I saw that the gate was fastened with a padlocked chain. No more visitors today, thank you.

# 17

I drove the twenty-odd miles back to town and ate lunch. While I ate I felt more and more silly over the whole deal. You just don't find people the way I was going about it. You meet interesting characters like Earl and Dr. Verringer, but you don't meet the man you are looking for. You waste tires, gasoline, words, and nervous energy in a game with no pay-off. You're not even betting table limit four ways on Black 28. With three names that started with V, I had as much chance of paging my man as I had of breaking Nick the Greek in a crap game.

Anyway the first one is always wrong, a dead end, a promising lead that blows up in your face with no music. But he shouldn't have said Slade instead of Wade. He was an intelligent man. He wouldn't forget that easy, and if he did he would just forget.

Maybe, and maybe not. It had not been a long acquaintance. Over my coffee I thought about Drs. Vukanich and Varley. Yes or no? They would kill most of the afternoon. By then I could call the Wade mansion in Idle Valley and be told the head of the household had returned to his domicile and all was gleaming bright for the time being.

Dr. Vukanich was easy. He was only half a dozen blocks down the line. But Dr. Varley was away to hell and gone in the Altadena hills, a long, hot, boring drive. Yes or no?

The final answer was yes. For three good reasons. One was that you can never know too much about the shadow line and the people who walk it. The second was that anything I could add to the file Peters had got out for me was just that much thanks and goodwill. The third reason was that I didn't have anything else to do.

I paid my check, left my car where it was, and walked the north side of the street to the Stockwell Building. It was an antique with a cigar counter in the entrance and a manually operated elevator that lurched and hated to level off. The corridor of the sixth floor was narrow and the doors had frosted glass panels. It was older and much dirtier than my own building. It was loaded with doctors, dentists, Christian

Science practitioners not doing too good, the kind of lawyers you hope the other fellow has, the kind of doctors and dentists who just scrape along. Not too skillful, not too clean, not too much on the ball, three dollars and please pay the nurse; tired, discouraged men who know just exactly where they stand, what kind of patients they can get and how much money they can be squeezed into paying. Please Do Not Ask For Credit. Doctor is In, Doctor is Out. That's a pretty shaky molar you have there, Mrs. Kazinski. Now if you want this new acrylic filling, every bit as good as a gold inlay, I can do it for you for $14. Novocain will be two dollars extra, if you wish it. Doctor is In, Doctor is Out. That will be Three Dollars. Please Pay the Nurse.

In a building like that there will always be a few guys making real money, but they don't look it. They fit into the shabby background, which is protective coloring for them. Shyster lawyers who are partners in a bail-bond racket on the side (only about two per cent of all forfeited bail bonds are ever collected). Abortionists posing as anything you like that explains their furnishings. Dope pushers posing as urologists, dermatologists, or any branch of medicine in which the treatment can be frequent, and the regular use of local anesthetics is normal.

Dr. Lester Vukanich had a small and ill-furnished waiting room in which there were a dozen people, all uncomfortable. They looked like anybody else. They had no signs on them. Anyway you can't tell a doper well under control from a vegetarian bookkeeper. I had to wait three quarters of an hour. The patients went in through two doors. An active ear, nose, and throat man can handle four sufferers at once, if he has enough room.

Finally I got in. I got to sit in a brown leather chair beside a table covered with a white towel on which was a set of tools. A sterilizing cabinet bubbled against the wall. Dr. Vukanich came in briskly with his white smock and his round mirror strapped to his forehead. He sat down in front of me on a stool.

"A sinus headache, is it? Very severe?" He looked at a folder the nurse had given him.

I said it was awful. Blinding. Especially when I first got up in the morning. He nodded sagely.

"Characteristic," he said, and fitted a glass cap over a thing that looked like a fountain pen.

He pushed it into my mouth. "Close the lips but not the teeth, please." While he said it he reached out and switched off the light. There was no window. A ventilating fan purred somewhere.

Dr. Vukanich withdrew his glass tube and put the lights back up. He looked at me carefully.

"No congestion at all, Mr. Marlowe. If you have a headache, it is not from a sinus condition. I'd hazard a guess that you never had sinus trouble in your life. You had a septum operation sometime in the past, I see."

"Yes, Doctor. Got a kick playing football."

He nodded. "There is a slight shelf of bone which should have been cut away. Hardly enough to interfere with breathing, however."

He leaned back on the stool and held his knee. "Just what did you expect me to do for you?" he asked. He was a thin-faced man with an uninteresting pallor. He looked like a tubercular white rat.

"I wanted to talk to you about a friend of mine. He's in bad shape. He's a writer. Plenty of dough, but bad nerves. Needs help. He lives on the sauce for days on end. He needs that little extra something. His own doctor won't co-operate any more."

"Exactly what do you mean by co-operate?" Dr. Vukanich asked.

"All the guy needs is an occasional shot to calm him down. I thought maybe we could work something out. The money would be solid."

"Sorry, Mr. Marlowe. It is not my sort of problem." He stood up. "Rather a crude approach, if I may say so. Your friend may consult me, if he chooses. But he'd better have something wrong with him that requires treatment. That will be ten dollars, Mr. Marlowe."

"Come off it, Doc. You're on the list."

Dr. Vukanich leaned against the wall and lit a cigarette. He was giving me time. He blew smoke and looked at it. I gave him one of my cards to look at instead. He looked at it.

"What list would that be?" he inquired.

"The barred-window boys. I figure you might know my friend already. His name's Wade. I figure you might have him stashed away somewhere in a little white room. The guy is missing from home."

"You are an ass," Dr. Vukanich told me. "I don't go in for penny ante stuff like four-day liquor cures. They cure nothing in any case. I have no little white rooms and I am not acquainted with the friend you mention—even if he exists. That will be ten dollars—cash—right now. Or would you rather I called the police and make a complaint that you solicited me for narcotics?"

"That would be dandy," I said. "Let's."

"Get out of here, you cheap grifter."

I stood up off the chair. "I guess I made a mistake, Doctor. The last time the guy broke parole he holed up with a doctor whose name began with V. It was strictly an undercover operation. They fetched him late at night and brought him back the same way when he was over the jumps. Didn't even wait long enough to see him go in the house. So when he hops the coop again and don't come back for quite a piece, naturally we check over our files for a lead. We come up with three doctors whose names begin with V."

"Interesting," he said with a bleak smile. He was still giving me time. "What is the basis of your selection?"

I stared at him. His right hand was moving softly up and down the upper part of his left arm on the inside of it. His face was covered with a light sweat.

"Sorry, Doctor. We operate very confidential."

"Excuse me a moment. I have another patient that—"

He left the rest of it hanging in the air and went out. While he was gone a nurse poked her head through the doorway, looked at me briefly and withdrew.

Then Dr. Vukanich came back in strolling happily. He was smiling and relaxed. His eyes were bright.

"What? Are you still here?" He looked very surprised or pretended to. "I thought our little visit had been brought to an end."

"I'm leaving. I thought you wanted me to wait."

He chuckled. "You know something, Mr. Marlowe? We live in extraordinary times. For a mere five hundred dollars I could have you put in the hospital with several broken bones. Comical, isn't it?"

"Hilarious," I said. "Shoot yourself in the vein, don't you, Doc? Boy, do you brighten up!"

I started out. "Hasta luego, amigo," he chirped. "Don't forget my ten bucks. Pay the nurse."

He moved to an intercom and was speaking into it as I left. In the waiting room the same twelve people or twelve just like them were being uncomfortable. The nurse was right on the job.

"That will be ten dollars, please, Mr. Marlowe. This office requires immediate cash payment."

I stepped among the crowded feet to the door. She bounded out of her chair and ran around the desk. I pulled the door open.

"What happens when you don't get it?" I asked her.

"You'll find out what happens," she said angrily.

"Sure. You're just doing your job. So am I. Take a gander at the card I left and you'll see what my job is."

I went on out. The waiting patients looked at me with disapproving eyes. That was no way to treat Doctor.

# 18

Dr. Amos Varley was a very different proposition. He had a big old house in a big old garden with big old oak trees shading it. It was a massive frame structure with elaborate scrollwork along the overhang of the porches and the white porch railings had turned and fluted uprights like the legs of an old-fashioned grand piano. A few frail elderly people sat in long chairs on the porches with rugs tucked around them.

The entrance doors were double and had stained-glass panels. The hall inside was wide and cool and the parquetry floor was polished and without a single rug. Altadena is a hot place in summer. It is pushed back against the hills and the breeze jumps clear over it. Eighty years ago people knew how to build houses for this climate.

A nurse in crisp white took my card and after a wait Dr. Amos Varley condescended to see me. He was a big bald-headed guy with a cheery smile. His long white coat was spotless, he walked noiselessly on crepe rubber soles.

"What can I do for you, Mr. Marlowe?" He had a rich soft voice to soothe the pain and comfort the anxious heart. Doctor is here, there is nothing to worry about, everything will be fine. He had that bedside manner, thick, honeyed layers of it. He was wonderful—and he was as tough as armor plate.

"Doctor, I am looking for a man named Wade, a well-to-do alcoholic who has disappeared from his home. His past history suggests that he is holed up in some discreet joint than can handle him with skill. My only lead is a reference to a Dr. V. You're my third Dr. V. and I'm getting discouraged."

He smiled benignly. "Only your third, Mr. Marlowe? Surely there must be a hundred doctors in and around the Los Angeles area whose names begin with V."

"Sure, but not many of them would have rooms with barred windows. I noticed a few upstairs here, on the side of the house."

"Old people," Dr. Varley said sadly, but it was a rich full sadness. "Lonely old people, depressed and unhappy old people, Mr. Marlowe. Sometimes—" He made an expressive gesture with his hand, a curving motion outwards, a pause, then a gentle falling, like a dead leaf fluttering to the ground. "I don't treat alcoholics here," he added precisely. "Now if you will excuse me—"

"Sorry, Doctor. You just happened to be on our list. Probably a mistake. Something about a run-in with the narcotics people a couple of years ago."

"Is that so?" He looked puzzled, then the light broke. "Ah, yes, an assistant I was unwise enough to employ. For a very short time. He abused my confidence badly. Yes, indeed."

"Not the way I heard it," I said. "I guess I heard it wrong."

"And how did you hear it, Mr. Marlowe?" He was still giving me the full treatment with his smile and his mellow tones.

"That you had to turn in your narcotic prescription book."

That got to him a little. He didn't quite scowl but he peeled off a few layers of the charm. His blue eyes had a chilly glint. "And the source of this fantastic information?"

"A large detective agency that has facilities for building files on that sort of thing."

"A collection of cheap blackmailers, no doubt."

"Not cheap, Doctor. Their base rate is a hundred dollars a day. It's run by a former colonel of military police. No nickel grabber, Doctor. He rates way up."

"I shall give him a piece of my mind," Dr. Varley said with cool distaste. "His name?" The sun had set in Dr. Varley's manner. It was getting to be a chilly evening.

"Confidential, Doctor. But don't give it a thought. All in the day's work. Name of Wade doesn't ring a bell at all, huh?"

"I believe you know your way out, Mr. Marlowe."

The door of a small elevator opened behind him. A nurse pushed a wheel chair out. The chair contained what was left of a broken old man. His eyes were closed, his skin had a bluish tinge. He was well wrapped up. The nurse wheeled him silently across the polished floor and out of a side door. Dr. Varley said softly:

"Old people. Sick old people. Lonely old people. Do not come back, Mr. Marlowe. You might annoy me. When annoyed I can be rather unpleasant. I might even say *very* unpleasant."

"Okay by me, Doctor. Thanks for the time. Nice little dying-in home you got here."

"What was that?" He took a step towards me and peeled off the remaining layers of honey. The soft lines of his face set themselves into hard ridges.

"What's the matter?" I asked him. "I can see my man wouldn't be here. I wouldn't look for anybody here that wasn't too frail to fight back. Sick old people. Lonely old people. You said it yourself, Doctor. Unwanted old people, but with money and hungry heirs. Most of them probably judged incompetent by the court."

"I am getting annoyed," Dr. Varley said.

"Light food, light sedation, firm treatment. Put them out in the sun, put them back in the bed. Bar some of the windows in case there's a little spunk left. They love you, Doctor, one and all. They die holding your hand and seeing the sadness in your eyes. It's genuine too."

"It certainly is," he said in a low throaty growl. His hands were fists now. I ought to knock it off. But he had begun to nauseate me.

"Sure it is," I said. "Nobody likes to lose a good paying customer. Especially one you don't even have to please."

"Somebody has to do it," he said. "Somebody has to care for these sad old people, Mr. Marlowe."

"Somebody has to clean out cesspools. Come to think of it that's a clean honest job. So long, Dr. Varley. When my job makes me feel dirty I'll think of you. It will cheer me up no end."

"You filthy louse," Dr. Varley said between his wide white teeth. "I ought to break your back. Mine is an honorable branch of an honorable profession."

"Yeah." I looked at him wearily. "I know it is. Only it smells of death."

He didn't slug me, so I walked away from him and out. I looked back from the wide double doors. He hadn't moved. He had a job to do, putting back the layers of honey.

# 19

I drove back to Hollywood feeling like a short length of chewed string. It was too early to eat, and too hot. I turned on the fan in my office. It didn't make the air any cooler, just a little more lively. Outside on the boulevard the traffic brawled endlessly. Inside my head thoughts stuck together like flies on flypaper.

Three shots, three misses. All I had been doing was seeing too many doctors.

I called the Wade home. A Mexican sort of accent answered

and said that Mrs. Wade was not at home. I asked for Mr. Wade. The voice said Mr. Wade was not home either. I left my name. He seemed to catch it without any trouble. He said he was the houseboy.

I called George Peters at The Carne Organization. Maybe he knew some more doctors. He wasn't in. I left a phony name and a right telephone number. An hour crawled by like a sick cockroach. I was a grain of sand on the desert of oblivion. I was a two-gun cowpoke fresh out of bullets. Three shots, three misses. I hate it when they come in threes. You call on Mr. A. Nothing. You call on Mr. B. Nothing. You call on Mr. C. More of the same. A week later you find out it should have been Mr. D. Only you didn't know he existed and by the time you found out, the client had changed his mind and killed the investigation.

Drs. Vukanich and Varley were scratched. Varley had it too rich to fool with hooch cases. Vukanich was a punk, a high-wire performer who hit the main line in his own office. The help must know. At least some of the patients must know. All it took to finish him was one sorehead and one telephone call. Wade wouldn't have gone within blocks of him, drunk or sober. He might not be the brightest guy in the world—plenty of successful people are far from mental giants—but he couldn't be dumb enough to fool with Vukanich.

The only possible was Dr. Verringer. He had the space and the seclusion. He probably had the patience. But Sepulveda Canyon was a long way from Idle Valley. Where was the point of contact, how did they know each other, and if Verringer owned that property and had a buyer for it, he was halfway to being pretty well heeled. That gave me an idea. I called a man I knew in a title company to find out the status of the property. No answer. The title company had closed for the day.

I closed for the day too, and drove over to La Cienaga to Rudy's Bar-B-Q, gave my name to the master of ceremonies, and waited for the big moment on a bar stool with a whiskey sour in front of me and Marek Weber's waltz music in my ears. After a while I got in past the velvet rope and ate one of Rudy's "world-famous" Salisbury steaks, which is hamburger on a slab of burnt wood, ringed with browned-over mashed potato, supported by fried onion rings and one of those mixed up salads which men will eat with complete docility in restaurants, although they would probably start yelling if their wives tried to feed them one at home.

After that I drove home. As I opened the front door the phone started to ring.

"This is Eileen Wade, Mr. Marlowe. You wanted me to call you."

"Just to find out if anything had happened at your end. I have been seeing doctors all day and have made no friends."

"No, I'm sorry. He still hasn't showed up. I can't help being rather anxious. Then you have nothing to tell me, I suppose." Her voice was low and dispirited.

"It's a big crowded county, Mrs. Wade."

"It will be four whole days tonight."

"Sure, but that's not too long."

"For me it is." She was silent for a while. "I've been doing a lot of thinking, trying to remember something," she went on. "There must be something, some kind of hint or memory. Roger talks a great deal about all sorts of things."

"Does the name Verringer mean anything to you, Mrs. Wade?"

"No, I'm afraid not. Should it?"

"You mentioned that Mr. Wade was brought home one time by a tall young man dressed in a cowboy outfit. Would you recognize this tall young man if you saw him again, Mrs. Wade?"

"I suppose I might," she said hesitantly, "if the conditions were the same. But I only caught the merest glimpse of him. Was his name Verringer?"

"No, Mrs. Wade. Verringer is a heavily built, middle-aged man who runs, or more accurately has run, some kind of guest ranch in Sepulveda Canyon. He has a dressed up fancy boy named Earl working for him. And Verringer calls himself a doctor."

"That's wonderful," she said warmly. "Don't you feel that you're on the right track?"

"I could be wetter than a drowned kitten. I'll call you when I know. I just wanted to make sure Roger hadn't come home and that you hadn't recalled anything definite."

"I'm afraid I haven't been of much help to you," she said sadly. "Please call me at any time, no matter how late it is."

I said I would do that and we hung up. I took a gun and a three-cell flashlight with me this time. The gun was a tough little short-barreled .32 with flat-point cartridges. Dr. Verringer's boy Earl might have other toys than brass knuckles. If he had, he was plenty goofy enough to play with them.

I hit the highway again and drove as fast as I dared. It was a moonless night, and would be getting dark by the time I reached the entrance to Dr. Verringer's estate. Darkness was what I needed.

The gates were still locked with the chain and padlock. I drove on past and parked well off the highway. There was still some light under the trees but it wouldn't last long. I climbed the gate and went up the side of the hill looking for a hiking path. Far back in the valley I thought I heard a quail. A mourning dove exclaimed against the miseries of life. There wasn't any hiking path or I couldn't find one, so I went back to the road and walked along the edge of the gravel. The eucalyptus trees gave way to the oaks and I crossed the ridge and far off I could see a few lights. It took me three quarters of an hour to work up behind the swimming pool and the tennis courts to a spot where I could look down on the main building at the end of the road. It was lighted up and I could hear music coming from it. And farther off in the trees another cabin showed light. There were small dark cabins dotted all over the place in the trees. I went along a path now and suddenly a floodlight went on at the back of the main cabin. I stopped dead. The floodlight was not looking for anything. It pointed straight down and made a wide pool of light on the back porch and the ground beyond. Then a door banged open and Earl came out. Then I knew I was in the right place.

Earl was a cowpoke tonight, and it had been a cowpoke who brought Roger Wade home the time before. Earl was spinning a rope. He wore a dark shirt stitched with white and a polka-dot scarf knotted loosely around his neck. He wore a wide leather belt with a load of silver on it and a pair of tooled leather holsters with ivory-handled guns in them. He wore elegant riding pants and boots cross-stitched in white and glistening new. On the back of his head was a white sombrero and what looked like a woven silver cord hanging loosely down his shirt, the ends not fastened.

He stood there alone under the white floodlight, spinning his rope around him, stepping in and out of it, an actor without an audience, a tall, slender, handsome dude wrangler putting on a show all by himself and loving every minute of it. Two-Gun Earl, the Terror of Cochise County. He belonged on one of those guest ranches that are so all-fired horsy the telephone girl wears riding boots to work.

All at once he heard a sound, or pretended to. The rope dropped, his hands swept the two guns from the holsters, and the crook of his thumbs was over the hammers as they came level. He peered into the darkness. I didn't dare move. The damn guns could be loaded. But the floodlight had blinded him and he didn't see anything. He slipped his guns back in the holsters, picked up the rope and gathered it loosely, went back into the house. The light went off, and so did I.

I moved around through the trees and got close to the small lighted cabin on the slope. No sound came from it. I reached a screened window and looked in. The light came from a lamp on a night table beside a bed. A man lay flat on his back in the bed, his body relaxed, his arms in pajama sleeves outside the covers, his eyes wide open and staring at the ceiling. He looked big. His face was partly shadowed, but I could see that he was pale and that he needed a shave and had needed one for just about the right length of time. The spread fingers of his hands lay motionless on the outside of the bed. He looked as if he hadn't moved for hours.

I heard steps coming along the path at the far side of the cabin. A screen door creaked and then the solid shape of Dr. Verringer showed in the doorway. He was carrying what looked like a large glass of tomato juice. He switched on a standing lamp. His Hawaiian shirt gleamed yellowly. The man in the bed didn't even look at him.

Dr. Verringer put the glass down on the night table and pulled a chair close and sat down. He reached for one of the wrists and felt a pulse. "How are you feeling now, Mr. Wade?" His voice was kindly and solicitous.

The man on the bed didn't answer him or look at him. He went on staring at the ceiling.

"Come, come, Mr. Wade. Let us not be moody. Your pulse is only slightly faster than normal. You are weak, but otherwise—"

"Tejjy," the man on the bed said suddenly, "tell the man that if he knows how I am, the son of a bitch needn't bother to ask me." He had a nice clear voice, but the tone was bitter.

"Who is Tejjy?" Dr. Verringer asked patiently.

"My mouthpiece. She's up there in the corner."

Dr. Verringer looked up. "I see a small spider," he said. "Stop acting, Mr. Wade. It is not necessary with me."

"*Tegenaria domestica*, the common jumping spider, pal. I like spiders. They practically never wear Hawaiian shirts."

Dr. Verringer moistened his lips. "I have no time for playfulness, Mr. Wade."

"Nothing playful about Tejjy." Wade turned his head slowly, as if it weighed very heavy, and stared at Dr. Verringer contemptuously. "Tejjy is dead serious. She creeps up on you. When you're not looking she makes a quick silent hop. After a while she's near enough. She makes the last jump. You get sucked dry, Doctor. Very dry. Tejjy doesn't eat you. She just sucks the juice until there's nothing left but the skin. If you plan to wear that shirt much longer, Doctor, I'd say it couldn't happen too soon."

Dr. Verringer leaned back in the chair. "I need five thousand dollars," he said calmly. "How soon could that happen?"

"You got six hundred and fifty bucks," Wade said nastily. "As well as my loose change. How the hell much does it cost in this bordello?"

"Chicken feed," Dr. Verringer said. "I told you my rates had gone up."

"You didn't say they had moved to Mount Wilson."

"Don't fence with me, Wade," Dr. Verringer said curtly. "You are in no position to get funny. Also you have betrayed my confidence."

"I didn't know you had any."

Dr. Verringer tapped slowly on the arms of the chair. "You called me up in the middle of the night," he said. "You were in a desperate condition. You said you would kill yourself if I didn't come. I didn't want to do it and you know why. I have no license to practice medicine in this state. I am trying to get rid of this property without losing it all. I have Earl to look after and he was about due for a bad spell. I told you it would cost you a lot of money. You still insisted and I went. I want five thousand dollars."

"I was foul with strong drink," Wade said. "You can't hold a man to that kind of bargain. You're damn well paid already."

"Also," Dr. Verringer said slowly, "you mentioned my name to your wife. You told her I was coming for you."

Wade looked surprised. "I didn't do anything of the sort," he said. "I didn't even see her. She was asleep."

"Some other time then. A private detective has been here asking about you. He couldn't possibly have known where to come, unless he was told. I stalled him off, but he may come back. You have to go home, Mr. Wade. But first I want my five thousand dollars."

"You're not the brightest guy in the world, are you, Doc? If my wife knew where I was, why would she need a detective? She could have come herself—supposing she cared that much. She could have brought Candy, our houseboy. Candy would cut your Blue Boy into thin strips while Blue Boy was making up his mind what picture he was starring in today."

"You have a nasty tongue, Wade. And a nasty mind."

"I have a nasty five thousand bucks too, Doc. Try and get it."

"You will write me a check," Dr. Verringer said firmly. "Now, at once. Then you will get dressed and Earl will take you home."

"A check?" Wade was almost laughing. "Sure I'll give you a check. Fine. How will you cash it?"

Dr. Verringer smiled quietly. "You think you will stop payment, Mr. Wade. But you won't. I assure you that you won't."

"You fat crook!" Wade yelled at him.

Dr. Verringer shook his head. "In some things, yes. Not in all. I am a mixed character like most people. Earl will drive you home."

"Nix. That lad makes my skin crawl," Wade said.

Dr. Verringer stood up gently and reached over and patted the shoulder of the man on the bed. "To me Earl is quite harmless, Mr. Wade. I have ways of controlling him."

"Name one," a new voice said, and Earl came through the door in his Roy Rogers outfit. Dr. Verringer turned smiling.

"Keep that psycho away from me," Wade yelled, showing fear for the first time.

Earl put his hands on his ornamented belt. His face was deadpan. A light whistling noise came from between his teeth. He moved slowly into the room.

"You shouldn't have said that," Dr. Verringer said quickly, and turned towards Earl. "All right, Earl. I'll handle Mr. Wade myself. I'll help him get dressed while you bring the car up here as close to the cabin as possible. Mr. Wade is quite weak."

"And he's going to be a lot weaker," Earl said in a whistling kind of voice. "Out of my way, fatso."

"Now, Earl—" he reached out and grabbed the handsome young man's arm—"you don't want to go back to Camarillo, do you? One word from me and—"

That was as far as he got. Earl jerked his arm loose and his right hand came up with a flash of metal. The armored fist crashed against Dr. Verringer's jaw. He went down as if shot through the heart. The fall shook the cabin. I started running.

I reached the door and yanked it open. Earl spun around, leaning forward a little, staring at me without recognition. There was a bubbling sound behind his lips. He started for me fast.

I jerked the gun out and showed it to him. It meant nothing. Either his own guns were not loaded or he had forgotten all about them. The brass knuckles were all he needed. He kept coming.

I fired through the open window across the bed. The crash of the gun in the small room seemed much louder than it should have been. Earl stopped dead. His head slewed around and he looked at the hole in the window screen. He looked back at me. Slowly his face came alive and he grinned.

"Wha' happen?" he asked brightly.

"Get rid of the knucks," I said, watching his eyes.

He looked surprisingly down at his hand. He slipped the mauler off and threw it casually in the corner.

"Now the gun belt," I said. "Don't touch the guns, just the buckle."

"They're not loaded," he said smiling. "Hell, they're not even guns, just stage money."

"The belt. Hurry it."

He looked at the short-barreled .32. "That a real one? Oh sure it is. The screen. Yeah, the screen."

The man on the bed wasn't on the bed any more. He was behind Earl. He reached swiftly and pulled one of the bright guns loose. Earl didn't like this. His face showed it.

"Lay off him," I said angrily. "Put that back where you got it."

"He's right," Wade said. "They're cap guns." He backed away and put the shiny pistol on the table. "Christ, I'm as weak as a broken arm."

"Take the belt off," I said for the third time. When you start something with a type like Earl you have to finish it. Keep it simple and don't change your mind.

He did it at last, quite amiably. Then, holding the belt, he walked over to the table and got his other gun and put it in the holster and put the belt right back on again. I let him do it. It wasn't until then that he saw Dr. Verringer crumpled on the floor against the wall. He made a sound of concern, went quickly across the room into the bathroom, and came back with a glass jug of water. He dumped the water on Dr. Verringer's head. Dr. Verringer sputtered and rolled over. Then he groaned. Then he clapped a hand to his jaw. Then he started to get up. Earl helped him.

"Sorry, Doc. I must have just let fly without seeing who it was."

"It's all right, nothing broken," Verringer said, waving him away. "Get the car up here, Earl. And don't forget the key for the padlock down below."

"Car up here, sure. Right away. Key for the padlock. I got it. Right away, Doc."

He went out of the room whistling.

Wade was sitting on the side of the bed, looking shaky.

"You the dick he was talking about?" he asked me. "How did you find me?"

"Just asking around from people who know about these things," I said. "If you want to get home, you might get clothes on."

Dr. Verringer was leaning against the wall, massaging his jaw. "I'll help him," he said thickly. "All I do is help people and all they do is kick me in the teeth."

"I know just how you feel," I said.

I went out and left them to work at it.


## 20

The car was close by when they came out, but Earl was gone. He had stopped the car, cut the lights, and walked back towards the big cabin without saying anything to me. He was still whistling, groping for some half-remembered tune.

Wade climbed carefully into the back seat and I got in beside him. Dr. Verringer drove. If his jaw hurt badly and his head ached, he didn't show it or mention it. We went over the ridge and down to the end of the graveled drive. Earl had already been down and unlocked the gate and pulled it open. I told Verringer where my car was and he pulled up close to it. Wade got into it and sat silent, staring at nothing. Verringer got out and went round beside him. He spoke to Wade gently.

"About my five thousand dollars, Mr. Wade. The check you promised me."

Wade slid down and rested his head on the back of the seat. "I'll think about it."

"You promised it. I need it."

"Duress, the word is, Verringer, a threat of harm. I have protection now."

"I fed and washed you," Verringer persisted. "I came in the night. I protected you, I cured you—for the time being, at least."

"Not five grand worth," Wade sneered. "You got plenty out of my pockets."

Verringer wouldn't let go. "I have a promise of a connection in Cuba, Mr. Wade. You are a rich man. You should help others in their need. I have Earl to look after. To avail myself of this opportunity I need the money. I will pay it back in full."

I began to squirm. I wanted to smoke, but I was afraid it would make Wade sick.

"Like hell you'd pay it back," Wade said wearily. "You won't live long enough. One of these nights Blue Boy will kill you in your sleep."

Verringer stepped back. I couldn't see his expression, but his voice hardened. "There are more unpleasant ways to die," he said. "I think yours will be one of them."

He walked back to his car and got into it. He drove in through his gates and was gone. I backed and turned and headed towards the city. After a mile or two Wade muttered: "Why should I give that fat slob five thousand dollars?"

"No reason at all."

"Then why do I feel like a bastard for not giving it to him?"

"No reason at all."

He turned his head just enough to look at me. "He handled me like a baby," Wade said. "He hardly left me alone for fear Earl would come in and beat me up. He took every dime I had in my pockets."

"You probably told him to."

"You on his side?"

"Skip it," I said. "This is just a job to me."

Silence for a couple of miles more. We went past the fringe of one of the outlying suburbs. Wade spoke again.

"Maybe I'll give it to him. He's broke. The property is foreclosed. He won't get a dime out of it. All on account of that psycho. Why does he do it?"

"I wouldn't know."

"I'm a writer," Wade said. "I'm supposed to understand what makes people tick. I don't understand one damn thing about anybody."

I turned over the pass and after a climb the lights of the

valley spread out endlessly in front of us. We dipped down to the highway north and west that goes to Ventura. After a while we passed through Encino. I stopped for a light and looked up towards the lights high on the hill where the big houses were. In one of them the Lennoxes had lived. We went on.

"The turn-off is pretty close now," Wade said. "Or do you know it?"

"I know it."

"By the way, you haven't told me your name."

"Philip Marlowe."

"Nice name." His voice changed sharply, saying: "Wait a minute. You the guy that was mixed up with Lennox?"

"Yeah."

He was staring at me in the darkness of the car. We passed the last buildings on the main drag of Encino.

"I knew her," Wade said. "A little. Him I never saw. Queer business, that. The law boys gave you the rough edge, didn't they?"

I didn't answer him.

"Maybe you don't like to talk about it," he said.

"Could be. Why would it interest you?"

"Hell, I'm a writer. It must be quite a story."

"Take tonight off. You must be feeling pretty weak."

"Okay, Marlowe. Okay. You don't like me. I get it."

We reached the turn-off and I swung the car into it and towards the low hills and the gap between them that was Idle Valley.

"I don't either like you or dislike you," I said. "I don't know you. Your wife asked me to find you and bring you home. When I deliver you at your house I'm through. Why she picked on me I couldn't say. Like I said, it's just a job."

We turned the flank of a hill and hit a wider, more firmly paved road. He said his house was a mile farther on, on the right side. He told me the number, which I already knew. For a guy in his shape he was a pretty persistent talker.

"How much is she paying you?" he asked.

"We didn't discuss it."

"Whatever it is, it's not enough. I owe you a lot of thanks. You did a great job, chum. I wasn't worth the trouble."

"That's just the way you feel tonight."

He laughed. "You know something, Marlowe? I could get to like you. You're a bit of a bastard—like me."

We reached the house. It was a two-story over-all shingle house with a small pillared portico and a long lawn from the entrance to a thick row of shrubs inside the white fence. There was a light in the portico. I pulled into the driveway and stopped close to the garage.

"Can you make it without help?"

"Of course." He got out of the car. "Aren't you coming in for a drink or something?"

"Not tonight, thanks; I'll wait here until you're in the house."

He stood there breathing hard. "Okay," he said shortly.

He turned and walked carefully along a flagged path to the front door. He held on to a white pillar for a moment, then tried the door. It opened, he went in. The door stayed open and light washed across the green lawn. There was a sudden flutter of voices. I started backing from the driveway, following the back-up light. Somebody called out.

I looked and saw Eileen Wade standing in the open doorway. I kept going and she started to run. So I had to stop. I cut the lights and got out of the car. When she came up I said:

"I ought to have called you, but I was afraid to leave him."

"Of course. Did you have a lot of trouble?"

"Well—a little more than ringing a doorbell."

"Please come in the house and tell me all about it."

"He should be in bed. By tomorrow he'll be as good as new."

"Candy will put him to bed," she said. "He won't drink tonight, if that's what you are thinking of."

"Never occurred to me. Goodnight, Mrs. Wade."

"You must be tired. Don't you want a drink yourself?"

I lit a cigarette. It seemed like a couple of weeks since I had tasted tobacco. I drank in the smoke.

"May I have just one puff?"

She came close to me and I handed her the cigarette. She drew on it and coughed. She handed it back laughing. "Strictly an amateur, as you see."

"So you knew Sylvia Lennox," I said. "Was that why you wanted to hire me?"

"I knew who?" She sounded puzzled.

"Sylvia Lennox." I had the cigarette back now. I was eating it pretty fast.

"Oh," she said, startled. "That girl that was—murdered. No, I didn't know her personally. I knew who she was. Didn't I tell you that?"

"Sorry, I'd forgotten just what you did tell me."

She was still standing there quietly, close to me, slim and tall in a white dress of some sort. The light from the open door touched the fringe of her hair and made it glow softly.

"Why did you ask me if that had anything to do with my wanting to, as you put it, hire you?" When I didn't answer at once she added, "Did Roger tell you he knew her?"

"He said something about the case when I told him my name. He didn't connect me with it immediately, then he did. He talked so damn much I don't remember half of what he said."

"I see. I must go in, Mr. Marlowe, and see if my husband needs anything. And if you won't come in—"

"I'll leave this with you," I said.

I took hold of her and pulled her towards me and tilted her head back. I kissed her hard on the lips. She didn't fight me and she didn't respond. She pulled herself away quietly and stood there looking at me.

"You shouldn't have done that," she said. "That was wrong. You're too nice a person."

"Sure. Very wrong," I agreed. "But I've been such a nice faithful well-behaved gun dog all day long, I got charmed into one of the silliest ventures I ever tackled, and damned if it didn't turn out just as though somebody had written a script for it. You know something? I believe you knew where he was all along—or at least knew the name of Dr. Verringer. You just wanted to get me involved with him, tangled up with him so I'd feel a sense of responsibility to look after him. Or am I crazy?"

"Of course you're crazy," she said coldly. "That is the most outrageous nonsense I ever listened to." She started to turn away.

"Wait a minute," I said. "That kiss won't leave a scar. You just think it will. And don't tell me I'm too nice a person. I'd rather be a heel."

She looked back. "Why?"

"If I hadn't been a nice guy to Terry Lennox, he would still be alive."

"Yes?" she said quietly. "How can you be so sure? Good-night, Mr. Marlowe. And thank you so very much for almost everything."

She walked back along the edge of the grass. I watched her into the house. The door closed. The porch light went off. I waved at nothing and drove away.

## 21

Next morning I got up late on account of the big fee I had earned the night before. I drank an extra cup of coffee, smoked an extra cigarette, ate an extra slice of Canadian bacon, and for the three hundredth time I swore I would never again use an electric razor. That made the day normal. I hit the office about ten, picked up some odds and ends of mail, slit the envelopes and let the stuff lie on the desk. I opened the windows wide to let out the smell of dust and dinginess that collected in the night and hung in the still air, in the corners of the room, in the slats of the venetian blinds. A dead moth was spread-eagled on a corner of the desk. On the window sill a bee with tattered wings was crawling along the woodwork, buzzing in a tired remote sort of way, as if she knew it wasn't any use, she was finished, she had flown too many missions and would never get back to the hive again.

I knew it was going to be one of those crazy days. Everyone has them. Days when nobody rolls in but the loose wheels, the dingoes who park their brains with their gum, the squirrels who can't find their nuts, the mechanics who always have a gear wheel left over.

The first was a big blond roughneck named Kuissenen or something Finnish like that. He jammed his massive bottom in the customer's chair and planted two wide horny hands on my desk and said he was a power-shovel operator, that he lived in Culver City, and the goddam woman who lived next door to him was trying to poison his dog. Every morning before he let the dog out for a run in the back yard he had to search the place from fence to fence for meatballs thrown over the potato vine from next door. He'd found nine of them so far and they were loaded with a greenish powder he knew was an arsenic weed killer.

"How much to watch out and catch her at it?" He stared at me as unblinkingly as a fish in a tank.

"Why not do it yourself?"

"I got to work for a living, mister. I'm losing four twenty-five an hour just coming up here to ask."

"Try the police?"

"I try the police. They might get around to it some time next year. Right now they're busy sucking up to MGM."

"S.P.C.A.? The Tailwaggers?"

"What's them?"

I told him about the Tailwaggers. He was far from interested. He knew about the S.P.C.A. The S.P.C.A. could take a running jump. They couldn't see nothing smaller than a horse.

"It says on the door you're an investigator," he said truculently. "Okay, go the hell out and investigate. Fifty bucks if you catch her."

"Sorry," I said. "I'm tied up. Spending a couple of weeks hiding in a gopher hole in your back yard would be out of my line anyway—even for fifty bucks."

He stood up glowering. "Big shot," he said. "Don't need the dough, huh? Can't be bothered saving the life of a itty-bitty dog. Nuts to you, big shot."

"I've got troubles too, Mr. Kuissenen."

"I'll twist her goddam neck if I catch her," he said, and I didn't doubt he could have done it. He could have twisted the hind leg off of an elephant. "That's what makes it I want somebody else. Just because the little tike barks when a car goes by the house. Sour-faced old bitch."

He started for the door. "Are you sure it's the dog she's trying to poison?" I asked his back.

"Sure I'm sure." He was halfway to the door before the nickel dropped. He swung around fast then. "Say that again, buster."

I just shook my head. I didn't want to fight him. He might hit me on the head with my desk. He snorted and went out, almost taking the door with him.

The next cookie in the dish was a woman, not old, not young, not clean, not too dirty, obviously poor, shabby, querulous and stupid. The girl she roomed with—in her set any woman who works out is a girl—was taking money out of her purse. A dollar here, four bits there, but it added up. She figured she was out close to twenty dollars in all. She couldn't afford it. She couldn't afford to move either. She couldn't afford a detective. She thought I ought to be willing to throw a scare into the roommate just on the telephone like, not mentioning any names.

It took her twenty minutes or more to tell me this. She kneaded her bag incessantly while telling it.

"Anybody you know could do that," I said.

"Yeah, but you bein' a dick and all."

"I don't have a license to threaten people I know nothing about."

"I'm goin' to tell her I been in to see you. I don't have to say it's her. Just that you're workin' on it."

"I wouldn't if I were you. If you mention my name she may call me up. If she does that, I'll tell her the facts."

She stood up and slammed her shabby bag against her stomach. "You're no gentleman," she said shrilly.

"Where does it say I have to be?"

She went out mumbling.

After lunch I had Mr. Simpson W. Edelweiss. He had a card to prove it. He was manager of a sewing machine agency. He was a small tired-looking man about forty-eight to fifty, small hands and feet, wearing a brown suit with sleeves too long, and a stiff white collar behind a purple tie with black diamonds on it. He sat on the edge of the chair without fidgeting and looked at me out of sad black eyes. His hair was black too and thick and rough without a sign of gray in it that I could see. He had a clipped mustache with a reddish tone. He could have passed for thirty-five if you didn't look at the backs of his hands.

"Call me Simp," he said. "Everybody else does. I got it coming. I'm a Jewish man married to a Gentile woman, twenty-four years of age, beautiful. She run away a couple of times before."

He got out a photo of her and showed it to me. She might have been beautiful to him. To me she was a big sloppy-looking cow of a woman with a weak mouth.

"What's your trouble, Mr. Edelweiss? I don't do divorce business." I tried to give him back the photo. He waved it away. "The client is always mister to me," I added. "Until he has told me a few dozen lies anyway."

He smiled. "Lies I got no use for. It's not a divorce matter. I just want Mabel back again. But she don't come back until I find her. Maybe it's a kind of game with her."

He told me about her, patiently, without rancor. She drank, she played around, she wasn't a very good wife by his standards, but he could have been brought up too strict. She had a heart as big as a house, he said, and he loved her. He didn't kid himself he was any dreamboat, just a steady worker bringing home the pay check. They had a joint bank account. She had drawn it all out, but he was prepared for that. He had a pretty good idea who she had lit out with, and if he was right the man would clean her out and leave her stranded.

"Name of Kerrigan," he said. "Monroe Kerrigan. I don't aim to knock the Catholics. There is plenty of bad Jews too. This Kerrigan is a barber when he works. I ain't knocking barbers either. But a lot of them are drifters and horse players. Not real steady."

"Won't you hear from her when she is cleaned out?"

"She gets awful ashamed. She might hurt herself."

"It's a Missing Persons job, Mr. Edelweiss. You should go down and make a report."

"No. I'm not knocking the police, but I don't want it that way. Mabel would be humiliated."

The world seemed to be full of people Mr. Edelweiss was not knocking. He put some money on the desk.

"Two hundred dollars," he said. "Down payment. I'd rather do it my way."

"It will happen again," I said.

"Sure." He shrugged and spread his hands gently. "But twenty-four years old and me almost fifty. How could it be different? She'll settle down after a while. Trouble is, no kids. She can't have kids. A Jew likes to have a family. So Mabel knows that. She's humiliated."

"You're a very forgiving man, Mr. Edelweiss."

"Well I ain't a Christian," he said. "And I'm not knocking Christians, you understand. But with me it's real. I don't just say it. I do it. Oh, I almost forgot the most important."

He got out a picture postcard and pushed it across the desk after the money. "From Honolulu she sends it. Money goes fast in Honolulu. One of my uncles had a jewelry business there. Retired now. Lives in Seattle."

I picked the photo up again. "I'll have to farm this one out," I told him. "And I'll have to have this copied."

"I could hear you saying that, Mr. Marlowe, before I got here. So I come prepared." He took out an envelope and it contained five more prints. "I got Kerrigan too, but only a snapshot." He went into another pocket and gave me another envelope. I looked at Kerrigan. He had a smooth dishonest face that did not surprise me. Three copies of Kerrigan.

Mr. Simpson W. Edelweiss gave me another card which had on it his name, his residence, his telephone number. He said he hoped it would not cost too much but that he would respond at once to any demand for further funds and he hoped to hear from me.

"Two hundred ought to pretty near do it if she's still in Honolulu," I said. "What I need now is a detailed physical description of both parties that I can put into a telegram. Height, weight, age, coloring, any noticeable scars or other identifying marks, what clothes she was wearing and had with her, and how much money was in the account she cleaned out. If you've been through this before, Mr. Edelweiss, you will know what I want."

"I got a peculiar feeling about this Kerrigan. Uneasy."

I spent another half hour milking him and writing things

down. Then he stood up quietly, shook hands quietly, bowed and left the office quietly.

"Tell Mabel everything is fine," he said as he went out.

It turned out to be routine. I sent a wire to an agency in Honolulu and followed it with an airmail containing the photos and whatever information I had left out of the wire. They found her working as a chambermaid's helper in a luxury hotel, scrubbing bathtubs and bathroom floors and so on. Kerrigan had done just what Mr. Edelweiss expected, cleaned her out while she was asleep and skipped, leaving her stuck with the hotel bill. She pawned a ring which Kerrigan couldn't have taken without violence, and got enough out of it to pay the hotel but not enough to buy her way home. So Edelweiss hopped a plane and went after her.

He was too good for her. I sent him a bill for twenty dollars and the cost of a long telegram. The Honolulu agency grabbed the two hundred. With a portrait of Madison in my office safe I could afford to be underpriced.

So passed a day in the life of a P.I. Not exactly a typical day but not totally untypical either. What makes a man stay with it nobody knows. You don't get rich, you don't often have much fun. Sometimes you get beaten up or shot at or tossed into the jailhouse. Once in a long while you get dead. Every other month you decide to give it up and find some sensible occupation while you can still walk without shaking your head. Then the door buzzer rings and you open the inner door to the waiting room and there stands a new face with a new problem, a new load of grief, and a small piece of money.

"Come in, Mr. Thingummy. What can I do for you?"

There must be a reason.

Three days later in the shank of the afternoon Eileen Wade called me up, and asked me to come around to the house for a drink the next evening. They were having a few friends in for cocktails. Roger would like to see me and thank me adequately. And would I please send in a bill?

"You don't owe me anything, Mrs. Wade. What little I did I got paid for."

"I must have looked very silly acting Victorian about it," she said. "A kiss doesn't seem to mean much nowadays. You will come, won't you?"

"I guess so. Against my better judgment."

"Roger is quite well again. He's working."

"Good."

"You sound very solemn today. I guess you take life pretty seriously."

"Now and then. Why?"

She laughed very gently and said goodbye and hung up. I sat there for a while taking life seriously. Then I tried to think of something funny so that I could have a great big laugh. Neither way worked, so I got Terry Lennox's letter of farewell out of the safe and reread it. It reminded me that I had never gone to Victor's for that gimlet he asked me to drink for him. It was just about the right time of day for the bar to be quiet, the way he would have liked it himself, if he had been around to go with me. I thought of him with a vague sadness and with a puckering bitterness too. When I got to Victor's I almost kept going. Almost, but not quite. I had too much of his money. He had made a fool of me but he had paid well for the privilege.

## 22

It was so quiet in Victor's that you almost heard the temperature drop as you came in at the door. On a bar stool a woman in a black tailormade, which couldn't at that time of year have been anything but some synthetic fabric like orlon, was sitting alone with a pale greenish-colored drink in front of her and smoking a cigarette in a long jade holder. She had that fine-drawn intense look that is sometimes neurotic, sometimes sex-hungry, and sometimes just the result of drastic dieting.

I sat down two stools away and the barkeep nodded to me, but didn't smile.

"A gimlet," I said. "No bitters."

He put the little napkin in front of me and kept looking at me. "You know something," he said in a pleased voice. "I heard you and your friend talking one night and I got me in a bottle of that Rose's Lime Juice. Then you didn't come back any more and I only opened it tonight."

"My friend left town," I said. "A double if it's all right with you. And thanks for taking the trouble."

He went away. The woman in black gave me a quick glance, then looked down into her glass. "So few people drink them around here," she said so quietly that I didn't realize at first that she was speaking to me. Then she looked my way again. She had very large dark eyes. She had the reddest fingernails I had ever seen. But she didn't look like a pickup and there was no trace of come-on in her voice. "Gimlets I mean."

"A fellow taught me to like them," I said.

"He must be English."

"Why?"

"The lime juice. It's as English as boiled fish with that awful anchovy sauce that looks as if the cook had bled into it. That's how they got called limeys. The English—not the fish."

"I thought it was more a tropical drink, hot weather stuff. Malaya or some place like that."

"You may be right." She turned away again.

The bartender set the drink in front of me. With the lime juice it has a sort of pale greenish yellowish misty look. I tasted it. It was both sweet and sharp at the same time. The woman in black watched me. Then she lifted her own glass towards me. We both drank. Then I knew hers was the same drink.

The next move was routine, so I didn't make it. I just sat there. "He wasn't English," I said after a moment. "I guess maybe he had been there during the war. We used to come in here once in a while, early like now. Before the mob started boiling."

"It's a pleasant hour," she said. "In a bar almost the only pleasant hour." She emptied her glass. "Perhaps I knew your friend," she said. "What was his name?"

I didn't answer her right away. I lit a cigarette and watched her tap the stub of hers out of the jade holder and fit another in its place. I reached across with a lighter. "Lennox," I said.

She thanked me for the light and gave me a brief searching

glance. Then she nodded. "Yes, I knew him very well. Perhaps a little too well."

The barkeep drifted over and glanced at my glass. "A couple more of the same," I said. "In a booth."

I got down off the stool and stood waiting. She might or might not blow me down. I didn't particularly care. Once in a while in this much too sex-conscious country a man and a woman can meet and talk without dragging bedrooms into it. This could be it, or she could just think I was on the make. If so, the hell with her.

She hesitated, but not for long. She gathered up a pair of black gloves and a black suede bag with a gold frame and clasp and walked across into a corner booth and sat down without a word. I sat down across the small table.

"My name is Marlowe."

"Mine is Linda Loring," she said calmly. "A bit of a sentimentalist, aren't you, Mr. Marlowe?"

"Because I came in here to drink a gimlet? How about yourself?"

"I might have a taste for them."

"So might I. But it would be a little too much coincidence."

She smiled at me vaguely. She had emerald earrings and an emerald lapel pin. They looked like real stones because of the way they were cut—flat with beveled edges. And even in the dim light of a bar they had an inner glow.

"So you're the man," she said.

The bar waiter brought the drinks over and set them down. When he went away I said: "I'm a fellow who knew Terry Lennox, liked him, and had an occasional drink with him. It was kind of a side deal, an accidental friendship. I never went to his home or knew his wife. I saw her once in a parking lot."

"There was a little more to it than that, wasn't there?"

She reached for her glass. She had an emerald ring set in a nest of diamonds. Beside it a thin platinum band said she was married. I put her in the second half of the thirties, early in the second half.

"Maybe," I said. "The guy bothered me. He still does. How about you?"

She leaned on an elbow and looked up at me without any particular expression. "I said I knew him rather too well. Too well to think it mattered much what happened to him. He had a rich wife who gave him all the luxuries. All she asked in return was to be let alone."

"Seems reasonable," I said.

"Don't be sarcastic, Mr. Marlowe. Some women are like that. They can't help it. It wasn't as if he didn't know in the beginning. If he had to get proud, the door was open. He didn't have to kill her."

"I agree with you."

She straightened up and looked hard at me. Her lip curled. "So he ran away and, if what I hear is true, you helped him. I suppose you feel proud about that."

"Not me," I said. "I just did it for the money."

"That is not amusing, Mr. Marlowe. Frankly I don't know why I sit here drinking with you."

"That's easily changed, Mrs. Loring." I reached for my glass and dropped the contents down the hatch. "I thought perhaps you could tell me something about Terry that I didn't know. I'm not interested in speculating why Terry Lennox beat his wife's face to a bloody sponge."

"That's a pretty brutal way to put it," she said angrily.

"You don't like the words? Neither do I. And I wouldn't be here drinking a gimlet if I believed he did anything of the sort."

She stared. After a moment she said slowly: "He killed himself and left a full confession. What more do you want?"

"He had a gun," I said. "In Mexico that might be enough excuse for some jittery cop to pour lead into him. Plenty of American police have done their killings the same way—some of them through doors that didn't open fast enough to suit them. As for the confession, I haven't seen it."

"No doubt the Mexican police faked it," she said tartly.

"They wouldn't know how, not in a little place like Otato-clán. No, the confession is probably real enough, but it doesn't prove he killed his wife. Not to me anyway. All it proves to me is that he didn't see any way out. In a spot like that a certain sort of man—you can call him weak or soft or sentimental if it amuses you—might decide to save some other people from a lot of very painful publicity."

"That's fantastic," she said. "A man doesn't kill himself or deliberately get himself killed to save a little scandal. Sylvia was already dead. As for her sister and her father—they could take care of themselves very efficiently. People with enough money, Mr. Marlowe, can always protect themselves."

"Okay, I'm wrong about the motive. Maybe I'm wrong all down the line. A minute ago you were mad at me. You want me to leave now—so you can drink *your* gimlet?"

Suddenly she smiled. "I'm sorry. I'm beginning to think you are sincere. What I thought then was that you were trying to justify yourself, far more than Terry. I don't think you are, somehow."

"I'm not. I did something foolish and I got the works for it. Up to a point anyway. I don't deny that his confession saved me a lot worse. If they had brought him back and tried him, I guess they would have hung one on me too. The least it would have cost me would have been far more money than I could afford."

"Not to mention your license," she said dryly.

"Maybe. There was a time when any cop with a hangover could get me busted. It's a little different now. You get a hearing before a commission of the state licensing authority. Those people are not too crazy about the city police."

She tasted her drink and said slowly: "All things considered, don't you think it was best the way it was? No trial, no sensational headlines, no mud-slinging just to sell newspapers without the slightest regard for truth or fairplay or for the feelings of innocent people."

"Didn't I just say so? And you said it was fantastic."

She leaned back and put her head against the upper curve of the padding on the back of the booth. "Fantastic that Terry Lennox should have killed himself just to achieve that. Not fantastic that it was better for all parties that there should be no trial."

"I need another drink," I said, and waved at the waiter. "I feel an icy breath on the back of my neck. Could you by any chance be related to the Potter family, Mrs. Loring?"

"Sylvia Lennox was my sister," she said simply. "I thought you would know."

The waiter drifted over and I gave him an urgent message. Mrs. Loring shook her head and said she didn't want anything more. When the waiter took off I said:

"With the hush old man Potter—excuse me, Mr. Harlan Potter—put on this affair, I would be lucky to know for sure that Terry's wife even had a sister."

"Surely you exaggerate. My father is hardly that powerful, Mr. Marlowe—and certainly not that ruthless. I'll admit he does have very old-fashioned ideas about his personal privacy. He never gives interviews even to his own newspapers. He is never photographed, he never makes speeches, he travels mostly by car or in his own plane with his own crew. But he is quite human for all that. He liked Terry. He said Terry was a gentleman twenty-four hours a day instead of for the fifteen minutes between the time the guests arrive and the time they feel their first cocktail."

"He slipped a little at the end. Terry did."

The waiter trotted up with my third gimlet. I tried it for flavor and then sat there with a finger on the edge of the round base of the glass.

"Terry's death was quite a blow to him, Mr. Marlowe. And you're getting sarcastic again. Please don't. Father knew it would all look far too neat to some people. He would much rather Terry had just disappeared. If Terry had asked him for help, I think he would have given it."

"Oh no, Mrs. Loring. His own daughter had been murdered."

She made an irritable motion and eyed me coldly.

"This is going to sound pretty blunt, I'm afraid. Father had written my sister off long ago. When they met he barely spoke to her. If he expressed himself, which he hasn't and won't, I feel sure he would be just as doubtful about Terry as you are. But once Terry was dead, what did it matter? They could have been killed in a plane crash or a fire or a highway accident. If she had to die, it was the best possible time for her to die. In another ten years she would have been a sex-ridden hag like some of these frightful women you see at Hollywood parties, or used to a few years back. The dregs of the international set."

All of a sudden I got mad, for no good reason. I stood up and looked over the booth. The next one was still empty. In the one beyond a guy was reading a paper all by himself, quietly. I sat down with a bump, pushed my glass out of the way, and leaned across the table. I had sense enough to keep my voice down.

"For hell's sake, Mrs. Loring, what are you trying to sell me? That Harlan Potter is such a sweet lovely character he wouldn't dream of using his influence on a political D.A. to drop the blanket on a murder investigation so that the murder was never really investigated at all? That he had doubts about Terry's guilt but didn't let anyone lift a finger to find out who was really the killer? That he didn't use the political power of his newspapers and his bank account and the nine hundred guys who would trip over their chins trying to guess what he wanted done before he knew himself? That he didn't arrange it so that a tame lawyer and nobody else, nobody from the D.A.'s office or the city cops, went down to Mexico to make sure Terry actually had put a slug in his head instead of being knocked off by some Indian with a hot gun just for kicks? Your old man is worth a hundred million bucks, Mrs. Loring. I wouldn't know just how he got it, but I know damn well he didn't get it without building himself a pretty far-reaching organization. He's no softie. He's a hard tough man. You've got to be in these days to make that kind of money. And you do business with some funny people. You may not meet them or shake hands with them, but they are there on the fringe doing business with you."

"You're a fool," she said angrily. "I've had enough of you."

"Oh sure. I don't make the kind of music you like to hear. Let me tell you something. Terry talked to your old man the night Sylvia died. What about? What did your old man say to him? 'Just run on down to Mexico and shoot yourself, old boy. Let's keep this in the family. I know my daughter is a tramp and that any one of a dozen drunken bastards might have blown his top and pushed her pretty face down her throat for her. But that's incidental, old boy. The guy will be sorry when he sobers up. You've had it soft and now is the time you pay back. What we want is to keep the fair Potter name as sweet as mountain lilac. She married you because she needed a front. She needs it worse than ever now she's dead. And you're it. If you can get lost and stay lost, fine. But if you get found, you check out. See you in the morgue.'"

"Do you really think," the woman in black asked with dry ice in her voice, "that my father talks like that?"

I leaned back and laughed unpleasantly. "We could polish up the dialogue a little if that helps."

She gathered her stuff together and slid along the seat. "I'd like to give you a word of warning," she said slowly and very carefully, "a very simple word of warning. If you think my father is that kind of man and if you go around broadcasting the kind of thoughts you have just expressed to me, your career in this city in your business or in any business is apt to be extremely short and terminated very suddenly."

"Perfect, Mrs. Loring. Perfect. I get it from the law, I get it from the hoodlum element, I get it from the carriage trade. The words change, but the meaning is the same. Lay off. I came in here to drink a gimlet because a man asked me to. Now look at me. I'm practically in the boneyard."

She stood up and nodded briefly. "Three gimlets. Doubles. Perhaps you're drunk."

I dropped too much money on the table and stood up beside her. "You had one and a half, Mrs. Loring. Why even that much? Did a man ask you too, or was it all your own idea? Your own tongue got a little loose."

"Who knows, Mr. Marlowe? Who knows? Who really knows anything? There's a man over there at the bar watching us. Would it be anyone you know?"

I looked around, surprised that she had noticed. A lean dark character sat on the end stool nearest the door.

"His name is Chick Agostino," I said. "He's a gun toter for a gambling boy named Menendez. Let's knock him down and jump on him."

"You certainly are drunk," she said quickly and started to walk. I went after her. The man on the stool swung around and looked to his front. When I came abreast I stepped up behind him and reached in under both his arms quickly. Maybe I *was* a little drunk.

He swung around angrily and slid off the stool. "Watch it, kiddo," he snarled. Out of the corner of my eye I saw that she had stopped just inside the door to glance back.

"No guns, Mr. Agostino? How reckless of you. It's almost dark. What if you should run into a tough midget?"

"Scram!" he said savagely.

"Aw, you stole that line from the *New Yorker*."

His mouth worked but he didn't move. I left him and followed Mrs. Loring out through the door into the space under the awning. A gray-haired colored chauffeur stood there talking to the kid from the parking lot. He touched his cap and went off and came back with a flossy Cadillac limousine. He opened the door and Mrs. Loring got in. He shut the door as though he was putting down the lid of a jewel box. He went around the car to the driver's seat.

She ran the window down and looked out at me, half smiling.

"Goodnight, Mr. Marlowe. It's been nice — or has it?"

"We had quite a fight."

"You mean you had — and mostly with yourself."

"It usually is. Goodnight, Mrs. Loring. You don't live around here, do you?"

"Not exactly. I live in Idle Valley. At the far end of the lake. My husband is a doctor."

"Would you happen to know any people named Wade?"

She frowned. "Yes, I know the Wades. Why?"

"Why do I ask? They're the only people in Idle Valley that I know."

"I see. Well, goodnight again, Mr. Marlowe."

She leaned back in the seat and the Cadillac purred politely and slid away into the traffic along the Strip.

Turning I almost bumped into Chick Agostino.

"Who's the doll?" he sneered. "And next time you crack wise, be missing."

"Nobody that would want to know you," I said.

"Okay, bright boy. I got the license number. Mendy likes to know little things like that."

The door of a car banged open and a man about seven feet high and four feet wide jumped out of it, took one look at

Agostino, then one long stride, and grabbed him by the throat with one hand.

"How many times I gotta tell you cheap hoods not to hang around where I eat?" he roared.

He shook Agostino and hurled him across the sidewalk against the wall. Chick crumpled up coughing.

"Next time," the enormous man yelled, "I sure as hell put the blast on you, and believe me, boy, you'll be holding a gun when they pick you up."

Chick shook his head and said nothing. The big man gave me a raking glance and grinned. "Nice night," he said, and strolled into Victor's.

I watched Chick straighten himself out and regain some of his composure. "Who's your buddy?" I asked him.

"Big Willie Magoon," he said thickly. "A vice squad bimbo. He thinks he's tough."

"You mean he isn't sure?" I asked him politely.

He looked at me emptily and walked away. I got my car out of the lot and drove home. In Hollywood anything can happen, anything at all.

# 23

A low-swung Jaguar swept around the hill in front of me and slowed down so as not to bathe me in the granite dust from the half mile of neglected paving at the entrance to Idle Valley. It seemed they wanted it left that way to discourage the Sunday drivers spoiled by drifting along on superhighways. I caught a glimpse of a bright scarf and a pair of sun goggles. A hand waved at me casually, neighbor to neighbor. Then the dust slid across the road and added itself to the white film already well spread over the scrub and the sunbaked grass. Then I was around the outcrop and the paving started up in proper shape and everything was smooth and cared for. Live oaks clustered towards the road, as if they were curious to see who went by, and sparrows with rosy heads hopped about pecking at things only a sparrow would think worth pecking at.

Then there were a few cottonwoods but no eucalyptus. Then a thick growth of Carolina poplars screening a white house. Then a girl walking a horse along the shoulder of the road. She had levis on and a loud shirt and she was chewing on a twig. The horse looked hot but not lathered and the girl was crooning to him gently. Beyond a fieldstone wall a gardener was guiding a power lawnmower over a huge undulating lawn that ended far back in the portico of a Williamsburg Colonial mansion, the large de luxe size. Somewhere someone was playing left-handed exercises on a grand piano.

Then all this wheeled away and the glisten of the lake showed hot and bright and I began to watch numbers on gateposts. I had seen the Wades' house only once and in the dark. It wasn't as big as it had looked by night. The driveway was full of cars, so I parked on the side of the road and walked in. A Mexican butler in a white coat opened the door for me. He was a slender neat good-looking Mexican and his coat fitted him elegantly and he looked like a Mexican who was getting fifty a week and not killing himself with hard work.

He said: "Buenas tardes, señor," and grinned as if he had put one over. "Su nombre de Usted, por favor?"

"Marlowe," I said, "and who are you trying to upstage, Candy? We talked on the phone, remember?"

He grinned and I went in. It was the same old cocktail party, everybody talking too loud, nobody listening, everybody hanging on for dear life to a mug of the juice, eyes very bright, cheeks flushed or pale and sweaty according to the amount of alcohol consumed and the capacity of the individual to handle it. Then Eileen Wade materialized beside me in a pale blue something which did her no harm. She had a glass in her hand but it didn't look as if it was more than a prop.

"I'm so glad you could come," she said gravely. "Roger wants to see you in his study. He hates cocktail parties. He's working."

"With this racket going on?"

"It never seems to bother him. Candy will get you a drink—or if you'd rather go to the bar—"

"I'll do that," I said. "Sorry about the other night."

She smiled. "I think you apologized already. It was nothing."

"The hell it was nothing."

She kept the smile long enough to nod and turn and walk away. I spotted the bar over in the corner by some very large french windows. It was one of those things you push around. I was halfway across the room, trying not to bump anybody, when a voice said: "Oh, Mr. Marlowe."

I turned and saw Mrs. Loring on a couch beside a prissy-looking man in rimless cheaters with a smear on his chin that might have been a goatee. She had a drink in her hand and looked bored. He sat still with his arms folded and scowled.

I went over there. She smiled at me and gave me her hand. "This is my husband, Dr. Loring. Mr. Philip Marlowe, Edward."

The guy with the goatee gave me a brief look and a still briefer nod. He didn't move otherwise. He seemed to be saving his energy for better things.

"Edward is very tired," Linda Loring said. "Edward is always very tired."

"Doctors often are," I said. "Can I get you a drink, Mrs. Loring? Or you, Doctor?"

"She's had enough," the man said without looking at either of us. "I don't drink. The more I see of people who do, the more glad I am that I don't."

"Come back, little Sheba," Mrs. Loring said dreamily.

He swung around and did a take. I got away from there and made it to the bar. In the company of her husband Linda Loring seemed like a different person. There was an edge to her voice and a sneer in her expression which she hadn't used on me even when she was angry.

Candy was behind the bar. He asked me what I would drink.

"Nothing right now, thanks. Mr. Wade wants to see me."

"Es muy occupado, señor. Very busy."

I didn't think I was going to like Candy. When I just looked at him he added: "But I go see. De pronto, señor."

He threaded his way delicately through the mob and was back in no time at all. "Okay, chum, let's go," he said cheerfully.

I followed him across the room the long way of the house. He opened a door, I went through, he shut it behind me, and a lot of the noise was dimmed. It was a corner room, big and cool and quiet, with french windows and roses outside and an airconditioner set in a window to one side. I could see the lake, and I could see Wade lying flat out on a long blond leather couch. A big bleached wood desk had a typewriter on it and there was a pile of yellow paper beside the typewriter.

"Good of you to come, Marlowe," he said lazily. "Park yourself. Did you have a drink or two?"

"Not yet." I sat down and looked at him. He still looked a bit pale and pinched. "How's the work going?"

"Fine, except that I get tired too quick. Pity a four-day drunk is so painful to get over. I often do my best work after one. In my racket it's so easy to tighten up and get all stiff and wooden. Then the stuff is no good. When it's good it comes easy. Anything you have read or heard to the contrary is a lot of mishmash."

"Depends who the writer is, maybe," I said. "It didn't come easy to Flaubert, and his stuff is good."

"Okay," Wade said, sitting up. "So you have read Flaubert, so that makes you an intellectual, a critic, a savant of the literary world." He rubbed his forehead. "I'm on the wagon and I hate it. I hate everybody with a drink in his hand. I've got to go out there and smile at those creeps. Every damn one of them knows I'm an alcoholic. So they wonder what I'm running away from. Some Freudian bastard has made that a commonplace. Every ten-year-old kid knows it by now. If I had a ten-year-old kid, which God forbid, the brat would be asking me, 'What are you running away from when you get drunk, Daddy?'"

"The way I got it, all this was rather recent," I said.

"It's got worse, but I was always a hard man with a bottle. When you're young and in hard condition you can absorb a lot of punishment. When you are pushing forty you don't snap back the same way."

I leaned back and lit a cigarette. "What did you want to see me about?"

"What do *you* think I'm running away from, Marlowe?"

"No idea. I don't have enough information. Besides, everybody is running away from something."

"Not everybody gets drunk. What are *you* running away from? Your youth or a guilty conscience or the knowledge that you're a small time operator in a small time business?"

"I get it," I said. "You need somebody to insult. Fire away, chum. When it begins to hurt I'll let you know."

He grinned and rumpled his thick curly hair. He speared his chest with a forefinger. "You're looking right at a small time operator in a small time business, Marlowe. All writers are punks and I am one of the punkest. I've written twelve best sellers, and if I ever finish that stack of magoozlum on the desk there I may possibly have written thirteen. And not a damn one of them worth the powder to blow it to hell. I have a lovely home in a highly restricted residential neighborhood that belongs to a highly restricted multimillionaire. I have a lovely wife who loves me and a lovely publisher who loves me and I love me the best of all. I'm an egotistical son of a bitch, a literary prostitute or pimp—choose your own word—and an all-round heel. So what can you do for me?"

"Well, what?"

"Why don't you get sore?"

"Nothing to get sore about. I'm just listening to you hate yourself. It's boring but it doesn't hurt my feelings."

He laughed roughly. "I like you," he said. "Let's have a drink."

"Not in here, chum. Not you and me alone. I don't care to watch you take the first one. Nobody can stop you and I don't guess anyone would try. But I don't have to help."

He stood up. "We don't have to drink in here. Let's go outside and glance at a choice selection of the sort of people you get to know when you make enough lousy money to live where they live."

"Look," I said. "Shove it. Knock it off. They're no different from anybody else."

"Yeah," he said tightly, "but they ought to be. If they're not, what use are they? They're the class of the county and they're no better than a bunch of truckdrivers full of cheap whiskey. Not as good."

"Knock it off," I said again. "You want to get boiled, get boiled. But don't take it out on a crowd that can get boiled without having to lie up with Dr. Verringer or get loose in the head and throw their wives down the stairs."

"Yeah," he said, and he was suddenly calm and thoughtful. "You pass the test, chum. How about coming to live here for a while? You could do me a lot of good just being here."

"I don't see how."

"But I do. Just by being here. Would a thousand a month interest you? I'm dangerous when I'm drunk. I don't want to be dangerous and I don't want to be drunk."

"I couldn't stop you."

"Try it for three months. I'd finish the damn book and then go far off for a while. Lie up some place in the Swiss mountains and get clean."

"The book, huh? Do you have to have the money?"

"No. I just have to finish something I started. If I don't I'm through. I'm asking you as a friend. You did more than that for Lennox."

I stood up and walked over close to him and gave him a hard stare. "I got Lennox killed, mister. I got him killed."

"Phooey. Don't go soft on me, Marlowe." He put the edge of his hand against his throat. "I'm up to here in the soft babies."

"Soft?" I asked. "Or just kind?"

He stepped back and stumbled against the edge of the couch, but didn't lose his balance.

"The hell with you," he said smoothly. "No deal. I don't blame you, of course. There's something I want to know, that I have to know. You don't know what it is and I'm not sure I know myself. All I'm positive of is that there *is* something, and I have to know it."

"About who? Your wife?"

He moved his lips one over the other. "I think it's about me," he said. "Let's go get that drink."

He walked to the door and threw it open and we went out.

If he had been trying to make me uncomfortable, he had done a first class job.

# 24

When he opened the door the buzz from the living room exploded into our faces. It seemed louder than before, if possible. About two drinks louder. Wade said hello here and there and people seemed glad to see him. But by that time they would have been glad to see Pittsburgh Phil with his custom-built icepick. Life was just one great big vaudeville show.

On the way to the bar we came face to face with Dr. Loring and his wife. The doctor stood up and stepped forward to face Wade. He had a look on his face that was almost sick with hatred.

"Nice to see you, Doctor," Wade said amiably. "Hi, Linda. Where have you been keeping yourself lately? No, I guess that was a stupid question. I—"

"Mr. Wade," Loring said in a voice that had a tremor to it, "I have something to say to you. Something very simple, and I hope very conclusive. Stay away from my wife."

Wade looked at him curiously. "Doctor, you're tired. And you don't have a drink. Let me get you one."

"I don't drink, Mr. Wade. As you very well know. I am here for one purpose and I have expressed that purpose."

"Well, I guess I get your point," Wade said, still amiable. "And since you are a guest in my house, I have nothing to say except that I think you are a little off the beam."

There had been a drop in the talk near by. The boys and girls were all ears. Big production. Dr. Loring took a pair of gloves out of his pocket, straightened them, took hold of one by the finger end, and swung it hard against Wade's face.

Wade didn't bat an eye. "Pistols and coffee at dawn?" he asked quietly.

I looked at Linda Loring. She was flushed with anger. She stood up slowly and faced the doctor.

"Dear God, what a ham you are, darling. Stop acting like a damn fool, will you, darling? Or would you rather stick around until somebody slaps *your* face?"

Loring swung around to her and raised the gloves. Wade

stepped in front of him. "Take it easy, Doc. Around here we only hit our wives in private."

"If you are speaking for yourself, I am well aware of it," Loring sneered. "And I don't need lessons in manners from you."

"I only take promising pupils," Wade said. "Sorry you have to leave so soon." He raised his voice. "Candy! Que el Doctor Loring salga de aqui en el acto!" He swung back to Loring. "In case you don't know Spanish, Doctor, that means the door is over there." He pointed.

Loring stared at him without moving. "I have warned you, Mr. Wade," he said icily. "And a number of people have heard me. I shall not warn you again."

"Don't," Wade said curtly. "But if you do, make it on neutral territory. Gives me a little more freedom of action. Sorry, Linda. But you married him." He rubbed his cheek gently where the heavy end of the glove had hit him. Linda Loring was smiling bitterly. She shrugged.

"We are leaving," Loring said. "Come, Linda."

She sat down again and reached for her glass. She gave her husband a glance of quiet contempt. "You are," she said. "You have a number of calls to make, remember."

"You are leaving with me," he said furiously.

She turned her back on him. He reached suddenly and took hold of her arm. Wade took him by the shoulder and spun him around.

"Take it easy, Doc. You can't win them all."

"Take your hand off me!"

"Sure, just relax," Wade said. "I have a good idea, Doctor. Why don't you see a good doctor?"

Somebody laughed loudly. Loring tensed like an animal all set to spring. Wade sensed it and neatly turned his back and moved away. Which left Dr. Loring holding the bag. If he went after Wade, he would look sillier than he looked now. There was nothing for him to do but leave, and he did it. He marched quickly across the room staring straight in front of him to where Candy was holding the door open. He went out. Candy shut the door, wooden-faced, and went back to the bar. I went over there and asked for some Scotch. I didn't see where Wade went. He just disappeared. I didn't see Eileen either. I turned my back on the room and let them sizzle while I drank my Scotch.

A small girl with mud-colored hair and a band around her forehead popped up beside me and put a glass on the bar and bleated. Candy nodded and made her another drink.

The small girl turned to me. "Are you interested in Communism?" she asked me. She was glassy-eyed and she was running a small red tongue along her lips as if looking for a crumb of chocolate. "I think everyone ought to be," she went on. "But when you ask any of the men here they just want to paw you."

I nodded and looked over my glass at her snub nose and sun-coarsened skin.

"Not that I mind too much if it's done nicely," she told me, reaching for the fresh drink. She showed me her molars while she inhaled half of it.

"Don't rely on me," I said.

"What's your name?"

"Marlowe."

"With an 'e' or not?"

"With."

"Ah, Marlowe," she intoned. "Such a sad beautiful name." She put her glass down damn nearly empty and closed her eyes and threw her head back and her arms out, almost hitting me in the eye. Her voice throbbed with emotion, saying:

> *"Was this the face that launch'd a thousand ships*
> *And burnt the topless towers of Ilium?*
> *Sweet Helen, make me immortal with a kiss."*

She opened her eyes, grabbed her glass, and winked at me. "You were pretty good in there, chum. Been writing any poetry lately?"

"Not very much."

"You can kiss me if you like," she said coyly.

A guy in a shantung jacket and an open neck shirt came up behind her and grinned at me over the top of her head. He had short red hair and a face like a collapsed lung. He was as ugly a guy as I ever saw. He patted the top of the little girl's head.

"Come on kitten. Time to go home."

She rounded on him furiously. "You mean you got to water those goddamned tuberous begonias again?" she yelled.

"Aw listen, kitten—"

"Take your hands off me, you goddamned rapist," she screamed, and threw the rest of her drink in his face. The rest wasn't more than a teaspoonful and two lumps of ice.

"For Chrissake, baby, I'm your husband," he yelled back, grabbing for a handkerchief and mopping his face. "Get it? Your husband."

She sobbed violently and threw herself into his arms. I stepped around them and got out of there. Every cocktail party is the same, even the dialogue.

The house was leaking guests out into the evening air now. Voices were fading, cars were starting, goodbyes were bouncing around like rubber balls. I went to the french windows and out onto a flagged terrace. The ground sloped towards the lake which was as motionless as a sleeping cat. There was a short wooden pier down there with a rowboat tied to it by a white painter. Towards the far shore, which wasn't very far, a black waterhen was doing lazy curves, like a skater. They didn't seem to cause as much as a shallow ripple.

I stretched out on a padded aluminum chaise and lit a pipe and smoked peacefully and wondered what the hell I was doing there. Roger Wade seemed to have enough control to handle himself if he really wanted to. He had done all right with Loring. I wouldn't have been too surprised if he had hung one on Loring's sharp little chin. He would have been out of line by the rules, but Loring was much farther out of line.

If the rules mean anything at all any more, they mean that you don't pick a roomful of people as the spot to threaten a man and hit him across the face with a glove when your wife is standing right beside you and you are practically accusing her of a little double time. For a man still shaky from a hard bout with the hard stuff Wade had done all right. He had done more than all right. Of course I hadn't seen him drunk. I didn't know what he would be like drunk. I didn't even know that he was an alcoholic. There's a big difference. A man who drinks too much on occasion is still the same man as he was sober. An alcoholic, a real alcoholic, is not the same man at all. You can't predict anything about him for sure except that he will be someone you never met before.

Light steps sounded behind me and Eileen Wade came across the terrace and sat down beside me on the edge of a chaise.

"Well, what did you think?" she asked quietly.

"About the gentleman with the loose gloves?"

"Oh no." She frowned. Then she laughed. "I hate people who make stagy scenes like that. Not that he isn't a fine doctor. He has played that scene with half the men in the valley. Linda Loring is no tramp. She doesn't look like one, talk like one, or behave like one. I don't know what makes Dr. Loring behave as if she was."

"Maybe he's a reformed drunk," I said. "A lot of them grow pretty puritanical."

"It's possible," she said, and looked towards the lake. "This is a very peaceful place. One would think a writer would be happy here—if a writer is ever happy anywhere." She turned to look at me. "So you won't be persuaded to do what Roger asked."

"There's no point in it, Mrs. Wade. Nothing I could do. I've said all this before. I couldn't be sure of being around at the right time. I'd have to be around *all* the time. That's impossible, even if I had nothing else to do. If he went wild, for example, it would happen in a flash. And I haven't seen any indications that he does get wild. He seems pretty solid to me."

She looked down at her hands. "If he could finish his book, I think things would be much better."

"I can't help him do that."

She looked up and put her hands on the edge of the chaise beside her. She leaned forward a little. "You can if he thinks you can. That's the whole point. Is it that you would find it distasteful to be a guest in our house and be paid for it?"

"He needs a psychiatrist, Mrs. Wade. If you know one that isn't a quack."

She looked startled. "A psychiatrist? Why?"

I knocked the ashes out of my pipe and sat holding it, waiting for the bowl to get cooler before I put it away.

"You want an amateur opinion, here it is. He thinks he has a secret buried in his mind and he can't get at it. It may be a guilty secret about himself, it may be about someone else. He thinks that's what makes him drink, because he can't get at this thing. He probably thinks that whatever happened, happened while he was drunk and he ought to find it wherever people go when they're drunk—really bad drunk, the way he gets. That's a job for a psychiatrist. So far, so good. If that is wrong, then he gets drunk because he wants to or can't help it, and the idea about the secret is just his excuse. He can't write his book, or anyway can't finish it. Because he gets drunk. That is, the assumption seems to be that he can't finish his book because he knocks himself out by drinking. It could be the other way around."

"Oh no," she said. "No. Roger has a great deal of talent. I feel quite sure that his best work is still to come."

"I told you it was an amateur opinion. You said the other morning that he might have fallen out of love with his wife. That's something else that could go the other way around."

She looked towards the house, then turned so that she had her back to it. I looked the same way. Wade was standing inside the doors, looking out at us. As I watched he moved behind the bar and reached for a bottle.

"There's no use interfering," she said quickly. "I never do. Never. I suppose you're right, Mr. Marlowe. There just isn't anything to do but let him work it out of his system."

The pipe was cool now and I put it away. "Since we're groping around in the back of the drawer, how about that other way around?"

"I love my husband," she said simply. "Not as a young girl loves, perhaps. But I love him. A woman is only a young girl once. The man I loved then is dead. He died in the war. His name, strangely enough, had the same initials as yours. It doesn't matter now—except that sometimes I can't quite believe that he is dead. His body was never found. But that happened to many men."

She gave me a long searching look. "Sometimes—not often, of course—when I go into a quiet cocktail lounge or the lobby of a good hotel at a dead hour, or along the deck of a liner early in the morning or very late at night, I think I may see him waiting for me in some shadowy corner." She paused and dropped her eyes. "It's very silly. I'm ashamed of it. We were very much in love—the wild, mysterious, improbable kind of love that never comes but once."

She stopped talking and sat there half in a trance looking out over the lake. I looked back at the house again. Wade was standing just inside the open french windows with a glass in his hand. I looked back at Eileen. For her I wasn't there any more. I got up and went into the house. Wade stood there with the drink and the drink looked pretty heavy. And his eyes looked wrong.

"How you making out with my wife, Marlowe?" It was said with a twist of the mouth.

"No passes, if you mean it that way."

"That's exactly the way I mean it. You got to kiss her the other night. Probably fancy yourself as a fast worker, but you're wasting your time, bud. Even if you had the right kind of polish."

I tried to move around him but he blocked me with a solid shoulder. "Don't hurry away, old man. We like you around. We get so few private dicks in our house."

"I'm the one too many," I said.

He hoisted the glass and drank from it. When he lowered it he leered at me.

"You ought to give yourself a little more time to build resistance," I told him. "Empty words, huh?"

"Okay, coach. Some little character builder, aren't you? You ought to have more sense than to try educating a drunk. Drunks don't educate, my friend. They disintegrate. And part of the process is a lot of fun." He drank from the glass again, leaving it nearly empty. "And part of it is damned awful. But if I may quote the scintillating words of the good Dr. Loring, a bastardly bastard with a little black bag, stay away from my wife, Marlowe. Sure you go for her. They all do. You'd like to sleep with her. They all would. You'd like to share her dreams and sniff the rose of her memories. Maybe I would too. But there is nothing to share, chum—nothing, nothing, nothing. You're all alone in the dark."

He finished his drink and turned the glass upside down.

"Empty like that, Marlowe. Nothing there at all. I'm the guy that knows."

He put the glass on the edge of the bar and walked stiffly to the foot of the stairs. He made about a dozen steps up, holding on to the rail, and stopped and leaned against it. He looked down at me with a sour grin.

"Forgive the corny sarcasm, Marlowe. You're a nice guy. I wouldn't want anything to happen to you."

"Anything like what?"

"Perhaps she didn't get around yet to that haunting magic of her first love, the guy that went missing in Norway. You wouldn't want to be missing, would you, chum? You're my own special private eye. You find me when I'm lost in the savage splendor of Sepulveda Canyon." He moved the palm of his hand in a circular motion on the polished wood banister. "It would hurt me to the quick if you got lost yourself. Like that character who hitched up with the limeys. He got so lost a man sometimes wonders if he ever existed. You figure she could have maybe just invented him to have a toy to play with?"

"How would I know?"

He looked down at me. There were deep lines between his eyes now and his mouth was twisted with bitterness.

"How would anybody know? Maybe she don't know herself. Baby's tired. Baby been playing too long with broken toys. Baby wants to go bye-bye."

He went on up the stairs.

I stood there until Candy came in and started tidying up around the bar, putting glasses on a tray, examining bottles to see what was left, paying no attention to me. Or so I thought. Then he said:

"Señor. One good drink left. Pity to waste him." He held up a bottle.

"You drink it."

"Gracias, señor, no me gusta. Un vaso de cerveza, no más. A glass of beer is my limit."

"Wise man."

"One lush in the house is enough," he said, staring at me. "I speak good English, not?"

"Sure, fine."

"But I think Spanish. Sometimes I think with a knife. The boss is my guy. He don't need any help, hombre. I take care of him, see."

"A great job you're doing, punk."

"Hijo de la flauta," he said between his white teeth. He picked up a loaded tray and swung it up on the edge of his shoulder and the flat of his hand, bus boy style.

I walked to the door and let myself out, wondering how an expression meaning 'son of a flute' had come to be an insult in Spanish. I didn't wonder very long. I had too many other things to wonder about. Something more than alcohol was the matter with the Wade family. Alcohol was no more than a disguised reaction.

Later that night, between nine-thirty and ten, I called the Wades' number. After eight rings I hung up, but I had only just taken my hand off the instrument when it started to ring me. It was Eileen Wade.

"Someone just rang here," she said. "I had a sort of hunch it might be you. I was just getting ready to take a shower."

"It was me, but it wasn't important, Mrs. Wade. He seemed a little woolly-headed when I left—Roger did. I guess maybe I feel a little responsibility for him by now."

"He's quite all right," she said. "Fast asleep in bed. I think Dr. Loring upset him more than he showed. No doubt he talked a lot of nonsense to you."

"He said he was tired and wanted to go to bed. Pretty sensible, I thought."

"If that is all he said, yes. Well, goodnight and thank you for calling, Mr. Marlowe."

"I didn't say it was all he said. I said he said it."

There was a pause, then: "Everyone gets fantastic ideas once in a while. Don't take Roger too seriously, Mr. Marlowe. After all, his imagination is rather highly developed. Naturally it would be. He shouldn't have had anything to drink so soon after the last time. Please try to forget all about it. I suppose he was rude to you among other things."

"He wasn't rude to me. He made quite a lot of sense. Your husband is a guy who can take a long hard look at himself and see what is there. It's not a very common gift. Most people go through life using up half their energy trying to protect a dignity they never had. Goodnight, Mrs. Wade."

She hung up and I set out the chess board. I filled a pipe, paraded the chessmen and inspected them for French shaves and loose buttons, and played a championship tournament game between Gortchakoff and Meninkin, seventy-two moves to a draw, a prize specimen of the irresistible force meeting the immovable object, a battle without armor, a war without blood, and as elaborate a waste of human intelligence as you could find anywhere outside an advertising agency.

## 25

Nothing happened for a week except that I went about my business which just then didn't happen to be very much business. One morning George Peters of The Carne Organization called me up and told me he had happened to be down Sepulveda Canyon way and had looked in on Dr. Verringer's place just out of curiosity. But Dr. Verringer was no longer there. Half a dozen teams of surveyors were mapping the tract for a subdivision. Those he spoke to had never even heard of Dr. Verringer.

"The poor sucker got closed out on a trust deed," Peters said. "I checked. They gave him a grand for a quitclaim just to save time and expense, and now somebody is going to make a million bucks clear, out of cutting the place up for residential property. That's the difference between crime and business. For business you gotta have capital. Sometimes I think it's the only difference."

"A properly cynical remark," I said, "but big time crime takes capital too."

"And where does it come from, chum? Not from guys that hold up liquor stores. So long. See you soon."

It was ten minutes to eleven on a Thursday night when Wade called me up. His voice was thick, almost gurgling, but I recognized it somehow. And I could hear short hard rapid breathing over the telephone.

"I'm in bad shape, Marlowe. Very bad. I'm slipping my anchor. Could you make it out here in a hurry?"

"Sure—but let me talk to Mrs. Wade a minute."

He didn't answer. There was a crashing sound, then a dead silence, then in a short while a kind of banging around. I yelled something into the phone without getting any answer. Time passed. Finally the light click of the receiver being replaced and the buzz of an open line.

In five minutes I was on the way. I made it in slightly over half an hour and I still don't know how. I went over the pass on wings and hit Ventura Boulevard with the light against me and made a left turn anyhow and dodged between trucks and generally made a damn fool of myself. I went through Encino at close to sixty with a spotlight on the outer edge of the parked cars so that it would freeze anyone with a notion to step out suddenly. I had the kind of luck you only get when you don't care. No cops, no sirens, no red flashers. Just visions of what might be happening in the Wade residence and not very pleasant visions. She was alone in the house with a drunken maniac, she was lying at the bottom of the stairs with her neck broken, she was behind a locked door and somebody was howling outside and trying to break it in, she was running down a moonlit road barefoot and a big buck Negro with a meat cleaver was chasing her.

It wasn't like that at all. When I swung the Olds into their driveway lights were on all over the house and she was standing in the open doorway with a cigarette in her mouth. I got out and walked over the flagstones to her. She had slacks on and a shirt with an open collar. She looked at me calmly. If there was any excitement around there I had brought it with me.

The first thing I said was as loony as the rest of my behavior. "I thought you didn't smoke."

"What? No, I don't usually." She took the cigarette out and looked at it and dropped it and stepped on it. "Once in a long while. He called Dr. Verringer."

It was a remote placid voice, a voice heard at night over water. Completely relaxed.

"He couldn't," I said. "Dr. Verringer doesn't live there any more. He called me."

"Oh really? I just heard him telephoning and asking some-one to come in a hurry. I thought it must be Dr. Verringer."

"Where is he now?"

"He fell down," she said. "He must have tipped the chair too far back. He's done it before. He cut his head on something. There's a little blood, not much."

"Well, that's fine," I said. "We wouldn't want a whole lot of blood. Where is he now, I asked you."

She looked at me solemnly. Then she pointed. "Out there somewhere. By the edge of the road or in the bushes along the fence."

I leaned forward and peered at her. "Chrissake, didn't you look?" I decided by this time that she was in shock. Then I looked back across the lawn. I didn't see anything but there was heavy shadow near the fence.

"No, I didn't look," she said quite calmly. "You find him. I've had all of it I can take. I've had more than I can take. You find him."

She turned and walked back into the house, leaving the door open. She didn't walk very far. About a yard inside the door she just crumpled to the floor and lay there. I scooped her up and spread her out on one of the two big davenports that faced each other across a long blond cocktail table. I felt her pulse. It didn't seem very weak or unsteady. Her eyes were closed and the lids were blue. I left her there and went back out.

He was there all right, just as she had said. He was lying on his side in the shadow of the hibiscus. He had a fast thumping pulse and his breathing was unnatural. Something on the back of his head was sticky. I spoke to him and shook him a little. I slapped his face a couple of times. He mumbled but didn't come to. I dragged him up into a sitting position and dragged one of his arms over my shoulder and heaved him up with my back turned to him and grabbed for a leg. I lost. He was as heavy as a block of cement. We both sat down on the grass and I took a short breather and tried again. Finally I got him hoisted into a fireman's lift position and plowed across the lawn in the direction of the open front door. It seemed about the same distance as a round trip to Siam. The two steps of the porch were ten feet high. I staggered over to the couch and went down on my knees and rolled him off. When I straightened up again my spine felt as if it had cracked in at least three places.

Eileen Wade wasn't there any more. I had the room to myself. I was too bushed at the moment to care where anybody was. I sat down and looked at him and waited for some breath. Then I looked at his head. It was smeared with blood. His hair was sticky with it. It didn't look very bad but you never know with a head wound.

Then Eileen Wade was standing beside me, quietly looking down at him with that same remote expression.

"I'm sorry I fainted," she said. "I don't know why."

"I guess we'd better call a doctor."

"I telephoned Dr. Loring. He is my doctor, you know. He didn't want to come."

"Try somebody else then."

"Oh he's coming," she said. "He didn't want to. But he's coming as soon as he can manage."

"Where's Candy?"

"This is his day off. Thursday. The cook and Candy have Thursdays off. It's the usual thing around here. Can you get him up to bed?"

"Not without help. Better get a rug or blanket. It's a warm night, but cases like this get pneumonia very easily."

She said she would get a rug. I thought it was damn nice of her. But I wasn't thinking very intelligently. I was too bushed from carrying him.

We spread a steamer rug over him and in fifteen minutes Dr. Loring came, complete with starched collar and rimless cheaters and the expression of a man who has been asked to clean up after the dog got sick.

He examined Wade's head. "A superficial cut and bruise," he said. "No chance of concussion. I should say his breath would indicate his condition rather obviously."

He reached for his hat. He picked up his bag.

"Keep him warm," he said. "You might bathe his head gently and get rid of the blood. He'll sleep it off."

"I can't get him upstairs alone, Doctor," I said.

"Then leave him where he is." He looked at me without interest. "Goodnight, Mrs. Wade. As you know I don't treat alcoholics. Even if I did, your husband would not be one of my patients. I'm sure you understand that."

"Nobody's asking you to treat him," I said. "I'm asking for some help to get him into his bedroom so that I can undress him."

"And just who are you?" Dr. Loring asked me freezingly.

"My name's Marlowe. I was here a week ago. Your wife introduced me."

"Interesting," he said. "In what connection do you know my wife?"

"What the hell does that matter? All I want is—"

"I'm not interested in what you want," he cut in on me. He turned to Eileen, nodded briefly, and started out. I got between him and the door and put my back to it.

"Just a minute, Doc. Must be a long time since you glanced at that little piece of prose called the Hippocratic Oath. This man called me on the phone and I live some way off. He sounded bad and I broke every traffic law in the state getting over here. I found him lying out on the ground and I carried him in here and believe me he isn't any bunch of feathers. The houseboy is away and there's nobody here to help me upstairs with Wade. How does it look to you?"

"Get out of my way," he said between his teeth. "Or I shall call the sheriff's substation and have them send over a deputy. As a professional man—"

"As a professional man you're a handful of flea dirt," I said, and moved out of his way.

He turned red—slowly but distinctly. He choked on his own bile. Then he opened the door and went out. He shut it carefully. As he pulled it shut he looked in at me. It was as nasty a look as I ever got and on as nasty a face as I ever saw.

When I turned away from the door Eileen was smiling.

"What's funny?" I snarled.

"You. You don't care what you say to people, do you? Don't you know who Dr. Loring is?"

"Yeah—and I know what he is."

She glanced at her wrist watch. "Candy ought to be home by now," she said. "I'll go see. He has a room behind the garage."

She went out through an archway and I sat down and

looked at Wade. The great big writer man went on snoring. His face was sweaty but I left the rug over him. In a minute or two Eileen came back and she had Candy with her.

## 26

The Mex had a black and white checked sport shirt, heavily pleated black slacks without a belt, two-tone black and white buckskin shoes, spotlessly clean. His thick black hair was brushed straight back and shining with some kind of hair oil or cream.

"Señor," he said, and sketched a brief sarcastic bow.

"Help Mr. Marlowe carry my husband upstairs, Candy. He fell and hurt himself a little. I'm sorry to trouble you."

"De nada, señora," Candy said smiling.

"I think I'll say goodnight," she said to me. "I'm tired out. Candy will get you anything you want."

She went slowly up the stairs. Candy and I watched her.

"Some doll," he said confidentially. "You stay the night?"

"Hardly."

"Es lástima. She is very lonely, that one."

"Get that gleam out of your eye, kid. Let's put this to bed."

He looked sadly at Wade snoring on the couch. "Pobrecito," he murmured as if he meant it. "Borracho como una cuba."

"He may be drunk as a sow but he sure ain't little," I said. "You take the feet."

We carried him and even for two he was as heavy as a lead coffin. At the top of the stairs we went along an open balcony past a closed door. Candy pointed to it with his chin.

"La señora," he whispered. "You knock very light maybe she let you in."

I didn't say anything because I needed him. We went on with the carcass and turned in at another door and dumped him on the bed. Then I took hold of Candy's arm high up near the shoulder where dug-in fingers can hurt. I made mine hurt him. He winced a little and then his face set hard.

"What's your name, cholo?"

"Take your hand off me," he snapped. "And don't call me a cholo. I'm no wetback. My name is Juan García de Soto y Sotomayor. I am Chileno."

"Okay, Don Juan. Just don't get out of line around here. Keep your nose and mouth clean when you talk about the people you work for."

He jerked loose and stepped back, his black eyes hot with anger. His hand slipped inside his shirt and came out with a long thin knife. He balanced it by the point on the heel of his hand, hardly even glancing at it. Then he dropped the hand and caught the handle of the knife while it hung in the air. It was done very fast and without any apparent effort. His hand went up to shoulder height, then snapped forward and the knife sailed through the air and hung quivering in the wood of the window frame.

"Cuidado, señor!" he said with a sharp sneer. "And keep your paws to yourself. Nobody fools with me."

He walked lithely across the room and plucked the knife out of the wood, tossed it in the air, spun on his toes and caught it behind him. With a snap it disappeared under his shirt.

"Neat," I said, "but just a little on the gaudy side."

He strolled up to me smiling derisively.

"And it might get you a broken elbow," I said. "Like this."

I took hold of his right wrist, jerked him off balance, swung to one side and a little behind him, and brought my bent forearm up under the back of his elbow joint. I bore down on it, using my forearm as a fulcrum.

"One hard jerk," I said, "and your elbow joint cracks. A crack is enough. You'd be out of commission as a knife thrower for several months. Make the jerk a little harder and you'd be through permanently. Take Mr. Wade's shoes off."

I let go of him and he grinned at me. "Good trick," he said. "I will remember."

He turned to Wade and reached for one of his shoes, then stopped. There was a smear of blood on the pillow.

"Who cut the boss?"

"Not me, chum. He fell and cut his head on something. It's only a shallow cut. The doctor has been here."

Candy let his breath out slowly. "You see him fall?"

"Before I got here. You like this guy, don't you?"

He didn't answer me. He took the shoes off. We got Wade undressed little by little and Candy dug out a pair of green and silver pajamas. We got Wade into those and got him inside the bed and well covered up. He was still sweaty and still snoring. Candy looked down at him sadly, shaking his sleek head from side to side, slowly.

"Somebody's got to take care of him," he said. "I go change my clothes."

"Get some sleep. I'll take care of him. I can call you if I need you."

He faced me. "You better take care of him good," he said in a quiet voice. "Very good."

He went out of the room. I went into the bathroom and got a wet washcloth and a heavy towel. I turned Wade over a little and spread the towel on the pillow and washed the blood off his head gently so as not to start the bleeding again. Then I could see a sharp shallow cut about two inches long. It was nothing. Dr. Loring had been right that much. It wouldn't have hurt to stitch it but it probably was not really necessary. I found a pair of scissors and cut the hair away enough so that I could put on a strip of adhesive. Then I turned him on his back and washed his face. I guess that was a mistake.

He opened his eyes. They were vague and unfocused at first, then they cleared and he saw me standing beside the bed. His hand moved and went up to his head and felt the adhesive. His lips mumbled something, then his voice cleared up also.

"Who hit me? You?" His hand felt for the adhesive.

"Nobody hit you. You took a fall."

"Took a fall? When? Where?"

"Wherever you telephoned from. You called me. I heard you fall. Over the wire."

"I called you?" He grinned slowly. "Always available, aren't you, fella? What time is it?"

"After one A.M."

"Where's Eileen?"

"Gone to bed. She had it rough."

He thought that over silently. His eyes were full of pain. "Did I—" He stopped and winced.

"You didn't touch her as far as I know. If that's what you mean. You just wandered outdoors and passed out near the fence. Quit talking. Go to sleep."

"Sleep," he said quietly and slowly, like a child reciting its lesson. "What would that be?"

"Maybe a pill would help. Got any?"

"In the drawer. Night table."

I opened it and found a plastic bottle with red capsules in it. Seconal, 1½ grains. Prescription by Dr. Loring. That nice Dr. Loring. Mrs. Roger Wade's prescription.

I shook two of them loose and put the bottle back and poured a glass of water from a thermos jug on the night table. He said one capsule would be enough. He took it and drank some water and lay back and stared at the ceiling again. Time passed. I sat in a chair and watched him. He didn't seem to get sleepy. Then he said slowly:

"I remember something. Do me a favor, Marlowe. I wrote some crazy stuff I don't want Eileen to see. It's on top of the typewriter under the cover. Tear it up for me."

"Sure. That all you remember?"

"Eileen is all right? Positive about that?"

"Yes. She's just tired. Let it ride, Wade. Stop thinking. I shouldn't have asked you."

"Stop thinking, the man says." His voice was a little drowsy now. He was talking as if to himself. "Stop thinking, stop dreaming, stop loving, stop hating. Goodnight, sweet prince. I'll take that other pill."

I gave it to him with some more water. He lay back again, this time with his head turned so that he could see me. "Look, Marlowe, I wrote some stuff I don't want Eileen—"

"You told me already. I'll attend to it when you go to sleep."

"Oh. Thanks. Nice to have you around. Very nice."

Another longish pause. His eyelids were getting heavy.

"Ever kill a man, Marlowe?"

"Yes."

"Nasty feeling, isn't it?"

"Some people like it."

His eyes went shut all the way. Then they opened again, but they looked vague. "How could they?"

I didn't answer. The eyelids came down again, very gradually, like a slow curtain in the theater. He began to snore. I waited a little longer. Then I dimmed the light in the room and went out.

## 27

I stopped outside Eileen's door and listened. I didn't hear any sound of movement inside, so I didn't knock. If she wanted to know how he was, it was up to her. Downstairs the living room looked bright and empty. I put out some of the lights. From over near the front door I looked up at the balcony. The middle part of the living room rose to the full height of the house walls and was crossed by open beams that also supported the balcony. The balcony was wide and edged on two sides by a solid railing which looked to be about three and a half feet high. The top and the uprights were cut square to match the cross beams. The dining room was through a square arch closed off by double louvered doors. Above it I guessed there were servants' quarters. This part of the second floor was walled off so there would be another stairway reaching it from the kitchen part of the house. Wade's room was in the corner over his study. I could see the light from his open door reflected against the high ceiling and I could see the top foot of his doorway.

I cut all the lights except in one standing lamp and crossed to the study. The door was shut but two lamps were lit, a standing lamp at the end of the leather couch and a cowled desk lamp. The typewriter was on a heavy stand under this and beside it on the desk there was a disorderly mess of yellow paper. I sat in a padded chair and studied the layout. What I wanted to know was how he had cut his head. I sat in his desk chair with the phone at my left hand. The spring was set very weak. If I tilted back and went over, my head might have caught the corner of the desk. I moistened my handkerchief and rubbed the wood. No blood, nothing there. There was a lot of stuff on the desk, including a row of books between bronze elephants, and an old-fashioned square glass inkwell. I tried that without result. Not much point to it anyway, because if someone else had slugged him, the weapon didn't have to be in the room. And there wasn't anyone else to do it. I stood up and switched on the cornice lights. They reached into the shadowy corners and of course the answer was simple enough after all. A square metal wastebasket was lying on its side over against the wall, with paper spilled. It couldn't have walked there, so it had been thrown or kicked. I tried its sharp corners with my moistened handkerchief. I got the red-brown smear of blood this time. No mystery at all. Wade had fallen over and struck his head on the sharp corner of the wastebasket—a glancing blow most likely—picked himself up and booted the damn thing across the room. Easy.

Then he would have another quick drink. The drinking liquor was on the cocktail table in front of the couch. An empty bottle, another three quarters full, a thermos jug of water and a silver bowl containing water which had been ice cubes. There was only one glass and it was the large economy size.

Having taken his drink he felt a little better. He noticed the phone off the hook in a bleary sort of way and very likely didn't remember any more what he had been doing with it. So he just walked across and put it back in its cradle. The time had been just about right. There is something compulsive about a telephone. The gadget-ridden man of our age loves it, loathes it, and is afraid of it. But he always treats it with respect, even when he is drunk. The telephone is a fetish.

Any normal man would have said hello into the mouthpiece before hanging up, just to be sure. But not necessarily a man who was bleary with drink and had just taken a fall. It didn't matter anyhow. His wife might have done it, she might have heard the fall and the bang as the wastebasket bounced against the wall and come into the study. About that time the last drink would kick him in the face and he would stagger out of the house and across the front lawn and pass out where I had found him. Somebody was coming for him. By this time he didn't know who it was. Maybe the good Dr. Verringer.

So far, so good. So what would his wife do? She couldn't handle him or reason with him and she might well be afraid to try. So she would call somebody to come and help. The servants were out, so it would have to be by the telephone. Well, she *had* called somebody. She had called that nice Dr. Loring. I'd just assumed she called him after I got there. She hadn't said so.

From here on it didn't quite add up. You'd expect her to look for him and find him and make sure he wasn't hurt. It wouldn't hurt him to lie out on the ground on a warm summer night for a while. She couldn't move him. It had taken all I had to do that. But you wouldn't quite expect to find her standing in the open doorway smoking a cigarette, not knowing except very vaguely where he was. Or would you? I didn't know what she had been through with him, how dangerous he was in that condition, how much afraid she might be to go near him. "I've had all of it I can take," she had said to me when I arrived. "You find him." Then she had gone inside and pulled a faint.

It still bothered me, but I had to leave it at that. I had to assume that when she had been up against the situation often enough to know there was nothing she could do about it except to let it ride, then that would be what she would do. Just that. Let it ride. Let him lie out there on the ground until somebody came around with the physical equipment to handle him.

It still bothered me. It bothered me also that she had checked out and gone into her own room while Candy and I got him upstairs to bed. She said she loved the guy. He was her husband, they had been married for five years, he was a very nice guy indeed when sober—those were her own words. Drunk, he was something else, something to stay away from because he was dangerous. All right, forget it. But somehow it still bothered me. If she was really scared, she wouldn't have been standing there in the open door smoking a cigarette. If she was just bitter and withdrawn and disgusted, she wouldn't have fainted.

There was something else. Another woman, perhaps. Then she had only just found out. Linda Loring? Maybe. Dr. Loring thought so and said so in a very public manner.

I stopped thinking about it and took the cover off the typewriter. The stuff was there, several loose sheets of typed yellow paper that I was supposed to destroy so Eileen wouldn't see them. I took them over to the couch and decided I deserved a drink to go with the reading matter. There was a half bath off the study. I rinsed the tall glass out and poured a libation and sat down with it to read. And what I read was really wild. Like this:

# 28

The moon's four days off the full and there's a square patch of moonlight on the wall and it's looking at me like a big blind milky eye, a wall eye. Joke. Goddam silly simile. Writers. Everything has to be like something else. My head is as fluffy as whipped cream but not as sweet. More similes. I could vomit just thinking about the lousy racket. I could vomit anyway. I probably will. Don't push me. Give me time. The worms in my solar plexus crawl and crawl and crawl. I would be better off in bed but there would be a dark animal underneath the bed and the dark animal would crawl around rustling and hump himself and bump the underside of the bed, then I would let out a yell that wouldn't make any sound except to me. A dream yell, a yell in a nightmare. There is nothing to be afraid of and I am not afraid because there is nothing to be afraid of, but just the same I was lying like that once in bed and the dark animal was doing it to me, bumping himself against the underside of the bed, and I had an orgasm. That disgusted me more than any other of the nasty things I have done.

I'm dirty. I need a shave. My hands are shaking. I'm sweating. I smell foul to myself. The shirt under my arms is wet and on the chest and back. The sleeves are wet in the folds of the elbows. The glass on the table is empty. It would take both hands to pour the stuff now. I could get one out of the bottle maybe to brace me. The taste of the stuff is sickening. And it wouldn't get me anywhere. In the end I won't be able to sleep even and the whole world will moan in the horror of tortured nerves. Good stuff, huh, Wade? More.

It's all right for the first two or three days and then it is negative. You suffer and you take a drink and for a little while it is better, but the price keeps getting higher and higher and what you get for it is less and less and then there is always the point where you get nothing but nausea. Then you call Verringer. All right, Verringer, here I come. There isn't any Verringer any more. He's gone to Cuba or he is dead. The queen has killed him. Poor old Verringer, what a fate, to die in bed with a queen—that kind of queen. Come on, Wade, let's get up and go places. Places where we haven't ever been and aren't ever going back to when we have been. Does this sentence make sense? No. Okay, I'm not asking any money for it. A short pause here for a long commercial.

Well, I did it. I got up. What a man. I went over to the couch and here I am kneeling beside the couch with my hands down on it and my face in my hands, crying. Then I prayed and despised myself for praying. Grade Three drunk despising himself. What the hell are you praying to, you fool? If a well man prays, that's faith. A sick man prays and he is just scared. Nuts to prayer. This is the world you made and you make it all by yourself and what little outside help you got—well you made that too. Stop praying, you jerk. Get up on your feet and take that drink. It's too late for anything else now.

Well, I took it. Both hands. Poured it in the glass too. Hardly spilled a drop. Now if I can hold it without vomiting. Better add some water. Now lift it slow. Easy, not too much at a time. It gets warm. It gets hot. If I could stop sweating. The glass is empty. It's down on the table again.

There's a haze over the moonlight but I set that glass down in spite of it, carefully, carefully, like a spray of roses in a tall vase. The roses nod their heads with dew. Maybe I'm a rose. Brother, have I got dew. Now to get upstairs. Maybe a short one straight for the journey. No? Okay, whatever you say. Take it upstairs when I get there. If I get there, something to look forward to. If I make it upstairs I am entitled to compensation. A token of regard from me to me. I have such a beautiful love for myself—and the sweet part of it—no rivals.

Double space. Been up and came down. Didn't like it upstairs. The altitude makes my heart flutter. But I keep hitting these typewriter keys. What a magician is the subconscious. If only it would work regular hours. There was moonlight upstairs too. Probably the same moon. No variety about the moon. It comes and goes like the milkman and the moon's milk is always the same. The milk's moon is always—hold it, chum. You've got your feet crossed. This is no time to get involved in the case history of the moon. You got enough case history to take care of the whole damn valley.

She was sleeping on her side without sound. Her knees drawn up. Too still I thought. You always make some sound when you sleep. Maybe not asleep, maybe just trying to sleep. If I went closer I would know. Might fall down too. One of her eyes opened—or did it? She looked at me or did she? No. Would have sat up and said, Are you sick, darling? Yes, I am sick, darling. But don't give it a thought, darling, because this sick is my sick and not your sick, and let you sleep still and lovely and never remember and no slime from me to you and nothing come near you that is grim and gray and ugly.

You're a louse, Wade. Three adjectives, you lousy writer. Can't you even stream-of-consciousness you louse without getting it in three adjectives for Chrissake? I came downstairs again holding on to the rail. My guts lurched with the steps and I held them together with a promise. I made the main floor and I made the study and I made the couch and I waited for my heart to slow down. The bottle is handy. One thing you can say about Wade's arrangements the bottle is always handy. Nobody hides it, nobody locks it up. Nobody says, Don't you think you've had enough, darling? You'll make yourself sick, darling. Nobody says that. Just sleep on side softly like roses.

I gave Candy too much money. Mistake. Should have started him with a bag of peanuts and worked up to a banana. Then a little real change, slow and easy, always keep him eager. You give him a big slug of the stuff to begin with and pretty soon he has a stake. He can live in Mexico for a month, live high wide and nasty, on what it costs here for a day. So when he gets that stake, what does he do? Well, does a man ever have enough money, if he thinks he can get more? Maybe it's all right. Maybe I ought to kill the shiny-eyed bastard. A good man died for me once, why not a cockroach in a white jacket?

Forget Candy. There's always a way to blunt a needle. The other I shall never forget. It's carved on my liver in green fire.

Better telephone. Losing control. Feel them jumping, jumping, jumping. Better call someone quick before the pink things crawl on my face. Better call, call, call. Call Sioux City Sue. Hello, Operator, give me Long Distance. Hello, Long Distance, get me Sioux City Sue. What's her number? No have number, just name, Operator. You'll find her walking along Tenth Street, on the shady side, under the tall corn trees with their spreading ears. . . . All right, Operator, all right. Just cancel the whole program and let me tell you some-thing, I mean, ask you something. Who's going to pay for all those snazzy parties Gifford is throwing in London, if you cancel my long distance call? Yeah, you think your job is solid. You think. Here, I better talk to Gifford direct. Get him on the line. His valet just brought in his tea. If he can't talk we'll send over somebody that can.

Now what did I write that for? What was I trying not to think about? Telephone. Better telephone now. Getting very bad, very, very . . .

That was all. I folded the sheets up small and pushed them down into my inside breast pocket behind the note case. I went over to the french windows and opened them wide and stepped out onto the terrace. The moonlight was a little spoiled. But it was summer in Idle Valley and summer is never quite spoiled. I stood there looking at the motionless color-less lake and thought and wondered. Then I heard a shot.

# 29

On the balcony two lighted doors were open now—Eileen's and his. Her room was empty. There was a sound of strug-gling from his and I came through the door in a jump to find her bending over the bed wrestling with him. The black gleam of a gun shot up into the air, two hands, a large male hand and a woman's small hand were both holding it, neither by the butt. Roger was sitting up in bed and leaning forward pushing. She was in a pale blue house coat, one of those quilted things, her hair was all over her face and now she had both hands on the gun and with a quick jerk she got it away from him. I was surprised that she had the strength, even dopey as he was. He fell back glaring and panting and she stepped away and bumped into me.

She stood there leaning against me, holding the gun with both hands pressed hard against her body. She was racked with panting sobs. I reached around her body and put my hand on the gun.

She spun around as if it took that to make her realize I was there. Her eyes widened and her body sagged against me. She let go of the gun. It was a heavy clumsy weapon, a Webley double-action hammerless. The barrel was warm. I held her with one arm, dropped the gun in my pocket, and looked past her head at him. Nobody said anything.

Then he opened his eyes and that weary smile played on his lips. "Nobody hurt," he muttered. "Just a wild shot into the ceiling."

I felt her go stiff. Then she pulled away. Her eyes were focused and clear. I let her go.

"Roger," she said in a voice not much more than a sick whisper, "did it have to be that?"

He stared owlishly, licked his lip and said nothing. She went and leaned against the dressing table. Her hand moved mechanically and threw the hair back from her face. She shuddered once from head to foot, shaking her head from side to side. "Roger," she whispered again. "Poor Roger. Poor miserable Roger."

He was staring straight up at the ceiling now. "I had a nightmare," he said slowly. "Somebody with a knife was leaning over the bed. I don't know who. Looked a little like Candy. Couldn't of been Candy."

"Of course not, darling," she said softly. She left the dressing table and sat down on the side of the bed. She put her hand out and began to stroke his forehead. "Candy has gone to bed long ago. And why would Candy have a knife?"

"He's a Mex. They all have knives," Roger said in the same remote impersonal voice. "They like knives. And he doesn't like me."

"Nobody likes you," I said brutally.

She turned her head swiftly. "Please—please don't talk like that. He didn't know. He had a dream—"

"Where was the gun?" I growled, watching her, not paying any attention to him.

"Night table. In the drawer." He turned his head and met my stare. There hadn't been any gun in the drawer, and he knew I knew it. The pills had been in there and some odds and ends, but no gun.

"Or under the pillow," he added. "I'm vague about it. I

shot once—" he lifted a heavy hand and pointed—"up there."

I looked up. There seemed to be a hole in the ceiling plaster all right. I went where I could look up at it. Yes. The kind of hole a bullet might make. From that gun it would go on through, into the attic. I went back close to the bed and stood looking down at him, giving him the hard eye.

"Nuts. You meant to kill yourself. You didn't have any nightmare. You were swimming in a sea of self-pity. You didn't have any gun in the drawer or under your pillow either. You got up and got the gun and got back into bed and there you were all ready to wipe out the whole messy business. But I don't think you had the nerve. You fired a shot not meant to hit anything. And your wife came running— that's what you wanted. Just pity and sympathy, pal. Nothing else. Even the struggle was mostly fake. She couldn't take a gun away from you if you didn't want her to."

"I'm sick," he said. "But you could be right. Does it matter?"

"It matters like this. They'd put you in the psycho ward, and believe me, the people who run that place are about as sympathetic as Georgia chain-gang guards."

Eileen stood up suddenly. "That's enough," she said sharply. "He *is* sick, and you know it."

"He wants to be sick. I'm just reminding him of what it would cost him."

"This is not the time to tell him."

"Go on back to your room."

Her blue eyes flashed. "How dare you—"

"Go on back to your room. Unless you want me to call the police. These things are supposed to be reported."

He almost grinned. "Yeah, call the police," he said, "like you did on Terry Lennox."

I didn't pay any attention to that. I was still watching her. She looked exhausted now, and frail, and very beautiful. The moment of flashing anger was gone. I put a hand out and touched her arm. "It's all right," I said. "He won't do it again. Go back to bed."

She gave him a long look and went out of the room. When

the open door was empty of her I sat down on the side of the bed where she had been sitting.

"More pills?"

"No thanks. It doesn't matter whether I sleep. I feel a lot better."

"Did I hit right about that shot? It was just a crazy bit of acting?"

"More or less." He turned his head away. "I guess I was light-headed."

"Nobody can stop you from killing yourself, if you really want to. I realize that. So do you."

"Yes." He was still looking away. "Did you do what I asked you—that stuff in the typewriter?"

"Uh huh. I'm surprised you remember. It's pretty crazy writing. Funny thing, it's clearly typed."

"I can always do that—drunk or sober—up to a point anyway."

"Don't worry about Candy," I said. "You're wrong about his not liking you. And I was wrong to say nobody did. I was trying to jar Eileen, make her mad."

"Why?"

"She pulled one faint already tonight."

He shook his head slightly. "Eileen never faints."

"Then it was a phony."

He didn't like that either.

"What did you mean—a good man died for you?" I asked.

He frowned, thinking about it. "Just rubbish. I told you I had a dream—"

"I'm talking about that guff you typed out."

He looked at me now, turning his head on the pillow as if it had enormous weight. "Another dream."

"I'll try again. What's Candy got on you?"

"Shove it, Jack," he said, and closed his eyes.

I got up and closed the door. "You can't run forever, Wade. Candy could be a blackmailer, sure. Easy. He could even be nice about it—like you and lift your dough at the same time. What is it—a woman?"

"You believe that fool, Loring," he said with his eyes closed.

"Not exactly. What about the sister—the one that's dead?"

It was a wild pitch in a sense but it happened to split the plate. His eyes snapped wide open. A bubble of saliva showed on his lips.

"Is that—why you're here?" he asked slowly, and in a whispering voice.

"You know better. I was invited. You invited me."

His head rolled back and forth on the pillow. In spite of the seconal he was eaten up by his nerves. His face was covered with sweat.

"I'm not the first loving husband who has been an adulterer. Leave me alone, damn you. Leave me alone."

I went into the bathroom and got a face towel and wiped his face off. I grinned at him sneeringly. I was the heel to end all heels. Wait until the man is down, then kick him and kick him again. He's weak. He can't resist or kick back.

"One of these days we'll get together on it," I said.

"I'm not crazy," he said.

"You just hope you're not crazy."

"I've been living in hell."

"Oh sure. That's obvious. The interesting point is why. Here—take this." I had another seconal out of the night table and another glass of water. He got up on one elbow and grabbed for the glass and missed it by a good four inches. I put it in his hand. He managed to drink and swallow his pill. Then he lay back flat and deflated, his face drained of emotion. His nose had that pinched look. He could almost have been a dead man. He wasn't throwing anybody down any stairs tonight. Most likely not any night.

When his eyelids got heavy I went out of the room. The weight of the Webley was against my hip, dragging at my pocket. I started back downstairs again. Eileen's door was open. Her room was dark but there was enough light from the moon to frame her standing just inside the door. She called out something that sounded like a name, but it wasn't mine. I stepped close to her.

"Keep your voice down," I said. "He's gone back to sleep."

"I always knew you would come back," she said softly. "Even after ten years."

I peered at her. One of us was goofy.

"Shut the door," she said in the same caressing voice. "All these years I have kept myself for you."

I turned and shut the door. It seemed like a good idea at the moment. When I faced her she was already falling towards me. So I caught her. I damn well had to. She pressed herself hard against me and her hair brushed my face. Her mouth came up to be kissed. She was trembling. Her lips opened and her teeth opened and her tongue darted. Then her hands dropped and jerked at something and the robe she was wearing came open and underneath it she was as naked as September Morn but a darn sight less coy.

"Put me on the bed," she breathed.

I did that. Putting my arms around her I touched bare skin, soft skin, soft yielding flesh. I lifted her and carried her the few steps to the bed and lowered her. She kept her arms around my neck. She was making some kind of a whistling noise in her throat. Then she thrashed about and moaned. This was murder. I was as erotic as a stallion. I was losing control. You don't get that sort of invitation from that sort of woman very often anywhere.

Candy saved me. There was a thin squeak and I swung around to see the doorknob moving. I jerked loose and jumped for the door. I got it open and barged out through it and the Mex was tearing along the hall and down the stairs. Halfway down he stopped and turned and leered at me. Then he was gone.

I went back to the door and shut it—from the outside this time. Some kind of weird noises were coming from the woman on the bed, but that's all they were now. Weird noises. The spell was broken.

I went down the stairs fast and crossed into the study and grabbed the bottle of Scotch and tilted it. When I couldn't swallow any more I leaned against the wall and panted and let the stuff burn in me until the fumes reached my brain.

It was a long time since dinner. It was a long time since anything that was normal. The whiskey hit me hard and fast and I kept guzzling it until the room started to get hazy and the furniture was all in the wrong places and the lamplight was like wildfire or summer lightning. Then I was flat out on the leather couch, trying to balance the bottle on my chest. It seemed to be empty. It rolled away and thumped on the floor.

That was the last incident of which I took any precise notice.

# 30

A shaft of sunlight tickled one of my ankles. I opened my eyes and saw the crown of a tree moving gently against a hazed blue sky. I rolled over and leather touched my cheek. An axe split my head. I sat up. There was a rug over me. I threw that off and got my feet on the floor. I scowled at a clock. The clock said a minute short of six-thirty.

I got up on my feet and it took character. It took will power. It took a lot out of me, and there wasn't as much to spare as there once had been. The hard heavy years had worked me over.

I plowed across to the half bath and stripped off my tie and shirt and sloshed cold water in my face with both hands and sloshed it on my head. When I was dripping wet I toweled myself off savagely. I put my shirt and tie back on and reached for my jacket and the gun in the pocket banged against the wall. I took it out and swung the cylinder away from the frame and tipped the cartridges into my hand, five full, one just a blackened shell. Then I thought, what's the use, there are always more of them. So I put them back where they had been before and carried the gun into the study and put it away in one of the drawers of the desk.

When I looked up Candy was standing in the doorway, spick and span in his white coat, his hair brushed back and shining black, his eyes bitter.

"You want some coffee?"

"Thanks."

"I put the lamps out. The boss is okay. Asleep. I shut his door. Why you get drunk?"

"I had to."

He sneered at me. "Didn't make her, huh? Got tossed out on your can, shamus."

"Have it your own way."

"You ain't tough this morning, shamus. You ain't tough at all."

"Get the goddam coffee," I yelled at him.

"Hijo de la puta!"

In one jump I had him by the arm. He didn't move. He just looked at me contemptuously. I laughed and let go of his arm.

"You're right, Candy. I'm not tough at all."

He turned and went out. In no time at all he was back with a silver tray and a small silver pot of coffee on it and sugar and cream and a neat triangular napkin. He set it down on the cocktail table and removed the empty bottle and the rest of the drinking materials. He picked another bottle off the floor.

"Fresh. Just made," he said, and went out.

I drank two cups black. Then I tried a cigarette. It was all right. I still belonged to the human race. Then Candy was back in the room again.

"You want breakfast?" he asked morosely.

"No, thanks."

"Okay, scram out of here. We don't want you around."

"Who's we?"

He lifted the lid of a box and helped himself to a cigarette. He lit it and blew smoke at me insolently.

"I take care of the boss," he said.

"You making it pay?"

He frowned, then nodded. "Oh yes. Good money."

"How much on the side—for not spilling what you know?"

He went back to Spanish. "No entendido."

"You understand all right. How much you shake him for? I bet it's not more than a couple of yards."

"What's that? Couple of yards?"

"Two hundred bucks."

He grinned. "You give me couple of yards, shamus. So I don't tell the boss you come out of her room last night."

"That would buy a whole busload of wetbacks like you."

He shrugged that off. "The boss gets pretty rough when he blows his top. Better pay up, shamus."

"Pachuco stuff," I said contemptuously. "All you're touching is the small money. Lots of men play around when they're lit. Anyhow she knows all about it. You don't have anything to sell."

There was a gleam in his eye. "Just don't come round any more, tough boy."

"I'm leaving."

I stood up and walked around the table. He moved enough to keep facing towards me. I watched his hand but he evidently wasn't wearing a knife this morning. When I was close enough I slapped a hand across his face.

"I don't get called a son of a whore by the help, greaseball. I've got business here and I come around whenever I feel like it. Watch your lip from now on. You might get pistol-whipped. That pretty face of yours would never look the same again."

He didn't react at all, not even to the slap. That and being called a greaseball must have been deadly insults to him. But this time he just stood there wooden-faced, motionless. Then without a word he picked up the coffee tray and carried it out.

"Thanks for the coffee," I said to his back.

He kept going. When he was gone I felt the bristles on my chin, shook myself, and decided to be on my way. I had had a skinful of the Wade family.

As I crossed the living room Eileen was coming down the stairs in white slacks and open-toed sandals and a pale blue shirt. She looked at me with complete surprise. "I didn't know you were here, Mr. Marlowe," she said, as though she hadn't seen me for a week and at that time I had just dropped in for tea.

"I put his gun in the desk," I said.

"Gun?" Then it seemed to dawn on her. "Oh, last night was a little hectic, wasn't it? But I thought you had gone home."

I walked over closer to her. She had a thin gold chain around her neck and some kind of fancy pendant in gold and blue on white enamel. The blue enameled part looked like a pair of wings, but not spread out. Against these there was a broad white enamel and gold dagger that pierced a scroll. I couldn't read the words. It was some kind of military insigne.

"I got drunk," I said. "Deliberately and not elegantly. I was a little lonely."

"You didn't have to be," she said, and her eyes were as clear as water. There wasn't a trace of guile in them.

"A matter of opinion," I said. "I'm leaving now and I'm not sure I'll be back. You heard what I said about the gun?"

"You put it in his desk. It might be a good idea to put it somewhere else. But he didn't really mean to shoot himself, did he?"

"I can't answer that. But next time he might."

She shook her head. "I don't think so. I really don't. You were a wonderful help last night, Mr. Marlowe. I don't know how to thank you."

"You made a pretty good try."

She got pink. Then she laughed. "I had a very curious dream in the night," she said slowly, looking off over my shoulder. "Someone I used to know was here in the house. Someone who has been dead for ten years." Her fingers went up and touched the gold and enamel pendant. "That's why I am wearing this today. He gave it to me."

"I had a curious dream myself," I said. "But I'm not telling mine. Let me know how Roger gets on and if there is anything I can do."

She lowered her eyes and looked into mine. "You said you were not coming back."

"I said I wasn't sure. I may have to come back. I hope I won't. There is something very wrong in this house. And only part of it came out of a bottle."

She stared at me, frowning. "What does that mean?"

"I think you know what I'm talking about."

She thought it over carefully. Her fingers were still touching the pendant gently. She let out a slow patient sigh. "There's always another woman," she said quietly. "At some time or other. It's not necessarily fatal. We're talking at cross purposes, aren't we? We are not even talking about the same thing, perhaps."

"Could be," I said. She was still standing on the steps, the third step from the bottom. She still had her fingers on the pendant. She still looked like a golden dream. "Especially if you have in mind that the other woman is Linda Loring."

She dropped her hand from the pendant and came down one more step of the stairs.

"Dr. Loring seems to agree with me," she said indifferently. "He must have some source of information."

"You said he had played that scene with half the males in the valley."

"Did I? Well—it was the conventional sort of thing to say at the time." She came down another step.

"I haven't shaved," I said.

That startled her. Then she laughed. "Oh, I wasn't expecting you to make love to me."

"Just what did you expect of me, Mrs. Wade—in the beginning, when you first persuaded me to go hunting? Why me—what have I got to offer?"

"You kept faith," she said quietly. "When it couldn't have been very easy."

"I'm touched. But I don't think that was the reason."

She came down the last step and then she was looking up at me. "Then what was the reason?"

"Or if it was—it was a damn poor reason. Just about the worst reason in the world."

She frowned a tiny frown. "Why?"

"Because what I did—this keeping faith—is something even a fool doesn't do twice."

"You know," she said lightly, "this is getting to be a very enigmatic conversation."

"You're a very enigmatic person, Mrs. Wade. So long and good luck and if you really care anything about Roger, you'd better find him the right kind of doctor—and quick."

She laughed again. "Oh, that was a mild attack last night. You ought to see him in a bad one. He'll be up and working by this afternoon."

"Like hell he will."

"But believe me he will. I know him so well."

I gave her the last shot right in the teeth and it sounded pretty nasty.

"You don't really want to save him, do you? You just want to look as if you are trying to save him."

"That," she said deliberately, "was a very beastly thing to say to me."

She stepped past me and walked through the dining room doors and then the big room was empty and I crossed to the front door and let myself out. It was a perfect summer morning in that bright secluded valley. It was too far from the city to get any smog and cut off by the low mountains from the dampness of the ocean. It was going to be hot later, but in a nice refined exclusive sort of way, nothing brutal like the heat of the desert, not sticky and rank like the heat of the city. Idle Valley was a perfect place to live. Perfect. Nice people with nice homes, nice cars, nice horses, nice dogs, possibly even nice children.

But all a man named Marlowe wanted from it was out. And fast.

## 31

I went home and showered and shaved and changed clothes and began to feel clean again. I cooked some breakfast, ate it, washed up, swept the kitchen and the service porch, filled a pipe and called the phone answering service. I shot a blank. Why go to the office? There would be nothing there but another dead moth and another layer of dust. In the safe would be my portrait of Madison. I could go down and play with that, and with the five crisp hundred dollar bills that still smelled of coffee. I could do that, but I didn't want to. Something inside me had gone sour. None of it really belonged to me. What was it supposed to buy? How much loyalty can a dead man use? Phooey: I was looking at life through the mists of a hangover.

It was the kind of morning that seems to go on forever. I was flat and tired and dull and the passing minutes seemed to fall into a void, with a soft whirring sound, like spent rockets. Birds chirped in the shrubbery outside and the cars went up and down Laurel Canyon Boulevard endlessly. Usually I wouldn't even hear them. But I was brooding and irritable and mean and oversensitive. I decided to kill the hangover.

Ordinarily I was not a morning drinker. The Southern California climate is too soft for it. You don't metabolize fast enough. But I mixed a tall cold one this time and sat in an easy chair with my shirt open and pecked at a magazine, reading a crazy story about a guy that had two lives and two psychiatrists, one was human and one was some kind of insect in a hive. The guy kept going from one to the other and the whole thing was as crazy as a crumpet, but funny in an offbeat sort of way. I was handling the drink carefully, a sip at a time, watching myself.

It was about noon when the telephone rang and the voice said: "This is Linda Loring. I called your office and your phone service told me to try your home. I'd like to see you."

"Why?"

"I'd rather explain that in person. You go to your office from time to time, I suppose."

"Yeah. From time to time. Is there any money in it?"

"I hadn't thought of it that way. But I have no objection, if you want to be paid. I could be at your office in about an hour."

"Goody."

"What's the matter with you?" she asked sharply.

"Hangover. But I'm not paralyzed. I'll be there. Unless you'd rather come here."

"Your office would suit me better."

"I've got a nice quiet place here. Dead-end street, no near neighbors."

"The implication does not attract me—if I understand you."

"Nobody understands me, Mrs. Loring. I'm enigmatic. Okay, I'll struggle down to the coop."

"Thank you so much." She hung up.

I was slow getting down there because I stopped on the way for a sandwich. I aired out the office and switched on the buzzer and poked my head through the communicating door and she was there already, sitting in the same chair where Mendy Menendez had sat and looking through what could have been the same magazine. She had a tan gabardine suit on today and she looked pretty elegant. She put the magazine aside, gave me a serious look and said:

"Your Boston fern needs watering. I think it needs repotting too. Too many air roots."

I held the door open for her. The hell with the Boston fern. When she was inside and I had let the door swing shut I held the customer's chair for her and she gave the office the usual once-over. I got around to my side of the desk.

"You're establishment isn't exactly palatial," she said. "Don't you even have a secretary?"

"It's a sordid life, but I'm used to it."

"And I shouldn't think very lucrative," she said.

"Oh I don't know. Depends. Want to see a portrait of Madison?"

"A what?"

"A five-thousand-dollar bill. Retainer. I've got it in the safe." I got up and started over there. I spun the knob and opened it and unlocked a drawer inside, opened an envelope, and dropped it in front of her. She stared at it in something like amazement.

"Don't let the office fool you," I said. "I worked for an old boy one time that would cash in at about twenty millions. Even your old man would say hello to him. His office was no better than mine, except he was a bit deaf and had that soundproofing stuff on the ceiling. On the floor brown linoleum, no carpet."

She picked the portrait of Madison up and pulled it between her fingers and turned it over. She put it down again.

"You got this from Terry, didn't you?"

"Gosh, you know everything, don't you Mrs. Loring?"

She pushed the bill away from her, frowning. "He had one. He carried it on him ever since he and Sylvia were married the second time. He called it his mad money. It was not found on his body."

"There could be other reasons for that."

"I know. But how many people carry a five-thousand-dollar bill around with them? How many who could afford to give you that much money would give it to you in this form?"

It wasn't worth answering. I just nodded. She went on brusquely.

"And what were you supposed to do for it, Mr. Marlowe? Or would you tell me? On that last ride down to Tijuana he had plenty of time to talk. You made it very clear the other evening that you didn't believe his confession. Did he give you a list of his wife's lovers so that you might find a murderer among them?"

I didn't answer that either, but for different reasons.

"And would the name of Roger Wade appear on that list by any chance?" she asked harshly. "If Terry didn't kill his wife, the murderer would have to be some violent and irresponsible man, a lunatic or a savage drunk. Only that sort of man could, to use your own repulsive phrase, beat her face into a bloody sponge. Is that why you are making yourself so very useful to the Wades—a regular mother's helper who comes on call to nurse him when he is drunk, to find him when he is lost, to bring him home when he is helpless?"

"Let me set you right on a couple of points, Mrs. Loring. Terry may or may not have given me that beautiful piece of engraving. But he gave me no list and mentioned no names. There was nothing he asked me to do except what you seem to feel sure I did do, drive him to Tijuana. My getting involved with the Wades was the work of a New York publisher who is desperate to have Roger Wade finish his book, which involves keeping him fairly sober, which in turn involves finding out if there is any special trouble that makes him get drunk. If there is and it can be found out, then the next step would be an effort to remove it. I say effort, because the chances are you couldn't do it. But you could try."

"I could tell you in one simple sentence why he gets drunk," she said contemptuously. "That anemic blond show piece he's married to."

"Oh I don't know," I said. "I wouldn't call her anemic."

"Really? How interesting." Her eyes glittered.

I picked up my portrait of Madison. "Don't chew too long on that one, Mrs. Loring. I am not sleeping with the lady. Sorry to disappoint you."

I went over to the safe and put my money away in the locked compartment. I shut the safe and spun the dial.

"On second thought," she said to my back, "I doubt very much that anyone is sleeping with her."

I went back and sat on the corner of the desk. "You're getting bitchy, Mrs. Loring. Why? Are you carrying a torch for our alcoholic friend?"

"I hate remarks like that," she said bitingly. "I hate them. I suppose that idiotic scene my husband made makes you think you have the right to insult me. No, I am not carrying a torch for Roger Wade. I never did—even when he was a sober man who behaved himself. Still less now that he is what he is."

I flopped into my chair, reached for a matchbox, and stared at her. She looked at her watch.

"You people with a lot of money are really something," I said. "You think anything you choose to say, however nasty, is perfectly all right. You can make sneering remarks about Wade and his wife to a man you hardly know, but if I hand you back a little change, that's an insult. Okay, let's play it low down. Any drunk will eventually turn up with a loose woman. Wade is a drunk, but you're not a loose woman. That's just a casual suggestion your high-bred husband drops to brighten up a cocktail party. He doesn't mean it, he's just saying it for laughs. So we rule you out, and look for a loose woman elsewhere. How far do we have to look, Mrs. Loring—to find one that would involve you enough to bring you down here trading sneers with me? It has to be somebody rather special, doesn't it—otherwise why should you care?"

She sat perfectly silent, just looking. A long half minute went by. The corners of her mouth were white and her hands were rigid on her gabardine bag that matched her suit.

"You haven't exactly wasted your time, have you?" she said at last. "How convenient that this publisher should have thought of employing you! So Terry named no names to you! Not a name. But it really didn't matter, did it, Mr. Marlowe? Your instinct was unerring. May I ask what you propose to do next?"

"Nothing."

"Why, what a waste of talent! How can you reconcile it with your obligation to your portrait of Madison? Surely there must be something you can do."

"Just between the two of us," I said, "you're getting pretty corny. So Wade knew your sister. Thanks for telling me, however indirectly. I already guessed it. So what? He's just one of what was most likely a fairly rich collection. Let's leave it there. And let's get around to why you wanted to see me. That kind of got lost in the shuffle, didn't it?"

She stood up. She glanced at her watch once more. "I have a car downstairs. Could I prevail upon you to drive home with me and drink a cup of tea?"

"Go on," I said. "Let's have it."

"Do I sound so suspicious? I have a guest who would like to make your acquaintance."

"The old man?"

"I don't call him that," she said evenly.

I stood up and leaned across the desk. "Honey, you're awful cute sometimes. You really are. Is it all right if I carry a gun?"

"Surely you're not afraid of an old man." She wrinkled her lip at me.

"Why not? I'll bet you are—plenty."

She sighed. "Yes, I'm afraid I am. I always have been. He can be rather terrifying."

"Maybe I'd better take two guns," I said, then wished I hadn't.

## 32

It was the damndest-looking house I ever saw. It was a square gray box three stories high, with a mansard roof, steeply sloped and broken by twenty or thirty double dormer windows with a lot of wedding cake decoration around them and between them. The entrance had double stone pillars on each side but the cream of the joint was an outside spiral staircase with a stone railing, topped by a tower room from which there must have been a view the whole length of the lake.

The motor yard was paved with stone. What the place really seemed to need was a half mile of poplar-lined driveway and a deer park and a wild garden and a terrace on three levels and a few hundred roses outside the library window and a long green vista from every window ending in forest and silence and quiet emptiness. What it had was a wall of fieldstone around a comfortable ten or fifteen acres, which is a fair hunk of real estate in our crowded little country. The driveway was lined with a cypress hedge trimmed round. There were all sorts of ornamental trees in clumps here and there and they didn't look like California trees. Imported stuff. Whoever built that place was trying to drag the Atlantic seaboard over the Rockies. He was trying hard, but he hadn't made it.

Amos, the middle-aged colored chauffeur, stopped the Caddy gently in front of the pillared entrance, hopped out, and came around to hold the open door for Mrs. Loring. I got out first and helped him hold it. I helped her get out. She had hardly spoken to me since we got into the car in front of my building. She looked tired and nervous. Maybe this idiotic hunk of architecture depressed her. It would have depressed a laughing jackass and made it coo like a mourning dove.

"Who built this place?" I asked her. "And who was he mad at?"

She finally smiled. "Hadn't you seen it before?"

"Never been this far into the valley."

She walked me over to the other side of the driveway and pointed up. "The man who built it jumped out of that tower room and landed about where you are standing. He was a French count named La Tourelle and unlike most French counts he had a lot of money. His wife was Ramona Desborough, who was not exactly threadbare herself. In the silent-picture days she made thirty thousand a week. La Tourelle built this place for their home. It's supposed to be a miniature of the Château de Blois. You know that, of course."

"Like the back of my hand," I said. "I remember now. It was one of those Sunday paper stories once. She left him and he killed himself. There was some kind of queer will too, wasn't there?"

She nodded. "He left his ex-wife a few millions for carfare and tied the rest up in a trust. The estate was to be kept on just as it was. Nothing was to be changed, the dining table was to be laid in style every night, and nobody was to be allowed inside the grounds except the servants and the lawyers. The will was broken, of course. Eventually the estate was carved up to some extent and when I married Dr. Loring my father gave it to me for a wedding present. It must have cost him a fortune merely to make it fit to live in again. I loathe it. I always have."

"You don't have to stay here, do you?"

She shrugged in a tired sort of way. "Part of the time, at least. One of his daughters has to show him some sign of stability. Dr. Loring likes it here."

"He would. Any guy who could make the kind of scene he made at Wade's house ought to wear spats with his pajamas."

She arched her eyebrows. "Why, thank you for taking such an interest, Mr. Marlowe. But I think enough has been said on that subject. Shall we go in? My father doesn't like to be kept waiting."

We crossed the driveway again and went up the stone steps and half of the big double doors swung open noiselessly and an expensive and very snooty looking character stood aside for us to enter. The hallway was bigger than all the floor space in the house I was living in. It had a tesselated floor and there seemed to be stained-glass windows at the back and if there had been any light coming through them I might have been able to see what else was there. From the hallway we went through some more double carved doors into a dim room that couldn't have been less than seventy feet long. A man was sitting there waiting, silent. He stared at us coldly.

"Am I late, Father?" Mrs. Loring asked hurriedly. "This is Mr. Philip Marlowe. Mr. Harlan Potter."

The man just looked at me and moved his chin down about half an inch.

"Ring for tea," he said. "Sit down, Mr. Marlowe."

I sat down and looked at him. He looked at me like an entomologist looking at a beetle. Nobody said anything. There was complete silence until the tea came. It was put down on a huge silver tray on a Chinese table. Linda sat at a table and poured.

"Two cups," Harlan Potter said. "You can have your tea in another room, Linda."

"Yes, Father. How do you like your tea, Mr. Marlowe?"

"Any way at all," I said. My voice seemed to echo off into the distance and get small and lonely.

She gave the old man a cup and then gave me a cup. Then she stood up silently and went out of the room. I watched her go. I took a sip of tea and got a cigarette out.

"Don't smoke, please. I am subject to asthma."

I put the cigarette back in the pack. I stared at him. I don't know how it feels to be worth a hundred million or so, but he didn't look as if he was having any fun. He was an enormous man, all of six feet five and built to scale. He wore a gray tweed suit with no padding. His shoulders didn't need any. He wore a white shirt and a dark tie and no display handkerchief. A spectacle case showed in the outside breast pocket. It was black, like his shoes. His hair was black too, no gray at all. It was brushed sideways across his skull in a MacArthur sweep. And I had a hunch there was nothing under it but bare skull. His eyebrows were thick and black. His voice seemed to come from a long way off. He drank his tea as if he hated it.

"It will save time, Mr. Marlowe, if I put my position before you. I believe you are interfering in my affairs. If I am correct, I propose to stop it."

"I don't know enough about your affairs to interfere in them, Mr. Potter."

"I disagree."

He drank some more tea and put the cup aside. He leaned back in the big chair he was sitting in and took me to pieces with his hard gray eyes.

"I know who you are, naturally. And how you make your living—if you make one—and how you became involved with Terry Lennox. It has been reported to me that you helped Terry get out of the country, that you have doubts about his guilt, and that you have since made contact with a man who was known to my dead daughter. For what purpose has not been explained to me. Explain it."

"If the man has a name," I said, "name it."

He smiled very slightly but not as if he was falling for me. "Wade. Roger Wade. Some sort of writer, I believe. A writer, they tell me, of rather prurient books which I should not be interested to read. I further understand that this man is a dangerous alcoholic. That may have given you a strange notion."

"Maybe you had better let me have my own notions, Mr. Potter. They are not important, naturally, but they're all I have. First, I do not believe Terry killed his wife, because of the way it was done and because I don't think he was that kind of man. Second, I didn't make contact with Wade. I was asked to live in his house and do what I could to keep him sober while he finished a job of writing. Third, if he is a dangerous alcoholic, I haven't seen any sign of it. Fourth, my first contact was at the request of his New York publisher and I didn't at that time have any idea that Roger Wade even knew your daughter. Fifth, I refused this offer of employment and then Mrs. Wade asked me to find her husband who was away somewhere taking a cure. I found him and took him home."

"Very methodical," he said dryly.

"I'm not finished being methodical, Mr. Potter. Sixth— you or someone on your instructions sent a lawyer named Sewell Endicott to get me out of jail. He didn't say who sent him, but there wasn't anyone else in the picture. Seventh, when I got out of jail a hoodlum named Mendy Menendez pushed me around and warned me to keep my nose clean and gave me a song and dance about how Terry had saved his life and the life of a gambler at Las Vegas named Randy Starr. The story could be true for all I know. Menendez pretended to be sore that Terry hadn't asked him for help getting to Mexico and had asked a punk like me instead. He, Menendez, could have done it two ways from the jack by lifting one finger, and done it much better."

"Surely," Harlan Potter said with a bleak smile, "you are not under the impression that I number Mr. Menendez and Mr. Starr among my acquaintances."

"I wouldn't know, Mr. Potter. A man doesn't make your kind of money in any way I can understand. The next person to warn me off the courthouse lawn was your daughter, Mrs. Loring. We met by accident at a bar and we spoke because we were both drinking gimlets, Terry's favorite drink, but an uncommon one around here. I didn't know who she was until she told me. I told her a little of how I felt about Terry and she gave me the idea that I would have a short unhappy career if I got you mad. Are you mad, Mr. Potter?"

"When I am," he said coldly, "you will not have to ask me. You will be in no uncertainty about it."

"What I thought. I've been kind of expecting the goon squad to drop around, but they haven't shown so far. I haven't been bothered by the cops either. I could have been. I could have been given a rough time. I think all you wanted, Mr. Potter, was quiet. Just what have I done to disturb you?"

He grinned. It was a sour kind of grin, but it was a grin. He put his long yellow fingers together and crossed a leg over his knee and leaned back comfortably.

"A pretty good pitch, Mr. Marlowe, and I have let you make it. Now listen to me. You are exactly right in thinking all I want is quiet. It's quite possible that your connection with the Wades may be incidental, accidental, and coincidental. Let it remain so. I am a family man in an age when it means almost nothing. One of my daughters married a Bostonian prig and the other made a number of foolish marriages, the last being with a complaisant pauper who allowed her to live a worthless and immoral life until he suddenly and for no good reason lost his self-control and murdered her. You think that impossible to accept because of the brutality with which it was done. You are wrong. He shot her with a Mauser automatic, the very gun he took with him to Mexico. And after he shot her he did what he did in order to cover the bullet wound. I admit the brutality of this, but remember the man had been in a war, had been badly wounded, had suffered a great deal and seen others suffer. He may not have intended to kill her. There may have been some sort of scuffle, since the gun belonged to my daughter. It was a small but powerful gun, 7.65 m/m caliber, a model called P.P.K. The bullet went completely through her head and lodged in the wall behind a chintz curtain. It was not found immediately and the fact was not published at all. Now let us consider the situation." He broke off and stared at me. "Are you very badly in need of a cigarette?"

"Sorry, Mr. Potter. I took it out without thinking. Force of habit." I put the cigarette back for the second time.

"Terry had just killed his wife. He had ample motive from

the rather limited police point of view. But he also had an excellent defense—that it was her gun in her possession and that he tried to take it away from her and failed and she shot herself with it. A good trial lawyer could have done a lot with that. He would probably have been acquitted. If he had called me up then, I would have helped him. But by making the murder a brutal affair to cover the traces of the bullet, he made it impossible. He had to run away and even that he did clumsily."

"He certainly did, Mr. Potter. But he called you up in Pasadena first, didn't he? He told me he did."

The big man nodded. "I told him to disappear and I would still see what I could do. I didn't want to know where he was. That was imperative. I could not hide a criminal."

"Sounds good, Mr. Potter."

"Do I detect a note of sarcasm? No matter. When I learned the details there was nothing to be done. I could not permit the sort of trial that kind of killing would result in. To be frank, I was very glad when I learned that he had shot himself in Mexico and left a confession."

"I can understand that, Mr. Potter."

He beetled his eyebrows at me. "Be careful, young man. I don't like irony. Can you understand now that I cannot tolerate any further investigation of any sort by any person? And why I have used all my influence to make what investigation there was as brief as possible and as little publicized as possible?"

"Sure—if you're convinced he killed her."

"Of course he killed her. With what intent is another matter. It is no longer important. I am not a public character and I do not intend to be. I have always gone to a great deal of trouble to avoid any kind of publicity. I have influence but I don't abuse it. The District Attorney of Los Angeles County is an ambitious man who has too much good sense to wreck his career for the notoriety of the moment. I see a glint in your eye, Marlowe. Get rid of it. We live in what is called a democracy, rule by the majority of the people. A fine ideal if it could be made to work. The people elect, but the party machines nominate, and the party machines to be effective must spend a great deal of money. Somebody has to give it to them, and that somebody, whether it be an individual, a financial group, a trade union or what have you, expects some consideration in return. What I and people of my kind expect is to be allowed to live our lives in decent privacy. I own newspapers, but I don't like them. I regard them as a constant menace to whatever privacy we have left. Their constant yelping about a free press means, with a few honorable exceptions, freedom to peddle scandal, crime, sex, sensationalism, hate, innuendo, and the political and financial uses of propaganda. A newspaper is a business out to make money through advertising revenue. That is predicated on its circulation and you know what the circulation depends on."

I got up and walked around my chair. He eyed me with cold attention. I sat down again. I needed a little luck. Hell, I needed it in carload lots.

"Okay, Mr. Potter, what goes from here?"

He wasn't listening. He was frowning at his own thoughts. "There's a peculiar thing about money," he went on. "In large quantities it tends to have a life of its own, even a conscience of its own. The power of money becomes very difficult to control. Man has always been a venal animal. The growth of populations, the huge costs of wars, the incessant pressure of confiscatory taxation—all these things make him more and more venal. The average man is tired and scared, and a tired, scared man can't afford ideals. He has to buy food for his family. In our time we have seen a shocking decline in both public and private morals. You can't expect quality from people whose lives are a subjection to a lack of quality. You can't have quality with mass production. You don't want it because it lasts too long. So you substitute styling, which is a commercial swindle intended to produce artificial obsolescence. Mass production couldn't sell its goods next year unless it made what it sold this year look unfashionable a year from now. We have the whitest kitchens and the most shining bathrooms in the world. But in the lovely white kitchen the average American housewife can't produce a meal fit to eat, and the lovely shining bathroom is mostly a receptacle for deodorants, laxatives, sleeping pills, and the products of that confidence racket called the cosmetic industry. We make the finest packages in the world, Mr. Marlowe. The stuff inside is mostly junk."

He took out a large white handkerchief and touched his temples with it. I was sitting there with my mouth open, wondering what made the guy tick. He hated everything.

"It's a little too warm for me in these parts," he said. "I'm used to a cooler climate. I'm beginning to sound like an editorial that has forgotten the point it wanted to make."

"I got your point all right, Mr. Potter. You don't like the way the world is going so you use what power you have to close off a private corner to live in as near as possible to the way you remember people lived fifty years ago before the age of mass production. You've got a hundred million dollars and all it has bought you is a pain in the neck."

He pulled the handkerchief taut by two opposite corners, then crumpled it into a ball and stuffed it in a pocket.

"And then?" he asked shortly.

"That's all there is, there isn't any more. You don't care who murdered your daughter, Mr. Potter. You wrote her off as a bad job long ago. Even if Terry Lennox didn't kill her, and the real murderer is still walking around free, you don't care. You wouldn't want him caught, because that would revive the scandal and there would have to be a trial and his defense would blow your privacy as high as the Empire State Building. Unless, of course, he was obliging enough to commit suicide, before there was any trial. Preferably in Tahiti or Guatemala or the middle of the Sahara Desert. Anywhere where the County would hate the expense of sending a man to verify what had happened."

He smiled suddenly, a big rugged smile with a reasonable amount of friendliness in it.

"What do you want from me, Marlowe?"

"If you mean how much money, nothing. I didn't ask myself here. I was brought. I told the truth about how I met Roger Wade. But he did know your daughter and he does have a record of violence, although I haven't seen any of it. Last night the guy tried to shoot himself. He's a haunted man. He has a massive guilt complex. If I happened to be looking for a good suspect, he might do. I realize he's only one of many, but he happens to be the only one I've met."

He stood up and standing up he was really big. Tough too. He came over and stood in front of me.

"A telephone call, Mr. Marlowe, would deprive you of your license. Don't fence with me. I won't put up with it."

"Two telephone calls and I'd wake up kissing the gutter— with the back of my head missing."

He laughed harshly. "I don't operate that way. I suppose in your quaint line of business it is natural for you to think so. I've given you too much of my time. I'll ring for the butler to show you out."

"Not necessary," I said, and stood up myself. "I came here and got told. Thanks for the time."

He held his hand out. "Thank you for coming. I think you're a pretty honest sort of fellow. Don't be a hero, young man. There's no percentage in it."

I shook hands with him. He had a grip like a pipe wrench. He smiled at me benignantly now. He was Mr. Big, the winner, everything under control.

"One of these days I might be able to throw some business your way," he said. "And don't go away thinking that I buy politicians or law enforcement officers. I don't have to. Goodbye, Mr. Marlowe. And thank you again for coming."

He stood there and watched me out of the room. I had my hand on the front door when Linda Loring popped out of a shadow somewhere.

"Well?" she asked me quietly. "How did you get on with Father?"

"Fine. He explained civilization to me. I mean how it looks to him. He's going to let it go on for a little while longer. But it better be careful and not interfere with his private life. If it does, he's apt to make a phone call to God and cancel the order."

"You're hopeless," she said.

"Me? I'm hopeless? Lady, take a look at your old man. Compared with him I'm a blue-eyed baby with a brand new rattle."

I went on out and Amos had the Caddy there waiting. He drove me back to Hollywood. I offered him a buck but he wouldn't take it. I offered to buy him the poems of T. S. Eliot. He said he already had them.

# 33

A week went by and I heard nothing from the Wades. The weather was hot and sticky and the acid sting of the smog had crept as far west as Beverly Hills. From the top of Mulholland Drive you could see it leveled out all over the city like a ground mist. When you were in it you could taste it and smell it and it made your eyes smart. Everybody was griping about it. In Pasadena, where the stuffy millionaires holed up after Beverly Hills was spoiled for them by the movie crowd, the city fathers screamed with rage. Everything was the fault of the smog. If the canary wouldn't sing, if the milkman was late, if the Pekinese had fleas, if an old coot in a starched collar had a heart attack on the way to church, that was the smog. Where I lived it was usually clear in the early morning and nearly always at night. Once in a while a whole day would be clear, nobody quite knew why.

It was on a day like that—it happened to be a Thursday—that Roger Wade called me up. "How are you? This is Wade." He sounded fine.

"Fine, and you?"

"Sober, I'm afraid. Scratching a hard buck. We ought to have a talk. And I think I owe you some dough."

"Nope."

"Well, how about lunch today? Could you make it here somewhere around one?"

"I guess so. How's Candy?"

"Candy?" He sounded puzzled. He must have blacked out plenty that night. "Oh, he helped you put me to bed that night."

"Yeah. He's a helpful little guy—in spots. And Mrs. Wade?"

"She's fine too. She's in town shopping today."

We hung up and I sat and rocked in my swivel chair. I ought to have asked him how the book was going. Maybe you always ought to ask a writer how the book is going. And then again maybe he gets damned tired of that question.

I had another call in a little while, a strange voice.

"This is Roy Ashterfelt. George Peters told me to call you up, Marlowe."

"Oh yes, thanks. You're the fellow that knew Terry Lennox in New York. Called himself Marston then."

"That's right. He was sure on the sauce. But it's the same guy all right. You couldn't very well mistake him. Out here I saw him in Chasen's one night with his wife. I was with a client. The client knew them. Can't tell you the client's name, I'm afraid."

"I understand. It's not very important now, I guess. What was his first name?"

"Wait a minute while I bite my thumb. Oh yeah, Paul. Paul Marston. And there was one thing more, if it interests you. He was wearing a British Army service badge. Their version of the ruptured duck."

"I see. What happened to him?"

"I don't know. I came west. Next time I saw him he was here too—married to Harlan Potter's somewhat wild daughter. But you know all that."

"They're both dead now. But thanks for telling me."

"Not at all. Glad to help. Does it mean anything to you?"

"Not a thing," I said, and I was a liar. "I never asked him about himself. He told me once he had been brought up in an orphanage. Isn't it just possible you made a mistake?"

"With that white hair and that scarred face, brother? Not a chance. I won't say I never forget a face, but not that one."

"Did he see you?"

"If he did, he didn't let on. Hardly expect him to in the circumstances. Anyhow he might not have remembered me. Like I said, he was always pretty well lit back in New York."

I thanked him some more and he said it was a pleasure and we hung up.

I thought about it for a while. The noise of the traffic outside the building on the boulevard made an unmusical obbligato to my thinking. It was too loud. In summer in hot weather everything is too loud. I got up and shut the lower part of the window and called Detective-Sergeant Green at Homicide. He was obliging enough to be in.

"Look," I said, after the preliminaries, "I heard something about Terry Lennox that puzzles me. A fellow I know used to know him in New York under another name. You check his war record?"

"You guys never learn," Green said harshly. "You just never learn to stay on your own side of the street. That matter is closed, locked up, weighted with lead and dropped in the ocean. Get it?"

"I spent part of an afternoon with Harlan Potter last week at his daughter's house in Idle Valley. Want to check?"

"Doing what?" he asked sourly. "Supposing I believe you."

"Talking things over. I was invited. He likes me. Incidentally, he told me the girl was shot with a Mauser P.P.K. 7.65 m/m. That news to you?"

"Go on."

"Her own gun, chum. Makes a little difference, maybe. But don't get me wrong. I'm not looking into any dark corners. This is a personal matter. Where did he get that wound?"

Green was silent. I heard a door close in the background. Then he said quietly, "Probably in a knife fight south of the border."

"Aw hell, Green, you had his prints. You sent them to Washington like always. You got a report back—like always. All I asked was something about his service record."

"Who said he had one?"

"Well, Mendy Menendez for one. Seems Lennox saved his life one time and that's how he got the wound. He was captured by the Germans and they gave him the face he had."

"Menendez, huh? You believe that son of a bitch? You got a hole in your own head. Lennox didn't have any war record. Didn't have any record of any kind under any name. You satisfied?"

"If you say so," I said. "But I don't see why Menendez would bother to come up here and tell me a yarn and warn me to keep my nose clean on account of Lennox was a pal of him and Randy Starr in Vegas and they didn't want anybody fooling around. After all Lennox was already dead."

"Who knows what a hoodlum figures?" Green asked bitterly. "Or why? Maybe Lennox was in a racket with them before he married all that money and got respectable. He was a floor manager at Starr's place in Vegas for a while. That's where he met the girl. A smile and a bow and a dinner jacket.

Keep the customers happy and keep an eye on the house players. I guess he had class for the job."

"He had charm," I said. "They don't use it in police business. Much obliged, Sergeant. How is Captain Gregorius these days?"

"Retirement leave. Don't you read the papers?"

"Not the crime news, Sergeant. Too sordid."

I started to say goodbye but he chopped me off. "What did Mr. Money want with you?"

"We just had a cup of tea together. A social call. He said he might put some business my way. He also hinted—just hinted, not in so many words—that any cop that looked cross-eyed at me would be facing a grimy future."

"He don't run the police department," Green said.

"He admits it. Doesn't even buy commissioners or D.A.'s, he said. They just kind of curl up in his lap when he's having a doze."

"Go to hell," Green said, and hung up in my ear.

A difficult thing, being a cop. You never know whose stomach it's safe to jump up and down on.

# 34

The stretch of broken-paved road from the highway to the curve of the hill was dancing in the noon heat and the scrub that dotted the parched land on both sides of it was flour-white with granite dust by this time. The weedy smell was almost nauseating. A thin hot acrid breeze was blowing. I had my coat off and my sleeves rolled up, but the door was too hot to rest an arm on. A tethered horse dozed wearily under a clump of live oaks. A brown Mexican sat on the ground and ate something out of a newspaper. A tumbleweed rolled lazily across the road and came to rest against a piece of granite outcrop, and a lizard that had been there an instant before disappeared without seeming to move at all.

Then I was around the hill on the blacktop and in another

country. In five minutes I turned into the driveway of the Wades' house, parked and walked across the flagstones and rang the bell. Wade answered the door himself, in a brown and white checked shirt with short sleeves, pale blue denim slacks, and house slippers. He looked tanned and he looked good. There was an inkstain on his hand and a smear of cigarette ash on one side of his nose.

He led the way into his study and parked himself behind his desk. On it there was a thick pile of yellow typescript. I put my coat on a chair and sat on the couch.

"Thanks for coming, Marlowe. Drink?"

I got that look on my face you get when a drunk asks you to have a drink. I could feel it. He grinned.

"I'll have a coke," he said.

"You pick up fast," I said. "I don't think I want a drink right now. I'll take a coke with you."

He pressed something with his foot and after a while Candy came. He looked surly. He had a blue shirt on and an orange scarf and no white coat. Two-tone black and white shoes, elegant high-waisted gabardine pants.

Wade ordered the cokes. Candy gave me a hard stare and went away.

"Book?" I said, pointing to the stack of paper.

"Yeah. Stinks."

"I don't believe it. How far along?"

"About two thirds of the way—for what it's worth. Which is damn little. You know how a writer can tell when he's washed up?"

"Don't know anything about writers." I filled my pipe.

"When he starts reading his old stuff for inspiration. That's absolute. I've got five hundred pages of typescript here, well over a hundred thousand words. My books run long. The public likes long books. The damn fool public thinks if there's a lot of pages there must be a lot of gold. I don't dare read it over. And I can't remember half of what's in it. I'm just plain scared to look at my own work."

"You look good yourself," I said. "From the other night I wouldn't have believed it. You've got more guts than you think you have."

"What I need right now is more than guts. Something you

don't get by wishing for it. A belief in yourself. I'm a spoiled writer who doesn't believe any more. I have a beautiful home, a beautiful wife, and a beautiful sales record. But all I really want is to get drunk and forget."

He leaned his chin in his cupped hands and stared across the desk.

"Eileen said I tried to shoot myself. Was it that bad?"

"You don't remember?"

He shook his head. "Not a damn thing except that I fell down and cut my head. And after a while I was in bed. And you were there. Did Eileen call you?"

"Yeah. Didn't she say?"

"She hasn't been talking to me very much this last week. I guess she's had it. Up to here." He put the edge of one hand against his neck just under his chin. "That show Loring put on here didn't help any."

"Mrs. Wade said it meant nothing."

"Well, she would, wouldn't she? It happened to be the truth, but I don't suppose she believed it when she said it. The guy is just abnormally jealous. You have a drink or two with his wife in the corner and laugh a little and kiss her goodbye and right off he assumes you are sleeping with her. One reason being that he isn't."

"What I like about Idle Valley," I said, "is that everybody is living just a comfortable normal life."

He frowned and then the door opened and Candy came in with two cokes and glasses and poured the cokes. He set one in front of me without looking at me.

"Lunch in half an hour," Wade said, "and where's the white coat?"

"This my day off," Candy said, deadpan. "I ain't the cook, boss."

"Cold cuts or sandwiches and beer will do," Wade said. "The cook's off today, Candy. I've got a friend to lunch."

"You think he is your friend?" Candy sneered. "Better ask your wife."

Wade leaned back in his chair and smiled at him. "Watch your lip, little man. You've got it soft here. I don't often ask a favor of you, do I?"

Candy looked down at the floor. After a moment he looked

up and grinned. "Okay, boss. I put the white coat on. I get the lunch, I guess."

He turned softly and went out. Wade watched the door close. Then he shrugged and looked at me.

"We used to call them servants. Now we call them domestic help. I wonder how long it will be before we have to give them breakfast in bed. I'm paying the guy too much money. He's spoiled."

"Wages—or something on the side?"

"Such as what?" he asked sharply.

I got up and handed him some folded yellow sheets. "You'd better read it. Evidently you don't remember asking me to tear it up. It was in your typewriter, under the cover."

He unfolded the yellow pages and leaned back to read them. The glass of coke fizzed unnoticed on the desk in front of him. He read slowly, frowning. When he came to the end he refolded the sheets and ran a finger along the edge.

"Did Eileen see this?" he asked carefully.

"I wouldn't know. She might have."

"Pretty wild, isn't it?"

"I liked it. Especially the part about a good man dying for you."

He opened the paper again and tore it into long strips viciously and dumped the strips into his wastebasket.

"I suppose a drunk will write or say or do anything," he said slowly. "It's meaningless to me. Candy's not blackmailing me. He likes me."

"Maybe you'd better get drunk again. You might remember what you meant. You might remember a lot of things. We've been through this before—that night when the gun went off. I suppose the seconal blanked you out too. You sounded sober enough. But now you pretend not to remember writing that stuff I just gave you. No wonder you can't write your book, Wade. It's a wonder you can stay alive."

He reached sideways and opened a drawer of his desk. His hand fumbled in it and came up with a three-decker check book. He opened it and reached for a pen.

"I owe you a thousand dollars," he said quietly. He wrote in the book. Then on the counterfoil. He tore the check out, came around the desk with it, and dropped it in front of me. "Is that all right?"

I leaned back and looked up at him and didn't touch the check and didn't answer him. His face was tight and drawn. His eyes were deep and empty.

"I suppose you think I killed her and let Lennox take the rap," he said slowly. "She was a tramp all right. But you don't beat a woman's head in just because she's a tramp. Candy knows I went there sometimes. The funny part of it is I don't think he would tell. I could be wrong, but I don't think so."

"Wouldn't matter if he did," I said. "Harlan Potter's friends wouldn't listen to him. Also, she wasn't killed with that bronze thing. She was shot through the head with her own gun."

"She maybe had a gun," he said almost dreamily. "But I didn't know she had been shot. It wasn't published."

"Didn't know or didn't remember?" I asked him. "No, it wasn't published."

"What are you trying to do to me, Marlowe?" His voice was still dreamy, almost gentle. "What do you want me to do? Tell my wife? Tell the police? What good would it do?"

"You said a good man died for you."

"All I meant was that if there had been any real investigation I might have been identified as one—but only one—of the possible suspects. It would have finished me in several ways."

"I didn't come here to accuse you of a murder, Wade. What's eating you is that you're not sure yourself. You have a record of violence to your wife. You black out when you're drunk. It's no argument to say you don't beat a woman's head in just because she's a tramp. That is exactly what somebody did do. And the guy who got credit for the job seemed to me a lot less likely than you."

He walked to the open french windows and stood looking out at the shimmer of heat over the lake. He didn't answer me. He hadn't moved or spoken a couple of minutes later when there was a light knock at the door and Candy came in wheeling a tea wagon, with a crisp white cloth, silver-covered dishes, a pot of coffee, and two bottles of beer.

"Open the beer, boss?" he asked Wade's back.

"Bring me a bottle of whiskey." Wade didn't turn around.

"Sorry, boss. No whiskey."

Wade spun around and yelled at him, but Candy didn't budge. He looked down at the check lying on the cocktail table and his head twisted as he read it. Then he looked up at me and hissed something between his teeth. Then he looked at Wade.

"I go now. This my day off."

He turned and went. Wade laughed.

"So I get it myself," he said sharply, and went.

I lifted one of the covers and saw some neatly trimmed three-cornered sandwiches. I took one and poured some beer and ate the sandwich standing up. Wade came back with a bottle and a glass. He sat down on the couch and poured a stiff jolt and sucked it down. There was the sound of a car going away from the house, probably Candy leaving by the service driveway. I took another sandwich.

"Sit down and make yourself comfortable," Wade said. "We have all afternoon to kill." He had a glow on already. His voice was vibrant and cheerful. "You don't like me, do you, Marlowe?"

"That question has already been asked and answered."

"Know something? You're a pretty ruthless son of a bitch. You'd do anything to find what you want. You'd even make love to my wife while I was helpless drunk in the next room."

"You believe everything that knife thrower tells you?"

He poured some more whiskey into his glass and held it up against the light. "Not everything, no. A pretty color whiskey is, isn't it? To drown in a golden flood—that's not so bad. 'To cease upon the midnight with no pain.' How does that go on? Oh, sorry, you wouldn't know. Too literary. You're some kind of a dick, aren't you? Mind telling me why you're here?"

He drank some more whiskey and grinned at me. Then he spotted the check lying on the table. He reached for it and read it over his glass.

"Seems to be made out to somebody named Marlowe. I wonder why, what for. Seems I signed it. Foolish of me. I'm a gullible chap."

"Stop acting," I said roughly. "Where's your wife?"

He looked up politely. "My wife will be home in due course. No doubt by that time I shall be passed out and she can entertain you at her leisure. The house will be yours."

"Where's the gun?" I asked suddenly.

He looked blank. I told him I had put it in his desk. "Not there now, I'm sure," he said. "You may search if it pleases you. Just don't steal any rubber bands."

I went to the desk and frisked it. No gun. That was something. Probably Eileen had hidden it.

"Look, Wade, I asked you where your wife was. I think she ought to come home. Not for my benefit, friend, for yours. Somebody has to look out for you, and I'll be goddamned if it's going to be me."

He stared vaguely. He was still holding the check. He put his glass down and tore the check across, then again and again, and let the pieces fall to the floor.

"Evidently the amount was too small," he said. "Your services come very high. Even a thousand dollars *and* my wife fail to satisfy you. Too bad, but I can't go any higher. Except on this." He patted the bottle.

"I'm leaving," I said.

"But why? You wanted me to remember. Well—here in the bottle is my memory. Stick around, pal. When I get lit enough I'll tell you about all the women I have murdered."

"All right, Wade. I'll stick around for a while. But not in here. If you need me, just smash a chair against the wall."

I went out and left the door open. I walked across the big living room and out to the patio and pulled one of the chaises into the shadow of the overhang and stretched out on it. Across the lake there was a blue haze against the hills. The ocean breeze had begun to filter through the low mountains to the west. It wiped the air clean and it wiped away just enough of the heat. Idle Valley was having a perfect summer. Somebody had planned it that way. Paradise Incorporated, and also Highly Restricted. Only the nicest people. Absolutely no Central Europeans. Just the cream, the top drawer crowd, the lovely, lovely people. Like the Lorings and the Wades. Pure gold.

# 35

I lay there for half an hour trying to make up my mind what to do. Part of me wanted to let him get good and drunk and see if anything came out. I didn't think anything much would happen to him in his own study in his own house. He might fall down again but it would be a long time. The guy had capacity. And somehow a drunk never hurts himself very badly. He might get back his mood of guilt. More likely, this time he would just go to sleep.

The other part of me wanted to get out and stay out, but this was the part I never listened to. Because if I ever had I would have stayed in the town where I was born and worked in the hardware store and married the boss's daughter and had five kids and read them the funny paper on Sunday morning and smacked their heads when they got out of line and squabbled with the wife about how much spending money they were to get and what programs they could have on the radio or TV set. I might even have got rich—small-town rich, an eight-room house, two cars in the garage, chicken every Sunday and the *Reader's Digest* on the living room table, the wife with a cast iron permanent and me with a brain like a sack of Portland cement. You take it, friend. I'll take the big sordid dirty crooked city.

I got up and went back to the study. He was just sitting there staring at nothing, the Scotch bottle more than half empty, a loose frown on his face and a dull glitter in his eyes. He looked at me like a horse looking over a fence.

"What d'you want?"

"Nothing. You all right?"

"Don't bother me. I have a little man on my shoulder telling me stories."

I got another sandwich off the tea wagon and another glass of beer. I munched the sandwich and drank the beer, leaning against his desk.

"Know something?" he asked suddenly, and his voice suddenly seemed much more clear. "I had a male secretary once. Used to dictate to him. Let him go. He bothered me sitting there waiting for me to create. Mistake. Ought to have kept him. Word would have got around I was a homo. The clever boys that write book reviews because they can't write anything else would have caught on and started giving me the buildup. Have to take care of their own, you know. They're all queers, every damn one of them. The queer is the artistic arbiter of our age, chum. The pervert is the top guy now."

"That so? Always been around, hasn't he?"

He wasn't looking at me. He was just talking. But he heard what I said.

"Sure, thousands of years. And especially in all the great ages of art. Athens, Rome, the Renaissance, the Elizabethan Age, the Romantic Movement in France—loaded with them. Queers all over the place. Ever read *The Golden Bough*? No, too long for you. Shorter version though. Ought to read it. Proves our sexual habits are pure conventions—like wearing a black tie with a dinner jacket. Me. I'm a sex writer, but with frills and straight."

He looked up at me and sneered. "You know something? I'm a liar. My heroes are eight feet tall and my heroines have callouses on their bottoms from lying in bed with their knees up. Lace and ruffles, swords and coaches, elegance and leisure, duels and gallant death. All lies. They used perfume instead of soap, their teeth rotted because they never cleaned them, their fingernails smelled of stale gravy. The nobility of France urinated against the walls in the marble corridors of Versailles, and when you finally got several sets of underclothes off the lovely marquise the first thing you noticed was that she needed a bath. I ought to write it that way."

"Why don't you?"

He chuckled. "Sure, and live in a five-room house in Compton—if I was that lucky." He reached down and patted the whiskey bottle. "You're lonely, pal. You need company."

He got up and walked fairly steadily out of the room. I waited, thinking about nothing. A speedboat came racketing down the lake. When it came in sight I could see that it was high out of the water on its step and towing a surfboard with a husky sunburned lad on it. I went over to the french windows and watched it make a sweeping turn. Too fast, the speedboat almost turned over. The surfboard rider danced on one foot trying to hold his balance, then went shooting off into the water. The speedboat drifted to a stop and the man in the water came up to it in a lazy crawl, then went back along the tow rope and rolled himself on to the surfboard.

Wade came back with another bottle of whiskey. The speedboat picked up and went off into the distance. Wade put his fresh bottle down beside the other. He sat down and brooded.

"Christ, you're not going to drink all that, are you?"

He squinted his eyes at me. "Take off, buster. Go on home and mop the kitchen floor or something. You're in my light." His voice was thick again. He had taken a couple in the kitchen, as usual.

"If you want me, holler."

"I couldn't get low enough to want you."

"Yeah, thanks. I'll be around until Mrs. Wade comes home. Ever hear of anybody named Paul Marston?"

His head came up slowly. His eyes focused, but with effort. I could see him fighting for control. He won the fight—for the moment. His face became expressionless.

"Never did," he said carefully, speaking very slowly. "Who's he?"

The next time I looked in on him he was asleep, with his mouth open, his hair damp with sweat, and reeking of Scotch. His lips were pulled back from his teeth in a loose grimace and the furred surface of his tongue looked dry.

One of the whiskey bottles was empty. A glass on the table had about two inches in it and the other bottle was about three quarters full. I put the empty on the tea wagon and rolled it out of the room, then went back to close the french windows and turn the slats of the blinds. The speedboat might come back and wake him. I shut the study door.

I wheeled the tea wagon out to the kitchen, which was blue and white and large and airy and empty. I was still hungry. I ate another sandwich and drank what was left of the beer, then poured a cup of coffee and drank that. The beer was flat but the coffee was still hot. Then I went back to the patio. It was quite a long time before the speedboat came tearing down the lake again. It was almost four o'clock when I heard its distant roar swell into an ear-splitting howl of noise. There ought to be a law. Probably was and the guy in the speedboat didn't give a damn. He enjoyed making a nuisance of himself, like other people I was meeting. I walked down to the edge of the lake.

He made it this time. The driver slowed just enough on the turn and the brown lad on the surfboard leaned far out against the centrifugal pull. The surfboard was almost out of the water, but one edge stayed in and then the speedboat straightened out and the surfboard still had a rider and they went back the way they had come and that was that. The waves stirred up by the boat came charging in towards the shore of the lake at my feet. They slapped hard against the piles of the short landing and jumped the tied boat up and down. They were still slapping it around when I turned back to the house.

As I reached the patio I heard a bell chiming from the direction of the kitchen. When it sounded again I decided that only the front door would have chimes. I crossed to it and opened it.

Eileen Wade was standing there looking away from the house. As she turned she said: "I'm sorry, I forgot my key." Then she saw me. "Oh—I thought it was Roger or Candy."

"Candy isn't here. It's Thursday."

She came in and I shut the door. She put a bag down on the table between the two davenports. She looked cool and also distant. She pulled off a pair of white pigskin gloves.

"Is anything wrong?"

"Well, there's a little drinking being done. Not bad. He's asleep on the couch in his study."

"He called you?"

"Yes, but not for that. He asked me to lunch. I'm afraid he didn't have any himself."

"Oh." She sat down slowly on a davenport. "You know, I completely forgot it was Thursday. The cook's away too. How stupid."

"Candy got the lunch before he left. I guess I'll blow now. I hope my car wasn't in your way."

She smiled. "No. There was plenty of room. Won't you have some tea? I'm going to have some."

"All right." I didn't know why I said that. I didn't want any tea. I just said it.

She slipped off a linen jacket. She hadn't worn a hat. "I'll just look in and see if Roger is all right."

I watched her cross to the study door and open it. She stood there a moment and closed the door and came back.

"He's still asleep. Very soundly. I have to go upstairs for a moment. I'll be right down."

I watched her pick up her jacket and gloves and bag and go up the stairs and into her room. The door closed. I crossed to the study with the idea of removing the bottle of hooch. If he was still asleep, he wouldn't need it.

# 36

The shutting of the french windows had made the room stuffy and the turning of the venetian blinds had made it dim. There was an acrid smell on the air and there was too heavy a silence. It was not more than sixteen feet from the door to the couch and I didn't need more than half of that to know a dead man lay on that couch.

He was on his side with his face to the back of the couch, one arm crooked under him and the forearm of the other lying almost across his eyes. Between his chest and the back of the couch there was a pool of blood and in that pool lay the Webley Hammerless. The side of his face was a smeared mask.

I bent over him, peering at the edge of the wide open eye, the bare and gaudy arm, at the inner curve of which I could see the puffed and blackened hole in his head from which the blood oozed still.

I left him like that. His wrist was warm but there was no doubt he was quite dead. I looked around for some kind of note or scribble. There was nothing but the pile of script on the desk. They don't always leave notes. The typewriter was uncovered on its stand. There was nothing in that. Otherwise everything looked natural enough. Suicides prepare themselves in all sorts of ways, some with liquor, some with elaborate champagne dinners. Some in evening clothes, some in no clothes. People have killed themselves on the tops of walls, in ditches, in bathrooms, in the water, over the water, on the water. They have hanged themselves in barns and gassed themselves in garages. This one looked simple. I hadn't heard the shot but it must have gone off when I was down by the lake watching the surfboard rider make his turn. There was plenty of noise. Why that should have mattered to Roger Wade I didn't know. Perhaps it hadn't. The final impulse had coincided with the run of the speedboat. I didn't like it, but nobody cared what I liked.

The torn pieces of the check were still on the floor but I left them. The torn strips of that stuff he had written that other night were in the wastebasket. These I did not leave. I picked them out and made sure I had them all and stuffed them into my pocket. The basket was almost empty, which made it easy. No use wondering where the gun had been. There were too many places to hide it in. It could have been in a chair or in the couch, under one of the cushions. It could have been on the floor, behind the books, anywhere.

I went out and shut the door. I listened. From the kitchen, sounds. I went out there. Eileen had a blue apron on and the kettle was just beginning to whistle. She turned the flame down and gave me a brief impersonal glance.

"How do you like your tea, Mr. Marlowe?"

"Just out of the pot as it comes."

I leaned against the wall and got a cigarette out just to have something to do with my fingers. I pinched and squeezed it and broke it in half and threw one half on the floor. Her eyes followed it down. I bent and picked it up. I squeezed the two halves together into a little ball.

She made the tea. "I always take cream and sugar," she said over her shoulder. "Strange, when I drink my coffee black. I learned tea drinking in England. They were using saccharin instead of sugar. When the war came they had no cream, of course."

"You lived in England?"

"I worked there. I stayed all through the Blitz. I met a man—but I told you about that."

"Where did you meet Roger?"

"In New York."

"Married there?"

She swung around, frowning. "No, we were not married in New York. Why?"

"Just talking while the tea draws."

She looked out of the window over the sink. She could see down to the lake from there. She leaned against the edge of the drainboard and her fingers fiddled with a folded tea towel.

"It has to be stopped," she said, "and I don't know how. Perhaps he'll have to be committed to an institution. Somehow I can't quite see myself doing that. I'd have to sign something, wouldn't I?"

She turned around when she asked that.

"He could do it himself," I said. "That is, he could have up to now."

The tea timer rang its bell. She turned back to the sink and poured the tea from one pot into another. Then she put the fresh pot on the tray she had already fixed up with cups. I went over and got the tray and carried it to the table between the two davenports in the living room. She sat down opposite me and poured two cups. I reached for mine and set it down in front of me for it to cool. I watched her fix hers with two lumps of sugar and the cream. She tasted it.

"What did you mean by that last remark?" she asked suddenly. "That he could have up to now—committed himself to some institution, you meant, didn't you?"

"I guess it was a wild pitch. Did you hide the gun I told you about? You know, the morning after he made that play upstairs."

"Hide it?" she repeated frowning. "No. I never do anything like that. I don't believe in it. Why are you asking?"

"And you forgot your house keys today?"

"I told you I did."

"But not the garage key. Usually in this kind of house the outside keys are mastered."

"I don't need a key for the garage," she said sharply. "It opens by a switch. There's a relay switch inside the front door you push up as you go out. Then another switch beside the garage operates that door. Often we leave the garage open. Or Candy goes out and closes it."

"I see."

"You are making some rather strange remarks," she said with acid in her voice. "You did the other morning."

"I've had some rather strange experiences in this house. Guns going off in the night, drunks lying out on the front lawn and doctors coming that won't do anything. Lovely women wrapping their arms around me and talking as if they thought I was someone else, Mexican houseboys throwing knives. It's a pity about that gun. But you don't really love your husband, do you? I guess I said that before too."

She stood up slowly. She was as calm as a custard, but her violet eyes didn't seem quite the same color, nor of quite the same softness. Then her mouth began to tremble.

"Is—is something—wrong in there?" she asked very slowly, and looked towards the study.

I barely had time to nod before she was running. She was at the door in a flash. She threw it open and darted in. If I expected a wild scream I was fooled. I didn't hear anything. I felt lousy. I ought to have kept her out and eased into that corny routine about bad news, prepare yourself, won't you sit down, I'm afraid something rather serious has happened. Blah, blah, blah. And when you have worked your way through it you haven't saved anybody a thing. Often enough you have made it worse.

I got up and followed her into the study. She was kneeling beside the couch with his head pulled against her breast, smearing herself with his blood. She wasn't making a sound of any kind. Her eyes were shut. She was rocking back and forth on her knees as far as she could, holding him tight.

I went back out and found a telephone and a book. I called the sheriff's substation that seemed to be nearest. Didn't matter, they'd relay it by radio in any case. Then I went out to the kitchen and turned the water on and fed the strips of yellow paper from my pocket down the electric garbage grinder. I dumped the tea leaves from the other pot after it. In a matter of seconds the stuff was gone. I shut off the water and switched off the motor. I went back to the living room and opened the front door and stepped outside.

There must have been a deputy cruising close by because he was there in about six minutes. When I took him into the study she was still kneeling by the couch. He went over to her at once.

"I'm sorry, ma'am. I understand how you must feel, but you shouldn't be touching anything."

She turned her head, then scrambled to her feet. "It's my husband. He's been shot."

He took his cap off and put it on the desk. He reached for the telephone.

"His name is Roger Wade," she said in a high brittle voice. "He's the famous novelist."

"I know who he is, ma'am," the deputy said, and dialed.

She looked down at the front of her blouse. "May I go upstairs and change this?"

"Sure." He nodded to her and spoke into the phone, then hung up and turned. "You say he's been shot. That mean somebody else shot him?"

"I think this man murdered him," she said without looking at me, and went quickly out of the room.

The deputy looked at me. He got a notebook out. He wrote something in it. "I better have your name," he said casually, "and address. You the one called in?"

"Yes." I told him my name and address.

"Just take it easy until Lieutenant Ohls gets here."

"Bernie Ohls?"

"Yeah. You know him?"

"Sure. I've known him a long time. He used to work out of the D.A.'s office."

"Not lately," the deputy said. "He's Assistant Chief of Homicide, working out of the L.A. Sheriff's office. You a friend of the family, Mr. Marlowe?"

"Mrs. Wade didn't make it sound that way."

He shrugged and half smiled. "Just take it easy, Mr. Marlowe. Not carrying a gun, are you?"

"Not today."

"I better make sure." He did. He looked towards the couch then. "In spots like this you can't expect the wife to make much sense. We better wait outside."

# 37

Ohls was a medium-sized thick man with short-cropped faded blond hair and faded blue eyes. He had stiff white eyebrows and in the days before he stopped wearing a hat you were always a little surprised when he took it off—there was so much more head than you expected. He was a hard tough cop with a grim outlook on life but a very decent guy underneath. He ought to have made captain years ago. He had passed the examination among the top three half a dozen times. But the Sheriff didn't like him and he didn't like the Sheriff.

He came down the stairs rubbing the side of his jaw. Flashlights had been going off in the study for a long time. Men had gone in and out. I had just sat in the living room with a plain-clothes dick and waited.

Ohls sat down on the edge of a chair and dangled his hands. He was chewing on an unlit cigarette. He looked at me broodingly.

"Remember the old days when they had a gatehouse and a private police force in Idle Valley?"

I nodded. "And gambling also."

"Sure. You can't stop it. This whole valley is still private property. Like Arrowhead used to be, and Emerald Bay. Long time since I was on a case with no reporters jumping around. Somebody must have whispered in Sheriff Petersen's ear. They kept it off the teletype."

"Real considerate of them," I said. "How is Mrs. Wade?"

"Too relaxed. She must of grabbed some pills. There's a dozen kinds up there—even demerol. That's bad stuff. Your friends don't have a lot of luck lately, do they? They get dead."

I didn't have anything to say to that.

"Gunshot suicides always interest me," Ohls said loosely. "So easy to fake. The wife says you killed him. Why would she say that?"

"She doesn't mean it literally."

"Nobody else was here. She says you knew where the gun was, knew he was getting drunk, knew he had fired off the gun the other night when she had to fight with him to get the gun away from him. You were there that night too. Don't seem to help much, do you?"

"I searched his desk this afternoon. No gun. I'd told her where it was and to put it away. She says now she didn't believe in that sort of thing."

"Just when would 'now' be?" Ohls asked gruffly.

"After she came home and before I phoned the substation."

"You searched the desk. Why?" Ohls lifted his hands and put them on his knees. He was looking at me indifferently, as if he didn't care what I said.

"He was getting drunk. I thought it just as well to have the gun somewhere else. But he didn't try to kill himself the other night. It was just show-off."

Ohls nodded. He took the chewed cigarette out of his mouth, dropped it into a tray, and put a fresh one in place of it.

"I quit smoking," he said. "Got me coughing too much. But the goddam things still ride me. Can't feel right without one in my mouth. You supposed to watch the guy when he's alone?"

"Certainly not. He asked me to come out and have lunch. We talked and he was kind of depressed about his writing not going well. He decided to hit the bottle. Think I should have taken it away from him?"

"I'm not thinking yet. I'm just trying to get a picture. How much drinking did you do?"

"Beer."

"It's your tough luck you were here, Marlowe. What was the check for? The one he wrote and signed and tore up?"

"They all wanted me to come and live here and keep him in line. All means himself, his wife, and his publisher, a man named Howard Spencer. He's in New York, I guess. You can check with him. I turned it down. Afterwards she came to me and said her husband was off on a toot and she was worried and would I find him and bring him home. I did that. Next thing I knew I was carrying him in off his front lawn and putting him to bed. I didn't want any part of it, Bernie. It just kind of grew up around me."

"Nothing to do with the Lennox case, huh?"

"Aw, for Pete's sake. There isn't any Lennox case."

"How true," Ohls said dryly. He squeezed his kneecaps. A man came in at the front door and spoke to the other dick, then came across to Ohls.

"There's a Dr. Loring outside, Lieutenant. Says he was called. He's the lady's doctor."

"Let him in."

The dick went back and Dr. Loring came in with his neat black bag. He was cool and elegant in a tropical worsted suit. He went past me without looking at me.

"Upstairs?" he asked Ohls.

"Yeah—in her room." Ohls stood up. "What you give her that demerol for, Doc?"

Dr. Loring frowned at him. "I prescribe for my patient as I think proper," he said coldly. "I am not required to explain why. Who says I gave Mrs. Wade demerol?"

"I do. The bottle's up there with your name on it. She's got a regular drugstore in her bathroom. Maybe you don't know it, Doc, but we have a pretty complete exhibit of the little pills downtown. Bluejays, redbirds, yellow jackets, goofballs, and all the rest of the list. Demerol's about the worst of the lot. That's the stuff Goering lived on, I heard somewhere. Took eighteen a day when they caught him. Took the army doctors three months to cut him down."

"I don't know what those words mean," Dr. Loring said frigidly.

"You don't? Pity. Bluejays are sodium amytal. Redbirds are seconal. Yellow jackets are nembutal. Goofballs are one of the barbiturates laced with benzedrine. Demerol is a synthetic narcotic that is very habit forming. You just hand 'em out, huh? Is the lady suffering from something serious?"

"A drunken husband can be a very serious complaint indeed for a sensitive woman," Dr. Loring said.

"You didn't get around to him, huh? Pity. Mrs. Wade's upstairs, Doc. Thanks for the time."

"You are impertinent, sir. I shall report you."

"Yeah, do that," Ohls said. "But before you report me, do something else. Keep the lady clear in her head. I've got questions to ask."

"I shall do exactly what I think best for her condition. Do you know who I am, by any chance? And just to make matters clear, Mr. Wade was not my patient. I don't treat alcoholics."

"Just their wives, huh?" Ohls snarled at him. "Yeah, I know who you are, Doc. I'm bleeding internally. My name is Ohls. Lieutenant Ohls."

Dr. Loring went on up the stairs. Ohls sat down again and grinned at me.

"You got to be diplomatic with this kind of people," he said.

A man came out of the study and came up to Ohls. A thin serious-looking man with glasses and a brainy forehead.

"Lieutenant."

"Shoot."

"The wound is contact, typically suicidal, with a good deal of distention from gas pressure. The eyes are exophthalmic from the same cause. I don't think there will be any prints on the outside of the gun. It's been bled on too freely."

"Could it be homicide if the guy was asleep or passed out drunk?" Ohls asked him.

"Of course, but there's no indication of it. The gun's a Webley Hammerless. Typically, this gun takes a very stiff pull to cock it, but a very light pull to discharge it. The recoil explains the position of the gun. I see nothing against suicide so far. I expect a high figure on alcoholic concentration. If it's high enough—" the man stopped and shrugged meaningly—"I might be inclined to doubt suicide."

"Thanks. Somebody call the coroner?"

The man nodded and went away. Ohls yawned and looked at his watch. Then he looked at me.

"You want to blow?"

"Sure, if you'll let me. I thought I was a suspect."

"We might oblige you later on. Stick around where you can be found, that's all. You were a dick once, you know how they go. Some you got to work fast before the evidence gets away from you. This one is just the opposite. If it was a homicide, who wanted him dead? His wife? She wasn't here. You? Fine, you had the house to yourself and knew where the gun was. A perfect setup. Everything but a motive, and we might perhaps give some weight to your experience. I figure if you wanted to kill a guy, you could maybe do it a little less obviously."

"Thanks, Bernie. I could at that."

"The help wasn't here. They're out. So it must have been somebody that just happened to drop by. That somebody had to know where Wade's gun was, had to find him drunk enough to be asleep or passed out, and had to pull the trigger when that speedboat was making enough noise to drown the shot, and had to get away before you came back into the house. That I don't buy on any knowledge I have now. The only person who had the means and opportunity was the one guy who wouldn't have used them—for the simple reason he *was* the one guy who had them."

I stood up to go. "Okay, Bernie. I'll be home all evening."

"There's just one thing," Ohls said musingly. "This man Wade was a big time writer. Lots of dough, lots of reputation. I don't go for his sort of crap myself. You might find nicer people than his characters in a whorehouse. That's a matter of taste and none of my business as a cop. With all this money he had a beautiful home in one of the best places to live in in the county. He had a beautiful wife, lots of friends, and no troubles at all. What I want to know is what made all that so tough that he had to pull a trigger? Sure as hell something did. If you know, you better get ready to lay it on the line. See you."

I went to the door. The man on the door looked back at Ohls, got the sign, and let me out. I got into my car and had to edge over on the lawn to get around the various official cars that jammed the driveway. At the gate another deputy looked me over but didn't say anything. I slipped my dark glasses on and drove back towards the main highway. The road was empty and peaceful. The afternoon sun beat down on the manicured lawns and the large roomy expensive houses behind them.

A man not unknown to the world had died in a pool of blood in a house in Idle Valley, but the lazy quiet had not been disturbed. So far as the newspapers were concerned it might have happened in Tibet.

At a turn of the road the walls of two estates came down to the shoulder and a dark green sheriff's car was parked there. A deputy got out and held up his hand. I stopped. He came to the window.

"May I see your driver's license, please?"

I took out my wallet and handed it to him open.

"Just the license, please. I'm not allowed to touch your wallet."

I took it out and gave it to him. "What's the trouble?"

He glanced into my car and handed me back my license.

"No trouble," he said. "Just a routine check. Sorry to have troubled you."

He waved me on and went back to the parked car. Just like a cop. They never tell you why they are doing anything. That way you don't find out they don't know themselves.

I drove home, bought myself a couple of cold drinks, went out to dinner, came back, opened the windows and my shirt and waited for something to happen. I waited a long time. It was nine o'clock when Bernie Ohls called up and told me to come in and not stop on the way to pick any flowers.

## 38

They had Candy in a hard chair against the wall of the Sheriff's anteroom. He hated me with his eyes as I went by him into the big square room where Sheriff Petersen held court in the middle of a collection of testimonials from a grateful public to his twenty years of faithful public service. The walls were loaded with photographs of horses and Sheriff Petersen made a personal appearance in every photograph. The corners of his carved desk were horses' heads. His inkwell was a mounted polished horse's hoof and his pens were planted in the mate to it filled with white sand. A gold plate on each of these said something or other about a date. In the middle of a spotless desk blotter lay a bag of Bull Durham and a pack of brown cigarette papers. Petersen rolled his own. He could roll one with one hand on horseback and often did, especially when leading a parade on a big white horse with a Mexican saddle loaded with beautiful Mexican silverwork. On horseback he wore a flat-crowned Mexican sombrero. He rode beautifully and his horse always knew exactly when to be quiet, when to act up so that the Sheriff with his calm inscrutable smile could bring the horse back under control with one hand. The Sheriff had a good act. He had a handsome hawklike profile, getting a little saggy under the chin by now, but he knew how to hold his head so it wouldn't show too much. He put a lot of hard work into having his picture taken. He was in his middle fifties and his father, a Dane, had left him a lot of money. The Sheriff didn't look like a Dane, because his hair was dark and his skin was brown and he had the impassive poise of a cigar store Indian and about the same kind of brains. But nobody had ever called him a crook. There had been crooks in his department and they had fooled him as well as they had fooled the public, but none of the crookedness rubbed off on Sheriff Petersen. He just went right on getting elected without even trying, riding white horses at the head of parades, and questioning suspects in front of cameras. That's what the captions said. As a matter of fact he never questioned anybody. He wouldn't have known how. He just sat at his desk looking sternly at the suspect, showing his profile to the camera. The flash bulbs would go off, the camera men would thank the Sheriff deferentially, and the suspect would be removed not having opened his mouth, and the Sheriff would go home to his ranch in the San Fernando Valley. There he could always be reached. If you couldn't reach him in person, you could talk to one of his horses.

Once in a while, come election time, some misguided politician would try to get Sheriff Petersen's job, and would be apt to call him things like The Guy With The Built-In Profile or The Ham That Smokes Itself, but it didn't get him anywhere. Sheriff Petersen just went right on getting re-elected, a living testimonial to the fact that you can hold an important public office forever in our country with no qualifications for it but a clean nose, a photogenic face, and a close mouth. If on top of that you look good on a horse, you are unbeatable.

As Ohls and I went in, Sheriff Petersen was standing behind his desk and the camera boys were filing out by another door. The Sheriff had his white stetson on. He was rolling a cigarette. He was all set to go home. He looked at me sternly.

"Who's this?" he asked in a rich baritone voice.

"Name's Philip Marlowe, Chief," Ohls said. "Only person in the house when Wade shot himself. You want a picture?"

The Sheriff studied me. "I don't think so," he said, and turned to a big tired-looking man with iron-gray hair. "If you need me, I'll be at the ranch, Captain Hernandez."

"Yes, sir."

Petersen lit his cigarette with a kitchen match. He lit it on his thumbnail. No lighters for Sheriff Petersen. He was strictly a roll-your-own-and-light-'em-with-one-hand type.

He said goodnight and went out. A deadpan character with hard black eyes went with him, his personal bodyguard. The door closed. When he was gone Captain Hernandez moved to the desk and sat in the Sheriff's enormous chair and a stenotype operator in the corner moved his stand out from the wall to get elbow room. Ohls sat at the end of the desk and looked amused.

"All right, Marlowe," Hernandez said briskly. "Let's have it."

"How come I don't get my photo taken?"

"You heard what the Sheriff said."

"Yeah, but why?" I whined.

Ohls laughed. "You know damn well why."

"You mean on account of I'm tall, dark, and handsome and somebody might look at me?"

"Cut it," Hernandez said coldly. "Let's get on with your statement. Start from the beginning."

I gave it to them from the beginning: my interview with Howard Spencer, my meeting with Eileen Wade, her asking me to find Roger, my finding him, her asking me to the house, what Wade asked me to do and how I found him passed out near the hibiscus bushes and the rest of it. The stenotype operator took it down. Nobody interrupted me. All of it was true. The truth and nothing but the truth. But not quite all the truth. What I left out was my business.

"Nice," Hernandez said at the end. "But not quite complete." This was a cool competent dangerous guy, this Hernandez. Somebody in the Sheriff's office had to be. "The night Wade shot off the gun in his bedroom you went into Mrs. Wade's room and were in there for some time with the door shut. What were you doing in there?"

"She called me in and asked me how he was."

"Why shut the door?"

"Wade was half asleep and I didn't want to make any noise. Also the houseboy was hanging around with his ear out. Also she asked me to shut the door. I didn't realize it was going to be important."

"How long were you in there?"

"I don't know. Three minutes maybe."

"I suggest you were in there a couple of hours," Hernandez said coldly. "Do I make myself clear?"

I looked at Ohls. Ohls didn't look at anything. He was chewing on an unlighted cigarette as usual.

"You are misinformed, Captain."

"We'll see. After you left the room you went downstairs to the study and spent the night on the couch. Perhaps I should say the rest of the night."

"It was ten minutes to eleven when he called me at home. It was long past two o'clock when I went into the study for the last time that night. Call it the rest of the night if you like."

"Get the houseboy in here," Hernandez said.

Ohls went out and came back with Candy. They put Candy in a chair. Hernandez asked him a few questions to establish who he was and so on. Then he said: "All right, Candy—we'll call you that for convenience—after you helped Marlowe put Roger Wade to bed, what happened?"

I knew what was coming more or less. Candy told his story in a quiet savage voice with very little accent. It seemed as if he could turn that on and off at will. His story was that he had hung around downstairs in case he was wanted again, part of the time in the kitchen where he got himself some food, part of the time in the living room. While in the living room sitting in a chair near the front door he had seen Eileen Wade standing in the door of her room and he had seen her take her clothes off. He had seen her put a robe on with nothing under it and he had seen me go into her room and I shut the door and stayed in there a long time, a couple of hours he thought. He had gone up the stairs and listened. He had heard the bedsprings making sounds. He had heard whispering. He made his meaning very obvious. When he had finished he gave me a corrosive look and his mouth was twisted tight with hatred.

"Take him out," Hernandez said.

"Just a minute," I said. "I want to question him."

"I ask the questions here," Hernandez said sharply.

"You don't know how, Captain. You weren't there. He's lying and he knows it and I know it."

Hernandez leaned back and picked up one of the Sheriff's pens. He bent the handle of the pen. It was long and pointed and made of stiffened horsehair. When he let go of the point it sprang back.

"Shoot," he said at last.

I faced Candy. "Where were you when you saw Mrs. Wade take her clothes off?"

"I was sitting down in a chair near the front door," he said in a surly tone.

"Between the front door and the two facing davenports?"

"What I said."

"Where was Mrs. Wade?"

"Just inside the door of her room. The door was open."

"What light was there in the living room?"

"One lamp. Tall lamp what they call a bridge lamp."

"What light was on the balcony?"

"No light. Light in her bedroom."

"What kind of light in her bedroom?"

"Not much light. Night table lamp, maybe."

"Not a ceiling light?"

"No."

"After she took her clothes off—standing just inside the door of her room, you said—she put on a robe. What kind of robe?"

"Blue robe. Long thing like a house coat. She tie it with a sash."

"So if you hadn't actually seen her take her clothes off you wouldn't know what she had on under the robe?"

He shrugged. He looked vaguely worried. "Sí. That's right. But I see her take her clothes off."

"You're a liar. There isn't any place in the living room from which you could see her take her clothes off right bang in her doorway, much less inside her room. She would have to come out to the edge of the balcony. If she had done that she would have seen you."

He just glared at me. I turned to Ohls. "You've seen the house. Captain Hernandez hasn't—or has he?"

Ohls shook his head slightly. Hernandez frowned and said nothing.

"There is no spot in that living room, Captain Hernandez, from which he could see even the top of Mrs. Wade's head— even if he was standing up—and he says he was sitting down—provided she was as far back as her own doorway or inside it. I'm four inches taller than he is and I could only see the top foot of an open door when I was standing just inside the front door of the house. She would have to come out to the edge of the balcony for him to see what he says he saw. Why would she do that? Why would she undress in her doorway even? There's no sense to it."

Hernandez just looked at me. Then he looked at Candy. "How about the time element?" he asked softly, speaking to me.

"That's his word against mine. I'm talking about what can be proved."

Hernandez spit Spanish at Candy too fast for me to understand. Candy just stared at him sulkily.

"Take him out," Hernandez said.

Ohls jerked a thumb and opened the door. Candy went out. Hernandez brought out a box of cigarettes, stuck one on his lip, and lit it with a gold lighter.

Ohls came back into the room. Hernandez said calmly: "I just told him that if there was an inquest and he told that story on the stand, he'd find himself doing a one-to-three up in Q for perjury. Didn't seem to impress him much. It's obvious what's eating him. An old-fashioned case of hot pants. If he'd been around and we had any reason to suspect murder, he'd make a pretty good pigeon—except that he would have used a knife. I got the impression earlier that he felt pretty bad about Wade's death. Any questions you want to ask, Ohls?"

Ohls shook his head. Hernandez looked at me and said: "Come back in the morning and sign your statement. We'll have it typed out by then. We ought to have a P.M. report by ten o'clock, preliminary anyway. Anything you don't like about this setup, Marlowe?"

"Would you mind rephrasing the question? The way you put it suggests there might be something I do like about it."

"Okay," he said wearily. "Take off. I'm going home."

I stood up.

"Of course I never did believe that stuff Candy pulled on us," he said. "Just used it for a corkscrew. No hard feelings, I hope."

"No feelings at all, Captain. No feelings at all."

They watched me go out and didn't say goodnight. I walked down the long corridor to the Hill Street entrance and got into my car and drove home.

No feelings at all was exactly right. I was as hollow and empty as the spaces between the stars. When I got home I mixed a stiff one and stood by the open window in the living room and sipped it and listened to the groundswell of the traffic on Laurel Canyon Boulevard and looked at the glare of the big angry city hanging over the shoulder of the hills through which the boulevard had been cut. Far off the banshee wail of police or fire sirens rose and fell, never for very long completely silent. Twenty-four hours a day somebody is running, somebody else is trying to catch him. Out there in the night of a thousand crimes people were dying, being maimed, cut by flying glass, crushed against steering wheels or under heavy tires. People were being beaten, robbed, strangled, raped, and murdered. People were hungry, sick, bored, desperate with loneliness or remorse or fear, angry, cruel, feverish, shaken by sobs. A city no worse than others, a city rich and vigorous and full of pride, a city lost and beaten and full of emptiness.

It all depends on where you sit and what your own private score is. I didn't have one. I didn't care.

I finished the drink and went to bed.

# 39

The inquest was a flop. The coroner sailed into it before the medical evidence was complete, for fear the publicity would die on him. He needn't have worried. The death of a writer—even a loud writer—is not news for long, and that summer there was too much to compete. A king abdicated and another was assassinated. In one week three large passenger planes crashed. The head man of a big wire service was shot to pieces in Chicago in his own automobile. Twenty-four convicts were burned to death in a prison fire. The Coroner of Los Angeles County was out of luck. He was missing the good things in life.

As I left the stand I saw Candy. He had a bright malicious grin on his face—I had no idea why—and as usual he was dressed just a little too well, in a cocoa brown gabardine suit with a white nylon shirt and a midnight blue bow tie. On the witness stand he was quiet and made a good impression. Yes, the boss had been pretty drunk lately a lot of times. Yes, he had helped put him to bed the night the gun went off upstairs. Yes, the boss had demanded whiskey before he, Candy, left on the last day, but he had refused to get it. No, he didn't know anything about Mr. Wade's literary work, but he knew the boss had been discouraged. He kept throwing it away and then getting it out of the wastebasket again. No, he had never heard Mr. Wade quarreling with anyone. And so on. The coroner milked him but it was thin stuff. Somebody had done a good coaching job on Candy.

Eileen Wade wore black and white. She was pale and spoke in a low clear voice which even the amplifier could not spoil. The coroner handled her with two pairs of velvet gloves. He talked to her as if he had trouble keeping the sobs out of his voice. When she left the stand he stood up and bowed and she gave him a faint fugitive smile that nearly made him choke on his saliva.

She almost passed me without a glance on the way out, then at the last moment turned her head a couple of inches and nodded very slightly, as if I was somebody she must have met somewhere a long time ago, but couldn't quite place in her memory.

Outside on the steps when it was all over I ran into Ohls. He was watching the traffic down below, or pretending to.

"Nice job," he said without turning his head. "Congratulations."

"You did all right on Candy."

"Not me, kid. The D.A. decided the sexy stuff was irrelevant."

"What sexy stuff was that?"

He looked at me then. "Ha, ha, ha," he said. "And I don't mean you." Then his expression got remote. "I been looking at them for too many years. It wearies a man. This one came out of the special bottle. Old private stock. Strictly for the carriage trade. So long, sucker. Call me when you start wearing twenty-dollar shirts. I'll drop around and hold your coat for you."

People eddied around us going up and down the steps. We just stood there. Ohls took a cigarette out of his pocket and looked at it and dropped it on the concrete and ground it to nothing with his heel.

"Wasteful," I said.

"Only a cigarette, pal. It's not a life. After a while maybe you marry the girl, huh?"

"Shove it."

He laughed sourly. "I been talking to the right people about the wrong things," he said acidly. "Any objection?"

"No objection, Lieutenant," I said, and went on down the steps. He said something behind me but I kept going.

I went over to a corn-beef joint on Flower. It suited my mood. A rude sign over the entrance said: "Men Only. Dogs and Women Not Admitted." The service inside was equally polished. The waiter who tossed your food at you needed a shave and deducted his tip without being invited. The food was simple but very good and they had a brown Swedish beer which could hit as hard as a martini.

When I got back to the office the phone was ringing. Ohls said: "I'm coming by your place. I've got things to say."

He must have been at or near the Hollywood substation because he was in the office inside twenty minutes. He planted himself in the customer's chair and crossed his legs and growled:

"I was out of line. Sorry. Forget it."

"Why forget it? Let's open up the wound."

"Suits me. Under the hat, though. To some people you're a wrong gee. I never knew you to do anything too crooked."

"What was the crack about twenty-dollar shirts?"

"Aw hell, I was just sore," Ohls said. "I was thinking of old man Potter. Like he told a secretary to tell a lawyer to tell District Attorney Springer to tell Captain Hernandez you were a personal friend of his."

"He wouldn't take the trouble."

"You met him. He gave you time."

"I met him, period. I didn't like him, but perhaps it was only envy. He sent for me to give me some advice. He's big and he's tough and I don't know what else. I don't figure he's a crook."

"There ain't no clean way to make a hundred million bucks," Ohls said. "Maybe the head man thinks his hands are clean but somewhere along the line guys got pushed to the wall, nice little businesses got the ground cut from under them and had to sell out for nickels, decent people lost their jobs, stocks got rigged on the market, proxies got bought up like a pennyweight of old gold, and the five per centers and the big law firms got paid hundred-grand fees for beating some law the people wanted but the rich guys didn't, on account of it cut into their profits. Big money is big power and big power gets used wrong. It's the system. Maybe it's the best we can get, but it still ain't any Ivory Soap deal."

"You sound like a Red," I said, just to needle him.

"I wouldn't know," he said contemptuously. "I ain't been investigated yet. You liked the suicide verdict, didn't you?"

"What else could it be?"

"Nothing else, I guess." He put his hard blunt hands on the desk and looked at the big brown freckles on the backs of them. "I'm getting old. Keratosis, they call those brown spots. You don't get them until you're past fifty. I'm an old cop and an old cop is an old bastard. I don't like a few things about this Wade death."

"Such as?" I leaned back and watched the tight sun wrinkles around his eyes.

"You get so you can smell a wrong setup, even when you know you can't do a damn thing about it. Then you just sit and talk like now. I don't like that he left no note."

"He was drunk. Probably just a sudden crazy impulse."

Ohls lifted his pale eyes and dropped his hands off the desk. "I went through his desk. He wrote letters to himself. He wrote and wrote and wrote. Drunk or sober he hit that typewriter. Some of it is wild, some of it kind of funny, and some of it is sad. The guy had something on his mind. He wrote all around it but he never quite touched it. That guy would have left a two-page letter if he knocked himself off."

"He was drunk," I said again.

"With him that didn't matter," Ohls said wearily. "The next thing I don't like is he did it there in that room and left his wife to find him. Okay, he was drunk. I still don't like it. The next thing I don't like is he pulled the trigger just when the noise of that speedboat could drown out the shot. What difference would it make to him? More coincidence, huh? More coincidence still that the wife forgot her door keys on the help's day off and had to ring the bell to get into the house."

"She could have walked around to the back," I said.

"Yeah, I know. What I'm talking about is a situation. Nobody to answer the door but you, and she said on the stand she didn't know you were there. Wade wouldn't have heard the bell if he had been alive and working in his study. His door is soundproofed. The help was away. That was Thursday. That she forgot. Like she forgot her keys."

"You're forgetting something yourself, Bernie. My car was in the driveway. So she knew I was there—or that somebody was there—before she rang the bell."

He grinned. "I forgot that, didn't I? All right, here's the picture. You were down at the lake, the speedboat was making all that racket—incidentally it was a couple of guys from Lake Arrowhead just visiting, had their boat on a trailer—Wade was asleep in his study or passed out, somebody took the gun out of his desk already, and she knew you had put it there because you told her that other time. Now suppose she didn't forget her keys, that she goes into the house, looks across and sees you down at the water, looks into the study and sees Wade asleep, knows where the gun is, gets it, waits for the right moment, plugs him, drops the gun where it was found, goes back outside the house, waits a little while for the speedboat to go away, and then rings the doorbell and waits for you to open it. Any objections?"

"With what motive?"

"Yeah," he said sourly. "That knocks it. If she wanted to slough the guy, it was easy. She had him over a barrel, habitual drunk, record of violence to her. Plenty alimony, nice fat property settlement. No motive at all. Anyhow the timing was too neat. Five minutes earlier and she couldn't have done it unless you were in on it."

I started to say something but he put his hand up. "Take it easy. I'm not accusing anybody, just speculating. Five minutes later and you get the same answer. She had ten minutes to pull it off."

"Ten minutes," I said irritably, "that couldn't possibly have been foreseen, much less planned."

He leaned back in the chair and sighed. "I know. You've got all the answers, I've got all the answers. And I still don't like it. What the hell were you doing with these people anyway? The guy writes you a check for a grand, then tears it up. Got mad at you, you say. You didn't want it anyway, wouldn't have taken it, you say. Maybe. Did he think you were sleeping with his wife?"

"Lay off, Bernie."

"I didn't ask were you, I asked did he think you were."

"Same answer."

"Okay, try this. What did the Mex have on him?"

"Nothing that I know of."

"The Mex has too much money. Over fifteen hundred in the bank, all kinds of clothes, a brand new Chevvy."

"Maybe he peddles dope," I said.

Ohls pushed himself up out of the chair and scowled down at me.

"You're an awful lucky boy, Marlowe. Twice you've slid out from under a heavy one. You could get overconfident. You were pretty helpful to those people and you didn't make a dime. You were pretty helpful to a guy named Lennox too, the way I hear it. And you didn't make a dime out of that one either. What do you do for eating money, pal? You got a lot saved so you don't have to work any more?"

I stood up and walked around the desk and faced him. "I'm a romantic, Bernie. I hear voices crying in the night and I go see what's the matter. You don't make a dime that way. You got sense, you shut your windows and turn up more sound on the TV set. Or you shove down on the gas and get far away from there. Stay out of other people's troubles. All it can get you is the smear. The last time I saw Terry Lennox we had a cup of coffee together that I made myself in my house, and we smoked a cigarette. So when I heard he was dead I went out to the kitchen and made some coffee and poured a cup for him and lit a cigarette for him and when the coffee was cold and the cigarette was burned down I said goodnight to him. You don't make a dime that way. *You* wouldn't do it. That's why you're a good cop and I'm a private eye. Eileen Wade is worried about her husband, so I go out and find him and bring him home. Another time he's in trouble and calls me up and I go out and carry him in off the lawn and put him to bed, and I don't make a dime out of it. No percentage at all. No nothing, except sometimes I get my face pushed in or get tossed in the can or get threatened by some fast money boy like Mendy Menendez. But no money, not a dime. I've got a five-thousand-dollar bill in my safe but I'll never spend a nickel of it. Because there was something wrong with the way I got it. I played with it a little at first and I still get it out once in a while and look at it. But that's all—not a dime of spending money."

"Must be a phony," Ohls said dryly, "except they don't make them that big. So what's your point with all this yap?"

"No point. I told you I was a romantic."

"I heard you. And you don't make a dime at it. I heard that too."

"But I can always tell a cop to go to hell. Go to hell, Bernie."

"You wouldn't tell me to go to hell if I had you in the back room under the light, chum."

"Maybe we'll find out about that some day."

He walked to the door and yanked it open. "You know something, kid? You think you're cute but you're just stupid. You're a shadow on the wall. I've got twenty years on the cops without a mark against me. I know when I'm being kidded and I know when a guy is holding out on me. The wise guy never fools anybody but himself. Take it from me, chum. I know."

He pulled his head back out of the doorway and let the door close. His heels hammered down the corridor. I could still hear them when the phone on my desk started to sound. The voice said in that clear professional tone:

"New York is calling Mr. Philip Marlowe."

"I'm Philip Marlowe."

"Thank you. One moment, please, Mr. Marlowe. Here is your party."

The next voice I knew. "Howard Spencer, Mr. Marlowe. We've heard about Roger Wade. It was a pretty hard blow. We haven't the full details, but your name seems to be involved."

"I was there when it happened. He just got drunk and shot himself. Mrs. Wade came home a little later. The servants were away—Thursday's the day off."

"You were alone with him?"

"I wasn't with him. I was outside the house, just hanging around waiting for his wife to come home."

"I see. Well, I suppose there will be an inquest."

"It's all over, Mr. Spencer. Suicide. And remarkably little publicity."

"Really? That's curious." He didn't exactly sound disappointed—more like puzzled and surprised. "He was so well known. I should have thought—well, never mind what I thought. I guess I'd better fly out there, but I can't make it before the end of next week. I'll send a wire to Mrs. Wade. There may be something I could do for her—and also about the book. I mean there may be enough of it so that we could get someone to finish it. I assume you did take the job after all."

"No. Although he asked me to himself. I told him right out I couldn't stop him from drinking."

"Apparently you didn't even try."

"Look, Mr. Spencer, you don't know the first damn thing about this situation. Why not wait until you do before jumping to conclusions? Not that I don't blame myself a little. I guess that's inevitable when something like this happens, and you're the guy on the spot."

"Of course," he said. "I'm sorry I made that remark. Most uncalled for. Will Eileen Wade be at her home now—or wouldn't you know?"

"I wouldn't know, Mr. Spencer. Why don't you just call her up?"

"I hardly think she would want to speak to anyone yet," he said slowly.

"Why not? She talked to the Coroner and never batted an eye."

He cleared his throat. "You don't sound exactly sympathetic."

"Roger Wade is dead, Spencer. He was a bit of a bastard and maybe a bit of a genius too. That's over my head. He was an egotistical drunk and he hated his own guts. He made me a lot of trouble and in the end a lot of grief. Why the hell should I be sympathetic?"

"I was talking about Mrs. Wade," he said shortly.

"So was I."

"I'll call you when I get in," he said abruptly. "Goodbye."

He hung up. I hung up. I stared at the telephone for a couple of minutes without moving. Then I got the phone book up on the desk and looked for a number.

## 40

I called Sewell Endicott's office. Somebody said he was in court and would not be available until late in the afternoon. Would I care to leave my name? No.

I dialed the number of Mendy Menendez's joint on the Strip. It was called El Tapado this year, not a bad name either. In American Spanish that means buried treasure among other things. It had been called other names in the past, quite a few other names. One year it was just a blue neon number on a blank high wall facing south on the Strip, with its back against the hill and a driveway curving around one side out of sight of the street. Very exclusive. Nobody knew much about it except vice cops and mobsters and people who could afford thirty bucks for a good dinner and any amount up to fifty grand in the big quiet room upstairs.

I got a woman who didn't know from nothing. Then I got a captain with a Mex accent.

"You wish to speak with Mr. Menendez? Who is calling?"

"No names, amigo. Private matter."

"Un momento, por favor."

There was a longish wait. I got a hard boy this time. He sounded as if he was talking through the slit in an armored car. It was probably just the slit in his face.

"Talk it up. Who wants him?"

"The name's Marlowe."

"Who's Marlowe?"

"This Chick Agostino?"

"No, this ain't Chick. Come on, let's have the password."

"Go fry your face."

There was a chuckle. "Hold the line."

Finally another voice said: "Hello, cheapie. What's the time by you?"

"You alone?"

"You can talk, cheapie. I been looking over some acts for the floor show."

"You could cut your throat for one."

"What would I do for an encore?"

I laughed. He laughed. "Been keeping your nose clean?" he asked.

"Haven't you heard? I got to be friends with another guy who suicided. They're going to call me the 'Kiss-of-Death Kid' from now on."

"That's funny, huh?"

"No, it isn't funny. Also the other afternoon I had tea with Harlan Potter."

"Nice going. I never drink the stuff myself."

"He said for you to be nice to me."

"I never met the guy and I don't figure to."

"He casts a long shadow. All I want is a little information, Mendy. Like about Paul Marston."

"Never heard of him."

"You said that too quick. Paul Marston was the name Terry Lennox used one time in New York before he came west."

"So?"

"His prints were checked through the F.B.I. files. No record. That means he never served in the Armed Forces."

"So?"

"Do I have to draw you a picture? Either that foxhole yarn of yours was all spaghetti or it happened somewhere else."

"I didn't say where it happened, cheapie. Take a kind word and forget the whole thing. You got told, you better stay told."

"Oh sure. I do something you don't like and I'm swimming to Catalina with a streetcar on my back. Don't try to scare me, Mendy. I've been up against the pros. You ever been in England?"

"Be smart, cheapie. Things can happen to a guy in this town. Things can happen to big strong boys like Big Willie Magoon. Take a look at the evening paper."

"I'll get one if you say so. It might even have my picture in it. What about Magoon?"

"Like I said—things can happen. I wouldn't know how except what I read. Seems Magoon tried to shake down four boys in a car with Nevada plates. Was parked right by his house. Nevada plates with big numbers like they don't have. Must have been some kind of a rib. Only Magoon ain't feeling funny, what with both arms in casts, and his jaw wired in three places, and one leg in high traction. Magoon ain't tough any more. It could happen to you."

"He bothered you, huh? I saw him bounce your boy Chick off the wall in front of Victor's. Should I ring up a friend in the Sheriff's office and tell him?"

"You do that, cheapie," he said very slowly. "You do that."

"And I'll mention that at the time I was just through having a drink with Harlan Potter's daughter. Corroborative evidence, in a sense, don't you think? You figure to smash her up too?"

"Listen to me careful, cheapie—"

"Were you ever in England, Mendy? You and Randy Starr and Paul Marston or Terry Lennox or whatever his name was? In the British Army perhaps? Had a little racket in Soho and got hot and figured the Army was a cooling-off spot?"

"Hold the line."

I held it. Nothing happened except that I waited and my arm got tired. I switched the receiver to the other side. Finally he came back.

"Now listen careful, Marlowe. You stir up that Lennox case and you're dead. Terry was a pal and I got feelings too. So you got feelings. I'll go along with you just this far. It was a Commando outfit. It was British. It happened in Norway, one of those islands off the coast. They got a million of them. November 1942. Now will you lie down and rest that tired brain of yours?"

"Thank you, Mendy. I will do that. Your secret is safe with me. I'm not telling it to anybody but the people I know."

"Buy yourself a paper, cheapie. Read and remember. Big tough Willie Magoon. Beat up in front of his own house. Boy, was he surprised when he come out of the ether!"

He hung up. I went downstairs and bought a paper and it was just as Menendez had said. There was a picture of Big Willie Magoon in his hospital bed. You could see half his face and one eye. The rest of him was bandages. Seriously but not critically injured. The boys had been very careful about that. They wanted him to live. After all he was a cop. In our town the mobs don't kill a cop. They leave that to the juveniles. And a live cop who has been put through the meat grinder is a much better advertisement. He gets well eventually and goes back to work. But from that time on something is missing—the last inch of steel that makes all the difference. He's a walking lesson that it is a mistake to push the racket boys too hard—especially if you are on the vice squad and eating at the best places and driving a Cadillac.

I sat there and brooded about it for a while and then I dialed the number of The Carne Organization and asked for George Peters. He was out. I left my name and said it was urgent. He was expected in about five-thirty.

I went over to the Hollywood Public Library and asked questions in the reference room, but couldn't find what I wanted. So I had to go back for my Olds and drive down-town to the Main Library. I found it there, in a smallish red-bound book published in England. I copied what I wanted from it and drove home. I called The Carne Organization again. Peters was still out, so I asked the girl to reroute the call to me at home.

I put the chessboard on the coffee table and set out a prob-lem called The Sphynx. It is printed on the end papers of a book on chess by Blackburn, the English chess wizard, prob-ably the most dynamic chess player who ever lived, although he wouldn't get to first base in the cold war type of chess they play nowadays. The Sphynx is an eleven-mover and it justifies its name. Chess problems seldom run to more than four or five moves. Beyond that the difficulty of solving them rises in almost geometrical progression. An eleven-mover is sheer unadulterated torture.

Once in a long while when I feel mean enough I set it out and look for a new way to solve it. It's a nice quiet way to go crazy. You don't even scream, but you come awfully close.

George Peters called me at five-forty. We exchanged pleasantries and condolences.

"You've got yourself in another jam, I see," he said cheerfully. "Why don't you try some quiet business like embalming?"

"Takes too long to learn. Listen, I want to become a client of your agency, if it doesn't cost too much."

"Depends what you want done, old boy. And you'd have to talk to Carne."

"No."

"Well, tell me."

"London is full of guys like me, but I wouldn't know one from the other. They call them private enquiry agents. Your outfit would have connections. I'd just have to pick a name at random and probably get hornswoggled. I want some infor-mation that should be easy enough to get, and I want it quick. Must have it before the end of next week."

"Spill."

"I want to know something about the war service of Terry Lennox or Paul Marston, whatever name he used. He was in the Commandos over there. He was captured wounded in

November 1942 in a raid on some Norwegian island. I want
to know what outfit he was posted from and what happened
to him. The War Office will have all that. It's not secret information, or I wouldn't think so. Let's say a question of
inheritance is involved."

"You don't need a P.I. for that. You could get it direct.
Write them a letter."

"Shove it, George. I might get an answer in three months.
I want one in five days."

"You have a thought there, pal. Anything else?"

"One thing more. They keep all their vital records over
there in a place they call Somerset House. I want to know
if he figures there in any connection—birth, marriage,
naturalization, anything at all."

"Why?"

"What do you mean, why? Who's paying the bill?"

"Suppose the names don't show?"

"Then I'm stuck. If they do, I want certified copies of
anything your man turns up. How much you soaking me?"

"I'll have to ask Carne. He may thumb it out altogether.
We don't want the kind of publicity you get. If he lets me
handle it, and you agree not to mention the connection, I'd
say three hundred bucks. Those guys over there don't get
much by dollar standards. He might hit us for ten guineas,
less than thirty bucks. On top of that any expenses he might
have. Say fifty bucks altogether and Carne wouldn't open a
file for less than two-fifty."

"Professional rates."

"Ha, ha. He never heard of them."

"Call me, George. Want to eat dinner?"

"Romanoff's?"

"All right," I growled, "if they'll give me a reservation—
which I doubt."

"We can have Carne's table. I happen to know he's dining
privately. He's a regular at Romanoff's. It pays off in the upper brackets of the business. Carne is a pretty big boy in this
town."

"Yeah, sure. I know somebody—and know him personally—who could lose Carne under his little fingernail."

"Good work, kid. I always knew you would come through

in the clutch. See you about seven o'clock in the bar at Romanoff's. Tell the head thief you're waiting for Colonel Carne. He'll clear a space around you so you don't get elbowed by any riffraff like screenwriters or television actors."

"See you at seven," I said.

We hung up and I went back to the chess board. But The Sphynx didn't seem to interest me any more. In a little while Peters called me back and said it was all right with Carne provided the name of their agency was not connected with my problems. Peters said he would get a night letter off to London at once.

# 41

Howard Spencer called me on the following Friday morning. He was at the Ritz-Beverly and suggested I drop over for a drink in the bar.

"Better make it in your room," I said.

"Very well, if you prefer it. Room 828. I've just talked to Eileen Wade. She seems quite resigned. She has read the script Roger left and says she thinks it can be finished off very easily. It will be a good deal shorter than his other books, but that is balanced by the publicity value. I guess you think we publishers are a pretty callous bunch. Eileen will be home all afternoon. Naturally she wants to see me and I want to see her."

"I'll be over in half an hour, Mr. Spencer."

He had a nice roomy suite on the west side of the hotel. The living room had tall windows opening on a narrow iron-railed balcony. The furniture was upholstered in some candy-striped material and that with the heavily flowered design of the carpet gave it an old-fashioned air, except that everything you could put a drink down on had a plate glass top and there were nineteen ash trays spotted around. A hotel room is a pretty sharp indication of the manners of the guests. The Ritz-Beverly wasn't expecting them to have any.

Spencer shook hands. "Sit down," he said. "What will you drink?"

"Anything or nothing. I don't have to have a drink."

"I fancy a glass of Amontillado. California is poor drinking country in the summer. In New York you can handle four times as much for one half the hangover."

"I'll take a rye whiskey sour."

He went to the phone and ordered. Then he sat down on one of the candy-striped chairs and took off his rimless glasses to polish them on a handkerchief. He put them back on, adjusted them carefully, and looked at me.

"I take it you have something on your mind. That's why you wanted to see me up here rather than in the bar."

"I'll drive you out to Idle Valley. I'd like to see Mrs. Wade too."

He looked a little uncomfortable. "I'm not sure that she wants to see you," he said.

"I know she doesn't. I can get in on your ticket."

"That would not be very diplomatic of me, would it?"

"She tell you she didn't want to see me?"

"Not exactly, not in so many words." He cleared his throat. "I get the impression that she blames you for Roger's death."

"Yeah. She said that right out—to the deputy who came the afternoon he died. She probably said it to the Sheriff's homicide lieutenant that investigated the death. She didn't say it to the Coroner, however."

He leaned back and scratched the inside of his hand with a finger, slowly. It was just a sort of doodling gesture.

"What good would it do for you to see her, Marlowe? It was a pretty dreadful experience for her. I imagine her whole life had been pretty dreadful for some time. Why make her live it over? Do you expect to convince her that you didn't miss out a little?"

"She told the deputy I killed him."

"She couldn't have meant that literally. Otherwise—"

The door buzzer rang. He got up to go to the door and open it. The room service waiter came in with the drinks and put them down with as much flourish as if he was serving a seven course dinner. Spencer signed the check and gave him four bits. The guy went away. Spencer picked up his glass of sherry and walked away as if he didn't want to hand me my drink. I let it stay where it was.

"Otherwise what?" I asked him.

"Otherwise she *would* have said something to the Coroner, wouldn't she?" He frowned at me. "I think we are talking nonsense. Just what did you want to see me about?"

"You wanted to see me."

"Only," he said coldly, "because when I talked to you from New York you said I was jumping to conclusions. That implied to me that you had something to explain. Well, what is it?"

"I'd like to explain it in front of Mrs. Wade."

"I don't care for the idea. I think you had better make your own arrangements. I have a great regard for Eileen Wade. As a businessman I'd like to salvage Roger's work if it can be done. If Eileen feels about you as you suggest, I can't be the means of getting you into her house. Be reasonable."

"That's all right," I said. "Forget it. I can get to see her without any trouble. I just thought I'd like to have somebody along with me as a witness."

"Witness to what?" he almost snapped at me.

"You'll hear it in front of her or you won't hear it at all."

"Then I won't hear it at all."

I stood up. "You're probably doing the right thing, Spencer. You want that book of Wade's—if it can be used. And you want to be a nice guy. Both laudable ambitions. I don't share either of them. The best of luck to you and goodbye."

He stood up suddenly and started towards me. "Now just a minute, Marlowe. I don't know what's on your mind but you seem to take it hard. Is there some mystery about Roger Wade's death?"

"No mystery at all. He was shot through the head with a Webley Hammerless revolver. Didn't you see a report of the inquest?"

"Certainly." He was standing close to me now and he looked bothered. "That was in the eastern papers and a couple of days later a much fuller account in the Los Angeles papers. He was alone in the house, although you were not far away. The servants were away, Candy and the cook, and Eileen had been uptown shopping and arrived home just after it happened. At the moment it happened a very noisy motor-boat on the lake drowned the sound of the shot, so that even you didn't hear it."

"That's correct," I said. "Then the motorboat went away, and I walked back from the lake edge and into the house, heard the doorbell ringing, and opened it to find Eileen Wade had forgotten her keys. Roger was already dead. She looked into the study from the doorway, thought he was asleep on the couch, went up to her room, then out to the kitchen to make some tea. A little later than she did I also looked into the study, noticed there was no sound of breathing, and found out why. In due course I called the law."

"I see no mystery," Spencer said quietly, all the sharpness gone from his voice. "It was Roger's own gun, and only the week before he had shot it off in his own room. You found Eileen struggling to get it away from him. His state of mind, his behavior, his depressions over his work—all that was brought out."

"She told you the stuff is good. Why should he be depressed over it?"

"That's just her opinion, you know. It may be very bad. Or he may have thought it worse than it was. Go on. I'm not a fool. I can see there is more."

"The homicide dick who investigated the case is an old friend of mine. He's a bulldog and a bloodhound and an old wise cop. He doesn't like a few things. Why did Roger leave no note—when he was a writing fool? Why did he shoot himself in such a way as to leave the shock of discovery to his wife? Why did he bother to pick the moment when I couldn't hear the gun go off? Why did she forget her house keys so that she had to be let in to the house? Why did she leave him alone on the day the help got off? Remember, she said she didn't know I would be there. If she did, those two cancel out."

"My God," Spencer bleated, "are you telling me the damn fool cop suspects Eileen?"

"He would if he could think of a motive."

"That's ridiculous. Why not suspect you? You had all after-noon. There could have been only a few minutes when she could have done it—and she had forgotten her house keys."

"What motive could I have?"

He reached back and grabbed my whiskey sour and swallowed it whole. He put the glass down carefully and got a handkerchief out and wiped his lips and his fingers where the chilled glass had moistened them. He put the handkerchief away. He stared at me.

"Is the investigation still going on?"

"Couldn't say. One thing is sure. They know by now whether he had drunk enough hooch to pass him out. If he had, there may still be trouble."

"And you want to talk to her," he said slowly, "in the presence of a witness."

"That's right."

"That means only one of two things to me, Marlowe. Either you are badly scared or you think she ought to be."

I nodded.

"Which one?" he asked grimly.

"I'm not scared."

He looked at his watch. "I hope to God you're crazy."

We looked at each other in silence.

# 42

North through Coldwater Canyon it began to get hot. When we topped the rise and started to wind down towards the San Fernando Valley it was breathless and blazing. I looked sideways at Spencer. He had a vest on, but the heat didn't seem to bother him. He had something else to bother him a lot more. He looked straight ahead through the windshield and said nothing. The valley had a thick layer of smog nuzzling down on it. From above it looked like a ground mist and then we were in it and it jerked Spencer out of his silence.

"My God, I thought Southern California had a climate," he said. "What are they doing—burning old truck tires?"

"It'll be all right in Idle Valley," I told him soothingly. "They get an ocean breeze in there."

"I'm glad they get something besides drunk," he said.

"From what I've seen of the local crowd in the rich suburbs I think Roger made a tragic mistake in coming out here to live. A writer needs stimulation—and not the kind they bottle. There's nothing around here but one great big sun-tanned hangover. I'm referring to the upper crust people of course."

I turned off and slowed down for the dusty stretch to the entrance of Idle Valley, then hit the paving again and in a little while the ocean breeze made itself felt, drifting down through the gap in the hills at the far end of the lake. High sprinklers revolved over the big smooth lawns and the water made a swishing sound as it licked at the grass. By this time most of the well-heeled people were away somewhere else. You could tell by the shuttered look of the houses and the way the gardener's truck was parked smack in the middle of the driveway. Then we reached the Wades' place and I swung through the gateposts and stopped behind Eileen's Jaguar. Spencer got out and marched solidly across the flagstones to the portico of the house. He rang the bell and the door opened almost at once. Candy was there in the white jacket and the dark good-looking face and the sharp black eyes. Everything was in order.

Spencer went in. Candy gave me a brief look and neatly shut the door in my face. I waited and nothing happened. I leaned on the bell and heard the chimes. The door swung wide and Candy came out snarling.

"Beat it! Turn blue. You want a knife in the belly?"

"I came to see Mrs. Wade."

"She don't want any part of you."

"Out of my way, peasant. I got business here."

"Candy!" It was her voice, and it was sharp.

He gave me a final scowl and backed into the house. I went in and shut the door. She was standing at the end of one of the facing davenports, and Spencer was standing beside her. She looked like a million. She had white slacks on, very high-waisted, and a white sport shirt with half sleeves, and a lilac-colored handkerchief budding from the pocket over her left breast.

"Candy is getting rather dictatorial lately," she said to Spencer. "It's so good to see you, Howard. And so nice of you to come all this way. I didn't realize you were bringing someone with you."

"Marlowe drove me out," Spencer said. "Also he wanted to see you."

"I can't imagine why," she said coolly. Finally she looked at me, but not as if not seeing me for a week had left an emptiness in her life. "Well?"

"It's going to take a little time," I said.

She sat down slowly. I sat down on the other davenport. Spencer was frowning. He took his glasses off and polished them. That gave him a chance to frown more naturally. Then he sat on the other end of the davenport from me.

"I was sure you would come in time for lunch," she told him, smiling.

"Not today, thanks."

"No? Well, of course if you are too busy. Then you just want to see that script."

"If I may."

"Of course. Candy! Oh, he's gone. It's on the desk in Roger's study. I'll get it."

Spencer stood up. "May I get it?"

Without waiting for an answer he started across the room. Ten feet behind her he stopped and gave me a strained look. Then he went on. I just sat there and waited until her head came around and her eyes gave me a cool impersonal stare.

"What was it you wanted to see me about?" she asked curtly.

"This and that. I see you are wearing that pendant again."

"I often wear it. It was given to me by a very dear friend a long time ago."

"Yeah. You told me. It's a British military badge of some sort, isn't it?"

She held it out at the end of the thin chain. "It's a jeweler's reproduction of one. Smaller than the original and in gold and enamel."

Spencer came back across the room and sat down again and put a thick pile of yellow paper on the corner of the cocktail table in front of him. He glanced at it idly, then his eyes were watching Eileen.

"Could I look at it a little closer?" I asked her.

She pulled the chain around until she could unfasten the clasp. She handed the pendant to me, or rather she dropped it in my hand. Then she folded her hands in her lap and just looked curious. "Why are you so interested? It's the badge of a regiment called the Artists Rifles, a Territorial regiment. The man who gave it to me was lost soon afterwards. At Andalsnes in Norway, in the spring of that terrible year—1940." She smiled and made a brief gesture with one hand. "He was in love with me."

"Eileen was in London all through the Blitz," Spencer said in an empty voice. "She couldn't get away."

We both ignored Spencer. "And you were in love with him," I said.

She looked down and then raised her head and our glances locked. "It was a long time ago," she said. "And there was a war. Strange things happen."

"There was a little more to it than that, Mrs. Wade. I guess you forget how much you opened up about him. 'The wild mysterious improbable kind of love that never comes but once.' I'm quoting you. In a way you're still in love with him. It's darn nice of me to have the same initials. I suppose that had something to do with your picking me out."

"His name was nothing like yours," she said coldly. "And he is dead, dead, dead."

I held the gold and enamel pendant out to Spencer. He took it reluctantly. "I've seen it before," he muttered.

"Check me on the design," I said. "It consists of a broad dagger in white enamel with a gold edge. The dagger points downwards and the flat of the blade crosses in front of a pair of upward-curling pale blue enamel wings. Then it crosses in back of a scroll. On the scroll are the words: WHO DARES WINS."

"That seems to be correct," he said. "What makes it important?"

"She says it's a badge of the Artists Rifles, a Territorial outfit. She says it was given to her by a man who was in that outfit and was lost in the Norwegian campaign with the British Army in the spring of 1940 at Andalsnes."

I had their attention. Spencer watched me steadily. I wasn't talking to the birds and he knew it. Eileen knew it too. Her tawny eyebrows were crimped in a puzzled frown which could have been genuine. It was also unfriendly.

"This is a sleeve badge," I said. "It came into existence because the Artists Rifles were made over or attached or seconded or whatever the correct term is into a Special Air Service Outfit. They had originally been a Territorial Regiment of infantry. This badge didn't even exist until 1947. Therefore nobody gave it to Mrs. Wade in 1940. Also, no Artists Rifles were landed at Andalsnes in Norway in 1940. Sherwood Foresters and Leicestershires, yes. Both Territorial. Artists Rifles, no. Am I being nasty?"

Spencer put the pendant down on the coffee table and pushed it slowly across until it was in front of Eileen. He said nothing.

"Do you think I wouldn't know?" Eileen asked me contemptuously.

"Do you think the British War Office wouldn't know?" I asked her right back.

"Obviously there must be some mistake," Spencer said mildly.

I swung around and gave him a hard stare. "That's one way of putting it."

"Another way of putting it is that I am a liar," Eileen said icily. "I never knew anyone named Paul Marston, never loved him or he me. He never gave me a reproduction of his regimental badge, he was never missing in action, he never existed. I bought this badge myself in a shop in New York where they specialize in imported British luxuries, things like leather goods, hand-made brogues, regimental and school ties and cricket blazers, knickknacks with coats of arms on them and so on. Would an explanation like that satisfy you, Mr. Marlowe?"

"The last part would. Not the first. No doubt somebody told you it was an Artists Rifles badge and forgot to mention what kind, or didn't know. But you did know Paul Marston and he did serve in that outfit, and he was missing in action in Norway. But it didn't happen in 1940, Mrs. Wade. It happened in 1942 and he was in the Commandos then, and it wasn't at Andalsnes, but on a little island off the coast where the Commando boys pulled a fast raid."

"I see no need to be so hostile about it," Spencer said in an executive sort of voice. He was fooling with the yellow sheets in front of him now. I didn't know whether he was trying to stooge for me or was just sore. He picked up a slab of yellow script and weighed it on his hand.

"You going to buy that stuff by the pound?" I asked him.

He looked startled, then he smiled a small difficult smile.

"Eileen had a pretty rough time in London," he said. "Things get confused in one's memory."

I took a folded paper out of my pocket. "Sure," I said. "Like who you got married to. This is a certified copy of a marriage certificate. The original came from Caxton Hall Registry Office. The date of the marriage is August 1942. The parties named are Paul Edward Marston and Eileen Victoria Sampsell. In a sense Mrs. Wade is right. There was no such person as Paul Edward Marston. It was a fake name because in the army you have to get permission to get married. The man faked an identity. In the army he had another name. I have his whole army history. It's a wonder to me that people never seem to realize that all you have to do is ask."

Spencer was very quiet now. He leaned back and stared. But not at me. He stared at Eileen. She looked back at him with one of those faint half deprecatory, half seductive smiles women are so good at.

"But he was dead, Howard. Long before I met Roger. What could it possibly matter? Roger knew all about it. I never stopped using my unmarried name. In the circumstances I had to. It was on my passport. Then after he was killed in action—" She stopped and drew a slow breath and let her hand fall slowly and softly to her knee. "All finished, all done for, all lost."

"You're sure Roger knew?" he asked her slowly.

"He knew something," I said. "The name Paul Marston had a meaning for him. I asked him once and he got a funny look in his eyes. But he didn't tell me why."

She ignored that and spoke to Spencer.

"Why, of course Roger knew all about it." Now she was smiling at Spencer patiently as if he was being a little slow on the take. The tricks they have.

"Then why lie about the dates?" Spencer asked dryly.

"Why say the man was lost in 1940 when he was lost in 1942? Why wear a badge that he couldn't have given you and make a point of saying that he did give it to you?"

"Perhaps I was lost in a dream," she said softly. "Or a nightmare, more accurately. A lot of my friends were killed in the bombing. When you said goodnight in those days you tried not to make it sound like goodbye. But that's what it often was. And when you said goodbye to a soldier —it was worse. It's always the kind and gentle ones that get killed."

He didn't say anything. I didn't say anything. She looked down at the pendant lying on the table in front of her. She picked it up and fitted it to the chain around her neck again and leaned back composedly.

"I know I haven't any right to cross-examine you, Eileen," Spencer said slowly. "Let's forget it. Marlowe made a big thing out of the badge and the marriage certificate and so on. Just for a moment I guess he had me wondering."

"Mr. Marlowe," she told him quietly, "makes a big thing out of trifles. But when it comes to a really big thing—like saving a man's life—he is out by the lake watching a silly speedboat."

"And you never saw Paul Marston again," I said.

"How could I when he was dead?"

"You didn't know he was dead. There was no report of his death from the Red Cross. He might have been taken prisoner."

She shuddered suddenly. "In October 1942," she said slowly, "Hitler issued an order that all Commando prisoners were to be turned over to the Gestapo. I think we all know what that meant. Torture and a nameless death in some Gestapo dungeon." She shuddered again. Then she blazed at me: "You're a horrible man. You want me to live that over again, to punish me for a trivial lie. Suppose someone you loved had been caught by those people and you knew what had happened, what must have happened to him or her? Is it so strange that I tried to build another kind of memory— even a false one?"

"I need a drink," Spencer said. "I need a drink badly. May I have one?"

She clapped her hands and Candy drifted up from nowhere as he always did. He bowed to Spencer.

"What you like to drink, Señor Spencer?"

"Straight Scotch, and plenty of it," Spencer said.

Candy went over in the corner and pulled the bar out from the wall. He got a bottle up on it and poured a stiff jolt into a glass. He came back and set it down in front of Spencer. He started to leave again.

"Perhaps, Candy," Eileen said quietly, "Mr. Marlowe would like a drink too."

He stopped and looked at her, his face dark and stubborn.

"No, thanks," I said. "No drink for me."

Candy made a snorting sound and walked off. There was another silence. Spencer put down half of his drink. He lit a cigarette. He spoke to me without looking at me.

"I'm sure Mrs. Wade or Candy could drive me back to Beverly Hills. Or I can get a cab. I take it you've said your piece."

I refolded the certified copy of the marriage license. I put it back in my pocket.

"Sure that's the way you want it?" I asked him.

"That's the way everybody wants it."

"Good." I stood up. "I guess I was a fool to try to play it this way. Being a big time publisher and having the brains to go with it—if it takes any—you might have assumed I didn't come out here just to play the heavy. I didn't revive ancient history or spend my own money to get the facts just to twist them around somebody's neck. I didn't investigate Paul Marston because the Gestapo murdered him, because Mrs. Wade was wearing the wrong badge, because she got mixed up on her dates, because she married him in one of those quickie wartime marriages. When I started investigating him I didn't know any of those things. All I knew was his name. Now how do you suppose I knew that?"

"No doubt somebody told you," Spencer said curtly.

"Correct, Mr. Spencer. Somebody who knew him in New York after the war and later on saw him out here in Chasen's with his wife."

"Marston is a pretty common name," Spencer said, and sipped his whiskey. He turned his head sideways and his right eyelid drooped a fraction of an inch. So I sat down again. "Even Paul Marstons could hardly be unique. There are nineteen Howard Spencers in the Greater New York area telephone directories, for instance. And four of them are just plain Howard Spencer with no middle initial."

"Yeah. How may Paul Marstons would you say had had one side of their faces smashed by a delayed-action mortar shell and showed the scars and marks of the plastic surgery that repaired the damage?"

Spencer's mouth fell open. He made some kind of heavy breathing sound. He got out a handkerchief and tapped his temples with it.

"How many Paul Marstons would you say had saved the lives of a couple of tough gamblers named Mendy Menendez and Randy Starr on that same occasion? They're still around, they've got good memories. They can talk when it suits them. Why ham it up any more, Spencer? Paul Marston and Terry Lennox were the same man. It can be proved beyond any shadow of a doubt."

I didn't expect anyone to jump six feet into the air and scream and nobody did. But there is a kind of silence that is almost as loud as a shout. I had it. I had it all around me, thick and hard. In the kitchen I could hear water run. Outside on the road I could hear the dull thump of a folded newspaper hit the driveway, then the light inaccurate whistling of a boy wheeling away on his bicycle.

I felt a tiny sting on the back of my neck. I jerked away from it and swung around. Candy was standing there with his knife in his hand. His dark face was wooden but there was something in his eyes I hadn't seen before.

"You are tired, amigo," he said softly. "I fix you a drink, no?"

"Bourbon on the rocks, thanks," I said.

"De pronto, señor."

He snapped the knife shut, dropped it into the side pocket of his white jacket and went softly away.

Then at last I looked at Eileen. She sat leaning forward, her hands clasped tightly. The downward tilt of her face hid her expression if she had any. And when she spoke her voice had the lucid emptiness of that mechanical voice on the telephone that tells you the time and if you keep on listening, which people don't because they have no reason to, it will keep on telling you the passing seconds forever, without the slightest change of inflection.

"I saw him once, Howard. Just once. I didn't speak to him at all. Nor he to me. He was terribly changed. His hair was white and his face—it wasn't quite the same face. But of course I knew him, and of course he knew me. We looked at each other. That was all. Then he was gone out of the room and the next day he was gone from her house. It was at the Lorings' I saw him—and her. One afternoon late. You were there, Howard. And Roger was there. I suppose you saw him too."

"We were introduced," Spencer said. "I knew who he was married to."

"Linda Loring told me he just disappeared. He gave no reason. There was no quarrel. Then after a while that woman divorced him. And still later I heard she found him again. He was down and out. And they were married again. Heaven knows why. I suppose he had no money and it didn't matter to him any more. He knew that I was married to Roger. We were lost to each other."

"Why?" Spencer asked.

Candy put my drink in front of me without a word. He looked at Spencer and Spencer shook his head. Candy drifted away. Nobody paid any attention to him. He was like the prop man in a Chinese play, the fellow that moves things around on the stage and the actors and audience alike behave as if he wasn't there.

"Why?" she repeated. "Oh, you wouldn't understand. What we had was lost. It could never be recovered. The Gestapo didn't get him after all. There must have been *some* decent Nazis who didn't obey Hitler's order about the Commandos. So he survived, he came back. I used to pretend to myself that I would find him again, but as he had been, eager and young and unspoiled. But to find him married to that redheaded whore—that was disgusting. I already knew about her and Roger. I have no doubt Paul did too. So did Linda Loring, who is a bit of a tramp herself, but not completely so. They all are in that set. You ask me why I didn't leave Roger and go back to Paul. After he had been in her arms and Roger had been in those same willing arms? No thank you. I need a little more inspiration than that. Roger I could forgive. He drank, he didn't know what he was doing. He worried about his work and he hated himself because he was just a mercenary hack. He was a weak man, unreconciled, frustrated, but understandable. He was just a husband. Paul was either much more or he was nothing. In the end he was nothing."

I took a swig of my drink. Spencer had finished his. He was scratching at the material of the davenport. He had forgotten the pile of paper in front of him, the unfinished novel of the very much finished popular author.

"I wouldn't say he was nothing," I said.

She lifted her eyes and looked at me vaguely and dropped them again.

"Less than nothing," she said, with a new note of sarcasm in her voice. "He knew what she was, he married her. Then because she was what he knew she was, he killed her. And then ran away and killed himself."

"He didn't kill her," I said, "and you know it."

She came upright with a smooth motion and stared at me blankly. Spencer let out a noise of some kind.

"Roger killed her," I said, "and you also know that."

"Did he tell you?" she asked quietly.

"He didn't have to. He did give me a couple of hints. He would have told me or someone in time. It was tearing him to pieces not to."

She shook her head slightly. "No, Mr. Marlowe. That was not why he was tearing himself to pieces. Roger didn't know he had killed her. He had blacked out completely. He knew something was wrong and he tried to bring it to the surface, but he couldn't. The shock had destroyed his memory of it. Perhaps it would have come back and perhaps in the last moments of his life it did come back. But not until then. Not until then."

Spencer said in a sort of growl: "That sort of thing just doesn't happen, Eileen."

"Oh yes, it does," I said. "I know of two well established instances. One was a blackout drunk who killed a woman he picked up in a bar. He strangled her with a scarf she was wearing fastened with a fancy clasp. She went home with him and what went on then is not known except that she got dead and when the law caught up with him he was wearing the fancy clasp on his own tie and he didn't have the faintest idea where he got it."

"Never?" Spencer asked. "Or just at the time?"

"He never admitted it. And he's not around any more to be asked. They gassed him. The other case was a head wound. He was living with a rich pervert, the kind that collects first editions and does fancy cooking and has a very expensive secret library behind a panel in the wall. The two of them had a fight. They fought all over the house, from room to room, the place was a shambles and the rich guy eventually got the low score. The killer, when they caught him, had dozens of bruises on him and a broken finger. All he knew for sure was that he had a headache and he couldn't find his way back to Pasadena. He kept circling around and stopping to ask directions at the same service station. The guy at the service station decided he was nuts and called the cops. Next time around they were waiting for him."

"I don't believe that about Roger," Spencer said. "He was no more psycho than I am."

"He blacked out when he was drunk," I said.

"I was there. I *saw* him do it," Eileen said calmly.

I grinned at Spencer. It was some kind of grin, not the cheery kind probably, but I could feel my face doing its best.

"She's going to tell us about it," I told him. "Just listen. She's going to tell us. She can't help herself now."

"Yes, that is true," she said gravely. "There are things no one likes to tell about an enemy, much less about one's own husband. And if I have to tell them publicly on a witness stand, you are not going to enjoy it, Howard. Your fine, talented, ever so popular and lucrative author is going to look pretty cheap. Sexy as all get out, wasn't he? On paper, that is. And how the poor fool tried to live up to it! All that woman was to him was a trophy. I spied on them. I should be ashamed of that. One has to say these things. I am ashamed of nothing. I saw the whole nasty scene. The guest house she used for her amours happens to be a nice secluded affair with its own garage and entrance on a side street, a dead end, shaded by big trees. The time came, as it must to people like Roger, when he was no longer a satisfactory lover. Just a little too drunk. He tried to leave but she came out after him screaming and stark naked, waving some kind of small statuette. She used language of a depth of filth and depravity I couldn't attempt to describe. Then she tried to hit him with the statuette. You are both men and you must know that nothing shocks a man quite so much as to hear a supposedly refined woman use the language of the gutter and the public urinal. He was drunk, he had had sudden spells of violence, and he had one then. He tore the statuette out of her hand. You can guess the rest."

"There must have been a lot of blood," I said.

"Blood?" She laughed bitterly. "You should have seen him when he got home. When I ran for my car to get away he was just standing there looking down at her. Then he bent and picked her up in his arms and carried her into the guest house. I knew then that the shock had partially sobered him. He got home in about an hour. He was very quiet. It shook him when he saw me waiting. But he wasn't drunk then. He was dazed. There was blood on his face, on his hair, all over the front of his coat. I got him into the lavatory off the study and got him stripped and cleaned off enough to get him upstairs into the shower. I put him to bed. I got an old suitcase and went downstairs and gathered up the bloody clothes and put them in the suitcase. I cleaned the basin and the floor and then I took a wet towel out and made sure his car was clean. I put it away and got mine out. I drove to the Chatsworth Reservoir and you can guess what I did with the suitcase full of bloody clothes and towels."

She stopped. Spencer was scratching at the palm of his left hand. She gave him a quick glance and went on.

"While I was away he got up and drank a lot of whiskey. And the next morning he didn't remember a single thing. That is, he didn't say a word about it or behave as if he had anything on his mind but a hangover. And I said nothing."

"He must have missed the clothes," I said.

She nodded. "I think he did eventually—but he didn't say

so. Everything seemed to happen at once about that time. The papers were full of it, then Paul was missing, and then he was dead in Mexico. How was I to know that would happen? Roger was my husband. He had done an awful thing, but she was an awful woman. And he hadn't known what he was doing. Then almost as suddenly as it began the papers dropped it. Linda's father must have had something to do with that. Roger read the papers, of course, and he made just the sort of comments one would expect from an innocent bystander who had just happened to know the people involved."

"Weren't you afraid?" Spencer asked her quietly.

"I was sick with fear, Howard. If he remembered, he would probably kill me. He was a good actor—most writers are—and perhaps he already knew and was just waiting for a chance. But I couldn't be sure. He might—just might—have forgotten the whole thing permanently. And Paul was dead."

"If he never mentioned the clothes that you had dumped in the reservoir, that proved he suspected something," I said. "And remember, in that stuff he left in the typewriter the other time—the time he shot the gun off upstairs and I found you trying to get it away from him—he said a good man had died for him."

"He said that?" Her eyes widened just the right amount.

"He wrote it—on the typewriter. I destroyed it, he asked me to. I supposed you had already seen it."

"I never read anything he wrote in his study."

"You read the note he left the time Verringer took him away. You even dug something out of the wastebasket."

"That was different," she said coolly. "I was looking for a clue to where he might have gone."

"Okay," I said, and leaned back. "Is there any more?"

She shook her head slowly, with a deep sadness. "I suppose not. At the very last, the afternoon he killed himself, he may have remembered. We'll never know. Do we want to know?"

Spencer cleared his throat. "What was Marlowe supposed to do in all this? It was your idea to get him here. You talked me into that, you know."

"I was terribly afraid. I was afraid of Roger and I was afraid *for* him. Mr. Marlowe was Paul's friend, almost the last person to see him who knew him. Paul might have told him something. I had to be sure. If he was dangerous, I wanted him on my side. If he found out the truth, there might still be some way to save Roger."

Suddenly and for no reason that I could see, Spencer got tough. He leaned forward and pushed his jaw out.

"Let me get this straight, Eileen. Here was a private detective who was already in bad with the police. They'd had him in jail. He was supposed to have helped Paul—I call him that because you do—jump the country to Mexico. That's a felony, if Paul was a murderer. So if he found out the truth and could clear himself, he would just sit on his hands and do nothing. Was that your idea?"

"I was afraid, Howard. Can't you understand that? I was living in the house with a murderer who might be a maniac. I was alone with him a large part of the time."

"I understand that," Spencer said, still tough. "But Marlowe didn't take it on, and you were still alone. Then Roger fired the gun off and for a week after that you were alone. Then Roger killed himself and very conveniently it was Marlowe who was alone that time."

"That is true," she said. "What of it? Could I help it?"

"All right," Spencer said. "Is it just possible you thought Marlowe might find the truth and with the background of the gun going off once already, just kind of hand it to Roger and say something like, 'Look, old man, you're a murderer and I know it and your wife knows it. She's a fine woman. She has suffered enough. Not to mention Sylvia Lennox's husband. Why not do the decent thing and pull the trigger and everybody will assume it was just a case of too much wild drinking? So I'll stroll down by the lake and smoke a cigarette, old man. Good luck and goodbye. Oh, here's the gun. It's loaded and it's all yours.' "

"You're getting horrible, Howard. I didn't think anything of the sort."

"You told the deputy Marlowe had killed Roger. What was that supposed to mean?"

She looked at me briefly, almost shyly. "I was very wrong to say that. I didn't know what I was saying."

"Maybe you thought Marlowe had shot him," Spencer suggested calmly.

Her eyes narrowed. "Oh no, Howard. Why? Why would he do that? That's an abominable suggestion."

"Why?" Spencer wanted to know. "What's abominable about it? The police had the same idea. And Candy gave them a motive. He said Marlowe was in your room for two hours the night Roger shot a hole in his ceiling—after Roger had been put to sleep with pills."

She flushed to the roots of her hair. She stared at him dumbly.

"And you didn't have any clothes on," Spencer said brutally. "That's what Candy told them."

"But at the inquest—" she began to say in a shattered kind of voice. Spencer cut her off.

"The police didn't believe Candy. So he didn't tell it at the inquest."

"Oh." It was a sigh of relief.

"Also," Spencer went on coldly, "the police suspected you. They still do. All they need is a motive. Looks to me like they might be able to put one together now."

She was up on her feet. "I think you had both better leave my house," she said angrily. "The sooner the better."

"Well, did you or didn't you?" Spencer asked calmly, not moving except to reach for his glass and find it empty.

"Did I or didn't I what?"

"Shoot Roger?"

She was standing there staring at him. The flush had gone. Her face was white and tight and angry.

"I'm just giving you the sort of thing you'd get in court."

"I was out. I had forgotten my keys. I had to ring to get into the house. He was dead when I got home. All that is known. What has got into you, for God's sake?"

He took a handkerchief out and wiped his lips. "Eileen, I've stayed in this house twenty times. I've never known that front door to be locked during the daytime. I don't say you shot him. I just asked you. And don't tell me it was impossible. The way things worked out it was easy."

"I shot my own husband?" she asked slowly and wonderingly.

"Assuming," Spencer said in the same indifferent voice, "that he *was* your husband. You had another when you married him."

"Thank you, Howard. Thank you very much. Roger's last book, his swan song, is there in front of you. Take it and go. And I think you had better call the police and tell them what you think. It will be a charming ending to our friendship. Most charming. Goodbye, Howard. I am very tired and I have a headache. I'm going to my room and lie down. As for Mr. Marlowe—and I suppose he put you up to all this—I can only say to him that if he didn't kill Roger in a literal sense, he certainly drove him to his death."

She turned to walk away. I said sharply: "Mrs. Wade, just a moment. Let's finish the job. No sense in being bitter. We are all trying to do the right thing. That suitcase you threw into the Chatsworth Reservoir—was it heavy?"

She turned and stared at me. "It was an old one, I said. Yes, it was very heavy."

"How did you get it over the high wire fence around the reservoir?"

"What? The fence?" She made a helpless gesture. "I suppose in emergencies one has an abnormal strength to do what has to be done. Somehow or other I did it. That's all."

"There isn't any fence," I said.

"Isn't any fence?" She repeated it dully, as if it didn't mean anything.

"And there was no blood on Roger's clothes. And Sylvia Lennox wasn't killed outside the guest house, but inside it on the bed. And there was practically no blood, because she was already dead—shot dead with a gun—and when the statuette was used to beat her face to a pulp, it was beating a dead woman. And the dead, Mrs. Wade, bleed very little."

She curled her lip at me contemptuously. "I suppose you were there," she said scornfully.

Then she went away from us.

We watched her go. She went up the stairs slowly, moving with calm elegance. She disappeared into her room and the door closed softly but firmly behind her. Silence.

"What was that about the wire fence?" Spencer asked me vaguely. He was moving his head back and forth. He was flushed and sweating. He was taking it gamely but it wasn't easy for him to take.

"Just a gag," I said. "I've never been close enough to the Chatsworth Reservoir to know what it looks like. Maybe it has a fence around it, maybe not."

"I see," he said unhappily. "But the point is she didn't know either."

"Of course not. She killed both of them."

# 43

Then something moved softly and Candy was standing at the end of the couch looking at me. He had his switch knife in his hand. He pressed the button and the blade shot out. He pressed the button and the blade went back into the handle. There was a sleek glitter in his eye.

"Million de pardones, señor," he said. "I was wrong about you. She killed the boss. I think I—" He stopped and the blade shot out again.

"No." I stood up and held my hand out. "Give me the knife, Candy. You're just a nice Mexican houseboy. They'd hang it onto you and love it. Just the kind of smoke screen that would make them grin with delight. You don't know what I'm talking about. But I do. They fouled it up so bad that they couldn't straighten it out now if they wanted to. And they don't want to. They'd blast a confession out of you so quick you wouldn't even have time to tell them your full name. And you'd be sitting on your fanny up in San Quentin with a life sentence three weeks from Tuesday."

"I tell you before I am not a Mexican. I am Chileno from Viña del Mar near Valparaíso."

"The knife, Candy. I know all that. You're free. You've got money saved. You've probably got eight brothers and sisters back home. Be smart and go back where you came from. This job here is dead."

"Lots of jobs," he said quietly. Then he reached out and dropped the knife into my hand. "For you I do this."

I dropped the knife into my pocket. He glanced up towards the balcony. "La señora—what do we do now?"

"Nothing. We do nothing at all. The señora is very tired. She has been living under a great strain. She doesn't want to be disturbed."

"We've got to call the police," Spencer said grittily.

"Why?"

"Oh my God, Marlowe—we have to."

"Tomorrow. Pick up your pile of unfinished novel and let's go."

"We've got to call the police. There is such a thing as law."

"We don't have to do anything of the sort. We haven't enough evidence to swat a fly with. Let the law enforcement people do their own dirty work. Let the lawyers work it out. They write the laws for other lawyers to dissect in front of other lawyers called judges so that other judges can say the first judges were wrong and the Supreme Court can say the second lot were wrong. Sure there's such a thing as law. We're up to our necks in it. About all it does is make business for lawyers. How long do you think the big-shot mobsters would last if the lawyers didn't show them how to operate?"

Spencer said angrily: "That has nothing to do with it. A man was killed in this house. He happened to be an author and a very successful and important one, but that has nothing to do with it either. He was a man and you and I know who killed him. There's such a thing as justice."

"Tomorrow."

"You're just as bad as she is if you let her get away with it. I'm beginning to wonder about you a little, Marlowe. You could have saved his life if you had been on your toes. In a sense you did let her get away with it. And for all I know this whole performance this afternoon has been just that—a performance."

"That's right. A disguised love scene. You could see Eileen is crazy about me. When things quiet down we may get married. She ought to be pretty well fixed. I haven't made a buck out of the Wade family yet. I'm getting impatient."

He took his glasses off and polished them. He wiped perspiration from the hollows under his eyes, replaced the glasses and looked at the floor.

"I'm sorry," he said. "I've taken a pretty stiff punch this afternoon. It was bad enough to know Roger had killed himself. But this other version makes me feel degraded—just knowing about it." He looked up at me. "Can I trust you?"

"To do what?"

"The right thing—whatever it is." He reached down and picked up the pile of yellow script and tucked it under his arm. "No, forget it. I guess you know what you are doing. I'm a pretty good publisher but this is out of my line. I guess what I really am is just a goddam stuffed shirt."

He walked past me and Candy stepped out of his way, then went quickly to the front door and held it open. Spencer went out past him with a brief nod. I followed. I stopped beside Candy and looked into his dark shining eyes.

"No tricks, amigo," I said.

"The señora is very tired," he said quietly. "She has gone to her room. She will not be disturbed. I know nothing, señor. No me acuerdo de nada . . . A sus órdenes, señor."

I took the knife out of my pocket and held it out to him. He smiled.

"Nobody trusts me, but I trust you, Candy."

"Lo mismo, señor. Muchas gracias."

Spencer was already in the car. I got in and started it and backed down the driveway and drove him back to Beverly Hills. I let him out at the side entrance of the hotel.

"I've been thinking all the way back," he said as he got out. "She must be a little insane. I guess they'd never convict her."

"They won't even try," I said. "But she doesn't know that."

He struggled with the batch of yellow paper under his arm, got it straightened out, and nodded to me. I watched him heave open the door and go on in. I eased up on the brake and the Olds slid out from the white curb, and that was the last I saw of Howard Spencer.

I got home late and tired and depressed. It was one of those nights when the air is heavy and the night noises seem muffled and far away. There was a high misty indifferent moon. I walked the floor, played a few records, and hardly heard them. I seemed to hear a steady ticking somewhere, but there wasn't anything in the house to tick. The ticking was in my head. I was a one-man death watch.

I thought of the first time I had seen Eileen Wade and the second and the third and the fourth. But after that something in her got out of drawing. She no longer seemed quite real. A murderer is always unreal once you know he is a murderer. There are people who kill out of hate or fear or greed. There are the cunning killers who plan and expect to get away with it. There are the angry killers who do not think at all. And there are the killers who are in love with death, to whom murder is a remote kind of suicide. In a sense they are all insane, but not in the way Spencer meant it.

It was almost daylight when I finally went to bed.

The jangle of the telephone dragged me up out of a black well of sleep. I rolled over on the bed, fumbled for slippers, and realized that I hadn't been asleep for more than a couple of hours. I felt like a half-digested meal eaten in a greasy-spoon joint. My eyes were stuck together and my mouth was full of sand. I heaved up on the feet and lumbered into the living room and pulled the phone off the cradle and said into it: "Hold the line."

I put the phone down and went into the bathroom and hit myself in the face with some cold water. Outside the window something went snip, snip, snip. I looked out vaguely and saw a brown expressionless face. It was the once-a-week Jap gardener I called Hardhearted Harry. He was trimming the tecoma—the way a Japanese gardener trims your tecoma. You ask him four times and he says, "next week" and then he comes by at six o'clock in the morning and trims it outside your bedroom window.

I rubbed my face dry and went back to the telephone.

"Yeah?"

"This is Candy, señor."

"Good morning, Candy."

"La señora es muerta."

Dead. What a cold black noiseless word it is in any language. The lady is dead.

"Nothing you did, I hope."

"I think the medicine. It is called demerol. I think forty,

fifty in the bottle. Empty now. No dinner last night. This morning I climb up on the ladder and look in the window. Dressed just like yesterday afternoon. I break the screen open. La señora es muerta. Frio como agua de nieve."

Cold as icewater. "You call anybody?"

"Sí. El Doctor Loring. He call the cops. Not here yet."

"Dr. Loring, huh? Just the man to come too late."

"I don't show him the letter," Candy said.

"Letter to who?"

"Señor Spencer."

"Give it to the police, Candy. Don't let Dr. Loring have it. Just the police. And one more thing, Candy. Don't hide anything, don't tell them any lies. We were there. Tell the truth. This time the truth and all the truth."

There was a little pause. Then he said: "Sí. I catch. Hasta la vista, amigo." He hung up.

I dialed the Ritz-Beverly and asked for Howard Spencer.

"One moment, please. I'll give you the desk."

A man's voice said: "Desk speaking. May I help you?"

"I asked for Howard Spencer. I know it's early, but it's urgent."

"Mr. Spencer checked out last evening. He took the eight o'clock plane to New York."

"Oh, sorry. I didn't know."

I went out to the kitchen to make coffee—yards of coffee. Rich, strong, bitter, boiling hot, ruthless, depraved. The lifeblood of tired men.

It was a couple of hours later that Bernie Ohls called me.

"Okay, wise guy," he said. "Get down here and suffer."

# 44

It was like the other time except that it was day and we were in Captain Hernandez's office and the Sheriff was up in Santa Barbara opening Fiesta Week. Captain Hernandez was there and Bernie Ohls and a man from the coroner's office and Dr. Loring, who looked as if he had been caught performing an abortion, and a man named Lawford, a deputy from the D.A.'s office, a tall gaunt expressionless man whose brother was vaguely rumored to be a boss of the numbers racket in the Central Avenue district.

Hernandez had some handwritten sheets of note paper in front of him, flesh-pink paper, deckle-edged, and written on with green ink.

"This is informal," Hernandez said, when everybody was as comfortable as you can get in hard chairs. "No stenotype or recording equipment. Say what you like. Dr. Weiss represents the coroner who will decide whether an inquest is necessary. Dr. Weiss?"

He was fat, cheerful, and looked competent. "I think no inquest," he said. "There is every surface indication of narcotic poisoning. When the ambulance arrived the woman was still breathing very faintly and she was in a deep coma and all the reflexes were negative. At that stage you don't save one in a hundred. Her skin was cold and respiration would not be noticed without close examination. The houseboy thought she was dead. She died approximately an hour after that. I understand the lady was subject to occasional violent attacks of bronchial asthma. The demerol was prescribed by Dr. Loring as an emergency measure."

"Any information or deduction about the amount of demerol taken, Dr. Weiss?"

"A fatal dose," he said, smiling faintly. "There is no quick way of determining that without knowing the medical history, the acquired or natural tolerance. According to her confession she took twenty-three hundred milligrams, four or five times the minimal lethal dose for a non-addict." He looked questioningly at Dr. Loring.

"Mrs. Wade was not an addict," Dr. Loring said coldly. "The prescribed dose would be one or two fifty-milligram tablets. Three or four during a twenty-four-hour period would be the most I'd permit."

"But you gave her fifty at a whack," Captain Hernandez said. "A pretty dangerous drug to have around in that quantity, don't you think? How bad was this bronchial asthma, Doctor?"

Dr. Loring smiled contemptuously. "It was intermittent,

like all asthma. It never amounted to what we term *status asthmaticus*, an attack so severe that the patient seems in danger of suffocating."

"Any comment, Dr. Weiss?"

"Well," Dr. Weiss said slowly, "assuming the note didn't exist and assuming we had no other evidence of how much of the stuff she took, it could be an accidental overdose. The safety margin isn't very wide. We'll know for sure tomorrow. You don't want to suppress the note, Hernandez, for Pete's sake?"

Hernandez scowled down at his desk. "I was just wondering. I didn't know narcotics were standard treatment for asthma. Guy learns something every day."

Loring flushed. "An emergency measure, I said, Captain. A doctor can't be everywhere at once. The onset of an asthmatic flareup can be very sudden."

Hernandez gave him a brief glance and turned to Lawford. "What happens to your office, if I give this letter to the press?"

The D.A.'s deputy glanced at me emptily. "What's this guy doing here, Hernandez?"

"I invited him."

"How do I know he won't repeat everything said in here to some reporter?"

"Yeah, he's a great talker. You found that out. The time you had him pinched."

Lawford grinned, then cleared his throat. "I've read that purported confession," he said carefully. "And I don't believe a word of it. You've got a background of emotional exhaustion, bereavement, some use of drugs, the strain of wartime life in England under bombing, this clandestine marriage, the man coming back here, and so on. Undoubtedly she developed a feeling of guilt and tried to purge herself of it by a sort of transference."

He stopped and looked around, but all he saw was faces with no expression. "I can't speak for the D.A. but my own feeling is that your confession would be no grounds to seek an indictment even if the woman had lived."

"And having already believed one confession you wouldn't

care to believe another that contradicted the first one," Hernandez said caustically.

"Take it easy, Hernandez. Any law enforcement agency has to consider public relations. If the papers printed that confession we'd be in trouble. That's for sure. We've got enough eager beaver reformer groups around just waiting for that kind of chance to stick a knife into us. We've got a grand jury that's already jittery about the working-over your vice squad lieutenant got last week—it's about ten days."

Hernandez said: "Okay, it's your baby. Sign the receipt for me."

He shuffled the pink deckle-edged pages together and Lawford leaned down to sign a form. He picked up the pink pages, folded them, put them in his breast pocket and walked out.

Dr. Weiss stood up. He was tough, good-natured, unimpressed. "We had the last inquest on the Wade family too quick," he said. "I guess we won't bother to have this one at all."

He nodded to Ohls and Hernandez, shook hands formally with Loring, and went out. Loring stood up to go, then hesitated.

"I take it that I may inform a certain interested party that there will be no further investigation of this matter?" he said stiffly.

"Sorry to have kept you away from your patients so long, Doctor."

"You haven't answered my question," Loring said sharply. "I'd better warn you—"

"Get lost, Jack," Hernandez said.

Dr. Loring almost staggered with shock. Then he turned and fumbled his way rapidly out of the room. The door closed and it was a half minute before anybody said anything. Hernandez shook himself and lit a cigarette. Then he looked at me.

"Well?" he said.

"Well what?"

"What are you waiting for?"

"This is the end, then? Finished? Kaput."

"Tell him, Bernie."

"Yeah, sure it's the end," Ohls said. "I was all set to pull her in for questioning. Wade didn't shoot himself. Too much alcohol in his brain. But like I told you, where was the motive? Her confession could be wrong in details, but it proves she spied on him. She knew the layout of the guest house in Encino. The Lennox frail had taken both her men from her. What happened in the guest house is just what you want to imagine. One question you forgot to ask Spencer. Did Wade own a Mauser P.P.K.? Yeah, he owned a small Mauser automatic. We talked to Spencer already today on the phone. Wade was a blackout drunk. The poor unfortunate bastard either thought he had killed Sylvia Lennox or he actually had killed her or else he had some reason to know his wife had. Either way he was going to lay it on the line eventually. Sure, he'd been hitting the hooch long before, but he was a he guy married to a beautiful nothing. The Mex knows all about it. The little bastard knows damn near everything. That was a dream girl. Some of her was here and now, but a lot of her was there and then. If she ever got hot pants, it wasn't for her husband. Get what I'm talking about?"

I didn't answer him.

"Damn near made her yourself, didn't you?"

I gave him the same no answer.

Ohls and Hernandez both grinned sourly. "Us guys aren't exactly brainless," Ohls said. "We knew there was something in that story about her taking her clothes off. You outtalked him and he let you. He was hurt and confused and he liked Wade and he wanted to be sure. When he got sure he'd have used his knife. This was a personal matter with him. He never snitched on Wade. Wade's wife did, and she deliberately fouled up the issue just to confuse Wade. It all adds. In the end I guess she was scared of him. And Wade never threw her down any stairs. That was an accident. She tripped and the guy tried to catch her. Candy saw that too."

"None of it explains why she wanted me around."

"I could think of reasons. One of them is old stuff. Every cop has run into it a hundred times. You were the loose end, the guy that helped Lennox escape, his friend, and probably to some extent his confidant. What did he know and what did he tell you? He took the gun that had killed her and he knew it had been fired. She could have thought he did it for her. That made her think he knew she had used it. When he killed himself she was sure. But what about you? You were still the loose end. She wanted to milk you, and she had the charm to use, and a situation ready-made for an excuse to get next to you. And if she needed a fall guy, you were it. You might say she was collecting fall guys."

"You're imputing too much knowledge to her," I said.

Ohls broke a cigarette in half and started chewing on one half. The other half he stuck behind his ear.

"Another reason is she wanted a man, a big, strong guy that could crush her in his arms and make her dream again."

"She hated me," I said. "I don't buy that one."

"Of course," Hernandez put in dryly. "You turned her down. But she would have got over that. And then you blew the whole thing up in her face with Spencer listening in."

"You two characters been seeing any psychiatrists lately?"

"Jesus," Ohls said, "hadn't you heard? We got them in our hair all the time these days. We've got two of them on the staff. This ain't police business any more. It's getting to be a branch of the medical racket. They're in and out of jail, the courts, the interrogation rooms. They write reports fifteen pages long on why some punk of a juvenile held up a liquor store or raped a schoolgirl or peddled tea to the senior class. Ten years from now guys like Hernandez and me will be doing Rohrschach tests and word associations instead of chin-ups and target practice. When we go out on a case we'll carry little black bags with portable lie detectors and bottles of truth serum. Too bad we didn't grab the four hard monkeys that poured it on Big Willie Magoon. We might have been able to unmaladjust them and make them love their mothers."

"Okay for me to blow?"

"What are you not convinced about?" Hernandez asked, snapping a rubber band.

"I'm convinced. The case is dead. She's dead, they're all dead. A nice smooth routine all around. Nothing to do but go home and forget it ever happened. So I'll do that."

Ohls reached the half cigarette from behind his ear, looked at it as if wondering how it got there, and tossed it over his shoulder.

"What are you crying about?" Hernandez said. "If she hadn't been fresh out of guns she might have made it a perfect score."

"Also," Ohls said grimly, "the telephone was working yesterday."

"Oh sure," I said. "You'd have come running and what you would have found would have been a mixed up story that admitted nothing but a few silly lies. This morning you have what I suppose is a full confession. You haven't let me read it, but you wouldn't have called in the D.A. if it was just a love note. If any real solid work had been done on the Lennox case at the time, somebody would have dug up his war record and where he got wounded and all the rest of it. Somewhere along the line a connection with the Wades would have turned up. Roger Wade knew who Paul Marston was. So did another P.I. I happened to get in touch with."

"It's possible," Hernandez admitted, "but that isn't how police investigations work. You don't fool around with an open-shut case, even if there's no heat on to get it finalized and forgotten. I've investigated hundreds of homicides. Some are all of a piece, neat, tidy, and according to the book. Most of them make sense here, don't make sense there. But when you get motive, means, opportunity, flight, a written confession, and a suicide immediately afterwards, you leave it lay. No police department in the world has the men or the time to question the obvious. The only thing against Lennox being a killer was that somebody thought he was a nice guy who wouldn't have done it and that there were others who could equally well have done it. But the others didn't take it on the lam, didn't confess, didn't blow their brains out. He did. And as for being a nice guy I figure sixty to seventy per cent of all the killers that end up in the gas chamber or the hot seat or on the end of a rope are people the neighbors thought were just as harmless as a Fuller Brush salesman. Just as harmless and quiet and well bred as Mrs. Roger Wade. You want to read what she wrote in that letter? Okay, read it. I've got to go down the hall."

He stood up and pulled a drawer open and put a folder on the top of the desk. "There are five photostats in here, Marlowe. Don't let me catch you looking at them."

He started for the door and then turned his head and said to Ohls: "You want to talk to Peshorek with me?"

Ohls nodded and followed him out. When I was alone in the office I lifted the cover of the file folder and looked at the white-on-black photostats. Then touching only the edges I counted them. There were six, each of several pages clipped together. I took one and rolled it up and slipped it into my pocket. Then I read over the next one in the pile. When I had finished I sat down and waited. In about ten minutes Hernandez came back alone. He sat down behind his desk again, tallied the photostats in the file folder, and put the file back in his desk.

He raised his eyes and looked at me without any expression. "Satisfied?"

"Lawford know you have those?"

"Not from me. Not from Bernie. Bernie made them himself. Why?"

"What would happen if one got loose?"

He smiled unpleasantly. "It won't. But if it did, it wouldn't be anybody in the Sheriff's office. The D.A. has photostat equipment too."

"You don't like District Attorney Springer too well, do you, Captain?"

He looked surprised. "Me? I like everybody, even you. Get the hell out of here. I've got work to do."

I stood up to go. He said suddenly: "You carry a gun these days?"

"Part of the time."

"Big Willie Magoon carried two. I wonder why he didn't use them."

"I guess he figured he had everybody scared."

"That could be it," Hernandez said casually. He picked up a rubber band and stretched it between his thumbs. He stretched it farther and farther. Finally with a snap it broke.

He rubbed his thumb where the loose end had snapped back against it. "Anybody can be stretched too far," he said. "No matter how tough he looks. See you around."

I went out of the door and got out of the building fast. Once a patsy, always a patsy.

# 45

Back in my dog house on the sixth floor of the Cahuenga Building I went through my regular double play with the morning mail. Mail slot to desk to wastebasket, Tinker to Evers to Chance. I blew a clear space on the top of the desk and unrolled the photostat on it. I had rolled it so as not to make creases.

I read it over again. It was detailed enough and reasonable enough to satisfy any open mind. Eileen Wade had killed Terry's wife in a fit of jealous fury and later when the opportunity was set up she had killed Roger because she was sure he knew. The gun fired into the ceiling of his room that night had been part of the setup. The unanswered and forever unanswerable question was why Roger Wade had stood still and let her put it over. He must have known how it would end. So he had written himself off and didn't care. Words were his business, he had words for almost everything, but none for this.

"I have forty-six demerol tablets left from my last prescription," she wrote. "I now intend to take them all and lie down on the bed. The door is locked. In a very short time I shall be beyond saving. This, Howard, is to be understood. What I write is in the presence of death. Every word is true. I have no regrets—except possibly that I could not have found them together and killed them together. I have no regrets for Paul whom you have heard called Terry Lennox. He was the empty shell of the man I loved and married. He meant nothing to me. When I saw him that afternoon for the only time after he came back from the war—at first I didn't know him. Then I did and he knew me at once. He should have died young in the snow of Norway, my lover that I gave to death. He came back a friend of gamblers, the husband of a rich whore, a spoiled and ruined man, and probably some kind of crook in his past life. Time makes everything mean and shabby and wrinkled. The tragedy of life, Howard, is not that the beautiful things die young, but that they grow old and mean. It will not happen to me. Goodbye, Howard."

I put the photostat in the desk and locked it up. It was time for lunch but I wasn't in the mood. I got the office bottle out of the deep drawer and poured a slug and then got the phone book off the hook at the desk and looked up the number of the *Journal*. I dialed it and asked the girl for Lonnie Morgan.

"Mr. Morgan doesn't come in until around four o'clock. You might try the press room at the City Hall."

I called that. And I got him. He remembered me well enough. "You've been a pretty busy guy, I heard."

"I've got something for you, if you want it. I don't think you want it."

"Yeah? Such as?"

"A photostat of a confession to two murders."

"Where are you?"

I told him. He wanted more information. I wouldn't give him any over the phone. He said he wasn't on a crime beat. I said he was still a newspaperman and on the only independent paper in the city. He still wanted to argue.

"Where did you get this whatever it is? How do I know it's worth my time?"

"The D.A.'s office has the original. They won't release it. It breaks open a couple of things they hid behind the icebox."

"I'll call you. I have to check with the brass."

We hung up. I went down to the drugstore and ate a chicken salad sandwich and drank some coffee. The coffee was overtrained and the sandwich was as full of rich flavor as a piece torn off an old shirt. Americans will eat anything if it is toasted and held together with a couple of toothpicks and has lettuce sticking out of the sides, preferably a little wilted.

At three-thirty or so Lonnie Morgan came in to see me. He was the same long thin wiry piece of tired and expressionless humanity as he had been the night he drove me home from the jailhouse. He shook hands listlessly and rooted in a crumpled pack of cigarettes.

"Mr. Sherman—that's the M.E.—said I could look you up and see what you have."

"It's off the record unless you agree to my terms." I unlocked the desk and handed him the photostat. He read the four pages rapidly and then again more slowly. He looked very excited—about as excited as a mortician at a cheap funeral.

"Gimme the phone."

I pushed it across the desk. He dialed, waited, and said: "This is Morgan. Let me talk to Mr. Sherman." He waited and got some other female and then got his party and asked him to ring back on another line.

He hung up and sat holding the telephone in his lap with the forefinger pressing the button down. It rang again and he lifted the receiver to his ear.

"Here it is, Mr. Sherman."

He read slowly and distinctly. At the end there was a pause. Then, "One moment, sir." He lowered the phone and glanced across the desk. "He wants to know how you got hold of this."

I reached across the desk and took the photostat away from him. "Tell him it's none of his goddam business how I got hold of it. Where is something else. The stamp on the back of the pages show that."

"Mr. Sherman, it's apparently an official document of the Los Angeles Sheriff's office. I guess we could check its authenticity easy enough. Also there's a price."

He listened some more and then said: "Yes, sir. Right here." He pushed the phone across the desk. "Wants to talk to you."

It was a brusque authoritative voice. "Mr. Marlowe, what are your terms? And remember the *Journal* is the only paper in Los Angeles which would even consider touching this matter."

"You didn't do much on the Lennox case, Mr. Sherman."

"I realize that. But at that time it was purely a question of scandal for scandal's sake. There was no question of who was guilty. What we have now, if your document is genuine, is something quite different. What are your terms?"

"You print the confession in full in the form of a photographic reproduction. Or you don't print it at all."

"It will be verified. You understand that?"

"I don't see how, Mr. Sherman. If you ask the D.A. he will either deny it or give it to every paper in town. He'd have to. If you ask the Sheriff's office they will put it up to the D.A."

"Don't worry about that, Mr. Marlowe. We have ways. How about your terms?"

"I just told you."

"Oh. You don't expect to be paid?"

"Not with money."

"Well, you know your own business, I suppose. May I have Morgan again?"

I gave the phone back to Lonnie Morgan.

He spoke briefly and hung up. "He agrees," he said. "I take that photostat and he checks it. He'll do what you say. Reduced to half size it will take about half of page 1A."

I gave him back the photostat. He held it and pulled at the tip of his long nose. "Mind my saying I think you're a damn fool?"

"I agree with you."

"You can still change your mind."

"Nope. Remember that night you drove me home from the City Bastille? You said I had a friend to say goodbye to. I've never really said goodbye to him. If you publish this photostat, that will be it. It's been a long time—a long, long time."

"Okay, chum." He grinned crookedly. "But I still think you're a damn fool. Do I have to tell you why?"

"Tell me anyway."

"I know more about you than you think. That's the frustrating part of newspaper work. You always know so many things you can't use. You get cynical. If this confession is printed in the *Journal*, a lot of people will be sore. The D.A., the coroner, the Sheriff's crowd, an influential and powerful private citizen named Potter, and a couple of toughies called

Menendez and Starr. You'll probably end up in the hospital or in jail again."

"I don't think so."

"Think what you like, pal. I'm telling you what *I* think. The D.A. will be sore because he dropped a blanket on the Lennox case. Even if the suicide and confession of Lennox made him look justified, a lot of people will want to know how Lennox, an innocent man, came to make a confession, how he got dead, did he really commit suicide or was he helped, why was there no investigation into the circumstances, and how come the whole thing died so fast. Also, if he has the original of this photostat he will think he has been double-crossed by the Sheriff's people."

"You don't have to print the identifying stamp on the back."

"We won't. We're pals with the Sheriff. We think he's a straight guy. We don't blame him because he can't stop guys like Menendez. Nobody can stop gambling as long as it's legal in all forms in some places and legal in some forms in all places. You stole this from the Sheriff's office. I don't know how you got away with it. Want to tell me?"

"No."

"Okay. The coroner will be sore because he buggered up the Wade suicide. The D.A. helped him with that too. Harlan Potter will be sore because something is reopened that he used a lot of power to close up. Menendez and Starr will be sore for reasons I'm not sure of, but I know you got warned off. And when those boys get sore at somebody he gets hurt. You're apt to get the treatment Big Willie Magoon got."

"Magoon was probably getting too heavy for his job."

"Why?" Morgan drawled. "Because those boys have to make it stick. If they take the trouble to tell you to lay off, you lay off. If you don't and they let you get away with it they look weak. The hard boys that run the business, the big wheels, the board of directors, don't have any use for weak people. They're dangerous. And then there's Chris Mady."

"He just about runs Nevada, I heard."

"You heard right, chum. Mady is a nice guy but he knows what's right for Nevada. The rich hoodlums that operate in

Reno and Vegas are very careful not to annoy Mr. Mady. If they did, their taxes would go up fast and their police co-operation would go down the same way. Then the top guys back East would decide some changes were necessary. An operator who can't get along with Chris Mady ain't operating correctly. Get him the hell out of there and put somebody else in. Getting him out of there means only one thing to them. Out in a wooden box."

"They never heard of me," I said.

Morgan frowned and whipped an arm up and down in a meaningless gesture. "They don't have to. Mady's estate on the Nevada side of Tahoe is right next to Harlan Potter's estate. Could be they say hello once in a while. Could be some character that is on Mady's payroll hears from another guy on Potter's payroll that a punk named Marlowe is buzzing too loud about things that are not any of his business. Could be that this passing remark gets passed on down to where the phone rings in some apartment in L.A. and a guy with large muscles gets a hint to go out and exercise himself and two or three of his friends. If somebody wants you knocked off or smashed, the muscle men don't have to have it explained why. It's mere routine to them. No hard feelings at all. Just sit still while we break your arm. You want this back?"

He held out the photostat.

"You know what I want," I said.

Morgan stood up slowly and put the photostat in his inside pocket. "I could be wrong," he said. "You may know more about it than I do. I wouldn't know how a man like Harlan Potter looks at things."

"With a scowl," I said. "I've met him. But he wouldn't operate with a goon squad. He couldn't reconcile it with his opinion of how he wants to live."

"For my money," Morgan said sharply, "stopping a murder investigation with a phone call and stopping it by knocking off the witnesses is just a question of method. And both methods stink in the nostrils of civilization. See you around —I hope."

He drifted out of the office like something blown by the wind.

# 46

I drove out to Victor's with the idea of drinking a gimlet and sitting around until the evening edition of the morning papers was on the street. But the bar was crowded and it wasn't any fun. When the barkeep I knew got around to me he called me by name.

"You like a dash of bitters in it, don't you?"

"Not usually. Just for tonight two dashes of bitters."

"I haven't seen your friend lately. The one with the green ice."

"Neither have I."

He went away and came back with the drink. I pecked at it to make it last, because I didn't feel like getting a glow on. Either I would get really stiff or stay sober. After a while I had another of the same. It was just past six when the kid with the papers came into the bar. One of the barkeeps yelled at him to beat it, but he managed one quick round of the customers before a waiter got hold of him and threw him out. I was one of the customers. I opened up the *Journal* and glanced at page 1A. They had made it. It was all there. They had reversed the photostat by making it black on white and by reducing it in size they had fitted it into the top half of the page. There was a short brusque editorial on another page. There was a half column by Lonnie Morgan with a by-line, on still another page.

I finished my drink and left and went to another place to eat dinner and then drove home.

Lonnie Morgan's piece was a straightforward factual recapitulation of the facts and happenings involved in the Lennox case and the "suicide" of Roger Wade—the facts as they had been published. It added nothing, deduced nothing, imputed nothing. It was clear concise businesslike reporting. The editorial was something else. It asked questions—the kind a newspaper asks of public officials when they are caught with jam on their faces.

About nine-thirty the telephone rang and Bernie Ohls said he would drop by on his way home.

"Seen the *Journal*?" he asked coyly, and hung up without waiting for an answer.

When he got there he grunted about the steps and said he would drink a cup of coffee if I had one. I said I would make some. While I made it he wandered around the house and made himself very much at home.

"You live pretty lonely for a guy that could get himself disliked," he said. "What's over the hill in back?"

"Another street. Why?"

"Just asking. Your shrubbery needs pruning."

I carried some coffee into the living room and he parked himself and sipped it. He lit one of my cigarettes and puffed at it for a minute or two, then put it out. "Getting so I don't care for the stuff," he said. "Maybe it's the TV commercials. They make you hate everything they try to sell. God, they must think the public is a halfwit. Every time some jerk in a white coat with a stethoscope hanging around his neck holds up some toothpaste or a pack of cigarettes or a bottle of beer or a mouthwash or a jar of shampoo or a little box of something that makes a fat wrestler smell like mountain lilac I always make a note never to buy any. Hell, I wouldn't buy the product even if I liked it. You read the *Journal*, huh?"

"A friend of mine tipped me off. A reporter."

"You got friends?" he asked wonderingly. "Didn't tell you how they got hold of the material, did he?"

"No. And in this state he doesn't have to tell you."

"Springer is hopping mad. Lawford, the deputy D.A. that got the letter this morning, claims he took it straight to his boss, but it makes a guy wonder. What the *Journal* printed looks like a straight reproduction from the original."

I sipped coffee and said nothing.

"Serves him right," Ohls went on. "Springer ought to have handled it himself. Personally I don't figure it was Lawford that leaked. He's a politician too." He stared at me woodenly.

"What are you here for, Bernie? You don't like me. We used to be friends—as much as anybody can be friends with a tough cop. But it soured a little."

He leaned forward and smiled—a little wolfishly. "No cop likes it when a private citizen does police work behind his back. If you had connected up Wade and the Lennox frail for me the time Wade got dead I'd have made out. If you had connected up Mrs. Wade and this Terry Lennox I'd have had her in the palm of my hand—alive. If you had come clean from the start Wade might be still alive. Not to mention Lennox. You figure you're a pretty smart monkey, don't you?"

"What would you like me to say?"

"Nothing. It's too late. I told you a wise guy never fools anybody but himself. I told you straight and clear. So it didn't take. Right now it might be smart for you to leave town. Nobody likes you and a couple of guys that don't like people do something about it. I had the word from a stoolie."

"I'm not that important, Bernie. Let's stop snarling at each other. Until Wade was dead you didn't even enter the case. After that it didn't seem to matter to you and to the coroner or to the D.A. or to anybody. Maybe I did some things wrong. But the truth came out. You could have had her yesterday afternoon—with what?"

"With what you had to tell us about her."

"Me? With the police work I did behind your back?"

He stood up abruptly. His face was red. "Okay, wise guy. She'd have been alive. We could have booked her on suspicion. You *wanted* her dead, you punk, and you know it."

"I wanted her to take a good long quiet look at herself. What she did about it was her business. I wanted to clear an innocent man. I didn't give a good goddam how I did it and I don't now. I'll be around when you feel like doing something about me."

"The hard boys will take care of you, buster. I won't have to bother. You think you're not important enough to bother them. As a P.I. named Marlowe, check. You're not. As a guy who was told where to get off and blew a raspberry in their faces publicly in a newspaper, that's different. That hurts their pride."

"That's pitiful," I said. "Just thinking about it makes me bleed internally, to use your own expression."

He went across to the door and opened it. He stood looking down the redwood steps and at the trees on the hill across the way and up the slope at the end of the street.

"Nice and quiet here," he said. "Just quiet enough."

He went on down the steps and got into his car and left. Cops never say goodbye. They're always hoping to see you again in the line-up.

# 47

For a short time the next day things looked like getting lively. District Attorney Springer called an early press conference and delivered a statement. He was the big florid black-browed prematurely gray-haired type that always does so well in politics.

"I have read the document which purports to be a confession by the unfortunate and unhappy woman who recently took her life, a document which may or may not be genuine, but which, if genuine, is obviously the product of a disordered mind. I am willing to assume that the *Journal* published this document in good faith, in spite of its many absurdities and inconsistencies, and these I shall not bore you with enumerating. If Eileen Wade wrote these words, and my office in conjunction with the staff of my respected coadjutor, Sheriff Petersen, will soon determine whether or no she did, then I say to you that she did not write them with a clear head, nor with a steady hand. It is only a matter of weeks since the unfortunate lady found her husband wallowing in his own blood, spilled by his own hand. Imagine the shock, the despair, the utter loneliness which must have followed so sharp a disaster! And now she has joined him in the bitterness of death. Is anything to be gained by disturbing the ashes of the dead? Anything, my friends, beyond the sale of a few copies of a newspaper which is badly in need of circulation? Nothing, my friends, nothing. Let us leave it at that. Like Ophelia in that great dramatic masterpiece called *Hamlet*, by the immortal William Shakespeare, Eileen Wade wore her rue with a difference. My political enemies would like to make much of that difference, but my friends and fellow voters will not be deceived. They know that this office has long stood for wise and mature law enforcement, for justice tempered with mercy, for solid, stable, and conservative government. The *Journal* stands for I know not what, and for what it stands I do not much or greatly care. Let the enlightened public judge for itself."

The *Journal* printed this guff in its early edition (it was a round-the-clock newspaper) and Henry Sherman, the

Managing Editor, came right back at Springer with a signed comment.

Mr. District-Attorney Springer was in good form this morning. He is a fine figure of a man and he speaks with a rich baritone voice that is a pleasure to listen to. He did not bore us with any facts. Any time Mr. Springer cares to have the authenticity of the document in question proved to him, the *Journal* will be most happy to oblige. We do not expect Mr. Springer to take any action to reopen cases which have been officially closed with his sanction or under his direction, just as we do not expect Mr. Springer to stand on his head on the tower of the City Hall. As Mr. Springer so aptly phrases it, is anything to be gained by disturbing the ashes of the dead? Or, as the *Journal* would prefer to phrase it less elegantly, is anything to be gained by finding out who committed a murder when the murderee is already dead? Nothing, of course, but justice and truth.

On behalf of the late William Shakespeare, the *Journal* wishes to thank Mr. Springer for his favorable mention of *Hamlet*, and for his substantially, although not exactly, correct allusion to Ophelia. 'You must wear your rue with a difference' was not said of Ophelia but by her, and just what she meant has never been very clear to our less erudite minds. But let that pass. It sounds well and helps to confuse the issue. Perhaps we may be permitted to quote, also from that officially approved dramatic production known as *Hamlet*, a good thing that happened to be said by a bad man: "And where the offence is let the great axe fall."

Lonnie Morgan called me up about noon and asked me how I liked it. I told him I didn't think it would do Springer any harm.

"Only with the eggheads," Lonnie Morgan said, "and they already had his number. I meant what about you?"

"Nothing about me. I'm just sitting here waiting for a soft buck to rub itself against my cheek."

"That wasn't exactly what I meant."

"I'm still healthy. Quit trying to scare me. I got what I wanted. If Lennox was still alive he could walk right up to Springer and spit in his eye."

"You did it for him. And by this time Springer knows that. They got a hundred ways to frame a guy they don't like. I don't figure what made it worth your time. Lennox wasn't that much man."

"What's that got to do with it?"

He was silent for a moment. Then he said: "Sorry, Marlowe. Shut my big mouth. Good luck."

We hung up after the usual goodbyes.

About two in the afternoon Linda Loring called me. "No names, please," she said. "I've just flown in from that big lake up north. Somebody up there is boiling over something that was in the *Journal* last night. My almost ex-husband got it right between the eyes. The poor man was weeping when I left. He flew up to report."

"What do you mean, almost ex-husband?"

"Don't be stupid. For once Father approves. Paris is an excellent place to get a quiet divorce. So I shall soon be leaving to go there. And if you have any sense left you could do worse than spend a little of that fancy engraving you showed me going a long way off yourself."

"What's it got to do with me?"

"That's the second stupid question you've asked. You're not fooling anyone but yourself, Marlowe. Do you know how they shoot tigers?"

"How would I?"

"They tie a goat to a stake and then hide out in a blind. It's apt to be rough on the goat. I like you. I'm sure I don't know why, but I do. I hate the idea of your being the goat. You tried so hard to do the right thing—as you saw it."

"Nice of you," I said. "If I stick my neck out and it gets chopped, it's still my neck."

"Don't be a hero, you fool," she said sharply. "Just because someone we knew chose to be a fall guy, you don't have to imitate him."

"I'll buy you a drink if you're going to be around long enough."

"Buy me one in Paris. Paris is lovely in the fall."

"I'd like to do that too. I hear it was even better in the spring. Never having been there I wouldn't know."

"The way you're going you never will."

"Goodbye, Linda. I hope you find what you want."

"Goodbye," she said coldly. "I always find what I want. But when I find it, I don't want it any more."

She hung up. The rest of the day was a blank. I ate dinner

and left the Olds at an all night garage to have the brake
linings checked. I took a cab home. The street was as empty
as usual. In the wooden mailbox was a free soap coupon. I
went up the steps slowly. It was a soft night with a little haze
in the air. The trees on the hill hardly moved. No breeze. I
unlocked the door and pushed it part way open and then
stopped. The door was about ten inches open from the frame.
It was dark inside, there was no sound. But I had the feeling
that the room beyond was not empty. Perhaps a spring
squeaked faintly or I caught the gleam of a white jacket across
the room. Perhaps on a warm still night like this one the room
beyond the door was not warm enough, not still enough. Perhaps there was a drifting smell of man on the air. And perhaps
I was just on edge.

I stepped sideways off the porch on to the ground and
leaned down against the shrubbery. Nothing happened. No
light went on inside, there was no movement anywhere that I
heard. I had a gun in a belt holster on the left side, butt
forward, a short-barreled Police .38. I jerked it out and it got
me nowhere. The silence continued. I decided I was a damn
fool. I straightened up and lifted a foot to go back to the
front door, and then a car turned the corner and came fast up
the hill and stopped almost without sound at the foot of my
steps. It was a big black sedan with the lines of a Cadillac. It
could have been Linda Loring's car, except for two things.
Nobody opened a door and the windows on my side were all
shut tight. I waited and listened, crouched against the bush,
and there was nothing to listen to and nothing to wait for.
Just a dark car motionless at the foot of my redwood steps,
with the windows closed. If its motor was still running I
couldn't hear it. Then a big red spotlight clicked on and the
beam struck twenty feet beyond the corner of the house. And
then very slowly the big car backed until the spotlight could
swing across the front of the house, across the hood and up.

Policemen don't drive Cadillacs. Cadillacs with red spotlights belong to the big boys, mayors and police commissioners, perhaps District Attorneys. Perhaps hoodlums.

The spotlight traversed. I went down flat, but it found me
just the same. It held on me. Nothing else. Still the car door
didn't open, still the house was silent and without light.

Then a siren growled in low pitch just for a second or two and stopped. And then at last the house was full of lights and a man in a white dinner jacket came out to the head of the steps and looked sideways along the wall and the shrubbery.

"Come on in, cheapie," Menendez said with a chuckle. "You've got company."

I could have shot him with no trouble at all. Then he stepped back and it was too late—even if I could have done it. Then a window went down at the back of the car and I could hear the thud as it opened. Then a machine pistol went off and fired a short burst into the slope of the bank thirty feet away from me.

"Come on in, cheapie," Menendez said again from the doorway. "There just ain't anywhere else to go."

So I straightened up and went and the spotlight followed me accurately. I put the gun back in the holster on my belt. I stepped up onto the small redwood landing and went in through the door and stopped just inside. A man was sitting across the room with his legs crossed and a gun resting sideways on his thigh. He looked rangy and tough and his skin had that dried-out look of people who live in sun-bleached climates. He was wearing a dark brown gabardine-type windbreaker and the zipper was open almost to his waist. He was looking at me and neither his eyes nor the gun moved. He was as calm as an adobe wall in the moonlight.

# 48

I looked at him too long. There was a brief half-seen move at my side and a numbing pain in the point of my shoulder. My whole arm went dead to the fingertips. I turned and looked at a big mean-looking Mexican. He wasn't grinning, he was just watching me. The .45 in his brown hand dropped to his side. He had a mustache and his head bulged with oily black hair brushed up and back and over and down. There was a dirty sombrero on the back of his head and the leather chin strap hung loose in two strands down the front of a stitched shirt that smelled of sweat. There is nothing tougher than a tough Mexican, just as there is nothing gentler than a gentle Mexican, nothing more honest than an honest Mexican, and above all nothing sadder than a sad Mexican. This guy was one of the hard boys. They don't come any harder anywhere.

I rubbed my arm. It tingled a little but the ache was still there and the numbness. If I had tried to pull a gun I should probably have dropped it.

Menendez held his hand out towards the slugger. Without seeming to look he tossed the gun and Menendez caught it. He stood in front of me now and his face glistened. "Where would you like it, cheapie?" His black eyes danced.

I just looked at him. There is no answer to a question like that.

"I asked you a question, cheapie."

I wet my lips and asked one back. "What happened to Agostino? I thought he was your gun handler."

"Chick went soft," he said gently.

"He was always soft—like his boss."

The man in the chair flicked his eyes. He almost but not quite smiled. The tough boy who had paralyzed my arm neither moved nor spoke. I knew he was breathing. I could smell that.

"Somebody bump into your arm, cheapie?"

"I tripped over an enchilada."

Negligently, not quite looking at me even, he slashed me across the face with the gun barrel.

"Don't get gay with me, cheapie. You're out of time for all that. You got told and you got told nice. When I take the trouble to call around personally and tell a character to lay off—he lays off. Or else he lays down and don't get up."

I could feel a trickle of blood down my cheek. I could feel the full numbing ache of the blow in my cheekbone. It spread until my whole head ached. It hadn't been a hard blow, but the thing he used was hard. I could still talk and nobody tried to stop me.

"How come you do your own slugging, Mendy? I thought that was coolie labor for the sort of boys that beat up Big Willie Magoon."

"It's the personal touch," he said softly, "on account of I had personal reasons for telling you. The Magoon job was strictly business. He got to thinking he could push me around—me that bought his clothes and his cars and stocked his safe deposit box and paid off the trust deed on his house. These vice squad babies are all the same. I even paid school bills for his kid. You'd think the bastard would have some gratitude. So what does he do? He walks into my private office and slaps me around in front of the help."

"On account of why?" I asked him, in the vague hope of getting him mad at somebody else.

"On account of some lacquered chippie said we used loaded dice. Seems like the bim was one of his sleepy-time gals. I had her put out of the club—with every dime she brought in with her."

"Seems understandable," I said. "Magoon ought to know no professional gambler plays crooked games. He doesn't have to. But what have I done to you?"

He hit me again, thoughtfully. "You made me look bad. In my racket you don't tell a guy twice. Not even a hard number. He goes out and does it, or you ain't got control. You ain't got control, you ain't in business."

"I've got a hunch that there's a little more to it than that," I said. "Excuse me if I reach for a handkerchief."

The gun watched me while I got one out and touched the blood on my face.

"A two-bit peeper," Menendez said slowly, "figures he can make a monkey out of Mendy Menendez. He can get me laughed at. He can get me the big razzoo—me, Menendez. I ought to use a knife on you, cheapie. I ought to cut you into slices of raw meat."

"Lennox was your pal," I said, and watched his eyes. "He got dead. He got buried like a dog without even a name over the dirt where they put his body. And I had a little something to do with proving him innocent. So that makes you look bad, huh? He saved your life and he lost his, and that didn't mean a thing to you. All that means anything to you is playing the big shot. You didn't give a hoot in hell for anybody but yourself. You're not big, you're just loud."

His face froze and he swung his arm back to slug me a

third time and this time with the power behind it. His arm was still going back when I took a half step forward and kicked him in the pit of the stomach.

I didn't think, I didn't plan, I didn't figure my chances or whether I had any. I just got enough of his yap and I ached and bled and maybe I was just a little punch drunk by this time.

He jackknifed, gasping, and the gun fell out of his hand. He groped for it wildly making strained sounds deep in his throat. I put a knee into his face. He screeched.

The man in the chair laughed. That staggered me. Then he stood up and the gun in his hand came up with him.

"Don't kill him," he said mildly. "We want to use him for live bait."

Then there was movement in the shadows of the hall and Ohls came through the door, blank-eyed, expressionless and utterly calm. He looked down at Menendez. Menendez was kneeling with his head on the floor.

"Soft," Ohls said. "Soft as mush."

"He's not soft," I said. "He's hurt. Any man can be hurt. Was Big Willie Magoon soft?"

Ohls looked at me. The other man looked at me. The tough Mex at the door hadn't made a sound.

"Take that goddam cigarette out of your face," I snarled at Ohls. "Either smoke it or leave it alone. I'm sick of watching you. I'm sick of you, period. I'm sick of cops."

He looked surprised. Then he grinned.

"That was a plant, kiddo," he said cheerfully. "You hurt bad? Did the nasty mans hit your facey-wacey? Well for my money you had it coming and it was damn useful that you had." He looked down at Mendy. Mendy had his knees under him. He was climbing out of a well, a few inches at a time. He breathed gaspingly.

"What a talkative lad he is," Ohls said, "when he doesn't have three shysters with him to button his lip."

He jerked Menendez to his feet. Mendy's nose was bleeding. He fumbled the handkerchief out of his white dinner jacket and held it to his nose. He said no word.

"You got crossed up, sweetheart," Ohls told him carefully. "I ain't grieving a whole lot over Magoon. He had it coming.

But he was a cop and punks like you lay off cops—always and forever."

Menendez lowered the handkerchief and looked at Ohls. He looked at me. He looked at the man who had been sitting in the chair. He turned slowly and looked at the tough Mex by the door. They all looked at him. There was nothing in their faces. Then a knife shot into view from nowhere and Mendy lunged for Ohls. Ohls side-stepped and took him by the throat with one hand and chopped the knife out of his hand with ease, almost indifferently. Ohls spread his feet and straightened his back and bent his legs slightly and lifted Menendez clear off the floor with one hand holding his neck. He walked him across the floor and pinned him against the wall. He let him down, but didn't let go of his throat.

"Touch me with one finger and I'll kill you," Ohls said. "One finger." Then he dropped his hands.

Mendy smiled at him scornfully, looked at his handkerchief, and refolded it to hide the blood. He held it to his nose again. He looked down at the gun he had used to hit me. The man from the chair said loosely: "Not loaded, even if you could grab it."

"A cross," Mendy said to Ohls. "I heard you the first time."

"You ordered three muscles," Ohls said. "What you got was three deputies from Nevada. Somebody in Vegas don't like the way you forget to clear with them. The somebody wants to talk to you. You can go along with the deputies or you can go downtown with me and get hung on the back of the door by a pair of handcuffs. There's a couple of boys down there would like to see you close up."

"God help Nevada," Mendy said quietly, looking around again at the tough Mex by the door. Then he crossed himself quickly and walked out of the front door. The tough Mex followed him. Then the other one, the dried out desert type, picked up the gun and the knife and went out too. He shut the door. Ohls waited motionless. There was a sound of doors banging shut, then a car went off into the night.

"You sure those mugs were deputies?" I asked Ohls.

He turned as if surprised to see me there. "They had stars," he said shortly.

"Nice work, Bernie. Very nice. Think he'll get to Vegas alive, you coldhearted son of a bitch?"

I went to the bathroom and ran cold water and held a soaked towel against my throbbing cheek. I looked at myself in the glass. The cheek was puffed out of shape and bluish and there were jagged wounds on it from the force of the gun barrel hitting against the cheekbone. There was a discoloration under my left eye too. I wasn't going to be beautiful for a few days.

Then Ohls' reflection showed behind me in the mirror. He was rolling his damn unlighted cigarette along his lips, like a cat teasing a half-dead mouse, trying to get it to run away just once more.

"Next time don't try to outguess the cops," he said gruffly. "You think we let you steal that photostat just for laughs? We had a hunch Mendy would come gunning for you. We put it up to Starr cold. We told him we couldn't stop gambling in the county, but we could make it tough enough to cut way into the take. No mobster beats up a cop, not even a bad cop, and gets away with it in our territory. Starr convinced us he had nothing to do with it, that the outfit was sore about it and Menendez was going to get told. So when Mendy called for a squad of out-of-town hard boys to come and give you the treatment, Starr sent him three guys he knew, in one of his own cars, at his own expense. Starr is a police comissioner in Vegas."

I turned around and looked at Ohls. "The coyotes out in the desert will get fed tonight. Congratulations. Cop business is wonderful uplifting idealistic work, Bernie. The only thing wrong with cop business is the cops that are in it."

"Too bad for you, hero," he said with a sudden cold savagery. "I could hardly help laughing when you walked into your own parlor to take your beating. I got a rise out of that, kiddo. It was a dirty job and it had to be done dirty. To make these characters talk you got to give them a sense of power. You ain't hurt bad, but we had to let them hurt you some."

"So sorry," I said. "So very sorry you had to suffer like that."

He shoved his taut face at me. "I hate gamblers," he said in a rough voice. "I hate them the way I hate dope pushers.

They pander to a disease that is every bit as corrupting as dope. You think those palaces in Reno and Vegas are just for harmless fun? Nuts, they're there for the little guy, the something-for-nothing sucker, the lad that stops off with his pay envelope in his pocket and loses the week-end grocery money. The rich gambler loses forty grand and laughs it off and comes back for more. But the rich gambler don't make the big racket, pal. The big steal is in dimes and quarters and half dollars and once in a while a buck or even a five-spot. The big racket money comes in like water from the pipe in your bathroom, a steady stream that never stops flowing. Any time anybody wants to knock off a professional gambler, that's for me. I like it. And any time a state government takes money from gambling and calls it taxes, that government is helping to keep the mobs in business. The barber or the beauty parlor girl puts two bucks on the nose. That's for the Syndicate, that's what really makes the profits. The people want an honest police force, do they? What for? To protect the guys with courtesy cards? We got legal horse tracks in this state, we got them all year round. They operate honest and the state gets its cut, and for every dollar laid at the track there's fifty laid with the bookies. There's eight or nine races on a card and in half of them, the little ones nobody notices, the fix can be in any time somebody says so. There's only one way a jock can win a race, but there's twenty ways he can lose one, with a steward at every eighth pole watching, and not able to do a damn thing about it if the jock knows his stuff. That's legal gambling, pal, clean honest business, state approved. So it's right, is it? Not by my book, it ain't. Because it's gambling and it breeds gamblers and when you add it all up there's one kind of gambling—the wrong kind."

"Feel better?" I asked him, putting some white iodine on my wounds.

"I'm an old tired beat-up cop. All I feel is sore."

I turned around and stared at him. "You're a damn good cop, Bernie, but just the same you're all wet. In one way cops are all the same. They all blame the wrong things. If a guy loses his pay check at a crap table, stop gambling. If he gets drunk, stop liquor. If he kills somebody in a car crash, stop making automobiles. If he gets pinched with a girl in a hotel room, stop sexual intercourse. If he falls downstairs, stop building houses."

"Aw shut up!"

"Sure, shut me up. I'm just a private citizen. Get off it, Bernie. We don't have mobs and crime syndicates and goon squads because we have crooked politicians and their stooges in the City Hall and the legislatures. Crime isn't a disease, it's a symptom. Cops are like a doctor that gives you aspirin for a brain tumor, except that the cop would rather cure it with a blackjack. We're a big rough rich wild people and crime is the price we pay for it, and organized crime is the price we pay for organization. We'll have it with us a long time. Organized crime is just the dirty side of the sharp dollar."

"What's the clean side?"

"I never saw it. Maybe Harlan Potter could tell you. Let's have a drink."

"You looked pretty good walking in that door," Ohls said.

"You looked better when Mendy pulled the knife on you."

"Shake," he said, and put his hand out.

We had the drink and he left by the back door, which he had jimmied to get in, having dropped by the night before for scouting purposes. Back doors are a soft touch if they open out and are old enough for the wood to have dried and shrunk. You knock the pins out of the hinges and the rest is easy. Ohls showed me a dent in the frame when he left to go back over the hill to where he had left his car on the next street. He could have opened the front door almost as easily but that would have broken the lock. It would have showed up too much.

I watched him climb through the trees with the beam of a torch in front of him and disappear over the rise. I locked the door and mixed another mild drink and went back to the living room and sat down. I looked at my watch. It was still early. It only seemed a long time since I had come home.

I went to the phone and dialed the operator and gave her the Lorings' phone number. The butler asked who was calling, then went to see if Mrs. Loring was in. She was.

"I was the goat all right," I said, "but they caught the tiger alive. I'm bruised up a little."

"You must tell me about it sometime." She sounded about as far away as if she had got to Paris already.

"I could tell you over a drink—if you had time."

"Tonight? Oh, I'm packing my things to move out. I'm afraid that would be impossible."

"Yes, I can see that. Well, I just thought you might like to know. It was kind of you to warn me. It had nothing at all to do with your old man."

"Are you sure?"

"Positive."

"Oh. Just a minute." She was gone for a time, then she came back and sounded warmer. "Perhaps I could fit a drink in. Where?"

"Anywhere you say. I haven't a car tonight, but I can get a cab."

"Nonsense, I'll pick you up, but it will be an hour or longer. What is the address there?"

I told her and she hung up and I put the porch light on and then stood in the open door inhaling the night. It had got much cooler.

I went back in and tried to phone Lonnie Morgan but couldn't reach him. Then just for the hell of it I put a call in to the Terrapin Club at Las Vegas, Mr. Randy Starr. He probably wouldn't take it. But he did. He had a quiet, competent, man-of-affairs voice.

"Nice to hear from you, Marlowe. Any friend of Terry's is a friend of mine. What can I do for you?"

"Mendy is on his way."

"On his way where?"

"To Vegas, with the three goons you sent after him in a big black Caddy with a red spotlight and siren. Yours, I presume?"

He laughed. "In Vegas, as some newspaper guy said, we use Cadillacs for trailers. What's this all about?"

"Mendy staked out here in my house with a couple of hard boys. His idea was to beat me up—putting it low—for a piece in the paper he seemed to think was my fault."

"Was it your fault?"

"I don't own any newspapers, Mr. Starr."

"I don't own any hard boys in Cadillacs, Mr. Marlowe."

"They were deputies maybe."

"I couldn't say. Anything else?"

"He pistol-whipped me. I kicked him in the stomach and used my knee on his nose. He seemed dissatisfied. All the same I hope he gets to Vegas alive."

"I'm sure he will, if he started this way. I'm afraid I'll have to cut this conversation short now."

"Just a second, Starr. Were you in on that caper at Otatoclán—or did Mendy work it alone?"

"Come again?"

"Don't kid, Starr. Mendy wasn't sore at me for why he said—not to the point of staking out in my house and giving me the treatment he gave Big Willie Magoon. Not enough motive. He warned me to keep my nose clean and not to dig into the Lennox case. But I did, because it just happened to work out that way. So he did what I've just told you. So there was a better reason."

"I see," he said slowly and still mildly and quietly. "You think there was something not quite kosher about how Terry got dead? That he didn't shoot himself, for instance, but someone else did?"

"I think the details would help. He wrote a confession which was false. He wrote a letter to me which got mailed. A waiter or hop in the hotel was going to sneak it out and mail it for him. He was holed up in the hotel and couldn't get out. There was a big bill in the letter and the letter was finished just as a knock came at his door. I'd like to know who came into the room."

"Why?"

"If it had been a bellhop or a waiter, Terry would have added a line to the letter and said so. If it was a cop, the letter wouldn't have been mailed. So who was it—and why did Terry write that confession?"

"No idea, Marlowe. No idea at all."

"Sorry I bothered you, Mr. Starr."

"No bother, glad to hear from you. I'll ask Mendy if he has any ideas."

"Yeah—if you ever see him again—alive. If you don't—find out anyway. Or somebody else will."

"You?" His voice hardened now, but it was still quiet.

"No, Mr. Starr. Not me. Somebody that could blow you out of Vegas without taking a long breath. Believe me, Mr. Starr. Just believe me. This is strictly on the level."

"I'll see Mendy alive. Don't worry about that, Marlowe."

"I figured you knew all about that. Goodnight, Mr. Starr."

# 49

When the car stopped out front and the door opened I went out and stood at the top of the steps to call down. But the middle-aged colored driver was holding the door for her to get out. Then he followed her up the steps carrying a small overnight case. So I just waited.

She reached the top and turned to the driver: "Mr. Marlowe will drive me to my hotel, Amos. Thank you for everything. I'll call you in the morning."

"Yes, Mrs. Loring. May I ask Mr. Marlowe a question?"

"Certainly, Amos."

He put the overnight case down inside the door and she went in past me and left us.

" 'I grow old . . . I grow old . . . I shall wear the bottoms of my trousers rolled.' What does that mean, Mr. Marlowe?"

"Not a bloody thing. It just sounds good."

He smiled. "That is from the 'Love Song of J. Alfred Prufrock.' Here's another one. 'In the room the women come and go/Talking of Michael Angelo.' Does that suggest anything to you, sir?"

"Yeah—it suggests to me that the guy didn't know very much about women."

"My sentiments exactly, sir. Nonetheless I admire T. S. Eliot very much."

"Did you say 'nonetheless'?"

"Why, yes I did, Mr. Marlowe. Is that incorrect?"

"No, but don't say it in front of a millionaire. He might think you were giving him the hotfoot."

He smiled sadly. "I shouldn't dream of it. Have you had an accident, sir?"

"Nope. It was planned that way. Goodnight, Amos."

"Goodnight, sir."

He went back down the steps and I went back into the house. Linda Loring was standing in the middle of the living room looking around her.

"Amos is a graduate of Howard University," she said. "You don't live in a very safe place—for such an unsafe man, do you?"

"There aren't any safe places."

"Your poor face. Who did that to you?"

"Mendy Menendez."

"What did you do to him?"

"Nothing much. Kicked him a time or two. He walked into a trap. He's on his way to Nevada in the company of three or four tough Nevada deputies. Forget him."

She sat down on the davenport.

"What would you like to drink?" I asked. I got a cigarette box and held it out to her. She said she didn't want to smoke. She said anything would do to drink.

"I thought of champagne," I said. "I haven't any ice bucket, but it's cold. I've been saving it for years. Two bottles. Cordon Rouge. I guess it's good. I'm no judge."

"Saving it for what?" she asked.

"For you."

She smiled, but she was still staring at my face. "You're all cut." She reached her fingers up and touched my cheek lightly. "Saving it for me? That's not very likely. It's only a couple of months since we met."

"Then I was saving it until we met. I'll go get it." I picked up her overnight bag and started across the room with it.

"Just where are you going with that?" she asked sharply.

"It's an overnight bag, isn't it?"

"Put it down and come back here."

I did that. Her eyes were bright and at the same time they were sleepy.

"This is something new," she said slowly. "Something quite new."

"In what way?"

"You've never laid a finger on me. No passes, no suggestive remarks, no pawing, no nothing. I thought you were tough, sarcastic, mean, and cold."

"I guess I am—at times."

"Now I'm here and I suppose without preamble, after we have had a reasonable quantity of champagne you plan to grab me and throw me on the bed. Is that it?"

"Frankly," I said, "some such idea did stir at the back of my mind."

"I'm flattered, but suppose I don't want it that way? I like you. I like you very much. But it doesn't follow that I want to go to bed with you. Aren't you rather jumping at con- clusions—just because I happen to bring an overnight bag with me?"

"Could be I made an error," I said. I went and got her overnight bag and put it back by the front door. "I'll get the champagne."

"I didn't mean to hurt your feelings. Perhaps you would rather save the champagne for some more auspicious occa- sion."

"It's only two bottles," I said. "A really auspicious occasion would call for a dozen."

"Oh, I see," she said, suddenly angry. "I'm just to be a fill-in until someone more beautiful and attractive comes along. Thank you so very much. Now you've hurt my feel- ings, but I suppose it's something to know that I'm safe here. If you think a bottle of champagne will make a loose woman out of me, I can assure you that you are very much mistaken."

"I admitted the mistake already."

"The fact that I told you I was going to divorce my hus- band and that I had Amos drop me by here with an overnight bag doesn't make me as easy as all that," she said, still angry.

"Damn the overnight bag!" I growled. "The hell with the overnight bag! Mention it again and I'll throw the damn thing down the front steps. I asked you to have a drink. I'm going out to the kitchen to get the drink. That's all. I hadn't the least idea of getting you drunk. You don't want to go to bed with me. I understand perfectly. No reason why you should. But we can still have a glass or two of champagne, can't we? This doesn't have to be a wrangle about who is going to get seduced and when and where and on how much champagne."

"You don't have to lose your temper," she said, flushing.

"That's just another gambit," I snarled. "I know fifty of them and I hate them all. They're all phony and they all have a sort of leer at the edges."

She got up and came over close to me and ran the tips of her fingers gently over the cuts and swollen places on my face. "I'm sorry. I'm a tired and disappointed woman. Please be kind to me. I'm no bargain to anyone."

"You're not tired and you're no more disappointed than most people are. By all the rules you ought to be the same sort of shallow spoiled promiscuous brat your sister was. By some miracle you're not. You've got all the honesty and a large part of the guts in your family. You don't need anyone to be kind to you."

I turned and walked out of the room down the hall to the kitchen and got one of the bottles of champagne out of the icebox and popped the cork and filled a couple of shallow goblets quickly and drank one down. The sting of it brought tears to my eyes, but I emptied the glass. I filled it again. Then I put the whole works on a tray and carted it into the living room.

She wasn't there. The overnight bag wasn't there. I put the tray down and opened the front door. I hadn't heard any sound of its opening and she had no car. I hadn't heard any sound at all.

Then she spoke from behind me. "Idiot, did you think I was going to run away?"

I shut the door and turned. She had loosened her hair and she had tufted slippers on her bare feet and a silk robe the color of a sunset in a Japanese print. She came towards me slowly with a sort of unexpectedly shy smile. I held a glass out to her. She took it, took a couple of sips of the champagne, and handed it back.

"It's very nice," she said. Then very quietly and without a

trace of acting or affectation she came into my arms and pressed her mouth against mine and opened her lips and her teeth. The tip of her tongue touched mine. After a long time she pulled her head back but kept her arms around my neck. She was starry-eyed.

"I meant to all the time," she said. "I just had to be difficult. I don't know why. Just nerves perhaps. I'm not really a loose woman at all. Is that a pity?"

"If I had thought you were I'd have made a pass at you the first time I met you in the bar at Victor's."

She shook her head slowly and smiled. "I don't think so. That's why I am here."

"Perhaps not that night," I said. "That night belonged to something else."

"Perhaps you don't ever make passes at women in bars."

"Not often. The light's too dim."

"But a lot of women go to bars just to have passes made at them."

"A lot of women get up in the morning with the same idea."

"But liquor is an aphrodisiac—up to a point."

"Doctors recommend it."

"Who said anything about doctors? I want my champagne."

I kissed her some more. It was light, pleasant work.

"I want to kiss your poor cheek," she said, and did. "It's burning hot," she said.

"The rest of me is freezing."

"It is not. I want my champagne."

"Why?"

"It'll get flat if we don't drink it. Besides I like the taste of it."

"All right."

"Do you love me very much? Or will you if I go to bed with you?"

"Possibly."

"You don't have to go to bed with me, you know. I don't absolutely insist on it."

"Thank you."

"I want my champagne."

"How much money have you got?"

"Altogether? How would I know? About eight million dollars."

"I've decided to go to bed with you."

"Mercenary," she said.

"I paid for the champagne."

"The hell with the champagne," she said.


# 50


An hour later she stretched out a bare arm and tickled my ear and said: "Would you consider marrying me?"

"It wouldn't last six months."

"Well, for God's sake," she said, "suppose it didn't. Wouldn't it be worth it? What do you expect from life—full coverage against all possible risks?"

"I'm forty-two years old. I'm spoiled by independence. You're spoiled a little—not too much—by money."

"I'm thirty-six. It's no disgrace to have money and no disgrace to marry it. Most of those who have it don't deserve it and don't know how to behave with it. But it won't be long. We'll have another war and at the end of that nobody will have any money—except the crooks and the chiselers. We'll all be taxed to nothing, the rest of us."

I stroked her hair and wound some of it around my finger. "You may be right."

"We could fly to Paris and have a wonderful time." She raised herself on an elbow and looked down at me. I could see the shine of her eyes but I couldn't read her expression. "Do you have something against marriage?"

"For two people in a hundred it's wonderful. The rest just work at it. After twenty years all the guy has left is a work bench in the garage. American girls are terrific. American wives take in too damn much territory. Besides—"

"I want some champagne."

"Besides," I said, "it would be just an incident to you. The first divorce is the only tough one. After that it's merely a problem in economics. No problem to you. Ten years from now you might pass me on the street and wonder where the hell you had seen me before. If you noticed me at all."

"You self-sufficient, self-satisfied, self-confident, untouchable bastard. I want some champagne."

"This way you will remember me."

"Conceited too. A mass of conceit. Slightly bruised at the moment. You think I'll remember you? No matter how many men I marry or sleep with, you think I'll remember you? Why should I?"

"Sorry. I overstated my case. I'll get you some champagne."

"Aren't we sweet and reasonable?" she said sarcastically. "I'm a rich woman, darling, and I shall be infinitely richer. I could buy you the world if it were worth buying. What have you now? An empty house to come home to, with not even a dog or cat, a small stuffy office to sit in and wait. Even if I divorced you I'd never let you go back to that."

"How would you stop me? I'm no Terry Lennox."

"Please. Don't let's talk about him. Nor about that golden icicle, the Wade woman. Nor about her poor drunken sunken husband. Do you want to be the only man who turned me down? What kind of pride is that? I've paid you the greatest compliment I know how to pay. I've asked you to marry me."

"You paid me a greater compliment."

She began to cry. "You fool, you utter fool!" Her cheeks were wet. I could feel the tears on them. "Suppose it lasted six months or a year or two years. What would you have lost except the dust on your office desk and the dirt on your venetian blinds and the loneliness of a pretty empty kind of life?"

"You still want some champagne?"

"All right."

I pulled her close and she cried against my shoulder. She wasn't in love with me and we both knew it. She wasn't crying over me. It was just time for her to shed a few tears.

Then she pulled away and I got out of bed and she went into the bathroom to fix her face. I got the champagne. When she came back she was smiling.

"I'm sorry I blubbered," she said. "In six months from now I won't even remember your name. Bring it into the living room. I want to see lights."

I did what she said. She sat on the davenport as before. I put the champagne in front of her. She looked at the glass but didn't touch it.

"I'll introduce myself," I said. "We'll have a drink together."

"Like tonight?"

"It won't ever be like tonight again."

She raised her glass of champagne, drank a little of it slowly, turned her body on the davenport and threw the rest in my face. Then she began to cry again. I got a handkerchief out and wiped my face off and wiped hers for her.

"I don't know why I did that," she said. "But for God's sake don't say I'm a woman and a woman never knows why she does anything."

I poured some more champagne into her glass and laughed at her. She drank it slowly and then turned the other way and fell across my knees.

"I'm tired," she said. "You'll have to carry me this time."

After a while she went to sleep.

In the morning she was still asleep when I got up and made coffee. I showered and shaved and dressed. She woke up then. We had breakfast together. I called a cab and carried her overnight case down the steps.

We said goodbye. I watched the cab out of sight. I went back up the steps and into the bedroom and pulled the bed to pieces and remade it. There was a long dark hair on one of the pillows. There was a lump of lead at the pit of my stomach.

The French have a phrase for it. The bastards have a phrase for everything and they are always right.

To say goodbye is to die a little.

## 51

Sewell Endicott said he was working late and I could drop around in the evening about seven-thirty.

He had a corner office with a blue carpet, a red mahogany desk with carved corners, very old and obviously very valuable, the usual glass-front bookshelves of mustard-yellow legal books, the usual cartoons by Spy of famous English judges, and a large portrait of Justice Oliver Wendell Holmes on the south wall, alone. Endicott's chair was quilted in black leather. Near him was an open rolltop desk jammed with papers. It was an office no decorator had had a chance to pansy up.

He was in his shirtsleeves and he looked tired, but he had that kind of face. He was smoking one of his tasteless cigarettes. Ashes from it had fallen on his loosened tie. His limp black hair was all over the place.

He stared at me silently after I sat down. Then he said: "You're a stubborn son of a bitch, if ever I met one. Don't tell me you're still digging into that mess."

"Something worries me a little. Would it be all right now if I assumed you were representing Mr. Harlan Potter when you came to see me in the birdcage?"

He nodded. I touched the side of my face gently with my fingertips. It was all healed up and the swelling was gone, but one of the blows must have damaged a nerve. Part of the cheek was still numb. I couldn't let it alone. It would get all right in time.

"And that when you went to Otatoclán you were temporarily deputized as a member of the D.A.'s staff?"

"Yes, but don't rub it in, Marlowe. It was a valuable connection. Perhaps I gave it too much weight."

"Still is, I hope."

He shook his head. "No. That's finished. Mr. Potter does his legal business through San Francisco, New York, and Washington firms."

"I guess he hates my guts—if he thinks about it."

Endicott smiled. "Curiously enough, he put all the blame on his son-in-law, Dr. Loring. A man like Harlan Potter has

to blame somebody. He couldn't possibly be wrong himself. He felt that if Loring hadn't been feeding the woman
dangerous drugs, none of it would have happened."

"He's wrong. You saw Terry Lennox's body in Otatoclán,
didn't you?"

"I did indeed. In the back of a cabinet maker's shop. They
have no proper mortuary there. He was making the coffin
too. The body was ice-cold. I saw the wound in the temple.
There's no question of identity, if you had any ideas along
those lines."

"No, Mr. Endicott, I didn't, because in his case it could
hardly be possible. He was disguised a little though, wasn't
he?"

"Face and hands darkened, hair dyed black. But the scars
were still obvious. And the fingerprints, of course, were easily
checked from things he had handled at home."

"What kind of police force do they have down there?"

"Primitive. The jefe could just about read and write. But he
knew about fingerprints. It was hot weather, you know. Quite
hot." He frowned and took his cigarette out of his mouth
and dropped it negligently into an enormous black basalt sort
of receptacle. "They had to get ice from the hotel," he added.
"Plenty of ice." He looked at me again. "No embalming
there. Things have to move fast."

"You speak Spanish, Mr. Endicott?"

"Only a few words. The hotel manager interpreted." He
smiled. "A well-dressed smoothie, that fellow. Looked tough,
but he was very polite and helpful. It was all over in no time."

"I had a letter from Terry. I guess Mr. Potter would know
about it. I told his daughter, Mrs. Loring. I showed it to her.
There was a portrait of Madison in it."

"A what?"

"Five-thousand-dollar bill."

He raised his eyebrows. "Really. Well, he could certainly
afford it. His wife gave him a cool quarter of a million the
second time they were married. I've an idea he meant to go
to Mexico to live anyhow—quite apart from what happened.
I don't know what happened to the money. I wasn't in on
that."

"Here's the letter, Mr. Endicott, if you care to read it."

I took it out and gave it to him. He read it carefully, the way lawyers read everything. He put it down on the desk and leaned back and stared at nothing.

"A little literary, isn't it?" he said quietly. "I wonder why he did it."

"Killed himself, confessed, or wrote me the letter?"

"Confessed and killed himself, of course," Endicott said sharply. "The letter is understandable. At least you got a reasonable recompense for what you did for him—and since."

"The mailbox bothers me," I said. "Where he says there was a mailbox on the street under his window and the hotel waiter was going to hold his letter up before he mailed it, so Terry could see that it was mailed."

Something in Endicott's eyes went to sleep. "Why?" he asked indifferently. He picked another of his filtered cigarettes out of a square box. I held my lighter across the desk for him.

"They wouldn't have one in a place like Otatoclán," I said.

"Go on."

"I didn't get it at first. Then I looked the place up. It's a mere village. Population say ten or twelve hundred. One street partly paved. The jefe has a Model A Ford as an official car. The post office is in the corner of a store, the chanceria, the butcher shop. One hotel, a couple of cantinas, no good roads, a small airfield. There's hunting around there in the mountains—lots of it. Hence the airfield. Only decent way to get there."

"Go on. I know about the hunting."

"So there's a mailbox on the street. Like there's a race course and a dog track and a golf course and a jai alai frontón and park with a colored fountain and a bandstand."

"Then he made a mistake," Endicott said coldly. "Perhaps it was something that looked like a mailbox to him—say a trash receptacle."

I stood up. I reached for the letter and refolded it and put it back in my pocket.

"A trash receptacle," I said. "Sure, that's it. Painted with the Mexican colors, green, white, red, and a sign on it stenciled in large clear print: KEEP OUR CITY CLEAN. In Spanish, of course. And lying around it seven mangy dogs."

"Don't get cute, Marlowe."

"Sorry if I let my brains show. Another small point I have already raised with Randy Starr. How come the letter got mailed at all? According to the letter the method was prearranged. So somebody told him about the mailbox. So somebody lied. So somebody mailed the letter with five grand in it just the same. Intriguing, don't you agree?"

He puffed smoke and watched it float away.

"What's your conclusion—and why ring Starr in on it?"

"Starr and a heel named Menendez, now removed from our midst, were pals of Terry's in the British Army. They are wrong gees in a way—I should say in almost every way—but they still have room for personal pride and so on. There was a cover-up here engineered for obvious reasons. There was another sort of cover-up in Otatoclán, for entirely different reasons."

"What's your conclusion?" he asked me again and much more sharply.

"What's yours?"

He didn't answer me. So I thanked him for his time and left.

He was frowning as I opened the door, but I thought it was an honest frown of puzzlement. Or maybe he was trying to remember how it looked outside the hotel and whether there was a mailbox there.

It was another wheel to start turning—no more. It turned for a solid month before anything came up.

Then on a certain Friday morning I found a stranger waiting for me in my office. He was a well-dressed Mexican or Suramericano of some sort. He sat by the open window smoking a brown cigarette that smelled strong. He was tall and very slender and very elegant, with a neat dark mustache and dark hair, rather longer than we wear it, and a fawn-colored suit of some loosely woven material. He wore those green sunglasses. He stood up politely.

"Señor Marlowe?"

"What can I do for you?"

He handed me a folded paper. "Un aviso de parte del Señor Starr en Las Vegas, señor. Habla Usted Español?"

"Yeah, but not fast. English would be better."

"English then," he said. "It is all the same to me."

I took the paper and read it. "This introduces Cisco Maioranos, a friend of mine. I think he can fix you up. S."

"Let's go inside, Señor Maioranos," I said.

I held the door open for him. He smelled of perfume as he went by. His eyebrows were awfully damned dainty too. But he probably wasn't as dainty as he looked because there were knife scars on both sides of his face.

# 52

He sat down in the customer's chair and crossed his knees. "You wish certain information about Señor Lennox, I am told."

"The last scene only."

"I was there at the time, señor. I had a position in the hotel." He shrugged. "Unimportant and of course temporary. I was the day clerk," He spoke perfect English but with a Spanish rhythm. Spanish—American Spanish that is—has a definite rise and fall which to an American ear seems to have nothing to do with the meaning. It's like the swell of the ocean.

"You don't look the type," I said.

"One has difficulties."

"Who mailed the letter to me?"

He held out a box of cigarettes. "Try one of these."

I shook my head. "Too strong for me. Colombian cigarettes I like. Cuban cigarettes are murder."

He smiled faintly, lit another pill himself, and blew smoke. The guy was so goddam elegant he was beginning to annoy me.

"I know about the letter, señor. The mozo was afraid to go up to the room of this Señor Lennox after the guarda was posted. The cop or dick, as you say. So I myself took the letter to the correo. After the shooting, you understand."

"You ought to have looked inside. It had a large piece of money in it."

"The letter was sealed," he said coldly. "El honor no se mueve de lado como los congrejos. That is, honor does not move sidewise like a crab, señor."

"My apologies. Please continue."

"Señor Lennox had a hundred-peso note in his left hand when I went into the room and shut the door in the face of the guarda. In his right hand was a pistol. On the table before him was the letter. Also another paper which I did not read. I refused the note."

"Too much money," I said, but he didn't react to the sarcasm.

"He insisted. So I took the note finally and gave it to the mozo later. I took the letter out under the napkin on the tray from the previous service of coffee. The dick looked hard at me. But he said nothing. I was halfway down the stairs when I heard the shot. Very quickly I hid the letter and ran back upstairs. The dick was trying to kick the door open. I used my key. Señor Lennox was dead."

He moved his fingertips gently along the edge of the desk and sighed. "The rest no doubt you know."

"Was the hotel full?"

"Not full, no. There were half a dozen guests."

"Americans?"

"Two Americanos del Norte. Hunters."

"Real Gringos or just transplanted Mexicans?"

He drew a fingertip slowly along the fawn-colored cloth above his knee. "I think one of them could well have been of Spanish origin. He spoke border Spanish. Very inelegant."

"They go near Lennox's room at all?"

He lifted his head sharply but the green cheaters didn't do a thing for me. "Why should they, señor?"

I nodded. "Well, it was damn nice of you to come in here and tell me about it, Señor Maioranos. Tell Randy I'm ever so grateful, will you?"

"No hay de que, señor. It is nothing."

"And later on, if he has time, he could send me somebody who knows what he is talking about."

"Señor?" His voice was soft, but icy. "You doubt my word?"

"You guys are always talking about honor. Honor is the

cloak of thieves—sometimes. Don't get mad. Sit quiet and let me tell it another way."

He leaned back superciliously.

"I'm only guessing, mind. I could be wrong. But I could be right too. These two Americanos were there for a purpose. They came in on a plane. They pretended to be hunters. One of them was named Menendez, a gambler. He registered under some other name or not. I wouldn't know. Lennox knew they were there. He knew why. He wrote me that letter because he had a guilty conscience. He had played me for a sucker and he was too nice a guy for that to rest easy on him. He put the bill—five thousand dollars it was—in the letter because he had a lot of money and he knew I hadn't. He also put in a little off-beat hint which might or might not register. He was the kind of guy who always wants to do the right thing but somehow winds up doing something else. You say you took the letter to the correo. Why didn't you mail it in the box in front of the hotel?"

"The box, señor?"

"The mailbox. The cajón cartero, you call it, I think."

He smiled. "Otatoclán is not Mexico City, señor. It is a very primitive place. A street mailbox in Otatoclán? No one there would understand what it was for. No one would collect letters from it."

I said: "Oh. Well, skip it. You did not take any coffee on any tray up to Señor Lennox's room, Señor Maioranos. You did not go into the room past the dick. But the two Americanos did go in. The dick was fixed, of course. So were several other people. One of the Americanos slugged Lennox from behind. Then he took the Mauser pistol and opened up one of the cartridges and took out the bullet and put the cartridge back in the breech. Then he put this gun to Lennox's temple and pulled the trigger. It made a nasty-looking wound, but it did not kill him. Then he was carried out on a stretcher covered up and well hidden. Then when the American lawyer arrived, Lennox was doped and packed in ice and kept in a dark corner of the carpintería where the man was making a coffin. The American lawyer saw Lennox there, he was ice-cold, in a deep stupor, and there was a bloody blackened wound in his temple. He looked plenty dead. The next day the coffin was buried with stones in it. The American lawyer went home with the fingerprints and some kind of document which was a piece of cheese. How do you like that, Señor Maioranos?"

He shrugged. "It would be possible, señor. It would require money and influence. It would be possible, perhaps, if this Señor Menendez was closely related to important people in Otatoclán, the alcalde, the hotel proprietor and so on."

"Well, that's possible too. It's a good idea. It would explain why they picked a remote little place like Otatoclán."

He smiled quickly. "Then Señor Lennox may still be alive, no?"

"Sure. The suicide had to be some kind of fake to back up the confession. It had to be good enough to fool a lawyer who had been a district attorney, but it would make a very sick monkey out of the current D.A. if it backfired. This Menendez is not as tough as he thinks he is, but he was tough enough to pistol-whip me for not keeping my nose clean. So he had to have reasons. If the fake got exposed, Menendez would be right in the middle of an international stink. The Mexicans don't like crooked police work any more than we do."

"All that is possible, señor, as I very well know. But you accused me of lying. You said I did not go into the room where Señor Lennox was and get his letter."

"You were already in there, chum—writing the letter."

He reached up and took the dark glasses off. Nobody can change the color of a man's eyes.

"I suppose it's a bit too early for a gimlet," he said.

# 53

They had done a wonderful job on him in Mexico City, but why not? Their doctors, technicians, hospitals, painters, architects are as good as ours. Sometimes a little better. A Mexican cop invented the paraffin test for powder nitrates. They couldn't make Terry's face perfect, but they had done plenty.

They had even changed his nose, taken out some bone and made it look flatter, less Nordic. They couldn't eliminate every trace of a scar, so they had put a couple on the other side of his face too. Knife scars are not uncommon in Latin countries.

"They even did a nerve graft up here," he said, and touched what had been the bad side of his face.

"How close did I come?"

"Close enough. A few details wrong, but they are not important. It was a quick deal and some of it was improvised and I didn't know myself just what was going to happen. I was told to do certain things and to leave a clear trail. Mendy didn't like my writing to you, but I held out for that. He undersold you a little. He never noticed the bit about the mailbox."

"You knew who killed Sylvia?"

He didn't answer me directly. "It's pretty tough to turn a woman in for murder—even if she never meant much to you."

"It's a tough world. Was Harlan Potter in on all this?"

He smiled again. "Would he be likely to let anyone know that? My guess is not. My guess is he thinks I am dead. Who would tell him otherwise—unless you did?"

"What I'd tell him you could fold into a blade of grass. How's Mendy these days—or is he?"

"He's doing all right. In Acapulco. He slipped by because of Randy. But the boys don't go for rough work on cops. Mendy's not as bad as you think. He has a heart."

"So has a snake."

"Well, what about that gimlet?"

I got up without answering him and went to the safe. I spun the knob and got out the envelope with the portrait of Madison on it and the five C notes that smelled of coffee. I dumped the lot out on the desk and then picked up the five C notes.

"These I keep. I spent almost all of it on expenses and research. The portrait of Madison I enjoyed playing with. It's all yours now."

I spread it on the edge of the desk in front of him. He looked at it but didn't touch it.

"It's yours to keep," he said. "I've got plenty. You could have let things lie."

"I know. After she killed her husband and got away with it she might have gone on to better things. He was of no real importance, of course. Just a human being with blood and a brain and emotions. He knew what happened too and he tried pretty hard to live with it. He wrote books. You may have heard of him."

"Look, I couldn't very well help what I did," he said slowly. "I didn't want anyone to get hurt. I wouldn't have had a dog's chance up here. A man can't figure every angle that quick. I was scared and I ran. What should I have done?"

"I don't know."

"She had a mad streak. She might have killed him anyway."

"Yeah, she might."

"Well, thaw out a little. Let's go have a drink somewhere where it's cool and quiet."

"No time right now, Señor Maioranos."

"We were pretty good friends once," he said unhappily.

"Were we? I forget. That was two other fellows, seems to me. You permanently in Mexico?"

"Oh yes. I'm not here legally even. I never was. I told you I was born in Salt Lake City. I was born in Montreal. I'll be a Mexican national pretty soon now. All it takes is a good law-yer. I've always liked Mexico. It wouldn't be much risk going to Victor's for that gimlet."

"Pick up your money, Señor Maioranos. It has too much blood on it."

"You're a poor man."

"How would you know?"

He picked the bill up and stretched it between his thin fingers and slipped it casually into an inside pocket. He bit his lip with the very white teeth you can have when you have a brown skin.

"I couldn't tell you any more than I did that morning you drove me to Tijuana. I gave you a chance to call the law and turn me in."

"I'm not sore at you. You're just that kind of guy. For a long time I couldn't figure you at all. You had nice ways and nice qualities, but there was something wrong. You had standards and you lived up to them, but they were personal. They had no relation to any kind of ethics or scruples. You were a nice guy because you had a nice nature. But you were just as happy with mugs or hoodlums as with honest men. Provided the hoodlums spoke fairly good English and had fairly acceptable table manners. You're a moral defeatist. I think maybe the war did it and again I think maybe you were born that way."

"I don't get it," he said. "I really don't. I'm trying to pay you back and you won't let me. I couldn't have told you any more than I did. You wouldn't have stood for it."

"That's as nice a thing as was ever said to me."

"I'm glad you like something about me. I got in a bad jam. I happened to know the sort of people who know how to deal with bad jams. They owed me for an incident that happened long ago in the war. Probably the only time in my life I ever did the right thing quick like a mouse. And when I needed them, they delivered. And for free. You're not the only guy in the world that has no price tag, Marlowe."

He leaned across the desk and snapped at one of my cigarettes. There was an uneven flush on his face under the deep tan. The scars showed up against it. I watched him spring a fancy gas cartridge lighter loose from a pocket and light the cigarette. I got a whiff of perfume from him.

"You bought a lot of me, Terry. For a smile and a nod and a wave of the hand and a few quiet drinks in a quiet bar here and there. It was nice while it lasted. So long, amigo. I won't say goodbye. I said it to you when it meant something. I said it when it was sad and lonely and final."

"I came back too late," he said. "These plastic jobs take time."

"You wouldn't have come at all if I hadn't smoked you out."

There was suddenly a glint of tears in his eyes. He put his dark glasses back on quickly.

"I wasn't sure about it," he said. "I hadn't made up my mind. They didn't want me to tell you anything. I just hadn't made up my mind."

"Don't worry about it, Terry. There's always somebody around to do it for you."

"I was in the Commandos, bud. They don't take you if you're just a piece of fluff. I got badly hurt and it wasn't any fun with those Nazi doctors. It did something to me."

"I know all that, Terry. You're a very sweet guy in a lot of ways. I'm not judging you. I never did. It's just that you're not here any more. You're long gone. You've got nice clothes and perfume and you're as elegant as a fifty-dollar whore."

"That's just an act," he said almost desperately.

"You get a kick out of it, don't you?"

His mouth dropped in a sour smile. He shrugged an expressive energetic Latin shrug.

"Of course. An act is all there is. There isn't anything else. In here—" he tapped his chest with the lighter—"there isn't anything. I've had it, Marlowe. I had it long ago. Well—I guess that winds things up."

He stood up. I stood up. He put out a lean hand. I shook it.

"So long, Señor Maioranos. Nice to have known you—however briefly."

"Goodbye."

He turned and walked across the floor and out. I watched the door close. I listened to his steps going away down the imitation marble corridor. After a while they got faint, then they got silent. I kept on listening anyway. What for? Did I want him to stop suddenly and turn and come back and talk me out of the way I felt? Well, he didn't. That was the last I saw of him.

I never saw any of them again—except the cops. No way has yet been invented to say goodbye to them.

PLAYBACK

*To Jean and Helga*

# I

THE VOICE on the telephone seemed to be sharp and pe-remptory, but I didn't hear too well what it said—partly because I was only half awake and partly because I was hold-ing the receiver upside down. I fumbled it around and grunted.

"Did you hear me? I said I was Clyde Umney, the lawyer."

"Clyde Umney, the lawyer. I thought we had several of them."

"You're Marlowe, aren't you?"

"Yeah. I guess so." I looked at my wrist watch. It was 6.30 A.M., not my best hour.

"Don't get fresh with me, young man."

"Sorry, Mr. Umney. But I'm not a young man. I'm old, tired and full of no coffee. What can I do for you, sir?"

"I want you to meet the Super Chief at eight o'clock, iden-tify a girl among the passengers, follow her until she checks in somewhere, and then report to me. Is that clear?"

"No."

"Why not?" he snapped.

"I don't know enough to be sure I could accept the case."

"I'm Clyde Um—"

"Don't," I interrupted. "I might get hysterical. Just tell me the basic facts. Perhaps another investigator would suit you better. I never was an FBI man."

"Oh. My secretary, Miss Vermilyea, will be at your office in half an hour. She will have the necessary information for you. She is very efficient. I hope you are."

"I'm more efficient when I've had breakfast. Have her come here, would you?"

"Where is here?"

I gave him the address of my place on Yucca Avenue, and told him how she would find it.

"Very well," he said grudgingly, "but I want one thing very clear. The girl is not to know she is being followed. This is very important. I am acting for a very influential firm of Washington attorneys. Miss Vermilyea will advance you some expense money and pay you a retainer of two hundred and fifty dollars. I expect a high degree of efficiency. And let's not waste time talking."

"I'll do the best I can, Mr. Umney."

He hung up. I struggled out of bed, showered, shaved and was nuzzling my third cup of coffee when the door bell rang.

"I'm Miss Vermilyea, Mr. Umney's secretary," she said in a rather chintzy voice.

"Please come in."

She was quite a doll. She wore a white belted raincoat, no hat, a well-cherished head of platinum hair, booties to match the raincoat, a folding plastic umbrella, a pair of blue-gray eyes that looked at me as if I had said a dirty word. I helped her off with her raincoat. She smelled very nice. She had a pair of legs—so far as I could determine—that were not painful to look at. She wore night sheer stockings. I stared at them rather intently, especially when she crossed her legs and held out a cigarette to be lighted.

"Christian Dior," she said, reading my rather open mind. "I never wear anything else. A light, please."

"You're wearing a lot more today," I said, snapping a lighter for her.

"I don't greatly care for passes this early in the morning."

"What time would suit you, Miss Vermilyea?"

She smiled rather acidly, inventoried her handbag and tossed me a manila envelope. "I think you'll find everything you need in this."

"Well—not quite everything."

"Get on with it, you goof. I've heard all about you. Why do you think Mr. Umney chose you? He didn't. I did. And stop looking at my legs."

I opened the envelope. It contained another sealed envelope and two checks made out to me. One, for $250, was marked "Retainer, as an advance against fees for professional services." The other was for $200 and was marked "Advance to Philip Marlowe for necessary expenses."

"You will account for the expenses to me, in exact detail," Miss Vermilyea said. "And buy your own drinks."

The other envelope I didn't open—not yet. "What makes Umney think I'll take a case I know nothing about?"

"You'll take it. You're not asked to do anything wrong. You have my word for that."

"What else do I have?"

"Oh, we might discuss that over a drink some rainy evening, when I'm not too busy."

"You've sold me."

I opened the other envelope. It contained a photograph of a girl. The pose suggested a natural ease, or a lot of experience in being photographed. It showed darkish hair which might possibly have been red, a wide clear forehead, serious eyes, high cheekbones, nervous nostrils and a mouth which was not giving anything away. It was a fine-drawn, almost a taut face, and not a happy one.

"Turn it over," Miss Vermilyea said.

On the back there was clearly typed material.

"Name: Eleanor King. Height five feet four inches. Age about 29. Hair dark reddish brown, thick, with a natural wave. Erect carriage, low distinct voice, well dressed but not overdressed. Conservative make-up. No visible scars. Characteristic mannerisms: habit of moving her eyes without moving her head when entering a room. Scratches palm of right hand when tense. Left-handed but adept in concealing it. Plays fast tennis, swims and dives beautifully, holds her liquor. No convictions, but prints on file."

"Been in the coop," I said, looking up at Miss Vermilyea.

"I have no information beyond what is there. Just follow your instructions."

"No name, Miss Vermilyea. At twenty-nine a dish like this would almost certainly have been married. There's no mention of a wedding ring or any other jewels. That makes me wonder."

She glanced at her watch. "Better do your wondering at the Union Station. You haven't much time." She stood up. I helped her on with her white raincoat and opened the door.

"You came in your own car?"

"Yes." She went halfway out and turned. "There's one thing I like about you. You don't paw. And you have nice manners—in a way."

"It's a rotten technique—to paw."

"And there's one thing I don't like about you. Guess what it is."

"Sorry. No idea—except that some people hate me for being alive."

"I didn't mean that."

I followed her down the steps and opened her car door for her. It was a cheap job, a Fleetwood Cadillac. She nodded briefly and slid down the hill.

I went back up and loaded a few things into an overnight bag, just in case.


## 2


There was nothing to it. The Super Chief was on time, as it almost always is, and the subject was as easy to spot as a kangaroo in a dinner jacket. She wasn't carrying anything but a paperback which she dumped in the first trash can she came to. She sat down and looked at the floor. An unhappy girl, if ever I saw one. After a while she got up and went to the book rack. She left it without picking anything out, glanced at the big clock on the wall and shut herself in a telephone booth. She talked to someone after putting a handful of silver into the slot. Her expression didn't change at all. She hung up and went to the magazine rack, picked up a *New Yorker*, looked at her watch again, and sat down to read.

She was wearing a midnight blue tailor-made suit with a white blouse showing at the neck and a big sapphire blue lapel pin which would probably have matched her earrings, if I could see her ears. Her hair was a dusky red. She looked like her photograph, but a little taller than I expected. Her dark blue ribbon hat had a short veil hanging from it. She was wearing gloves.

After a while she moved across the arches outside of which the taxis wait. She looked left at the coffee shop, turned and went into the main waiting room, glanced at the drugstore and newsstand, the information booth, and the people sitting on the clean wooden benches. Some of the ticket windows were open, some not. She wasn't interested in them. She sat down again and looked up at the big clock. She pulled off her right glove and set her wrist watch, a small plain platinum toy without jewels. Mentally I put Miss Vermilyea beside her. She didn't look soft or prissy or prudish, but she made the Vermilyea look like a pick-up.

She didn't stay long sitting down this time, either. She got up and strolled. She went out into the patio and came back and went into the drugstore and stayed some time at the paper-book rack. Two things were obvious. If anyone was going to meet her, the date hadn't been for train time. She looked like a girl waiting between trains. She went into the coffee shop. She sat down at one of the plastic top tables, read the menu, and then started to read her book. A waitress came with the inevitable glass of ice water, and the menu. The subject gave an order. The waitress went away, the subject went on reading her book. It was about nine-fifteen.

I went out through the arches to where a redcap was waiting by the taxi starter. "You work the Super Chief?" I asked him.

"Yeah. Part of it." He glanced without too deep interest at the buck I was teasing with my fingers.

"I was expecting someone on the Washington–San Diego through car. Anybody get off?"

"You mean get off permanent, baggage and all?"

I nodded.

He thought about it, studying me with intelligent chestnut eyes. "One passenger get off," he said at last. "What your friend look like?"

I described a man. Someone who looked something like Edward Arnold. The redcap shook his head.

"Can't help you, mister. What got off don't look like that at all. Your friend probably still on the train. They don't have to get off the through car. She gets hitched on to Seventy-Four. Leaves here eleven-thirty. The train ain't made up yet."

"Thanks," I said, and gave him the dollar. The subject's baggage was still on the train, which was all I wanted to know.

I went back to the coffee shop and looked in through the glass wall.

Subject was reading her paperback and toying with coffee and a snail. I moved over to a phone booth and called a

garage I knew well and asked them to send somebody for my
car if I didn't call again by noon. They'd done this often
enough to have a spare key on hand. I went out to the car
and got my overnight bag out of it and into a two-bit locker.
In the enormous waiting room, I bought a round trip to San
Diego and trotted back to the coffee shop once again.

Subject was in place, but no longer alone. A guy was across
the table from her smiling and talking, and one look was
enough to show that she knew him and regretted it. He
was California from the tips of his port wine loafers to the
buttoned and tieless brown and yellow checked shirt inside
his rough cream sports jacket. He was about six feet one,
slender, with a thin conceited face and too many teeth. He
was twisting a piece of paper in his hand.

The yellow handkerchief in his outside breast pocket
sprayed out like a small bunch of daffodils. And one thing was
as clear as distilled water. The girl didn't want him there.

He went on talking and twitching the paper. Finally he
shrugged and got up from his chair. He reached over and ran
a fingertip down her cheek. She jerked back. Then he opened
the twisted paper and laid it carefully down in front of her.
He waited, smiling.

Her eyes went down to it very, very slowly. Her eyes held
on it. Her hand moved to take it, but his was quicker. He put
it away in his pocket, still smiling. Then he took out one of
those pocket notebooks with perforated pages, and wrote
something with a clip pen and tore the sheet out and put that
down in front of her. That she could have. She took it, read
it, put it in her purse. At last she looked at him. And at last
she smiled at him. My guess was that it took quite an effort.
He reached across to pat her hand, then walked away from
the table and out.

He shut himself in a phone booth, dialed, and talked for
quite a while. He came out, found himself a redcap and went
with the redcap to a locker. Out came a light oyster-white
suitcase and a matching overnight case. The redcap carried
them through the doors to the parking lot and followed him
to a sleek two-toned Buick Roadmaster, the solid top convertible type that isn't convertible. The redcap put the stuff in
behind the tipped seat, took his money, went away. The guy

in the sports coat and yellow handkerchief got in and backed his car out and then stopped long enough to put on dark glasses and light a cigarette. After that he was gone. I wrote down the license number and went back into the station.

The next hour was three hours long. The girl left the coffee shop and read her book in the waiting room. Her mind wasn't on it. She kept turning back to see what she had read. Part of the time she didn't read at all, just held the book and looked at nothing. I had an early morning edition of the evening paper and behind it I watched her and added up what I had in my head. None of it was solid fact. It just helped to pass the time.

The guy who had sat at the table with her had come off the train, since he had baggage. It could have been her train and he could have been the passenger that got off her car. Her attitude made it pretty clear that she didn't want him around, and his that that was too bad but if she would glance at his piece of paper she would change her mind. And apparently she did. Since this happened after they got off the train when it could have happened more quietly before, then it followed that he didn't have his piece of paper on the train.

At this point the girl got up abruptly and went to the news-stand and came back with a pack of cigarettes. She tore it open and lit one. She smoked awkwardly as if she wasn't used to it, and while she smoked her attitude seemed to change, to become more flashy and hard, as if she was deliberately vul-garizing herself for some purpose. I looked at the wall clock: 10.47. I went on with my thinking.

The twist of paper had looked like a newspaper clipping. She had tried to grab it, he hadn't let her. Then he had writ-ten some words on a piece of blank paper and given them to her and she had looked at him and smiled. Conclusion: the dreamboat had something on her and she had to pretend to like it.

Next point was that earlier on he had left the station and gone somewhere, perhaps to get his car, perhaps to get the clipping, perhaps anything you like. That meant he wasn't afraid that she would run out on him, and that reinforced the idea that he hadn't at that time disclosed everything he was holding up his sleeve but had disclosed some of it. Could be he wasn't sure himself. Had to check. But now having shown her his hole card he had gone off in a Buick with his baggage. Therefore he was no longer afraid of losing her. Whatever held them together was strong enough to keep on holding them.

At 11.05 I tossed all this out of the window and started with a fresh premise. I got nowhere. At 11.10 the public address system said Number Seventy-Four on Track Eleven was now ready to receive passengers for Santa Ana, Oceanside, Del Mar and San Diego. A bunch of people left the waiting room, including the girl. Another bunch was already going through the gate. I watched her through and went back to the phone booths. I dropped my dime and dialed the number of Clyde Umney's office.

Miss Vermilyea answered by giving the phone number only.

"This is Marlowe. Mr. Umney in?"

Her voice was formal saying: "I'm sorry, Mr. Umney is in court. May I take a message?"

"Am in contact and leaving by train for San Diego, or some intermediate stop. Can't tell which yet."

"Thank you. Anything else?"

"Yeah, the sun's shining and our friend is no more on the lam than you are. She ate breakfast in the coffee shop which has a glass wall towards the concourse. She sat in the waiting room with a hundred and fifty other people. And she could have stayed on the train out of sight."

"I have all that, thank you. I'll get it to Mr. Umney as soon as possible. You have no firm opinion then?"

"I have one firm opinion. That you're holding out on me."

Her voice changed abruptly. Somebody must have left the office. "Listen, chum, you were hired to do a job. Better do it and do it right. Clyde Umney draws a lot of water in this town."

"Who wants water, beautiful? I take mine straight with a beer chaser. I might make sweeter music if I was encouraged."

"You'll get paid, shamus—if you do a job. Not otherwise. Is that clear?"

"That's the nicest thing you ever said to me, sweetheart. Goodbye now."

"Listen, Marlowe," she said with sudden urgency. "I didn't mean to be rough with you. This is very important to Clyde Umney. If he doesn't come through, he might lose a very valuable connection. I was just sounding off."

"I liked it, Vermilyea. It did things to my subconscious. I'll call in when I can."

I hung up, went through the gate, down the ramp, walked about from here to Ventura to get to Track Eleven and climbed aboard a coach that was already full of the drifting cigarette smoke that is so kind to your throat and nearly always leaves you with one good lung. I filled and lit a pipe and added to the general frowst.

The train pulled out, dawdled interminably through the yards and the back stretches of East L.A., picked up a little speed and made its first stop at Santa Ana. Subject did not get off. At Oceanside and Del Mar the same. At San Diego I hopped off quickly, chartered a cab, and then waited eight minutes outside the old Spanish station for the redcaps to come out with the baggage. Then the girl came out too.

She didn't take a cab. She crossed the street and rounded the corner to a U-Drive outfit and after a longish interval came out again looking disappointed. No driver's license, no U-Drive. You'd think she would have known that.

She took a cab this time and it did a U turn and started north. Mine did the same. I had a little difficulty with my driver about the tail job.

"That's something you read about in books, mister. We don't do it in Dago."

I passed him a fin and the $4 \times 2\frac{1}{2}$ photostat of my license. He looked them over, both of them. He looked off up the block.

"Okay, but I report it," he said. "The dispatcher may report it to the Police Business Office. That's the way it is here, chum."

"Sounds like the kind of city I ought to live in," I said. "And you've lost the tail. He turned left two blocks ahead."

The driver handed me back my wallet. "Lost my left eye," he said tersely. "What you think a two-way radiophone is for?" He picked it up and talked into it.

He turned left at Ash Street to Highway 101 and we

merged with the traffic and kept going at a peaceable forty. I stared at the back of his head.

"You don't have a worry in the world," the driver told me over his shoulder. "This five is on top of the fare, huh?"

"Right. And why don't I have a worry in the world?"

"The passenger's going to Esmeralda. That's twelve miles north of here on the ocean front. Destination, unless changed en route—and if it is I'll get told—a motel hotel joint called the Rancho Descansado. That's Spanish for relax, take it easy."

"Hell, I didn't need a cab at all," I said.

"You got to pay for the service, mister. We ain't buying groceries giving it away."

"You Mexican?"

"We don't call ourselves that, mister. We call ourselves Spanish-Americans. Born and raised in the USA. Some of us don't hardly speak Spanish any more."

*"Es gran lástima,"* I said. *"Una lengua muchísima hermosa."*

He turned his head and grinned. *"Tiene Vd. razón, amigo. Estoy muy bien de acuerdo."*

We went on to Torrance Beach, through there and swung out towards the point. From time to time the hackie talked into his radiophone. He turned his head enough to speak to me again.

"You want to keep out of sight?"

"What about the other driver? Will he tell his passenger she's being tailed?"

"He ain't been told hisself. That's why I asked you."

"Pass him and get there ahead, if you can. That's five more on the top."

"A cinch. He won't even see me. I can rib him later on over a bottle of Tecate."

We went through a small shopping center, then the road widened and the houses on one side looked expensive and not new, while the houses on the other side looked very new and still not cheap. The road narrowed again and we were in a 25 mile zone. My driver cut to the right, wound through some narrow streets, jumped a stop sign, and before I had had time to size up where we were going, we were sliding down into a canyon with the Pacific glinting off to the left beyond a wide shallow beach with two lifeguard stations on open metal towers. At the bottom of the canyon the driver started to turn in through the gates, but I stopped him. A large sign, gold script on a green background, said: *El Rancho Descansado*.

"Get out of sight," I said. "I want to make sure."

He swung back on the highway, drove fast down beyond the end of the stucco wall, then cut into a narrow winding road on the far side and stopped. A gnarled eucalyptus with a divided trunk hung over us. I got out of the cab, put dark glasses on, strolled down to the highway and leaned against a bright red jeep with the name of a service station painted on it. A cab came down the hill and turned into the Rancho Descansado. Three minutes passed. The cab came out empty and turned back up the hill. I went back to my driver.

"Cab No. 423," I said. "That check?"

"That's your pigeon. What now?"

"We wait. What's the layout over there?"

"Bungalows with car ports. Some single, some double. Office in a small one down front. Rates pretty steep in season. This is slack time around here. Half price probably and plenty of room."

"We wait five minutes. Then I check in, drop my suitcase, and look for a car to rent."

He said that was easy. In Esmeralda there were three places that rented cars, time and mileage, any make you wanted.

We waited the five minutes. It was now just past three o'clock. I was empty enough to steal the dog's dinner.

I paid my driver off, watched him leave, and went across the highway and into the office.

# 3

I leaned a polite elbow on the counter and looked across at the happy-faced young guy in the polka-dotted bow tie. I looked from him to the girl at the small PBX against the side wall. She was an outdoorsy type with shiny make-up and a horse tail of medium blond hair sticking out at the back of her noodle. But she had nice large soft eyes and when they looked at the clerk they glistened. I looked back at him and choked back a snarl. The girl at the PBX swung her horse tail in an arc and put the eye on me also.

"I'd be glad to show you what we have vacant, Mr. Marlowe," the young guy said politely. "You can register later, if you decide to stay here. About how long would you be likely to want accommodations?"

"Only as long as she does," I said. "The girl in the blue suit. She just registered. Using what name I wouldn't know."

He and the PBX girl stared at me. Both their faces had the same expression of distrust mixed with curiosity. There are a hundred ways of playing this scene. But this was a new one for me. In no city hotel in the world would it work. It might work here. Mostly because I didn't give a damn.

"You don't like that, do you?" I said.

He shook his head slightly. "At least you're frank about it."

"I'm tired of being cagey. I'm worn out with it. Did you notice her ring finger?"

"Why no, I didn't." He looked at the PBX girl. She shook her head and kept her eyes on my face.

"No wedding ring," I said. "Not any more. All gone. All broken up. All the years—ah, the hell with it. I've followed her all the way from—well, never mind where. She won't even speak to me. What am I doing here? Making a damn fool of myself." I turned away quickly and blew my nose. I had their attention. "I'd better go somewhere else," I said, turning back.

"You want to make it up and she won't," the PBX girl said quietly.

"Yes."

"I'm sympathetic," the young guy said. "But you know how it is, Mr. Marlowe. A hotel has to be very careful. These situations can lead to anything—even shootings."

"Shootings?" I looked at him with wonder. "Good God, what sort of people do that?"

He leaned both arms on the desk. "Just what would you like to do, Mr. Marlowe?"

"I'd like to be near her—in case she needs me. I wouldn't

speak to her. I wouldn't even knock at her door. But she would know I was there and she'd know why. I'd be waiting. I'll always be waiting."

The girl loved it now. I was up to my neck in the soft corn. I took a deep slow breath and shot for the grand prize. "And I don't somehow like the look of the guy who brought her here," I said.

"Nobody brought her here—except a cabdriver," the clerk said. But he knew what I meant all right.

The PBX girl half smiled. "He doesn't mean that, Jack. He means the reservation."

Jack said, "I kind of gathered as much, Lucille. I'm not so dumb." Suddenly he brought a card out from the desk and put it down in front of me. A registration card. Across the corner diagonally was written the name Larry Mitchell. In a very different writing in the proper places: (Miss) Betty Mayfield, West Chatham, New York. Then in the top left-hand corner in the same writing as Larry Mitchell a date, a time, a price, a number.

"You're very kind," I said. "So she's gone back to her maiden name. It's legal, of course."

"Any name is legal, if there's no intent to defraud. You would like to be next door to her?"

I widened my eyes. Maybe they glistened a little. Nobody ever tried harder to make them glisten.

"Look," I said, "it's damn nice of you. But you can't do it. I'm not going to make any trouble, but you can't be sure. It's your job if I pulled anything."

"Okay," he said. "I've got to learn some day. You look all right to me. Just don't tell anybody." He took the pen from its cup and held it out. I signed my name with an address on East Sixty-first Street, New York City.

Jack looked at it. "That's near Central Park, isn't it?" he asked idly.

"Three blocks and a bit," I said. "Between Lexington and Third Avenue."

He nodded. He knew where it was. I was in. He reached for a key.

"I'd like to leave my suitcase here," I said, "and go get something to eat and maybe rent a car, if I can. You could have it put in the room for me?"

Sure. He could do that for me easy. He took me outside and pointed up through a grove of saplings. The cottages were allover shingled, white with green roofs. They had porches with railings. He showed me mine through the trees. I thanked him. He started back in and I said, "Look, there's one thing. She may check out when she knows."

He smiled. "Of course. Nothing we can do about that, Mr. Marlowe. Lots of our guests only stay a night or two—except in summer. We don't expect to be filled up this time of year."

He went on into the office cottage and I heard the girl say to him: "He's kind of cute, Jack—but you shouldn't have done it."

I heard his answer too. "I hate that guy Mitchell—even if he is a pal of the owner."

# 4

The room was bearable. It had the usual concrete couch, chairs without cushions, a small desk against the front wall, a walk-in closet with a built-in chest, a bathroom with a Holly-wood bath and neon shaving lights beside the mirror over the basin, a small kitchenette with a refrigerator and a white stove, a three-burner electric. In a wall cupboard over the sink enough dishes and stuff. I got some ice cubes and made my-self a drink with the bottle from my suitcase, sipped it and sat in a chair listening, leaving the windows shut and the venetian blinds dark. I heard nothing next door, then I heard the toilet flush. Subject was in residence. I finished the drink, killed a cigarette and studied the wall heater on the party wall. It con-sisted of two long frosted bulbs in a metal box. It didn't look as if it would throw out much heat, but in the closet there was a plug-in fan heater with a thermostat and a three-way plug, which made it 220 volts. I slipped off the chromium grille guard of the wall heater and twisted out the frosted bulbs. I got a doctor's stethoscope out of my suitcase and held it against the metal backing and listened. If there was another similar heater back against it in the next room, and there almost certainly would be, all I had between the two rooms was a metal panel and some insulation, probably a bare minimum of that.

I heard nothing for a few minutes, then I heard a telephone being dialed. The reception was perfect. A woman's voice said: "Esmeralda 4-1499, please."

It was a cool contained voice, medium pitch, very little expression in it except that it sounded tired. It was the first time I had heard her voice in all the hours I had been following her.

There was a longish pause, then she said: "Mr. Larry Mitchell, please."

Another pause, but shorter. Then: "This is Betty Mayfield, at the Rancho Descansado." She pronounced the "a" in Descansado wrong. Then: "Betty Mayfield, I said. Please don't be stupid. Do you want me to spell it for you?"

The other end had things to say. She listened. After a while she said: "Apartment 12C. You ought to know. You made the reservation . . . Oh. I see . . . Well, all right. I'll be here."

She hung up. Silence. Complete silence. Then the voice in there said slowly and emptily: "Betty Mayfield, Betty Mayfield, Betty Mayfield. Poor Betty. You were a nice girl once—long ago."

I was sitting on the floor on one of the striped cushions with my back to the wall. I got up carefully, laid the stethoscope down on the cushion and went to lie on the day bed. After a while he would arrive. She was in there waiting for him, because she had to. She'd had to come there for the same reason. I wanted to know what it was.

He must have been wearing crepe soles because I didn't hear anything until the buzzer sounded next door. Also, he hadn't driven his car up to the cottage. I got down on the floor and went to work with the stethoscope.

She opened the door, he came in and I could imagine the smile on his face as he said: "Hello, Betty. Betty Mayfield is the name, I believe. I like it."

"It was my name originally." She closed the door.

He chuckled. "I suppose you were wise to change it. But how about the initials on your luggage?"

I didn't like his voice any better than his smile. It was high

and cheerful, almost bubbly with sly good humor. There was
not quite a sneer in it, but close enough. It made me clamp
my teeth.

"I suppose," she said dryly, "that was the first thing you
noticed."

"No, baby. *You* were the first thing I noticed. The mark of
a wedding ring but no wedding ring was the second. The
initials were only the third."

"Don't call me 'baby,' you cheap blackmailer," she said
with a sudden muted fury.

It didn't faze him in the least. "I may be a blackmailer,
honey, but—" another conceited chuckle—"I'm certainly
not cheap."

She walked, probably away from him. "Do you want a
drink? I see you have a bottle with you."

"It might make me lascivious."

"There's only one thing about you I'm afraid of, Mr.
Mitchell," the girl said coolly. "Your big loose mouth. You
talk too much and you like yourself too well. We'd better
understand each other. I like Esmeralda. I've been here before and I always wanted to come back. It's nothing but sheer
bad luck that you live here and that you were on the train that
was taking me here. It was the worst kind of luck that you
should have recognized me. But that's all it is—bad luck."

"Good luck for me, honey," he drawled.

"Perhaps," she said, "if you don't put too much pressure
on it. If you do, it's liable to blow up in your face."

There was a brief silence. I could see them in my imagination, staring at each other. His smile might be getting a little
nervous, but not much.

"All I've got to do," he said quietly, "is pick up the phone
and call the San Diego papers. You want publicity? I can
arrange it for you."

"I came here to get rid of it," she said bitterly.

He laughed. "Sure, by an old coot of a judge falling to
pieces with senile decay, and in the only state in the Union—
and I've checked on that—where it could happen after the
jury said otherwise. You've changed your name twice. If your
story got printed out here—and it's a pretty good story,
honey—I guess you'd have to change your name again—

and start traveling a little more. Gets kind of tiresome, doesn't it?"

"That's why I'm here," she said. "That's why you're here. How much do you want? I realize it will only be a down payment."

"Have I said anything about money?"

"You will," she said. "And keep your voice down."

"The cottage is all yours, honey. I walked around it before I came in. Doors closed, windows shut, blinds drawn, car ports empty. I can check with the office, if you're nervous. I've got friends around here—people you need to know, people who can make life pleasant for you. Socially this is a tough town to break into. And it's a damn dull town if you're on the outside looking in."

"How did *you* get in, Mr. Mitchell?"

"My old man is a big shot in Toronto. We don't get on and he won't have me around home. But he's still my old man and he's still the real thing, even if he does pay me to stay away."

She didn't answer him. Her steps went away. I heard her in the kitchen making the usual sounds connected with getting ice out of a tray of cubes. The water ran, the steps came back.

"I'd like one myself," she said. "Perhaps I've been rude to you. I'm tired."

"Sure," he said equably. "You're tired." A pause. "Well, here's to when you're not tired. Say about seven-thirty this evening at The Glass Room. I'll pick you up. Nice place for dinner. Dancing. Quiet. Exclusive, if that means anything any more. Belongs to the Beach Club. They don't have a table unless they know you. I'm among friends there."

"Expensive?" she asked.

"A little. Oh yes—and that reminds me. Until my monthly check comes in, you could let me have a couple of dollars." He laughed. "I'm surprised at myself. I did mention money after all."

"A couple of dollars?"

"A couple of hundred would be better."

"Sixty dollars is all I have—until I can open an account or cash some traveler's checks."

"You can do that at the office, baby."

"So I can. Here's fifty. I don't want to spoil you, Mr. Mitchell."

"Call me Larry. Be human."

"Should I?" Her voice had changed. There was a hint of invitation in it. I could imagine the slow smile of pleasure on his face. Then I guessed from the silence that he had grabbed her and she had let him. Finally her voice was a little muffled, saying: "That's enough, Larry. Be nice now and run along. I'll be ready at seven-thirty."

"One more for the road."

In a moment the door opened and he said something I didn't catch. I got up and went to the window and took a careful look through the slats of the blind. A floodlight was turned on in one of the tall trees. Under it I saw him stroll off up the slope and disappear. I went back to the heater panel and for a while I heard nothing and wasn't sure what I was listening for. But I knew soon enough.

There was quick movement back and forth, the sound of drawers being pulled open, the snap of a lock, the bump of a lifted lid against something.

She was packing up to leave.

I screwed the long frosted bulbs back into the heater and replaced the grille and put the stethoscope back in my suit-case. The evening was getting chilly. I slipped my jacket on and stood in the middle of the floor. It was getting dark and no light on. I just stood there and thought it over. I could go to the phone and make a report and by that time she could be on her way in another cab to another train or plane to another destination. She could go anywhere she liked, but there would always be a dick to meet the train if it meant enough to the big important people back in Washington. There would always be a Larry Mitchell or a reporter with a good memory. There would always be the little oddness to be noticed and there would always be somebody to notice it. You can't run away from yourself.

I was doing a cheap sneaky job for people I didn't like, but — that's what you hire out for, chum. They pay the bills, you dig the dirt. Only this time I could taste it. She didn't look like a tramp and she didn't look like a crook. Which meant only that she could be both with more success than if she had.

# 5

I opened the door and went along to the next and pushed the little buzzer. Nothing moved inside. There was no sound of steps. Then came the click of a chain set in the groove and the door opened a couple of inches on light and emptiness. The voice said from behind the door: "Who is it?"

"Could I borrow a cup of sugar?"

"I haven't any sugar."

"Well how about a couple of dollars until my check comes in?"

More silence. Then the door opened to the limit of the chain and her face edged into the opening and shadowed eyes stared out at me. They were just pools in the dark. The flood-light set high in the tree glinted on them obliquely.

"Who are you?"

"I'm your next door neighbor. I was having a nap and voices woke me. The voices spoke words. I was intrigued."

"Go somewhere else and be intrigued."

"I could do that, Mrs. King—pardon me, Miss Mayfield—but I'm not sure you'd want me to."

She didn't move and her eyes didn't waver. I shook a cigarette out of a pack and tried to push up the top of my Zippo with my thumb and rotate the wheel. You should be able to do it one-handed. You can too, but it's an awkward process. I made it at last and got the cigarette going, yawned, and blew smoke out through my nose.

"What do you do for an encore?" she asked.

"To be strictly kosher I should call L.A. and tell the party who sent me. Maybe I could be talked out of it."

"God," she said fervently, "two of them in one afternoon. How lucky can a girl get?"

"I don't know," I said. "I don't know anything. I think I've been played for a sucker, but I'm not sure."

"Wait a minute." She shut the door in my face. She wasn't gone long. The chain came out of the groove inside and the door came open.

I went in slowly and she stepped back and away from me. "How much did you hear? And shut the door, please."

I shut it with my shoulder and leaned against it.

"The tag end of a rather nasty conversation. The walls here are as thin as a hoofer's wallet."

"You in show business?"

"Just the opposite of show business. I'm in the hide-and-seek business. My name is Philip Marlowe. You've seen me before."

"Have I?" She walked away from me in little cautious steps and went over by her open suitcase. She leaned against the arm of a chair. "Where?"

"Union Station in L.A. We waited between trains, you and I. I was interested in you. I was interested in what went on between you and Mr. Mitchell—that's his name, isn't it? I didn't hear anything and I didn't see much because I was outside the coffee shop."

"So what interested you, you great big lovable something or other?"

"I've just told you part of it. The other thing that interested me was how you changed after your talk with him. I watched you work at it. It was very deliberate. You made yourself over into just another flip hardboiled modern cutie. Why?"

"What was I before?"

"A nice quiet well-bred girl."

"That was the act," she said. "The other was my natural personality. Which goes with something else." She brought a small automatic up from her side.

I looked at it. "Oh guns," I said. "Don't scare me with guns. I've lived with them all my life. I teethed on an old Derringer, single-shot, the kind the riverboat gamblers used to carry. As I got older I graduated to a lightweight sporting rifle, then a .303 target rifle and so on. I once made a bull at nine hundred yards with open sights. In case you don't know, the whole target looks the size of a postage stamp at nine hundred yards."

"A fascinating career," she said.

"Guns never settle anything," I said. "They are just a fast curtain to a bad second act."

She smiled faintly and transferred the gun to her left hand. With her right she grabbed the edge of her blouse at the collar line and with a quick decisive motion tore it to the waist.

"Next," she said, "but there's no hurry about it, I turn the gun in my hand like this"—she put it back in her right hand, but held it by the barrel—"I slam myself on the cheekbone with the butt. I do a beautiful bruise."

"And after that," I said, "you get the gun into its proper position and release the safety catch and pull the trigger, just about the time I get through the lead column in the Sports Section."

"You wouldn't get halfway across the room."

I crossed my legs and leaned back and lifted the green glass ash tray from the table beside the chair and balanced it on my knee and held the cigarette I was smoking between the first and second fingers of my right hand.

"I wouldn't get any of the way across the room. I'd be sitting here like this, quite comfortable and relaxed."

"But slightly dead," she said. "I'm a good shot and it isn't nine hundred yards."

"Then you try to sell the cops your account of how I tried to attack you and you defended yourself."

She tossed the gun into her suitcase and laughed. It sounded like a genuine laugh with real amusement in it. "Sorry," she said. "You sitting there with your legs crossed and a hole in your head and me trying to explain how I shot you to defend my honor—the picture makes me a little lightheaded."

She dropped into a chair and leaned forward with her chin cupped in a hand, the elbow propped on her knee, her face taut and drained, her dark red hair framing it too luxuriantly, so that her face looked smaller than it should have.

"Just what are you doing to me, Mr. Marlowe? Or is it the other way around—what I can do for you in return for you not doing anything at all?"

"Who is Eleanor King? What was she in Washington, D.C.? Why did she change her name somewhere along the way and have the initials taken off her bag? Odds and ends like that are what you could tell me. You probably won't."

"Oh, I don't know. The porter took the initials off my things. I told him I had had a very unhappy marriage and was divorced and had been given the right to resume my unmarried name. Which is Elizabeth or Betty Mayfield. That could all be true, couldn't it?"

"Yeah. But it doesn't explain Mitchell."

She leaned back and relaxed. Her eyes stayed watchful. "Just an acquaintance I made along the way. He was on the train."

I nodded. "But he came down here in his own car. He made the reservation here for you. He's not liked by the people here, but apparently he is a friend of someone with a lot of influence."

"An acquaintance on a train or a ship sometimes develops very quickly," she said.

"So it seems. He even touched you for a loan. Very fast work. And I got the impression you didn't care for him too well."

"Well," she said, "so what? But as a matter of fact I'm crazy about him." She turned her hand over and looked down at it. "Who hired you, Mr. Marlowe, and for what?"

"A Los Angeles lawyer, acting on instructions from back east. I was to follow you and check you in somewhere. Which I did. But now you're getting ready to move out. I'm going to have to start over again."

"But with me knowing you're there," she said shrewdly. "So you'll have a much harder job of it. You're a private detective of some sort, I gather."

I said I was. I had killed my cigarette some time back. I put the ash tray back on the table and stood up.

"Harder for me, but there are lots of others, Miss Mayfield."

"Oh, I'm sure there are, and all such nice little men. Some of them are even fairly clean."

"The cops are not looking for you. They'd have had you easily. It was known about your train. I even got a photo of you and a description. But Mitchell can make you do just what he wants. Money isn't all he'll want."

I thought she flushed a little, but the light didn't strike her face directly. "Perhaps so," she said. "And perhaps I don't mind."

"You mind."

She stood up suddenly and came near me. "You're in a business that doesn't pay fortunes, aren't you?"

I nodded. We were very close now.

"Then what would it be worth to you to walk out of here and forget you ever saw me?"

"I'd walk out of here for free. As for the rest, I have to make a report."

"How much?" She said it as if she meant it. "I can afford a substantial retainer. That's what you call it, I've heard. A much nicer word than blackmail."

"It doesn't mean the same thing."

"It could. Believe me, it can mean just that—even with some lawyers and doctors. I happen to know."

"Tough break, huh?"

"Far from it, shamus. I'm the luckiest girl in the world. I'm alive."

"I'm on the other side. Don't give it away."

"Well, what do you know," she drawled. "A dick with scruples. Tell it to the seagulls, buster. On me it's just confetti. Run along now, Mr. PI Marlowe, and make that little old phone call you're so anxious about. I'm not restraining you."

She started for the door, but I caught her by the wrist and spun her around. The torn blouse didn't reveal any startling nakedness, merely some skin and part of a brassière. You'd see more on the beach, far more, but you wouldn't see it through a torn blouse.

I must have been leering a little, because she suddenly curled her fingers and tried to claw me.

"I'm no bitch in heat," she said between tight teeth. "Take your paws off me."

I got the other wrist and started to pull her closer. She tried to knee me in the groin, but she was already too close. Then she went limp and pulled her head back and closed her eyes. Her lips opened with a sardonic twist to them. It was a cool evening, maybe even cold down by the water. But it wasn't cold where I was.

After a while she said with a sighing voice that she had to dress for dinner.

I said, "Uh-huh."

After another pause she said it was a long time since a man had unhooked her brassière. We did a slow turn in the direction of one of the twin day beds. They had pink and silver covers on them. The little odd things you notice.

Her eyes were open and quizzical. I studied them one at a time because I was too close to see them together. They seemed well matched.

"Honey," she said softly, "you're awful sweet, but I just don't have the time."

I closed her mouth for her. It seems that a key slid into the door from the outside, but I wasn't paying too close attention. The lock clicked, the door opened, and Mr. Larry Mitchell walked in.

We broke apart. I turned and he looked at me droopy-eyed, six feet one and tough and wiry.

"I thought to check at the office," he said, almost absently. "Twelve B was rented this afternoon, very soon after this was occupied. I got faintly curious, because there are a lot of vacancies here at the moment. So I borrowed the other key. And who is this hunk of beef, baby?"

"She told you not to call her 'baby,' remember?"

If that meant anything to him, he didn't show it. He swung a knotted fist gently at his side.

The girl said: "He's a private eye named Marlowe. Somebody hired him to follow me."

"Did he have to follow you as close as all that? I seem to be intruding on a beautiful friendship."

She jerked away from me and grabbed the gun out of her suitcase. "What we've been talking is money," she told him.

"Always a mistake," Mitchell said. His color was high and his eyes too bright. "Especially in that position. You won't need the gun, honey."

He poked at me with a straight right, very fast and well sprung. I stepped inside it, fast, cool and clever. But the right wasn't his meal ticket. He was a lefty too. I ought to have noticed that at the Union Station in L.A. Trained observer, never miss a detail. I missed him with a right hook and he didn't miss with his left.

It snapped my head back. I went off balance just long enough for him to lunge sideways and lift the gun out of the girl's hand. It seemed to dance through the air and nestle in his left hand.

"Just relax," he said. "I know it sounds corny, but I could drill you and get away with it. I really could."

"Okay," I said thickly. "For fifty bucks a day I don't get shot. That costs seventy-five."

"Please turn around. It would amuse me to look at your wallet."

I lunged for him, gun and all. Only panic could have made him shoot and he was on his home field and nothing to panic about. But it may be that the girl wasn't so sure. Dimly at the extreme edge of vision I saw her reach for the whiskey bottle on the table.

I caught Mitchell on the side of the neck. His mouth yapped. He hit me somewhere, but it wasn't important. Mine was the better punch, but it didn't win the wrist watch, because at that moment an army mule kicked me square on the back of my brain. I went zooming out over a dark sea and exploded in a sheet of flame.

# 6

The first sensation was that if anybody spoke harshly to me I should burst out crying. The second, that the room was too small for my head. The front of the head was a long way from the back, the sides were an enormous distance apart, in spite of which a dull throbbing beat from temple to temple. Distance means nothing nowadays.

The third sensation was that somewhere not far off an insistent whining noise went on. The fourth and last was that ice water was running down my back. The cover of a day bed proved that I had been lying on my face, if I still had one. I rolled over gently and sat up and a rattling noise ended in a thump. What rattled and thumped was a knotted towel full of melting ice cubes. Somebody who loved me very much had put them on the back of my head. Somebody who loved me less had bashed in the back of my skull. It could have been the same person. People have moods.

I got up on my feet and lunged for my hip. The wallet was

there in the left pocket, but the flap was unbuttoned. I went through it. Nothing was gone. It had yielded its information, but that was no secret any more. My suitcase stood open on the stand at the foot of the day bed. So I was home in my own quarters.

I reached a mirror and looked at the face. It seemed familiar. I went to the door and opened it. The whining noise was louder. Right in front of me was a fattish man leaning against the railing. He was a middle-sized fat man and the fat didn't look flabby. He wore glasses and large ears under a dull gray felt hat. The collar of his topcoat was turned up. His hands were in the pockets of his coat. The hair that showed at the sides of his head was battleship gray. He looked durable. Most fat men do. The light from the open door behind me bounced back from his glasses. He had a small pipe in his mouth, the kind they call a toy bulldog. I was still foggy but something about him bothered me.

"Nice evening," he said.

"You want something?"

"Looking for a man. You're not him."

"I'm alone in here."

"Right," he said. "Thanks." He turned his back on me and leaned his stomach against the railing of the porch.

I went along the porch to the whining noise. The door of 12C was wide open and the lights were on and the noise was a vacuum cleaner being operated by a woman in a green uniform.

I went in and looked the place over. The woman switched off the vacuum and stared at me. "Something you wanted?"

"Where's Miss Mayfield?"

She shook her head.

"The lady who had this apartment," I said.

"Oh, that one. She checked out. Half an hour ago." She switched the vacuum on again. "Better ask at the office," she yelled through the noise. "This apartment is on change."

I reached back and shut the door. I followed the black snake of the vacuum cord over to the wall and yanked the plug out. The woman in the green uniform stared at me angrily. I went over and handed her a dollar bill. She looked less angry.

"Just want to phone," I said.

"Ain't you got a phone in your room?"

"Stop thinking," I said. "A dollar's worth."

I went to the phone and lifted it. A girl's voice said: "Office. Your order, please."

"This is Marlowe. I'm very unhappy."

"What? . . . Oh yes, Mr. Marlowe. What can we do for you?"

"She's gone. I never even got to talk to her."

"Oh, I'm sorry, Mr. Marlowe," she sounded as if she meant it. "Yes, she left. We couldn't very well——"

"She say where to?"

"She just paid up and left, sir. Quite suddenly. No forwarding address at all."

"With Mitchell?"

"I'm sorry, sir. I didn't see anyone with her."

"You must have seen something. How did she leave?"

"In a taxi. I'm afraid——"

"All right. Thank you." I went back to my apartment.

The middle-sized fat man was sitting comfortably in a chair with his knees crossed.

"Nice of you to drop in," I said. "Anything in particular I could do for you?"

"You could tell me where Larry Mitchell is."

"Larry Mitchell?" I thought it over carefully. "Do I know him?"

He opened a wallet and extracted a card. He struggled to his feet and handed it to me. The card read: Goble and Green, Investigators, 310 Prudence Building, Kansas City, Missouri.

"Must be interesting work, Mr. Goble."

"Don't get funny with me, buster. I get annoyed rather easy."

"Fine. Let's watch you get annoyed. What do you do— bite your mustache?"

"I ain't got no mustache, stupid."

"You could grow one. I can wait."

He got up on his feet much more rapidly this time. He looked down at his fist. Suddenly a gun appeared in his hand. "You ever get pistol-whipped, stupid?"

"Breeze off. You bore me. Mudheads always bore me."

His hand shook and his face turned red. Then he put the gun back in the shoulder holster and wobbled towards the door. "You ain't through with me," he snarled over his shoulder.

I let him have that one. It wasn't worth topping.

# 7

After a while I went down to the office.

"Well, it didn't work," I said. "Does either one of you happen to have noticed the cabdriver who took her away?"

"Joe Harms," the girl said promptly. "You ought to maybe find him at the stand halfway up Grand. Or you could call the office. A pretty nice guy. He made a pass at me once."

"And missed by from here to Paso Robles," the clerk sneered.

"Oh, I don't know. You didn't seem to be there."

"Yeah," he sighed. "You work twenty hours a day trying to put enough together to buy a home. And by the time you have, fifteen other guys have been smooching your girl."

"Not this one," I said. "She's just teasing you. She glows every time she looks at you."

I went out and left them smiling at each other.

Like most small towns, Esmeralda had one main street from which in both directions its commercial establishments flowed gently for a short block or so and then with hardly a change of mood became streets with houses where people lived. But unlike most small California towns it had no false fronts, no cheesy billboards, no drive-in hamburger joints, no cigar counters or poolrooms, and no street corner toughs to hang around in front of them. The stores on Grand Street were either old and narrow but not tawdry or else well modernized with plate glass and stainless steel fronts and neon lighting in clear crisp colors. Not everybody in Esmeralda was prosperous, not everybody was happy, not everybody drove a Cadillac, a Jaguar or a Riley, but the percentage of obviously prosperous living was very high, and the stores that sold luxury goods were as neat and expensive-looking as those in Beverly Hills and far less flashy. There was another small difference too. In Esmeralda what was old was also clean and sometimes quaint. In other small towns what is old is just shabby.

I parked midway of the block and the telephone office was right in front of me. It was closed of course, but the entrance was set back and in the alcove which deliberately sacrificed money space to style were two dark green phone booths, like sentry boxes. Across the way was a pale buff taxi, parked diagonally to the curb in slots painted red. A gray-haired man sat in it reading the paper. I crossed to him.

"You Joe Harms?"

He shook his head. "He'll be back after a while. You want a cab?"

"No, thanks."

I walked away from him and looked in at a store window. There was a checked brown and beige sport shirt in the window which reminded me of Larry Mitchell. Walnut brogues, imported tweeds, ties, two or three, and matching shirts for them set out with plenty of room to breathe. Over the store the name of a man who was once a famous athlete. The name was in script, carved and painted in relief against a redwood background.

A telephone jangled and the cabdriver got out of the taxi and went across the sidewalk to answer it. He talked, hung up, got in his cab and backed out of the slot. When he was gone, the street was utterly empty for a minute. Then a couple of cars went by, then a good-looking well dressed colored boy and his prettied up cutie came strolling the block looking in at the windows and chattering. A Mexican in a green bellhop's uniform drove up in somebody's Chrysler New Yorker—it could be his for all I knew—went into the drugstore and came out with a carton of cigarettes. He drove back towards the hotel.

Another beige cab with the name Esmeralda Cab Company tooled around the corner and drifted into the red slot. A big bruiser with thick glasses got out and checked on the wall phone, then got back into his cab and pulled a magazine out from behind his rear-view mirror.

I strolled over to him and he was it. He was coatless and had his sleeves rolled up past the elbows, although this was no Bikini suit weather.

"Yeah. I'm Joe Harms." He stuck a pill in his kisser and lit it with a Ronson.

"Lucille down at the Rancho Descansado thought maybe you'd give me a little information." I leaned against his cab and gave him my big warm smile. I might as well have kicked the curbing.

"Information about what?"

"You picked up a fare this evening from one of their cottages. Number 12C. A tallish girl with reddish hair and a nice shape. Her name's Betty Mayfield but she probably didn't tell you that."

"Mostly they just tell me where they want to go. Quaint, isn't it?" He blew a lungful of smoke at his windshield and watched it flatten out and float around in the cab. "What's the pitch?"

"Girl friend walked out on me. We had a little argument. All my fault. I'd like to tell her I'm sorry."

"Girl friend got a home somewhere?"

"A long way from here."

He knocked ash from his cigarette by flicking his little finger at it still in his mouth.

"Could be she planned it that way. Could be she don't want you to know where she went. Could be you were lucky at that. They can drop the arm on you for shacking up in a hotel in this town. I'll admit it has to be pretty flagrant."

"Could be I'm a liar," I said, and got a business card out of my wallet. He read it and handed it back.

"Better," he said. "Some better. But it's against the company rules. I'm not driving this hack just to build muscle."

"A five interest you? Or is that against the rules too?"

"My old man owns the company. He'd be pretty sore if I was on the chisel. Not that I don't like money."

The phone on the wall jangled. He slid out of the cab and went over to it in about three long strides. I just stood planted, gnawing my lip. He talked and came back and stepped into the cab and was sitting behind the wheel all in one motion.

"Have to blow," he said. "Sorry. I'm kind of behind schedule. Just got back from Del Mar, the seven forty-seven to L.A. makes a flag stop there. Most people from here go that way."

He started his motor and leaned out of the cab to drop his cigarette in the street.

I said, "Thanks."

"For what?" He backed out and was gone.

I looked at my watch again. Time and distance checked. It was all of twelve miles to Del Mar. It would take almost an hour to ferry someone to Del Mar and drop him or her off at the railroad station and turn around and come back. He had told me in his own way. There was no point in telling me at all unless it meant something.

I watched him out of sight and then crossed the street to the booths outside the telephone company's office. I left the booth door open and dropped my dime and dialed the big O.

"I'd like to make a collect call to West Los Angeles, please." I gave her a Bradshaw number. "Person to person, Mr. Clyde Umney. My name is Marlowe and I'm calling from Esmeralda 4-2673, a pay phone."

She got him a lot quicker than it took me to tell her all that. He came on sharp and quick.

"Marlowe? It's about time you reported in. Well—let's have it."

"I'm in San Diego. I've lost her. She slipped away while I was taking a nap."

"I just knew I'd picked a smart cookie," he said unpleasantly.

"It's not as bad as it sounds, Mr. Umney. I have a rough idea where she went."

"Rough ideas are not good enough for me. When I hire a man I expect him to deliver exactly what I order. And just what do you mean by a rough idea?"

"Would it be possible for you to give me some notion of what this is all about, Mr. Umney? I grabbed it off kind of quick on account of meeting the train. Your secretary gave me a lot of personality but very little information. You want me to be happy in my work, don't you, Mr. Umney?"

"I gathered that Miss Vermilyea told you all there is to know," he grumbled. "I am acting at the request of an important law firm in Washington. Their client desires to remain anonymous for the present. All you have to do is trace this party to a stopping place, and by stopping place I do not mean a rest room or a hamburger stand. I mean a hotel, apartment house, or perhaps the home of someone she knows. That's all. How much simpler do you want it?"

"I'm not asking for simplicity, Mr. Umney. I'm asking for background material. Who the girl is, where she came from, what she's supposed to have done to make this job necessary."

"Necessary?" he yapped at me. "Who the hell are you to decide what is necessary? Find that girl, pin her down, and phone me her address. And if you expect to be paid, you better do it damn quick. I'll give you until ten o'clock tomorrow morning. After that I'll make other arrangements."

"Okay, Mr. Umney."

"Where are you exactly and what is your telephone number?"

"I'm just kind of wandering around. I got hit on the head with a whiskey bottle."

"Well, that's too bad," he said acidly. "I presume you had already emptied the bottle."

"Oh it might have been worse, Mr. Umney. It might have been *your* head. I'll call you around ten A.M. at your office. Don't worry about anybody losing anybody. There's two other guys working the same side of the street. One's a local boy named Mitchell and the other is a Kansas City shamus name of Goble. He carries a gun. Well good night, Mr. Umney."

"Hold it!" he roared. "Wait a minute! What does that mean—two other operatives?"

"You asking me what it means? I'm the guy that asked you. Looks like you only got a piece of the job."

"Hold it! Hold it right there!" There was a silence. Then in a steady voice that didn't bluster any more: "I'll call Washington the first thing in the morning, Marlowe. Excuse me if I sounded off. It begins to look as though I am entitled to a little more information about this project."

"Yeah."

"If you make contact again, call me here. At any hour. Any hour at all."

"Yeah."

"Good night, then." He hung up.

I put the phone back on the hook and took a deep breath. My head still ached but the dizziness was gone. I breathed in the cool night air laced with sea fog. I pushed out of the booth and looked across the street. The old guy who had been in the taxi slot when I arrived was back again. I strolled across and asked him how to get to The Glass Room, which was where Mitchell had promised to take Miss Betty Mayfield to dinner—whether she liked it or not. He told me, I thanked him, recrossed the empty street and climbed into my rented car, and started back the way I had come.

It was still possible that Miss Mayfield had grabbed the 7.47 for Los Angeles or some way station. It was a lot more likely that she had not. A cabdriver taking a fare to the station doesn't stick around to watch the fare get on the train. Larry Mitchell wouldn't be that easy to shake. If he had enough on her to make her come to Esmeralda, he had enough on her to keep her there. He knew who I was and what I was doing. He didn't know why, because I didn't know myself. If he had half a brain, and I gave him credit for a good deal more, he would have to assume I could trace her movements as far as a taxi took her. The first guess I was working on was that he would have driven to Del Mar, parked his big Buick somewhere in the shadows, and waited for her taxi to drive up and unload. When it turned around and started back, he would pick her up and drive her back to Esmeralda. The second guess I was working on was that she wouldn't tell him anything he didn't already know. I was a Los Angeles private eye, unknown parties had hired me to follow her, I had done so and then made the mistake of trying to get too close. That would bother him because it suggested he didn't have the field to himself. But if his information, whatever it was, came from a press clipping, he could hardly expect to have it to himself forever. Anybody with enough interest and enough patience could turn it up in time. Anybody with enough reason to hire a private dick probably knew it already. And that in turn meant that whatever kind of bite he planned to put on Betty Mayfield, financial or amatory or both, would have to be put on fast.

A third of a mile down the canyon a small illuminated sign

with an arrow pointing seaward said in script *The Glass Room*.
The road wound down between cliffside houses with warm
lights in the windows, manicured gardens, stucco walls
and one or two of fieldstone or brick inset with tiles in the
Mexican tradition.

I drove down the last curve of the last hill and the smell of
raw seaweed filled my nostrils and the fog-veiled lights of The
Glass Room swelled to amber brightness and the sound of
dance music drifted across the paved parking lot. I parked
with the sea growling out of sight almost at my feet. There
was no attendant. You just locked your car and went in.

A couple of dozen cars, no more. I looked them over.
One hunch at least had paid off. The Buick Roadmaster
solid top bore a license number I had in my pocket. It was
parked almost at the entrance and next to it in the very last
space near the entrance was a pale green and ivory Cadillac
convertible with oyster-white leather seats, a plaid traveling
rug thrown over the front seat to keep it dry, and all the
gadgets a dealer could think of, including two enormous
spotlights with mirrors on them, a radio aerial almost long
enough for a tuna boat, a folding chromium luggage rack to
help out the boot if you wanted to travel far and in style, a
sun visor, a prism reflector to pick up traffic lights obscured
by the visor, a radio with enough knobs on it for a control
panel, a cigarette lighter into which you dropped your cigarette and it smoked it for you, and various other trifles
which made me wonder how long it would be before they
installed radar, sound-recording equipment, a bar, and an
anti-aircraft battery.

All this I saw by the light of a clip-on flash. I moved it to
the license holder and the name was Clark Brandon, Hotel
Casa del Poniente, Esmeralda, California.

# 8

The entrance lobby was on a balcony which looked down
over the bar and a dining room on two levels. A curving car-

peted staircase led down to the bar. Nobody was upstairs but the hat-check girl and an elderly party in a phone booth whose expression suggested that nobody better fool with him.

I went down the stairs to the bar and tucked myself in a small curved space that commanded a view of the dance floor. One side of the building was an enormous glass window. Outside of it was nothing but fog, but on a clear night with a moon low over the water it would have been sensational. A three-piece Mexican band was making the kind of music a Mexican band always makes. Whatever they play, it all sounds the same. They always sing the same song, and it always has nice open vowels and a drawn out sugary lilt, and the guy who sings it always strums on a guitar and has a lot to say about *amor, mi corazón*, a lady who is "linda" but very hard to convince, and he always has too long and too oily hair and when he isn't making with the love stuff he looks as if his knife work in an alley would be efficient and economical.

On the dance floor half a dozen couples were throwing themselves around with the reckless abandon of a night watchman with arthritis. Most of them were dancing cheek to cheek, if dancing is the word. The men wore white tuxedos and the girls wore bright eyes, ruby lips, and tennis or golf muscles. One couple was not dancing cheek to cheek. The guy was too drunk to keep time and the girl was too busy not getting her pumps walked on to think of anything else. I needn't have worried about losing Miss Betty Mayfield. She was there and with Mitchell, but far from happy. Mitchell's mouth was open, he was grinning, his face was red and shiny, and his eyes had that glazed look. Betty was holding her head as far as she could get away from him without breaking her neck. It was very obvious that she had had about all of Mr. Larry Mitchell that she could take.

A Mexican waiter in a short green jacket and white pants with a green stripe down the side came up and I ordered a double Gibson and asked if I could have a club sandwich where I was. He said, *"Muy bien, señor,"* smiled brightly, and disappeared.

The music stopped, there was desultory clapping. The orchestra was deeply moved, and played another number. A dark-haired headwaiter who looked like a road company Herbert Marshall circulated among the tables offering his intimate smile and stopping here and there to polish an apple. Then he pulled out a chair and sat down opposite a big handsome Irish type character with gray in his hair and just enough of it. He seemed to be alone. He wore a dark dinner jacket with a maroon carnation in the lapel. He looked like a nice guy if you didn't crowd him. At that distance and in that light I couldn't tell much more, except that if you did crowd him, you had better be big, fast, tough and in top condition.

The headwaiter leaned forward and said something and they both looked towards Mitchell and the Mayfield girl. The captain seemed concerned, the big guy didn't seem to care much one way or another. The headwaiter got up and left. The big guy fitted a cigarette into a holder and a waiter popped a lighter at him as if he had been waiting all evening for the opportunity. The big guy thanked him without looking up.

My drink came and I grabbed it and drank. The music stopped and stayed stopped. The couples divided and strolled back to their tables. Larry Mitchell still had hold of Betty. He was still grinning. Then he began to pull her close. He put his hand behind her head. She tried to shake him off. He pulled harder and pushed his flushed face down on hers. She struggled but he was too strong for her. He chewed her face some more. She kicked him. He jerked his head up, annoyed.

"Let go of me, you drunken slob," she said breathlessly but very distinctly.

His face got a nasty look. He grabbed her arms hard enough to bruise her and slowly using his strength he pulled her tight against his body and held her there. People looked hard, but nobody moved.

"Whassa matta, baby, you no love poppa no more?" he inquired loudly and thickly.

I didn't see what she did to him with her knee but I could guess and it hurt him. He pushed her away and his face went savage. Then he hauled off and slapped her across the mouth forehand and backhand. The red showed on her skin at once.

She stood quite still. Then in a voice the whole joint could hear she said clearly and slowly: "Next time you do that, Mr. Mitchell—be sure to wear a bullet-proof vest."

She turned and walked away. He just stood there. His face had gone glistening white—whether from pain or rage I couldn't tell. The headwaiter walked softly up to him and murmured something with an inquiring lift of the eyebrow.

Mitchell brought his eyes down and looked at the man. Then without a word he walked right through him and the headwaiter had to stagger out of his way. Mitchell followed Betty, and on the way he bumped a man in a chair and didn't stop to apologize. Betty was sitting down now at a table against the glass wall right next to the big dark guy in the dinner jacket. He looked at her. He looked at Mitchell. He took his cigarette holder out of his mouth and looked at that. His face was quite expressionless.

Mitchell reached the table. "You hurt me, sweetness," he said thickly but loudly. "I'm a bad man to hurt. Catch on? Very bad. Want to apologize?"

She stood up, jerked a wrap off the back of the chair and faced him.

"Shall I pay the check, Mr. Mitchell—or will you pay it with what you borrowed from me?"

His hand went back for another swing at her face. She didn't move. The guy at the next table did. He came up on his feet in one smooth movement and grabbed Mitchell's wrist.

"Take it easy, Larry. You've got a skinful." His voice was cool, almost amused.

Mitchell jerked his wrist loose and spun around. "Stay out of this, Brandon."

"Delighted, old man. I'm not in it. But you'd better not slug the lady again. They don't often throw people out of here—but it could happen."

Mitchell laughed angrily. "Why don't you go spit in your hat, mister?"

The big man said softly, "Take it easy, Larry, I said. I won't say it again."

Mitchell glared at him. "Okay, see you later," he said in a sulky voice. He started off and stopped. "Much later," he added, half turning. Then he went out—unsteadily but quickly, looking at nothing.

Brandon just stood there. The girl just stood there. She looked uncertain about what to do next.

She looked at him. He looked at her. He smiled, just polite and easygoing, no come-on. She didn't smile back.

"Anything I could do?" he asked. "Drop you anywhere?" Then he half turned his head. "Oh, Carl."

The headwaiter came up to him quickly.

"No check," Brandon said. "You know, in the circumstances—"

"Please," the girl said sharply. "I don't want other people paying my bills."

He shook his head slowly. "Custom of the house," he said. "Nothing to do with me personally. But may I send you a drink?"

She looked at him some more. He had what it took all right. "Send?" she asked.

He smiled politely. "Well, bring then—if you care to sit down."

And this time he pulled out the chair at his own table. And she sat down. And at that moment, not a second before, the headwaiter signaled the orchestra and they began to play another number.

Mr. Clark Brandon seemed to be the sort of man who got what he wanted without raising his voice.

After a while my club sandwich came. It was nothing to brag about, but eatable. I ate it. I stuck around for half an hour. Brandon and the girl seemed to be doing all right. They were both quiet. After a while they danced. Then I left and sat in the car outside and smoked. She could have seen me although she didn't show it. I knew Mitchell hadn't. He had turned too quickly up the stairs, he had been too mad to see anything.

About ten-thirty, Brandon came out with her and they got into the Cadillac convertible with the top down. I followed it away without trying to hide because the way they went would be the way anybody would go back to the downtown part of Esmeralda. Where they went was to the Casa del Poniente, and Brandon drove down the ramp to the garage.

There was only one thing more to find out. I parked in the side lot and went through the lobby to the house phones.

"Miss Mayfield, please. Betty Mayfield."

"One moment, please—" slight pause— "Oh yes, she just checked in. I'm ringing the room, sir."

Another and much longer pause.

"I'm sorry, Miss Mayfield's room does not answer."

I thanked her and hung up. I beat it out of there fast in case she and Brandon should get off at the lobby.

I went back to my rented chariot, and poked my way along the canyon through the fog to the Rancho Descansado. The cottage where the office was seemed to be locked up and empty. A single hazy light outside showed the position of a night bell. I groped my way up to 12C, tucked the car in the car port, and yawned my way into my room. It was cold and damp and miserable. Someone had been in and taken the striped cover off the day bed and removed the matching pillowcases.

I undressed and put my curly head on the pillow and went to sleep.


# 9


A tapping sound awoke me. It was very light but it was also persistent. I had the feeling that it had been going on a long time and that it had very gradually penetrated my sleep. I rolled over and listened. Somebody tried the door and then the tapping started again. I glanced at my wrist watch. The faint phosphorescence showed it was past three o'clock. I got up on my feet and moved over to my suitcase and reached down into it for the gun. I went over to the door and opened it a crack.

A dark figure in slacks stood there. Some kind of windbreaker also. And a dark scarf knotted around the head. It was a woman.

"What do you want?"

"Let me in—quickly. Don't put any light on."

So it was Betty Mayfield. I pulled the door back and she slid in like a wisp of the fog. I shut the door. I reached for my bathrobe and pulled it on.

"Anybody else outside?" I asked. "There's nobody next door."

"No. I'm alone." She leaned against the wall and breathed quickly. I fumbled my pen flash out of my coat and poked a small beam around and found the heater switch. I shone the little light on her face. She blinked away from it and raised a hand. I put the light down on the floor and trailed it over to the windows and shut them both and lowered and turned the blinds. Then I went back and switched on the lamp.

She let out a gasp, then said nothing. She was still leaning against the wall. She looked as if she needed a drink. I went out to the kitchenette and poured some whiskey into a glass and carried it to her. She waved it away, then changed her mind and grabbed the glass and emptied it.

I sat down and lit a cigarette, the always mechanical reaction that gets so boring when someone else does it. Then I just sat there and looked at her and waited.

Our eyes met across great gulfs of nothing. After a while she reached slowly into the slanted pocket of the windbreaker and pulled out the gun.

"Oh no," I said. "Not that again."

She looked down at the gun. Her lip twitched. She wasn't pointing it anywhere. She pushed herself away from the wall and crossed to lay the gun down at my elbow.

"I've seen it," I said. "We're old friends. Last time I saw it Mitchell had it. So?"

"That's why I knocked you out. I was afraid he would shoot you."

"That would have fouled up all his plans—whatever his plans were."

"Well, I couldn't be sure. I'm sorry. Sorry I hit you."

"Thanks for the ice cubes," I said.

"Aren't you going to look at the gun?"

"I have looked at it."

"I walked all the way over here from the Casa. I'm staying there now. I—moved in this afternoon."

"I know. You took a taxi to the Del Mar station to catch an evening train and then Mitchell picked you up there and drove you back. You had dinner together and danced and there was a little ill-feeling. A man named Clark Brandon took you back to the hotel in his convertible."

She stared. "I didn't see you there," she said finally, in a voice that was thinking of other things.

"I was in the bar. While you were with Mitchell you were too busy getting your face slapped and telling him to wear a bullet-proof vest next time he came around. Then at Brandon's table you sat with your back to me. I left before you did and waited outside."

"I'm beginning to think you *are* a detective," she said quietly. Her eyes went to the gun again. "He never gave it back to me," she said. "Of course I couldn't prove that."

"That means you'd like to be able to."

"It might help a little. It probably wouldn't help quite enough. Not when they found out about me. I guess you know what I'm talking about."

"Sit down and stop grinding your teeth."

She moved slowly to a chair and sat down on the edge and leaned forward. She stared at the floor.

"I know there's something to find out," I said. "Because Mitchell found it out. So I could find it out too—if I tried. Anyone could who knows there is something to find. I don't know at this moment. All I was hired to do was to keep in touch and report back."

She looked up briefly. "And you've done that?"

"I reported in," I said after a pause. "I'd lost contact at the time. I mentioned San Diego. He'd get that from the operator anyway."

"You'd lost contact," she repeated dryly. "He must think a lot of you, whoever he is." Then she bit her lip. "I'm sorry. I didn't mean to say that. I'm trying to make up my mind about something."

"Take your time," I said. "It's only twenty past three A.M."

"Now *you're* sneering."

I looked towards the wall heater. It didn't show a thing, but there seemed to be a lessening of the chill if no more. I decided I needed a drink. I went out to the kitchen and got it. I put it down, poured some more and came back.

She had a small imitation leather folder in her hand now. She showed it to me.

"I have five thousand dollars in American Express checks in this—one hundred dollar size. How far would you go for five grand, Marlowe?"

I took a sip of whiskey. I thought about it with a judicial expression. "Assuming a normal rate of expenses, that would buy me full time for several months. That is, if I happened to be for sale."

She tapped on the chair arm with the folder. I could see that her other hand was almost pulling her kneecap off.

"You're for sale all right," she said. "And this would be merely a down payment. I can buy big. I've got more money than you ever dreamed of. My last husband was so rich that it was pitiful. I got a cool half million dollars out of him."

She put a hardboiled sneer on her face and gave me plenty of time to get used to it.

"I take it I wouldn't have to murder anybody?"

"You wouldn't have to murder anybody."

"I don't like the way you say that."

I looked sideways at the gun that I hadn't so far laid a finger on. She had walked over from the Casa in the middle of the night to bring it to me. I didn't have to touch it. I stared at it. I bent over and sniffed it. I still didn't have to touch it, but I knew I was going to.

"Who's wearing the bullet?" I asked her. The cold in the room had got into my blood. It ran ice water.

"Just one bullet? How did you know?"

I picked up the gun then. I slipped the magazine out, looked at it, slipped it back. It snapped home in the butt.

"Well, it could have been two," I said. "There are six in the magazine. This gun holds seven. You could jack one into the chamber and then add another to the magazine. Of course you could fire the whole supply and then put six in the magazine."

"We're just talking, aren't we?" she said slowly. "We don't quite want to say it in plain words."

"All right. Where is he?"

"Lying across a chaise on the balcony of my room. All the rooms on that side have balconies. They have concrete walls across them, and the end walls—between the rooms or suites, that is—are slanted outward. I guess a steeplejack or a mountain climber might get around one of the end walls, but not carrying a weight. I'm on the twelfth floor. There's nothing any higher but the penthouse floor." She stopped and frowned, then made a sort of helpless gesture with the hand that had been squeezing her kneecap. "This is going to sound a little corny," she went on. "He could only have got there through my room. And I didn't let him through my room."

"But you're sure he's dead?"

"Quite sure. Quite dead. Stone cold dead. I don't know when it happened. I didn't hear a sound. Something woke me all right. But it wasn't any sound like a shot. Anyhow he was already cold. So I don't know what woke me. And I didn't get up right away. I just lay there, thinking. I didn't go back to sleep, so after a while I put the light on and got up and walked around and smoked. Then I noticed the fog was gone and it was moonlight. Not down on the ground, but up there on my floor. I could still see fog down below when I went out on the balcony. It was damned cold. The stars seemed enormous. I stood there near the wall for quite a while before I even saw him. I guess that sounds pretty corny too—or pretty unlikely. I can't imagine the police taking it very seriously—even at first. And afterwards—well, just take it this way. I haven't a chance in a million—unless I get help."

I stood up, tossed down what whiskey was left in the glass and walked over to her.

"Let me tell you two or three things. First off, you're not taking this with normal reactions. You're not icy cool, but you're too cool. No panic, no hysteria, no nothing. You're fatalistic. Next, I heard the entire conversation between you and Mitchell this afternoon. I took those bulbs out—" I pointed to the wall heater—"and used a stethoscope against the partition at the back. What Mitchell had on you was a knowledge of who you were, and that knowledge was something that if published could drive you into another switch of names and another dodge to some other town somewhere. You said you were the luckiest girl in the world because you were alive. Now a man is dead on your balcony, shot with your gun, and the man of course is Mitchell. Right?"

She nodded. "Yes, it's Larry."

"And you didn't kill him, you say. And the cops would hardly believe that even at first, you say. And later on not at all. My guess is that you've been there before."

She was still looking up at me. She came slowly to her feet. Our faces were close, we stared hard into each other's eyes. It didn't mean a thing.

"Half a million dollars is a lot of money, Marlowe. You're not too hard to take. There are places in the world where you and I could have a beautiful life. In one of those tall apartment houses along the ocean front in Rio. I don't know how long it would last, but things can always be arranged, don't you think?"

I said: "What a lot of different girls you are. Now you're making like a moll. When I first saw you, you were a quiet well-bred little lady. You didn't like dreamboats like Mitchell making a pitch at you. Then you bought yourself a pack of cigarettes and smoked one as if you hated it. Then you let him cuddle you—after you got down here. Then you tore your blouse at me ha, ha, ha, cynical as a Park Avenue pet after her butter and egg man goes home. Then you let me cuddle you. Then you cracked me on the head with a whiskey bottle. Now you're talking about a beautiful life in Rio. Which one of you would have her head on the next pillow when I woke up in the morning?"

"Five thousand dollars down. And a lot more to come. The police wouldn't give you five toothpicks. If you think different, you have a telephone."

"What do I do for the five grand?"

She let her breath out slowly as if a crisis was past. "The hotel is built almost on the edge of the cliff. At the foot of the wall there's only a narrow walk, very narrow. Below the cliffs are rocks and the sea. It's almost high tide. My balcony hangs right over all that."

I nodded. "Are there fire stairs?"

"From the garage. They start just beside the basement elevator landing, which is up two or three steps from the garage floor. But it's a long hard climb."

"For five grand I'd climb it in a diver's suit. Did you come out through the lobby?"

"Fire stairs. There's an all night man in the garage but he was asleep in one of the cars."

"You said Mitchell is lying on a chaise. Is there a lot of blood?"

She winced. "I—I didn't notice. I suppose there must be."

"You didn't notice? You went near enough to find out he was stone cold dead. Where was he shot?"

"Nowhere that I saw. It must have been under him."

"Where was the gun?"

"It was lying on the floor of the porch—beside his hand."

"Which hand?"

She widened her eyes slightly. "Does it matter? I don't know which hand. He's sort of lying across the chaise with his head hanging on one side and his legs on the other. Do we have to keep on talking about it?"

"All right," I said. "I don't know a damn thing about the tides and currents around here. He might wash up on the beach tomorrow and he might not show up for two weeks. Assuming, of course, we bring it off. If it's a long time they may not even find out he was shot. Then I guess there's some possibility that he won't be found at all. Not much, but some. There are barracuda in these waters, and other things."

"You certainly do a thorough job of making it revolting," she said.

"Well, I had a running start. Also I was thinking if there was any chance of suicide. Then we'd have to put the gun back. He was left-handed, you know. That's why I wanted to know which hand."

"Oh. Yes, he was left-handed. You're right. But not suicide. Not that smirking, self-satisfied gentleman."

"Sometimes a man kills the dearest thing he loves, they say. Couldn't it be himself?"

"Not this character," she said briefly and finally. "If we are very lucky, they will probably think he fell off the balcony. God knows he was drunk enough. And by that time I'll be in South America. My passport is still valid."

"In what name is your passport?"

She reached out and drew her fingertips down my cheek.

"You'll know all about me soon enough. Don't be impatient. You'll know all the intimate things about me. Can't you wait a little?"

"Yeah. Start getting intimate with those American Express checks. We have another hour or two of darkness and more than that of fog. You play with the checks while I get dressed."

I reached into my jacket and gave her a fountain pen. She sat down near the light and began to sign them with the second signature. Her tongue peeped out between her teeth. She wrote slowly and carefully. The name she wrote was Elizabeth Mayfield.

So the switch of names had been planned before she left Washington.

While I dressed I wondered if she was really foolish enough to think I'd help her dispose of a body.

I carried the glasses out to the kitchenette and scooped the gun up on the way. I let the swing door close and slipped the gun and the magazine into the tray under the broiler of the stove. I rinsed out the glasses and wiped them off. I went back into the living room and threw my clothes on. She didn't even look at me.

She went on signing the checks. When she had finished, I took the folder of checks and flipped them over one by one, checking the signatures. The big money meant nothing to me. I shoved the folder into my pocket, put the lamp out and moved to the door. I opened it and she was beside me. She was close beside me.

"Sneak out," I said. "I'll pick you up on the highway just above where the fence ends."

She faced me and leaned a little towards me. "Can I trust you?" she asked softly.

"Up to a point."

"You're honest at least. What happens if we don't get away with it? If somebody reported a shot, if he has been found, if we walk in on that and the place is full of policemen?"

I just stood there with my eyes on her face and didn't answer her.

"Just let me guess," she said very softly and slowly. "You'll sell me out fast. And you won't have any five thousand dollars. Those checks will be old newspaper. You won't dare cash a single one of them."

I still didn't say anything.

"You son of a bitch." She didn't raise her voice even a semitone. "Why did I ever come to you?"

I took her face between my hands and kissed her on the lips. She pulled away.

"Not for that," she said. "Certainly not for that. And one more small point. It's terribly small and unimportant, I know. I've had to learn that. From expert teachers. Long hard painful lessons and a lot of them. It just happens that I really didn't kill him."

"Maybe I believe you."

"Don't bother to try," she said. "Nobody else will."

She turned and slid along the porch and down the steps. She flitted off through the trees. In thirty feet the fog hid her.

I locked up and got into the rent car and drove it down the silent driveway past the closed office with the light over the night bell. The whole place was hard asleep, but trucks were rumbling up through the canyon with building materials and oil and the big closed up jobs with and without trailers, full of anything and everything that a town needs to live on. The fog lights were on and the trucks were slow and heavy up the hill.

Fifty yards beyond the gate she stepped out of the shadows at the end of the fence and climbed in. I switched on my headlights. Somewhere out on the water a foghorn was moaning. Upstairs in the clear reaches of the sky a formation of jets from North Island went over with a whine and a whoosh and a bang of the shock wave and were gone in less time than it took me to pull the lighter out of the dash and light a cigarette.

The girl sat motionless beside me, looking straight ahead and not speaking. She wasn't seeing the fog or the back of a truck we were coming up behind. She wasn't seeing anything. She was just sitting there frozen in one position, stony with despair, like somebody on the way to be hanged.

Either that or she was the best little scene stealer I had come across in a long long time.

## 10

The Casa del Poniente was set on the edge of the cliffs in about seven acres of lawn and flower beds, with a central patio on the sheltered side, tables set out behind a glass screen, and a trellised walk leading through the middle of it to an entrance. There was a bar on one side, a coffee shop on the other, and at each end of the building blacktop parking lots partly hidden behind six-foot hedges of flowering shrubs. The parking lots had cars in them. Not everyone bothered to use the basement garage, although the damp salt air down there is hard on chromium.

I parked in a slot near the garage ramp and the sound of the ocean was very close and you could feel the drifting spray and smell it and taste it. We got out and moved over to the garage entrance. A narrow raised walk edged the ramp. A sign hung midway of the entrance said: Descend in Low Gear. Sound Horn. The girl grabbed me by the arm and stopped me.

"I'm going in by the lobby. I'm too tired to climb the stairs."

"Okay. No law against it. What's the room number?"

"Twelve twenty-four. What do we get if we're caught?"

"Caught doing what?"

"You know what. Putting—putting it over the balcony wall. Or somewhere."

"I'd get staked out on an anthill. I don't know about you. Depends what else they have on you."

"How can you talk like that before breakfast?"

She turned and walked away quickly. I started down the ramp. It curved as they all do and then I could see a glassed-in cubbyhole of an office with a hanging light in it. A little farther down and I could see that it was empty. I listened for sounds of somebody doing a little work on a car, water in a washrack, steps, whistling, any little noise to indicate where the night man was and what he was doing. In a basement garage you can hear a very small noise indeed. I heard nothing.

I went on down and was almost level with the upper end of the office. Now by stooping I could see the shallow steps up into the basement elevator lobby. There was a door marked: To Elevator. It had glass panels and I could see light beyond it, but little else.

I took three more steps and froze. The night man was looking right at me. He was in a big Packard sedan in the back seat. The light shone on his face and he wore glasses and the light shone hard on the glasses. He was leaning back comfortably in the corner of the car. I stood there and waited for him to move. He didn't move. His head was against the car cushions. His mouth was open. I had to know why he didn't move. He might be just pretending to be asleep until I got out of sight. When that happened he would beat it across to the phone and call the office.

Then I thought that was silly. He wouldn't have come on the job until evening and he couldn't know all the guests by sight. The sidewalk that bordered the ramp was there to walk on. It was almost 4 A.M. In an hour or so it would begin to get light. No hotel prowler would come around that late.

I walked straight over to the Packard and looked in on him. The car was shut up tight, all windows. The man didn't move. I reached for the door handle and tried to open the door without noise. He still didn't move. He looked like a very light colored man. He also looked asleep and I could hear him snoring even before I got the door open. Then I got it full in the face—the honeyed reek of well-cured marijuana. The guy was out of circulation, he was in the valley of peace, where time is slowed to a standstill, where the world is all colors and music. And in a couple of hours from now he wouldn't have a job, even if the cops didn't grab him and toss him into the deep freeze.

I shut the car door again and crossed to the glass-paneled door. I went through into a small bare elevator lobby with a concrete floor and two blank elevator doors and beside them, opening on a heavy door closer, the fire stairs. I pulled that open and started up. I went slowly. Twelve stories and a basement take a lot of stairs. I counted the fire doors as I passed them because they were not numbered. They were heavy and solid and gray like the concrete of the steps. I was sweating and out of breath when I pulled open the door to the twelfth-floor corridor. I prowled along to Room 1224 and tried the knob. It was locked, but almost at once the door was opened, as if she had been waiting just behind it. I went in past her and flopped into a chair and waited to get some breath back. It was a big airy room with french windows opening on a balcony. The double bed had been slept in or arranged to look that way. Odds and ends of clothing on chairs, toilet articles on the dresser, luggage. It looked about twenty bucks a day, single.

She turned the night latch in the door. "Have any trouble?"

"The night man was junked to the eyes. Harmless as a kitten." I heaved myself out of the chair and started across to the french doors.

"Wait!" she said sharply. I looked back at her. "It's no use," she said. "Nobody could do a thing like that."

I stood there and waited.

"I'd rather call the police," she said. "Whatever it means for me."

"That's a bright idea," I said. "Why ever didn't we think of it before?"

"You'd better leave," she said. "There's no need for you to be mixed up in it."

I didn't say anything. I watched her eyes. She could hardly keep them open. It was either delayed shock or some kind of dope. I didn't know which.

"I swallowed two sleeping pills," she said, reading my mind. "I just can't take any more trouble tonight. Go away from here. Please. When I wake I'll call room service. When the waiter comes I'll get him out on the balcony somehow and he'll find—whatever he'll find. And I won't know a damn thing about it." Her tongue was getting thick. She shook herself and rubbed hard against her temples. "I'm sorry about the money. You'll have to give it back to me, won't you?"

I went over close to her. "Because if I don't you'll tell them the whole story?"

"I'll have to," she said drowsily. "How can I help it? They'll get it out of me. I'm—I'm too tired to fight any more."

I took hold of her arm and shook her. Her head wobbled. "Quite sure you only took two capsules?"

She blinked her eyes open. "Yes. I never take more than two."

"Then listen. I'm going out there and have a look at him. Then I'm going back to the Rancho. I'm going to keep your money. Also I have your gun. Maybe it can't be traced to me but— Wake up! Listen to me!" Her head was rolling sideways again. She jerked straight and her eyes widened, but they looked dull and withdrawn. "Listen. If it can't be traced to you, it certainly can't be traced to me. I'm working for a lawyer and my assignment is you. The traveler's checks and the gun will go right where they belong. And your story to the cops won't be worth a wooden nickel. All it will do is help to hang you. Understand that?"

"Ye-es," she said. "And I don't g-give a damn."

"That's not you talking. It's the sleeping medicine."

She sagged forward and I caught her and steered her over to the bed. She flopped on it any old way. I pulled her shoes off and spread a blanket over her and tucked her in. She was asleep at once. She began to snore. I went into the bathroom and groped around and found a bottle of Nembutal on the shelf. It was almost full. It had a prescription number and a date on it. The date was a month old, the drugstore was in Baltimore. I dumped the yellow capsules out into my palm and counted them. There were forty-seven and they almost filled the bottle. When they take them to kill themselves, they take them all— except what they spill, and they nearly always spill some. I put the pills back in the bottle and put the bottle in my pocket.

I went back and looked at her again. The room was cold. I turned the radiator on, not too much. And finally at long last I opened the french doors and went out on the balcony. It was as cold as hell out there. The balcony was about twelve by fourteen feet, with a thirty-inch wall across the front and a low iron railing sprouting out of that. You could jump off easy enough, but you couldn't possibly fall off accidentally. There were two aluminum patio chaises with padded cushions, two armchairs of the same type. The dividing wall to the left stuck out the way she had told me. I didn't think even a steeplejack could get around the projection without climbing tackle. The wall at the other end rose sheer to the edge of what must be one of the penthouse terraces.

Nobody was dead on either of the chaises, nor on the floor of the balcony, nor anywhere at all. I examined them for traces of blood. No blood. No blood on the balcony. I went along the safety wall. No blood. No signs of anything having been heaved over. I stood against the wall and held on to the metal railing and leaned out as far as I could lean. I looked straight down the face of the wall to the ground. Shrubs grew close to it, then a narrow strip of lawn, then a flagstone footpath, then another strip of lawn and then a heavy fence with more shrubs growing against that. I estimated the distance. At that height it wasn't easy, but it must have been at least thirty-five feet. Beyond the fence the sea creamed on some half-submerged rocks.

Larry Mitchell was about half an inch taller than I was but weighed about fifteen pounds less, at a rough guess. The man wasn't born who could heave a hundred and seventy-five pound body over that railing and far enough out to fall into the ocean. It was barely possible that a girl wouldn't realize that, just barely possible, about one tenth of one per cent possible.

I opened the french door and went through and shut it and crossed to stand beside the bed. She was still sound asleep. She was still snoring. I touched her cheek with the back of my hand. It was moist. She moved a little and mumbled. Then she sighed and settled her head into the pillow. No stertorous breathing, no deep stupor, no coma, and therefore no overdose.

She had told me the truth about one thing, and about damned little else.

I found her bag in the top drawer of the dresser. It had a zipper pocket at the back. I put her folder of traveler's checks in it and looked through it for information. There was some crisp folding money in the zipper pocket, a Santa Fe timetable, the folder her ticket had been in and the stub of the railroad ticket and the Pullman reservation. She had had Bedroom E on Car 19, Washington, D.C., to San Diego, California. No letters, nothing to identify her. That would be locked up in the luggage. In the main part of the bag was what a woman carries, a lipstick, a compact, a change purse, some silver, and a few keys on a ring with a tiny bronze tiger hanging from it. A pack of cigarettes that seemed just about full but had been opened.

A matchbook with one match used. Three handkerchiefs with no initials, a packet of emery boards, a cuticle knife, and some kind of eyebrow stuff, a comb in a leather case, a little round jar of nail polish, a tiny address book. I pounced on that. Blank, not used at all. Also in the bag were a pair of sun glasses with spangled rims in a case, no name on the case; a fountain pen, a small gold pencil, and that was all. I put the bag back where I had found it. I went over to the desk for a piece of hotel stationery and an envelope.

I used the hotel pen to write: "Dear Betty: So sorry I couldn't stay dead. Will explain tomorrow. Larry."

I sealed the note in the envelope, wrote *Miss Betty Mayfield* on it, and dropped it where it might be if it had been pushed under the door.

I opened the door, went out, shut the door, and went back to the fire stairs, then said out loud: "The hell with it," and rang for the elevator. It didn't come. I rang again and kept on ringing. Finally it came up and a sleepy-eyed young Mexican opened the doors and yawned at me, then grinned apologetically. I grinned back and said nothing.

There was nobody at the desk, which faced the elevators. The Mexican parked himself in a chair and went back to sleep before I had taken six steps. Everybody was sleepy but Marlowe. He works around the clock, and doesn't even collect.

I drove back to the Rancho Descansado, saw nobody awake there, looked longingly at the bed, but packed my suitcase — with Betty's gun in the bottom of it — put twelve bucks in an envelope and on the way out put that through the slot in the office door, with my room key.

I drove to San Diego, turned the rent car in, and ate breakfast at a joint across from the station. At seven-fifteen I caught the two-car diesel job that makes the run to L.A. nonstop and pulls in at exactly 10 A.M.

I rode home in a taxi and shaved and showered and ate a second breakfast and glanced through the morning paper. It was near on eleven o'clock when I called the office of Mr. Clyde Umney, the lawyer.

He answered himself. Maybe Miss Vermilyea hadn't got up yet.

"This is Marlowe. I'm home. Can I drop around?"

"Did you find her?"

"Yeah. Did you call Washington?"

"Where is she?"

"I'd like to tell you in person. Did you call Washington?"

"I'd like your information first. I have a very busy day ahead." His voice was brittle and lacked charm.

"I'll be there in half an hour." I hung up fast and called the place where my Olds was.

## II

There are almost too many offices like Clyde Umney's office. It was paneled in squares of combed plywood set at right angles one to the other to make a checkerboard effect. The lighting was indirect, the carpeting wall to wall, the furniture blond, the chairs comfortable, and the fees probably exorbitant. The metal window frames opened outward and there was a small but neat parking lot behind the building, and every slot in it had a name painted on a white board. For some reason Clyde Umney's stall was vacant, so I used it. Maybe he had a chauffeur drive him to his office. The building was four stories high, very new, and occupied entirely by doctors and lawyers.

When I entered, Miss Vermilyea was just fixing herself for a hard day's work by touching up her platinum blond coiffure. I thought she looked a little the worse for wear. She put away her hand mirror and fed herself a cigarette.

"Well, well. Mr. Hard Guy in person. To what may we attribute this honor?"

"Umney's expecting me."

"*Mister* Umney to you, buster."

"Boydie-boy to you, sister."

She got raging in an instant. "Don't call me 'sister,' you cheap gumshoe!"

"Then don't call me buster, you very expensive secretary.

What are you doing tonight? And don't tell me you're going out with four sailors again."

The skin around her eyes turned whiter. Her hand crisped into a claw around a paperweight. She just didn't heave it at me. "You son of a bitch!" she said somewhat pointedly. Then she flipped a switch on her talk box and said to the voice: "Mr. Marlowe is here, Mr. Umney."

Then she leaned back and gave me the look. "I've got friends who could cut you down so small you'd need a stepladder to put your shoes on."

"Somebody did a lot of hard work on that one," I said. "But hard work's no substitute for talent."

Suddenly we both burst out laughing. The door opened and Umney stuck his face out. He gestured me in with his chin, but his eyes were on the platinum girl.

I went in and after a moment he closed the door and went behind his enormous semicircular desk, with a green leather top and just piles and piles of important documents on it. He was a dapper man, very carefully dressed, too short in the legs, too long in the nose, too sparse in the hair. He had limpid brown eyes which, for a lawyer, looked very trustful.

"You making a pass at my secretary?" he asked me in a voice that was anything but limpid.

"Nope. We were just exchanging pleasantries."

I sat down in the customer's chair and looked at him with something approaching politeness.

"She looked pretty mad to me." He squatted in his executive vice-president type chair and made his face tough.

"She's booked up for three weeks," I said. "I couldn't wait that long."

"Just watch your step, Marlowe. Lay off. She's private property. She wouldn't give you the time of day. Besides being a lovely piece of female humanity, she's as smart as a whip."

"You mean she can type and take dictation as well?"

"As well as what?" He reddened suddenly. "I've taken enough lip from you. Just watch your step. Very carefully. I have enough influence around this town to hang a red light on you. Now let me have your report and make it short and to the point."

"You talk to Washington yet?"

"Never mind what I did or didn't do. I want your report as of right now. The rest is my business. What's the present location of the King girl?" He reached for a nice sharp pencil and a nice clean pad. Then he dropped the pencil and poured himself a glass of water from a black and silver thermos jug.

"Let's trade," I said. "You tell me why you want her found and I'll tell you where she is."

"You're my employee," he snapped. "I don't have to give you any information whatsoever." He was still tough but beginning to shred a little around the edge.

"I'm your employee if I want to be, Mr. Umney. No check has been cashed, no agreement has been made."

"You accepted the assignment. You took an advance."

"Miss Vermilyea gave me a check for two hundred and fifty as an advance, and another check for two hundred for expenses. But I didn't bank them. Here they are." I took the two checks out of my pocketbook and laid them on the desk in front of him. "Better keep them until you make up your mind whether you want an investigator or a yes man, and until I make up my mind whether I was offered a job or was being suckered into a situation I knew nothing about."

He looked down at the checks. He wasn't happy. "You've already had expenses," he said slowly.

"That's all right, Mr. Umney. I had a few dollars saved up—and the expenses are deductible. Also I've had fun."

"You're pretty stubborn, Marlowe."

"I guess, but I have to be in my business. Otherwise I wouldn't be in business. I told you the girl was being black-mailed. Your Washington friends must know why. If she's a crook, fine. But I have to get told. And I have an offer you can't match."

"For more money you are willing to switch sides?" he asked angrily. "That would be unethical."

I laughed. "So I've got ethics now. Maybe we're getting somewhere."

He took a cigarette out of a box and lit it with a pot-bellied lighter that matched the thermos and the pen set.

"I still don't like your attitude," he growled. "Yesterday I didn't know any more than you did. I took it for granted that a reputable Washington law firm would not ask me to do any-thing against legal ethics. Since the girl could have been ar-rested without difficulty, I assumed it was some sort of domestic mix-up, a runaway wife or daughter, or an impor-tant but reluctant witness who was already outside the juris-diction where she could be subpoenaed. That was just guessing. This morning things are a little different."

He got up and walked to the big window and turned the slats of the blinds enough to keep the sun off his desk. He stood there smoking, looking out, then came back to the desk and sat down again.

"This morning," he went on slowly and with a judicious frown, "I talked to my Washington associates and I am in-formed that the girl was confidential secretary to a rich and important man—I'm not told his name—and that she ab-sconded with certain important and dangerous papers from his private files. Papers that might be damaging to him if made public. I'm not told in what way. Perhaps he has been fudging his tax returns. You never know these days."

"She took this stuff to blackmail him?"

Umney nodded. "That is the natural assumption. They had no value to her otherwise. The client, Mr. A we will call him, didn't realize that the girl had left until she was already in another state. He then checked his files and found that some of his material was gone. He was reluctant to go to the police. He expects the girl to go far enough away to feel safe and from that point to start negotiations with him for the return of the material at a heavy price. He wants to peg her down somewhere without her knowing it, walk in and catch her off balance and especially before she contacts some sharp lawyer, of whom I regret to say there are far too many, and with the sharp lawyer works out a scheme that would make her safe from prosecution. Now you tell me someone is blackmailing her. On what grounds?"

"If your story stood up, it could be because he is in a posi-tion to spoil her play," I said. "Maybe he knows something that could hang a pinch on her without opening up the other box of candy."

"You say if the story stood up," he snapped. "What do you mean by that?"

"It's as full of holes as a sink strainer. You're being fed a line, Mr. Umney. Where would a man keep material like the important papers you mention—if he had to keep them at all? Certainly not where a secretary could get them. And unless he missed the stuff before she left, how did he get her followed to the train? Next, although she took a ticket to California, she could have got off anywhere. Therefore she would have to be watched on the train, and if that was done, why did someone need me to pick her up here? Next, this, as you tell it, would be a job for a large agency with nation-wide connections. It would be idiotic to take a chance on one man. I lost her yesterday. I could lose her again. It takes a bare minimum of six operatives to do a standard tail job in any sizable place, and that's just what I mean—a bare minimum. In a really big city you'd need a dozen. An operative has to eat and sleep and change his shirt. If he's tailing by car he has to be able to drop a man while he finds a place to park. Department stores and hotels may have half a dozen entrances. But all this girl does is hang around Union Station here for three hours in full view of everybody. And all your friends in Washington do is mail you a picture, call you on the phone, and then go back to watching television."

"Very clear," he said. "Anything else?" His face was deadpan now.

"A little. Why—if she didn't expect to be followed—would she change her name? Why if she did expect to be followed would she make it so easy? I told you two other guys were working the same side of the street. One is a Kansas City private detective named Goble. He was in Esmeralda yesterday. He knew just where to go. Who told him? I had to follow her and bribe a taxi driver to use his R/T outfit to find out where her cab was going so that I wouldn't lose her. So why was I hired?"

"We'll come to that," Umney said curtly. "Who was the other party you say was working the same side of the street?"

"A playboy named Mitchell. He lives down there. He met the girl on the train. He made a reservation for her in Esmeralda. They're just like that—" I held up two touching fingers—"except that she hates his guts. He's got something on her and she is afraid of him. What he has on her is a knowledge of who she is, where she came from, what happened to her there, and why she is trying to hide under another name. I overheard enough to know that, but not enough to give me exact information."

Umney said acidly: "Of course the girl was covered on the train. Do you think you are dealing with idiots? You were nothing more than a decoy—to determine whether she had any associates. On your reputation—such as it is—I relied on you to grandstand just enough to let her get wise to you. I guess you know what an open shadow is."

"Sure. One that deliberately lets the subject spot him, then shake him, so that another shadow can pick him up when he thinks he is safe."

"You were it." He grinned at me contemptuously. "But you still haven't told me where she is."

I didn't want to tell him, but I knew I'd have to. I had up to a point accepted the assignment, and giving him back his money was only a move to force some information out of him.

I reached across the desk and picked up the $250 check. "I'll take this as payment in full, expenses included. She is registered as Miss Betty Mayfield at the Casa del Poniente in Esmeralda. She is loaded with money. But of course your expert organization must know all this already."

I stood up. "Thanks for the ride, Mr. Umney."

I went out and shut his door. Miss Vermilyea looked up from a magazine. I heard a faint muffled click from somewhere in her desk.

"I'm sorry I was rude to you," I said. "I didn't get enough sleep last night."

"Forget it. It was a stand-off. With a little practice I might get to like you. You're kind of cute in a low down sort of way."

"Thanks," I said and moved to the door. I wouldn't say she looked exactly wistful, but neither did she look as hard to get as a controlling interest in General Motors.

I turned back and closed the door.

"I guess it's not raining tonight, is it? There was something we might have discussed over a drink, if it had been a rainy night. And if you had not been too busy."

She gave me a cool amused look. "Where?"

"That would be up to you."

"Should I drop by your place?"

"It would be damn nice of you. That Fleetwood might help my credit standing."

"I wasn't exactly thinking of that."

"Neither was I."

"About six-thirty perhaps. And I'll take good care of my nylons."

"I was hoping you would."

Our glances locked. I went out quickly.


## 12


At half past six the Fleetwood purred to the front door and I had it open when she came up the steps. She was hatless. She wore a flesh-colored coat with the collar turned up against her platinum hair. She stood in the middle of the living room and looked around casually. Then she slipped the coat off with a lithe movement and threw it on the davenport and sat down.

"I didn't really think you'd come," I said.

"No. You're the shy type. You knew darned well I'd come. Scotch and soda, if you have it."

"I have it."

I brought the drinks and sat down beside her, but not close enough for it to mean anything. We touched glasses and drank.

"Would you care to go to Romanoff's for dinner?"

"And then what?"

"Where do you live?"

"West Los Angeles. A house on a quiet old street. It happens to belong to me. I asked you, and then what, remember?"

"That would be up to you, naturally."

"I thought you were a tough guy. You mean I don't have to pay for my dinner?"

"I ought to slap your face for that crack."

She laughed suddenly and stared at me over the edge of her glass.

"Consider it slapped. We had each other a bit wrong. Romanoff's could wait a while, couldn't it?"

"We could try West Los Angeles first."

"Why not here?"

"I guess this will make you walk out on me. I had a dream here once, a year and a half ago. There's still a shred of it left. I'd like it to stay in charge."

She stood up quickly and grabbed her coat. I managed to help her on with it.

"I'm sorry," I said, "I should have told you before."

She swung around with her face close to mine, but I didn't touch her.

"Sorry that you had a dream and kept it alive? I've had dreams too, but mine died. I didn't have the courage to keep them alive."

"It's not quite like that. There was a woman. She was rich. She thought she wanted to marry me. It wouldn't have worked. I'll probably never see her again. But I remember."

"Let's go," she said quietly. "And let's leave the memory in charge. I only wish I had one worth remembering."

On the way down to the Cadillac I didn't touch her either. She drove beautifully. When a woman is a really good driver she is just about perfect.

# 13

The house was on a curving quiet street between San Vincente and Sunset Boulevard. It was set far back and had a long driveway and the entrance to the house was at the back with a small patio in front of it. She unlocked the door and switched on lights all over the house and then disappeared without a word. The living room had nicely mixed furniture and a feeling of comfort. I stood waiting until she came back with two tall glasses. She had taken her coat off.

"You've been married, of course," I said.

"It didn't take. I got this house and some money out of it, but I wasn't gunning for anything. He was a nice guy, but we were wrong for each other. He's dead now—plane crash—he was a jet pilot. Happens all the time. I know a place between here and San Diego that is full of girls who were married to jet pilots when they were alive."

I took a single sip of my drink and put it down.

I lifted her glass out of her hand and put it down too.

"Remember yesterday morning when you told me to stop looking at your legs?"

"I seem to remember."

"Try and stop me now."

I took hold of her and she came into my arms without a word. I picked her up and carried her and somehow found the bedroom. I put her down on the bed. I peeled her skirt up until I could see the white thighs above her long beautiful nylon-clad legs. Suddenly she reached up and pulled my head down against her breast.

"Beast! Could we have a little less light?"

I went to the door and switched the light off in the room. There was still a glow from the hall. When I turned she was standing by the bed as naked as Aphrodite, fresh from the Aegean. She stood there proudly and without either shame or enticement.

"Damn it," I said, "when I was young you could undress a girl slowly. Nowadays she's in the bed while you're struggling with your collar button."

"Well, struggle with your goddam collar button."

She pulled the bedcovers back and lay on the bed shamelessly nude. She was just a beautiful naked woman completely unashamed of being what she was.

"Satisfied with my legs?" she asked.

I didn't answer.

"Yesterday morning," she said, half dreamily, "I said there was something about you I liked—you didn't paw—and something I didn't like. Know what it was?"

"No."

"That you didn't make me do this then."

"Your manner hardly encouraged it."

"You're supposed to be a detective. Please put out all the lights now."

Then very soon in the dark she was saying, "Darling, darling, darling" in that very special tone of voice a woman uses only in those special moments. Then a slow gentle relaxing, a peace, a quietness.

"Still satisfied with my legs?" she asked dreamily.

"No man ever would be. They would haunt him, no matter how many times he made love to you."

"You bastard. You complete bastard. Come closer."

She put her head on my shoulder and we were very close now.

"I don't love you," she said.

"Why would you? But let's not be cynical about it. There are sublime moments—even if they are only moments."

I felt her tight and warm against me. Her body surged with vitality. Her beautiful arms held me tight.

And again in the darkness that muted cry, and then again the slow quiet peace.

"I hate you," she said with her mouth against mine. "Not for this, but because perfection never comes twice and with us it came too soon. And I'll never see you again and I don't want to. It would have to be forever or not at all."

"And you acted like a hardboiled pick-up who had seen too much of the wrong side of life."

"So did you. And we were both wrong. And it's useless. Kiss me harder."

Suddenly she was gone from the bed almost without sound or movement.

After a little while the light went on in the hallway and she stood in the door in a long wrapper.

"Goodbye," she said calmly. "I'm calling a taxi for you. Wait out in front for it. You won't see me again."

"What about Umney?"

"A poor frightened jerk. He needs someone to bolster his ego, to give him a feeling of power and conquest. I give it to him. A woman's body is not so sacred that it can't be used—especially when she has already failed at love."

She disappeared. I got up and put my clothes on and listened before I went out. I heard nothing. I called out, but there was no answer. When I reached the sidewalk in front of the house the taxi was just pulling up. I looked back. The house seemed completely dark.

No one lived there. It was all a dream. Except that someone had called the taxi. I got into it and was driven home.

# 14

I left Los Angeles and hit the superhighway that now bypassed Oceanside. I had time to think.

From Los Angeles to Oceanside were eighteen miles of divided six-lane superhighway dotted at intervals with the carcasses of wrecked, stripped, and abandoned cars tossed against the high bank to rust until they were hauled away. So I started thinking about why I was going back to Esmeralda. The case was all backwards and it wasn't my case anyway. Usually a PI gets a client who, for too little money, wants too much information. You get it or you don't, depending on circumstances. The same with your fee. But once in a while you get the information and too much else, including a story about a body on a balcony which wasn't there when you went to look. Common sense says go home and forget it, no money coming in. Common sense always speaks too late. Common sense is the guy who tells you you ought to have had your brakes relined last week before you smashed a front end this week. Common sense is the Monday morning quarterback who could have won the ball game if he had been on the team. But he never is. He's high up in the stands with a flask on his hip. Common sense is the little man in a gray suit who never makes a mistake in addition. But it's always somebody else's money he's adding up.

At the turn-off I dipped down into the canyon and ended up at the Rancho Descansado. Jack and Lucille were in their usual positions. I dropped my suitcase and leaned on the desk.

"Did I leave the right change?"

"Yes, thanks," Jack said. "And now you want the room back, I suppose."

"If possible."

"Why didn't you tell us you were a detective?"

"Now, what a question." I grinned at him. "Does a detective ever tell anyone he's a detective? You watch TV, don't you?"

"When I get a chance. Not too often here."

"You can always tell a detective on TV. He never takes his hat off. What do you know about Larry Mitchell?"

"Nothing," Jack said stiffly. "He's a friend of Brandon's. Mr. Brandon owns this place."

Lucille said brightly: "Did you find Joe Harms all right?"

"Yes, thanks."

"And did you—?"

"Uh-huh."

"Button the lip, kid," Jack said tersely. He winked at me and pushed the key across the counter. "Lucille has a dull life, Mr. Marlowe. She's stuck here with me and a PBX. And an itty-bitty diamond ring—so small I was ashamed to give it to her. But what can a man do? If he loves a girl, he'd like it to show on her finger."

Lucille held her left hand up and moved it around to get a flash from the little stone. "I hate it," she said. "I hate it like I hate the sunshine and the summer and the bright stars and the full moon. That's how I hate it."

I picked up the key and my suitcase and left them. A little more of that and I'd be falling in love with myself. I might even give myself a small unpretentious diamond ring.

## 15

The house phone at the Casa del Poniente got no reply from Room 1224. I walked over to the desk. A stiff-looking clerk was sorting letters. They are always sorting letters.

"Miss Mayfield is registered here, isn't she?" I asked.

He put a letter in a box before he answered me. "Yes, sir. What name shall I say?"

"I know her room number. She doesn't answer. Have you seen her today?"

He gave me a little more of his attention, but I didn't really send him. "I don't think so." He glanced over his shoulder. "Her key is out. Would you care to leave a message?"

"I'm a little worried. She wasn't well last night. She could be up there sick, not able to answer the phone. I'm a friend of hers. Marlowe's the name."

He looked me over. His eyes were wise eyes. He went behind a screen in the direction of the cashier's office and spoke to somebody. He came back in a short time. He was smiling.

"I don't think Miss Mayfield is ill, Mr. Marlowe. She ordered quite a substantial breakfast in her room. And lunch. She has had several telephone calls."

"Thanks a lot," I said. "I'll leave a message. Just my name and that I'll call back later."

"She might be out in the grounds or down on the beach," he said. "We have a warm beach, well sheltered by a breakwater." He glanced at the clock behind him. "If she is, she won't be there much longer. It's getting cool by now."

"Thanks. I'll be back."

The main part of the lobby was up three steps and through an arch. There were people in it just sitting, the dedicated hotel lounge sitters, usually elderly, usually rich, usually doing nothing but watching with hungry eyes. They spend their lives that way. Two old ladies with severe faces and purplish permanents were struggling with an enormous jigsaw puzzle set out on a specially built king-size card table. Farther along there was a canasta game going—two women, two men. One of the women had enough ice on her to cool the Mojave Desert and enough make-up to paint a steam yacht. Both women had cigarettes in long holders. The men with them looked gray and tired, probably from signing checks. Farther along, still sitting where they could look out through the glass, a young couple were holding hands. The girl had a diamond and emerald sparkler and a wedding ring which she kept touching with her fingertips. She looked a little dazed.

I went out through the bar and poked around in the gardens. I went along the path that threaded the cliff top and had no trouble picking out the spot I had looked down on the night before from Betty Mayfield's balcony. I could pick it out because of the sharp angle.

The bathing beach and small curved breakwater were a hundred yards along. Steps led down to it from the cliff. People were lying around on the sand. Some in swim suits or trunks, some just sitting there on rugs. Kids ran around screaming. Betty Mayfield was not on the beach.

I went back into the hotel and sat in the lounge.

I sat and smoked. I went to the newsstand and bought an evening paper and looked through it and threw it away. I strolled by the desk. My note was still in Box 1224. I went to the house phones and called Mr. Mitchell. No answer. I'm sorry. Mr. Mitchell does not answer his telephone.

A woman's voice spoke behind me: "The clerk said you wanted to see me. Mr. Marlowe—" she said. "Are you Mr. Marlowe?"

She looked as fresh as a morning rose. She was wearing dark green slacks and saddle shoes and a green windbreaker over a white shirt with a loose Paisley scarf around that. A bandeau on her hair made a nice wind-blown effect.

The bell captain was hanging out his ear six feet away. I said: "Miss Mayfield?"

"I'm Miss Mayfield."

"I have the car outside. Do you have time to look at the property?"

She looked at her wrist watch. "Ye-es, I guess so," she said. "I ought to change pretty soon, but—oh, all right."

"This way, Miss Mayfield."

She fell in beside me. We walked across the lobby. I was getting to feel quite at home there. Betty Mayfield glanced viciously at the two jigsaw puzzlers.

"I hate hotels," she said. "Come back here in fifteen years and you would find the same people sitting in the same chairs."

"Yes, Miss Mayfield. Do you know anybody named Clyde Umney?"

She shook her head. "Should I?"

"Helen Vermilyea? Ross Goble?"

She shook her head again.

"Want a drink?"

"Not now, thanks."

We came out of the bar and went along the walk and I held the door of the Olds for her. I backed out of the slot and pointed it straight up Grand Street towards the hills. She slipped dark glasses with spangled rims on her nose. "I found the traveler's checks," she said. "You're a queer sort of detective."

I reached in my pocket and held out her bottle of sleeping pills. "I was a little scared last night," I said. "I counted these but I didn't know how many had been there to start with. You said you took two. I couldn't be sure you wouldn't rouse up enough to gulp a handful."

She took the bottle and stuffed it into her windbreaker. "I had quite a few drinks. Alcohol and barbiturates make a bad combination. I sort of passed out. It was nothing else."

"I wasn't sure. It takes a minimum of thirty-five grains of that stuff to kill. Even then it takes several hours. I was in a tough spot. Your pulse and breathing seemed all right but maybe they wouldn't be later on. If I called a doctor, I might have to do a lot of talking. If you had taken an overdose, the homicide boys would be told, even if you snapped out of it. They investigate all suicide attempts. But if I guessed wrong, you wouldn't be riding with me today. And where would I be then?"

"It's a thought," she said. "I can't say I'm going to worry about it terribly. Who are these people you mentioned?"

"Clyde Umney's the lawyer who hired me to follow you—on instructions from a firm of attorneys in Washington, D.C. Helen Vermilyea is his secretary. Ross Goble is a Kansas City private eye who says he is trying to find Mitchell." I described him to her.

Her face turned stony. "Mitchell? Why should he be interested in Larry?"

I stopped at the corner of Fourth and Grand for an old coot in a motorized wheel chair to make a left turn at four miles an hour. Esmeralda is full of the damn things.

"Why should he be looking for Larry Mitchell?" she asked bitterly. "Can't anybody leave anybody else alone?"

"Don't tell me anything," I said. "Just keep on asking me questions to which I don't know the answers. It's good for my inferiority complex. I told you I had no more job. So why am I here? That's easy. I'm groping for that five grand in traveler's checks again."

"Turn left at the next corner," she said, "and we can go up into the hills. There's a wonderful view from up there. And a lot of very fancy homes."

"The hell with them," I said.

"It's also very quiet up there." She picked a cigarette out of the pack clipped to the dash and lit it.

"That's two in two days," I said. "You're hitting them hard. I counted your cigarettes last night too. And your matches. I went through your bag. I'm kind of snoopy when I get roped in on a phony like that one. Especially when the client passes out and leaves me holding the baby."

She turned her head to stare at me. "It must have been the dope and the liquor," she said. "I must have been a little off base."

"Over at the Rancho Descansado you were in great shape. You were hard as nails. We were going to take off for Rio and live in luxury. Apparently also in sin. All I had to do was get rid of the body. What a letdown! No body."

She was still staring at me, but I had to watch my driving. I made a boulevard stop and a left turn. I went along another dead-end street with old streetcar tracks still in the paving.

"Turn left up the hill at that sign. That's the high school down there."

"Who fired the gun and what at?"

She pressed her temples with the heels of her hands. "I guess *I* must have. I must have been crazy. Where is it?"

"The gun? It's safe. Just in case your dream came true, I might have to produce it."

We were climbing now. I set the pointer to hold the Olds in third. She watched that with interest. She looked around her at the pale leather seats and the gadgets.

"How can you afford an expensive car like this? You don't make a lot of money, do you?"

"They're all expensive nowadays, even the cheap ones. Fellow might as well have one that can travel. I read somewhere that a dick should always have a plain dark inconspicuous car that nobody would notice. The guy had never been to L.A. In L.A. to be conspicuous you would have to drive a flesh-pink Mercedes-Benz with a sun porch on the roof and three pretty girls sunbathing."

She giggled.

"Also," I labored the subject, "it's good advertising. Maybe I dreamed I was going to Rio. I could sell it there for more than it set me back new. On a freighter it wouldn't cost too much to ferry."

She sighed. "Oh, stop teasing me about that. I don't feel funny today."

"Seen your boy friend around?"

She sat very still. "Larry?"

"You got others?"

"Well—you might have meant Clark Brandon, although I hardly know him. Larry was pretty drunk last night. No—I haven't seen him. Perhaps he's sleeping it off."

"Doesn't answer his phone."

The road forked. One white line curved to the left. I kept straight on, for no particular reason. We passed some old Spanish houses built high on the slope and some very modern houses built downhill on the other side. The road passed these and made a wide turn to the right. The paving here looked new. The road ran out to a point of land and a turning circle. There were two big houses facing each other across the turning circle. They were loaded with glass brick and their seaward windows were green glass. The view was magnificent. I looked at it for all of three seconds. I stopped against the end curb and cut the motor and sat. We were about a thousand feet up and the whole town was spread out in front of us like a 45 degree air photo.

"He might be sick," I said. "He might have gone out. He might even be dead."

"I told you—" She began to shake. I took the stub of the cigarette away from her and put it in the ash tray. I ran the car windows up and put an arm around her shoulders and pulled her head down on my shoulder. She was limp, unresisting; but she still shook.

"You're a comfortable man," she said. "But don't rush me."

"There's a pint in the glove compartment. Want a snort?"

"Yes."

I got it out and managed to pull the metal strip loose with one hand and my teeth. I held the bottle between my knees and got the cap off. I held it to her lips. She sucked some in and shuddered. I recapped the pint and put it away.

"I hate drinking from the bottle," she said.

"Yeah. Unrefined. I'm not making love to you, Betty. I'm worried. Anything you want done?"

She was silent for a moment. Then her voice was steady, saying: "Such as what? You can have those checks back. They were yours. I gave them to you."

"Nobody gives anybody five grand like that. It makes no sense. That's why I came back down from L.A. I drove up there early this morning. Nobody goes all gooey over a character like me and talks about having half a million dollars and offers me a trip to Rio and a nice home complete with all the luxuries. Nobody drunk or sober does that because she dreamed a dead man was lying out on her balcony and would I please hurry around and throw him off into the ocean. Just what did you expect me to do when I got there—hold your hand while you dreamed?"

She pulled away and leaned in the far corner of the car. "All right, I'm a liar. I've always been a liar."

I glanced at the rear view mirror. Some kind of small dark car had turned into the road behind and stopped. I couldn't see who or what was in it. Then it swung hard right against the curbing and backed and made off the way it had come. Some fellow took the wrong road and saw it was a dead end.

"While I was on the way up those damn fire stairs," I went on, "you swallowed your pills and then faked being awfully terribly sleepy and then after a while you actually did go to sleep—I think. Okay. I went out on the balcony. No stiff. No blood. If there had been, I might have managed to get him over the top of the wall. Hard work, but not impossible, if you know how to lift. But six trained elephants couldn't have thrown him far enough to land in the ocean. It's thirty-five feet to the fence and you'd have to throw him so far out that he would clear the fence. I figure an object as heavy as a man's body would have to be thrown a good fifty feet outward to clear the fence."

"I told you I was a liar."

"But you didn't tell me why. Let's be serious. Suppose a man had been dead on your balcony. What would you expect me to do about it? Carry him down the fire stairs and get him into the car I had and drive off into the woods somewhere and bury him? You do have to take people into your confidence once in a while when bodies are lying around."

"You took my money," she said tonelessly. "You played up to me."

"That way I might find out who was crazy."

"You found out. You should be satisfied."

"I found out nothing—not even who you are."

She got angry. "I told you I was out of my mind," she said in a rushing voice. "Worry, fear, liquor, pills—why can't you leave me alone? I told you I'd give you back that money. What more do you want?"

"What do I do for it?"

"Just take it." She was snapping at me now. "That's all. Take it and go away. Far, far away."

"I think you need a good lawyer."

"That's a contradiction in terms," she sneered. "If he was good, he wouldn't be a lawyer."

"Yeah. So you've had some painful experience along those lines. I'll find out in time, either from you or some other way. But I'm still being serious. You're in trouble. Apart from what happened to Mitchell, if anything, you're in enough trouble to justify hiring yourself a lawyer. You changed your name. So you had reasons. Mitchell was putting the bite on you. So *he* had reasons. A firm of Washington attorneys is looking for you. So *they* have reasons. And their client has reasons to have them looking for you."

I stopped and looked at her as well as I could see her in the freshly darkening evening. Down below, the ocean was getting a lapis lazuli blue that somehow failed to remind me of Miss Vermilyea's eyes. A flock of gulls went south in a fairly compact mass but it wasn't the kind of tight formation North Island is used to. The evening plane from L.A. came down the coast with its port and starboard lights showing, and then the winking light below the fuselage went on and it swung out to sea for a long lazy turn into Lindbergh Field.

"So you're just a shill for a crooked lawyer," she said nastily, and grabbed for another of my cigarettes.

"I don't think he's very crooked. He just tries too hard. But that's not the point. You can lose a few bucks to him without screaming. The point is something called privilege. A licensed investigator doesn't have it. A lawyer does, provided his concern is with the interests of a client who has retained him. If the lawyer hires an investigator to work in those interests, then the investigator has privilege. That's the only way he can get it."

"You know what you can do with your privilege," she said. "Especially as it was a lawyer that hired you to spy on me."

I took the cigarette away from her and puffed on it a couple of times and handed it back.

"It's all right, Betty. I'm no use to you. Forget I tried to be."

"Nice words, but only because you think I'll pay you more to be of use to me. You're just another of them. I don't want your damn cigarette either." She threw it out of the window. "Take me back to the hotel."

I got out of the car and stamped on the cigarette. "You don't do that in the California hills," I told her. "Not even out of season." I got back into the car and turned the key and pushed the starter button. I backed away and made the turn and drove back up the curve to where the road divided. On the upper level where the solid white line curved away a small car was parked. The car was lightless. It could have been empty.

I swung the Olds hard the opposite way from the way I had come, and flicked my headlights on with the high beam. They swept the car as I turned. A hat went down over a face, but not quick enough to hide the glasses, the fat broad face, the outjutting ears of Mr. Ross Goble of Kansas City.

The lights went on past and I drove down a long hill with lazy curves. I didn't know where it went except that all roads around there led to the ocean sooner or later. At the bottom there was a T-intersection. I swung to the right and after a few blocks of narrow street I hit the boulevard and made another right turn. I was now driving back towards the main part of Esmeralda.

She didn't speak again until I got to the hotel. She jumped out quickly when I stopped.

"If you'll wait here, I'll get the money."

"We were tailed," I said.

"What—?" She stopped dead, with her head half turned.

"Small car. You didn't notice him unless you saw my lights brush him as I made the turn at the top of the hill."

"Who was it?" Her voice was tense.

"How would I know? He must have picked us up here, therefore he'll come back here. Could he be a cop?"

She looked back at me, motionless, frozen. She took a slow step, and then she rushed at me as if she was going to claw my face. She grabbed me by the arms and tried to shake me. Her breath came whistling.

"Get me out of here. Get me out of here, for the love of Christ. Anywhere. Hide me. Get me a little peace. Somewhere where I can't be followed, hounded, threatened. He swore he would do it to me. He'd follow me to the ends of the earth, to the remotest island of the Pacific—"

"To the crest of the highest mountain, to the heart of the loneliest desert," I said. "Somebody's been reading a rather old-fashioned book."

She dropped her arms and let them hang limp at her sides.

"You've got as much sympathy as a loan shark."

"I'll take you nowhere," I said. "Whatever it is that's eating you, you're going to stay put and take it."

I turned and got into the car. When I looked back, she was already halfway to the bar entrance, walking with quick strides.

# 16

If I had any sense, I would pick up my suitcase and go back home and forget all about her. By the time she made up her mind which part she was playing in which act of which play, it would probably be too late for me to do anything about it except maybe get pinched for loitering in the post office.

I waited and smoked a cigarette. Goble and his dirty little jalopy ought to show up and slip into a parking slot almost any moment. He couldn't have picked us up anywhere else, and since he knew that much he couldn't have followed us for any reason except to find out where we went.

He didn't show. I finished the cigarette, dropped it overboard, and backed out. As I turned out of the driveway towards the town, I saw his car on the other side of the street, parked left-hand to the curb. I kept going, turned right at the boulevard and took it easy so he wouldn't blow a gasket trying to keep up. There was a restaurant about a mile along called The Epicure. It had a low roof, and a red brick wall to shield it from the street and it had a bar. The entrance was at the side. I parked and went in. It wasn't doing any business yet. The barkeep was chatting with the captain and the captain didn't even wear a dinner jacket. He had one of those high desks where they keep the reservation book. The book was open and had a list of names in it for later in the evening. But it was early now. I could have a table.

The dining room was dim, candlelit, divided by a low wall into two halves. It would have looked crowded with thirty people in it. The captain shoved me in a corner and lit my candle for me. I said I would have a double Gibson. A waiter came up and started to remove the place setting on the far side of the table. I told him to leave it, a friend might join me. I studied the menu, which was almost as large as the dining room. I could have used a flashlight to read it, if I had been curious. This was about the dimmest joint I was ever in. You could be sitting at the next table from your mother and not recognize her.

The Gibson arrived. I could make out the shape of the glass and there seemed to be something in it. I tasted it and it wasn't too bad. At that moment Goble slid into the chair across from me. In so far as I could see him at all, he looked about the same as he had looked the day before. I went on peering at the menu. They ought to have printed it in braille.

Goble reached across for my glass of ice water and drank. "How you making out with the girl?" he asked casually.

"Not getting anywhere. Why?"

"Whatcha go up on the hill for?"

"I thought maybe we could neck. She wasn't in the mood. What's your interest? I thought you were looking for some guy named Mitchell."

"Very funny indeed. Some guy named Mitchell. Never heard of him, I believe you said."

"I've heard of him since. I've seen him. He was drunk. Very drunk. He damn near got himself thrown out of a place."

"Very funny," Goble said, sneering. "And how did you know his name?"

"On account of somebody called him by it. That would be *too* funny, wouldn't it?"

He sneered. "I told you to stay out of my way. I know who you are now. I looked you up."

I lit a cigarette and blew smoke in his face. "Go fry a stale egg."

"Tough, huh," he sneered. "I've pulled the arms and legs off bigger guys than you."

"Name two of them."

He leaned across the table, but the waiter came up.

"I'll have bourbon and plain water," Goble told him. "Bonded stuff. None of that bar whiskey for me. And don't try to fool me. I'll know. And bottled water. The city water here is terrible."

The waiter just looked at him.

"I'll have another of these," I said, pushing my glass.

"What's good tonight?" Goble wanted to know. "I never bother with these billboards." He flicked a disdainful finger at the menu.

"The *plat du jour* is meat loaf," the waiter said nastily.

"Hash with a starched collar," Goble said. "Make it meat loaf."

The waiter looked at me. I said the meat loaf was all right

with me. The waiter went away. Goble leaned across the table again, after first taking a quick look behind him and on both sides.

"You're out of luck, friend," he said cheerfully. "You didn't get away with it."

"Too bad," I said. "Get away with what?"

"You're bad out of luck, friend. Very bad. The tide was wrong or something. Abalone fisher—one of those guys with frog feet and rubber masks—stuck under a rock."

"The abalone fisher stuck under a rock?" A cold prickly feeling crawled down my back. When the waiter came with the drinks, I had to fight myself not to grab for mine.

"Very funny, friend."

"Say that again and I'll smash your goddam glasses for you," I snarled.

He picked up his drink and sipped it, tasted it, thought about it, nodded his head.

"I came out here to make money," he mused. "I didn't nowise come out to make trouble. Man can't make money making trouble. Man can make money keeping his nose clean. Get me?"

"Probably a new experience for you," I said. "Both ways. What was that about an abalone fisher?" I kept my voice controlled, but it was an effort.

He leaned back. My eyes were getting used to the dimness now. I could see that his fat face was amused.

"Just kidding," he said. "I don't know any abalone fishers. Only last night I learned how to pronounce the word. Still don't know what the stuff is. But things are kind of funny at that. I can't find Mitchell."

"He lives at the hotel." I took some more of my drink, not too much. This was no time to dive into it.

"I know he lives at the hotel, friend. What I don't know is where he is at right now. He ain't in his room. The hotel people ain't seen him around. I thought maybe you and the girl had some ideas about it."

"The girl is screwy," I said. "Leave her out of it. And in Esmeralda they don't say 'ain't seen.' That Kansas City dialect is an offense against public morals here."

"Shove it, Mac. When I want to get told how to talk

English I won't go to no beat-up California peeper." He turned his head and yelled: "Waiter!"

Several faces looked at him with distaste. The waiter showed up after a while and stood there with the same expression as the customers.

"Hit me again," Goble said, snapped a finger at his glass.

"It is not necessary to yell at me," the waiter said. He took the glass away.

"When I want service," Goble yelped at his back, "service is what I want."

"I hope you like the taste of wood alcohol," I told Goble.

"Me and you could get along," Goble said indifferently, "if you had any brains."

"And if you had any manners and were six inches taller and had a different face and another name and didn't act as if you thought you could lick your weight in frog spawn."

"Cut the doodads and get back to Mitchell," he said briskly. "And to the dish you was trying to fumble up the hill."

"Mitchell is a man she met on a train. He had the same effect on her that you have on me. He created in her a burning desire to travel in the opposite direction."

It was a waste of time. The guy was as invulnerable as my great-great-grandfather.

"So," he sneered, "Mitchell to her is just a guy she met on a train and didn't like when she got to know him. So she ditched him for you? Convenient you happened to be around."

The waiter came with the food. He set it out with a flourish. Vegetables, salad, hot rolls in a napkin.

"Coffee?"

I said I'd rather have mine later. Goble said yes and wanted to know where his drink was. The waiter said it was on the way—by slow freight, his tone suggested. Goble tasted his meat loaf and looked surprised. "Hell, it's good," he said. "What with so few customers I thought the place was a bust."

"Look at your watch," I said. "Things don't get moving until much later. It's that kind of town. Also, it's out of season."

"Much later is right," he said, munching. "An awful lot

later. Two, three in the A.M. sometimes. People go calling on their friends. You back at the Rancho, friend?"

I looked at him without saying anything.

"Do I have to draw you a picture, friend? I work long hours when I'm on a job."

I didn't say anything.

He wiped his mouth. "You kind of stiffened up when I said that about the guy stuck under a rock. Or could I be wrong?"

I didn't answer him.

"Okay, clam up," Goble sneered. "I thought maybe we could do a little business together. You got the physique and you take a good punch. But you don't know nothing about nothing. You don't have what it takes in my business. Where I come from you got to have brains to get by. Out here you just got to get sun-burned and forget to button your collar."

"Make me a proposition," I said between my teeth.

He was a rapid eater even when he talked too much. He pushed his plate away from him, drank some of his coffee and got a toothpick out of his vest.

"This is a rich town, friend," he said slowly. "I've studied it. I've boned up on it. I've talked to guys about it. They tell me it's one of the few spots left in our fair green country where the dough ain't quite enough. In Esmeralda you got to belong, or you're nothing. If you want to belong and get asked around and get friendly with the right people you got to have class. There's a guy here made five million fish in the rackets back in Kansas City. He bought up property, sub-divided, built houses, built some of the best properties in town. But he didn't belong to the Beach Club because he didn't get asked. So he bought it. They know who he is, they touch him big when they got a fund-raising drive, he gets service, he pays his bills, he's a good solid citizen. He throws big parties but the guests come from out of town unless they're moochers, no-goods, the usual trash you always find hopping about where there's money. But the class people of the town? He's just a nigger to them."

It was a long speech and while he made it he glanced at me casually from time to time, glanced around the room, leaned back comfortably in his chair and picked his teeth.

"He must be breaking his heart," I said. "How did they find out where his dough came from?"

Goble leaned across the small table. "A big shot from the Treasury Department comes here for a vacation every spring. Happened to see Mr. Money and know all about him. He spread the word. You think it's not breaking his heart? You don't know these hoods that have made theirs and gone respectable. He's bleeding to death inside, friend. He's found something he can't buy with folding money and it's eating him to a shell."

"How did you find out all this?"

"I'm smart. I get around. I find things out."

"All except one," I said.

"Just what's that?"

"You wouldn't know if I told you."

The waiter came up with Goble's delayed drink and took dishes away. He offered the menu.

"I never eat dessert," Goble said. "Scram."

The waiter looked at the toothpick. He reached over and deftly flicked it out from between Goble's fingers. "There's a Men's Room here, chum," he said. He dropped the toothpick into the ash tray and removed the ash tray.

"See what I mean?" Goble said to me. "Class."

I told the waiter I would have a chocolate sundae and some coffee. "And give this gentleman the check," I added.

"A pleasure," the waiter said. Goble looked disgusted. The waiter drifted. I leaned across the table and spoke softly.

"You're the biggest liar I've met in two days. And I've met a few beauties. I don't think you have any interest in Mitchell. I don't think you ever saw or heard of him until yesterday when you got the idea of using him as a cover story. You were sent here to watch a girl and I know who sent you—not who hired you, but who had it done. I know why she is being watched and I know how to fix it so that she won't be watched. If you've got any high cards, you'd better play them right away quick. Tomorrow could be too late."

He pushed his chair back and stood up. He dropped a folded and crimped bill on the table. He looked me over coolly.

"Big mouth, small brain," he said. "Save it for Thursday

when they set the trash cans out. You don't know from nothing, friend. My guess is you never will."

He walked off with his head thrust forward belligerently.

I reached across for the folded and crimped bill Goble had dropped on the table. As I expected it was only a dollar. Any guy who would drive a jalopy that might be able to do forty-five miles an hour downhill would eat in joints where the eighty-five cent dinner was something for a wild Saturday night.

The waiter slid over and dumped the check on me. I paid up and left Goble's dollar in his plate.

"Thanks," the waiter said. "That's guy's a real close friend of yours, huh?"

"The operative word is close," I said.

"The guy might be poor," the waiter said tolerantly. "One of the choice things about this town is that the people who work here can't afford to live here."

There were all of twenty people in the place when I left, and the voices were beginning to bounce down off the low ceiling.

# 17

The ramp down to the garage looked just the same as it had looked at four o'clock in the morning, but there was a swishing of water audible as I rounded the curve. The glassed-in cubicle office was empty. Somewhere somebody was washing a car, but it wouldn't be the attendant. I crossed to the door leading into the elevator lobby and held it open. The buzzer sounded behind me in the office. I let the door close and stood outside it waiting and a lean man in a long white coat came around the corner. He wore glasses, had a skin the color of cold oatmeal and hollow tired eyes. There was something Mongolian about his face, something south-of-the-border, something Indian, and something darker than that. His black hair was flat on a narrow skull.

"Your car, sir? What name, please?"

"Mr. Mitchell's car in? The two-tone Buick hardtop?"

He didn't answer right away. His eyes went to sleep. He had been asked that question before.

"Mr. Mitchell took his car out early this morning."

"How early?"

He reached for a pencil that was clipped to his pocket over the stitched-on scarlet script with the hotel name. He took the pencil out and looked at it.

"Just before seven o'clock. I went off at seven."

"You work a twelve-hour shift? It's only a little past seven now."

He put the pencil back in his pocket. "I work an eight-hour shift but we rotate."

"Oh. Last night you worked eleven to seven."

"That's right." He was looking past my shoulder at something far away. "I'm due off now."

I got out a pack of cigarettes and offered him one.

He shook his head.

"I'm only allowed to smoke in the office."

"Or in the back of a Packard sedan."

His right hand curled, as if around the haft of a knife.

"How's your supply? Needing anything?"

He stared.

"You should have said 'Supply of what?'" I told him.

He didn't answer.

"And I would have said I wasn't talking about tobacco," I went on cheerfully. "About something cured with honey."

Our eyes met and locked. Finally he said softly: "You a pusher?"

"You snapped out of it real nice, if you were in business at seven A.M. this morning. Looked to me as if you would be out of circulation for hours. You must have a clock in your head—like Eddie Arcaro."

"Eddie Arcaro," he repeated. "Oh yes, the jockey. Has a clock in his head, has he?"

"So they say."

"We might do business," he said remotely. "What's your price?"

The buzzer sounded in the office. I had heard the elevator in the shaft subconsciously. The door opened and the couple

I had seen holding hands in the lobby came through. The girl
had on an evening dress and the boy wore a tux. They stood
side by side, looking like two kids who had been caught kissing. The attendant glanced at them and went off and a car
started and came back. A nice new Chrysler convertible. The
guy handed the girl in carefully, as if she was already pregnant. The attendant stood holding the door. The guy came
around the car and thanked him and got in.

"Is it very far to The Glass Room?" he asked diffidently.

"No, sir." The attendant told them how to get there.

The guy smiled and thanked him and reached in his pocket
and gave the attendant a dollar bill.

"You could have your car brought around to the entrance,
Mr. Preston. All you have to do is call down."

"Oh thanks, but this is fine," the guy said hurriedly. He
started carefully up the ramp. The Chrysler purred out of
sight and was gone.

"Honeymooners," I said. "They're sweet. They just don't
want to be stared at."

The attendant was standing in front of me again with the
same flat look in his eyes.

"But there's nothing sweet about us," I added.

"If you're a cop, let's see the buzzer."

"You think I'm a cop?"

"You're some kind of nosy bastard." Nothing he said
changed the tone of his voice at all. It was frozen in B Flat.
Johnny One-Note.

"I'm all of that," I agreed. "I'm a private star. I followed
somebody down here last night. You were in a Packard right
over there—" I pointed—"and I went over and opened the
door and sniffed the weed. I could have driven four Cadillacs
out of here and you wouldn't have turned over in bed. But
that's your business."

"The price today," he said. "I'm not arguing about last
night."

"Mitchell left by himself?"

He nodded.

"No baggage?"

"Nine pieces. I helped him load it. He checked out.
Satisfied?"

"You checked with the office?"

"He had his bill. All paid up and receipted."

"Sure. And with that amount of baggage a hop came with him naturally."

"The elevator kid. No hops on until seven-thirty. This was about one A.M."

"Which elevator kid?"

"A Mex kid we call Chico."

"You're not Mex?"

"I'm part Chinese, part Hawaiian, part Filipino, and part nigger. You'd hate to be me."

"Just one more question. How in hell do you get away with it? The muggles, I mean."

He looked around. "I only smoke when I feel extra special low. What the hell's it to you? What the hell's it to anybody? Maybe I get caught and lose a crummy job. Maybe I get tossed in a cell. Maybe I've been in one all my life, carry it round with me. Satisfied?" He was talking too much. People with unstable nerves are like that. One moment monosyllables, next moment a flood. The low tired monotone of his voice went on.

"I'm not sore at anybody. I live. I eat. Sometimes I sleep. Come around and see me some time. I live in a flea bag in an old frame cottage on Polton's Lane, which is really an alley. I live right behind the Esmeralda Hardware Company. The toilet's in a shed. I wash in the kitchen, at a tin sink. I sleep on a couch with broken springs. Everything there is twenty years old. This is a rich man's town. Come and see me. I live on a rich man's property."

"There's a piece missing from your story about Mitchell," I said.

"Which one?"

"The truth."

"I'll look under the couch for it. It might be a little dusty."

There was the rough noise of a car entering the ramp from above. He turned away and I went through the door and rang for the elevator. He was a queer duck, the attendant, very queer. Kind of interesting, though. And kind of sad, too. One of the sad, one of the lost.

The elevator was a long time coming and before it came I

had company waiting for it. Six feet three inches of handsome, healthy male named Clark Brandon. He was wearing a leather windbreaker and a heavy roll-collar blue sweater under it, a pair of beat-up Bedford cord breeches, and the kind of high laced boots that field engineers and surveyors wear in rough country. He looked like the boss of a drilling crew. In an hour from now, I had no doubt he would be at The Glass Room in a dinner suit and he would look like the boss of that too, and perhaps he was. Plenty of money, plenty of health and plenty of time to get the best out of both, and wherever he went he would be the owner.

He glanced at me and waited for me to get into the elevator when it came. The elevator kid saluted him respectfully. He nodded. We both got off at the lobby. Brandon crossed to the desk and got a big smile from the clerk—a new one I hadn't seen before—and the clerk handed him a fistful of letters. Brandon leaned against the end of the counter and tore the envelopes open one by one and dropped them into a wastebasket beside where he was standing. Most of the letters went the same way. There was a rack of travel folders there. I picked one off and lit a cigarette and studied the folder.

Brandon had one letter that interested him. He read it several times. I could see that it was short and handwritten on the hotel stationery, but without looking over his shoulder that was all I could see. He stood holding the letter. Then he reached down into the basket and came up with the envelope. He studied that. He put the letter in his pocket and moved along the desk. He handed the clerk the envelope.

"This was handed in. Did you happen to see who left it? I don't seem to know the party."

The clerk looked at the envelope and nodded. "Yes, Mr. Brandon, a man left it just after I came on. He was a middle-aged fat man with glasses. Gray suit and topcoat and gray felt hat. Not a local type. A little shabby. A nobody."

"Did he ask for me?"

"No, sir. Just asked me to put the note in your box. Anything wrong, Mr. Brandon?"

"Look like a goof?"

The clerk shook his head. "He just looked what I said. Like a nobody."

Brandon chuckled. "He wants to make me a Mormon bishop for fifty dollars. Some kind of nut, obviously." He picked the envelope up off the counter and put it in his pocket. He started to turn away, then said: "Seen Larry Mitchell around?"

"Not since I've been on, Mr. Brandon. But that's only a couple of hours."

"Thanks."

Brandon walked across to the elevator and got in. It was a different elevator. The operator grinned all over his face and said something to Brandon. Brandon didn't answer him or look at him. The kid looked hurt as he whooshed the doors shut. Brandon was scowling. He was less handsome when he scowled.

I put the travel folder back in the rack and moved over to the desk. The clerk looked at me without interest. His glance said I was not registered there. "Yes, sir?"

He was a gray-haired man who carried himself well.

"I was just going to ask for Mr. Mitchell, but I heard what you said."

"The house phones are over there." He pointed with his chin. "The operator will connect you."

"I doubt it."

"Meaning what?"

I pulled my jacket open to get at my letter case. I could see the clerk's eyes freeze on the rounded butt of the gun under my arm. I got the letter case out and pulled a card.

"Would it be convenient for me to see your house man? If you have one."

He took the card and read it. He looked up. "Have a seat in the main lobby, Mr. Marlowe."

"Thank you."

He was on the phone before I had done a complete turn away from the desk. I went through the arch and sat against the wall where I could see the desk. I didn't have very long to wait.

The man had a hard straight back and a hard straight face, with the kind of skin that never tans but only reddens and pales out again. His hair was almost a pompadour and mostly reddish blond. He stood in the archway and let his eyes take in the lobby slowly. He didn't look at me any longer than at anybody else. Then he came over and sat down in the next chair to me. He wore a brown suit and a brown and yellow bow tie. His clothes fitted him nicely. There were fine blond hairs on his cheeks high up. There was a grace note of gray in his hair.

"My name's Javonen," he said without looking at me. "I know yours. Got your card in my pocket. What's your trouble?"

"Man named Mitchell. I'm looking for him. Larry Mitchell."

"You're looking for him why?"

"Business. Any reason why I shouldn't look for him?"

"No reason at all. He's out of town. Left early this morning."

"So I heard. It puzzled me some. He only got home yesterday. On the Super Chief. In L.A. he picked up his car and drove down. Also, he was broke. Had to make a touch for dinner money. He ate dinner at The Glass Room with a girl. He was pretty drunk—or pretended to be. It got him out of paying the check."

"He can sign his checks here," Javonen said indifferently. His eyes kept flicking around the lobby as if he expected to see one of the canasta players yank a gun and shoot his partner or one of the old ladies at the big jigsaw puzzle start pulling hair. He had two expressions—hard and harder. "Mr. Mitchell is well known in Esmeralda."

"Well, but not favorably," I said.

He turned his head and gave me a bleak stare. "I'm an assistant manager here, Mr. Marlowe. I double as security officer. I can't discuss the reputation of a guest of the hotel with you."

"You don't have to. I know it. From various sources. I've observed him in action. Last night he put the bite on somebody and got enough to blow town. Taking his baggage with him, is my information."

"Who gave this information to you?" He looked tough asking that.

I tried to look tough not answering it. "On top of that I'll give you three guesses," I said. "One, his bed wasn't slept in last night. Two, it was reported to the office sometime today that his room had been cleaned out. Three, somebody on your night staff won't show for work tonight. Mitchell couldn't get all his stuff out without help."

Javonen looked at me, then prowled the lobby again with his eyes. "Got something that proves you are what the card reads? Anyone can have a card printed."

I got my wallet out and slipped a small photostat of my license from it and passed it over. He glanced at it and handed it back. I put it away.

"We have our own organization to take care of skipouts," he said. "They happen—in any hotel. We don't need your help. And we don't like guns in the lobby. The clerk saw yours. Somebody else could see it. We had a stickup attempted here nine months ago. One of the heist guys got dead. I shot him."

"I read about it in the paper," I said. "It scared me for days and days."

"You read some of it. We lost four or five thousand dollars worth of business the week following. People checked out by the dozen. You get my point?"

"I let the clerk see my gunbutt on purpose. I've been asking for Mitchell all day and all I got was the runaround. If the man checked out, why not say so? Nobody had to tell me he had jumped his bill."

"Nobody said he jumped his bill. His bill, Mr. Marlowe, was paid in full. So where does that leave you?"

"Wondering why it was a secret he had checked out."

He looked contemptuous. "Nobody said that either. You don't listen good. I said he was out of town on a trip. I said his bill was paid in full. I didn't say how much baggage he took. I didn't say he had given up his room. I didn't say that what he took was all he had . . . Just what are you trying to make out of all this?"

"Who paid his bill?"

His face got a little red. "Look, buster, I told you *he* paid it. In person, last night, in full and a week in advance as well. I've been pretty patient with you. Now you tell me something. What's your angle?"

"I don't have one. You've talked me out of it. I wonder why he paid a week in advance."

Javonen smiled—very slightly. Call it a down payment on a smile. "Look, Marlowe, I put in five years in Military Intelligence. I can size up a man—like for instance the guy we're talking about. He pays in advance because we feel happier that way. It has a stabilizing influence."

"He ever pay in advance before?"

"God damn it . . . !"

"Watch yourself," I cut in. "The elderly gent with the walking stick is interested in your reactions."

He looked halfway across the lobby to where a thin, old, bloodless man sat in a very low round-backed padded chair with his chin on gloved hands and the gloved hands on the crook of a stick. He stared unblinkingly in our direction.

"Oh, him," Javonen said. "He can't even see this far. He's eighty years old."

He stood up and faced me. "Okay, you're clammed," he said quietly. "You're a private op, you've got a client and instructions. I'm only interested in protecting the hotel. Leave the gun home next time. If you have questions, come to me. Don't question the help. It gets told around and we don't like it. You wouldn't find the local cops friendly if I suggested you were being troublesome."

"Can I buy a drink in the bar before I go?"

"Keep your jacket buttoned."

"Five years in Military Intelligence is a lot of experience," I said looking up at him admiringly.

"It ought to be enough." He nodded briefly and strolled away through the arch, back straight, shoulders back, chin in, a hard lean well set-up piece of man. A smooth operator. He had milked me dry—of everything that was printed on my business card.

Then I noticed that the old party in the low chair had lifted a gloved hand off the crook of his stick and was curving a finger at me. I pointed a finger at my chest and looked the question. He nodded, so over I went.

He was old, all right, but a long way from feeble and a long way from dim. His white hair was neatly parted, his nose was long and sharp and veined, his faded-out blue eyes were still keen, but the lids drooped wearily over them. One ear held the plastic button of a hearing aid, grayish pink like his ear.

The suede gloves on his hands had the cuffs turned back. He wore gray spats over polished black shoes.

"Pull up a chair, young man." His voice was thin and dry and rustled like bamboo leaves.

I sat down beside him. He peered at me and his mouth smiled. "Our excellent Mr. Javonen spent five years in Military Intelligence, as no doubt he told you."

"Yes, sir. CIC, a branch of it."

"Military Intelligence is an expression which contains an interior fallacy. So you are curious about how Mr. Mitchell paid his bill?"

I stared at him. I looked at the hearing aid. He tapped his breast pocket. "I was deaf long before they invented these things. As the result of a hunter balking at a fence. It was my own fault. I lifted him too soon. I was still a young man. I couldn't see myself using an ear trumpet, so I learned to lip-read. It takes a certain amount of practice."

"What about Mitchell, sir?"

"We'll come to him. Don't be in a hurry." He looked up and nodded.

A voice said, "Good evening, Mr. Clarendon." A bellhop went by on his way to the bar. Clarendon followed him with his eyes.

"Don't bother with that one," he said. "He's a pimp. I have spent many many years in lobbies, in lounges and bars, on porches, terraces and ornate gardens in hotels all over the world. I have outlived everyone in my family. I shall go on being useless and inquisitive until the day comes when the stretcher carries me off to some nice airy corner room in a hospital. The starched white dragons will minister to me. The bed will be wound up, wound down. Trays will come with that awful loveless hospital food. My pulse and temperature will be taken at frequent intervals and invariably when I am dropping off to sleep. I shall lie there and hear the rustle of the starched skirts, the slurring sound of the rubber shoe soles on the aseptic floor, and see the silent horror of the doctor's smile. After a while they will put the oxygen tent over me and draw the screens around the little white bed and I shall, without even knowing it, do the one thing in the world no man ever has to do twice."

He turned his head slowly and looked at me. "Obviously, I talk too much. Your name, sir?"

"Philip Marlowe."

"I am Henry Clarendon IV. I belong to what used to be called the upper classes. Groton, Harvard, Heidelberg, the Sorbonne. I even spent a year at Uppsala. I cannot clearly remember why. To fit me for a life of leisure, no doubt. So you are a private detective. I do eventually get around to speaking of something other than myself, you see."

"Yes, sir."

"You should have come to me for information. But of course you couldn't know that."

I shook my head. I lit a cigarette, first offering one to Mr. Henry Clarendon IV. He refused it with a vague nod.

"However, Mr. Marlowe, it is something you should have certainly learned. In every luxury hotel in the world there will be half a dozen elderly idlers of both sexes who sit around and stare like owls. They watch, they listen, they compare notes, they learn everything about everyone. They have nothing else to do, because hotel life is the most deadly of all forms of boredom. And no doubt I'm boring you equally."

"I'd rather hear about Mitchell, sir. Tonight at least, Mr. Clarendon."

"Of course. I'm egocentric, and absurd, and I prattle like a schoolgirl. You observe that handsome dark-haired woman over there playing canasta? The one with too much jewelry and the heavy gold trim on her glasses?"

He didn't point or even look. But I picked her out. She had an overblown style and she looked just a little hardboiled. She was the one with the ice, the paint.

"Her name is Margo West. She is seven times a divorcee. She has stacks of money and reasonably good looks, but she can't hold a man. She tries too hard. Yet she's not a fool. She would have an affair with a man like Mitchell, she would give him money and pay his bills, but she would never marry him. They had a fight last night. Nevertheless I believe she may have paid his bill. She often has before."

"I thought he got a check from his father in Toronto every month. Not enough to last him, huh?"

Henry Clarendon IV gave me a sardonic smile. "My dear

fellow, Mitchell has no father in Toronto. He gets no monthly check. He lives on women. That is why he lives in a hotel like this. There is always some rich and lonely female in a luxury hotel. She may not be beautiful or very young, but she has other charms. In the dull season in Esmeralda, which is from the end of the race meet at Del Mar until about the middle of January, the pickings are very lean. Then Mitchell is apt to travel — Majorca or Switzerland if he can make it, to Florida or one of the Caribbean islands if he is not in rich funds. This year he had poor luck. I understand he only got as far as Washington."

He brushed a glance at me. I stayed deadpan polite, just a nice youngish guy (by his standards) being polite to an old gentleman who liked to talk.

"Okay," I said. "She paid his hotel bill, maybe. But why a week in advance?"

He moved one gloved hand over the other. He tilted his stick and followed it with his body. He stared at the pattern in the carpet. Finally he clicked his teeth. He had solved the problem. He straightened up again.

"That would be severance pay," he said dryly. "The final and irrevocable end of the romance. Mrs. West, as the English say, had had it. Also, there was a new arrival in Mitchell's company yesterday, a girl with dark red hair. Chestnut red, not fire red or strawberry red. What I saw of their relationship seemed to me a little peculiar. They were both under some sort of strain."

"Would Mitchell blackmail a woman?"

He chuckled. "He would blackmail an infant in a cradle. A man who lives on women always blackmails them, although the word may not be used. He also steals from them when he can get his hands on any of their money. Mitchell forged two checks with Margo West's name. That ended the affair. No doubt she has the checks. But she won't do anything about it except keep them."

"Mr. Clarendon, with all due respect, how in hell would you know all these things?"

"She told me. She cried on my shoulder." He looked toward the handsome dark-haired woman. "She does not at the moment look as if I could be telling the truth. Nevertheless I am."

"And why are you telling it to me?"

His face moved into a rather ghastly grin. "I have no delicacy. I should like to marry Margo West myself. It would reverse the pattern. Very small things amuse a man of my age. A hummingbird, the extraordinary way a strellitzia bloom opens. Why at a certain point in its growth does the bud turn at right angles? Why does the bud split so gradually and why do the flowers emerge always in a certain exact order, so that the sharp unopened end of the bud looks like a bird's beak and the blue and orange petals make a bird of paradise? What strange deity made such a complicated world when presumably he could have made a simple one? Is he omnipotent? How could he be? There's so much suffering and almost always by the innocent. Why will a mother rabbit trapped in a burrow by a ferret put her babies behind her and allow her throat to be torn out? Why? In two weeks more she would not even recognize them. Do you believe in God, young man?"

It was a long way around, but it seemed I had to travel it. "If you mean an omniscient and omnipotent God who intended everything exactly the way it is, no."

"But you should, Mr. Marlowe. It is a great comfort. We all come to it in the end because we have to die and become dust. Perhaps for the individual that is all, perhaps not. There are grave difficulties about the afterlife. I don't think I should really enjoy a heaven in which I shared lodgings with a Congo pygmy or a Chinese coolie or a Levantine rug peddler or even a Hollywood producer. I'm a snob, I suppose, and the remark is in bad taste. Nor can I imagine a heaven presided over by a benevolent character in a long white beard locally known as God. These are foolish conceptions of very immature minds. But you may not question a man's religious beliefs however idiotic they may be. Of course I have no right to assume that I shall go to heaven. Sounds rather dull, as a matter of fact. On the other hand how can I imagine a hell in which a baby that died before baptism occupies the same degraded position as a hired killer or a Nazi death-camp commandant or a member of the Politburo? How strange it is that man's finest aspirations, dirty little animal that he is, his finest actions also, his great and unselfish heroism, his constant daily courage in a harsh world—how strange that these things should be so much finer than his fate on this earth. That has to be somehow made reasonable. Don't tell me that honor is merely a chemical reaction or that a man who deliberately gives his life for another is merely following a behavior pattern. Is God happy with the poisoned cat dying alone in convulsions behind the billboard? Is God happy that life is cruel and that only the fittest survive? The fittest for what? Oh no, far from it. If God were omnipotent and omniscient in any literal sense, he wouldn't have bothered to make the universe at all. There is no success where there is no possibility of failure, no art without the resistance of the medium. Is it blasphemy to suggest that God has his bad days when nothing goes right, and that God's days are very, very long?"

"You're a wise man, Mr. Clarendon. You said something about reversing the pattern."

He smiled faintly. "You thought I had lost the place in the overlong book of my words. No sir, I had not. A woman like Mrs. West almost always ends up marrying a series of pseudo-elegant fortune hunters, tango dancers with handsome sideburns, skiing instructors with beautiful blond muscles, faded French and Italian aristocrats, shoddy princelings from the Middle East, each worse than the one before. She might even in her extremity marry a man like Mitchell. If she married me, she would marry an old bore, but at least she would marry a gentleman."

"Yeah."

He chuckled. "The monosyllable indicates a surfeit of Henry Clarendon IV. I don't blame you. Very well, Mr. Marlowe, why are you interested in Mitchell? But I suppose you can't tell me."

"No sir, I can't. I'm interested in knowing why he left so soon after coming back, who paid his bill for him and why, if Mrs. West or, say, some well-heeled friend like Clark Brandon paid for him, it was necessary to pay a week in advance as well."

His thin worn eyebrows curved upwards. "Brandon could easily guarantee Mitchell's account by lifting the telephone.

Mrs. West might prefer to give him the money and have him pay the bill himself. But a week in advance? Why would our Javonen tell you that? What does it suggest to you?"

"That there's something about Mitchell the hotel doesn't want known. Something that might cause the sort of publicity they hate."

"Such as?"

"Suicide and murder are the sort of things I mean. That's just by way of example. You've noticed how the name of a big hotel is hardly ever mentioned when one of the guests jumps out of a window? It's always a midtown or a downtown hotel or a well-known exclusive hotel — something like that. And if it's rather a high class place, you never see any cops in the lobby, no matter what happened upstairs."

His eyes went sideways and mine followed his. The canasta table was breaking up. The dolled-up and well-iced woman called Margo West strolled off towards the bar with one of the men, her cigarette holder sticking out like a bowsprit.

"So?"

"Well," I said, and I was working hard, "if Mitchell keeps his room on the records, whatever room he had — "

"Four-eighteen," Clarendon put in calmly. "On the ocean side. Fourteen dollars a day out of season, eighteen in season."

"Not exactly cheap for a guy on his uppers. But he still has it, let's say. So whatever happened, he's just away for a few days. Took his car out, put his luggage in around seven A.M. this morning. A damn funny time to leave when he was as drunk as a skunk late last night."

Clarendon leaned back and let his gloved hands hang limp. I could see that he was getting tired. "If it happened that way, wouldn't the hotel prefer to have you think he had left for good? Then you'd have to search for him somewhere else. That is, if you really are searching for him."

I met his pale stare. He grinned.

"You're not making very good sense to me, Mr. Marlowe. I talk and talk, but not merely to hear the sound of my voice. I don't hear it naturally in any case. Talking gives me an opportunity to study people without seeming altogether rude. I have studied you. My intuition, if such be the correct word, tells me that your interest in Mitchell is rather tangential. Otherwise you would not be so open about it."

"Uh-huh. Could be," I said. It was a spot for a paragraph of lucid prose. Henry Clarendon IV would have obliged. I didn't have a damn thing more to say.

"Run along now," he said. "I'm tired. I'm going up to my room and lie down a little. A pleasure to have met you, Mr. Marlowe." He got slowly to his feet and steadied himself with the stick. It was an effort. I stood up beside him.

"I never shake hands," he said. "My hands are ugly and painful. I wear gloves for that reason. Good evening. If I don't see you again, good luck."

He went off, walking slowly and keeping his head erect. I could see that walking wasn't any fun for him. The two steps up from the main lobby to the arch were made one at a time, with a pause in between. His right foot always moved first. The cane bore down hard beside his left. He went out through the arch and I watched him move towards an elevator. I decided Mr. Henry Clarendon IV was a pretty smooth article.

I strolled along to the bar. Mrs. Margo West was sitting in the amber shadows with one of the canasta players. The waiter was just setting drinks before them. I didn't pay too much attention because farther along in a little booth against the wall was someone I knew better. And alone.

She had the same clothes on except that she had taken the bandeau off her hair and it hung loose around her face.

I sat down. The waiter came over and I ordered. He went away. The music from the invisible record player was low and ingratiating.

She smiled a little. "I'm sorry I lost my temper," she said. "I was very rude."

"Forget it. I had it coming."

"Were you looking for me in here?"

"Not especially."

"Were you—oh, I forgot." She reached for her bag and put it in her lap. She fumbled in it and then passed something rather small across the table, something not small enough for her hand to hide that it was a folder of traveler's checks. "I promised you these."

"No."

"Take them, you fool! I don't want the waiter to see."

I took the folder and slipped it into my pocket. I reached into my inside pocket and got out a small receipt book. I entered the counterfoil and then the body of the receipt. "Received from Miss Betty Mayfield, Hotel Casa del Poniente, Esmeralda, California, the sum of $5000 in American Express Company traveler's checks of $100 denomination, countersigned by the owner, and remaining her property, subject to her demand at any time until a fee is arranged with, and an employment accepted by me, the undersigned."

I signed this rigmarole and held the book for her to see it.

"Read it and sign your name in the lower left-hand corner."

She took it and held it close to the light.

"You make me tired," she said. "Whatever are you trying to spring?"

"That I'm on the level and you think so."

She took the pen I held out and signed and gave the stuff back to me. I tore out the original and handed it to her. I put the book away.

The waiter came and put my drink down. He didn't wait to be paid. Betty shook her head at him. He went away.

"Why don't you ask me if I have found Larry?"

"All right. Have you found Larry, Mr. Marlowe?"

"No. He has skipped the hotel. He had a room on the fourth floor on the same side as your room. Must be fairly nearly under it. He took nine pieces of luggage and beat it in his Buick. The house peeper, whose name is Javonen—he calls himself an assistant manager and security officer—is satisfied that Mitchell paid his bill and even a week in advance for his room. He has no worries. He doesn't like me, of course."

"Does somebody?"

"You do—five thousand dollars worth."

"Oh, you *are* an idiot. Do you think Mitchell will come back?"

"I told you he paid a week in advance."

She sipped her drink quietly. "So you did. But that could mean something else."

"Sure. Just spitballing, for example, I might say it could mean that he didn't pay his bill, but someone else did. And that the someone else wanted time to do something—such as getting rid of that body on your balcony last night. That is, if there was a body."

"Oh, stop it!"

She finished her drink, killed her cigarette, stood up and left me with the check. I paid it and went back through the lobby, for no reason that I could think of. Perhaps by pure instinct. And I saw Goble getting into the elevator. He seemed to have a rather strained expression. As he turned he caught my eye, or seemed to, but he gave no sign of knowing me. The elevator went up.

I went out to my car and drove back to the Rancho Descansado. I lay down on the couch and went to sleep. It had been a lot of day. Perhaps if I had a rest and my brain cleared, I might have some faint idea of what I was doing.

# 18

An hour later I was parked in front of the hardware store. It wasn't the only hardware store in Esmeralda, but it was the only one that backed on the alley called Polton's Lane. I walked east and counted the stores. There were seven of them to the corner, all shining with plate glass and chromium trim. On the corner was a dress shop with mannequins in the windows, scarves and gloves and costume jewelry laid out under the lights. No prices showing. I rounded the corner and went south. Heavy eucalyptus trees grew out of the sidewalk. They branched low down and the trunks looked hard and heavy, quite unlike the tall brittle stuff that grows around Los Angeles. At the far corner of Polton's Lane there was an automobile agency. I followed its high blank wall, looking at broken crates, piles of cartons, trash drums, dusty parking spaces, the back yard of elegance. I counted the buildings. It was easy. No questions to ask. A light burned in the small window of a tiny frame cottage that had long ago been somebody's simple home. The cottage had a wooden porch with a broken railing. It had been painted once, but that was in the remote past before the shops swallowed it up. Once it may even have had a garden. The shingles of the roof were warped. The front door was a dirty mustard yellow. The window was shut tight and needed hosing off. Behind part of it hung what remained of an old roller blind. There were two steps up to the porch, but only one had a tread. Behind the cottage and halfway to the loading platform of the hardware store there was what had presumably been a privy. But I could see where a water pipe cut through the sagging side. A rich man's improvements on a rich man's property. A one-unit slum.

I stepped over the hollow place where a step should have been and knocked on the door. There was no bell push. Nobody answered. I tried the knob. Nobody had locked the door. I pushed it open and went in. I had that feeling. I was going to find something nasty inside.

A bulb burned in a frayed lamp crooked on its base, the paper shade split. There was a couch with a dirty blanket on it. There was an old cane chair, a Boston rocker, a table covered with a smeared oilcloth. On the table spread out beside a coffee cup was a copy of *El Diario*, a Spanish language newspaper, also a saucer with cigarette stubs, a dirty plate, a tiny radio which emitted music. The music stopped and a man began to rattle off a commercial in Spanish. I turned it off. The silence fell like a bag of feathers. Then the clicking of an alarm clock from beyond a half open door. Then the clank of a small chain, a fluttering sound and a cracked voice said rapidly: *"Quién es? Quién es? Quién es?"* This was followed by the angry chattering of monkeys. Then silence again.

From a big cage over in the corner the round angry eye of a parrot looked at me. He sidled along the perch as far as he could go.

*"Amigo,"* I said.

The parrot let out a screech of insane laughter.

"Watch your language, brother," I said.

The parrot crabwalked to the other end of the perch and pecked into a white cup and shook oatmeal from his beak contemptuously. In another cup there was water. It was messy with oatmeal.

"I bet you're not even housebroken," I said.

The parrot stared at me and shuffled. He turned his head and stared at me with his other eye. Then he leaned forward and fluttered his tail feathers and proved me right.

*"Necio!"* he screamed. *"Fuera!"*

Somewhere water dripped from a leaky faucet. The clock ticked. The parrot imitated the ticking amplified.

I said: "Pretty Polly."

*"Hijo de la chingada,"* the parrot said.

I sneered at him and pushed the half-open door into what there was of a kitchen. The linoleum on the floor was worn through to the boards in front of the sink. There was a rusty three-burner gas stove, an open shelf with some dishes and the alarm clock, a riveted hot water tank on a support in the corner, the antique kind that blows up because it has no safety valve. There was a narrow rear door, closed, with a key in the lock, and a single window, locked. There was a light bulb hanging from the ceiling. The ceiling above it was cracked and stained from roof leaks. Behind me the parrot shuffled aimlessly on his perch and once in a while let out a bored croak.

On the zinc drainboard lay a short length of black rubber tubing, and beside that a glass hypodermic syringe with the plunger pushed home. In the sink were three long thin empty tubes of glass with tiny corks near them. I had seen such tubes before.

I opened the back door, stepped to the ground and walked to the converted privy. It had a sloping roof, about eight feet high in front, less than six at the back. It opened outward, being too small to open any other way. It was locked but the lock was old. It did not resist me much.

The man's scuffed toes almost touched the floor. His head was up in the darkness inches from the two by four that held up the roof. He was hanging by a black wire, probably a piece of electric light wire. The toes of his feet were pointed down as if they reached to stand on tiptoe. The worn cuffs of his khaki denim pants hung below his heels. I touched him enough to know that he was cold enough so that there was no point in cutting him down.

He had made very sure of that. He had stood by the sink in his kitchen and knotted the rubber tube around his arm, then clenched his fist to make the vein stand out, then shot a syringeful of morphine sulphate into his blood stream. Since all three of the tubes were empty, it was a fair guess that one of them had been full. He could not have taken in less than enough. Then he had laid the syringe down and released the knotted tube. It wouldn't be long, not a shot directly into the blood stream. Then he had gone out to his privy and stood on the seat and knotted the wire around his throat. By that time he would be dizzy. He could stand there and wait until his knees went slack and the weight of his body took care of the rest. He would know nothing. He would already be asleep.

I closed the door on him. I didn't go back into the house. As I went along the side towards Polton's Lane, that handsome residential street, the parrot inside the shack heard me and screeched: *"Quién es? Quién es? Quién es?"*

Who is it? Nobody, friend. Just a footfall in the night.

I walked softly, going away.

# 19

I walked softly, in no particular direction, but I knew where I would end up. I always did. At the Casa del Poniente. I climbed back into my car on Grand and circled a few blocks aimlessly, and then I was parked as usual in a slot near the bar entrance. As I got out I looked at the car beside mine. It was Goble's shabby dark little jalopy. He was as adhesive as a band-aid.

At another time I would have been racking my brains for some idea of what he was up to, but now I had a worse problem. I had to go to the police and report the hanging man. But I had no notion what to tell them. Why did I go to his house? Because, if he was telling the truth, he had seen Mitchell leave early in the morning. Why was that of significance? Because I was looking for Mitchell myself. I wanted to have a heart to heart talk with him. About what? And from there on I had no answers that would not lead to Betty

Mayfield, who she was, where she came from, why she changed her name, what had happened back in Washington, or Virginia or wherever it was, that made her run away.

I had $5000 of her money in traveler's checks in my pocket, and she wasn't even formally my client. I was stuck, but good.

I walked over to the edge of the cliff and listened to the sound of the surf. I couldn't see anything but the occasional gleam of a wave breaking out beyond the cove. In the cove the waves don't break, they slide in politely, like floorwalkers. There would be a bright moon later, but it hadn't checked in yet.

Someone was standing not far away, doing what I was doing. A woman. I waited for her to move. When she moved I would know whether I knew her. No two people move in just the same way, just as no two sets of fingerprints match exactly.

I lit a cigarette and let the lighter flare in my face, and she was beside me.

"Isn't it about time you stopped following me around?"

"You're my client. I'm trying to protect you. Maybe on my seventieth birthday someone will tell me why."

"I didn't ask you to protect me. I'm not your client. Why don't you go home—if you have a home—and stop annoying people?"

"You're my client—five thousand dollars worth. I have to do something for it—even if it's no more than growing a mustache."

"You're impossible. I gave you the money to let me alone. You're impossible. You're the most impossible man I ever met. And I've met some dillies."

"What happened to that tall exclusive apartment house in Rio? Where I was going to lounge in silk pajamas and play with your long lascivious hair, while the butler set out the Wedgwood and the Georgian silver with that faint dishonest smile and those delicate gestures, like a pansy hair stylist fluttering around a screen star?"

"Oh, shut up!"

"Wasn't a firm offer, huh? Just a passing fancy, or not even that. Just a trick to make me slaughter my sleeping hours and trot around looking for bodies that weren't there."

"Did anybody ever give you a swift poke in the nose?"

"Frequently, but sometimes I make them miss."

I grabbed hold of her. She tried to fight me off, but no fingernails. I kissed the top of her head. Suddenly she clung to me and turned her face up.

"All right. Kiss me, if it's any satisfaction to you. I suppose you would rather have this happen where there was a bed."

"I'm human."

"Don't kid yourself. You're a dirty low-down detective. Kiss me."

I kissed her. With my mouth close to hers I said: "He hanged himself tonight."

She jerked away from me violently. "Who?" she asked in a voice that could hardly speak.

"The night garage attendant here. You may never have seen him. He was on mesca, tea, marijuana. But tonight he shot himself full of morphine and hanged himself in the privy behind his shack in Polton's Lane. That's an alley behind Grand Street."

She was shaking now. She was hanging on to me as if to keep from falling down. She tried to say something, but her voice was just a croak.

"He was the guy that said he saw Mitchell leave with his nine suitcases early this morning. I wasn't sure I believed him. He told me where he lived and I went over this evening to talk to him some more. And now I have to go to the cops and tell them. And what do I tell them without telling them about Mitchell and from then on about you?"

"Please—please—*please* leave me out of it," she whispered. "I'll give you more money. I'll give you all the money you want."

"For Pete's sake. You've already given me more than I'd keep. It isn't money I want. It's some sort of understanding of what the hell I'm doing and why. You must have heard of professional ethics. Some shreds of them still stick to me. Are you my client?"

"Yes. I give up. They all give up to you in the end, don't they?"

"Far from it. I get pushed around plenty."

I got the folder of traveler's checks out of my pocket and

put a pencil flash on them and tore out five. I refolded it and handed it to her. "I've kept five hundred dollars. That makes it legal. Now tell me what it's all about."

"No. You don't have to tell anybody about that man."

"Yes, I do. I have to go to the cop house just about now. I have to. And I have no story to tell them that they won't bust open in three minutes. Here, take your goddam checks—and if you ever push them at me again, I'll smack your bare bottom."

She grabbed the folder and tore off into the darkness to the hotel. I just stood there and felt like a damn fool. I don't know how long I stood there, but finally I stuffed the five checks into my pocket and went wearily back to my car and started off to the place where I knew I had to go.

## 20

A man named Fred Pope who ran a small motel had once told me his views on Esmeralda. He was elderly, talkative, and it always pays to listen. The most unlikely people sometimes drop a fact or two that means a lot in my business.

"I been here thirty years," he said. "When I come here I had dry asthma. Now I got wet asthma. I recall when this town was so quiet dogs slept in the middle of the boulevard and you had to stop your car, if you had a car, and get out and push them out of the way. The bastards just sneered at you. Sundays it was like you was already buried. Everything shut up as tight as a bank vault. You could walk down Grand Street and have as much fun as a stiff in the morgue. You couldn't even buy a pack of cigarettes. It was so quiet you could of heard a mouse combin' his whiskers. Me and my old woman—she's been dead fifteen years now—used to play cribbage in a little place we had down on the street that goes along the cliff, and we'd listen in case something exciting would happen—like an old geezer taking a walk and tapping with a cane. I don't know if the Hellwigs wanted it that way or whether old man Hellwig done it out of spite. In them years he didn't live here. He was a big shot in the farm equipment business."

"More likely," I said, "he was smart enough to know that a place like Esmeralda would become a valuable investment in time."

"Maybe," Fred Pope said. "Anyhow, he just about created the town. And after a while he come to live here—up on the hill in one of them great big stucco houses with tile roofs. Pretty fancy. He had gardens with terraces and big green lawns and flowering shrubs, and wrought iron gates—imported from Italy, I heard, and Arizona fieldstone walks, and not just one garden, half a dozen. And enough land to keep the neighbors out of his hair. He drank a couple bottles of hooch a day and I heard he was a pretty rough customer. He had one daughter, Miss Patricia Hellwig. She was the real cream and still is.

"By that time Esmeralda had begun to fill up. At first it was a lot of old women and their husbands, and I'm tellin' you the mortician business was real good with tired old men that died and got planted by their loving widows. The goddam women last too long. Mine didn't."

He stopped and turned his head away for a moment, before he went on.

"There was a streetcar from San Diego by then, but the town was still quiet—too quiet. Not hardly anybody got born here. Child-bearing was thought kind of too sexy. But the war changed all that. Now we got guys that sweat, and tough school kids in levis and dirty shirts, and artists and country club drunks and them little gifte shoppes that sell you a two-bit highball glass for eight-fifty. We got restaurants and liquor stores, but we still don't have no billboards or pool-rooms or drive-ins. Last year they tried to put in a dime-in-the-slot telescope in the park. You ought to of heard the town council scream. They killed it for sure, but the place ain't no bird refuge any more. We got as smart stores as Beverly Hills. And Miss Patricia, she spent her whole life working like a beaver to give things to the town. Hellwig died five years ago. The doctors told him he would have to cut down on the booze or he wouldn't live a year. He cussed them out and said if he couldn't take a drink when he wanted to, morning, noon or night, he'd be damned if he'd take one at all. He quit—and he was dead in a year.

"The docs had a name for it—they always have—and I guess Miss Hellwig had a name for them. Anyway, they got bumped off the staff of the hospital and that knocked them loose from Esmeralda. It didn't matter a whole lot. We still got about sixty doctors here. The town's full of Hellwigs, some with other names, but all of the family one way or another. Some are rich and some work. I guess Miss Hellwig works harder than most. She's eighty-six now, but tough as a mule. She don't chew tobacco, drink, smoke, swear or use no make-up. She give the town the hospital, a private school, a library, an art center, public tennis courts, and God knows what else. And she still gets driven in a thirty-year-old Rolls-Royce that's about as noisy as a Swiss watch. The mayor here is two jumps from a Hellwig, both downhill. I guess she built the municipal center too, and sold it to the city for a dollar. She's some woman. Of course we got Jews here now, but let me tell you something. A Jew is supposed to give you a sharp deal and steal your nose, if you ain't careful. That's all bunk. A Jew enjoys trading; he likes business, but he's only tough on the surface. Underneath a Jewish businessman is usually real nice to deal with. He's human. If you want cold-blooded skinning, we got a bunch of people in this town now that will cut you down to the bone and add a service charge. They'll take your last dollar from you between your teeth and look at you like you stole it from them."

## 21

The cop house was part of a long modernistic building at the corner of Hellwig and Orcutt. I parked and went into it, still wondering how to tell my story, and still knowing I had to tell it.

The business office was small but very clean, and the duty officer on the desk had two sharp creases in his shirt, and his uniform looked as if it had been pressed ten minutes before.

A battery of six speakers on the wall was bringing in police and sheriff's reports from all over the county. A tilted plaque on the desk said the duty officer's name was Griddell. He looked at me the way they all look, waiting.

"What can we do for you, sir?" He had a cool pleasant voice, and that look of discipline you find in the best ones.

"I have to report a death. In a shack behind the hardware store on Grand, in an alley called Polton's Lane, there's a man hanging in a sort of privy. He's dead. No chance to save him."

"Your name, please?" He was already pressing buttons.

"Philip Marlowe. I'm a Los Angeles private detective."

"Did you notice the number of this place?"

"It didn't have one that I could see. But it's right smack behind the Esmeralda Hardware Company."

"Ambulance call, urgent," he said into his mike. "Possible suicide in a small house behind the Esmeralda Hardware Store. Man hanging in a privy behind the house."

He looked up at me. "Do you know his name?"

I shook my head. "But he was the night garage man at the Casa del Poniente."

He flicked some sheets of a book. "We know him. Has a record for marijuana. Can't figure how he held the job, but he may be off it now, and his sort of labor is pretty scarce here."

A tall sergeant with a granite face came into the office, gave me a quick glance and went out. A car started.

The duty officer flicked a key on a small PBX. "Captain, this is Griddell on the desk. A Mr. Philip Marlowe has reported a death in Polton's Lane. Ambulance moving. Sergeant Green is on his way. I have two patrol cars in the vicinity."

He listened for a moment, then looked at me. "Captain Alessandro would like to speak to you, Mr. Marlowe. Down the hall, last door on the right, please."

He was on the mike again before I was through the swinging door.

The last door on the right had two names on it. Captain Alessandro in a plaque fastened to the wood, and Sergeant Green on a removable panel. The door was half open, so I knocked and went in.

The man at the desk was as immaculate as the desk officer. He was studying a card through a magnifying glass, and a tape recorder beside him was telling some dreary story in a crumpled, unhappy voice. The captain was about six feet three inches tall and had thick dark hair and a clear olive skin. His uniform cap was on the desk near him. He looked up, cut off the tape recorder and put down the magnifying glass and the card.

"Have a seat, Mr. Marlowe."

I sat down. He looked at me for a moment without speaking. He had rather soft brown eyes, but his mouth was not soft.

"I understand you know Major Javonen at the Casa."

"I've met him, Captain. We are not close friends."

He smiled faintly. "That's hardly to be expected. He wouldn't enjoy private detectives asking questions in the hotel. He used to be in the CIC. We still call him Major. This is the politest goddam town I was ever in. We are a goddam smooth bunch around here, but we're police just the same. Now about this Ceferino Chang?"

"So that's his name. I didn't know."

"Yes. We know him. May I ask what you are doing in Esmeralda?"

"I was hired by a Los Angeles attorney named Clyde Umney to meet the Super Chief and follow a certain party until that party came to a stop somewhere. I wasn't told why, but Mr. Umney said he was acting for a firm of Washington attorneys and he didn't know why himself. I took the job because there is nothing illegal in following a person, if you don't interfere with that person. The party ended up in Esmeralda. I went back to Los Angeles and tried to find out what it was all about. I couldn't, so I took what I thought was a reasonable fee, two hundred and fifty, and absorbed my own expenses. Mr. Umney was not very pleased with me."

The captain nodded. "That doesn't explain why you are here or what you have to do with Ceferino Chang. And since you are not now working for Mr. Umney, unless you are working for another attorney you have no privilege."

"Give me a break, if you can, Captain. I found out that the party I was following was being blackmailed, or there was an attempt at blackmail, by a man named Larry Mitchell. He lives or lived at the Casa. I have been trying to get in touch with him, but the only information I have is from Javonen and this Ceferino Chang. Javonen said he checked out, paid his bill, and a week in advance for his room. Chang told me he left at seven A.M. this morning with nine suitcases. There was something a bit peculiar about Chang's manner, so I wanted to have another talk with him."

"How did you know where he lived?"

"He told me. He was a bitter man. He said he lived on a rich man's property, and he seemed angry that it wasn't kept up."

"Not good enough, Marlowe."

"Okay, I didn't think it was myself. He was on the weed. I pretended to be a pusher. Once in a while in my business a man has to do a good deal of faking."

"Better. But there's something missing. The name of your client—if you have one."

"Could it be in confidence?"

"Depends. We never disclose the names of blackmail victims, unless they come out in court. But if this party has committed or been indicted for a crime, or has crossed a state line to escape prosecution, then it would be my duty as an officer of the law to report her present whereabouts and the name she is using."

"Her? So you know already. Why ask me? I don't know why she ran away. She won't tell me. All I know is she is in trouble and in fear, and that somehow Mitchell knew enough to make her say uncle."

He made a smooth gesture with his hand and fished a cigarette out of a drawer. He stuck it in his mouth but didn't light it.

He gave me another steady look.

"Okay, Marlowe. For now I'll let it lay. But if you dig anything up, here is where you bring it."

I stood up. He stood up too and held his hand out.

"We're not tough. We just have a job to do. Don't get too hostile with Javonen. The guy who owns that hotel draws a lot of water around here."

"Thanks, Captain. I'll try to be a nice little boy—even to Javonen."

I went back along the hall. The same officer was on the desk. He nodded to me and I went out into the evening and got into my car. I sat with my hands tight on the steering wheel. I wasn't too used to cops who treated me as if I had a right to be alive. I was sitting there when the desk officer poked his head out of the door and called that Captain Alessandro wanted to see me again.

When I got back to Captain Alessandro's office, he was on the telephone. He nodded me to the customer's chair and went on listening and making quick notes in what looked like the sort of condensed writing that many reporters use. After a while he said: "Thanks very much. We'll be in touch."

He leaned back and tapped on his desk and frowned.

"That was a report from the sheriff's substation at Escondido. Mitchell's car has been found—apparently abandoned. I thought you might like to know."

"Thanks, Captain. Where was this?"

"About twenty miles from here, on a country road that leads to Highway 395, but is not the road a man would naturally take to get to 395. It's a place called Los Peñasquitos Canyon. Nothing there but outcrop and barren land and a dry river bed. I know the place. This morning a rancher named Gates went by there with a small truck, looking for fieldstone to build a wall. He passed a two-tone Buick hardtop parked off the side of the road. He didn't pay much attention to the Buick, except to notice that it hadn't been in a wreck, so somebody just parked it there.

"Later on in the day, around four, Gates went back to pick up another load of fieldstone. The Buick was still there. This time he stopped and looked it over. No keys in the lock, but the car wasn't locked up. No sign of any damage. Just the same, Gates wrote down the license number and the name and address on the registration certificate. When he got back to his ranch he called the substation at Escondido. Of course the deputies knew Los Peñasquitos Canyon. One of them went over and looked at the car. Clean as a whistle. The deputy managed to trick the trunk open. Empty except for a spare tire and a few tools. So he went back to Escondido and called in here. I've just been talking to him."

I lit a cigarette and offered one to Captain Alessandro. He shook his head.

"Got any ideas, Marlowe?"

"No more than you have."

"Let's hear them anyway."

"If Mitchell had some good reason to get lost and had a friend who would pick him up—a friend nobody here knew anything about—he would have stored his car in some garage. That wouldn't have made anyone curious. There wouldn't be anything to make the garage curious. They would just be storing a car. Mitchell's suitcases would already have been in his friend's car."

"So?"

"So there wasn't any friend. So Mitchell disappeared into thin air—with his nine suitcases—on a very lonely road that was hardly ever used."

"Go on from there." His voice was hard now. It had an edge to it. I stood up.

"Don't bully me, Captain Alessandro. I haven't done anything wrong. You've been very human so far. Please don't get the idea that I had anything to do with Mitchell's disappearance. I didn't—and still don't—know what he had on my client. I just know that she is a lonely and frightened and unhappy girl. When I know why, if I do manage to find out, I'll let you know or I won't. If I don't, you'll just have to throw the book at me. It wouldn't be the first time it's happened to me. I don't sell out—even to good police officers."

"Let's hope it doesn't turn out that way, Marlowe. Let's hope."

"I'm hoping with you, Captain. And thanks for treating me the way you have."

I walked back down the corridor, nodded to the duty officer on the desk and climbed back into my car again. I felt twenty years older.

I knew—and I was pretty damn sure Captain Alessandro knew too—that Mitchell wasn't alive, that he hadn't driven his car to Los Peñasquitos Canyon, but somebody had driven him there, with Mitchell lying dead on the floor of the back seat.

There was no other possible way to look at it. There are

things that are facts, in a statistical sense, on paper, on a tape recorder, in evidence. And there are things that are facts because they have to be facts, because nothing makes any sense otherwise.

## 22

It is like a sudden scream in the night, but there is no sound. Almost always at night, because the dark hours are the hours of danger. But it has happened to me also in broad daylight— that strange, clarified moment when I suddenly know something I have no reason for knowing. Unless out of the long years and the long tensions, and in the present case, the abrupt certainty that what bullfighters call "the moment of truth" is here.

There was no other reason, no sensible reason at all. But I parked across from the entrance to the Rancho Descansado, and cut my lights and ignition, and then drifted about fifty yards downhill and pulled the brake back hard.

I walked up to the office. There was the small glow of light over the night bell, but the office was closed. It was only ten-thirty. I walked around to the back and drifted through the trees. I came on two parked cars. One was a Hertz rent car, as anonymous as a nickel in a parking meter, but by bending down I could read the license number. The car next to it was Goble's little dark jalopy. It didn't seem very long since it was parked by the Casa del Poniente. Now it was here.

I went on through the trees until I was below my room. It was dark, soundless. I went up the few steps very slowly and put my ear to the door. For a little while I heard nothing. Then I heard a strangled sob—a man's sob, not a woman's. Then a thin, low cackling laugh. Then what seemed to be a hard blow. Then silence.

I went back down the steps and through the trees to my car. I unlocked the trunk and got out a tire iron. I went back to my room as carefully as before—even more carefully. I listened again. Silence. Nothing. The quiet of the night. I reached out my pocket flash and flicked it once at the window, then slid away from the door. For several minutes nothing happened. Then the door opened a crack.

I hit it hard with my shoulder and smashed it wide open. The man stumbled back and then laughed. I saw the glint of his gun in the faint light. I smashed his wrist with the tire iron. He screamed. I smashed his other wrist. I heard the gun hit the floor.

I reached back and switched the lights on. I kicked the door shut.

He was a pale-faced redhead with dead eyes. His face was twisted with pain, but his eyes were still dead. Hurt as he was, he was still tough.

"You ain't going to live long, boy," he said.

"You're not going to live at all. Get out of my way."

He managed to laugh.

"You've still got legs," I said. "Bend them at the knees and lie down—face down—that is, if you want a face."

He tried to spit at me, but his throat choked. He slid down to his knees, holding his arms out. He was groaning now. Suddenly he crumpled. They're so goddam tough when they hold the stacked deck. And they never know any other kind of deck.

Goble was lying on the bed. His face was a mass of bruises and cuts. His nose was broken. He was unconscious and breathing as if half strangled.

The redhead was still out, and his gun lay on the floor near him. I wrestled his belt off and strapped his ankles together. Then I turned him over and went through his pockets. He had a wallet with $670 in it, a driver's license in the name of Richard Harvest, and the address of a small hotel in San Diego. His pocketbook contained numbered checks on about twenty banks, a set of credit cards, but no gun permit.

I left him lying there and went down to the office. I pushed the button of the night bell, and kept on pushing it. After a while a figure came down through the dark. It was Jack in a bathrobe and pajamas. I still had the tire iron in my hand.

He looked startled. "Something the matter, Mr. Marlowe?"

"Oh, no. Just a hoodlum in my room waiting to kill me.

Just another man beaten to pieces on my bed. Nothing the matter at all. Quite normal around here, perhaps."

"I'll call the police."

"That would be awfully damn nice of you, Jack. As you see, I am still alive. You know what you ought to do with this place? Turn it into a pet hospital."

He unlocked the door and went into the office. When I heard him talking to the police I went back to my room. The redhead had guts. He had managed to get into a sitting position against the wall. His eyes were still dead and his mouth was twisted into a grin.

I went over to the bed. Goble's eyes were open.

"I didn't make it," he whispered. "Wasn't as good as I thought I was. Got out of my league."

"The cops are on their way. How did it happen?"

"I walked into it. No complaints. This guy's a life-taker. I'm lucky. I'm still breathing. Made me drive over here. He cooled me, tied me up, then he was gone for a while."

"Somebody must have picked him up, Goble. There's a rent car beside yours. If he had that over at the Casa, how did he get back there for it?"

Goble turned his head slowly and looked at me. "I thought I was a smart cookie. I learned different. All I want is back to Kansas City. The little guys can't beat the big guys—not ever. I guess you saved my life."

Then the police were there.

First two prowl car boys, nice cool-looking serious men in the always immaculate uniforms and the always deadpan faces. Then a big tough sergeant who said his name was Sergeant Holzminder, and that he was the cruising sergeant on the shift. He looked at the redhead and went over to the bed.

"Call the hospital," he said briefly, over his shoulder.

One of the cops went out to the car. The sergeant bent down over Goble. "Want to tell me?"

"The redhead beat me up. He took my money. Stuck a gun into me at the Casa. Made me drive him here. Then he beat me up."

"Why?"

Goble made a sighing sound and his head went lax on the

pillow. Either he passed out again or faked it. The sergeant straightened up and turned to me. "What's your story?"

"I haven't any, Sergeant. The man on the bed had dinner with me tonight. We'd met a couple of times. He said he was a Kansas City PI. I never knew what he was doing here."

"And this?" The sergeant made a loose motion towards the redhead, who was still grinning a sort of unnatural epileptic grin.

"I never saw him before. I don't know anything about him, except that he was waiting for me with a gun."

"That your tire iron?"

"Yes, Sergeant."

The other cop came back into the room and nodded to the sergeant. "On the way."

"So you had a tire iron," the sergeant said coldly. "So why?"

"Let's say I just had a hunch someone was waiting for me here."

"Let's try it that you didn't have a hunch, that you already knew. And knew a lot more."

"Let's try it that you don't call me a liar until you know what you're talking about. And let's try it that you don't get so goddam tough just because you have three stripes. And let's try something more. This guy may be a hood, but he still has two broken wrists, and you know what that means, Sergeant? He'll never be able to handle a gun again."

"So we book you for mayhem."

"If you say so, Sergeant."

Then the ambulance came. They carried Goble out first and then the intern put temporary splints on the two wrists of the redhead. They unstrapped his ankles. He looked at me and laughed.

"Next time, pal, I'll think of something original—but you did all right. You really did."

He went out. The ambulance doors clanged shut and the growling sound of it died. The sergeant was sitting down now, with his cap off. He was wiping his forehead.

"Let's try again," he said evenly. "From the beginning.

Like as if we didn't hate each other and were just trying to understand. Could we?"

"Yes, Sergeant. We could. Thanks for giving me the chance."

# 23

Eventually I landed back at the cop house. Captain Alessandro had gone. I had to sign a statement for Sergeant Holzminder.

"A tire iron, huh?" he said musingly. "Mister, you took an awful chance. He could have shot you four times while you were swinging on him."

"I don't think so, Sergeant. I bumped him pretty hard with the door. And I didn't take a full swing. Also, maybe he wasn't supposed to shoot me. I don't figure he was in business for himself."

A little more of that, and they let me go. It was too late to do anything but go to bed, too late to talk to anyone. Just the same I went to the telephone company office and shut myself in one of the two neat outdoor booths and dialed the Casa del Poniente.

"Miss Mayfield, please. Miss Betty Mayfield. Room 1224."

"I can't ring a guest at this hour."

"Why? You got a broken wrist?" I was a real tough boy tonight. "Do you think I'd call if it wasn't an emergency?"

He rang and she answered in a sleepy voice.

"This is Marlowe. Bad trouble. Do I come there or do you come to my place?"

"What? What kind of trouble?"

"Just take it from me for just this once. Should I pick you up in the parking lot?"

"I'll get dressed. Give me a little time."

I went out to my car and drove to the Casa. I was smoking my third cigarette and wishing I had a drink when she came quickly and noiselessly up to the car and got in.

"I don't know what this is all about," she began, but I interrupted her.

"You're the only one that does. And tonight you're going to tell me. And don't bother getting indignant. It won't work again."

I jerked the car into motion and drove fast through silent streets and then down the hill and into the Rancho Descansado and parked under the trees. She got out without a word and I unlocked my door and put the lights on.

"Drink?"

"All right."

"Are you doped?"

"Not tonight, if you mean sleeping pills. I was out with Clark and drank quite a lot of champagne. That always makes me sleepy."

I made a couple of drinks and gave her one. I sat down and leaned my head back.

"Excuse me," I said. "I'm a little tired. Once in every two or three days I have to sit down. It's a weakness I've tried to get over, but I'm not as young as I was. Mitchell's dead."

Her breath caught in her throat and her hand shook. She may have turned pale. I couldn't tell.

"Dead?" she whispered. "Dead?"

"Oh, come off it. As Lincoln said, you can fool all of the detectives some of the time, and some of the detectives all the time, but you can't—"

"Shut up! Shut up right now! Who the hell do you think you are?"

"Just a guy who has tried very hard to get where he could do you some good. A guy with enough experience and enough understanding to know that you were in some kind of jam. And wanted to help you out of it, with no help from you."

"Mitchell's dead," she said in a low breathless voice. "I didn't mean to be nasty. Where?"

"His car has been found abandoned in a place you wouldn't know. It's about twenty miles inland, on a road that's hardly used. A place called Los Peñasquitos Canyon. A place of dead land. Nothing in his car, no suitcases. Just an empty car parked at the side of a road hardly anybody ever uses."

She looked down at her drink and took a big gulp. "You said he was dead."

"It seems like weeks, but it's only hours ago that you came over here and offered me the top half of Rio to get rid of his body."

"But there wasn't—I mean, I must just have dreamed—"

"Lady, you came over here at three o'clock in the morning in a state of near-shock. You described just where he was and how he was lying on the chaise on your little porch. So I went back with you and climbed the fire stairs, using the infinite caution for which my profession is famous. And no Mitchell, and then you asleep in your little bed with your little sleeping pill cuddled up to you."

"Get on with your act," she snapped at me. "I know how you love it. Why didn't *you* cuddle up to me? I wouldn't have needed a sleeping pill—perhaps."

"One thing at a time, if you don't mind. And the first thing is that you were telling the truth when you came here. Mitchell *was* dead on your porch. But someone got his body out of there while you were over here making a sucker out of me. And somebody got him down to his car and then packed his suitcases and got them down. All this took time. It took more than time. It took a great big reason. Now who would do a thing like that—just to save you the mild embarrassment of reporting a dead man on your porch?"

"Oh, shut up!" She finished her drink and put the glass aside. "I'm tired. Do you mind if I lie down on your bed?"

"Not if you take your clothes off."

"All right—I'll take my clothes off. That's what you've been working up to, isn't it?"

"You might not like that bed. Goble was beaten up on it tonight—by a hired gun named Richard Harvest. He was really brutalized. You remember Goble, don't you? The fat sort of man in the little dark car that followed us up the hill the other night."

"I don't know anybody named Goble. And I don't know anybody named Richard Harvest. How do you know all this? Why were they here—in your room?"

"The hired gun was waiting for me. After I heard about

Mitchell's car I had a hunch. Even generals and other important people have hunches. Why not me? The trick is to know when to act on one. I was lucky tonight—or last night. I acted on a hunch. He had a gun, but I had a tire iron."

"What a big strong unbeatable man you are," she said bitterly. "I don't mind the bed. Do I take my clothes off now?"

I went over and jerked her to her feet and shook her. "Stop your nonsense, Betty. When I want your beautiful white body, it won't be while you're my client. I want to know what you are afraid of. How the hell can I do anything about it if I don't know? Only you can tell me."

She began to sob in my arms.

Women have so few defenses, but they certainly perform wonders with those they have.

I held her tight against me. "You can cry and cry and sob and sob, Betty. Go ahead, I'm patient. If I wasn't that—well, hell, if I wasn't that—"

That was as far as I got. She was pressed tight to me trembling. She lifted her face and dragged my head down until I was kissing her.

"Is there some other woman?" she asked softly, between my teeth.

"There have been."

"But someone very special?"

"There was once, for a brief moment. But that's a long time ago now."

"Take me. I'm yours—all of me is yours. Take me."

# 24

A banging on the door woke me. I opened my eyes stupidly. She was clinging to me so tightly that I could hardly move. I moved her arms gently until I was free. She was still sound asleep.

I got out of bed and pulled a bathrobe on and went to the door; I didn't open it.

"What's the matter? I was asleep."

"Captain Alessandro wants you at the office right away. Open the door."

"Sorry, can't be done. I have to shave and shower and so on."

"Open the door. This is Sergeant Green."

"I'm sorry, Sergeant. I just can't. But I'll be along just as soon as I can make it."

"You got a dame in there?"

"Sergeant, questions like that are out of line. I'll be there."

I heard his steps go down off the porch. I heard someone laugh. I heard a voice say, "This guy is really rich. I wonder what he does on his day off."

I heard the police car going away. I went into the bathroom and showered and shaved and dressed. Betty was still glued to the pillow. I scribbled a note and put it on my pillow. "The cops want me. I have to go. You know where my car is. Here are the keys."

I went out softly and locked the door and found the Hertz car. I knew the keys would be in it. Operators like Richard Harvest don't bother about keys. They carry sets of them for all sorts of cars.

Captain Alessandro looked exactly as he had the day before. He would always look like that. There was a man with him, an elderly stony-faced man with nasty eyes.

Captain Alessandro nodded me to the usual chair. A cop in uniform came in and put a cup of coffee in front of me. He gave me a sly grin as he went out.

"This is Mr. Henry Cumberland of Westfield, Carolina, Marlowe. North Carolina. I don't know how he found his way out here, but he did. He says Betty Mayfield murdered his son."

I didn't say anything. There was nothing for me to say. I sipped the coffee which was too hot, but good otherwise.

"Like to fill us in a little, Mr. Cumberland?"

"Who's this?" He had a voice as sharp as his face.

"A private detective named Philip Marlowe. He operates out of Los Angeles. He is here because Betty Mayfield is his client. It seems that you have rather more drastic ideas about Miss Mayfield than he has."

"I don't have any ideas about her, Captain," I said. "I just like to squeeze her once in a while. It soothes me."

"You like being soothed by a murderess?" Cumberland barked at me.

"Well, I didn't know she was a murderess, Mr. Cumberland. It's all news to me. Would you care to explain?"

"The girl who calls herself Betty Mayfield—and that was her maiden name—was the wife of my son, Lee Cumberland. I never approved of the marriage. It was one of those wartime idiocies. My son received a broken neck in the war and had to wear a brace to protect his spinal column. One night she got it away from him and taunted him until he rushed at her. Unfortunately, he had been drinking rather heavily since he came home, and there had been quarrels. He tripped and fell across the bed. I came into the room and found her trying to put the brace back on his neck. He was already dead."

I looked at Captain Alessandro. "Is this being recorded, Captain?"

He nodded. "Every word."

"All right, Mr. Cumberland. There's more, I take it."

"Naturally. I have a great deal of influence in Westfield. I own the bank, the leading newspaper, most of the industry. The people of Westfield are my friends. My daughter-in-law was arrested and tried for murder and the jury brought in a verdict of guilty."

"The jury were all Westfield people, Mr. Cumberland?"

"They were. Why shouldn't they be?"

"I don't know, sir. But it sounds like a one-man town."

"Don't get impudent with me, young man."

"Sorry, sir. Would you finish?"

"We have a peculiar law in our state, and I believe in a few other jurisdictions. Ordinarily the defense attorney makes an automatic motion for a directed verdict of not guilty and it is just as automatically denied. In my state the judge may reserve his ruling until after the verdict. The judge was senile. He reserved his ruling. When the jury brought in a verdict of guilty, he declared in a long speech that the jury had failed to consider the possibility that my son had in a drunken rage removed the brace from his neck in order to terrify his wife. He said that where there was so much bitterness anything was possible, and that the jury had failed to consider the possibility that my daughter-in-law might have been doing exactly what she said she was doing—trying to put the brace back on my son's neck. He voided the verdict and discharged the defendant.

"I told her that she had murdered my son and that I would see to it that she had no place of refuge anywhere on this earth. That is why I am here."

I looked at the captain. He looked at nothing. I said: "Mr. Cumberland, whatever your private convictions, Mrs. Lee Cumberland, whom I know as Betty Mayfield, has been tried and acquitted. You have called her a murderess. That's a slander. We'll settle for a million dollars."

He laughed almost grotesquely. "You small-town nobody," he almost screamed. "Where I come from you would be thrown into jail as a vagrant."

"Make it a million and a quarter," I said. "I'm not so valuable as your ex-daughter-in-law."

Cumberland turned on Captain Alessandro. "What goes on here?" he barked. "Are you all a bunch of crooks?"

"You're talking to a police officer, Mr. Cumberland."

"I don't give a good goddam what you are," Cumberland said furiously. "There are plenty of crooked police."

"It's a good idea to be sure—before you call them crooked," Alessandro said, almost with amusement. Then he lit a cigarette and blew smoke and smiled through it.

"Take it easy, Mr. Cumberland. You're a cardiac case. Prognosis unfavorable. Excitement is very bad for you. I studied medicine once. But somehow I became a cop. The war cut me off, I guess."

Cumberland stood up. Spittle showed on his chin. He made a strangled sound in his throat. "You haven't heard the last of this," he snarled.

Alessandro nodded. "One of the interesting things about police work is that you never hear the last of anything. There are always too many loose ends. Just what would you like me to do? Arrest someone who has been tried and acquitted, just because you are a big shot in Westfield, Carolina?"

"I told her I'd never give her any peace," Cumberland said

furiously. "I'd follow her to the end of the earth. I'd make sure everyone knew just what she was!"

"And what is she, Mr. Cumberland?"

"A murderess that killed my son and was let off by an idiot of a judge — that's what she is!"

Captain Alessandro stood up, all six feet three inches of him. "Take off, buster," he said coldly. "You annoy me. I've met all kinds of punks in my time. Most of them have been poor stupid backward kids. This is the first time I've come across a great big important man who was just as stupid and vicious as a fifteen-year-old delinquent. Maybe you own Westfield, North Carolina, or think you do. You don't own a cigar butt in my town. Get out before I put the arm on you for interfering with an officer in the performance of his duties."

Cumberland almost staggered to the door and groped for the knob, although the door was wide open. Alessandro looked after him. He sat down slowly.

"You were pretty rough, Captain."

"It's breaking my heart. If anything I said makes him take another look at himself — oh well, hell!"

"Not his kind. Am I free to go?"

"Yes. Goble won't make charges. He'll be on his way back to Kansas City today. We'll dig up something on this Richard Harvest, but what's the use? We put him away for a while, and a hundred just like him are available for the same work."

"What do I do about Betty Mayfield?"

"I have a vague idea that you've already done it," he said, deadpan.

"Not until I know what happened to Mitchell." I was just as deadpan as he was.

"All I know is that he's gone. That doesn't make him police business."

I stood up. We gave each other those looks. I went out.

# 25

She was still asleep. My coming in didn't wake her. She slept like a little girl, soundlessly, her face at peace. I watched her for a moment, then lit a cigarette and went out to the kitchen. When I had put coffee on to percolate in the handsome paper-thin dime store aluminum percolator provided by the management, I went back and sat on the bed. The note I had left was still on the pillow with my car keys.

I shook her gently and her eyes opened and blinked.

"What time is it?" she asked stretching her bare arms as far as she could. "God, I slept like a log."

"It's time for you to get dressed. I have some coffee brewing. I've been down to the police station—by request. Your father-in-law is in town, Mrs. Cumberland."

She shot upright and stared at me without breathing.

"He got the brush, but good, from Captain Alessandro. He can't hurt you. Was that what all the fear was about?"

"Did he say—say what happened back in Westfield?"

"That's what he came here to say. He's mad enough to jump down his own throat. And what of it? You didn't, did you? Do what they said?"

"I did not." Her eyes blazed at me.

"Wouldn't matter if you had—now. But it wouldn't make me very happy about last night. How did Mitchell get wise?"

"He just happened to be there or somewhere nearby. Good heavens, the papers were full of it for weeks. It wasn't hard for him to recognize me. Didn't they have it in the papers here?"

"They ought to have covered it, if only because of the unusual legal angle. If they did, I missed it. The coffee ought to be ready now. How do you take it?"

"Black, please. No sugar."

"Fine. I don't have any cream or sugar. Why did you call yourself Eleanor King? No, don't answer that. I'm stupid. Old man Cumberland would know your unmarried name."

I went out to the kitchen and removed the top of the percolator, and poured us both a cup. I carried hers to her. I sat down in a chair with mine. Our eyes met and were strangers again.

She put her cup aside. "That was good. Would you mind looking the other way while I gather myself together?"

"Sure." I picked a paperback off the table and made a pretense of reading it. It was about some private eye whose idea of a hot scene was a dead naked woman hanging from the shower rail with the marks of torture on her. By that time Betty was in the bathroom. I threw the paperback into the wastebasket, not having a garbage can handy at the moment. Then I got to thinking there are two kinds of women you can make love to. Those who give themselves so completely and with such utter abandonment that they don't even think about their bodies. And there are those who are self-conscious and always want to cover up a little. I remembered a girl in a story by Anatole France who insisted on taking her stockings off. Keeping them on made her feel like a whore. She was right.

When Betty came out of the bathroom she looked like a fresh-opened rose, her make-up perfect, her eyes shining, every hair exactly in place.

"Will you take me back to the hotel? I want to speak to Clark."

"You in love with him?"

"I thought I was in love with you."

"It was a cry in the night," I said. "Let's not try to make it more than it was. There's more coffee out in the kitchen."

"No, thanks. Not until breakfast. Haven't you ever been in love? I mean enough to want to be with a woman every day, every month, every year?"

"Let's go."

"How can such a hard man be so gentle?" she asked wonderingly.

"If I wasn't hard, I wouldn't be alive. If I couldn't ever be gentle, I wouldn't deserve to be alive."

I held her coat for her and we went out to my car. On the way back to the hotel she didn't speak at all. When we got there and I slid into the now familiar parking slot, I took the five folded traveler's checks out of my pocket and held them out to her.

"Let's hope it's the last time we pass these back and forth," I said. "They're wearing out."

She looked at them, but didn't take them. "I thought they were your fee," she said rather sharply.

"Don't argue, Betty. You know very well that I couldn't take money from you."

"After last night?"

"After nothing. I just couldn't take it. That's all. I haven't done anything for you. What are you going to do? Where are you going? You're safe now."

"I've no idea. I'll think of something."

"Are you in love with Brandon?"

"I might be."

"He's an ex-racketeer. He hired a gunman to scare Goble off. The gunman was ready to kill me. Could you really love a man like that?"

"A woman loves a man. Not what he is. And he may not have meant it."

"Goodbye, Betty. I gave it what I had, but it wasn't enough."

She reached her hand out slowly and took the checks. "I think you're crazy. I think you're the craziest man I ever met." She got out of the car and walked away quickly, as she always did.

# 26

I gave her time to clear the lobby and go up to her room, and then I went into the lobby myself and asked for Mr. Clark Brandon on a house phone. Javonen came by and gave me a hard look, but he didn't say anything.

A man's voice answered. It was his all right.

"Mr. Brandon, you don't know me, although we shared an elevator the other morning. My name is Philip Marlowe. I'm a private detective from Los Angeles, and I'm a friend of Miss Mayfield. I'd like to talk to you a little, if you'll give me the time."

"I seem to have heard something about you, Marlowe. But

I'm all set to go out. How about a drink around six this evening?"

"I'd like to get back to Los Angeles, Mr. Brandon. I won't keep you long."

"All right," he said grudgingly. "Come on up."

He opened the door, a big, tall, very muscular man in top condition, neither hard nor soft. He didn't offer to shake hands. He stood aside, and I went in.

"You alone here, Mr. Brandon?"

"Sure. Why?"

"I wouldn't want anyone else to hear what I have to say."

"Well say it and get done."

He sat in a chair and put his feet up on an ottoman. He flicked a gold lighter at a gold-tipped cigarette. Big deal.

"I first came down here on the instructions of a Los Angeles lawyer to follow Miss Mayfield and find out where she went, and then report back. I didn't know why and the lawyer said he didn't either, but that he was acting for a reputable firm of attorneys in Washington. Washington, D.C."

"So you followed her. So what?"

"So she made contact with Larry Mitchell, or he with her, and he had a hook of some sort into her."

"Into a lot of women from time to time," Brandon said coldly. "He specialized in it."

"He doesn't any more, does he?"

He stared at me with cool blank eyes. "What's that mean?"

"He doesn't do anything any more. He doesn't exist any more."

"I heard he left the hotel and went off in his car. What's it to do with me?"

"You didn't ask me how I know he doesn't exist any more."

"Look, Marlowe." He flicked ash from his cigarette with a contemptuous gesture. "It could be that I don't give a damn. Get to what concerns me, or else get out."

"I also got involved down here, if involved is the word, with a man named Goble who said he was a private eye from Kansas City, and had a card which may or may not have proved it. Goble annoyed me a good deal. He kept following me around. He kept talking about Mitchell. I couldn't figure what he was after. Then one day at the desk you got an anonymous letter. I watched you read it over and over. You asked the clerk who left it. The clerk didn't know. You even picked the empty envelope out of the wastebasket. And when you went up in the elevator you didn't look happy."

Brandon was beginning to look a little less relaxed. His voice had a sharper edge.

"You could get too nosy, Mr. PI. Ever think of that?"

"That's a silly question. How else would I make a living?"

"Better get out of here while you can still walk."

I laughed at him, and that really burned him. He shot to his feet and came striding over to where I was sitting.

"Listen, boy friend. I'm a pretty big man in this town. I don't get pushed around much by small-time operators like you. Out!"

"You don't want to hear the rest?"

"I said, out!"

I stood up. "Sorry. I was prepared to settle this with you privately. And don't get the idea that I'm trying to put a bite on you—like Goble. I just don't do those things. But if you toss me out—without hearing me out—I'll have to go to Captain Alessandro. He'll listen."

He stood glowering for a long moment. Then a curious sort of grin appeared on his face.

"So he'll listen to you. So what? I could get him transferred with one phone call."

"Oh, no. Not Captain Alessandro. He's not brittle. He got tough with Henry Cumberland this morning. And Henry Cumberland isn't a man that's used to having anyone get tough with him, any place, any time. He just about broke Cumberland in half with a few contemptuous words. You think you could get that guy to lay off? You should live so long."

"Jesus," he said, still grinning, "I used to know guys like you once. I've lived here so long now I must have forgotten they still make them. Okay. I'll listen."

He went back to the chair and picked another gold-tipped cigarette from a case and lit it. "Care for one?"

"No thanks. This boy Richard Harvest—I think he was a mistake. Not good enough for the job."

"Not nearly good enough, Marlowe. Not nearly. Just a cheap sadist. That's what comes of getting out of touch. You lose your judgment. He could have scared Goble silly without laying a finger on him. And then taking him over to your place—what a laugh! What an amateur! And look at him now. No good for anything any more. He'll be selling pencils. Would you care for a drink?"

"I'm not on that kind of terms with you, Brandon. Let me finish. In the middle of the night—the night I made contact with Betty Mayfield, and the night you chased Mitchell out of The Glass Room—and did it very nicely, I might add—Betty came over to my room at the Rancho Descansado. One of your properties, I believe. She said Mitchell was dead on a chaise on her porch. She offered me large things to do something about it. I came back over here and there was no man dead on her porch. The next morning the night garage man told me Mitchell had left in his car with nine suitcases. He'd paid his bill and a week in advance to hold his room. The same day his car was found abandoned in Los Peñasquitos Canyon. No suitcases, no Mitchell."

Brandon stared hard at me, but said nothing.

"Why was Betty Mayfield afraid to tell me what she was afraid of? Because she had been convicted of murder in Westfield, North Carolina, and then the verdict was reversed by the judge, who has that power in that state, and used it. But Henry Cumberland, the father of the husband she was accused of murdering, told her he would follow her anywhere she went and see that she had no peace. Now she finds a dead man on her porch. And the cops investigate and her whole story comes out. She's frightened and confused. She thinks she couldn't be lucky twice. After all, a jury did convict her."

Brandon said softly: "His neck was broken. He fell over the end wall of my terrace. She couldn't have broken his neck. Come out here. I'll show you."

We went out on the wide sunny terrace. Brandon marched to the end wall and I looked down over it and I was looking straight down on a chaise on Betty Mayfield's porch.

"This wall isn't very high," I said. "Not high enough to be safe."

"I agree," Brandon said calmly. "Now suppose he was

standing like this—" he stood with his back against the wall, and the top of it didn't come very much above the middle of his thighs. And Mitchell had been a tall man too—"and he goads Betty into coming over near enough so that he can grab her, and she pushes him off hard, and over he goes. And he just happens to fall in such a way—by pure chance—that his neck snaps. And that's exactly how her husband died. Do you blame the girl for getting in a panic?"

"I'm not sure I blame anybody, Brandon. Not even you."

He stepped away from the wall and looked out to sea and was silent for a moment. Then he turned.

"For nothing," I said, "except that you managed to get rid of Mitchell's body."

"Now, how in hell could I do that?"

"You're a fisherman, among other things. I'll bet that right here in this apartment you have a long strong cord. You're a powerful man. You could get down to Betty's porch, you could put that cord under Mitchell's arms, and you have the strength to lower him to the ground behind the shrubbery. Then, already having his key out of his pocket, you could go to his room and pack up all his stuff, and carry it down to the garage, either in the elevator, or down the fire stairs. That would take three trips. Not too much for you. Then you could drive his car out of the garage. You probably knew the night man was a doper and that he wouldn't talk, if he knew you knew. This was in the small hours of the night. Of course the garage man lied about the time. Then you could drive the car as near as possible to where Mitchell's body was, and dump him into it, and drive off to Los Peñasquitos Canyon."

Brandon laughed bitterly. "So I am in Los Peñasquitos Canyon with a car and a dead man and nine suitcases. How do I get out of there?"

"Helicopter."

"Who's going to fly it?"

"You. They don't check much on helicopters yet, but they soon will, because they are getting more and more numerous. You could have one brought to you in Los Peñasquitos Canyon, having arranged in advance, and you could have had someone come along to pick up the pilot. A man in your position can do almost anything, Brandon."

"And then what?"

"You loaded Mitchell's body and his suitcases into the helicopter and flew out to sea and set the helicopter hovering close to the water, and then you could dump the body and the suitcases, and drift on back to wherever the helicopter came from. A nice clean well-organized job."

Brandon laughed raucously—too raucously. The laugh had a forced sound.

"You think I'd actually be idiot enough to do all this for a girl I had only just met?"

"Uh-uh. Think again, Brandon. You did it for you. You forget Goble. Goble came from Kansas City. Didn't *you*?"

"What if I did?"

"Nothing. End of the line. But Goble didn't come out here for the ride. And he wasn't looking for Mitchell, unless he already knew him, and between them, they figured they had a gold mine. You were the gold mine. But Mitchell got dead and Goble tried to go it alone, and he was a mouse fighting with a tiger. But would you want to explain how Mitchell fell off your terrace? Would you want an investigation of your background? What so obvious as for the police to think you had thrown Mitchell over the wall? And even if they couldn't prove it, where would you be in Esmeralda from then on?"

He walked slowly to the far end of the terrace and back. He stood in front of me, his expression completely blank.

"I could have you killed, Marlowe. But in some strange way in the years I have lived here, I don't seem to be that kind of guy any more. So you have me licked. I don't have any defense, except to have you killed. Mitchell was the lowest kind of man, a blackmailer of women. You could be right all along the line, but I wouldn't regret it. And it's just possible, believe me, just possible that I too went out on a limb for Betty Mayfield. I don't expect you to believe it, but it *is* possible. Now, let's deal. How much?"

"How much for what?"

"For not going to the cops."

"I already told you how much. Nothing. I just wanted to know what happened. Was I approximately right?"

"Dead right, Marlowe. Right on the nose. They may get me for it yet."

"Maybe. Well, I'll take myself out of your hair now. Like I said—I want to get back to Los Angeles. Somebody might offer me a cheap job. I have to live, or do I?"

"Would you shake hands with me?"

"No. You hired a gun. That puts you out of the class of people I shake hands with. I might be dead today, if I hadn't had a hunch."

"I didn't mean him to kill anyone."

"You hired him. Goodbye."

# 27

I got out of the elevator and Javonen seemed to be waiting for me. "Come into the bar," he said. "I want to talk to you."

We went into the bar, which was very quiet at that hour. We sat at a corner table. Javonen said quietly: "You think I'm a bastard, don't you?"

"No. You have a job. I have a job. Mine annoyed you. You didn't trust me. That doesn't make you a bastard."

"I try to protect the hotel. Who do you try to protect?"

"I never know. Often, when I do know, I don't know how. I just fumble around and make a nuisance of myself. Often I'm pretty inadequate."

"So I heard—from Captain Alessandro. If it's not too personal, how much do you make on a job like this?"

"Well, this was a little out of the usual line, Major. As a matter of fact, I didn't make anything."

"The hotel will pay you five thousand dollars—for protecting its interests."

"The hotel, meaning Mr. Clark Brandon."

"I suppose. He's the boss."

"It has a sweet sound—five thousand dollars. A very sweet sound. I'll listen to it on my way back to Los Angeles." I stood up.

"Where do I send the check, Marlowe?"

"The Police Relief Fund could be glad to have it. Cops don't make much money. When they get in trouble they have to borrow from the Fund. Yes, I think the Police Relief Fund would be very grateful to you."

"But not you?"

"You were a major in the CIC. You must have had a lot of chances to graft. But you're still working. I guess I'll be on my way."

"Listen, Marlowe. You're being a damn fool. I want to tell you—"

"Tell yourself, Javonen. You have a captive audience. And good luck."

I walked out of the bar and got into my car. I drove to the Descansado and picked up my stuff and stopped at the office to pay my bill. Jack and Lucille were in their usual positions. Lucille smiled at me.

Jack said: "No bill, Mr. Marlowe. I've been instructed. And we offer you our apologies for last night. But they're not worth much, are they?"

"How much would the bill be?"

"Not much. Twelve-fifty maybe."

I put the money on the counter. Jack looked at it and frowned. "I said there was no bill, Mr. Marlowe."

"Why not? I occupied the room."

"Mr. Brandon—"

"Some people never learn, do they? Nice to have known you both. I'd like a receipt for this. It's deductible."

# 28

I didn't do more than ninety back to Los Angeles. Well, perhaps I hit a hundred for a few seconds now and then. Back on Yucca Avenue I stuck the Olds in the garage and poked at the mailbox. Nothing, as usual. I climbed the long flight of redwood steps and unlocked my door. Everything was the same. The room was stuffy and dull and impersonal as it always was. I opened a couple of windows and mixed a drink in the kitchen. I sat down on the couch and stared at the wall. Wherever I went, whatever I did, this was what I would come back to. A blank wall in a meaningless room in a meaningless house.

I put the drink down on a side table without touching it. Alcohol was no cure for this. Nothing was any cure but the hard inner heart that asked for nothing from anyone.

The telephone started to ring. I picked it up and said emptily: "Marlowe speaking."

"Is this Mr. Philip Marlowe?"

"Yes."

"Paris has been trying to reach you, Mr. Marlowe. I'll call you back in a little while."

I put the phone down slowly and I think my hand shook a little. Driving too fast, or not enough sleep.

The call came through in fifteen minutes: "The party calling you from Paris is on the line, sir. If you have any difficulty, please flash your operator."

"This is Linda. Linda Loring. You remember me, don't you, darling?"

"How could I forget?"

"How are you?"

"Tired—as usual. Just came off a very trying sort of case. How are you?"

"Lonely. Lonely for you. I've tried to forget you. I haven't been able to. We made beautiful love together."

"That was a year and a half ago. And for one night. What am I supposed to say?"

"I've been faithful to you. I don't know why. The world is full of men. But I've been faithful to you."

"I haven't been faithful to you, Linda. I didn't think I'd ever see you again. I didn't know you expected me to be faithful."

"I didn't. I don't. I'm just trying to say that I love you. I'm asking you to marry me. You said it wouldn't last six months. But why not give it a chance? Who knows—it might last forever. I'm begging you. What does a woman have to do to get the man she wants?"

"I don't know. I don't even know how she knows she wants him. We live in different worlds. You're a rich woman, used to being pampered. I'm a tired hack with a doubtful future. Your father would probably see to it that I didn't even have that."

"You're not afraid of my father. You're not afraid of anyone. You're just afraid of marriage. My father knows a man when he sees one. Please, please, please. I'm at the Ritz. I'll send you a plane ticket at once."

I laughed. "You'll send *me* a plane ticket? What sort of guy do you think I am? I'll send *you* a plane ticket. And that will give you time to change your mind."

"But, darling, I don't need you to send me a plane ticket. I have—"

"Sure. You have the money for five hundred plane tickets. But this one will be *my* plane ticket. Take it, or don't come."

"I'll come, darling. I'll come. Hold me in your arms. Hold me close in your arms. I don't want to own you. Nobody ever will. I just want to love you."

"I'll be here. I always am."

"Hold me in your arms."

The phone clicked, there was a buzzing sound, and then the line went dead.

I reached for my drink. I looked around the empty room—which was no longer empty. There was a voice in it, and a tall slim lovely woman. There was a dark hair on the pillow in the bedroom. There was that soft gentle perfume of a woman who presses herself tight against you, whose lips are soft and yielding, whose eyes are half blind.

The telephone rang again. I said: "Yes?"

"This is Clyde Umney, the lawyer. I don't seem to have had any sort of satisfactory report from you. I'm not paying you to amuse yourself. I want an accurate and complete account of your activities at once. I demand to know in full detail exactly what you have been doing since you returned to Esmeralda."

"Having a little quiet fun—at my own expense."

His voice rose to a sharp cackle. "I demand a full report from you at once. Otherwise I'll see that you get bounced off your license."

"I have a suggestion for you, Mr. Umney. Why don't you go kiss a duck?"

There were sounds of strangled fury as I hung up on him. Almost immediately the telephone started to ring again.

I hardly heard it. The air was full of music.

# DOUBLE INDEMNITY

*Screenplay by Billy Wilder and Raymond Chandler*
*From the Novel by James M. Cain*

# Double Indemnity

## PART ONE

A DOWNTOWN INTERSECTION in Los Angeles fades in: It is night, about two o'clock, very light traffic. — At the left and in the immediate foreground a semaphore traffic signal stands at GO. Approaching it at about thirty miles per hour is a Dodge 1938 coupe. It is driven erratically and weaving a little, but not out of control. When the car is about forty feet away, the signal changes to STOP. The car makes no attempt to stop but comes on through as a light NEWSPAPER TRUCK is seen crossing the intersection at right angles. It swerves and skids to avoid the Dodge, which goes on as though nothing had happened. The truck stops with a panicky screech of tires. There is a large sign on the truck: "READ THE LOS ANGELES TIMES." The truck driver's infuriated face stares after the coupe.

The COUPE continues along the street, still weaving, then slows down and pulls over toward the curb in front of a tall office building. — The COUPE stops. The headlights are turned off. For a second nothing happens, then the car door opens slowly. A man eases himself out onto the sidewalk and stands a moment leaning on the open door to support himself. He's a tall man, about thirty-five years old. From the way he moves there seems to be something wrong with his left shoulder. He straightens up and painfully lowers his left hand into his jacket pocket. He leans into the car. He brings out a light-weight overcoat and drapes it across his shoulders. He shuts the car door and walks toward the building.

The ENTRANCE of the building comes into view. Above the closed, double-plate glass doors is lettered: PACIFIC BUILDING. To the left of the entrance there is a drugstore, closed, dark except for a faint light in the back. The man comes stiffly up to the doors. He tries the doors. They are locked. He knocks on the glass. Inside, over his shoulder, the lobby of the building is visible: a side entrance to the drugstore on the left, in the rear a barber shop and cigar and magazine stand closed up for the night, and to the right two

875

elevators. One elevator is open and its dome light falls across the dark lobby.

The man knocks again. The night watchman sticks his head out of the elevator and looks toward the entrance. He comes out with a newspaper in one hand and a half-eaten sandwich in the other. He finishes the sandwich on the way to the doors, looks out and recognizes the man outside, unlocks the door and pulls it open.

NIGHT WATCHMAN. Why, hello there, Mr. Neff.

Neff walks in past him without answering. Then he crosses the LOBBY, heading for the elevator. The night watchman looks after him, relocks the door, and follows him to the elevator. Neff enters it.

In the ELEVATOR: Neff stands leaning against the wall. He is pale and haggard with pain, but "deadpans" as the night watchman joins him.

NIGHT WATCHMAN. Working pretty late aren't you, Mr. Neff?

NEFF (*tight-lipped*). Late enough.

NIGHT WATCHMAN. You look kind of all in at that.

NEFF. I'm fine. Let's ride.

The night watchman pulls the lever; the doors close and the elevator rises.

NIGHT WATCHMAN. How's the insurance business, Mr. Neff?

NEFF. Okay.

NIGHT WATCHMAN. They wouldn't ever sell me any. They say I've got something loose in my heart. I say it's rheumatism.

NEFF (*scarcely listening*). Uh-huh.

The night watchman looks around at him, turns away again, and the elevator stops.

NIGHT WATCHMAN (*surly*). Twelve.

The door opens. Across a small dark reception room a pair

of frosted glass doors are lettered: PACIFIC ALL-RISK
INSURANCE   COMPANY—FOUNDED   1906—MAIN
OFFICE. There is a little light beyond the glass doors. Neff
straightens up and walks heavily out of the elevator, across
the reception room to the doors. He pushes them open. The
night watchman stares after him morosely, works the lever,
and the elevator doors start to close.

The TWELFTH FLOOR INSURANCE OFFICE: (The Insurance
Company occupies the entire eleventh and twelfth floors of
the building. On the twelfth floor are the executive offices
and claims and sales departments. These all open off a balcony
which runs all the way around. From the balcony one can see
the eleventh floor below: one enormous room filled with
desks, typewriters, filing cabinets, business machines, etc.)
—Neff comes through the double entrance doors from the
reception room. The twelfth floor is dark. Some light shines
up from the eleventh floor. Neff takes a few steps then holds
on to the balcony railing and looks down and we see:

The ELEVENTH FLOOR, from Neff's point-of-view. Two colored women are cleaning the offices. One is dry-mopping the
floor, the other is moving chairs back into position. A colored
man is emptying waste baskets into a big square box. He
shuffles a little dance step as he moves, and hums a little tune.

NEFF moves away from the railing with a faint smile on his
face, and walks past two or three offices toward a glass door
with number twenty-seven on it and three names: HENRY
B. ANDERSON, WALTER NEFF, LOUIS L. SCHWARTZ.
Neff opens the door.

NEFF'S OFFICE: Three desks, filing cabinets, one typewriter
on a stand, one dictaphone on a fixed stand are against the
wall with a rack of records underneath. There are telephones
on all three desks. We see a water cooler with an inverted
bottle and paper cup holder beside it. There are two windows
facing toward the front of the building—venetian blinds, no
curtains. The waste basket is full—ash trays unemptied. The
office has not been cleaned.

Neff enters, switches on the desk lamp. He looks across at
the dictaphone, goes heavily to it and lifts off the fabric cover.
He leans down hard on the dictaphone stand as if feeling
faint. Then he turns away, takes a few uncertain steps and falls

heavily into a swivel chair. His head goes far back, his eyes close, cold sweat shows on his face. For a moment he stays like this, exhausted, then his eyes open slowly and look down at his left shoulder. His good hand flips the overcoat back; he unbuttons his jacket, loosens his tie and shirt. This was quite an effort. He rests for a second, breathing hard. With the help of his good hand he edges his left elbow up on the arm-rest of the chair, supports it there and then pulls his jacket wide. A heavy patch of dark blood shows on his shirt. He pushes his chair along the floor toward the water cooler, using his feet and his right hand against the desk, takes out a handkerchief, presses with his hand against the spring faucet of the cooler, soaks the handkerchief in water and tucks it, dripping wet, against the wound inside his shirt. Next, he gets a handful of water and splashes it on his face. The water runs down his chin and drips. He breathes heavily, with closed eyes. He fingers a pack of cigarettes in his shirt pocket, pulls it out, looks at it. There is blood on it. He wheels himself back to the desk and dumps the loose cigarettes out of the packet. Some are bloodstained, a few are clean. He takes one, puts it between his lips, gropes around for a match, then lights the cigarette. He takes a deep drag and lets smoke out through his nose.

He pulls himself toward the dictaphone again, still in the swivel chair, reaches it, lifts the horn off the bracket and the dictaphone makes a low buzzing sound. He presses the button switch on the horn. The sound stops, the record revolves on the cylinder. He begins to speak:

NEFF. Office memorandum, Walter Neff to Barton Keyes, Claims Manager. Los Angeles, July 16th, 1938. Dear Keyes: I suppose you'll call this a confession when you hear it. I don't like the word confession. I just want to set you right about one thing you couldn't see, because it was smack up against your nose. You think you're such a hot potato as a claims manager, such a wolf on a phony claim. Well, maybe you are, Keyes, but let's take a look at this Dietrichson claim, Accident and Double Indemnity. You were pretty good in there for a while, all right. You said it wasn't an accident. Check. You said it wasn't suicide. Check. You said it was murder. Check and double check. You thought you had it cold, all wrapped up in tissue paper, with pink ribbons around it. It was perfect, except that it wasn't, because you made a mistake, just one tiny little mistake. When it came to picking the killer, you picked the wrong guy, if you know what I mean. Want to know who killed Dietrichson? Hold tight to that cheap cigar of yours, Keyes. I killed Dietrichson. Me, Walter Neff, insurance agent, 35 years old, unmarried, no visible scars — (*He glances down at his wounded shoulder.*) — until a little while ago, that is. Yes, I killed him. I killed him for money — and a woman — and I didn't get the money and I didn't get the woman. Pretty, isn't it?

He interrupts the dictation, lays down the horn on the desk. He takes his lighted cigarette from the ash tray, puffs it two or three times, and kills it. He picks up the horn again.

NEFF (*his voice now quiet and contained*). It all began last May. Around the end of May, it was. I'd been out to Glendale to deliver a policy on some dairy trucks. On the way back I remembered this auto renewal on Los Feliz Boulevard. So I drove over there.

As he goes on speaking, the scene slowly dissolves to the DIETRICHSON HOME in the LOS FELIZ DISTRICT: Palm trees line the street of middle-class houses mostly in Spanish style. Some kids are throwing a baseball back and forth across a couple of front lawns. An ice cream wagon dawdles along the block. Neff's coupe meets and passes the ice cream wagon and stops before one of the Spanish houses. Neff gets out.

He carries a briefcase, his hat is a little on the back of his head. His movements are easy and full of ginger. He inspects the house, checks the number, goes up on the front porch and rings the bell.

NEFF'S VOICE (*synchronized with the scene*). It was one of those California Spanish houses everyone was nuts about ten or fifteen years ago. This one must have cost somebody about 30,000 bucks — that is, if he ever finished paying for it.

The DIETRICHSON HOME: We see the entrance door as Neff rings the bell again and waits. The door opens. A maid, about forty-five, rather slatternly, opens the door.

NEFF. Mr. Dietrichson in?

MAID. Who wants to see him?

NEFF. The name is Neff. Walter Neff.

MAID. If you're selling something—

NEFF. Look, it's Mr. Dietrichson I'd like to talk to, and it's not magazine subscriptions.

He pushes past her into the house, and enters the HALLWAY. It is "Spanish" in style, as is the house throughout. A wrought-iron staircase curves down from the second floor. A fringed Mexican shawl hangs down over the landing. A large tapestry hangs on the wall. Downstairs, the dining room to one side, living room on the other side are visible through a wide archway. All of this—architecture, furniture, decorations, etc.—is genuine early Leo Carrillo period. . . . Neff has edged his way in past the maid who still holds the door open.

MAID. Listen, Mr. Dietrichson's not in.

NEFF. How soon do you expect him?

MAID. He'll be home when he gets here, if that's any help to you.

At this point a woman's voice comes from the top of the stairs.

VOICE. What is it, Nettie? Who is it?

As Neff looks up, the scene cuts to the UPPER LANDING of the STAIRCASE, as seen from below. Phyllis Dietrichson, a blonde woman in her early thirties, stands there looking down. She holds a large bath-towel around her very appetizing torso, down to about two inches above her knees. Her legs are bare. She wears a pair of high-heeled bedroom slippers with pompons, on her left ankle a gold anklet.

MAID'S VOICE. It's for Mr. Dietrichson.

PHYLLIS (*looking down at Neff*). I'm Mrs. Dietrichson. What is it?

Neff looks up, and takes his hat off.

NEFF. How do you do, Mrs. Dietrichson. I'm Walter Neff, Pacific All-Risk.

Following this we see PHYLLIS and NEFF alternately, each of them in the previous setting.

PHYLLIS. Pacific all-what?

NEFF. Pacific All-Risk Insurance Company. It's about some renewals on the automobiles, Mrs. Dietrichson. I've been trying to contact your husband for the past two weeks. He's never at his office.

PHYLLIS. Is there anything I can do?

NEFF. The insurance ran out on the fifteenth. I'd hate to think of your getting a smashed fender or something while you're not—uh—fully covered.

PHYLLIS (*glancing over her towel costume; with a little provocative smile*). Perhaps I know what you mean, Mr. Neff. I've just been taking a sun bath.

NEFF. No pigeons around, I hope. . . . About those policies, Mrs. Dietrichson—I hate to take up your time—

PHYLLIS. That's all right. If you can wait till I put something on, I'll be right down. Nettie, show Mr. Neff into the living room.

She turns away as gracefully as one can with a towel for a wrapper, following which the scene cuts to the ENTRANCE HALL as Neff watches Phyllis out of sight. He speaks to the maid while still looking up.

NEFF. Where would the living room be?

MAID. In there, but they keep the liquor locked up.

NEFF. That's okay. I always carry my own keys.

He goes through the archway, while the maid goes off the other way, and the scene cuts to the LIVING ROOM, as the Narrator's Voice (that is, Neff's talking into the dictaphone) starts again:

NEFF'S VOICE (*synchronized with the scene*). The living room was still stuffy from last night's cigars. The windows were closed and the sunshine coming in through the Venetian blinds showed up the dust in the air. The furniture was kind of corny and old-fashioned, but it had a comfortable look, as if people really sat in it. On the piano, in a couple of fancy frames, were Mr. Dietrichson and Lola, his daughter by his first wife. They had a bowl of those little red goldfish on the table behind the davenport, but, to tell you the truth, Keyes, I wasn't a whole lot interested in goldfish right then, nor in auto renewals, nor in Mr. Dietrichson and his daughter Lola. I was thinking about that dame upstairs, and the way she had looked at me, and I wanted to see her again, close, without that silly staircase between us.

Neff comes into the room and throws his briefcase on the plush davenport and tosses his hat on top of it. He looks around the room, then moves over to a baby grand piano with a sleazy Spanish shawl dangling down one side and two cabinet photographs standing in a staggered position on top. Neff glances them over: Mr. Dietrichson, age about fifty-one, a big, blocky man with glasses and a Rotarian look about him; Lola Dietrichson, age nineteen, wearing a filmy party dress and a yearning look in her pretty eyes. Neff walks away from the piano and takes a few steps back and forth across the rug. His eyes fall on a wrinkled corner. He carefully straightens it out with his foot. His back is to the archway as he hears high heels clicking on the staircase. He turns and looks through the arch.

The scene cuts to the STAIRCASE, from Neff's point of view, as Phyllis Dietrichson is coming downstairs. First we see her feet, with pompon slippers and the gold anklet on her left ankle. Then the view pulls back slowly as she descends, until we see all of her. She is wearing a pale blue summer dress.

PHYLLIS' VOICE. I wasn't long, was I?

NEFF'S VOICE. Not at all, Mrs. Dietrichson.

PHYLLIS (*as the scene pulls back with her into the living room*). I hope I've got my face on straight.

NEFF. It's perfect for my money.

PHYLLIS (*crossing to the mirror over the fireplace*). Won't you sit down, Mr. — Neff is the name, isn't it?

NEFF. With two f's, like in Philadelphia, if you know the story.

PHYLLIS. What story?

NEFF. The Philadelphia story. What are we talking about?

PHYLLIS (*working with her lipstick*). About the insurance. My husband never tells me anything.

NEFF. It's on your two cars, the La Salle and the Plymouth.

He crosses to the davenport to get the policies from his briefcase. She turns away from the mirror and sits in a big chair with her legs drawn up sideways, the anklet now clearly visible.

NEFF. We've been handling this insurance for three years for Mr. Dietrichson . . . (*His eyes have caught the anklet.*) That's a honey of an anklet you're wearing, Mrs. Dietrichson. (*Phyllis smiles faintly and covers the anklet with her dress.*) We'd hate to see the policies lapse. Of course, we give him thirty days. That's all we're allowed to give.

PHYLLIS. I guess he's been too busy down at Long Beach in the oil fields.

NEFF. Could I catch him home some evening for a few minutes?

PHYLLIS. I suppose so. But he's never home much before eight.

NEFF. That would be fine with me.

PHYLLIS. You're not connected with the Automobile Club, are you?

NEFF. No, the All-Risk, Mrs. Dietrichson. Why?

PHYLLIS. Somebody from the Automobile Club has been trying to get him. Do they have a better rate?

NEFF. If your husband's a member.

PHYLLIS. No, he isn't.

NEFF (*as Phyllis rises and walks up and down, paying less and less attention*). Well, he'd have to join the club and pay a membership fee to start with. The Automobile Club is fine. I never knock the other fellow's merchandise, Mrs. Dietrichson, but I can do just as well for you. I have a very attractive policy here. It wouldn't take me two minutes to put it in front of your husband. (*He consults the policies he is holding.*) For instance, we're writing a new kind of fifty percent retention feature in the collision coverage.

PHYLLIS (*stopping in her walk*). You're a smart insurance man, aren't you, Mr. Neff?

NEFF. I've had eleven years of it.

PHYLLIS. Doing pretty well?

NEFF. It's a living.

PHYLLIS. You handle just automobile insurance, or all kinds? (*She sits down again, in the same position as before.*)

NEFF. All kinds. Fire, earthquake, theft, public liability, group insurance, industrial stuff and so on right down the line.

PHYLLIS. Accident insurance?

NEFF. Accident insurance? Sure, Mrs. Dietrichson. (*His eyes fall on the anklet again.*) I wish you'd tell me what's engraved on that anklet.

PHYLLIS. Just my name.

NEFF. As for instance?

PHYLLIS. Phyllis.

NEFF. Phyllis. I think I like that.

PHYLLIS. But you're not sure?

NEFF. I'd have to drive it around the block a couple of times.

PHYLLIS (*standing up again*). Mr. Neff, why don't you drop by tomorrow evening about eight-thirty. He'll be in then.

NEFF. Who?

PHYLLIS. My husband. You were anxious to talk to him, weren't you?

NEFF. Sure, only I'm getting over it a little. If you know what I mean.

PHYLLIS. There's a speed limit in this state, Mr. Neff. Forty-five miles an hour.

NEFF. How fast was I going, officer?

PHYLLIS. I'd say about ninety.

NEFF. Suppose you get down off your motorcycle and give me a ticket.

PHYLLIS. Suppose I let you off with a warning this time.

NEFF. Suppose it doesn't take.

PHYLLIS. Suppose I have to whack you over the knuckles.

NEFF. Suppose I bust out crying and put my head on your shoulder.

PHYLLIS. Suppose you try putting it on my husband's shoulder.

NEFF. That tears it. (*Neff takes his hat and briefcase.*) Eight-thirty tomorrow evening then, Mrs. Dietrichson.

PHYLLIS. That's what I suggested.

As they both move toward the archway, the scene cuts to the HALLWAY, and PHYLLIS and NEFF are seen going toward the ENTRANCE DOOR.

NEFF. Will you be here, too?

PHYLLIS. I guess so. I usually am.

NEFF. Same chair, same perfume, same anklet?

PHYLLIS (*opening the door*). I wonder if I know what you mean.

NEFF (*walking out*). I wonder if you wonder.

Outside the DIETRICHSON HOME, looking past Neff's

parked car toward the entrance door, which is just closing: Neff comes toward the car, swinging his briefcase. He opens the car door and looks back with a confident smile. — Next we see the ENTRANCE DOOR, as the peep window in the upper panel opens and Phyllis looks out after him. NEFF sits in his car and presses the starter button, looking back toward the little window in the ENTRANCE DOOR, as the peep window is quickly closed from the inside. And then we see the STREET as Neff makes a U-turn and drives back down the block.

NEFF'S VOICE (*over the scene*). She liked me. I could feel that. The way you feel when the cards are falling right for you, with a nice little pile of blue and yellow chips in the middle of the table. Only what I didn't know then was that I wasn't playing her. She was playing me — with a deck of marked cards — and the stakes weren't any blue and yellow chips. They were dynamite. It was a hot afternoon and I can still remember the smell of honeysuckle all along the street. How could I have known that murder can sometimes smell like honeysuckle. Maybe you would have known, Keyes, the minute she mentioned accident insurance, but I didn't. I felt like a millionaire.

The scene dissolves to the INSURANCE OFFICE on the TWELFTH FLOOR. There is activity on the eleventh floor below: typewriters working, adding machines, filing clerks, secretaries, and so forth. Neff, wearing his hat and carrying his briefcase, enters from the vestibule. He walks toward his office. He passes a few salesmen. There is an exchange of greetings.

NEFF'S VOICE: I went back to the office to see if I had any mail. It was the day you had that truck driver from Inglewood on the carpet. — Remember, Keyes?

Just as Neff reaches his office a secretary comes out. She stops.

SECRETARY. Oh, Mr. Neff, Mr. Keyes wants to see you. He's been yelling for you all afternoon.

NEFF. Is he sore, or just frothing at the mouth a little? Here, park these for me, sweetheart.

He hands her his hat and briefcase and the scene moves with him as he continues to a door lettered: BARTON KEYES—

CLAIMS MANAGER. Keyes' voice is heard inside, quite loud. Neff grins as he opens the door and goes in. Then the scene cuts to KEYES' OFFICE: It is a minor executive office, not too tidy: a large desk across one corner, good carpet, several chairs, filing cabinet against one wall, a dictaphone on the corner of the desk. — Keyes is sitting behind the desk with his coat off but his hat on. A cigar is clamped in his mouth, ashes falling like snow down his vest, a gold chain and elk's tooth across it. On the other side of the desk sits Sam Gorlopis. He is a big, dumb bruiser, six feet three inches tall — rough, untidy hair, broad face, small piggish eyes — wearing a dirty work shirt and corduroy pants. He holds a sweat-soaked hat on his knee with a hairy hand. He is chewing gum rapidly. As Neff opens the door, Keyes is giving it to Gorlopis, the truck driver.

KEYES. Come on, come on, Gorlopis. You're not kidding anybody with that line of bull. You're in a jam and you know it.

GORLOPIS. Sez you. All I want is my money.

KEYES. Sez you. All you're gonna get is the cops.

He sees Neff standing inside the door.

KEYES. Come in, Walter. This is Sam Gorlopis from Inglewood.

NEFF. Sure, I know Mr. Gorlopis. Wrote a policy on his truck. How are you, Mr. Gorlopis?

GORLOPIS. I ain't so good. My truck burned down. (*He looks sideways cautiously at Keyes.*)

KEYES. Yeah, he just planted his big foot on the starter and the whole thing blazed up in his face.

GORLOPIS. Yes, sir.

KEYES. And didn't even singe his eyebrows.

GORLOPIS. No sir. Look, mister. I got twenty-six hundred bucks tied up in that truck. I'm insured with this company and I want my money.

KEYES. You got a wife, Gorlopis?

GORLOPIS. Sure I got a wife.

KEYES. You got kids?

GORLOPIS. Two kids.

KEYES. What you got for dinner tonight?

GORLOPIS. We got meat loaf.

KEYES. How do you make your meat loaf, Gorlopis?

GORLOPIS. Veal and pork and bread and garlic. Greek style.

KEYES. How much garlic?

GORLOPIS. Lotsa garlic, Mr. Keyes.

KEYES. Okay, Gorlopis. Now listen here. Let's say you just came up here to tell me how to make meat loaf. That's all, understand? Because if you came up here to claim on that truck, I'd have to turn you over to the law, Gorlopis, and they'd put you in jail. No wife. No kids—

GORLOPIS. What for?

KEYES (*yelling*). —And no meat loaf, Gorlopis!

GORLOPIS. I didn't do nothin'.

KEYES. Yeah? Now, look, Gorlopis. Every month hundreds of claims come to this desk. Some of them are phonies, and I know which ones. How do I know, Gorlopis? (*He speaks as if to a child.*) Because my little man tells me.

GORLOPIS. What little man?

KEYES. The little man in here. (*He pounds the pit of his stomach.*) Every time one of those phonies comes along he ties knots in my stomach. And yours was one of them, Gorlopis. That's how I knew your claim was crooked. So what did I do? I sent a tow car out to your garage this afternoon and they jacked up that burned-out truck of yours. And what did they find, Gorlopis? They found what was left of a neat pile of shavings.

GORLOPIS. What shavings?

KEYES. The ones you soaked with kerosene and dropped a match on.

GORLOPIS (*cringing under the impact*). Look, Mr. Keyes, I'm just a poor man. Maybe I made a mistake.

KEYES. Well, that's one way of putting it.

GORLOPIS (*starting to leave*). I ain't feelin' so good, Mr. Keyes.

KEYES. Here, just a minute. Sign this and you'll feel fine. (*He puts a blank form in front of him and points.*) Right there. It's a waiver on your claim. (*Gorlopis hesitates, then signs laboriously.*) Now you're an honest man again.

GORLOPIS. But I ain't got no more truck.

KEYES. Goodbye, Gorlopis.

GORLOPIS (*still bewildered*). Goodbye, Mr. Keyes. (*He stands up and goes slowly to the door and turns there.*) Twenty-six hundred bucks. That's a lot of dough where I live.

KEYES. What's the matter, Gorlopis? Don't you know how to open the door? Just put your hand on the knob, turn it to the right, now pull it toward you—

GORLOPIS (*doing just as Keyes says*). Like this, Mr. Keyes?

KEYES. That's the boy. Now the same thing from the outside.

GORLOPIS (*stupefied*). Thank you, Mr. Keyes.

He goes out, closing the door after him. Keyes takes his cigar stub from his mouth and turns it slowly in the flame of a lighted match. He turns to Neff.

KEYES. What kind of an outfit is this anyway? Are we an insurance company, or a bunch of dimwitted amateurs, writing a policy on a mugg like that?

NEFF. Wait a minute, Keyes. I don't rate this beef. I clipped a note to that Gorlopis application to have him thoroughly investigated before we accepted the risk.

KEYES. I know you did, Walter. I'm not beefing at you. It's the company. The way they do things. The way they don't do things. The way they'll write anything just to get it down on the sales sheet. And I'm the guy that has to sit here up to my neck in phony claims so they won't throw more money out of the window than they take in at the door.

NEFF (*grinning*). Okay, turn the record over and let's hear the other side.

KEYES. I get darn sick of picking up after a gang of fast-talking salesmen dumb enough to sell life insurance to a guy that sleeps in the same bed with four rattlesnakes. I've had twenty-six years of that, Walter, and I—

NEFF. And you loved every minute of it, Keyes. You love it, only you worry about it too much, you and your little man. You're so darn conscientious you're driving yourself crazy. You wouldn't even say today is Tuesday without you looked at the calendar, and then you would check if it was this year's or last year's calendar, and then you would find out what company printed the calendar, then find out if their calendar checks with the World Almanac's calendar.

KEYES. That's enough from you, Walter. Get out of here before I throw my desk at you.

NEFF. I love you, too.

He walks out, still grinning, and we next see the exterior of the OFFICES. Neff comes out of Keyes' office and walks back along the balcony, where there is great activity of secretaries going in and out of doors.—Neff enters his own office. Anderson, a salesman, is sitting at one of the desks, filling out a report. Neff goes to his own desk. He looks down at some mail. On top there is a typewritten note. He reads it, sits down, and leafs through his desk calendar.

We get a closeup of a CALENDAR PAGE showing the date:

THURSDAY

23

May

and five or six appointments pencilled in tightly on the page.

NEFF'S VOICE (*over the scene*). I really did, too, you old crab, always yelling your fat head off, always sore at everyone. But behind the cigar ashes on your vest I kind of knew you had a heart as big as a house . . . Back in my office there was a phone message from Mrs. Dietrichson about the renewals. She didn't want me to come tomorrow evening. She wanted me to come Thursday afternoon at three-thirty instead. I had a lot of stuff lined up for that Thursday afternoon, including a trip down to Santa Monica to see a couple of live prospects about some group insurance. But I kept thinking about Phyllis Dietrichson and the way that anklet of hers cut into her leg.

The ENTRANCE HALL of the DIETRICHSON HOME fades in. There is a moving view of Phyllis Dietrichson's feet and ankles as she comes down the stairs, her high heels clicking on the tiles. The anklet glistens on her leg as she moves. Phyllis reaches the entrance hall, and as she walks toward the front door her whole body becomes visible. She wears a gay print dress with a wide sash over her hips. She opens the door. Outside is Neff, wearing a sport coat and flannel slacks. He takes his hat off.

PHYLLIS. Hello, Mr. Neff. (*As he stands there with a little smile*) Aren't you coming in?

NEFF (*starting to go inside*). I'm considering it.

PHYLLIS. I hope you didn't mind my changing the appointment. Last night wasn't so convenient.

NEFF. That's okay. I was working on my stamp collection.

Phyllis leads Neff toward the living room, and they go in through the archway. She then heads toward the davenport, in front of which is a low tea table holding tall glasses, ice cubes, lemon and a pot of tea.

PHYLLIS. I was just fixing some iced tea. Would you like a glass?

NEFF. Unless you have a bottle of beer that's not working.

PHYLLIS. There might be some. I never know what's in the ice box. (*Calling*) Nettie! . . . . (*She pours herself a glass of tea.*) About those renewals, Mr. Neff. I talked to my husband about it.

NEFF. You did?

PHYLLIS. Yes. He'll renew with you, he told me. In fact, I thought he'd be here this afternoon.

NEFF. But he's not?

PHYLLIS. No.

NEFF. That's terrible.

PHYLLIS (*calling again, impatiently*). Nettie! . . *Nettie!* . . . . Oh, I forgot, it's the maid's day off.

NEFF. Don't bother, Mrs. Dietrichson. I'd like some iced tea very much.

PHYLLIS. Lemon? Sugar?

NEFF. Fix it your way.

She fixes him a glass of tea while he looks around. He sits down slowly. (We see them together and separately in close shots throughout the conversation.)

NEFF. Seeing it's the maid's day off maybe there's something I can do for you. (*As she hands him the tea*) Like running the vacuum cleaner.

PHYLLIS. Fresh.

NEFF. I used to peddle vacuum cleaners. Not much money but you learn a lot about life.

PHYLLIS. I didn't think you'd learned it from a correspondence course.

NEFF. Where did you pick up this tea drinking? You're not English, are you?

PHYLLIS. No. Californian. Born right here in Los Angeles.

NEFF. They say native Californians all come from Iowa.

PHYLLIS. I wanted to ask you something, Mr. Neff.

NEFF. Make it Walter.

PHYLLIS. Walter?

NEFF. That's right.

PHYLLIS. Tell me, Walter, on this insurance—how much commission do you make?

NEFF. Twenty percent. Why?

PHYLLIS. I thought maybe I could throw a little more business your way.

NEFF. I can always use it.

PHYLLIS. I was thinking about my husband. I worry a lot about him, down in those oil fields. It's very dangerous.

NEFF. Not for an executive, is it?

PHYLLIS. He doesn't just sit behind a desk. He's right down there with the drilling crews. It's got me worried sick.

NEFF. You mean a crown block might fall on him some rainy night?

PHYLLIS. Please don't talk like that.

NEFF. But that's the idea.

PHYLLIS. The other day a casing line snapped and caught the foreman. He's in the hospital with a broken back.

NEFF. Bad.

PHYLLIS. It's got me jittery just thinking about it. Suppose something like that happened to my husband?

NEFF. It could.

PHYLLIS. Don't you think he ought to have accident insurance?

NEFF. Uh huh.

PHYLLIS. What kind of insurance could he have?

NEFF. Enough to cover doctors' and hospital bills. Say a hundred and twenty-five a week cash benefit. And he'd rate around fifty thousand capital sum.

PHYLLIS. Capital sum? What's that?

NEFF. In case he gets killed. Maybe I shouldn't have said that.

PHYLLIS. I suppose you have to think of everything in your business.

NEFF. Well, your husband would understand. I'm sure I could sell him on the idea of some accident protection. Why don't I talk to him about it?

PHYLLIS. You could try. But he's pretty tough going.

NEFF. They're all tough at first.

PHYLLIS. He has a lot on his mind. He doesn't want to listen to anything except maybe a baseball game on the radio. Sometimes we sit all evening without saying a word to each other.

NEFF. Sounds pretty dull.

PHYLLIS (*shrugging*). So I just sit and knit.

NEFF. Is that what you married him for?

PHYLLIS. Maybe I like the way his thumbs hold up the wool.

NEFF. Any time his thumbs get tired— Only with me around you wouldn't have to knit.

PHYLLIS. Wouldn't I?

NEFF. You bet your life you wouldn't.—(*After taking a sip of the iced tea*) I wonder if a little rum would get this up on its feet!

PHYLLIS. I want to ask you something, Walter. Could I get an accident policy for him—without bothering him at all?

NEFF. How's that again?

PHYLLIS. That would make it easier for you, too. You wouldn't even have to talk to him. I have a little allowance of my own. I could pay for it and he needn't know anything about it.

NEFF. Why shouldn't he know?

PHYLLIS. Because he doesn't want accident insurance. He's superstitious about it.

NEFF. A lot of people are. Funny, isn't it?

PHYLLIS. If there was a way to get it like that, all the worry would be over. You see what I mean, Walter?

NEFF. Sure. I've got good eyesight. You want him to have the policy without him knowing it. And that means without the insurance company knowing that he doesn't know. That's the set-up, isn't it?

PHYLLIS. Is there anything wrong with it?

NEFF. No, I think it's lovely. And then, some dark wet night, if that crown block did fall on him—

PHYLLIS. What crown block?

NEFF. Only sometimes they have to have a little help. They can't quite make it on their own.

PHYLLIS. I don't know what you're talking about.

NEFF. Of course, it doesn't have to be a crown block. It can be a car backing over him, or he can fall out of an upstairs window. Any little thing like that, as long as it's a morgue job.

PHYLLIS. Are you crazy?

NEFF. Not that crazy. Goodbye, Mrs. Dietrichson. (*He picks up his hat.*)

PHYLLIS (*jumping up*). What's the matter?

NEFF (*starting to leave*). Look, baby, you can't get away with it.

PHYLLIS. Get away with what?

NEFF. You want to knock him off, don't you, baby.

PHYLLIS. That's a horrible thing to say!

NEFF. What'd you think I was, anyway? A guy that walks into a good-looking dame's front parlor and says "Good afternoon, I sell accident insurance on husbands. You got one that's been around too long? Somebody you'd like to turn into a little hard cash? Just give me a smile and I'll help you collect." Boy, what a dope you must think I am.

PHYLLIS. I think you're rotten.

NEFF. I think you're swell. So long as I'm not your husband.

PHYLLIS. Get out of here.

NEFF. You bet I will. You bet I'll get out of here, baby. But quick. (*He goes out.*)

She looks after him and we then see the outside of the DIETRICHSON HOUSE, Neff's voice coming over this, as he talks into the dictaphone.

NEFF'S VOICE (*over the scene*). So I let her have it, straight between the eyes. She didn't fool me for a minute, not this time. I knew I had hold of a red-hot poker and the time to drop it was before it burned my hand off. I stopped at a drive-in for a bottle of beer, the one I had wanted all along, only I wanted it worse now, to get rid of the sour taste of her iced tea, and everything that went with it. I didn't want to go back to the office, so I dropped by a bowling alley at Third and Western and rolled a few lines to get my mind thinking about something else for a while.

As Neff bangs the front door shut, walks quickly to his car and drives away, the scene dissolves to the DRIVE-IN of a RESTAURANT, "shooting" past Neff sitting behind the wheel of his car. The car hop hangs a tray on the door and serves him a bottle of beer.—This dissolves to the interior of a BOWLING ALLEY where Neff is bowling. He rolls the ball with an effort at concentration, but his mind is not really on the game. This dissolves to the exterior of an APARTMENT HOUSE. It is late afternoon. The apartment house is called the LOS OLIVOS APARTMENTS. It is a six-story building in the Normandie-Wilshire district, with a basement garage. The view moves up the front of the building to the top floor windows, as a little rain starts to fall.

NEFF'S VOICE (*continuing*). I didn't feel like eating dinner when I left, and I didn't feel like a show, so I drove home, put the car away and went up to my apartment.

We now see the LIVING ROOM of NEFF'S APARTMENT at dusk. It is a double apartment of conventional design, with kitchen, dinette, and bathroom, square-cut overstuffed borax furniture. Gas logs are lit in the imitation fireplace. Neff stands by the window with his coat off and his tie loose. Raindrops strike against the glass. He turns away impatiently, paces up and down past a caddy bag with golf clubs in it, pulls one out at random, makes a couple of short swings, throws the club on the couch, and paces again. —

NEFF'S VOICE (*continuing*). It had begun to rain outside and I watched it get dark and didn't even turn on the light. That didn't help me either. I was all twisted up inside, and I was still holding on to that red-hot poker. And right then it came over me that I hadn't walked out on anything at all, that the hook was too strong, that this wasn't the end between her and me. It was only the beginning. So at eight o'clock the bell would ring and I would know who it was without even having to think, as if it was the most natural thing in the world.

The doorbell rings. Neff goes to the door and opens it, revealing Phyllis standing there.

PHYLLIS. Hello. (*As Neff just looks at her in amazement*) You forgot your hat this afternoon. (*She has nothing in her hands but her bag.*)

NEFF. Did I? (*He looks down at her hands.*)

PHYLLIS. Don't you want me to bring it in?

NEFF. Sure. Put it on the chair. (*She comes in. He closes the door.*) How did you know where I live?

PHYLLIS. It's in the phone book. (*Neff switches on the standing lamp.*) It's raining.

NEFF. So it is. Peel off your coat and sit down. (*She starts to take off her coat.*) Your husband out?

PHYLLIS. Long Beach. They're spudding in a new well. He phoned he'd be late. About nine-thirty. (*He takes her coat and lays it across the back of a chair.*) It's about time you said you're glad to see me.

NEFF. I knew you wouldn't leave it like that.

PHYLLIS. Like what?

NEFF. Like it was this afternoon.

PHYLLIS. I must have said something that gave you a terribly wrong impression. You must surely see that. You must never think anything like that about me, Walter.

NEFF. Okay.

PHYLLIS. It's not okay. Not if you don't believe me.

NEFF. What do you want me to do?

PHYLLIS. I want you to be nice to me. Like the first time you came to the house.

NEFF. It can't be like the first time. Something has happened.

PHYLLIS. I know it has. It's happened to us.

NEFF. That's what I mean.

Phyllis has moved over to the window. She stares out through the wet windowpane.

NEFF. What's the matter now?

PHYLLIS. I feel as if he was watching me. Not that he cares about me. Not any more. But he keeps me on a leash. So tight I can't breathe. I'm scared.

NEFF. What of? He's in Long Beach, isn't he?

PHYLLIS. I oughtn't to have come.

NEFF. Maybe you oughtn't.

PHYLLIS. You want me to go?

NEFF. If you want to.

PHYLLIS. Right now?

NEFF. Sure. Right now.

By this time, he has hold of her wrists. He draws her to him slowly and kisses her. Her arms tighten around him. After a moment he pulls his head back, still holding her close. — Then they break away from each other, and she puts her head on his shoulder.

NEFF. I'm crazy about you, baby.

PHYLLIS. I'm crazy about you, Walter.

NEFF. That perfume on your hair. What's the name of it?

PHYLLIS. I don't know. I bought it down at Ensenada.

NEFF. We ought to have some of that pink wine to go with it. The kind that bubbles. But all I have is bourbon.

PHYLLIS. Bourbon is fine, Walter.

He lets her go and moves toward the dinette. We then see the DINETTE and KITCHEN, which contains a small table and some chairs. A low glass-and-china cabinet is built between the dinette and kitchen, leaving a space like a doorway. The kitchen is the usual apartment house kitchen, with stove, ice-box, sink, etc. It is quite small. — Neff goes to the ice-box and Phyllis drifts in after him.

NEFF. Soda?

PHYLLIS. Plain water, please.

NEFF. Get a couple of glasses, will you.

He points at the china closet. He has taken a tray of ice cubes from the refrigerator and is holding it under the hot-water faucet.

NEFF. You know, about six months ago a guy slipped on the soap in his bathtub and knocked himself out cold and drowned. Only he had accident insurance. So they had an autopsy and she didn't get away with it.

Phyllis has the glasses now. She hands them to him. He dumps some ice cubes into the glasses.

PHYLLIS. Who didn't?

NEFF. His wife. (*He reaches for the whiskey bottle on top of the china closet.*) And there was a case of a guy found shot and his wife said he was cleaning a gun and his stomach got in the way. All she collected was a three-to-ten stretch in Tehachapi.

PHYLLIS. Perhaps it was worth it to her.

Neff hands her a glass.

NEFF. See if you can carry this as far as the living room. (*They move back toward the living room.*)

The LIVING ROOM as Phyllis and Neff go toward the davenport: she is sipping her drink and looking around.

PHYLLIS. It's nice here, Walter. Who takes care of it for you?

NEFF. A colored woman comes in twice a week.

PHYLLIS. You get your own breakfast?

NEFF. Once in a while I squeeze a grapefruit. The rest I get at the corner drugstore. (*They sit on the davenport, fairly close together.*)

PHYLLIS. It sounds wonderful. Just strangers beside you. You don't know them. You don't hate them. You don't have to sit across the table and smile at him and that daughter of his every morning of your life.

NEFF. What daughter? Oh, that little girl on the piano.

PHYLLIS. Yes. Lola. She lives with us. He thinks a lot more of her than he does of me.

NEFF. Ever think of a divorce?

PHYLLIS. He wouldn't give me a divorce.

NEFF. I suppose because it would cost him money.

PHYLLIS. He hasn't got any money. Not since he went into the oil business.

NEFF. But he had when you married him?

PHYLLIS. Yes, he had. And I wanted a home. Why not? But

that wasn't the only reason. I was his wife's nurse. She was sick for a long time. When she died, he was all broken up. I pitied him so.

NEFF. And now you hate him.

PHYLLIS. Yes, Walter. He's so mean to me. Every time I buy a dress or a pair of shoes he yells his head off. He won't let me go anywhere. He keeps me shut up. He's always been mean to me. Even his life insurance all goes to that daughter of his. That Lola.

NEFF. Nothing for you at all, huh?

PHYLLIS. No. And nothing is just what I'm worth to him.

NEFF. So you lie awake in the dark and listen to him snore and get ideas.

PHYLLIS. Walter, I don't want to kill him. I never did. Not even when he gets drunk and slaps my face.

NEFF. Only sometimes you wish he was dead.

PHYLLIS. Perhaps I do.

NEFF. And you wish it was an accident, and you had that policy. For fifty thousand dollars. Is that it?

PHYLLIS. Perhaps that too. (*She takes a long drink.*) The other night we drove home from a party. He was drunk again. When we got into the garage he just sat there with his head on the steering wheel and the motor still running. And I thought what it would be like if I didn't switch it off, just closed the garage door and left him there.

NEFF. I'll tell you what it would be like, if you had that accident policy, and tried to pull a monoxide job. We have a guy in our office named Keyes. For him a set-up like that would be just like a slice of rare roast beef. In three minutes he'd know it wasn't an accident. In ten minutes you'd be sitting under the hot lights. In half an hour you'd be signing your name to a confession.

PHYLLIS. But, Walter, I didn't do it. I'm not going to do it.

NEFF. Not if there's an insurance company in the picture, baby. So long as you're honest they'll pay you with a smile, but you just try to pull something like that and you'll find out. They know more tricks than a carload of monkeys. And if there's a death mixed up in it, you haven't got a prayer. They'll hang you as sure as ten dimes will buy a dollar, baby. (*She begins to cry, and he puts his arms around her and kisses her.*) Just stop thinking about it, will you.

He holds her tight. Their heads touch, side by side, as the scene slowly starts to recede and then dissolves to NEFF's OFFICE at night. — Neff is sitting in the swivel chair, talking into the dictaphone. He has hooked the wastebasket under his feet to sit more comfortably. As he talks, a little cough shakes him now and then.

NEFF. So we just sat there, and she kept on crying softly, like the rain on the window, and we didn't say anything. Maybe she had stopped thinking about it, but I hadn't. I couldn't. Because it all tied up with something I had been thinking about for years, since long before I ever ran into Phyllis Dietrichson. Because, in this business you can't sleep for trying to figure out the tricks they could pull on you. You're like the guy behind the roulette wheel, watching the customers to make sure they don't crook the house. And then one night, you get to thinking how you could crook the house yourself. And do it smart. Because you've got that wheel right under your hands. And you know every notch in it by heart. And you figure all you need is a plant out in front, a shill to put down the bet. And suddenly the doorbell rings and the whole set-up is right there in the room with you . . . Look, Keyes, I'm not trying to whitewash myself. I fought it, only maybe I didn't fight it hard enough. The stakes were fifty thousand dollars, but they were the life of a man, too, a man who'd never done me any dirt. Except he was married to a woman he didn't care anything about, and I did . . .

The scene dissolves back to NEFF's LIVING ROOM and the view moves slowly toward the davenport again. Neff sits in one corner with his feet on the low table. He is smoking his cigarette and staring at the ceiling. Phyllis has been sitting fairly close to him. She gets up slowly and crosses to her rain coat, lying over the chair.

PHYLLIS. I've got to go now, Walter. (*Neff does not answer. He keeps on staring at the ceiling. She starts to put the raincoat on.*) Will you phone me, Walter? (*As Neff still does not answer*) Walter! (*He looks at her slowly, almost absently.*) I hate him. I loathe going back to him. You believe me, don't you, Walter?

NEFF. Sure I believe you.

PHYLLIS. I can't stand it anymore. What if they did hang me?

NEFF. You're not going to hang, baby—

PHYLLIS. It's better than going on this way.

NEFF. —you're not going to hang, baby. Not ever. Because you're going to do it the smart way. Because I'm going to help you.

PHYLLIS. You!

NEFF. Me.

PHYLLIS. Do you know what you're saying?

NEFF. Sure I know what I'm saying.

He gets up and grips her arm.

NEFF. We're going to do it together. We're going to do it right. And I'm the guy that knows how.

There is fierce determination in his voice. His fingers dig into her arm.

PHYLLIS. Walter, you're hurting me.

NEFF. There isn't going to be any slip-up. Nothing sloppy. Nothing weak. It's got to be perfect. (*He kisses her.*) You go now. (*He leads her toward the door.*) Call me tomorrow. But not from your house. From a booth. And watch your step. Every single minute. It's got to be perfect, understand. Straight down the line.

They have now reached the door. Neff opens it. Phyllis stands in the doorway, her lips white.

PHYLLIS. Straight down the line.

She goes quietly. He watches her down the corridor. Slowly he closes the door and goes back into the room. He moves across to the window and opens it wide. He stands there, looking down into the dark street. From below comes the sound of a car starting and driving off. The rain drifts in against his face. He just stands there motionless. His mind is going a hundred miles a minute, and the scene fades out.

NEFF'S VOICE (*synchronized with the scene*). That was it, Keyes. The machinery had started to move and nothing could stop it.


PART TWO

NEFF'S OFFICE fades in at night. Neff sits slumped in his chair before the dictaphone. On the desk next to him stands a used record. The cylinder on the dictaphone is not turning. He is smoking a cigarette. He puts it down then lifts the needle and slides off the record which is on the machine and stands it on end on the desk beside the other used record. He reaches down painfully to take another record from the rack beneath the dictaphone, looks at it against the light to make sure it has not been used, then slides it into place on the machine and resets the needle. He lifts the horn and resumes his dictation.

NEFF. The first thing we had to do was to fix him up with that accident policy. I knew he wouldn't buy, but all I wanted was his signature on an application. So I had to make him sign without his knowing what he was signing. And I wanted a witness other than Phyllis to hear me give him the sales talk. I was trying to think with your brains, Keyes. I wanted all the answers ready for all the questions you were going to spring as soon as Dietrichson was dead.

Neff takes a last drag on his cigarette and kills it by running it under the ledge of the dictaphone stand. He drops the stub on the floor and resumes.

NEFF. A couple of nights later I went to the house. Everything looked fine, except I didn't like the witness Phyllis had brought in. It was Dietrichson's daughter Lola, and it made me feel a little queer in the belly to have her right there in the room, playing Chinese checkers, as if nothing was going to happen.

This dissolves to a BOARD of CHINESE CHECKERS. The view then moves back and gradually reveals the DIETRICHSON LIVING ROOM at night. The checker-board is on the davenport between Phyllis and Lola. Mr. Dietrichson sits in a big easy chair. His coat and tie are over the back of the chair, and the evening paper is lying tumbled on the floor beside him. He is smoking a cigar with the band on it. He has a drink in front of him and several more inside him. In another chair sits Neff, his briefcase on the floor, leaning against his chair. He holds his rate book partly open, with a finger in it for a marker. He is going full swing.

NEFF. I suppose you realize, Mr. Dietrichson, that, not being an employee, you are not covered by the State Compensation Insurance Act. The only way you can protect yourself is by having a personal policy of your own.

DIETRICHSON. I know all about that. The next thing you'll tell me I need earthquake insurance and lightning insurance and hail insurance.

Phyllis looks up from the checker-board and cuts in on the dialogue. Lola listens without much interest.

PHYLLIS (*to Dietrichson*). If we bought all the insurance they can think up, we'd stay broke paying for it, wouldn't we, honey?

DIETRICHSON. What keeps us broke is you going out and buying five hats at a crack. Who needs a hat in California?

NEFF. I always say insurance is a lot like a hot water bottle. It looks kind of useless and silly hanging on a hook, but when you get that stomachache in the middle of the night, it comes in mighty handy.

DIETRICHSON. Now you want to sell me a hot water bottle.

NEFF. Dollar for dollar, accident insurance is the cheapest coverage you can buy, Mr. Dietrichson.

DIETRICHSON. Maybe some other time, Mr. Neff. I had a tough day.

NEFF. Just as you say Mr. Dietrichson.

DIETRICHSON. Suppose we just settle that automobile insurance tonight.

NEFF. Sure. All we need on that is for you to sign an application for renewal.

Phyllis throws a quick glance at Neff. As she looks back she sees that Lola is staring down at her wrist watch.

LOLA. Phyllis, do you mind if we don't finish this game? It bores me stiff.

PHYLLIS. Got something better to do?

LOLA (*getting up*). Yes, I have. (*To Dietrichson*) Father, is it all right if I run along now?

DIETRICHSON. Run along where? Who with?

LOLA. Just Anne. We're going roller skating.

DIETRICHSON. Anne who?

LOLA. Anne Matthews.

PHYLLIS. It's not that Nino Zachette again?

DIETRICHSON. It better not be that Zachette guy. If I ever catch you with him —

LOLA. It's Anne Matthews, I told you. I also told you we're going roller skating. I'm meeting her at the corner of Vermont and Franklin — the north-west corner, in case you're interested. And I'm late already. I hope that is all clear. Good night, father. Good night, Phyllis. (*She starts to go.*)

NEFF. Good night, Miss Dietrichson.

LOLA. Oh, I'm sorry. Good night, Mr. —

NEFF. Neff.

LOLA. Good night, Mr. Neff.

PHYLLIS. Now you're not going to take my car again.

LOLA. No thanks. I'd rather be dead. (*She goes out through the archway.*)

DIETRICHSON. A great little fighter for her weight.

Dietrichson sucks down a big swallow of his drink. Neff has taken two blank forms from his briefcase. He puts the briefcase on Mr. Dietrichson's lap and lays the forms on top. Phyllis is watching closely.

NEFF. This is where you sign, Mr. Dietrichson.

DIETRICHSON. Sign what?

NEFF. The applications for your auto renewals. So you'll be protected until the new policies are issued.

DIETRICHSON. When will that be?

NEFF. In about a week.

DIETRICHSON. Just so I'm covered when I drive up North.

Neff takes out his fountain pen.

NEFF. San Francisco, Mr. Dietrichson?

DIETRICHSON. Palo Alto.

PHYLLIS. He was a Stanford man, Mr. Neff. And he still goes to his class reunion every year.

DIETRICHSON. What's wrong with that? Can't I have a little fun even once a year?

NEFF. Great football school, Stanford. Did you play football, Mr. Dietrichson?

DIETRICHSON. Left guard. Almost made the varsity, too.

Neff has unscrewed his fountain pen. He hands it to Mr. Dietrichson. Dietrichson puts on his glasses.

NEFF. On that bottom line, Mr. Dietrichson. (*Dietrichson signs. Neff's and Phyllis' eyes meet for a split second.*) Both copies, please.

He withdraws the top copy barely enough to expose the signature line on the supposed duplicate.

DIETRICHSON. Sign twice, huh?

NEFF. One is the agent's copy. I need it for my files.

DIETRICHSON (*in a mutter*). Files. Duplicates. Triplicates.

Dietrichson grunts and signs again. Again Neff and Phyllis exchange a quick glance.

NEFF. No hurry about the check, Mr. Dietrichson. I can pick it up at your office some morning. (*Casually Neff lifts the briefcase and signed applications off Dietrichson's lap.*)

DIETRICHSON. How much you taking me for?

NEFF. One forty-seven fifty, Mr. Dietrichson.

Dietrichson stands up. He is about Neff's height but a little heavier.

PHYLLIS. I guess that's enough insurance for one evening, Mr. Neff.

DIETRICHSON. Plenty.

Dietrichson has poured some more whisky into his glass. He tries the siphon but it is empty. He gathers up his coat and tie and picks up his glass.

DIETRICHSON. Good night, Mr. Neff.

NEFF (*zipping up his briefcase*). Good night, Mr. Dietrichson. Good night, Mrs. Dietrichson.

DIETRICHSON. Bring me some soda when you come up, Phyllis. (*Dietrichson trundles off toward the archway.*)

PHYLLIS (*to Neff*). I think you left your hat in the hall.

Phyllis leads the way and Neff goes after her, his briefcase under his arm. The scene then cuts to the HALLWAY of the

Dietrichson residence as Phyllis enters through the living room archway with Neff behind her. She leads him toward the door. On the way he picks up his hat. In the background Dietrichson begins to ascend the stairs, carrying his coat and glass. Phyllis and Neff move close to the door. They speak in very low voices.

PHYLLIS. All right, Walter?

NEFF. Fine.

PHYLLIS. He signed it, didn't he?

NEFF. Sure he signed it. You saw him.

Phyllis opens the door a crack. Both look at the stairs, where Dietrichson is going up. Phyllis takes her hand off the doorknob and holds on to Neff's arm.

NEFF (*looking up*). Watch it, will you.

Phyllis slowly drops her hand from his arm. Both look up as Dietrichson goes across the balcony and out of sight.

NEFF. Listen. That trip to Palo Alto. When does he go?

PHYLLIS. End of the month.

NEFF. He drives, huh?

PHYLLIS. He always drives.

NEFF. Not this time. You're going to make him take the train.

PHYLLIS. Why?

NEFF. Because it's all worked out for a train.

For a second they stand listening and looking up as if they had heard a sound.

PHYLLIS. It's all right. Go on, Walter.

NEFF. Look, baby. There's a clause in every accident policy, a little something called double indemnity. The insurance companies put it in as a sort of come-on for the customers. It means they pay double on certain accidents. The kind that almost never happen. Like for instance if a guy got killed on a train, they'd pay a hundred thousand instead of fifty.

PHYLLIS. I see. (*Her eyes widen with excitement.*)

NEFF. We're hitting it for the limit, baby. That's why it's got to be a train.

PHYLLIS. It's going to be a train, Walter. Just the way you say. Straight down the line.

They look at each other. The look is like a long kiss. Neff goes out. Slowly Phyllis closes the door and leans her head against it as she looks up the empty stairway.

Outside the DIETRICHSON RESIDENCE: Neff, briefcase under his arm, comes down the steps to the street, where his Dodge coupé is parked at the curb. He opens the door and stops, looking in.—Sitting there in the dark corner of the car, away from the steering wheel, is Lola. She wears a coat but no hat.

LOLA. Hello, Mr. Neff. It's me. (*She gives him a sly smile.*)

NEFF (*a little annoyed*). Something the matter?

LOLA. I've been waiting for you.

NEFF. For me? What for?

LOLA. I thought you could let me ride with you, if you're going my way.

NEFF (*who doesn't like the idea very much*). Which way would that be?

LOLA. Down the hill. Down Vermont.

NEFF (*remembering*). Oh, sure. Vermont and Franklin. North-west corner, wasn't it? Be glad to, Miss Dietrichson.

As Neff gets into the car, the scene cuts to the interior of the COUPE; Neff puts the briefcase on the ledge behind the driver's seat. He closes the door and starts the car. They drift down the hill.

NEFF. Roller skating, eh? You like roller skating?

LOLA. I can take it or leave it. (*Neff looks at her curiously, and Lola meets his glance.*)

NEFF. Only tonight you're leaving it? (*This is an embarrassing moment for Lola.*)

LOLA. Yes, I am. You see, Mr. Neff, I'm having a very tough time at home. My father doesn't understand me and Phyllis hates me.

NEFF. That does sound tough, all right.

LOLA. That's why I have to lie sometimes.

NEFF. You mean it's not Vermont and Franklin.

LOLA. It's Vermont and Franklin all right. Only it's not Anne Matthews. It's Nino Zachette. You won't tell on me, will you?

NEFF. I'd have to think it over.

LOLA. Nino's not what father says at all. He just had bad luck. He was doing pre-med at U.S.C. and working nights as an usher in a theatre downtown. He got behind in his credits and flunked out. Then he lost his job for talking back. He's so hot-headed.

NEFF. That comes expensive, doesn't it?

LOLA. I guess my father thinks nobody's good enough for his daughter except maybe the guy that owns Standard Oil. Would you like a stick of gum?

NEFF. Never use it, thanks.

LOLA (*putting a stick of gum in her mouth*). I can't give Nino up. I wish father could see it my way.

NEFF. It'll straighten out all right, Miss Dietrichson.

LOLA. I suppose it will sometime. (*Looking out*) This is the corner right here, Mr. Neff. (*As Neff brings the car to a stop by the curb*) There he is. By the bus stop.

As Neff looks out, the scene cuts to the CORNER of Vermont and Franklin where Zachette stands waiting, hands in trousers pockets. He is about twenty-five, Italian-looking, open shirt, not well dressed.

Back in the COUPE we see LOLA and NEFF.

LOLA. He needs a haircut, doesn't he. Look at him. No job, no car, no money, no prospects, no nothing.—I love him. (*She leans over and honks on the horn.*) Nino!

We get a close view of ZACHETTE as he turns and looks toward the car.

LOLA'S VOICE. Over here, Nino.

Zachette walks toward the car, and the scene cuts to the COUPE: Lola has opened the door. Zachette comes up.

LOLA. This is Mr. Neff, Nino.

NEFF. Hello, Nino.

ZACHETTE (*belligerent from the first word*). The name is Zachette.

LOLA. Nino, please. Mr. Neff gave me a ride from the house. I told him all about us.

ZACHETTE. Why does he have to get told about us?

LOLA. We don't have to worry about Mr. Neff, Nino.

ZACHETTE. I'm not doing any worrying. Just don't you broadcast so much.

LOLA. What's the matter with you, Nino? He's a friend.

ZACHETTE. I don't have any friends. And if I did, I like to pick them myself.

NEFF. Look, sonny, she needed the ride and I brought her along. Is that anything to get tough about?

ZACHETTE. All right, Lola, make up your mind. Are you coming or aren't you?

LOLA. Of course I'm coming. Don't mind him, Mr. Neff. (*Lola steps out of the car.*) Thanks a lot. You've been very sweet.

Lola catches up with Zachette, and as they walk away together the scene cuts to the COUPE while Neff's dictation is heard. Neff looks after them. Slowly he puts the car in gear and drives on. His face is tight. Behind his head, light catches the metal of the zipper on the briefcase.

NEFF'S VOICE. She was a nice kid, and maybe he was a little better than he sounded. I kind of hoped so for her sake, but right then it gave me a nasty feeling to be thinking about them at all, with that briefcase right behind my head and her father's signature on it—and what that signature meant. It meant that he was a dead pigeon, and it was only a question of time, and not very much time at that. You know that big market in Los Feliz, Keyes? That's the place Phyllis and I had picked for a meeting place.

This dissolves to the SUPER-MARKET. There is a fair amount of activity but the place is not crowded. Neff comes along the sidewalk into the scene. He passes in front of the fruit and vegetable display and goes between the stalls into the market.

NEFF'S VOICE (*continued*). I already had most of the plan in my head, but a lot of details had to be worked out, and she had to know them all by heart when the time came.

Inside the MARKET: Neff stops by the cashier's desk and buys a pack of cigarettes. As he is opening the pack he looks back casually beyond the turnstile into the rear part of the market.

NEFF'S VOICE. We had to be very careful from now on. We couldn't let anybody see us together—we couldn't even talk to each other on the telephone—not from her house or at my office, anyway. So she was to be in the market every morning about eleven o'clock, buying stuff, and I could sort of run into her there any day I wanted to, sort of accidentally on purpose.

We see ROWS OF HIGH SHELVES in the market: The shelves are loaded with canned goods and other merchandise. Customers move around selecting articles and putting them in their baskets. Phyllis is seen among them, standing by the soap section. Her basket is partly filled. She wears a simple house dress, no hat, and has a large envelope pocketbook under her arm.—And now Neff spots Phyllis. Without haste he passes through the turnstile toward the back. Back at the SHELVES, Phyllis is putting a can of cleaning powder into her basket. Neff enters the scene and moves along the shelves toward her, very slowly, pretending to inspect the goods. A customer passes and goes on out of the scene. Phyllis and Neff are now very close. During the ensuing low-spoken dialogue, they continue to face the shelves, not looking at each other.

PHYLLIS. Walter—

NEFF. Not so loud.

PHYLLIS. I wanted to talk to you, Walter. Ever since yesterday.

NEFF. Let me talk first. It's all set. The accident policy came through. I've got it in my pocket. I got his check too. I saw him down in the oil fields. He thought he was paying for the auto insurance. The check's just made out to the company. It could be for anything. But you have to send a check for the auto insurance, see. It's all right that way, because one of the cars is yours.

PHYLLIS. But listen, Walter!

NEFF. Quick, open your bag.

She hesitates, then opens it. Neff looks around quickly, slips the policy out of his pocket and drops it into her bag. She snaps the bag shut.

NEFF. Can you get into his safe deposit box?

PHYLLIS. Yes. We both have keys.

NEFF. Fine. But don't put the policy in there yet. I'll tell you when. And listen, you never touched it or even saw it, understand?

PHYLLIS. I'm not a fool.

NEFF. Okay. When is he taking the train?

PHYLLIS. Walter, that's just it. He isn't going.

NEFF. What?

PHYLLIS. That's what I've been trying to tell you. The trip is off.

NEFF. What's happened?

He breaks off as a short, squatty woman, pushing a child in a walker, comes into sight and approaches. She stops beside Neff, who is pretending to read a label on a can. Phyllis puts a few cakes of soap into her basket.

WOMAN (*to Neff*). Mister, could you reach me that can of coffee? (*She points.*) That one up there.

NEFF (*reaching up*). This one?

She nods. Neff reaches a can down from the high shelf, and hands it to her.

WOMAN. I don't see why they always have to put what I want on the top shelf.

She moves away with her coffee and her child. Out of the corner of his eye Neff watches her go. He moves closer to Phyllis again.

NEFF. Go ahead. I'm listening.

PHYLLIS. He had a fall down at the well. He broke his leg. It's in a cast.

NEFF. That knocks it on the head all right.

PHYLLIS. What do we do, Walter?

NEFF. Nothing. Just wait.

PHYLLIS. Wait for what?

NEFF. Until he can take a train. I told you it's got to be a train.

PHYLLIS. We can't wait. I can't go on like this.

NEFF. We're not going to grab a hammer and do it quick, just to get it over with.

PHYLLIS. There are other ways.

NEFF. Only we're not going to do it other ways.

PHYLLIS. But we can't leave it like this. What do you think would happen if he found out about this accident policy?

NEFF. Plenty. But not as bad as sitting in that death-house.

PHYLLIS. Don't ever talk like that, Walter.

NEFF. Just don't let's start losing our heads.

PHYLLIS. It's not our heads. It's our nerve we're losing.

NEFF. We're going to do it right. That's all I said.

PHYLLIS. Walter, maybe it's *my* nerves. It's the waiting that gets me.

NEFF. It's getting me just as bad, baby. But we've got to wait.

PHYLLIS. Maybe we have, Walter. Only it's so tough without you. It's like a wall between us.

Neff looks at his watch.

NEFF. Good-bye, baby. I'm thinking of you every minute.

He goes off. She stares after him, as the scene dissolves to NEFF'S OFFICE. He is wearing a light gray suit and has his hat on. He is standing behind his desk opening some mail, taking a few papers out of his briefcase, checking something in his rate book, making a quick telephone call. But nothing of this is heard.

NEFF'S VOICE. After that a full week went by and I didn't see her once. I tried to keep my mind off her and off the whole idea. I kept telling myself that maybe those fates they say watch over you had gotten together and broken his leg to give me a way out. Then it was the fifteenth of June. You may remember that date, Keyes. I do too, only for a very different reason. You came into my office around three in the afternoon.

NEFF (*as Keyes enters with some papers in his hand*). Hello, Keyes.

KEYES. I just came from Norton's office. The semi-annual sales records are out. You're high man, Walter. That's twice in a row. Congratulations.

NEFF. Thanks. How would you like a cheap drink?

KEYES. How would you like a fifty dollar cut in salary?

NEFF. How would I— Do I laugh now, or wait until it gets funny?

KEYES. No, I'm serious. I've been talking to Norton. There's too much stuff piling up on my desk. Too much pressure on my nerves. I spend half the night walking up and down in my bed. I've got to have an assistant. I thought that you—

NEFF. Me? Why pick on me?

KEYES. Because I've got a crazy idea you might be good at the job.

NEFF. That's crazy all right. I'm a salesman.

KEYES. Yeah. A peddler, a glad-hander, a back-slapper. You're too good to be a salesman.

NEFF. Nobody's too good to be a salesman.

KEYES. Phooey. All you guys do is ring doorbells and dish out a smooth line of monkey talk. What's bothering you is that fifty buck cut, isn't it?

NEFF. Well, it'd trouble anybody.

KEYES. Now, look, Walter. The job I'm talking about takes brains and integrity. It takes more guts than there is in fifty salesmen. It's the hottest job in the business.

NEFF. It's still a desk job. I don't want a desk job.

KEYES. A desk job. Is that all you can see in it? Just a hard chair to park your pants on from nine to five. Just a pile of papers to shuffle around, and five sharp pencils and a scratch pad to make figures on, with maybe a little doodling on the side. That's not the way I see it, Walter. To me a claims man is a surgeon, and that desk is an operating table, and those pencils are scalpels and bone chisels. And those papers are not just forms and statistics and claims for compensation. They're alive, they're packed with drama, with twisted hopes and crooked dreams. A claims man, Walter, is a doctor and a blood-hound and a cop and a judge and a jury and a father confessor, all in one.

The telephone rings on Neff's desk. Automatically Keyes grabs the phone and answers.

KEYES. Who? Okay, hold the line. (*He puts the phone down on the desk and continues to Neff:*) And you want to tell me you're not interested. You don't want to work with your brains. All you want to work with is your finger on a doorbell. For a few bucks more a week. There's a dame on your phone.

NEFF (*picking the phone up and answering*). Walter Neff speaking.

The scene cuts to a PHONE BOOTH in the market: Phyllis is on the phone.

PHYLLIS. I had to call you, Walter. It's terribly urgent. Are you with somebody?

Back in NEFF'S OFFICE: Neff is at the phone. His eye catches Keyes', who is walking up and down.

NEFF. Of course I am. Can't I call you back . . . Margie?

PHYLLIS at the phone:

PHYLLIS. Walter, I've only got a minute. It can't wait. Listen. He's going tonight. On the train. Are you listening, Walter? Walter!

NEFF at the PHONE: His eyes are on Keyes. He speaks into the phone as calmly as possible.

NEFF. I'm listening. Only make it short . . . Margie.

PHYLLIS at the PHONE:

PHYLLIS. He's on crutches. The doctor says he can go if he's careful. The change will do him good. It's wonderful, Walter. Just the way you wanted it. Only with the crutches it's ever so much better, isn't it?

NEFF'S OFFICE, Neff on the phone:

NEFF. One hundred percent better. Hold the line a minute. (*He covers the receiver with his hand and turns to Keyes, who is now standing at the window.*) Suppose I join you in your office, Keyes—

He makes a gesture as if expecting Keyes to leave. Keyes stays right where he is.

KEYES. I'll wait. Only tell Margie not to take all day.

Neff looks at Keyes' back with a strained expression, then lifts the phone again.

NEFF. Go ahead.

PHYLLIS at the PHONE:

PHYLLIS. It's the ten-fifteen from Glendale. I'm driving him. Is it still that same dark street?

Back in the office, NEFF is still watching Keyes cautiously.

NEFF. Yeah—sure.

A closeup of PHYLLIS at the PHONE:

PHYLLIS. The signal is three honks on the horn. Is there anything else?

A closeup of NEFF at the phone:

NEFF. What color did you pick out?

PHYLLIS (*seen again*). Color? (*She catches on.*) Oh, sure. The blue suit, Walter. Navy blue. And the cast on his left leg.

NEFF (*seen again*). Navy blue. I like that fine.

PHYLLIS (*seen again*). This is it, Walter. I'm shaking like a leaf. But it's straight down the line now for both of us. I love you, Walter. Goodbye.

NEFF'S OFFICE: Neff is still on the phone.

NEFF. So long, Margie.

He hangs up. His mouth is grim, but he forces a smile as Keyes turns.

NEFF. I'm sorry, Keyes.

KEYES. What's the matter? The dames chasing you again? Or still? Or is it none of my business?

NEFF (*with a sour smile*). If I told you it was a customer —

KEYES. Margie! I bet she drinks from the bottle. Why don't you settle down and get married, Walter?

NEFF. Why don't you, for instance?

KEYES. I almost did, once. A long time ago.

NEFF (*getting up from his desk*). Look, Keyes, I've got a prospect to call on. (*But Keyes drives right ahead:*)

KEYES. We even had the church all picked out, the dame and I. She had a white satin dress with flounces on it. And I was on my way to the jewelry store to buy the ring. Then suddenly that little man in here started working on me. (*He punches his stomach with his fist.*)

NEFF. So you went back and started investigating her. That it?

KEYES (*nodding slowly, a little sad and a little ashamed*). And the stuff that came out. She'd been dyeing her hair ever since she was sixteen. And there was a manic-depressive in her family, on her mother's side. And she already had one husband, a professional pool player in Baltimore. And as for her brother —

NEFF. I get the general idea. She was a tramp from a long line of tramps. (*He picks up some papers impatiently.*)

KEYES. All right, I'm going. What am I to say to Norton? How about that job I want you for?

NEFF. I don't think I want it. Thanks, Keyes, just the same.

KEYES. Fair enough. Just get this: I picked you for the job, not because I think you're so darn smart, but because I thought maybe you were a shade less dumb than the rest of the outfit. I guess I was all wet. You're not smarter, Walter. You're just a little taller.

He goes out, and now Neff is alone. He watches the door close, then turns and goes slowly to the water cooler. He fills a paper cup and stands holding it. His thoughts are somewhere else. After a moment he absently throws the cupful of water into the receptacle under the cooler. He goes back to the desk . . . He takes his rate book out of his brief case and puts it on the desk. He buttons the top button of his shirt, and pulls his tie right. He leaves the office, with his briefcase under his arm.

NEFF'S VOICE (*synchronized with the above scene*). That was it, Keyes, and there was no use kidding myself any more. Those fates I was talking about had only been stalling me off. Now they had thrown the switch. The gears had meshed. The machinery had started to move and nothing could stop it. The time for thinking had all run out. From here on it was a question of following the time table, move by move, just as we had it rehearsed. I wanted my time all accounted for for the rest of the afternoon and up to the last possible moment in the evening. So I arranged to call on a prospect in Pasadena about a public liability bond. When I left the office I put my rate book on the desk as if I had forgotten it. That was part of the alibi.

The scene dissolves to NEFF'S APARTMENT HOUSE as Neff's coupé comes down the street, swings into the garage and goes down the ramp into the basement.

NEFF'S VOICE (*continuing*). I got home about seven and drove right into the garage. This was another item to establish my alibi.

This cuts to the GARAGE. There are about eight cars parked. A colored attendant in coveralls and rubber boots is washing a car with a hose and sponge. Neff's car comes in and stops near the attendant. Neff gets out with his briefcase under his arm.

ATTENDANT. Hiya there, Mr. Neff.

NEFF. How about a wash job on my heap, Charlie?

ATTENDANT. How soon you want it, Mr. Neff? I got two cars ahead of you.

NEFF. Anytime you get to it, Charlie. I'm staying in tonight.

ATTENDANT. Okay, Mr. Neff. Be all shined up for you in the morning.

NEFF (*crossing to the elevator, and speaking back over his shoulder*). That left front tire looks a little soft. Check it, will you?

ATTENDANT. You bet. Check 'em all round. Always do.

Neff enters the elevator and the scene dissolves to NEFF'S APARTMENT as Neff comes in. He walks straight to the phone, dials, and starts speaking into the mouthpiece, but only his dictation is heard.

NEFF'S VOICE. Up in my apartment I called Lou Schwartz, one of the salesmen that shared my office. He lived in Westwood. That made it a toll call and there'd be a record of it. I told him I had forgotten my rate book and needed some dope on the public liability bond I was figuring. I asked him to call me back. This was another item in my alibi, so that later on I could prove that I had been home.

The scene dissolves to NEFF'S LIVING ROOM. Neff comes into the living room from the bedroom, putting on the jacket of his blue suit. The phone rings. He picks up the receiver and starts talking, unheard, as before. He makes notes on a pad.

NEFF'S VOICE. I changed into a navy blue suit like Dietrichson was going to wear. Lou Schwartz called me back and gave me a lot of figures . . . . . . . .

Now he is seen folding a hand towel and stuffing it into his jacket pocket. He then takes a large roll of adhesive tape and puts that into his pants pocket. — This scene dissolving, we see a TELEPHONE BELL BOX (on the baseboard) and a DOORBELL above the entrance door as Neff's hand places a small card against the bell clapper in each of these; and this dissolves to the FIRE STAIRS of the apartment house at night as the view moves with Neff going down the stairs in his blue suit, with a hat pulled down over his eyes. — And this scene dissolving, we next get a distant view of the DIETRICHSON HOME at night.

There is no traffic.—Some windows are lit. Neff comes into view and approaches cautiously. He looks around and then slides open the garage door.

NEFF'S VOICE. I stuffed a hand towel and a big roll of adhesive tape into my pockets, so I could fake something that looked like a cast on a broken leg . . . Next I fixed the telephone and the doorbell, so that the cards would fall down if the bells rang. That way I would know there had been a phone call or visitor while I was away. I left the apartment house by the fire stairs and side door. Nobody saw me. It was already getting dark. I took the Vermont Avenue bus to Los Feliz and walked from there up to the Dietrichson house. There was that smell of honeysuckle again, only stronger, now that it was evening.

We see the interior of the GARAGE as Neff closes the door. A very faint light comes in at a side window. He opens the rear door of the sedan, gets in and closes the door after him. The dark interior of the car has swallowed him up.

NEFF'S VOICE. Then I was in the garage. His car was backed in, just the way I told Phyllis to have it. It was so still I could hear the ticking of the clock on the dashboard. I kept think- ing of the place we had picked out to do it, that dark street on the way to the station, and the three honks on the horn that were to be the signal . . . About ten minutes later they came down.

Outside the DIETRICHSON HOUSE: The front door has opened and Dietrichson is halfway down the steps. He is walking with crutches, wearing the dark blue suit and a hat. The cast is on his left leg. There is no shoe on his left foot. Only the white plaster shows. Phyllis comes after him, carry- ing his suitcase and his overcoat. She wears a camel's-hair coat and no hat. She catches up with him.

PHYLLIS. You all right, honey? I'll have the car out in a second.

Dietrichson just grunts. She passes him moving toward the garage, and slides the door open. Then we again see the GARAGE, as we get a low view from the sedan.
(The camera is very low inside the sedan, shooting slightly

upward from Neff's hiding place.) The garage door has just been opened. Phyllis comes to the car, and opens the rear door. She looks down, (seen very close) and a tight, cool smile flashes across her face. Then, very calmly, she puts the suitcase and overcoat in back on the seat. She closes the door again.

Outside the garage, Dietrichson stands watching Phyllis as she gets into the car and drives out to pick him up. She stops beside him and opens the right-hand door. Dietrichson climbs in with difficulty. She helps him, watching him closely.

PHYLLIS. Take it easy, honey. We've got lots of time.

DIETRICHSON. Just let me do it my own way. Grab that crutch.

She takes one of the crutches from him.

DIETRICHSON. They ought to make these things so they fold up.

For a moment, as he leans his hand on the back of the seat, there is danger that he may see Neff. He doesn't. He slides awkwardly into the seat and pulls the second crutch in after him. He closes the door. The car moves off, and this dissolves to the interior of the CAR as Phyllis is driving and Dietrichson is beside her. Dietrichson has a partly smoked cigar between his teeth. They are in the middle of a conversation.

DIETRICHSON. Aw, stop squawkin' can't you, Phyllis? No man takes his wife along to a class reunion. That's what class reunions are for.

PHYLLIS. Mrs. Tucker went along with her husband last year, didn't she?

DIETRICHSON. Yeah, and what happened to her? She sat in the hotel lobby for four days straight. Never even saw the guy until we poured him back on the train.

We get a close view of NEFF'S FACE, low down in the corner behind Dietrichson. His face is partly covered by the edge of a traveling rug which he has pulled up over him. He looks up at Dietrichson and Phyllis in the front seat.

PHYLLIS' VOICE. All right, honey. Just so long as you have a good time.

DIETRICHSON'S VOICE. I won't do much dancing, I can tell you that.

PHYLLIS (*as we now see their heads and shoulders as observed by Neff*). Remember what the doctor said. If you get careless you might end up with a shorter leg.

DIETRICHSON. So what? I could break the other one and match them up again.

PHYLLIS. It makes you feel pretty good to get away from me, doesn't it?

DIETRICHSON. It's only for four days. I'll be back Monday at the latest.

PHYLLIS. Don't forget we're having the Hobeys for dinner on Monday.

DIETRICHSON. The Hobeys? We had them last. They owe us a dinner, don't they?

PHYLLIS. Maybe they do but I've already asked them for Monday.

DIETRICHSON. Well, I don't want to feed the Hobeys.

We get a closeup of PHYLLIS' FACE only: there is a look of tension in her eyes now. She glances around quickly. The car has reached the dark street Neff and she picked out.

DIETRICHSON'S VOICE. And I don't want to eat at their house either. The food you get there, and that rope he hands out for cigars. Call it off, can't you?—This is not the right street! Why did you turn here?

Phyllis does not answer. She doesn't even breathe. Her hand goes down on the horn button. She honks three times. —A closeup shows Dietrichson reacting with surprise.

DIETRICHSON. What are you doing that for? What're you honking the horn for?

This is as far as his voice will ever get, as Neff starts to pull himself up. It breaks off and dies down in a muffled groan. There are struggling noises and a dull sound of something breaking. Phyllis drives on and never turns her head. She stares straight in front of her. Her teeth are clenched.

This dissolves to a PARKING SPACE adjoining Glendale Station, at night. The station is visible about sixty yards away. There is no parking attendant. Ten or twelve cars are parked diagonally, not crowded. The train is not in yet, but there is activity around the station from passengers and their friends, redcaps and baggage men and news vendors.

The Dietrichson sedan comes into view and parks in the foreground at the outer end of the line, several spaces from the next car, facing away from the camera. Both front doors are open. Phyllis gets out and from the other side crutches emerge, and a man (seen entirely from behind, and apparently Dietrichson) climbs out awkwardly. While he is steadying himself on the ground with the crutches, Phyllis has taken out Dietrichson's suitcase and overcoat. She walks around the car and rolls up the right front window. She closes and locks the car door. She tries the right rear door and takes a last look into the dim interior of the car. Then she and the man walk slowly away from the car to the end of the station platform and along it toward the station building. Phyllis walks several steps ahead of the man.

PHYLLIS and the MAN are then seen walking a little to one side, so that Phyllis is clearly seen but the man's face is not.

MAN (*in a subdued voice*). You handle the redcap and the conductor.

PHYLLIS. Don't worry.

MAN. Keep them away from me as much as you can. I don't want to be helped.

PHYLLIS. I said don't worry, Walter.

PHYLLIS and the MAN are now walking down the platform (facing front), and at this point it is quite clear that the man is NEFF.

NEFF. You start just as soon as the train leaves. At the dairy sign you turn off the highway onto the dirt road. From there it's exactly eight-tenths of a mile to the dump beside the tracks. Remember?

PHYLLIS. I remember everything.

NEFF. You'll be there a little ahead of the train. No speeding. You don't want any cops stopping you—with him in the back.

PHYLLIS. Walter, we've been through all that so many times.

NEFF. When you turn off the highway, cut all your lights. I'm going to be back on the observation platform. I'll drop off as close to the spot as I can. Wait for the train to pass, then blink your lights twice.

Phyllis nods. They go on. Over them is heard the noise of the train coming into the station and its lights are seen.

At the GLENDALE STATION PLATFORM: the train is just coming to a stop. The passengers move forward to the tracks. Phyllis, carrying the suitcase and overcoat, and Neff, still a little behind her, come toward us. A redcap sees them and runs up. He takes the suitcase out of Phyllis' hand.

REDCAP. San Francisco train, lady?

Phyllis takes an envelope containing Dietrichson's ticket from the pocket of the overcoat. She reads from the envelope.

PHYLLIS. Car nine, section eleven. Just my husband going.

REDCAP. Car nine, section eleven. Yessum, this way please.

Phyllis hands the overcoat to the redcap, who leads her and Neff toward car number nine. Neff still hangs back and keeps his head down, the way a man using crutches might naturally do.

Outside CAR NUMBER NINE: the pullman conductor and porter stand at the steps. The conductor is checking the tickets of passengers getting on. The redcap leads Phyllis and Neff into view. The conductor and porter see Neff on his crutches and move to help him.

PHYLLIS. It's all right, thanks. My husband doesn't like to be helped.

The redcap goes up the steps into the car. Neff laboriously swings himself up onto the box and from there up on the steps, keeping his head down. Meantime, Phyllis is holding the attention of the conductor and porter by showing them the ticket.

CONDUCTOR. Car nine, section eleven. The gentleman only. Thank you.

Phyllis nods and takes the ticket back. Neff has reached the top of the steps. She goes up after him and gives him the ticket. They are now close together.

PHYLLIS. Goodbye, honey. Take awful good care of yourself with that leg.

NEFF. Sure, I will. Just you take it easy going home.

PHYLLIS. I'll miss you, honey.

She kisses him. There are shouts of "All Aboard." The redcap comes from inside the car.

REDCAP. Section eleven, suh.

Phyllis takes a quarter from her bag and gives it to the redcap.

PORTER (*shouting*). All aboard!

The redcap descends. Phyllis kisses Neff again quickly.

PHYLLIS. Good luck, honey.

She runs down the steps. The porter picks up the box. He and the conductor get on board the train. Phyllis stands there waving goodbye as the train starts moving, and the porter begins to close the car door. Phyllis turns and walks out of sight in the direction of the parked car.

The scene then cuts to the PLATFORM as the train moves on. The light is dim.—The conductor is going on into the car. Neff is half turned away from the porter.

NEFF. Can you make up my berth right away?

PORTER. Yes, sir.

NEFF. I'm going back to the observation car for a smoke.

PORTER. This way, sir. Three cars back. (*He holds the vestibule door open, and Neff hobbles through.*)

This dissolves to the PULLMAN CAR, which is dimly lit. Most of the berths are made up. As Neff hobbles along, another porter and some passengers make way for the crippled man solicitously.—This dissolves to the PLATFORM between two cars as the train conductor meets Neff, opens the door for him, and Neff hobbles on through. This in turn dissolves to the PARLOR CAR, where four or five passengers are reading or writing. As Neff comes through on his crutches they pull in their feet to make room for him. One old lady, seeing that he is headed for the observation platform, opens the door for him. He thanks her with a nod and hobbles through.

And now the scene cuts to the OBSERVATION PLATFORM. It is dark except for a little light coming from inside the parlor car. The train is going about fifteen miles an hour between Glendale and Burbank. Neff has come out and hobbled to the railing. He stands looking back along the rails. Suddenly a man's voice speaks from behind him.

MAN'S VOICE. Can I pull a chair out for you?

Neff looks around. He sees a man sitting in the corner smoking a hand-rolled cigarette. He is about fifty-five years old, with white hair, and a broad-brimmed Stetson hat. He looks like a small town lawyer or maybe a mining man. Neff does not like the man's presence there very much. He turns to him just enough to answer.

NEFF. No thanks, I'd rather stand.

MAN. You going far?

NEFF. Palo Alto.

MAN. My name's Jackson. I'm going all the way to Medford. Medford, Oregon. Had a broken arm myself once.

NEFF. Uh-huh.

JACKSON. That darn cast sure itches something fierce, don't it? I thought I'd go crazy with mine. (*Neff stands silent. His mind is feverishly thinking of how to get rid of Jackson.*) Palo Alto's a nice little town. You a Stanford man?

NEFF. Used to be. (*He starts patting his pockets as if looking for something.*)

JACKSON. I bet you left something behind. I always do.

NEFF. My cigar case. Must have left it in my overcoat back in the section.

JACKSON (*taking out a small bag of tobacco and a packet of cigarette papers*). Care to roll yourself a cigarette, Mr.—?

NEFF. Dietrichson. Thanks. I really prefer cigars. (*Looking around*) Maybe the porter—

JACKSON. I could get your cigars for you. Be glad to, Mr. Dietrichson.

NEFF. That's darn nice of you. It's car nine, section eleven. If you're sure it's not too much trouble.

JACKSON. Car nine, section eleven. A pleasure.

He rises and walks into the parlor car. Neff turns slowly and watches Jackson go back through the car. Then he moves to one side of the platform and looks ahead along the track to orientate himself. He gives one last glance back into the parlor car to make sure no one is watching him. He slips the crutches from under his arms and stands on both feet. He drops the crutches off the train onto the tracks, then quickly swings his body over the rail.

We then see the OBSERVATION CAR, with Neff hanging onto the railing. He looks down, then lets go and drops to the right-of-way. The train recedes slowly into the night. Neff has fallen on the tracks. He picks himself up, rubs one knee and looks back along the line of the tracks and off to one side.

A dark landscape comes into view, and we see the RAILROAD TRACKS. Close beyond the edge of the right-of-way, the silhouette of a dump shows up. Beside it looms the dark bulk of the Dietrichson sedan. The headlights blink twice and go out.—NEFF, seen close, starts running toward the car. He runs a little awkwardly because of the improvised cast on his left foot. Then we see the CAR in the dark as the front door opens and Phyllis steps out. She closes the door and looks in the direction of the tracks. The uneven steps of Neff running toward her are heard. She opens the back door of the car and leans in. She pulls the rug off the corpse (which is not visible) and stands looking into the car, unable to take her eyes off what she sees, while at the same time her hands mechanically begin to fold the rug. The running steps grow louder and Neff comes into view, breathing hard. He reaches her.

NEFF. Okay. This has to go fast. Take his hat and pick up the crutches.

Neff points back toward the tracks. He reaches into the car and begins to drag out the body by the armpits. Phyllis coolly reaches past him and takes the hat off the dead man's head. She turns to go.

NEFF. Hang on to that rug. I'll need it.

Phyllis moves out of sight carrying the hat and rug, while NEFF gets a stronger hold on the dead Dietrichson and drags him free of the car and toward the tracks. The corpse is not seen.

PHYLLIS reaches the point where one of the crutches lies. She picks it up and goes for the other crutch a short distance away. She carries both crutches, the hat and the rug toward Neff.

NEFF has reached the railroad tracks. The corpse is lying beside the tracks, face down. Phyllis comes up to Neff. He takes the crutches and the hat from her. He throws the crutches beside the corpse. He takes the hat from Phyllis and tosses it carelessly along the track.

NEFF. Let's go. Stay behind me.

He takes the rug from her and they move back toward the car, Phyllis first, then Neff walking almost backwards, sweeping the ground over which the body was dragged with the rug as they go. — Then we see the CAR as they reach it together.

NEFF. Get in. You drive.

She gets in. Neff sweeps the ground after him as he goes around the car to get in beside her. He throws the rug into the back of the car.

Inside the CAR: Phyllis is behind the wheel. Neff beside her is just closing the door. He props his wrapped foot against the dashboard and begins to tear off the adhesive tape while at the same time Phyllis presses the starter button. The starter grinds, but the motor doesn't catch. She tries again. It still doesn't catch. Neff looks at her. She tries a third time. The starter barely turns over. The battery is very low.

Phyllis leans back. They stare at each other desperately. After a moment Neff bends forward slowly and turns the ignition key to the OFF position. He holds his left thumb poised over the starter button. There is a breathless moment. Then he presses the starter button with swift decision. The starter grinds with nerve-wracking sluggishness. Neff twists the ignition key to ON and instantly pulls the hand-throttle wide open. With a last feeble kick of the starter, the motor catches and races. He eases the throttle down and slides back into his place. They look at each other again. The tenseness of the moment still shows in their faces.

NEFF. Let's go, baby.

Phyllis releases the hand brake and puts the car in reverse. Neff is again busy unwrapping the tape from his leg.—Then the car, with the headlights out, backs up, swings around and moves off along the dirt road the way it came.

We see the SEDAN driving along a HIGHWAY in traffic, and again Neff's voice is heard over the scene. Phyllis and Neff are facing forward. Neff is bent over, peeling the towel and plaster off his foot, which is out of sight. Phyllis is calm, almost relaxed. Neff straightens up. They are talking to each other. Their lips are seen moving but what they say is not heard. They stop talking. Phyllis stares straight ahead. Neff is pulling adhesive tape off the wrapped towel that was on his foot. He folds the adhesive into a tight ball, rolls the towel up, puts both into his pockets.

NEFF'S VOICE (*synchronized with the scene*). On the way back we went over once more what she was to do at the inquest, if they had one, and about the insurance, when that came up. I was afraid she might go to pieces a little, now that we had done it, but she was perfect. No nerves. Not a tear, not even a blink of the eyes. . . .

This dissolves to a DARK STREET near Neff's house as the sedan comes into view and stops without pulling over to the curb.

NEFF'S VOICE. She dropped me a block from my apartment house.

The car door opens. Neff starts to get out.

PHYLLIS. Walter— (*Neff turns back to her.*) What's the matter, Walter. Aren't you going to kiss me?

NEFF. Sure, I'm going to kiss you.

PHYLLIS (*bending toward him and putting her arms around him*). It's straight down the line, isn't it? (*She kisses him. He is passive in the kiss.*) I love you, Walter.

NEFF. I love you, baby.

This dissolves to the FIRE STAIRS. Neff is seen going up.

NEFF'S VOICE. It was two minutes past eleven as I went up the fire stairs again. Nobody saw me this time either.

This dissolves to a closeup of NEFF'S HAND opening the telephone bell box and the door bell. The cards are still in position. Neff's hand takes them out.

NEFF'S VOICE. In the apartment I checked the bells. The cards hadn't moved. No calls. No visitors.

This dissolves to the LIVING ROOM, in which the lights are still on. Neff comes from the bedroom, wearing the light grey suit he wore before the murder, only without a tie. He buttons his jacket, looks around the room, and opens the corridor door.

NEFF'S VOICE. I changed the blue suit. There was one last thing to do. I wanted the garage man to see me again.

This dissolves to the BASEMENT GARAGE, where fifteen or twenty cars are now parked. Charlie, the attendant has washed Neff's car and is now polishing the glass and metal-work. Neff comes from the elevator. Charlie sees him. He straightens up.

CHARLIE. You going to need it after all, Mr. Neff? I'm not quite through.

NEFF. It's okay, Charlie. Just walking down to the drug store for something to eat. Been working upstairs all evening. My stomach's getting sore at me.

CHARLIE. Yes, sir, Mr. Neff.

He walks up the ramp toward the garage entrance, and the scene dissolves to the STREET outside the apartment house. Neff comes out at the top of the ramp and starts to walk down the street, not too fast. He walks about ten or fifteen yards. At first his steps sound hard and distinct on the sidewalk and echo in the deserted street. But slowly, as he goes on, they fade into utter silence. He walks a few feet without sound, then becomes aware of the silence. He stops rigidly and looks back. He stands like that for a moment, then turns forward again. There is a look of horror on his face now. He walks on again, and still his steps make no sound, as the scene fades out.

NEFF'S VOICE (*synchronized with the scene*). That was all there was to it. Nothing had slipped, nothing had been overlooked, there was nothing to give us away. And yet, Keyes, as I was walking down the street to the drug store, suddenly it came over me that everything would go wrong. It sounds crazy, Keyes, but it's true, so help me: I couldn't hear my own footsteps. It was the walk of a dead man.


PART THREE

NEFF'S OFFICE fades in at night. Neff still sits before the dictaphone. There are four cylinders on end on the desk next to him. He gets up from the swivel chair with great effort and stands a moment unsteadily. The wound in his shoulder is paining him. He is very weak as he slowly crosses to the water cooler. He takes the blood stained handkerchief from inside his shirt and soaks it with fresh water.—The office door opens behind him. He turns, hiding the handkerchief behind his back. In the doorway stands the colored man who has been cleaning up downstairs. He is carrying his big trash box by a rope handle.

COLORED MAN. Didn't know anybody was here, Mr. Neff. We ain't cleaned your office yet.

NEFF. Let it go tonight. I'm busy.

COLORED MAN. Whatever you say, Mr. Neff.

He closes the door slowly, staring at Neff with an uneasy expression. Neff puts the soaked handkerchief back on his wounded shoulder, then walks heavily over to his swivel chair and lowers himself into it. He takes the dictaphone horn and speaks into it again.

NEFF. That was the longest night I ever lived through, Keyes, and the next day was worse, when the story broke in the papers, and they were talking about it at the office, and the day after that when you started digging into it. I kept my hands in my pockets because I thought they were shaking, and I put on dark glasses so people couldn't see my eyes, and then I took them off again so people wouldn't get to wondering why I wore them. I was trying to hold myself together, but I could feel my nerves pulling me to pieces . . .

This dissolves to the INSURANCE OFFICE on the TWELFTH FLOOR. Neff comes through the reception room doors on the balcony with his hat on and his briefcase under his arm. He walks toward his office, but half way there he runs into Keyes. Keyes is wearing his vest and hat, no coat. He is carrying a file of papers and smoking a cigar.

KEYES. Come on, Walter. The big boss wants to see us.

NEFF. Okay. (*He turns and walks beside Keyes.*) That Dietrichson case?

KEYES. Must be.

NEFF. Anything wrong?

KEYES. The guy's dead, we had him insured and it's going to cost us money. That's always wrong.

He stops by a majolica jar full of sand and takes a pencil from his vest. He stands over the jar extinguishing his cigar carefully so as not to damage it.

NEFF. What have you got so far?

KEYES. Autopsy report. No heart failure, no apoplexy, no predisposing medical cause of any kind. He died of a broken neck.

NEFF. When is the inquest?

KEYES. They had it this morning. His wife and daughter made the identification. The train people and some passengers told how he went through to the observation car . . . It was all over in forty-five minutes. Verdict, accidental death.

Keyes puts the half-smoked cigar into his vest pocket with the pencil. They move on.

NEFF. What do the police figure?

KEYES. That he got tangled up in his crutches and fell off the train. They're satisfied. It's not their dough.

They stop at a door lettered in embossed chromium letters: EDWARD S. NORTON, JR. PRESIDENT. Keyes opens the door, and they go in.—We then see the RECEPTION ROOM of Mr. Norton's office. A secretary is sitting behind a desk. As Keyes and Neff enter, the door to Norton's private office is opened. From inside, Mr. Norton is letting out three legal-looking gentlemen. Norton is about forty-five, very well groomed, rather pompous in manner.

NORTON (*to the men who are leaving*). I believe the legal position is now clear, gentlemen. Please stand by. I may need you later. (*He sees Keyes and Neff.*) Come in, Mr. Keyes. You too, Mr. Neff.

Neff has put down his hat and briefcase. He and Keyes pass the legal-looking men and follow Norton into his office.

In NORTON'S OFFICE: Naturally it is the best office in the building; modern but not modernistic, spacious, very well furnished; flowers, smoking stands, easy chairs, etc. Norton has gone behind his desk. Keyes has come in, and Neff after him closes the door quietly. Norton looks disapprovingly at Keyes' shirt sleeves.

NORTON. You find this an uncomfortably warm day, Mr. Keyes? (*At this Keyes takes his hat off but holds it in his hands.*)

KEYES. Sorry, Mr. Norton. I didn't know this was formal.

NORTON (*smiling frostily*). Sit down, gentlemen. (*To Keyes*) Any new developments? (*Keyes and Neff sit down, Norton remains standing.*)

KEYES. I just talked to this Jackson long distance. Up in Medford, Oregon.

NORTON. Who's Jackson?

KEYES. The last guy that saw Dietrichson alive. They were out on the observation platform together talking. Dietrichson wanted a cigar and Jackson went to get Dietrichson's cigar case for him. When he came back to the observation platform, no Dietrichson. Jackson didn't think anything was wrong until a wire caught up with the train at Santa Barbara. They had found Dietrichson's body on the tracks near Burbank.

NORTON. Very interesting, about the cigar case. (*He walks up and down behind his desk thinking hard.*) Anything else?

KEYES. Not much. Dietrichson's secretary says she didn't know anything about the policy. There is a daughter, but all she remembers is Neff talking to her father about accident insurance at their house one night.

NEFF. I couldn't sell him at first. Mrs. Dietrichson opposed it. He told me he'd think it over. Later on I went down to the oil fields and closed him. He signed the application and gave me his check.

NORTON (*dripping with sarcasm*). A fine piece of salesmanship that was, Mr. Neff.

KEYES. There's no sense in pushing Neff around. He's got the best sales record in the office. Are your salesmen supposed to know that the customer is going to fall off a train?

NORTON. Fall off a train? Are we sure Dietrichson fell off a train? (*There is a charged pause.*)

KEYES. I don't get it.

NORTON. You don't, Mr. Keyes? Then what *do* you think of this case? This policy might cost us a great deal of money. As you know, it contains a double indemnity clause. Just what is your opinion?

KEYES. No opinion at all.

NORTON. Not even a hunch? One of those interesting little hunches of yours?

KEYES. Nope. Not even a hunch.

NORTON. I'm surprised, Mr. Keyes. I've formed a very definite opinion. I think I know—in fact I know I know what happened to Dietrichson.

KEYES. You know you know what?

NORTON. I know it was not an accident. (*He looks from Keyes to Neff and back to Keyes.*) What do you say to that?

KEYES. Me? You've got the ball. Let's see you run with it.

NORTON. There's a widespread feeling that just because a man has a large office —

The dictograph on his desk buzzes. He reaches over and depresses a key and puts the earpiece to his ear.

NORTON (*into the dictograph*). Yes? . . . Have her come in, please.—(*He replaces the earpiece. He turns back to Keyes and Neff.*)—that just because a man has a large office he must be an idiot. I'm having a visitor, if you don't mind. (*Keyes and Neff start to get up.*) No, no. I want you to stay and watch me handle this.

SECRETARY (*opening the door and ushering someone in*). Mrs. Dietrichson.

Neff stands staring at the door. He relaxes with an obvious effort of will. Phyllis comes in. She wears a gray tailored suit, small black hat with a veil, black gloves, and carries a black bag. The secretary closes the door behind her. Mr. Norton goes to meet her.

NORTON. Thank you very much for coming, Mrs. Dietrichson. I assure you I appreciate it. (*He turns a little toward Keyes.*) This is Mr. Keyes.

KEYES. How do you do.

PHYLLIS. How do you do.

NORTON. And Mr. Neff.

PHYLLIS. I've met Mr. Neff. How do you do.

Norton has placed a chair near her. Phyllis sits down. Norton goes behind his desk.

NORTON. Mrs. Dietrichson, I assure you of our sympathy in your bereavement. I hesitated before asking you to come here so soon after your loss. (*Phyllis nods silently.*) But now that you're here I hope you won't mind if I plunge straight into business. You know why we asked you to come, don't you?

PHYLLIS. No. All I know is that your secretary made it sound very urgent.

Keyes sits quietly in his chair with his legs crossed. He has hung his hat on his foot and thrust his thumbs in the arm-holes of his vest. He looks a little bored. Neff, behind him, stands leaning against the false mantel, completely dead-pan.

NORTON. Your husband had an accident policy with this company. Evidently you don't know that, Mrs. Dietrichson.

PHYLLIS. No. I remember some talk at the house—(*looking toward Neff*)—but he didn't seem to want it.

NEFF. He took it out a few days later, Mrs. Dietrichson.

PHYLLIS. I see.

NORTON. You'll probably find the policy among his personal effects.

PHYLLIS. His safe deposit box hasn't been opened yet. It seems a tax examiner has to be present.

NORTON. Please, Mrs. Dietrichson, I don't want you to think you are being subjected to any questioning. But there are a few things we should like to know.

PHYLLIS. What sort of things?

NORTON. We have the report of the coroner's inquest. Accidental death. We are not entirely satisfied. In fact, we are not satisfied at all. (*Phyllis looks at him coolly; Keyes looks vaguely interested; Neff is staring straight at Phyllis.*) Frankly Mrs. Dietrichson, we suspect suicide. (*Phyllis doesn't bat an eyelash.*) I'm sorry. Would you like a glass of water?

PHYLLIS. Please.

NORTON. Mr. Neff.

He indicates a thermos on a stand near Neff. Neff pours a glass of water and carries it over to Phyllis. She has lifted her veil a little. She takes the glass from his hand.

PHYLLIS. Thank you. (*Their eyes meet for a fraction of a second.*)

NORTON. Had your husband been moody or depressed lately, Mrs. Dietrichson? Did he seem to have financial worries, for instance?

PHYLLIS. He was perfectly all right and I don't know of any financial worries.

NORTON. There must have been something, Mrs. Dietrichson. Let us examine this so-called accident. First, your husband takes out this policy in absolute secrecy. Why? Because he doesn't want his family to suspect what he intends to do.

PHYLLIS. Do what?

NORTON. Commit suicide. Next, he goes on this trip entirely alone. He has to be alone. He hobbles all the way out to the observation platform, very unlikely with his leg in a cast, unless he has a very strong reason. Once there, he finds he is not alone. There is a man there. What was his name, Keyes?

(*Norton flips his fingers impatiently at Keyes who doesn't even bother to look up.*)

KEYES. His name was Jackson. Probably still is.

NORTON. Jackson. So your husband gets rid of this Jackson with some flimsy excuse about cigars. And then he is alone. And then he does it. He jumps. Suicide. In which case the company is not liable.—You know that, of course. We could go to court—

PHYLLIS. I don't know anything. In fact I don't know why I came here. (*She makes as if to rise indignantly.*)

NORTON. Just a moment, please. I said we *could* go to court. I didn't say we want to. Not only is it against our practice, but it would involve a great deal of expense, a lot of lawyers, a lot of time, perhaps years. (*As Phyllis rises coldly*) So what I want to suggest is a compromise on both sides. A settlement for a certain sum, a part of the policy value—

PHYLLIS. Don't bother, Mr. Norton. When I came in here I had no idea you owed me any money. You told me you did. Then you told me you didn't. Now you tell me you want to pay me a part of it, whatever it is. You want to bargain with me, at a time like this. I don't like your insinuations about my husband, Mr. Norton, and I don't like your methods. In fact I don't like you, Mr. Norton. Goodbye, gentlemen.

She turns and walks out. The door closes after her. There is a pregnant pause. Keyes straightens up in his chair.

KEYES. Nice going, Mr. Norton. You sure carried that ball. (*As Norton pours himself a glass of water and stands holding it*) Only you fumbled on the goal line. Then you heaved an illegal forward pass and got thrown for a forty-yard loss. Now you can't pick yourself up because you haven't got a leg to stand on.

NORTON. I haven't eh? Let her claim. Let her sue. We can prove it was suicide.

KEYES (*standing up*). Can we? Mr. Norton, the first thing that hit me was that suicide angle. Only I dropped it in the wastepaper basket just three seconds later. You ought to look at the statistics on suicide sometime. You might learn a little something about the insurance business.

NORTON. I was raised in the insurance business, Mr. Keyes.

KEYES. Yeah. In the front office. Come on, you never read an actuarial table in your life. I've got ten volumes on suicide alone. Suicide by race, by color, by occupation, by sex, by seasons of the year, by time of day. Suicide, how committed: by poisons, by fire-arms, by drowning, by leaps. Suicide by poison, subdivided by types of poison, such as corrosive, irritant, systemic, gaseous, narcotic, alkaloid, protein, and so forth. Suicide by leaps, subdivided by leaps from high places, under wheels of trains, under wheels of trucks, under the feet of horses, from steamboats. But, Mr. Norton, of all the cases on record there's not one single case of suicide by leap from the rear end of a moving train. And do you know how fast that train was going at the point where the body was found? Fifteen miles an hour. Now how could anybody jump off a slow moving train like that with any kind of expectation that he would kill himself? No soap, Mr. Norton. We're sunk, and we're going to pay through the nose, and you know it. May I have this?

Keyes' throat is dry after the long speech. He grabs the glass of water out of Norton's hand and drains it in one big gulp. Norton is watching him almost stupefied. Neff stands with the shadow of a smile on his face. Keyes puts the glass down noisily on Norton's desk.

KEYES. Come on, Walter.

Norton doesn't move or speak. Keyes puts his hat on and crosses toward the door, Neff after him. With the doorknob in his hands Keyes turns back to Norton with a glance down at his own shirt sleeves.

KEYES. Next time I'll rent a tuxedo.

They go out and the scene dissolves to NEFF at the dictaphone at night. There is a tired grin on his face as he talks into the horn.

NEFF. I could have hugged you right then and there, Keyes, you and your statistics. You were the only one we were really scared of, and instead you were almost playing on our team . . .

This dissolves to NEFF'S APARTMENT. It is almost dark in the room. The corridor door opens letting the light in. Neff enters with his hat on and his briefcase under his arm. He switches the lights on, closes the door, puts the key in his pocket. At this moment the telephone rings. He picks up the phone.

NEFF'S VOICE (*his dictation synchronized with the scene*). That evening when I got home my nerves had eased off. I could feel the ground under my feet again, and it looked like easy going from there on in.

NEFF (*at the telephone*). Hello . . . Hello, baby. . . . Sure, everything is fine . . . You were wonderful in Norton's office.

A TELEPHONE BOOTH in a drug store: Phyllis is on the phone. She is not dressed as in Norton's office.

PHYLLIS. I felt so funny. I wanted to look at you all the time.

NEFF (*at the telephone in his apartment*). How do you think I felt? Where are you, baby?

PHYLLIS (*at the phone*). At the drug store. Just a block away. Can I come up?

NEFF'S APARTMENT, with Neff at the phone:

NEFF. Okay. But be careful. Don't let anybody see you.

He hangs up, takes off his hat and drops hat and briefcase on the davenport. He looks around the room and crosses to lower the venetian blinds and draw the curtains. He gathers up the morning paper which is lying untidily on the floor and puts it in the wastepaper basket.—The door bell rings.—Neff stops in sudden alarm. It can't be Phyllis. The time is too short. For a second he stands there motionless, then crosses to the door and opens it.—In the door stands Keyes.

NEFF. Hello, Keyes.

Keyes walks past him into the room. His hands are clasped behind his back. There is a strange, absent-minded look in his eyes. Neff closes the door without taking his eyes off Keyes.

NEFF. What's on your mind?

KEYES (*stopping in the middle of the room and turning*). That broken leg. The guy broke his leg.

NEFF. What are you talking about?

KEYES. Talking about Dietrichson. He had accident insurance, didn't he? Then he broke his leg, didn't he?

NEFF. So what?

KEYES. And he didn't put in a claim. Why didn't he put in a claim? Why?

NEFF. What the dickens are you driving at?

KEYES. Walter, there's something wrong. I ate dinner two hours ago. It stuck half way. (*He prods his stomach with his thumb.*) The little man is acting up again. Because there's something wrong with that Dietrichson case.

NEFF. Because he didn't put in a claim? Maybe he just didn't have time.

KEYES. Or maybe he just didn't know he was insured.

He has stopped in front of Neff. They look at each other for a tense moment. Neff hardly breathes. Then Keyes shakes his head suddenly.

KEYES. No. That couldn't be it. You delivered the policy to him personally, didn't you, Walter? And you got his check.

NEFF (*stiff-lipped, but his voice is as well under control as he can manage*). Sure, I did.

KEYES (*prodding his stomach again*). Got any bicarbonate of soda?

NEFF. No, I haven't.

KEYES (*resuming his pacing*). Listen, Walter. I've been living with this little man for twenty-six years. He's never failed me yet. There's got to be something wrong.

NEFF. Maybe Norton was right. Maybe it was suicide, Keyes.

KEYES. No. Not suicide.—But not accident either.

NEFF. What else?

There is another longer pause, agonizing for Neff. Finally Keyes continues:

KEYES. Look. A man takes out an accident policy that is worth a hundred thousand dollars, if he is killed on a train. Then, two weeks later, he *is* killed on a train. And not in a train accident, mind you, but falling off some silly observation car. Do you know what the mathematical probability of that is, Walter? One out of I don't know how many billions. And add to that the broken leg. It just can't be the way it looks, Walter. Something has been worked on us.

NEFF. Such as what?

Keyes doesn't answer. He goes on pacing up and down. Finally Neff can't stand the silence any longer.

NEFF. Murder?

KEYES (*prodding his stomach again*). Don't you have any peppermint or anything?

NEFF. I'm sorry. (*After a pause*) Who do you suspect?

KEYES. Maybe I like to make things easy for myself. But I always tend to suspect the beneficiary.

NEFF. The wife?

KEYES. Yeah. That wide-eyed dame that didn't know anything about anything.

NEFF. You're crazy, Keyes. She wasn't even on the train.

KEYES. I know she wasn't, Walter. I don't claim to know how it was worked, or who worked it, but I know that it *was* worked. (*He crosses to the corridor door.*) I've got to get to a drug store. It feels like a hunk of concrete inside me.

As he puts his hand on the knob to open the door, the scene cuts to the CORRIDOR. The lighted hallway is empty except for Phyllis who has been standing close to the door of Neff's apartment, listening. The door has just started to open. Phyllis moves away quickly and flattens herself against the wall behind the opening door. Keyes is coming out.

KEYES. Good night, Walter.

Neff, behind him, looks anxiously down the hallway for Phyllis. Suddenly his eye catches a glimpse of her through the crack of the partly opened door. He pushes the door wide so as to hide her from Keyes.

NEFF. Good night, Keyes.

KEYES. See you at the office in the morning. (*He has reached the elevator. He pushes the call button and turns.*) But I'd like to move in on her right now, tonight, if it wasn't for Norton and his stripe-pants ideas about company policy. I'd have the cops after her so quick her head would spin. They'd put her through the wringer, and, brother, what they would squeeze out.

NEFF. Only you haven't got a single thing to go on, Keyes.

KEYES (*as the elevator comes up and stops*). Not too much. Twenty-six years experience, all the percentage there is, and this lump of concrete in my stomach.

He pulls back the elevator door and turns to Neff with one last glance of annoyance.

KEYES (*almost angrily*). No bicarbonate of soda.

Keyes gets into the elevator. The door closes. The elevator goes down.—Neff stands numb, looking at the spot where Keyes was last visible. Without moving his eyes he pulls the door around toward him with his left hand. Phyllis slowly comes out.—Neff motions quickly to her to go into the apartment. She crosses in front of him and enters. He steps in backwards after her.

NEFF'S APARTMENT: Phyllis has come a few steps into the room. Neff, backing in after her, closes the door from inside and turns slowly. They look at each other for a long moment in complete silence.

PHYLLIS. How much does he know?

NEFF. It's not what he knows. It's those stinking hunches of his.

PHYLLIS. But he can't prove anything, can he?

NEFF. Not if we're careful. Not if we don't see each other for a while.

PHYLLIS. For how long a while? (*She moves toward him but he does not respond.*)

NEFF. Until all this dies down. You don't know Keyes the way I do. Once he gets his teeth into something he won't let go. He'll investigate you. He'll have you shadowed. He'll watch you every minute from now on. Are you afraid, baby?

PHYLLIS. Yes, I'm afraid. But not of Keyes. I'm afraid of us. We're not the same any more. We did it so we could be together, but instead of that it's pulling us apart. Isn't it, Walter?

NEFF. What are you talking about?

PHYLLIS. And you don't really care whether we see each other or not.

NEFF. Shut up, baby.

He pulls her close and kisses her as the scene fades out.


## PART FOUR

The ANTEROOM of the INSURANCE OFFICE fades in. Two telephone operators and a receptionist are at work. Several visitors are waiting in chairs. Lola Dietrichson is one of them. She's wearing a simple black suit and hat, indicating mourning. Her fingers nervously pick at a handkerchief and her eyes are watching the elevator doors anxiously. (Now and then the telephone operators in the background are heard saying, "Pacific All-Risk. Good Afternoon.")—The elevator comes up and the doors open. Several people come out, among them Neff, carrying his briefcase. Lola sees him and stands up, and, as he is about to pass through the anteroom without recognizing her, she stops him.

LOLA. Hello, Mr. Neff.

NEFF (*looking at her, a little startled*). Hello— (*His voice hangs in the air.*)

LOLA. Lola Dietrichson. Don't you remember me?

NEFF (*on his guard*). Yes. Of course.

LOLA. Could I talk to you, just for a few minutes? Somewhere where we can be alone?

NEFF. Sure. Come on into my office.

He pushes the swing door open and holds it for her. As she passes in front of him his eyes narrow in uneasy speculation.—This cuts to the twelfth floor BALCONY as Neff comes up level with Lola and leads her toward his office.

NEFF. Is it something to do with—what happened?

LOLA. Yes, Mr. Neff. It's about my father's death.

NEFF. I'm terribly sorry, Miss Dietrichson.

He opens the door of his office and holds it for her. She enters and the scene cuts to the interior of NEFF'S OFFICE where Lou Schwartz, one of the other salesmen, is working at his desk.

NEFF (*to Schwartz*). Lou, do you mind if I use the office alone for a few minutes?

SCHWARTZ. It's all yours, Walter.

He gets up and goes out. Lola has walked over to the window and is looking out so Schwartz won't stare at her. Neff places a chair beside his desk.

NEFF. Won't you sit down?

At the sound of the closing door she turns and speaks with a catch in her voice.

LOLA. Mr. Neff, I can't help it, but I have such a strange feeling that there is something queer about my father's death.

NEFF. Queer? Queer in what way?

LOLA. I don't know why I should be bothering you with my troubles, except that you knew my father and knew about the insurance he took out. And you were so nice to me that evening in your car.

NEFF. Sure. We got along fine, didn't we.

He sits down. His face is grim and watchful.

LOLA. Look at me, Mr. Neff. I'm not crazy. I'm not hysterical. I'm not even crying. But I have the awful feeling that something is wrong, and I had the same feeling once before—when my mother died.

NEFF. When your mother died?

LOLA. We were up at Lake Arrowhead. That was six years ago. We had a cabin there. It was winter and very cold and my mother was very sick with pneumonia. She had a nurse with her. There were just the three of us in the cabin. One night I got up and went into my mother's room. She was delirious with fever. All the bed covers were on the floor and the windows were wide open. The nurse wasn't in the room. I ran and covered my mother up as quickly as I could. Just then I heard a door open behind me. The nurse stood there. She didn't say a word, but there was a look in her eyes I'll never forget. Two days later my mother was dead. (*After a pause*) Do you know who that nurse was?

Neff stares at her tensely. He knows only too well who the nurse was.

NEFF. No. Who?

LOLA. Phyllis. I tried to tell my father, but I was just a kid then and he wouldn't listen to me. Six months later she married him and I kind of talked myself out of the idea that she could have done anything like that. But now it's all back again, now that something has happened to my father, too.

NEFF. You're not making sense, Miss Dietrichson. Your father fell off a train.

LOLA. Yes, and two days before he fell off that train what was Phyllis doing? She was in her room in front of a mirror, with a black hat on, and she was pinning a black veil to it, as if she couldn't wait to see how she would look in mourning.

NEFF. Look. You've had a pretty bad shock. Aren't you just imagining all this?

LOLA. I caught her eyes in the mirror, and they had that look in them they had before my mother died. That same look.

NEFF. You don't like your step-mother, do you? Isn't it just because she *is* your step-mother?

LOLA. I loathe her. Because she did it. She did it for the money. Only you're not going to pay her, are you, Mr. Neff? She's not going to get away with it this time. I'm going to speak up. I'm going to tell everything I know.

NEFF. You'd better be careful, saying things like that.

LOLA. I'm not afraid. You'll see.

She turns again to the window so he won't see that she is crying. Neff gets up and goes to her.

LOLA. I'm sorry. I didn't mean to act like this.

NEFF. All this that you've been telling me—who else have you told?

LOLA. No one.

NEFF. How about your step-mother?

LOLA. Of course not. I'm not living in the house any more. I moved out.

NEFF. And you didn't tell that boyfriend of yours? Zachette.

LOLA. I'm not seeing him any more. We had a fight.

NEFF. Where are you living then?

LOLA. I got myself a little apartment in Hollywood.

NEFF. Four walls, and you just sit and look at them, huh?

LOLA (*turning from the window with a pathetic little nod; through her tears*). Yes, Mr. Neff.

The scene dissolves to LA GOLONDRINA at night. In the foreground, Neff and Lola are having dinner. In the background the usual activity of Olvera Street—sidewalk peddlers, guitar players, etc.—This dissolves to NEFF'S COUPE. Neff and Lola are driving along the beach near Santa Monica. Neff is wearing a light summer suit, very much in contrast to Lola's mourning. Apparently she is telling him a story and now and then she laughs, but there is no sound. (The view moves past her to a closeup of Neff behind the steering wheel.) He is only half listening to Lola. His mind is full of other thoughts.

NEFF'S VOICE (*synchronized with the above scene*). So I took her to dinner that evening at a Mexican joint down on Olvera Street where nobody would see us. I wanted to cheer her up . . . Next day was Sunday and we went for a ride down to the beach. She had loosened up a bit and she was even laughing . . . I had to make sure she wouldn't tell that stuff about Phyllis to anybody else. It was dynamite, whether it was true or not. And I had no chance to talk to Phyllis. You were watching her like a hawk, Keyes. I couldn't even phone her for fear you had the wires tapped.

This dissolves to the INSURANCE OFFICE as Neff, with his hat on and no briefcase, is walking toward Keyes' office. As he comes up close to the door, he stops with a startled expression on his face. On a chair beside the door sits a familiar figure. He is Jackson, the man from the observation platform of the train. He is wearing his Stetson hat and smoking a cigar. He is studying something in the file folder. Neff recognizes him immediately but Jackson does not look up. Neff controls his expression and goes on to open the door to Keyes' office.

NEFF'S VOICE (*over the above scene*). Monday morning there was a note on my desk that you wanted to see me, Keyes. For a minute I wondered if it could be about Lola. It was worse. Outside your door was the last guy in the world I wanted to see.

Inside KEYES' OFFICE: Neff is just closing the door from the inside. Keyes, his coat off, is lying on his office couch, chewing on a cigar, as usual.

KEYES. Come in. Come in, Walter. I want to ask you something. After all the years we've known each other, do you mind if I make a rather blunt statement?

NEFF. About what?

KEYES. About me. Walter, I'm a very great man. This Dietrichson business. It's murder, and murders don't come any neater. As fancy a piece of homicide as anybody ever ran into. Smart and tricky and almost perfect, *but*—(*bouncing off the couch like a rubber ball*)—but, I think Papa has it all figured out, figured out and wrapped up in tissue paper with pink ribbons on it.

NEFF. I'm listening.

KEYES (*levelling a finger at him*). You know what? That guy Dietrichson was never on the train.

NEFF. He wasn't?

KEYES. No, he wasn't, Walter. Look, you can't be sure of killing a man by throwing him off a train that's going fifteen miles an hour. The only way you can be sure is to kill him first and then throw his body on the tracks. That would mean either killing him on the train, or—and this is where it really gets fancy—you kill him somewhere else and put him on the tracks. Two possibilities, and I personally buy the second.

NEFF. You're way ahead of me, Keyes.

KEYES. Look, it was like this. They killed the guy—the wife and somebody else—and then the somebody else took the crutches and went on the train as Dietrichson, and then the somebody else jumped off, and then they put the body on the tracks where the train had passed. An impersonation, see. And a cinch to work. Because it was night, very few people were about, they had the crutches to stare at, and they never really looked at the man at all.

NEFF. It's fancy all right, Keyes. Maybe it's a little too fancy.

KEYES. Is it? I tell you it fits together like a watch. And now let's see what we have in the way of proof. The only guy that really got a good look at this supposed Dietrichson is sitting right outside my office. I took the trouble to bring him down here from Oregon. Let's see what he has to say. (*Keyes goes to the door and opens it.*) Come in, Mr. Jackson.

JACKSON (*entering with the file folder*). Yes sir, Mr. Keyes. These are fine cigars you smoke. (*He indicates the cigar he himself is smoking.*)

KEYES. Two for a quarter.

JACKSON. That's what I said.

KEYES. Never mind the cigar, Jackson. Did you study those photographs? What do you say?

JACKSON. Yes, indeed, I studied them thoroughly. Very thoroughly.

KEYES. Well? Did you make up your mind?

JACKSON. Mr. Keyes, I'm a Medford man. Medford, Oregon. Up in Medford we take our time making up our minds—

KEYES. Well you're not in Medford now. I'm in a hurry. Let's have it.

JACKSON (*indicating the file folder he is holding*). Are these photographs of the late Mr. Dietrichson?

KEYES. Yes.

JACKSON. Then my answer is no.

KEYES. What do you mean no?

JACKSON. I mean this is not the man that was on the train.

KEYES. Will you swear to that?

JACKSON. I'm a Medford man. Medford, Oregon. And if I say it, I mean it, and if I mean it, of course I'll swear it.

KEYES. Thank you. (*Turning to Neff*) There you are, Walter. There's your proof. (*Keyes remembers he forgot to introduce Jackson.*) Oh, Mr. Jackson, this is Mr. Neff, one of our salesmen.

JACKSON. Pleased to meet you, Mr. Neff. Pleased indeed.

NEFF. How do you do?

JACKSON. Very fine, thank you. Never was better.

KEYES. Mr. Jackson, how would you describe the man you saw on that observation platform?

JACKSON. Well, I'm pretty sure he was a younger man, about ten or fifteen years younger than the man in these photographs.

KEYES. Dietrichson was about fifty, wasn't he, Walter?

NEFF. Fifty-one, according to the policy.

JACKSON. The man I saw was nothing like fifty-one years old. Of course, it was pretty dark on that platform and, come to think of it, he tried to keep his back toward me. But I'm positive just the same.

KEYES. That's fine, Jackson. Now you understand this matter is strictly confidential. We may need you again down here in Los Angeles, if the case comes to court.

JACKSON. Any time you need me, I'm at your entire disposal, gentlemen. Expenses paid, of course.

KEYES (*picking up the telephone on his desk and speaking into it*). Get me Lubin, in the cashier's office.

Meanwhile, Jackson crosses over to Neff and, during the ensuing dialogue between him and Neff, we hear Keyes' low voice on the phone in the background. We do not hear what he says.

JACKSON (*to Neff*). Ever been in Medford, Mr. Neff?

NEFF. Never.

JACKSON. Wait a minute. Do you go trout fishing? Maybe I saw you up Klamath Falls way.

NEFF. Nope. Never fish.

JACKSON. Neff. Neff. I've got it! It's the name. There's a family of Neffs in Corvallis.

NEFF. No relation.

JACKSON. Let me see. This man's an automobile dealer in Corvallis. Very reputable man, too, I'm told.

KEYES (*rejoining them at this point*). All right, Mr. Jackson. Suppose you go down to the cashier's office—room twenty-seven on the eleventh floor. They'll take care of your expense account and your ticket for the train tonight.

JACKSON. Tonight? Tomorrow morning would suit me better. There's a very good osteopath down here I want to see before I leave.

KEYES (*having opened the door for Jackson*). Okay, Mr. Jackson. Just don't put her on the expense account.

JACKSON (*doesn't get it*). Goodbye, gentlemen. A pleasure. (*He goes out.*)

KEYES. There it is, Walter. It's beginning to come apart at the seams already. A murder's never perfect. It always comes apart sooner or later. And when two people are involved it's usually sooner. We know the Dietrichson dame is in it, and somebody else. Pretty soon we're going to know who that somebody else is. He'll show. He's got to show. Sometime, somewhere, they've got to meet. Their emotions are all kicked up. Whether it's love or hate doesn't matter. They can't keep away from each other. They think it's twice as safe because there are two of them. But it's not twice as safe. It's ten times twice as dangerous. They've committed a murder and that's not like taking a trolley ride together where each one can get off at a different stop. They're stuck with each other. They've got to ride all the way to the end of the line. And it's a one-way trip, and the last stop is the cemetery. (*He puts a cigar in his mouth and starts tapping his pockets for matches.*) She put in her claim and I'm going to throw it right back at her. (*Patting his pockets again*) Have you got one of those?

Neff strikes a match for him. Keyes takes the match out of his hand and lights his cigar.

KEYES. Let her sue us if she dares. I'll be ready for her—and that somebody else. They'll be digging their own graves.

The scene dissolves to a TELEPHONE BOOTH in Jerry's market. Neff is in the booth dialing a number, and as he waits he looks around to make sure he is not watched.

NEFF (*into the phone*). Mrs. Dietrichson? . . . This is Jerry's market. We just got in a shipment of that English soap you were asking about. Will you be coming by this morning? . . . Thank you, Mrs. Dietrichson. (*Neff hangs up.*)

This dissolves to the exterior of JERRY'S MARKET. The LaSalle stops in front of the market. Phyllis steps out and goes into the market, looking around. Then we see the SHELVES in the rear of the market.

Neff is moving slowly along them, outwardly calm but with his nerves on edge. From beyond him Phyllis approaches. She stops beside him, facing the same way, with a couple of feet separating them.

PHYLLIS. Hello, Walter.

NEFF (*in a harsh whisper*). Come closer.

PHYLLIS (*moving closer to him*). What's the matter?

NEFF. Everything's the matter. Keyes is rejecting your claim. He's sitting back with his mouth watering, waiting for you to sue. He wants you to sue. But you're not going to.

PHYLLIS. What's he got to stop me?

NEFF. He's got the goods. He's figured out how it was

worked. He knows it was somebody else on the train. He's dug up a witness he thinks will prove it.

PHYLLIS. Prove it how? Listen, if he rejects that claim, I *have* to sue.

NEFF. Yeah? And then you're in court and a lot of other things are going to come up. Like, for instance, about you and the first Mrs. Dietrichson.

PHYLLIS (*looking at him sharply*). What about me and the first Mrs. Dietrichson?

NEFF. The way she died. And about that black hat you were trying on — before you needed a black hat.

A customer comes along the aisle toward them. They move apart. The customer passes. Phyllis draws close again.

PHYLLIS. Walter, Lola's been telling you some of her cock-eyed stories. She's been seeing you.

NEFF. I've been seeing her, if you want to know. So she won't yell her head off about what *she* knows.

PHYLLIS. Yes, she's been putting on an act for you, crying all over your shoulder, that lying little —

NEFF. Keep her out of it. All I'm telling you is we're not going to sue.

PHYLLIS. Because you don't want the money any more, even if you could get it? Because she's made you feel like a heel all of a sudden.

NEFF. It isn't the money any more. It's our necks now. We're pulling out, understand.

PHYLLIS. Because of what Keyes can do? You're not fooling me, Walter. It's because of Lola. What you did to her father. You can't take it that she might find out some day.

NEFF. I said, leave her out of it.

PHYLLIS. Walter, it's me I'm talking about. *I* don't want to be left out of it.

NEFF. Stop saying that. It's just that it hasn't worked out the way we wanted. We can't have the money. We can't go through with it, that's all.

PHYLLIS. We have gone through with it, Walter. The tough part is all behind us. We just have to hold on now and not go soft inside, and stick together, close, the way we started out.

Phyllis takes his arm, forgetting where she is. He pulls away.

NEFF. Watch it, will you. Someone's coming.

One of the market help, pushing a small hand-truck loaded with packaged goods, comes along the aisle. He stops and begins to restock a shelf very close to Neff and Phyllis. They go off slowly in opposite directions. The view moves with Neff as he walks toward another shelf, one that stands away from the wall. Phyllis appears on the opposite side of the shelf and stops, facing him. They now continue their low-voiced dialogue through the piled-up merchandise.

PHYLLIS. I loved you, Walter. And I hated him. But I wasn't going to do anything about it, not until I met you. It was you had the plan. I only wanted him dead.

NEFF. Yeah, and I was the one that fixed him so he was dead. Is that what you're telling me?

Phyllis takes off her dark glasses for the first time and looks at him with cold, hard eyes.

PHYLLIS. Yes. And nobody's pulling out. We went into it together, and we're coming out at the end together. It's straight down the line for both of us, remember.

Phyllis puts the glasses on again and goes out.
This dissolves to NEFF'S OFFICE where Neff is dictating into the dictaphone.

NEFF. Yeah, I remembered it all right. Just as I remembered what you had told me, Keyes, about that trolley car ride, and how there was no way to get off until the end of the line, where the cemetery was. And I got to thinking what cemeteries are for. They're to put dead people in. I guess that was the first time I ever thought about Phyllis that way. Dead, I mean, and how things would be if she was dead. Because the way it was now she had me by the throat. She could hang me higher than a kite any day she felt like it. And there was nothing I could do, except hold my breath and watch that day come closer and closer, and maybe pray a little, if I still knew how to pray . . . I saw Lola three or four times that week. I guess it sounds crazy, Keyes, after what I had done, but it was only with her that I could relax and let go a little. Then one night we drove up into the hills above Hollywood Bowl . . .

This dissolves to HOLLYWOOD HILLS. Neff and Lola are climbing over a low hill in the foreground. The sky is starlit and music from the Bowl comes over the scene from below. As he helps her climb up, the view moves with them and shows the expanse of the Bowl below, a packed audience, and the orchestra on the lighted shell. They sit down on the grass. Neff sits near her, not too close. It is very dark and they are silhouetted against the shell lights. Neff puts a cigarette in his mouth and strikes a match. The flame lights up Lola's face. Neff glances at her. She is crying. He lights his cigarette and blows out the match. A pause follows.

NEFF. Why are you crying? (*As Lola doesn't answer*) You won't tell me?

LOLA (*in a choked voice*). Of course I will, Walter. I wouldn't tell anybody else but you. It's about Nino.

NEFF. Zachette? What about him?

LOLA. They killed my father together. He and Phyllis. He helped her do it. I know he did.

NEFF. What makes you say that?

LOLA. I've been following him. He's at her house, night after night. It was Phyllis and him all the time. Maybe he was going with me just for a blind. And the night of the murder—

NEFF. You promised not to talk that way any more.

LOLA. —he was supposed to pick me up after a lecture at U.C.L.A.—but he never showed up. He said he was sick. Sick! He couldn't show up, because the train was leaving with my father on it. (*She begins to cry again.*) Maybe I'm just crazy. Maybe it's all just in my mind.

NEFF. Sure, it's all in your mind.

LOLA. I only wish it was, Walter, because I still love him.

Over Neff's face, as he listens to the music comes the dictation:

NEFF'S VOICE. Zachette. That's funny. Phyllis and Zachette. What was he doing up at her house? I couldn't figure that one out. I tried to make sense out of it and got nowhere. But the real brain-twister came the next day. You sprang it on me, Keyes, after office hours, when you caught me down in the lobby of the building.

This dissolves to the LOBBY of the Pacific Building, about 5:00 P.M. or a little later. A stream of office employees is coming out of an elevator; a second elevator reaches the lobby and some more office employees come out, among them Neff, wearing his hat and carrying his briefcase. The view precedes him as he walks toward the entrance doors. He is stopped by Keyes' voice, off to one side.

KEYES' VOICE. Oh, Walter, just a minute.

Neff stops and looks toward the cigar counter, as he moves toward him. Keyes is standing there buying cigars. He is stuffing them into his pockets.

NEFF. Hello, Keyes.

KEYES. Hang onto your hat, Walter.

NEFF. What for?

KEYES. Nothing much. The Dietrichson case just busted wide open.

NEFF. How do you mean?

KEYES. The guy showed. That's how.

NEFF. The somebody else?

KEYES. Yeah. The guy that did it with her.

NEFF. No kidding?

KEYES. She's filed suit against us, and it's okay by me. When we get into that courtroom I'll tear them apart, both of them. Come on — I'll buy you a martini.

NEFF. No thanks, Keyes.

KEYES. With two olives.

NEFF. I've got to get a shave and a shoeshine. I've got a date.

KEYES. Margie. I still bet she drinks from the bottle.

He bites off the end of the cigar and puts the cigar into his mouth. He starts tapping his pockets for a match, as usual. Neff strikes a match for him.

NEFF. They give you matches when they sell you cigars, Keyes. All you have to do is ask for them.

KEYES. I don't like them. They always explode in my pockets. So long, Walter.

Keyes goes toward the street and out of the scene. Neff moves back into the lobby. As he reaches the elevator, he looks back over his shoulder, to make sure Keyes is gone, then steps into the empty elevator.

NEFF (*entering the elevator*). Twelve.

This dissolves to the ENTRANCE of the office on the 12TH FLOOR as Neff comes out of the elevator. The receptionist is just tidying up her desk. She has her hat on and is preparing to leave. Neff passes on through the swinging doors to the twelfth floor balcony. — This cuts to the 12TH FLOOR BALCONY as Neff enters from the reception room. A couple of belated employees are leaving for the day. Neff goes toward Keyes' office, looks around to make sure he is unobserved, and enters.
KEYES' OFFICE: Neff has just come in. He goes over to Keyes' desk and searches the papers on it. He tries the desk drawers and finds them locked. His eye falls on the dictaphone on the stand beside the desk. A record is on it, the needle is

about two thirds of the way toward the end. He lifts the needle and sets it back to the beginning of the record, sets the switch to play-back position. He lifts the arm off the bracket and starts the machine. Keyes voice is heard coming from the horn:

KEYES' VOICE. Memo to Mr. Norton. Confidential. Dietrichson File. With regard to your proposal to put Walter Neff under surveillance, I disagree absolutely. I have investigated his movements on the night of the crime, and he is definitely placed in his apartment from 7:15 P.M. on. In addition to this, I have known Neff intimately for eleven years, and I personally vouch for him, without reservation . . . .

Neff stops the machine. He sits down slowly, still holding the horn. He is deeply moved. After a moment, he presses the switch again.

KEYES' VOICE (*from the dictaphone*) . . . Furthermore, no connection whatsoever has been established between Walter Neff and Mrs. Phyllis Dietrichson, whereas I am now able to report that such a connection has been established between her and another man. This man has been observed to visit the Dietrichson home on the night of July 9th, 10th, 11th, 12th and 13th. We have succeeded in identifying him as one Nino Zachette, former medical student, aged twenty-eight, residing at Lilac Court Apartments, 1228½ N. La Brea Avenue. We have checked Zachette's movements on the night of the crime and have found that they cannot be accounted for. I am preparing a more detailed report for your consideration and it is my belief that we already have sufficient evidence against Zachette and Mrs. Dietrichson to justify police action. I strongly urge that this whole matter be turned over to the office of the District Attorney. Respectfully, Barton Keyes.

Neff sits, staring blankly at the wall. The cylinder goes on revolving, but no more voice comes—only the whir of the needle on the empty record. At last he remembers to replace the horn. He hangs it back on its hook. The machine stops. Neff gets up from the chair, walks slowly to the door and goes out.

We see the 12TH FLOOR BALCONY as Neff comes out of

Keyes' office. He walks slowly back toward the reception room entrance, then stands there looking out through the glass doors. All the employees have now left. Neff is entirely alone. He moves as if to go out, then stops rigidly as his face lights up with excitement at a sudden idea. He turns quickly and walks on to his own office and enters.—Then NEFF'S OFFICE comes into view as Neff walks across to his desk, lifts the telephone and dials a number. (During the ensuing telephone conversation, only what he says is heard. The pauses indicate speeches at the other end of the line.)

NEFF. Phyllis? Walter. I've got to see you . . . Tonight . . . Yes, it has to be tonight . . . How's eleven o'clock? Don't worry about Keyes. He's satisfied . . . Leave the door on the latch and put the lights out. No, nobody's watching the house . . . I told you Keyes is satisfied. It's just for the neighbors . . . That's what I said. Yeah. Eleven o'clock. Goodbye, baby.

Neff hangs up and stands beside the desk with a grim expression on his face, takes a handkerchief out and wipes perspiration from his forehead and the palms of his hands. The gesture has a symbolic quality, as if he were trying to wipe away the murder.

NEFF'S VOICE. I guess I don't have to tell you what I was going to do at eleven o'clock, Keyes. For the first time I saw a way to get clear of the whole mess I was in, and of Phyllis, too, all at the same time. Yeah, that's what I thought. But what I didn't know was that she was all set for me. That she had outsmarted me again, just like she always had . . .

This dissolves to the HALL STAIRWAY of the DIETRICHSON HOME at night. The lights are turned on. Phyllis is coming down the stairs. She wears white lounging pajamas, and she is carrying something small and heavy concealed in a scarf in her right hand. She reaches the front door, opens it slightly, fixes the catch so that the door can be opened from the outside. She switches off the porch light and the hall light. She moves toward the living room, where there is still a light on.

NEFF'S VOICE. She was all set and waiting for me. It could have been something in my voice when I called her up that tipped her off. And it could have been that she had the idea already. And an idea wasn't the only thing she had waiting for me.

The scene cuts to the LIVING ROOM. On the long table behind the davenport, one of the lamps is lit. The only other light in the room is a standing lamp beside the desk. A window toward the back is open, and through it comes the sound of music, probably a neighboring radio.—Phyllis enters and crosses to the table. She puts out the lamp, then moves over to the desk and puts out the lamp there. The room is filled with bright moonlight coming in at the windows.—Phyllis crosses to the chair by the fireplace (the one she sat in the first time Neff came to the house). She lifts the loose cushion and puts what was in the scarf behind it. As she withdraws the scarf, there is a brief glint of something metallic before she covers the hidden object with the cushion again.—She turns to the low table in front of the davenport and takes a cigarette from the box. She takes a match and is about to strike it when, just then, she hears a car coming up the hill. She listens, motionless. The car stops. A car door is slammed.—Calmly, Phyllis strikes the match and lights her cigarette. She drops the match casually into a tray, goes back to the chair, sits down and waits, quietly smoking. There are footsteps outside the house.—Over the chair in which Phyllis is sitting the hallway is visible through the arch. The front door opens. Neff comes in. He is silhouetted against the moonlight as he stands there. He closes the door again.

PHYLLIS (*in the foreground*). In here, Walter.

Neff comes through the arch and walks slowly toward her.

NEFF. Hello, baby. Anybody else in the house?

PHYLLIS. Nobody. Why?

NEFF. What's that music?

PHYLLIS. A radio up the street.

NEFF (*sitting down on the arm of the davenport, close to her*). Just like the first time I was here. We were talking about automobile insurance. Only you were thinking about murder. And I was thinking about that anklet.

PHYLLIS. And what are you thinking about now?

NEFF. I'm all through thinking. This is goodbye.

PHYLLIS. Goodbye? Where are you going?

NEFF. It's you that's going, baby. Not me. I'm getting off the trolley car right at this corner.

PHYLLIS. Suppose you stop being fancy. Let's have it, whatever it is.

NEFF. I have a friend who's got a funny theory. He says when two people commit a murder they're kind of on a trolley car, and one can't get off without the other. They're stuck with each other. They have to go on riding clear to the end of the line. And the last stop is the cemetery.

PHYLLIS. Maybe he's got something there.

NEFF. You bet he has. Two people are going to ride to the end of the line, all right. Only I'm not going to be one of them. I've got another guy to finish my ride for me.

PHYLLIS. So you've got it all arranged, Walter.

NEFF. You arranged it for me. I didn't have to do a thing.

PHYLLIS. Just who are you talking about?

NEFF. An acquaintance of yours. A Mr. Zachette. Come on, baby, I just got into this because I knew a little something about insurance, didn't I? I was just a sucker. I'd have been brushed-off as soon as you got your hands on the money.

PHYLLIS. What are you talking about?

NEFF. Save it. I'm telling this. It's been you and that Zachette guy all along, hasn't it?

PHYLLIS. That's not true.

NEFF. It doesn't make any difference whether it's true or not. The point is Keyes believes Zachette is the guy he's been looking for. He'll have him in the gas chamber before he knows what happened to him.

PHYLLIS. And what's happening to me all this time?

NEFF. Don't be silly. What do you expect to happen to you? You helped him do the murder, didn't you? That's what Keyes thinks. And what's good enough for Keyes is good enough for me.

PHYLLIS. Maybe it's not good enough for me, Walter. Maybe I don't go for the idea. Maybe I'd rather talk.

NEFF. Sometimes people are where they can't talk. Under six feet of dirt, for instance. And if it was you, they'd just charge it up to Zachette, wouldn't they. One more item on his account. Sure they would. That's just what they're going to do. Especially since he's coming here tonight . . . Oh, in about fifteen minutes from now, baby. With the cops right behind him. It's all taken care of.

PHYLLIS. And that'd make everything lovely for you, wouldn't it?

NEFF. Right. And it's got to be done before that suit of yours comes to trial, and Lola gets a chance to sound off, and they trip you up on the stand, and you start to fold up and drag me down with you.

PHYLLIS. Listen, Walter. Maybe I had Zachette here so they won't get a chance to trip me up. So we can get that money and be together.

NEFF. That's cute. Say it again.

PHYLLIS. He came here the first time just to ask where Lola was. I made him come back. I was working on him. He's a crazy sort of guy, quick-tempered. I kept hammering into him that she was with another man, so he'd get into one of his jealous rages, and then I'd tell him where she was. And you know what he'd have done to her, don't you, Walter.

NEFF. Yeah, and for once I believe you. Because it's just rotten enough.

PHYLLIS. We're both rotten, Walter.

NEFF. Only you're just a little more rotten. You're rotten clear through. You got me to take care of your husband, and then you got Zachette to take care of Lola, and maybe take care of me too, and then somebody else would have come along to take care of Zachette for you. That's the way you operate isn't it, baby.

PHYLLIS. Suppose it is, Walter. Is what you've cooked up for tonight any better?

NEFF (*getting up from the davenport, listening to the music for a moment*). I don't like this music anymore. It's too close. Do you mind if I shut the window?

Phyllis just stares at him. He goes quietly over to the window and shuts it and draws the curtain. Phyllis speaks to his back:

PHYLLIS (*her voice low and urgent*). Walter!

Neff turns; something changes in his face. There is the report of a gun. He stands motionless for a moment, then very slowly starts toward her. Phyllis stands with the gun in her hand. Neff stops after he has taken a few steps.

NEFF. What's the matter? Why don't you shoot again? Maybe if I came a little closer? (*Taking a few more steps toward her and stopping again*) How's that. Do you think you can do it now?

Phyllis is silent. She doesn't shoot. Her expression is tortured. Neff goes on until he is close to her. Quietly he takes the gun out of her unresisting hand.

NEFF. Why didn't you shoot, baby? (*In reply Phyllis puts her arms around him in complete surrender.*) Don't tell me it's because you've been in love with me all this time.

PHYLLIS. No. I never loved you, Walter. Not you, or anybody else. I'm rotten to the heart. I used you, just as you said. That's all you ever meant to me—until a minute ago. I didn't think anything like that could ever happen to me.

NEFF. I'm sorry, baby. I'm not buying.

PHYLLIS. I'm not asking you to buy. Just hold me close.

Neff draws her close to him. She reaches up to his face and kisses him on the lips. As she comes out of the kiss there is realization in her eyes that this is the final moment.

NEFF. Goodbye, baby.

Out of sight the gun explodes once, twice. Phyllis quivers in his arms. Her eyes fill with tears. Her head falls limp against his shoulder. Slowly he lifts her and carries her to the davenport. He lays her down on it carefully, almost tenderly. The moonlight coming in at the French doors shines on the anklet. He looks at it for the last time and slowly turns away. As he does so, he puts his hand inside his coat and it comes out with blood on it. Only then is it apparent that Phyllis' shot actually did hit him. He looks at the blood on his fingers with a dazed expression and quickly goes out of the room, the way he came.

And now Neff comes out of the DIETRICHSON HOME. He closes the front door with his right hand. His left arm hangs limp. He takes a few steps down the walk, then suddenly hears somebody approaching. He moves behind the palm tree near the walk.

A man comes up the steps toward the front door—Zachette. Just as he reaches the door, Neff calls to him.

NEFF. Hey you. Come here a minute. I said come here, Zachette. (*Zachette turns and approaches him slowly.*) The name is Neff.

ZACHETTE. Yeah? And I still don't like it. What do you want?

NEFF. Look, kid, I want to give you a present. (*He takes some loose change out of his pocket and holds out a coin.*) Here's a nice new nickel.

ZACHETTE. What's the gag?

NEFF. Suppose you go back down the hill to a drug store and make a phone call.

Neff starts to drop the nickel into Zachette's handkerchief pocket. Zachette knocks his hand away.

ZACHETTE. Keep your nickel and buy yourself an ice cream cone.

NEFF. The number is Granite 0386. Ask for Miss Dietrichson. The first name is Lola.

ZACHETTE. Lola? She isn't worth a nickel. And if I ever talk to her, it's not going to be over any telephone.

NEFF. Tough, aren't you? Take the nickel. Take it and call her. She wants you to.

ZACHETTE. Yeah? She doesn't want any part of me.

NEFF. I know who told you that, and it's not true. She's in love with you. Always has been. Don't ask me why. I couldn't even guess.

Zachette just stares at him. Neff moves again to put the nickel into Zachette's pocket. This time Zachette allows him to do it.

NEFF. Now beat it. Granite 0386, I told you. (*He motions toward the street below.*) That way.

Zachette goes slowly past him. Neff grabs him and pushes him almost violently down the walk. Zachette goes out of view. The sound of his steps dies away as Neff looks after him, and, far off in the distance, the siren of a police car is heard. Then Neff moves off through the shrubbery toward the side of the house where he parked his car.

This dissolves to NEFF'S OFFICE at night. The desk lamp is still lighted; outside the windows, the dawn is slowly breaking. Neff is still clutching the horn of the dictaphone. There are eight or nine used cylinders on the desk beside him. A widening stain of blood shows on the left shoulder of his gray jacket. He is very weak by now, and his voice holds a note of utter exhaustion.

NEFF. It's almost four-thirty now, Keyes. It's cold. I wonder if she's still lying there alone in that house, or whether they've found her by now. I wonder a lot of things, but they don't matter any more, except I want to ask you to do me a favor. I want you to be the one to tell Lola, kind of gently, before it breaks wide open . . . Yes, and I'd like you to look after her and that guy Zachette, so he doesn't get pushed around too much. Because . . .

Suddenly he stops his dictation with an instinctive feeling that he is not alone in the room.

As he turns in his chair the view draws back slowly. The office door is wide open. Keyes is standing a few steps inside it. Behind him, on the balcony outside, stands the night watchman and the colored janitor, peering curiously into the room over Keyes' shoulder. Slowly, and without taking his eyes off Neff's face, Keyes reaches back and pushes the door shut. — Neff hangs up the dictaphone horn. He looks at Keyes with a faint, tired grin and speaks very slowly.

NEFF. Hello, Keyes. (*Keyes moves toward him a few steps and stands without answering.*) Up pretty early, aren't you? I always wondered what time you got down to work. (*Keyes, staring at him, still does not answer.*) Or did your little man pull you out of bed.

KEYES. The janitor did. Seems you leaked a little blood on the way in here.

NEFF. Wouldn't be surprised. (*Neff makes a motion indicating the used cylinders standing on the desk.*) I wanted to straighten out that Dietrichson story for you.

KEYES. So I gather.

NEFF. How long have you been standing there?

KEYES. Long enough.

NEFF. Kind of a crazy story with a crazy twist to it. One you didn't quite figure out.

KEYES. You can't figure them all, Walter.

NEFF. That's right. You can't, can you? And now I suppose I get the big speech, the one with all the two-dollar words in it. Let's have it, Keyes.

KEYES. You're all washed up, Walter.

NEFF. Thanks, Keyes. That was short anyway.

They stare at each other for a long moment, then, with an intense effort Neff gets up on his feet and stands there swaying a little. His face is covered with sweat. His shoulder is bleeding. He is on the verge of collapse.

KEYES. Walter, I'm going to call a doctor.

NEFF (*bitterly*). What for? So they can patch me up? So they can nurse me along till I'm back on my feet? So I can walk under my own power into that gas chamber up in San Quentin? Is that it, Keyes?

KEYES. Something like that, Walter.

NEFF. Well, I've got a different idea. Look here. Suppose you went back to bed and didn't find these cylinders till tomorrow morning, when the office opens. From then on you can play it any way you like. Would you do that much for me, Keyes?

KEYES. Give me one good reason.

NEFF. I need four hours to get where I'm going.

KEYES. You're not going anywhere, Walter.

NEFF. You bet I am. I'm going across the border.

KEYES. You haven't got a chance.

NEFF. Good enough to try for.

KEYES. You'll never make the border.

NEFF. That's what you think. Watch me.

Neff starts to move toward the door, staggering a little, holding himself upright with great effort.

KEYES (*in a voice of stony calm*). You'll never even make the elevator.

Neff has reached the door. He twists the knob and drags the door open. He turns in it to look back at Keyes' implacable face.

NEFF. So long, Keyes.

Neff goes out, leaving the door wide open. The view follows his staggering walk along the balcony toward the elevator lobby. The sound of his breathing is so harsh and loud that for a moment it dominates the scene. Finally he reaches the swing doors leading into the lobby and starts to push them open. At this moment he collapses. He clutches the edge of the door and as it swings around with him he falls to the floor. He tries to struggle up but cannot rise. In the background comes the sound of a telephone being dialed.

KEYES' VOICE. Hello . . . Send an ambulance to the Pacific Building on Olive Street . . . Yeah . . . It's a police job.

There is the sound of the phone being replaced in its cradle. Then there are footsteps growing louder along the balcony and Keyes walks slowly into view. He kneels down beside Neff.

KEYES. How you doing, Walter?

Neff manages a faint smile.

NEFF. I'm fine. Only somebody moved the elevator a couple of miles away.

KEYES. They're on their way.

NEFF (*slowly and with great difficulty*). You know why you didn't figure this one, Keyes? Let me tell you. The guy you were looking for was too close. He was right across the desk from you.

KEYES. Closer than that, Walter. (*The eyes of the two men meet in a moment of silence.*)

NEFF. I love you too.

Neff fumbles for the handkerchief in Keyes' pocket, pulls it out and clumsily wipes his face with it. The handkerchief drops from his hand. He gets a loose cigarette out of his pocket and puts it between his lips. Then with great difficulty he gets out a match, tries to strike it, but is too weak. Keyes takes the match out of his hand, strikes it for him and lights his cigarette. The scene fades out.

# SELECTED ESSAYS

# Contents

# The Simple Art of Murder

Fiction in any form has always intended to be realistic. Old-fashioned novels which now seem stilted and artificial to the point of burlesque did not appear that way to the people who first read them. Writers like Fielding and Smollett could seem realistic in the modern sense because they dealt largely with uninhibited characters, many of whom were about two jumps ahead of the police, but Jane Austen's chronicles of highly inhibited people against a background of rural gentility seem real enough psychologically. There is plenty of that kind of social and emotional hypocrisy around today. Add to it a liberal dose of intellectual pretentiousness and you get the tone of the book page in your daily paper and the earnest and fatuous atmosphere breathed by discussion groups in little clubs. These are the people who make best-sellers, which are promotional jobs based on a sort of indirect snob-appeal, carefully escorted by the trained seals of the critical fraternity, and lovingly tended and watered by certain much too powerful pressure groups whose business is selling books, although they would like you to think they are fostering culture. Just get a little behind in your payments and you will find out how idealistic they are.

The detective story for a variety of reasons can seldom be promoted. It is usually about murder and hence lacks the element of uplift. Murder, which is a frustration of the individual and hence a frustration of the race, may have, and in fact has, a good deal of sociological implication. But it has been going on too long for it to be news. If the mystery novel is at all realistic (which it very seldom is) it is written in a certain spirit of detachment; otherwise nobody but a psychopath would want to write it or read it. The murder novel has also a depressing way of minding its own business, solving its own problems and answering its own questions. There is nothing left to discuss, except whether it was well enough written to be good fiction, and the people who make up the half-million sales wouldn't know that anyway. The detection of quality in writing is difficult enough even for those who make a career of the job, without paying too much attention to the matter of advance sales.

The detective story (perhaps I had better call it that, since the English formula still dominates the trade) has to find its public by a slow process of distillation. That it does do this, and holds on thereafter with such tenacity, is a fact; the reasons for it are a study for more patient minds than mine. Nor is it any part of my thesis to maintain that it is a vital and significant form of art. There are no vital and significant forms of art; there is only art, and precious little of that. The growth of populations has in no way increased the amount; it has merely increased the adeptness with which substitutes can be produced and packaged.

Yet the detective story, even in its most conventional form, is difficult to write well. Good specimens of the art are much rarer than good serious novels. Rather second-rate items outlast most of the high velocity fiction, and a great many that should never have been born simply refuse to die at all. They are as durable as the statues in public parks and just about that dull. This is very annoying to people of what is called discernment. They do not like it that penetrating and important works of fiction of a few years back stand on their special shelf in the library marked "Best-Sellers of Yesteryear," and nobody goes near them but an occasional shortsighted customer who bends down, peers briefly and hurries away; while old ladies jostle each other at the mystery shelf to grab off some item of the same vintage with a title like *The Triple Petunia Murder Case*, or *Inspector Pinchbottle to the Rescue*. They do not like it that "really important books" get dusty on the reprint counter, while *Death Wears Yellow Garters* is put out in editions of fifty or one hundred thousand copies on the news-stands of the country, and is obviously not there just to say goodbye.

To tell you the truth, I do not like it very much myself. In my less stilted moments I too write detective stories, and all this immortality makes just a little too much competition. Even Einstein couldn't get very far if three hundred treatises of the higher physics were published every year, and several thousand others in some form or other were hanging around in excellent condition, and being read too. Hemingway says somewhere that the good writer competes only with the dead. The good detective story writer (there must after all be a few) competes not only with all the unburied dead but with all the hosts of the living as well. And on almost equal terms; for it is one of the qualities of this kind of writing that the thing that makes people read it never goes out of style. The hero's tie may be a little off the mode and the good gray inspector may arrive in a dogcart instead of a streamlined sedan with siren screaming, but what he does when he gets there is the same old futzing around with timetables and bits of charred paper and who trampled the jolly old flowering arbutus under the library window.

I have, however, a less sordid interest in the matter. It seems to me that production of detective stories on so large a scale, and by writers whose immediate reward is small and whose need of critical praise is almost nil, would not be possible at all if the job took any talent. In that sense the raised eyebrow of the critic and the shoddy merchandizing of the publisher are perfectly logical. The average detective story is probably no worse than the average novel, but you never see the average novel. It doesn't get published. The average—or only slightly above average—detective story does. Not only is it published but it is sold in small quantities to rental libraries, and it is read. There are even a few optimists who buy it at the full retail price of two dollars, because it looks so fresh and new, and there is a picture of a corpse on the cover. And the strange thing is that this average, more than middling dull, pooped-out piece of utterly unreal and mechanical fiction is not terribly different from what are called the masterpieces of the art. It drags on a little more slowly, the dialogue is a little grayer, the cardboard out of which the characters are cut is a shade thinner, and the cheating is a little more obvious; but it is the same kind of book. Whereas the good novel is not at all the same kind of book as the bad novel. It is about entirely different things. But the good detective story and the bad detective story are about exactly the same things, and they are about them in very much the same way. There are reasons for this too, and reasons for the reasons; there always are.

I suppose the principal dilemma of the traditional or classic

or straight-deductive or logic—and—deduction novel of detection is that for any approach to perfection it demands a
combination of qualities not found in the same mind. The
cool-headed constructionist does not also come across with
lively characters, sharp dialogue, a sense of pace and an acute
use of observed detail. The grim logician has as much atmosphere as a drawing-board. The scientific sleuth has a nice
new shiny laboratory, but I'm sorry I can't remember the
face. The fellow who can write you a vivid and colorful prose
simply won't be bothered with the coolie labor of breaking
down unbreakable alibis. The master of rare knowledge is living psychologically in the age of the hoop skirt. If you know
all you should know about ceramics and Egyptian needle-
work, you don't know anything at all about the police. If you
know that platinum won't melt under about 2800 degrees F.
by itself, but will melt at the glance of a pair of deep blue eyes
when put close to a bar of lead, then you don't know how
men make love in the twentieth century. And if you know
enough about the elegant flânerie of the pre-war French Riviera to lay your story in that locale, you don't know that a
couple of capsules of barbital small enough to be swallowed
will not only not kill a man—they will not even put him to
sleep, if he fights against them.

Every detective story writer makes mistakes, and none will
ever know as much as he should. Conan Doyle made mistakes
which completely invalidated some of his stories, but he was a
pioneer, and Sherlock Holmes after all is mostly an attitude
and a few dozen lines of unforgettable dialogue. It is the
ladies and gentlemen of what Mr. Howard Haycraft (in his
book *Murder for Pleasure*) calls the Golden Age of detective
fiction that really get me down. This age is not remote. For
Mr. Haycraft's purpose it starts after the first World War and
lasts up to about 1930. For all practical purposes it is still here.
Two-thirds or three-quarters of all the detective stories published still adhere to the formula the giants of this era created,
perfected, polished and sold to the world as problems in logic
and deduction. These are stern words, but be not alarmed.
They are only words. Let us glance at one of the glories of the
literature, an acknowledged masterpiece of the art of fooling
the reader without cheating him. It is called *The Red House*

*Mystery*, was written by A. A. Milne, and has been named by
Alexander Woollcott (rather a fast man with a superlative)
"one of the three best mystery stories of all time." Words of
that size are not spoken lightly. The book was published in
1922, but is quite timeless, and might as easily have been published in July 1939, or, with a few slight changes, last week. It
ran thirteen editions and seems to have been in print, in the
original format, for about sixteen years. That happens to few
books of any kind. It is an agreeable book, light, amusing in
the *Punch* style, written with a deceptive smoothness that is
not as easy as it looks.

It concerns Mark Ablett's impersonation of his brother
Robert, as a hoax on his friends. Mark is the owner of the
Red House, a typical laburnum-and-lodge-gate English country house, and he has a secretary who encourages him and
abets him in this impersonation, because the secretary is going to murder him, if he pulls it off. Nobody around the Red
House has ever seen Robert, fifteen years absent in Australia,
known to them by repute as a no-good. A letter from Robert
is talked about, but never shown. It announces his arrival, and
Mark hints it will not be a pleasant occasion. One afternoon,
then, the supposed Robert arrives, identifies himself to a
couple of servants, is shown into the study, and Mark (according to testimony at the inquest) goes in after him. Robert
is then found dead on the floor with a bullet hole in his face,
and of course Mark has vanished into thin air. Arrive the police, suspect Mark must be the murderer, remove the debris
and proceed with the investigation, and in due course, with
the inquest.

Milne is aware of one very difficult hurdle and tries as well
as he can to get over it. Since the secretary is going to murder
Mark once he has established himself as Robert, the impersonation has to continue on and fool the police. Since, also,
everybody around the Red House knows Mark intimately,
disguise is necessary. This is achieved by shaving off Mark's
beard, roughening his hands ("not the hands of a manicured
gentlemen"—testimony) and the use of a gruff voice and
rough manner. But this is not enough. The cops are going to
have the body and the clothes on it and whatever is in the
pockets. Therefore none of this must suggest Mark. Milne

therefore works like a switch engine to put over the motivation that Mark is such a thoroughly conceited performer that he dresses the part down to the socks and underwear (from all of which the secretary has removed the maker's labels), like a ham blacking himself all over to play Othello. If the reader will buy this (and the sales record shows he must have) Milne figures he is solid. Yet, however light in texture the story may be, it is offered as a problem of logic and deduction. If it is not that, it is nothing at all. There is nothing else for it to be. If the situation is false, you cannot even accept it as a light novel, for there is no story for the light novel to be about. If the problem does not contain the elements of truth and plausibility, it is no problem; if the logic is an illusion, there is nothing to deduce. If the impersonation is impossible once the reader is told the conditions it must fulfill, then the whole thing is a fraud. Not a deliberate fraud, because Milne would not have written the story if he had known what he was up against. He is up against a number of deadly things, none of which he even considers. Nor, apparently, does the casual reader, who wants to like the story, hence takes it at its face value. But the reader is not called upon to know the facts of life; it is the author who is the expert in the case. Here is what this author ignores:

1. The coroner holds formal jury inquest on a body for which no competent legal identification is offered. A coroner, usually in a big city, will sometimes hold inquest on a body that *cannot* be identified, if the record of such an inquest has or may have a value (fire, disaster, evidence of murder, etc.). No such reason exists here, and there is no one to identify the body. A couple of witnesses said the man said he was Robert Ablett. This is mere presumption, and has weight only if nothing conflicts with it. Identification is a condition precedent to an inquest. Even in death a man has a right to his own identity. The coroner will, wherever humanly possible, enforce that right. To neglect it would be a violation of his office.

2. Since Mark Ablett, missing and suspected of the murder, cannot defend himself, all evidence of his movements before and after the murder is vital (as also whether he has money to run away on); yet all such evidence is given by the man closest

to the murder, and is without corroboration. It is automatically suspect until proved true.

3. The police find by direct investigation that Robert Ablett was not well thought of in his native village. Somebody there must have known him. No such person was brought to the inquest. (The story couldn't stand it.)

4. The police know there is an element of threat in Robert's supposed visit, and that it is connected with the murder must be obvious to them. Yet they make no attempt to check Robert in Australia, or find out what character he had there, or what associates, or even if he actually came to England, and with whom. (If they had, they would have found out he had been dead three years.)

5. The police surgeon examines the body with a recently shaved beard (exposing unweathered skin), artificially roughened hands, yet the body of a wealthy, soft-living man, long resident in a cool climate. Robert was a rough individual and had lived fifteen years in Australia. That is the surgeon's information. It is impossible he would have noticed nothing to conflict with it.

6. The clothes are nameless, empty, and have had the labels removed. Yet the man wearing them asserted an identity. The presumption that he was not what he said he was is overpowering. Nothing whatever is done about this peculiar circumstance. It is never even mentioned as being peculiar.

7. A man is missing, a well-known local man, and a body in the morgue closely resembles him. It is impossible that the police should not at once eliminate the chance that the missing man *is* the dead man. Nothing would be easier than to prove it. Not even to think of it is incredible. It makes idiots of the police, so that a brash amateur may startle the world with a fake solution.

The detective in the case is an insouciant gent named Antony Gillingham, a nice lad with a cheery eye, a cozy little flat in London, and that airy manner. He is not making any money on the assignment, but is always available when the local gendarmerie loses its notebook. The English police seem to endure him with their customary stoicism; but I shudder to think of what the boys down at the Homicide Bureau in my city would do to him.

There are less plausible examples of the art than this. In *Trent's Last Case* (often called "the perfect detective story") you have to accept the premise that a giant of international finance, whose lightest frown makes Wall Street quiver like a chihuahua, will plot his own death so as to hang his secretary, and that the secretary when pinched will maintain an aristocratic silence; the old Etonian in him maybe. I have known relatively few international financiers, but I rather think the author of this novel has (if possible) known fewer. There is one by Freeman Wills Crofts (the soundest builder of them all when he doesn't get too fancy) wherein a murderer by the aid of makeup, split second timing, and some very sweet evasive action, impersonates the man he has just killed and thereby gets him alive and distant from the place of the crime. There is one of Dorothy Sayers' in which a man is murdered alone at night in his house by a mechanically released weight which works because he always turns the radio on at just such a moment, always stands in just such a position in front of it, and always bends over just so far. A couple of inches either way and the customers would get a rain check. This is what is vulgarly known as having God sit in your lap; a murderer who needs that much help from Providence must be in the wrong business. And there is a scheme of Agatha Christie's featuring M. Hercule Poirot, that ingenius Belgian who talks in a literal translation of school-boy French, wherein, by duly messing around with his "little gray cells," M. Poirot decides that nobody on a certain through sleeper could have done the murder alone, therefore everybody did it together, breaking the process down into a series of simple operations, like assembling an egg-beater. This is the type that is guaranteed to knock the keenest mind for a loop. Only a halfwit could guess it.

There are much better plots by these same writers and by others of their school. There may be one somewhere that would really stand up under close scrutiny. It would be fun to read it, even if I did have to go back to page 47 and refresh my memory about exactly what time the second gardener potted the prize-winning tea-rose begonia. There is nothing new about these stories and nothing old. The ones I mentioned are all English only because the authorities (such as they are) seem to feel the English writers had an edge in this dreary routine, and that the Americans, (even the creator of Philo Vance—probably the most asinine character in detective fiction) only made the Junior Varsity.

This, the classic detective story, has learned nothing and forgotten nothing. It is the story you will find almost any week in the big shiny magazines, handsomely illustrated, and paying due deference to virginal love and the right kind of luxury goods. Perhaps the tempo has become a trifle faster, and the dialogue a little more glib. There are more frozen daiquiris and stingers ordered, and fewer glasses of crusty old port; more clothes by *Vogue*, and décors by the *House Beautiful*, more chic, but not more truth. We spend more time in Miami hotels and Cape Cod summer colonies and go not so often down by the old gray sundial in the Elizabethan garden. But fundamentally it is the same careful grouping of suspects, the same utterly incomprehensible trick of how somebody stabbed Mrs. Pottington Postlethwaite III with the solid platinum poignard just as she flatted on the top note of the Bell Song from *Lakmé* in the presence of fifteen ill-assorted guests; the same ingenue in fur-trimmed pajamas screaming in the night to make the company pop in and out of doors and ball up the timetable; the same moody silence next day as they sit around sipping Singapore slings and sneering at each other, while the flat-feet crawl to and fro under the Persian rugs, with their derby hats on.

Personally I like the English style better. It is not quite so brittle, and the people as a rule, just wear clothes and drink drinks. There is more sense of background, as if Cheesecake Manor really existed all around and not just the part the camera sees; there are more long walks over the Downs and the characters don't all try to behave as if they had just been tested by MGM. The English may not always be the best writers in the world, but they are incomparably the best dull writers.

There is a very simple statement to be made about all these stories: they do not really come off intellectually as problems, and they do not come off artistically as fiction. They are too contrived, and too little aware of what goes on in the world. They try to be honest, but honesty is an art. The poor writer is dishonest without knowing it, and the fairly good one can be dishonest because he doesn't know what to be honest about. He thinks a complicated murder scheme which baffles the lazy reader, who won't be bothered itemizing the details, will also baffle the police, whose business is with details. The boys with their feet on the desks know that the easiest murder case in the world to break is the one somebody tried to get very cute with; the one that really bothers them is the murder somebody only thought of two minutes before he pulled it off. But if the writers of this fiction wrote about the kind of murders that happen, they would also have to write about the authentic flavor of life as it is lived. And since they cannot do that, they pretend that what they do is what should be done. Which is begging the question—and the best of them know it.

In her introduction to the first *Omnibus of Crime*, Dorothy Sayers wrote: "It (the detective story) does not, and by hypothesis never can, attain the loftiest level of literary achievement." And she suggested somewhere else that this is because it is a "literature of escape" and not "a literature of expression." I do not know what the loftiest level of literary achievement is: neither did Aeschylus or Shakespeare; neither does Miss Sayers. Other things being equal, which they never are, a more powerful theme will provoke a more powerful performance. Yet some very dull books have been written about God, and some very fine ones about how to make a living and stay fairly honest. It is always a matter of who writes the stuff, and what he has in him to write it with. As for literature of expression and literature of escape, this is critics' jargon, a use of abstract words as if they had absolute meanings. Everything written with vitality expresses that vitality; there are no dull subjects, only dull minds. All men who read escape from something else into what lies behind the printed page; the quality of the dream may be argued, but its release has become a functional necessity. All men must escape at times from the deadly rhythm of their private thoughts. It is part of the process of life among thinking beings. It is one of the things that distinguish them from the three-toed sloth; he apparently—one can never be quite sure—is perfectly content hanging upside down on a branch, and not even reading

Walter Lippmann. I hold no particular brief for the detective story as the ideal escape. I merely say that *all* reading for pleasure is escape, whether it be Greek, mathematics, astronomy, Benedetto Croce, or *The Diary of the Forgotten Man.* To say otherwise is to be an intellectual snob, and a juvenile at the art of living.

I do not think such considerations moved Miss Dorothy Sayers to her essay in critical futility.

I think what was really gnawing at her mind was the slow realization that her kind of detective story was an arid formula which could not even satisfy its own implications. It was second-grade literature because it was not about the things that could make first-grade literature. If it started out to be about real people (and she could write about them—her minor characters show that), they must very soon do unreal things in order to form the artificial pattern required by the plot. When they did unreal things, they ceased to be real themselves. They became puppets and cardboard lovers and papier mâché villains and detectives of exquisite and impossible gentility. The only kind of writer who could be happy with these properties was the one who did not know what reality was. Dorothy Sayers' own stories show that she was annoyed by this triteness; the weakest element in them is the part that makes them detective stories, the strongest the part which could be removed without touching the "problem of logic and deduction." Yet she could not or would not give her characters their heads and let them make their own mystery. It took a much simpler and more direct mind than hers to do that.

In the *Long Week-End*, which is a drastically competent account of English life and manners in the decade following the first World War, Robert Graves and Alan Hodge gave some attention to the detective story. They were just as traditionally English as the ornaments of the Golden Age, and they wrote of the time in which these writers were almost as well-known as any writers in the world. Their books in one form or another sold into the millions, and in a dozen languages. These were the people who fixed the form and established the rules and founded the famous Detection Club, which is a Parnassus of English writers of mystery. Its roster includes practically every important writer of detective fiction since Conan Doyle. But Graves and Hodge decided that during this whole period only one first-class writer had written detective stories at all. An American, Dashiell Hammett. Traditional or not, Graves and Hodge were not fuddy-duddy connoisseurs of the second rate; they could see what went on in the world and that the detective story of their time didn't; and they were aware that writers who have the vision and the ability to produce real fiction do not produce unreal fiction.

How original a writer Hammett really was, it isn't easy to decide now, even if it mattered. He was one of a group, the only one who achieved critical recognition, but not the only one who wrote or tried to write realistic mystery fiction. All literary movements are like this; some one individual is picked out to represent the whole movement; he is usually the culmination of the movement. Hammett was the ace performer, but there is nothing in his work that is not implicit in the early novels and short stories of Hemingway. Yet for all I know, Hemingway may have learned something from Hammett, as well as from writers like Dreiser, Ring Lardner, Carl Sandburg, Sherwood Anderson and himself. A rather revolutionary debunking of both the language and material of fiction had been going on for some time. It probably started in poetry; almost everything does. You can take it clear back to Walt Whitman, if you like. But Hammett applied it to the detective story, and this, because of its heavy crust of English gentility and American pseudo-gentility, was pretty hard to get moving. I doubt that Hammett had any deliberate artistic aims whatever; he was trying to make a living by writing something he had first hand information about. He made some of it up; all writers do; but it had a basis in fact; it was made up out of real things. The only reality the English detection writers knew was the conversational accent of Surbiton and Bognor Regis. If they wrote about dukes and Venetian vases, they knew no more about them out of their own experience than the well-heeled Hollywood character knows about the French Modernists that hang in his Bel-Air château or the semi-antique Chippendale-cum-cobbler's bench that he uses for a coffee table. Hammett took murder out of the Venetian vase and dropped it into the alley; it doesn't have to stay there forever, but it was a good idea to begin by getting as far as possible from Emily Post's idea of how a well-bred debutante gnaws a chicken wing. He wrote at first (and almost to the end) for people with a sharp, aggressive attitude to life. They were not afraid of the seamy side of things; they lived there. Violence did not dismay them; it was right down their street.

Hammett gave murder back to the kind of people that commit it for reasons, not just to provide a corpse; and with the means at hand, not with hand-wrought duelling pistols, curare, and tropical fish. He put these people down on paper as they are, and he made them talk and think in the language they customarily used for these purposes. He had style, but his audience didn't know it, because it was in a language not supposed to be capable of such refinements. They thought they were getting a good meaty melodrama written in the kind of lingo they imagined they spoke themselves. It was, in a sense, but it was much more. All language begins with speech, and the speech of common men at that, but when it develops to the point of becoming a literary medium it only looks like speech. Hammett's style at its worst was almost as formalized as a page of Marius the Epicurean; at its best it could say almost anything. I believe this style, which does not belong to Hammett or to anybody, but is the American language (and not even exclusively that any more), can say things he did not know how to say or feel the need of saying. In his hands it had no overtones, left no echo, evoked no image beyond a distant hill. He is said to have lacked heart, yet the story he thought most of himself is the record of a man's devotion to a friend. He was spare, frugal, hardboiled, but he did over and over again what only the best writers can ever do at all. He wrote scenes that seemed never to have been written before.

With all this he did not wreck the formal detective story. Nobody can; production demands a form that can be produced. Realism takes too much talent, too much knowledge, too much awareness. Hammett may have loosened it up a little here, and sharpened it a little there. Certainly all but the stupidest and most meretricious writers are more conscious of their artificiality than they used to be. And he demonstrated that the detective story can be important writing. *The Maltese Falcon* may or may not be a work of genius, but an art which is capable of it is not "by hypothesis" incapable of anything. Once a detective story can be as good as this, only the pedants will deny that it *could* be even better. Hammett did something else, he made the detective story fun to write, not an exhausting concatenation of insignificant clues. Without him there might not have been a regional mystery as clever as Percival Wilde's *Inquest*, or an ironic study as able as Raymond Postgate's *Verdict of Twelve*, or a savage piece of intellectual double-talk like Kenneth Fearing's *The Dagger of the Mind*, or a tragi-comic idealization of the murderer as in Donald Henderson's *Mr. Bowling Buys a Newspaper*, or even a gay and intriguing Hollywoodian gambol like Richard Sale's *Lazarus No. 7*.

The realistic style is easy to abuse: from haste, from lack of awareness, from inability to bridge the chasm that lies between what a writer would like to be able to say and what he actually knows how to say. It is easy to fake; brutality is not strength, flipness is not wit, edge-of-the-chair writing can be as boring as flat writing; dalliance with promiscuous blondes can be very dull stuff when described by goaty young men with no other purpose in mind than to describe dalliance with promiscuous blondes. There has been so much of this sort of thing that if a character in a detective story says, "Yeah," the author is automatically a Hammett imitator.

And there are still quite a few people around who say that Hammett did not write detective stories at all, merely hard-boiled chronicles of mean streets with a perfunctory mystery element dropped in like the olive in a martini. These are the flustered old ladies—of both sexes (or no sex) and almost all ages—who like their murders scented with magnolia blossoms and do not care to be reminded that murder is an act of infinite cruelty, even if the perpetrators sometimes look like playboys or college professors or nice motherly women with softly graying hair. There are also a few badly-scared champions of the formal or the classic mystery who think no story is a detective story which does not pose a formal and exact problem and arrange the clues around it with neat labels on them. Such would point out, for example, that in reading *The*

*Maltese Falcon* no one concerns himself with who killed Spade's partner, Archer (which is the only formal problem of the story) because the reader is kept thinking about something else. Yet in *The Glass Key* the reader is constantly reminded that the question is who killed Taylor Henry, and exactly the same effect is obtained; an effect of movement, intrigue, cross-purposes and the gradual elucidation of character, which is all the detective story has any right to be about anyway. The rest is spillikins in the parlor.

But all this (and Hammett too) is for me not quite enough. The realist in murder writes of a world in which gangsters can rule nations and almost rule cities, in which hotels and apartment houses and celebrated restaurants are owned by men who made their money out of brothels, in which a screen star can be the fingerman for a mob, and the nice man down the hall is a boss of the numbers racket; a world where a judge with a cellar full of bootleg liquor can send a man to jail for having a pint in his pocket, where the mayor of your town may have condoned murder as an instrument of money-making, where no man can walk down a dark street in safety because law and order are things we talk about but refrain from practising; a world where you may witness a hold-up in broad daylight and see who did it, but you will fade quickly back into the crowd rather than tell anyone, because the hold-up men may have friends with long guns, or the police may not like your testimony, and in any case the shyster for the defense will be allowed to abuse and vilify you in open court, before a jury of selected morons, without any but the most perfunctory interference from a political judge.

It is not a very fragrant world, but it is the world you live in, and certain writers with tough minds and a cool spirit of detachment can make very interesting and even amusing patterns out of it. It is not funny that a man should be killed, but it is sometimes funny that he should be killed for so little, and that his death should be the coin of what we call civilization. All this still is not quite enough.

In everything that can be called art there is a quality of redemption. It may be pure tragedy, if it is high tragedy, and it may be pity and irony, and it may be the raucous laughter of the strong man. But down these mean streets a man must go who is not himself mean, who is neither tarnished nor afraid. The detective in this kind of story must be such a man. He is the hero, he is everything. He must be a complete man and a common man and yet an unusual man. He must be, to use a rather weathered phrase, a man of honor, by instinct, by inevitability, without thought of it, and certainly without saying it. He must be the best man in his world and a good enough man for any world. I do not care much about his private life; he is neither a eunuch nor a satyr; I think he might seduce a duchess and I am quite sure he would not spoil a virgin; if he is a man of honor in one thing, he is that in all things. He is a relatively poor man, or he would not be a detective at all. He is a common man or he could not go among common people. He has a sense of character, or he would not know his job. He will take no man's money dishonestly and no man's insolence without a due and dispassionate revenge. He is a lonely man and his pride is that you will treat him as a proud man or be very sorry you ever saw him. He talks as the man of his age talks, that is, with rude wit, a lively sense of the grotesque, a disgust for sham, and a contempt for pettiness. The story is his adventure in search of a hidden truth, and it would be no adventure if it did not happen to a man fit for adventure. He has a range of awareness that startles you, but it belongs to him by right, because it belongs to the world he lives in.

If there were enough like him, I think the world would be a very safe place to live in, and yet not too dull to be worth living in.

# Writers in Hollywood

HOLLYWOOD is easy to hate, easy to sneer at, easy to lampoon. Some of the best lampooning has been done by people who have never been through a studio gate, some of the best sneering by egocentric geniuses who departed huffily—not forgetting to collect their last pay check—leaving behind them nothing but the exquisite aroma of their personalities and a botched job for the tired hacks to clean up.

Even as far away as New York, where Hollywood assumes all really intelligent people live (since they obviously do not live in Hollywood), the disease of exaggeration can be caught. The motion picture critic of one of the less dazzled intellectual weeklies, commenting recently on a certain screenplay, remarked that it showed "how dull a couple of run-of-the-mill $3000-a-week writers can be." I hope this critic will not be startled to learn that 50 per cent of the screenwriters of Hollywood made less than $10,000 last year, and that he could count on his fingers the number that made a steady income anywhere near the figure he so contemptuously mentioned. I don't know whether they could be called run-of-the-mill writers or not. To me the phrase suggests something a little easier to get hold of.

I hold no brief for Hollywood. I have worked there a little over two years, which is far from enough to make me an authority, but more than enough to make me feel pretty thoroughly bored. That should not be so. An industry with such vast resources and such magic techniques should not become dull so soon. An art which is capable of making all but the very best plays look trivial and contrived, all but the very best novels verbose and imitative, should not so quickly become wearisome to those who attempt to practice it with something else in mind than the cash drawer. The making of a picture ought surely to be a rather fascinating adventure. It is not; it is an endless contention of tawdry egos, some of them powerful, almost all of them vociferous, and almost none of them capable of anything much more creative than credit-stealing and self-promotion.

Hollywood is a showman's paradise. But showmen make nothing; they exploit what someone else has made. The publisher and the play producer are showmen too; but they exploit what is already made. The showmen of Hollywood control the making—and thereby degrade it. For the basic art of motion pictures is the screenplay; it is fundamental, without it there is nothing. Everything derives from the screenplay, and most of that which derives is an applied skill which, however adept, is artistically not in the same class with the creation of a screenplay. But in Hollywood the screenplay is written by a salaried writer under the supervision of a producer—that is to say, by an employee without power or decision over the uses of his own craft, without ownership of it, and, however extravagantly paid, almost without honor for it.

I am aware that there are colorable economic reasons for the Hollywood system of "getting out the script." But I am not much interested in them. Pictures cost a great deal of money—true. The studio spends the money; all the writer spends is his time (and incidentally his life, his hopes, and all the varied experiences, most of them painful, which finally made him into a writer)—this also is true. The producer is charged with the salability and soundness of the project—true. The director can survive few failures; the writer can stink for ten years and still make his thousand a week—true also. But entirely beside the point.

I am not interested in why the Hollywood system exists or persists, nor in learning out of what bitter struggles for prestige it arose, nor in how much money it succeeds in making out of bad pictures. I am interested only in the fact that as a result of it there is no such thing as an art of the screenplay, and there never will be as long as the system lasts, for it is the essence of this system that it seeks to exploit a talent without permitting it the right to be a talent. It cannot be done; you can only destroy the talent, which is exactly what happens—when there is any to destroy.

Granted that there isn't much. Some chatty publisher (probably Bennett Cerf) remarked once that there are writers in Hollywood making two thousand dollars a week who haven't had an idea in ten years. He exaggerated—backwards: there are writers in Hollywood making two thousand a week who never had an idea in their lives, who have never written a photographable scene, who could not make two cents a word in the pulp market if their lives depended on it. Hollywood is full of such writers, although there are few at such high salaries. They are, to put it bluntly, a pretty dreary lot of hacks, and most of them know it, and they take their kicks and their salaries and try to be reasonably grateful to an industry which permits them to live much more opulently than they could live anywhere else.

And I have no doubt that most of them, also, would like to be much better writers than they are, would like to have force and integrity and imagination—enough of these to earn a decent living at some art of literature that has the dignity of a free profession. It will not happen to them, and there is not much reason why it should. If it ever could have happened, it will not happen now. For even the best of them (with a few rare exceptions) devote their entire time to work which has no more possibility of distinction than a Pekinese has of becoming a Great Dane: to asinine musicals about technicolor legs and the yowling of night-club singers; to "psychological" dramas with wooden plots, stock characters, and that persistent note of fuzzy earnestness which suggests the conversation of schoolgirls in puberty; to sprightly and sophisticated comedies (we hope) in which the gags are as stale as the attitudes, in which there is always a drink in every hand, a butler in every doorway, and a telephone on the edge of every bathtub; to historical epics in which the male actors look like female impersonators, and the lovely feminine star looks just a little too starry-eyed for a babe who has spent half her life swapping husbands; and last but not least, to those pictures of deep social import in which everybody is thoughtful and grown-up and sincere and the more difficult problems of life are wordily resolved into a unanimous vote of confidence in the inviolability of the Constitution, the sanctity of the home, and the paramount importance of the streamlined kitchen.

And these, dear readers, are the million-dollar babies—the cream of the crop. Most of the boys and girls who write for the screen never get anywhere near this far. They devote their sparkling lines and their structural finesse to horse operas, cheap gun-in-the-kidney melodramas, horror items about mad scientists and cliffhangers concerned with screaming blondes and circular saws. The writers of this tripe are licked before they start. Even in a purely technical sense their work is doomed for lack of the time to do it properly. The challenge of screenwriting is to say much in little and then take half of that little out and still preserve an effect of leisure and natural movement. Such a technique requires experiment and elimination. The cheap pictures simply cannot afford it.

2

Let me not imply that there are no writers of authentic ability in Hollywood. There are not many, but there are not many anywhere. The creative gift is a scarce commodity, and patience and imitation have always done most of its work. There is no reason to expect from the anonymous toilers of the screen a quality which we are very obviously not getting from the publicized litterateurs of the best-seller list, from the compilers of fourth-rate historical novels which sell half a million copies, from the Broadway candy butchers known as playwrights, or from the sulky maestri of the little magazines.

To me the interesting point about Hollywood's writers of talent is not how few or how many they are, but how little of worth their talent is allowed to achieve. Interesting—but hardly unexpected, once you accept the premise that writers are employed to write screenplays on the theory that, being writers, they have a particular gift and training for the job, and are then prevented from doing it with any independence or finality whatsoever, on the theory that, being merely writers, they know nothing about making pictures; and of course if they don't know how to make pictures, they couldn't possibly know how to write them. It takes a producer to tell them that.

I do not wish to become unduly vitriolic on the subject of producers. My own experience does not justify it, and after all, producers too are slaves of the system. Also, the term "producer" is of very vague definition. Some producers are powerful in their own right, and some are little more than legmen for the front office; some—few, I trust—receive less money than some of the writers who work for them. It is even said that in one large Hollywood studio there are producers who are lower than writers; not merely in earning power, but in prestige, importance, and aesthetic ability. It is, of course, a *very* large studio where all sorts of unexplained things could happen and hardly be noticed.

For my thesis the personal qualities of a producer are rather beside the point. Some are able and humane men and some are low-grade individuals with the morals of a goat, the artistic integrity of a slot machine, and the manners of a floorwalker with delusions of grandeur. In so far as the writing of the screenplay is concerned, however, the producer is the boss; the writer either gets along with him and his ideas (if he has any) or gets out. This means both personal and artistic subordination, and no writer of quality will long accept either without surrendering that which made him a writer of quality, without dulling the fine edge of his mind, without becoming little by little a conniver rather than a creator, a supple and facile journeyman rather than a craftsman of original thought.

It makes very little difference how a writer feels towards his producer as a man; the fact that the producer can change and destroy and disregard his work can only operate to diminish that work in its conception and to make it mechanical and indifferent in execution. The impulse to perfection cannot exist where the definition of perfection is the arbitrary decision of authority. That which is born in loneliness and from the heart cannot be defended against the judgment of a committee of sycophants. The volatile essences which make literature cannot survive the clichés of a long series of story conferences. There is little magic of word or emotion or situation which can remain alive after the incessant bone-scraping revisions imposed on the Hollywood writer by the process of rule by decree. That these magics do somehow, here and there, by another and even rarer magic, survive and reach the screen more or less intact is the infrequent miracle which keeps Hollywood's handful of fine writers from cutting their throats.

Hollywood has no right to expect such miracles, and it does not deserve the men who bring them to pass. Its conception of what makes a good picture is still as juvenile as its treatment of writing talent is insulting and degrading. Its idea of "production value" is spending a million dollars dressing up a story that any good writer would throw away. Its vision of the rewarding movie is a vehicle for some glamorpuss with two expressions and eighteen changes of costume, or for some male idol of the muddled millions with a permanent hangover, six worn-out acting tricks, the build of a lifeguard, and the mentality of a chicken-strangler. Pictures for such purposes as these, Hollywood lovingly and carefully makes. The good ones smack it in the rear when it isn't looking.

### 3

For all this too there are colorable economic reasons. The motion picture is a great industry as well as a defeated art. Its technicians are now in their third generation, its investments are world-wide, its demand for material is insatiable. Five hundred pictures a year must be made or the theaters will be dark, countless people will be thrown out of work, financial organizations will totter, and bankers will start jumping out of their office windows again. Hollywood does not possess enough real talent to make one tenth of five hundred pictures, even if it could find stories to base them on. But the rest must be made somehow, and they are made—with great effort and bitter struggle, with the hardening of many arteries and the graying of many hairs, and with the slow deadening of such real ability as could have been saved by happier tasks.

And the men who turn out this essentially dreary product are well paid by the standards of other industries. This reward is not, of course, due to any big-heartedness on the part of the financial big shots who control the working capital. The men with the money and the ultimate power can do anything they like with Hollywood—as long as they don't mind losing their investment. They can destroy any studio executive overnight, contract or no contract; any star, any producer, any director—as an individual. What they cannot destroy is the Hollywood system. It may be wasteful, absurd, even dishonest, but it is all there is, and no cold-blooded board of directors can replace it. It has been tried, but the showmen always win. They always win against mere money. What in the long run—the very long run—they can never defeat is talent, even writing talent.

It is, I am afraid, a *very* long run indeed. There is no present indication whatever that the Hollywood writer is on the point of acquiring any real control over his work, any right to choose what that work shall be (other than refusing jobs, which he can only do within narrow limits), or even any right to decide how the values in the producer-chosen work shall be brought out. There is no present guarantee that his best lines, best ideas, best scenes will not be changed or omitted on the set by the director or dropped on the floor during the later process of cutting—for the simple but essential reason that the best things in any picture, artistically speaking, are invariably the easiest to leave out, mechanically speaking.

There is no attempt in Hollywood to exploit the writer as an artist of meaning to the picture-buying public; there is every attempt to keep the public uninformed about his vital contribution to whatever art the movie contains. On the billboards, in the newspaper advertisements, his name will be smaller than that of the most insignificant bit-player who achieves what is known as billing; it will be the first to disappear as the size of the ad is cut down toward the middle of the week; it will be the last and least to be mentioned in any word-of-mouth or radio promotion.

The first picture I worked on was nominated for an Academy award (if that means anything), but I was not even invited to the press review held right in the studio. An extremely successful picture made by another studio from a story I wrote used verbatim lines out of the story in its promotional campaign, but my name was never mentioned once in any radio, magazine, billboard, or newspaper advertising that I saw or heard—and I saw and heard a great deal. This neglect is of no consequence to me personally; to any writer of books a Hollywood by-line is trivial. To those whose whole work is in Hollywood it is not trivial, because it is part of a deliberate and successful plan to reduce the professional screenwriter to the status of an assistant picture-maker, superficially deferred to (while he is in the room), essentially ignored, and even in his most brilliant achievements carefully pushed out of the way of any possible accolade which might otherwise fall to the star, the producer, the director.

## 4

If all this is true, why then should any writer of genuine ability continue to work in Hollywood at all? The obvious reason is not enough: few screenwriters possess homes in Bel-Air, illuminated swimming pools, wives in full-length mink coats, three servants, and that air of tired genius gone a little sour. Money buys pathetically little in Hollywood beyond the pleasure of living in an unreal world, associating with a narrow group of people who think, talk, and drink nothing but pictures, most of them bad, and the doubtful pleasure of watching famous actors and actresses guzzle in some of the rudest restaurants in the world.

I do not mean that Hollywood society is any duller or more dissipated than moneyed society anywhere: God knows it couldn't be. But it is a pretty thin reward for a lifetime devoted to the essential craft of what might be a great art. I suppose the truth is that the veterans of the Hollywood scene do not realize how little they are getting, how many dull egotists they have to smile at, how many shoddy people they have to treat as friends, how little real accomplishment is possible, how much gaudy trash their life contains. The superficial friendliness of Hollywood is pleasant—until you find out that nearly every sleeve conceals a knife. The companionship during working hours with men and women who take the business of fiction seriously gives a pale heat to the writer's lonely soul. It is so easy to forget that there is a world in which men buy their own groceries and, if they choose, think their own thoughts. In Hollywood you don't even write your own checks—and what you think is what you hope some producer or studio executive will like.

Beyond this I suppose there is hope; there are several hopes. The cold dynasty will not last forever, the dictatorial producer is already a little unsure, the top-heavy director has long since become a joke in his own studio; after a while even technicolor will not save him. There is hope that a decayed and make-shift system will pass, that somehow the flatulent moguls will learn that only writers can write screenplays and only proud and independent writers can write good screen-plays, and that present methods of dealing with such men are destructive of the very force by which pictures must live.

And there is the intense and beautiful hope that the Holly-wood writers themselves—such of them as are capable of it—will recognize that writing for the screen is no job for amateurs and half-writers whose problems are always solved by somebody else. It is the writers' own weakness as crafts-men that permits the superior egos to bleed them white of initiative, imagination, and integrity. If even a quarter of the *highly paid* screenwriters in Hollywood could produce a com-pletely integrated and photographable screenplay under their own power, with only the amount of interference and discus-sion necessary to protect the studio's investment in actors and ensure a reasonable freedom from libel and censorship troubles, then the producer would assume his proper function of coördinating and conciliating the various crafts which com-bine to make a picture; and the director—heaven help his strutting soul—would be reduced to the ignominious task of making pictures as they are conceived and written—and not as the director would try to write them, if only he knew how to write.

Certainly there are producers and directors—although how pitifully few—who are sincere enough to want such a change, and talented enough to have no fear of its effect on their own position. Yet it is only a little over three years since the major (and only this very year the minor) studios were forced, after prolonged and bitter struggle, to agree to treat the writers according to some reasonable standard of business ethics. In this struggle the writers were not really fighting the motion picture industry at all; they were only fighting certain power-ful elements in it—employees like themselves—who had hitherto glommed off all the glory and prestige and most of the money, and could only continue to do so by selling them-selves to the world as the true makers of pictures.

This struggle is still going on; in a sense it will always go on, in a sense it always *should* go on. But so far the cards are stacked against the writer. If there is no art of the screenplay, the reason is at least partly that there exists no available body of technical theory and practice by which it can be learned. There is no available library of screenplay literature, because the screenplays belong to the studios, and they will only show them within their guarded walls. There is no body of critical opinion, because there are no critics of the screenplay; there are only critics of motion pictures as entertainment, and most of these critics know nothing whatever of the means whereby the motion picture is created and put on celluloid. There is no teaching, because there is no one to teach. If you do not know how pictures are made, you cannot speak with any authority on how they should be constructed; if you do, you are busy enough trying to do it.

There is no correlation of crafts within the studio itself; the average—and far better than average—screenwriter knows hardly anything of the technical problems of the director, and nothing at all of the superlative skill of the trained cutter. He spends his effort in writing shots that cannot be made, or which if made would be thrown away; in writing dialogue that cannot be spoken, sound effects that cannot be heard, and nuances of mood and emotion which the camera cannot reproduce. His idea of an effective scene is something that has to be shot down a stair well or out of a gopher hole; or a conversation so static that the director, in order to impart a sense of motion to it, is compelled to photograph it from nine different angles.

In fact, no part of the vast body of technical knowledge which Hollywood contains is systematically and as a matter of course made available to the new writer in a studio. They tell him to look at pictures—which is to learn architecture by staring at a house. And then they send him back to his rabbit hutch to write little scenes which his producer, in between telephone calls to his blondes and his booze-companions, will tell him ought to have been written quite differently. The producer is probably correct; the scene ought to have been written differently. It ought to have been written right. But first it had to be written. The producer didn't do that. He wouldn't know how. Anyway he's too busy. And he's making too much money. And the atmosphere of intellectual squalor in which the salaried writer operates would offend his dignity.

I have kept the best hope of all for the last. In spite of all I have said, the writers of Hollywood *are* winning their battle for prestige. More and more of them are becoming showmen in their own right, producers and directors of their own screenplays. Let us be glad for their additional importance and power, and not examine the artistic result too critically. The boys make good (and some of them might even make good pictures). Let us rejoice together, for the tendency to become showmen is well in the acceptable tradition of the literary art as practiced among the cameras.

For the very nicest thing Hollywood can possibly think of to say to a writer is that he is too good to be only a writer.

# Twelve Notes on the Mystery Story

I. IT MUST be credibly motivated, both as to the original situation and the denouement; it must consist of the plausible actions of plausible people in plausible circumstances, it being remembered that plausibility is largely a matter of style. This requirement rules out most trick endings and a great many "closed circle" stories in which the least likely character is forcibly made over into the criminal, without convincing anybody. It also rules out such elaborate mises-en-scène as Christie's *Murder in a Calais Coach*, where the whole setup for the crime requires such a fluky set of happenings that it could never seem real.

2. It must be technically sound as to the methods of murder and detection. No fantastic poisons or improper effects from poison such as death from nonfatal doses, etc. No use of silencers on revolvers (they won't work) or snakes climbing bellropes ("The Speckled Band"). Such things at once destroy the foundation of the story. If the detective is a trained policeman, he must act like one, and have the mental and physical equipment that go with the job. If he is a private investigator or amateur, he must at least know enough about police methods not to make an ass of himself. When a policeman is made out to be a fool, as he always was in the Sherlock Holmes stories, this not only deprecates the accomplishment of the detective but it makes the reader doubt the author's knowledge of his own field. Conan Doyle and Poe were primitives in this art and stand in relation to the best modern writers as Giotto does to da Vinci. They did things which are no longer permissible and exposed ignorances that are no longer tolerated. Also, police art, itself, was rudimentary in their time. "The Purloined Letter" would not fool a modern cop for four minutes. Conan Doyle showed no knowledge whatever of the organization of Scotland Yard's men. Christie commits the same stupidities in our time, but that doesn't make them right. Contrast Austin Freeman, who wrote a story about a forged fingerprint ten years before police method realized such things could be done.

3. It must be honest with the reader. This is always said, but the implications are not realized. Important facts not only must not be concealed, they must not be distorted by false emphasis. Unimportant facts must not be projected in such a way as to make them portentous. (This creation of red herrings and false menace out of trick camera work and mood shots is the typical Hollywood mystery picture cheat.) Inferences from the facts are the detective's stock in trade; but he should disclose enough to keep the reader's mind working. It is arguable, although not certain, that inferences arising from special knowledge (e.g., Dr. Thorndyke) are a bit of a cheat, because the basic theory of all good mystery writing is that at some stage not too late in the story the reader did have the materials to solve the problem. If special scientific knowledge was necessary to interpret the facts, the reader did not have the solution unless he had the special knowledge. It may have been Austin Freeman's feeling about this that led him to the invention of the inverted detective story, in which the reader knows the solution from the beginning and takes his pleasure from watching the detective trace it out a step at a time.

4. It must be realistic as to character, setting, and atmosphere. It must be about real people in a real world. Very few mystery writers have any talent for character work, but that doesn't mean it is not necessary. It makes the difference between the story you reread and remember and the one you skim through and almost instantly forget. Those like Valentine Williams who say the problem overrides everything are merely trying to cover up their own inability to create character.

5. It must have a sound story value apart from the mystery element; i.e., the investigation itself must be an adventure worth reading.

6. To achieve this it must have some form of suspense, even if only intellectual. This does not mean menace and especially it does not mean that the detective must be menaced by grave personal danger. This last is a trend and like all trends will exhaust itself by overimitation. Nor need the reader be kept hanging onto the edge of his chair. The overplotted story can be dull too; too much shock may result in numbness to shock. But there must be conflict, physical, ethical or emotional, and

there must be some element of danger in the broadest sense of the word.

7. It must have color, lift, and a reasonable amount of dash. It takes an awful lot of technical adroitness to compensate for a dull style, although it has been done, especially in England.

8. It must have enough essential simplicity to be explained easily when the time comes. (This is possibly the most often violated of all the rules). The ideal denouement is one in which everything is revealed in a flash of action. This is rare because ideas that good are always rare. The explanation need not be very short (except on the screen), and often it cannot be short; but it must be interesting in itself, it must be something the reader is anxious to hear, and not a new story with a new set of characters, dragged in to justify an overcomplicated plot. Above all the explanation must not be merely a long-winded assembling of minute circumstances which no ordinary reader could possibly be expected to remember. To make the solution dependent on this is a kind of unfairness, since here again the reader did not have the solution within his grasp, in any practical sense. To expect him to remember a thousand trivialities and from them to select that three that are decisive is as unfair as to expect him to have a profound knowledge of chemistry, metallurgy, or the mating habits of the Patagonian anteater.

9. It must baffle a reasonably intelligent reader. This opens up a very difficult question. Some of the best detective stories ever written (those of Austin Freeman, for example) seldom baffle an intelligent reader to the end. But the reader does not guess the *complete solution* and could not himself have made a logical demonstration of it. Since readers are of many minds, some will guess a cleverly hidden murder and some will be fooled by the most transparent plot. (Could "The Red-Headed League" ever really fool a modern reader?) It is not necessary or even possible to fool to the hilt the real aficionado of mystery fiction. A mystery story that consistently did that and was honest would be unintelligible to the average fan; he simply would not know what the story was all about. But there must be some important elements of the story that elude the most penetrating reader.

10. The solution must seem inevitable once revealed. This is the least often emphasized element of a good mystery, but it is one of the important elements of all fiction. It is not enough merely to fool or elude or sidestep the reader; you must make him feel that he ought not to have been fooled and that the fooling was honorable.

11. It must not try to do everything at once. If it is a puzzle story operating in a rather cool, reasonable atmosphere, it cannot also be a violent adventure or a passionate romance. An atmosphere of terror destroys logical thinking; if the story is about the intricate psychological pressures that lead apparently ordinary people to commit murder, it cannot then switch to the cool analysis of the police investigator. The detective cannot be hero and menace at the same time; the murderer cannot be a tormented victim of circumstance and also a heavy.

12. It must punish the criminal in one way or another, not necessarily by operation of the law. Contrary to popular (and Johnston Office) belief, this requirement has nothing much to do with morality. It is a part of the logic of detection. If the detective fails to resolve the consequences of the crime, the story is an unresolved chord and leaves irritation behind it.

## Addenda

1. The perfect detective story cannot be written. The type of mind which can evolve the perfect problem is not the type of mind that can produce the artistic job of writing. It would be nice to have Dashiell Hammett and Austin Freeman in the same book, but it just isn't possible. Hammett couldn't have the plodding patience and Freeman couldn't have the verve for narrative. They don't go together. Even a fair compromise such as Dorothy Sayers is less satisfying than the two types taken separately.

2. The most effective way to conceal a simple mystery is behind another mystery. This is literary legerdemain. You do not fool the reader by hiding clues or faking character à la Christie but by making him solve the wrong problem.

3. It has been said that "nobody cares about the corpse."

This is bunk. It is throwing away a valuable element. It is like saying the murder of your aunt means no more to you than the murder of an unknown man in an unknown part of a city you never visited.

4. Flip dialogue is not wit.

5. A mystery serial does not make a good mystery novel. The "curtains" depend for their effect on your not having the next chapter to read at once. In book form these curtains give the effect of a false suspense and tend to be merely irritating. The magazines have begun to find that out.

6. Love interest nearly always weakens a mystery story because it creates a type of suspense that is antagonistic and not complementary to the detective's struggle to solve the problem. The kind of love interest that works is the one that complicates the problem by adding to the detective's troubles but which at the same time you instinctively feel will not survive the story. A really good detective never gets married. He would lose his detachment, and this detachment is part of his charm.

7. The fact that love interest is played up in the big magazines and on the screen doesn't make it artistic. Women are supposed to be the targets of magazine fiction and movies. The magazines are not interested in mystery writing as an art. They are not interested in any kind of writing as an art.

8. The hero of the mystery story is the detective. Everything hangs on his personality. If he hasn't one, you have very little. And you have *very few* really good mystery stories. Naturally.

9. The criminal cannot be the detective. This is an old rule and has once in a while been violated successfully, but it is sound as it ever was. For this reason: the detective by tradition and definition is the seeker after truth. He can't be that if he already knows the truth. There is an implied guarantee to the reader that the detective is on the level.

10. The same remark applies to the story where the first-person narrator is the criminal. I should personally have to qualify this by saying that for me the first-person narration can always be accused of subtle dishonesty because of its appearance of candor and its ability to suppress the detective's ratiocination while giving a clear account of his words and

acts. Which opens up the much larger question of what honesty really is in this context; is it not a matter of degree rather than an absolute? I think it is and always will be. Regardless of the candor of the first-person narrative there comes a time when the detective has made up his mind and yet does not communicate this to the reader. He holds some of his thinking out for the denouement or explanation. He tells the facts but not the reaction in his mind to those facts. Is this a permissible convention of deceit? It must be; otherwise the detective telling his own story could not have solved the problem in advance of the technical denouement. Once in a lifetime a story such as *The Big Sleep* holds almost nothing back; the denouement is an action which the reader meets as soon as the detective. The theorizing from that action follows immediately. There is only a momentary concealment of the fact that Marlowe loaded the gun with blanks when he gave it to Carmen down by the oil sump. But even this is tipped off to the reader when he says, "If she missed the can, which she was certain to do, she would probably hit the wheel. That would stop a small slug completely. However she wasn't going to hit even that." He doesn't say why, but the action follows so quickly that you don't feel any real concealment.

11. The murderer must not be a loony. The murderer is not a murderer unless he commits murder in the legal sense.

12. There is, as has been said, no real possibility of absolute perfection in writing a mystery story. Why? For two main reasons, one of which has been stated above in Addenda Note 1. The second is the attitude of the reader himself. Readers are of too many kinds and too many levels of culture. The puzzle addict, for instance, regards the story as a contest of wits between himself and the writer; if he guesses the solution, he has won, even though he could not document his guess or justify it by solid reasoning. There is something of this competitive spirit in all readers, but the reader in whom it predominates sees no value beyond the game of guessing the solution. There is the reader, again, whose whole interest is in sensation, sadism, cruelty, blood, and the element of death. Again there is some in all of us, but the reader in whom it predominates will care nothing for the so-called deductive story, however meticulous. A third class of reader is the worrier-about-the-

characters; this reader doesn't care so much about the solution; what really gets her upset is the chance that the silly little heroine will get her neck twisted on the spiral staircase. Fourth, and most important, there is the intellectual literate reader who reads mysteries because they are almost the only kind of fiction that does not get too big for its boots. This reader savors style, characterization, plot twists, all the virtuosities of the writing much more than he bothers about the solution. You cannot satisfy all these readers completely. To do so involves contradictory elements. I, in the role of reader, almost never try to guess the solution to a mystery. I simply don't regard the contest between the writer and myself as important. To be frank I regard it as the amusement of an inferior type of mind.

13. As has been suggested above, all fiction depends on some form of suspense. But the study of the mechanics of that extreme type called menace reveals the curious psychological duality of the mind of a reader or audience which makes it possible on the one hand to be terrified about what is hiding behind the door and at the same time to know that the heroine or leading lady is not going to be murdered once she is established as the heroine or leading lady. If the character played by Claudette Colbert is in awful danger, we also know absolutely that Miss Colbert is not going to be hurt for the simple reason that she is Miss Colbert. How does the audience's mind get upset by menace in view of this clear knowledge? Of the many possible reasons I suggest two. The intelligence and the emotions function on different levels. The emotional reaction to visual images and sounds, or their evocation in descriptive writing, is independent of reasonableness. The primitive element of fear is never far from the surface of our thoughts; anything that calls to it can defeat reason for the time being. Hence menace makes its appeal to a very ancient and very irrational emotion. Few men are beyond its influence. The other reason I suggest is that in any intense kind of literary or other projection the part is greater than the whole. The scene before the eyes dominates the thought of the audience; the normal individual makes no attempt to reconcile it with the pattern of the story. He is swayed by what is in the actual scene. When you have finished

the book, it may, not necessarily will, fall into focus as a whole and be remembered by its merit so considered; but for the time of reading, the chapter is the dominating factor. The vision of the emotional imagination is very short but also very intense.

# Notes (very brief, please) on English and American Style

---

THE MERITS of American style are less numerous than its defects and annoyances, but they are more powerful.

It is a fluid language, like Shakespearean English, and easily takes in new words, new meanings for old words, and borrows at will and at ease from the usages of other languages, for example, the German free compounding of words and the use of noun or adjective as verb; the French simplification of grammar, the use of one, he, etc.

Its overtones and undertones are not stylized into a social conventional kind of subtlety which is in effect a class language. If they exist at all, they have a real impact.

It is more alive to clichés. Consider the appalling, because apparently unconscious, use of clichés by as good a writer as Maugham in *The Summing Up*, the deadly repetition of pet words until they almost make you scream. And the pet words are always little half-archaic words like *jejune* and *umbrage* and *vouchsafe*, none of which the average educated person could even define correctly.

Its impact is sensational rather than intellectual. It expresses things experienced rather than ideas.

It is a mass language only in the same sense that its baseball slang is born of baseball players. That is, it is a language which is being molded by writers to do delicate things and yet be within the grasp of superficially educated people. It is not a natural growth, much as its proletarian writers would like to think so. But compared with it at its best, English has reached the Alexandrian stage of formalism and decay.

## It has Disadvantages.

It overworks its catchphrases until they not merely become meaningless playtalk, like English catchphrases, but sickening, like overworked popular songs.

Its slang, being invented by writers and palmed off on simple hoodlums and ballplayers, often has a phony sound, even when fresh.

The language has no awareness of the continuing stream of culture. This may or may not be due to the collapse of classical education and it may or may not happen also in English. It is certainly due to a lack of the historical sense and to shoddy education, because American is an ill-at-ease language, without manner or self-control.

It has too great a fondness for the *faux naïf*, by which I mean the use of a style such as might be spoken by a very limited sort of mind. In the hands of a genius like Hemingway this may be effective, but only by subtly evading the terms of the contract, that is, by an artistic use of the telling detail which the speaker never would have noted. When not used by a genius it is as flat as a Rotarian speech.

The last noted item is very probably the result of the submerged but still very strong homespun revolt against English cultural superiority. "We're just as good as they are, even if we don't talk good grammar." This attitude is based on complete ignorance of the English people as a mass. Very few of them talk good grammar. Those that do probably speak more correctly than the same type of American, but the homespun Englishman uses as much bad grammar as the American, some of it being as old as *Piers Ploughman*, but still bad grammar. But you don't hear English professional men making elementary mistakes in the use of their own language. You do hear that constantly in America. Of course anyone who likes can put up an argument against any other person's ideas of correctness. Naturally this is historical up to a point and contemporary up to a point. There must be some compromise, or we should all be Alexandrians or boors. But roughly and ordinarily and plainly speaking, you hear American doctors and lawyers and schoolmasters talking in such a way that it is very clear they have no real understanding of their own language and its good or bad form. I'm not referring to the deliberate use of slang and colloquialisms; I'm referring to the pathetic attempts of such people to speak with unwonted correctness and horribly failing.

You don't hear this sort of collapse of grammar in England among the same kind of people.

It's fairly obvious that American education is a cultural flop. Americans are not a well-educated people culturally, and their vocational education often has to be learned all over again after they leave school and college. On the other hand they have open quick minds and if their education has little sharp positive value, it has not the stultifying effects of a more rigid training. Such tradition as they have in the use of their language is derived from English tradition, and there is just enough resentment about this to cause perverse use of ungrammaticalities—"just to show 'em."

Americans, having the most complex civilization the world has seen, still like to think of themselves as plain people. In other words they like to think the comic-strip artist is a better draftsman than Leonardo—just because he is a comic-strip artist and the comic strip is for plain people.

American style has no cadence. Without cadence a style has no harmonics. It is like a flute playing solo, an incomplete thing, very dexterous or very stupid as the case may be, but still an incomplete thing.

Since political power still dominates culture, American will dominate English for a long time to come. English, being on the defensive, is static and cannot contribute anything but a sort of waspish criticism of forms and manners. America is a land of mass production which has only just reached the concept of quality. Its style is utilitarian and essentially vulgar. Why then can it produce great writing or, at any rate, writing as great as this age is likely to produce? The answer is, it can't. All the best American writing has been done by men who are, or at some time were, cosmopolitans. They found here a certain freedom of expression, a certain richness of vocabulary, a certain wideness of interest. But they had to have European taste to use the material.

Final note—out of order— The tone quality of English speech is usually overlooked. This tone quality is infinitely variable and contributes infinite meaning. The American voice is flat, toneless, and tiresome. The English tone quality makes a thinner vocabulary and a more formalized use of language capable of infinite meanings. Its tones are of course read into written speech by association. This makes good English a class language, and that is its fatal defect. The English writer is a gentleman (or not a gentleman) first and a writer second.

# Introduction to "The Simple Art of Murder"

S OME literary antiquarian of a rather special type may one day think it worth while to run through the files of the pulp detective magazines which flourished during the late twenties and early thirties, and determine just how and when and by what steps the popular mystery story shed its refined good manners and went native. He will need sharp eyes and an open mind. Pulp paper never dreamed of posterity and most of it must be a dirty brown color by now. And it takes a very open mind indeed to look beyond the unnecessarily gaudy covers, trashy titles and barely acceptable advertisements and recognize the authentic power of a kind of writing that, even at its most mannered and artificial, made most of the fiction of the time taste like a cup of luke-warm consommé at a spinsterish tearoom.

I don't think this power was entirely a matter of violence, although far too many people got killed in these stories and their passing was celebrated with a rather too loving attention to detail. It certainly was not a matter of fine writing, since any attempt at that would have been ruthlessly blue-penciled by the editorial staff. Nor was it because of any great originality of plot or character. Most of the plots were rather ordinary and most of the characters rather primitive types of people. Possibly it was the smell of fear which these stories managed to generate. Their characters lived in a world gone wrong, a world in which, long before the atom bomb, civilization had created the machinery for its own destruction, and was learning to use it with all the moronic delight of a gangster trying out his first machine gun. The law was something to be manipulated for profit and power. The streets were dark with something more than night. The mystery story grew hard and cynical about motive and character, but it was not cynical about the effects it tried to produce nor about its technique of producing them. A few unusual critics recognized this at the time, which was all one had any right to expect. The average critic never recognizes an achievement when it happens. He explains it after it has become respectable.

The emotional basis of the standard detective story was and had always been that murder will out and justice will be done. Its technical basis was the relative insignificance of everything except the final denouement. What led up to that was more or less passage-work. The denouement would justify everything. The technical basis of the *Black Mask* type of story on the other hand was that the scene outranked the plot, in the sense that a good plot was one which made good scenes. The ideal mystery was one you would read if the end was missing. We who tried to write it had the same point of view as the film makers. When I first went to work in Hollywood a very intelligent producer told me that you couldn't make a successful motion picture from a mystery story, because the whole point was a disclosure that took a few seconds of screen time while the audience was reaching for its hat. He was wrong, but only because he was thinking of the wrong kind of mystery.

As to the emotional basis of the hard-boiled story, obviously it does not believe that murder will out and justice will be done—unless some very determined individual makes it his business to see that justice is done. The stories were about the men who made that happen. They were apt to be hard men, and what they did, whether they were called police officers, private detectives or newspaper men, was hard, dangerous work. It was work they could always get. There was plenty of it lying around. There still is. Undoubtedly the stories about them had a fantastic element. Such things happened, but not so rapidly, nor to so close-knit a group of people, nor within so narrow a frame of logic. This was inevitable because the demand was for constant action; if you stopped to think you were lost. When in doubt have a man come through a door with a gun in his hand. This could get to be pretty silly, but somehow it didn't seem to matter. A writer who is afraid to overreach himself is as useless as a general who is afraid to be wrong.

As I look back on my own stories it would be absurd if I did not wish they had been better. But if they had been much better they would not have been published. If the formula had been a little less rigid, more of the writing of that time might have survived. Some of us tried pretty hard to break out of the formula, but we usually got caught and sent back. To exceed the limits of a formula without destroying it is the dream of every magazine writer who is not a hopeless hack. There are things in my stories which I might like to change or leave out altogether. To do this may look simple, but if you try, you find you cannot do it at all. You will only destroy what is good without having any noticeable effect on what is bad. You cannot recapture the mood, the state of innocence, much less the animal gusto you had when you had very little else. Everything a writer learns about the art or craft of fiction takes just a little away from his need or desire to write at all. In the end he knows all the tricks and has nothing to say.

As for the literary quality of these exhibits, I am entitled to assume from the imprint of a distinguished publisher that I need not be sickeningly humble. As a writer I have never been able to take myself with that enormous earnestness which is one of the trying characteristics of the craft. And I have been fortunate to escape what has been called "that form of snobbery which can accept the Literature of Entertainment in the Past, but only the Literature of Enlightenment in the Present." Between the one-syllable humors of the comic strip and the anemic subtleties of the litterateurs there is a wide stretch of country, in which the mystery story may or may not be an important landmark. There are those who hate it in all its forms. There are those who like it when it is about nice people ("that charming Mrs. Jones, whoever would have thought she would cut off her husband's head with a meat saw? Such a handsome man, too!"). There are those who think violence and sadism interchangeable terms, and those who regard detective fiction as sub-literary on no better grounds than that it does not habitually get itself jammed up with subordinate clauses, tricky punctuation and hypothetical subjunctives. There are those who read it only when they are tired or sick, and, from the number of mystery novels they consume, they must be tired and sick most of the time. There are the aficionados of deduction (with whom I have had words, see pp. 977–992) and the aficionados of sex who can't get it into their hot little heads that the fictional detective is a catalyst, not a Casanova. The former demand a ground plan of Greythorpe Manor, showing the study, the gun room, the main hall and staircase and the passage to that grim little room where the butler polishes the Georgian silver, thin-lipped and silent, hearing the murmur of doom. The latter think the shortest distance between two points is from a blonde to a bed.

No writer can please them all, no writer should try. The stories in this book certainly had no thought of being able to please anyone ten or fifteen years after they were written. The mystery story is a kind of writing that need not dwell in the shadow of the past and owes little if any allegiance to the cult of the classics. It is a good deal more than unlikely that any writer now living will produce a better historical novel than *Henry Esmond*, a better tale of children than *The Golden Age*, a sharper social vignette than *Madame Bovary*, a more graceful and elegant evocation than *The Spoils of Poynton*, a wider and richer canvas than *War and Peace* or *The Brothers Karamazov*. But to devise a more plausible mystery than *The Hound of the Baskervilles* or *The Purloined Letter* should not be too difficult. Nowadays it would be rather more difficult not to. There are no "classics" of crime and detection. Not one. Within its frame of reference, which is the only way it should be judged, a classic is a piece of writing which exhausts the possibilities of its form and can hardly be surpassed. No story or novel of mystery has done that yet. Few have come close. Which is one of the principal reasons why otherwise reasonable people continue to assault the citadel.

La Jolla, California
February 15, 1950

# SELECTED LETTERS

## To Dale Warren

January 7th. 1945

Dear Warren:

I finally unearthed your kind letter from a tangled mass of correspondence dating back to the Civil War, spurred on by your letter in the *Atlantic* about my little tirade. Do not think I have not meant to write to you. My wife regards you as a somewhat rare bird, since you wrote to me twice without mentioning the fact that you were connected with a publishing firm. The *Atlantic* article has got me into a lot of trouble. Mr. P. Marlowe, a simple alcoholic vulgarian who never sleeps with his clients while on duty, is trying to go refined on me. "What the hell," he says, "do you mean by keeping me in the basement all this time. Here you are unmasked as a guy who can write English — after a fashion — so get busy and write some about me." I can imagine the result. I suppose, if I write another article in the *Atlantic*, if there is one, he will demand spats and a monocle and start collecting old pewter.

There are certain acute disadvantages in attracting attention, even the small amount that has come my way. People start telling you how you do things and then you start trying to do them that way. All I wanted when I began was to play with a fascinating new language, and trying, without anybody noticing it, to see what it would do as a means of expression which might remain on the level of unintellectual thinking and yet acquire the power to say things which are usually only said with a literary air. I didn't really care a hell of a lot what kind of story I wrote; I wrote melodrama because when I looked around me it was the only kind of writing I saw that was relatively honest and yet was not trying to put over somebody's party line. So now there are guys talking about prose and other guys telling me I have a social conscience. P. Marlowe has as much social conscience as a horse. He has a personal conscience, which is an entirely different matter. There are people who think I dwell on the ugly side of life. God help them! If they had any idea how little I have told them about it! P. Marlowe doesn't give a damn who is president; neither do I, because I know he will be a politician. There was even a bird who informed me I could write a good proletarian novel; in my limited world there is no such animal, and if there were, I am the last mind in the world to like it, being by tradition and long study a complete snob. P. Marlowe and I do not despise the upper classes because they take baths and have money; we despise them because they are phoney. And so on. And now I see ahead of me either an acute self-consciousness about simple things which I never had any idea of explaining, or a need to explain them at length, and with fury, in the very lingo I had been trying to forget. Because that is the only lingo people who can understand explanations of the sort will accept them in.

I have a note from a friend of yours, Mary Lasswell. Have to answer it, but have never read anything she wrote, which makes it embarrassing. I also have a letter from a lady in Caracas, Venezuela, who asks me if I would like to be her friend when she comes to New York. It has a faint suggestion about it of another letter I had once from a girl in Seattle who said that she was interested in music and sex, and gave me the impression that, if I was pressed for time, I need not even bother to bring my own pajamas. She probably had spots.

RAYMOND CHANDLER

"IT DOESN'T MATTER A DAMN WHAT
A NOVEL IS ABOUT"

## To Charles Morton

6520 Drexel Ave.
Los Angeles 36, Calif.
Dec. 12th. 1945

Dear Charles:

I've owed you a letter for so damn long that I suppose you wonder whether I am still alive. So do I, at times. Before I delve into your two letters to see if there are any questions you wanted replies to, let me report that my blast at Hollywood was received here in frozen silence. I don't think any local paper or trade-paper even mentioned it (but can't be sure); Irving Hoffman did in his column, briefly, but he doesn't function here, although his stuff appears in the *Hollywood Reporter*. In view of the subject matter, and quite regardless of the reputation of the writer, and in view of the *Atlantic*, it seems to me reasonable to think there was a suppression of the subject by request of the studio publicity heads. I could be wrong, but that is what I'm inclined to think. In various roundabout ways I heard that the piece was not received with favor. My agent was told by the Paramount story editor that it had done me a lot of harm with the producers at Paramount. Charlie Brackett, that fading wit, said: "Chandler's books are not good enough, nor his pictures bad enough, to justify that article." I wasted a little time trying to figure out what that meant. It seems to mean that the only guy who can speak his mind about Hollywood is either (a) a failure in Hollywood, or (b) a celebrity somewhere else. I would reply to Mr. Brackett that if my books had been any worse, I should not have been invited to Hollywood, and that if they had been any better, I should not have come. Of course, as you and I know, the only kind of man qualified to deal with Hollywood in any such drastic fashion is one who has enough reputation to get a hearing, has not been in Hollywood long enough to lose his sense of proportion, but has been there long enough and has accomplished enough there so that it could not be said of him he was merely knocking a racket he couldn't lick.

I noticed that (unlike the *Post*) you did not open my fan mail. Too bad you didn't raise the point so that you could have. There wasn't much, but there was a very charming letter from Beirne Lay and also one from Studs Lonigan which I have still to answer. He thinks I didn't go far enough, that I should have coordinated Hollywood with the social problems of the time. That's the worst of these deep thinkers. They can't let you speak your piece, then put your hat on and go home. Everything to them is just a chapter in the unfolding of the human struggle for decent expression, or like another volume from Jules Romains. Of course they're right in a way, more right than Wolcott Gibbs, for example, who seems to take the view, intellectually unsound, that an art which is practised badly is simply a bad art (I wonder if he ever read *Clarissa Harlowe*) and the view, socially and factually unsound, that a man is of necessity more intelligent than his cook. I liked his piece because I like the way he says things; I like but do not crave to practise the somewhat arctic style of the *New Yorker*. It has made *New Yorker* writers out of too many people who might have been their own writers. But I should somehow like to ask Wolcott whether he really believes the medium which has produced *The Last Laugh*, *Variety*, *M.*, *Mayerling*, *Night Must Fall*, *Intolerance*, *The Little Foxes* (screen version), *The More the Merrier*, etc. etc. is really inferior to the medium which has produced *Dear Ruth*, *The Voice of the Turtle*, *Mrs. Tanqueray's Past*, *The Lion and the Mouse*, *Oklahoma*, *Dear Brutus*, *Getting Married*, etc. etc. And if he agrees that it is not, I should further like to ask him whether criticism has any function whatsoever in the development and self-education of an art; because if it has, all he is really saying is that he does not want to review pictures because they are bad and bore him, whereas he does want to review plays because they are good and do not bore him. That may be his privilege, but it is certainly not a critical opinion.

In case you are still planning to use this article in your anthology, I should like, if there is time, to point out a few errors. They are not very important, but we might as well get the thing right. Whom do I address? Some of them are probably actual typographical errors of a sort. There is one I should like to mention, because it is the kind of thing I never can understand. It is the 9th. line from the end of the piece. It reads: "and not examine the artistic result too critically. The." What I wrote was; "and not too critically examine the artistic result." I believe, but am not certain, that it was this last way in the original proofs, perhaps not in the revised proof. It is obvious that somebody, for no reason save that he thought he was improving the style, changed the order of the words. The length is the same, therefore that could not enter into it. I confess myself completely flabbergasted by the literary attitude this expresses. Because it is the attitude that gets me, the assumption on the part of some editorial hireling that he can write better than the man who sent the stuff in, that he knows more about phrase and cadence and the placing of words, and that he actually thinks that a clause with a strong (stressed) syllable at the end, which was put there because it was strong, is improved by changing the order so that the clause ends in a weak adverbial termination. I don't mind the guy being wrong about this. That's nothing. It could even, within limits, be a matter of opinion, although I do not agree. But here is somebody who apparently decided in his own mind that Chandler was using a rhetorical word order, which he was, and that he didn't know what the hell he was doing, didn't even know he was being rhetorical, and that he, Joe Doakes with the fat red pencil, is the boy to show him how wrong he is, by changing it back to the way the editor of the Weehawken County Gazeteer would have written it in his weekly editorial about the use of steel floss to clean chicken dirt off Grade AA eggs. Christ!

While still coughing hysterically into my kidney basin I thank you for your kind remarks from the wife of the Harvard Nieman Fellow, and I am still a bit dizzy from some remarks your pal Dale Warren made about *The Maltese Falcon*, which he apparently regards as quite inferior to *The Leavenworth Case* (Read it for laughs, if you haven't). I reread the *Falcon* not long ago, and I give up. Somebody in this room has lost a straitjacket. It must be me. Frankly, I can conceive of better writing than the *Falcon*, and a more tender and warm attitude to life, and a more flowery ending; but by God, if you can show me twenty books written approximately 20 years back that have as much guts and life now, I'll eat them between slices of Edmund Wilson's head. Really I'm beginning to wonder quite seriously whether anybody knows what writing is anymore, whether they haven't got the whole bloody business so completely mixed up with subject matter and significance and who's going to win the peace and what they gave him for the screen rights and if you're not a molecular physicist, you're illiterate, and so on, that there simply isn't anybody around who can read a book and say that the guy knew how to write or didn't. Even poor old Edmund Wilson, who writes as if he had a loose upper plate (was it DeVoto who said that?) dirtied his pants in the *New Yorker* a few short weeks ago in reviewing Marquand's last book. He wrote: "A novel by Sinclair Lewis, however much it may be open to objection, is at least a book by a writer—that is, a work of the imagination that imposes its atmosphere, a creation that shows the color and modelling of a particular artist's hand." Is that all a good writer has to do? Hell, I always thought it was, but hell, I didn't know Wilson knew it.

Can I do a piece for you entitled *The Insignificance of Significance*, in which I will demonstrate in my usual whorehouse style that it doesn't matter a damn what a novel is about, that the only fiction of any moment in any age is that which does magic with words, and that the subject matter is merely the springboard for the writer's imagination; that the art of fiction, if it can any longer be called that, has grown from nothing to an artificial synthesis in a mere matter of 300 years, and has now reached such a degree of mechanical perfection that the only way you can tell the novelists apart is by whether they write about miners in Butte, coolies in China, Jews in the Bronx, or stockbrokers on Long Island, or whatever it is; that all the women and most of the men write exactly the same, or at least choose one of half a dozen thoroughly standardized procedures; and that in spite of certain inevitable slight differences (very slight indeed on the long view) the whole damn business could be turned out by a machine just as well, and will be almost any day now; and that the only writers left who have *anything* to say are those who write about practically nothing and monkey around with odd ways of doing it.

I think you're all crazy. I'm going into the motion picture business. I might even get to be a producer.

RAY

"THE MOST DURABLE THING IN WRITING IS STYLE"

## To Mrs. Robert Hogan

March 8th. 1947

Dear Mrs. Hogan:

Thank you for your elegant letter. It was charming of you to write at such length. I'm pleased to find someone else than myself who writes long letters. A few notes on your question-naire. I might say that my first piece of writing was a poem. I had extensive experience writing for daily papers and weekly reviews in England when quite young, but although I made as much at it as most people, I still did not make a decent living. So went into business when I came to this country. Started writing pulp during the depression as my highly paid executive job went by the board. Particular medium I picked was due to a belief on my part that (a) some of the pulps at that time had very honest and forthright stuff in them; (b) that the literary standard was flexible and there was a chance to get "paid while learning"; (c) that although the average story in the *Black Mask* was not too good, there was a possibility of writing them very much better without hurting their chances of being read.

I have never written but one story for a slick magazine. It was sold to the *Post* and they liked it and wanted more about the same character. But in spite of my agent's advice (later objurgation and finally almost fury) I had a conviction that the superficial neatness of slick writing was only natural when it was feminine, and that if I got good at it (which as I look back seems easy, but did not seem so then), I would eventu-ally be damn sorry. Mine was of course a losing game, on the surface. I wrote pulp stories with as much care as slick stories. It was very poor pay for the work I put into them. I obeyed the formula because I honestly liked it, but I was always try-ing to stretch it, trying to get in bits of peripheral writing which were not necessary but which I felt would have a sub-conscious effect even on the semi-literate readers; I felt some-how that the thing to get in this kind of story was a kind of richness of texture, and that you couldn't get it in a slick story. Or at least I couldn't. In the end I did get it, and it is quite clear now that when men of the quality of, say Charles Morton of the *Atlantic* say they think any one of my novel-ettes is better than anything Hammett ever wrote, they are not talking about the quality of mystery or violence or plot, but about this richness of texture. I myself don't like the sto-ries any more and am a bit apprehensive about their being published in a collected edition. But I do like what I was trying to do in them.

One of my peculiarities and difficulties as a writer is that I won't discard anything. I have heard this is unprofessional and that it is a weakness of the amateur not to be able to tell when his stuff is not coming off. I can tell that all right, as to the matter in hand, but I can't overlook the fact that I had a reason, a feeling, for starting to write it, and I'll be damned if I won't lick it. I have lost months of time because of this stubbornness. However, after working in Hollywood, where the analysis of plot and motivation is carried on daily with an utter ruthlessness, I realize that it was always a plot difficulty that held me up. I simply would not plot far enough ahead. I'd write something I liked and then I would have a hell of a time making it fit in to the structure. This resulted in some rather startling oddities of construction, about which I care nothing, being fundamentally rather uninterested in plot.

Another of my oddities (and this one I believe in absolutely) is that you never quite know where your story is until you have written the first draft of it. So I always regard the first draft as raw material. What seems to be alive in it is what belongs in the story. Even if the neatness has to be lost, I will still keep whatever has that effect of getting up on its own feet and marching. A good story cannot be devised; it has to be distilled. In the long run, however little you talk or even think about it, the most durable thing in writing is style, and style is the most valuable investment a writer can make with his time. It pays off slowly, your agent will sneer at it, your publisher will misunderstand it, and it will take people you never heard of to convince them by slow degrees that the writer who puts his individual mark on the way he writes will always pay off. He can't do it by trying, because the kind of style I am thinking about is a projection of personality and you have to have a personality before you can project it. But granted that you have one, you can only project it on paper by thinking of something else. This is ironical in a way; it is the reason, I suppose, why in a generation of "made" writers I still say you can't make a writer. Preoccupation with style will not produce it. No amount of editing and polishing will have any appreciable effect on the flavor of how a man writes. It is the product of the quality of his emotion and perception; it is the ability to transfer these to paper which makes him a writer, in contrast to the great number of people who have just as good emotions and just as keen perceptions, but cannot come within a googol of miles of putting them on paper. I know several made writers. Hollywood, of course, is full of them; their stuff often has an immediate impact of competence and sophistication, but it is hollow underneath, and you never go back to it. I don't, anyway.

If anyone asked me to give advice to beginning writers, I should probably say quite sincerely that I don't know enough to give advice of a general nature. You are largely preoccupied with the problem of showing people how to make their material marketable. You probably, or certainly, know a lot more about that than I do. Anyhow, I've never had any luck helping anyone to do it. Such wisdom as I may have acquired through my own struggles is only useful for the long pull, since it rather goes to the belief that too much preoccupation with the mechanics of writing is a sure sign of a weak talent or none at all.

Sincerely,<br>RAYMOND CHANDLER

"THAT DAMN LITTLE PAPER CLIP
KEPT SLIPPING AWAY"

## To Frederick Lewis Allen

May 7, 1948

Dear Mr. Allen:

Thanks for the kind words spoken in connection with your P. and O. notes on Eric Bentley. I did not rise to the occasion. I was afraid to try. This sort of thing can become a back-scratching routine of which the public tires very damn fast.

Just the same, I think Bentley's round-up of the plays was everything that anyone could desire. It would be invidious for me to remark (even if I knew what I was talking about) that Bentley is probably the best dramatic critic in the U.S. and, with the possible exception of Mary McCarthy, the *only* dramatic critic in the U.S. The rest of the boys are just think-piece writers whose subject happens to be a play. They are interested in exploiting their own personal brand of verbal glitter. They are witty and readable and sometimes cute, but they tell you next to nothing about the dramatic art and the relationship of the play in question to that art.

It is not enough for a critic to be right, since he will occasionally be wrong. It is not enough for him to give colorable reasons. He must create a reasonable world into which his reader may enter blindfold and feel his way to the chair by the fire without barking his shins on the unexpected dust mop. The barbed phrase, the sedulously rare word, the highbrow affectation of style—these are amusing, but useless. They place nothing and reveal not the temper of the times. The great critics, of whom there are piteously few, build a home for the truth.

In his review of *The Iceman Cometh* that fading wit and tired needlepoint worker, George Jean Nathan says: "With the appearance of this long awaited work our theatre has become dramatically alive again. It makes most of the plays . . . produced during the more than twelve-year period of O'Neill's absence look comparatively like so much damp tissue paper." Cute and quite easy, and with two sentences the spuriousness of an entire career seems to stand revealed. A critic who could write that drivel about O'Neill's drivel is hors concours. It would be charitable to say he has lost contact with his brains; it would be far more accurate to say he has merely made public a truth which was privately known from the beginning: that George Jean Nathan's critical reputation is not founded on his knowing what he is talking about, since obviously he doesn't now and most probably never did, but on a certain personal dexterity with the choice and order of words.

This play, *The Iceman Cometh*, is a sort of touchstone. If that fools you, you are a knuckle-headed sucker for pretentiousness. That's all there is to say; it is quite simple, quite devastating, and there is no retrieving the position. I shall probably never read another line of Nathan. I know there is nothing there. I suspect there never was.

The current year's touchstone is *A Streetcar Named Desire*. Bentley knocks it for a loop, so does McCarthy. O'Neill with a better shooting script. That's all. Zero in art, A or possibly A plus in adaptation to the circumstance that where there is no art, it is possible for an ingenious fellow to simulate it without losing money.

It is wrong to be harsh with the New York critics, unless one admits in the same breath that it is a condition of their existence that they should write entertainingly about something which is rarely worth writing about at all. This leads or forces them to develop a technique of pseudo-subtlety and abstruseness which, when acquired, permits them to deal with trivial things as though they were momentous. This is the basis of all successful advertising copy writing. Criticism is impossible in a world where the important thing is not to be right, or even to know the reasons for being right, but to write a column about a play—any damn play at all—which column however insignificant the ostensible subject, never lets down on the significance of the references to the subject. These people do not write about plays; they write about their neuroses. How else could they keep the ball in the air? Good critical writing is measured by the perception and evaluation of the subject; bad critical writing by the necessity of maintaining the professional standing of the critic.

I thought De Voto's piece about the drinking habits of the Great American Yahoo was quite wonderful. So indirectly, and yet so devastatingly, he exposes that awful truth that where a civilization is in the process of going rotten, you will always find the symbols of this rottenness in the suburbs, in the lives and homes of supposedly rather ordinary decent people. When they begin to break up into devil worship, the disease is probably too far gone for a cure. Or would be, in any country but this.

Auden leaves me lost and groping. His piece about detective stories was brilliant in the clear cold classical manner. But why drag me in? I'm just a fellow who jacked up a few pulp novelettes into book form. How could I possibly care a button about the detective story as a form? All I'm looking for is an excuse for certain experiments in dramatic dialogue. To justify them I have to have plot and situation; but fundamentally I care almost nothing about either. All I really care about is what Errol Flynn calls "the music," the lines he has to speak. Here I am halfway through a Marlowe story and having a little fun (until I got stuck) and along comes this fellow Auden and tells me I am interested in writing serious studies of a criminal milieu. So now I look at everything I put down and say to myself, Remember, old boy, this has to be a serious study of a criminal milieu. Are you serious? No. Is this a criminal milieu? No, just average corrupt living with the melodramatic angle over-emphasized, not because I am crazy about melodrama for its own sake, but because I am realistic enough to know the rules of the game.

A long time ago when I was writing for pulps I put into a story a line like "he got out of the car and walked across the sun-drenched sidewalk until the shadow of the awning over the entrance fell across his face like the touch of cool water." They took it out when they published the story. Their readers didn't appreciate this sort of thing: just held up the action. And I set out to prove them wrong. My theory was they just *thought* they cared nothing about anything but the action; that really, although they didn't know it, they cared very little about the action. The things they really cared about, and that I cared about, were the creation of emotion through dialogue and description; the things they remembered, that haunted them, were not for example that a man got killed, but that in the moment of his death he was trying to pick a paper clip up off the polished surface of a desk, and it kept slipping away from him, so that there was a look of strain on his face and his mouth was half open in a kind of tormented grin, and the last thing in the world he thought about was death. He didn't even hear death knock on the door. That damn little paper clip kept slipping away from his fingers and he just wouldn't push it to the edge of the desk and catch it as it fell.

With kindest regards,

# To James Sandoe

6005 Camino de la Costa
La Jolla, California
April 14th. 1949

Dear Sandoe:

Have read *The Moving Target* by John Macdonald and am a good deal impressed by it, in a peculiar way. In fact I could use it as a springboard for a sermon on How Not to be a Sophisticated Writer. What you say about pastiche is of course quite true, and the materials of the plot situations are borrowed here and there. E.g. the opening set up is lifted more or less from *The Big Sleep*, mother paralyzed instead of father, money from oil, atmosphere of corrupted wealth, and the lawyer-friend villain is lifted straight out of *The Thin Man*; but I personally am a bit Elizabethan about such things, do not think they greatly matter, since all writers must imitate to begin with, and if you attempt to cast yourself in some accepted mould, it is natural to go to the examples that have attained some notice or success.

What strikes me about the book (and I guess I should not be writing about it if I didn't feel that the author had something) is first an effect that is rather repellant. There is nothing to hitch to; here is a man who wants the public for the mystery story in its primitive violence and also wants it to be clear that he, individually, is a highly literate and sophisticated character. A car is "acned with rust" not spotted. Scribblings on toilet walls are "graffiti" (we know Italian yet, it says); one refers to "podex osculation" (medical Latin too, ain't we hell?). "The seconds piled up precariously like a tower of poker chips," etc. The simile that does not quite come off because it doesn't understand what the purpose of the simile is.

The scenes are well handled, there is a lot of experience of some kind behind this writing, and I should not be surprised to find the name was a pseudonym for a novelist of some performance in another field. The thing that interests me is whether this pretentiousness in the phrasing and choice of words makes for better writing. It does not. You could only justify it if the story itself were devised on the same level of sophistication, and you wouldn't sell a thousand copies, if it was. When you say, "spotted with rust," (or pitted, and I'd almost but not quite go for "pimpled") you convey at once a simple visual image. But when you say, "acned with rust" the attention of the reader is instantly jerked away from the thing described to the pose of the writer. This is of course a very simple example of the stylistic misuse of language, and I think that certain writers are under a compulsion to write in re-cherché phrases as a compensation for a lack of some kind of natural animal emotion. They feel nothing, they are literary eunuchs, and therefore they fall back on an oblique terminol-ogy to prove their distinction. It is the sort of mind that keeps avant garde magazines alive, and it is quite interesting to see an attempt to apply it to the purposes of this kind of story.

R.C.


"YOU CAN'T WRITE JUST BECAUSE YOU HAVE READ ALL THE BOOKS"

## To Hamish Hamilton

6005 Camino de la Costa
La Jolla, California
June 17, 1949

Dear Jamie:            .            .            .

I am very uneasy in mind. I seem to have lost ambition and have no ideas any more. I don't really want to do anything, or rather one part of me does and the other doesn't. One of the penalties of even a mild success is an indifference to it, and the effort to do something that will attract interest and praise is really something it is a pity to lose. I read these profound discussions, say in *The Partisan Review*, about art, what it is, literature what it is, and the good life and liberalism and what is the definitive position of Rilke or Kafka, and the scrap about Ezra Pound getting the Bollingen award, and it all seems so meaningless to me. Who cares? Too many good men have been dead too long for it to matter what any of these people do or don't do. What does a man work for? Money? Yes, but in a purely negative way. Without some money nothing else is possible, but once you have the money (and I don't mean a fortune, just a few thousand quid a year) you don't sit and count it and gloat over it. Everything you attain removes a reason for wanting to attain anything. Do I wish to be a great writer? Do I wish to win the Nobel Prize? Not, if it takes much hard work. What the hell, they give the Nobel Prize to too many second-raters for me to get excited about it. Besides, I'd have to go to Sweden and dress up and make a speech. Is the Nobel Prize worth all that? Hell, no. Or I read in some book like Haycraft's *Art of the Mystery Story* various so-called critical essays on the detective novel—and what second-rate stuff it all is! The whole business is on a plane of diminished values, there is a constant haste to deprecate the mystery story as literature for fear the writer of the piece should be assumed to think it important writing. This conditioned approach might well be the result of the decay of the classics, a sort of intellectual insularity which has no historical perspective. People are always suggesting to writers of my sort, "You write so well why don't you attempt a serious novel?" By which they mean something by Marquand or Betty Smith. They would probably be insulted if one suggested that the aesthetic gap, if any, between a good mystery and the best serious novel of the last ten years is hardly measurable on any scale that could measure the gap between the serious novel and any representative piece of Attic writing of the Fourth Century B.C., any ode of Pindar or Horace or Sappho, any chorus of Sophocles, and so on. You cannot have art without a public taste and you cannot have a public taste without a sense of style and quality throughout the social structure. Curiously enough this sense of style seems to have very little to do with refinement or even with humanity. It can exist in a savage and dirty age, but it cannot exist in the age of Milton Berle, Mary Margaret McBride, the Book of the Month Club, the Hearst press, and the Coca-Cola machine. You can't produce art by trying, by setting up exacting standards, by talking about critical minutiae, by the Flaubert method. It is produced with great ease, in an almost offhand manner, and without self-consciousness. You can't write just because you have read all the books.

•     •     •

All the best,<br>RAY

## "MARLOWE IS A MORE HONORABLE MAN THAN YOU OR I"

### To John Houseman

Your article in *Vogue* was much admired here. I think it was beautifully written and had a lot of style. For me personally it had an effect (after-taste is a better word) of depression and it aroused my antagonism. It is artistically patronizing, intellectually dishonest and logically unsound. It is the last whimper of the Little Theatre mind in you. However, I'm all for your demand that pictures, even tough pictures, and especially tough pictures, have a moral content. (Because *The Big Sleep* had none I feel a little annoyed with you for not realizing that the book had a high moral content.) *Time* this week calls Philip Marlowe "amoral." This is pure nonsense. Assuming that his intelligence is as high as mine (it could hardly be higher), assuming his chances in life to promote his own interest are as numerous as they must be, why does he work for such pittance? For the answer to that is the whole story, the story that is always being written by indirection and yet never is written completely or even clearly. It is the struggle of all fundamentally honest men to make a decent living in a corrupt society. It is an impossible struggle; he can't win. He can be poor and bitter and take it out in wisecracks and casual amours, or he can be corrupt and amiable and rude like a Hollywood producer. Because the bitter fact is that outside of two or three technical professions which require long years of preparation, there is absolutely no way for a man of this age to acquire a decent affluence in life without to some degree corrupting himself, without accepting the cold, clear fact that success is always and everywhere a racket.

The stories I wrote were ostensibly mysteries. I did not write the stories behind those stories, because I was not a good enough writer. That does not alter the fact that Marlowe is a more honorable man than you or I. I don't mean Bogart playing Marlowe and I don't mean because I created him. I didn't create him at all; I've seen dozens like him in all essentials except the few colorful qualities he needed to be in a book. (A few even had those.) They were all poor; they will always be poor. How could they be anything else.

When you have answered that question, you can call him a zombie.

Love,<br>Ray

*c. October 1949*

---

## "I THINK I AM A BIT OF AN ANOMALY"

## *To Hamish Hamilton*

6005 Camino de la Costa<br>La Jolla, California<br>November 10, 1950

Dear Jamie:

.        .        .

Why do people want biographical material? Why does it matter? And why does a writer have to talk about himself as a person? It's all such a bore. I was born in Chicago, Illinois, so damned long ago that I wish I had never told anybody when. Both my parents were of Quaker descent. Neither was a practicing Quaker. My mother was born in Waterford, Ireland, where there was a very famous Quaker school, and perhaps still is. My father came of a Pennsylvania farming family, probably one of the batch that settled with William Penn. At the age of seven I had scarlet fever in a hotel, and I understand this is a very rare accomplishment. I remember principally the ice cream and the pleasure of pulling the loose skin off during convalescence. I spent five years in Dulwich and thereafter lived in France and Germany for a couple more years. At that time I was thought to be a British subject, since my mother had regained her British nationality while I was still a minor. So that when I returned to the United States, the record shows that I was admitted as a British subject. It took a long, long struggle, and finally a law suit against the Attorney General of the United States to get it changed. The point of law was that a minor cannot be expatriated, and I don't know why they found it so hard to accept this. It cost me quite a lot of money to force it on them. I had done several years free lancing in London in a rather undistinguished way. I did book reviews, essays, etc., for the old *Academy*, sketches and verses for the *Westminster Gazette*, odd paragraphs here and there, etc. I served in the First Division of the Canadian Expeditionary Force in what used to be called the Great War, and was later attached to the R.A.F., but had not completed flight training when the Armistice came. So far I had shown very little talent for writing, and that little was riddled with intellectual snobbery. I arrived in California with a beautiful wardrobe, a public school accent, no practical gifts for earning a living, and a contempt for the natives which, I am sorry to say, has in some measure persisted to this day. I had a pretty hard time trying to make a living. Once I worked on an apricot ranch ten hours a day, twenty cents an hour. Another time I worked for a sporting goods house, stringing tennis rackets for $12.50 a week, 54 hours a week. I taught myself bookkeeping and from there on my rise was as rapid as the growth of a sequoia. I detested business life, but in spite of that I finally became an officer or director of half a dozen independent oil corporations. The depression finished that. I was much too expensive a luxury for those days. Wandering up and down the Pacific Coast in an automobile, I began to read pulp magazines, because they were cheap enough to throw away and because I never had any taste at any time for the kind of thing which is known as women's magazines. This was in the great days of the *Black Mask* (if I may call them great days) and it struck me that some of the writing was pretty forceful and honest, even though it had its crude aspect. I decided that this might be a good way to try to learn to write fiction and get paid a small amount of money at the same time. I spent five months over an 18,000 word novelette and sold it for $180. After that I never looked back, although I had a good many uneasy periods looking forward. I wrote *The Big Sleep* in three months, but a lot of the material in it was revamped from a couple of novelettes. This gave it body but didn't make it any easier to write. I was always a slow worker. In the best month I ever had, I wrote two 18,000 word novelettes and a short story which was sold to the *Post*. For Gardner this would be the work of a couple of days, but for me it was a terrific production and I have never approached it since. I went to Hollywood in 1943 to work with Billy Wilder on *Double Indemnity*. This was an agonizing experience and has probably shortened my life; but I learned from it as much about screen writing as I am capable of learning, which is not very much. I was under contract to Paramount after that and did several pictures for them, including one original screen play, *The Blue Dahlia*, which was written from scratch (that is without any basic story) and shot complete in twenty weeks. I was told at the time that this was some sort of a record for a high budget picture. All my books, except *The Little Sister*, have been made into pictures, two of them twice. Like every writer, or almost every writer, who goes to Hollywood, I was convinced in the beginning that there must be some discoverable method of working in pictures which would not be completely stultifying to whatever creative talent one might happen to possess. But like others before me I discovered that this was a dream. It's nobody's fault; it's part of the structure of the industry. Too many people have too much to say about a writer's work. It ceases to be his own. And after a while he ceases to care about it. He has brief enthusiasms, but they are destroyed before they can flower. People who can't write tell him how to write. He meets clever and interesting people and may even form lasting friendships, but all this is incidental to his proper business of writing. The wise screen writer is he who wears his second-best suit, artistically speaking, and doesn't take things too much to heart. He should have a touch of cynicism, but only a touch. The complete cynic is as useless to Hollywood as he is to himself. He should do the best he can without straining at it. He should be scrupulously honest about his work, but he should not expect scrupulous honesty in return. He won't get it. And when he has had enough, he should say good-bye with a smile, because for all he knows he may want to go back.

By the end of 1946 I had had enough. I moved to La Jolla. Since then I have written two screen plays, one of them with only occasional visits to a studio to talk over the story, and one without any visits to the studio at all. I shall probably do others, and if so I shall do them as well as I know how; but I shall keep my heart to myself.

I have been married since 1924 and have no children. I am supposed to be a hard-boiled writer, but that means nothing. It is merely a method of projection. Personally I am sensitive and even diffident. At times I am extremely caustic and pugnacious; at other times very sentimental. I am not a good mixer because I am very easily bored, and to me the average never seems good enough, in people or in anything else. I am a spasmodic worker with no regular hours, which is to say I only write when I feel like it. I am always surprised at how very easy it seems at the time, and at how very tired one feels afterwards. As a mystery writer, I think I am a bit of an anomaly, since most mystery writers of the American school are only semi-literate; and I am not only literate but intellectual, much as I dislike the term. It would seem that a classical education might be rather a poor basis for writing novels in a hard-boiled vernacular. I happen to think otherwise. A classical education saves you from being fooled by pretentiousness, which is what most current fiction is too full of. In this country the mystery writer is looked down on as sub-literary merely because he is a mystery writer, rather than for instance a writer of social significance twaddle. To a classicist—even a very rusty one—such an attitude is merely a parvenu insecurity. When people ask me, as occasionally they do, why I don't try my hand at a serious novel, I don't argue with them; I don't even ask them what they mean by a serious novel. It would be useless. They wouldn't know. The question is parrot-talk. The problem of what is significant literature I leave to fat bores like Edmund Wilson—a man of many distinctions—among which personally I revere most highly (in the *Chronicles of Hecate County*) that of having made fornication as dull as a railroad time table.

Reading over some of the above, I seem to detect a rather supercilious tone here and there. I am afraid this is not altogether admirable, but unfortunately it is true. It belongs. I am, as a matter of fact, rather a supercilious person in many ways. I shouldn't be at all surprised if it shows in what I write. And it may well be this which arouses such flailing anger in pip-squeaks like John Dickson Carr and Anthony Boucher.

.       .       .

Yours ever,
RAY

"THE FACTS OF PHILIP MARLOWE'S LIFE"

## To D. J. Ibberson

April 19, 1951

Dear Mr. Ibberson:

It is very kind of you to take such an interest in the facts of Philip Marlowe's life. The date of his birth is uncertain. I think he said somewhere that he was thirty-eight years old, but that was quite awhile ago and he is no older today. This is just something you will have to face. He was not born in a Midwestern town but in a small California town called Santa Rosa, which your map will show you to be about fifty miles north of San Francisco. Santa Rosa is famous as the home of Luther Burbank, a fruit and vegetable horticulturist, once of considerable renown. It is perhaps less widely known as the background of Hitchcock's picture *Shadow of a Doubt*, most of which was shot right in Santa Rosa. Marlowe has never spoken of his parents, and apparently he has no living relatives. This could be remedied if necessary. He had a couple of years of college, either at the University of Oregon at Eugene, or Oregon State University at Corvallis, Oregon. I don't know why he came to Southern California, except that eventually most people do, although not all of them remain. He seems to have had some experience as an investigator for an insurance company and later as investigator for the district attorney of Los Angeles county. This would not necessarily make him a police officer nor give him the right to make an arrest. The circumstances in which he lost that job are well known to me but I cannot be very specific about them. You'll have to be satisfied with the information that he got a little too efficient at a time and in a place where efficiency was the last thing desired by the persons in charge. He is slightly over six feet tall and weighs about thirteen stone eight. He has dark brown hair, brown eyes, and the expression "passably good looking" would not satisfy him in the least. I don't think he looks tough. He can be tough. If I had ever had an opportunity of selecting the movie actor who could best represent him to my mind, I think it would have been Cary Grant. I think he dresses as well as can be expected. Obviously he hasn't very much money to spend on clothes, or on anything else for that matter. The horn-rimmed sunglasses do not make him distinctive. Practically everyone in Southern California wears sunglasses at some time or other. When you say he wears 'pyjamas' even in summer, I don't know what you mean. Who doesn't? Were you under the impression that he wore a nightshirt? Or did you mean that he might sleep raw in hot weather? The last is possible, although our weather here is very seldom hot at night. You are quite right about his smoking habits, although I don't think he insists on Camels. Almost any sort of cigarette will satisfy him. The use of cigarette cases is not as common here as in England. He definitely does not use bookmatches which are always safety matches. He uses either large wooden matches, which we call kitchen matches, or a smaller match of the same type which comes in small boxes and can be struck anywhere, including on the thumbnail if the weather is dry enough. In the desert or in the mountains it is quite easy to strike a match on your thumbnail, but the humidity around Los Angeles is pretty high. Marlowe's drinking habits are much as you state. I don't think he prefers rye to bourbon, however. He will drink practically anything that is not sweet. Certain drinks, such as Pink Ladies, Honolulu cocktails and crème de menthe highballs, he would regard as an insult. Yes, he makes good coffee. Anyone can make good coffee in this country, although it seems quite impossible in England. He takes cream, and sugar with his coffee, not milk. He will also drink it black without sugar. He cooks his own breakfast, which is a simple matter, but not any other meal. He is a late riser by inclination, but occasionally an early riser by necessity. Aren't we all? I would not say that his chess comes up to tournament standard. I don't know where he got the little paper-bound book of tournament games published in Leipzig, but he likes it because he prefers the continental method of designating the squares on the chess board. Nor do I know that he is something of a card player. This has slipped my mind. What do you mean he is "moderately fond of animals"? If you live in an apartment house, moderately is about as fond of them as you can get. It seems to me that you have an inclination to interpret any chance remark as an indication of a fixed taste. As to his interest in women as "frankly carnal", these are your words, not mine.

.       .       .

Marlowe cannot recognize a Bryn Mawr accent, because there is no such thing. All he implies by that expression is a toplofty way of speaking. I doubt very much that he can tell genuine old furniture from fakes. And I also beg leave to doubt that many experts can do it either, if the fakes are good enough. I pass the Edwardian furniture and pre-Raphaelite art. I just don't recall where you get your facts. I would not say that Marlowe's knowledge of perfume stops at Chanel Number 5. That again is merely a symbol of something that is expensive and at the same time reasonably restrained. He likes all the slightly acrid perfumes, but not the cloying or overspiced type. He is, as you may have noticed, a slightly acrid person. Of course he knows what the Sorbonne is, and he also knows where it is. Of course he knows the difference between a tango and a rumba, and also between a conga and a samba, and he knows the difference between a samba and a mamba, although he does not believe that the mamba can overtake a galloping horse. I doubt if he knows the new dance called a mambo, because it seems to be only recently discovered or developed.

Now let's see, how far does that take us? Fairly regular

film-goer, you say, dislikes musicals. Check. May be an admirer of Orson Welles. Possibly, especially when Orson is directed by someone other than himself. Marlowe's reading habits and musical tastes are just as much a mystery to me as they are to you, and if I tried to improvise, I'm afraid I would get him confused with my own tastes. If you ask me why he is a private detective, I can't answer you. Obviously there are times when he wishes he were not, just as there are times when I would rather be almost anything than a writer. The private detective of fiction is a fantastic creation who acts and speaks like a real man. He can be completely realistic in every sense but one, that one sense being that in life as we know it such a man would not be a private detective. The things which happen to him might still happen to him, but they would happen as the result of a peculiar set of chances. By making him a private detective, you skip the necessity for justifying his adventures.

Where he lives: in *The Big Sleep* and some earlier stories he apparently lived in a single apartment with a pull-down bed, a bed that folds up into the wall and it has a mirror on the under side of it. Then he moved into an apartment similar to that occupied by a character named Joe Brody in *The Big Sleep*. It may have been the same apartment, he may have got it cheap because a murder had taken place in it. I think, but I'm not sure, that this apartment is on the fourth floor. It contains a living room which you enter directly from the hallway, and opposite are French windows opening on an ornamental balcony, which is just something to look at, certainly not anything to sit out on. Against the right-hand wall as you stand in the doorway is a davenport. In the left-hand wall, nearest to the hallway of the apartment house, there is a door that leads to an interior hall. Beyond that, against the left-hand wall, there is this oak drop leaf desk, an easy chair, etc; beyond that, an archway entrance to the dinette and kitchen. The dinette, as known in American apartment houses or at any rate in California apartment houses, is simply a space divided off from the kitchen proper by an archway or a built-in china closet. It would be very small, and the kitchen would also be very small. As you enter the hallway from the living room (the interior hallway) you would come on your right to the bathroom door and continuing straight on you would come to the bedroom. The bedroom would contain a walk-in closet. The bathroom in a building of this type would contain a shower in the tub and a shower curtain. None of the rooms is very large. The rent of the apartment, furnished, would have been about sixty dollars a month when Marlowe moved into it. God knows what it would be now. I shudder to think. I should guess not less than ninety dollars a month, probably more.

As to Marlowe's office, I'll have to take another look at it sometime to refresh my memory. It seems to me it's on the sixth floor in a building which faces north, and that his office window faces east. But I'm not certain about this. As you say, there is a reception room which is a half-office, perhaps half the space of a corner office, converted into two reception rooms with separate entrances and communicating doors right and left respectively. Marlowe has a private office which communicates with his reception room, and there is a connection which causes a buzzer to ring in his private office when the door of the reception room is opened. But this buzzer can be switched off by a toggle switch. He has not, and never has had, a secretary. He could very easily subscribe to a telephone answering service, but I don't recall mentioning that anywhere. And I do not recall that his desk has a glass top, but I may have said so. The office bottle is kept in the filing drawer of the desk,—a drawer, standard in American office desks (perhaps also in England) which is the depth of two ordinary drawers, and is intended to contain file folders, but very seldom does, since most people keep their file folders in filing cases. It seems to me that some of these details flit about a good deal. His guns have also been rather various. He started out with a German Luger automatic pistol. He seems to have had Colt automatics of various calibers, but not larger than .38, and when last I heard he has a Smith & Wesson .38 special, probably with a four-inch barrel. This is a very powerful gun, although not the most powerful made, and has the advantage over an automatic of using a lead cartridge. It will not jam or discharge accidentally, even if dropped on a hard surface, and is probably just as effective a weapon at short range as a .45 caliber automatic. It would be better with a six-inch barrel, but that would make it much more awkward to carry. Even a four-inch barrel is not too convenient, and the detective branch of the police usually carries a gun with only a two and a half-inch barrel. This is about all I have for you now, but if there is anything else you want to know, please write to me again. The trouble is, you really seem to know a good deal more about Philip Marlowe than I do, and perhaps I shall have to ask you questions instead of your asking me.

With kindest regards,

Yours ever,

"I DON'T SEEM TO CARE WHO CONKED<br>SIR MORTIMER WITH THE POKER"

## To Frederic Dannay

July 10, 1951

Dear Frederic Dannay:

No, I would not care to nominate the ten best living detective-story writers. I don't mind sticking my neck out, but the point is, one has to agree on a few fundamentals before one starts picking lists of ten bests. For instance, does the category include writers of suspense stories in which there is little mystery, or none at all? If it does not, you eliminate some of the best performers, such as Elisabeth Sanxay Holding, certainly one of my favorites. And if it does, why call them detective stories? Charlotte Armstrong's *Mischief* contains no puzzle element whatever. On the other hand, some puzzle merchants, the people who have timetables and ground plans and pay the most meticulous attention to details, can't write a lick. There is a saying that a good plot will make a good detective story, but I personally question whether you can have a good plot if you can't create any believable characters or situations. My list, if I made it, would probably leave out some of those names which will inevitably appear on your ten best list. I just don't think they're any good, because by my standards they can't write. And it may also happen that a single book, such as *The 31st of February* by Julian Symons, or *Walk the Dark Streets* by William Krasner,

CHRONOLOGY

NOTE ON THE TEXTS

NOTES

# Chronology

1888    Born Raymond Thornton Chandler on July 23 in Chi-
        cago, only child of Florence Dart Thornton Chandler and
        Maurice Benjamin Chandler. (Mother was immigrant
        from Waterford, Ireland, to Nebraska. Father, born in
        Philadelphia in 1859, studied engineering at the University
        of Pennsylvania before moving to Nebraska to work for
        a railroad company. Parents were married in Laramie,
        Wyoming, in July 1887.)

1889–94  Father drinks heavily and is often absent. Chandler spends
        summers with mother in Plattsmouth, Nebraska, as guests
        of aunt Grace Thornton Fitt and her family. Parents even-
        tually divorce. Father disappears and provides no support.

1895–99  Moves to England with mother in 1895. Lives with
        mother, grandmother Annie Thornton, and aunt Ethel
        Thornton in Upper Norwood, suburb south of London
        (later recalls that he and his mother were treated coldly by
        his grandmother and aunt). Spends summers in Water-
        ford, Ireland, with uncle Ernest Thornton. Attends
        Church of England and goes to local school.

1900    Household moves to nearby Dulwich. Chandler enters
        Dulwich College as day student. Studies mathematics,
        music, Latin, French, divinity, and English history.

1901–2  Plays rugby and cricket. Studies French, German, and
        Spanish in preparation for career in business. Ranks at top
        of his form and wins prizes for general achievement and
        mathematics.

1903–4  Resumes study of classics, reading Virgil, Cicero, Caesar,
        Livy, and Ovid in Latin and Thucydides, Plato, Aris-
        tophanes, and the Gospel of St. Mark in Greek.

1905–6  Leaves Dulwich in April 1905 when family decides to send
        him abroad for further study in foreign languages. Studies
        commercial French at business college in Paris, then goes
        to Munich and studies German with a tutor. Visits
        Nuremberg and Vienna.

1907–8   Returns to England and lives with mother in Streatham in southwest London, where she had moved following death of her mother. Becomes naturalized British subject on May 20, 1907, in order to qualify for civil service examination. Takes examination in June 1907 and places third among six hundred candidates. Works as clerk in naval supplies office of the Admiralty. Resigns after six months.

1909–11  Works briefly as journalist for the *Daily Express,* then joins staff of the *Westminster Gazette.* Writes articles on European affairs and contributes sketches and poems. Lives with mother in Forest Hill in southeast London. Begins contributing literary essays to *The Academy* in 1911.

1912     Borrows £500 from uncle Ernest Thornton and returns to America. Becomes friends with Warren Lloyd, a Los Angeles attorney, during Atlantic crossing. Stays with aunt Grace Thornton Fitt in Nebraska before settling in Los Angeles. Works on apricot ranch and strings tennis racquets for sporting goods store. Lives in furnished rooms.

1913–14  Studies bookkeeping. Obtains job as accountant and bookkeeper for the Los Angeles Creamery with help of Warren Lloyd. Spends time with the Lloyd family and their friends, who are interested in literature, music, psychology, and the occult. Meets pianist and composer Julian Pascal and his wife Cecilia (Cissy), also a pianist, through Lloyd.

1915–16  Lives at 311 Loma Drive near Pershing Square with his mother, who has returned to America.

1917     Goes to Victoria, British Columbia, in August and enlists in the Canadian Army. Sails for England in November after three months of training.

1918     Assigned on March 18 to 7th Battalion, 2nd Infantry Brigade, 1st Canadian Division, and is sent to France. Serves in trenches in Lens-Arras sector (later writes: "Once you have had to lead a platoon into direct machine-gun fire, nothing is ever the same again"). Returned to England with rank of acting sergeant after receiving concussion during German artillery bombardment. Transfers in July to Royal Air Force and is in training school when war ends on November 11.

1919        Returns to Vancouver and is discharged from military service on February 20. Takes job in San Francisco office of an English bank. Returns to Los Angeles and works for the *Daily Express* for six weeks. Begins love affair with Cissy Pascal (born Pearl Eugenie Hurlburt in Perry, Ohio, in 1870). Cissy files for divorce from Julian Pascal in July.

1920–23     Settles with mother in Redondo Beach (later moves with her to Santa Monica), while Cissy lives in Hermosa Beach. Pascal divorce becomes final in October 1920, but Chandler delays marriage with Cissy because of his mother's disapproval of the difference in their ages. Begins working as bookkeeper for Dabney Oil Syndicate, company owned by Joseph Dabney and Ralph Lloyd, Warren Lloyd's brother.

1924        Mother dies of cancer in January. Chandler marries Cissy Pascal on February 6. Becomes auditor of Dabney Oil Syndicate (later South Basin Oil Company) and is soon promoted to vice-president in charge of Los Angeles office.

1925–31     Lives with Cissy in various apartments around Los Angeles, moving frequently. Enjoys playing tennis and attending college football games with friends. Becomes increasingly aware of his age difference with Cissy. Drinks heavily, behaves erratically (sometimes threatening suicide), and has affairs with younger women working in oil company office.

1932        Fired from South Basin Oil Company for drunkenness and absenteeism. Goes to Seattle and stays with army friends, then returns to Los Angeles when Cissy is hospitalized with pneumonia. After her recovery, they move to an apartment in Hollywood Hills. Chandler assists Edward Lloyd, son of Warren Lloyd, in lawsuit against South Basin Oil Company for misappropriation of revenues from Ventura Avenue oil fields once owned by Lloyd family. Receives allowance from Edward Lloyd of $100 a month, which allows him to devote himself to writing. Stops excessive drinking.

film version of *Farewell, My Lovely*, directed by Edward Dmytryk and starring Dick Powell as Philip Marlowe, is released by RKO. Consulted during filming of *The Big Sleep* at Warner Brothers by director Howard Hawks. Publishes essay "The Simple Art of Murder" in December *Atlantic Monthly*.

1945    Begins writing original screenplay *The Blue Dahlia* for Paramount, which wants to make a film starring Alan Ladd before Ladd enters military service. Shooting begins before screenplay is finished; when Chandler falls seriously behind schedule, he proposes to producer John Houseman that he finish the script while drunk. Houseman agrees, and Chandler completes the screenplay in eight days, dictating to secretaries provided by the studio while receiving regular glucose injections from his doctor. (Film, directed by George Marshall, is released in 1946; Chandler receives Academy Award nomination and Edgar award from Mystery Writers of America for his screenplay.) Works for MGM on screenplay for *The Lady in the Lake*, directed by actor Robert Montgomery, who also plays Philip Marlowe. Leaves after disagreements with studio, and screenplay is completed by Steve Fisher with Chandler receiving no screen credit. Article "Writers in Hollywood" published in November *Atlantic Monthly*.

1946    Film version of *The Big Sleep* is released; Chandler is pleased by Humphrey Bogart's performance as Philip Marlowe ("so much better than any other tough-guy actor"). Works for Paramount on adaptation of novel *The Innocent Mrs. Duff* by Elisabeth Sanxay Holding, but ends relationship with studio before screenplay is completed. Angered by inclusion of story "The Man Who Liked Dogs," which he had "cannibalized" for *Farewell, My Lovely*, by Joseph T. Shaw in his anthology *The Hard-Boiled Omnibus*. Buys house for $40,000 at 6005 Camino de la Costa in La Jolla, where he and Cissy, who is increasingly frail, live in relative seclusion. Stops excessive drinking. Purchases dictation machine which he uses to carry on extensive correspondence (his frequent correspondents include mystery writer Erle Stanley Gardner; James Sandoe, book reviewer and librarian at University of Colorado; British publisher Hamish Hamilton; and Dale Warren, publicity director of Houghton Mifflin).

Ends connection with long-time literary agent Sydney Sanders in November.

1947    Begins writing original screenplay *Playback,* set in Vancouver, for Universal. Radio program featuring Van Heflin as Philip Marlowe is broadcast on NBC. *The Brasher Doubloon,* film version of *The High Window* directed by John Brahm and starring George Montgomery as Philip Marlowe, is released.

1948    Chandler completes *Playback* screenplay, but studio decides that filming in Vancouver is too expensive, and film is not produced. Works on novel *The Little Sister.* Becomes client of literary agency Brandt and Brandt in New York, and conducts extensive correspondence with agent Carl Brandt and his associate Bernice Baumgarten. Essay "Oscar Night in Hollywood" published in June *Atlantic Monthly.* Leaves Knopf over disagreements about copyrights, earnings from paperback editions, and other issues, and signs contract with Houghton Mifflin for *The Little Sister.* Finishes novel in September. Offers guidelines to scriptwriters for CBS radio series "The Adventures of Philip Marlowe," starring Gerald Mohr, but is otherwise uninvolved with program.

1949    Suffers from ailments, including bronchitis, skin allergies, and shingles, that become chronic conditions. *The Little Sister* is published in Britain by Hamish Hamilton in June and in the U.S. by Houghton Mifflin in September. Agrees to publication of collection of his pulp magazine stories proposed by Houghton Mifflin, but writes to editor Paul Brooks: "I am going to have to revise and edit this trash. There are crudities here and there which I can no longer tolerate."

1950    Works with director Alfred Hitchcock on screen adaptation of Patricia Highsmith's novel *Strangers on a Train* for Warner Brothers. Fantasy story "Professor Bingo's Snuff" published in *Park East* in August. Hitchcock becomes unhappy with Chandler's work on screenplay, and he is replaced by Czenzi Ormonde (Chandler and Ormonde share screenwriting credit when film is released in 1951, though little of Chandler's work remains in final version). *The Simple Art of Murder,* collection of early stories, published by Houghton Mifflin in September and by Hamish Hamilton in November. Chandler and Cissy are saddened by death of their black Persian cat Taki ("so much a part of our lives that even now we dread to come into the silent empty house after being out at night").

1951    Works on new novel, *Summer in Idle Valley* (later retitled *The Long Goodbye*). Visited in February by English novelist and playwright J. B. Priestley and during the summer by American humorist S. J. Perelman.

1952    Publishes "Ten Per Cent of Your Life," article on literary agents, in February *Atlantic Monthly*. Sends draft of *The Long Goodbye* to agents Carl Brandt and Bernice Baumgarten in May, and is troubled when they criticize "softness" of Marlowe in the novel. Begins making extensive revisions. Sails to England with Cissy in August, and sees publisher Hamish Hamilton, J. B. Priestley, film critic Dilys Powell, etymologist Eric Partridge, and others in London. Returns to United States in October. Breaks off relations with Brandt and Brandt agency in November. Cissy's health worsens.

1953    Works on novel loosely based on *Playback* screenplay but puts it aside. Resumes heavy drinking. Finishes *The Long Goodbye* in July. Cissy is acutely ill with respiratory and heart trouble. *The Long Goodbye* published in Britain by Hamish Hamilton in November.

1954    Houghton Mifflin publishes *The Long Goodbye* in the U.S. in March. After repeated hospitalizations throughout the year, Cissy dies on December 12.

1955    Chandler writes to Hamilton in January: "For thirty years, ten months and four days, she was the light of my life, my whole ambition. Anything else I did was just the fire for her to warm her hands at. That is all there is to say." Drinks heavily and suffers from deep depression. Attempts suicide with revolver while drunk on February 22; fires bullet into bathroom ceiling, then surrenders gun when police arrive. After being placed in county hospital for psychiatric observation, spends six days in a private sanitarium. Sells La Jolla house in March and leaves California. Visits friends in Chicago and Old Chatham, New

York. Drinks heavily while in New York City and recovers in New York Hospital. Sails to England in April. Learns onboard ship that he has won Edgar award from the Mystery Writers of America for *The Long Goodbye*. In London receives attention from press and other writers. Forms friendships with pianist Natasha Spender (wife of poet Stephen Spender), Helga Greene (who becomes his literary agent), and thriller writer Ian Fleming. Returns to America in September, then goes back to London in November after learning that Natasha Spender is ill. Visits Spain and Morocco with her and then returns to London, where she undergoes a successful operation. Chandler drinks heavily and is hospitalized for two weeks in a London clinic, where he is diagnosed as having malaria.

1956    Rents small apartment in St. John's Wood, London. Suffers from infatuation with Natasha Spender. Returns to America in May to avoid British taxes. Drinks heavily in New York, collapses, and is hospitalized for exhaustion and malnutrition. Returns to La Jolla in June and rents an apartment. Continues heavy drinking. Briefly considers marrying Louise Landis Loughner, San Francisco woman who had written him an admiring letter in 1955. Sees Natasha Spender in Arizona and California in December.

1957    Becomes involved in personal life of his divorced Australian secretary and her two children. Revises "English Summer," short story written in the 1930s, but abandons plans to expand it into a novel or play. Becomes involved in complex dispute with British authorities over taxes owed because of extended residence in England in 1955. Resumes work on *Playback* with encouragement from Helga Greene. Hospitalized again for drinking in August. Visited in November by Helga Greene. Completes *Playback* in late December.

1958    Begins novel "Poodle Springs," in which Philip Marlowe marries Linda Loring from *The Long Goodbye* (completes only a few chapters). Travels to England in February. At suggestion of Ian Fleming, goes to Capri with Helga Greene to interview deported American Mafia leader "Lucky" Luciano for the London *Sunday Times* (resulting article "My Friend Luco" is not published for legal reasons). Hospitalized in London for drinking in May.

*Playback* is published by Hamish Hamilton in July and by Houghton Mifflin in October. Returns to La Jolla in August and is rejoined by his Australian secretary. Works on "The Pencil," short story featuring Philip Marlowe. Chandler's health declines from his continued drinking; he is cared for by Kay West, a former neighbor in London.

1959      Visited in February by Helga Greene, who has him hospitalized. While in the hospital Chandler proposes marriage to Greene; she accepts. Visits New York at beginning of March with Greene to accept presidency of Mystery Writers of America. Returns alone to La Jolla while Greene goes on to London, where they intend to live. Drinks heavily, develops pneumonia, and is hospitalized on March 23. Dies in Scripps Clinic at 3:50 P.M. on March 26. Buried on March 30 at Mount Hope Cemetery in San Diego.

# Note on the Texts

This volume contains four novels by Raymond Chandler, *The Lady in the Lake*, *The Little Sister*, *The Long Goodbye*, and *Playback*, published between 1945 and 1958; the screenplay for the film *Double Indemnity*, released in 1944; and a selection of Chandler's essays, journal entries, and letters.

The texts of the novels printed here are those of the first American editions: *The Lady in the Lake* (New York: Alfred A. Knopf, 1945); *The Little Sister* (Boston: Houghton Mifflin, 1949); *The Long Goodbye* (Boston: Houghton Mifflin, 1954); and *Playback* (Boston: Houghton Mifflin, 1958). *The Long Goodbye* and *Playback* were published in Britain by Hamish Hamilton several months before the American editions appeared, but the texts of the British and American editions are identical except for differences in spelling. Chandler did not revise these novels following publication.

The screenplay of *Double Indemnity* was adapted from James M. Cain's 1936 novella by Chandler and the director Billy Wilder. Of their collaboration, Chandler later wrote: "Working with Billy Wilder was an agonizing experience and has probably shortened my life, but I learned from it about as much about screen writing as I am capable of learning, which is not very much." The text of the screenplay printed here was published in *Best Film Plays—1945*, edited by John Gassner and Dudley Nichols (New York: Crown Publishers, 1946). Significant differences between the published screenplay and the released version of the film are indicated in the notes to this volume.

"The Simple Art of Murder" was originally published in *Atlantic Monthly* in December 1944 and was included in Howard Haycraft's anthology *The Art of the Mystery Story* (New York: Simon & Schuster, 1946) in a version described by Haycraft as "specially revised by Mr. Chandler for this publication." The version of the essay included in Chandler's short-story collection *The Simple Art of Murder* (Boston: Houghton Mifflin, 1950) is apparently an independent revision of the *Atlantic Monthly* version, since it incorporates only a few of the changes made for the Haycraft anthology. The text printed here is that published in *The Art of the Mystery Story*.

"Writers in Hollywood" was published in *Atlantic Monthly* in November 1945 and was never revised by Chandler. The *Atlantic Monthly* text is printed here.

"Twelve Notes on the Mystery Story" and "Notes (very brief,

# *Notes*

In the notes below, the reference numbers denote page and line of this volume (the line count includes chapter headings). No note is made for material included in standard desk-reference books such as Webster's *Collegiate*, *Biographical*, and *Geographical* dictionaries. For references to other studies and further biographical background than is contained in the Chronology, see Frank MacShane, *The Life of Raymond Chandler* (New York: E. P. Dutton, 1976); *Selected Letters of Raymond Chandler* (New York: Columbia University Press, 1981), edited by Frank MacShane; *Raymond Chandler Speaking* (Boston: Houghton Mifflin, 1962), edited by Dorothy Gardiner and Kathrine Sorley Walker; and *The Notebooks of Raymond Chandler and English Summer: A Gothic Romance* (New York: Ecco Press, 1976), edited by Frank MacShane.

## THE LADY IN THE LAKE

3.4−5    rubber blocks . . . the government]  In June 1942 the U.S. government initiated a national scrap-rubber drive.

15.36    Capehart]  Expensive brand of radio.

26.33    rat rolls]  Pads used for styling hair.

65.28    celotex]  A wallboard made of sugar-cane residue, used for insulation.

84.13    Philo Vance]  Fastidious and erudite hero of a series of detective novels by S. S. Van Dine (Willard Huntington Wright, 1888−1939), including *The Canary Murder Case* (1928), *The Greene Murder Case* (1928), and *The Kennel Murder Case* (1933).

## THE LITTLE SISTER

266.12    Margaret O'Brien]  Child actress (b. 1937) featured in films including *Journey for Margaret* (1942), *Jane Eyre* (1944), and *Meet Me in St. Louis* (1944).

274.5−6    "You seen that in a picture,"]  The scene described occurs in Howard Hawks' *To Have and Have Not* (1944), starring Humphrey Bogart.

300.34    redhot]  Gunman.

302.10    wire recorder]  A sound-recording device using magnetized steel wire.

409.7    muggle-smoker."]  Marijuana smoker.

## THE LONG GOODBYE

425.8 vag] Vagrant.

428.30 Musso's] Musso and Frank's Grill on Hollywood Boulevard, which opened in 1919.

443.8 Connie] Lockheed Constellation, four-engine propeller plane.

478.15 Costello] Frank Costello (1891–1973; real name Francesco Castiglia), New York underworld figure associated with "Lucky" Luciano and Meyer Lansky, who was investigated by the Kefauver Committee of the U.S. Senate in 1951 and subsequently convicted of tax evasion.

479.11 *Frank Merriwell*] Fictional athletic hero at Yale, the protagonist of a series of dime novels, the first published in 1895.

486.20 mozo] Boy; servant.

488.14 Ruy Lopez] Chess opening, named after 16th-century chess writer Ruy Lopez de Sigura.

488.17–18 Khachaturyan . . . violin concerto.] Aram Khachaturian (1903–78), Soviet composer; his violin concerto was composed in 1940.

490.7 Hattie Carnegie] Carnegie (1886–1956) was a leading American fashion designer of 1930s and 1940s.

491.14 Lucrezia's . . . vial.] Lucrezia Borgia (1480–1519), Renaissance aristocrat and patron of art, often accused of poisoning her enemies.

500.3 Arthur Murray] Dancer (1895–1991) and founder of chain of dance-instruction studios.

500.11–12 Monogram] Hollywood studio (1930–53) specializing in low-budget westerns and crime pictures.

506.19–20 *The Last Tycoon*] Fitzgerald's novel of Hollywood was left unfinished at the time of his death and appeared posthumously in 1941.

531.36 Marek Weber] Popular band leader.

537.19 Camarillo] State mental hospital in southern California.

561.29 "Come back, little Sheba,"] Title of a play (1950) by William Inge about an alcoholic.

567.27–29 "*Was. . . kiss.*"] Marlowe, *The Tragical History of Doctor Faustus*, scene vi.

594.11 September Morn] Painting (1912) by French salon artist Paul Emile Chabas (1869–1937); it was widely reproduced, and was banned in some American cities.

616.15 ruptured duck."] Emblem signifying honorable discharge from the U.S. armed services.

623.31    'To cease . . . no pain.'] John Keats, "Ode to a Nightingale."

626.13–14    *The Golden Bough*. . . Shorter version] Sir James Frazer's an-
thropological study *The Golden Bough* was originally published in 12 volumes
(1890–1915); a one-volume abridgment was published in 1922.

634.22    Arrowhead . . . Emerald Bay.] Arrowhead Springs, resort in San
Bernardino National Forest; Emerald Bay, cove on the southwest side of
Lake Tahoe, reserved as a state park.

692.9–10    Tinker to Evers to Chance] Celebrated double-play combination of Chicago Cubs players Joe Tinker, Johnny Evers, and Frank Chance,
popularized in a 1908 poem by Franklin P. Adams.

701.28–29    wore . . . difference] Cf. *Hamlet*, IV.v.183.

702.24–25    "And . . . fall."] *Hamlet*, IV.v.219.

723.7    Spy] Pseudonym of the English caricaturist Sir Leslie Ward
(1841–1913).


PLAYBACK

737.16    Super Chief] Luxury train running between Los Angeles and
Chicago.

741.28    Edward Arnold] Character actor featured in dozens of films including *Diamond Jim* (1935), *The Glass Key* (1935), *Easy Living* (1937), *Mr.
Smith Goes to Washington* (1939), and *Meet John Doe* (1941).

772.2    Herbert Marshall] English actor (1890–1966) featured in many
films including *Trouble in Paradise* (1932), *The Painted Veil* (1934), and
*Foreign Correspondent* (1940).

818.33    Eddie Arcaro] Jockey (b. 1916) who raced for 30 years, winning
the Triple Crown twice and the Kentucky Derby five times.

819.27    Johnny One-Note] Song (1937) by Richard Rodgers and Lorenz
Hart, featured in the musical *Babes in Arms*.

826.8    CIC] Counter Intelligence Corps.

861.4–6    some private eye . . . torture on her.] The reference is to
Mickey Spillane's *One Lonely Night* (1951).


DOUBLE INDEMNITY

873.1    DOUBLE INDEMNITY] The film, produced by Joseph Sistrom,
was released by Paramount in 1944. It was directed by Billy Wilder, with
cinematography by John F. Seitz and music by Miklos Rozsa; the editor was
Doane Harrison. The cast included Fred MacMurray (Walter Neff), Barbara
Stanwyck (Phyllis Dietrichson), Edward G. Robinson (Barton Keyes), Porter

Hall (Mr. Jackson), Jean Heather (Lola Dietrichson), Tom Powers (Mr. Dietrichson), Byron Barr (Nino Zachette), Richard Gaines (Mr. Norton), and Fortunio Bonanova (Sam Gorlopis). The film received six Academy Award nominations, including best picture and best screenplay.

873.3    *Novel. . . Cain*]   Cain's novella was published in 1936. Of the extensive changes made in the book's dialogue by Chandler and Wilder, Chandler wrote in a letter to Cain in March 1944: "A curious matter I'd like to call to your attention . . . is your dialogue. Nothing could be more natural and easy and to the point on paper, and yet it doesn't quite play. We tried it out by having a couple of actors do a scene right out of the book. It had a sort of remote effect that I was at a loss to understand. It came to me then that the effect of your written dialogue is only partly sound and sense. The rest of the effect is the appearance on the page. These unevenly shaped hunks of quick-moving speech hit the eye with a sort of explosive effect. You read the stuff in batches, not in individual speech and counterspeech. On the screen this is all lost, and the essential mildness of the phrasing shows up as lacking in sharpness."

880.14    Leo Carrillo]   Carrillo (1880–1961) played stereotypical Latin characters in many films including *Viva Villa!* (1934), *In Caliente* (1935), and *The Gay Desperado* (1936); he later played Pancho on the television series *The Cisco Kid.*

883.5    The Philadelphia story]   Reference to play (1939) by Philip Barry, filmed in 1940.

886.10–16    She liked . . . dynamite]   This passage does not appear in the released version of the film.

887.26–888.17    KEYES. Yeah . . . do nothin.']   This dialogue does not appear in the released version.

905.31–35    NEFF. I . . . bottle.]   This dialogue does not appear in the released version.

907.3–4    PHYLLIS. Now . . . dead.]   This dialogue does not appear in the released version.

912.4–5    LOLA. He . . . him.]   Omitted in the released version.

924.12–15    DIETRICHSON. Just . . . up.]   In the released version, Dietrichson replies: "Yeah."

924.23–30    DIETRICHSON. Aw . . . train.]   This dialogue does not appear in the released version.

925.1–4    PHYLLIS' VOICE. . . you that.]   This dialogue does not appear in the released version.

925.14–20    PHYLLIS. Don't . . . Hobeys.]   This dialogue does not appear in the released version.

925.24–26    DIETRICHSON'S VOICE. . . you?—]   Omitted in the released version.

934.29–935.11    He gets . . . into it.]   Omitted in the released version, in which the scene begins by fading in on Neff speaking into the dictaphone.

948.32–949.11    NEFF. Won't . . . watchful.]   Omitted in the released version, which cuts from Schwartz leaving the room to Lola, who is already seated, beginning to speak.

959.3–7    Because . . . pray . . . ]   Omitted in the released version.

961.17–29    Neff moves . . . enters.]   In the released version, Neff stands in the lobby, then turns and boards the elevator as Neff's voice is heard saying: "I was scared stiff, Keyes. Maybe you were playing cat and mouse with me. Maybe you knew all along I was the somebody else. I had to find out. And I knew where to look—in your office." The film then cuts to Neff entering Keyes' office.

963.26–27    was all . . . had . . . ]   In the released version: "had plans of her own."

963.36–964.3    NEFF'S VOICE. She . . . for me.]   Omitted in the released version.

## SELECTED ESSAYS

984.2    *Trent's Last Case*]   By E. C. Benson, published in 1912.

984.10    Freeman Wills Crofts]   Crofts (1879–1957) was the author of many novels notable for their elaborate use of timetables and alibis, including *The Cask* (1920), *The Pit-Prop Syndicate* (1925), and *The Loss of the Jane Vosper* (1936).

984.15    Dorothy Sayers']   Sayers (1893–1957) wrote a series of detective novels featuring Lord Peter Wimsey, including *The Unpleasantness at the Bellona Club* (1928), *Murder Must Advertise* (1933), and *Gaudy Night* (1936).

984.23    a scheme of Agatha Christie's]   The plot referred to is that of *Murder in the Calais Coach* (1934; American title, *Murder on the Orient Express*).

985.2–3    creator . . . Vance]   S. S. Van Dine (pseudonym of Willard Huntington Wright, 1888–1939).

986.16    *Omnibus of Crime*]   Anthology of short crime fiction published in 1928.

987.39    Detection Club]   The Detection Club was founded in London in 1928 by the novelist Anthony Berkeley (also known as Francis Iles); its first president was G. K. Chesterton.

989.22    Marius the Epicurean]   Novel (1885) by Walter Pater.

991.10     all this (and Hammett too)]   Cf. Rachel Fields' novel *All This and Heaven Too* (filmed 1940).

994.37     Bennett Cerf]   Cerf (1898–1971), co-founder of Random House, was also known as an anthologist and television personality.

1003.5     and not . . . too critically.]   For Chandler's comments on this passage, see 1026.29–1027.16.

1004.10    Christie's *Murder in a Calais Coach*]   See note 984.23.

1004.17    "The Speckled Band"]   Story by Arthur Conan Doyle, collected in *The Adventures of Sherlock Holmes* (1892).

1004.31    "The Purloined Letter"]   Story by Edgar Allan Poe, first published in 1844.

1004.35–36    Austin Freeman . . . fingerprint]   *The Red Thumb Mark* (1907).

1005.11    Dr. Thorndyke]   The forensic analyst who is the detective hero of most of R. Austin Freeman's novels.

1005.27    Valentine Williams]   Author (1883–1946) of mystery novels including *The Eye in Attendance* (1927) and *Death Answers the Bell* (1932).

1006.33–34    "The Red-Headed League"]   Story by Arthur Conan Doyle, collected in *The Adventures of Sherlock Holmes* (1892).

1007.19    Johnston Office]   Eric A. Johnston succeeded Will Hays in 1941 as president of the Motion Picture Association of America and administrator of its production code.

1017.6     *Black Mask*]   Pulp crime magazine whose contributors, besides Chandler, included Dashiell Hammett, Paul Cain, Carroll John Daly, and Erle Stanley Gardner.

SELECTED LETTERS

1025.13    Charlie Brackett]   Charles Brackett (1892–1969), producer and screenwriter, best known for collaborations with Billy Wilder, including *Ninotchka* (1939), *The Lost Weekend* (1945), and *Sunset Boulevard* (1950).

1025.31    Beirne Lay . . . Studs Lonigan]   Beirne Lay Jr. (1909–82) was a wartime bomber group commander whose screenplays included *I Wanted Wings* (1941) and *Twelve O'Clock High* (1949); "Studs Lonigan" refers to James T. Farrell (1904–79), author of the fictional trilogy of that name.

1025.38    Jules Romains]   French author (1885–1972) best known for 27-volume cycle of novels *Les Hommes de Bonne Volonté* (*Men of Good Will*), 1932–46.

1025.39    Wolcott Gibbs]   Gibbs (1902–58) was drama critic for *The New Yorker* from 1940 until his death.

1026.9–11    *The Last Laugh. . . The More the Merrier*]    *The Last Laugh* (dir. F. W. Murnau, Germany, 1924); *Variety* (dir. E. A. Dupont, Germany, 1925); *M* (dir. Fritz Lang, Germany, 1931); *Mayerling* (dir. Anatole Litvak, France, 1936); *Night Must Fall* (dir. Richard Thorpe, U.S., 1937); *Intolerance* (dir. D. W. Griffith, U.S., 1916); *The Little Foxes* (dir. William Wyler, U.S., 1941); *The More the Merrier* (dir. George Stevens, U.S., 1943).

1026.12–14    *Dear Ruth. . . Getting Married*]    *Dear Ruth* (1944) by Joseph M. Hyman and Bernard Hart; *The Voice of the Turtle* (1943) by John Van Druten; *The Second Mrs. Tanqueray* (1893) by Arthur Wing Pinero; *The Lion and the Mouse* (1905) by Charles Klein; *Oklahoma!* (1943) by Richard Rodgers and Oscar Hammerstein II; *Dear Brutus* (1917) by J. M. Barrie; *Getting Married* (1908) by George Bernard Shaw.

1027.20    Dale Warren]    Publicity director of Houghton Mifflin, Chandler's publisher at the time.

1027.21–22    *The Leavenworth Case*]    Novel (1878) by Anna Katharine Green.

1027.38    DeVoto]    Bernard De Voto (1897–1955), historian and columnist for *Harper's Magazine*.

1027.40    Marquand's last book]    John P. Marquand's *Repent in Haste* (1945).

1031.23    *Frederick Lewis Allen*]    Allen (1890–1954) was editor of *Harper's Magazine* and author of bestselling historical works such as *Only Yesterday* (1931) and *The Big Change* (1952).

1031.27    Eric Bentley]    Eric Bentley (b. 1916), author of *The Playwright as Thinker* (1946) and other works.

1031.35    Mary McCarthy]    McCarthy (1912–89) was drama critic for *The Partisan Review* from 1937 to 1956.

1032.16    *The Iceman Cometh*]    Eugene O'Neill's play opened on Broadway in October 1946.

1032.17    George Jean Nathan]    Nathan (1882–1958) was co-editor with H. L. Mencken of *The Smart Set* and *The American Mercury*; he was the author of *The Popular Theatre* (1918), *The Critic and the Drama* (1922), *Since Ibsen* (1933), and other books.

1033.32–33    Auden . . . detective stories]    "The Guilty Vicarage" was published in *Harper's Magazine* in May 1948.

1035.2    *James Sandoe*]    Librarian at the University of Colorado and a reviewer of crime fiction.

1035.7    John Macdonald]    Pseudonym of Kenneth Millar (1915–83), who after the publication of *The Moving Target* changed his pseudonym to Ross Macdonald at the request of mystery writer John D. MacDonald.

1036.20     *Hamish Hamilton*]   Chandler's British publisher.

1036.34     Pound . . . Bollingen]   Pound was awarded the $10,000 prize in February 1949 by a panel of judges that included T. S. Eliot, W. H. Auden, Conrad Aiken, Louise Bogan, Allen Tate, and Robert Lowell. At the time, Pound was confined to St. Elizabeth's Hospital in Washington, D.C., after being judged insane and hence unable to stand trial for treason in connection with his broadcasts from Italy during World War II.

1037.25     Betty Smith]   Smith (1904–72) was the author of *A Tree Grows in Brooklyn* (1943), *Tomorrow Will Be Better* (1948), and other novels.

1037.37     Mary Margaret McBride]   Popular radio personality.

1038.8     John Houseman]   Houseman (1902–88) co-founded the Mercury Theatre with Orson Welles and later produced such Hollywood films as *The Blue Dahlia* (1946), *Letter from an Unknown Woman* (1948), and *They Live By Night* (1949).

1041.10     Gardner]   Erle Stanley Gardner (1889–1970), prolific author of novels featuring lawyer Perry Mason.

1043.1     *Chronicles of Hecate County*]   *Memoirs of Hecate County* (1946).

1043.9     John Dickson Carr . . . Anthony Boucher]   Carr (1905–77), who also wrote under the name Carter Dickson, was the author of many detective novels including *Poison in Jest* (1932), *The Three Coffins* (1935), and *The Case of the Constant Suicides* (1941); Boucher (pseudonym of William Anthony Parker White, 1911–68) was a well-known reviewer of detective fiction and author of novels including *The Case of the Seven of Calvary* (1937) and *The Case of the Seven Sneezes* (1942).

1048.13     *Frederic Dannay*]   Co-author (1905–82) with Manfred B. Lee of many detective novels published under the pseudonym Ellery Queen, including *The Roman Hat Mystery* (1928), *Calamity Town* (1942), and *Ten Days' Wonder* (1948), and co-editor of *Ellery Queen's Mystery Magazine* (first issue 1941) and of many anthologies of crime fiction.

1048.22–23     Elisabeth Sanxay Holding]   American crime writer (1889–1955), author of *Miasma* (1928), *Net of Cobwebs* (1945), *The Innocent Mrs. Duff* (1946), and other novels.

1049.40     Edmund Wilson]   Wilson discussed crime fiction in "Why Do People Read Detective Stories?" (*The New Yorker*, October 14, 1944) and "Who Cares Who Killed Roger Ackroyd?" (*The New Yorker*, January 20, 1945), concluding that "the reading of detective stories is simply a kind of vice that, for silliness and minor harmfulness, ranks somewhere between smoking and crossword puzzles."

1051.14     Hornblower . . . Forester]   Series of novels about Captain Horatio Hornblower, a British naval commander in the Napoleonic period.

1051.22    G. A. Henty] George Alfred Henty (1832–1902), popular writer of boys' adventure stories including *The Young Francs-Tireurs* (1872), *Redskin and Cowboy* (1892), and *With Roberts to Pretoria* (1902).

1051.30–31    Popski's *Private Army*] World War II memoir published in 1950 by Lieutenant Colonel Vladimir Peniakoff (1897–1951), a British officer widely known as "Popski," who had commanded a small special forces unit in North Africa and Italy that became known as "Popski's Private Army."

1051.35    Rex Stout] Stout (1886–1975) was the author of novels about detective Nero Wolfe, including *Fer-de-Lance* (1932), *The Red Box* (1937), and *Too Many Cooks* (1938).

CATALOGING INFORMATION

Chandler, Raymond, 1888–1959
  (Selections)
  Novels and other writings / Raymond Chandler.
     p.  cm.  — (The Library of America ; 80)
  Contents: The lady in the lake—The little sister—The long
goodbye—Playback—Double indemnity—Selected essays and letters.
    1. Marlowe, Philip (Fictitious character)—Fiction.  2. Private
investigators—California—Los Angeles—Fiction.  3. Detective
and mystery stories, American.  4. Los Angeles (Calif.)—Fiction.
I. Title.  II. Title. The lady in the lake.  III. Title. The little sister.
IV. Title. The long goodbye.  V. Title.  Playback.
VI. Title.  Double indemnity.  VII. Series.
PS3505.H3224A6    1995c     94–43705
813'.52—dc20
ISBN 1–883011–08–6

This book is set in 10 point Linotron Galliard,
a face designed for photocomposition by Matthew Carter
and based on the sixteenth-century face Granjon. The paper is
acid-free Ecusta Nyalite and meets the requirements for permanence
of the American National Standards Institute. The binding
material is Brillianta, a woven rayon cloth made by
Van Heek-Scholco Textielfabrieken, Holland.
The composition is by The Clarinda
Company. Printing and binding by
R.R.Donnelley & Sons Company.
Designed by Bruce Campbell.

# HIDING
# IN THE
# BATHROOM

# HIDING
# IN THE
# BATHROOM

## An Introvert's Roadmap
## to Getting Out There
### (When You'd Rather Stay Home)

## Morra Aarons-Mele

**DEY ST.**
*An Imprint of* WILLIAM MORROW

"Are You An Introvert?" on pages xvi–xvi courtesy of QuietRev.com.

Work+Life Fit is trademarked property of FlexStrategy Group/Work+Life Fit Inc. and used with permission.

"Social Anxiety versus Introversion" in Chapter 1 courtesy of Dr. Ellen Hendriksen.

"Collaborative Negotiation Prep Worksheet" in Chapter 12 reprinted with permission from Tanya Tarr.

"Own Your Expertise" exercise from the Op Ed project reprinted with permission from Katie Orenstein.

HarperCollins books may be purchased for educational, business, or sales promotional use. For information, please e-mail the Special Markets Department at SPsales@harpercollins.com.

FIRST EDITION

Designed by Paula Russell Szafranski
Title page background by phokin/Shutterstock, Inc.

Library of Congress Cataloging-in-Publication Data has been applied for.

ISBN 978-0-06-266608-6

17 18 19 20 21   LSC   10 9 8 7 6 5 4 3 2 1

*To my husband Nicco Mele,*
*who I love so deeply and learn from every day.*

*And to Rachel Sklar and Glynnis MacNicol of TheLi.st,*
*two women who lead fearlessly and give generously.*

*And finally to my mom, Pamela Aarons,*
*who taught me how to be strong.*

# CONTENTS

# HIDING
# IN THE
# BATHROOM

# INTRODUCTION

N etwork your way to the top."
"Always say yes."
"Never eat lunch alone."
"Get out there!"

If you're an overachiever like me, you've definitely heard this advice. And, if you're ambitious, you also probably believe that to be successful, you have to be out there 24/7, tirelessly pressing the flesh, doing deals, tweeting, and keynoting conferences. That there's a successful "type"—the intense, sleepless mover and shaker, the person who "leans in" and musters endless amounts of grit. And if you don't fit that type, well, you're out of luck.

I call bullshit.

Much of what we think we must do to succeed is unnecessary and even counterproductive. I've interviewed over one hundred fifty successful entrepreneurs and executives, and I can tell you that most of them aren't the always-on, outgoing superstars we would assume. One new media CEO whose viral videos have garnered over a hundred million views told me that she experiences major anxiety being in a room where she doesn't know anyone. "I go straight into awkward middle schooler mode," she confessed. The founder of a biotech firm who just received Series A financing confessed that she hides in the bathroom at conferences, "usually because I am crying." A former Wall Street banker who now runs a successful tech start-up has to "take beta-blockers for public speaking."

And then there's me. I'm a hermit by nature, an extreme introvert, more comfortable at home, with my kids, my cats, and my kitchen than out there selling to a room. I'll admit it: facilitating meetings and giving speeches intimidate and exhaust me. When I fly to meet a potential client or to give a talk, I take so much anxiety-fighting Xanax that I'm barely conscious. I manage my social media feeds very tightly, doing just enough to keep me in the game. And yet I own and run a successful business in which I am the primary sales driver.

"Hiding in the bathroom" has become my shorthand for hacking and faking my way to appearing like a typical successful business-person. Given my natural inclinations, I would hide almost all the time. I would rarely choose to leave my house. But as extensive as my online network is, I could not sustain a business that way. So I've learned to get out there, building in strategies and tricks that allay my anxieties and introversion while I'm at a professional gathering or client meeting, then creating home time to recharge, be on my own, and do the work.

I used to beat myself up about needing to hide in the bathroom. I would walk into a huge crowd, panic at the number of strangers, and head immediately for the ladies'. But over time I've learned that I often need a moment to reset during a busy workday. Now I know it's okay to take a moment to breathe. Then I put on some lipstick, look in the mirror, and tell myself, *You can do it. Get out there.*

## Becoming My Own Kind of Entrepreneur

When I was a kid, I told everyone, "I want to be a media mogul." I had a photo of famed Paramount boss Sherry Lansing on my bedroom wall. I wrote my tenth-grade economics paper on the inside story of Barry Diller's bid to own Universal Studios. And, because I had the good fortune of coming of age during the Clinton years, when jobs were plentiful for precocious twentysomethings, I was well on my way. After graduating from college, I worked a series of high-profile jobs in the marketing world and was even recognized in a prominent national "top 30 under 30" list.

There was one problem: secretly (or perhaps not so secretly), I was miserable. I tried on many different personas, and adopted countless ad hoc coping mechanisms, but nothing helped. I kept torpedoing my success at every turn. I drank too much at office happy hours and acted inappropriately. My weight constantly went up and down as I bounced between bingeing and barely eating at all. I was anxious almost every day, and had frequent panic attacks. Quite often, I was so depressed that I called in sick to work and hid in bed all day.

At my last job, I was asked to start a department from scratch, and I was too prideful, anxious, and shortsighted to secure allies. Eventually the New York office tried to get me fired. Did this girl stand up and fight like a plucky heroine in a novel? No, she did not. She cried in the bathroom and started working from home as often as she could.

But, when she eventually quit and started freelancing, she became an accidental entrepreneur who focuses more on making time for life than making millions.

I run a business called Women Online. We are a social-impact marketing agency with the sole mission of creating campaigns that mobilize women for social good. I like to say we are small but mighty: even though we have fewer than ten people—and are virtual at that!—we help the largest organizations in the world with digital strategy. For example, we helped President Obama's campaign reach mom bloggers and get them to the polls, and we created digital tools that inspired American families to learn about and support the work of Malala Yousafzai and the United Nations, both on a mission to educate girls worldwide.

Over the last decade, I've built a life that allows me to earn enough money and find just enough recognition without driving myself crazy and sacrificing my homebody self. I learned to play to my strengths and nourish my introversion, focusing less on the long-term outcome of "success" and more on the everyday. Today, thanks to the deliberate way I've organized my business, I can literally be at the UN one day and home with the boys digging in the dirt the next. On the days I'm at a client's office, pitching new business or giving a speech, you'll probably find me in the ladies' in between sessions. Every single day I build in lots of breaks and alone time for myself, even if it's just five minutes in a quiet room. Of course, this best-of-both-worlds lifestyle comes at a cost. It has meant sacrifices, less success than some peers, and a slower path. But it's my version of success, and I love it.

The "aha" moment came when I learned to redefine my vision of success. The old vision was media mogul. My new vision was less focused on some far-off notion of success attained. I traded "someday" for "today." For me, it's the choice to be a hermit entrepreneur: a mostly tongue-in-cheek term I use to describe my choice to mostly work at home in my yoga pants.

What if you became the kind of success you wanted to be? What if you could enjoy the everyday of your work life? What if you stopped all that networking? What if you distilled your business development to the bare minimum, and still managed to grow your business or your income? What if instead of getting out there, you could simply stay in?

The good news is that you can learn and practice the skills you need to achieve a version of success that's right for you, and make enough money. And I'll give you strategies and concrete career-development and management tools to get there.

These strategies begin with setting a vision and developing realistic goals that satisfy all of your needs, even if it means accepting a more modest career or slower business growth trajectory. Then, manage around your goals in ways that allow for an enjoyable, "hermit" lifestyle. To maximize your impact with the least amount of face time, you carve out a strong professional niche and digital footprint for yourself. If you own a small business or work freelance, you price your offerings slightly above market rate. You determine the right client, project mix, or type of work that allows you the time you need for yourself. No matter where you work, you create a long-term, professional "franchise" for yourself that assures you of future jobs, freelance gigs, and business opportunities as well as even more free time in the future. You engage in high-impact, smart networking and only attend a few strategically selected conferences. You track your work flow and scope your work more carefully so as to protect your time for family, friends, and self. And finally, you recalibrate expectations with bosses, spouses, family members, and others.

In this book, we're going to talk a lot about emotions, particularly anxiety. As a business owner and entrepreneur with serious mental health challenges, I've often found myself hiding out in the bathroom. We've all been there, but few of us actually talk about it.

But part and parcel of being a successful introvert is allowing those emotions to be an opportunity to gain knowledge, and to make them work for you, instead of driving your work. As my friend Dr. Kim Leary, associate professor at Harvard Medical School says, "Think about what you give up if you aren't attuned to your emotions." Life would indeed be dull and gray, and you can use that anxiety to help you in your career, not harm it.

Now that I've realized my anxiety is part of who I am, and that, rather than fight it all the time, I embrace what it gives me, like excellent people skills, empathy, and drive. I like to think my anxiety and I are business partners, frequently negotiating, sometimes arguing, but often creating great work. Later on, we'll examine what I call the "gift of anxiety"—the secret skills anxiety gives us in our work lives—and we'll detail specific strategies to manage it when it gets unruly.

Ultimately, hiding in the bathroom means relentlessly attending to the care and feeding of your *whole* being. It means vigorously reinforcing your personal boundaries, even when others pressure you to grow faster or make more money. You will not garner accolades for growing your career or business slowly, or for enjoying your life. You won't be featured in magazines, and you probably won't keynote conferences. Even worse, everyone in your life, from your accountant to your graphic designer to maybe even your spouse, will question your strategy. It's not sexy to develop slowly. But hermit professionals know the truth: it's better. Committed to what will make them happy over the long term, they do what it takes to stay home and make each day rich, meaningful, and fulfilling.

All this might sound unrealistic, but in fact the successful professionals I've interviewed for this book and for my *Forbes* podcast all share one thing in common: they have managed to integrate work with personal passion and interest. Some of them, like me, are extreme introverts—they have social anxiety and hate to fly. These men and women don't follow the traditional rules. They have made their own rules and honed their skills accordingly. You can, too.

Leaning in is great, but not everyone can lean in all the time. It makes us too tired. It's also not that fun. More fun is nerding out on your own for hours, just thinking and doing—engaging in what investor Paul Graham terms "rich, solitary, germinative time." It might be picking your kids up from school every day or taking care of your aging parents. It might be tinkering in your garden or cultivating other hobbies. The dirty little secret of success is that you can grow your business, build your career, and do the work you love while still making room for outside interests. You can hang out at home more and keep travel, networking, and extracurriculars to a minimum. I hope *Hiding in the Bathroom* will show you how.

# ARE YOU AN INTROVERT?

Susan Cain's excellent book *Quiet* is the bible for the modern introvert. If you haven't read it, I really recommend it. (There's also the excellent sister website, QuietRev.com.) Here are a list of traits common to introverts to help you discover if you're one, too. (Adapted with thanks from *Quiet,* and amended to my own research.)

*I do my best work in a quiet environment.*

*Too much exposure to noise or light leaves me feeling drained, spacey, or headachy. (Fluorescents!)*

*Being out and about in a social or work setting leaves me feeling drained, even if I have a great time.*

*In large social gatherings, I need to take frequent breaks to be by myself or with a trusted friend.*

*Large crowds drain me.*

*I recharge and draw energy through alone time.*

*I like to think before I speak, and I like to feel prepared before I speak.*

*I have an active interior monologue, and I tend to ruminate a lot on events and decisions.*

*People would describe me as quiet. (Note: No one would describe me as quiet. In fact, I'm extremely talkative, sometimes loud, and I love public speaking. I'm still an introvert and you can be, too.)*

*I need a lot of alone time.*

*Working in an open-plan office is very draining, and I seek quiet spaces to hide out.*

*I work better at home.*

*(Courtesy QuietRev.com)*

# My Life as an Unhappy Overachiever

The idea for this book began when I gave a speech at my alma mater, Brown University. I was nervous before the speech (as was the Brown Alumni Relations staff!) because I planned to get raw. In front of a room of two hundred successful women, I was going to share the story of how I became happy at work only after I realized that the idea of who I wanted to be was making me anxious, destructive, and depressed.

I was nervous but also elated as I approached the podium. As I began to command the large hall I'd walked by many times as an anxious, and often sad, undergraduate, I felt free. "If you knew me at Brown, I don't think you'd have expected I'd be keynoting the dinner," I opened.

"I have the dubious distinction," I continued, diving in, "of being an ambitious risk taker who also struggles with anxiety and depression. This has forced me to learn some very helpful coping mechanisms, and I want to share some today with you."

But first, I told them, there were the panic attacks. That time sophomore year I couldn't get out of bed for a week. Hiding in my dorm room, and then, when I graduated, in my apartments. How

I sought geographical cures, moving to different cities, like London, and even farther-away continents, like Africa. How I did a fair amount of drugs—the worst of which, ironically, were by prescription. (Okay, I didn't mention that in the speech.)

I talked about how, as a young woman, I wanted so badly to be liked, and to do everything right. I felt it was expected of me. I had been the kid who cried at sleepaway camp and wouldn't let my mother and sister leave my first night at college. I only wanted home, and comfort. Instead I dealt with its absence like many young people do: through eating, drinking, and hookups.

I told them how, because I was very ambitious and driven, I went for every big job and opportunity I could—how I ran marketing for Europe's largest online travel company when I was twenty-five. How I kept getting promoted, and I kept being miserable. The work was easy, but the office politics, the hours, the pace, networking, and rules of getting ahead rubbed up against my very temperament. I was living out someone else's climb up the ladder, and I was fighting a losing battle.

I had quit nine jobs, I wasn't even thirty, and I cried in the bathroom almost every day.

I talked about the day I realized that who I was and what I was doing every day were completely mismatched.

It was during my final corporate job, when, under the ubiquitous fluorescent lights, I realized I was *allergic* to them. They give me migraines. And as long as I had to show up and sit under those lights for ten-plus hours a day simply because I was expected to, I could never be happy.

"I see now," I told the audience, "that I was caught in a cycle of achievement, of working hard for someone else's dreams or expectations, and not my own." It was only when I accepted that I needed a quieter life, needed to reframe success on my own terms, and figure out the tool kit I needed to get there, that I could find joy at work. Becoming "less successful" set me free.

Not exactly your typical go-get-'em women's leadership speech.

I looked around the room and was terrified. Would the undergrads and alumnae think I was a nutjob? I had worked so hard on the speech, and it was the first real keynote I had delivered. (It's still one of the few.)

The speech got a standing ovation, and I felt like Oprah.

Many of the women in the room came up to me. Some were crying. Thank you, they said. We're so anxious all the time, and no one tells us the truth.

I'll never forget one young woman, a senior who was an economics major. She said to me: "I'm just so tired of trying to be this perfect person." Like me, and many in the audience, she was on both antidepressants and antianxiety medication.

I felt her pain. Growing up, I was sent to the best private schools, and it never occurred to me to do anything less than achieve. Those of us fortunate enough to be raised with expectations of academic or financial success learn that when we achieve, we garner praise and positive attention—even if we're faking our own enjoyment. Through childhood, adolescence, and into adulthood, we keep achieving, craving the external validation that comes when we get all As or are chosen to captain the team. I was, and am, extremely ambitious. But the more we achieve in order to win the approval of others, the further we get from our own goals—and happiness.

In the twenty-two years since I entered college, it has only gotten worse. The achievement pressure starts at birth, and snowballs from there. When a good friend, my commiserator in the high-stakes process of applying to private kindergarten in Los Angeles, visited her alma mater, the admissions director told her, "You wouldn't recognize the program. It's much more challenging than it was when you were here."

For similar reasons, even to this day, I don't like to visit college campuses—and my husband is a professor! I can feel the echoes of anxiety and profound loneliness so strongly. And it's not only me. A recent Duke study found that women who graduated in the 1970s were much happier than those graduating now, and had far more self-confidence. The report concluded that the women who graduated in the seventies cared less about what people thought about them, and were able to take risks—such as pursuing a nontraditional career or starting their own business. In fact, women seem to be increasingly less happy, even as they achieve more professionally.

Ambitious and privileged young people on the path to college are raised with a narrative of achievement—a surround-sound, multi-faceted version—that no generation has experienced before. Do the most extracurriculars. Have the perfect internship. Get a great first job. Build your personal brand. Run that marathon. Eat organic. Get perfectly hairless and smooth. Fuck perfectly. Navigate dating. Enter your thirties, find a partner, conceive, and give birth (naturally, of course). Make your pregnant body the perfect temple for your perfect newborn, who will become a precociously perfect toddler. With the addition of social media, you're supposed to share it all, too—as you suffer the FOMO of watching everyone else seemingly sail through life.

I've found that it is especially hard to achieve in a traditional career ladder scenario if you are an introvert, and if you need more control over your space, pace, and place of work than others. Let me be clear: this has nothing to do with laziness, or lack of ambition. Your need for a different kind of workday has nothing to do with the level of effort you will put in, or the drive you possess. That's ingrained in who you are just as much as your need for quiet or alone time. When you work differently, it may even mean you work harder than someone who's spending plenty of time at the office surfing Gilt.com. I may be a hermit who rarely eats lunch with anyone, but ask anyone who knows me and they will agree: I work hard and I am driven as hell. (They don't know I'm usually working in bed.)

# THE OVERACHIEVER INDEX

Are you addicted to achievement? No score needed here; you know it when you see it.

*You regularly get nine hours of sleep, and you feel guilty.*

*You're really sick. But no one needs to know. (Cough.)*

*You only got 720 on your GMAT.*

*You lost five pounds. Time for the next five.*

*You've actually made up boyfriends for your parents. They'd worry if you were single.*

*Work isn't enough: you need to join a board or volunteer or start a nonprofit.*

*You hired a designer for your three-year-old's preschool project.*

*You don't let anyone over unless the house is perfectly clean.*

*Nothing store-bought will tarnish your Thanksgiving table.*

*After your (99 percent glowing) performance review, you can't stop thinking about the one piece of negative feedback you got from your boss.*

*Reading about your former college roommate's new start-up totally ruins your day, but you obsessively search Google for more news.*

# THE TWIN PLAGUES:
# FOMO AND ACHIEVEMENT PORN

You're sitting in your home office, scanning Facebook. Friends and colleagues are giving TED Talks, being featured in interviews, and posting pictures of fabulous events. You're not even dressed. Another day, another professional conference, keynote, or viral event that's not yours. Why aren't you out there? What's wrong with you?

FOMO is the curse of our social media moment. According to Wikipedia[1] (and who better to define the digital age?) it's a "pervasive apprehension that others might be having rewarding experiences from which one is absent." (As Mindy Kaling succinctly puts it, "Why is everyone hanging out without me?") You always know what colleagues and competitors are up to—as long as it's good.

When I launched my podcast series for *Forbes*, I obsessively tracked how many "likes" other hosts got on their social media. At least once a week I lie on my bed in the dead silence of my workday and scroll through Twitter, just to feel bad about my choice to be a hermit entrepreneur. And even though I'm a middle-aged married lady who's off the dating market, social media FOMO still causes me anxiety, except now it's about my feed's professional accomplishments and political activism ("Such an honor to receive the alumni achievement award!"); amazing exotic vacations with kids who don't seem to whine or bitch on the plane; or marathons run.

I don't know any human being, introverted, extroverted, or in-between, who doesn't fall prey to FOMO on a regular basis. It's the most human thing in the world to compare oneself to others. Not to sound like a thirteen-year-old, but it sucks, no matter what kind of personality you have.

## If I'm an Introvert, Why Do I Feel FOMO?

But wait a minute: Didn't you make a choice to be in your home of-fice and not out there socializing? You hate the idea of giving a TED Talk! So why do you feel so left out?

If you're an anxious introvert, in conflict over where you belong in the rat race, an Instagram picture can turn into a dagger. *If only I were different,* you might think, *I, too, would be invited to that party. I'd be getting that award. Instead I'm hiding.*

But remember—actually, this feeling isn't about you at all. It's *the whole point* of social media. The creators of Instagram, Twitter, Facebook, and other FOMO-inducing sites specifically developed a product that would be addictive because it preys on our most hu-man emotions.[2] When you feel different and lesser than the per-fect vignettes filling your feed, social media is cruel indeed—and it makes you want to come back for more.

Caterina Fake, who cofounded the groundbreaking Flickr *and* coined the term *FOMO* (she is my hero), explains how social soft-ware both "creates and cures FOMO. If you didn't know that party was going on, you'd be home contentedly reading your latest *New Yorker.* But since you do, you hungrily watch each new tweet. It gives you a sense that you're missing out, even when you aren't." Your FOMO isn't about your failure. It's actually the marketing strategy of Instagram, Facebook, Snapchat, and Twitter.

And I'm not innocent. When I have something fabulous to share, what do I do? Show off—the speaking gig, a VIP invite, a great photo where I look awesome, or my adorable baby. I understand the rush of endorphins a really well-received social media post brings. It's almost more fun than the event itself.

But, while posting gourmet meals or a fun night out is one thing, tech writer Brian Solis reminds us that all of us who use social net-works and apps channel the "'accidental narcissist'" in us. We act out roles, ignoring our own enjoyment.

I call this syndrome "achievement porn." I know using the term *porn* is controversial, and yet I can think of no other word that quite describes what I'm talking about: airbrushed, glossy images of successful people in made-for-coveting environments. Social media like blogs or Instagram allows fledgling achievers to craft powerful narratives about their potential, and rise. (My least favorite? The "mompreneur" who just happens to whip up a million-dollar business while messing around in the kitchen.) By consuming ever-higher levels of broadcast, digital, and social media, we've come to believe the impossible. And we watch it all unfold, feeling jealous it's not ours.

No one likes to feel jealous—and in a world in which social media has made subtle showing off the default, we now have an opportunity to feel jealous several times a day. In tweets and awards and magazine spreads, achievement is fetishized, and logging onto Facebook can lead to a paralyzing wave of FOMO. By the time you've reached the workplace, chances are you've internalized it so deeply you don't even question it. You're so busy performing so others can validate you, you forget to notice if you're working toward your own goals.

Still, FOMO is a clever tool, and every businessperson cultivates it. In his brilliant podcast series *StartUp*, Alex Blumberg notes that FOMO drives Silicon Valley investing; if a potential investor doesn't feel a sense of FOMO when learning of a new investment opportunity, then the rich guy will find another idea to throw his money at. The object that inspires FOMO is imbued with an aura of success.

Like FOMO, achievement can be an illusion and publicity doesn't pay the bills (nor do TED Talks). Take Theranos founder Elizabeth Holmes. She built a company that promised to simplify blood tests, and she raised at least $750 million in backing. We all wanted to believe the incredible story of the tenacious, glamorous blonde who disrupted an industry and became a billionaire. Too bad it wasn't true.

## Bea Arthur's Story

It's crucial to remember that thousands of follows on an Instagram feed or a *Fast Company* feature isn't money in your bank account. Bea Arthur learned that in Silicon Valley, when solid revenue, TV appearances, accolades, and tons of PR still didn't pay the bills for her second start-up, the online therapy company In Your Corner.

The child of entrepreneur immigrants from Ghana, Bea Arthur was brave and confident, and by all appearances, a Silicon Valley success story: the first African American woman invited to Y Combinator, the famous Silicon Valley start-up incubator. She had a TEDx Talk in her pocket, multiple TV appearances, and glowing press. And, unlike most start-ups, her company actually earned money.

But, in real life, as she scaled, her start-up was failing, and she was living on loans. "I'd have to get up and smile and do these talks and go on TV," Bea says, "and it was raining inside my soul."

Here's where the irony gets even deeper: the more Silicon Valley courted her, providing venture capital and media attention, the more she abandoned her original mission and overspent. "I fell for all of the start-up scene's charms," she says. "I loved how they knew the best apps to get analytics, and the best places to get burritos."

She also wanted to look like them: swanky, even when it didn't make sense for the kind of company she was running. "When I got back to New York, I got a super-nice, superexpensive office, even though my team was small and mostly remote, and I worked from home a lot," she says.

As Bea told *Forbes*, she drank the "Start-up Kool-Aid."

Ironically, as her business was failing, her personal visibility hit new heights: no one could imagine a Y Combinator pick failing; after all, Y Combinator had discovered Airbnb and Dropbox. In private, she took out a disastrous loan, stopped paying herself, and let go of her favorite employees. But in public, she put on a brave face, trying to raise more money for the company, and spending money to keep up appearances.

People want to believe the hype, because, she says, "We're in the age of crushing it."

The good news: the pain of closing reconnected Bea to her roots as a therapist, and her company's original mission, which had been to make sure people "don't have to suffer alone." Now Bea is focused on what the future of therapy will be and is founding a think tank to discover just that. Her new nonprofit, The Difference, will be devoted to innovations in mental health research and resources, and based on the belief that the right talk at the right time can make all The Difference.

## CONNECTING VERSUS "CURATION"

### Dadvertising and Public Parenting

At a low point in our marriage, I accused my husband of being a dad "only for Facebook" because he frequently posted only the cutest images and stories. His social feed portrayed a superdad, and only I knew the truth: at the time, Nicco was actually spending very little time with our kids. But his social media narrative made it seem otherwise. He knew that men who are cute daddies are rewarded by society, and he knew how to play the game. In his own way, he created a narrative of achievement porn that was irresistible: a successful man with a big book coming out, with adorable children he doted on. If I was his publicist, I'd give him an A-plus.

That's right: on social media, people are often faking it. And, when you fake it, suddenly you're all about reaching someone else's goals instead of working toward achieving your own.

Parenting on the Internet didn't start with performing. In 2005, at the first BlogHer conference, blogger Alice Bradley stood up and declared, "Mommy blogging is a radical act." At the time she was right. The very act of giving voice publicly to the everyday struggles of parents was incredibly brave, not least because writing about parenthood—especially motherhood—had always been dismissed. Now social media was giving moms and dads a chance to connect and be heard.

But along the way, something nefarious happened. As online parenting culture evolved, it became less about community and more about curation. Instead of sharing real stories about our lives, we began to curate them in adorable images and anecdotes. Instead of turning to each other for information, support, and expertise, we started to judge and compare. We had been using the Internet to share stressful moments during what can be a lonely, isolating experience. Now public parenting was becoming a competitive sport.

And, as social media emerged as a platform where people could build influence and social currency, parents became strategic about what they posted. Instagrams emphasize the aesthetic, using filters, airbrushing, and retouching, and personal family photo shoots are par for the course. People edit their 140 Twitter characters like each is a novel. And Facebook posts highlight only the best in our lives—down to awesome parenting bloopers that become book deals.

When social media makes us our own personal PR firms, it's only natural that we begin to worry we don't measure up. It also means that the online world becomes less a place for community and more a world of personal advertisements.

For working mothers, online community is a double-edged sword. For me, the mere act of posting a snippet of work-life conflict on Facebook can feel so healing. But the more we share, the more we create a public narrative of what life *should* look like for a working parent—not what it actually *does* look like. My mother frequently served up Cheerios for dinner when I was growing up. Now there are endless blog posts and Instagrams and Pinterest pages featuring perfectly composed organic meals for the perfect working mom to feed her kids. Seeing into the exquisite bento box lunches of the world is a pretty pressure-filled way to spend your morning.

In addition, there's a tremendous taboo about talking about child-care help. When she was doing press for *Lean In,* Facebook COO and wonder woman Sheryl Sandberg barred any reporter from commenting about her nannies (emphasis on the plural). But, as Julia LeStage, a former TV producer who commissioned the very first *Big Brother* and then sold the world's first crowdsourced weather app, says, "If you're working, someone else is taking care of the children." They're not hiding under the table in the conference room! That parents are expected to hide the help they get while humblebragging their adorable kids at the same time, makes it even worse.

Posting parenting now starts as early as conception. (I'm looking at you, "baby bump" watchers and Facebook Gender Reveal All-Stars.) Writer Chimamanda Ngozi Adichie, who quietly had a baby without announcing she was even pregnant, explained why in a recent interview on Jezebel: "I just feel like we live in an age when women are supposed to perform pregnancy."[3]

And that's too bad. Rather than being an opportunity for more achievement posting, the reality of a baby at home can just as easily make the expectations of the rest of our world matter so much less.

We guilty hermits can take a breath and stop searching for the perfect job to make us happy, stop going out every night, stop performing for an external audience. Which is great practice for the hermit at work. Whether it's about parenting, success, or any other kind of achievement, FOMO distracts us from what we really want and need.

## The "Belfie" Trap

In 2001, when I was marketing manager at iVillage.co.uk, the Shape Up Challenge was the cutting edge of community weight loss. On message boards, women came together in a six-week program to lose weight and get fit. Every day participants checked in to cheer each other on. I loved the pure support the women showed for each other.

Now my sensible middle-aged friends are more likely to post pictures of their run rather than belfies (look it up). You know the post: "Nancy ran six miles and felt great." Good for Nancy. Except, now I feel a subtle sense of competition. Nancy ran six miles, and I'm sitting here surfing Facebook like a lump, reading about it. I feel FOMO.

Many of the young women I spoke to at my Brown lecture, and at many other talks thereafter, talked about body pressure. When I was in college, my (perfect . . . really, she was my idol) friend Jenny once said to me, "I think I'm addicted to running. It makes me feel in control." Now we can post our fitness and weight-loss milestones online and get even more validation of our achievement. Any overachiever knows that this external validation intensifies the feeling of being in control, and we want more of it. After all, what feels better than being told how great you look, or how hard you must work out?

Body image is one of the most powerful ways we internalize achievement porn. Now amplified by the media, poor body image affects everything from self-esteem to academic performance.[4] But when it comes to the impact of social media, we are living out an experiment in real time. Women (and men) who share their bodies online take two forms: empowered and disturbing. On the one hand, social media is a medium to fight back against fat-shaming and to challenge stereotypical portraits of beauty, including lack of diversity. Think about videos that reveal Photoshop tricks or that have become social media movements to resist these beauty stereotypes. Conversely, on any given day, I'm exposed (and I'm sure I'm not alone) to up to a hundred images of my social-network friends flaunting their hard work on those hot bods. Do I cheer them on? Feel jealous? Or both? I find myself having to take a step back, and consider how all the bodies online make me feel about my own.

The support of online community when you achieve that great body, or you run every day, can feel wonderful. But it can also be a Band-Aid to cover a deeper sense of unease—both for the person

doing the posting and the person reading it. That's why I've followed the latest iteration, hashtag-driven community "challenges"
and social media stars' diet programs, with great interest.

Among the latter, Kayla Itsines is—no pun intended—perhaps the
biggest. Her #BBG, or Bikini Body Guide, brings over three million
people united by a hashtag and a regimen to get—yes—beach-body
ready. Participants regularly thank Kayla for inspiring them to find
their best selves (and their hidden six-packs), and the beautiful-by-
any-standard Kayla posts inspiring Instagrams like "I'm not beautiful like you. I'm beautiful like me."

# How Much Do You Need Validation?

**How much do you know about your peers?**

**a)** I have Google alerts set up for all of them.

**b)** I try to scope out the competition, but I have confidence in my own
projects, too.

**c)** You can't win the race if you're always looking at the other lane. My day is
spent on my own product.

**How often do you compare yourself to someone else?**

**a)** Do they have five kids and fifty employees? Were they on the radio
yesterday? Did they lose the baby weight in three months? I'm always
comparing myself to other people.

**b)** I do feel bad when I see how much other people get done, but I try not to
get bogged down in it.

**c)** I definitely have career idols I try to live up to, but as for professional peers,
I know we all go up and down.

**When you get good professional news or feedback, is your first call to
one of your parents?**

**a)** Yes. I don't feel like an accomplishment is truly mine until someone related to me gives their stamp of approval.

**b)** I like to share things that make me happy and proud, because the people I share them with will be, too.

**c)** I'll include it in my holiday letter.

***You realize you forgot a big presentation in your office, and your boss and clients are waiting in the conference room. You:***

**a)** Apologize eighteen times and run to your office to get it. Afterwards, you apologize again. And again.

**b)** Apologize, book it to your stuff, then set up quickly. If all goes well, they'll remember the presentation, not your flub.

**c)** Who cares? You're there to show them your work. Nobody's perfect.

***An e-mail from a new client lands in your in-box. You:***

**a)** Are terrified. You're always afraid someone's going to yell at you.

**b)** Have no idea what it is, but flag it to make sure you get back to the client that day.

**c)** Are excited. You really have some good ideas on how to move forward.

***You have what you think is a great proposal. Everyone hates it. You:***

**a)** Are devastated. You've failed. Probably you shouldn't have this job. In fact, they're probably coming to fire you this minute.

**b)** Feel like a failure. But time has shown you that feedback can be very useful, and that it's usually not personal.

**c)** Still think it's a pretty good idea. Hopefully, you can sell it to someone else at some point.

***You're about to meet your significant other's parents. In the past week, you:***

**a)** Dieted, bought a new outfit, and quizzed your partner on his parents' likes and dislikes relentlessly.

**b)** Are kind of scared, but looking forward. But you Googled them, and got a haircut. You're not crazy.

**c)** Hope you don't have a big political argument at the table. But you're sure everyone will survive.

*Your profits dropped by 50 percent this year. You:*

**a)** Need to find an entirely different field.

**b)** Will assess what happened. You might need to get a new job, but maybe not.

**c)** Take a deep breath. That's what savings are for.

*Someone asks you what you do at a party. You:*

**a)** Always feel like you're explaining something you messed up.

**b)** Have a set answer. No one cares THAT much; it's just chitter-chatter.

**c)** Like to hear what other people do. You have to think about yourself ALL DAY.

*You get your work back. It's been marked up with red ink. You:*

**a)** Have failed again. They are coming to yell at you, tell you how much better everyone else is doing, that you are on Google too much, that your partner's parents think you should go on a diet, that the fact that you apologize so much means even you know you should be fired, and that you're fired.

**b)** Er . . . okay. Did you do something wrong? Or did she just really want something else?

**c)** Try to put a positive spin on it. After all, edits from someone else actually mean less work for you!

*You ran a 5K.*

**a)** Your friends ran a 10K. You'll start training tomorrow.

**b)** You ran a 5K! And now . . . brunch!

**c)** You will never understand this whole 5K thing.

## Mostly a's

Whoa! You need to take a step back. Not only are you working overtime to please other people, you're terrified what will happen if you don't. News flash: Sometimes you'll make other people unhappy (even as I write this I know I can't take my own advice here). Sometimes you'll fail. But if you don't take that risk, and take it on your own terms, you'll spend your whole life apologizing for decisions you didn't even believe in.

See Chapter 5 for some tools on determining the work you want to do—and learning how to cope with people who disagree. (And they will.) And delete those Google alerts.

### Mostly b's

You're the middle child in the validation family—you're capable of suddenly needing the world to love you, but you're pretty sure that's not realistic. (Most of the time.) What's great is that you're open to learning from what the world dishes out. But, because you're open to others' opinions, your task is to always take them for what they are: other people's opinions. That means needing to remind yourself that no one's perfect, but other people can have useful things to say. Life is a collaboration. That sometimes makes you want to hide in the bathroom.

### Mostly c's

I'd say you should learn to take other people's opinions to heart, but not only would you ignore me—maybe you don't need to. There will always be people who believe in themselves so thoroughly that they can devote themselves entirely to their own vision. If you become a total despot, that's a problem. But if you can take the hard knocks when no one agrees and go forward anyway, kudos to you.

Browsing the #BBG online commentary, like so much else in social media, provokes a confusing mix of envy, voyeurism, and "you go, girl"-ing. Kayla and her #BBGs present an aspiration of perfection. Anyone can look and feel and act like Kayla, she promises, if you just work hard enough: there are tons of perfect #BBG bikini photos online, posted by ordinary, nonceleb women. And with those abs, it seems, you can get Kayla's magical self-assurance.

No doubt, looking thin and fit creates incredible social feedback. I've been chunky, and I've been thin, and it shocks me how differently I am treated when I am thin. And if there's a great skinny-looking photo of me—I am the FIRST person out there, sharing it. #notproudbuthonest.

Body-image FOMO is tough for everyone, but if you're sensitive to achievement porn because deep down you know traditional "achievement" is not for you, think about exactly what you're feeling the next time you see a photo of a friend looking ripped and feel envious, or when you yourself post that photo, hoping to feel . . . what?

# GETTING STARTED

## *Turning FOMO into a Friend*

FOMO is human and universal; it will never go away completely. But you can get it under control. Ultimately, the best cure for FOMO is feeling secure in your own day-to-day life. It won't happen overnight. Every single time I feel left out or a twinge of envy, I have to consciously say to myself, *Stop. Here's why what you're doing is right for you.* (Yes, even if it means I'm lying on the couch and haven't exercised in days.)

It might take years to erase FOMO from your vocabulary, but here are some ways to start tackling the challenge for the long haul:

❑ **Use FOMO as a tool, not a cudgel.** Don't beat yourself up when you feel it. Give yourself the opportunity to take stock of your vision and your career. Are you feeling FOMO because you're not doing what you want in the moment, or because you're fundamentally heading in the wrong direction? Momentary jealousy over a friend's glam Saturday night is far different from a consistent gnawing when keeping up with a colleague who's getting a master's degree, for example. Learn to differentiate FOMO (ego) from a true desire to grow and push yourself.

❑ **Turn objects of envy into role models and mentors.** FOMO sometimes means you really want something *for yourself.* That colleague who's getting a degree or writing a book: How did she do it? What are her tips? Just because someone is a couple years ahead of you doesn't mean her accomplishments are unattainable for you!

❑ **Praise somebody.** When you tell someone how amazing they are, you'll be surprised how often they were impressed by something you did, too. When you know you're not just in competition, you can see that you're both working to make your entire field better.

❑ **Set your own pace.** I felt jealous of friends writing books for years, but I knew it wasn't yet my time. Well, the day I decided I was going to write this book, I worked twelve hours a day for three straight days to get a proposal off the ground. I'd never done that before! I was driven by a force within, and it felt good.

❑ **Turn FOMO into JOMO—Joy of Missing Out.** "Think of it as a lifestyle shift, in which you feel grateful for what you have, instead of resentment of what you're missing." Anil Dash, a tech entrepreneur and the dad who coined the term *JOMO,* says there's a practical angle, too: "Cultivating JOMO came from parenthood. It's pragmatic. I can't do everything I would like to do, so I'd better find some joy in what I have."

❑ **Everyone feels FOMO.** That's why there's a word for it (and a hashtag). We're not insecure, and we're not failures. We're just human.

## Use FOMO to Find Yourself

I have a colleague I adore whose Facebook notifications nonetheless generate a cloud of noxious FOMO for me. Every time I read her business has won an award or announced a new hire (which is often), I'm filled with envy, even anger. Why isn't my business doing as well? After all, we're in the same field. We even collaborate. I was plugging along happily, and suddenly I feel like a failure.

We used to be able to live in blissful ignorance of our friends' successes, at least on a daily basis. With social media, we can't. But here's the thing: once you get in touch with your FOMO, it can be a powerful diagnostic tool. Don't judge yourself, don't feel petty. Merely observe.

Everyone has a particular FOMO trigger. Do you feel jealous of how much money other people are making? How often they appear in print? How their achievements stack up against yours? How many social media followers they have, or how often they're checking in from exotic places? If they have kids and a partner—or if they don't? It's true that you may never be on the cover of *Wired,* but maybe you've realized that eventually, you want to do something worth writing home about.

Like a sore muscle or overused tendon, excessive FOMO is also a sign that a behavior has to change. Do you want the boss's praise? Do you want to sell your product to the company? Train people in workplace politics? Design the table in the conference room? Buy the company? Build the company? Or just be the boss? Focus not only on your career, but on the kind of power you want.

Finally, analyze. After my husband heard me bitch about my colleague for the umpteenth time, he asked why I felt so personally affronted by her success. I sat with it for a while and realized: it wasn't about her, it was about me. I was feeling guilty about my firm's earnings, which were lower than I felt they should be. I was feeling guilty that I hadn't given my team a raise in a while, that we hadn't been hiring, and that earnings were stagnant. "But, sweetie," my husband said, "you try to maximize your flexibility."

So I had a tough conversation with myself about my goals both for my personal time and for my company. I came to realize I had made a choice to earn less money and grow more slowly than other firms, and it was a choice I was comfortable with. Ironically, once I wrote publicly about my choice, I was interviewed about choosing flexibility over maximizing earnings for the *Wall Street Journal.* (I bragged so much, it's possible I created some FOMO myself. You can't win.) But once I used the FOMO to find out something about myself instead of beat myself up, I was able to stop feeling that anger, and even to move forward in my own career.

## Career-Boosting FOMO

What's amazing is that reframing FOMO into the warm wishes of an acknowledgment or repost is actually a great business development tool for hermits. Plus, it can create community. A single mom of one toddler recently told me she had no idea how, with three kids, I managed to work so much—and I told her I had just been thinking I couldn't believe how much she worked as a single mom! We both felt better—instead of less than. Here are some healthy and advantageous ways to deal with those FOMO moments:

- ❑ **Break the cycle of bragging.** Use online community for what it was invented for: advice! You have really smart friends (and clearly they are perfect parents or amazing social activists), so why not gain counsel and conversation? Facebook can be annoying, but it's also an incredible place to engage both strong and weak ties on your silly and tough questions alike.

- ❑ **Use Shine Theory.** Ann Friedman, who, along with Aminatou Sow, the two brilliant writers, entrepreneurs, and podcasters who coined the term *Shine Theory,* suggests befriending the girl who intimidates you most, because it doesn't make you look worse by comparison—it actually makes you look better.[5] As Ann says, "I don't shine if you don't shine." It's a fantastic cure for your own jealousy—and also a way of quashing the damaging stereotype of the "mean girl."

- ❑ **Do what privileged white men do.** Use the achievement of those you associate with as a symptom of your own greatness. (My husband is a master of this technique.) Name-dropping builds credibility for you by doing nothing.

❑ **You are who you hang out with.** I use this technique a lot in my work in mobilizing online audiences for social good. It's called social proofing—a theory that people gain social capital and credibility when they are have special access or are privy to special information. For example, I'm part of an online community of women called The List. And one of the rules is that we cheer (publicly, on social media) for any Lister who does something good. It's success by association, but it's also loving, kind, and creates a great community.

❑ **Share FOMO with a friend.** That friend who triggers your FOMO? Chances are if you asked her, she would list off similar characteristics in you that trigger her. When you constantly feel you don't do enough, share that with a friend. I promise you, it's hilarious.

❑ **Get out of your head.** Flip the script. If you are prone to rumination about how little you do, do some good for someone. As ABC News reporter Claire Shipman, a ruminator, too, says, "I think that's a real confidence boost for women." The simple act of getting outside yourself to acknowledge the needs or good work— even with a quick tweet—of someone else can literally shift your whole day.

## BEFORE WE DIVE IN

When I say "entrepreneur," chances are you think two words: Mark Cuban. A billionaire tech founder, Cuban is also a prolific speaker who provides stirring advice about how to become a successful entrepreneur. He is smart and charismatic, and embodies the macho, always closing, "sleep when I'm dead" (and seemingly extroverted) business persona so popular today. He's a classic extrovert—exactly the kind of person who would make an anxious introvert think they could never succeed.

And then there's Gary Vaynerchuk. Already a legend in the social media world for having transformed a family wine store into a multimillion-dollar business, Gary was on fire and my client's editor had just published his bestseller *Crush It*. As one of the first social media celebrities to break through, he was everywhere, all the time. I admired what he had accomplished. He seemed to embody what a digital-age entrepreneur *should* be: an energetic, larger-than-life, frenetic personality who was simultaneously a master salesman and a people pleaser.

When first starting my business, I was in a planning meeting with a client and her publisher. It was a big, well-respected house on Avenue of the Americas. And guess who was involved in the planning, as a favor to my client's editor?

Gary Vaynerchuk.

We tried to schedule a meeting to talk about ideas, and Gary put us on speakerphone with his assistant. "Well, I can offer you three A.M. on Wednesday," she said. We all laughed. "Yes," she continued, "that's literally the only free space on Gary's calendar."

Curious about how Gary had built a massive social media following and a big business, I pulled up one of his YouTube instructional videos a few days later. In the video, he was sitting on the toilet. With his laptop. Yes, he told viewers, "I do e-mail when I poop."

My heart sank. And you know what? That was when I knew I was never going to be like Gary Vaynerchuk—or Mark Cuban, for that matter. Nor would I be like all those fabulous women leaders I saw onstage at conferences like Women in the World or TED Women. I wouldn't be like Kara Goldin, who grew the healthy soda-alternative Hint Water into a $90 million company while raising four children. I wouldn't be like my colleague Cheryl Contee, who helped build a consulting firm and a tech platform that has helped so many progressive organizations. (Oh, and she's also a single mom.)

I love a good *Shark Tank* episode as much as anyone, and I have tremendous respect for Sheryl Sandberg. But we have to lose the idea that there's one, unique blueprint for success. Think of all the amazing potential business owners out there who never take the plunge because they believe they're not "the type." Think of all the unhappy executives who put relentless pressure on themselves to build a vast network and achieve boundless growth and sales, but who too soon burn out and leave their professions (I've talked to more than a few). Think of the many successful professionals everywhere who suffer in silence, performing work that consumes their lives and smothers their souls.

I wouldn't be like all those friends and colleagues who have rocketed past me in their careers, getting big promotions, making lots of money, winning awards, and getting interviewed in *Fast Company*. I could feel envious—and I did—but I had to accept that being on and out there all the time just wasn't right for me, and that it was making me unhappy. Yes, I wanted to work hard and make an impact in the world, but I also wanted to stay close to my natural equilibrium, which involves being at home, where I feel content, surrounded by my family, animals, and kitchen.

As I joked to the audience at Brown, if you spend enough time on the American Airlines shuttle between New York, Boston, and Washington, D.C., you'll learn all about successful people's anxieties. During delays or jumbled boarding calls, I'm often sharing flying anxiety and other stories with fellow road warriors. All of us look ambitious, together, and successful on the outside. And we are! But on the inside we may struggle with anxiety every time we "get out there." We may be introverts who have to learn how to work a room. We may be hermits by choice, heading home for some quality time working in a home office. These intricacies don't stop you, but they do force you to work differently, to learn strategies and coping skills. Most of all, they force you to ask, is this the best life for me? I hope the techniques, stories, and tips that follow will be as helpful to you as they are to me.

# 2

# *Lean in Less*

Like almost every female entrepreneur, I have a huge amount of respect for Sheryl Sandberg, author of *Lean In* and *Option B*. She's everything I admire: accomplished, groundbreaking, successful, and generous. She's turned the story of the endless juggling of the working mom's life into a bestseller, and made it critical for alpha-dog men to sit up and listen.

And, until *Lean In* came out, I felt pretty smug. At thirty-six, I was doing work that I loved, occasionally dipping into the spotlight, then returning home to chill with my precious family. I could handle a demanding business trip, and get through difficult situations with my head held high. I could congratulate friends on their rise and not feel jealous (mostly), because I liked the formula I'd figured out for my life. I was so much happier than when I was conventionally successful. And I didn't cry every day at work.

But when *Lean In* was published, accompanied by a barrage of media stories and think pieces, I felt disheartened, even angry. I was thrilled that the book tackled the very real barriers women face in the workplace. But most of the women I knew could not work any harder. They simply could not lean in more.

And suddenly I was forced to reckon with a choice that now had a name: Was I leaning *out*?

## The Sandberg Freak-Out

I began to worry about my own career trajectory. I had left corporate America at twenty-nine and had worked from home ever since. I only networked when I absolutely needed to, and made sure I schmoozed in very small doses. All that hiding in the bathroom meant that what had started out like a rocket seemed to be flattening out. Although I ran a fairly successful business, I wasn't getting rich by any measure. Sure, I'd feel "in the game" when I was invited to give a big speech, or won an important new contract. But that would pass, and I'd lose the burst of adrenaline. I had my yoga pants, but while friends got big jobs, I stayed status quo.

Had I given up? Let the sisterhood down? Would I be a disappointment to Sheryl?

I'd like to say I resolved my self-doubt quickly, but in truth it stayed with me for several years after *Lean In*'s publication. And the questions were occupying not only me, but so many women who had read Sheryl's significant book.

## Leaning Out: Sara Critchfield and Jessica Jackley's Stories

As the founding Editorial Director of Upworthy, the fastest-growing media company of all time, Sara Critchfield achieved social-media-legend status through her team's ability to make almost anything go viral. But four months into maternity leave with her first baby, Sara realized she wanted to spend more time with her daughter.

When we first met, her anxiety was palpable. Like me, she was convinced she would be eclipsed in the marketplace by up-and-comers, become irrelevant, and no one would hire her six months from now. She didn't want to lean into her career in digital media and it scared her to death.

Jessica Jackley, who cofounded the revolutionary online micro-lender Kiva while still in her twenties, had a similar story. When the incredible superconnector Susan McPherson (more on her later) introduced us, I was both nervous and thrilled. I was nervous because Jessica intimidated me, and also because I had recently moved to Los Angeles, a city where it seems everyone is vegan, skinny, and gorgeous.

Susan suggested we meet for lunch with several other women who worked in social impact. Over our vegan lunch, Jessica and I bonded: we were both nursing new babies (neither of us felt very skinny or gorgeous), and we both have sons named Asa. But as we got to talking, I learned something about Jessica few would ever guess: she was *leaning out.*

"When we were launching Kiva, my work pace was unhealthy, unsustainable, and ruined my first marriage," she told me. In her new work life, she says, "I put on grown-up clothes twice a week."

What I immediately loved about Jessica's story, and what I tell myself now when I feel like I'm working on autopilot, is that it's a gift to do just enough work sometimes, and it doesn't hurt you to change your pace. It doesn't mean your rocket-ship days are over.

After burning out with Kiva, getting divorced, then getting re-married and having three children in the following five years, Jessica used her reputation to cultivate a successful consulting and speaking practice that focuses on her experience with Kiva. Leveraging her core of knowledge with fifteen to twenty lectures a year, "I can sustain myself," she told me. And, particularly important for a parent, she added, "And because speaking comes particularly easy to me, it's actually a low-stress activity. At this point I can give a talk backwards, inside out, standing on my head. Or while nursing, which I've actually done a few times!"

As we know, ambitious women are under constant pressure to produce and achieve, much of it self-inflicted. If you're a size six, get to four! If you get $1 million in sales, go for $1.5!

Life, however, demands adaptation—which means our generation, however ambitious, doesn't always benefit from the *Lean In* message. You're in grad school while working full-time, a toddler needs you at home, you have a sick parent needing your care, and you need to keep your day job, even though you don't like it. Because the concept of leaning in is binary, if you don't keep working harder and doing more, you've failed. This creates a tremendous amount of pressure on a single individual to achieve a whole lot. Lean in too far, and you can fall on your face.

If you've been conditioned to achieve, *compromise* is a dirty word. It's not something they teach in business school, and it's never going to put you on the cover of *Forbes*. But you will get things done, and in doing so you will learn skills and tactics that prepare you for success. My extroverted friend Samantha calls my approach to compromise perfect for those of us "who don't want to lean in, but want to stay in."

No two people have the same ideal mix of work and life. That's why in this book, we'll refer to **Work+Life Fit** (no balance!).[1] Work+Life Fit was developed by Cali Yost, an international workplace strategy expert. It honors the notion that no two people want the exact same integration of work and personal life. (Which is why your boss may be e-mailing you at midnight, not because she thinks you need to work harder, but because she's a night owl.)

Because that's what it's about: what really matters to *you*! Your definition of success. My version of success might very well be the ability to earn a good living while rarely having to leave my home office, while someone else might consider leaning in less the very definition of failing. Both definitions are legitimate.

And as for Sara, she sat with her anxiety for a while, and realized she wanted to go back to where she started out: faith-based organizing. Instead of following the money, she is, as she puts it, "following the energy." She takes on fifteen hours a week of consulting work to pay the bills, and saves the rest of her work time for reengaging in community organizing. A compromise for now, but Sara says, "I feel like I'm playing. The pressure is gone."

# LEANING OUT

## *It's Not Just for Parents*

The notion of working less by choice has gotten seriously mommy-tracked. Work-life balance and flexible work arrangements are so strongly correlated with parenthood that we assume a successful childless person prioritizes career advancement over anything else.

But leaning out is not just a mommy issue. Some working parents want to work all the time; some professionals without children want a less draining schedule.

Consider the idea of "holistic success." Twenty-seven-year-old Rhonesha Byng, founder of the media company HerAgenda, who coined the term, is on a mission to promote holistic success. Her ambition is to make sure the professionals she reaches through her community don't ignore their personal lives, even if they are only in their early twenties.

"I didn't understand it at first when my mentors would tell me, 'Take breaks, make sure you make time to go out on dates,'" Rhonesha says. "But I realized that, looking back, they realized what they had given up by spending all their time and energy focused on work."

Integrating work and everything else in your life is not just for moms and dads. After all, some parents may want to work all the time, while some nonparents choose to spend the minimum in the office in favor of other pursuits. Your goal may not be to make room for kids, but for a side hustle or another project such as graduate school or writing. I quit my last full-time job years before I got pregnant, because, as we know, I didn't like showing up for work. It wasn't about parenting for me.

In fact, it's optimal to determine your work+life fit before you have kids, which is why Rhonesha's message is so important. When her mentors encouraged her to go out on dates, to prioritize her stated goal of having a family one day, what they were really telling her was, "Think ahead. Prepare. There's more to life than your day job."

## My Managed-Growth Story

My last job was running the digital public affairs division of a large PR firm. Over the years, in tons of political campaigns and start-ups, I had worked twelve-hour (and more) days. Now, if I left before six thirty, I felt that I was letting people down.

I was twenty-nine, and I looked at the women ten years ahead of me, and at the sacrifices they'd made to manage family and work. I knew I didn't want to be in the same position in ten years. Why was being in the office a measure of how effective you were at your job, anyway? There had to be a better way.

That's how I became obsessed with work: not with doing it, but with how to make it better for people like me who love what they do but hate going to the office.

So I went back to school for a degree in clinical social work and a master's in public administration at Harvard, where I immersed myself in the data of work life. The literature confirmed what I'd observed: rich or poor, workers can no longer set ordinary boundaries to protect their time and personal lives—even though it doesn't lead to higher productivity.

My own boundaries were about to take a hit. The plan for my new, flexible career was to continue with a social work degree at Boston College, then specialize in work-life consulting. But I got pregnant with my first son two months before I finished my MPA, and then the economy crashed. My husband's small business hit rocky terrain, and everyone around me, it seemed, had lost much of their life savings. And though I was still struggling with antenatal depression, now I was panicking, too. I had to earn money, quick.

So back I went to digital consulting full-time, but now with an agenda. I wanted to work for myself and have more control over my time while still doing meaningful work. I knew I needed to take care of my physical and mental health. I wanted to optimize my stress-to-income ratio.

Ellen Galinsky, who cofounded the Families and Work Institute, gave me my start. Knowing my interest in workplace flexibility practices, she offered to mentor me in work life while I helped her with social media. Ellen is a legend in the field, and she opened many doors. By 2011, I had turned that freelance consulting into Women Online. By 2012, I had a team of four employees, plus four contractors staffed on individual projects. I worked four days a week, and was pretty disciplined about controlling my time.

When people started to call me an entrepreneur, at first, I drank the Kool-Aid. I began to dream of the kind of growth that was entirely ridiculous for a firm my size. I spent too much money on the business with expensive dinners out, always picking up the tab, not to mention on my own travel. I bought another small firm and invested in a software product. I was "playing start-up," as Bea Arthur calls it, and the result wasn't good.

When the 2012 Obama campaign hired us to do women's outreach online, it was an amazing validation of our work. But the same day I went to the bank. I was an extra (and unaccounted for) $60,000 deep into my line of credit, and I didn't know how I would pay it back.

Everyone says that's a natural feeling for an entrepreneur—you're always on the edge. But the push and pull of my feelings that day sticks with me: excitement at landing such a big client, and fear that I owed so much money. I vowed then I'd stop playing start-up, and control workload and finances as much as possible.

So what did I do? I began to keep the scope of the services we offer very specialized, rather than expanding offerings into a full-service digital marketing or PR firm. I kept the staff small, and even now I try constantly to manage everyone's expectations, including my own.

This was my journey toward accepting growth . . . with compromise.

Sometimes it sucks. It's much sexier in a culture that idealizes the entrepreneur to be always hungry, always wanting to grow faster. You know, to *lean in*. When other firms grow their staffs, I feel tremendous FOMO. Many times we've lost contracts to larger firms with bigger offerings and bigger names. There have been so many smart people I've wanted to hire, or opportunities I had to turn down, because they would place too much pressure on me to earn, earn, earn. And sometimes I end up in that situation anyway, because business is fickle and I have bills to pay.

Growth with compromise requires constant recalibration. If the sales pipeline is slow, or if I have an opportunity to nail down future work, I have to take it. Every new child (I have three) has altered my work+life fit. When my third baby, Josephine, was due, I was grounded. I couldn't fly or attend many new business meetings. I only took one week of maternity leave. But I socked away five months of cash—and I did work from bed!

So, that's my story. People call businesses like Women Online "managed growth." But that's too fancy a term. Because I wanted time, and to have work that meant something to me, I set limits on my goals—and I surprised myself by managing to earn a good living. In fact, my limits actually helped Women Online specialize, and grow.

## GETTING STARTED

### *Think About Compromise as Your Friend, Not Your Enemy*

To set limits on the pace of your growth, you have to figure out what you will and won't give up. HelloFlo founder Naama Bloom provides a great example: "Instead of staying in a big corporate job just because it was responsible, I realized I'd rather compromise on savings, exercise and a social life."

Like Naama suggests, first, establish some nonnegotiables in your work life. Be specific! Below is an example list with some typical career goals, but feel free to create your own. Once you know your nonnegotiables, it's much easier to figure out what you can compromise on and manage your growth intentionally.

## RENOWN

*I want magazine covers!*

## MONEY

*I have a target salary and savings plan, and I won't budge.*

## EXCITEMENT

*I need to be inspired by my work.*

## TITLE

*My goal is to eventually be CTO (sole business owner, management, etc. . . . )*

## PROMINENCE IN YOUR FIELD

*It's important to me that my work is honored by colleagues.*

Now write down what you are willing to give up to achieve your goals; be specific. Again, below are some examples.

## SOCIAL LIFE

*I can miss a few Saturday nights with my friends.*

## SAVINGS

*My work now is important enough to suspend future security.*

**DISPOSABLE INCOME**

*Shoes? Starbucks? I can live without it for a while.*

**WHERE I LIVE**

*My job is in Cleveland, but my heart is in New York.*

**THE CAR I DRIVE**

*Walking is great exercise.*

**VACATIONS**

*I'm okay only getting a week off a year.*

And some biggies. Do these fit you now, or can you take them or leave them?

**FAMILY**

*I want a healthy family life, and that means being in the office at nine and out by five / I'm not focused on family right now.*

**PERSONAL SPACE**

*I can't be on all the time—no texting from the boss at 10 P.M. / I live for Slack.*

**WORK ENVIRONMENT**

*I want to be in a supportive, friendly work space / I love competition—work isn't for friends.*

**STABILITY**

*I want a job for the long haul/I like to switch it up.*

You can also think in terms of ratios. Juliette Kayyem, Harvard professor, national security adviser, and public speaker, talks about her "influence-to-stress ratio." (The minute I heard that, I thought,

*I'm stealing it!*) After a day of running around in her yoga pants, in the evenings she often goes on CNN to provide spot-on national security analysis. That is high influence to low stress!

You could also think about your ideal *income*-to-stress ratio, or your personal-space-to-work-environment ratio. Would you give up a little of one to have a lot of the other?

Once you have your list, think about your pace. What are your targets? Do you want to be management in the next five years? Start a family by thirty-five? Buy a house next year? You don't necessarily have control over timing, but setting some specifics down will help you assess where you need to add and take away. (For instance, if you want to take a four-month trip around the world, you may need to be frugal for a year—and cultivate a really good relationship with your boss!)

## EXPECTATIONS CHART

There's a famous poem by Kenneth Koch about how impossible it is to have a social life, a love life, and a productive work life. ("You Want a Social Life, with Friends.") You *can* have them all, of course—but probably not all at the same time.

A great way to figure out if you're on the right path is to actually write down your expectations for the future, how you're handling them right now, and how life intrudes. What might you have to give up? What do you need to put off? Make a column for each heading, and fill in your answers.

### FAMILY

*I'd like to spend all Sunday with my kids.*
*I'd like one night out with my partner a week.*
*I'd like to start college funds and put [X] in them.*

### WORK

*I'd like to bill [X amount] this year.*

*I'd like to get closer to a senior position.*

*I'd like to increase my earnings by [X] percent.*

**INFRASTRUCTURE**

*I'd like to buy a house in the next five years.*

*I'd like to upgrade my apartment next year.*

*I'd like to move to a larger city.*

**LIFE**

*I'd like to save 10 percent of my income for retirement.*

*I'd like to take a two-week vacation to China.*

*I'd like to see at least three plays/concerts/movies with friends.*

Now make a column called **costs/time**. How much will you have to save for each? How much time for family and friends do you have to give up that you currently spend working, and vice versa? What will each require from you?

## COST / TIME ANALYSIS

| MY EXPECTATIONS | MY COSTS/TIME | WHAT MIGHT I HAVE TO GIVE UP/TAKE ON |
|---|---|---|
| BUY A HOUSE IN 5 YEARS | $30K DOWN PAYMENT | EATING OUT ($300 SAVINGS A MONTH)<br>CABLE ($150 A MONTH)<br>GYM ($60 A MONTH) |
| TRIP TO CHINA IN 2 YEARS | $3,000 | FREELANCE CONSULTING PROJECT |

Ideally, use a program like Mint to put your spending in categories. Once you know roughly what you spend your money on ($400 a month on restaurants?!) you can cut it down intentionally.

For instance, can you save for college at the same time you save for a house? Can you see friends as much as you want and grow your business? Do you have the extra money required for an extended vacation, or the extra time to attend every soccer match?

Once you know your goals and desires and what they will cost, you can rejigger them a bit. You won't feel guilty for not meeting your own expectations—and you can't do everything—if you have a realistic plan for your life right now.

## Appropriate Effort

Last week, in the midst of a deadline, running two extremely demanding client campaigns, recovering from a bad cold, and managing three children, I cooked beef bourguignon for a Tuesday-night dinner party.

Why? Why didn't I just order in Chinese food? Everyone at the dinner was a good friend. No one would have been offended.

I don't know about you, but achievement porn's profound effect means I struggle daily with the idea that I might not do everything perfectly—and I mean *everything,* from my first grader's class project to a pitch deck for a new six-figure client. That's why the concept of "appropriate effort" has been so freeing for me.

Appropriate effort is the opposite of our culture's expectation to always do your best. Instead it's doing something well, but removing any emotional investment. Buddhist teacher Sally Kempton, who has done much to popularize the concept, explains that appropriate effort is any effort that doesn't involve struggle. For Sally, the secret of acting with appropriate effort is to ask herself, *If this were the last act of my life, how would I want to do it?*

It's an incredible tool to cultivate if you're a perfectionist or groomed to overachieving. (Especially if, like me, you've found a way to be a perfectionist even at yoga.) And practicing AE regularly can give you some healthy breathing room to accomplish the goals on your big list. By removing fear of the outcome, you bring your whole self into what you're doing—and savor the process.

For example, when I am writing a blog post, client proposal, or even this book, I often fixate so intensely on the outcome (Will it be any good? Will anyone read it?) that the writing becomes merely a chore to get the damn thing done. I have to tell myself over and over: *You love writing, so enjoy this. You can worry about the statistics later.*

By removing the stress of outcome, I am also better able to really focus on pieces that matter, and try to care less about things I cannot change. For example, I hate my head shot, but after agonizing over it for days, I realized my reaction was well beyond appropriate effort, and I tried to channel my energy back into editing, not stressing over my image (which is the height of achievement porn).

## How Can You Bring Appropriate Effort into Your Life?

**What if you only gave 89 percent?** A work project or a homemade cake for your kid's birthday may not need you to pull out the big guns. The key is to acknowledge the outcome. Will what you do be good enough for them? Will what you achieve be good enough for you? The answer to both is: almost surely.

❑ **Remember that the challenge of being always on is universal.** Forty-three percent of highly skilled women with children leave their jobs voluntarily at some point in their careers. Sheryl Sandberg wrote *Lean In* with the benefits of a staff, and an in-office nursery, something most of us can only dream of.

❑ **Compromise between caregiving and work may be unavoidable.** Your kid is throwing up at school. You have to look into nursing homes. A sister far away is getting chemo. Don't torment yourself about taking time for the other important things in your life. The world won't disappear if you're away for two weeks, and if people in your workplace make you feel you're slacking off, consider the bigger picture.

❑ **Nothing is forever.** Remember Jessica Jackley and Sara Critchfield. Giving yourself room by leaning in a bit less—whether it's to spend more time with a kid or take a trip to Rio—doesn't necessarily mean leaving the work you've mastered forever. You're not out of the game, you're recalibrating.

❑ **Reality bites.** Sometimes, you will need to do less. You get tired. You will say no. You will fuck up. You won't get a promotion or your business might never earn you millions of dollars. You will accept less. If you've been conditioned to achieve, this will make you feel like a failure. Know that it's okay to make your dreams and your career a little smaller in order to have the complete life you want.

## CAN WE ALL JUST SLEEP?

The cult of achievement porn says that the successful person relentlessly drives forward, with little time to rest, recharge, or unplug. We expect successful people to be like presidents: on 24/7/365.

Achievement porn articles contribute to the illusion that successful people don't sleep. But, as CEO coach Meredith Fineman puts it, we must get rid of all the articles titled "Twelve things eight of the most productive people (you won't believe how productive they are!) in the world do before 6 A.M." or "You'll never believe how the most productive people go to bed (they hang upside down like fruit bats)." "Here are sixteen reasons why getting up before 4 A.M. increases your productivity, and also some oatmeal recipes." I'm waiting for the moment a hugely successful leader (besides Arianna Huffington, and I don't even believe her) admits that they get enough sleep.

Sleep is like work+life fit: everyone's is different. My husband, bless him, usually doesn't need more than six hours a night. (Just like Barack Obama.) He gets up at five to work out and goes all day. He always naps on the weekend. On my perfect day, I wake around six thirty, nap at four, and then work again until about nine thirty. I need nine hours of sleep.

I used to be embarrassed about this, and I lied to everyone I knew because if they didn't sleep, why should I? But it's important to understand your sleep needs and be honest about them. Arianna Huffington (of course) reviewed the book *Rest* by Alex Soojung-Kim Pang in the *New York Times*, and pointed out something valuable: it was actually the industrial revolution that created a drastic separation of work and leisure, which are now perpetually in conflict with each other.

Before the industrial revolution, when most people worked where they lived, work and rest patterns were very different from our own. Many people went to sleep when the sun went down, only to rise in the middle of the night for a few hours to work, have sex, or talk with their partner—even visit with neighbors. And then they would wake again with the sun.

If you ask around, you might find this to be the preferred sleep pattern of some of the most productive people you know. Others nap. When I called Wharton's Stew Friedman to interview him for this book, he proudly stated, "I've just woken up from my nap." It was a Tuesday. But indeed, a nap is part of his work routine, because it energizes him, and tons of data back him up: a nap on the job can increase productivity and reduce workplace accidents.

Not all of us can nap at work, but we can try to get in touch with our natural sleep rhythms and determine how to better meet our rest needs. We can also resist the pressure to conform to an ideal of success that equates lack of sleep with ambition. I like to laugh at profiles of successful women who share that they often get up at four thirty or 5 A.M. for some "me time." To me, that sounds like torture, but it may for work them (apparently it works for Michelle Obama).

In *Rest,* Pang points out that rest and work aren't opposites, like "black and white or good and evil. They're more like different points on life's wave." I love this notion of a life in motion, with gentle breaks for rest in between crashes and peaks. Imagine if you had a work life where you could sleep the hours you need to, and also work the hours you prefer to. When we work to our natural sleep schedules, and don't feel like we need to lie about them to maintain our professional credibility, everyone is better off.

# WELCOME TO YOUR IMPERFECT LIFE

The very nature of success—perhaps an old remnant from the Calvinist heritage that informed the good old Protestant work ethic and ensuing industrial revolution—is to think about reaching a goal: "When I achieve X, I can finally live a life I enjoy." But growing your career is merely one element of your existence. And ironically, focusing solely on growing your career can blind you to other equally generative opportunities.

In *Composing a Life,* author Mary Catherine Bateson emphasizes that women's lives so often veer from the paths we may intend them to take. This is a wonderful thing, but sadly we're not taught to think of it that way. Bateson writes of the huge creative potential of a life that twists and turns, and is not "pointed towards a single ambition."

If you fear leaning out (and really, how could you not), consider Bateson's wise nudge about how the huge creative potential of the twists and valleys in your work life.

Dreams and great success can get sparked unexpectedly, if you give yourself the space and time. The seed for Kiva was planted in Jessica Jackley's head when she was working in administration at the Stanford Graduate School of Business. This wasn't her dream job, but it was way to pay the bills while she figured things out.

One night she decided to stay late and watch Nobel laureate Muhammad Yunus give a lecture on microfinance. Yunus's speech jolted her thinking. "It seemed like magic," Jackley said, "that a tiny amount of capital could fast-forward the businesses of people living in extreme poverty, through the work they were already doing."[2]

Over the next few years, Jackley explored this new thinking, traveling to Africa, enrolling in business school, learning Swahili. She took the time she needed to create work that would answer her questions about poverty and entrepreneurship. That curiosity helped create Kiva.

When I last caught up with Sara Critchfield, she was in her car heading to the Lake Shrine near Malibu, a famous spot for practitioners of self-realization meditation. "I don't know how helpful I'm going to be for your interview," she said with a laugh. "Why?" I asked; what was she doing? "Piloting a new program for Airbnb," she told me. The lodging giant created special programs to hang out in a city with someone with shared interests, so Sara volunteered to curate a spiritual journey around Los Angeles, including visits to special mosques, synagogues, churches, and meditation fellowships

(Gandhi's ashes are buried at the Lake Shrine). "I've been having a lot of energy for what I started out doing, which is faith-based work. At some point I'll have to do what gives me money, but for now I'm playing," she said. I could hear the joy in her voice.

Sara gave herself permission to play and learn what she might want to do next. We don't get many chances as adults to unleash the joy and curiosity we had as children. Sometimes, being taken off course and getting a moment to breathe can open up new and deeply generative twists in our lives. This could be phoning in a job in order to focus on a side hustle, taking time when you have small children at home, or finding a safe space to land when you know you need a change but still have bills to pay. Some call it leaning out, but I think it's growing something new.

# 3

## *The Gift of Anxiety*

B e fearless." I listened as Warren Buffett exhorted the crowd of five thousand women at the first United State of Women Summit. Everyone cheered. I felt left out.

You've heard this before; it transcends cultures and gender. Fearlessness, it seems, is the ticket to success. But what about the rest of us?

In our society, we conflate leadership with fearlessness, and we are quick to ignore or reject anxiety as a sign of weakness. But I think fear is a powerful clue, and anxiety can be a gift.

### *Jesus, Morra, Why Would You Ever Say Anxiety Is a Gift?!*

Almost everyone experiences anxiety at some point. Life is stressful. And often anxiety will pass, or therapy and medication can help.

But there are those of us for whom anxiety is a constant companion. Whether you are tightly wound, sensitive by nature, or experiencing anxiety caused by a specific circumstance, anxiety is constantly with you. Over the years I've tried everything for mine:

benzodiazepines, meditation, hypnotherapy, Freudian analysis. And even when I find myself happy and relaxed, after ten minutes I think, *Wait, aren't I supposed to be anxious about something?*

I've come to think my anxiety and I are actually in successful negotiation, and we're trying to make this relationship work. Yes, anxiety can be a gift—if you make it a tool to guide you. After all, if anxiety is going to be with you anyway, you might as well make it useful. And when you are attuned to the clues your psyche is giving you, you can use them to propel yourself forward.

When I asked Christina Wallace if she ever considered her anxiety a gift, she didn't waste a second answering: "Absolutely." Wallace is a graduate of Harvard Business School, two-time start-up founder, accomplished executive, and creator of an innovative STEM education program. She is extremely intimidating on paper and in person, because, like me, she's really tall.

Christina had severe childhood trauma, and has done a lot of work to manage the aftereffects. Even so, she says, "Situations where I feel like I can't trust the other person or the rug has been pulled out from under me throw me into fight-or-flight mode." She will have panic attacks and crippling anxiety. She's learned that she needs to work with her managers and her colleagues to find a way that allows her to see feedback ahead of time, for example, so she processes it and prepares instead of feeling blindsided and anxious.

Anxiety has been a gift, says Christina, because "it's made me an incredible manager (according to the dozen or so employees I've managed across my last three start-ups) because I am much more aware of how [my employees] like feedback and how to help them show their best selves." Christina is incredibly attuned to people around her, and she can navigate almost any situation.

Anxiety is never a simple gift, though. Christina notes that being an "achiever on steroids" has propelled her career far, and fast. But, she adds, "I have to make sure I don't just do things for medals or résumé bullets, but things that make me happy and fill me emotionally and spiritually."

Like any special gift, anxiety must be managed. But as you can see from Christina, modulating your work life to better suit your emotional needs doesn't mean hiding in an ashram. Work is demanding, and there will always be times when you have to suck it up, put on your big-girl panties, and walk into that room. But work also demands a healthy scaffolding of support and self-care. With practice and intention, you can minimize the scary stuff and play to your strengths.

## Finding Her Voice: Alicia Lutes's Story

Sometimes, a trait that comes up at work for a hermit or an introvert can be key toward helping with management. Writer and editor Alicia Lutes calls her anxiety the "base for [her] creativity," and it makes her a terrific boss. At just thirty, Alicia is Managing Editor of Nerdist and host of Fangirling!, and was previously the Associate Editor at Legendary Digital Networks, which includes Nerdist, Geek and Sundry, and Amy Poehler's Smart Girls.

Like Christina Wallace, Morgan Shanahan, and me (and you?), Alicia is "crazy ambitious," and uses the anxiety that goes along with it to her benefit. "If I want something," she says, "I try and work at it, because I can't deal with the what-ifs and the regrets." This trait has also allowed her to be a better, more empathetic boss. "I think that because of my anxiety and depression, I am better at managing other people than I might be at managing myself. I don't want my staff to get stressed out."

Her own boss returns the favor to Alicia. "If there are moments where I'm being too self-deprecating, she'll say, 'Please don't talk about my friend that way.'" I love that, and I wish sometimes I had a boss like Alicia's!

As a writer, Alicia finds that allowing herself to show her own personality is key to her appeal. "The whole reason I am successful is that I have a distinct voice," she says. "And a big piece of it stems from my anxiety, and my neurosis, and the self-deprecation." Obviously, it's found a huge audience with readers, even those who don't have pervasive anxiety. "It's a very human thing, and even if jokes seem especially relevant to someone who has anxiety or depression, there is a kernel there that is universal," she says.

## Going for Broke

Since I was a girl, I've had what's usually referred to as generalized anxiety disorder: an ambient and pervasive sense of anxiety. At three, I developed agoraphobia and refused to go outside for a whole summer. I had migraines. At nineteen, a car accident sent me into a crippling and major depression. One psychiatrist diagnosed me with mild bipolar disorder. Now, at forty, I have mild social anxiety and fear of flying. Oh—and I worry everyone I love is going to die.

I am not fearless. I am fearful. I am an entrepreneur who finds the daily tasks of being an entrepreneur scary and hard. I have panic attacks on planes, at large events, and during the meetings required to get out there and sell my business. It's the rare business trip where I don't make an escape plan. I've run for the airport immediately after showing my face at a conference. I always need to call my poor husband for a pep talk. Every day is a tug-of-war between my ambition and my anxiety.

Still, in terms of my work, my anxiety is a love-hate situation. I am literally often scared to leave the house. But like Christina, my anxiety has gotten me where I am today. I hustle. My anxiety also gives me extreme bag-lady syndrome. I always think my bank account will hit zero, that I won't have a job, and that I'll wind up on the streets. So my anxiety forces me to manage my schedule and workload. The anxiety drives my work ethic. It keeps me asking more of myself. It keeps me hungry. It helps make me successful.

Once you've been through clinical depressions and panic attacks, you're never completely free of them. Anticipating the return can be tough. But, in truth, now my anxiety is almost like a friend to me.

It's forced me to build an excellent infrastructure to remain functional when I really feel like hiding under the covers, and part of my achievement comes from keeping it in check.

## Making Your Obsession Work for You: Morgan Shanahan's Story

When I started thinking some more about anxiety, I called up a lot of friends and asked, "How does managing anxiety fit into your career trajectory?" Some had no idea what I was talking about. (Lucky them!) But Morgan Shanahan, senior editor at BuzzFeed, gave a great cackling laugh. Then she said, "From what I gather, the world views me as functional. I don't view myself that way at all."

Early in her career, as a twenty-seven-year-old up-and-coming screenwriter in L.A., she found out she was pregnant. That day she also got fired. Her postpartum depression and anxiety made it impossible for her to keep freelance jobs, while the medication she took for the depression made her nonfunctional in meetings.

As an outlet, she began blogging about her struggle at the818. com. Her writing made it become one of the most powerful—and self-supporting—mom blogs. Now she covers parenting at BuzzFeed, where she is supported by a team, and takes on special projects focusing on mental health.

"Now I'm not obsessed with how horrible I am," Shanahan says. "I'm obsessing about something that I can help people with. You can function with high anxiety and obsessive-compulsive disorder, if you find something positive to be obsessed with."

Even better, Morgan is using her creative voice, passion, and drive to create original content about depression for BuzzFeed video. And it's going viral, which makes her bosses happy.

## ANXIETY BY THE NUMBERS

According to the National Institutes of Health, the spectrum of anxiety disorders includes generalized anxiety disorder (GAD), panic disorder (PD) and agoraphobia, obsessive-compulsive disorder (OCD), phobic disorder (including social phobia or anxiety), and post-traumatic stress disorder (PTSD). Anxiety and depression are often comorbid conditions (they go together).[1]

Globally, one in thirteen people suffers from anxiety. Clinical anxiety affects around 10 percent of people in North America, Western Europe, and Australia/New Zealand compared to about 8 percent in the Middle East and 6 percent in Asia.[2]

Social anxiety is the third most common psychological disorder, right after the big boys of depression and alcoholism.[3]

Up to 25 percent of American adults will fit the clinical description of anxiety during their lifetimes.[4]

A typical panic attack lasts between fifteen and thirty minutes.[5]

More than a quarter of Americans take SSRIs or benzodiazepines for anxiety, depression, or other mental health disorders.[6]

Women are far more likely to take this medication, with over 25 percent of American women treated vs. 15 percent of men.[7]

Around 15 percent of all new mothers have postpartum depression, anxiety, or OCD (PPD), and it is treatable.[8]

Cognitive behavioral therapy is the most widely used technique in combating anxiety.[9]

Mindfulness is an effective tool to combat anxiety and excessive rumination.[10]

## Breaking the Vicious Cycle

Obsessing about failure is a deadly prescription, and it's especially hard because successful people are supposed to be bold and brave. When anxiety makes us question if we deserve what we want, it creates a self-defeating cycle.

Sometimes the obsessing is about what a failed loser you are: FOMO on steroids. Morgan describes it as "thinking about what a fucking failure I am, and how much better every other parent is than me, how much better every person I've ever met is than me. Looking at the cars of people driving by and being like, well, they have a nicer car, they're more successful, they're a better parent, they can provide for their child."

Another feature of anxiety is globalization: one small worry cascades into a giant one. When my husband was an entrepreneur, it was difficult for us to have conversations about the state of his company. A few rough conversations when he was starting out made me convinced he was about to declare bankruptcy . . . every single month for ten years.

But I think the hardest part of the anxiety-depression combination is constant ruminating and obsessing. You obsess about things you'd never want to admit to anyone, and these little worries become constant fears. That can include obsessing about how much you're obsessing. Writer and Editor Alicia Lutes jokes, "I'm, like, none of these things are actually really anything. You're just a nightmare human that is obsessed with yourself."

And when it comes to career, feeling that an obsession with failure is selfish can be very, very challenging when you're trying to become a "success." Duh. But thinking about the positive effects of your anxiety can help break the cycle, and make anxiety into one of your tools.

## CRYING IN THE BATHROOM—AM I ALONE?

The answer to that question is no, you're not—and women's bathrooms have a storied history. Jessica Bennett, a *New York Times* journalist and author of the great book *Feminist Fight Club*, says that women's bathrooms often serve as secret feminist bunkers, good for "hiding tears, planning internal revolts, and figuring out how to ask for a raise." *Newsweek* reporters planned the first class-action sexual discrimination lawsuit largely in the ladies' room, and it was depicted in the book and TV series *Good Girls Revolt*.

But if you're not planning any revolts, you might need to figure out what your tears are telling you. Everyone needs an occasional break to cry, but the women's bathroom is fertile ground for so many emotions. Try to use them to figure out what kind of a work space you want when you open the door.

A nonprofit development director told me of a time at her organization when she was aware that several of her staff were frequently crying in the bathroom. Some less enlightened managers would ignore this, or even shame the staff for their bathroom trips. Not this one: she took it as a sign that something was wrong with the organizational culture, spoke to the staff one-on-one, did some sleuthing, and created a plan to address the culprit (a toxic and abusive board chair). All that crying in the bathroom was an important clue for the leadership.

Is your crying a symptom of a situation you can resolve by approaching a manager or making a change? Is it a situational sadness, such as a breakup or dealing with a loved one's illness or trauma? Are you still depressed and crying when you're out of the office, say, for a business trip, or an off-site meeting? If you work at home, how do you feel? I have experienced the sadness of an ambient depression, and I have experienced the need to be in another role, or in another place. Don't think of crying in the bathroom as hiding—think of it as an opportunity to tune into what your crying is telling you.

## The Bright Side: Making Anxiety Work for You

I am not sugarcoating anxiety in the least, but at work, your anxious nature can offer secret skills like social attunement, attention to detail, organization, drive, and the biggest: empathy.

According to leadership guru Marcus Buckingham, data show that working on weaknesses is far less effective than working from strengths. I've come to accept my nature, and value its strengths, like the fact that I have strong empathy and interpersonal skills, and I always get a good night's sleep, 'cause I'm never out late partying.

It was the former LinkedIn senior executive and current Silicon Valley tech CEO Arvind Rajan who told me about Buckingham's observation, and he used his own life as an example. Arvind is a skilled practitioner of cultivating leadership without pressing the flesh, and he has coped with his social anxiety through a very successful twenty-year career in Silicon Valley.

"I didn't even realize how much anxiety I had until I started to go to cocktail parties for work," Arvind says. "I'd make an appearance and find a reason to go to the bathroom and sneak out." (See: men hide in the bathroom, too.)

His simple suggestion: reframe your expectations of yourself as a leader. "Networking is a skill we learn just like we learn how to do Excel," he says. "At some level you need to master the basics. But you're better off playing to your strengths."

This knowledge leads to more security—and being more comfortable revealing your true self. "If you'd asked me to do this interview in my twenties, I would have worried it would make me seem weak," Arvind says. "Now, I don't mind admitting where I have weaknesses."

Most entrepreneurs in Silicon Valley are, in fact, introverts, and a bit socially awkward, Arvind told me. But they know their stuff. They may worry about how they're perceived on a personal level, but professionally, they are 100 percent assured in what they're pitching. It's ironic to me that the leaders we idolize in Silicon Valley are largely introverted, socially awkward, and probably anxious. They certainly play to their strengths.

I love to watch the fantastic example of Richard, the nerdy tech CEO on HBO's *Silicon Valley*. His usual demeanor is so awkward, and he suffers so much anxiety, that in the moments when he does spring into expressing surprising strength and force, he throws everyone off their game, and wins the moment. What a great tactic. Identify your strengths as a leader who has some anxiety, and play to those.

## SOCIAL ANXIETY VERSUS INTROVERSION

Introversion and social anxiety are different, but often conflated. Here are a couple of tells to see if you have some social anxiety:

- ❑ My fear of social activities can cause tension in my personal and professional relationships.

- ❑ I feel anxious before picking up the phone or arriving at a meeting.

- ❑ It can be difficult for me to leave my house when I need to attend a social event or work event.

- ❑ I fear getting rejected or made fun of if I enter a conversation.

- ❑ I'm driven to get everything perfect, otherwise I might be harshly judged.

*(Courtesy Dr. Ellen Hendriksen)*

**Social Anxiety.** Social anxiety can be a wonderful gift at work, because those of us who have it are exquisitely attuned to other people's needs.[11] I always joke that the reason I am so good at client services is that I am deathly afraid my clients will be unhappy.

But as psychologist Ellen Hendriksen writes,[12] for anxious introverts, "the social antennae are too sensitive." Ironically, we can read a room, even if we can't walk into it with confidence. We may imagine people judging us, or pick up negative judgments that aren't there. People like me with social anxiety think there is something wrong with us, and, as a result, we hide in the bathroom, thus avoiding situations that we might even enjoy.

Dr. Hendriksen notes that social anxiety is a learned behavior, usually stemming from a childhood situation where we learned we did not fit. I know for me, I forever feel like an outcast because until I was about nine, I was one. I had no friends, and no one would have lunch with me because I was weird and my mom never packed me anything good to trade. My height didn't help.

But I'm a grown-up now, and with care and intention, I've learned to make anxiety into a useful tool. I tell myself that people do like me now, and I use those attunement skills for good.

**Preparation, Organization, and Attention to Detail.** I bet you were never the type to wing it! Anticipatory anxiety means you rehearse before doing, and plan for the big events. You plan your body language and practice your tone of voice, in addition to your facts and figures. Perhaps fear of not being good enough means you prepare for every line of a speech and transition in a slide. People get a lot of flak for being prepared (remember Donald Trump's nasty accusation that Hillary Clinton actually prepared for their debates). This is a healthy adaptation to anxiety, and it means you are in control of your work and yourself when it matters.

And, because you're attuned and you can read a room, if your perfectly prepared remarks fall flat, you can pivot on a dime and meet the tone the audience wants.

**Time Management.** You have no time for time wasters! You don't procrastinate. You know the best way to quell the fear and anxiety is to tackle something head-on, so you start the day with the scariest thing on your to-do list. Then, you give yourself a little treat.

You also use your avoidance to be more judicious in choosing the times when you actually do press the flesh.

You know the people who spend all their time at conferences or lunches? There's a plus in putting yourself out there, but a lot of it is expensive hype.

Being early for meetings, even if you did so because you were terrified, makes clients happy. Also, hello: if you always arrive at the airport an extra hour early, you're much more likely to get upgraded.

**Drive.** The drive of anxiety can come from a dark place. Morgan Shanahan notes, "I'm an obsessive, so how do I get it all done? I fucking obsess. It's been a blessing and a curse." This is different from a drive that gets fed by the validation of others, one that yields achievement that isn't truly about what you want. A drive born of anxiety is generative and forces us to create solutions. After all, behind every rags-to-riches or unlikely-origin story of success is a deep anxiety: the threat of poverty, loss, and failure drive something great. Anxiety means that every day you have something to prove. Hard to live with; great in business.

**Structure.** Putting in place a support system for your anxiety also means you have a support system for setbacks. You've built a network of employees, friends, family, and a kitchen cabinet (more on that one in Chapter 4) to keep you going. You're probably good at managing your personal infrastructure and know how to build the scaffolding: the fact that you need to rehearse a scenario (say a business trip in which your kids will be in others' care) in order to survive it means you have the mechanisms in place for healthy transitions!

My colleague has just been treated for her ADHD as a forty-year-old. The tactics she's recently been taught to manage her daily life sound very much like mine: lots of lists, practice at prioritization, and breaking down the work of the day into bearable chunks. For example, something that feels unbearable comes first, and then is followed by completely bearable tasks (for example, a scary call with a client would be followed by busywork like filing receipts or something enjoyable, like writing). It's all about the structure that works for you.

**Empathy.** The old chestnut for stage fright is to imagine everyone in the audience in their underwear. When you struggle with social anxiety, you can automatically see everyone in their underwear—

figuratively, at least. You can flip the script from being about yourself ("Does anyone like me? Am I stupid?") to tune into how other people feel. Perhaps they're anxious themselves, faking their extroversion or enjoyment, or simply having a bad day. Or perhaps they're really enjoying themselves with you and think you're pretty smart. Can you let go and enjoy with them? Nonverbal cues and mirroring others' signals win friends and influence people. Plus, they help you get out of your head.

Your own struggles with anxiety, and how they affect you at work, can also give you insight into other employees' struggles, whether they're dealing with a new baby or a broken leg. Giving support can lead to getting support, and a healthier, more empathetic office for everyone.

## GETTING STARTED

### Working with Your Anxiety

Imagine you have a business trip coming up. You know that it's going to be all the things you hate: flying, being separated from your kids, your partner, or your space, lots of schmoozing. You can feel the anticipatory anxiety building up.

Your anxiety is part of you, and it can be a valuable piece. But that doesn't mean you should let it take over. Ignoring anxiety can hurt you, and succumbing to it can quash your dreams. You need an excellent scaffolding to support your ambition.

**Structure** is an anxious person's best friend. I make a schedule with all the details of the day. (*I will shower. I will call the dentist. I will write six e-mails. I will jog for fifteen minutes.*) Even when I'm on top of the world, I keep them up. They help me feel in control, and prevent me from going global.

**Team.** I've chosen to give up some income because I know that support is crucial to my functioning. My life changed when I decided to hire a full-time assistant, who handles my schedule and even structures "break time," which frees me up to concentrate on our P&L, especially when what Winston Churchill, a major depressive, called "the black dog" hits.

But you don't need to hire help. Colleagues, mentors, e-mail lists, and Facebook groups—any support structure—give you a safe space outside your job that you can use for advice, opinions, grousing, networking, and celebrating. When I feel less alone at work, I feel less anxious. And when I don't trust my own opinion or work, I have colleagues whose opinion I really value and who cover my weaknesses.

**Save the environment.** If your environment is out of control, you will feel out of control. Left to my own devices, I would putter around all day and clean the house. Since this is not productive— and more than a little obsessive—I allot myself thirty minutes every morning and evening to clean up, usually while I'm on a routine work call. And, if your anxiety makes you leave your house a disaster, try giving a deep clean to one room a week.

**Self-care.** Building in self-care—exercise, massage, alone time —is not selfish. It's a key part of managing your anxiety. Even a ten-minute walk or a cup of coffee with a friend can calm your nerves. There's a great quote from activist and attorney April Reign: "Everyone is finite"—meaning you won't have anything to give if you never take care of yourself. I wish it was tattooed on my hand.

**Pep talks.** You can give these to yourself, or you can reach out to a trusted confidant. The key is to find what motivates you to reach past your anxiety.

My husband is my official pep talker. He is really good at it. He knows my most ridiculous and minute fears, and he knows the drill. I blub to him, and he simply listens. He asks me important questions when I'm hiding in a bathroom, waiting to run for the exit and next flight home. He'll ask me if I have important client work and *can't* leave. When I give pep talks to myself, it's most often when I am sitting on a plane, ready for takeoff. I remind myself that my children need money just as much as they need me around. This is not a choice; it's not fun. I'm doing what I need to do.

Pep talks are important, because they keep you in the game when it matters. For instance, when I attended the White House summit on the United State of Women, it was one of the most important days of my life. I cheered and teared up as I watched heroes and role models from President Obama to Cecile Richards take the stage. But my palms were sweating with panic. There could be bombings, or shootings. My children were three thousand miles away. In between Joe Biden and Oprah, I tried to rebook my flight home.

But I called my husband for a pep talk, and went through my day and my goals. Hearing the words out of my own mouth made me feel more in control, more empowered. I told him to tell me to stay. And I stayed.

**Label your anxiety.** Sometimes, simply noting what's making you anxious and acknowledging it can help you calm down. For example, my psychiatrist Dr. Carol Birnbaum taught me to observe my anxiety:*I'm feeling flooded with anxiety because I'm separated from my kids and I can't see them.* Then I remind myself, *You're just like all these other mothers in the world. They're anxious, too.*

**Ask for updates.** Worrying takes you out of whatever you're doing at the time—not a great plan at work. So build in reassurances. Away from your kids? Get your babysitter to send you pictures. Meeting going on without you? Ask your colleague to shoot you an e-mail. It's much harder to obsess about what's going wrong when you know what's going on.

**You're not alone.** Besides us garden-variety anxiety experts, there are a ton of people suffering small- to large-scale anxiety at any given time. People are afraid of bugs, mice, spiders, water, death, sharks, clowns, hospitals, blood, elevators. People in their twenties are panicking because they're trying to figure it all out. People in their middle age are having midlife crises. People in their eighties are wondering why they wasted so much time worrying.

The point is, if you're panicking on the runway, you're only human. A bunch of other people on the plane are panicked about something, too.

**Send a substitute.** If all else fails, remember that *everyone* on your team is a brand ambassador, and every single appearance doesn't need to be made by you. You probably have a colleague who loves being in the press or pressing the flesh. Shift your thinking from "I need to be out there" to a sense of distributed leadership. Send that person out there and bask in the glow!

## FLYING HIGH

For those of us whose work demands a lot of air travel, flying anxiety can be very limiting. And for those of us who are more sensitive or need more control, it can be even more intense.

Captain Tom Bunn, an air-force veteran, an airline captain, and a licensed therapist, was part of the first fear-of-flying program, which was started at Pan Am in 1975. Now he's president and founder of SOAR, Inc., which has helped over five thousand people overcome their fear of flying.

"Being on the ground," Bunn says, "is our most basic way of controlling things. When you get lifted up in the air, you don't have control, and you don't have escape, and these are the ways we usually calm ourselves on the ground."

His method involves simple exercises and a lot of oxytocin, powerful tools you can use to ease your fears without drugs or alcohol. (I'm not judging. I've been there.)

**Practice vagal maneuvers.** The vagus nerve literally controls our fight-or-flight instincts. Signals that we are physically safe stimulate the vagus nerve—which is in charge of panic attacks and other stress responses in the parasympathetic nervous system—to slow your heart rate and calm you down.

So, before you get on the plane, build in a calming presence and link it directly to the challenges you will face on the plane. Imagine the face of someone who loves you: your lover, your partner, your baby, even your dog.

**Flood your oxytocin.** When you're flooded with oxytocin, a deep sense of well-being will shut down your anxiety. To find your oxytocin, imagine a triggering moment: amazing sex, nursing your new baby, even something like closing a deal. Try to remember every detail and talk yourself through it. I have to admit, I imagine nursing, where I can even feel a "phantom letdown." Captain Tom notes that men who have flying anxiety do better imagining moments of afterglow after great sex.

For a more advanced exercise, you can try to train your brain to link the oxytocin with the elements of flying. When you hear the announcement for boarding, trigger your oxytocin. When you hear the click of the seat belt or the flight attendant asking for devices to be turned off, trigger your oxytocin. In time, your memories will become automatically linked to the flight ritual, and slow down your stress hormones.

**Practice "loving-kindness."** Buddhists use a simple meditation in which you picture someone you love in front of you, someone who fills you with a sense of security, and imagine them wishing you well. The words of the meditation are, "May I feel safe. May I feel content. May I feel strong. May I live with ease." You can use any words that are natural to you as well: "You are fine," or, "you are safe," for example.

**Meditation for the time-challenged.** You don't have to spend an hour on a cushion every day or visit a yogi to use meditation for your flight. YouTube is filled with simple breathing exercises, meditations, and thought exercises, some as short as five minutes, to provide a quick burst of calm, as are several free apps, such as 10% Happier.

**Medicate.** Anne Parris traveled for years working for a large accounting company. Because medication was frowned upon in her family, it never occurred to her to ask for an antianxiety pill from her doctor. So for literally twenty years, on every flight, she sat there, awake, afraid to have any alcohol because she could not lose control, and feared she would die.

She laughed when she told me, "I took Ativan for the first time on a flight a few months ago and it was literally a joyful experience. I still had to do my preflight ritual but at least I didn't worry I was going to die once I boarded the plane."

I think it's safe to say that I have not really been conscious on a flight since 2008. It doesn't mean I don't fly—I do almost every week. It's not joyous, even with medication. Sometimes it gets hairy.

I was at Washington Reagan Airport, awaiting my flight home after forty-eight hours of a presentation to the Council on Foreign Relations, business development meetings and meals, and a five-hour client retreat I'd run and directed. I'd paid for multiple breakfasts, lunches, and Starbucks with former or prospective colleagues or clients. All I wanted to do was pass out in coach, then wake up in Los Angeles.

I performed my time-tested ritual for the perfect medicated flight. One Xanax fifty minutes before takeoff. Except this time . . . I decided to take two. I was really anxious. Forty-five minutes before takeoff, just about to board, I popped two pills, swigged some water, and pulled out my neck roll. Here we go.

Then, a tarmac delay was announced over the loudspeaker. Panic. Would I fall asleep in the boarding area? Who would make sure I get home? I don't remember anything else. I think some kind stranger woke me up when we finally boarded.

If you take a lot of medication to fly (assuming, like I did, some kind stranger helps you make it to your destination!) you may not be able to drive a rental car when you arrive, and you may need to adjust your schedule. You can say no to a client dinner if you're recovering from catatonia when you arrive. At the end of the day, when it comes to coping with the anxiety of travel with medication, it's way more important that you're prepared for the big meeting the next day.

**Be choosy.** I feel much safer on a 747 than I do on a regional jet. I always do better in business class. As a result, I have worked hard to build up loyalty points on the airlines I feel most comfortable with. Because I have loyalty points, I get upgraded more often, which also makes my flying experience more palatable. If you have the money and being in first class diminishes your anxiety, allow yourself to upgrade.

**Lucky charms.** I'm not superstitious, but I do have a lucky charm from each of my children that I have to have in my purse when I get on the plane. Having a concrete object, like a picture or piece of jewelry, can help with triggering oxytocin, or be a visual stimulus for your own pep talk.

## What Your Body Is Telling You

I am the queen of psychosomatic illness and injury. I get migraines when I work too much or travel. In a job I hated, I developed horrible wrist tendonitis and had to go on leave to get surgery. I get sick when I'm stressed. Every few months I just have to go to bed for a few days.

Over the years I've finally accepted that a dysfunctional body is a clue that something needs to change at work.

Workstations are not natural places for our bodies, and squinting at our smartphones is even worse. My migraines are caused by muscle tension and resulting musculoskeletal dysfunction, all from hunching over my laptop, peering down at my iPhone, clenching my jaw on a plane, or worrying about traffic in the back of a New York City taxi.

Posture is also a clue. Feeling under attack at work, even unconsciously, elicits a fear response: we crouch down to protect the vital organs. Not only can the fear-response posture cause pain, it can affect the digestive system. Even if it's not caused by posture, many women suffer from irritable or irregular bowels or IBS, which can have its root in persistent, low-level anxiety.

My women's community is chock-full of migraine sufferers, all of us type A overachievers who literally send stress and fear to our jaws, shoulders, and backs. We're hurting ourselves, and most of the time we don't do anything to try to stop it.

I have been on a five-year journey to cure mine. It turns out, clenching my jaw 24/7 for years has created the upper body's version of a system failure. Everything is crunched, and what I think are migraines are actually frozen fascia and muscles. After thousands of dollars and countless appointments with neurologists, ENTs, hormone specialists, chiropractors, Botox-administering dentists, orthodontists, and energy healers, I found a solution in the Center for Craniofacial Pain at Tufts Dental School. A plastic jaw appliance that prevents me from clenching—a fancy version of a retainer—and physical therapy have made it better.

Ultimately, my worst enemy in my pain is myself. When you feel pain, take it seriously. And if it's anxiety and stress causing the pain, take that seriously, too. I've learned to take time to respond to my own pain. And now, if I need to avoid a stressful situation or spend half the day lying prone on a heating pad, it's no one's business but my own.

## The Listen-to-Your-Body Scan

This two-part exercise can help you see how stress is affecting your body.

First, sit upright in a chair. Put your feet flat on the floor and your hands on your lap. Keep your chin neutral. Note which part of the body you can immediately feel. Then, with your eyes closed, scan through the following:

**Your head**      **Your stomach**

**Your jaw**       **Your hips**

**Your neck cords**    **Hamstrings and butt**

**Your shoulders**     **Your calves, ankles, and feet**

**Your wrists and forearms**

**Your upper back**

**Your lower back**

Note which feel tight, and, in order to gain some relief, breathe into the area of tightness or pain.

Next, keep a diary for a week. (Don't choose a week in which you have a huge project due.)

❑ Note how you feel at 9 A.M., noon, three, and 6 P.M. How does your body change over the course of the day?

❑ What part or parts of your body hurt at the end of the workday?

❑ When you think about work, is there a part of the body you immediately feel?

❑ How often during the week do you rely on a drink, muscle relaxant, or over-the-counter pain relief, if at all?

❑ Note how often you exercise, do yoga, dance, or take a walk. (The stairs count!) How do you feel afterward?

❑ Note how your body feels on the weekend. Is it different from how it feels at work?

Now you should have a sense of your level of pain response to your work, as well as what times you feel it, and where it is located in the body. The next step is to link corresponding activities to your feelings. Are the feelings triggered by people? Tasks? What relieves those feelings, and what exacerbates them? Do you dread your ten o'clock meeting, but feel thrilled after each phone call with a client? Use your body's signals to find out how your work is treating you.

## Stand up Straight

In a famous study, slumped participants used more negative words, spoke with lower affect, and expressed poorer self-esteem than the ones who sat up straight. If you want a quick fix, you can help change your emotions, as well as your mood, by changing your posture.

**Wall angels.** Here is my number one trick for helping regain good posture and instantly (I swear) quashing a tension migraine or sore shoulders.

Lean against a wall if you can, or simply stand up straight. Make sure your neck is neutral and your eyes are looking straight ahead, not at the floor. Raise your arms to the side to make a T, your elbows bent at ninety degrees. Bring your shoulders back and retract your shoulder blades, trying to make them touch. Keeping your shoulder blades together, move your arms up and down like a set of angel wings. Do three sets of fifteen (it's hard!).

**Belly breath.** To gain calm, sit in a chair with your feet flat on the ground, hands at your sides. Breathe in and relax your upper body and legs. Then practice moving the breath down from your neck cords to your abdomen. Swell out your belly so you can see it, and visualize moving the breath down from your throat, your diaphragm, and into your abdomen.

**Dance party.** Put on your favorite music and dance or move for five minutes. Simply swoop your arms over your head to get your energy moving. Roll your neck and shoulders and shift your weight and energy from your neck, jaw, and shoulders into your legs and feet.

## Taking the Leap: Therapy

It's hard for successful people to admit they're struggling; or that they don't know what to do; or what they could be doing better. Therapy can be expensive, and it can be daunting to try to find the right person. But what if therapy was like working out at the gym—a preventive measure? It is a crucial part of your tool kit if you struggle with mental health issues.

Some of us need some privacy in order to open up. Whatever you can't say out loud to your friends, colleagues, parents, you can say to a therapist. Trust me, you don't want to wait until crisis strikes. I'll never forget my very first panic attack, when I was nineteen. I collapsed on the floor of the college library and my wonderful roommate walked me home. For some months after, I thought I'd been stricken with an illness or had a bad reaction to medication, because that's what the psychiatrist treating me quickly surmised (he wasn't much for conversation). It wasn't until several months later that I saw a therapist who suggested I'd had a panic attack. She gave me a definition, a framework for identifying and coping with later attacks, and helped me piece together an important puzzle. Therapy doesn't have to be about lying on a couch discussing your childhood; it can be useful and practical, a sensible part of your life repertoire.

There's no doubt about it, though: therapy is expensive. For those whose insurance doesn't cover it, many therapists offer sliding scales, or can recommend a practitioner who does. Also, there are now online and text-only therapists, who can provide a measure of relief for those who may not have time to go in person. And even if you don't plan to go every week, you can see a therapist a few times, and you will always have someone to call if you need urgent help.

Taking the step of going on medication is a personal choice. Don't listen to the opinions of your friends or your hairstylist or anyone else. It's *your* mental health. For me, antidepressants and antianxiety medication have been crucial to my functioning, and can also be a lifesaver for those having a hard time or in transition.

The most important thing is to find a psychiatrist or prescriber you trust, and to work closely on a plan. Don't simply let your GP prescribe the medication—you need a specialist on the case. Finding the right medication cocktail can take time, so don't get discouraged if you have to try a few. And don't be afraid to speak up about side effects. I've been on almost every antidepressant. Some affect your libido, and some make you gain weight. It doesn't make you petty to worry about this!

## Parenthood and Anxiety

In today's world, when bombs go off willy-nilly and basic safety at schools isn't even certain, sometimes even the everyday separation from my kids can be excruciating. When my children are out with their nanny and I'm working at home, I can hear sirens in the distance and freeze up. There is not a single time I get on an airplane without worrying I'll never see my children again.

Forget about the crazy hormones and physical changes: your world will never be the same once it's inhabited by precious little people you created, and this can be extremely anxiety provoking.

It can start as soon as you get pregnant. It's not as well-known, but antenatal depression is postpartum depression's ugly sibling. All three of my children gestated on Prozac, because perhaps the worst depression I ever experienced was during the first trimester of my first pregnancy. I hated everything, especially my poor little fetus. I'll never forget the day my mom suggested that perhaps I shouldn't go through with the pregnancy.

After I went back on meds at three months, I gave birth to my beloved and cherished first son, Asa. All along, I worked with a psychiatrist who specialized in pregnant women (sometimes called a reproductive psychiatrist), and so I felt better about any risk to the fetus.

Like me, Morgan Shanahan became pregnant with her first child during the economic crash of 2008. After vomiting multiple times a day the first three months, she found herself simply too sad to function. "I really truly believed that motherhood was going to put a screeching halt on all of my plans, and my plans were already not going the way I wanted them to," Morgan says. "I was like, 'This is it. This is where life goes off the rails. It's over.'"

For some, postpartum depression (PPD) is their first experience of mental illness. Many of us have experienced episodes of anxiety or depression in the past, and pregnancy brings on an episode in full force.

After PPD, when you finally make it back to work, you may find the formerly mundane aspects of work-life (travel, being out of the home) scary. When you are torn between demands at work and those at home, it's normal to ask yourself, *Am I present enough? Am I giving enough to my children?*

I am a huge proponent of never dismissing these feelings. It's important to use them as a barometer and to trust your instincts. It's also important, though, to differentiate between mild mom-FOMO and your true parenting priorities. For instance, I have a dear friend who is a stay-at-home mom. I crave her beautifully made dinners and long neighborhood playdates. But when I leave her house, I don't chew over it.

When I enter a stage of feeling constantly guilty about being out of touch with my kids, which does happen, I say, *Self, nothing is permanent. You are not ruining your children.* For that very reason, every six months or so I reevaluate my work+life fit. If things feel really skewed in one direction or another (for example, too much work and not enough time with my kids, or too much time with my kids and not enough client work) I try to come up with a plan to shift things.

## THE BEARABILITY SPECTRUM

In a world where ambient anxiety reigns, the most important thing you need to decide is that your anxiety is not your boss. My wonderful psychiatrist Dr. Birnbaum stresses, "You can't protect yourself from all the anxiety that's out there. But you can get into such a hyperaroused state that it feels almost impossible to calm down. Something really scary may make you anxious. Then your body gets so hypercharged that you don't sleep well, and you don't get refreshed." Which, of course, makes it harder to deal with your anxiety.

A great way to break the cycle is to chop up tasks that make you extremely anxious into bearable pieces. You can also move something from completely unbearable to slightly bearable. For example, you might nudge along your fear of flying from "I can't get on a plane" to "I'm going to pack." "I'm going to make a plan to keep in touch with my kids." "I'm going to order a Lyft and call my friend while I'm stuck in traffic en route to the airport." And finally, once on the plane: "I'm going to take a Xanax, do a calming meditation, and survive."

I use a bearability practice to manage my anxiety, especially around business travel. I get very anxious when I am working far away from home and I haven't heard from my nanny or husband. I worry something bad has happened, and it distracts me and takes me away from my work. So I set up a system: I ask my husband or the caregiver to text me every three hours. I don't want to have to ask them for updates, because they might be driving with the kids in the car and it might be dangerous to respond. (#anxious.)

How can you build in reassurances you need to get through your day and minimize the anxiety?

# CHUNKING

Chunking helps manage any act that paralyzes you or gives you panic attacks. Chunking is a simple way to divide any task or block of time into manageable pieces.

**Leave time.** Once you've got a hold on what predictably makes you scared, you have to give yourself enough space to chunk it. One of the worst ways to handle something that scares you is to put it off to the last minute. That's what causes you to panic on a plane, or obsess in a meeting, or go off the rails when you have to talk to your boss.

**Find the fear.** Usually, there's a peak moment in any task that terrifies you. That exact moment is what you have to work toward, but you have to locate it first. Is it when you're packing for the trip or boarding the flight? Is it when the project is due or when you sign up for it in the first place? What's the part that puts your heart in your throat?

**How can you make that better?** Here's the part where you put some of your bodywork to good use, and try out some practical ideas. Maybe you need to work on the project every other day instead of one big burst (hence the time thing). Maybe you need to work in a pep talk from your friend the night before the trip. Maybe you need to put a list of things you predictably find funny, or find adorable (here's where YouTube videos are really handy) to watch before you go into that meeting. Be creative, and try some things out. You're one step closer to finding what works.

**Reconsider brave.** So maybe you can't deal with making presentations. What did someone once tell you *they* thought was brave about you? Maybe a best friend can't believe you routinely speak in front of crowds. Maybe someone's amazed at how you're not affected by heights, or that you got a degree in poetry as well as business. The truth is, things we take for granted often seem brave to others, and things we can't do are a breeze for some. Remembering that it's all relative can be very helpful when you're feeling defined by what (you think) you can't do.

When you're in the moment, find that brave thing. Let yourself feel proud and brave (or amused and shaking your head at your friend) instead of nuts.

**Always be breathing.** You lucked out: the human body, full stop, is always calmed by breathing when brainwork won't make it happen. And let's face it—when things are bad, often nothing seems like it will work. Start by simply taking a few deep breaths. Find a breathing exercise that works for you. You can use Google, YouTube, apps. There are a million. At first, it will seem silly. But anytime, anywhere, it will work.

**Make it a practice.** Part of paying attention to your feelings is not re-inventing the wheel each time you're upset. You can't control your feelings, but you can control how you respond to them. If watching cat videos helps you fly, do it. If going through high school yearbooks the night before a meeting lets you remember that This Too Shall Pass, do that. If making a pie chart of your past clients lets you see you'll get more clients, do that.

Sometimes shame or denial makes you try to ignore your feelings in the hopes that you'll be able to push past them. You don't need to push past them—these are your feelings. You should honor them, not avoid them.

**Lay off yourself.** If you have tried everything—and I mean everything —acknowledge that this is something you can't do, and figure out how you can live without it. If your job requires flying and you *really can't fly,* have a talk with your boss (or yourself). If you are better at doing than pitching, be excellent at executing. You're not superwoman; you don't have to master every single task that scares you. Sometimes not being able to is actually a sign that it's time for a change in your circumstances, not in you.

## YOU HAVE TO DEAL WITH IT

So many of us walk around with anxiety that we express through de-structive behavior: binge eating, drinking, drugs, spending, random sex, you name it.

I wrote this chapter because I want you to understand that a life with anxiety can be productive and great—and yes, stressful—and it can be an essential piece of who you are at work and life. It is a lion that can be tamed, even channeled. But to get there, you must have the courage to take the first step toward a treatment plan, and the willingness to accept yourself as you are.

# 4

## *Loving Your Inner Hermit*

Once, I broke my little toe and worked at home for a week. My boss was flummoxed: he couldn't comprehend why an employee who could be such a powerhouse would stay home for a wonky toe. A few months later I tried to quit the job, and he asked me to stay. He said, "Do you want to work from home three days a week?"

How did he know?

Here's the truth: I took so many sick days at so many jobs that I'm embarrassed. At some, I barely went to work. But once I started freelancing, I had a revelation: though my actual productivity didn't change, I loved the feeling of coming in and out of clients' offices, working my own hours, and not having to be "on" all the time.

Being a hermit is different from being an introvert. While introverts can go out and build billion-dollar companies, hermits understand and accept what makes them thrive, and that might be giving themselves lots of space and alone time at work. It's fundamentally a lifestyle choice. Introversion is a character trait. You are born with it. Choosing to be a hermit usually happens after several years in the working world, when you say to yourself, *This just isn't working for me*. You make a choice to alter the place, pace, or space of your work to better suit your need for quiet. You're also willing to accept some limitations to growth (for example, that billion dollars) in order to control your everyday. Being a hermit is saying, "I need to manage my time and boundaries, like being able to be at home in my yoga pants three days a week. And I am willing to banish FOMO from my vocabulary to get there."

Often, we hermits suffer through years of stress and anxiety before finding our work+life fit, because we're not paying attention to our "tell." That's the emotional or physical state that lets you know you're penned in and strained by a work environment that's wrong for your temperament.

My tell was anxiety. And as we know, my anxiety has been my gift and my curse. It's made me work harder to get to where I need to go while trying to keep the monsters at bay, and it's also helped me become very good at saying no. Most important, it's made me be creative in designing a life that can support my family without ruining my spirit. I love to be in the big world, but only so much. Now, though I have been doing the same work for two decades, I set the terms of my time, space, and schedule.

You can be a hermit and be tremendously influential and successful (and I'm not just talking about a Salinger-like recluse writer in the woods). And, though you may not be able to be a hermit all the time or for your whole career, you can work toward building the time and space you need.

## Claire Shipman's story

A role model of mine is "secret slacker" and former *Good Morning America* correspondent Claire Shipman. She's a Peabody Award–winning journalist and former White House correspondent for NBC, and she covered the fall of the Soviet Union for CNN. Her first book, *Womenomics*, written with the BBC's Katty Kay, was a *New York Times* bestseller, and her new work is about cultivating confidence.

A real slacker, right? Except most days, she works from home.

About ten years ago, Claire realized her adrenaline-filled work life wasn't working for her anymore. She only found a work+life fit when she "tuned into what I like about work," cut out the constant demands to travel, and was extremely judicious about what she took on.

*Womenomics,* in fact, began as a bond between Katty and Claire, who felt like misfits in their field. "Instead of comparing notes about our TV careers," Claire says, "we would literally talk about how we could get out of work the next day, or how we hoped we weren't going to have to do a story that night, so we could get home early and be with the kids."

That wasn't, Claire explains, what you're supposed to want in television, where the premium is being on as much as possible.

"After my second child, I kept saying no to reporting trips," Claire says. "An executive and mentor of mine told me, 'Everybody else at the company jumps when we say jump. You don't.'"

Once Claire realized she had to be realistic about what demands she placed on herself and decide what she was willing to sacrifice, it was crucial to tune out other people when they asked things like, "Don't you want to be anchoring a show?'"

Going part-time meant sacrificing high-profile opportunities abroad and at home, including the "seven-year adrenaline rush" of covering the White House. But, she realized, "there is life out here, and I don't have to be exhausted and half-brain-dead."

"Sometimes I look at people who seem to have endless energy, who aren't sitting around ruminating, who just move through, and I'm in awe," Claire says. "But you have to recognize who you are as a person. It's taken me a long time to be able to say to myself, *You don't need to do everything.*" Claire is still an incredibly high-achieving person, but she has been able to lessen some of her own internal expectations of achievement.

# Are You a Hermit?

When I think of jobs like airline pilot or surgeon, in which you have to be at the top of your game because lives depend on it, I can't understand how people manage. Not wanting to run an ER doesn't make you a hermit. It might be that you just dislike your boss, your team, or your work product. You might just dislike your whole field. Still, take a moment to consider if it is simply that you love your work, but feel chafed by your work life. Is your stress about what you do, or about how you do it?

**1. You've finally taken the leap to a new field/role you think fits you better. You . . .**

**a)** Were right. Your new tasks and environment are much more suited to you.

**b)** Have the same amount of challenges you always have at work, but feel like you've advanced and are on the right track.

**c)** Are still miserable. And this is your third switch.

**2. You have a meeting with a new client, and the whole team will be there. You are . . .**

**a)** Glad to have them see you do your thing!

**b)** Terrified about what they'll think you're doing wrong, but glad to have them as backup.

**c)** Who cares about this meeting? Why do you have to go? Argh . . .

**3. You get a day off. Finally you can . . .**

**a)** See the movie you've been wanting to see. You guys did a great job on that contract.

**b)** Do some work! You always feel weird about closing the door.

**c)** Dream about what life would be like if every day were a day off.

**4. The best part of your work is . . .**

**a)** You love your work, but you also love the office. You have great coworkers.

**b)** It's amazing when you finish a project you are really proud of.

**c)** Leaving.

**5. You have to meet with the CEO. You are . . .**

**a)** Thrilled. This is a big honor.

**b)** Terrified. There will be a lot of judging.

**c)** Terrified. Will she see what a fraud you are?

### Mostly a's

You love your field AND you love where you work! Lucky you! The best part is that since you've found a great workplace, you'll always be able to judge when somewhere or some role isn't a fit.

### Mostly b's

You're into the work you do, but your personality contains characteristics of a hermit—you like to stay at home, you prefer to be your own boss, and you feel pressured by the go-getter elements of the job. It's important for you to think about what parts of your job you dread so you can try to turn your environment into a place where you can be productive without too much strain. There's no way to be in the wrong work environment without its doing some harm to your work AND your life.

### Mostly c's

You hate your work! Why on earth are you doing it, and does it pay enough to make it worth it? You need to start thinking about a field that may make you less miserable. The good news is that even though switching is scary, you'll find your work more fulfilling when you hit the right field, and more skills will transfer than you thought. Then, and only then, will you be able to tell if you're ALSO, God forbid, a hermit.

# GETTING STARTED

## The Digital Challenge

There is a premium placed on social interaction and networking, but the workplace is changing, as are social norms about working from home and networking online. There's good news for the ambitious hermit. Here's the wonderful thing about the digital age: it's hermit-friendly.

I love being able to engage in thoughtful conversations via e-mail or Facebook throughout the day. When it comes to this hermit-friendly digital space, the pleasure of a sustained conversation over text should not be quickly dismissed. As much as I struggle with IRL social stuff, I have an incredible community of friends and acquaintances online who ensure I'm supported, mentally stimulated, and kept au courant, all from my home office.

Best of all, it feels completely low pressure. As psychologist and digital media scholar Yalda Uhls says, "When you don't have the social pressure of having to immediately respond to another person, when you have time to write versus speak, you can be more articulate and thoughtful."

However, that digital revolution is a gift and a curse. I can't remember the last time I worked with a large organization whose team was in the same office. Our conference calls are always a jumble of areas codes and muted cell phones. For jobs that rely on a computer, the workplace doesn't need to be in a specific location, and you can get face time from FaceTime.

In fact, 20 percent of American workers "telework" most of the time. Census data show that 50 percent of workers have jobs that are compatible with working remotely. And, unsurprisingly, 90 percent of workers say they would like to be able to telework[1] two or three days a week, with "on" days for meetings with colleagues and clients.

Sounds like the ideal hermit schedule, right?

But for every hour we gain working remotely, our smartphone overcompensates. Constant contact with our work—via mobile technology—is eroding any sense of separation between home and work. Sometimes the race to respond to a colleague's e-mail overwhelms any rational sense of how urgent that e-mail actually is.

Sadly, this is not something that can be changed by implementing a flexible work policy. It's bigger than any of us. Harvard Business School's Leslie Perlow studies time at work, most notably what happens when teams have more freedom to control their time. Spoiler alert: they are happier, more productive, and more engaged. Teams whose managers create and enforce clear boundaries about when to be "on" reduce burnout, turnover, and mistakes made by stress.

Perlow notes even as managers struggle with being "on," they expect it from those they manage. Über-connectivity, in our minds, still equals performance, and the ideal worker is always on. Workers that resist the ideal pay a price.

What's more, as flexibility quickly evolves, we're working without a map. "A strict separation between work and life requires setting micro-boundaries daily," Perlow explains. "Will I answer e-mail now or not? Can I turn off my phone on weekends? Many people don't know where to draw the line."[2]

For a hermit, the tether is a double-edged sword. When the choice is between being chained to our iPhones in the quiet of our own space or working in an open-plan office, we choose the chains.

I made my peace with my smartphone a while ago. The majority of my day, I'm on conference calls and checking e-mail compulsively, just like the rest of us. But I'm doing it in bed or while making soup. And I don't have to talk to anyone during lunch. I control the space, pace, and place of my work.

The flexible workplace is still in its adolescence. But it may help us finally learn that the world doesn't end if you let an e-mail go unanswered for an hour. As Claire Shipman says, simply breaking the cycle of adrenaline we get into when we work in an always-on environment lends tremendous perspective and, ultimately, freedom.

## A Hermit's Challenges: Strong Ties and Loose Ties

I don't like socializing, and even though I love my friends, I get nervous before dates. I like to be alone with my family or with myself. As I have gotten older, I've become even more introverted. Because picking up the phone or making a date feels hard, I'm not great at forming close friendships. It's often easier for me to maintain a large network of casual acquaintances on the Internet than see my very close friends in real life.

But there are two types of relationships we must maintain as a functional adult: strong ties and loose ties. Strong ties are your closest social group, your real friends or intimate colleagues. Loose ties are acquaintances, occasional colleagues, and members of your community, such as other parents at school or your neighbors.

Being a hermit is challenging to both kinds of relationship. If you're an introvert, you may love to be with friends and socialize, but doing so drains you of energy, so you have to limit it. Sprinkle in a little social anxiety, and you've got a lot to overcome, because you may find it tough to be a good friend to strong ties and avoid being seen as rude to loose ones. But forcing yourself to work at strong and loose ties is important, first because having good friends is wonderful and healthy, and second because loose ties are the key to your success, especially if you're a hermit. In my experience, relationships with loose ties, ballasted by online conversations, are the secret strategy for a successful hermit to advance or bring in new business without having to get out there too often.

I used to feel tremendously guilty about this, until I learned a lesson from my minister, Claire Feingold Thoryn, who leads my Unitarian Universalist congregation. Funny and charming, capable of commanding a crowd, Claire seemed like the last person to be a secret hermit.

But, as she told us in one of her sermons, when her friend was about to give birth for the first time, and struggling, Claire kept putting off calling and checking in, even though her friend had specifically asked her to. Instead she sent half-hearted texts about plans that never came to fruition. With two young children and a busy congregation, she had no energy to talk on the phone and engage.

But when Claire's friend, having trouble nursing, texted, "I need your help," Claire cleared her day, got in her car, and drove to see her friend. And, as she told us from the pulpit, "I never did make that call, but I helped her latch the baby. Being there in a pinch made up for my lack of follow-through."

Claire's story is useful to think about if you feel guilty for needing alone time and space, even if it's from your good friends. It doesn't mean you don't love them. So maybe you're not great at staying in touch or remembering birthdays. Concentrate on being a good friend when it really matters.

## Maintaining Close Ties

Because I need so much alone time, I have a hard time giving over leisure time to others.

I avoid the phone, and the people I love and respect most. I don't call them back not because I don't love them or I don't care, but because I feel anxious doing it.

How silly is that? You're my friend, I love you, but I feel anxious picking up the phone to dial you. I can't really explain it. So I asked Dr. Ellen Hendriksen, the social anxiety expert. It's called anticipatory anxiety, and it's a common behavior if social settings make you anxious. Dr. Hendriksen says she can even feel this anxiety before she hits send on an e-mail, which I can totally relate to. So what's her advice?

"I tell myself to be brave for ten seconds. You can do anything for ten seconds. That's the amount of time it takes to dial a number. That's the amount of time it takes to hit send. That's the amount of time it takes to walk in the door. So, if you can just get over that initial hump, you'll get into the rhythm of talking to your friend and forget you were anxious."

I also like to give myself guidelines I know I can keep to. For example, perhaps quick check-ins are easier for you than heart-to-hearts. Or you can make space only to call one friend a week. Don't forget that a little goes a long way; leave a voice mail if having a conversation is too time-consuming.

Reverend Claire likens being a friend to prayer: pray as you can, not as you can't. She also notes that it's common to have stronger relationships with people who live nearby. It's easy to lose touch with your friends who live far away, but it's meaningful to build your support network where you are.

I am lucky in that my friends persist. Over the years the people I truly value are those who don't let me hide. They don't let me get away with my own bullshit. If I don't return their calls, they keep calling me and calling me.

But over the years, as I've identified this trait in myself, I have gone from slamming myself as a "bad friend" to calling myself an "atypical" friend. Remember: Facebook, e-mail, and texting have brought out the hermit in all of us. Making time in person, even if it's once a year, is the best of all.

The trick behind dealing with your hermit behaviors while still maintaining those close ties is to be a wonderful friend in batches you can handle. And give yourself a little credit, even when you fail.

## Maintaining Loose Ties

I love the listening-and-thinking part of church. I was not raised in a faith community, and it is something I want badly for my children. But I hate the coffee hour that immediately follows.

After we'd attended church for a few months, my husband (who grew up going to church several times a week) delivered some bad news to me: coffee hour is how you build community. It, not the sermon, is the key.

And what happens when you throw community out the window isn't pretty. In her essay "Am I an Introvert, or Just Rude?" self-confessed hermit KJ Dell'Antonia[3] tried embracing her desire to skip out. At first, she writes, saying no "brought with it a keen, almost illicit pleasure." She left meetings and assemblies early, and once sat in the car and read a book while her children attended a family athletic event. "I'd spent so long accommodating the world's demand that I get out there and participate," she writes. "Finally, the world seemed willing to accommodate me."

As it turns out, it wasn't. Her friends took her "tortoiseshell" as rudeness, and her kids were enraged. It also wasn't good for her. Data prove that even a small interaction with another person outside your family unit increases personal and group happiness (yes, even for introverts).[4] Giving in to her own discomfort was ruining her friendships, her family life, and the internal life she was working so hard to protect.

But how to engage when you just want to put in your earbuds and disappear? Smile! A warm expression goes far at school drop-off or a professional association mixer. Smiles also serve a social purpose: a warm, genuine smile puts everyone at ease, signaling altruism and community mindedness.[5] It's the first step in striking up a conversation. Ask the dry cleaner how she's doing. Joke with the barista. You'll be surprised at how quickly even greeting the dad you say hi to on the street as you bring your own kid to school develops into a pleasant ritual. And then, when you see him at church, you'll have someone to talk to over the coffee.

## The Loose-Ties Payoff

When you're out in a world of strangers, it can be hard to stay open, especially when your phone and headphones are there to give you a perfectly good excuse to shut off from the world. But loose ties leave you open to chance and serendipity, important in both career and community.

As I've said before, I'm never at my best in airports, especially after a flight from Dubai or some other faraway place my work takes me. But I have to remind myself that you never know who you'll meet if you're open and friendly in public. I met Steve, who runs a big division of a giant technology company, in line at Logan Airport— and literally just as I was outlining this chapter, he e-introduced me to his new colleague, who's in charge of women's leadership programming at the tech company. I e-mailed back about the serendipitous moment: "As it happens, I was just working on including a piece about the need to unplug and be present where you are . . ."

Some breaks are also a great way to meet kindred spirits and establish loose ties. Kenny Lao, who founded Rickshaw Dumpling Company, told me he met his most useful connections in front of his headquarters in Madison Square Park—including his future husband—on one of his many smoke breaks. (Kenny wants you to know he has now quit. Cigarettes are the really unhealthy version of hiding in the bathroom.)

I met one of my dearest colleagues and best hires on a smoke break, back when I was young and stupid and smoked. Mike Krempasky and I bonded outside a dive bar in D.C. after the bitter election of 2004. He is a fierce conservative, I am a fierce liberal, and we'd never have become friends were it not for my needing a lighter. A few months later, when I needed to hire a supersmart conservative strategist, he was my first call, and the introduction was easy.

If you don't smoke (and you shouldn't!), you may just have to pluck up your courage to make the first move when it comes to meeting new loose ties—whether it's starting to say "good morning" to the person you pass every day in the street, chatting with the barista, or leaving your house keys with a neighbor. It almost always pays off. The *New York Times's* KJ Dell'Antonia laughed as she told me a story about meeting Nicholas Kristof, the esteemed journalist and activist, at the copier on one of her rare trips to the *Times* headquarters in Manhattan.

Kristof and Dell'Antonia are colleagues, but KJ was still nervous to talk to him in person, although they had e-mailed. "I wanted to meet him," she said. "I'm a great admirer of his. I took a deep breath, turned around, pulled myself together and said, 'Hi.' That's a lot of harder than sending an e-mail or tagging someone on Facebook." But for KJ, that small moment cemented the bond of two colleagues in a visceral way.

Sometimes, a hi is all it takes.

## ADOPT AN EXTROVERT

My husband, Nicco, is not only the love of my life, he is also my greatest teacher and mentor. He's helped me temper my reclusive tendencies; to think more expansively; to take risks. And I have literally stolen my entire playbook from him.

Nicco is naturally an extrovert and superconnector. He loves nothing better than a good cocktail party or community event. He would like to be out every night. (It's actually amazing we're still married.)

An extrovert partner has two great uses: he or she can serve both as a model and as a "pipeline for opportunities," as financial therapist Amanda Clayman says about hers. "When I'm feeling inadequate, I think, what would Greg do in this situation?" He's also a constant source of connections for her. "I don't feel like I need to go out and try to socialize all the time," she says.

Of course, your adopted extrovert doesn't need to be a romantic partner. (Sometimes, it's easier if he isn't!) They can be your colleague, business partner, or friend. Play anthropologist: What are the characteristics or traits in your adopted extrovert you'd most like to borrow, if only for a few hours? Perhaps it's being able to enter a group discussion with ease, or recount your hilarious stories to a captivated audience.

I think often of one of my earliest bosses, Betty Hudson. The only six-foot-two-inch cheerleader in the history of the University of Georgia, I'm sure, she was taller than me, but so elegant and graceful. Betty had Ted Turner and half of the most powerful people in media on speed dial, and made you feel like her best friend within five minutes. She would walk into a room and crack a joke (often at her own expense), and everyone melted. I studied her like a book. And on a good day, I think she'd be proud of how I can work a room—even if I have to force myself to take on those traits I don't instinctively have.

## Your Kitchen Cabinet

When I set out to interview people for this book, I didn't have to do much research. Just like Mitt Romney had his "binders full of women," I have a digital sisterhood—my kitchen cabinet—of subject-matter experts and wise confidantes. We might see each other once or twice a year, or even less, but we keep in touch in a meaningful way online. (By the way, did you know Mitt Romney actually did have real binders?)

Your kitchen cabinet is separate from supportive colleagues or senior mentors—those are people to whom you might not want to show your vulnerabilities. A kitchen cabinet is made up of people of different skills and professional backgrounds who will push you in different directions and into different arenas—and, ideally, become true friends. Diversity is key: no pale, male, and stale group-think here!

Time, place, and circumstance can work wonders when it comes to creating kinship, and it need not be in person. My friend Allyson Downey created a fantastic Google group for working moms of children under five in order to research her book *Here's the Plan*. She plumbed us for wisdom, and we plumbed each other. When my daughter was eight months old, that group was the only place I felt I could turn when debating whether to wean.

For now, ask yourself, *Who's in your kitchen cabinet? Who could be?* Here are some people to consider . . .

☐  A financial expert
☐  Your personal-brand guru
☐  Someone who will always tell you the truth
☐  A master negotiator
☐  Your friend with amazing personal style
☐  A friend with a similar parenting philosophy, with older kids

## Get Out of Your Head

I would wager that if you're a hermit, you're prone to stewing. Ruminating. Dwelling. But if you're a natural ruminator, you have to practice getting out of your head because when you're too much in your head, little gets done and moods get dark. Stepping outside our own feelings gets us in a better frame of mind than wondering how we are coming up short or what other people are thinking.

Here are three simple tricks to get out of your head and engage in the world.

**Link into meaning:** If you're feeling stuck in a negative pattern and want to retreat from the world, Claire Shipman recommends consciously giving more thought to how your work ties into a larger mission or movement, or how you can help other people. This is similar to the practice of snapping out of FOMO by recognizing a colleague's great work. Meaning in work is very important; sometimes equal to salary or even happiness in surveys of engaged employees.[6] So if you're feeling like a lowly cog in the wheel compared to a superstar friend, remember that wheel is important, and your cog is a crucial piece of getting it done.

**Just say hi, or smile to a stranger.** Sometimes a smile is all it takes to snap out of rumination. As KJ Dell'Antonia says, "No one wants to be trapped on a plane for six hours looking at your seat mate's grandchildren, but a simple smile and a 'how are you' really is not a lot to ask." She cites a study showing that even though commuters insist they prefer solitude on their journey, when they briefly connect with another commuter—a smile or a pleasantry—they report greater pleasure and a more positive experience.[7]

**Send a thinking-of-you text, leave a kind voice mail, endorse a colleague on LinkedIn, or make a small online donation to your favorite charity.** Wharton's Adam Grant has repeatedly shown that small but frequent acts of giving fuel productivity and generativity. Giving gets you out of your head.[8] It's a small and nonthreatening way to snap out of it.

## THE WAY OF . . . GOING OUT OF YOUR WAY

Love your hermit self, but remember that it's not your entire self. When you love, love hard, and when you choose to communicate outward, do it with your whole self. Every day you can push yourself to be a healthy hermit, protecting your time and space while still engaging positively with the world.

You are not being selfish; you're saving the best for when it's really needed. No one says it better than this wonderful quote from the Indian teachings of Samkhya: "This stopping of the movement outwards is not self-defense, but rather an effort to have the response come from within, from the deepest part of one's being."

Still, when self-defense feels like disengaging, or when my anxiety or depression or even a bad news cycle gets the better of me, I remember that goodness happens when you're engaged in the world, and the very loosest of ties are often in your corner, too.

In February 2015, I was at my wit's end, a five-week-old baby wrapped around me, two screaming boys behind, in line at the local Ralph's grocery store with a giant cart of pantry staples. We'd moved from Boston to Los Angeles exactly three days before, and were sleeping on air mattresses and eating on the floor, awaiting our furniture from the East Coast. I was disoriented, but I was more than that. I was depressed, anxious, postpartum, and in a fog of rage at my husband for moving us all 2,592 miles and promptly disappearing into his exciting new job.

But I must have looked up from my fog and vaguely smiled (or teared up) at the woman in line ahead of me, because she moved aside to let me go in front of her. Then, giving me a sympathetic smile, she asked, "Can I help you with anything?"

"Yes," I blurted. "I need a preschool for my four-year-old."

She didn't miss a beat: call this one, she said, and wrote the name down on a coupon. Sure enough, I called, and they accepted my son Tom to start the following week.

That small act of kindness welcomed me to California in the best possible way.

# 5

# *Vision Quest*

I t's not a shock: people who wake up with the sense that their lives are guided by a larger plan feel better. Doctors have even found it increases health. And having a strong vision works. A recent survey of 2,631 successful CEOs who ran companies with at least $1 million in yearly revenue found it was the single trait that rose above all others in importance.[1]

But for sensitive souls who are tormented by achievement porn and a poor work+life fit, "purpose" can feel like just one more unrealistic burden. Just think back to perfect-looking Kayla Itsines and her "motivational" Instagram posts ("I hope you feel beautiful today," she grams, next to a selfie of her concave thighs and stunning abs).

Your vision for your career doesn't need to be grand, and I'm not big on the single, overwhelming goal. (Though I like to think that Taylor Swift, whom my son Tom is obsessed with, knew she was going to be the world's biggest pop star when she was only six.) I am big on the nitty-gritty. After all, my vision includes not getting dressed for work until noon and cooking between meetings.

A vision is your core set of principles, aligning your work to the reasons you live your life the way you do. Vision means executing, growing, and managing your own definition of success. It means imagining a work life you really want. Yes, purpose equals power— but if your purpose isn't right for you, the power will not come. Consider a vision that gives you room to be happy *and* imperfect.

## Vision vs. Achievement Porn

For many people, achieving a long-term goal is *more* important than being happy every day. That is a wonderful quality and is, I'm sure, characteristic of many people who are tremendous leaders and who work to change the world. It's okay if you're not one of those people. I certainly am not.

We assume a vision has to mean deciding to win Olympic gold or having a *New York Times* bestseller. But your true vision is probably less dramatic in scope. Visions are small, and particular. A great vision is: I want to wake up happy Monday morning.

In fact, creating your vision is mostly an exercise in self-acceptance, and even a decidedly un-fancy one can make you happy and successful. That means you don't need a shaman or a life coach to find one, but you do need to be honest with yourself.

I might want to be a billionaire or live in a castle, but these are fantasies, not visions. A vision is that castle, downsized: a certain level of financial freedom; meaningful work (in my case, a successful small business that allows me to work at home); and room to accomplish a few personal goals, like having children or writing a book.

It's also not about material things. Sometimes when I close my eyes, my vision seems to involve—cough—luxury cars and expensive handbags. When it does, I say to myself, *That's great, Morra, and you should work hard because you like nice things, but your vision for your life is not about Chanel.* It involves never having to go work in an office that uses fluorescent lights again.

## WHAT'S WRONG WITH HAVING PURPOSE?

The "double bottom-line business"—one that is successful and does good—is a great innovation, and it deserves its global visibility. But, like achievement porn, widespread social entrepreneurship has had the unintended consequence of convincing young people they are not doing enough if their work does not have a larger global purpose.

But when "purpose" becomes one more box to tick off on the achievement list, it can lose all meaning. There's even pressure for one's extracurricular life to be socially conscious.

But I say, as someone who earns a large portion of my income from helping organizations advertise their purpose, valuing good business practices doesn't have to mean imbuing everything—from what you buy at Safeway to your business plan—with purpose.

If you have not started an organic tampon business by age twenty-five, do not beat yourself up. Please. Do good work, be kind to people, support the causes that truly move you, and your purpose will evolve naturally.

## *My Company's Vision Story*

Sometimes your vision will come to you in a flash, but more often you must create space to let it emerge.

My vision arrived after a tumultuous time: a crippling depression, the birth of my first child, the Great Recession, a move to a new city, and many fruitless applications to doctoral programs. It came when I realized I'd been pursuing a completely financially unviable dream.

Here's how it came about.

Because I was an experienced blogger and expert in women's online community thanks to years at iVillage.com and BlogHer.com, my freelance clients were particularly intrigued by my expertise. I knew a lot about connecting women through online community—and identifying influential women online for my client organizations to partner with. Word started getting around that there was a good consultant who focused on helping organizations reach women online.

About a year in, I was making good money, spending a lot of time with my son, and enjoying my work. I was blogging about women, work, and leadership, which fulfilled my need to be engaged in civic work and discourse, and got me a tiny bit of visibility, which fulfilled both my ego and business development goals. I worked from home unless I was traveling, which meant I put on makeup and nice clothes. Otherwise I was in yoga pants.

And one morning I woke up and it hit me: this was going to be my business. It was going to be called Women Online. We would be the first digital marketing agency focusing on creating online campaigns that mobilized women for good causes. I registered the domain that morning and began thinking about a logo. My first logo was awful. But I was so excited about the idea I couldn't think of anything else.

One month later I knew that my consulting firm was going to be different. Many online leaders build influencer databases, but mine had a key difference: it was database of women bloggers who cared about social change. I called it the Mission List.

Because my vision was about women's advancement, I was committed to my employees having the kind of flexible, manageable workload I set for myself. We wouldn't have an office, and everyone who worked for me would be able to keep their own hours and plan their own days. It would be small and profitable, meaningful and manageable.

But visions are tricky, and you have to give them time to materialize.

Right when we started, it pretty much came to a halt. I got pregnant with my second son when my first was only thirteen months old, and my father was diagnosed with terminal cancer. Although my sister assumed the major portion of caretaking duties, 2010 and half of 2011 were taken up with my dad's care, death, and estate, as well as my wonderful new son Tom. Growing a company was just not on the agenda; it was all about subsistence, paying the bills, and preserving time for Dad, toddler, and baby.

Still, things slowly picked back up.

Now we have worked for two presidential campaigns, for the world's largest charitable foundation, the nation's largest labor union, the nation's largest not-for-profit organization, and even America's largest bank. We've helped the United Nations and Malala Yousafzai get their messages out. There was even a brief, intoxicating period where I flirted with an acquisition offer for the firm. (I felt like I was in a movie—it was sexy and fun, but completely unrealistic.) We have now grown to eight employees.

There's a wonderful British saying: "Start as you mean to go on." I like to think setting a strong vision creates real strength and intention. Through three children, two cross-country moves, and countless other life changes, Women Online's vision has stayed wonderfully consistent.

And I will say, the vision paid off.

## WOMEN ONLINE'S VISION STATEMENT

When I started online, I had a clear mission: to work with influential women's communities online; to work with organizations that genuinely had a mission to improve women's lives; and to help empower them so they could take action—because women vote more, we advocate more, and we dominate social media channels. That was key to crafting our vision statement.

**"WE'RE A SMALL SHOP, BUT WE HAVE HUGE CLIENTS."**

*We aim to be a hugely profitable, high-impact boutique firm.*

*We deliver the absolute best client service and smart thinking.*

*We sit at the grown-ups' table. We work with clients who value us.*

*We work with clients whose values we share.*

*We have a distinct voice, we advocate for social change and social responsibility, and we manage a community of women with the same goals.*

*All WO team members get to have a life and build a sustainable business.*

*We focus on what we can achieve and do well, and don't get upset about what we should be doing or what others are doing.*

*We define success for us.*

# GETTING STARTED

## Setting Your Vision

There are a million books on setting your vision, but before you get overwhelmed, here are some simple steps to coax your vision from its hiding place.

**Put It in Writing.** Write down a vision statement for your next five years at work, or for your business. It's about putting on paper (or iPad) what you want to carry through on in your life. There are no rules here. Just try to capture a vision that encompasses not only how you want to feel about your work or business, but what you want to do. Shut off your inner critic!

**Ask, what motivates me?** It may take you a while to arrive at the answer . . . or at least, to arrive at your honest answer. To get started, look at the categories on the next page. How close are you to each category? What are the specifics of your contribution? Your control? Your salary?

- ❑ **Passion maximizer:** It's very important to me to love my work and feel like I am making a valuable contribution to something I care about. I'd rather work like crazy at a job I love than earn tons of money (although money is fine, too!).

- ❑ **Income maximizer:** I am motivated by money. I will sacrifice short-term happiness, time, or flexibility to earn the most money I can.

- ❑ **Flexibility maximizer:** I am motivated by control over my schedule and work flow. It's most important to me to call my own shots and work at the place, pace, and time I want.

- ❑ **Prestige maximizer:** I need to feel important. I want to be in the thick of it, and feel like a crucial player.

**Ask, do my short-term and long-term goals for career and life match up?** Goals are complex, and involve an integration of life, work, and leisure. It's important to make sure your short- and long-term goals can work together.

Take a piece of paper and brainstorm responses to the following statements. Be as detailed as you can.

- ❑ In the short term, I want to work X way and accomplish X, Y, and Z.

- ❑ In the next ten or fifteen years, I want to do X and I want to have done X, Y, and Z.

If your short-and long-term goals are at a disconnect, you need to rethink things. For example, if you want to take a year off and travel around the world, but also want to be a millionaire in five years, that might need a rethink. But working hard for five years on your income could open up that year off down the line.

**More/less exercise.** My friend and colleague Christine Koh is a huge intention-setter, and I've learned from her. I asked Christine about the vision she guides her life by, and she shared this exercise:

Take a piece of paper. Make two columns, "More" and "Less." In each column, make a list: What do I want more of? What do I want less of? Look at the list to see what items elicit a really strong reaction. For the items that elicit the strongest reactions, jot down action items to help move them forward. Then, revisit every six months.

**What's my vision for the everyday?** It's important to have a long-term plan, but you need to stick to those goals in order to achieve them! If you hate your work in the day-to-day, chances are you won't stick to your goals. You need to be sure the actual work you do is the right fit for your temperament and wishes.

When Christine was preparing to write her dissertation, she saw the academic journal articles stacked around her and she felt despair. She hated academic journals. She still powered through and got her Ph.D., but it took her years to realize it was a terrible fit. She wanted to be with people, and to be creative—she just hadn't paid attention to how her work made her feel in the moment.

Another friend of mine had a similar realization after making a ton of money as a recruiter on Wall Street. After years, it finally hit her: she hated the bulk of her workday, which she spent talking on the phone.

So ask yourself some specific questions. Do you want to be at a computer, writing alone? Never in front of a computer? Running around on sales calls?

Do you like to be with people, constantly working in teams? Or do you need lots of alone time? How much flexibility do you like? Deadlines? Needing to be somewhere at a certain time? This stuff matters. How do you feel about flying? I'm serious. Do you love it? Hate it?

A fundamental misfit might necessitate a new career. But I'd wager that there are elements of your work you love (after all, you chose it) and that you might need to shift time, place, content, or pace in order to make work enjoyable again.

If this is the case, then . . .

## Tweak It

Cali Yost coined this term, and it's a fantastic way to find your work+life fit without making a 180-degree shift.

Assuming you like the meat of what you do, think about the tasks that are part of your day job that fill you with dread or make you nervous. What kind of scaffolding do you need to make that dread manageable? If you are a hermit or an introvert, how can you shift your work to make it less stressful?

Once I left the 24/7 nature of political campaigns and the stressful and draining, brightly lit corporate office life, I realized I absolutely loved the substance of my work. I could tweak my skill set, my relationships and network, and my professional credibility to meet a new vision for my work life.

## So How Do You Start?

My friend Mitra Kalita is a powerhouse media executive. I asked her how she prepares for a big change in her life, and she said, "Haircut. Buy a house. Get the closets done. New me." Her risk profile is definitely not mine, but, as Mitra said, "I stress more over my hair than real estate."

Everyone has a different definition of risk and different triggers for stress. Everything stresses me out, so I have learned to build in self-care tactics to keep the old cortisol down.

For those of us who are prone to high stress and anxiety, building in a calming or meditative habit is crucial, especially when you're entering a period of change. Stanford brain surgeon Dr. James Doty notes, "People don't appreciate the power of their intention to change everything. Even short periods of time where you are attentive, if you will, or mindful, and have intention to open your heart, have a profound effect."[2]

One of my favorite techniques is guided visualization. I'm too anxious and fidgety to sit still and meditate in silence, but I love to listen to a good guided meditation. (Tara Brach's podcasts are favorites, because she had a good sense of humor.)

## KITCHEN CABINET WISDOM

Building in self-care as you contemplate change is key. It can be as simple as a walk alone, or time in quiet. I asked some of my most grounded and wise Facebook friends to imagine they were about to embark on a new chapter. What advice they would give? Here are their favorite tools, tricks, and resources:

*"I like the idea of thinking of this kind of time as a 'fertile void.' You don't exactly know what's next, but the possibilities are manifold."*

**—Cynthia Freeman**

*"I don't ask my kids to figure out what they want to be when they grow up. I ask them to imagine what a happy day would look like. I try to take that advice, too. The trick is not ever asking yourself what you want to BE, but what you want to DO!"*

**—Dottie Enrico**

*"I make sure to book time for myself in a setting I can concentrate in and bring along banner paper, a black Sharpie, some colored Mr. Sketch markers, Tony Buzan's Mind Map technique, and some quality time wringing out my brain to squeeze all the ideas out."*

**—Stephanie Goodell**

*"Triangulate with insights from your head, heart, and soul. Head: talk with your most analytical advisers! Heart: ask those who know and love you truly, especially your kids. Soul: tap into your inner wisdom."*

**—Carolyn Ou**

*"Ask for coffee or lunch dates with people you admire for advice and counsel. Buy a new nice notebook, and take notes on EVERYTHING."*

**—Leah Russin**

> *"Follow your curiosity and spend time doing things you enjoy. They often lead directly, or indirectly, to new opportunities."*
>
> **—Britt Bravo**
>
> *"A weekend away before or during a transition is the best. Stay at the hotel. Do not leave. Actually be quiet and rest. And, always, eat ice cream."*
>
> **—Jennie O'Hagan Korneychuk**

## GET SERIOUS

Just because your vision seems less ambitious than the stereotypical business powerhouse doesn't mean you can take it less seriously. Take the space and time to set intentions, to marinate in them, and to write them down. Give yourself the gift of stillness as you enter a period of transition.

Even more important, try to turn off the achievement supersizer. This is really hard to do! It may take you weeks or even months of writing, talking to trusted friends and counselors, and daydreaming to get to the true kernel of your vision. Every time it feels too small, you'll be tempted to beef it up or reframe it in a more societally acceptable way. For example: you may say your vision is to be an entrepreneur, while in truth your vision is to have more control over your work life. Those are two very different things! One is glamorous and the other feels prosaic. So work hard at being honest with yourself.

# 6

## *Setting Boundaries*

I t's easy for billionaire geniuses like Steve Jobs to say no. It's not easy for people who hide in bathrooms. Why? Because every cultural message says success means saying yes. And I envy every extroverted go-getter out there because I also think I would be thirty-seven times more successful if I actually liked to go to cocktail parties.

But for a hermit, creating healthy boundaries—meaning, saying no—is key.

After my father died in 2010 and I thought I was done having kids, I felt compelled to say yes to almost everything. Deliver a proposal for a potential client by tomorrow morning? Absolutely! Fly to Texas to join a panel discussion for free? Sure. It's business development! Agree to write an eight-hundred-word, unpaid blog post for a barely read website? Count me in!

But the day before that panel in Texas, I'd suffer a crippling anxiety attack. Not to mention, my Amex bill could top $10,000 a month with all that uncompensated travel in the name of "business development."

Although I had the best of intentions when I said yes, I burned a few bridges with last-minute cancellations. I ducked out during meetings. Once, I canceled an important three-day meeting in D.C. when a giant blizzard was predicted to hit Boston and I wanted to return home to my kids. I had reached my personal limit, but it was awkward for me and for my client.

It wasn't merely that giving too much time to pointless efforts strained essential work hours and time with family. Being an entrepreneurial doormat stripped me of an essential strength: the ability to maintain the healthy boundaries I needed.

After too many years of regretting saying yes or being unable to follow through, I learned my lesson. Saying yes too much wreaks havoc on my mental and physical health, my time, and my finances. I had to respect my personal limits, even if I didn't like them.

## Tuning In

My dear friend, psychologist Rebecca Harley, tells me that the people who come to see her often have just one question: "How the hell did I get here?" The answer, she thinks, is that they tuned out a lot of messages.

It's very difficult to give yourself permission to get off a path, especially if getting on that path has been hard. It's difficult to say, after years of work, that you are in a place that you really don't recognize. But every time I suffered an anxiety attack on a trip or felt depressed while standing in the middle of a cocktail party, my personal boundaries were being crossed. I just wasn't tuning in.

That's the challenge: to tune into these messages, and then define your boundaries.

Not tuning into anxiety or depression comes at a cost. In my case, the message was my constant, debilitating migraines and pain in my entire upper body. By 4 P.M., I'd be downing Motrin and lying on an ice pack, in terrible pain. That's to say nothing of that retainer I needed to unclench my jaw. Other "messages" your body might be sending you could be an aching back or neck, irritable bowels, panic attacks, inability to sleep . . . I could go on.

This begs the question, why can crossing boundaries cripple you? Because boundaries are a *big deal*. Your physical boundaries control your safety by establishing your level of comfort with touching and interaction, and your emotional boundaries protect you from being crushed by toxic personalities or enmeshed by codependent ones.

Your boundaries around work are equally important, and they encompass every other kind. As Darlene Lancer, licensed marriage and family therapist puts it, "Boundaries are your bottom line."[1] Limits are the rules you put in place to maintain your boundaries, so to stay successful in your job, you might need to set limits on your personal time or distance yourself from coworkers who get too close. You might need to set limits on clients who are discourteous or even abusive, or work that overstimulates you or creates emotional turmoil.

You need permission to feel when your boundaries are being crossed—and it's not a one-shot deal. I give you permission to say, "That's not going to work for me." Find your boundaries and your limits so you can define the terms of your work and success.

## What's the Difference Between a Limit and a Boundary?

Understanding the difference between a limit and a boundary has always been difficult for me. So I turned to my wise therapist friend Rebecca to explain them, and she led me through a helpful exercise. She told me to imagine I was in a swimming pool with a rope dividing the shallow from the deep end. Wherever I was unable to stand securely, the boundary was being crossed. A limit, on the other hand, is a declaration of a boundary—it's the rope itself. Limits are tactical: I will not check e-mail after 5 P.M. on a Friday, because working during the weekend sends me off into the deep end—the boundary.

Once you understand what your boundaries are, you can set limits—although they may not make you the most popular girl on the block. Leah Ginsberg, a former travel editor at Yahoo, has a boundary many of us may relate to. On trips with fellow journalists—which often meant hours of group activity—she was always the one to go back to her room after dinner, skipping drinks and socializing. "I think everyone thought I was a bitch, basically. But I literally can't function if I don't have some time to myself." Even if you're not stuck on a tour bus with colleagues twelve hours a day, you may feel overwhelmed by frequent socializing with coworkers. Once you realize that that's a boundary, you can politely set a limit: "No, I can't go to your happy hour tonight." I will leave you here with something to chew on, courtesy of workplace expert Erica Keswin: "When Gallup found that having a "best friend" (not "close" or "good" but "best") at work was correlated to higher performance, they were pointing to something that introverts excel at—making meaningful connections." Focus on the quality of your connections at work, not the quantity!

## Setting and Maintaining Your Boundaries

You can't feel 100 percent comfortable keeping your boundaries and your work life in sync unless you feel you are satisfying the expectations of other people in your life. Your efficacy in maintaining your limits is as much about managing your emotions and anxieties around other people's expectations as it is about you actually getting things done. The magic is realizing you don't just have to fulfill expectations. You can meet your boundaries and make others understand your needs.

Whether managing a team at work or a toddler at home, making peace with others' expectations of you is an important skill. And here's the truth: The people in your life may not respect your boundaries! They may want more time, or for you to climb faster, or to make more money.

Living out your own terms of success requires intense focus and self-regulation, as well as practice, with everyone from your romantic partner, to your family, to your team at work, to your boss, and to your clients—even Facebook. (But sorry in advance, I can't really help with toddlers.)

# GETTING STARTED

## *I'm Ready to Tune In. How Do I Start?*

Engaging proactively with your feelings can give you, as Rebecca Harley says, an "early warning system" for your boundaries being crossed. She suggests two emotional cues to tune in on: discomfort and resentment.

Both of these emotions are common signals that your personal boundaries are being threatened, but they are also emotions we are taught to suppress and question. When an interaction or situation triggers either emotion, examine the interaction or expectation, and ask why. When your boss texts you at 9 P.M. for a quick urgent matter, you may feel a moment's twinge of resentment but you can understand it's a reasonable request and quickly move on. When she continually texts you just because she can, your resentment is probably growing strong because your boundaries have been crossed.

Rebecca Harley tells us, "We have our feelings not just to communicate outward but to communicate inward." She suggests a mindfulness exercise to begin to tune in. First, simply observe. What doesn't feel quite right? What is arising? Next, try to put words onto the emotion you're feeling. They don't have to be specific.

Once you're paying attention, you're on the road to knowing what comes next. Rebecca says that by virtue of paying attention, you're getting a closer approximation to what the right decision is for you. Give yourself a baseline permission to recognize that your feelings might mean something, then allow a willingness to observe until they start to resolve themselves into a clearer directional message.

Even though I cried in the bathroom and had migraines, it was my hatred of fluorescent lights that allowed me to tune into my feelings—and it's recognizing those signals in yourself that will allow you to tune into yours so you can set the boundaries you need.

## THE BOUNDARY TEST

Before I take on a new task, client engagement, trip, or project, I ask these questions of myself and the team. If the project makes us say yes to enough of them, game on.

**Is this something I can do from home or with some autonomy in scheduling?** I need to feel autonomy over my time, workplace, and the personal space I can maintain from clients or coworkers.

**Is the organization or client representative of Women Online's mission?** It's very important to our team to feel motivated by what we're doing, and it's crucial that clients support women's advancement.

**Is the organization or client someone I respect and look forward to working with?** If a potential client or colleague sets off alarm bells or icky feelings, I step away.

**Is the person or organization I am assisting fulfilling an important social good, or is it personally or professionally meaningful to me?** Sometimes a project won't expressly fulfill our mission, but will hit my personal sweet spot of advancing better and more equitable workplaces for all.

### DOES THIS FULFILL ONE OF THE FOLLOWING OBJECTIVES?

- ❑ Earn meaningful money
- ❑ Create powerful new relationships or business development opportunities
- ❑ Raise my professional visibility among a desirable or new audience
- ❑ Advance the company to a higher level

**Is this essential to my bottom line?** What am I giving up to take this on? This is a business, so sometimes we take on work that simply supports our bottom line. Conversely, sometimes we need to turn down compelling work that we will lose money on.

**Will I learn something new?** Even though you run a business, you deserve to satisfy your curiosity and keep learning (at least most of the time). Sometimes the least likely projects have the most to teach, so keep your radar attuned to a new challenge or skill-building opportunity.

**Does this advance my vision?** Projects advance your vision for many different reasons; some pay the bills for months in advance, while others thrust your company into the spotlight for a much-needed business development boost. I keep it simple: I always love a project where I don't have to travel.

## Setting Boundaries with Family

My husband, who should be the national chair of Overcommitters Anonymous, is always pushing me to grow more and try harder. He does it out of love. He knows how much I care about my work and he believes in me. It's unfathomable to him that I would not push myself as hard as he pushes himself.

Years ago, a couples therapist gave us a great gift. She taught us that, in addition to marriage matters (dates, sex, kids), we needed to make time for "the corporation." The corporation involves finances, scheduling, childcare, planning, and reviewing our careers and goals.

I try to be very open with Nicco in these conversations. It's taken years to show him I'm strategic about my work choices. And since I take on more of the child rearing, I'm honest about my work+life fit, and whether I feel in control, or am hurtling into the void. (I like to think that I've taught Nicco something, too, and that's the ability to set boundaries and limits. He proudly comes home and reports back all the times he's said no in a week. And I am proud!)

Being honest helps me see my changing limits, and also helps me to set boundaries. When Nicco and I can discuss the work-life equation and reach an explicit understanding of which value is greater, I can let go of my insecurity, and, thereafter, proudly tell him I spent the day not working. On the flip side, good boundaries for your children are important, too. It's hard not to feel guilty when your kids want your attention and you can't give it to them, but if you're clear about when you're "on" and when you're off as a parent, the guilt will lessen. Years ago, a woman I met randomly at an event told me a simple and excellent method of keeping boundaries as a parent who worked at home. She had two signs for her office door. One sign was a smiley face, and the other had the smiley face with a red strike-though (imagine the *Ghostbusters* logo). She trained her daughter to enter the home office or knock only when the smiley sign was up. Kids love rules.

Pleasing my parents and stepparent is another story. Raised to maximize their opportunities, they were mystified when I quit so many jobs in my twenties, and, as I got older, were mystified by my refusal to maximize my income. Now my mom thinks I work too much and it makes me a lousy mother. (You can't win.)

My expectations for my life rarely align with those my mother has for me, which is fine, because I'm over forty years old. But even though I can write this, I still feel bad when I don't meet her expectations. If that sentence resonates with you, it might be helpful to think about the people in your life who really matter to you. Next, consider the primary expectations you have for yourself. Then think about what expectations other people have. For example, you might expect your partner to be the main breadwinner, leaving you the freedom to earn less. But does she agree? Is it worth discussing with her? Here's a commonly mismatched expectation about boundaries that seems silly but can have deep impact: my partner and I will not use smartphones after 8 P.M. Do you both agree?

You don't need your family to understand your motives, or to justify your workday to them. But it can be helpful to review others' expectations in your mind, and think about where misalignments may occur. When you're making a change, it's really helpful for your nearest and dearest to understand why and how you're making it. As long as you're clear about your boundaries, you have freedom to create limits.

## Setting Expectations at Work

Last year I gave an interview about work+life fit for a new book on working mothers. When the author asked me how I manage my mommy guilt, I paused to think, then blurted, "I don't feel guilty about my kids. I feel guilty about my staff!"

I have a wonderful team at Women Online. We have worked together for years, and I feel lucky to have such talented people with me. The team enjoys incredible flexibility, work with wonderful clients, and its members are treated with respect.

But the truth is, they could all find higher-paying and higher-profile jobs. Similar firms grow more quickly. No one has received a raise in the past three years. I bring in all the business, and, while we won't turn down big, exciting new clients, we won't necessarily seek them out either. I try to be clear: this is part of the deal. Sometimes, however, I can feel them itching for a change. But since I tell them my boundaries, they can set limits, and I can, too.

When you work for someone else, setting limits can be challenging. That doesn't mean you shouldn't try, though. Work+life fit expert Cali Yost offers some valuable advice: "Your boss cares about two things: can they reach you if they need you, and if they need you, will you come through." People who look at the big picture, she says, are generally able to set reasonable limits in other ways.

As the boss, I like to keep my boundaries clear with my clients, too. I am direct when I need to put family or personal matters first. But I'm happy to have clients ask me personal questions and call me in the evening, and I accept that I'm attached to my iPhone and will work weekends. Being choosy about my clients and extracurricular responsibilities makes this easier.

I learned about setting boundaries from powerful women who'd figured it all out before me—from pollster and business owner Margie Omero, who took Fridays off with her father when she was well under thirty, to my client who left the office each day at four thirty and expected her staff to be ready with their questions for her well before three so she would not get stuck and miss her train home.

Because I had come from start-ups, politics, and a huge client services firm, for many years I had no idea it was even permissible for anyone below the CEO to state they might be unavailable or unwilling to work at any moment. When I began to pay attention, to study about workplace flexibility, and, most importantly, to ask lots of questions to those leaders who seemed to have good limits, I realized the world wouldn't end if I didn't always answer an e-mail immediately.

## Setting Boundaries with Social Media

Shonda Rhimes, the legendary TV producer, has a signature on her e-mail that says, "Please Note: I will not engage in work e-mails after 7 P.M. or on weekends. If I am your boss, may I suggest: PUT DOWN YOUR PHONE."

When leaders are open and clear and unapologetic about the lines they draw, the rest of us have permission to consider our own boundaries. It's a gift to everyone. But, as people whose bosses are not as enlightened as Shonda Rhimes know, your workplace can tank your e-mail boundaries. Harvard's Leslie Perlow, the author of *Sleeping with Your Smartphone,* writes, "When you innocently clear out your inbox on Saturday morning, think about your subordinate who's on the soccer field with their kids."

Perlow calls this the cycle of responsiveness, and has wonderful suggestions on how to break it—starting with teamwork, like agreeing to not answer phones on Saturday mornings. And bosses and employees both need to examine the in-box addiction: Is the lack of boundaries driven by urgency, habit, disorganization, or a lack of clear limits?

Social media is another minefield, especially now that corporations regularly use platforms like Twitter and Instagram for personal branding. Everyone has different boundaries regarding self-exposure, which means everyone needs to set different limits. As Leah Ginsberg says, "You have to put yourself out there and you have to play a role, and I'm not good at either of those things." For hermits, just keeping a toe in someplace like LinkedIn may be the solution.

Phone usage is another source of conflict. The phone is an ever-present appendage for my husband, Nicco, and though he doesn't mind if I check mine, the fact that he's always checking his can fill me with rage. So we've set some boundaries on phone usage. We don't during family time, or even when he and I are driving together.

Many introverts or people who struggle with social anxiety in face-to-face situations absolutely love social media. In fact, the best community managers I have ever worked with are usually introverts who tend to avoid face-to-face socializing. They come alive online. However, other introverts feel conflicted about our society's decreasing boundaries between personal and professional space and time, and how this affects our social media profiles.

Is it even possible these days to maintain, say, a personal Facebook community while having LinkedIn and Twitter profiles that are explicitly public facing? I don't think you can, to be honest—just remember Election 2016 and hacked gmails. Nor do I even think it's advisable if you're planning to be a hermit entrepreneur, because building your online brand on all platforms is a wonderful way to develop business when you don't want to physically get out there. Any sense of privacy you feel online is fake, so by all means try to keep your Facebook profile among friends, but don't ever assume it won't go public. Be conscious about that, especially when it comes to sharing personal news and information that can make you squirrelly.

Social media for work may have more interpersonal impact than we think. Christine Koh notes that if being active on social media is key to your professional status, boundary issues may, as a result, arise with your partner or family. In her case, a "front-facing" life requires vigilance. "My husband and I came to an explicit agreement about how much the kids will be on social media," she says. "You'll see them from the side. You will see them from the back. You will see them in sunglasses, but you actually never see their faces."

## Being Flexible . . . Even with Boundaries

However firmly we set our own boundaries, all of us constantly break our own rules. Sometimes you just need to; for instance, answering e-mail after hours during a busy time at work. But it's also a worthwhile way to see if the limits you've set are really necessary.

If you say you're not going to check Facebook during work, but you still get your work done when you do check it, maybe that's not a limit you need to set. Or, if you realize you're leaving yourself enough time for personal responsibilities at work, maybe you can lighten up on work at home. (I work late every night!) Being comfortable with breaking your own rules is actually really liberating.

That flexibility also leaves room for life changes. Once you are aware of them, your boundaries are likely to stay put, but limits might vary over time. A new mom with an infant may set completely different limits on e-mail hours than an empty nester, who won't feel upset with weekend or evening e-mail. Or maybe a new mom wants the e-mail for distraction, while the empty nester wants to read a book! Either way, use your life changes as an opportunity to switch it up.

# SAYING NO WELL

Learning to say no without guilt is the greatest gift you can give yourself, and one of the hardest things to do, especially for women. If you're going to succeed in setting boundaries, you need to learn how to say no. (And think twice about the next time you start a no with "I'm sorry." You don't have to be sorry just because you're saying no.)

That's where a framework comes in. I asked my community on Facebook for their words of wisdom on saying no with grace and strength.

Beth Monaghan, founder of the hundred-person PR agency Inkhouse, learned to say no by writing down her goals for the year, and literally carrying them around. "Every time something comes up, I can ask, 'Does this help me achieve a goal?' If the answer is no, I say no. And if I'm trying to convince myself to say yes, it's still probably a no."

MBA coach Andrea Sparrey envisions some of her fondest mentors in her head and imagines what they would counsel her to do if she explained the yes/no dilemma to them.

Entrepreneur Lauren Bacon's method: "I always respond with a variant of 'Thanks so much for the invitation! Let me sleep on it and get back to you first thing tomorrow.' That allows me time to step back, look at my goal list, and figure out how I really want to answer."

Author Samantha Ettus, the queen of anti-guilt, told me, "Guilt never creates good decisions. I would not want someone to say yes to me out of guilt, so I don't allow guilt to determine my decisions."

Podcast entrepreneur Molly Beck says no as quickly as possible and then suggests another person to take her place, trying especially to offer opportunities to people who might not otherwise get them.

For Elisa Camahort Page *no* can mean *not right now.* I really agree with this. A good, firm no allows you to maintain a relationship with the other person, and you never know where that will lead. Any businessperson will tell you that a no can turn into a yes over time. And, if you're feeling anxious about saying no to someone with whom you'd like to have a long-term business relationship, it's okay to reconsider and say yes to something that will eat up your time without compensation.

Many in my kitchen cabinet suggest practicing your noes, or having a few ready-made responses. I love Deb Roby's script for a graceful no: "Thank you for thinking of me; I am honored. However, this project does not line up with my goals for this (cycle/quarter/season/year), so I will have to decline."

Here's a final note for those of us with anxiety: sometimes you can talk yourself into a no when you really mean yes. Practice tuning into your gut reaction upon hearing an invitation. If you're excited about an opportunity at first, only to let anxiety set in later, let the excitement win over anxiety. For example, you're invited to a wonderful conference in a faraway city, and you're thrilled. You say yes, and immediately feel anxiety: What if your plane crashes on the way? What if you make a fool of yourself? Try to work through this and tune back to your excitement. Anxiety can be negotiated with.

## THE BEAUTY OF BOUNDARIES

Steve Jobs famously said, "Innovation is saying no to 1,000 things."

Saying no and setting strong boundaries makes you powerful! I know it feels scary, especially if you're starting out or starting again. In my case, learning to say no meant realizing that my inability to do it stemmed from insecurity. I feared that turning down any opportunity was pure hubris. If I turned down an opportunity, certainly few other chances would come along, right? I'm no Steve Jobs.

It doesn't matter. Every no is time you can put to good use and innovate, or further your own work.

I love to think of Steve Jobs brusquely turning down invitations to focus on creating the devices that would change the world. Maybe he got invited to attend a tech networking hour on Sandhill Road but instead said, "Nah, I've got a little computer I'm working on." Don't waste your "no" time second-guessing your decision or feeling guilty. Use the time well, and you, too, will innovate.

# 7

# *Time Is on Your Side*

'm obsessed with reading articles about how luminaries use their time. For example, the *New York Times* tells me Italian luxury design magnate Brunello Cucinelli starts his day by swimming laps in his pool for an hour, and finishes it by reading some Socrates. Meanwhile, *Forbes* let me know Alice + Olivia founder Stacey Bendet wakes up at 4:45 A.M. for a bowl of quinoa, then does an hour of ashtanga yoga.

I will never have enough freedom or brain cells to end my day with Socrates, and stealing me time from sleep time, as Stacey does, would make me miserable. For those of us with far more plebeian lives, gaining control of our time usually comes from adjusting work patterns. Study after study shows that the most engaged and productive workers are those who feel a sense of autonomy and control over their work lives.

I always joke that if tomorrow someone promised to pay me over $500,000 a year in salary alone, I would consider going back to full-time work in an office environment. But right now, unless something drastic changes, control over my time is worth more to me than a fat salary.

Because, as with everything else, there's no free lunch. For every chunk of time you take back from work or other people's expectations, you'll probably lose something else: money, prestige, career advancement, or that feeling of being in the thick of it.

Although there are many, there are a few different methods of pacing I regularly consider: building in flexibility; bursting and leapfrogging; chunking your day; and finding the right level of busy.

Your time is yours, and you can be strategic in how you use it. I call it pacing your career, and it means thinking about how can you creatively seize control over your time—both in the minute and over the long term.

## The Flexible Worker

Let's say your company has invested a lot in you. Your boss is grooming you. You're grateful, and you've always seen yourself reaching a certain level of success. But now you realize your schedule is actually making you anxious and miserable. You've decided you want to pare down. So how do you have that conversation? And how do you set yourself up for success?

Workplace expert Cali Yost tells us that, first, you need to ask yourself, *What do I need? What does it look like, and how does flexibility help me do that?* while taking into account those who have control over your time, work, and money.

One of Yost's clients, a woman who worked in the financial services industry, was very much on the fast track. But, nine months pregnant with her third child, she burst into tears as she told Cali, "I'm quitting."

Instead of agreeing, Yost told her she needed to propose a different way of working. The woman said her boss would never go for it. Yost replied, "The worst thing that can happen is she says no. And she's likely to listen if you come in with a plan."

They sat down at Starbucks and went over every aspect of the new work paradigm, detailing, as Yost told her, "what parts of your job you're going to let go, what you're going to keep, how you're going to keep contributing, how your compensation's going to change, how you're going to supervise people." Yost encouraged her to present it, but the woman was still dubious.

The next day the woman called Yost and told her, "I'm mad!" Yost began to apologize, and the woman interrupted. "No, I'm mad because my boss said okay. I went through every talking point. I had every argument. And it was just . . .'okay!'"

If Yost's client's experiences resonate with you—whether you are experiencing a life change or acknowledging new boundaries or limits—consider what you would ask your boss, and what your plan would be. Do you want one afternoon a week? How can you stack your business development schedule to accomplish what you need to in four days? What meetings can you move? What responsibilities could you give up, and how can you keep the ones you have?

Here are a few starters:

- ❑ Reduce your commute by working at home.
- ❑ Adjust your hours worked during the day.
- ❑ Change the number of days each week you work.
- ❑ Lessen business travel.
- ❑ Cut out some meetings so you can have alone time.
- ❑ Reshuffle your day to maximize productivity.
- ❑ Reduce the number of professional events you attend.
- ❑ Cut down "extracurriculars" like serving on committees or boards or in internal working groups, or writing/doing social media, to a bare minimum.

Having a plan means you're coming from a position of strength not weakness. As Cali says, "Your boss wants to know where you are, and can you get the work done." Bosses also prefer that your flexible schedule doesn't create more work for them or the team. So when you present a case for flexibility, assure your manager you will be reachable, you will copiously communicate with your peers or clients to make sure the transition is seamless, and, of course, you'll get the work done. After all, who doesn't get more work done out of the office and in the quiet of home or their favorite coffee shop?

You have to show you've thought it all through. "It's not enough to just figure out what you do when. You have to go to the how, where, and with whom," Cali says. "Be clear: Where am I going to do it? I'm doing it in my home office in the basement. With whom am I coordinating this? I'm going to let my family know that I'm going to be working for these four hours in the basement office. I'm going to have to tell my team, 'These four hours are meant to be my focus time. If you really need me, I am available. Here's the technology I'd like you to use to get in touch with me.'"

After the baby came, Cali's client in financial services managed her new schedule, working four days a week, with one day a week working from home. But here's the rub: because she was a senior leader in a traditional environment, she had to give something up. "You can't keep all the good things, and then pass off the crap you don't want," Cali told her. "What part of your job is awesome but takes up a lot of time and somebody else could do it?"

Flexibility will always require redefining success for yourself. Which is another way of saying: compromise.

## DON'T LET "FLEXIBILITY" RUIN YOUR DAY

Until about three years ago, I was constantly pulling over to the side of the road to dial into conference calls, or balancing a Lego in one hand while answering an e-mail with the other. I thought this was freedom. Instead it made me crazy. And because I didn't have a set work schedule, I was always carving out time for life during the workweek.

I had to have an honest conversation with myself, and say: *You are not delivering the best to your clients, your team, or to your children.*

Those of us who run flexible workplaces share some of the blame for an always-on culture. But companies have begun making changes. Leaders from the president of a hip Hollywood digital studio to the work-life director at accounting giant Ernst & Young suggested creating a basic scaffolding for flexibility, and tweaking from there. For example, as long as there aren't pressing client deadlines, create two or three core business days when people are expected to be in the office for meetings, and let people work flexibly the other days of the week.

Here's how I decided to change how we at Women Online operate during the nine-to-five.

❑ Work core business hours four days a week (nine to five). If you have a dedicated day or afternoon off, let the team know, and mark it on the shared company calendar.

❑ Schedule personal appointments or time on the calendar, and don't be ashamed (thank you, Cali Yost).

❑ Make a concerted effort to do work calls on a landline, or ensure you have a good cell connection so conference calls are doable. If you have to be in transit during a call, let the client or team know beforehand.

❑ Don't send external e-mails after business hours. Clients deserve a life, too!

❑ Schedule time for a phone call; don't let e-mail chains drag on or get complicated.

❑ Here's the hardest one: unless it's to a quick yes or no question, if you are working out of office or on your iPhone, resist the urge to respond quickly or less thoughtfully than you might while sitting at your desk. A good answer is usually better than a quick one.

Forcing myself to be fully present at work actually reduced my anxiety. I could get into "flow" and focus on the work I love, and the team felt more cohesive.

Even in the digital age, structure and boundaries are key. If you're a manager, be honest about your bad habits, and work flexibly—with guidelines.

# Strategic Time Use

We develop strategies for career advancement in order to save money, even to find love. But time underpins everything else, and it's finite.

To use the time you gain constructively, it's important to know what you want the time for—and what you're willing to give up for it. Take a minute to jot down some goals, and arrange them in terms of priority.

## GOAL

*EXAMPLES:*

*Time with kids when I'm not so exhausted*

*Time to exercise*

*Study for my GRE*

*Time to cook dinner instead of ordering out*

*Use my vacation time*

*Have one night out a week*

*Work from home one day a week*

*Take a longer maternity leave*

*NOTES:*

_____

_____

_____

_____

## SACRIFICE

*Will I get promoted if I give less time?*

*Take it out of work day or sleep time*

*Sleep*

*No working around the clock*

*Will be out of the loop*

*Sleep*

*Salary? Advancement?*

*Salary, advancement, out of the loop*

_____

_____

_____

_____

# GETTING STARTED

## *Leapfrogging and Bursting*

Early in her career, Sheryl Sandberg received some important advice from Google CEO Eric Schmidt. "When companies are growing quickly and they are having a lot of impact, careers take care of themselves," he said. "If you're offered a seat on a rocket ship, don't ask what seat. Just get on."

That brings us to leapfrogging.

People who leapfrog work in bursts, channeling their skills, energy, and joie de vivre into short periods of time, taking advantage of slow times at work to recover and recharge. Leapfrogging is how I learned that a career doesn't have to be linear, and you can be successful and still get a rest.

Some people do this strategically, as an unconventional way to grow their careers rapidly. I met my first leapfroggers working in politics. D.C.'s staffers work 24/7 on yearlong or eighteen-month campaigns, then, after Election Day, turn to lucrative private-sector consulting work to refill their coffers. The bigger the race they work on (a presidential or major senate race, say), the higher the fees they can command in the private sector, with their pick of plum jobs. Check out the flow of Obama staffers who went to Silicon Valley's hottest companies or to teach at Harvard and Stanford Business Schools, for example. The glow of their high-profile and, frankly, sexy election work meant they could raise their prices and coast on some major laurels for a while.

My first leapfrog came from working on the Kerry-Bush presidential campaign for two years. I wasn't high level, or even very talented, but because I worked on the digital side at a time when politics was going online, I was in demand. Near the end of the campaign, a former staffer for Bill Clinton told me I had a window of time, and that I should be strategic about how I used it. "You're hot right now, and you have a lot of opportunities. They won't be there forever."

He was right. I became a VP at a large company, the youngest VP in a company of thousands of people. Sure, I hated it and I quit after sixteen months, but by then I had leapfrogged several levels in my career, and was able to command good rates as a freelancer—plus, I could be more of a hermit.

Twelve years after that fateful lunch, I still use the leapfrogging strategy to grow my business without having to work too hard. How? I try to work on one or two "marquee" clients per year, no matter how low-paying. High-profile work boosts my business development, so I can get business through the door even in slow periods. When you say, "When I was working for so-and-so," the mic drops. If you're running your own business and want to find a way to enable a hermit lifestyle, get out there and land a big-kahuna client, or a viral campaign or a hot product. Then tell everyone you know.

Obviously, leapfrogging makes the most sense early in your career, when you have the least to lose. Kiva founder Jessica Jackley advises, "Try something big and bold and crazy right out of the gate. Give your life away for two years. If it works, it opens a lot of doors. Once you're older, it's a harder calculus to make." For Jessica, it was building a project she started in graduate school into a multinational organization. For others, it might be working at an investment bank for a few years, joining a start-up or political campaign, or any other high-risk, high-reward type venture.

There's tremendous joy, Jackley says, to being so deeply immersed in one's work, when it's for a limited period of time. Sometimes she misses the passion. "What if I don't get to be a part of something like that again?" she asks, almost wistfully. Now that she has three children, her priorities have changed. "I didn't think twice about throwing my life into something in that way. What if that's what's required to have such a big impact?"

I understand where Jessica is coming from. She feels limited and apprehensive. But look around: there are many stars of all ages in politics, tech, and innovation who take crazy moon shot jobs for short periods of time. When I worked in politics, our digital teams comprised young men in hoodies (which you'd expect) and older people who'd been through three or four careers already, all working insane hours. And not for the money!

## Chunking Your Day

If you like your daily work schedule, you'll enjoy work more. Yes, a radical four-hour-workweek level of control is not realistic. But if your default is hiding in the bathroom, taking charge of your schedule to better fit your energy and moods can really help.

Lindy Huang Werges, whose financial services staffing firm grew 300 percent last year, has one of the most insightful takes on her workday I've ever seen.

Lindy schedules "clusters" each day. Her calendar is blocked out for production hours in two parts each day: 9–11 A.M. and 2–4:30 P.M. The production hours are her intense, revenue generating hours. Everything else is "non-production" time, the non-revenue generating work that is essential but allows her time to breathe a little bit. Lindy has a "blackout" on her calendar from four-thirty to eight. (But not necessarily because she's with her kids; because her brain is full by then.) Because Lindy is an incredibly vibrant, nonhermit person, seeing and hearing about the way she works felt like a sort of permission to schedule my day to suit my state of mind—so I thought about how I perform best.

What I found was, for my own schedule, I like to work in intense bursts, with two or three days of intense activity, and then days with a lot of alone time and quiet.

I have a job that demands a lot of engagement. It's embarrassing, but before I get on a call, I often have to give myself a pep talk, because picking up the phone can trigger social anxiety. On a bad day, even anticipating a phone call can make me feel like hiding. Although once I'm on the call and hooked into the other people or the work, I'm fine and happy, I schedule myself in a way that doesn't fill me with nerves when I review my schedule in the morning.

I have a similar strategy with my week. I've learned that to deal with my anxieties and reclusive tendencies, I have to dive in and keep going until I'm exhausted, and then schedule time to recharge by building in alone work time. My ideal week will have me tightly scheduled for two or three days with external-facing meetings, out-of-town travel, and lots of interaction and engagement with existing clients or potential clients, such as meetings or speaking engagements.

When I'm in the zone, dressed up, makeup on, I'm good. I forget I'm a hermit and get engaged in the work and people. The sheer act of looking like a grown-up reminds me I can do it. On the road, I'll do as many meetings as I can. On busy client days, I'll also try to schedule as many back-to-back phone calls as possible, so I don't have time to ruminate. And once I get on the plane or train, I turn off.

On quieter days, I'm a putterer. I try to schedule calls and meetings in the morning, when my energy level is higher. I work, then break, work, then break. I don't like to leave the house except for errands or kid stuff. Ideally, I will have at least a two-hour block with nothing scheduled so I can have some maker time to write proposals or memos and work on projects that don't demand interaction. And then I finish early, around 3 P.M. so that my brain and body can recharge. I'll usually log back on around 8 P.M. I love to write or really dig into projects at night, when it's quiet. I also use a service called Boomerang to schedule e-mails to be delivered during working hours so that a client won't expect me to work all the time, and my team won't feel obligated to respond.

My weekly podcast also demands a lot of personality, which means a lot of energy. When I recorded it from home, I was so reluctant to do it that the hours before we recorded would be ruined by anticipatory anxiety. But I realized that if I left the house to record and went to a real studio, I could get into the zone easily without losing my morning.

Christine Koh, my colleague at Women Online in addition to being an author, blogger, lifestyle influencer, podcast host, and Ph.D., is my hero and opposite, but she also knows her work style. She is focused and task driven and, unlike me, doesn't let a bad day send her back to bed. She puts in a solid nine-to-five, and then she's done. Her husband told her, with love, "You are like a robot. You go into your office and you just destroy, and then you come out and you look glazed, but you have conquered the day." Christine says her ability to switch quickly into parenting mode comes from feeling "the flock has been tended accordingly," just like mine comes from feeling I don't have to keep regular hours to do good work.

# Get Your Ideal Workday

Only you can figure out the cadence of your ideal day, but to start, ask yourself some questions. Let your answers be as specific as possible; for example, "I'm most productive at five, when the people in my house are still asleep," or "I get my best work done on the train." Remember, your dream day may be very different from the actual workday that will make you happy, or the workday you get to do. But a specific list can help you develop ideas for maximizing your time.

*1. When in the day do you feel most productive?*

*2. How long are you able to concentrate on any given project? Do you work best by doing one big one a day, or doing a little work on several?*

*3. Do you work on weekends? Do you feel resentful, or that you're finally getting a chance to catch up?*

*4. Do meetings inspire you, or feel like a waste of time?*

*5. On what tasks do you really shine? What work do you get praised for? Are they the same?*

*6. When you procrastinate, do you still manage to get your work in, or is procrastinating really having a detrimental effect on your productivity? How do you usually procrastinate, and when?*

*7. What distracts you? In what zone do you feel no distraction?*

*8. What are the tasks you dread?*

*9. What are the tasks you like?*

*10. At what time of day are you just done?*

*11. Do you get more work done around people? Alone? Do you waste time with colleagues, or do colleagues help you get motivated?*

*12. What tasks really bring in the bulk of your income? How are your earnings distributed?*

Now, what are the limitations that affect your workday? For instance, you may have a boss who wants you on 24/7, or you may be a freelancer with monthly deadlines and little client support. A sample list might look like this.

*1. I have to pick up my kids at five.*

*2. My job has project meetings every other day, and they go on forever.*

*3. My clients call me at all hours.*

*4. I need to set aside time for business development at least once a week in order to bring in enough work.*

*5. My boss wants me in at seven every day, and I can't leave until six.*

*6. I need to bring in [X] amount of clientele.*

*7. My job has a lot of paperwork that keeps me from my real work, but I have to do it.*

Now make a wish list for the parts of your life that get affected by work. Go crazy!

*1. I wish my house weren't such a disaster.*

*2. I wish I had time to go to my kid's soccer class.*

*3. I wish I made more money—I have no disposable income.*

*4. I wish I had more time. I have plenty of money, but nowhere to spend it.*

*5. I want to build up some savings for retirement, or to buy an [X].*

*6. I want to take one big vacation a year.*

*7. I wish I could go out on a Wednesday night once in a while.*

Now give yourself some credit!

*1. At work, I really get praised for*_____.

*2. Strangers are impressed when they hear I do*_____.

*3. My secret hack for getting things done is*_____.

*4. In recommendations, people cite my*_____.

*5. I feel most proud of myself when I*_____.

Okay, you've got an enormous list now. Take some time with it. Use the information to think specifically about your hours, your goals, your productivity, and what's in the way. You may not be able to achieve the workday you want entirely right now, and you certainly won't always stick to it, but when you're stuck at work, go back to the list and use it for guidance.

## Levels of Busy

Christine Koh notes the power of what she calls finding the "Goldilocks level of busy." (See later for my Goldilocks contract-size method. I guess Goldilocks was pretty smart: there is a perfect fit for most of us.)

**Too big:** You are overwhelmed—your inner hermit is in distress. You can't figure out how to structure your days. Review your calendar for the past couple of months. What weeks had too much? How many events were there? What pushed you over the edge?

**Too few:** What were too few events? When did you actually start to get antsy?

**What was just right?** Figuring out the happy number as a target and shooting for it is a good feeling. I can't take more than five meetings a week, with one evening event max. Christine notes, "There's always more work to do, so part of the challenge is giving yourself the permission to take the time you need. Try to build it into your routine." When you know what you want more of, you can craft it into your intentions.

## THERE IS NO RULE BOOK

I've already shared my very strong opinions on establishing a vision, developing strong boundaries, and taking your time seriously. Lest you think I'm immune to doubt about all this, let me tell you a little about my friend Meighan Stone.

When I'm feeling frustrated with just how limited my boundaries can be, I think of her incredible work with some envy. When Meighan was president of the Malala Fund, she traveled the world with the Nobel Peace Prize winner to raise funds and implement programs that educate girls. A normal month for Meighan might find her opening a school in Nigeria, meeting with CENTCOM generals in Jordan, staffing Malala for an interview with Oprah, or fund-raising for the organization with the billionaire "unicorn" founders of Silicon Valley. She worked in different time zones, many hours a week.

The mother of a seven-year-old, Meighan does incredible work in global development, and her passion fuels everything she does. In her week off, she organized a faith community protest to support refugees at the National Prayer Breakfast in Washington, D.C., and helped an upstart candidate launch his gubernatorial campaign. But Meighan makes sacrifices to do her work, definitely with her time, and sometimes even with her health and her personal security. I admire her tremendously, and I would never have the fortitude or courage, or, frankly, the energy to do what she does. I just followed her updates with awe from the comfort of my couch.

She and I laugh about this. Sometimes I feel jealous of Meighan:

her impact, her role in such a powerful movement, her travels. I see what's she's accomplishing and I feel envy and admiration. She's building a school in a Syrian refugee camp; I feel hopelessly bourgeois and suburban. But even if I had her skills, I would not be happy doing what she does. It would tax me to the limit and defy all my boundaries about time and control. Knowing this feels good.

We're going to get really practical in the next chapter, and talk about how to find your niche at work. When you know exactly what you stand for and what you're here to do, you can channel your passion efficiently, then take a break. It's the opposite of always being on. If, like me, you find yourself feeling envious of someone like Meighan, but know that controlling your boundaries and time is essential to your well-being, you'll love developing a strong niche.

# 8

# *Go Niche*

n January 2005, on top of a Mayan pyramid in Oaxaca, Mexico, I had a life-changing experience. I met Lisa Stone, the founder of BlogHer, the first community for women who blog.

At the time I was a political consultant in Washington, D.C. I had just finished three years in the trenches, working in Internet marketing for the Democratic National Committee and John Kerry's presidential campaign. I was beaten down by politics and its (mostly male) egos.

Every week I'd go to a gathering of young male "netizens": bloggers, activists, and pundits who were mostly under twenty-five. Now many have become famous. They shape Beltway opinions, and those gatherings are the stuff of political nerd legend. But back then, I'd sit at these meetings and boil at their myopia and ignorant swagger. ("I don't get why health care is a big deal to voters," is an actual quote. I wanted to scream! Only I was usually the single woman in the room . . . ) I had no outlet, and I was frustrated and insecure.

But BlogHer changed all that. Writing about politics as BlogHer's first political director gave me a platform to share women's points of view—then and still now in short supply in Beltway culture, no matter how important women are as a voting bloc.

BlogHer came at a time when blogs were changing news and political coverage. In 2005, Facebook was a one-year-old platform for college students, and YouTube was brand-new. But suddenly blog-based activists and reporters were threatening the authority of major outlets and changing the media landscape. Which meant that all of a sudden a blogger like me and a reporter for the *Washington Post* were publishing major scoops.

I will never forget the moment when I got front-row seats at the YouTube presidential primary town hall in South Carolina next to Adam Nagourney. I sat there and I thought, *I'm a blogger, and I have the same access as the political reporter for the New York Times.*

I didn't know it then, but as one of the few female bloggers who covered politics, I had lucked into a powerful niche. As blogging gained popularity and authority, I often found myself fielding questions from curious political, marketing, and communications professionals: What was this blogging and citizen journalism thing all about, and could I explain it to them? Even better, I could blog from anywhere, and this allowed me more time to myself while still building professional influence. I knew I was onto something.

## The Hermit on the Web

Contrary to what you might think, a strong online presence is a hermit's best friend. Indeed, if you're shy, a strong digital presence and online brand is especially critical, because it creates a powerful digital footprint that separates you from the competition and does your networking for you, even when you're away from your iPhone.

The best way for a hermit to build a strong online presence (besides saying smart things and creating great content, of course) is to focus on gaining expertise and awareness within a specific niche of your business or professional field. You spin fewer wheels when your offering is focused and your expertise is sharply defined. You also spend less time comparing yourself to others and trying to compete with bigger budgets and more business development resources. This is equally powerful whether you work for yourself or within an organization.

That doesn't mean tweeting every two minutes or constantly posting to Instagram. A meandering and banal Twitter account, for example, will not do you any favors. Nor will a company blog no one reads (I've been there). But a strategically crafted online presence is a potent business development tool.

That means the more niche, the better. Georgetown University's Cal Newport, a computer science professor who studies how to perform productive, valuable, and meaningful work in the digital age, argues that the market "rewards things that are rare and valuable. Social media use is decidedly not. Any 16-year-old with a smartphone can invent a hashtag or repost a viral article."[1] A hermit gains value from her unique online footprint and its smart content, not its popularity. Showcasing your niche allows you to stand out in a sea of blog posts and search engine optimization (SEO).

## Go Hyperniche: Ana Flores's Story

Ana Flores, a former TV producer, created the "hyperniche" #WeAllGrow Latina Network, a powerful online community focusing on Latina social media influencers. By "owning that we are unapologetically about the Latina woman's experience," she's created a powerful business, unlike any in the marketplace. Laughing, she says, "With platforms and apps bombarding us all the time, the natural instinct is to compete with influencer marketplaces that are all about reaching everybody. But I think there is much more of a need for expert voices."

This extends to her specific brand: We All Grow Latina. The name derives from the company's mission, stated by Ana in a 2010 blog post: when one of us grows, we all grow. This reflects the open, almost sisterly vibe of the company's events both online and off. "Everything you see about us, from the pinkish colors, to the way that we speak to our audience, the way that we manage our community, what our events are about, the inspirational messages: They're not crafted through market research. They're crafted because that's who we are and that's how we want to be spoken to."

When she worked in TV, Ana created content for massive multinational companies like MTV and Univision, where, she says, "You are validated by their brand names." But even after the recession, she turned down job offers to stick with her blog, Spanglish Baby. "I just knew," Ana says, "that if I hung on to it for a little bit longer, it would bring me something. And my mom and everybody were like, 'Are you crazy? Take the job.'"

My beloved husband refers to my business, Women Online, as Vag.org. Every time I talk about my business, people remark condescendingly, "Oh, what a great niche." (Never mind the fact that women are 52 percent of the global population.) But I just smile and nod. If I decided to be a full-service marketing and PR firm, the pool of companies I'd be competing with would be much larger, and their resources far greater than mine. Not to mention I'd have to pay a lot more to market my services. The truth is, owning a niche is powerful.

Like Ana, I learned about the power of the niche by growing up professionally in online community culture, where people find others who share their very particular passions. I started my career at iVillage.com, the web's largest destination for women, where my job was to highlight stories of women's connections for the media and public-affairs campaigns. Our members were dealing with breast cancer, cranky toddlers, or divorce, and I could tell the connections were real, even though I was a twenty-two-year-old who knew very little about these topics.

Ten years later, BlogHer was the amazing natural evolution of iVillage.com, as well as the natural evolution of BlogHer cofounder Lisa Stone's work as editor of Women.com. Both early sites relied on message-board technology to connect women seeking advice and sharing stories. (For a taste of community culture's size and power, just check out Hermione Granger fanfiction communities.) And, like Ana, my niche business is driven by passion as well as intuition.

As a small-business owner who has built her credibility through her social media platform, I can say that the more authentic your online voice, the more response you will receive. You can take your life experience, distill the most meaningful pieces, and create a narrative that compels others. The key to building a strong online presence is ownership. You need to know what you want to say, who you want to say it to, and most important, *why* you are the right person to carry the message. You need conviction.

As Ana puts it, "It really has to be something that comes from you, that belongs to you, and that you are that topic—that *you* live it."

The thing that is so wonderful about creating your digital brand is that it truly is personal. I have interviewed many successful bloggers with millions of readers, and time and again they tell me that they view their blog or website as an extension of their living room, or perhaps as a small boutique or storefront. It's their personal space, a true piece of their life that is open for others to visit, as long as the visitors behave.

## Why Women (Especially Women Introverts) Need a Strong Digital Brand

For women of any age, becoming social-network savvy isn't just about connecting with friends. It's about creating and maintaining the critical connections that establish your expertise and leadership, regardless of whether you're employed or own your own business. And even more than for men, it is critical for women to establish a strong online brand. While your career path may wax and wane as you start a family, care for relatives, and deal with any of the myriad of issues that can disrupt your climb up the career ladder, your digital brand stays with you. It is a crucial piece of your credibility as a professional and as a leader.

What do I mean by digital brand? I simply mean how someone finds you online, and what they find when they do.

The first step in a digital brand is a simple website or a blog that curates all of your professional accomplishments, interests, and opinions. You control the content, you control the message, and the site changes as your career grows. Think of it as your digital CV. It might include participating in marketing channels such as Twitter, LinkedIn, Facebook, or Pinterest, which are excellent places to find like-minded people. But ultimately, you cannot control the content of a site owned by someone else. And therefore, you need your own home on the web.

The Internet gives us the space to showcase the accomplishments of our less-than-linear lives, create new networks and professional opportunities that bolster our careers, and highlight our unique brands, all from the comfort of home. (I do always blog in bed.)

The web allows you to maintain relationships with colleagues and to forge new connections with thought leaders in your space—from *home*, at the time and place that's convenient for you. This is important for women who are on a break from a career path because of caretaking or childbearing, and for women who are introverts or hermits, who need to get out there without always getting out there.

It's important to establish a digital footprint to . . .

**Access new networks.** Research shows that women's social and professional networks are different from men's, and this can hurt us professionally. Women tend to have fewer weak ties, more all-female reference groups, more contacts who are peers, and fewer who are superiors. We're much more likely to form tight-knit groups of equals among ourselves. The way we form ties isn't necessarily wrong, but it can hinder our progress professionally. For the same reason finding male mentors at work is important, building a diverse online social network can really help boost your career. Having an online brand isn't just about creating Facebook, Twitter, and Pinterest pages; it's about forging relationships online that can propel your leadership potential.

**Engage from anywhere.** Women are still responsible for the majority of caretaking and domestic work in American homes, regardless of whether they hold a paying job. Our caretaking responsibilities can prevent us from being able to participate fully in the work culture outside of regular business hours. As the network scholar Howard Aldrich writes, after work, "Men head for cocktails, women head for the dry cleaner." But online media fundamentally changes this equation. Women can be at home and still engage in the virtual cocktail party happening across social networks.

**Build a portable, permanent brand.** Women can lose out professionally because most of us take some time out of the paid workforce to raise children. If you take time off to have a baby or opt out of a typical career-ladder progression, your online presence can still grow and burnish your professional reputation. Your online brand is layoff-proof and it can grow with you as your expertise and interests grow. In fact, according to the Families and Work Institute, jumping in and out of the traditional workforce is the new normal for all ages. Keeping up a strong professional profile online allows you to stay engaged even if you're not officially working.

**Establish expertise and credentials.** By creating a strong online brand through digital publishing, you establish expertise in your field while bypassing the traditional gatekeepers or barriers to success. A strong Google rank, along with links to your work, establishes credentials in the digital age. Research shows women feel the need to be more credentialed before assuming or asking for greater responsibilities or positions of power much more than men. Strong use of social media allows us to build credentials without having to break into traditional networks. (If we are part of those networks, even better—we can use our position to link out to more women.)

**Create strong community ties.** We get by with a little help from our online friends. These connections not only build social capital, they're also a wonderful addition to life. My entrepreneurial networks do everything from referring clients to helping me find resources like tax assistance and trademark advice, and I don't have to leave my house. Online communities can help busy people feel connected, listened to, and recharged. Online community ties help keep us from feeling isolated when our family and home responsibilities surround us. Perhaps more practically, staying connected to a professional community helps women stay on top of current trends in their professional space, helping us better prepare to reenter the workforce when the time comes.

# GETTING STARTED

## *Twitter for Dummies (You're Not)*

Twice a year I give a workshop at the Harvard Kennedy School to encourage students to think about using digital and social media to establish their professional brand online. I can't tell you how many really brilliant people have heard me speak about building an online brand, and responded sheepishly, "I'm not smart enough to do social media." Or "I'm too old." One was, I kid you not, an M.D./ Ph.D. Another was a former member of Special Forces.

This mind-set is total crap. First of all, if you're a professional you are definitely smart enough to create content online. If a nine-year-old can make a YouTube video, so can you. Second, don't be ageist against yourself! The stereotype that only young people are good at social media and web stuff is damaging and untrue. Figure out which pieces you want to take on yourself, don't be afraid to hire help for the rest (freelance web design and social media help is copious), and get going. Here's my advice:

## Morra's Guide to Owning Your Corner of the Internet

**Identify your ecosystem.** Your ecosystem is the unique set of players, circumstances, and organizations that create a professional field or topic area.

**Define the work or mission of the marketplace.** In this case, it helps to get as narrow as possible. You may think your ecosystem's work is accounting or public relations consulting, but it's a lot more effort to become a big fish in a giant pond, and tough on hermits. Get granular: perhaps the work of your ecosystem is accountants with a specialty in not-for-profit management, or public relations management for American cities trying to attract tourists from China.

**Know the players.** In any field, there are players. These could be individuals or firms. If you've worked long enough, you know them. You see them quoted and you see them receive awards and accolades. Get to know the players in your chosen field intimately. This is your competitive set. Review their websites, follow them on Twitter, understand their pricing and staffing, and suss out the secrets of their success as well as their vulnerabilities.

**Think about how you or your firm would pitch against a player, and how you'd highlight your advantages over theirs.** Once you find your target audience, and the specific tactics they are using to promote their brand, chew on what they are missing. There's your opportunity. Drill down as much as you can. If you're a company providing flexible jobs for moms, see who blogs about these issues both locally and nationwide. Check out the content, tweeting, and LinkedIn groups about your field. What aren't they covering that you could?

**Establish your expertise and POV.** Even though you're a hermit, you're still hard-core! Negotiation coach Tanya Tarr is a fan of using a portfolio as "hard evidence" of your accomplishments to establish credibility in the marketplace. When I started Women Online, I borrowed case studies from past client work, because Women Online itself didn't have any work to show yet. I was only partially bullshitting, because I'd actually done the work, and I knew my trade. The difference was now I could sell past results with a new edge.

**Find some "boast bitches."** But you don't need to brag yourself. In her book *Feminist Fight Club,* Jessica Bennett says to let these validators vouch for you. Your status also depends on praise from your peers, and with it, your status in the ecosystem will rise quickly. With peers you admire, you can return the favor.

**What does your audience need more of, or what are they missing?** Just as shoppers in search of homemade wedding favors are served by Etsy, your audience is served by the specific online ecosystem you're part of. Think about your brand in the narrowest sense, and identify your target audience. Even more important than understanding your marketplace and your competition is understanding your audience. What do they have plenty of and what do they need or wish they had more of? Where is the gap in the larger marketplace, and crucially, where is the gap in marketing and communicating the offering? This is where your online brand comes in. Do you know how much time I spent online searching for customized Easter basket liners for my kids? There are about three or four small online businesses who specialize in that offering. I bet they make a lot of money.

**Where does your audience hang out?** Define your audience's media choices. Understand where the audience hangs out online (even IRL), who influences their decisions, and what media you need to have a presence in. My clients are mission-driven organizations, but the consumer audience I need to work with every day is the vast and powerful community of women in social media who want to learn about and promote my clients. You might also have a consumer and a trade audience, or some other combination. Make sure you're considering everybody.

**How can you reach them?** So, for all potential audiences you need to reach, what conferences do you need to attend? What trade journals or B2B publications must you have a presence in? I literally draw a map and create circles for all the various points of contact I need to influence, from press to events to social media to professionals or thought leaders in my field. Use this research as a learning tool to enhance your strategies. The key to success here is to identify where your passions intersect with what's missing.

## Finding the "Blue Ocean"

Normally I hate business school jargon, but this is a great one. Created by INSEAD professors W. Chan Kim and Renée Mauborgne, the Blue Ocean strategy is "the simultaneous pursuit of differentiation and low cost to open up a new market space and create new demand." In English: understand the marketplace and what the players aren't providing. Use your expertise to create a solution, and technology to price it well.

The theory goes that when you identify and create an offering in the Blue Ocean, competition doesn't matter, and your costs to entry are lower. You're not paying for as much advertising, and you've got far less competition. Widely available technology (such as WordPress or an app builder) allows you to create a minimum viable product with little cash or expertise. In other words, it's a great approach for an entrepreneur who wants to do purposeful work and have a life. And it's especially helpful when you're in a large field, such as public relations, hair care, or apparel.

Swivel is an app that connects women of color with expert hair stylists, whether they wear their hair naturally or straighten it, and it seems to define Blue Ocean opportunity. "It's for when you put your hair in a bun after you get it done and say to yourself: 'Did she even use a flat iron? It's still so puffy,' says Jihan Thompson, a former magazine editor and founder of the app. "So many times I've left the salon feeling like I wasted my money."[2]

Now, that's a clear mission, a well-defined audience, and a big opportunity!

## Create Your Offering

When I founded Women Online, I had a Blue Ocean: there are lots of marketing firms that specialize in reaching women, there are lots of digital firms that work with online communities, and there are lots of firms that specialize in mission-driven marketing campaigns, but to my knowledge, there still is no other digital marketing firm that helps mission-driven organizations and campaigns connect with influential communities of women online. I would be a service consulting firm but I also intended to build a product, a database of influential women online who care about social change. I could do that cheaply thanks to open-source software and blogs.

I made a little triangle diagram to define the intersection:

My research showed that, though our offering was specialized, the addressable market was huge. There are over four million mom blogs in the United States alone, at every income bracket, and the majority of Facebook's 1.6 billion daily users are women.[3] Women

Women

Social
Change

Social
Media

are 1.5 times more likely than men to sign an online petition, and women make more frequent charitable donations.[4] My ideal clients were also an enormous field: political campaigns, not-for-profit organizations, foundations, and even companies whose issues and products women naturally cared about.

Still, I knew I would compete against three different kinds of firms: public relations firms that specialize in influencer marketing; digital agencies that also specialize in social media and content marketing; and social-impact firms that specialize in working for nonprofits, foundations, and political campaigns.

I defined a competitive set of about eight firms that I always seemed to be competing for business with, or that seemed to be winning clients I wanted. I set up a tracking system on Google Alerts, Mention, and Newsle to monitor the work of competitors, collaborators, and role models, and to know who was talking about us and what they were saying. This "oppo" research keeps us smart. Sometimes it causes a lot of FOMO. That is a very helpful reality check.

And in my weekly rounds with folks in my industry, I made sure to always be on the lookout for the scoop and gossip about my competitive set. What were they doing well? What were people saying about them that wasn't so great? And above all, how could we stand out? Defining the niche that only we owned against these bigger firms was most important of all.

## Make Your Networking Niche

Even your networking can be niche—and hypereffective. This means small, specialized, curated groups for your field or niche might be a better use of time than a giant fancy conference with a famous keynoter—an especially great perk for introverts and hermits! Michelle Madhok, founder of SheFinds.com and MomFinds .com, notes, "I'm a member of a small, invite-only group for owners of websites in key content verticals. It's very specialized, and it's both networking and learning information from peers that isn't publicly out there."

Starting these private conversations can be as easy as retweeting an insightful tweet, commenting regularly on an active blog related to your work, or engaging others in an online group or forum. You can also invite friends in your field to write a guest post for your blog or invite a few colleagues to participate in a blog roundtable where they each share their perspective on a particular topic. If you're involved in an issue with public-policy or global implications, or cultural impact, you can organize a live tweet of an upcoming speech or event. Use a hashtag so others can participate, too.

## Create Content That Supports Your Niche

Chances are, potential clients are going to Google you. Your search engine return page is frontline for your business or brand. Google juice and word of mouth are two of the most powerful allies you have as a hermit entrepreneur. And if you Google "Women Online"— guess who you see.

To ensure your search leads to accurate, useful, and professional results, you need strong content that supports searches for your name and related key words a potential customer might use to search for you.

**Find your friends.** Pick which platforms work best for what you do. For example, if you're a media commentator, Twitter will likely be much more useful for you than Pinterest. If you're a photographer, image-heavy sites like Tumblr and Pinterest will showcase your work brilliantly. Updating your social networks and blogging regularly will improve your SEO—search engine optimization— which is important for establishing your expertise and credentials. Remember, though, to be a good host at the party. Don't just promote yourself and your opinions. Acknowledge others, respond, and foster relationships. It makes for good karma and good business.

**Start small.** Maybe you don't want to commit to having your own blog or site just yet—and that's fine. Check out local online publications and volunteer to write a weekly or monthly column related to your work. You can also look for online publications related to your field and volunteer to write for them.

**Stay current.** Facebook and Twitter are the best places to post quick updates and interact on a personal level with your audience. Creating a fabulous e-mail newsletter, or using your Twitter feed or Facebook page or Instagram to "push" content to people, is important. Use your website or blog for posting the most important information you wish to expand upon. People don't often visit websites or blogs anymore without being prompted by a link in a social media field or an e-mail. However, quality is more important than quantity. Updating your content simply for the sake of updating could bury your best and most important updates, which you want to showcase.

**Don't get stuck in traffic.** Build influence by guiding audiences through the chaos of so much content. If your customers hang out in several places, target them where they are. Stacey Ferguson, founder of the social media community and conference Blogalicious, reminds us that now "everything is so divided up—you've got your blog, then Facebook, Instagram, Pinterest." By the same token, do your research! Creating profiles on every social network is not necessary, and trying to keep them all updated will drive you crazy.

**Online PR.** Even though you've rejected it personally, remember that you want to create a bit of FOMO in your potential customers, bosses, or investors. You can do this online without even having to speak in public or attend an event! The fact that I blog at prestigious outlets like the *Harvard Business Review* lends me an aura of credibility, and no one has to know I write my pieces in bed. Guest blogging, getting quoted as an expert, or freelance writing in a relevant business publication has a long digital footprint, and it's not just you talking about how great you are: it's a valid third party or a journalist. Resources like HARO (a free service that sends out multiple journalist queries every day) make it easier to get in front of media looking for experts.

**Long form.** Tweeting is great, Facebook is our home away from home, and we adore Pinterest, but the act of sitting down and giving voice to your opinions is crucial. Blogging is still a wonderful format to be smart and insightful. So is podcasting. Medium.com makes it possible for anyone to write on a forum shared by Melinda Gates and Bono. It's much harder on other platforms that contain your thoughts to a few characters. Telling the world what you think, but, more importantly, doing the work and asking the hard questions, is incredible for your professional credibility and your business development.

**Think about a simple newsletter.** Sending out a monthly or quarterly newsletter is a great way to update members of your audience who might not visit your website regularly but still want to be kept in the loop. And there's no better way to track influence than producing an e-mail people will actually open.

I'm a big fan of creating a delectable newsletter and building a CRM (customer-relationship-management database) to track customers. I have built up a "biz dev" list in my MailChimp with over nine hundred names of past clients, colleagues, and possible future clients. Everyone on that list has the potential to connect me to a new client for Women Online. And when I want to try to gin up some business quickly, I draft a witty newsletter.

There are several online services and templates you can use to create e-mail newsletters. My company loves MailChimp. Once you have a newsletter, know that your subscribers likely receive similar update e-mails from other organizations, so it's important that yours contains relevant content that is easy to read quickly. Make sure it has a fabulous voice.

Hermit freelancer, host of the popular podcast *Call Your Girl-*

*friend,* and feminist journalist Ann Friedman is the absolute gold standard. The popular and influential Ann Friedman Weekly is a must-read and gives her an instant way to connect with editors and TV bookers. Friedman's newsletters feel like sitting down to catch up and chat at the end of the week with your friend. She mixes links to her personal work with the best writing from around the web over the past week, plus funny pie charts, GIFs, and jokes. And she has used it to build a powerful business and platform as a feminist pundit, thinker, and writer.

She also has a great, no-stress method: she writes it partly for herself. "This is a nice way to give myself structure at end of week . . . what did I read? What did I produce? If you're not consuming interesting things, you won't produce interesting things."

If all this content participation is too much for your hermit nature, feel free to hire someone who loves it! That is okay. Many successful entrepreneurs with large digital presences outsource their social media communications and writing to someone who they trust, who can channel their voice.

## WHAT'S YOUR FRANCHISE?

Many people I meet are simply scared to be as open and authentic as you need to be to be successful online. And it *is* scary! This is why the professional "franchise" approach can be helpful. Instead of simply tweeting, creating a franchise allows you to use a social platform to build something helpful for your entire field. Consider how to develop a digital franchise that shows off your unique smarts: something online that people love and rely on.

❑ Founded and hosted by Susan McPherson, head of McPherson Strategies, #CSRChat, a biweekly Twitter conversation, is a fantastic resource for anyone active in the world of corporate social responsibility, sustainability, and the place where social change meets the corporate world. As host of the franchise, Susan convenes the most important players in CSR to answer her questions. It's a PR win for participants, and for Susan, who "has proven to be the ultimate source of lead generation." It also began as a one-off, but after the first show, somebody e-mailed and said, "When's the next one?" Pay attention to what people respond to: you may have a possible franchise.

❑ Amy Webb is a prolific writer and creates more smart content than I can believe (her book *Data: A Love Story* was optioned by a Hollywood studio). Her company, Webb Media, helps clients determine the future, and how to cope with it. Each year, the firm produces a comprehensive "curated guide to digital media, design, and journalism conferences" that rates cost against the chance you'll actually learn something new. Webb Media also produces a great trend guide. These two franchises capture Webb Media's brand ("the future") and allow the company to reach new business leads without Amy having to get on a plane or train and hold a meeting. And—proof of the power of the franchise—you don't even have to provide an e-mail address to download them.

❑ Podcasting is the new blogging (and that is a huge compliment). I'm a huge fan, and I have one myself. If talking, not writing, is your thing, consider Carrie Kerpen's approach. In her podcast *All the Social Ladies*, Carrie interviews women in digital media about their careers, along with any advice they have for women trying to break into the field. Carrie says, "It was an easy way to overcome shyness about speaking to women in positions of power, and I also thought it would help with leading the next generation. I started getting business when guests and fans would refer me to clients. Now I have over 1,000,000 downloads of the podcast."

## What's in the Name?

When I was twenty-three and working in London, a bunch of very cool ad guys taught me a saying I love: "Does what it says on the tin." Originally a slogan for wood sealant, the phrase means that the name on the packaging should never veer too far from the product's actual use. I always think of this when trying to name a project or help a client name a new brand. When clients are trying to be fancy, I stop and ask them, "Does the name do what it says on the tin?" In other words, does the name offer a clear promise of what you're offering?

Now, Women Online does what it says on the tin. The company is about connecting and mobilizing women online. However, my Google Analytics results frequently tell me that some of my most frequent visitors are those searching for mail-order brides and Eastern European women online. I bet they're disappointed to find my marketing agency! Oh, well. So much for the tin.

Still, another vote in favor of "does what it says on the tin" is the very prevalence of key words. In fact, when I was trying to develop the subtitle for this book, the very wise people at my publishing imprint, Dey Street, stressed the importance of using relevant and popular key words. How else, they pointed out, would the right audience find the book? That's why you see "introvert" in the subtitle: people often search for advice with that word.

So if you're struggling to create a name for your business or personal brand, use Google AdWords and trend data to find out what keywords your target audience actually uses when trying to find content like yours. If your company's brand name doesn't reflect such words, then ensure that supporting copy does. For example, leaders in the work-life field have fought for years to change public adoption of *work-life balance* as the term of art, because, as we've discussed, they think the idea of balance is a pointless exercise. Here's the problem: that's not what the public uses. It's not what the media uses. Everyone except leaders in the field uses *work-life balance*. For someone like Cali Yost, her leader branding might include her term *Work+Life Fit,* but you can bet supporting copy on her website references *work-life balance,* because that's how people will find her via Google.

## You Must Also Buy Your Name

Owning your name online is a critical first step toward fully owning your online presence. Leave no stone unturned when it comes to establishing your name online across all possible social media platforms even if you don't use them now. Register a few domain names and all possible extensions. This can be done using sites like GoDaddy, BlueHost, or HostGator, or, if you have an existing site hosted on Squarespace (my personal favorite), WordPress, .me, or Blogger, you can register your domain name and host your blog there. Using Google's App Suite, you can give contractors or part-time workers an e-mail address at your firm in about two minutes, which is fantastic for branding and communicating with clients.

Also, be sure to use the same name across platforms. If possible, use the same name for your URL, Twitter handle, Facebook fan page, YouTube channel, etc. This will make it easy for clients to find you online and gives you a professional, streamlined image.

## Your Look Must Also Be Consistent

For this one, you need to spend money to make money. If you're a hermit, your online look needs to do a lot of work for you. And so do photos of yourself on the web. Please invest in photography and a logo that are chic and professional. Graphics and image matter. Get a gorgeous head shot and use it for all your online properties. It is money well spent.

## But People Online Are Mean!

In 2007 and 2008, I had a pretty good run as a pundit on CNN. But the worst part was the online comments after segments, because, when you appear on TV as a female political commentator, all commenters care about is how you look. I was informed on right-wing blogs that (a) I was completely unfuckable, and (b) I look like John Malkovich. (I suppose the two are related.) It didn't help that I was often paired against the Megababe of the Right Wing, Mary Katherine Brewer.

And that was nothing compared to one of my colleagues, who had to get an FBI detail because she and her kids kept getting death threats. She was an outspoken political blogger, and she was extremely in-your-face. She paid a heavy price, and I've seen a lot of friends braver than me go through scary, scary times.

The Internet isn't always a safe place, especially when you are a person with strong views. I realized that being a woman who wrote and spoke publicly about things like abortion rights and gun control meant strangers would say hateful things about me.

As of this moment I only have 6242 followers on Twitter. Certainly the owner of a social media firm should have more than six thousand followers on Twitter, no? But I am the least tough person out there. My skin is thin! Keeping my online presence narrow is deliberate. While I am turned off by trolls, the art of curating a gorgeous visual feed, say, on Instagram, almost scares me more. I just cannot be that fabulous.

But I know I have to accept some exposure, because every article I write that impresses potential clients means I can stay home extra days and not get on a plane.

Balancing my reluctance by consistently writing insightful (I hope) and professionally relevant blogs for elite online publications helps protect my professional credibility and keeps up my Google juice online. It also allows me the flexibility I crave, because I'm letting my online content work for me, even if I'm hiding at home or hanging out with my kids.

Writing professionally doesn't feel scary to me. It feels necessary. And when parties in power and policies change, it can feel *really* necessary. I had to find credibility in a way I can handle, which for many years meant staying out of personal or political discussions online, and keeping it strictly professional.

The challenge for you is to quit thinking of your online presence as a #FOMO-inducing Instagram feed of fabulousity, and shift your thinking into carving out your own unique space online. Your voice is valuable, professionally advantageous, and once you get into creating online content, it can be addictive. Best of all, you can do it anytime, anywhere, and especially from your couch.

# 9

# *The Hermit Entrepreneur*

I n the next two chapters, we'll discuss how to maximize your flexibility and quiet time and minimize stressors at work. This chapter focuses on entrepreneurs, while Chapter 10 addresses the hermit who works within an organization.

If you feel like you aren't cut out to be an entrepreneur because you don't have a huge appetite for risk or you're not willing to sacrifice your personal life, I'm here to tell you that's crap. If you have a vision for your life, your work, and the impact you want to make, a small business just might be the right strategy.

Here's the truth: running a business is a skill, not an inherent gift. And it's not the exclusive province of extroverts or the carefree. With the right tools, you can grow your business, land new clients, and do the work you love, while keeping travel, networking, and extracurriculars to a minimum. In fact, being a small-business owner is actually a fantastic career for the hermit, once you know how to sustain it.

A hermit entrepreneur maximizes control over her pace, place, and space so she can do as much work from the quiet of home as possible. But a day in the life of a hermit entrepreneur might look different every day! One day you might be running around from business appointment to appointment, hustling as hard as you can, in full makeup and wardrobe, while the next might find you in sweats, working from your home office and venturing outside only to check the mail. That day might be full of back-to-back calls, or it might feature chunks of unclaimed time for writing on deeper-thinking work. For me, a good week sees me out and about two days and working from home for three. On top of that, at least one of the "home" days needs to feature almost no conference calls or web meetings.

## Small Is Sexy

The media just loves an iconoclastic entrepreneur. That is, as long as their company is a "unicorn"—meaning, valued at a billion dollars.

But those million breathless articles and magazine covers are very far from the true story of successful entrepreneurs. These small-business owners actually create a thriving, innovative economy, and their companies reflect their values, not just their valuation.

Silicon Valley veteran Gina Bianchini, whose start-up Ning was once valued at over $800 million but never made that unicorn exit, has a different growth plan for her new company, Mighty Networks.

With Mighty Networks, Gina has kept her team at about 20 people and built a profitable business. The company creates social-networking software for professional communities. *Wired* notes, "As the current unicorns—from Dropbox to Snapchat—grapple with skyrocketing burn rates and build out expensive enterprise sales-forces to help them grow into their valuations, Bianchini is adding customers and banking revenues."[1]

The smaller the company, the more control you (the owner) have. This may mean you can keep better hours because you contain your workload, or it can mean you decide how to spend your company's resources or give back to the community. You can run a mission-driven business simply by directing dollars you would already spend in a good direction. Lindy Huang Werges started her executive recruiting firm, Integritas Resources, after years of working for both large corporations and start-ups. It's a revenue-driven firm that is focused on accounting and finance, and she controls how her firm's dollars get spent.

"Philanthropy is important to me," Huang Werges says. "I wasn't able to do it in larger companies. We are a woman- and minority-owned business, and we invest in minority- and women-owned companies." In 2015, her firm invested 33 percent of its earnings in giving back, and her revenues still grew by 500 percent. "We even try to take our clients out to lunch at local restaurants," Huang Werges says.

In a culture that idealizes the entrepreneur who's always hungry, it's hard to feel that small is, truly, sexy. Often I feel I'm letting people down by passing up opportunities to expand rapidly. I see colleagues and competitors staffing up, and can feel a twinge of envy and insecurity. But then I have to pinch myself and remember this is a choice. And it *is* a choice.

That's why the enterprising hermit must, above all, be realistic. Part of being realistic is having the systems and knowledge in place to control growth, whether to stimulate it or slow it down. Your career may not be a rocket ship. But it will keep rising steadily, and even if it's not a thrill ride, it will give you a great sense of satisfaction.

## GETTING STARTED

To value your product, you have to figure out your finances, growth, and business type. Here's a step-by-step guide.

### "The McKinsey of Mommybloggers"

Positioning your business means creating the desired perception of it, and when I was starting out, I hadn't positioned mine. I simply tried to price myself fairly enough to get hired. But after about a year of working and competing against other momblogger agencies or influencer marketing firms, I realized I wanted to be different. I jokingly said I was going to be "The McKinsey of Mommybloggers."

The phrase is tongue-in-cheek, but it means we hold ourselves to a high standard in a field that's completely unregulated and full of firms of varying quality. McKinsey is a legendary, elite, and high-priced strategy consulting firm. They hire the best, work with the best, and, in the market's view, do the best work.

That's how I wanted Women Online to be perceived—a challenge, since the company is about moms (undervalued in the marketplace), social media (a field with no barriers to entry), and digital marketing (again, not exactly Nobel Prize–level work).

Pricing is one of the most powerful tools to control your work life, and your choice is also a positioning statement. Like everything else in business, it's more art than science, and you need to be flexible. Here are the metrics we use to price our services:

**Price:** We are not the least expensive firm in our space, and that's on purpose. However, because we often work with nonprofit organizations, our fees are flexible and are managed on a sliding scale.

**Clientele:** We are extremely choosy about who we take on. If I wouldn't work for this client for free, I won't do it.

**Quality vs. volume:** Our sales approach, our pitch, and our very presentation is niche. Some pitches use low prices, some are about technology, some feature giant numbers of ad impressions, or sheer volume of business. Ours emphasizes our quality, our excellent strategy and field knowledge, and the fact that we work with world-renowned clients. It's social proofing. This approach says: if we're good enough for them, surely we're good enough for you.

**Staying low-tech:** My firm will never earn awards for its infrastructure or tracking. Our website is, frankly, meh. I'd like a better website, but the investment required for such infrastructure would strain me as much as bringing on extra staff, and it's not part of my plan.

I know other small firms run by hermits who have done the opposite: invested up front in incredible technology, high-tech websites, databases, and tracking for pitches that use metrics and results to get business. It works beautifully. I think the key is knowing what kind of business you're going to run.

Six years in, my business has stayed small while competitors have grown exponentially, sold to big firms, or taken on outside capital. We are not for everyone, and we lose as much business as we win. That's okay, though, because our clients tend to stay with us, and they refer other new clients to us.

That's where the aspirational piece of pricing comes in, and why it's important for hermits. When you price your goods or services slightly higher than market average, you can shoot for clients you want instead of shooting for volume, which helps stave off work-life conflicts right out of the gate.

## Pricing 101

First, you need to learn the landscape. Having some basic guidelines on how to price your work is very helpful, especially if you bill by the hour or on a project basis. If you are starting a business in a field you currently work in, this won't be too hard. If you're doing something new, creating a competitive set is really helpful, much as you did when developing your brand niche.

You can make this set both aspirational (building in some profit, or competing with the players) and realistic (making sure it covers your monthly nut—and we'll define that and learn how to figure that out in this chapter).

What kind of firms do you want to be considered alongside?

What kind of firms are you actually competing against?

This is really important because clients or hiring managers will group you in a cohort, consciously or unconsciously. And if you are responding to RFPs or government contracts, you'll need a solid sense of pricing.

## Women and the Underpricing Trap

I have a tough time being taken seriously as an expensive strategist because I work in a space that's entirely about reaching women. I still have to fight all the time to get paid the rates I want. (You know that pay gap between men and women? There's also a pricing gap for women entrepreneurs.) Obviously, if you're undercharging for your work, you have to work more! That makes it difficult to be a successful hermit.

One counterintuitive way to get a sense of what to charge? Ask some men.

Data show men set higher reference points on income: they always aim higher, and they often get it. Traditionally, when pricing, women tend to consult more female reference groups. Our fellow entrepreneurs, clients, or experts in your field—that is, our professional networks—look more like us. This can be a real disadvantage when it comes to evaluating your worth in the marketplace. (Later, in Chapter 12, on negotiation, we'll learn the basic tool kit to ensure you're paid your worth.)

## Do the Hustle

Yes, you have to value your work, but sometimes you'll have to compromise. That's where hustling comes in.

Real estate mogul Clelia Peters explains it well: "I define hustling as what happens when you realistically survey the marketplace and strategically choose to offer your services at a discount or with more favorable terms than competitors 'purely to gain a foothold among new clients.'"

Hustling can also mean doing whatever it takes to win new business or establish your foothold, but should not be about selling yourself short. There's the kind of hustling that verges on being taken advantage of, like doing work on spec, and there's hustling with a contingency plan. If a potential client asks you to do some free work, you can say yes if you like. But sometimes what you think might be hustling is someone taking advantage just because they can. I think our record for putting together and then tweaking new proposals for a potential client lies at four iterations. That's about twenty hours of work, all unbillable. When it all comes to naught, you can feel angry.

This effort is key, so either build time that you may never win back into your budgeting, or build in a hustle with contingencies, for example by writing free articles or planning an event from which you can draw lasting credibility and accolades, whether or not the client comes through.

Going all out is also a way to develop a portfolio. A blogger I know began by simply doing that: blogging about her passion for free. But, because she entered the fray just as blogging was started, she was able to establish a foothold in the field, which led to several high-profile paid gigs writing, teaching, and speaking, as well as a full-time job to support her and provide health care as she built her business. In time, that exposure led to a book deal—one entirely unrelated to her blog—and she was able to go freelance full-time.

Hustling is part of the life of an entrepreneur, hermit or not, and it's essential when you're starting out (and probably when you're well established, too). You'll have to take less than you're worth at some point, but make sure it's only a short-term strategy. Be careful not to price yourself too low, though: in my experience being too "cheap" often suggests to clients that you are not good enough at what you do.

Remember, too, that you can hustle from home. It's great to get out there and meet potential clients or customers face-to-face, but follow-ups and relationship development via phone or e-mail works well. Most important, hustling is a state of mind. Even the most introverted entrepreneur needs to hustle. If you love your work and you feel in control, you won't mind it, and you'll probably even enjoy it.

## Feathering Your Nest

A wonderful lifestyle is a curse if you wake up ten years later with no financial security.

Financial planners will tell you that you must have a cash cushion of six months while also saving for retirement, a house, or college, and paying yourself. This might not be realistic for small-business owners; I have never done it. Feathering your nest is being intentional and smart about where all your money is going, and making sure your business venture is really taking care of you.

Too many people have escaped the reality of their daily work lives to create an entrepreneurial dream that not only fails, but strips them of whatever financial security they have built up. Remember, you are becoming a hermit entrepreneur to try to reduce stress and anxiety in your life. If you don't have the money saved to float yourself for six months while your business ramps up, reconsider why you're doing it. If you're launching a product or opening a store and you're planning on cashing out your kids' college funds or refinancing the house, reconsider.

Start-up veteran Lane Wood puts it like this: "Entrepreneurship is something we sell motivated individuals in the same way the beauty industry sells women makeup or shoes." Like *Sex and the City*'s Carrie Bradshaw, who realizes she's spent over $40,000 on shoes with nothing to show for it, people may be buying a dream with damaging effects. Smart people quite literally mortgage their futures.

This is because sustainability works both ways. Your lifestyle must be sustainable emotionally, physically, and financially! I might be an anxious wreck full of migraines if I'm on the road selling every day of the week, but if I stay home and hide for too long, I can't pay the bills. That's pretty stressful, too.

So how to take care of your finances and your emotional health? Feathering your own nest could look as simple as pulling out pretax dollars every month to fund a SEP-IRA. It could mean keeping up a highly paid consulting gig while you're launching your business so you can keep earning cash and maintaining your health insurance. It could mean keeping a job while you work every night on growing your business, with your living room filled with boxes of your product. You'll know what's right; just don't ignore your finances.

## *Having a* Knippel

My most powerful early experiences around money were shaped by my father's moving out when I was eleven and sometimes refusing to pay the bills (simply because he felt like it).

Like many women of her generation, my mother is an educator. She earned a good living as a learning-disabilities consultant. And, like many middle- and upper-middle-class women of her generation, she stopped working when my sister and I were born.

As privileged as my childhood was, it was peppered by constant stress about money: Would we ever have enough? When I was accepted early into Brown University, an Ivy League school, I called my father excitedly to let him know. "That's great, honey, but you have to go to Rutgers [the state university of New Jersey]," he said. That's a good problem to have, but it also highlighted the truth that my sister, mother, and I were completely dependent on men. I hated that feeling, and I was determined never to depend on a man for my own income. Thankfully, the Brown volleyball coach magically made some funding appear, and indeed I packed up and left for Rhode Island.

When I was about twenty-eight and getting serious about a man, my mom told me about her *knippel*. It's a concept that is crucial for women entrepreneurs . . . and in fact, for everyone.

In Yiddish, a *knippel* is a knot, like the kind you might make in a handkerchief. The phrase comes from the old country, where women would hide jewels or a few coins in those knots or in the seams of their dress. That way, in case their husband died, left, or they had to flee during a pogrom, there would be a little cash. Now a *knippel* just means a little money on the side that your partner doesn't know about.

In my mom's case, her *knippel* was a secret stock account. Her friend Barbara's *knippel,* Mom proudly reported, had recently done very well in an AT&T stock split. But when she advised me to have one, I recoiled, because my marriage would never be toxic like my parents'.

I'm happy to report my marriage is not toxic. It's great. But I still have a *knippel* and so does my husband (I think).

You don't need to be married to have a *knippel*—you don't even need to be in a relationship. Think of it as your own knot for your future self. It's another way to feather a nest, because life brings us surprises, and sometimes, as hard as it can be, we have to handle them alone.

## GIVE YOUR MONEY A GOAL

There's a common saying: the only difference between an entrepreneur and someone with a dream is money. But all money isn't equal, and to figure that out, first, you need to accept that money is an emotional topic. Think of money as the principal element in how you make choices, and how you establish what your financial values and priorities are.

I've learned the hard way that, for an entrepreneur, emotions and money don't mix. In my case, my emotions revolved around credit use. I had a serious shopping problem in my twenties. (I was interviewed on TV about my staggering $12,000 debt!) That's why the first time my bank gave me a line of credit, I felt ashamed to use it. It felt like running up debt on Daddy's credit card.

Then my stepfather, an accomplished businessman, told me this wasn't debt: it was growth. Was I ready for it?

Well, at the time, I wasn't, and that's why I was anxious about using the credit line. My money didn't have a goal.

The advice of financial therapist Amanda Clayman is something to take to heart. She stresses that a goal, when budgeting your business, can be transformative. She recommends choosing one even before you launch that business.

Paying attention to how money comes in and out is key to stress. For instance, in my case, when I was younger, failing to set appropriate boundaries in my work made me spend impulsively on expensive self-care. In effect, I was reinforcing the system, because the more money you spend, the more chained you are to your job.

By the same token, not budgeting can lead to overwork, another violation of boundaries. "We put such a high value on being a hard worker," Amanda says, but people also need to give themselves permission to say, "I only need this much money."

Any money that doesn't have a direction is vulnerable to being misspent. That's why, Amanda says, it's so important to set an intention. Money set aside will still actually change our behavior in the moment, if it doesn't have a goal.

That doesn't mean you'll find the solution or answer immediately. Realizing what goal to give your money takes time and experience. But allowing yourself to reflect how your emotions affect your spending or saving is the first step to letting your finances make you happy, which is the goal of an entrepreneur.

## Figure out Your Monthly Nut

My husband's great-uncle John had a funny story about how we spend money. When his father-in-law remarked that John must be doing well if he could afford a new Cadillac, John replied, "Of course I can't afford it," then added, "If I could afford a Cadillac, I'd be driving a Rolls-Royce."

We might chuckle, but how true is this for you? I know it is for me. (See my aforementioned TV interview about my shopping-inspired debt.) The American Dream is built on overextending ourselves. Symbols of success like cars, watches, and handbags are expensive, and, unfortunately, there's a very eager consumer credit industry to enable us. Endless exposure to American Express commercials in my youth—"Membership has its privileges"—had me whipping out my Amex with way too much gusto. I thought the color of the card signified something about what I'd achieved in life. I'm much better now, though I would be lying if I said I was left with a huge amount of money at the end of every month.

I can't tell you how many people have told me the biggest barrier they feel to launching a business is dealing with cash flow. They're right to take it seriously, because control over your cash flow is what buys you freedom and flexibility. If you're going to be a hermit, you need to figure out how to pay for it!

So, before striking out on your own, figuring that out is certainly important. That's where a "monthly nut" comes in. Here is how it works if you own a small business. Your monthly nut is all of your business expenses, and the cash you need to generate in order to cover the nut.

Your accountant might use a financial statement for this, but I find accounting-speak, even after all these years, confusing, so I put the terms in my own basic language.

Set up a spreadsheet (I use Google Docs) and add a line for all your fixed expenses.

| ITEM | COST (ESTIMATES ARE OK) |
|---|---|
| **SALARIES** | |
| **RENT + CAPITAL EXPENSES** | |
| **ADMINISTRATIVE (AN AVERAGE OF YEARLY LEGAL, ACCOUNTING, INSURANCE PAYMENTS, DUES, ETC.)** | |
| **TAXES (ESTIMATE QUARTERLY PAYMENTS)** | |
| **CREDIT CARD/TRAVEL & ENTERTAINING (PUT IN A HEALTHY AMOUNT BASED ON YEARLY AVERAGE)** | |

The total is your nut. If your business's nut is $34,000, you know that every month, to break even, you need to earn at least $34,000 in revenue.

Other expenses will come and go, of course. For example, I usually have several contractors working on projects; I pay them out of the specific contract fee they are assigned to. I might have a trip that comes up that I need to pay for. You can handle these kinds of things as they arise. The nut is simply those bills you need to pay every month. Once you know this number, you know how much you need to earn.

The comfortable monthly nut keeps you motivated, but not stretched too thin. If you are consistently going into debt to cover your monthly basic expenses, you have four options:

1. Get a new job and earn more money, or keep on your current path if you're due for a big promotion.

2. Cut down your expenses.

3. If you have one, ask your partner to float more of the expenses while you figure things out.

4. Win the lottery.

If you want to be a successful hermit, I suggest number two: try to pare down your expenses. This is good discipline while you figure things out. Then, once you know how much you need, you can put systems in place to earn it.

Here's a way to calculate your personal monthly nut that is especially helpful if you are a freelancer, or your business income and personal income are one and the same. I realized I was never going to download receipts or actualize my spending into Quicken or another budgeting platform. But every six months or so, I adjust our monthly personal budget and make sure it's as accurate as possible.

(Feel free to swap out for relevant categories.)

| ITEM | COST (ESTIMATES ARE OK) |
|---|---|
| MORTGAGE OR RENT | |
| UTILITIES (HEAT, CABLE, PHONE, WATER/SEWER, LAWN) | |
| GROCERIES | |
| TAXES (ESTIMATE QUARTERLY PAYMENTS) | |
| CAR + GAS + AUTO INSURANCE | |
| DINING OUT/ENTERTAINMENT | |
| STUDENT LOANS | |
| 529/401(K) OR SEP (IF NOT TAKEN FROM PAYCHECK) | |
| LIFE INSURANCE | |
| DRY CLEANING | |
| GYM | |
| PERSONAL (CLOTHES, FUN) | |
| CHILDCARE OR SCHOOL | |
| HOUSEKEEPER | |

## Scoping Your Work

Scoping is the key to maintaining your boundaries as a hermit entrepreneur. According to the business dictionary, the "scope of work," whether you are in a service business or producing product, means, "The division of work to be performed under a contract or subcontract in the completion of a project, typically broken out into specific tasks with deadlines." Usually contracts will have a Scope of Work attached, which holds one accountable.

But I also like to think of scoping as an everyday discipline that allows me to protect my time and sanity. Scoping is basically boundary setting. You could even scope out the work involved in throwing a dinner party, a kid's birthday, or in planning a vacation.

One of the keys to scoping effectively as a homebody entrepreneur is right-sizing your contracts. (Goldilocks again.) The first step is a more global decision than creating a scope for a particular project. Every project has a specific impact on your time management and your boundaries, and you have to be honest with yourself about what pace you thrive on. At some level, only experience in your business will truly teach you how to create the work product that's right for you.

Over the years, my team has learned how to sniff out the right-sized project for us. Our contracts tend to be smaller than those of other digital marketing firms, but we can do a lot of our work independently, and we don't usually do work that is super-deadline-driven. At kickoff, we set up milestones. When we meet those milestones, it means no frantic calls from our clients, no working weekends, but also no huge rush when we finish a giant, stressful project. My colleagues running huge social media projects or planning major events or building amazing websites get the glory and a bigger seat at the table, but they often have to go 24/7, and and the work is stressful the whole time. It's an emotional trade-off I willingly make.

Scoping can also be seasonal. In your business, when to grow and when to stay status quo probably has a rhythm all its own. I know that the period from Christmas to Valentine's Day is always quiet.

Work wraps up at the end of the year, and new business doesn't really get going until mid-February. Summer and fall are usually very busy and profitable. I never get to take a summer vacation! So I try to save cash for winter, and also know I need to pump up business development in early February. Then, instead of panicking, I work less in January and try to enjoy it.

The scoping process, in which you determine how you're going to get a task completed, is crucial for hermits. Whether creating a product or offering a service, I'm shocked to hear how many business owners continually overpromise, erase all their boundaries, and fail because they're not being honest about the kind of work they need to do and the scope of their work. Now, we all fail; it's a natural part of work. But incorrectly scoping is a correctable failure. You miss deadlines, can't deliver what's promised, and feel miserable. Your boundaries are erased because you think about stressful work all the time. Even worse, your valuable word-of-mouth referral pipeline can get damaged, which means you need to start the hunt for more work from scratch. This makes you feel you have to overcompensate in business development. It is no fun.

Here are four steps to consider:

❑ The meta-question: What kind of work product do you want to deliver? Learn to specify the kind of project your business does, and the impact it will have on your schedule and boundaries.
❑ Determine what you are good at and what you can safely say good-bye to.
❑ Find the right tools to plan, and learn to be realistic about scope.
❑ Determine what you have the capacity to deliver—and again, be realistic.

There are lots of web-based or SAAS tools out there to help you scope a project. Most are designed for creative agency or service-based teams. Software company 10000ft offers several versions of an easy-to-use and comprehensive online tool for scoping and project management.

A simple spreadsheet will do. You want to list every aspect of the job, line by line, and estimate how many hours you think each element will take.

Every element of the project should be accounted for in terms of hours and cost estimates, low to high. That allows the development firm to budget the project and allocate staff resources. As the proj-

## EXAMPLE: SCOPE CHART
## FOR A DIGITAL MARKETING AGENCY

| EXPENSE | HOURS | COST ESTIMATE | SPENT TO DATE | EST. TO COMPLETE | NOTES |
|---|---|---|---|---|---|
| PROJECT MANAGEMENT | | | | | |
| CLIENT MEETINGS | | | | | |
| STRATEGIC PLAN DEVELOPMENT | | | | | |
| EDITORIAL CALENDAR | | | | | |
| DESIGN | | | | | |
| SHARE GRAPHICS FOR SOCIAL MEDIA | | | | | |
| CONTENT CREATION | | | | | |
| COPYWRITING FOR FACEBOOK | | | | | |
| TOTAL | | | | | |

ect evolves, keep accounting for hours and costs up-to-date so you know how you're pacing.

While it's essential to scope out a project so you know how much to charge, it's also essential to scope a project so you know how the work will affect your life for the next six months or so.

It's also helpful to think about how you can scale production or a client engagement without adding too much extra labor or time to the scope of work. Ask yourself as you're preparing a contract, *How big should the project be, and how can I scale without including too much extra labor?*

I can scale a project in my field (social media–content creation) without adding too many extra woman-hours. The fee for a campaign that produces forty pieces of content isn't four times higher than one that produces ten pieces, but the volume of social media impressions the client gets will be much higher. On the other hand, there are project tasks a client could double or triple, and it would impact the budget and time spent by a corresponding amount.

For example, if you develop software for one customer and new customers want the same exact software, you can probably scale up without too much impact on time management or the bottom line. That's why companies that scale and can produce lots of work product without adding much extra labor make a lot of money! Unfortunately, that is not my business and I am not rich. But I have learned how to realize my own little economies of scale.

# THE WORLD'S MOST BASIC SCOPING TOOL

Total project budget: $25,200
Length of project: four weeks

| TEAM MEMBER | TASK | HOURS/ WEEK | COST/ WEEK | TOTAL COST | % OF BUDGET |
|---|---|---|---|---|---|
| JEN | METRICS AND TRACKING | 3 | 450 | 1800 | 6% |
| AMANDA | SOCIAL MEDIA– CONTENT CREATION AND COPYWRITING | 20 | 3,000 | 12,000 | 48% |
| JAMES | LANDING PAGE DEVELOPMENT AND GRAPHICS | 15 | 2,250 | 9,000 | 36% |
| ANA | PROJECT MANAGEMENT AND MEETING FACILITATION | 5 | 600 | 2,400 | 10% |

## Capacity Plan

Your capacity plan is the total sum of all your scopes of work. It details your current workload, and when individual tasks begin and end, to determine what you actually have the capacity to do. For instance, if you have ten clients and ten people, the capacity plan should, at a glance, reflect how those people are using their time. It's key to maximizing your profits, because you can actually lose profit when you overpromise and underplan. For instance, the artisan sellers on Etsy.com are full of cautionary tales of business owners who scaled quickly, experienced great demand for their products, and simply didn't have the staff time or resources (such as a hard-to-source ingredient) to meet the demand. There's even a term for it: "handmade business burnout."[2]

For simplicity's sake, say you have four employees, and four projects at your company.

| (HOURS PER MONTH) | EMPLOYEE 1 | EMPLOYEE 2 | EMPLOYEE 3 | EMPLOYEE 4 |
|---|---|---|---|---|
| CLIENT 1 | 10 | 40 | 20 | |
| CLIENT 2 | | 40 | | 80 |
| CLIENT 3 | 70 | 20 | | 65 |
| CLIENT 4 | | 40 | 60 | |
| BIZ DEV | 60 | | | 10 |
| ADMIN | 20 | 20 | 20 | 5 |

If everyone works 160 hours a month, then who has capacity for a new project? Answer: it's Employee 3—she still has forty hours free per month. The next question is whether I can staff Employee 3 on this new project. If the scope of the project is more than she can take on and the other staff can accommodate, then I need to bring in new staff to service the client. Now, this question is a personal and financial one. Is bringing on someone new worth potential added stress? Or is the upside of winning this new client going to pay dividends in future business development—say, if it's a vanity client or high margin?

Jen Vento, the managing director of Women Online, also warns about "scope creep"—when you wind up providing much more on a project than originally specified. "Be very prescriptive," she advises. "If we're going to post five original pieces of content per week on a project, and then we're going to curate another ten or fifteen, I'm going to plan that out to the individual piece."

After every engagement, we also like to look at the hours we actually spent on a project and divide it by the budget so we can figure out our effective hourly rate. Meeting what we set is our goal. It doesn't mean you have to meet the budget exactly for every project, as long as your overall time sheet balances out.

Jen and I both tend to offer too much for free, so we have built in traps to catch ourselves. One of these is sussing out our future clients before we even sign the contract. "The personal dynamics between a customer and your firm can hugely impact scoping," she says. Take note of the process leading up to the signing: Do you have to micromanage already? How many people are you working with on a regular basis? How many group meetings will there be a week? On some level, Jen says, you just have to trust your gut. "Is this a person I want to be with?" she asks. "There are some clients we have a relationship with. And some I never want to talk to again."

## Choosing Your Clients

Not all clients are equal. Part of growth is choosing clients that will allow you to maintain boundaries but also earn money. This is not about "reaching scale." It's about sustainability and profitability. Your client mix can also help the introvert with business development, because your clients speak for you.

Here's how I think about my client mix in terms of public perception and business development:

❑ **Vanity clients.** These are the big names I can brag about. They instantly give me credibility in the marketplace and increase my firm's value. They are less about income maximizing and more about doing a fantastic job. Nothing is better biz dev than a happy, big-name client.

❑ **LTRs.** Long-term relationships. Just like in marriage, sometimes things can get a little stale and eyes might wander. But you're always there for each other, and you have deep ties and institutional memory. These are usually multiyear, retainer contracts.

❑ **High margin.** I'm not going to brag about these clients. However, they pay really well, are low churn (meaning they don't turn over often), and are wonderful for a cash infusion in uncertain times. Last year I had a large corporate client who paid us $50,000 for about thirty hours of work. All the work we proposed got stuck in legal and bureaucracy and no one seemed to mind. And of course, good work is always great for word of mouth, so make sure to do your best for these clients. You never know who knows whom.

❑ **Just for the love.** You would do this for free, because you love the cause or client, or you want the experience. Price it low, or do it pro bono, and dive in. Because Women Online works with many not-for-profits of varying size, I have learned how to "mix" clients so I can make a profit while working for both small nonprofits, who offer a lower hourly rate, and large companies with bigger budgets.

❑ **Short term.** These are a lot of work to set up and are high churn, but they can lead to long-term work.

For me, the ideal mix is 50 percent long-term retainer clients, with a contract of six months or twelve months. Another 40 percent of the client work will be short-term engagements—six-week or three-month projects. Then I always save 10 percent for pro bono work, just for the love (and the brand boost it can give to my firm). For you, this might be totally different: you might want to do 30 percent pro bono work and 70 percent short-term projects, with a complete stoppage in the summer so you can take time off. (Ken, a highly skilled database developer in Seattle and a friend of my husband's, works ten months a year because he likes to save the summers for camping.) Acknowledge your hermit self, and decide what percentage of work you can devote to what.

## Realization and Utilization

Even short-term clients or work products are not all created equal. I may have a short-term client that is very profitable, and one that is a money loser. The difference comes in how long it takes to win the business, from first meeting to contract signing (sales cycle), and how many hours I spend on work winning the project. It's very simple math. Figure out the hourly rate for the project, then multiply that by the hours you spent wooing them. That's deducted from your total profit.

See below. Not only is Client A less profitable because I'm spending valuable hermit time wooing them, I have to wait six agonizing months to know if they even sign the contract or not! Also, don't forget

|          | CONTRACT VALUE | SALES CYCLE | BIZ DEV HOURS | EXECUTION HOURS | IMPACT ON PROFIT |
|----------|----------------|-------------|---------------|-----------------|------------------|
| CLIENT A | $30,000        | 6 MONTHS    | 15            | 150             | ($3,000)         |
| CLIENT B | $30,000        | 3 WEEKS     | 3             | 150             | ($600)           |

the paperwork time it takes to get a customer signed up in your system. Factor that in. For instance, six hours of contract negotiation is a lot less painful on a six-month client than a one-month engagement.

And because the time you spend to develop a client or customer relationship is unpaid, you need to guard that time carefully. Every hour spent courting a client in person, on the phone, or by writing a proposal is an hour lost to earning revenue or spending time at home.

I refer to this as utilization rate; it's also sometimes called billability or profitability. This is how much of you and your staff's time is being billed to clients vs. being spent on business development, overhead costs, or administrative time (time that comes out of your pocket, not from client projects). If I work two thousand hours during the year, for instance, and one thousand of that is billable to the client, my utilization is 50 percent. My accountant, Alicia, says that for a midlevel worker, you should shoot for 65 percent utilization (meaning 65 percent of their time is directly billable back to clients) and about 50 percent once they're senior, while brand-new staff should be at least 75 percent, because they're not doing development and sales.

So how do you plan for utilization? Alicia says it's complicated, and depends on how many clients you have for the year, and what your goals are. "Say that it's my first year and I only have two clients signed up," Alicia says. "I know that my utilization is going to be very low. My goal is to have ten clients by the end of the year. So I should only be spending 20 percent on utilization, while 80 percent should be working on closing those new deals. That means I've got to have enough cash in the bank to cover for the fact that I'm only billable 20 percent of the time."

My biggest lesson on the big picture of sales came when I started a new department at a large communications firm. My boss told me I'd have to bring in a certain figure of revenue in order to be able to hire more people for my fledgling department. I expected the revenue number to simply cover the salaries of my new hires, but that wasn't the case. My boss told me that for every new hire I brought in, I would need to earn 2.5 times that person's salary! This was to cover business development time, overhead expenses, and administrative costs. Never forget the hidden costs.

## Putting Systems in Place

I have four different financial reports that I consult at all times. These reports are applicable if you run a business, work freelance or are self-employed, or work on any sort of commission structure. Here they are:

- ❑ **Cash in the bank.** Know your cash position at all times. This can be as simple as logging into your online account frequently to check, or setting up a daily alert to send you your balance in the morning. You can even set an alert for every transaction. If you want to take it one step further and have decent projections and a good system for cash-flow management, you can use a simple document called a FINMO, which stands for something like "financial info monthly."

- ❑ **Accounts receivable, or AR.** Use a simple online software program such as QuickBooks or FreshBooks. Especially if you're a service business, it's essential to know your booked revenue.

- ❑ **Accounts payable, or AP.** These are the invoices you owe. Obviously, these are important to keep current.

- ❑ **Pipeline or biz dev planning doc.** My wonderful accountant, Alicia, taught me this one. I use a spreadsheet and I also keep a pipeline at the bottom of my FINMO, with a cell estimating the likelihood that business will close. For every proposal or strong indication of interest I get in a new project, I log the client, contact, last meeting date, scope of work and contract size, and potential to close (WARM, COLD, DEAD, CLOSED). I can quickly scan it and see, for example, that I might have $250,000 in biz dev prospects but only $25,000 in my bank account. Time to get moving and close some of those prospects! If I have $250,000 in my bank account but only $25,000 in prospects, I need to turn up some business development levers, although I might take a few days off to enjoy in the short term. The pipeline document extends years back, and so it not only shows me what potential new clients are in play, but also allows me to review my "win" rate over time.

Michael Ansara, founder of the Share Group and Upsource Inc, who actually lives my fantasy of owning a horse farm and making jam, notes that business people who only look at their numbers backward are missing something. Once you're halfway into the next month, he says, "It's kind of hard to do much about the previous one." Instead you should be projecting a few months forward, then asking, "Whoops, we've got a hole. How are we going to fill that?"

"We're not doing this as an exercise in accounting," Michael says. "We're doing this to see where the opportunities are, and where [there] are problems we need to correct. There's hundreds of numbers, but what are the really critical ratios? And which ones drive profitability and success? And now, how do we move them the way we want to move them?"

The thing I like about Michael's approach is its humanness and practicality. I don't have an MBA, and I've always been intimidated by those who have them. But it's in talking to experienced entrepreneurs like Michael that you realize, running a business is mostly common sense.

Speaking of common sense, I want to talk now about a topic that seems to defy it: growth. It's easy to all assume that the purpose of starting a business is to grow. But for the hermit entrepreneur, this may not make sense. Ask yourself, whether you're about to start or you already have a business, how much bigger do you want to get? How much risk can you handle? If the answer is "not a lot!," read on.

## Are You Building to Delegate or Staying Small?

There are two basic models for a hermit entrepreneur who's starting small.

1. Use your own labor and time to earn the bulk of your income.

2. Manage others' time, delegating tasks to them and earning a percentage of others' revenue.

Successful solo players I know have two strategies to keep boundaries and coffers well balanced. They almost always have a strong administrative assistant or junior person to take on tasks that suck time and don't earn money. This is a powerful opportunity for you to secure your future by investing a little bit of money into something that will pay dividends.

They also have a network of colleagues whom they can team up with, and to whom they can refer extra business with confidence or subcontract overflow. If you're a solopreneur or a small-business owner, your Rolodex of fellow travelers is key. If a client suddenly demands time you do not have, or needs a skill set you do not possess, you can phone a friend, and maintain your limits.

You can base your monthly earning on available time. And about this, too, you must be realistic. My friend Margie Cader runs a successful PR consultancy and is rigorous about turning down new work if she is booked. "What works for me is to charge by the hour, or to really base a retainer on hours—but not go over," she says. "There have been times that I have overserviced clients, of course. And sometimes you do this at the start of a relationship. But I've gotten better at it over the years and I never lose my shirt. So, I'm less concerned with a big retainer or a big contract than I am with making sure I am being properly compensated for my hours."

It may seem counterintuitive that someone who wants to avoid interaction as much as possible would want to choose a life in which they constantly manage others, but there's a wonderful magic to it. The less time you personally need to bill and the more time you can delegate to your staff, the more free time you have to pursue the work you want to do and maintain the boundaries you need. Become your own delegator in chief. This is not an income-maximizing approach, but it is a flexibility-maximizing approach.

You could build a business with a small number of employees whom you really trust and still maintain most of your boundaries. However, you cannot micromanage, and you cannot expect perfection. If you set up a system where you bring in the majority of the new business (say that's ten hours a week) and work on clients with a light touch (say that's twenty hours a week), with another ten hours for admin, you're working forty hours a week on what should be a pretty profitable and well-run business, as long as your staff is billing enough to support their time as well as most of yours. That means you must ask, if, say, your firm's blended hourly rates equal $150 per hour, how many hours a month does everyone need to bill to pay for the whole company? Your staff should be billing more time than you are, and the numbers need to account for that.

Here's a very simple way of looking at it:

Your business has a $45,000 monthly nut (this includes all salaries, taxes, expenses, and administrative and capital costs).

After doing your research and determining your pricing strategy, you have arrived at a rate of $150 per hour for your company's services, based on the marketplace. This is a "blended" rate: a junior person might only be worth $50 per hour and you as the owner are worth $300, but it works out to a good average rate of $150 per hour.

At $150 per hour, a team of five needs to bill three hundred hours to meet the $45,000 threshold.

Say you earn $8,000 per month, but your time is only 50 percent billable (you work twenty hours a week on billable client work, or $12,000 per month in revenue).

The other four people need to reliably bill fifty-five hours a month (or $33,000) each to make up your monthly nut.

That's pretty manageable, and actually, they should bill more. But this model shows how you can build a pretty successful business while controlling your hours.

Now, using this model, you can size up or size down. Probably you wouldn't have five full-time staff at this level of income, but you might have consultants who work on specific projects for you.

If you manage other people, the key is to understand how much revenue each person is responsible for, including yourself, and to be laser-focused on and realistic about how everyone is using their time.

Once your business reaches about fifteen employees or more (and mine never has), it is hard to take time away. I have interviewed several small-business owners about this shift, and the truth is, once a critical mass of income, staff, and clients is reached, the business becomes more consuming.

Assuming they don't have start-up capital, most businesses follow a pattern of growth that looks like a staircase: one or two employees at first, working for a while, and then growing to more. But I have known many service consulting firms, for example, that staff up quickly because they start off with a large client, and then actually shrink over time because that may prove easier to sustain. There is no single right answer. Be realistic about your revenue, monthly nut, and your boundaries, and you'll find the right number for you.

## BRINGING IT ALL TOGETHER

Don't ever let anyone tell you that you can't be an entrepreneur because you're risk-averse, like to be at home, or because you are allergic to working twenty-four hours a day. (I have heard it all a hundred times. Still do.) You may not be able to be *their* definition of an entrepreneur, but you can be your own.

I hope that the chapters of this book feel like building blocks. Your vision to live out the success that's right for you requires strong boundaries, control over your time, a strong niche, and the basic skills to make a business run. Add hustle, craftsmanship, and subject-matter knowledge to the mix, and you can absolutely build a wonderful and strong small business while protecting your time and emotional needs.

And now let's talk about the hermit at work in a larger organization.

# **10**

# *The Corporate Hermit*

Many years ago I interviewed at a large corporation where all employees literally had to clock in and out via a swipe card, all day long. Everyone I asked about the company raved about the incredible cafeteria. But all the free food in the world couldn't get me to focus in my interview because I was stuck on the swipe cards. Every instinct in me said, *Forget this*, while the good girl in me kept saying, *This is a very prestigious place to work*.

I've always been frustrated by glowing press for companies like Google that offer employees lots of time to think, and encourage introverts and quiet-seekers to use nap pods and to play pool while creating brilliant products. But that organic sushi at the cafeteria comes at a cost. What Google and its perk-ridden Silicon Valley compatriots don't offer is freedom.

A lot of us are work-life rebels. It pains us to show up every day somewhere at the expected hour. Unfortunately, in overachieving circles, it's socially unacceptable to say that. You seem lazy. And admitting you try to work as few hours in the office as possible can be corporate suicide.

So what's a hermit at work to do?

I admit, I had to work really hard to find stories of successful corporate hermits. I'm not sure if it's because people didn't want to admit they are hermits, or because it's very hard to achieve. After all, if I had been able to build one alone day into my ambitious schedule without feeling like a loser, perhaps I wouldn't have left corporate work at twenty-nine.

So those who advance in their career while replenishing their resources have incredible skills to teach the rest of us—whether we're hermits, or introverts, or both. These are work-life leaders who have learned how to feel they have space and alone time, even within a large organization, and they keep a low profile while also rising in the ranks.

The successful corporate hermit knows that to do her best work, she needs more control over her schedule and space than the average person. This could be as simple as having a day a week to work from home, coming in a bit later or leaving early, or chucking a meeting-heavy culture in favor of creating more "maker time." It's control over place, space, and pace.

Being a hermit at work isn't about being mediocre, and being an introvert doesn't condemn you to making a less-than-stellar impression. It's not about working less hard than your colleagues, but about working differently. It's about being awesome when you need to be so you can earn the autonomy, alone time, and freedom you need in order to thrive.

## Making the Change

We learned many years ago that in the workplace, autonomy and control help engage people. It doesn't matter whether or not you're a parent. It doesn't matter whether you're married or single. Doesn't matter whether you're Gen Y or a Boomer. For example, accounting giant EY has measured retention from a flexibility perspective for a decade, and they know that the top 25 percent of teams in terms of levels of flexibility—meaning team members can determine where, when, and how the work gets done—have five points better retention than the bottom 25 percent.[1]

Work culture is changing, and breaking the hermit's way. Technology, of course, has ushered it along. Since many office workers don't literally need to be together to get work done, it's now much more acceptable to work away from the office. Things that would have been considered shocking just twenty years ago (replying to your boss at eleven thirty at night in a nonemergency situation, for example) are now quite normal. And here's what's really interesting: Americans don't seem to mind feeling tethered to office work by their devices as long as they don't have to physically be at the office. Gallup polling finds that among U.S. workers who report they frequently check e-mail away from work, 86 percent say it is a somewhat or strongly positive development to be able to do so. The same poll finds that when "asked how much time in a typical seven-day week they spend working remotely using a computer or other electronic device, such as a smartphone or tablet, employees who report checking their e-mail frequently say they spend nearly 10 hours working remotely."[2]

Many freelancers can also live with it. Talia Borodin, who recently opened her own consultancy, has a policy that directly addresses her life as a freelancer: "I frequently respond to e-mails after hours," she says, "but since I work one tenth the hours I did when I was full-time, it seems like a fair trade."

Perhaps the biggest change is the sheer variety of working styles we have now, from people who happily work at coworking spaces like WeWork or Workbar, to full-time office workers, to people like me who are 100 percent work from home. Indeed, all three work styles may even be collaborating on the same project or working for the same company! Maryella Gockel, who has pioneered flexible work at accounting giant Ernst & Young for years, likens the evolution of work styles to the famous "quiet car" on commuter trains and Amtrak. Some love it, some hate it, but it's a great option to have. In innovative environments, she says, work is moving away from "all day, every day." Instead there are all-hands-on-deck times, and time-off times.

In newer companies where digital natives increasingly prevail, "flexibility" can be baked in. Kathryn Schotthoefer, President of Heavenspot, a part of advertising giant M&C Saatchi, notes that in her fast-moving digital entertainment company, "As long as everyone gets their job done and can work collaboratively with other people, it doesn't really matter to me when they're in the office."

When you're just starting out in an office environment, of course, you most likely will need to put in the face time, especially when you're in an environment where being present means being committed. But as you advance in your career, you can negotiate from a position of power. And if you're an executive with hermit tendencies, you do have the power of changing culture at your company.

Mighty Networks' Gina Bianchini laughed when I asked her if she knew any powerful hermits in Silicon Valley. "Everyone I know is a hermit," she said. At Mighty, employees weekly work from home, coming into the office for scheduled meetings and check-ins.

## SLUDGE

We've all heard it:
   "Nice of you to finally join us!"
   "Leaving early?"
   "Is he ever at his desk?"
   "Must be great to work from home every Friday."
   "Another sick day?"
There's a very specific kind of workplace passive aggression: sludge. The term was coined by workplace innovators and consultants Cali Ressler and Jody Thompson, who write, "Sludge is the workplace chatter that reinforces the idea that people can't be trusted with complete autonomy."[4]
   If you are an office hermit, you're probably familiar with it. In work

systems where rules and rewards are based on traditional values, someone who tries to make her own schedule and rules of engagement is going to get some flak. (There's even social sludging: if you don't want to go out to the office lunch, or you skip happy hour, you get a reputation as a pill.)

Maryella Gockel smiles at how her firm's quest to create a flexible environment sometimes backfired. "We put in these great, comfy chairs where you could put your feet up with your laptop," she says. "But the minute folks said to people, 'Gee, you look comfortable,' people stopped using those comfy chairs. It was code for 'Are you really working?'"

You can try to ignore the criticism, knowing your results are great, or engage your colleagues to change their view of commitment. But let's face it: people can be petty assholes, and there's only so much you can do to change others' perspectives. It's probably easiest to try to understand that sludging is often unconscious, and their comments have less to do with you than with their own insecurities or their own business practices.

Or, you can always sludge back. One great suggestion from Thompson and Ressler: if a coworker says, "Leaving early?" say, "Oh, I'm sorry, did you need my help?"

In such a short amount of time, the concept of working from home has changed so dramatically and allowed for a hermit lifestyle in the corporate world. From 1998 to 2010, tech giant Sun Microsystems' philosophy of "open work" meant around twenty thousand Sun employees spent an average of three to four days out of the office, wherever they wanted to work. When they wanted to get out of the house, remote employees could check in at Sun "drop-in" stations, plug a data card into the system, and pick back up on their work. This innovation helped pioneer cloud computing! And the company saved over hundreds of millions in energy and real estate costs.[5]

Now, mega-corporations like Deloitte, IBM, Dell, and United Health Group not only have strong percentages of employees who work remotely, they have assigned aggressive targets to make half their workforce remote in coming years.[6] My friend Casey Carlson, for example, manages a thirty-person Deloitte team in India from her home office in suburban Boston.

Work+life fit is becoming less gendered, and that's essential. Take for example Nirad Jain, a New York City–based partner at Bain, an elite consulting firm where the average partner earns $1 million per year. He is proudly quoted bragging about his work+life fit: When his two-year-old daughter, Isha, woke up with a temperature of 104, he stayed home from an important client meeting while another partner "insisted on flying to the meeting, both to help keep the project on track and to support Nirad's parenting needs."[7]

If a high-status executive dad can brag in a national magazine about taking time for his children, a person in middle management should be able to point out that the world won't end if she misses a meeting, too. We can only hope that what's happening at Bain bodes well for the rest of us looking for flexibility when we need it most.

## Finding the Right Role, in the Right Environment

My mom, an only child who grew up feeling lonely, loved working in a hospital because, as she said, "It's like working in a family." She thrived in that committed group in an intensely human setting, and loved teaching for the same reason. My father, at the other extreme, always said to me, "The best boss in the world is an asshole." He was a labor arbitrator and an art dealer on the weekends, and was proud to be self-employed. I can still hear the tap-tap-tap of his typewriter and smell the cigarette smoke as he wrote briefs from his home office in the attic.

Both my parents liked their work well enough, but they especially liked the environment in which they worked—even though, in my dad's case, his freedom came with enormous financial instability. For the workplace hermit, environment is key, and some workplaces are far more hermit-friendly than others.

Leah Ginsberg, now Deputy Editor of *Forbes* Women's Digital

Network, started out in a very "old-school" media company. "It was ten to six on the dot," she says, "and if you were two seconds late, it was, 'Where were you?'"

Leah loves her work as an editor, because "You're in your own head a lot," she says. "I love to just fall down a research rabbit hole." She also understands that her best ideas don't come in meetings. "I don't work exactly the way other people do in terms of brainstorming," she says. "I prefer to be able to think about things on my own beforehand."

A great deal of Leah's satisfaction is because she knows herself well. She's an introvert, not a morning person, and she doesn't like her every movement tracked by a boss. She has a lot in common with many of us hermits, and she's made her corporate job work for her; she found the right kind of role, and she knows exactly what kind of office culture she thrives in.

# GETTING STARTED

## The Questions to Ask

Like Leah, I've talked myself into many jobs that weren't a fit because I was a fan of the company or attracted by the prestige or the money. But when, like Leah, you know your own boundaries, you can avoid a bad fit right from the start by tuning into signals even before the interview.

Mercedes De Luca, COO of Basecamp, says e-mail can be the first sign. "If the HR rep is e-mailing you at midnight and scheduling interviews for Saturday afternoons, those are red flags," she says. Another warning sign is the immediate e-mail response. "You know they have an always-on-e-mail culture," she says. "It can be hard to work in that environment, and people often wind up catching up weekends and nights." Social media chatter is also revealing. "If your candidate company skews negative on platforms like Twitter, LinkedIn, or Glassdoor, reach out to your networks and raise questions in your interview to fact-check your findings."[8]

It's also important to simply observe the office on your first visit, Leah says. In one job she took, "When I went in to interview, you could hear a pin drop. It could've been a clue for me." A sneaky trip is to schedule a meeting very early or very late to see how full the office is. Best of all is to have a friend or the friend of a colleague give you the inside scoop.

Then, once you're in the interview, it may be beneficial to ask what a day in the office is like, or how many meetings you would typically have in a week. Most of us can't just say, "I want to be able to come in when I want and I want to do this," but you can listen for code words. *Entrepreneurial*, Leah says, can mean managers encourage innovation—or that you're expected to have no life outside of work. Having to interview with an HR gatekeeper first may be another sign of corporate inflexibility.

One of the biggest bullets I ever dodged was being turned down for a CMO role because I asked to temporarily work from home a few days a week while nursing my four-month-old baby. Even though I lived ten minutes from the office, even though half the company was located in another state, and even though they were ready to make me an offer!

## THE JOB SHARE

It's not always about switching careers. If you're in the right role for you, it's picking the rhythm and pace you need. And finding a creative way to shift your pace when you know you're in the right job can be the key to a happy work life.

Take Maisie Pollard. She's a C-level executive at a major hospital, a powerful role. She defies the stereotype that an atypical work schedule automatically means less prestige or salary.

Maisie was one of the youngest-ever chief administrative officers at Beth Israel Deaconess Medical Center in Boston, working a typical sixty to seventy hours a week, when she had her first child. She wanted to cut her hours, so her boss suggested she dial down to four days a week in the office.

The problem was, she says, "It was sixty or seventy hours in four days instead of five days. So I thought I needed to switch careers. I went to a career counselor, and we circled my ideal jobs from the newspaper. Lo and behold, it kept coming back to, I'm in the right job and I'm in the right career, but it wasn't right for my work-life balance."

The woman who had held Maisie's job before was still on as an internal consultant. Slowly, this position started to evolve into a job share. "She knew everything, and it allowed me to work less," Maisie says. "She did a lot of clinical work. I did more of the management and business side." Maisie saved budget on additional roles that weren't needed because she and her partner could do so much more.

"The other wonderful thing," Maisie says, "was that our kids were at different points in their lives. Hers were older, mine were little. We evolved into [working less] when the kids needed us in different ways."

Maisie's story highlights an important thing to consider: You might be in the right job, but you simply have to alter the structure of that job to keep going. Or, you might be in the right field, but in the wrong position. To me, this is the true definition of flexibility: crafting the day-to-day realities of your work so you can thrive and be amazing at what you do.

## Finding Your Team and Communicating Well

The hermit executive can do a lot to create a culture that empowers people to work in the way that makes them thrive. Good teams understand their members' work styles, and, like good teachers, create an environment that encourages tolerance and collaboration. And the corporate hermit must seek that kind of environment.

We all know the difference a bad boss and a bad team can make. (Think of Gary Cole in *Office Space*, surveilling the floor and taunting staff if they aren't there when he's looking.) Flexible work environments have less tolerance for bad managers and poor communication because tyranny doesn't work well. Maryella Gockel explains how work at innovative companies is changing from merely creating policies for flexible work to helping managers create teams that can thrive as a flexible unit. "You've got a raging extrovert who gets energy from office conversations, and someone who needs more space and quiet," she says. "How do you create that inclusive team where people understand how people do their best work?"

You may be lucky and work in an environment with flexibility and autonomy baked in. Workplace expert Cali Yost calls them high-performance flexible environments. In this kind of flexible work culture, employees don't ask for permission, but they are proactive in planning and communicating. "Everyone has a responsibility for their plan," she says. "You've got to make sure you're updating them on where you are and what's going on. Expectations have to be clear with your manager and your team."

## STAYING ALERT

**"I'll be online later."**

We all say it, and we all feel we have to. These four little words that make us feel better for taking time out during the day or finishing early. They're like an insurance policy against being sludged.

But, if you're a work+life rebel, you do mind the expectation that even though you're leaving at a reasonable time, or on a flexible schedule, you have to be available whenever, wherever.

Because smartphone technology is fairly new, we're still creating norms and ways to cope with the always-on expectation. There is no single answer. But if those four words are ruining your happiness at work, here are some enlightened approaches to curbing your accessibility.

***Core hours/norms.*** Blocking off availability is the first step to freedom. Web-development business owner Lauren Bacon sets the norm for client expectations up front: her firm doesn't return calls after business hours. (She and her cofounder make sure to model respect for the rule: if they do work late, they take the equivalent amount of time off.) At the business accelerator Bionic, founders have established a company norm that staff are only available via e-mail/phone/text between 7 A.M. and 7 P.M., Monday through Friday. Other firms set core meetings hours from 10 A.M. to 4 P.M. One friend has an easy-to-follow "go dark" rule: if it's dark out, she is not expected to be on call.

*Schedule your e-mail traffic.* My life changed when I discovered Boomerang, a software tool that allows me to schedule my e-mails. (Basecamp has a similar feature.) This means I can work late at night or Saturday morning (my favorite), but recipients won't see my e-mails until Monday morning. Scheduling your e-mails is a wonderful gift, because, as we know, one sent e-mail can start a hamster wheel of activity. Professional services firm JDI's CEO Josh Jones-Dilworth uses the Slack program to indicate team availability: he knows that if he e-mails a client late at night, what started as a simple message can escalate into a late-night full-on work session.[3]

*Institute a "Sabbath."* Nowadays, renowned business leaders are all about the "digital Sabbath," when you unplug from Friday night to Saturday night. If you're in a position to do so, pilot a Sabbath with your team. If not, take one yourself, and talk about how wonderful and healing it was. People might get the message.

*Find a job where extra time costs extra money.* Most salaried positions don't pay overtime, so your management doesn't care how many hours a week you work or how many e-mails they send you at midnight. But for jobs with overtime, any work above a certain number of hours must be approved. When your boss has to pay more to e-mail you, suddenly your time off becomes sacred to her. You can institute "overtime" into your work as well. Lauren Bacon considers contact outside of office hours to be overtime, so her core hours save her clients money.

Own your time. Until every country adopts a version of the French "right to disconnect" law in which employees have a legal right to take a break from e-mail and accessibility (and I'm not holding my breath), office hermits may have to cobble together solutions. But remember expert Cali Yost's advice: your boss doesn't want you to be so unhappy that you're at risk of leaving. So here's an idea: take control, and just stop responding after hours unless it's really urgent. Don't send texts after appointed off time, don't promise you'll be available. Be the work+life rebel. My team at

Women Online has done this for years. I must admit it annoyed me until I just accepted it and gave up. If I really need them, I call.

***Skip "shallow work."*** As Dr. Cal Newport says, "No one ever got promoted because they were great at answering e-mail." Newport argues that maintaining your in-box, or posting basic social media content, is low-value, or "shallow," work. Shallow work might help pay the bills and manage your logistics, but deleting e-mails is not adding your unique skill or voice to the world. To maintain a true competitive advantage, you should be engaging in "deep work," which Cal defines as a skilled activity applied at a high level—in other words, your expertise. I don't know about you, but I don't get many e-mails at 10 P.M. that require me to dive right into deep work.

## Try a Hermit Pilot

As you know, I'm a big believer in the value of pacing and cycles. If you're a hermit executive, you probably don't want to be White House press secretary or an ER physician. Talk about extreme working environments. If you're an ambitious corporate hermit, it's crucial to find not only the right culture but the right pace at work.

The successful hermit works in a flexible team that doesn't sludge, and also takes advantage of the cycles of a typical office job. For example, if you are in professional services, different clients will have different expectations, and it's hard for most managers to defy those expectations. If you have a very demanding client, flexibility may be limited for the duration of that engagement. On another assignment, a client might be okay with letting you set the pace. Of course there are intense times, but honestly, if there's a crisis every single day at your white-collar office job, something is seriously wrong with the company.

Even if you have a rigid manager—one who doesn't understand why anyone might want to work from home, you can set up a pilot. It can begin with one person saying, "You know, I need four hours of unbroken time this week, and here's how I'm going to do it." Don't be afraid to ask for a "hermit pilot," where you try the job for three months or some other specified period of time. It may be that with some tweaks, you're able to find a rhythm you all agree with—and you may even get some company. (And probably some sludging.)

"You don't say, 'I want to be a hermit,'" Cali says, "because many people can't fathom why you would want that. So you want to say, 'Hey, I'm more productive if I get these chunks of time where I can just focus. Here's how it's going to help me, here's how I'm going to do it, and here's how people can reach me if you need me.' " In her experience, being responsive and accountable is the main thing managers want. If you are able to be 100 percent committed when you're required to be on, you can earn a lot of slack to control your time and place.

Cali says there's a common problem among workplace hermits: they quit before even asking. She says, "I have had managers tear up and say to me, 'I absolutely would have listened. I didn't know!'"

Failing to negotiate a better schedule with a boss before leaving is like getting divorced without telling your partner you're unhappy. But Cali notes that our work culture makes people afraid to ask for what they specifically need. Instead they go global. "They'll come into the office and say, 'I can't travel anymore,'" Cali says.

Cali has interviewed hundreds of managers, and she knows what they want from their employees: a plan. "What are you going to do on your out-of-office day? Who is covering for you? If people do need you, how do they communicate to you?" You must advocate for yourself, she says, because another thing managers want from their employees is to not have to micromanage. Cali says, "You've got to think first, 'What do I need? What does it look like this week? How, when, and where can flexibility help me do that?'"

There also needs to be a check-in in place. "Across the team, there needs to be a mechanism to make sure everyone's tasks are coordinated, and that expectations are clear," Cali says. In other words, making sure stakeholders don't feel like you're a pain in the ass.

Remember, other people on your team may have work+life fit goals, too! Your team can change as you do. Your best team doesn't care that the next day after you're wiped out from a huge pitch you're working from home. They think, 'Wow. She did a great job on that pitch.'

Obviously, it also helps to do your job really well. Think of it like this: the most successful salesmen might spend a hell of a lot of time on the golf course (or in strip clubs). No one judges them for it because they bring in a lot of revenue.

## Sales: A Hermit's Paradise

Being on the road and pressing the flesh may not seem like the obvious choice for a hermit, but for making your own hours and being free of supervision, it can't be beat.

Anne Greenwood, who managed hundreds of people in the brokerage industry on Wall Street notes that her sales staff "had total freedom." What she focused on was results. "As long as you're building your business and keeping your clients happy, it's up to you. I literally had people who I didn't see for two weeks."

She adds, "If you're in sales, you will never have to miss a kid's soccer game, a school play, or the tea party with the teacher in first grade on Fridays. And no one is going to ask you where you are."

Another great job is pharmaceutical sales rep. (I'm sure you've seen them while at a doctor's office, with a little rolling suitcase and a nice car.) In fact, pharmaceutical sales gets top marks as the best overall job for working mothers, according to *Forbes*.[9] In a survey of 250 pharmaceutical sales reps this quote stood out to me: "Feeling like I'm self-employed, because I have flexibility in my job."[10] They get the perks of being self-employed, but they have the back-office support and compensation that small-business owners rarely achieve.

If sales scares you, change how you think about selling (we'll tackle this in Chapter 11). Being judged on the revenue you bring into a firm is a lot of responsibility, but the flip side is control and freedom.

## Surviving the Open Plan

I can't tell you how many times I've been at a client's office space and needed to pump breast milk, and I've found the reserved and private "wellness" rooms occupied by workers seeking refuge from their open-plan offices. Indeed, "how to survive an open office" is a very popular search on Google.

So here are some strategies.

Open-plan offices became en vogue in the postwar era as architects and management theorists tried to break down social and human barriers by removing doors and walls.[11] The first iterations of open plan featured rows and rows of desks in a line. In the 1960s, cubicles came into fashion, sort of a compromise effort to offer junior workers some privacy, while employees of a certain status had private offices that ringed the cubicles. Now trends are leading back to desks and tables without any barriers, often referred to as "pods," that are even for senior leaders. After all, open plan saves money and space and increases transparency (it's tough to check Facebook or shop for shoes when everyone can see your monitor). A recent meta-analysis of open-plan workers found that open office spaces cause conflict, high blood pressure, and increased staff turnover.[12]

Office design changes with time, and it has an enormous effect on how an office culture functions. Alan Dandron, a design principal at the Architecture and Interior Design firm Mancini Duffy, says that the hierarchical and transactional layout of many offices is gone—and Alan says he's seeing more offices without desks entirely. Now, he says, spaces reflect how work is more collaborative, "but the design industry has been slow to take introverts into account."

A few tips from the experts:

"Face outward," says Geoffrey James, contributing editor at *Inc.* magazine. This gives you a sense of privacy, and you can't be taken by surprise by a coworker sneaking up on you or reading over your shoulder, which can trigger a cortisol-upping startle. I'll never forget the day I was instant messaging a colleague about what a "dumb fuck" the new CEO of my start-up was when, of course, he instantly appeared over my shoulder. It was a move worthy of Ilana in *Broad City,* and needless to say, I left the job soon after the incident.

The stress of an open-plan office led Elan Morgan, who was working in development at a local university, to crack her molars from anxiety-driven jaw clenching. But she loved her work, so she tried to adopt a new philosophy to manage her cubicle. She bought a coat stand to create the illusion of a wall (some people buy plants or another curtain-like object). She built in time for walks and lunches outside or at places she enjoyed, and she created signals (such as wearing headphones) to make sure colleagues knew she couldn't be bothered. A colleague in her office taught her a true pro tip: observe the pattern of the week. There are quiet times you can count on. "It turned out that Wednesday afternoons were when everyone in her office was out at meetings," she says. Elan's colleague took that time to lie down in her cubicle and meditate.

"One day it occurred to me that no rule said that meeting rooms could only be booked for groups, so I booked myself a room for two hours and worked alone without interruptions. They were the two most blissful hours of my open-plan office life." Booking a small conference room on a regular basis, just for yourself, could provide the decompressing time you need in the workplace.

Office design trends are shifting in response to a zest for "collaboration" and also to the way technology is changing work styles, but office designer Alan Dandron says there's a bit of a backlash against all that open, collaborative space. His clients want more small rooms and hideaways. His challenge is to balance corporations' desire for efficiency with humans' desire for some privacy.

Spaces are specifically designed to support a behavior, which means there's less waste, Dandron says, "but also we know you need support spaces that make the open spaces work." In private offices, his clients frequently "request a little living room set up—sofa and all. They want offices to feel more homey, and they know they need to create private spaces for phone calls and conversations within the open plan. At the same time meditation rooms, gyms, and lactation rooms are becoming more and more common."

One day, I hope, all companies will design work to suit many different temperaments, including neurodiversity and those of us who react strongly to sensory stimulation. Imagine if you got to choose what kind of physical space you worked in every day, just like you might choose your health-plan option or order office supplies. Someone who needs quiet could be in a quiet space, and the extroverts could all sit around a big table. Then everyone could come together for meetings or very focused sessions. As demand for highly skilled high-tech talent and high connectivity further impacts how we work, those days can't be too far off!

Until then, if you must work open plan, there are ways to hack it. The good news for hermits: what's really shifting is that offices are becoming about places to meet, and much work can be done anywhere.

## When Corporate Life Just Doesn't Fit

Sometimes, even the most flexible environment isn't right for you. But, when even a schedule can't change, there are still ways to keep the relationship. Think about becoming a consultant to your current organization—this can be a great strategy when you need to dial down but aren't ready to completely change things up. You'd be surprised at how many organizations are open to employees going 1099 (e.g. becoming a consultant) or part time. Think about particular tasks you could continue to do as a freelancer, from home. Perhaps there's one part of job you are spectacular at, and everyone would be fine with you continuing solely on that.

I counsel many people who leave steady and prestigious jobs for the unknown of freelancing or small business. I try to help them be realists and not fantasists, because even the happiest hermits can have a bittersweet relationship with their new, leaner life. Just like any job, working for yourself provides good and bad days. Just remember, if you're ready to make the leap, you don't have to storm out the door and never return. You can ease your way out of the nine to five and learn if self-employment is for you.

## EARN IT. THEN OWN IT.

I believe that if you do a great job and work hard, you've earned the right to control your own time and location at work. You're a grown-up, you'll do what you need to do and show up when you need to. Autonomy shouldn't be a perk. And yet: I can't tell you how many very senior and acclaimed professionals I've interviewed who show up, day after day, at the office, simply because that's the norm.

Here's the thing: taking control of your time might actually earn you more power at work. Next time you feel cowed in the face of a culture of face time, channel the privileged white male.

In my career, I've always known successful men who come in early to prove their eagerness, then disappear for much of the afternoon. It's assumed they're off doing something important. Patriarchy wins again. Watch the senior executives in an organization (who, let's face it, are probably privileged white men). They work hard, but at any given time, do you know where they are? No! They could be out on a sales call, on the golf course, or at home napping, for all you know. And they like it that way.

High-status men understand how to use the system to have their cake and eat it, too. Recently, a study of 726 MBA men and women showed that though both sexes preferred flexible hours, the men did not take advantage of formal telecommuting programs as frequently as the women.[13] Instead, when they wanted to work from home or remotely, they simply did. They didn't feel the need to ask permission. Perhaps they understood that simply being flexible without asking for it maintains their power.

Most professional women only begin to take advantage of official workplace flexibility policies when they have a caregiving crisis, whether for a baby, partner, or elderly relative. This automatically positions their flexibility as a perk.[14] It strips power from the worker who uses it. It mommy-tracks us, when instead, our autonomy should be valued and rewarded.

I'm going to say it again: control over pace, place, and space is NOT a mommy issue! Everyone has their own work+life fit, and if you're an introvert, yours may not include sitting in an open-plan office fifty hours a week. If you love your career and you want to stay in it, don't let lack of flexibility or a poor work+life fit chase you out! Remember what workplace expert Cali Yost says: most managers feel shocked when employees quit over a work+life fit conflict. They don't want you to leave. So next time you're chafing against silly face-time rules, think like a boss and take what you need. Try a stealth pilot and start working from home more. Do an even better job while you're taking what you need, and I promise you, no one will complain. Build in what you need, communicate wisely, kick some butt, and bring your manager along.

Finally, if you're just starting out, this all may seem unrealistic—and it might be. You might have a few more years of proving yourself. I started out as an executive assistant, and for the first few years of my career it was my job to be chained to a desk (so my bosses could come and go as they wanted!). That doesn't mean you can't prepare for more flexibility a few years on. For now, spy on the more senior people you respect. Monitor their comings and goings. Are there any who seem to have worked out a really great gig? Ask them how they did it.

When you know what you want, and you see role models who've figured it out, you'll be on a much quicker path to autonomy and your happier hermit work life.

# 11

## *Sell Like Yourself!*

Get out there!"

"Dominate."

"Always be closing."

When we think of sales, we think of the iconic image of Alec Baldwin in the film *Glengarry Glen Ross*. "Put that coffee down!" he yells at a terrified Jack Lemmon, Baldwin's alpha lumbering over Lemmon's beta male with Donald Trump–like predation. "You can't close shit, you are shit," he sums up, wearing a watch that costs more than Lemmon's car.

I call this the "fuck you" stance of sales.

Like the patriarchy, the image of the salesman as an alpha male asshole is internalized into our work culture. Worse, the obnoxious, dominant salesperson can be extremely effective in communicating power. As Courtney Nichols Gould, CEO of SmartyPants Vitamins, an eight-figure company she started in her house, puts it, "What makes you a great entrepreneur can make you a crappy person."

Because we think success is about being a shark, we forget that kindness, caring, and pride in your work is one of the most powerful tools. We worry we'll be stereotyped and our work devalued. But the gifted introvert salesperson is a secret weapon for any organization or small business.

My heroes don't use fancy watches to win business. They own their worth and their expertise, and get paid. Pride in your craft is one of the most successful selling points anyone can have. It beats a hundred hours of schmoozing. It inspires clients, drives word of mouth, and it keeps your shop humming, because the easiest new business to win comes from someone who is already your customer.

Bathroom-hiders face many common hurdles when it comes to selling a product or negotiating a deal. But know that your wonderful empathy plus a commitment to doing great work make you a strong salesperson and negotiator. You just need to stop trying to be someone else.

## Suiting Up

When Courtney Nichols Gould was a new media executive, she modeled her sales technique after the top performers in her field, which meant taking her clients to strip clubs. She was competitive about it, too; she even knew the names of all the strippers. "I was going to out-dude every dude there," she says.

But, once she was flying high as the top salesperson at her company, Courtney says, "It felt wrong. Wrong like, 'This isn't me.'" She didn't feel dominant. She felt sorry for the women working in the strip clubs.

"So much of what we are taught in sales comes from a place of scarcity," Courtney says. But as CEO of SmartyPants, her perspective has changed. "I believe when you're pursuing your passion, you're not selling as much as you're inviting customers to join you."

Like Courtney, I learned how to sell by watching people around me; when I ran marketing departments I was constantly being sold to, and I tried to pay attention. As a client of ad agencies and digital publishers, I, too, was invited along to strip clubs (I said good-bye at the door and let the guys go on without me) and enjoyed some great steak-house dinners.

Many gifted salespeople come up through the ranks selling like everyone else, until they reach a point where they're confident enough to sell like themselves. And that doesn't have to mean always playing hardball, like the real estate agents we watch on *Million Dollar Listing* or the cast of any number of films and TV shows about Wall Street or Washington, D.C. When I started my own business and had to start selling rather than being sold to, I tried to mimic everything I'd learned. I tried to act like an alpha dog.

The problem was, I always felt like I was playing dress-up in someone else's clothes. As a green entrepreneur, I was definitely selling out of someone else's playbook, and I'm pretty sure people could tell I was new to the game. It finally hit me that I needed to own my sales style at a meeting with a potential client at Henrietta's Table, the power breakfast spot for much of Boston and all of Harvard.

The client I was courting was a wealthy man pushing sixty. He ran a cool new "one for one" start-up (think TOMS shoes: buy one, and the company will donate one to a person in need). I had been working for some time to get his digital marketing business. In fact, by the time of the breakfast we were on proposal version four—i.e., four executions of my free ideas—for him to consider. (Talk about taking advantage of hustle.)

In my mind, this breakfast meant we were finally sealing the deal. When the check came, I reached for it. "I always pick up the check for my clients," I said. "And you're my client now, right?"

He looked at me as if his teenage daughter had offered to pay.

After years of watching my husband and past vendors always treat at client dinners, I thought it was how it was done. But this client didn't respond to me when I mimicked being an alpha male. We had both internalized the patriarchy, me by mimicking "male" negotiating, and he by seeing me as a thirteen-year-old.

Needless to say, I didn't get the business. And that was the moment that convinced me I had to sell like myself.

As I grew as a salesperson, I kept pieces I really respected from past mentors (always be responsive; turn around proposals quickly; play the long game; and don't be afraid to act against your best interests if you think it's right for your client). Slowly, I stopped trying to change personalities in a sales meeting, and I began to I use my tune-in skills to read situations. Closing the deals became much easier.

## Passion as a Sales Tool

You've got to be hungry to close a sale, but we're trained to play it cool. (There's always another customer waiting in the wings, right?) Selling, we're taught, is like dating: play a little hard to get (i.e., create FOMO) and they'll want to be on board.

Well, I don't roll that way. In fact, the thing I hear most when I'm pitching is, "You are so passionate!" And I'm not afraid to show I'm hungry: I've even been known to say, "I want to work with you so badly," or "You are my dream client."

I used to take the comments about my passionate pitching as a compliment. After all, I love what I do and I am proud of what I know, and it makes me excited to talk about it. But displaying passion runs counter to our cultural norm of playing it cool, never wanting something too badly.

When I started talking to other entrepreneurs and leaders, I started to see that noting someone's passion can be dismissive, whether it's a man saying it to a woman, or even a woman to a woman. Tereza Nemessanyi, one of Microsoft's entrepreneurs-in-residence, points out when someone invokes your passion, it can be condescending, and, ultimately, dismissive. "There's a fine line between passion and 'crazy.' And passion and collaboration imply emotion—which isn't seen as bankable." (Why are we so scared of emotions in business?)

After all, Tereza says, you never see a male thought-leader or market-mover lauded for his "passion." (Think of calling the president or Bill Gates "passionate.") Men are celebrated for their courage, strength, and acumen. As Tereza points out, they don't have "passion," they have "focus." They're not "collaborative," they pull together an A-team.

I think this is less about gender, than about the dominant alpha-dog "fuck you" sales stance we all inherit. I know many authentically passionate men who absolutely love what they sell. And I know many men and women who are absolutely talented—and terrifying—at playing hardball during a sales process. What matters is selling like yourself, and not assuming a posture. And, after all, if you're an introvert or a hermit, owning your passion is essential. You don't need to schmooze clients over dinner if your product is going to rock their worlds when you talk about it on the phone.

I've also found that if you own your passion in the moment because you truly take pride in your work, you cultivate an infectious quality that drives incredible referrals from your current customers. You can also have personal passion for the relationships you develop along the way. If you care for your clients as you do your colleagues and friends, you will find your clients actually do become friends.

I have been with my clients through cancer, deaths in the family, babies, miscarriages, frustrations with bosses, desires to quit, and everything else in between. I try to convey to them that it is a privilege to work with them and share the journey. And I believe, in most cases, people buy the products and work with the proprietors they feel good about.

Susan McPherson, owner of McPherson Strategies, is one of the most generous and caring people I know. She owns a leading corporate social responsibility consultancy, and she's an angel investor and board member of the UNHCR's nonprofit arm. She's *also* a powerful superconnector and an incredible networker. When I asked her how she got most of her business, she told me it was almost all inbound: people came to her. When I asked her what her secret was, she told me it was being good to people (and I can personally vouch for the fact that she is!).

And the connections she built weren't all necessarily face-to-face. "Years ago, before the Internet," she says, "I used to go through my Rolodex once a month, call my clients, and say, 'Just want to thank you for your business.' It was a human touch point. And because I was on the phone, it wasn't as scary as going to an event."

And way before Twitter, she was clipping articles and stuffing them in an envelope. Now social media lets her find a new platform to showcase the wins of others. "I know it's commonplace now to tweet something somebody says, but I've been doing that since the dawn of time."

So now, when people call me "passionate" and "collaborative," I say thank you. I own my niche, and I take pride in the clients that sign me up.

## The Ask . . . Without Asking

When I meet someone, even a client, and I can tell they aren't happy where they are, my brain starts creating new career opportunities for them. Ironically, this has turned out to be a great skill for biz dev. Sometimes I have even placed clients in a new role—and then I get to work with them again.

Stew Friedman, a renowned leadership professor at the Wharton School, notes that the connections we make through the sales process, networking, or negotiating are actually foundations of the social capital that drive our world. "When you approach a social encounter as an opportunity for you to discover something about other people that you can help them with, as opposed to take something from them, then you are inducing long-term reciprocity," he says.

The most successful business owners I know always go the extra mile and build toward that longer-term relationship. But it's not always directly related to their business. Some are excellent sources of recipes, travel ideas, child-rearing techniques . . . even tarot-card readings.

Even if it's unconscious, working toward that long-term relationship and discovering the interconnection between client work and life can foster both professional and personal success. Christine Koh has brought her love of blogging to several clients of ours, and helped them find their online voices. But, more importantly, her instinct for helping stressed-out parents pare down (beautifully expressed in her book *Minimalist Parenting*) has helped so many people in our professional network manage the overload. She's so passionate about her work and about helping other people that the interconnection between "client work" and life projects feels seamless.

Like Christine, Michael Ansara, a successful entrepreneur who's built and sold two companies in call-center and customer-service technology, believes in getting to know the real person behind the client, and sparking a relationship that leads into a sale. And this is the key for introverts in order to sell with authenticity—that passion we spoke about earlier. Michael is also a feminist hero. When his daughter Meg was battleground states director for Hillary Clinton's 2016 presidential campaign, she delivered her third baby six weeks before Election Day. Michael stayed with Meg those six weeks in her tiny Brooklyn rental, taking care of the newborn and bringing it to campaign HQ for Meg to nurse, seventeen hours a day, seven days a week.

As Michael explains, he builds loyalty by being interested in the actual client and what's going on in their world. "I'm a great believer in sending articles, books, magazines—anything that you think will be of interest to either a past client, current client, or prospective client—with no ask attached to it." Paradoxically, that leads to more sales than a hard ask ever would. "I always found that when you could become pretty much an indispensable source of ideas, many of which had nothing directly to do with your specific service that you were selling, then it becomes very easy to sell it," Michael says.

Mixing your business goals with your real passions means you'll enjoy the sales process more and remove any remaining ick factor. SmartyPants's Courtney Nichols Gould puts it perfectly: "I went from doing sales as selling something into doing something I believe in and inviting people to join me in what I love."

## Craftspersonship

Imagine your passion was building houses. If you knew a wonderful family planned to live in one, to raise their children there, you wouldn't treat the building as just a job. You would pour your heart and soul into the work, and after it was built, you'd check on it.

That's being a craftsperson. Craftspeople care about their work long after the contract is signed, while salespeople just cash the check and move on.

There is a firm that I consider a competitor, although they barely know who I am. Still, we share some clients and we have competed against each other for work. This firm wins big contracts and I often feel very envious of them. But over and over, I hear that they don't fulfill the promises they make. They're all razzle-dazzle. The firm focuses on selling, but not on their craft. And their clients don't leave happy.

Hillary Moglen, principal at the issue advocacy firm Rally, which helped win marriage equality, has won a reputation as a must-hire in a very niche but key field. She hates networking and "selling," and actually left a firm that wanted her to be more "market-y, shmooze-y, and network-y." They parted because she had proved herself in work, but not in bringing in business.

"Since then," she says, "I've had to find my own way of bringing in business. My philosophy is to find opportunities to talk specifically about the work we've done, and work that I've been particularly involved in. When I'm having to talk about our company and what we do broadly, that's less comfortable."

Hillary has cultivated craftsmanship, not salesmanship. She's no schmoozer. But get her in a room of public policy nerds (who are exactly the people who will hire her) and she is like a movie star. And almost 100 percent of her new business comes from referrals from past or current clients who love her work.

# GETTING STARTED

## Cultivate the Craftsperson in Yourself

Hands down, the easiest way for a hermit to keep business going is to do great work and then figure out some painless ways to drive word of mouth among happy customers or clients. Here are four steps toward building a craft-based business.

**Check your sales.** Obviously, you shouldn't lie to a client (although a little embellishment is expected), but it's just as important not to lie to yourself. You need to look at how you feel while you're actually *pitching*. Do you feel like you're saying what you think the client wants to hear, or faking what you think you should be saying? Does getting the project give you a sinking feeling? Sales are about more than a healthy spreadsheet (though that's great!).

**Check in.** Not only should you check in with clients as a good business practice, you should want to check in—to see how they're doing, to let them know what you're doing, and, most important, to see if they're happy. If not, you should offer to fix what they're unhappy about. A good craftsperson wants what they build to be working for the client, not only to lock down the sale.

**Deliver.** It's better to set clear boundaries about resources and time right from the beginning, because, in the long term, a client respects a contractor who can deliver the work, not only a promise.

**Examine your clientele.** Are you proud of those you work with? If you're not, chances are you're not proud of the work either. This doesn't mean everything you do needs to be glamorous and high profile, or the work you've always dreamed of. (You can even take on a stinker for the pay from time to time.) But you should take as much pride in a teeny, low-paying, low-profile project as you do a major one—and treat the client the same.

## Pitching for Introverts

As BlogHer cofounder Elisa Camahort Page puts it, the first part of a great pitch is owning your expertise. When you own your expertise, you are very clear in why you are an expert in what you do, you express it clearly, people feel it, and the benefits of working with you become clear. Being a master craftsperson means you know exactly why and how you own your expertise.

Selling like yourself requires a lot of practice. It must feel authentic, but it must also be effective. However you feel it, you have to be able to put it into words, and these words should be flexible. And you must be able to pitch for your company, a specific product you sell, or your professional services—for instance, as an expert speaker, writer, or teacher.

How? One of the most effective tools an early boss taught me was to develop a "boilerplate" pitch. This is about two hundred words of focused bio sentences mixed with a lot of specifics. It's your "who I am and what I will do for you." If you have the basic language, you'll be amazed how it will carry you through many growth experiences in your career.

And, if you're worried it makes you a braggart to sell yourself, don't. Experts offer good counsel and get things done.

# OWN YOUR EXPERTISE IN TWO MINUTES

### by Katie Orenstein, Founder of the Op-Ed Project[2]

Begin by filling these in. Don't overthink!

Hello, my name is_____

I am an expert in_____

Because_____

I admit, when I first did this exercise in a workshop, I said I was an expert in . . . "cats." It was funny, but it was also a cop-out. That answer was a way to defuse any bragging or hubris I might feel. But owning your expertise isn't hubris. It's what your client hires you for. When someone pays me tens of thousands of dollars or more in professional fees for my expertise in marketing and mobilizing women, they're not interested in how modest and self-effacing I am.

When you first do the exercise, you might find yourself adding qualifiers, like "I think I'm an expert because . . ." or "I suppose it's because . . ." Take those out. It's hard to be declarative and it feels weird, but it's the first step, and it's good practice for your pitching. Even your language in this exercise should own your expertise.

Once you have your basic pitch of who you are and why you're awesome, you'll need to develop some talking points that work effectively in a sales situation. Talking points support your expertise and give clients concrete evidence about why you're worth it. One example might be, "Our approach will save you X percent, because we are so much more efficient that other firms. In fact, when we worked for [insert impressive client example X] we saved them X percent over six months and increased their customer satisfaction." Talking points are some sales numbers, some razzle-dazzle names to drop, and some major successes. Focus. Quality beats quantity.

Think of your boilerplate as your outfit, and talking points as accessories.

My basic pitch is below. Talking points I might throw in vary. All are time-tested, and while they speak to different strengths, they reassure potential customers.

### BOILERPLATE:

*I'm the founder of the award-winning social-impact agencies Women Online and the Mission List. I can help your organization create an effective and efficient digital campaign that will mobilize your women consumers and turn them into advocates. I've been working with women online since 1999 and (fun fact) I helped Hillary Clinton log on for her first Internet chat. I've worked on over 175 online action campaigns, including four presidential campaigns, and raised over $100 million in online donations in my time. I've helped President Obama, Malala Yousafzai, the United Nations, the Bill and Melinda Gates Foundation, and many other leading figures and organizations create effective campaigns that mobilize women. I'm also a blogger, author, and podcast host. Online community changed my life, and I'm extremely loyal to it. I was founding political director for BlogHer.com, and have written for the* Harvard Business Review, *the* Huffington Post, MomsRising, *the* Wall Street Journal, *the* New York Times, *and the* Guardian.

Here's a guide to how I've developed the talking points for Women Online. You can apply them to your own:

**Numbers and efficacy:** Our work offers serious return on investment (ROI), and it's often more effective than traditional advertising. I like to have some impressive numbers to throw in here.

**Authenticity and deep community expertise:** I've been blogging since I got my start at iVillage, the original online community for women. All of my staff are content creators and influential bloggers, so we not only understand what moves women online, we work in a community we are part of and value deeply. Our work is built on relationships, not pitches.

**We're grown-ups:** When you hire us, you work with the senior-level talent, including me. You're not passed off to a junior account executive.

**We're experienced, and that experience translates:** We helped X organization build their entire online strategy, because our experience raising money for nonprofits and political campaigns meant we had a unique understanding of how to build a communications campaign that supports the growth of your donor base.

**Here's how we help clients solve problems:** Harvard Law School called us when they needed to get more women in their executive ed program, so we devised a strategy that reached women decision makers through the business media they consume. (This is a great one. Remember Michael Ansara's tactic? Throw in some relevant examples of how you helped past clients solve thorny issues.)

Now that I've been pitching for almost twenty years, I'm here to tell you, I could do it in my sleep. I still get nervous with in-between strategy talk and negotiating, and cocktail-hour banter makes me hide in the bathroom . . . but I can get up in front of any-size room and talk about my work.

That means it takes practice. Sketch a draft of your pitch. Show it to friends and trusted colleagues to make sure you're showcasing all your accomplishments. (You'd be surprised at how many you can forget!) Practice your pitch in front of a few friends, and get their feedback. Pitching them is more nerve-rattling than any future client will ever be.

## The Ask . . . for Money

If, like Alec Baldwin in *Glengarry Glen Ross,* you drive around in an $80,000 BMW and wear a watch that costs more than most cars, folks will assume you're worth whatever you ask. The "fuck you" method works here, too: when you assume that stance, your clients immediately assume you're worth every penny, whether you're in a hoodie or Céline. I always marvel at competitors who successfully charge triple what I do, simply because they assume the "fuck you" stance.

When you're passionate and nice, people can forget you actually need to earn a living. Doing incredible work for clients who love you doesn't ensure you're paid top dollar, or even what you're worth in the marketplace.

As the kinder, gentler seller, you need different strategies to ensure you're paid what you're worth. Here are three of my favorites:

**Invoke the cause.** Women experience 15 percent more success in a negotiation if they negotiate on behalf of someone else.[1] (I know, I know, it's ridiculous!) After maternity leave, women who state clearly to their bosses, "I need to work to support my family," get better opportunities and are paid more. (Don't get me started.) I find it helpful to remind people that my business is not for vanity and that my household depends on me, and I talk about the larger impact of supporting women's businesses. Women on average get paid seventy-seven cents on the dollar, and you don't want to be one of them.

You can even invoke the cause to yourself: if I'm feeling insecure or even greedy about quoting a high rate, I remember the people who are relying on me getting paid.

**Name-drop.** You may have noticed that in my pitch, I drop some pretty heavy names. Don't think of it as obnoxious, like it might be in a regular conversation. Putting forward strong credentials or clients is a great way to communicate how much you're worth. People want to be in good company. And it reassures them to know that other large outfits have trusted you. A brand name will do more for your market price and business development than a year of networking, and it prevents you from being devalued. If I'm sensing a potential client isn't taking me seriously, or we're negotiating on fee and they don't want to pay my rate, I'll make sure to weave in, "Well, when I worked for President Obama," or "When we won the award for promoting Malala's film."

**Be matter-of-fact.** Hillary Moglen, principal at the issue advocacy firm Rally, is not cheap. She knows exactly how much work goes into the end product, she knows how to make it successful, and she knows how much it costs. You get what you pay for in her shop, and it's not an emotional decision.

To get your facts in place, know your market and how much competitors charge. Scope carefully so you feel confident in your price. If you need to cut off 5 or 10 percent to get the job, fine. Then *be* confident. Sometimes you will try to achieve a certain sales price and you will fail. And sometimes you'll be pleasantly surprised.

I like to think that I'm evolving after years of invoking causes and dropping names. The older I get, the more I just want to say, *This is what I cost: take it or leave it.*

But as an anxious introvert, my ruminative nature can be difficult when I'm trying to sell, because I always second-guess everything and am convinced my client thinks I'm not worth the price I'm asking. Even worse, my general anxiety about money and bag-lady fears can make me feel desperate while I'm trying to sell, which is never good for the outcome. In my head I'm saying to myself, *If I don't get this contract I'm going to have to shut down the business,* while on the outside I'm trying to smile and close the deal. It's never a good combo.

If you get anxious when asking for money, channel the facts. You've done your homework, you know what you or your product is worth. If you get anxious, say in your head, *This is a fair price.*

**Most important, be yourself.** If you're a generous person, be generous in business. If you have a tendency to be Mama Bear, be Mama Bear with customers. If you're anxious, don't hide behind a fake set of armor. Your authentic self can drive your success. Listening to your authentic self is probably why you run a P&L in the first place. Some inner drive and sharp instinct brought you to this place. Now learn to define that instinct and make it work for your business and your life.

Whether you're selling a product, a service, or your company, use these strategies to see yourself past salesmanship and into craftsmanship and selling like yourself.

## Accepting "No" When You Feel Things in Technicolor

When I was working in corporate jobs, whenever a boss would give me negative feedback, I'd cry. They'd get upset or uncomfortable (of course). But whether the criticism was slight or major, I cared about the work, and hearing I was less than perfect literally made me feel like they were ripping my heart out.

Entrepreneur Christina Wallace calls this "feeling in Technicolor," and it's something we sensitive Hermits need to accept—and plan for.

Because here's the deal: if you're selling something, you will be turned down. It's a fact of life. If you're an anxious, introverted overachiever, though, you need to prepare yourself. A no can be made for any multitude of reasons, but chances are, you will hear no as "you're not good enough." Everyone hates rejection, but if you're already prone to rumination and overanalysis, the effect can feel like personal failure. You may catastrophize and blow things way out of proportion. (If I get negative feedback from a client, get passed over for a big new contract, or a client doesn't renew, I immediately assume I'm going broke.) Add your passion and craftsmanship to the mix, and you're likely to feel like they're turning down *you*.

But this is a moment that you can't let being über-sensitive win.

You can't grow in your career until you get rejected. Frankly, rejection is actually a sign your business is healthy—because it means you're casting a wide enough net both to get clients and to get important feedback.

If you're a Technicolor feeler, you've got to practice getting rejection and negative feedback. The best way is to find a trusted counselor who feels in black and white—ideally, a successful extrovert. (Mine is my husband.) They respond to rejection in a way we hermits can learn from. I have watched my Nicco and his alpha-dog colleagues shake off noes and think it's the other party's loss (even their fault!) because they don't let the no disturb the solid inner core of who they are.

When I'm castigating myself over a rejection, I try to remember all the guys who run our country. (Privileged white men, or PWM, as we call them in my house.) These men come from a world of abundance, so if they encounter a no, they assume it's just a temporary roadblock, and a yes is just around the corner.

And you know what? Even though they screw up right and left, say ridiculous things, and even commit crimes, they just keep going, rising to higher and higher levels of power.

So the next time a no sends you questioning the viability of your entire financial future or existence, brush it off. Instead of imagining you're going to get fired, lose everything, and become a bag lady, force yourself to be generous and expansive. Channel your inner PWM. Give yourself a break. Tell yourself, *That's okay. There's plenty more.*

**12**

# *Claim Your Negotiation Style*

The stereotype about a negotiation is that it's a game of chicken: someone has to leave the table or die. This approach is called combative, or positional, negotiation, and it's the alpha-dog territory we see in my personal favorite reality-TV genre: real estate shows. Think of the real estate agents saying "Do we have a deal? on *Million Dollar Listing* or any real estate reality show; think (gulp) of President Trump's bloviating tweets and what he calls "the art of the deal." It sounds like macho bullshit to me, but, apparently, many of our countrymen think that's what strong negotiation skills sound like. (I blame the patriarchy!)

Guess what: bathroom-hiders, counterintuitively, actually have a great advantage in negotiations, since we're strongly attuned to both others and ourselves, and we can sniff out bullshit. This lets us adjust to diverse situations and other people's expectations, which is crucial to successful negotiating. We know we need to prepare for several different outcomes because that lessens our anxiety. We want everyone to leave happy, and so we are great at making that happen.

Now I know to trust my gut and handle negotiations in my own introvert style: by doing my homework, asking lots of questions, and finding a common thread between me and my client.

I used to think negotiating was just for alpha dogs, and so when I did it, I quickly became a puddle. Meaning, I was so nervous that I said yes too quickly, and didn't fight for my terms. Instead of understanding that a negotiation isn't personal, and that a counteroffer doesn't mean the other party doubts your worth, I'd take everything personally. And give in. I left a lot of opportunity and financial benefit at the table simply because I was too scared to ask.

When I own my own style, I still don't always get exactly what I want. But at least I'm not a puddle.

## What's the Deal?

Nothing brings out my impostor syndrome more than asking for money to do work. When people balk at my figure, I'm usually pretty sure they're right: I don't deserve it. Even worse, it's hard to find a model negotiator, since most examples show you can only get what you want by being a shark.

Before I found my own style, the stress of negotiating made me so eager to get it over with (or avoid it altogether) that I usually left with less than I needed. This wasn't only about lining my own pockets; it also meant less for my employees and our consumer audience: the bloggers and content creators we hire. My insecurities were hurting my business.

Negotiation coach (and my personal guru) Tanya Tarr notes that the way we think about negotiating is as a "sledgehammer form of power." But there's a more flexible form of power, she says, one in which you are not married to options, but "inventive and imaginative, which makes it easier for another party to make a decision." This is called collaborative, or value-based, negotiation.

In value-based negotiation, unlike a shark, writes expert Natalie Reynolds, you want the other party to feel like they've won. "Otherwise," she explains, you'll have a client who leads with dissatisfaction. "They'll start asking for more, making late payments, not prioritizing your requests, or just being generally uncooperative."[1]

# GETTING STARTED

## Get Emotional

You may think that emotions and negotiations go together like chalk and cheese, but when it comes to emotions in negotiation, says Harvard Medical School associate professor Dr. Kimberlyn Leary, we don't have a choice. "You're always engaged emotionally if you're relating to other human beings," she says. The key is to use your emotions as a tool.

Dr. Leary says, "Emotions are really like a set of sensors that give you all kinds of valuable information about the other person, about yourself, about the interaction. If you can learn to use those as sources of data, you will get better outcomes."

If you're not a psychologist with years of training, how do you get in touch with your emotions and then determine how to handle them? Here's Leary's advice:

**Locate the trigger.** First you need to understand what emotions a negotiation is triggering (mad, sad, nervous, ashamed). If you can identify and regulate your emotions, you'll be more in control of how to handle the person or scenario. As the "getting to yes" guru Roger Fisher says, "Just because you're mad with your negotiating partner doesn't mean that the only thing you can do is raise your voice."

**Write about it.** Psychologist James Pennebaker has shown that as little as fifteen minutes of writing a night can help people significantly to understand their emotions, make connections between this event and that event, and actually contribute to their overall mental health.

**Picture it.** Harvard Business School's Mike Wheeler suggests using question prompts such as, what emotions do you typically feel before a negotiation? What would you like to feel? What are the ways that you can typically cultivate that feeling in your life? How could you adapt that behavior into the scenario?

**Tune in to your body.** Because often a negotiation happens fast, you can't analyze in real time, and your physical feelings are an actual clue.

**Check in, even at the table.** "As you're calculating the figures, calculate the emotional equation. Then you can catch up to yourself with the next thing that you say or offer, or don't say or don't offer."

**Talk back.** Negotiations and challenging conversations bring up all kinds of memories and baggage: of past bosses, stressful situations, and even your parents yelling at you. When you know what sets you off, you can set it aside. "So, this reminds me of my father, ex-boss, professor," Leary says. "Tell yourself strongly: they are not my father, grandfather, and professor!"

## GENDER'S ROLE

The weight of thousands of years of patriarchy manifests in every deal we try to make, and the system is rigged against us. Ask for too much, and it can backfire. (Even while negotiating with women.) And if you are anxious *and* asking for more, you are even more likely to be penalized.

I fondly call this the Bitch Tax.

Unfortunately, I'm not alone in doing this. According to Linda Babcock and Sara Laschever, authors of *Women Don't Ask:*

❑ Men initiate negotiations about four times as often as women.
❑ Women are more pessimistic about the how much is available when they do negotiate and so they typically ask for and get less when they do negotiate—on average, 30 percent less than men.
❑ 20 percent of adult women (twenty-two million people) say they never negotiate at all, even though they often recognize negotiation as appropriate and even necessary.[3]

Blech.

It's hard not to feel like a feminist traitor when you negotiate "like a woman"— i.e., think about communal benefits and shared values, and hold back from asking for the moon and stars. (Yes, it shouldn't be this way! Screw the patriarchy.) But negotiating "like a man" or judging yourself when you negotiate "like a woman" can be a mistake.

More and more, data show that acting like a man disadvantages you because either you don't seem authentic, or another party might punish you for assuming a traditionally male stance (the Bitch Tax). However, avoiding negotiation is very damaging for women. The key to staying at the negotiating table and achieving your desired outcome is to negotiate like your true self, accepting the role of gender norms and making them work for you.

Hannah Riley Bowles, one of the world's leading scholars on women and negotiation, has immensely helpful words of wisdom to make you feel okay about the tendency to be nice instead of a shark.

First, deliberately trying *not* to act like what Bowles calls the feminine ideal can backfire: "If acting forceful is your personality, great," she says, "but many times women change who they are in negotiations because they believe it's the only way to be successful. But if you start to say things that sound different than who you are, that's a red flag to the other party."

And avoiding certain negotiations may be an act of wisdom, not fear. A 2014 Harvard Business School study shows that though women avoid negotiations more often than men, it may be because they instinctively know when to negotiate and when to hold back.[4] They avoid strategically—either because the situations are not favorable to their negotiating style or because they're not experienced enough to negotiate that deal successfully. Whatever the reason, being attuned—not blindly ambitious—kept them from wasting time.

What matters is you getting what you need and deserve. I try to bring in a larger sense of purpose and use my natural self-deprecation as a tool. Few of my negotiations are about me becoming richer, much to the chagrin of those who depend on me for income. (Oh, well.) But that style translates as authentic to the client, who is more likely to respond positively—and actually make the negotiation successful—and I have become confident about rejecting negotiations that may not be fruitful before they begin.

## Collaborative Negotiation 101

What if you thought about a negotiation not as a win but as a success—one that makes both the client and you happy?

The first step toward a successful collaboration is attuning yourself—both to the situation, to your needs, and to the needs of your client. This work sheet by Tanya Tarr is an excellent way to lay out the basics of any negotiation.[2]

# Collaborative Negotiation Prep Worksheet
*Courtesy of Tanya Tarr*

Goal:

Objective: What's being negotiated:

## PEOPLE

| PARTY 1 | PARTY 2 |
|---|---|

### Interests: What are my motivations, needs, concerns and fears?

| | |
|---|---|
| Motivation: | Motivation: |
| Needs: | Needs: |
| Concerns: | Concerns: |
| Fears: | Fears: |

### What standards or values will guide making a decision?
(Ex. Fairness, accessibility, utility, tradition, market value, etc.)

| | |
|---|---|
| | |

### What happens if no agreement is reached?

| | |
|---|---|
| | |

**What is the minimum set of options that MUST be included for an agreement to occur?**

**What are the maximum resources available for an agreement to occur?**

**Do we have a NOPE situation? (No Options for Possible Engagement)**

**What are the potential options that could be a part of the final agreement?**

**Final Outcome?**

## Shooting the Moon

Once you realize negotiating isn't just for Mark Cuban wannabes and you can use your fantastic negotiation skills to align with organizations that share your values, not just maximize your money haul . . . you'll probably get what you always wanted. Because the bro-tastic (as Tanya Tarr calls it) version of negotiating is asking for the moon and stars, the rest of us may feel like we need to raise our price just to keep up. But actually, doing your research and being realistic is more likely to place you in an organization that shares those values—and where you can advance.

Tanya Tarr relates a story in which she and a "tall, good-looking white male" were candidates for the same, very competitive job. "We had roughly the same qualifications," she says. After doing her research, Tanya asked for $75,000, smack in the middle of the pay range for the job, but a healthy bump up from what she was already making.

The other candidate asked for $95,000 a year. Tanya found out later that that's why she had gotten the job, since when the other candidate overshot the range by $15,000, it made the company feel like he didn't know the sector and lacked expertise.

"P.S., in two years," Tanya adds, "I was making $95,000."

If the organization does reward the candidate with blind ambition with the job, Tanya suggests, "Think of that as a clarifying event that helps you understand that you probably don't have the same values the organization does. Is that really somewhere you want to work?"

## Your Negotiation Tool Kit

If you negotiate without a plan or a firm grasp on your emotional investment, you're much more likely to turn into a puddle, or try to act tough and be caught out. These steps can make sure everyone emerges happy.

**What motivates you?** First, you must know what's motivating you to get to the table. Tanya Tarr says, "If you don't know what truly motivates you, you really don't know what will satisfy you." The first question is tactical. Are you gunning for a new job for the salary? The new title? The opportunity to work with a new boss, or escape an old one? The second is what fundamentally motivates you as a person. For example, in working with Tanya, I learned I was less motivated by money or status than by the need to protect the ones I loved and those I care about.

**Know your BATNA.** BATNA, or best alternative to a negotiated agreement, is especially important when you're very attached to the outcome, and gives you a sense of power even in the most risky negotiation. For example, if you're negotiating for salary in a prospective new job, your BATNA could be that you'll remain in your current job quite happily.

**Know the zone of possible agreement.** Tanya Tarr interviewed ten CEOs about their approach in naming the first figure in a negotiation, termed *anchoring* in negotiation-speak. Half said never name the first number, and half said always do. Advice from your elders can help. Keeping it realistic is a strength, not a weakness. The zone of possible agreement gives you a basis from which to operate, however you negotiate; so you can feel comfortable being flexible.

**Remind yourself of your mission.** As you sit at the table, ground yourself by remembering your values and the larger purpose of your work. You should feel confident in what you're asking for, not just because you deserve it, but because it's right. Then, before you're tempted to say to yourself, *I'm asking for too much,* you can remind yourself that getting a raise sets a great precedent for others in the firm, or you can help pay off student loans, or provide a better life for your kids.

**Give evidence.** You may not feel empowered or deserving in the moment, and so it's important to have your reasons nailed down. Evidence might be that employees who work part-time in your field have focused contributions, or that your fee for a certain service is the lowest on the market. And it's not only valuable for the other side of the table: Tanya notes that the best way to squelch impostor syndrome is to have evidence ready of why you're asking what you're asking. Remember the idea of a "portfolio" of great facts about your work and awesomeness, or Jessica Bennett's concept of a Boast Bitch—an outside validator who can vouch for your worth.

**Practice**. Like most things in life, negotiating gets easier the more you do it. That said, no two negotiations are alike, and your stance might change given different scenarios. So role-play your terms with someone you trust, and in real life, experiment with different situations and personas. Negotiate everywhere! You might see what works best when seeking a lower price at the consignment store, for instance, or a better seat on the plane. When flying, I've learned that I can get an upgrade when I'm sweet and kind at the counter, not tough and threatening. I've been an upgrade queen ever since.

**Find your lucky socks.** Tanya Tarr wears Wonder Woman socks to situations that make her anxious. I have my go-to outfits, and believe me, the woman wearing them looks much richer and put-together than I actually am. Find the outfit that gives your confidence—even if it's superhero socks.

**Understand your counterpart's motivations**. Here's where being an anxious, hypersensitive soul really works for you. Put your attunement to work. When does the other person sound fearful? Angry? Relieved? Bored? What aspects of the situation seem to motivate them in conversation? Your observations can steer your responses and your strategy.

**Research, research, research.** Buying a car is one of the most dreaded negotiations out there, but I'm awesome at it. Why? USAA, to which I have a family membership, tells members the wholesale price of any car, features and all. I walk into the dealership armed with objective, bulletproof data, and I automatically win.

# YOUR EMOTIONAL BATNA

When I was younger, I went through a months-long, multiple-interview process at a hot start-up. I had to sneak out of my day job to meet them, and every time I got on the subway, I felt nauseated. When an e-mail from the hiring manager came into my in-box, my first instinct was to hit delete. I was so caught up in the notion of winning, I was ignoring its effect on me.

There's an emotional BATNA to every negotiation, too, and listening to it will keep you from wasting their time and yours. For example, if your asking price is keeping you up at night, consider lowering it. If negotiating a huge fee out of a contract is going to give you crippling performance anxiety, take less. Advice from Wall Street and Sheryl Sandberg notwithstanding, your emotional well-being is part of the cost-benefit ratio.

I'm going to contradict myself right now. Sometimes you need to toughen up and let go of fears that hold you back while still acknowledging and accommodating for the very real triggers that create unnecessary anxiety. My mentor Lisa Stone, cofounder of BlogHer and self-confessed "shy girl," reminded me that introverts especially have to get tough when it really matters.

Before she started BlogHer, Lisa was a journalist and reporter. When her divorce made her a single mother and her fear of the spotlight kept her from the managerial roles she needed to support herself and her son, her little brother gave her a talking-to, armed with his own facts. "Get over your desire not to lead teams. It's the only way you'll be able to support your son in Silicon Valley," he said.

Lisa realized her comfort zone behind the reporter's notebook would only get her so far. When she stopped being a solo contributor and became Executive Producer, she was supervising thirty-five people within the year. In the next decade, she would cofound BlogHer.com, the largest community for women in social media. In addition to the financial pressure, realizing her ultimate purpose, to break into the males-only zone of digital media, was key: "My discomfort was overcome by the need to actually change things."

## Always Consult Before Deciding (ACBD)

The bestseller *Beyond Reason,* by Roger Fisher and Dan Shapiro, discusses how we shouldn't pretend negotiating can or should be separated from emotions and interpersonal relationships. Consulting with others—whether they are involved in the negotiation or not—has three crucial benefits.

1. Other parties feel included in the decision making.

2. You might learn something through a consultation.

3. You still maintain veto power in a negotiation, but consulting another person allows them to give input, which can be valuable.

But more than even these points, ACBD provides checks and balances and a clear strategy for those of us who don't trust our instincts.

When I was in graduate school at Harvard, I cofounded a skills-building series for women graduate students called Effective Strategies for Powerful Women. A core team of women students convened six sessions led by big-name Harvard professors on everything from negotiating to strengthening communications skills. I loved working on it so much. I was a very gung ho member of the group, and at times I went too far on my own without consulting my other team members. As a result, the de facto leader of the team, who originally conceived the idea, froze me out, and I got none of the credit for organizing the sessions. By going too far on my own steam, I accidentally ensured I'd reap none of the rewards of my great work.

Like much of business, ACBD isn't rocket science, and it strengthens the notion that having a strong kitchen cabinet is one of your best strategies for success. If you're an introvert or a hermit, it may be hard for you to reach out, and in the middle of a tough time, you may be feeling low or depressed, making asking for advice even harder. One of the key signs of depression is a sense that you're not worth considering, so my telling you to consult someone for advice on a tough question at a tough time may feel rich indeed. But trust me, try to force yourself. Write out a script if you have to; ask for solid advice and engage another party in a big decision.

**We're in this together.** Columbia University scholar Beth Fisher-Yoshida lays out this intuitive approach, which I love to try to apply to negotiations and sales. It's simple: seek to establish an interdependence of goals. Meaning: if I succeed, you succeed, and if I fail, so do you. It's the opposite of a zero-sum shark negotiation, in which one person succeeds at the other person's loss. Fisher-Yoshida writes, "When we have familiar interests and attitudes, it is easier to believe we share common goals. This alignment is more likely to induce cooperative behaviors."[5]

**Use appreciative inquiry.** The practice of appreciative inquiry seeks to search for and activate the best in people. Tanya Tarr frames it this way: "Imagine how much fun a negotiation with a potential customer could be if you could activate your counterpart's sense of pride and wonder, because you feel it, too? Imagine if you put your natural sense of curiosity and interpersonal radar to use in a negotiation?"

Wharton's Stew Friedman reminds us that in any transaction, you can find a way to change it from taking to giving—to help the other party, either directly by serving them, or indirectly by connecting them to other people that you may know. This induces reciprocity, the engine of any good relationship. You can apply the relationship building to negotiations, because it's so important to engage the other party and learn about what makes them tick.

"One of the basic tenets of all modern negotiation theorists," Friedman says, "is 'the more you know about your partner's interests, the more likely you're going to get a better outcome for yourself.' What do you care about? What are you interested in? What matters to you? The more I know about that, the easier it is for me to fashion ideas for resolution that work for both of us."

## NEGOTIATING ISN'T EVERYTHING

I want to stress that yes, you can negotiate a great deal by employing your intuitive introvert skills. Your anxiety might drive you to prepare so well that you achieve an absolutely phenomenal outcome.

You might also decide to negotiate for just enough, and be happy anyway. Like so many things, the concept of negotiation is deeply affected by achievement porn. Real life isn't *Million Dollar Listing* or *Shark Tank,* and negotiating the most killer deal doesn't have to be a badge of honor. Think of Tanya's story; she didn't push for the absolute maximum salary in her initial salary negotiation, but she soon ended up making it anyway. She wanted to make sure she aligned with the organization, where, after all, she'd be spending at least nine hours a day.

The idea of settling for less in favor of achieving an outcome that would make you content feels foreign, I know. But if you decide that, as an anxious introvert, you want to minimize unnecessary stressors, or in a move to commit to a hermit lifestyle you also want to reduce maximizing your output, getting to just enough might be great. I often think of negotiating the way I think about setting the scope of work in a contract: I want enough work to feel committed and well compensated, but not too much to lose sleep or control over my time. All that matters in the negotiation is that you and your counterpart walk away feeling good. If you're trying to create a life for yourself that doesn't have you running for the bathroom, or suffering anxiety every day, just enough is perfect.

# 13

## *Be a Player from Your Home Office*

One of my superconnectors (you know, the person who always introduces you to the people who power your career forward), a former client, now a friend, invited me to the White House Correspondents' Dinner, aka "nerd prom." I was ten weeks pregnant and so sick I could barely focus. The thought of swanning around with five hundred people more important than me filled me with existential dread.

But I did it. I squeezed into a fancy dress, ate some saltines, and had a good time. I really did. And, when I went to hide in the bathroom, which I did quite often during the terrifying predinner cocktail period, legendary journalist Andrea Mitchell and I bonded over our mutual dislike of high heels. And I peed next to Sofia Vergara.

In the months to come, as I headed into pregnancy's familiar weight gain, lethargy, and anxiety about my business future, the image of me at that event, literally rubbing shoulders with my heroes, gave me faith in my ability to succeed. A ticket to that event is hard to come by, and I felt honored that my former client thought of me as someone worthy to introduce to his professional network.

Your superconnectors are probably not your best friends or closest colleagues, because they share a similar network with you. Your best superconnectors may simply be acquaintances—in social-networking theory, "weak ties." And in a network, they're much more important than your closest ones.

## How to Create a Great Social Network Even If You're Not That Social

Networking for hermits can be summed up in one sentence uttered by a fellow small business owner, who observed, "I don't know why I bother to go anywhere. The same ten people always refer me all my business."

We all have superconnectors: folks with large and diverse social networks who are key to our success, though we might not have noticed it. There are three events a year that I will always attend, because year after year they are intellectually stimulating and they enhance my professional network. I meet people who drive my business forward in a superconcentrated time frame. Not surprisingly, two of these events are hosted by my superconnectors.

Superconnectors are generous and helpful because that's who they are. And, if you cultivate powerful superconnectors and nurture a strong online social network, you can keep actual in-person networking to a minimum while still advancing in your career (ideally from bed).

Any social network is made up of nodes. These are the individual actors or people in the network. Some of the nodes in your network are more powerful than others in introducing new relationships. My superconnector from the White House Correspondents' Dinner was a node with a lot of access to other nodes.

Networks aren't only for our personal lives. They build our civic society because they form social capital and interpersonal ties. As defined by Wayne Baker, professor at the Ross School of Business at University of Michigan, *social capital* refers to the resources available in and through personal and business networks. When it comes to work, social capital is pretty much everything that propels careers forward: relationships, financial resources, leads or new job opportunities, mentorship, and Baker notes, intangibles like trust, goodwill, and cooperation.[1]

## Can I Have Strong Social Capital When I'm Not That Social?

Absolutely! Even the biggest hermit needs strong social networks.

Building networks is a skill I had to learn. When I left college, I felt so sad that no professor had ever taken an interest in me, and that I had no relationships with anyone besides my small group of friends. I looked in wonder at friends who got recommended for scholarships or great opportunities, who had dinner at professors' houses. How did they do it? I knew I was smart, but I had no idea how to nurture professional relationships (I wasn't so great with personal ones either).

Why hadn't I formed those social networks? Well, I was convinced that no one older or important would ever want to spend time with me. I never wanted to ask for their time or attention. I was socially anxious, and when I did reach out, my tactics were artless. In my early career, I was mentored by some incredible people, but I never kept in touch. I didn't reach out or offer to help others naturally. It wasn't because I was a mean person, it was because I was scared. I felt worthless and very alone professionally, outside family and friends.

Even if you were born into privileged circles, networking can be very very stressful if you're shy. The secret is that, for hermits, front-loading the hard work of building strong relationships actually means you have to travel and work less when it comes to business development for your job or company. And for introverts, knowing your superconnectors and having them in your corner can save you a lot of networking angst. If you can develop close relationships with a few superconnectors with access to diverse networks, they'll do the connecting for you.

Sometimes a superconnection doesn't even need to be a person. It can be a passion project.

For my beloved editor, Lizzie Skurnick, it turned out that the biggest superconnector in her career was her blog. (I totally relate to this, because blogging changed my life forever, too.) Her inspiration to launch one of the first literary blogs, Old Hag, led to her career as an author, publisher, *New York Times* columnist, and much more—and, most important, let her make her living in the book world. Lizzie says, "My entire professional life and my dearest closest friends spring from a blog. If I hadn't started it, and connected with the three people who also shared my passion, I wouldn't have the life I have now."

In 2003, Lizzie was sitting in her apartment, forty pounds overweight, recently fired from her job, her only income coming from a still-new relationship writing about books for a local indie paper. But from a major writer she profiled, she learned about blogs, and joined the fledgling world of literary bloggers. At the time, she says, "You could get fired for blogging, and we all either hated our jobs, or were about to get fired." None of them had any idea the media was about to become obsessed with blogging, and she and her friends were swept up in it, some founding new Gawker blogs, some going to *The Daily Show*, some making a splash in print media.

For Lizzie, it led to writing reviews for the *New York Times Book Review*. It also, through a friend who read her blog, put her on the radar of a local teen-girls magazine that let her work part-time but still gave her health care. Another blogging friend introduced her to the new editor in chief of Jezebel, and she launched a column on YA books that the major author (remember her?) recommended to her editor. That became a book, as did her *New York Times Magazine* column, which another blogger friend had recommended her for.

*That* in turn led to her YA imprint, Lizzie Skurnick Books, which put her in the *Times* again, but now as a subject.

"Everything, everything I have came from the blog," she says, "but I was just noodling around. At the time, using a blog to be ambitious would have been crazy. So never underestimate the value of just fooling around with what you love."

## When Hiding Changes Your Life: Cheryl Contee's Story

Cheryl Contee isn't a hermit, but for years circumstances forced her to hide her real identity behind a pseudonym—"Jill Tubman"—on the influential blog Jack and Jill Politics, which she cocreated. "Outspoken black people have a pretty long history in America of getting shot at, or hung," Cheryl says. "Blogging was very new then. Certainly being an outspoken black person taking on the Congressional Black Caucus or the Bush administration had not been done before."

Working eighteen-hour days, Cheryl was passed over for a promotion and finally decided it was worth it to take in a fraction of her former salary to work for herself. One tweet announcing her free-agent status led to her future tech-founder and business partner, and to a shift: she started managing her identity as Jill, shifting that identity into her real self.

"I think there were a lot of people who were surprised," she adds, "including one friendship that I almost lost because he felt that he had a relationship with Jill Tubman, and didn't realize it was me."

Jill, who, Cheryl says, is "probably funnier than me," was more confrontational, angrier, and blunter, as well. But the blog and the business allowed her to put the two together: "I felt the need to move forward in one direction rather than having a semicompartmentalized life."

Bringing them together was more rewarding than the corporate job had ever been. "I never dreamed that by launching the blog I would one day shake the president's hand and that he would know who I was and thank me."

Having to hide was, Cheryl says, very similar to the process of becoming an entrepreneur. "When we were starting, and my family was concerned for my safety, I decided that it was worth the cost, and I think, as an entrepreneur, it's a similar process. You're going to pay a heavy price in some ways. You have to be willing to go to the mat. Am I willing to put it all on the table in order to achieve my dream and the dreams of the people who joined me in this venture?"

Cheryl is truly a brave and original thinker. But her adoption of an alter ego who was just a little more out there than her true self at the time helped her grow into her current life as a leader and tech entrepreneur. Being anonymous gave her the courage that she couldn't give her true self.

Although it wasn't her goal, Cheryl's brave dive into the world of politics and cultural commentary opened up entirely new networks for her. By the time she was "outed" in the press, she was ready to leave her corporate job and start a company, and her bold voice and online leadership had paved the way, even though, ironically, it had been constructed under a fictitious identity.

## GETTING STARTED

## Find Your Superconnectors

Ask people how they got to where they are and you'll hear, over and over again, that they built on their relationships.

Connecting dots is what superconnectors do all the time, and you can learn a lot from them. One of the quickest ways to do it yourself is to start identifying the superconnectors already in your network. (If you seem a bit light on them, don't worry—we'll talk about building your superconnector stable in a minute.)

❑ Think about the last five years of work, or school, or the last ten projects you've worked on. Write down everyone who introduced you to a new boss, job opportunity, or client; recommended you for a speaking gig, professional organization, board, or blogging opportunity; or introduced you to a new community or social network that has added value.

❑ Go through the past few years of customer engagements, or look at your biggest contracts. Think about who introduced you to new employers, recruiters, or strong connections for advancement. In the cases where someone referred you to a customer, who was it? Is there a pattern?

❑ Take a large piece of paper or a whiteboard and draw circles; these are your nodes. Write down all the nodes that refer you business— don't be strict with the definition. Here a node can be a person, but it can also be an event, a professional organization, someone's website you're listed on, or a partner firm. Is there one client who always sends you new prospects? An event that results in new clients?

❑ Look back over the signature moments in your professional life: Which people helped facilitate them? Whose faces pop into your mind?

Eye what you've written critically. Is there one particular "superconnector" in your life that has widened your world? This could be a person, a yearly event, an organization. You will see common threads; I guarantee it. Challenge yourself to look critically at who is in your network, and if the list is not diverse enough or full of enough weak ties, you'll need to work harder to expand it.

## What If I Don't Have Any Superconnectors?

Don't worry if you're reading this and feel like you don't have any superconnectors. It sounds so trite, but if you do things you like to do and seek out places (online and offline) where people with shared values tend to be, pay close attention to possible kindred spirits, and take a small risk now and then; you'll build the network that's right for you.

When I researched articles and books on building strong networks and making superconnections, everything seemed to be written by white men, which disappointed but didn't surprise me. The very spirit and language of networking and leadership culture in this country is what I like to call "enlightened bro." (Tim Ferriss, I'm talking about you.)

But in truth, the art of making wonderful connections through acquaintances or strangers is introvert-friendly, because it's about being attuned to another person and reading subtle signals. It's the risk part where you may need to practice.

In his book *Achieving Success Through Social Capital*, eminent social-network scholar Wayne Baker tells a great story about how his wife, Cheryl, forged a superconnection (I will use quite a bit of Baker's theory in this chapter, because I think it's great and enlightened). New to a city and unsure of her next career move, she bonded with her superconnector when she admired the flyer the woman was printing at Kinko's.[2] "The page that faced up was the woman's picture, along with her bio," Baker recounts. "Here was someone who had her own unique path. Here is someone who had done it." She asked for a copy of the brochure, and called the lady out of the blue. It turned out she and Cheryl shared many professional and spiritual interests—ones that created further relationships and connections.

To forge a connection with a stranger or someone you don't know well, you have to take a risk. You have to strike up a conversation, as Baker's wife did in Kinko's, or as KJ Dell'Antonia did when she chatted up Nicholas Kristof in the hallways of the *New York Times*. And for every great connection, you'll face a rejection, or simply a nod, and you'll have to move on. The good news is that superconnectors tend to adopt people, so you may only have to make the first move, and you'll be in good hands thereafter.

My favorite failed-connection story is very typical of D.C., which is why I don't live there anymore. I was invited to an exclusive Georgetown party at the home of Nancy Jacobson, a legendary political fund-raiser, and her husband, Mark Penn, famous pollster, CEO of PR giant Burson Marsteller, and, at the time, top adviser to Hillary Clinton.

As host, Mark was making the rounds, and he came upon me. I was very eager to meet him because I really wanted a job with Hillary Clinton's 2008 presidential campaign. I wasn't wearing a name tag, not that it would have mattered. He asked me, "Who are you?" but then got quickly distracted. When he asked again, clearly not interested, I simply replied, "I'm no one you need to know." He seemed relieved, and quickly moved on.

The point is, your superconnectors may not be who you think they will be, or even who you hope they will be. No matter. I still worked for Hillary in the end, because another one of my connections brought me in.

## Calendaring Your Superconnections

Once you've found your superconnectors, whether personal or professional, you must tend your network like a garden. Relationships from past jobs, past schooling, industry events, and even kindred spirits are the soil from which your business will grow.

When I met Nicco, I was amazed. Here was someone who kept in touch with everyone from his first job onward, and beyond that, who had the richest network of experiences, friends, and supporters

I'd ever seen. It spanned generations, and included a diverse set of people, some very important. Many in his professional community were real, dear friends.

I also saw how Nicco puts a tremendous amount of work into keeping up his relationships, and is never scared to pick up the phone. He values everyone in his life and he works hard for them.

Nicco is an avid reader and poetry aficionado, and he loves to send people books. When I first met him, it seemed sort of crazy, to meet someone and then after just spending a few hours with them to send them a book. But I realized over time that that's how he loves to connect with people (they always end up talking books) and it's a passion he loves to share.

In our digital era, you can even tag someone with love and consideration. Susan McPherson is wonderful at surfacing a useful or compelling article on Facebook and tagging someone with a "thought of you." This tiny gesture feels generous and helps people stay in the know. Likewise, you could go through LinkedIn once a week, check in on what your contacts are doing, and comment on a few of their updates, endorse a few more. A digital acknowledgment of someone's worth is meaningful and builds social capital.

Camille Preston, who coaches people on finding their flow, sends past clients, friends, and colleagues articles or little snippets of information that she believes will help them work toward their personal goals, or conquer their personal demons. For her, it's a daily practice, and she sends a few people a "nugget" each day, just via e-mail.

If I have twenty free minutes, the last thing I'm inclined to do is pick up the phone and call someone. But what I have learned from Nicco, and practiced hard, is to honor my professional colleagues and work hard for them. I often have to go outside my comfort zone to do it, but I always end up having a good time. And I've adapted ways that I can stay in touch and tend my relationships in a manner that doesn't give me too much angst. Technology and online tools really help. I'll never be like Nicco, but no longer do I feel alone professionally. Instead I feel deeply blessed and supported.

I think the key is that your effort must be authentic to who you are and what you care about. It can't feel phony. Review those contacts, consolidate them, and develop a CRM. Message them with love, respect, and great stuff.

## The "Ten Touches" Rule

Nicco owned a small business for years. As the company grew, the team considered how much to invest in sales and marketing: maybe hire a PR firm, or develop sales collateral, or host events. Before they made a decision, he tried to figure out what made the business come in and go out.

"It became pretty clear that my relationships with people and the amount of contact I had in a week had a direct impact on how much business came in," he says.

So he made a new rule: check in with ten people from his Rolodex—i.e., Facebook, LinkedIn, and e-mail—a week. "Maybe the exchange is an e-mail, maybe it's a phone call, maybe it's lunch or dinner or coffee—maybe it's sending them a book or an interesting article," he told me. "It very rarely leads directly to business. But imagine you reach out to someone in your network and have a good conversation. Then, the next day that person is having lunch with a colleague looking for help. You are the top-of-mind recommendation."

This method doesn't just work for small-business owners. Silicon Valley entrepreneur and power saleswoman Joanna Bloor noted a senior vice president at a tech company in San Francisco whose sales team had a target of over $200 million per year. This leader worked four days a week. She had figured out that if she made the requisite number of contacts and dates between Monday and Thursday, she'd meet her sales goals and be able to take Fridays off.

## Is Managing My Social Network Slimy?

In *Achieving Success Through Social Capital*, Wayne Baker asks this question flat out: "Is it unethical to consciously 'manage' a social network?"[3] In essence, what kind of mercenary would treat relationships and human beings as useful tools for bettering her own life?

It is not unethical.

Thinking that managing our network is slimy assumes we are only using people for our own ends. But in true networking, that's a happy side effect, not the point.

Wharton's Stew Friedman says, "When you approach a social encounter as an opportunity for you to discover something about other people that you can help them with, as opposed to taking something from them, then you don't feel slimy. And if I find whatever resource I can provide, then you're going to want to help me in the future."

Your network doesn't have to be a scary thing; play to your strengths. As Stew Friedman tells us, "Think about networking as a contribution to your capacity to make the world better some way, to use your particular talents, skills, passion, interests to create value, to be of use, to have a life of significance."

And think about it: you are managing relationships throughout the day. You take your partners' clothes to the dry cleaners to do something nice for them; you flex a little to make room for a colleague's scheduling needs. You drop an endorsement on LinkedIn for someone you don't know well, just because. If you needed the favor returned, you hope they'll do the same for you. But this expectation of "ongoing reciprocity" isn't greedy. It's a positive view of how we operate in the world. As Friedman simply puts it, "We try to help each other."

Managing a relationship is as simple as learning about another person, being attuned to their goals and needs, and staying open to chances to help. It's bringing people, ideas, and resources together in a way that helps everyone involved. Consider Wayne Baker's take:

"It's not the management of relationships that is unethical. It's what we do with our knowledge that makes the practices ethical or not."

There's another positive side effect to managing networks. Generosity, as we've discussed throughout the book, is not only an underappreciated value in business, it's an incredibly effective tactic for reducing anxiety. If you flip the script in your life from trying to prove how interesting, intelligent, or effective you are into an inquiry into another person's needs, you forget yourself. You get out of your head and into relating to another person. You use your skills as an empath and a sensitive soul to attune to another, not to beat yourself up or force yourself to be something you're not. It's the social-capital equivalent of bringing homemade cookies into the office.

My favorite hermit social-capital discipline is to connect people to jobs or opportunities. When I see a posting on one of my networks, I'll think of five people to whom I could send it. It feels great, is great, and it's bringing good energy into the world.

## The Power of Online Professional Social Networks

No doubt, the digital age is a blessing and a curse. For hermits, it's mostly a blessing, because it means we can build an empire from bed (which is where I wrote this sentence from). The digitally connected member of society can meaningfully participate in the world in yoga pants.

But for that, you need an online social network.

This is much more serious than your Facebook page. An online professional social network is your entry point to the world, to news, to opportunities and connections far beyond your home office. To be effective, it must have many of the characteristics we just talked about in relation to superconnectors: diversity, weak ties, access to new opportunities, and social networks beyond our own.

Now we'll focus on the key digital skills and tools to build and foster powerful online networks from the comfort of your laptop.

An online network can be just powerful as one in real life—and the people you find in it may surprise you.

## Why Women Need Great Online Social Networks

I had a bitter laugh recently with my husband as he told me about the great new after-work cocktail spots in Harvard Square. "I wouldn't know about that," I said dryly. "I'm usually at home with the kids, drinking alone."

Work-related networks have traditionally been less effective for women because women tend to move in and out of the workforce due to childcare and family responsibilities. Instead of a wide-ranging group of weak ties, we have strong support networks. That means we have wonderful friends to call for advice on diaper rash, but fewer contacts who can put us in touch with a potential investor or patent lawyer.

Conversely, men benefit from an organized social life that promotes entrepreneurship. This network of weak ties contains valuable advisers who are their lawyers, accountants, business partners, or other power brokers.

But now online social networks, accessible from anywhere, prevent women's work networks from being interrupted by childcare. They can even create entrepreneurs: mom-blogging culture was built from online friends from Facebook or Twitter who only caught up in person once or twice a year at BlogHer or other community conferences.

Here's more good news. All-female reference groups have garnered power because of the vast marketing and political organizing opportunities they represent, and because online networking allows women to ignore barriers of place and life stage and connect with people from many walks of life. In the old days, power and access to capital was traded at the Yale Club, or on the golf course, among small groups of white men. Now women can form their own clubs, online. Some easy ways to start:

**Find your online colleagues.** Tapping into professional networks in your field requires sleuthing and research more than anything. You don't need to start from scratch. Once you find one hub of activity, others will follow. It could be a blog, a Twitter feed, a message board. If you attend a professional conference you really like, research the conference organizers and speakers online, and see where they hang out. As in any social situation, you want to be with people you like and respect, so be choosy and take your time to find the right community.

**Follow your bliss.** Often, professional communities evolve from other passion projects you take part in. I think of Pantsuit Nation and a myriad of other pro–Hillary Clinton online communities that developed during Election 2016 and grew from there. The power of Facebook showed us all the professional colleagues who were part of our political networks, and gave us a great deal in common with new weak ties.

You may find the same if you get involved in a more local or regional issue, such as a municipal funding push, volunteering effort, or civic campaign. A few in-person meetings can pave the way for a strong online network, even if it's just conducted via e-mails. I find that I tend to bond with other working mothers who fly a lot, and I love the community we created. I've even met some by commenting on blogs or following women on Twitter who cover travel and working motherhood.

**Contribute content.** Andrea Sparrey, now the immediate past president of AIGAC, the Association of International Graduate Admissions Consultants, began her career by editing the trade association's blog when she was just starting out as an MBA admissions consultant. In so doing, she met everyone influential and powerful in the field of business school admissions—her chosen field, because she interviewed and edited them.

At the time Andrea didn't have much choice: she needed to conduct most of her networking online. Because of her husband's job, she'd uprooted her life and moved from New York City to San Diego, far from the locus of elite business schools and the consultants, bankers, and entrepreneurs who applied to them. "I was willing to write articles—and it gave me a platform to call up the most important people! I then helped organize the conferences, and then I had the chance to go out and meet people at all levels of the field," Andrea says.

**Find, or create, communities of practice.** I would not be where I am today were it not for several specific, professionally driven online communities. These are simple listservs or Facebook groups, invite-only, and they not only keep me up-to-date on professional development and trends, they continuously supply weak ties to my social network. And, because we're bound together by "The List," we all go the extra mile to help each other.

Scholar Wayne Baker calls these "networks of practice": a formal or informal network of people who work in the same function or process but are geographically distributed.[4] Until I had my lists, my social networks were limited. I had a personal CRM and I went to the same events each year; everyone knew each other and everyone ran in the same professional circles, so at some point, getting new business and new clients tapped out. When I joined my "lists," all of a sudden my network broadened.

**Use the algorithms.** We're all used to finding the "People You May Know" feature on Facebook creepy (and when it pops up an old boyfriend from high school, it kind of is), but when you're a businessperson, it's free research. Ditto for Twitter's "Who to Follow," LinkedIn's similar feature, and any other social-network algorithm. That doesn't mean you should follow people blindly—it means you have an opportunity to find some people you really would like to know.

Mighty Networks founder and Silicon Valley executive Gina Bianchini calls these identity networks, and believes they are the future. "No matter where you are in the world, you should be able to instantly connect with people with a shared identity, a shared interest, a shared condition. And software is now smart enough to play the role of the fabulous host." No more endless searching through the web forms on alumni or professional directories. My wrists hurt just thinking about that.

**Use social proofing.** Earlier I mentioned the concept of social proofing, which means that people tend to "assume the actions of others in an attempt to reflect the correct behavior for a situation." This concept has been co-opted by marketers and social-change agents alike. Think about it the next time everyone in your social network turns their Facebook avatar a certain color for a cause. If I post "Je Suis Paris," or if I "Stand with Planned Parenthood" and change my Facebook profile to reflect my stance, chances are other people in my social network will see the change, assume it's what's expected, and turn their profiles, too. This adds power and currency to online social movements, but you can use it in business development and in online networking. (And I will say that sharing your social activism on your online profile can enhance your appeal to like-minded clients or employers, and scare off those who might be a bad fit.)

You can use social proofing to align your work with the people, organizations, and places that command the most respect in your given field. If you are part of a community with inherent value, others will assume you have professional value, too. It's the equivalent of why people carry status tote bags: they want others to know where they've been and who they've been with without having to actually say it.

You can even use social proofing "aspirationally," optimizing your LinkedIn and Facebook profile to sound as prestigious as possible by aligning with groups, institutions, and people who are desirable in your field. And you can be in the know on new trends, actions, or other acts of meaning that will advance your currency among your online networks. All this sends subtle signals to online connections that you're *someone*. Even if you're in your sweats.

**Peak event and the power of the online keynote.** If you are at a point in your career where you're asked to speak publicly, write, and offer expertise, you might feel compelled to give lots of talks and fly all over the country to enhance your market value. But Gina Bianchini believes we're at "peak event," and she's done her own analysis of why an important keynote isn't nearly as fruitful for her business development as a well-crafted blog or Q&A session on Quora.com.

Unless it's on video a live talk doesn't have as much staying power as an article, which is easily re-shared. And preparation is a multi-day process. Gina says, "I need to think of the presentation, write out all the slides, write out the script, memorize the script. Not to mention I have to sit in traffic, get my hair and makeup done, arrive early so I can sit there for an hour because they want me to be there early and mic'd up, practice my speech."

Gina can get a million views for a Q&A on Quora, her online keynote equivalent of sending out a fundraising email to raise $4 million instead of a political candidate going to a four-hour-long rubber chicken dinner. That's why political campaigns love online fund-raising—entrepreneurs should love online visibility.

**Social capital online.** There are about six professional friends in my life who I will do anything for, no matter what. Two are on-again, off-again clients, two are colleagues I frequently collaborate with, one is a longtime friend who helped launch me way back when, and one I have never met IRL! (We e-mail and have chatted a few times by phone.)

When I took his class in 2008, legendary social theorist Robert Putnam was unconvinced that computer-mediated communication could make our investments in social capital more productive. More recent scholarship suggests information technology enhances place-based community and the generation of bridging social capital.[5] Increased participation in social-network sites such as Facebook or blogs seems both to predict and contribute to increased interaction in offline social networks.

In short: online communities are not for losers.

Social scientists such as Harold Rheingold argue that not only can one truly care about online "friends" and neighbors as passionately as the real thing, the anonymity and invisibility of Internet communications prevent some of the biases and discriminations of face-to-face contact. Online communities grow and deepen through years. Strong online communities have the power to replace many lost community elements. They also have the power to invent new ideas and allow ordinary citizens to drive social change.

## ONLINE SELF-CARE

I could not be a hermit entrepreneur if it weren't for my strong online networks and incredible superconnectors (made easier to maintain because of my clear, strong niche and online brand). They have been the lifeblood of my business, allowing me to build my little fiefdom while in my pj's.

But as an introvert and someone who gets nervous when I engage too deeply, there are pros and cons to connecting online. As more and more of our social lives gets conducted online or via mobile, digital connections begin to feel just like IRL ones. You need to respond right away; the sheer volume of communication can be overwhelming. And then there's our old friend FOMO. The more you engage in high-quality online social networks, the more you will be daily faced with the incredible accomplishments of colleagues and friends.

I've talked about The List, the incredible online community of businesswomen I belong to. I truly love this community, which is technically just a Google group. Still, I have a secret way of coping with all the wonderfulness, which is sometimes too much for me to take in. If I'm having a melancholy day or need some quiet, I turn my e-mail settings to digest and only get the updates in my in-box once a day. It's the digital version of shutting out the world.

So as much as I advocate cultivating your online network, I also advocate turning it off or tuning it out every once in a while. In the same way as going out to a function every single night, engaging online professional communities each day can wear you thin. After the contentious 2016 presidential election, many people quit Facebook and Twitter for a period of time, simply because they were overstimulating at a time when they needed to be quiet, to grieve, and to take stock. I encourage you to use the same intention with your online professional engagement, monitoring your own reactions for burnout, and recognizing when you're overstimulated by all the energy of online conversations these days. Turn your feeds to digest, guilt-free.

And hey, you might even call a friend and take a walk, IRL.

# 14

## *Getting Out There (When You Have To)*

I have a secret: sometimes, if there is a professional event I should be at but can't attend, I just use the hashtag and tweet as if I'm there.

This is because I'm torn about these events. I never want to go. When I'm there, I have to force myself to go into rooms, and my anxiety has made me get straight into a cab and head to the airport, days early. But if there is an important gathering and I'm not invited, I have insane FOMO.

Sometimes even the most committed hermit has to get out there. Meeting clients, attending conferences, giving speeches; face time matters. But if you have a plan and you know how to take care of yourself, you can make the most of your time in the wild. Whether it's choosing the conferences that pay off, knowing how to make your speeches count, and—yes—figuring out when to say no, identifying the characteristics of going public gives you space to psych yourself up.

Choose wisely and prepare well, and you might even enjoy yourself.

## The Temporary Extrovert

The star speaker you heard during the plenary session? Hiding in the bathroom during cocktail hour. Those superstars holding drinks, laughing and charming everyone? Also angling for the exit. The only difference between them and you is that these leaders can tune in to a room and direct their energy outward in short bursts. They pitch, charm, and emote with the best of them. They just know to book in some quiet time afterward.

Life is not high school or a popularity contest. You don't need to be BFFs with your colleagues, or make sure there's a party to hit each Saturday night. (Isn't being a grown-up great?)

However, good social skills really, really help in business. And ironically, the more out there you are when you're out there, the more downtime you can pack into your schedule when you're "off." So I don't want you to feel you need to transform into a schmoozer. You just need to practice being a great extrovert for short amounts of time, and learn some powerful coping skills for when you simply must get out there.

# GETTING STARTED

## Morra's Fourteen-Point Plan for Surviving Events

By this point, you've learned to think about selling and negotiating in a way that's true to yourself and doesn't spike your cortisol. Now, what if you could do the same at cocktail hour? There's a way to work a room and leave a calling card that's authentic to you—and lets you banish stay-at-home FOMO.

**Channel your inner Oprah.** BlogHer cofounder and CEO Lisa Stone's former career as a journalist was key to helping her learn to work a room in Silicon Valley. "I've always been that person behind the reporter's notebook, asking other people their opinions," she told me. "What I don't like is the spotlight." If you feel alien, unworthy, shy, or nervous in a room full of powerful players, pretend you're there to report a story. Ask people lots of questions—this is your strength as an introvert! Listen actively. Draw them out. Even the most powerful person enjoys telling their own story. You can even use it to produce content. And the truth is, when you ask people lots of questions about themselves, you're remembered as a great conversationalist!

**Wear your battle gear.** My therapist once said to me, "The world doesn't have to know you feel like shit." Before I head to a business trip or a long day of meetings in the city, I wear one of my three fabulous outfits, get my hair blown out, and put on tons of makeup. This armor helps me transform from my homebody self into someone confident and open enough to make friends and charm people. I look like the best version of myself, and, often, I can actually be her.

**Be prepared.** On the few occasions I have been asked to give a keynote speech, I've channeled Hillary Clinton, who once said, "If you're not comfortable with public speaking—and nobody starts out comfortable; you have to learn how to be comfortable—practice." When I have to go out in public and be awesome, I'm training for the Olympics. I rehearse every word. I rehearse the room. I find my inner Gary, Julia Louis-Dreyfus's body man in HBO's *Veep*, and create a briefing book of attendee details for small talk. I even practice names before I walk in.

**Only connect.** Professional superconnector Susan McPherson says introducing others (known as the "cocktail bump") is the kindest and fastest means of escape for a hermit. "One of the reasons I love to host parties is I can introduce everybody else, and then I can run away. The conversation can go on without me, and people feel good being brought together."

**Chunk your time.** When you are at a conference, set a minimum target, pace yourself, and then give yourself a time-out treat. "One hour on earns one hour off," says Kate Gardiner. If you schmooze for an hour and meet three new people, you can allow yourself to go hide in your hotel room. The same goes for attending sessions, which can be a great way to learn new skills and meet people in a less pressured environment. One big chunk works, too. If I have to fly to New York or Washington for a client meeting or conference, I force myself to schedule five meetings that day. I'd rather be exhausted than fly back again.

**Remember, you are there to work, not make people like you.** For all of sixth grade, none of the girls in my class would eat lunch with me. Twenty-nine years later, the memories of sitting by myself for a year come flooding back when I enter a professional networking event. But here's the great thing: you're a grown-up, it's not middle school, and you don't need everyone to sit with you anymore. "I make it a point to ask questions and chat with the speakers during sessions specifically so that I can duck the networking," says financial therapist Amanda Clayman. "Then I don't have to feel like the unpopular high school dork."

**Find a conference "spouse."** When you're alone, establish a power duo with someone else for cocktail chatter, attending events, and standing in lines. Conference BFFs also work, as do actual partners, whom you can call for a quick pep talk when you're alone at the bar. (They'll be glad you're not off with your conference spouse.)

**Never, ever be afraid to hide in the bathroom.** Whether your kindred spirits are also hiding or they're just in there to pee, something about being in that shared space lets people's guard down. Either way, you can strike up the most informal and interesting conversations while putting on your lipstick. Even a short, friendly conversation by the sink will get your social juices flowing and make entering that large room easier. All you need to do is smile at someone in the mirror.

Once, I was feeling particularly bad about myself. I had been eclipsed on a client team by someone new, younger, and cooler, and I felt left out. Suddenly I recognized the woman at the sink next to me from her Twitter photo. We began chatting. She knew who I was. I remembered that indeed, I had a good professional reputation, relationships that had lasted years, and I would survive. Even better, I had someone to walk out of that room with into the fray.

**Make someone else comfortable.** BlogHer's Lisa Stone recalled something her mother told her as a girl, as Lisa was working on her own shyness. "You can take the responsibility to help other people feel like they belong, and make them feel good just by smiling at them." She adds, "Asking a stranger 'how are you?' is the gateway drug to feeling comfortable." Research backs Lisa up: the mere act of smiling at a stranger makes you feel more socially connected to others immediately after.[1] So even if the person you're smiling at doesn't notice, you'll feel more confident and connected when you emerge from the bathroom.

**Have a job to do.** Silicon Valley veteran Arvind Rajan, former executive at LinkedIn, the mother ship of networking, has social anxiety. "I can speak in front of two thousand people with no problem, but if there's a chitchat session after, I get anxious and drained." Arvind has learned that for him, structure is key to his comfort level. For the cocktail party, build in structure in an unstructured situation. It can be as easy as finding a person you've been meaning to meet. Talk, exchange e-mails, and then you're free to leave.

**Share your expertise.** It's counterintuitive, but, as with Arvind, for a shy person, sometimes the best position to be is in the front of the room. Remember Hillary Moglen, who hates networking events but excels at talking about her specific work in a room of people who will understand it? "I find opportunities to be in a thought-sharing position as opposed to just meeting people and having to explain myself to them," she says.

**Find something to like.** Journalist Claire Shipman says, "I dread the four hours leading up to a trip. But the minute I'm in the car headed toward the airport, I like the time to myself, and I like to get ready for my event. I try to focus on that. It's like when I'm looking at a new project. I try to remember the parts of the process that I enjoy, and remind myself I will get through it, even if there are some parts I don't love as much."

**Showcase something authentic to you.** Emily McKhann and Cooper Monroe founded a very successful social media agency called the Motherhood. For years, they made charming cloth bags just the size to hold business cards, and other goodies to hand out at conferences. I first got mine in 2007 and I still carry it in my purse today. They were so perfectly perfect for the brand and for Emily and Cooper: generous, beautiful, feminine. It was always a perfect and disarming way to begin or end what could be an awkward transaction.

**Know what comes next.** Are you attending the plenary session? Is there a dinner party the second night? The more you plan your schedule so you know you're hitting what you need to, the calmer you'll be (and the quicker you can exit).

**Follow up.** The magic of networking is that you can follow up from behind your screen. When I come home from an event, I put all the new business cards I have gathered in a safe place. I write down next steps for each; it could be everything from suggesting a phone call or coffee meeting to sending an article we discussed or a helpful introduction or link. Then, when I'm in a strong mood, I'll reach out via e-mail and suggest a next step.

It's also a good way to stop second-guessing what you said or didn't say, or beat yourself up for leaving early or feeling too shy to meet many people. A one-on-one conversation with someone new—regardless of who they are—is probably more valuable than any number of banal group conversations or short hellos, says Kate Gardiner.

**Finally, give yourself a reward at the end of the day.** You want to leave the event day with a positive memory, so you lower your internal stress response for planning the next one. If room service and a movie works for you, great. Don't judge yourself. Train yourself to push through the public time and then recharge.

## Be Ruthlessly Strategic About Events: What's Worth It?

The conference and event industry is thriving; indeed, for many struggling news organizations and publishers, it's become a cash cow. You could attend a regular old conference to network every other day. And, increasingly, invite-only conferences on a ship in the Bahamas or in Utah at a ski resort seem invented purely to create FOMO and raise the value of exclusivity. But all that ego gratification—I'm cool enough to join the club!—is expensive, and all that glad-handing is time-consuming. How much of it is truly valuable to your career?

There may be some events you choose to attend in hopes of cultivating new business or relationships, and you will pay to attend those. If you have target clients, Google their brand name and "conference," or Google the name of a key executive at a target client and "conference." You're not stalking! You're conducting valuable reconnaissance. Even better, try to speak at the conference as well. If you're both speakers, you're more likely to feel confident and make a good connection. If not, try to find a smaller venue, or invite your target to speak or moderate something you're planning.

Simply being in the room for some invite-only events is worth it. You don't need the spotlight; I have never been invited even to attend a TED event, but former speakers have told me that giving a talk on the main stage requires Oscar-night levels of preparation. TED veteran Nilofer Merchant notes, "Relish the opportunity that not-speaking presents. TED attendees who have used it only as part of the professional get-ahead checklist are not beloved members of the community." So be sure, if you attend an invite-only event, these are communities you want to be part of for the long term.

A quick "Is it Worth It?" conference checklist:

❑ Will your superconnectors be there? That alone is a reason to attend.

❑ Will it serve your ego or drive biz dev? Arvind Rajan spent many uncomfortable hours at swanky tech gatherings until he realized, "It doesn't make a difference to my success or failure at work."

❑ Did it pay off before? Write down the new business contacts, or even contracts, from the past couple years of events and conferences you've attended. It will quickly become clear which were valuable and which were a waste of time. Then you can build your calendar.

❑ Is it a need-to-go event in your field? If so, make it count: book tons of meetings, chunk your time, and psych yourself up. This is where social media is incredibly helpful. Some events have a private Facebook group for attendees, or an "alumni" listserv that keeps connections growing throughout the years.

❑ Is there a chance to build your team? SheFinds founder Michelle Madhok looks at it from a holistic standpoint: "I'll go to an event because a decision maker is there, or if I can go with one of my staffers. If we're going to go and use our energy, we better get as much out of it."

❑ Will it pay off in the future? "It's just like in budgeting," says Amanda Clayman. "Review what happened, predict what's going to come up, and then come up with a plan for it."

❑ Last but not least: Does it pay? Kate Gardiner, veteran of many bro-heavy New York and Silicon Valley media conferences, believes if you are being paid to speak, consult, or add value, you will be more purposeful in a room. And you will be much less anxious because you will know your job.

## The Power of Being Ambivalently Ambitious

When I sold this book and realized I was actually going to be a published author, I was thrilled and proud. But ten minutes later, I had an anxiety attack. I told my husband, "I'm going to have to get on lots of planes and hold lots of book events to promote it. I'm going to have to *ask* people to help me!"

I think perhaps out of all the moments in our eleven-year marriage, this was the one instance in which my husband truly thought I was insane. "So why the hell did you do it?" he asked, honestly flummoxed.

So why did I?

It was my goal to write a book for us hermits, introverts, and anxious people who struggle with success and do battle with our ambition.

But once I had the idea and set my mind to it, I needed a publisher to publish it. And every day of writing the book, my anticipatory anxiety has been high, thinking of how much I'm going to hate getting out there (getting on those flights won't be any easier . . . ) and promoting the book. I dread its success as much as its failure.

If you have made it this far in the book, I know you can relate to this ambivalence. Your ambition and creative energy drive you and set you apart. And yet every time you need to push yourself outside your introvert or hermit comfort zone, you want to hide. And, because you're not going to magically cure your ambivalence or introverted nature, and as long as you retain your wonderful ambition, every day might present a new opportunity for conflict because *each step forward in your career will demand you leave you hermitage and push against your introversion.* And with each step forward, your Technicolor feelings will feel less like a burden and more like a resource.

The good news is, once you have tools and strategies to get out there, you'll be more resilient. Don't be afraid to push yourself, when it's worth it.

See you in the bathroom.

# CONCLUSION

On my weekly podcast, I always ask my guests, "When is the last time you hid in the bathroom?"

The more extroverted think it's an amusing question. Their experiences are situational, like getting away from their whiny kids or surreptitiously checking their cell phones during a meeting.

The guests who struggle with shyness and introversion understand the question instinctively. Daily, their ambition clashes with their anxiety. A work presentation or speech at a conference becomes a minefield. Though they are great contributors and coworkers, they need their own space to get work done.

And yet most of us work in environments where we have to sneak into the lactation room or book a fake meeting just to get some alone time, or wait until we have a major life event like a baby in order to work from home on a regular basis. We hide in the bathroom if we're feeling emotional, and would more likely engage in a trust fall with our boss than admit that we have an anxiety disorder.

By now, you know that by tuning in, you can pay attention to the patterns in your own work life about what works and what doesn't, and figure out if it's possible to set up your life in a way that fits. If you're a powerful entrepreneur, it's easy. But what about the rest of us? Who said it's okay to ask to work from home without expecting a ding on career advancement? Most of us, myself included, can't ignore pushback from our managers, clients, and colleagues, no matter how subtle it may be.

There's a simple answer, but it's not easy: work needs to catch up with us.

In the twenty-first century, human capital is the most valuable resource in our economy. As we recognize neurological and emotional diversity in all its forms, workplace culture needs to begin to make room for the Technicolor range of emotion. Although so much has been done (rightly) to promote diversity at work, there's a giant hole in the understanding of how temperament and emotions play not just into our daily grind at the office, but into the very trajectory of success.

Think of all the talent companies lose because hermits need more control over their place, pace, and space. Think of all the potentially great entrepreneurs who feel discouraged from starting their businesses because "getting out there" is a trial. When one employee leaves a job, the typical cost of replacement is three months of salary. Think of the cost when a whole slice of the population struggles with the dominant workplace paradigm.

Recently, I've begun to think about the power of autonomy as it affects my own family. My eight-year-old son, Asa, has always had difficulty at school. It's hard for him to sit still. When he's passionate about a project, he gets obsessed. Small-group projects, he says, are the worst. (Wonder where he got all that?)

For three years, we changed his schools, hoping to find the right fit. Finally we did. In his current classroom, he has the ability to dialogue with his teachers when he needs a moment to manage his anxiety or is having trouble working in a group. He can take the space he needs, at the pace he needs.

School is changing to better fit the needs of students all along the temperament and neurological spectrum. It's my fondest wish that managers and HR professionals also begin to recognize the ambivalence and inner conflict that many insanely talented people feel. Because when they get the space they need, great employees have no reason to quit or feel miserable.

When I lived in Los Angeles, I often worked at the Santa Monica WeWork, the hippest coworking space I can imagine. Although the crowd made me feel old and extremely uncool, I loved experiencing the new and revolutionary optional office. People were only at WeWork because they wanted to be there. No one tracked their comings and goings, whether they were part of a four-person team or employed at a multinational corporation. Now the shared workplace is booming: in 2005, there was one coworking space in the United States. Today, there over seven thousand spaces globally, with thousands more added each year. It's not for everyone, but for introverts and hermits, a coworking space offers a delicious cocktail of freedom and structure.

Introversion, anxiety, and hiding in the bathroom are not weaknesses. They can, in fact, be the keys to your strength and success as a businessperson, whether it's using your sensitivity to attune to clients, your anxiety to be a better boss, or your need for space to forge new and interesting paths. They can help you attune to yourself, making your business life a more holistic part of your personal beliefs and goals. And, as a self-accepting hermit or introvert, you can show the business world how great things happen when teams are truly diverse and team members can be honest about who they truly are.

# ACKNOWLEDGMENTS

To my editor Alieza Schvimer, thank you for seeing this book through, making it better, and always taking my anxious phone calls! Thanks to the wonderful team at HarperCollins: Lisa Sharkey, Lynn Grady, Michael Barrs and Kendra Newton, Lauren Janiec and Shelby Meizlik, Stephanie Vallejo, Jeanne Reina, and Paula Szafranski.

Thank you to the incredible Lizzie Skurnick: editor extraordinaire, fellow toddler mom, and wonderful creative partner.

I'm grateful to my wonderful agent, Lorin Rees, for both years of great conversations and friendship and also for assuring me always that the book proposal was "getting close." Thanks to Seth Schulman for helping get the book idea ready for the light of day.

To my wonderful husband, Nicco, for Saturdays, and to Jessie Nunez, who I truly depend on and who is a gift in our lives. We are blessed to have you as well as the incredible teachers who provide such a strong foundation for Asa, Tom, and JJ.

More thanks to:

To Christina Vuleta, Lilly Knoepp, and the team at *Forbes*, thank you for supporting the Hiding in the Bathroom podcast! To Molly Beck: you helped me start this all. The team at Podcast Garage in

Boston offer the very best place to podcast and think about all matters *Hiding in the Bathroom*.

To Susan Cain for writing *Quiet* and continuing the conversation about introversion at her wonderful website, QuietRev.com.

To my sisters in work and life: Julia LeStage, Rebecca Harley, Andrea Sparrey, Hillary Moglen, Amy Farley, Chrysula Winegar, Emily McKhann, Kristin Chalmers, Samantha Ettus, Camille Preston, Meighan Stone, Tanya Tarr, Susan McPherson, and Cali Yost, and of course my real sisters Georgia Aarons and Gabrielle Eisele who I love and treasure. And to the women of The Li.st for wisdom always.

To Christine Koh, what can I say? Every day you teach me so much and make me laugh.

To Jen Vento, my partner at work.

To Kaitlyn Dowling. I still miss you.

To Lisa Stone, for being the best role model.

To Dr. Carol Birnbaum, for everything.

To Donna Curry, who asked me to give the Women's Launchpad Keynote and changed my life.

To the smart people who lent their wisdom to the book: Amanda Clayman, Claire Shipman, Carrie Kerpen, Cari Sommer, Dr. Kim Leary, Kenny Lao, Morgan Shanahan, Naama Bloom, Christina Wallace, Sara Critchfield, Elan Morgan, Cheryl Contee, Mitra Kalita, Ana Flores, Anil Dash, Cal Newport, Anne Greenwood, Lauren Bacon, Alicia Lutes, Bea Arthur, Lane Wood, Courtney Nichols Gould, Nilofer Merchant, Jessica Jackley, Rhonesha Byng, Meredith Fineman, Gina Bianchini, Arvind Rajan, Dr. Hannah Riley Bowles, Talia Borodin, Kelsey Wirth, Aaron Sherinian, Steve Cunningham, Erica Keswin, Alicia Chevalier, Leah Ginsberg, Michael Ansara, Leah Russin, Kathryn Schotthoefer, Katie Orenstein, Maisie Pollard, Stephanie Goodell, Yalda Uhls, Reverend Claire Feingold Thoryn, Elisa Camahort Page, Tereza Nemessanyi, Stew Friedman, Dr. Ellen Hendriksen, Kate Gardiner, Juliette Kayyem,

Alan Dandron, Maryella Gockel, Lindy Huang Werges, Britt Bravo, and Clelia Peters.

And to my very first bosses, who taught me so much: Sarah Eaton, Betty Hudson, Nancy Evans (for introducing me to *Composing a Life* years ago) Selia Bellanca, and to my first clients Ellen Galinsky and Leslie Tullio, who took a chance.

Finally, a huge thank you to my children Asa, Tom, and Josephine, who dealt with way too many hours of mommy buried in her laptop. I love you so much.

# NOTES

**CHAPTER 1**

1. H. Anderson, "Never Heard of FOMO? You're So Missing Out," *Observer*, April 16, 2011. https://en.wikipedia.org/wiki/Fear_of_missing_out.
2. Cal Newport, M.D., personal interview by Morra Aarons-Mele, *Hiding in the Bathroom* podcast episode, Forbes One Production, January 4, 2017.
3. J. E. Reich, "Chimamanda Ngozi Adichie Quietly Gave Birth, Refused to 'Perform Pregnancy,'" *Jezebel*, Gizmodo Media Group, July 5, 2016. http://jezebel.com/chimamanda-ngozi-adichie-quietly-gave-birth-refused-to-1783171806.
4. Y. Yamamiya, T. F. Cash, S. E. Melnyk, H. D. Posavac, and S. S. Posavac, "Women's Exposure to Thin-and-Beautiful Media Images: Body Image Effects of Media Ideal Internalization and Impact-Reduction Interventions," *Body Image* 2(1): 74–80. PMID: 18089176 DOI: 10.1016/j.bodyim.2004.11.001.
5. Ann Friedman, "Shine Theory: Why Powerful Women Make the Greatest Friends," *New York*, May 31, 2013. http://nymag.com/thecut/2013/05/shine-theory-how-to-stop-female-competition.html.

**CHAPTER 2**

1. Work+Life Fit is trademarked property of FlexStrategy Group/Work+Life Fit Inc. and is used with permission.
2. Vox Creative and Cadillac, "Where KIVA Founder Jessica Jackley Works and Finds Balance with Her Family," Vox Media, Inc., 2017. http://www.theverge.com/sponsored/8379807/jessica-jackley.

**CHAPTER 3**

1. Giovanni B. Cassano, M.D., Nicolò Baldini Rossi, M.D., and Stefano Pini, M.D., "Psychopharmacology of Anxiety Disorders," *Dialogues in Clinical Neuroscience* 4(3): 271–285, Sept. 2002. PMCID: PMC3181684.
2. Vanessa Coppard-Queensland, "Globally, 1 in 13 Suffers from Anxiety," *Fu-

*turity,* Sept. 5, 2012. http://www.futurity.org/globally-1-in-13-suffers-from -anxiety/.

3. Thomas A. Richards, "What Is Social Anxiety?," *Social Anxiety Institute,* 2017. https://socialanxietyinstitute.org/what-is-social-anxiety.

4. Giovanni B. Cassano, M.D., Nicolò Baldini Rossi, M.D., and Stefano Pini, M.D., "Psychopharmacology of Anxiety Disorders," *Dialogues in Clinical Neuroscience* 4(3): 271–285, Sept. 2002. PMCID: PMC3181684.

5. A.D.A.M., Inc., "Anxiety In-Depth Report," *New York Times,* 2008. http:// www.nytimes.com/health/guides/symptoms/stress-and-anxiety/print.html.

6. Medco Health Solutions, Inc., "America's State of Mind," *Medco Health Solutions, Inc.* (n.d.). http://apps.who.int/medicinedocs/documents/s19032en /s19032en.pdf.

7. Ibid.

8. Postpartum Progress Inc., "Statistics," Postpartum Progress Inc., 2016. http://postpartumprogress.org/the-facts-about-postpartum-depression/.

9. Anxiety and Depression Association of America, "Therapy," *ADAA,* 2010– 2016. https://www.adaa.org/finding-help/treatment/therapy.

10. Shian-Ling Keng, Moria J. Smoski, and Clive J. Robins, "Effects of Mindfulness on Psychological Health: A Review of Empirical Studies," May 13, 2013, *Clinical Psychology Review* (6): 1041–1056, Aug. 31, 2011. doi: 10.1016/j .cpr.2011.04.006.

11. Y. Tibi-Elhanany and S. G.Shamay-Tsoory, "Social Cognition in Social Anxiety: First Evidence for Increased Empathic Abilities," *Israel Journal of Psychiatry and Related Sciences* 48(2): 98–106, 2011. PMID: 22120444. https:// www.ncbi.nlm.nih.gov/pubmed/22120444.

12. Ellen Hendriksen, "The Differences Between Introversion and Social Anxiety," Quiet Revolution, 2017. http://www.quietrev.com/the-4-differences -between-introversion-and-social-anxiety/.

## CHAPTER 4

1. Global Workplace Analytics, "Latest Telecommuting Statistics," GlobalWorkPlaceAnalytics.com, 2016. http://globalworkplaceanalytics.com/tel ecommuting-statistics.

2. Laura Vanderkam, "Why and How Managers Should Help Workers Set Boundaries, *Fortune,* April 8, 2015. http://fortune.com/2015/04/08/work-life-setting-boundaries/.

3. KJ Dell'Antonia, "Am I Introverted or Just Rude?," *New York Times,* Sept. 24, 2016. http://www.nytimes.com/2016/09/25/opinion/sunday/am-i-introverted -or-just-rude.html.

4. Nicholas Epley and Juliana Schroeder, "Mistakenly Seeking Solitude," *Journal of Experimental Psychology: General* 143(5), Oct. 2014, 1980–1999. http:// dx.doi.org/10.1037/a0037323.

5. Eric Jaffe. "The Psychological Study of Smiling," Association for Psychological Science, Dec. 2010. http://www.psychologicalscience.org/index.php/pub lications/observer/2010/December-10/the-psychological-study-of-smiling .html.

6. Jessica Amortegui, "Why Finding Meaning at Work Is More Important

Than Feeling Happy," Fast Company & Inc., June 24, 2014. https://www
.fastcompany.com/3032126/how-to-find-meaning-during-your-pursuit-of
-happiness-at-work.

7. Nicholas Epley and Juliana Schroeder, "Mistakenly Seeking Solitude," *Journal of Experimental Psychology: General* 143(5), Oct. 2014, 1980–1999. http://
dx.doi.org/10.1037/a0037323.

8. Susan Dominus, "Is Giving the Secret to Getting Ahead?," *New York Times*,
March 27, 2013. http://www.nytimes.com/2013/03/31/magazine/is-giving
-the-secret-to-getting-ahead.html.

## CHAPTER 5

1. Ryan Westwood, "What Traits Do We Need to Succeed as Entrepreneurs?,"
*Forbes*, Sept. 4, 2015. http://www.forbes.com/sites/ryanwestwood/2015/09/04
/what-traits-Do-we-Need-to-succeed-as-entrepreneurs/#60401e127f8f.

2. Krista Tippett, "James Doty—the Magic Shop of the Brain," *On Being*, Feb.
11, 2016. https://www.onbeing.org/programs/james-doty-the-magic-shop
-of-the-brain/.

## CHAPTER 6

1. Darlene Lancer, "What Are Personal Boundaries? How Do I Get Some?,"
*Psych Central*. https://psychcentral.com/lib/what-are-personal-boundaries
-how-do-i-get-some/.

## CHAPTER 8

1. Cal Newport, "Quit Social Media. Your Career May Depend on It," *New
York Times*, Nov. 19, 2016. http://www.nytimes.com/2016/11/20/jobs/quit
-social-media-your-career-may-depend-on-it.html.

2. Crystal Martin, "An App to Help Black Women with Hair Care," *New York
Times*, Dec. 29, 2016, p. D5. http://www.nytimes.com/2016/12/26/fashion
/black-hair-care-app-swivel.html.

3. Maeve Duggan, "Demographics of Social Media Users," *Pew Research Center, Washington, D.C.*, Aug. 19, 2015. http://www.pewinternet.org/2015/08/19
/the-demographics-of-social-media-users/.

4. Georgina Pearce, "100 Women 2016: How Women Are Winning Online,"
*BBC News*, December 8, 2016. http://www.bbc.com/news/world-37255004.
Lisa Witter and Lisa Chen, "The She Spot: Why Women Are the Market for
Changing the World—and How to Reach Them," San Francisco: Berrett-
Koehler Publishers, June 1, 2008.

## CHAPTER 9

1. Jess Hempel, "A Unicorn Is the Last Thing This Web 2.0 Survivor
Wants," *Wired Business*, Condé Nast, Feb. 29, 2016. https://www.wired
.com/2016/02/unicorn-last-thing-web-2–0-survivor-wants/.

2. Donna Maria Coles Johnson, "7 Ways to Avoid Handmade Business Burnout," *Handmade Business, Small Business Trends LLC.*, Aug. 4, 2016. https://
smallbiztrends.com/2016/08/how-to-avoid-burnout-handmade-business
.html.

## CHAPTER 10

1. Maryella Gockel, EY Global Flexibility Leader, *Personal Interview* by Morra Aarons-Mele, Nov. 9, 2016.
2. Jim Harter, Sangeeta Agrawal, and Susan Sorenson, "Most U.S. Workers See Upside to Staying Connected to Work," *Gallup*, April 30, 2014. http://www.gallup.com/poll/168794/workers-upside-staying-connected-work.aspx.
3. Sara Holoubek, "I'll Be Online Later," LinkedIn Corporation, Oct. 10, 2016. https://www.linkedin.com/pulse/ill-online-later-sara-holoubek.
4. Jody Thompson and Cali Ressler, "3 Ways to Change Toxic Tendencies at Work," *Management Innovation eXchange,* Nov. 20, 2013. http://www.managementexchange.com/blog/3-ways-change-toxic-tendencies-work.
5. Phil Montero, "For Sun Microsystems, Open Work Is Working," *Anywhere Office*, Sept. 12, 2008. http://theanywhereoffice.com/mobile-work/for-sun-microsystems-open-work-is-working.htm.
6. Sara Sutton Fell, "Office, Schmoffice: How 3 Big-Name Companies Succeed with Remote Working," *Entrepreneur Media, Inc,* March 7, 2016. https://www.entrepreneur.com/article/270585.
7. Katheryn Reynolds-Lewis, "How Men Flex," *Working Mother, Bonnier Corporation Company,* Oct. 18, 2016. http://www.workingmother.com/content/how-men-flex.
8. Jessica Stillman, "Red Flags That New Job Will Give You No Work-Life Balance," *Baltimore Sun,* Oct. 28, 2016. http://www.baltimoresun.com/business/success/inc/tca-red-flags-that-new-job-will-give-you-no-work-life-balance-20161028-story.html.
9. Jenna Goudreau, "The Happiest Jobs for Working Moms," *Forbes,* May 6, 2011. http://www.forbes.com/sites/jennagoudreau/2011/05/06/the-happiest-jobs-for-working-moms/#7a09747d25d1.
10. Med Reps, "Love It or Leave It: Medical Sales Job Satisfaction Study," featured in On the Job, *MedReps,* Oct. 4, 2013. https://www.medreps.com/medical-sales-careers/love-it-or-leave-it-medical-sales-job-satisfaction-study/.
11. George Musser, "The Origin of Cubicles and the Open-Plan Office," *Scientific American,* Aug. 17, 2009. https://www.scientificamerican.com/article/the-origin-of-cubicles-an/.
12. Vinesh G. Oommen, Mike Knowles, and Isabella Zhao, "Should Health Service Managers Embrace Open Plan Work Environments? A Review," *Asia Pacific Journal of Health Management* 3(2): 37–43.
13. Nanette Fondas, "How Women and Men Use Flexible Work Policies Differently," *Atlantic,* July 19, 2013. http://www.theatlantic.com/sexes/archive/2013/07/how-women-and-men-use-flexible-work-policies-differently/277954/.
14. Pamela Stone and Lisa Ackerly-Hernandez, "The All-or-Nothing Workplace: Flexibility Stigma and 'Opting Out' Among Professional-Managerial Women," *Journal of Social Issues* 69: 235–256, June 12, 2013. doi:10.1111/josi.12013.

## CHAPTER 11

1. Hannah Riley Bowles and Kathleen L. McGinn, "When Does Gender Matter in Negotiation?," *John F. Kennedy School of Government Harvard University Faculty*

*Research Working Papers Series* RWP02–036, Sept. 2002). https://research.hks .harvard.edu/publications/getFile.aspx?Id=51.

2. Katie Orenstein, "Own Your Own Expertise," http://www.theopedproject .org/. Used with permission.

**CHAPTER 12**

1. Natalie Reynolds, "Deal or No Deal? Five Common Mistakes People Make When Negotiating Deals," *Guardian News and Media Limited,* April 28, 2014. https://www.theguardian.com/women-in-leadership/2014/apr/28/five-com mon-mistakes-made-by-negotiators.

2. Tanya Tarr, "Negotiate This!" negotiate-this.com, Jan. 17, 2017.

3. Linda Babcock and Sara Laschever, "Women Don't Ask: Negotiation and the Gender Divide," Princeton, NJ: Princeton University Press, 2003.

4. Olga Khazan, "Women Know When Negotiating Isn't Worth It," *Atlantic,* Jan. 6, 2017. https://www.theatlantic.com/business/archive/2017/01/women -negotiating/512174/.

5. Beth Fisher-Yoshida, "Climate Change and the Need for Collaboration," in P. T. Coleman, M. Deutsch, and E. C. Marcus, eds., *The Handbook of Conflict Resolution: Theory and Practice.* San Francisco: Jossey-Bass, *2014.* https://beth fisheryoshida.wordpress.com/tag/deutschs-crude-law-of-social-relations/.

**CHAPTER 13**

1. Wayne E. Baker, *Achieving Success Through Social Capital.* New York: John Wiley & Sons, Inc., 2000.

2. Ibid.

3. Ibid., p. 20.

4. Wayne E. Baker, *Achieving Success Through Social Capital,* New York: John Wiley & Sons, 2000, p. 20.

5. Christopher E. Beaudoin, "Explaining the Relationship Between Internet Use and Interpersonal Trust: Taking into Account Motivation and Informa- tion Overload," *Journal of Computer-Mediated Communication Association* 13, 2008, 550–568. doi:10.1111/j.1083–6101.2008.00410.x.

**CHAPTER 14**

1. Stephanie Pappas, "Why You Should Smile at Strangers," *Live Science— PURCH,* May 25, 2012. http://www.livescience.com/20578-social-connec tion-smile-strangers.html.

# ABOUT THE AUTHOR

**MORRA AARONS-MELE** is the founder of the award-winning social impact agency Women Online, hosts the *Forbes* podcast *Hiding in the Bathroom,* and created the influencer network the Mission List. She was founding political director of BlogHer.com, and has written for the *Harvard Business Review,* the Huffington Post, MomsRising, the *Wall Street Journal,* the *New York Times,* and the *Guardian.* She has lectured at the Yale Women's Campaign School, the Harvard Kennedy School, and at the World Economic Forum for Young Global Leaders. Aarons-Mele is a graduate of Brown University and the Harvard Kennedy School, and lives in her pajamas in Boston, Massachusetts.